D.H. Lawrence
Three Complete Novels

Lady Chatterley's Lover

The Rainbow

Sons and Lovers

JG PRESS

This edition published in the USA by JG Press and
distributed by World Publications, Inc, by arrangement
with Parragon Book Service Ltd in 1995, Unit 13-17
Avonbridge Trading Estate, Atlantic Road, Avonmouth, Bristol
BS11 9QD

Produced by Magpie Books Ltd, London

The JG Press Imprint is a Trademark of
JG Press, Inc
455 Somerset Avenue
North Dighton
MA 02764

ISBN 1 57215 127 7

A copy of the British Library Cataloguing in Publication
Data is available from the British Library.

Printed in Great Britain.

Contents

Introduction

The dark, sooty coal mines near Eastwood, England, where D.H. Lawrence lived for the first twenty-three years of his life, left an indelible
impression on his thoughts. Throughout his writings, he continually
returned to the miners and their lives in the pits. There was something unknown, something mysterious about the substance of coal and the work of the
miners. In an August, 1925, letter, Lawrence wrote that "Coal is a symbol of
something in the soul, old and dark and silky and natural." Elsewhere in the
same letter, reflecting on his early visions, he describes the colliers as "gods in
the underworld, or as elementals." From such observations, it is not difficult to
imagine the young Lawrence seeing the colliers trooping home from work,
swinging their pit bottles, while stained head-to-toe with black dust, as subterranean, elemental workers involved in some titanic struggle to release from the
earth's underworld its chthonic forces. Even though acutely aware of their extremely perilous working conditions and the depressing environment of the
local villages, Lawrence's interest is understandable as the efforts of the colliers
matched in many ways his own effort to liberate into consciousness the essence
and energy of the unconscious primal nature in man.

Consequently, his writings did not seek to establish their narrative through
"the old stable ego of character," but sought to capture the psychological instincts of his characters, their immediate emotional or irrational response to
things, events, or other people. Lawrence, in a letter to Edward Garnett,
claimed to be totally disinterested in subjecting his characters to one broad,
encompassing moral scheme. "The certain moral scheme is what I object to. In
Turgenev, and in Tolstoi, and in Dostoyevsky, the moral scheme into which all
the characters fit—and it is nearly the same scheme—is, whatever the extraor-
dinariness of the characters themselves, dull, old, dead." Yet this is not entirely
true. Lawrence doesn't present any Christian moral scheme of what is right or
wrong, as there is in *The Brothers Karamazov,* but his narratives do follow what
could be called certain laws of desire.

Desire, as often in Lawrence, is a desire influenced by elements larger than
the individual self, and in his letters and essays, he often comments on what he
sees as corruptive or procreative, repulsive or attractive, or as destructive or
beneficial in man's desires. The disintegration Lawrence finds in Edgar Allen
Poe, for instance, is not necessarily "evil," as "the old white psyche has to be
gradually broken down before anything else can come to pass," but it is extremely important that this decomposition has its end result in something positive or promising.

This moral scheme of Lawrence's does not judge one's actions solely as they may pertain to an afterlife as in a fundamentalist Christian morality, but judges how one's actions relate to life as it is being lived. Lawrence constantly emphasized the obscure and esoteric Christian doctrine of the resurrection of the body in the flesh—not just the spirit.

What Lawrence saw as being truly corruptive was those individuals who followed out their passions and desires while clinging to their old notions of selfhood. Allowing for no inner transformations, this desire creates only a shell, whose beauty does not affect the soul. Lawrence's favorite metaphor to describe this state of decomposition was the beetle.

> It is like a blow of triumphant decay, when I meet Birrell or the others. . . . It makes a form of inward corruption which truly makes me scarce able to live. . . . There is something nasty about him, like black-beetles. . . . I feel as if I should go mad, if I think of your set, D. G. and K. and B. It makes me dream of beetles.

Though he often complained of moralists, Lawrence continually comments on what he believes is proper or obscene about sex. "The evil thing that daytime love-making is, and all sex-palaver!" Or, as it is often called by Lawrence, this "sex in the head" betrays the chaste pleasures and corrupts that otherness, the mystery of sex, its unknowable element that continually provides for one's renewal to the wonders in life. This Lawrencian moral scheme of desire, if it can be called that, has close affinities with a sort of "alchemy of the soul." The characters in Lawrence's works are put through their trials of separation, conflict, environmental changes, and sexual encounters to get to the core of their being. This process results in a narrative where there is little between the effects of matter on the body and soul or in the response of the soul and body to events as they materialize. Aldous Huxley, in writing of Lawrence's work, termed this response between the psyche and matter "a kind of mystical materialism" and a "psychological reality, like physical reality, . . . determined by our mental and bodily make-up."

In a well-known description of his work, Lawrence compares the composition of his characters to the composition of a piece of coal or diamond which both have carbon as their inner element. "The ordinary novel would trace the history of the diamond—but I say, 'Diamond, what! This is carbon.' And my diamond might be coal or soot, and my theme is carbon." One is coal, the other, soot, but both have an inner reality, a logic that connects them: carbon.

This link between his characters that is both an inner reality as well as something physical gives substance to Lawrence's controversial notion of "blood consciousness." Criticized as "dangerous" as well as "frankly rubbish," Lawrence believed that the essence of such a consciousness found in his writing could revitalize and strengthen modern man just as the rituals of rejuvenation did in the primitive world.

Similar to other visions of light and dark realities, such as Blake's "Marriage of Heaven and Hell," Lawrence sought to combine the dark, animal, instinctual, and emotional nature of the blood with the enlightening, constructive, and attentive nature of consciousness. This concept would allow him to realize his source of creative powers without touching on any systems of thought that might repress his immediate desires or feelings.

Lady Chatterley's Lover, Lawrence's last major novel, combines his ideologies of blood consciousness, sexual awareness, and social commentary of England in the 1920s. By exaggerating the sorry state of Britain's aristocracy through Clifford Chatterley's impotence, and by portraying Mellors' and Lady Chatterly's explicit sexuality, Lawrence brings his causes to the reader's attention with the forcefulness of a manifesto.

In many ways the embodiment of Lawrence's ideals, Oliver Mellors stands for "the touch of bodily awareness between human beings—against the world, machines, and money's hand." Warmth, courage, emotions, blood, and a procreative sexuality are poised throughout Lawrence's writings against a cold, hard, and mechanical society.

Similar to Lawrence's affairs before he met his wife, Frieda, Mellors' affairs prior to Lady Chatterley involve a "pure," literary-cultured woman and a passionate, common woman. And, as Mellors conducts his occupation as groundskeeper of Wagby Manor's gardens and forest grounds with military efficiency and a naturalist's knowledgeable sensibility, he is again like Lawrence, both a modern Pan and a solitary voice in the wilderness.

The tragedy of the era from the story's opening line is in many ways the tragedy of Clifford Chatterley, who was severely injured in the First World War. Clifford, paralyzed from the hips down and rendered impotent, closely follows what Lawrence must have seen in post-war England as the helplessness of the British aristocracy to revitalize the spiritual and physical well-being of an industrial nation. The solution of this tragedy, the elopement of Lady Chatterley and Mellors, the marriage of a baroness to a groundskeeper who watches over a portion of England's ancient Sherwood Forest, signifies an attempt by Lawrence to reestablish the phenomenal beauty of nature found in the old aristocracy that industry's mechanical reasoning destroyed.

Lacking in the mysticism of *The Rainbow* and in the long detailed observations of *Sons and Lovers*, *Lady Chatterley's Lover* is Lawrence's most accessible and popular work. Though sometimes labelled as "perverse" and "obscene" by critics, *Lady Chatterley's Lover* clearly and thoroughly draws the line between Lawrence's ideas for an affirmative sexuality against what he saw as a corruption of life in an increasingly mechanized world. The naming of Mellors' and Lady Chatterley's sexual organs as "John Thomas" and "Lady Jane," the title to his second edition of this same work, is not so much a perversion, but a conceptual act that moves their sexuality from the self-centered ego and its social consciousness to an otherness of the self belonging to the imagination with its affinities to both the spiritual and the absurd.

The Rainbow also looks at agricultural and industrial England, but from a different perspective. Easily the most encompassing of Lawrence's works, this novel traces the story of four generations of Brangwens, whose ancestral families have worked the land of their farm for over two hundred years. In chronicling the story of the Brangwens, Lawrence often adopts the language of the King James Bible along with ancestral pagan references to strengthen the novel's themes that blend the ways of the land and the heavens.

The Brangwens work the Marsh Farm in the northeast section of Britain and, while never growing wealthy, they labor in the fields and take what the land yields them. They experience the plentifulness of the land throughout the day, and by night, sleep peacefully, knowing the fields will yield them tomorrow's harvest. The earth surrounding their farm house is alive, active, soft, and "heavy with the accumulation of the living day," and they work it "feeling the pulse and body of the soil."

In a single scene, Lawrence describes the magic of the Brangwens' life that gives their home and farm its confidence:

> *Two miles away, a church-tower stood on a hill, the houses of the little country town climbing assiduously up to it. Whenever one of the Brangwens in the fields lifted his head from his work, he saw the church-tower at Ilkeston in the empty sky. So that as he turned again to the horizontal land, he was aware of something standing above him and beyond him in the distance.*

With the church above them retelling the story of the heavenly cycle of creation, of His death in winter and resurrection in spring, and the land below them with the earth's cycle of creation, the fields they work have their place both in heaven and on earth.

But then a canal is built, dividing the land in two. The traffic of boats along its waters is soon followed by the development of the railroads, which in turn aids in the proliferation of the coal industry. The influx of new trade from the coal industry widens the horizons of the local community, at the same time, it dwarfs and belittles them.

Once the Brangwens' farm life, with the church above them, moved with the heavens under the sun, but as the coal industry takes over the main aspirations of the community during the day, the farm land no longer holds its once sovereign connection with the heavens of the church. As the farm life is symbolically pushed into the night and the shadows of the earth, its place in the heavens now with the moon, the Brangwens must now look to themselves to provide for this correspondence between the heavens and their place in society. Thus, the Brangwens' quest to reestablish their relationship to the heavens becomes mingled with the night, the magic of the harvest, and the mysteries of love.

Ursula Brangwen, the last generation of Brangwens described in the novel, experiences the most difficult trials as she seeks to advance further away from the Marsh farm than any previous Brangwen. Her affair with her lover begins in the stackyard of corn at harvest time, but their relationship later dissolves into a clash of ego-centered wills. Far from the farm and its heavenly correspondence, their wedding engagement culminates in a violent sexual encounter that causes their final separation.

After such a disastrous result in an affair that had once experienced a touch of the marvelous, Ursula is stranded and a cold wave of fear rises in her. Is there any return to that wonder existing between the heavens and earth in a modern world where the individual will is so supreme? Staring out from her window, she finds her answer in that one bright arch of prismed light that seems to exemplify what Lawrence once called the novel itself—"one bright book of life."

If there was any answer to overcoming the perils of modern life for Lawrence, it was the act of writing. Putting his pen to paper allowed him to rediscover past feelings and thoughts that could then be reviewed and transformed to benefit his current life. In a letter to his devotée, Dorothy Brett, he writes: "One sheds one's sicknesses in books—repeats and presents again one's emotions, to be master of them." With *Sons and Lovers,* Lawrence came to realize the truth of his relationships in a psychological context that provided him with an impetus for his later work.

In this autobiographical work, Paul Morel, modeled on the young Lawrence, struggles against the circumstances of growing up in a coal mining village with a dominating mother involved in a disastrous marriage. His mother, the strongest person in the household, consumes his being so thoroughly that he finds it difficult to engage in a lasting relationship with another woman.

As Jeffrey Meyers says in his biography of Lawrence, *Sons and Lovers* describes the destructive power of love. Gertrude Morel, in her courtship with Mr. Morel, is attracted to his vigorous behavior, confidence, and seemingly financial stability. But once she discovers his poverty and love of drink, she begins to loathe him. Thus begin the unfortunate circumstances that reverberate throughout the novel like a Greek tragedy.

Rejecting her husband, Mrs. Morel turns to her children, giving them the love that she has denied her husband. The children grow up learning to despise their father, so that as Mr. Morel grows old he becomes an unwanted stranger in his own home.

In this first mature novel of Lawrence's, as in later works, he sees the strength of individuals involved in sexual relationships as being rooted in the vitality of their physical being or in that individual's visionary view of life. Overwhelmed by the vitality of Mr. Morel, who delights in the strength required to work the mines, Mrs. Morel seeks the power of knowledge, her cloth, to cover the strength of his nakedness.

William Morel, the oldest son and his mother's favorite, advances successfully in the world. But as his inner self is still unable to leave his mother, he marries a women who is overly concerned with external things. This aberration of his body and soul weakens and cripples William, so that he succumbs to pneumonia at an early age.

With her favorite child gone, Mrs. Morel focuses all her attention on her son, Paul. Miriam, Paul's first girlfriend, is modeled after Lawrence's first love, Jessie Chambers, and the life of young Paul Morel describes the cultural and philosophical upbringing of Lawrence. Clara Dawes, Paul's suffragette girlfriend, depicts Alice Dax, Lawrence's active, passionate woman who helped liberate him from his dominating mother's maternal care and from Jessie's stifling spiritual love.

In many ways, *Sons and Lovers* is a portrait of the artist as a young man as important as James Joyce's as it is different. Where Joyce defined his position as an artist among his classroom friends, Lawrence, as portrayed in *Sons and Lovers,* seeks to become more of himself as a man and artist through his relationships with women.

The conflict between the sexes chronicled throughout Lawrence's work almost always reflects a philosophical or psychological note. For him, the otherness and unknown between the sexual attraction and conflict of men and women was an important means for his art. The differences between the sexes were for Lawrence an important and supreme way for couples to achieve a sense of self-discovery and enrichment. In the act of love, the soul experiences the otherness of the flesh and the flesh, the otherness of the soul. Thus, this divine union, this merging of two bodies, two souls, opens and reveals the unknown, those mysteries of love and life, for the artist who chooses such a theme.

Lawrence completed *Sons and Lovers* in 1912 at the age of twenty-seven while residing in Gargnano, Italy. Three years later, *The Rainbow* was published in England. After traveling to Ceylon, Australia, New Mexico, and Oaxaca, Mexico, he returned to Italy to write his first version of *Lady Chatterley's Lover,* which was completed in 1928, two years before his death.

Lawrence, who sought for a spirit-in-the-flesh union of men and women with the mysteries of nature and the procreative impulse of sexuality, never gained the popularity or widespread recognition in his lifetime that his writings would later achieve. For it was not until after his death that his work would make its full impact on society. In 1960, both the American and British publishers of *Lady Chatterley's Lover* won landmark cases for the unexpurgated version of the book to be published and distributed legally, ushering in a revolutionary decade that heralded many of the causes Lawrence championed. Though it is doubtful he would have applauded the entire era, the struggles initiated at that time against the cold and unreal systems of thought lost to the sensitive laws of nature and human touch would have encouraged him. For like Byron before him, the writings of Lawrence occupy a place in literature where the passionate heart will always find its hold on life.

Robert Yagley
1993

Lady Chatterley's Lover

I

Ours is essentially a tragic age, so we refuse to take it tragically. The cataclysm has happened, we are among the ruins, we start to build up new little habits, to have new little hopes. It is rather hard work: there is now no smooth road into the future: but we go round, or scramble over the obstacles. We've got to live, no matter how many skies have fallen.

This was more or less Constance Chatterley's position. The war had brought the roof down over her head. And she had realized that one must live and learn.

She married Clifford Chatterley in 1917, when he was home for a month on leave. They had a month's honeymoon. Then he went back to Flanders: to be shipped over to England again six months later, more or less in bits. Constance, his wife, was then twenty-three years old, and he was twenty-nine.

His hold on life was marvellous. He didn't die, and the bits seemed to grow together again. For two years he remained in the doctor's hands. Then he was pronounced a cure, and could return to life again, with the lower half of his body, from the hips down, paralyzed for ever.

This was in 1920. They returned, Clifford and Constance, to his home, Wragby Hall, the family "seat." His father had died, Clifford was now a baronet, Sir Clifford, and Constance was Lady Chatterley. They came to start housekeeping and married life in the rather forlorn home of the Chatterleys on a rather inadequate income. Clifford had a sister, but she had departed. Otherwise there were no near relatives. The elder brother was dead in the war. Crippled for ever, knowing he could never have any children, Clifford came home to the smoky Midlands to keep the Chatterley name alive while he could.

He was not really downcast. He could wheel himself about in a wheeled chair, and he had a bath-chair with a small motor attachment, so he could drive himself slowly round the garden and into the fine melancholy park, of which he was really so proud, though he pretended to be flippant about it.

Having suffered so much, the capacity for suffering had to some extent left him. He remained strange and bright and cheerful, almost, one might say, chirpy, with his ruddy, healthy-looking face, and his pale-blue, challenging bright eyes. His shoulders were broad and strong, his hands were very strong. He was expensively dressed, and wore handsome neckties from Bond Street. Yet still in his face one saw the watchful look, the slight vacancy of a cripple.

He had so very nearly lost his life, that what remained was wonderfully precious to him. It was obvious in the anxious brightness of his eyes, how proud he was, after the great shock, of being alive. But he had been so much hurt that something inside him had perished, some of his feelings had gone. There was a blank of insentience.

Constance, his wife, was a ruddy, country-looking girl with soft brown hair and sturdy body, and slow movements, full of unusual energy. She had big, wondering eyes, and a soft mild voice, and seemed just to have come from her native village. It was not so at all. Her father was the once well-known R.A., old Sir Malcolm Reid. Her mother had been one of the cultivated Fabians in the palmy, rather pre-Raphaelite days. Between artists and cultured socialists, Constance and her sister Hilda had had what might be called an aesthetically unconventional upbringing. They had been taken to Paris and Florence and Rome to breathe in art, and they had been taken also in the other direction, to the Hague and Berlin, to great Socialist conventions, where the speakers spoke in every civilized tongue, and no one was abashed.

The two girls, therefore, were from an early age not the least daunted by either art or ideal politics. It was their natural atmosphere. They were at once cosmopolitan and provincial, with the cosmopolitan provincialism of art that goes with pure social ideals.

They had been sent to Dresden at the age of fifteen, for music among other things. And they had had a good time there. They lived freely among the students, they argued with the men over philosophical, sociological and artistic matters, they were just as good as the men themselves: only better, since they were women. And they tramped off to the forests with sturdy youths bearing guitars, twang-twang! They sang the Wandervogel songs, and they were free. Free! That was the great word. Out in the open world, out in the forests of the morning, with lusty and splendid-throated young fellows, free to do as they liked, and—above all—to say what they liked. It was the talk that mattered supremely: the impassioned interchange of talk. Love was only a minor accompaniment.

Both Hilda and Constance had had their tentative love-affairs by the time they were eighteen. The young men with whom they talked so passionately and sang so lustily and camped under the trees in such freedom wanted, of course, the love connection. The girls were doubtful, but then the thing was so much talked about, it was supposed to be so important. And the men were so humble and craving. Why couldn't a girl be queenly, and give the gift of herself?

So they had given the gift of themselves, each to the youth with whom she had the most subtle and intimate arguments. The arguments, the discussions were the great thing: the love-making and connection were only a sort of primitive reversion and a bit of an anti-climax. One was less in love with the boy afterwards, and a little inclined to hate him, as if he had trespassed on one's privacy and inner freedom. For, of course, being a girl, one's whole dignity and meaning in life consisted in the achievement of an absolute, a perfect, a pure and noble freedom. What else did a girl's life mean? To shake off the old and sordid connections and subjections.

And however one might sentimentalize it, this sex business was one of the most ancient, sordid connections and subjections. Poets who glorified it were mostly men. Women had always known there was something better, something higher. And now they knew it more definitely than ever. The beautiful pure freedom of a woman was infinitely more wonderful than any sexual love. The only unfortunate thing was that men lagged so far behind women in the matter. They insisted on the sex thing like dogs.

And a woman had to yield. A man was like a child with his appetites. A woman had to yield him what he wanted, or like a child he would probably turn nasty and flounce away and spoil what was a very pleasant connection. But a woman could yield to a man without yielding her inner, free self. That the poets and talkers about sex did not seem to have taken sufficiently into account. A woman could take a man without really giving herself away. Certainly she could take him without giving herself into his power. Rather she could use this sex thing to have power over him. For she only had to hold herself back in sexual intercourse, and let him finish and expend himself without herself coming to the crisis: and then she could prolong the connection and achieve her orgasm and her crisis while he was merely her tool.

Both sisters had had their love experience by the time the war came, and they were hurried home. Neither was ever in love with a young man unless he and she were verbally very near: that is unless they were profoundly interested, TALKING to one another. The amazing, the profound, the unbelievable thrill there was in passionately talking to some really clever young man by the hour, resuming day after day for months . . . this they had never realized till it happened! The paradisal promise: Thou shalt have men to talk to!—had never been uttered. It was fulfilled before they knew what a promise it was.

And if after the roused intimacy of these vivid and soul-enlightened discussions the sex thing became more or less inevitable, then let it. It marked the end of a chapter. It had a thrill of its own too: a queer vibrating thrill inside the body, a final spasm of self-assertion, like the last word, exciting, and very like the row of asterisks that can be put to show the end of a paragraph, and a break in the theme.

When the girls came home for the summer holidays of 1913, when Hilda was twenty and Connie eighteen, their father could see plainly that they had had the love experience.

L'amour avait passé par là, as somebody puts it. But he was a man of experience himself, and let life take its course. As for the mother, a nervous invalid in the last few months of her life, she only wanted her girls to be "free," and to "fulfill themselves." She herself had never been able to be altogether herself: it had been denied her. Heaven knows why, for she was a woman who had her own income and her own way. She blamed her husband. But as a matter of fact, it was some old impression of authority on her own mind or soul that she could not get rid of. It had nothing to do with Sir Malcolm, who left his nervously hostile, high-spirited wife to rule her own roost, while he went his own way.

So the girls were "free," and went back to Dresden, and their music, and the university and the young men. They loved their respective young men, and their respective young men loved them with all the passion of mental attraction. All the wonderful things the young men thought and expressed and wrote, they thought and expressed and wrote for the young women. Connie's young man was musical, Hilda's was technical. But they simply lived for their young women. In their minds and their mental excitements, that is. Somewhere else they were a little rebuffed, though they did not know it.

It was obvious in them too that love had gone through them: that is, the physical experience. It is curious what a subtle but unmistakable transmutation it makes, both in the body of men and women: the women more blooming, more subtly rounded, her young angularities softened, and her expression either anxious or triumphant: the man much quieter, more inward, the very shapes of his shoulders and his buttocks less assertive, more hesitant.

In the actual sex-thrill within the body, the sisters nearly succumbed to the strange male power. But quickly they recovered themselves, took the sex-thrill as a sensation, and remained free. Whereas the men, in gratitude to the women for the sex experience, let their souls go out to her. And afterwards looked rather as if they had lost a shilling and found sixpence. Connie's man could be a bit sulky, and Hilda's a bit jeering. But that is how men are! Ungrateful and never satisfied. When you don't have them they hate you because you won't; and when you do have them they hate you again, for some other reason. Or for no reason at all, except that they are discontented children, and can't be satisfied whatever they get, let a woman do what she may.

However, came the war, Hilda and Connie were rushed home again after having been home already in May, to their mother's funeral. Before Christmas of 1914 both their German young men were dead: whereupon the sisters wept, and loved the young men passionately, but underneath forgot them. They didn't exist any more.

Both sisters lived in their father's, really their mother's Kensington house, and mixed with the young Cambridge group, the group that stood for "freedom" and flannel trousers, and flannel shirts open at the neck, and a well-bred sort of emotional anarchy, and a whispering, murmuring sort of voice, and an ultra-sensitive sort of manner. Hilda, however, suddenly married a man ten years older than herself, an elder member of the same Cambridge group, a man with a fair amount of money, and a comfortable family job in the government: he also wrote philosophical essays. She lived with him in a smallish house in Westminster, and moved in that good sort of society of people in the government who are not tip-toppers, but who are, or would be, the real intelligent power in the nation: people who know what they're talking about, or talk as if they did.

Connie did a mild form of war-work, and consorted with the flannel-trousered Cambridge intransigeants, who gently mocked at everything, so far. Her "friend" was a Clifford Chatterley, a young man of twenty-two, who had hurried home from Bonn, where he was studying the technicalities of coal-mining. He had previously spent two years at Cambridge. Now he had become a first lieutenant in a smart regiment, so he could mock at everything more becomingly in uniform.

Clifford Chatterley was more upper-class than Connie. Connie was well-to-do intelligentsia, but he was aristocracy. Not the big sort, but still it. His father was a baronet, and his mother had been a viscount's daughter.

But Clifford, while he was better bred than Connie, and more "society," was in his own way more provincial and more timid. He was at his ease in the narrow "great world," that is, landed aristocracy society, but he was shy and nervous of all that other big world which consists of the vast hordes of the middle and lower classes, and foreigners. If the truth must be told, he was a little bit frightened of middle and lower class humanity, and of foreigners not of his own class. He was, in some paralyzing way, conscious of his own defenselessness, though he had all the defense of privilege. Which is curious, but a phenomenon of our day.

Therefore the peculiar soft assurance of a girl like Constance Reid fascinated him. She was so much more mistress of herself in that outer world of chaos than he was master of himself.

Nevertheless he too was a rebel: rebelling even against his class. Or perhaps rebel is too strong a word; far too strong. He was only caught in the general, popular recoil of the young against convention and against any sort of real authority. Fathers were ridiculous: his own obstinate one supremely so. And governments were ridiculous: our own wait-and-see sort especially so. And armies were ridiculous, and old buffers of generals altogether, the red-faced Kitchener supremely. Even the war was ridiculous, though it did kill rather a lot of people.

In fact everything was a little ridiculous, or very ridiculous: certainly everything connected with authority, whether it were in the army or the government or the universities, was ridiculous to a degree. And as far as the governing class made any pretensions to govern, they were ridiculous too. Sir Geoffrey, Clifford's father, was intensely ridiculous, chopping down his trees, and weeding men out of his colliery to shove them into the war: and himself being so safe and patriotic; but, also, spending more money on his country than he'd got.

When Miss Chatterley—Emma—came down to London from the Midlands to do some nursing work, she was very witty in a quiet way about Sir Geoffrey and his determined patriotism. Herbert, the elder brother and heir, laughed outright, though it was his trees that were falling for trench props. But Clifford only smiled a little uneasily. Everything was ridiculous, quite true. But when it came too close and oneself became ridiculous too . . . ? At least people of a different class, like Connie, were earnest about something. They believed in something.

They were rather earnest about the Tommies, and the threat of conscription, and the shortage of sugar and toffee for the children. In all these things, of course, the authorities were ridiculously at fault. But Clifford could not take it to heart. To him the authorities were ridiculous *ab ovo*, not because of toffee or Tommies.

And the authorities felt ridiculous, and behaved in a rather ridiculous fashion, and it was all a mad hatter's tea-party for a while. Till things developed over there, and Lloyd George came to save the situation over here. And this surpassed even ridicule, the flippant young laughed no more.

In 1916 Herbert Chatterley was killed, so Clifford became heir. He was terrified even of this. His importance as son of Sir Geoffrey and child of Wragby was so ingrained in him, he could never escape it. And yet he knew that this too, in the eyes of the vast seething world, was ridiculous. Now he was heir and responsible for Wragby. Was that not terrible? And also splendid and at the same time, perhaps, purely absurd?

Sir Geoffrey would have none of the absurdity. He was pale and tense, withdrawn into himself, and obstinately determined to save his country and his own position, let it be Lloyd George or who it might. So cut off he was, so divorced from the England that was really England, so utterly incapable, that he even thought well of Horatio Bottomley. Sir Geoffrey stood for England and Lloyd George as his forebears had stood for England and St. George: and he never knew there was a difference. So Sir Geoffrey felled timber and stood for Lloyd George and England, England and Lloyd George.

And he wanted Clifford to marry and produce an heir. Clifford felt his father was a hopeless anachronism. But wherein was he himself any further ahead, except in a wincing sense of the ridiculousness of everything, and the paramount ridiculousness of his own position? For willy-nilly he took his baronetcy and Wragby with the last seriousness.

The gay excitement had gone out of the war . . . dead. Too much death and horror. A man needed support and comfort. A man needed to have an anchor in the safe world. A man needed a wife.

The Chatterleys, two brothers and a sister, had lived curiously isolated, shut in with one another at Wragby, in spite of all their connections. A sense of isolation intensified the family tie, a sense of the weakness of their position, a sense of defenselessness, in spite of, or because of the title and the land. They were cut off from those industrial Midlands in which they passed their lives. And they were cut off from their own class by the brooding, obstinate, shut-up nature of Sir Geoffrey, their father, whom they ridiculed but whom they were so sensitive about.

The three had said they would all live together always. But now Herbert was dead, and Sir Geoffrey wanted Clifford to marry. Sir Geoffrey barely mentioned it: he spoke very little. But his silent, brooding insistence that it should be so was hard for Clifford to bear up against.

But Emma said No! She was ten years older than Clifford, and she felt his marrying would be a desertion and a betrayal of what the young ones of the family had stood for.

Clifford married Connie, nevertheless, and had his month's honeymoon with her. It was the terrible year 1917, and they were intimate as two people who stand together on a sinking ship. He had been virgin when he married: and the sex part did not mean much to him. They were so close, he and she, apart from that. And Connie exulted a little in this intimacy which was beyond sex, and beyond a man's "satisfaction." Clifford anyhow was not just keen on his "satisfaction," as so many men seemed to be. No, the intimacy was deeper, more personal than that. And sex was merely an accident, or an adjunct, one of the curious obsolete, organic processes which persisted in its own clumsiness, but was not really necessary. Though Connie did want children: if only to fortify her against her sister-in-law Emma.

But early in 1918 Clifford was shipped home smashed, and there was no child. And Sir Geoffrey died of chagrin.

II

Connie and Clifford came home to Wragby in the autumn of 1920. Miss Chatterley, still disgusted at her brother's defection, had departed and was living in a little flat in London.

Wragby was a long low old house in brown stone, begun about the middle of the eighteenth century, and added on to, till it was a warren of a place without much distinction. It stood on an eminence in a rather fine old park of oak trees, but alas, one could see in the near distance the chimney of Tevershall pit, with its clouds of steam and smoke, and on the damp, hazy distance of the hill the raw straggle of Tevershall village, a village which began almost at the park gates, and trailed in utter hopeless ugliness for a long and gruesome mile: houses, rows of wretched, small, begrimed, brick houses, with black slate roofs for lids, sharp angles and wilful, blank dreariness.

Connie was accustomed to Kensington or the Scottish hills or the Sussex downs: that was her England. With the stoicism of the young she took in the utter, soulless ugliness of the coal-and-iron Midlands at a glance, and left it at what it was: unbelievable and not to be thought about. From the rather dismal rooms at Wragby she heard the rattle-rattle of the screens at the pit, the puff of the winding-engine, the clink-clink of shunting trucks, and the hoarse little whistle of the colliery locomotives. Tevershall pit-bank was burning, had been burning for years, and it would cost thousands to put it out. So it had to burn. And when the wind was that way, which was often, the house was full of the stench of this sulphurous combustion of the earth's excrement. But even on windless days the air always smelt of something under-earth: sulphur, iron, coal, or acid. And even on the Christmas roses the smuts settled persistently, incredible, like black manna from skies of doom.

Well, there it was: fated like the rest of things! It was rather awful, but why kick? You couldn't kick it away. It just went on. Life, like all the rest! On the low dark ceiling of cloud at night red blotches burned and quavered, dappling and swelling and contracting, like burns that give pain. It was the furnaces. At first they fascinated Connie with a sort of horror; she felt she was living underground. Then she got used to them. And in the morning it rained.

Clifford professed to like Wragby better than London. This country had a grim will of its own, and the people had guts. Connie wondered what else they had: certainly neither eyes nor minds. The people were as haggard, shapeless, and dreary as the countryside, and as unfriendly. Only there was something in their deep-mouthed slurring of the dialect, and the thresh-thresh of their hobnailed pit-boots as they trailed home in gangs on the asphalt from work, that was terrible and a bit mysterious.

There had been no welcome home for the young squire, no festivities, no deputation, not even a single flower. Only a dank ride in a motor-car up a dark, damp drive, burrowing through gloomy trees, out to the slope of the park where grey damp sheep were feeding, to the knoll where the house spread its dark brown façade, and the housekeeper and her husband were hovering, like unsure tenants on the face of the earth, ready to stammer a welcome.

There was no communication between Wragby Hall and Tevershall village, none. No caps were touched, no curtseys bobbed. The colliers merely stared; the tradesmen lifted their caps to Connie as to an acquaintance, and nodded awkwardly to Clifford; that was all. Gulf impassable, and a quiet sort of resentment on either side. At first Connie suffered from the steady drizzle of resentment that came from the village. Then she hardened herself to it, and it became a sort of tonic, something to live up to. It was not that she and Clifford were unpopular, they merely belonged to another species altogether from the colliers. Gulf impassable, breach indescribable, such as is perhaps non-existent south of the Trent. But in the Midlands and the industrial North gulf impassable, across which no communication could take place. You stick to your side, I'll stick to mine! A strange denial of the common pulse of humanity.

Yet the village sympathized with Clifford and Connie in the abstract. In the flesh it was—You leave me alone!—on either side.

The rector was a nice man of about sixty, full of his duty, and reduced, personally, almost to a nonentity by the silent—You leave me alone!—of the village. The miners' wives were nearly all Methodists. The miners were nothing. But even so much official uniform as the clergyman wore was enough to obscure entirely the fact that he was a man like any other man. No, he was Mester Ashby, a sort of automatic preaching and praying concern.

This stubborn, instinctive—We think ourselves as good as you, if you *are* Lady Chatterley—puzzled and baffled Connie at first extremely. The curious, suspicious, false amiability with which the miners' wives met her overtures; the curiously offensive tinge of—Oh dear me! I *am* somebody now, with Lady Chatterley talking to me! But she needn't think I'm not as good as her for all that!—which she always heard twanging in the women's half-fawning voices, was impossible. There was no getting past it. It was hopelessly and offensively nonconformist.

Clifford left them alone, and she learnt to do the same: she just went by without looking at them, and they stared as if she were a walking wax figure. When he had to deal with them, Clifford was rather haughty and contemptuous; one could no longer afford to be friendly. In fact he was altogether rather supercilious and contemptuous of anyone not in his own class. He stood his ground, without any attempt at conciliation. And he was neither liked nor disliked by the people; he was just part of things, like the pit-bank and Wragby itself.

But Clifford was really extremely shy and self-conscious now he was lamed. He hated seeing anyone except just the personal servants. For he had to sit in a wheeled chair or a sort of bath-chair. Nevertheless he was just as carefully dressed as ever, by his expensive tailors, and he wore the careful Bond Street neckties just as before, and from the top he looked just as smart and impressive as ever. He had never been one of the modern ladylike young men: rather bucolic even, with his ruddy face and broad shoulders. But his very quiet, hesitating voice, and his eyes, at the same time bold and frightened, assured and uncertain, revealed his nature. His manner was often offensively supercilious, and then again modest and self-effacing, almost tremulous.

Connie and he were attached to one another, in the aloof modern way. He was much too hurt in himself, the great shock of his maiming, to be easy and flippant. He was a hurt thing. And as such Connie stuck to him passionately.

But she could not help feeling how little connection he really had with people. The miners were, in a sense, his own men; but he saw them as objects rather than men, parts of the pit rather than parts of life, crude raw phenomena rather than human beings along with him. He was in some way afraid of them, he could not bear to have them look at him now he was lame. And their queer, crude life seemed as unnatural as that of hedgehogs.

He was remotely interested; but like a man looking down a microscope, or up a telescope. He was not in touch. He was not in actual touch with anybody, save, traditionally, with Wragby, and, through the close bond of family defense, with Emma. Beyond this nothing really touched him. Connie felt that she herself didn't really, not really touch him; perhaps there was nothing to get at ultimately; just a negation of human contact.

Yet he was absolutely dependent on her, he needed her every moment. Big and strong as he was, he was helpless. He could wheel himself about in a wheeled chair, and he had a sort of bath-chair with a motor attachment, in which he could puff slowly round the park. But alone he was like a lost thing. He needed Connie to be there, to assure him he existed at all.

Still he was ambitious. He had taken to writing stories; curious, very personal stories about people he had known. Clever, rather spiteful, and yet, in some mysterious way, meaningless. The observation was extraordinary and peculiar. But there was no touch, no actual contact. It was as if the whole thing took place in a vacuum. And since the field of life is largely an artificially-lighted stage today, the stories were curiously true to modern life, to the modern psychology, that is.

Clifford was almost morbidly sensitive about these stories. He wanted everyone to think them good, of the best, *ne plus ultra*. They appeared in the most modern magazines, and were praised and blamed as usual. But to Clifford the blame was torture, like knives goading him. It was as if the whole of his being were in his stories.

Connie helped him as much as she could. At first she was thrilled. He talked everything over with her monotonously, insistently, persistently, and she had to respond with all her might. It was as if her whole soul and body and sex had to rouse up and pass into these stories of his. This thrilled her and absorbed her.

Of physical life they lived very little. She had to superintend the house. But the housekeeper had served Sir Geoffrey for many years, and the dried-up, elderly, superlatively correct female . . . you could hardly call her a parlor-maid, or even a woman . . . who waited at table, had been in the house for forty years. Even the very housemaids were no longer young. It was awful! What could you do with such a place, but leave it alone! All these endless rooms that nobody used, all the Midlands routine, the mechanical cleanliness and the mechanical order! Clifford had insisted on a new cook, an experienced woman who had served him in his rooms in London. For the rest the place seemed run by mechanical anarchy. Everything went on in pretty good order, strict cleanliness, and strict punctuality; even pretty strict honesty. And yet, to Connie, it was a methodical anarchy. No warmth of feeling united it organically. The house seemed as dreary as a disused street.

What could she do but leave it alone . . . ? So she left it alone. Miss Chatterley came sometimes, with her aristocratic thin face, and triumphed, finding nothing altered. She would never forgive Connie for ousting her from her union in consciousness with her brother. It was she, Emma, who should be bringing forth the stories, these books, with him; the Chatterley stories, something new in the world, that *they,* the Chatterleys, had put there. There was no other standard. There was no organic connection with the thought and expression that had gone before. Only something new in the world: the Chatterley books, entirely personal.

Connie's father, when he paid a flying visit to Wragby, said in private to his daughter: As for Clifford's writing, it's smart, but there's nothing in it. It won't last! . . . Connie looked at the burly Scottish knight who had done himself well all his life, and her eyes, her big, still-wondering blue eyes became vague. Nothing in it! What did he mean by *nothing in it?* If the critics praised it, and Clifford's name was almost famous, and it even brought in money . . . what did her father mean by saying there was nothing in Clifford's writing? What else could there be?

For Connie had adopted the standard of the young: what there was in the moment was everything. And moments followed one another without necessarily belonging to one another.

It was in her second winter at Wragby her father said to her: "I hope, Connie, you won't let circumstances force you into being a *demi-vierge.*"

"A *demi-vierge!*" replied Connie vaguely. "Why? Why not?"

"Unless you like it, of course!" said her father hastily. To Clifford he said the same, when the two men were alone: "I'm afraid it doesn't quite suit Connie to be a *demi-vierge.*"

"A half-virgin!" replied Clifford, translating the phrase to be sure of it.

He thought for a moment, then flushed very red. He was angry and offended.

"In what way doesn't it suit her?" he asked stiffly.

"She's getting thin . . . angular. It's not her style. She's not the pilchard sort of little slip of a girl, she's a bonny Scotch trout."

"Without the spots, of course!" said Clifford.

He wanted to say something later to Connie about the demi-vierge business . . . the half-virgin state of her affairs. But he could not bring himself to do it. He was at once too intimate with her and not intimate enough. He was so very much at one with her, in his mind and hers, but bodily they were non-existent to one another, and neither could bear to drag in the corpus delicti. They were so intimate, and utterly out of touch.

Connie guessed, however, that her father had said something, and that something was in Clifford's mind. She knew that he didn't mind whether she were demi-vierge or demi-monde, so long as he didn't absolutely know, and wasn't made to see. What the eye doesn't see and the mind doesn't know, doesn't exist.

Connie and Clifford had now been nearly two years at Wragby, living their vague life of absorption in Clifford and his work. Their interests had never ceased to flow together over his work. They talked and wrestled in the throes of composition, and felt as if something were happening, really happening, really in the void.

And thus far it was a life: in the void. For the rest it was non-existence. Wragby was there, the servants . . . but spectral, not really existing. Connie went for walks in the park, and in the woods that joined the park, and enjoyed the solitude and the mystery, kicked the brown leaves of autumn, and picked the primroses of spring. But it was all a dream; or rather it was like the simulacrum of reality. The oak-leaves were to her like oak-leaves seen ruffling in a mirror, she herself was a figure somebody had read about, picking primroses that were only shadows or memories, or words. No substance to her or anything . . . no touch, no contact! Only this life with Clifford, this endless spinning of webs of yarn, of the minutiae of consciousness, these stories Sir Malcolm said there was nothing in, and they wouldn't last. Why should there be anything in them, why should they last? Sufficient unto the day is the evil thereof. Sufficient unto the moment is the *appearance* of reality.

Clifford had quite a number of friends, acquaintances really, and he invited them to Wragby. He invited all sorts of people, critics and writers, people who would help to praise his books. And they were flattered at being asked to Wragby, and they praised. Connie understood it all perfectly. But why not? This was one of the fleeting patterns in the mirror. What was wrong with it?

She was hostess to these people . . . mostly men. She was hostess also to Clifford's occasional aristocratic relations. Being a soft, ruddy, country-looking girl, inclined to freckles, with big blue eyes, and curling, brown hair, and a soft voice and rather strong, female loins she was considered a little old-fashioned and "womanly." She was not a "little pilchard sort of fish," like a boy. She was too feminine to be quite smart.

So the men, especially those no longer young, were very nice to her indeed. But, knowing what torture poor Clifford would feel at the slightest sign of flirting on her part, she gave them no encouragement at all. She was quiet and vague, she had no contact with them and intended to have none. Clifford was extraordinarily proud of himself.

His relatives treated her quite kindly. She knew that the kindliness indicated a lack of fear, and that these people had no respect for you unless you could frighten them a little. But again she had no contact. She let them be kindly and disdainful, she let them feel they had no need to draw their steel in readiness. She had no real connection with them.

Time went on. Whatever happened, nothing happened, because she was so beautifully out of contact. She and Clifford lived in their ideas and his books. She entertained . . . there were always people in the house. Time went on as the clock does, half-past eight instead of half-past seven.

III

Connie was aware, however, of a growing restlessness. Out of her discon-
nection, a restlessness was taking possession of her like madness. It
twitched her limbs when she didn't want to twitch them, it jerked her spine
when she didn't want to jerk upright but preferred to rest comfortably. It
thrilled inside her body, in her womb, somewhere, till she felt she must jump
into water and swim to get away from it; a mad restlessness. It made her heart
beat violently for no reason. And she was getting thinner.

It was just restlessness. She would rush off across the park, and abandon
Clifford, and lie prone in the bracken. To get away from the house . . . she must
get away from the house and everybody. The wood was her one refuge, her
sanctuary.

But it was not really a refuge, a sanctuary, because she had no connection
with it. It was only a place where she could get away from the rest. She never
really touched the spirit of the wood itself . . . if it had any such nonsensical
thing.

Vaguely she knew herself that she was going to pieces in some way. Vaguely
she knew she was out of connection: she had lost touch with the substantial and
vital world. Only Clifford and his books, which did not exist . . . which had
nothing in them! Void to void. Vaguely she knew. But it was like beating her
head against a stone.

Her father warned her again: "Why don't you get yourself a beau, Connie?
Do you all the good in the world."

That winter Michaelis came for a few days. He was a young Irishman who
had already made a large fortune by his plays in America. He had been taken up
quite enthusiastically for a time by smart society in London, for he wrote smart
society plays. Then gradually smart society realized that it had been made ridiculous at the hands of a down-at-heel Dublin street-rat, and revulsion came.
Michaelis was the last word in what was caddish and bounderish. He was discovered to be anti-English, and to the class that made this discovery this was
worse than the dirtiest crime. He was cut dead, and his corpse thrown into the
refuse-can.

Nevertheless Michaelis had his apartment in Mayfair, and walked down
Bond Street the image of a gentleman, for you cannot get even the best tailors
to cut their low-down customers, when the customers pay.

Clifford was inviting the young man of thirty at an inauspicious moment in
that young man's career. Yet Clifford did not hesitate. Michaelis had the ear of
a few million people, probably; and, being a hopeless outsider, he would no
doubt be grateful to be asked down to Wragby at this juncture, when the rest of
the smart world was cutting him. Being grateful, he would no doubt do Clifford
"good" over there in America. Kudos! A man gets a lot of kudos, whatever that
may be, by being talked about in the right way, especially "over there." Clifford
was a coming man; and it was remarkable what a sound publicity instinct he
had. In the end Michaelis did him most nobly in a play, and Clifford was a sort
of popular hero. Till the reaction, when he found he had been made ridiculous.

Connie wondered a little over Clifford's blind, imperious instinct to become
known: known, that is, to the vast amorphous world he did not himself know,
and of which he was uneasily afraid; known as a writer, as a first-class modern

writer. Connie was aware from successful, old, hearty, bluffing Sir Malcolm, that artists did advertise themselves, and exert themselves to put their goods over. But her father used channels ready-made, used by all the other R.A.'s who sold their pictures. Whereas Clifford discovered new channels of publicity, all kinds. He had all kinds of people at Wragby, without exactly lowering himself. But, determined to build himself a monument of a reputation quickly, he used any handy rubble in the making.

Michaelis arrived duly, in a very neat car, with a chauffeur and a manservant. He was absolutely Bond Street! But at sight of him something in Clifford's country soul recoiled. He wasn't exactly . . . not exactly . . . in fact, he wasn't at all, well, what his appearance intended to imply. To Clifford this was final and enough. Yet he was very polite to the man; to the amazing success in him. The bitch-goddess, as she is called, of Success, roamed, snarling and protective, round the half-humble, half-defiant Michaelis' heels, and intimidated Clifford completely: for he wanted to prostitute himself to the bitch-goddess Success also, if only she would have him.

Michaelis obviously wasn't an Englishman, in spite of all the tailors, hatters, barbers, booters of the very best quarter of London. No, no, he obviously wasn't an Englishman: the wrong sort of flattish, pale face and bearing; and the wrong sort of grievance. He had a grudge and a grievance: that was obvious to any true-born English gentleman, who would scorn to let such a thing appear blatant in his own demeanor. Poor Michaelis had been much kicked, so that he had a slightly tail-between-the-legs look even now. He had pushed his way by sheer instinct and sheerer effrontery on to the stage and to the front of it, with his plays. He had caught the public. And he had thought the kicking days were over. Alas, they weren't. . . . They never would be. For he, in a sense, asked to be kicked. He pined to be where he didn't belong . . . among the English upper classes. And how they enjoyed the various kicks they got at him! And how he hated them!

Nevertheless he traveled with his manservant and his very neat car, this Dublin mongrel.

There was something about him that Connie liked. He didn't put on airs to himself; he had no illusions about himself. He talked to Clifford sensibly, briefly, practically about all the things Clifford wanted to know. He didn't expand or let himself go. He knew he had been asked down to Wragby to be made use of, and like an old, shrewd, almost indifferent business man, or big-business man, he let himself be asked questions, and he answered with as little waste of feeling as possible.

"Money!" he said. "Money is a sort of instinct. It's a sort of property of nature in a man to make money. It's nothing you do. It's no trick you play. It's a sort of permanent accident of your own nature; once you start, you make money, and you go on; up to a point, I suppose."

"But you've got to begin," said Clifford.

"Oh, quite! You've got to get in. You can do nothing if you are kept outside. You've got to beat your way in. Once you've done that, you can't help it!"

"But could you have made money except by plays?" asked Clifford.

"Oh, probably not! I may be a good writer or I may be a bad one, but a writer and a writer of plays is what I am, and I've got to be. There's no question of that."

"And you think it's a writer of popular plays that you've got to be?" asked Connie.

"There, exactly!" he said, turning to her in a sudden flash. "There's nothing in it! There's nothing in popularity. There's nothing in the public, if it comes to that. There's nothing really in my plays to *make* them popular. It's not that. They just are, like the weather . . . the sort that will *have* to be . . . for the time being."

He turned his slow, rather full eyes, that had been drowned in such fathomless disillusion, on Connie, and she trembled a little. He seemed so old . . . endlessly old, built up of layers of disillusion, going down in him generation after generation, like geological strata; and at the same time he was forlorn like a child. An outcast, in a certain sense; but with the desperate bravery of his rat-like existence.

"At least it's wonderful what you've done at your time of life," said Clifford contemplatively.

"I'm thirty . . . yes, I'm thirty!" said Michaelis, sharply and suddenly, with a curious laugh; hollow, triumphant, and bitter.

"And are you alone?" asked Connie.

"How do you mean? Do I live alone? I've got my servant. He's a Greek, so he says, and quite incompetent. But I keep him. And I'm going to marry. Oh, yes, I must marry."

"It sounds like going to have your tonsils cut," laughed Connie. "Will it be an effort?"

He looked at her admiringly. "Well, Lady Chatterley, somehow it will! I find . . . excuse me . . . I find I can't marry an Englishwoman, not even an Irishwoman. . . ."

"Try an American," said Clifford.

"Oh, American!" he laughed a hollow laugh. "No, I've asked my man if he will find me a Turk or something . . . something nearer to the Oriental."

Connie really wondered at this queer, melancholy specimen of extraordinary success; it was said he had an income of fifty thousand dollars from America alone. Sometimes he was handsome: sometimes as he looked sideways, downwards, and the light fell on him, he had the silent, enduring beauty of a carved ivory negro mask, with his rather full eyes, and the strong queerly-arched brows, the immobile compressed mouth; that momentary but revealed immobility, an immobility, a timelessness which the Buddha aims at, and which negroes express sometimes without even aiming at it; something old, old, and acquiescent in the race! Aeons of acquiescence in race destiny, instead of our individual resistance. And then a swimming through, like rats in a dark river. Connie felt a sudden, strange leap of sympathy for him, a leap mingled with compassion, and tinged with repulsion, amounting almost to love. The outsider! The outsider! And they called him a bounder! How much more bounderish and assertive Clifford looked! How much stupider!

Michaelis knew at once he had made an impression on her. He turned his full, hazel, slightly prominent eyes on her in a look of pure detachment. He was estimating her, and the extent of the impression he had made. With the English nothing could save him from being the eternal outsider, not even love. Yet women sometimes fell for him. . . . Englishwomen too.

He knew just where he was with Clifford. They were two alien dogs which would have liked to snarl at one another, but which smiled instead, perforce. But with the woman he was not quite so sure.

Breakfast was served in the bedrooms; Clifford never appeared before lunch, and the dining-room was a little dreary. After coffee Michaelis, restless and ill-sitting soul, wondered what he should do. It was a fine November day . . . fine for Wragby. He looked over the melancholy park. My God! What a place!

He sent a servant to ask, could he be of any service to Lady Chatterley: he thought of driving into Sheffield. The answer came, would he care to go up to Lady Chatterley's sitting-room?

Connie had a sitting-room on the third floor, the top floor of the central portion of the house. Clifford's rooms were on the ground floor, of course. Michaelis was flattered by being asked up to Lady Chatterley's own parlor. He followed blindly after the servant . . . he never noticed things, or had contact with his surroundings. In her room he did glance vaguely round at the fine German reproductions of Renoir and Cézanne.

"It's very pleasant up here," he said, with his queer smile, as if it hurt him to smile, showing his teeth. "You are wise to get up to the top."

"Yes, I think so," she said.

Her room was the only gay, modern one in the house, the only spot in Wragby where her personality was at all revealed. Clifford had never seen it, and she asked very few people up.

Now she and Michaelis sat on opposite sides of the fire and talked. She asked him about himself, his mother and father, his brothers . . . other people were always something of a wonder to her, and when her sympathy was awakened she was quite devoid of class feeling. Michaelis talked frankly about himself, quite frankly, without affectation, simply revealing his bitter, indifferent, stray-dog's soul, then showing a gleam of revengeful pride in his success.

"But why are you such a lonely bird?" Connie asked him; and again he looked at her, with his full, searching, hazel look.

"Some birds *are* that way," he replied. Then, with a touch of familiar irony: "But, look here, what about yourself? Aren't you by way of being a lonely bird yourself?" Connie, a little startled, thought about it for a few moments, and then she said: "Only in a way! Not altogether, like you!"

"Am I altogether a lonely bird?" he asked, with his queer grin of a smile, as if he had toothache; it was so wry, and his eyes were so perfectly unchangingly melancholy, or stoical, or disillusioned, or afraid.

"Why?" she said, a little breathless, as she looked at him. "You are, aren't you?"

She felt a terrible appeal coming to her from him, that made her almost lose her balance.

"Oh, you're quite right!" he said, turning his head away, and looking sideways, downwards, with that strange immobility of an old race that is hardly here in our present day. It was that that really made Connie lose her power to see him detached from herself.

He looked up at her with the full glance that saw everything, registered everything. At the same time, the infant crying in the night was crying out of his breast to her, in a way that affected her very womb.

"It's awfully nice of you to think of me," he said laconically.

"Why shouldn't I think of you?" she exclaimed, with hardly breath to utter it.

He gave the wry, quick hiss of a laugh.

"Oh, in that way! . . . May I hold your hand for a minute?" he asked suddenly, fixing his eyes on her with almost hypnotic power, and sending out an appeal that affected her direct in the womb.

She stared at him, dazed and transfixed, and he went over and kneeled beside her, and took her two feet close in his two hands, and buried his face in her lap, remaining motionless. She was perfectly dim and dazed, looking down in a sort of amazement at the rather tender nape of his neck, feeling his face pressing against her. In all her burning dismay, she could not help putting her hand, with tenderness and compassion, on the defenseless nape of his neck, and he trembled, with a deep shudder.

Then he looked up at her with that awful appeal in his full, glowing eyes. She was utterly incapable of resisting it. From her breast flowed the answering, immense yearning over him; she must give him anything, anything.

He was a curious and very gentle lover, very gentle with the woman, trembling uncontrollably, and yet at the same time detached, aware, aware of every sound outside.

To her it meant nothing except that she gave herself to him. And at length he ceased to quiver any more, and lay quite still, quite still. Then, with dim, compassionate fingers, she stroked his head, that lay on her breast.

When he rose, he kissed both her hands, then both her feet, in their suede slippers, and in silence went away to the end of the room, where he stood with his back to her. There was silence for some minutes. Then he turned and came to her again as she sat in her old place by the fire.

"And now, I suppose you'll hate me!" he said in a quiet, inevitable way. She looked up at him quickly.

"Why should I?" she asked.

"They mostly do," he said; then he caught himself up. "I mean . . . a woman is supposed to."

"This is the last moment when I ought to hate you," she said resentfully.

"I know! I know! It should be so! You're *frightfully* good to me . . ." he cried miserably.

She wondered why he should be miserable. "Won't you sit down again?" she said. He glanced at the door.

"Sir Clifford!" he said, "won't he . . . won't he be . . . ?"

She paused a moment to consider. "Perhaps!" she said. And she looked up at him. "I don't want Clifford to know . . . not even to suspect. It would hurt him so much. But I don't think it's wrong, do you?"

"Wrong! Good God, no! You're only too infinitely good to me. . . . I can hardly bear it."

He turned aside, and she saw that in another moment he would be sobbing.

"But we needn't let Clifford know, need we?" she pleaded. "It *would* hurt him so. And if he never knows, never suspects, it hurts nobody."

"Me!" he said, almost fiercely; "he'll know nothing from me! You see if he does. Me give myself away! Ha! Ha!" he laughed hollowly, cynically at such an idea. She watched him in wonder. He said to her: "May I kiss your hand and go? I'll run into Sheffield I think, and lunch there, if I may, and be back to tea. May I do anything for you? May I be sure you don't hate me—and that you won't?"—he ended with a desperate note of cynicism.

"No, I don't hate you," she said. "I think you're nice."

"Ah!" he said to her fiercely, "I'd rather you said that to me than that you love me! It means such a lot more. . . . Till afternoon then. I've plenty to think about till then." He kissed her hands humbly and was gone.

"I don't think I can stand that young man," said Clifford at lunch.

"Why?" asked Connie.

"He's such a bounder underneath his veneer . . . just waiting to bounce us "

"I think people have been so unkind to him," said Connie.

"Do you wonder? And do you think he employs his shining hours doing deeds of kindness?"

"I think he has a certain sort of generosity."

"Towards whom?"

"I don't quite know."

"Naturally you don't. I'm afraid you mistake unscrupulousness for generosity."

Connie paused. Did she? It was just possible. Yet the unscrupulousness of Michaelis had a certain fascination for her. He went whole lengths where Clifford only crept a few timid paces. In his way he had conquered the world, which was what Clifford wanted to do. Ways and means . . . ? Were those of Michaelis more despicable than those of Clifford? Was the way the poor outsider had shoved and bounced himself forward in person, and by the back doors, any worse than Clifford's way of advertising himself into prominence? The bitch-goddess, Success, was trailed by thousands of gasping dogs with lolling tongues. The one that got her first was the real dog among dogs, if you go by success! So Michaelis could keep his tail up.

The queer thing was, he didn't. He came back towards tea-time with a large handful of violets and lilies, and the same hang-dog expression. Connie wondered sometimes if it were a sort of mask to disarm opposition, because it was almost too fixed. Was he really such a sad dog?

His sad-dog sort of extinguished self persisted all the evening, though through it Clifford felt the inner effrontery. Connie didn't feel it, perhaps because it was not directed against woman; only against men, and their presumptions and assumptions. That indestructible, inward effrontery in the meager fellow was what made men so down on Michaelis. His very presence was an affront to a man of society, cloak it as he might in an assumed good manner.

Connie was in love with him, but she managed to sit with her embroidery and let the men talk, and not give herself away. As for Michaelis, he was perfect; exactly the same melancholic, attentive, aloof young fellow of the previous evening, millions of degrees remote from his hosts, but laconically playing up to them to the required amount, and never coming forth to them for a moment. Connie felt he must have forgotten the morning. He had not forgotten. But he knew where he was . . . in the same old place outside, where the born outsiders are. He didn't take the love-making altogether personally. He knew it would not change him from an ownerless dog, whom everybody begrudges its golden collar, into a comfortable society dog.

The final fact being that at the very bottom of his soul he *was* an outsider, and anti-social, and he accepted the fact inwardly, no matter how Bond-Streety he was on the outside. His isolation was a necessity to him; just as the appearance of conformity and mixing-in with the smart people was also a necessity.

But occasional love, as a comfort and soothing, was also a good thing, and he was not ungrateful. On the contrary, he was burningly, poignantly grateful for a piece of natural, spontaneous kindness: almost to tears. Beneath his pale, immobile, disillusioned face, his child's soul was sobbing with gratitude to the woman, and burning to come to her again; just as his outcast soul was knowing he would keep really clear of her.

He found an opportunity to say to her, as they were lighting the candles in the hall:

"May I come?"

"I'll come to you," she said.

"Oh, good!"

He waited for her a long time . . . but she came.

He was the trembling excited sort of lover, whose crisis soon came, and was finished. There was something curiously childlike and defenseless about him. His defenses were all in his wits and cunning, his very instincts of cunning, and when these were in abeyance he seemed doubly naked and like a child, of unfinished, tender flesh, and somehow struggling helplessly.

He aroused in the woman a wild sort of compassion and yearning, and a wild, craving physical desire. The physical desire he did not satisfy in her; he was always come and finished so quickly, then shrinking down on her breast, and recovering somewhat his effrontery while she lay dazed, disappointed, lost.

But then she soon learnt to hold him, to keep him there inside her when his crisis was over. And there he was generous and curiously potent; he stayed firm inside her, given to her, while she was active . . . wildly, passionately active, coming to her own crisis. And as he felt the frenzy of her achieving her own orgasmic satisfaction from his hard, erect passivity, he had a curious sense of pride and satisfaction.

"Ah, how good!" she whispered tremulously, and she became quite still, clinging to him. And he lay there in his own isolation, but somehow proud.

He stayed that time only the three days, and to Clifford was exactly the same as on the first evening; to Connie also. There was no breaking down his external man.

He wrote to Connie with the same plaintive melancholy note as ever, sometimes witty, and touched with a queer, sexless affection. A kind of hopeless affection he seemed to feel for her, and the essential remoteness remained the same. He was hopeless at the very core of him, and he wanted to be hopeless. He rather hated hope. *"Une immense espérance an traversé la terre,"* he read somewhere, and his comment was: "—and it's darned-well drowned everything worth having."

Connie never really understood him, but in her way, she loved him. And all the time she felt the reflection of his hopelessness in her. She couldn't quite, quite love in hopelessness. And he, being hopeless, couldn't ever quite love at all.

So they went on for quite a time, writing, and meeting occasionally in London. She still wanted the physical, sexual thrill she could get with him by her own activity, his little orgasm being over. And he still wanted to give it her. Which was enough to keep them connected.

And enough to give her a subtle sort of self-assurance, something blind and a little arrogant. It was an almost mechanical confidence in her own powers, and went with a great cheerfulness.

She was terrifically cheerful at Wragby. And she used all her aroused cheerfulness and satisfaction to stimulate Clifford, so that he wrote his best at this time, and was almost happy in his strange blind way. He really reaped the fruits of the sensual satisfaction she got out of Michaelis' male passivity erect inside her. But of course he never knew it, and, if he had, he wouldn't have said thank-you!

Yet when those days of her grand joyful cheerfulness and stimulus were gone, quite gone, and she was depressed and irritable, how Clifford longed for them again! Perhaps if he'd known he might even have wished to get her and Michaelis together again.

IV

Connie always had a foreboding of the hopelessness of her affair with Mick, as people called him. Yet other men seemed to mean nothing to her. She was attached to Clifford. He wanted a good deal of her life and she gave it to him. But she wanted a good deal from the life of a man, and this Clifford did not give her; could not. There were occasional spasms of Michaelis. But, as she knew by foreboding, that would come to an end. Mick *couldn't* keep anything up. It was part of his very being that he must break off any connection, and be loose, isolated, absolutely lone dog again. It was his major necessity, even though he always said: She turned me down!

The world is supposed to be full of possibilities, but they narrow down to pretty few in most personal experience. There's lots of good fish in the sea . . . maybe . . . but the vast masses seem to be mackerel or herring, and if you're not mackerel or herring yourself, you are likely to find very few good fish in the sea.

Clifford was making strides into fame, and even money. People came to see him. Connie nearly always had somebody at Wragby. But if they weren't mackerel they were herring, with an occasional cat-fish, or conger-eel.

There were a few regular men, constants; men who had been at Cambridge with Clifford. There was Tommy Dukes, who had remained in the army, and was a Brigadier-General. "The army leaves me time to think, and saves me from having to face the battle of life," he said.

There was Charles May, an Irishman, who wrote scientifically about stars. There was Hammond, another writer. All were about the same age as Clifford; the young intellectuals of the day. They all believed in the life of the mind. What you did apart from that was your private affair, and didn't much matter. No one thinks of enquiring of another person at what hour he retires to the privy. It isn't interesting to anyone but the person concerned.

And so with most of the matters of ordinary life . . . how you make your money, or whether you love your wife, or if you have "affairs." All these matters concern only the person concerned, and, like going to the privy, have no interest for anyone else.

"The whole point about the sexual problem," said Hammond, who was a tall thin fellow with a wife and two children, but much more closely connected with a typewriter, "is that there is no point to it. Strictly there is no problem. We don't want to follow a man into the W.C., so why should we want to follow him into bed with a woman? And therein lies the problem. If we took no more notice of the one thing than the other, there'd be no problem. It's all utterly senseless and pointless; a matter of misplaced curiosity."

"Quite, Hammond, quite! But if someone starts making love to Julia, you begin to simmer; and if he goes on, you are soon at boiling point." . . . Julia was Hammond's wife.

"Why, exactly! So I should be if he began to urinate in a corner of my drawing-room. There's a place for all these things."

"You mean you wouldn't mind if he made love to Julia in some discreet alcove?"

Charlie May was slightly satirical, for he had flirted a very little with Julia, and Hammond had cut up very roughly.

"Of course I should mind. Sex is a private thing between me and Julia; and of course I should mind anyone else trying to mix in."

"As a matter of fact," said the lean and freckled Tommy Dukes, who looked much more Irish than May, who was pale and rather fat: "as a matter of fact, Hammond, you have a strong property instinct, and a strong will to self-assertion, and you want success. Since I've been in the army definitely, I've got out of the way of the world, and now I see how inordinately strong the craving for self-assertion and success is in men. It is enormously over-developed. All our individuality has run that way. And of course men like you think you'll get through better with a woman's backing. That's why you're so jealous. That's what sex is to you . . . a vital little dynamo between you and Julia to bring success. If you began to be unsuccessful you'd begin to flirt, like Charlie, who isn't successful. Married people like you and Julia have labels on you, like travellers' trunks. Julia is labelled *Mrs. Arnold B. Hammond* . . . just like a trunk on the railway that belongs to somebody. And you are labelled Arnold B. Hammond, c/o *Mrs. Arnold B. Hammond*. Oh, you're quite right, you're quite right! The life of the mind needs a comfortable house and decent cooking. You're quite right. It even needs posterity. But it all hinges on the instinct for success. That is the pivot on which all things turn."

Hammond looked rather piqued. He was rather proud of the integrity of his mind, and of his *not* being a time-server. None the less, he did want success.

"It's quite true, you can't live without cash," said May. "You've got to have a certain amount of it to be able to live and get along . . . even to be free to *think* you must have a certain amount of money, or your stomach stops you. But it seems to me you might leave the labels off sex. We're free to talk to anybody; so why shouldn't we be free to make love to any woman who inclines us that way?"

"There speaks the lascivious Celt," said Clifford.

"Lascivious! Well, why not? I can't see I do a woman any more harm by sleeping with her than by dancing with her . . . or even talking to her about the weather. It's just an interchange of sensations instead of ideas, so why not?"

"Be as promiscuous as the rabbits!" said Hammond.

"Why not? What's wrong with rabbits? Are they any worse than a neurotic, revolutionary humanity, full of nervous hate?"

"But we're not rabbits, even so," said Hammond.

"Precisely! I have my mind: I have certain calculations to make in certain astronomical matters that concern me almost more than life or death. Sometimes indigestion interferes with me. Hunger would interfere with me disastrously. In the same way starved sex interferes with me. What then?"

"I should have thought sexual indigestion from surfeit would have interfered with you more seriously," said Hammond satirically.

"Not it! I don't over-eat myself, and I don't over-fuck myself. One has a choice about eating too much. But you would absolutely starve me."

"Not at all. You can marry."

"How do you know I can? It may not suit the process of my mind. Marriage might . . . and would . . . stultify my mental processes. I'm not properly pivoted that way . . . and so must I be chained in a kennel like a monk? All rot and funk, my boy. I must live and do my calculations. I need women sometimes. I refuse to make a mountain of it, and I refuse anybody's moral condemnation or prohibition. I'd be ashamed to see a woman walking around with my name-label on her, address and railway station, like a wardrobe trunk."

These two men had not forgiven each other about the Julia flirtation.

"It's an amusing idea, Charlie," said Dukes, "that sex is just another form of talk, where you act the words instead of saying them. I suppose it's quite true. I suppose we might exchange as many sensations and emotions with women as we do ideas about the weather, and so on. Sex might be a sort of normal, physical conversation between a man and a woman. You don't talk to a woman unless you have ideas in common: that is you don't talk with any interest. And in the same way, unless you had some emotion or sympathy in common with a woman you wouldn't sleep with her. But if you had. . . ."

"If you *have* the proper sort of emotion or sympathy with a woman, you *ought* to sleep with her," said May. "It's the only decent thing to do with her. Just as, when you are interested talking to someone, the only decent thing is to have the talk out. You don't prudishly put your tongue between your teeth and bit it. You just say out your say. And the same the other way."

"No," said Hammond. "It's wrong. You, for example, May, you squander half your force with women. You'll never really do what you should do, with a fine mind such as yours. Too much of you goes the other way."

"Maybe it does. . . . and too little of you goes that way, Hammond, my boy, married or not. You can keep the purity and integrity of your mind, but it's going damned dry. Your pure mind is going as dry as fiddlesticks, from what I see of it. You're simply talking it down."

Tommy Dukes burst into a laugh.

"Go it, you two minds!" he said. "Look at me . . . I don't do any high and pure mental work, nothing but jot down a few ideas. And yet I neither marry nor run after women. I think Charlie's quite right; if he wants to run after the women, he's quite free not to run too often. But I wouldn't prohibit him from running. As for Hammond, he's got a property instinct, so naturally the straight road and the narrow gate are right for him. You'll see he'll be an English Man of Letters before he's done, A. B. C. from top to toe. Then there's me. I'm nothing. Just a squib. And what about you, Clifford? Do you think sex is a dynamo to help a man on to success in the world?"

Clifford rarely talked much at these times. He never held forth; his ideas were really not vital enough for it, he was too confused and emotional. Now he blushed and looked uncomfortable.

"Well!" he said, "being myself *hors de combat,* I don't see I've anything to say on the matter."

"Not at all," said Dukes; "the top of you's by no means *hors de combat.* You've got the life of the mind sound and intact. So let us hear your ideas."

"Well," stammered Clifford, "even then I don't suppose I have much idea. . . . I suppose marry-and-have-done-with-it would pretty well stand for what I think. Though of course between a man and woman who care for one another, it is a great thing."

"What sort of great thing?" said Tommy.

"Oh, . . . it perfects the intimacy," said Clifford, uneasy as a woman in such talk.

"Well, Charlie and I believe that sex is a sort of communication like speech. Let any woman start a sex conversation with me, and it's natural for me to go to bed with her to finish it, all in due season. Unfortunately no woman makes any particular start with me, so I go to bed by myself; and am none the worse for it. . . . I hope so anyway, for how should I know? Anyhow I've no starry calculations to be interfered with, and no immortal works to write. I'm merely a fellow skulking in the army. . . ."

Silence fell. The four men smoked. And Connie sat there and put another stitch in her sewing. . . . Yes, she sat there! She had to sit mum. She had to be quiet as a mouse, not to interfere with the immensely important speculations of these highly-mental gentlemen. But she had to be there. They didn't get on so well without her; their ideas didn't flow so freely. Clifford was much more edgy and nervous, he got cold feet much quicker in Connie's absence, and the talk didn't run. Tommy Dukes came off best; he was a little inspired by her presence. Hammond she didn't really like; he seemed so selfish in a mental way. And Charles May, though she Lked something about him, seemed a little distasteful and messy, in spite of his stars.

How many evenings had Connie sat and listened to the manifestations of these four men! these, and one or two others. That they never seemed to get anywhere didn't trouble her deeply. She liked to hear what they had to say, especially when Tommy was there. It was fun. Instead of men kissing you, and touching you, they revealed their minds to you. It was great fun! But what cold minds!

And also it was a little irritating. She had more respect for Michaelis, on whose name they all poured such withering contempt, as a little mongrel arriviste, and uneducated bounder of the worst sort. Mongrel and bounder or not, he jumped to his own conclusions. He didn't merely walk round them with millions of words, in the parade of the life of the mind.

Connie quite liked the life of the mind, and got a great thrill out of it. But she did think it overdid itself a little. She loved being there, amidst the tobacco smoke of those famous evenings of the cronies, as she called them privately to herself. She was infinitely amused, and proud too, that even their talking they could not do without her silent presence. She had an immense respect for thought . . . and these men, at least, tried to think honestly. But somehow there was a cat, and it wouldn't jump. They all alike talked at something, though what it was, for the life of her she couldn't say. It was something that Mick didn't clear, either.

But then Mick wasn't trying to do anything, but just get through his life, and put as much across other people as they tried to put across him. He was really anti-social, which was what Clifford and his cronies had against him. Clifford and his cronies were not anti-social; they were more or less bent on saving mankind, or on instructing it, to say the least.

There was a gorgeous talk on Sunday evening, when the conversation drifted again to love.

"Blest be the tie that binds
Our hearts in kindred something-or-other"—

said Tommy Dukes. "I'd like to know what the tie is. . . . The tie that binds us just now is mental friction on one another. And, apart from that, there's damned little tie between us. We bust apart, and say spiteful things about one another, like all the other damned intellectuals in the world. Damned everybodies, as far as that goes, for they all do it. Else we bust apart, and cover up the spiteful things we feel against one another by saying false sugaries. It's a curious thing that the mental life seems to flourish with its roots in spite, ineffable and fathomless spite. Always has been so! Look at Socrates, in Plato, and his bunch round him! The sheer spite of it all, just sheer joy in pulling somebody else to bits. . . . Protagoras, or whoever it was! And Alcibiades, and all the other little disciple dogs joining in the fray! I must say it makes one prefer Buddha, quietly sitting under a bo-tree, or Jesus, telling his disciples little Sunday stories, peacefully, and without any mental fireworks. No, there's something wrong with the mental life, radically. It's rooted in spite and envy, envy and spite. Ye shall know the tree by its fruit."

"I don't think we're altogether so spiteful," protested Clifford.

"My dear Clifford, think of the way we talk each other over, all of us. I'm rather worse than anybody else, myself. Because I infinitely prefer the spontaneous spite to the concocted sugaries; now they *are* poison; when I begin saying what a fine fellow Clifford is, etc.,etc., then poor Clifford is to be pitied. For God's sake, all of you, say spiteful things about me, then I shall know I mean something to you. Don't say sugaries, or I'm done."

"Oh, but I do think we honestly like one another," said Hammond.

"I tell you we must . . . we say such spiteful things to one another, about one another, behind our backs! I'm the worst."

"And I do think you confuse the mental life with the critical activity. I agree with you, Socrates gave the critical activity a grand start, but he did more than that," said Charlie May, rather magisterially. The cronies had such a curious pomposity under their assumed modesty. It was all so *ex cathedra,* and it all pretended to be so humble.

Dukes refused to be drawn out about Socrates.

"That's quite true, criticism and knowledge are not the same thing," said Hammond.

"They aren't, of course," chimed in Berry, a brown, shy young man, who had called to see Dukes, and was staying the night.

They all looked at him as if the ass had spoken.

"I wasn't talking about knowledge. . . . I was talking about the mental life," laughed Dukes. "Real knowledge comes out of the whole corpus of the consciousness; out of your belly and your penis as much as out of your brain and mind. The mind can only analyze and rationalize. Set the mind and the reason to cock it over the rest, and all they can do is criticize, and make a deadness. I say *all* they can do. It is vastly important. My God, the world needs criticizing to death. Therefore let's live the mental life, and glory in our spite, and strip the rotten old show. But, mind you, it's like this; while you *live* your life, you are in some way an organic whole with all life. But once you start the mental life you pluck the apple. You've severed the connection between the apple and the tree: the organic connection. And if you've got nothing in your life *but* the mental life, then you yourself are a plucked apple . . . you've fallen off the tree. And then it is a logical necessity to be spiteful, just as it's a natural necessity for a plucked apple to go bad."

Clifford made big eyes: it was all stuff to him. Connie secretly laughed to herself.

"Well then, we're all plucked apples," said Hammond, rather acidly and petulantly.

"So let's make cider of ourselves," said Charlie.

"But what do you think of Bolshevism?" put in the brown Berry, as if everything had led up to it.

"Bravo!" roared Charlie. "What do you think of Bolshevism?"

"Come on! Let's make hay of Bolshevism!" said Dukes.

"I'm afraid Bolshevism is a large question," said Hammond, shaking his head seriously.

"Bolshevism, it seems to me," said Charlie, "is just a superlative hatred of the thing they call the bourgeois; and what the bourgeois is, isn't quite defined. It is Capitalism, among other things. Feelings and emotions are also so decidedly bourgeois that you have to invent a man without them.

"Then the individual, especially the *personal* man, is bourgeois: so he must be suppressed. You must submerge yourselves in the great thing, the Soviet-social thing. Even an organism is bourgeois: so the ideal must be mechanical. The only thing that is a unit, non-organic, composed of many different, and equally essential parts, is the machine. Each man a machine-part, and the driving power of the machine, hate . . . hate of the bourgeois. That, to me, is Bolshevism."

"Absolutely!" said Tommy. "But also, it seems to me a perfect description of the whole of the industrial ideal. It's the factory-owner's ideal in a nut-shell; except that he would deny that the driving power was hate. Hate it is, all the same: hate of life itself. Just look at these Midlands, if it isn't plainly written up . . . but it's all part of the life of the mind, it's a logical development."

"I deny that Bolshevism is logical, it rejects the major part of the premises," said Hammond.

"My dear man, it allows the material premise; so does the pure mind . . . exclusively."

"At least Bolshevism has got down to rock bottom," said Charlie.

"Rock bottom! The bottom that has no bottom! The Bolshevists will have the finest army in the world in a very short time, with the finest mechanical equipment."

"But this thing can't go on . . . this hate business. There must be a reaction . . ." said Hammond.

"Well, we've been waiting for years . . . we wait longer. Hate's a growing thing like anything else. It's the inevitable outcome of forcing ideas on to life, of forcing one's deepest instincts; our deepest feelings we force according to certain ideas. We drive ourselves with a formula, like a machine. The logical mind pretends to rule the roost, and the roost turns into pure hate. We're all Bolshevists, only we are hypocrites. The Russians are Bolshevists without hypocrisy."

"But there are many other ways," said Hammond, "than the Soviet way. The Bolshevists aren't really intelligent."

"Of course not. But sometimes it's intelligent to be half-witted: if you want to make your end. Personally, I consider Bolshevism half-witted; but so do I consider our social life in the west half-witted. So I even consider our far-famed mental life half-witted. We're all as cold as crétins, we're all as passionless as idiots. We're all of us Bolshevists, only we give it another name. We think we're gods . . . men like gods! It's just the same as Bolshevism. One has to be human, and have a heart and a penis, if one is going to escape being either a god or a bolshevist . . . for they are the same thing: they're both too good to be true."

Out of the disapproving silence came Berry's anxious question:

"You do believe in love then, Tommy, don't you?"

"You lovely lad!" said Tommy. "No, my cherub, nine times out of ten, no! Love's another of those half-witted performances to-day. Fellows with swaying waists fucking little jazz girls with small-boy buttocks, like two collar studs! Do you mean that sort of love? Or the joint-property, make-a-success-of-it, my-husband-my-wife sort of love? No, my fine fellow, I don't believe in it at all!"

"But you do believe in something?"

"Me? Oh, intellectually I believe in having a good heart, a chirpy penis, a lively intelligence, and the courage to say 'shit!' in front of a lady."

"Well, you've got them all," said Berry.

Tommy Dukes roared with laughter. "You angel boy! If only I had! If only I had! No; my heart's as numb as a potato, my penis droops and never lifts its head up, I dare rather cut him clean off than say 'shit!' in front of my mother or my aunt . . . they are real ladies, mind you; and I'm not really intelligent, I'm only a 'mental-lifer.' It would be wonderful to be intelligent: then one would be alive in all the parts mentioned and unmentionable. The penis rouses his head and says: How do you do? to any really intelligent person. Renoir said he painted his pictures with his penis . . . he did too, lovely pictures! I wish I did something with mine. God! when one can only talk! Another torture added to Hades! And Socrates started it."

"There are nice women in the world," said Connie, lifting her head up and speaking at last.

The men resented it . . . she should have pretended to hear nothing. They hated her admitting she had attended so closely to such talk.

"My God!— *'If they be not nice to me*
What care I how nice they be?'—

No, it's hopeless! I just simply can't vibrate in unison with a woman. There's no woman I can really want when I'm faced with her, and I'm not going to start forcing myself to it . . . My God, no! I'll remain as I am, and lead the mental life. It's the only honest thing I can do. I can be quite happy *talking* to women; but it's all pure, hopelessly pure. Hopelessly pure! What do you say, Hildebrand, my chicken?"

"It's much less complicated if one stays pure," said Berry.

"Yes, life is all too simple!"

V

On a frosty morning with a little February sun, Clifford and Connie went for a walk across the park to the wood. That is, Clifford chuffed in his motor-chair, and Connie walked beside him.

The hard air was still sulphurous, but they were both used to it. Round the near horizon went the haze, opalescent with frost and smoke, and on the top lay the small blue sky; so that it was like being inside an enclosure, always inside. Life always a dream or a frenzy, inside an enclosure.

The sheep coughed in the rough, sere grass of the park, where frost lay bluish in the sockets of the tufts. Across the park ran a path to the wood-gate, a fine ribbon of pink. Clifford had had it newly gravelled with sifted gravel from the pit-bank. When the rock and refuse of the underworld had burned and given off its sulphur, it turned bright pink, shrimp-colored on dry days, darker, crab-colored on wet. Now it was pale shrimp-color, with a bluish-white hoar of frost. It always pleased Connie, this underfoot of sifted, bright pink. It's an ill-wind that brings nobody good.

Clifford steered cautiously down the slope of the knoll from the hall, and Connie kept her hand on the chair. In front lay the wood, the hazel thicket nearest, the purplish density of oaks beyond. From the wood's edge rabbits bobbed and nibbled. Rooks suddenly rose in a black train and went trailing off over the little slope.

Connie opened the wood-gate, and Clifford puffed slowly through into the broad riding that ran up an incline between the clean-whipped thickets of the hazel. The wood was a remnant of the great forest where Robin Hood hunted, and this riding was an old, old thoroughfare coming across country. But now, of course, it was only a riding through the private wood. The road from Mansfield swerved round to the north.

In the wood everything was motionless, the old leaves on the ground keeping the frost on their underside. A jay called harshly, many little birds fluttered. But there was no game; no pheasants. They had been killed off during the war, and the wood had been left unprotected, till now Clifford had got his gamekeeper again.

Clifford loved the wood; he loved the old oak trees. He felt they were his own through generations. He wanted to protect them. He wanted this place inviolate, shut off from the world.

The chair chuffed slowly up the incline, rocking and jolting on the frozen clods. And suddenly, on the left, came a clearing where there was nothing but a ravel of dead bracken, a thin and spindling sappling leaning here and there, big sawn stumps showing their tops and their grasping roots, lifeless. And patches of blackness where the woodmen had burned the brushwood and rubbish.

This was one of the places that Sir Geoffrey had cut during the war for trench timber. The whole knoll, which rose softly on the right of the riding, was denuded and strangely forlorn. On the crown of the knoll where the oaks had stood, now was bareness; and from there you could look out over the trees to the colliery railway, and the new works at Stacks Gate. Connie had stood and looked, it was a breach in the pure seclusion of the wood. It let in the world. But she didn't tell Clifford.

This denuded place always made Clifford curiously angry. He had been through the war, had seen what it meant. But he didn't get really angry till he saw this bare hill. He was having it re-planted. But it made him hate Sir Geoffrey.

Clifford sat with a fixed face as the chair slowly mounted. When they came to the top of the rise he stopped; he would not risk the long and very jolty downslope. He sat looking at the greenish sweep of the riding downwards, a clear way through the bracken and oaks. It swerved at the bottom of the hill and disappeared; but it had such a lovely easy curve, of knights riding and ladies on palfreys.

"I consider this is really the heart of England," said Clifford to Connie, as he sat there in the dim February sunshine.

"Do you?" she said, seating herself, in her blue knitted dress, on a stump by the path.

"I do! This is the old England, the heart of it; and I intend to keep it intact."

"Oh, yes!" said Connie. But, as she said it she heard the eleven-o'clock hooters at Stacks Gate colliery. Clifford was too used to the sound to notice.

"I want this wood perfect . . . untouched. I want nobody to trespass in it," said Clifford.

There was a certain pathos. The wood still had some of the mystery of wild, old England; but Sir Geoffrey's cuttings during the war had given it a blow. How still the trees were, with their crinkly, innumerable twigs against the sky, and their grey, obstinate trunks rising from the brown bracken! How safely the birds flitted among them! And once there had been deer, and archers, and monks paddling along on asses. The place remembered, still remembered.

Clifford sat in the pale sun, with the light on his smooth, rather blond hair, his reddish full face inscrutable.

"I mind more, not having a son, when I come here, than any other time," he said.

"But the wood is older than your family," said Connie gently.

"Quite!" said Clifford. "But we've preserved it. Except for us it would go . . . it would be gone already, like the rest of the forest. One must preserve some of the Old England!"

"Must one?" said Connie. "If it has to be preserved, and preserved against the new England? It's sad, I know."

"If some of the old England isn't preserved, there'll be no England at all," said Clifford. "And we who have this kind of property, and the feeling for it, *must* preserve it."

There was a sad pause.

"Yes, for a little while," said Connie.

"For a little while! It's all we can do. We can only do our bit. I feel every man of my family has done his bit here, since we've had the place. One may go against convention, but one must keep up tradition." Again there was a pause.

"What tradition?" asked Connie.

"The tradition of England! of this!"

"Yes," she said slowly.

"That's why having a son helps; one is only a link in a chain," he said.

Connie was not keen on chains, but she said nothing. She was thinking of the curious impersonality of his desire for a son.

"I'm sorry we can't have a son," she said.

He looked at her steadily, with his full, pale-blue eyes.

"It would almost be a good thing if you had a child by another man," he said. "If we brought it up at Wragby, it would belong to us and to the place. I don't believe very intensely in fatherhood. If we had the child to rear, it would be our own, and it would carry on. Don't you think it's worth considering?"

Connie looked up at him at last. The child, her child, was just an "it" to him. It . . . it . . . it!

"But what about the other man?" she asked.

"Does it matter very much? Do these things really affect us very deeply? . . . You had that lover in Germany . . . what is it now? Nothing almost. It seems to me that it isn't these little acts and little connections we make in our lives that matter so very much. They pass away, and where are they? Where . . . Where are the snows of yesteryear? . . . It's what endures through one's life that matters; my own life matters to me, in its long continuance and development. But what do the occasional connections matter? And the occasional sexual connections specially. If people don't exaggerate them ridiculously, they pass like the mating of birds. And so they should. What does it matter? It's the life-long companionship that matters. It's the living together from day to day, not the sleeping together once or twice. You and I are married, no matter what happens to us. We have the habit of each other. And habit, to my thinking, is more vital than any occasional excitement. The long, slow, enduring thing . . . that's what we live by . . . not the occasional spasm of any sort. Little by little, living together, two people fall into a sort of unison, they vibrate so intricately to one another. That's the real secret of marriage, not sex; at least not the simple function of sex. You and I are interwoven in a marriage. If we stick to that we ought to be able to arrange this sex thing, as we arrange going to the dentist; since fate has given us a checkmate physically there."

Connie sat and listened in a sort of wonder, and a sort of fear. She did not know if he was right or not. There was Michaelis, whom she loved; so she said to herself. But her love was somehow only an excursion from her marriage with Clifford; the long, slow habit of intimacy, formed through years of suffering and patience. Perhaps the human soul needs excursions, and must not be denied them. But the point of an excursion is that you come home again.

"And wouldn't you mind *what* man's child I got?" she asked.

"Why, Connie, I should trust your natural instinct of decency and selection. You just wouldn't let the wrong sort of fellow touch you."

She thought of Michaelis! He was absolutely Clifford's idea of the wrong sort of fellow.

"But men and women may have different feelings about the wrong sort of fellow," she said.

"No," he replied. "You cared for me. I don't believe you would ever care for a man who was purely antipathetic to me. Your rhythm wouldn't let you."

She was silent. Logic might be unanswerable because it was so absolutely wrong.

"And should you expect me to tell you?" she asked, glancing up at him almost furtively.

"Not at all. I'd better not know. . . . But you do agree with me, don't you, that the casual sex thing is nothing, compared to the long life lived together? Don't you think one can just subordinate the sex thing to the necessities of a long life? Just use it, since that's what we're driven to? After all, *do* these temporary excitements matter? Isn't the whole problem of life the slow building up of an integral personality, through the years? living an integrated life? There's no point in a disintegrated life. If lack of sex is going to disintegrate you, then go out and have a love affair. If lack of a child is going to disintegrate you, then have a child if you possibly can. But only do these things so that you have an integrated life, that makes a long harmonious thing. And you and I can do that together. . . . don't you think? . . . if we adapt ourselves to the necessities, and at the same time weave the adaptation together into a piece with our steadily-lived life. Don't you agree?"

Connie was a little overwhelmed by his words. She knew he was right theoretically. But when she actually touched her steadily-lived life with him she hesitated. . . . Was it actually her destiny to go on weaving herself into his life all the rest of her life? Nothing else?

Was it just that? She was to be content to weave a steady life with him, all one fabric, but perhaps brocaded with the occasional flower of an adventure. But how could she know what she would feel next year? How could one ever know? How could one say Yes? for years and years? The little yes, gone on a breath! Why should one be pinned down by that butterfly word? Of course it had to flutter away and be gone, to be followed by other yes's and no's! Like the straying of butterflies.

"I think you're right, Clifford. And as far as I can see I agree with you. Only life may turn quite a new face on it all."

"But until life turns a new face on it all, you do agree?"

"Oh, yes! I think I do, really."

She was watching a brown spaniel that had run out of a side-path, and was looking toward them with lifted nose, making a soft, fluffy bark. A man with a gun strode swiftly, softly out after the dog, facing their way as if about to attack them; then stopped instead, saluted, and was turning down hill. It was only the new gamekeeper, but he had frightened Connie, he seemed to emerge with such a swift menace. That was how she had seen him, like a sudden rush of a threat out of nowhere.

He was a man in dark green velveteens and gaiters . . . the old style, with a red face and red moustache and distant eyes. He was going quickly down hill.

"Mellors!" called Clifford.

The man faced lightly round, and saluted with a quick little gesture, a soldier! "Will you turn the chair round and get it started? That makes it easier," said Clifford.

The man at once slung his gun over his shoulder, and came forward with the same curious swift, yet soft movements, as if keeping invisible. He was moderately tall and lean, and was silent. He did not look at Connie at all, only at the chair.

"Connie, this is the new gamekeeper, Mellors. You haven't spoken to her ladyship yet, Mellors?"

"No, Sir!" came the ready, neutral words.

The man lifted his hat as he stood, showing his thick, almost fair hair. He stared straight into Connie's eyes, with a perfect, fearless, impersonal look, as if he wanted to see what she was like. He made her feel shy. She bent her head to him shyly, and he changed his hat to his left hand and made her a slight bow, like a gentleman; but he said nothing at all. He remained for a moment still, with his hat in his hand.

"But you've been here some time, haven't you?" Connie said to him.

"Eight months, Madam . . . your Ladyship!" he corrected himself calmly.

"And do you like it?"

She looked him in the eyes. His eyes narrowed a little, with irony, perhaps with impudence.

"Why, yes, thank you, your Ladyship! I was reared here. . . ." He gave another slight bow, turned, put his hat on, and strode to take hold of the chair. His voice on the last words had fallen into the heavy broad drag of the dialect . . . perhaps also in mockery, because there had been no trace of dialect before. He might almost be a gentleman. Anyhow, he was a curious, quick, separate fellow, alone, but sure of himself.

Clifford started the little engine, the man carefully turned the chair, and set it nose-forwards to the incline that curved gently to the dark hazel thicket.

"Is that all then, Sir Clifford?" asked the man.

"No, you'd better come along in case she sticks. The engine isn't really strong enough for the uphill work." The man glanced round for his dog . . . a thoughtful glance. The spaniel looked at him and faintly moved its tail. A little smile, mocking or teasing her, yet gentle, came into his eyes for a moment, then faded away, and his face was expressionless. They went fairly quickly down the slope, the man with his hand on the rail of the chair, steadying it. He looked like a free soldier rather than a servant. And something about him reminded Connie of Tommy Dukes.

When they came to the hazel grove, Connie suddenly ran forward and opened the gate into the park. As she stood holding it, the two men looked at her in passing. Clifford critically, the other man with a curious, cool wonder; impersonally wanting to see what she looked like. And she saw in his blue, impersonal eyes a look of suffering and detachment, yet a certain warmth. But why was he aloof, apart?

Clifford stopped the chair, once through the gate, and the man came quickly, courteously to close it.

"Why did you run to open?" asked Clifford in his quiet, calm voice, that showed he was displeased. "Mellors would have done it."

"I thought you would go straight ahead," said Connie.

"And leave you to run after us?" said Clifford.

"Oh, well, I like to run sometimes!"

Mellors took the chair again, looking perfectly unheeding, yet Connie felt he noted everything. As he pushed the chair up the steepish rise of the knoll in the park, he breathed rather quickly, through parted lips. He was rather frail, really. Curiously full of vitality, but a little frail and quenched. Her woman's instinct sensed it.

Connie fell back, let the chair go on. The day had greyed over: the small blue sky that had poised low on its circular rims of haze was closed in again, the lid was down, there was a raw coldness. It was going to snow. All grey, all grey! the world looked worn out.

The chair waited at the top of the pink path. Clifford looked around for Connie.

"Not tired, are you?" he asked.

"Oh, no!" she said.

But she was. A strange, weary yearning, a dissatisfaction had started in her. Clifford did not notice: those were not things he was aware of. But the stranger knew. To Connie, everything in her world and life seemed worn out, and her dissatisfaction was older than the hills.

They came to the house, and round to the back, where there were no steps. Clifford managed to swing himself over on to the low, wheeled house-chair; he was very strong and agile with his arms. Then Connie lifted the burden of his dead legs after him.

The keeper, waiting at attention to be dismissed, watched everything narrowly, missing nothing. He went pale, with a sort of fear, when he saw Connie lifting the inert legs of the man in her arms, into the other chair, Clifford pivoting round as she did so. He was frightened.

"Thanks, then, for the help, Mellors," said Clifford casually, as he began to wheel down the passage to the servants' quarters.

"Nothing else, Sir?" came the neutral voice, like one in a dream.

"Nothing. Good-morning!"

"Good-morning, Sir."

"Good-morning! It was kind of you to push the chair up that hill. . . . I hope it wasn't too heavy for you," said Connie, looking back at the keeper outside the door.

His eyes came to her in an instant, as if wakened up. He was aware of her.

"Oh, no, not heavy!" he said quickly. Then his voice dropped again into the broad sound of the vernacular: "Good-mornin' to your ladyship!"

"Who is your gamekeeper?" Connie asked at lunch.

"Mellors! You saw him," said Clifford.

"Yes, but where did he come from?"

"Nowhere! He was a Tevershall boy . . . son of a collier, I believe."

"And was he a collier himself?"

"Blacksmith on the pit-bank, I believe: overhead smith. But he was keeper here for two years before the war . . . before he joined up. My father always had a good opinion of him, so when he came back, and went to the pit for a blacksmith's job, I just took him back here as keeper. I was really very glad to get him . . . it's almost impossible to find a good man round here, for a gamekeeper . . . and it needs a man who knows the people."

"And isn't he married?"

"He was. But his wife went off with . . . with various men . . . but finally with a collier at Stacks Gate, and I believe she's living there still."

"So this man is alone?"

"More or less! He has a mother in the village . . . and a child, I believe."

Clifford looked at Connie, with his pale, slightly prominent blue eyes, in which a certain vagueness was coming. He seemed alert in the foreground, but the background was like the Midlands atmosphere, haze, smoky mist. And the haze seemed to be creeping forward. So when he stared at Connie in his peculiar way, giving her his peculiar, precise information, she felt all the background of his mind filling up with mist, with nothingness. And it frightened her. It made him seem impersonal, almost to idiocy.

And dimly she realized one of the great laws of the human soul: that when the emotional soul receives a wounding shock, which does not kill the body, the soul seems to recover as the body recovers. But this is only appearance. It is really only the mechanism of the reassumed habit. Slowly, slowly the wound to the soul begins to make itself felt, like a bruise, which only slowly deepens its terrible ache, till it fills all the psyche. And when we think we have recovered and forgotten, it is then that the terrible after-effects have to be encountered at their worst.

So it was with Clifford. Once he was "well," once he was back at Wragby, and writing his stories, and feeling sure of life, in spite of all, he seemed to forget, and to have recovered all his equanimity. But now, as the years went by, slowly, slowly, Connie felt the bruise of fear and horror coming up, and spreading in him. For a time it had been so deep as to be numb, as it were non-existent. Now slowly it began to assert itself in a spread of fear, almost paralysis. Mentally he still was alert. But the paralysis, the bruise of the too great shock was gradually spreading in his affective self.

And as it spread in him, Connie felt it spread in her. An inward dread, an emptiness, an indifference to everything gradually spread in her soul. When Clifford was aroused, he could still talk brilliantly, and, as it were, command the future: as when, in the wood, he talked about her having a child, and giving an heir to Wragby. But the day after, all the brilliant words seemed like dead leaves, crumpling up and turning to powder, meaning really nothing, blown away on any gust of wind. They were not the leafy words of an effective life, young with energy and belonging to the tree. They were the hosts of fallen leaves of a life that is ineffectual.

So it seemed to her everywhere. The colliers at Tevershall were talking again of a strike, and it seemed to Connie there again it was not a manifestation of energy, it was the bruise of the war that had been in abeyance, slowly rising to the surface and creating the great ache of unrest, and stupor of discontent. The bruise was deep, deep, deep . . . the bruise of the false inhuman war. It would take many years for the living blood of the generations to dissolve the vast black clot of bruised blood, deep inside their souls and bodies. And it would need a new hope.

Poor Connie! As the years drew on it was the fear of nothingness in her life that affected her. Clifford's mental life and hers gradually began to feel like nothingness. Their marriage, their integrated life based on a habit of intimacy, that he talked about: there were days when it all became utterly blank and nothing. It was words, just so many words. The only reality was nothingness, and over it a hypocrisy of words.

There was Clifford's success: the bitch-goddess! It was true he was almost famous, and his books brought him in a thousand pounds. His photograph appeared everywhere. There was a bust of him in one of the galleries, and a portrait of him in two galleries. He seemed the most modern of modern voices. With his uncanny lame instinct for publicity, he had become in four or five years one of the best known of the young "intellectuals." Where the intellect came in, Connie did not quite see. Clifford was really clever at that slightly humorous analysis of people and motives which leaves everything in bits at the end. But it was rather like puppies tearing the sofa cushions to bits; except that it was not young and playful, but curiously old, and rather obstinately conceited. It was weird and it was nothing. This was the feeling that echoed and re-echoed at the bottom of Connie's soul: it was all nothing, a wonderful display of nothingness. At the same time a display. A display! a display! a display!

Michaelis had seized upon Clifford as the central figure for a play; already he had sketched in the plot, and written the first act. For Michaelis was even better than Clifford at making a display of nothingness. It was the last bit of passion left in these men: the passion for making a display. Sexually they were passionless, even dead. And now it was not money that Michaelis was after. Clifford had never been primarily out for money, though he made it where he could, for money is the seal and stamp of success. And success was what they wanted. They wanted, both of them, to make a real display . . . a man's own very display of himself, that should capture for a time the vast populace.

It was strange . . . the prostitution to the bitch-goddess. To Connie, since she was really outside of it, and since she had grown numb to the thrill of it, it was again nothingness. Even the prostitution to the bitch-goddess was nothingness, though the men prostituted themselves innumerable times. Nothingness even that.

Michaelis wrote to Clifford about the play. Of course she knew about it long ago. And Clifford was again thrilled. He was going to be displayed again, this time somebody was going to display him, and to advantage. He invited Michaelis down to Wragby with Act I.

Michaelis came: in summer, in pale-colored suit and white suède gloves, with mauve orchids for Connie, very lovely, and Act I was a great success. Even Connie was thrilled . . . thrilled to what bit of marrow she had left. And Michaelis, thrilled by his power to thrill, was really wonderful . . . and quite beautiful, in Connie's eyes. She saw in him that ancient motionlessness of a race that can't be disillusioned any more, an extreme, perhaps, of impurity that is pure. On the far side of his supreme prostitution to the bitch-goddess he seemed pure, pure as an African ivory mask that dreams impurity into purity, in its ivory curves and planes.

His moment of sheer thrill with the two Chatterleys, when he simply carried Connie and Clifford away, was one of the supreme moments of Michaelis' life. He had succeeded: he had carried them away. Even Clifford was temporarily in love with him . . . if that is the way one can put it.

So next morning Mick was more uneasy than ever: restless, devoured, with his hands restless in his trouser pockets. Connie had not visited him the night . . . and he had not known where to find her. Coquetry! . . . at his moment of triumph.

He went up to her sitting-room in the morning. She knew he would come. And his restlessness was evident. He asked her about his play . . . did she think it good? He *had* to hear it praised. That affected him with the last thin thrill of passion beyond any sexual orgasm. And she praised it rapturously. Yet all the while, at the bottom of her soul, she knew it was nothing.

"Look here!" he said suddenly at last. "Why don't you and I make a clean thing of it? Why don't we marry?"

"But I am married," she said amazed, and yet feeling nothing.

"Oh, that! . . . he'll divorce you all right. . . . Why don't you and I marry? I want to marry. I know it would be the best thing for me . . . marry and lead a regular life. I lead the deuce of a life, simply tearing myself to pieces. Look here, you and I, we're made for one another . . . hand and glove. Why don't we marry? Do you see any reason why we shouldn't?"

Connie looked at him amazed: and yet she felt nothing. These men, they were all alike, they left everything out. They just went off from the top of their heads as if they were squibs, and expected you to be carried heavenwards along with their own thin sticks.

"But I am married already," she said. "I can't leave Clifford, you know."

"Why not? But why not?" he cried. "He'll hardly know you've gone, after six months. He doesn't know that anybody exists, except himself. Why, the man has no use for you at all, as far as I can see; he's entirely wrapped up in himself."

Connie felt there was truth in this. But she also felt that Mick was hardly making a display of selflessness.

"Aren't all men wrapped up in themselves?" she asked.

"Oh, more or less, I allow. A man's got to be, to get through. But that's not the point. The point is, what sort of a time can a man give a woman? Can he give her a damn good time, or can't he? If he can't he's no right to the woman. . . ." He paused and gazed at her with his full, hazel eyes, almost hypnotic. "Now, I consider," he added, "I can give a woman the darndest good time she can ask for. I think I can guarantee myself."

"And what sort of a good time?" asked Connie, gazing on him still with a sort of amazement, that looked like thrill; and underneath feeling nothing at all.

"Every sort of a good time, damn it, every sort! Dress, jewels up to a point, any night-club you like, know anybody you want to know, live the pace . . . travel and be somebody wherever you go. . . . Darn it, every sort of good time."

He spoke it almost in a brilliancy of triumph, and Connie looked at him as if dazzled, and really feeling nothing at all. Hardly even the surface of her mind was tickled at the glowing prospects he offered her. Hardly even her most outside self responded, that at any other time would have been thrilled. She just got no feeling from it all, she couldn't "go off." She just sat and stared and looked dazzled, and felt nothing, only somewhere she smelt the extraordinary unpleasant smell of the bitch-goddess.

Mick sat on tenterhooks, leaning forward in his chair, glaring at her almost hysterically: and whether he was more anxious out of vanity for her to say Yes! or whether he was more panic-stricken for fear she *should* say Yes—who can tell?

"I should have to think about it," she said. "I couldn't say now. It may seem to you Clifford doesn't count, but he does. When you think how disabled he is. . . ."

"Oh, damn it all! if a fellow's going to trade on his disabilities, I might begin to say how lonely I am, and always have been, and all the rest of the my-eye-Betty-Martin sob-stuff! Damn it all, if a fellow's got nothing but disabilities to recommend him. . . ."

He turned aside, working his hands furiously in his trouser pockets. That evening he said to her:

"You're coming round to my room tonight, aren't you? I don't darned know where your room is."

"All right!" she said.

He was a more excited lover that night, with his strange, small boy's frail nakedness. Connie found it impossible to come to her crisis before he had really finished his. And he roused a certain craving passion in her, with his little boy's nakedness and softness; she had to go on after he had finished, in the wild tumult and heaving of her loins, while he heroically kept himself up, and present in her, with all his will and self-offering, till she brought about her own crisis, with weird little cries.

When at last he drew away from her, he said, in a bitter, almost sneering little voice:

"You couldn't go off at the same time as a man, could you? You'd have to bring yourself off! You'd have to run the show!"

This little speech, at the moment, was one of the shocks of her life. Because that passive sort of giving himself was so obviously his only real mode of intercourse.

"What do you mean?" she said.

"You know what I mean. You keep on for hours after I've gone off . . . and I have to hang on with my teeth till you bring yourself off by your own exertions."

She was stunned by this unexpected piece of brutality, at the moment when she was glowing with a sort of pleasure beyond words, and a sort of love for him. Because after all, like so many modern men, he was finished almost before he had begun. And that forced the woman to be active.

"But you want me to go on, to get my own satisfaction?" she said.

He laughed grimly: "I want it!" he said. "That's good! I want to hang on with my teeth clenched, while you go for me!"

"But don't you?" she insisted.

He avoided the question. "All the darned women are like that," he said. "Either they don't go off at all, as if they were dead in there . . . or else they wait till a chap's really done, and then they start in to bring themselves off, and a chap's got to hang on. I never had a woman yet who went off just at the same moment as I did."

Connie only half heard this piece of novel, masculine information. She was only stunned by his feeling against her . . . his incomprehensible brutality. She felt so innocent.

"But you want me to have my satisfaction too, don't you?" she repeated.

"Oh, all right! I'm quite willing. But I'm darned if hanging on waiting for a woman to go off is much of a game for a man. . . ."

This speech was one of the crucial blows of Connie's life. It killed something in her. She had not been so very keen on Michaelis; till he started it, she did not want him. It was as if she never positively wanted him. But once he had started her, it seemed only natural for her to come to her own crisis with him. Almost she had loved him for it . . . almost that night she loved him, and wanted to marry him.

Perhaps instinctively he knew it, and that was why he had to bring down the whole show with a smash; the house of cards. Her whole sexual feeling for him, or for any man, collapsed that night. Her life fell apart from his as completely as if he had never existed.

And she went through the days drearily. There was nothing now but this empty treadmill of what Clifford called the integrated life, the long living to-

gether of two people, who are in the habit of being in the same house with one
another.

Nothingness! To accept the great nothingness of life seemed to be the one
end of living. All the many busy and important little things that make up the
grand sum-total of nothingness!

VI

"Why don't men and women really like one another nowadays?" Connie
asked Tommy Dukes, who was more or less her oracle.

"Oh, but they do! I don't think since the human species was invented, there
has ever been a time when men and women have liked one another as much as
they do today. Genuine liking! Take myself. . . . I really *like* women better than
men; they are braver, one can be more frank with them."

Connie pondered this.

"Ah, yes, but you never have anything to do with them!" she said.

"I? What am I doing but talking perfectly sincerely to a woman at this moment?"

"Yes, talking. . . ."

"And what more could I do if you were a man, than talk perfectly sincerely
to you?"

"Nothing perhaps. But a woman. . . ."

"A woman wants you to like her and talk to her, and at the same time love
her and desire her; and it seems to me the two things are mutually exclusive."

"But they shouldn't be!"

"No doubt water ought not to be so wet as it is; it overdoes it in wetness. But
there it is! I like women and talk to them, and therefore I don't love them and
desire them. The two things don't happen at the same time in me."

"I think they ought to."

"All right. The fact that things ought to be something else than what they are
is not my department."

Connie considered this. "It isn't true," she said. "Men can love women and
talk to them. I don't see how they can love them *without* talking, and being
friendly and intimate. How can they?"

"Well," he said, "I don't know. What's the use of my generalizing? I only
know my own case. I like women, but I don't desire them. I like talking to
them; but talking to them, though it makes me intimate in one direction, sets
me poles apart from them as far as kissing is concerned. So there you are! But
don't take me as a general example, probably I'm just a special case: one of the
men who like women, but don't love women, and even hate them if they force
me into a pretense of love, or an entangled appearance."

"But doesn't it make you sad?"

"Why should it? Not a bit! I look at Charlie May, and the rest of the men
who have affairs. . . . No, I don't envy them a bit! If fate sent me a woman I
wanted, well and good. Since I don't know any woman I want, and never see
one . . . why, I presume I'm cold, and really *like* some women very much."

"Do you like me?"

"Very much! And you see there's no question of kissing between us, is
there?"

"None at all!" said Connie. "But oughtn't there to be?"

"*Why*, in God's name? I like Clifford, but what would you say if I went and kissed him?"

"But isn't there a difference?"

"Where does it lie, as far as we're concerned? We're all intelligent human beings, and the male and female business is in abeyance. Just in abeyance. How would you like me to start acting up like a continental male at this moment, and parading the sex thing?"

"I should hate it."

"Well then! I tell you, if I'm really a male thing at all, I never run across the female of my species. And I don't miss her, I just *like* women. Who's going to force me into loving, or pretending to love them, working up the sex game?"

"No, I'm not. But isn't something wrong?"

"You may feel it, I don't."

"Yes, I feel something is wrong between men and women. A woman has no glamor for a man any more."

"Has a man for a woman?"

She pondered the other side of the question.

"Not much," she said truthfully.

"Then let's leave it alone, and just be decent and simple, like proper human beings with one another. Be damned to the artificial sex-compulsion! I refuse it!"

Connie knew he was right, really. Yet it left her feeling so forlorn, so forlorn and stray. Like a chip on a dreary pond, she felt. What was the point, of her or anything?

It was her youth which rebelled. These men seemed so old and cold. Everything seemed old and cold. And Michaelis let one down so; he was no good. The men didn't want one; they just didn't really want a woman, even Michaelis didn't.

And the bounders who pretended they did, and started working the sex game, they were worse than ever.

It was just dismal, and one had to put up with it. It was quite true, men had no real glamor for a woman: if you could fool yourself into thinking they had, even as she had fooled herself over Michaelis, that was the best you could do. Meanwhile you just lived on and there was nothing to it. She understood perfectly well why people had cocktail parties, and jazzed, and Charlestoned till they were ready to drop. You had to take it out some way or other, your youth, or it ate you up. But what a ghastly thing, this youth!

"What is your name?" she said playfully to the child. "Won't you tell me your name?"

Sniffs; then very affectedly in a piping voice: "Connie Mellors!"

"Connie Mellors! Well, that's a nice name! And did you come out with your Daddy; and he shot a pussy? But it was a bad pussy!"

The child looked at her, with bold, dark eyes of scrutiny, sizing her up, and her condolence.

"I wanted to stop with my Gran," said the little girl.

"Did you? But where is your Gran?"

The child lifted an arm, pointing down the drive. "At th' cottage."

"At the cottage! And would you like to go back to her?"

Sudden, shuddering quivers of reminiscent sobs. "Yes!"

"Come then, shall I take you? Shall I take you to your Gran? Then your

Daddy can do what he has to do." She turned to the man. "It is your little girl, isn't it?"

He saluted, and made a slight movement of the head in affirmation.

"I suppose I can take her to the cottage?"

"If your Ladyship wishes."

Again he looked into her eyes, with that calm, searching detached glance. A man very much alone, and on his own.

"Would you like to come with me to the cottage, to your Gran, dear?"

The child peeped up again. "Yes!" she simpered.

Connie disliked her; the spoilt, false little female. Nevertheless she wiped her face, and took her hand. The keeper saluted in silence.

"Good morning!" said Connie.

It was nearly a mile to the cottage, and Connie senior was well bored by Connie junior by the time the gamekeeper's picturesque little home was in sight. The child was already as full to the brim with tricks as a little monkey, and so self-assured.

At the cottage the door stood open, and there was a rattling heard inside. Connie lingered, the child slipped her hand, and ran indoors.

"Gran! Gran!"

"Why, are yer back a'ready!"

The grandmother had been blackleading the stove, it was Saturday morning. She came to the door in her sacking apron, a blacklead-brush in her hand, and a black smudge on her nose. She was a little, rather dry woman.

"Why, whatever?" she said, hastily wiping her arm across her face as she saw Connie standing outside.

"Good morning!" said Connie. "She was crying, so I just brought her home."

The grandmother looked round swiftly at the child:

"Why, wheer was yer Dad?"

The little girl clung to her grandmother's skirts and simpered.

"He was there," said Connie, "but he'd shot a poaching cat, and the child was upset."

"Oh, you'd no right t'ave bothered, Lady Chatterley, I'm sure! I'm sure it was very good of you, but you shouldn't 'ave bothered. Why, did ever you see!"—and the old woman turned to the child. "Fancy Lady Chatterley takin' all that trouble over yer! Why, she shouldn't 'ave bothered!"

"It was no bother, just a walk," said Connie, smiling.

"Why, I'm sure 'twas very kind of you, I must say! So she was crying! I knew there'd be something afore they got far. She's frightened of 'im, that's wheer it is. Seems 'e's almost a stranger to 'er, fair a stranger, and I don't think they're two as'd hit it off very easy. He's got funny ways."

Connie didn't know what to say.

"Look, Gran!" simpered the child.

The old woman looked down at the sixpence in the little girl's hand.

"An' sixpence an' all! Or, your Ladyship, you shouldn't, you shouldn't. Why, isn't Lady Chatterley good to yer! My word, you're a lucky girl this morning!"

She pronounced the name, as all the people did: Chat'ley. "Isn't Lady Chat'-ley *good* to you!" Connie couldn't help looking at the old woman's nose, and the latter again vaguely wiped her face with the back of her wrist, but missed the smudge.

Connie was moving away. "Well, thank you ever so much, Lady Chat'ley, I'm sure. Say thank you to Lady Chat'ley!"—this last to the child.

"Thank you," piped the child.

"There's a dear!" laughed Connie, and she moved away, saying "Good morning," heartily relieved to get away from the contact. Curious, she thought, that that thin, proud man should have that little, sharp woman for a mother!

And the old woman, as soon as Connie was gone, rushed to the bit of mirror in the scullery, and looked at her face. Seeing it, she stamped her foot with impatience. "Of *course,* she had to catch me in my coarse apron, and a dirty face! Nice idea she'd get of me!"

Connie went slowly home to Wragby. "Home!" . . . it was a warm word to use for that great, weary warren. But then it was a word that had had its day. It was somehow cancelled. All the great words, it seemed to Connie, were cancelled for her generation: love, joy, happiness, home, mother, father, husband, all these great dynamic words were half dead now, and dying from day to day. Home was a place you lived in, love was a thing you didn't fool yourself about, joy was a word you applied to a good Charleston, happiness was a term of hypocrisy used to bluff other people, a father was an individual who enjoyed his own existence, a husband was a man you lived with and kept going in spirits. As for sex, the last of the great words, it was just a cocktail term for an excitement that bucked you up for a while, then left you more raggy than ever. Frayed! It was as if the very material you were made of was cheap stuff, and was fraying out to nothing.

All that really remained was a stubborn stoicism: and in that there was a certain pleasure. In the very experience of the nothingness of life, phase after phase, *étape* after *étape,* there was a certain grisly satisfaction. So that's *that!* Always this was the last utterance: home, love, marriage, Michaelis: So that's *that!*—And when one died, the last words to life would be: So that's *that!*—

Money? Perhaps one couldn't say the same there. Money one always wanted. Money, success, the bitch-goddess, as Tommy Dukes persisted in calling it, after Henry James, that was a permanent necessity. You couldn't spend your last sou, and say finally: So that's *that!*—No, if you lived even another ten minutes, you wanted a few more sous for something or other. Just to keep the business mechanically going, you needed money. You had to have it. Money you *have* to have. You needn't really have anything else. So that's *that!*—

Since, of course, it's not your own fault you are alive. Once you are alive, money is a necessity, and the only absolute necessity. All the rest you can get along without, at a pinch. But not money. Emphatically, that's *that!*—

She thought of Michaelis, and the money she might have had with him; and even that she didn't want. She preferred the lesser amount which she helped Clifford to make by his writing. That she actually helped to make.—"Clifford and I together, we make twelve hundred a year out of writing"; so she put it to herself. Make money! Make it! Out of nowhere! Wring it out of the thin air! The last feat to be humanly proud of! The rest all-my-eye-Betty-Martin.

So she plodded home to Clifford, to join forces with him again, to make another story out of nothingness: and a story meant money. Clifford seemed to care very much whether his stories were considered first-class literature or not. Strictly, she didn't care. Nothing in it! said her father. Twelve hundred pounds last year! was the retort simple and final.

If you were young, you just set your teeth, and bit on and held on, till the money began to flow from the invisible; it was a question of power. It was a

question of will; a subtle, subtle, powerful emanation of will out of yourself
brought back to you the mysterious nothingness of money: a word on a bit of
paper. It was a sort of magic, certainly it was triumph. The bitch-goddess! Well,
if one had to prostitute oneself, let it be to a bitch-goddess! One could always
despise her even while one prostituted oneself to her, which was good.

Clifford, of course, had still many childish taboos and fetishes. He wanted to
be thought "really good," which was all cock-a-hoopy nonsense. What was
really good was what actually caught on. It was no good being really good and
getting left with it. It seemed as if most of the "really good" men just missed the
bus. After all you only lived one life, and if you missed the bus, you were just left
on the pavement, along with the rest of the failures.

Connie was contemplating a winter in London with Clifford, next winter.
He and she had caught the bus all right, so they might as well ride on top for a
bit, and show it.

The worst of it was, Clifford tended to become vague, absent, and to fall into
fits of vacant depression. It was the wound to his psyche coming out. But it
made Connie want to scream. Oh, God, if the mechanism of the consciousness
itself was going to go wrong, then what was one to do? Hang it all, one did
one's bit! Was one to be let down *absolutely?*

Sometimes she wept bitterly, but even as she wept she was saying to herself:
Silly fool, wetting hankies! As if that would get you anywhere!

Since Michaelis, she had made up her mind she wanted nothing. That
seemed the simplest solution of the otherwise insoluble. She wanted nothing
more than what she'd got; only she wanted to get ahead with what she'd got:
Clifford, the stories, Wragby, the Lady Chatterley business, money and fame,
such as it was . . . she wanted to go ahead with it all. Love, sex, all that sort of
stuff, just water-ices! Lick it up and forget it. If you don't hang on to it in your
mind, it's nothing. Sex especially . . . nothing! Make up your mind to it, and
you've solved the problem. Sex and a cocktail: they both lasted about as long,
had the same effect, and amounted to about the same thing.

But a child, a baby! that was still one of the sensations. She would venture
very gingerly on that experiment. There was the man to consider, and it
was curious, there wasn't a man in the world whose children you wanted.
Mick's children! Repulsive thought! As lief have a child to a rabbit! Tommy
Dukes? . . . he was very nice, but somehow you couldn't associate him with a
baby, another generation. He ended in himself. And out of all the rest of Clifford's pretty wide acquaintance, there was not a man who did not rouse her
contempt, when she thought of having a child by him. There were several who
would have been quite possible as lovers, even Mick. But as people to have
children with! Ugh! Humiliation and abomination.

So that was that!

Nevertheless, Connie had the child at the back of her mind. Wait! Wait! She
would sift the generations of men through her sieve, and see if she couldn't find
one who would do.—"Go ye into the streets and byways of Jerusalem, and see
if ye can find *a man.*" It had been impossible to find a man in the Jerusalem of
the prophet, though there were thousands of male humans. But *a man!* C'est
une autre chose!

She had an idea that he would have to be a foreigner: not an Englishman, still
less an Irishman. A real foreigner.

But wait! wait! Next winter she would get Clifford to London; the following
winter she would get him abroad to the South of France, Italy. Wait! She was in

no hurry about the child. That was her own private affair, and the one point on
which, in her own queer, female way, she was serious to the bottom of her soul.
She was not going to risk any chance comer, not she! One might take a lover
almost at any moment, but a man who should beget a child on one . . . wait!
wait! it's a very different matter.—"Go ye into the streets and byways of Jerusalem. . . ." It was not a question of love; it was a question of *a man*. Why, one
might even rather hate him, personally. Yet if he was the man, what would
one's personal hate matter? This business concerned another part of oneself.

It had rained as usual, and the paths were too sodden for Clifford's chair, but
Connie would go out. She went out alone every day now, mostly in the wood,
where she was really alone. She saw nobody there.

This day, however, Clifford wanted to send a message to the keeper, and as
the boy was laid up with influenza—somebody always seemed to have influenza
at Wragby—Connie said she would call at the cottage.

The air was soft and dead, as if all the world were slowly dying. Grey and
clammy and silent, even from the shuffling of the collieries, for the pits were
working short time, and today they were stopped altogether. The end of all
things!

In the wood all was utterly inert and motionless, only great drops fell from
the bare boughs, with a hollow little crash. For the rest, among the old trees was
depth within depth of grey, hopeless inertia, nothingness.

Connie walked dimly on. From the old wood came an ancient melancholy,
somehow soothing to her, better than the harsh insentience of the outer world.
She liked the *inwardness* of the remnant of forest, the unspeaking reticence of the
old trees. They seemed a very power of silence, and yet a vital presence. They,
too, were waiting: obstinately, stoically waiting, and giving off a potency of
silence. Perhaps they were only waiting for the end; to be cut down, cleared
away, the end of the forest, for them the end of all things. But perhaps their
strong and aristocratic silence, the silence of strong trees, meant something else.

As she came out of the wood on the north side, the keeper's cottage, a rather
dark, brown stone cottage, with gables and a handsome chimney, looked uninhabited, it was so silent and alone. But a thread of smoke rose from the chimney,
and the little railed-in garden in the front of the house was dug and kept very
tidy. The door was shut.

Now she was here she felt a little shy of the man, with his curious far-seeing
eyes. She did not like bringing him orders, and felt like going away again. She
knocked softly, no one came. She knocked again, but still not loudly. There was
no answer. She peeped through the window, and saw the dark little room, with
its almost sinister privacy, not wanting to be invaded.

She stood and listened, and it seemed to her she heard sounds from the back
of the cottage. Having failed to make herself heard, her mettle was roused, she
would not be defeated.

So she went around the side of the house. At the back of the cottage the land
rose steeply, so the back yard was sunken, and enclosed by a low stone wall. She
turned the corner of the house and stopped. In the little yard two paces beyond
her, the man was washing himself, utterly unaware. He was naked to the hips,
his velveteen breeches slipping down over his slender loins. And his white slim
back was curved over a big bowl of soapy water, in which he ducked his head,
shaking his head with a queer, quick little motion, lifting his slender white arms,
and pressing the soapy water from his ears, quick, subtle as a weasel playing with
water, and utterly alone. Connie backed away round the corner of the house,

and hurried away to the wood. In spite of herself, she had had a shock. After all, merely a man washing himself; commonplace enough. Heaven knows!

Yet in some curious way it was a visionary experience: it had hit her in the middle of the body. She saw the clumsy breeches slipping down over the pure, delicate, white loins, the bones showing a little, and the sense of aloneness, of a creature purely alone, overwhelmed her. Perfect, white, solitary nudity of a creature that lives alone, and inwardly alone. And beyond that, a certain beauty of a pure creature. Not the stuff of beauty, not even the body of beauty, but a lambency, the warm, white flame of a single life, revealing itself in contours that one might touch: a body!

Connie had received the shock of vision in her womb, and she knew it; it lay inside her. But with her mind she was inclined to ridicule. A man washing himself in a backyard! No doubt with evil-smelling yellow soap!—She was rather annoyed; why should she be made to stumble on these vulgar privacies?

So she walked away from herself, but after a while she sat down on a stump. She was too confused to think. But in the coil of her confusion, she was determined to deliver her message to the fellow. She would not be balked. She must give him time to dress himself, but not time to go out. He was probably preparing to go out somewhere.

So she sauntered slowly back, listening. As she came near, the cottage looked just the same. A dog barked, and she knocked at the door, her heart beating in spite of herself.

She heard the man coming lightly downstairs. He opened the door quickly, and startled her. He looked uneasy himself, but instantly a laugh came on his face.

"Lady Chatterley!" he said. "Will you come in?"

His manner was so perfectly easy and good, she stepped over the threshold into the rather dreary little room.

"I only called with a message from Sir Clifford," she said in her soft, rather breathless voice.

The man was looking at her with those blue, all-seeing eyes of his, which made her turn her face aside a little. He thought her comely, almost beautiful, in her shyness, and he took command of the situation himself at once.

"Would you care to sit down?" he asked, presuming she would not. The door stood open.

"No thanks! Sir Clifford wondered if you would . . ." and she delivered her message, looking unconsciously into his eyes again. And now his eyes looked warm and kind, particularly to a woman, wonderfully warm, and kind, and at ease.

"Very good, your Ladyship. I will see to it at once."

Taking an order, his whole self had changed, glazed over with a sort of hardness and distance. Connie hesitated, she ought to go. But she looked round the clean, tidy, rather dreary little sitting-room with something like dismay.

"Do you live here quite alone?" she asked.

"Quite alone, your Ladyship."

"But your mother . . . ?"

"She lives in her own cottage in the village."

"With the child?" asked Connie.

"With the child!"

And his plain, rather worn face took on an indefinable look of derision. It was a face that changed all the time, baffling.

"No," he said, seeing Connie stand at a loss, "my mother comes and cleans up for me on Saturdays; I do the rest myself."

Again Connie looked at him. His eyes were smiling again, a little mockingly, but warm and blue, and somehow kind. She wondered at him. He was in trousers and flannel shirt and a grey tie, his hair soft and damp, his face rather pale and worn-looking. When the eyes ceased to laugh they looked as if they had suffered a great deal, still without losing their warmth. But a pallor of isolation came over him, she was not really there for him.

She wanted to say so many things, and she said nothing. Only she looked up at him again, and remarked:

"I hope I didn't disturb you?"

The faint smile of mockery narrowed his eyes.

"Only combing my hair, if you don't mind. I'm sorry I hadn't a coat on, but then I had no idea who was knocking. Nobody knocks here, and the unexpected sounds ominous."

He went in front of her down the garden path to hold the gate. In his shirt, without the clumsy velveteen coat, she saw again how slender he was, thin, stooping a little. Yet, as she passed him, there was something young and bright in his fair hair, and his quick eyes. He would be a man about thirty-seven or eight.

She plodded on into the wood, knowing he was looking after her; he upset her so much, in spite of herself.

And he, as he went indoors, was thinking: "She's nice, she's real! she's nicer than she knows."

She wondered very much about him; he seemed so unlike a gamekeeper, so unlike a working-man anyhow; although he had something in common with the local people. But also something very uncommon.

"The gamekeeper, Mellors, is a curious kind of person," she said to Clifford: "he might almost be a gentleman."

"Might he?" said Clifford. "I hadn't noticed."

"But isn't there something special about him?" Connie insisted.

"I think he's quite a nice fellow, but I know very little about him. He only came out of the army last year, less than a year ago. From India, I rather think. He may have picked up certain tricks out there; perhaps he was an officer's servant, and improved on his position. Some of the men were like that. But it does them no good, they have to fall back into their old places when they get home again."

Connie gazed at Clifford contemplatively. She saw in him the peculiar tight rebuff against anyone of the lower classes who might be really climbing up, which she knew was characteristic of his breed.

"But don't you think there is something special about him?" she asked.

"Frankly, no! Nothing I had noticed."

He looked at her curiously, uneasily, half-suspiciously. And she felt he wasn't telling her the real truth; he wasn't telling himself the real truth, that was it. He disliked any suggestion of a really exceptional human being. People must be more or less at his level, or below it.

Connie felt again the tightness, niggardliness of the men of her generation. They were so tight, so scared of life!

VII

When Connie went up to her bedroom she did what she had not done for a long time: took off all her clothes, and looked at herself naked in the huge mirror. She did not know what she was looking for, or at, very definitely, yet she moved the lamp till it shone full on her.

And she thought, as she had thought so often, . . . what a frail, easily hurt, rather pathetic thing a human body is, naked; somehow a little unfinished, incomplete!

She had been supposed to have a rather good figure, but now she was out of fashion: a little too female, not enough like an adolescent boy. She was not very tall, a bit Scottish and short; but she had a certain fluent, down-slipping grace that might have been beauty. Her skin was faintly tawny, her limbs had a certain stillness, her body should have had a full, down-slipping richness; but it lacked something.

Instead of ripening its firm, down-running curves, her body was flattening and going a little harsh. It was as if it had not had enough sun and warmth; it was a little greyish and sapless.

Disappointed of its real womanhood, it had not succeeded in becoming boyish, and unsubstantial, and transparent; instead it had gone opaque.

Her breasts were rather small, and dropping pear-shaped. But they were unripe, a little bitter, without meaning hanging there. And her belly had lost the fresh, round gleam it had had when she was young, in the days of her German boy, who had really loved her physically. Then it was young and expectant, with a real look of its own. Now it was going slack, and a little flat, thinner, but with a slack thinness. Her thighs, too, that used to look so quick and glimpsey in their female roundness, somehow they too were going flat, slack, meaningless.

Her body was going meaningless, going full and opaque, so much insignificant substance. It made her feel immensely depressed and hopeless. What hope was there? She was old, old at twenty-seven, with no gleam and sparkle in the flesh. Old through neglect and denial, yes denial. Fashionable women kept their bodies bright like delicate porcelain, by external attention. There was nothing inside the porcelain; but she was not even as bright as that. The mental life! Suddenly she hated it with a rushing fury, the swindle!

She looked in the other mirror's reflection at her back, her waist, her loins. She was getting thinner, but to her it was not becoming. The crumple of her waist at the back, as she bent back to look, was a little weary; and it used to be so gay-looking. And the longish slope of her haunches and her buttocks had lost its gleam and its sense of richness. Gone! Only the German boy had loved it, and he was ten years dead, very nearly. How time went by! Ten years dead, and she was only twenty-seven. That healthy boy with his fresh, clumsy sensuality that she had then been so scornful of! Where would she find it now? It was gone out of men. They had their pathetic, two-seconds spasms like Michaelis; but no healthy human sensuality, that warms the blood and freshens the whole being.

Still she thought the most beautiful part of her was the long-sloping fall of the haunches from the socket of the back, and the slumberous, round stillness of the buttocks. Like hillocks of sand the Arabs say, soft and downward-slipping with a long slope. Here the life still lingered hoping. But here too she was thinner, and going unripe, astringent.

But the front of her body made her miserable. It was already beginning to slacken, with a slack sort of thinness, almost withered, going old before it had ever really lived. She thought of the child she might somehow bear. Was she fit, anyhow?

She slipped into her nightdress, and went to bed, where she sobbed bitterly. And in her bitterness burned a cold indignation against Clifford, and his writings and his talk: against all the men of his sort who defrauded a woman even of her own body.

Unjust! Unjust! The sense of deep physical injustice burned to her very soul.

But in the morning, all the same, she was up at seven, and going downstairs to Clifford. She had to help him in all the intimate things, for he had no man, and refused a woman-servant. The housekeeper's husband, who had known him as a boy, helped him, and did any heavy lifting; but Connie did the personal things, and she did them willingly. It was a demand on her, but she had wanted to do what she could.

So she hardly ever went away from Wragby, and never for more than a day or two; when Mrs. Betts, the housekeeper, attended to Clifford. He, as was inevitable in the course of time, took all the service for granted. It was natural he should.

And yet, deep inside herself, a sense of injustice, of being defrauded, began to burn in Connie. The physical sense of injustice is a dangerous feeling, once it is awakened. It must have outlet, or it eats away the one in whom it is aroused. Poor Clifford, he was not to blame. His was the greater misfortune. It was all part of the general catastrophe.

And yet was he not in a way to blame? This lack of warmth, this lack of the simple, warm, physical contact, was he not to blame for that? He was never really warm, nor even kind, only thoughtful, considerate, in a well-bred, cold sort of way! But never warm as a man can be warm to a woman, as even Connie's father could be warm to her, with the warmth of a man who did himself well, and intended to, but who still could comfort a woman with a bit of his masculine glow.

But Clifford was not like that. His whole race was not like that. They were all inwardly hard and separate, and warmth to them was just bad taste. You had to get on without it, and hold your own; which was all very well if you were of the same class and race. Then you could keep yourself cold and be very estimable, and hold your own, and enjoy the satisfaction of holding it. But if you were of another class and another race it wouldn't do; there was no fun merely holding your own, and feeling you belonged to the ruling class. What was the point, when even the smartest aristocrats had really nothing positive of their own to hold, and their rule was really a farce, not rule at all? What was the point? It was all cold nonsense.

A sense of rebellion smoldered in Connie. What was the good of it all? What was the good of her sacrifice, her devoting her life to Clifford? What was she serving, after all? A cold spirit of vanity, that had no warm human contacts, and that was as corrupt as any low-born Jew, in craving for prostitution to the bitch-goddess, Success. Even Clifford's cool and contactless assurance that he belonged to the ruling class didn't prevent his tongue lolling out of his mouth, as he panted after the bitch-goddess. After all, Michaelis was really more dignified in the matter, and far, far more successful. Really, if you looked closely at Clifford, he was a buffoon, and a buffoon is more humiliating than a bounder.

As between the two men, Michaelis really had far more use for her than

Clifford had. He had even more need of her. Any good nurse can attend to crippled legs! And as for the heroic effort, Michaelis was an heroic rat, and Clifford was very much of a poodle showing off.

There were people staying in the house, among them Clifford's Aunt Eva, Lady Bennerley. She was a thin woman of sixty, with a red nose, a widow, and still something of a "grande dame." She belonged to one of the best families, and had the character to carry it off. Connie liked her, she was so perfectly simple and frank, as far as she intended to be frank, and superficially kind. Inside herself she was a past-mistress in holding her own, and holding other people a little lower. She was not at all a snob: far too sure of herself. She was perfect at the social sport of coolly holding her own, and making other people defer to her.

She was kind to Connie, and tried to worm into her woman's soul with the sharp gimlet of her well-born observations.

"You're quite wonderful, in my opinion," she said to Connie. "You've done wonders for Clifford. I never saw any budding genius myself, and there he is all the rage."—Aunt Eva was quite complacently proud of Clifford's success. Another feather in the family cap. She didn't care a straw about his books, but why should she?

"Oh, I don't think it's my doing," said Connie.

"It must be! Can't be anybody else's. And it seems to me you don't get enough out of it."

"How?"

"Look at the way you are shut up here. I said to Clifford: 'If that child rebels one day, you'll have yourself to thank!' "

"But Clifford never denies me anything," said Connie.

"Look here, my dear child"—and Lady Bennerley laid her thin hand on Connie's arm. "A woman has to live her life, or live to repent not having lived it. Believe me!" And she took another sip of brandy, which maybe was her form of repentance.

"But I do live my life, don't I?"

"Not in my idea! Clifford should bring you to London and let you go about. His sort of friends are all right for him, but what are they for you? If I were you I should think it wasn't good enough. You'll let your youth slip by, and you'll spend your old age, and your middle age too, repenting it."

Her ladyship lapsed into contemplative silence, soothed by th∂ brandy.

But Connie was not keen on going to London, and being steered into the smart world by Lady Bennerley. She didn't feel really smart, it wasn't interesting. And she did feel the peculiar, withering coldness under it all; like the soil of Labrador, which has gay little flowers on its surface, and a foot down is frozen.

Tommy Dukes was at Wragby, and another man, Harry Winterslow, and Jack Strangeways with his wife Olive. The talk was much more desultory than when only the cronies were there, and everybody was a bit bored, for the weather was bad and there was only billiards, and the pianola to dance to.

Olive was reading a book about the future, when babies would be bred in bottles, and women would be "immunized."

"Jolly good thing too!" she said. "Then a woman can live her own life." Strangeways wanted children, and she didn't.

"How'd you like to be immunized?" Winterslow asked her with an ugly smile.

"I hope I am; naturally," she said. "Anyhow the future's going to have more sense, and a woman needn't be dragged down by her *functions*."

"Perhaps she'll float off into space altogether," said Dukes.

"I do think sufficient civilization ought to eliminate a lot of the physical disabilities," said Clifford. "All the love business, for example; it might just as well go. I suppose it would if we could breed babies in bottles."

"No!" cried Olive. "That might leave all the more room for fun."

"I suppose," said Lady Bennerley, contemplatively, "if the love-business went, something else would take its place. Morphia, perhaps. A little morphine in all the air. It would be wonderfully refreshing for everybody."

"The government releasing ether into the air on Saturdays, for a cheerful weekend!" said Jack. "Sounds all right, but where should we be by Wednesday?"

"So long as you can forget your body you are happy," said Lady Bennerley. "And the moment you begin to be aware of your body, you are wretched. So, if civilization is any good, it has to help us forget our bodies, and then time passes happily without our knowing it."

"Help us to get rid of our bodies altogether," said Winterslow. "It's quite time man began to improve on his own nature, especially the physical side of it."

"Imagine if we floated like tobacco smoke," said Connie.

"It won't happen," said Dukes. "Our old show will come flop; our civilization is going to fall. It's going down the bottomless pit, down the chasm. And, believe me, the only bridge across the chasm will be the phallus!"

"Oh! do, *do* be impossible, General!" cried Olive.

"I believe our civilization is going to collapse," said Aunt Eva.

"And what will come after it?" asked Clifford.

"I haven't the faintest idea; but something, I suppose," said the elderly lady.

"Connie says people like wisps of smoke, and Olive says immunized women and babies in bottles, and Dukes says the phallus is the bridge to what comes next. I wonder what it will really be?" said Clifford.

"Oh, don't bother! Let's get on with today," said Olive. "Only hurry up with the breeding bottle, and let us poor women off."

"There might even be real men, in the next phase," said Tommy. "Real, intelligent, wholesome men, and wholesome nice women! Wouldn't that be a change, an enormous change from us? *We're* not men, and the women aren't women. We're only cerebrating makeshifts, mechanical and intellectual experiments. There may even come a civilization of genuine men and women, instead of our little lot of cleverjacks, all at the intelligence-age of seven. It would be even more amazing than men of smoke or babies in bottles."

"Oh, when people begin to talk about real women, I give up," said Olive.

"Certainly nothing but the spirit in us is worth having," said Winterslow.

"Spirits!" said Jack, drinking his whiskey-and-soda.

"Think so? Give me the resurrection of the body!" said Dukes. "But it'll come, in time, when we've shoved the cerebral stone away a bit, the money and the rest. Then we'll get a democracy of touch, instead of a democracy of pocket."

Something echoed inside Connie: "Give me the democracy of touch, the resurrection of the body!" She didn't at all know what it meant, but it comforted her, as meaningless things may do.

Anyhow everything was terribly silly, and she was exasperatedly bored by it all, by Clifford, by Aunt Eva, by Olive and Jack, and Winterslow, and even by

Dukes. Talk, talk, talk! What hell it was, the continual rattle of it!

Then, when all the people went, it was no better. She continued plodding on, but exasperation and irritation had got hold of her body, she couldn't escape. The days seemed to grind by, with curious painfulness, yet nothing happened. Only she was getting thinner; even the housekeeper noticed it, and asked her about herself. Even Tommy Dukes insisted she was not well, though she said she was all right. Only she began to be afraid of the ghastly white tombstones, that peculiar loathsome whiteness of Carrara marble, detestable as false teeth, which stuck up on the hillside, under Tevershall Church, and which she saw with such grim plainness from the park. The bristling of the hideous false teeth of tombstones on the hill affected her with a grisly kind of horror. She felt the time not far off when she would be buried there, added to the ghastly host under the tombstones and the monuments, in these filthy Midlands.

She needed help, and she knew it; so she wrote a little *cri de coeur* to her sister, Hilda. "I'm not well lately, and I don't know what's the matter with me."

Down posted Hilda from Scotland, where she had taken up her abode. She came in March, alone, driving herself in a nimble two-seater. Up the drive she came, tooting up the incline, then sweeping round the oval of grass, where the two great wild beech-trees stood, on the flat in front of the house.

Connie had run out to the steps. Hilda pulled up her car, got out, and kissed her sister.

"But Connie!" she cried. "Whatever is the matter?"

"Nothing!" said Connie, rather shame-facedly; but she knew how she had suffered in contrast to Hilda. Both sisters had the same rather golden, glowing skin, and soft brown hair, and naturally strong, warm physique. But now Connie was thin and earthy-looking, with a scraggy, yellowish neck, that stuck out of her jumper.

"But you're ill, child!" said Hilda, in the soft, rather breathless voice, that both sisters had alike. Hilda was nearly, but not quite, two years older than Connie.

"No, not ill. Perhaps I'm bored," said Connie a little pathetically.

The light of battle glowed in Hilda's face: she was a woman, soft and still as she seemed, of the old amazon sort, not made to fit with men.

"This wretched place!" she said softly, looking at poor old, lumbering Wragby with real hate. She looked soft and warm herself, as a ripe pear, and she was an amazon of the real old breed.

She went quietly in to Clifford. He thought how handsome she looked, but also he shrank from her. His wife's family did not have his sort of manners, or his sort of etiquette. He considered them rather outsiders, but once they got inside they made him jump through the hoop.

He sat square and well-groomed in his chair, his hair sleek and blond, and his face fresh, his blue eyes pale, and a little prominent, his expression inscrutable, but well-bred. Hilda thought it sulky and stupid, and he waited. He had an air of aplomb, but Hilda didn't care what he had an air of; she was up in arms, and if he'd been Pope or Emperor it would have been just the same.

"Connie's looking awfully unwell," she said in her soft voice, fixing him with her beautiful, glowering grey eyes. She looked so maidenly, so did Connie; but he well knew the stone of Scottish obstinacy underneath.

"She's a little thinner," he said.

"Haven't you done anything about it?"

"Do you think it necessary?" he asked, with his suavest English stiffness, for the two things often go together.

Hilda only glowered at him without replying; repartee was not her forte, nor Connie's; so she glowered, and he was much more uncomfortable than if she had said things.

"I'll take her to a doctor," said Hilda at length. "Can you suggest a good one round here?"

"I'm afraid I can't."

"Then I'll take her to London, where we have a doctor we trust."

Though boiling with rage, Clifford said nothing.

"I suppose I may as well stay the night," said Hilda, pulling off her gloves, "and I'll drive her to town tomorrow."

Clifford was yellow at the gills with anger, and at evening the whites of his eyes were a little yellow too. He ran to liver. But Hilda was consistently modest and maidenly.

"You must have a nurse or somebody to look after you personally. You should really have a man-servant," said Hilda as they sat, with apparent calmness, at coffee after dinner. She spoke in her soft, seemingly gentle way, but Clifford felt she was hitting him on the head with a bludgeon.

"You think so?" he said coldly.

"I'm sure! It's necessary. Either that, or father and I must take Connie away for some months. This can't go on."

"What can't go on?"

"Haven't you looked at the child?" asked Hilda, gazing at him full stare. He looked rather like a huge, boiled crayfish, at the moment; or so she thought.

"Connie and I will discuss it," he said.

"I've already discussed it with her," said Hilda.

Clifford had been long enough in the hands of nurses; he hated them, because they left him no real privacy. And a man-servant! . . . he couldn't stand a man hanging round him. Almost better any woman. But why not Connie?

The two sisters drove off in the morning, Connie looking rather like an Easter lamb, rather small beside Hilda, who held the wheel. Sir Malcolm was away, but the Kensington house was open.

The doctor examined Connie carefully, and asked her all about her life. "I see your photograph, and Sir Clifford's, in the illustrated papers sometimes. Almost notorieties, aren't you? That's how the quiet little girls grow up, though you're only a quiet little girl even now, in spite of the illustrated papers. No, no! There's nothing organically wrong, but it won't do! It won't do! Tell Sir Clifford he's got to bring you to town, to take you abroad, and amuse you. You've got to be amused, got to! Your vitality is much too low; no reserves, no reserves. The nerves of the heart a bit queer already: oh, yes. Nothing but nerves; I'd put you right in a month at Cannes or Biarritz. But it mustn't go on, *mustn't,* I tell you, or I won't be answerable for consequences. You're spending your life without renewing it. You've got to be amused, properly, healthily amused. You're spending your vitality without making any. Can't go on, you know. Depression! avoid depression!"

Hilda set her jaw, and that meant something.

Michaelis heard they were in town, and came running with roses. "Why, whatever's wrong?" he cried. "You're a shadow of yourself. Why, I never saw such a change! Why ever didn't you let me know? Come to Nice with me! Come down to Sicily! Go on, come to Sicily with me, it's lovely there just now. You want sun! You want life! Why, you're wasting away! Come away with me! Come to Africa! Oh, hang Sir Clifford! Chuck him, and come along with me. I'll marry you the minute he divorces you. Come along and try a life! God's

love! That place Wragby would kill anybody. Beastly place! Foul place! Kill
anybody! Come away with me into the sun! It's the sun you want, of course,
and a bit of normal life."

But Connie's heart simply stood still at the thought of abandoning Clifford
there and then. She couldn't do it. No . . . no! She just couldn't. She had to go
back to Wragby.

Michaelis was disgusted. Hilda didn't like Michaelis, but she *almost* preferred
him to Clifford. Back went the sisters to the Midlands.

Hilda talked to Clifford, who still had yellow eyeballs when they got back.
He, too, in his way was overwrought; but he had to listen to all Hilda said, to all
the doctor had said, not to what Michaelis had said, of course, and he sat mum
through the ultimatum.

"Here is the address of a good man-servant, who was with an invalid patient
of the doctor's till he died last month. He is really a good man, and fairly sure to
come."

"But I'm *not* an invalid, and I will *not* have a man-servant," said Clifford,
poor devil.

"And here are the addresses of two women; I saw one of them, she would
do very well; a woman of about fifty, quiet, strong, kind, and in her way cultured. . . ."

Clifford only sulked, and would not answer.

"Very well, Clifford. If we don't settle something by tomorrow, I shall telegraph to father, and we shall take Connie away."

"Will Connie go?" asked Clifford.

"She doesn't want to, but she knows she must. Mother died of cancer,
brought on by fretting. We're not running any risks."

So next day Clifford suggested Mrs. Bolton, the Tevershall parish nurse.
Apparently Mrs. Betts had thought of her. Mrs. Bolton was just retiring from
her parish duties to take up private nursing jobs. Clifford had a queer dread of
delivering himself into the hands of a stranger, but this Mrs. Bolton had once
nursed him through scarlet fever, and he knew her.

The two sisters at once called on Mrs. Bolton, in a newish house in a row,
quite select for Tevershall. They found a rather good-looking woman of forty-
odd, in a nurse's uniform, with a white collar and apron, just making herself tea,
in a small, crowded sitting-room.

Mrs. Bolton was most attentive and polite, seemed quite nice, spoke with a
bit of a broad slur, but in heavily correct English, and from having bossed the
sick colliers for a good many years, had a very good opinion of herself, and a fair
amount of assurance. In short, in her tiny way, one of the governing class in the
village, very much respected.

"Yes, Lady Chatterley's not looking at all well! Why she used to be that
bonny, didn't she now? But she's been failing all winter! Oh, it's hard, it is. Poor
Sir Clifford! Eh, that war, it's a lot to answer for."

And Mrs. Bolton would come to Wragby at once, if Dr. Shardlow would let
her off. She had another fortnight's parish nursing to do, by rights, but they
might get a substitute, you know.

Hilda posted off to Dr. Shardlow, and on the following Sunday Mrs. Bolton
drove up in Leiver's cab to Wragby, with two trunks. Hilda had talks with her;
Mrs. Bolton was ready at any moment to talk. And she seemed so young! the
way the passion would flush in her rather pale cheek. She was forty-seven.

Her husband, Ted Bolton, had been killed in the pit, twenty-two years ago,

twenty-two years last Christmas, just at Christmas time, leaving her with two
children, one a baby in arms. Oh, the baby was married now—Edith—to a
young man in Boots Cash Chemists in Sheffield. The other one was a school-
teacher in Chesterfield, she came home week-ends, when she wasn't asked out
anywhere. Young folks enjoyed themselves nowadays; not like when she, Ivy
Bolton, was young.

Ted Bolton was twenty-eight when he was killed in an explosion down th'
pit. The butty in front shouted to them all to lie down quick; there were four of
them. And they all lay down in time, only Ted, and it killed him. Then at the
enquiry, on the masters' side they said Ted had been frightened, and trying to
run away, and not obeying orders, so it was like his fault really. So the compensation was only three hundred pounds, and they made out as if it was more of a
gift than legal compensation, because it was really the man's own fault. And they
wouldn't let her have the money down; she wanted to have a little shop. But
they said she'd no doubt squander it, perhaps in drink! So she had to draw it
thirty shillings a week. Yes, she had to go every Monday morning down to the
offices, and stand there a couple of hours waiting her turn; yes, for almost four
years she went every Monday. And what could she do with two little children
on her hands? But Ted's mother was very good to her. When the baby could
toddle she'd keep both the children for the day, while she, Ivy Bolton, went to
Sheffield, and attended classes in ambulance, and then the fourth year she even
took a nursing course and got qualified. She was determined to be independent
and keep her children. So she was assistant at Uthwaite hospital, just a little
place, for a while. But when the Company, the Tevershall Colliery Company,
really Sir Geoffrey, saw that she could get on by herself, they were very good to
her, gave her the parish nursing, and stood by her, she would say that for them.
And she'd done it ever since, till now it was getting a bit too much for her, she
needed something a bit lighter, there was such a lot of traipsing round if you
were a district nurse.

"Yes, the Company's been very good to *me,* I always say it. But I should
never forget what they said about Ted, for he was as steady and fearless a chap as
ever set foot on the cage, and it was as good as branding him a coward. But
there, he was dead, and could say nothing to none of 'em."

It was a queer mixture of feelings the woman showed as she talked. She liked
the colliers, whom she had nursed for so long; but she felt very superior to them.
She felt almost upper class; and at the same time a resentment against the ruling
class smoldered in her. The masters! In a dispute between masters and men, she
was always for the men. But when there was no question of contest, she was
pining to be superior, to be one of the upper class. The upper classes fascinated
her, appealing to her peculiar English passion for superiority. She was thrilled to
come to Wragby, thrilled to talk to Lady Chatterley; my word, different from
the common colliers' wives! She said so in so many words. Yet one could see a
grudge against the Chatterleys peep out in her; the grudge against the masters.

"Why, yes, of course, it would wear Lady Chatterley out! It's a mercy she has
a sister to come and help her. Men don't think; high and low alike, they take
what a woman does for them for granted. Oh, I've told the colliers off about it
many a time. But it's very hard for Sir Clifford, you know, crippled like that.
They were always a haughty family, stand-offish in a way, as they've a right to
be. But then, to be brought down like that! And it's very hard on Lady Chatterley, perhaps harder on her. What she misses! I only had Ted three years, but my
word, while I had him I had a husband I could never forget. He was one in a

thousand, and jolly as the day. Who'd ever have thought he'd get killed? I don't believe it to this day, somehow; I've never believed it, though I washed him with my own hands. But he was never dead for me, he never was. I never took it in."

This was a new voice in Wragby, very new for Connie to hear; it roused a new ear in her.

For the first week or so, Mrs. Bolton, however, was very quiet at Wragby; her assured, bossy manner left her, and she was nervous. With Clifford she was shy, almost frightened and silent. He liked that, and soon recovered his self-possession, letting her do things for him without even noticing her. "She's a useful nonentity!" he said. Connie opened her eyes in wonder, but did not contradict him. So different are impressions on two different people!

And he soon became rather superb, somewhat lordly with the nurse. She had rather expected it, and he played up without knowing. So susceptible we are to what is expected of us! The colliers had been so like children, talking to her, and telling her what hurt them, while she bandaged them, or nursed them. They had always made her feel so grand, almost superhuman in her administrations. Now Clifford made her feel small, and like a servant, and she accepted it without a word, adjusting herself to the upper classes.

She came very mute, with her long, handsome face, and downcast eyes, to administer to him. And she said very humbly: "Shall I do this now, Sir Clifford? Shall I do that?"

"No, leave it for a time, I'll have it done later."

"Very well, Sir Clifford."

"Come in again in half-an-hour."

"Very well, Sir Clifford."

"And just take those old papers out, will you?"

"Very well, Sir Clifford."

She went softly, and in half-an-hour she came softly again. She was bullied, but she didn't mind. She was experiencing the upper classes. She neither resented nor disliked Clifford; he was just part of a phenomenon, the phenomenon of the high-class folks, so far unknown to her, but now to be known. She felt more at home with Lady Chatterley, and after all it's the mistress of the house matters most.

Mrs. Bolton helped Clifford to bed at night, and slept across the passage from his room, and came if he rang for her in the night. She also helped him in the morning, and soon valeted him completely, even shaving him, in her soft, tentative woman's way. She was very good and competent, and she soon knew how to have him in her power. He wasn't so very different from the colliers after all, when you lathered his chin, and softly rubbed the bristles. The stand-offishness and the lack of frankness didn't bother her, she was having a new experience.

Clifford, however, inside himself, never quite forgave Connie for giving up her personal care of him to a strange hired woman. It killed, he said to himself, the real flower of the intimacy between him and her. But Connie didn't mind that. The fine flower of their intimacy was to her rather like an orchid, a bulb stuck parasitic on her tree of life, and producing, to her eyes, a rather shabby flower.

Now she had more time to herself she could softly play the piano, up in her room, and sing: "Touch not the nettle . . . for the bonds of love are ill to loose." She had not realized till lately how ill to loose they were, these bonds of love.

But thank heaven she had loosened them! She was so glad to be alone, not always to have to talk to him. When he was alone he tapped-tapped-tapped on a typewriter, to infinity. But when he was not "working," and she was there, he talked, always talked; infinite small analysis of people and motives, and results, characters and personalities, till now she had had enough. For years she had loved it, until she had enough, and then suddenly it was too much. She was thankful to be alone.

It was as if thousands and thousands of little roots and threads of consciousness in him and her had grown together into a tangled mass, till they could crowd no more, and the plant was dying. Now quietly, subtly she was unravelling the tangle of his consciousness and hers, breaking the threads gently, one by one, with patience and impatience to get clear. But the bonds of such love are more ill to loose even than most bonds; though Mrs. Bolton's coming had been a great help.

But he still wanted the old intimate evenings of talk with Connie: talk or reading aloud. But now she could arrange that Mrs. Bolton should come at ten to disturb them. At ten o'clock Connie could go upstairs and be alone. Clifford was in good hands with Mrs. Bolton.

Mrs. Bolton ate with Mrs. Betts in the housekeeper's room, since they were all agreeable. And it was curious how much closer the servants' quarters seemed to have come; right up to the doors of Clifford's study, when before they were so remote. For Mrs. Betts would sometimes sit in Mrs. Bolton's room, and Connie heard their lowered voices, and felt somehow the strong, outer vibration of the working people almost invading the sitting-rooms, when she and Clifford were alone. So changed was Wragby merely by Mrs. Bolton's coming.

And Connie felt herself released, in another world; she felt she breathed differently. But still she was afraid of how many of her roots, perhaps mortal ones, were tangled with Clifford's. Yet still, she breathed freer, a new phase was going to begin in her life.

VIII

Mrs. Bolton also kept a cherishing eye on Connie, feeling she must extend to her her female and professional protection. She was always urging her ladyship to walk out, to drive to Uthwaite, to be in the air. For Connie had got into the habit of sitting still by the fire, pretending to read, or to sew feebly, and hardly going out at all.

It was a blowy day soon after Hilda had gone, that Mrs. Bolton said: "Now, why don't you go for a walk through the wood, and look at the daffs behind the keeper's cottage? They're the prettiest sight you'd see in a day's march. And you could put some in your room, wild daffs are always so cheerful-looking, aren't they?"

Connie took it in good part, even daffs for daffodils. Wild daffodils! After all, one should not stew in one's own juice. The spring came back. . . . "Seasons return, but not to me returns Day, or the sweet approach of Ev'n or Morn."

And the keeper, his thin, white body, like a lonely pistil of an invisible flower! She had forgotten him in her unspeakable depression. But now something roused . . . "Pale beyond porch and portal" . . . the thing to do was to pass the porches and the portals.

She was stronger, she could walk better, and in the wood the wind would not be so tiring as it was across the park, flattening against her. She wanted to forget, to forget the world, and all the dreadful carrion-bodied people. "Ye must be born again! I believe in the resurrection of the body! Except a grain of wheat fall into the earth and die, it shall by no means bring forth. When the crocus cometh forth I too will emerge and see the sun!" In the wind of March endless phrases swept through her consciousness.

Little gusts of sunshine blew, strangely bright, and lit up the celandines at the wood's edge, under the hazel-rods, they spangled out bright and yellow. And the wood was still, stiller, but yet gusty with crossing sun. The first windflowers were out, and all the wood seemed pale with the pallor of endless little anemones, sprinkling the shaken floor. "The world has grown pale with thy breath." But it was the breath of Persephone, this time; she was out of hell on a cold morning. Cold breaths of wind came, and overhead there was an anger of entangled wind caught among the twigs. It, too, was caught and trying to tear itself free, the wind, like Absalom. How cold the anemones looked, bobbing their naked white shoulders over crinoline skirts of green. But they stood it. A few first bleached little primroses, too, by the path, and yellow buds unfolding themselves.

The roaring and swaying was overhead, only cold currents came down below. Connie was strangely excited in the wood, and the color flew in her cheeks, and burned blue in her eyes. She walked ploddingly, picking a few primroses and the first violets, that smelled sweet and cold, sweet and cold. And she drifted on without knowing where she was.

Till she came to the clearing, at the far end of the wood, and saw the green-stained stone cottage, looking almost rosy, like the flesh underneath a mushroom, its stone warmed in a burst of sun. And there was a sparkle of yellow jasmine by the door; the closed door. But no sound; no smoke from the chimney; no dog barking.

She went quietly round to the back, where the bank rose up; she had an excuse, to see the daffodils.

And they were there, the short-stemmed flowers, rustling and fluttering and shivering, so bright and alive, but with nowhere to hide their faces, as they turned them away from the wind.

They shook their bright, sunny little rags in bouts of distress. But perhaps they liked it really; perhaps they really liked the tossing.

Constance sat down with her back to a young pine-tree, that swayed against her with curious life, elastic and powerful, rising up. The erect, alive thing, with its top in the sun! And she watched the daffodils turn golden, in a burst of sun that was warm on her hands and lap. Even she caught the faint, tarry scent of the flowers. And then, being so still and alone, she seemed to get into the current of her own proper destiny. She had been fastened by a rope, and jagging and snarring like a boat at its moorings; now she was loose and adrift.

The sunshine gave way to chill; the daffodils were in shadow, dipping silently. So they would dip through the day and the long cold night. So strong in their frailty!

She rose, a little stiff, took a few daffodils, and went down. She hated breaking the flowers, but she wanted just one or two to go with her. She would have to go back to Wragby and its walls, and now she hated it, especially its thick walls. Walls! Always walls! Yet one needed them in this wind.

When she got home Clifford asked her:

"Where did you go?"

"Right across the wood! Look, aren't the little daffodils adorable? To think they should come out of the earth!"

"Just as much out of the air and sunshine," he said.

"But modelled in the earth," she retorted, with a prompt contradiction, that surprised her a little.

The next afternoon she went to the wood again. She followed the broad riding that swerved round and up through the larches to a spring called John's Well. It was cold on this hillside, and not a flower in the darkness of larches. But the icy little spring softly pressed upwards from its tiny well-bed of pure, reddish-white pebbles. How icy and clear it was! brilliant! The new keeper had no doubt put in fresh pebbles. She heard the faint tinkle of water, as the tiny overflow trickled over and downhill. Even above the hissing boom of the larchwood, that spread its bristling, leafless, wolfish darkness on the down-slope, she heard the tinkle as of tiny water-bells.

This place was a little sinister, cold, damp. Yet the well must have been a drinking-place for hundreds of years. Now no more. Its tiny cleared space was lush and cold and dismal.

She rose and went slowly towards home. As she went she heard a faint tapping away on the right, and stood still to listen. Was it hammering, or a woodpecker? It was surely hammering.

She walked on, listening. And then she noticed a narrow track between young fir-trees, a track that seemed to lead nowhere. But she felt it had been used. She turned down it adventurously, between the thick young firs, which gave way soon to the old oak wood. She followed the track, and the hammering drew nearer, in the silence of the windy wood, for trees make a silence even in their noise of wind.

She saw a secret little clearing, and a secret little hut made of rustic poles. And she had never been here before! She realized it was the quiet place where the growing pheasants were reared; the keeper in his shirt-sleeves was kneeling, hammering. The dog trotted forward with a short, sharp bark, and the keeper lifted his face suddenly and saw her. He had a startled look in his eyes.

He straightened himself and saluted, watching her in silence, as she came forward with weakening limbs. He resented the intrusion, he cherished his solitude as his only and last freedom in life.

"I wondered what the hammering was," she said, feeling weak and breathless, and a little afraid of him, as he looked so straight at her.

"Ah'm gettin' th' coops ready for th' young bods," he said, in broad vernacular.

She did not know what to say, and she felt weak.

"I should like to sit down a bit," she said.

"Come and sit 'ere i' th' 'ut," he said, going in front of her to the hut, pushing aside more timber and stuff, and drawing out a rustic chair, made of hazel sticks.

"Am Ah t'light yer a little fire?" he asked, with the curious naïveté of the dialect.

"Oh, don't bother," she replied.

But she looked at her hands: they were rather blue. So he quickly took some larch twigs to the little brick fireplace in the corner, and in a moment the yellow flame was running up the chimney. He made a place by the brick hearth.

"Sit 'ere then a bit, and warm yer," he said.

She obeyed him. He had that curious kind of protective authority she obeyed at once. So she sat and warmed her hands at the blaze, and dropped logs on the fire, whilst outside he was hammering again. She did not really want to sit, poked in a corner by the fire; she would rather have watched from the door, but she was being looked after, so she had to submit.

The hut was quite cozy, panelled with unvarnished deal, having a little rustic table and stool besides her chair, and a carpenter's bench, then a big box, tools, new boards, nails; and many things hung from pegs: axe, hatchet, traps, things in sacks, his coat. It had no window, the light came in through the open door. It was a jumble, but also it was a sort of little sanctuary.

She listened to the tapping of the man's hammer; it was not so happy. He was oppressed. Here was a trespass on his privacy, and a dangerous one! A woman! He had reached the point where all he wanted on earth was to be alone. And yet he was powerless to preserve his privacy; he was a hired man, and these people were his masters.

Especially he did not want to come into contact with a woman again. He feared it; for he had a big wound from old contacts. He felt if he could not be alone, and if he could not be left alone, he would die. His recoil away from the outer world was complete; his last refuge was this wood; to hide himself there!

Connie grew warm by the fire, which she had made too big: then she grew hot. She went and sat on the stool in the doorway, watching the man at work. He seemed not to notice her, but he knew. Yet he worked on, as if absorbedly, and his brown dog sat on her tail near him, and surveyed the untrustworthy world.

Slender, quiet and quick, the man finished the coop he was making, turned it over, tried the sliding door, then set it aside. Then he rose, went for an old coop, and took it to the chopping-log where he was working. Crouching, he tried the bars; some broke in his hands; he began to draw the nails. Then he turned the coop over and deliberated, and he gave absolutely no sign of awareness of the woman's presence.

So Connie watched him fixedly. And the same solitary aloneness she had seen in him naked, she now saw in him clothed: solitary, and intent, like an animal that works alone, but also brooding, like a soul that recoils away, away from all human contact. Silently, patiently, he was recoiling away from her even now. It was the stillness, and the timeless sort of patience, in a man impatient and passionate, that touched Connie's womb. She saw it in his bent head, the quick, quiet hands, the crouching of his slender, sensitive loins; something patient and withdrawn. She felt his experience had been deeper and wider than her own; much deeper and wider, and perhaps more deadly. And this relieved her of herself; she felt almost irresponsible.

So she sat in the doorway of the hut in a dream, utterly unaware of time and of particular circumstances. She was so drifted away that he glanced up at her quickly, and saw the utterly still, waiting look on her face. To him it was a look of waiting. And a little thin tongue of fire suddenly flickered in his loins, at the root of his back, and he groaned in spirit. He dreaded, with a repulsion almost of death, any further close human contact. He wished above all things she would go away, and leave him to his own privacy. He dreaded her will, her female will, and her modern female insistency. And above all he dreaded her cool, upper-class impudence of having her own way. For after all he was only a hired man. He hated her presence there.

Connie came to herself with sudden uneasiness. She rose. The afternoon was turning to evening, yet she could not go away. She went over to the man, who stood up at attention, his worn face stiff and blank, his eyes watching her.

"It is so nice here, so restful," she said. "I have never been here before."

"No?"

"I think I shall come and sit here sometimes."

"Yes!"

"Do you lock the hut when you're not here?"

"Yes, your Ladyship."

"Do you think I could have a key too, so that I could sit here sometimes? Are there two keys?"

"Not as Ah know on, ther' isna."

He had lapsed into the vernacular. Connie hesitated; he was putting up an opposition. Was it his hut, after all?

"Couldn't we get another key?" she asked in her soft voice, that underneath had the ring of a woman determined to get her way.

"Another!" he said, glancing at her with a flash of anger, touched with derision.

"Yes, a duplicate," she said, flushing.

" 'Appen Sir Clifford 'ud know," he said, putting her off.

"Yes!" she said, "he might have another. Otherwise we could have one made from the one you have. It would only take a day or so, I suppose. You could spare your key for so long."

"Ah canna tell yer, m'lady! Ah know nob'dy as ma'es keys round 'ere."

Connie suddenly flushed with anger.

"Very well!" she said. "I'll see to it."

"All right, your Ladyship."

Their eyes met. His had a cold, ugly look of dislike and contempt, and indifference to what would happen. Hers were hot with rebuff.

But her heart sank, she saw how utterly he disliked her, when she went against him. And she saw him in a sort of desperation.

"Good afternoon!"

"Afternoon, my Lady!" He saluted and turned abruptly away. She had wakened the sleeping dogs of old voracious anger in him, anger against the self-willed female. And he was powerless, powerless. He knew it!

And she was angry against the self-willed male. A servant too! She walked sullenly home.

She found Mrs. Bolton under the great beech tree on the knoll, looking for her.

"I just wondered if you'd be coming, my Lady," the woman said brightly.

"Am I late?" asked Connie.

"Oh . . . only Sir Clifford was waiting for his tea."

"Why didn't *you* make it then?"

"Oh, I don't think it's hardly my place. I don't think Sir Clifford would like it at all, my Lady."

"I don't see why not," said Connie.

She went indoors to Clifford's study, where the old brass kettle was simmering on the tray.

"Am I late, Clifford?" she said, putting down the few flowers and taking up the tea-caddy, as she stood before the tray in her hat and scarf. "I'm sorry! Why didn't you let Mrs. Bolton make the tea?"

"I didn't think of it," he said ironically. "I don't quite see her presiding at the tea-table."

"Oh, there's nothing sacrosanct about a silver tea-pot," said Connie.

He glanced up at her curiously.

"What did you do all afternoon?" he said.

"Walked and sat in a sheltered place. Do you know there are still berries on the big holly-tree?"

She took off her scarf, but not her hat, and sat down to make tea. The toast would certainly be leathery. She put the tea-cosy over the tea-pot, and rose to get a little glass for her violets. The poor flowers hung over, limp on their stalks.

"They'll revive again!" she said, putting them before him in their glass for him to smell.

"Sweeter than the lids of Juno's eyes," he quoted.

"I don't see a bit of connection with the actual violets," she said. "The Elizabethans are rather upholstered."

She poured him his tea.

"Do you think there is a second key to that little hut not far from John's Well, where the pheasants are reared?" she said.

"There may be. Why?"

"I happened to find it today—and I'd never seen it before. I think it's a darling place. I could sit there sometimes, couldn't I?"

"Was Mellors there?"

"Yes! That's how I found it; his hammering. He didn't seem to like my intruding at all. In fact he was almost rude when I asked about a second key."

"What did he say?"

"Oh, nothing: just his manner; and he said he knew nothing about keys."

"There may be one in father's study. Betts knows them all; they're all there. I'll get him to look."

"Oh, do!" she said.

"So Mellors was almost rude?"

"Oh, nothing, really! But I don't think he wanted me to have the freedom of the castle, quite."

"I don't suppose he did."

"Still, I don't see why he should mind. It's not his home, after all! It's not his private abode. I don't see why I shouldn't sit there if I want to."

"Quite!" said Clifford. "He thinks too much of himself, that man."

"Do you think he does?"

"Oh, decidedly! He thinks he's something exceptional. You know he had a wife he didn't get on with, so he joined up in 1915 and was sent out to India, I believe. Anyhow he was blacksmith to the cavalry in Egypt for a time; always was connected with horses, a clever fellow that way. Then some Indian colonel took a fancy to him, and he was made a lieutenant. Yes, they gave him a commission. I believe he went back to India with his colonel, and up to the northwest frontier. He was ill; he has a pension. He didn't come out of the army till last year, I believe, and then, naturally, it isn't easy for a man like that to get back to his own level. He's bound to flounder. But he does his duty all right, as far as I'm concerned. Only, I'm not having any of the Lieutenant Mellors touch."

"How could they make him an officer when he speaks broad Derbyshire?"

"He doesn't . . . except by fits and starts. He can speak perfectly well, for him. I suppose he has an idea if he's come down to the ranks again, he'd better speak as the ranks speak."

"Why didn't you tell me about him before?"

"Oh, I've no patience with these romances. They're the ruin of all order. It's a thousand pities they ever happened."

Connie was inclined to agree. What was the good of discontented people who fitted in nowhere?

In the spell of fine weather Clifford, too, decided to go to the wood. The wind was cold, but not so tiresome, and the sunshine was like life itself, warm and full.

"It's amazing," said Connie, "how different one feels when there's a really fresh fine day. Usually one feels the very air is half dead. People are killing the very air."

"Do you think people are doing it?" he asked.

"I do. The steam of so much boredom, and discontent and anger out of all the people, just kills the vitality in the air. I'm sure of it."

"Perhaps some condition of the atmosphere lowers the vitality of the people?" he said.

"No, it's man that poisons the universe," she asserted.

"Fouls his own nest," remarked Clifford.

The chair puffed on. In the hazel copse catkins were hanging pale gold, and in sunny places the wood-anemones were wide open, as if exclaiming with the joy of life, just as good as in past days, when people could exclaim along with them. They had a faint scent of apple-blossom. Connie gathered a few for Clifford.

He took them and looked at them curiously.

"Thou still unravished bride of quietness," he quoted. "It seems to fit flowers so much better than Greek vases."

"Ravished is such a horrid word!" she said. "It's only people who ravish things."

"Oh, I don't know . . . snails and things," he said.

"Even snails only eat them, and bees don't ravish."

She was angry with him, turning everything into words. Violets were Juno's eyelids, and windflowers were unravished brides. How she hated words, always coming between her and life: they did the ravishing, if anything did: ready-made words and phrases, sucking all the life-sap out of living things.

The walk with Clifford was not quite a success. Between him and Connie there was a tension that each pretended not to notice, but there it was. Suddenly, with all the force of her female instinct, she was shoving him off. She wanted to be clear of him, and especially of his consciousness, his words, his obsession with himself, his endless treadmill obsession with himself, and his own words.

The weather came rainy again. But after a day or two she went out in the rain, and she went to the wood. And once there, she went towards the hut. It was raining, but not so cold, and the wood felt so silent and remote, inaccessible in the dusk of rain.

She came to the clearing. No one there! The hut was locked. But she sat on the log doorstep, under the rustic porch, and snuggled into her own warmth. So she sat, looking at the rain, listening to the many noiseless noises of it, and to the strange soughings of wind in upper branches, when there seemed to be no wind. Old oak trees stood around, grey, powerful trunks, rain-blackened, round and vital, throwing off reckless limbs. The ground was fairly free of undergrowth, the anemones sprinkled, there was a bush or two, elder, or guelder-rose, and a purplish tangle of bramble; the old russet of bracken almost vanished under green anemone ruffs. Perhaps this was one of the unravished places. Unravished! The whole world was ravished.

Some things can't be ravished. You can't ravish a tin of sardines. And so many women are like that; and men. But the earth . . . !

The rain was abating. It was hardly making darkness among the oaks any more. Connie wanted to go; yet she sat on. But she was getting cold; yet the overwhelming inertia of her inner resentment kept her there as if paralyzed.

Ravished! How ravished one could be without ever being touched. Ravished by dead words become obscene, and dead ideas become obsessions.

A wet brown dog came running and did not bark, lifting a wet feather of a tail. The man followed in a wet black oilskin jacket, like a chauffeur, and face flushed a little. She felt him recoil in his quick walk, when he saw her. She stood up in the handbreath of dryness under the rustic porch. He saluted without speaking, coming slowly near. She began to withdraw.

"I'm just going," she said.

"Was yer waitin' to get in?" he asked, looking at the hut, not at her.

"No, I only sat a few minutes in the shelter," she said, with quiet dignity.

He looked at her. She looked cold.

"Sir Clifford 'adn't got no other key then?" he asked.

"No, but it doesn't matter. I can sit perfectly dry under this porch. Good afternoon!" She hated the excess of vernacular in his speech.

He watched her closely, as she was moving away. Then he hitched up his jacket, and put his hand in his breeches pocket, taking out the key of the hut.

" 'Appen yer'd better 'ave this key, an' mun fend for t'bods some other road."

"What do you mean?" she asked.

"I mean as 'appen Ah can find anuther pleece as'll du for rearin' th' pheasants. If yer want ter be 'ere, yo'll non want me messin' abaht a' th' time."

She looked at him, getting his meaning through the fog of the dialect.

"Why don't you speak ordinary English?" she said coldly.

"Me! Ah thowt it *wor* ordinary."

She was silent for a few moments in anger.

"So if yer want t' key, yer'd better ta'e it. Or 'appen Ah'd better gi'e 't yer termorrer, an' clear all t' stuff aht fust. Would that du for yer?"

She became more angry.

"I didn't want your key," she said. "I don't want you to clear anything out at all. I don't in the least want to turn you out of your hut, thank you! I only wanted to be able to sit here sometimes, like today. But I can sit perfectly well under the porch, so please say no more about it."

He looked at her again with his wicked blue eyes.

"Why," he began, in the broad slow dialect, "your Ladyship's as welcome as Christmas ter th' hut an' th' key an' iverythink as it. On'y this time o' th' year ther's bods ter set, an' Ah've got ter be potterin' abaht a good bit, seein' after 'em, an' a'. Winter time Ah need 'ardly come nigh th' pleece. But what wi' spring, an' Sir Clifford wantin' ter start th' pheasants. . . . An' your Ladyship'd non want me tinkerin' around an' about when she was 'ere, all th' time."

She listened with a dim kind of amazement.

"Why should I mind your being here?" she asked.

He looked at her curiously.

"T' nuisance on me!" he said briefly, but significantly.

She flushed. "Very well!" she said finally. "I won't trouble you. But I don't think I should have minded at all sitting and seeing you look after the birds. I should have liked it. But since you think it interferes with you, I won't disturb you, don't be afraid. You are Sir Clifford's keeper, not mine."

The phrase sounded queer, she didn't know why. But she let it pass.

"Nay, your Ladyship. It's your Ladyship's own 'ut. It's as your Ladyship likes an' pleases, every time. Yer can turn me off at a wik's notice. It wor only . . ."

"Only what?" she asked, baffled.

He pushed back his hat in an odd comic way.

"On'y as 'appen yo'd like the place ter yersen, when yer did come, an' not me messin' abaht."

"But why?" she said, angry. "Aren't you a civilized human being? Do you think I ought to be afraid of you? Why should I take any notice of you and your being here or not? Why is it important?"

He looked at her, all his face glimmering with wicked laughter.

"It's not, your Ladyship. Not in the very least," he said.

"Well, why then?" she asked.

"Shall I get your Ladyship another key then?"

"No, thank you! I don't want it."

"Ah'll get it anyhow. We'd best 'ave two keys ter th' place."

"And I consider you are insolent," said Connie, with her color up, panting a little.

"Nay, nay!" he said quickly. "Dunna yer say that! Nay, nay! I niver meant nuthink. Ah on'y thought as if yo' come 'ere, Ah s'd 'ave ter clear out, an' it'd mean a lot o' work, settin' up somewheres else. But if your Ladyship isn't going ter take no notice o' me, then . . . it's Sir Clifford's 'ut, an' everythink is as your Ladyship likes, everythink is as your Ladyship likes an' pleases, barrin' yer take no notice o' me, doin' the bits of jobs as Ah've got ter do."

Connie went away completely bewildered. She was not sure whether she had been insulted and mortally offended, or not. Perhaps the man really only meant what he said; that he thought she would expect him to keep away. As if she would dream of it! And as if he could possibly be so important, he and his stupid presence.

She went home in confusion, not knowing what she thought or felt.

IX

Connie was surprised at her own feeling of aversion for Clifford. What is more, she felt she had always really disliked him. Not hate: there was no passion in it. But a profound physical dislike. Almost it seemed to her, she had married him because she disliked him, in a secret, physical sort of way. But of course, she had married him really because in a mental way he attracted her and excited her. He had seemed, in some way, her master, beyond her.

Now the mental excitement had worn itself out and collapsed, and she was aware only of the physical aversion. It rose up in her from her depths: and she realized how it had been eating her life away.

She felt weak and utterly forlorn. She wished some help would come from outside. But in the whole world there was no help. Society was terrible because it was insane. Civilized society is insane. Money and so-called love are its two great manias; money a long way first. The individual asserts himself in his disconnected insanity in these two modes: money and love. Look at Michaelis! His life and activity were just insanity. His love was a sort of insanity.

And Clifford the same. All that talk! All that writing! All that wild struggling to push himself forward! It was just insanity. And it was getting worse, really maniacal.

Connie felt washed-out with fear. But at least, Clifford was shifting his grip from her on to Mrs. Bolton. He did not know it. Like many insane people, his insanity might be measured by the things he was *not* aware of; the great desert tracts in his consciousness.

Mrs. Bolton was admirable in many ways. But she had that queer sort of bossiness, endless assertion of her own will, which is one of the signs of insanity in modern woman. She *thought* she was utterly subservient and living for others. Clifford fascinated her because he always, or so often, frustrated her will, as if by a finer instinct. He had a finer, subtler will of self-assertion than herself. This was his charm for her.

Perhaps that had been his charm, too, for Connie.

"It's a lovely day, today!" Mrs. Bolton would say in her caressive, persuasive voice. "I should think you'd enjoy a little run in your chair today, the sun's just lovely."

"Yes? Will you give me that book—there, that yellow one. And I think I'll have those hyacinths taken out."

"Why, they're so beautiful!" She pronounced it with the "y" sound: be-yutiful!—"And the scent is simply gorgeous."

"The scent is what I object to," he said. "It's a little funereal."

"Do you think so!" she exclaimed in surprise, just a little offended, but impressed. And she carried the hyacinths out of the room, impressed by his higher fastidiousness.

"Shall I shave you this morning, or would you rather do it yourself?" Always the same soft, caressive, subservient, yet managing voice.

"I don't know. Do you mind waiting a while. I'll ring when I'm ready."

"Very good, Sir Clifford!" she replied, so soft and submissive, withdrawing quietly. But every rebuff stored up new energy of will in her.

When he rang, after a time, she would appear at once. And then he would say:

"I think I'd rather you shaved me this morning."

Her heart gave a little thrill, and she replied with extra softness:

"Very good, Sir Clifford!"

She was very deft, with a soft, lingering touch, a little slow. At first he had resented the infinitely soft touch of her fingers on his face. But now he liked it, with a growing voluptuousness. He let her shave him nearly every day: her face near his, her eyes so very concentrated, watching that she did it right. And gradually her fingertips knew his cheeks and lips, his jaw and chin and throat perfectly. He was well-fed and well-groomed, his face and throat were handsome enough, and he was a gentleman.

She was handsome, too, pale, her face rather long and absolutely still, her eyes bright, but revealing nothing. Gradually, with infinite softness, almost with love, she was getting him by the throat, and he was yielding to her.

She now did almost everything for him, and he felt more at home with her, less ashamed of accepting her menial offices, than with Connie. She liked handling him. She loved having his body in her charge, absolutely, to the last menial offices. She said to Connie one day: "All men are babies, when you come to the bottom of them. Why, I've handled some of the toughest customers as ever went down Tevershall pit. But let anything ail them so that you have to do for them, and they're babies, just big babies. Oh, there's not much difference in men!"

At first Mrs. Bolton had thought there really was something different in a gentleman, a *real* gentleman, like Sir Clifford. So Clifford had got a good start of her. But gradually, as she came to the bottom of him, to use her own term, she found he was like the rest, a baby grown to man's proportions: but a baby with a queer temper and a fine manner and power in its control, and all sorts of odd knowledge that she had never dreamed of, with which he could still bully her.

Connie was sometimes tempted to say to him: "For God's sake, don't sink so horribly into the hands of that woman!" But she found she didn't care for him enough to say it, in the long run.

It was still their habit to spend the evening together, till ten o'clock. Then they would talk, or read together, or go over his manuscript. But the thrill had gone out of it. She was bored by his manuscripts. But she still dutifully typed them out for him. But in time Mrs. Bolton would do even that.

For Connie had suggested to Mrs. Bolton that she should learn to use a typewriter. And Mrs. Bolton, always ready, had begun at once, and practiced assiduously. So now Clifford would sometimes dictate a letter to her, and she would take it down rather slowly, but correctly. And he was very patient, spelling for her the difficult words, or the occasional phrases in French. She was so thrilled, it was almost a pleasure to instruct her.

Now Connie would sometimes plead a headache as an excuse for going up to her room after dinner.

"Perhaps Mrs. Bolton will play piquet with you," she said to Clifford.

"Oh, I shall be perfectly all right. You go to your own room and rest, darling."

But no sooner had she gone, than he rang for Mrs. Bolton, and asked her to take a hand at piquet or bezique, or even chess. He had taught her all these games. And Connie found it curiously objectionable to see Mrs. Bolton, flushed and tremulous like a little girl, touching her queen or her knight with uncertain fingers, then drawing away again. And Clifford, faintly smiling with a half-teasing superiority, saying to her:

"You must say j'adoube!"

She looked up at him with bright, startled eyes, then murmured shyly, obediently:

"J'adoube"!

Yes, he was educating her. And he enjoyed it, it gave him a sense of power. And she was thrilled. She was coming bit by bit into possession of all that the gentry knew, all that made them upper class: apart from the money. That thrilled her. And at the same time, she was making him want to have her there with him. It was a subtle deep flattery to him, her genuine thrill.

To Connie, Clifford seemed to be coming out in his true colors: a little vulgar, a little common, and uninspired; rather fat. Ivy Bolton's tricks and humble bossiness were also only too transparent. But Connie did wonder at the genuine thrill which the woman got out of Clifford. To say she was in love with him would be putting it wrongly. She was thrilled by her contact with a man of the upper class, this titled gentleman, this author who could write books and poems, and whose photograph appeared in the illustrated newspapers. She was thrilled to a weird passion. And his "educating" her roused in her a passion of excitement and response much deeper than any love affair could have done. In truth, the very fact that there could be no love affair left her free to thrill to her very marrow with this other passion, the peculiar passion of knowing, knowing as he knew.

There was no mistake that the woman was in some way in love with him: whatever force we give to the word love. She looked so handsome and so

young, and her grey eyes were sometimes marvellous. At the same time, there
was a lurking soft satisfaction about her, even of triumph, and private satisfaction. Ugh, that private satisfaction! How Connie loathed it!

But no wonder Clifford was caught by the woman! She absolutely adored
him, in her persistent fashion, and put herself absolutely at his service, for him to
use as he liked. No wonder he was flattered!

Connie heard long conversations going on between the two. Or rather, it
was mostly Mrs. Bolton talking. She had unloosed to him the stream of gossip
about Tevershall village. It was more than gossip. It was Mrs. Gaskell and
George Eliot and Miss Mitford all rolled in one, with a great deal more, that
these women left out. Once started, Mrs. Bolton was better than any book,
about the lives of the people. She knew them all so intimately, and had such a
peculiar, flamey zest in all their affairs, it was wonderful, if just a *trifle* humiliating to listen to her. At first she had not ventured to "talk Tevershall," as she
called it, to Clifford. But once started, it went. Clifford was listening for "material," and he found it in plenty. Connie realized that his so-called genius was just
this: a perspicuous talent for personal gossip, clever and apparently detached.
Mrs. Bolton, of course, was very warm when she "talked Tevershall." Carried
away, in fact. And it was marvellous, the things that happened and that she
knew about. She would have run to dozens of volumes.

Connie was fascinated, listening to her. But afterwards always a little
ashamed. She ought not to listen with this queer rabid curiosity. After all, one
may hear the most private affairs of other people, but only in a spirit of respect
for the struggling, battered thing which any human soul is, and in a spirit of fine,
discriminative sympathy. For even satire is a form of sympathy. It is the way our
sympathy flows and recoils that really determines our lives. And here lies the
vast importance of the novel, properly handled. It can inform and lead into new
places the flow of our sympathetic consciousness, and it can lead our sympathy
away in recoil from things gone dead. Therefore, the novel, properly handled,
can reveal the most secret places of life: for it is in the *passional* secret places of
life, above all, that the tide of sensitive awareness needs to ebb and flow, cleans-
ing and freshening.

But the novel, like gossip, can also excite spurious sympathies and recoils,
mechanical and deadening to the psyche. The novel can glorify the most corrupt feelings, so long as they are *conventionally* "pure." Then the novel, like
gossip, becomes at last vicious, and, like gossip, all the more vicious because it is
always ostensibly on the side of the angels. Mrs. Bolton's gossip was always on
the side of the angels. "And he was such a *bad* fellow, and she was such a *nice*
woman." Whereas, as Connie could see even from Mrs. Bolton's gossip, the
woman had been merely a mealy-mouthed sort, and the man angrily honest.
But angry honesty made a "bad man" of him, and mealy-mouthedness made a
"nice woman" of her, in the vicious, conventional channeling of sympathy by
Mrs. Bolton.

For this reason, the gossip was humiliating. And for the same reason, most
novels, especially popular ones, are humiliating too. The public responds now
only to an appeal to its vices.

Nevertheless, one got a new vision of Tevershall village from Mrs. Bolton's
talk. A terrible, seething welter of ugly life it seemed: not at all the flat drabness
it looked from outside. Clifford of course knew by sight most of the people
mentioned; Connie knew only one or two. But it sounded really more like a
Central African jungle than an English village.

"I suppose you heard as Miss Allsopp was married last week! Would you ever! Miss Allsopp, old James's daughter, the boot-and-shoe Allsopp. You know, they built a house up at Pye Croft. The old man died last year from a fall: eighty-three, he was, an' nimble as a lad. An' then he slipped on Bestwood Hill, on a slide as the lad's 'ad made last winter, an' broke his thigh, and that finished him, poor old man, it did seem a shame. Well, he left all his money to Tattie: didn't leave the boys a penny. An' Tattie, I know, is five years . . . yes, she's fifty-three last autumn. And you know they were such Chapel people, my word! She taught Sunday School for thirty years, till her father died. And then she started carrying on with a fellow from Kinbrook, I don't know if you know him, an oldish fellow with a red nose, rather dandified, Willcock, as works in Harrison's woodyard. Well, he's sixty-five if he's a day, yet you'd have thought they were a pair of young turtledoves, to see them, arm-in-arm, and kissing at the gate: yes, an' she sitting on his knee right in the bay window on Pye Croft Road, for anybody to see. And he's got sons over forty: only lost his wife two years ago. If old James Allsopp hasn't risen from his grave, it's because there is no rising: for he kept her that strict! Now they're married and gone to live down at Kinbrook, and they say she goes round in a dressing-gown from morning to night, a veritable sight. I'm sure it's awful, the way the old ones go on! Why, they're a lot worse than the young, and a sight more disgusting. I lay it down to the pictures, myself. But you can't keep them away. I was always saying: go to a good instructive film, but do for goodness sake keep away from these melo-dramas and love films. Anyhow keep the children away! But there you are, the grown-ups are worse than the children: and the old ones beat the band. Talk about morality; nobody cares a thing. Folks does as they like, and much better off they are for it, I must say. But they're having to draw their horns in nowa-days, now th' pits are working so bad, and they haven't got the money. And the grumbling they do, it's awful, especially the women. The men are so good and patient! What can they do, poor chaps! But the women, oh, they do carry on! They go and show off, giving contributions for a wedding present for Princess Mary, and then when they see all the grand things that's been given, they simply rave: who's she, any better than anybody else! Why doesn't Swan & Edgar give me *one* fur coat, instead of giving her six? I wish I'd kept my ten shillings! What's she going to give *me*, I should like to know? Here I can't get a new spring coat, my dad's working that bad, and she gets van-loads. It's time as poor folks had some money to spend, rich ones 'as 'ad it long enough. I want a new spring coat, I do, an' wheer am I going to get it?—I say to them, be thankful you're well fed and well clothed, without all the new finery you want!—And they fly back at me: "Why isn't Princess Mary thankful to go about in her old rags, then, an' have nothing? Folks like *her* get van-loads, an' I can't have a new spring coat. It's a damned shame. Princess! bloomin' rot about Princess! It's munney as matters, an' cos she's got lots, they give her more! Nobody's givin' me any, an' I've as much right as anybody else. Don't talk to me about education. It's munney as matters. I want a new spring coat, I do, an' I shan't get it, cos there's no mun-ney.'—That's all they care about, clothes. They think nothing of giving seven or eight guineas for a winter coat—collier's daughters, mind you—and two guineas for a child's summer hat. And then they go to the Primitive Chapel in their two-guinea hat, girls as would have been proud of a three-and-sixpenny one in my day. I heard that at the Primitive Methodist anniversary this year, when they have a built-up platform for the Sunday School children, like a grandstand going almost up to th' ceiling, I heard Miss Thompson, who has the first class of girls in the Sunday School, say there'd be over a thousand pounds in new Sunday clothes sitting on that platform! And times are what they are! But you can't stop them. They're mad for clothes. And boys the same. The lads spend every penny on themselves, clothes, smoking, drinking in the Miner's Welfare, jaunting off to Sheffield two or three times a week. Why, it's another world. And they fear nothing, and they respect nothing, the young don't. The older men are that patient and good, really, they let the women take everything. And this is what it leads to. The women are positive demons. But the lads aren't like their dads. They're sacrificing nothing, they aren't: they're all for self. If you tell them they ought to be putting a bit by, for a home, they say: That'll keep, that will, I'm goin' t' enjoy mysen while I can. Owt else'll keep!—Oh, they're rough an' selfish, if you like. Everything falls on the older men, an' it's a bad lookout all round."

Clifford began to get a new idea of his own village. The place had always frightened him, but he had thought it more or less stable. Now—?

"Is there much socialism, bolshevism, among the people?" he asked.

"Oh!" said Mrs. Bolton. "You hear a few loud-mouthed ones. But they're mostly women who've got into debt. The men take no notice. I don't believe you'll ever turn our Tevershall men into reds. They're too decent for that. But the young ones blether sometimes. Not that they care for it really. They only want a bit of money in their pocket, to spend at the Welfare, or go gadding to Sheffield. That's all they care. When they've got no money, they'll listen to the reds spouting. But nobody believes in it, really."

"So you think there's no danger?"

"Oh, no! Not if trade was good, there wouldn't be. But if things were bad for a long spell, the young ones might go funny. I tell you, they're a selfish, spoilt lot. But I don't see how they'd ever do anything. They aren't ever serious about anything, except showing off on motorbikes and dancing at the Palais-de-danse in Sheffield. You can't *make* them serious. The serious ones dress up in evening clothes and go off to the Pally to show off before a lot of girls and dance these new Charlestons and what not. I'm sure sometimes the bus'll be full of young fellows in evening suits, collier lads, off to the Pally: let alone those that have gone with their girls in motors or on motor-bikes. They don't give a serious thought to a thing—save Doncaster races, and the Derby: for they all of them bet on every race. And football! But even football's not what it was, not by a long chalk. It's too much like hard work, they say. No, they'd rather be off on motor-bikes to Sheffield or Nottingham, Saturday afternoons."

"But what do they do when they get there?"

"Oh, hang round—and have tea in some fine tea-place like the Mikado—and go to the Pally or the Pictures or the Empire, with some girl. The girls are as free as the lads. They do just what they like."

"And what do they do when they haven't the money for these things?"

"They seem to get it, somehow. And they begin talking nasty then. But I don't see how you're going to get bolshevism, when all the lads want is just money to enjoy themselves, and the girls the same, with fine clothes: and they don't care about another thing. They haven't the brains to be socialists. They haven't enough seriousness to take anything really serious, and they never will have."

Connie thought, how extremely like all the rest of the classes the lower classes sounded. Just the same thing over again, Tevershall or Mayfair or Kensington. There was only one class nowadays: moneyboys. The moneyboy and the moneygirl, the only difference was how much you'd got, and how much you wanted.

Under Mrs. Bolton's influence, Clifford began to take a new interest in the mines. He began to feel he belonged. A new sort of self-assertion came into him. After all, he was the real boss in Tevershall, he was really the pits. It was a new sense of power, something he had till now shrunk from with dread.

Tevershall pits were running thin. There were only two collieries: Tevershall itself, and New London. Tevershall had once been a famous mine, and had made famous money. But its best days were over. New London was never very rich, and in ordinary times just got along decently. But now times were bad, and it was pits like New London that got left.

"There's a lot of Tevershall men left and gone to Stacks Gate and Whiteover," said Mrs. Bolton. "You've not seen the new works at Stacks Gate, opened after the war, have you, Sir Clifford? Oh, you must go one day, they're something quite new: great big chemical works at the pit-head, doesn't look a bit like a colliery. They say they get more money out of the chemical by-products than out of the coal—I forget what it is. And the grand new houses for the men, fair mansions! But a lot of Tevershall men got on there, and doin' well, a lot better than our own men. They say Tevershall's done, finished: only a question of a few more years, and it'll have to shut down. And New London'll go first. My word, won't it be funny, when there's no Tevershall pit working. It's bad enough during a strike, but my word, if it closes for good, it'll be like the end of the world. Even when I was a girl it was the best pit in the country, and a man counted himself lucky if he could work here. Oh, there's been some money made in Tevershall. And now the men say it's a sinking ship, and it's time they all got out. Doesn't it sound awful! But of course there's a lot as'll never go till they have to. They don't like these new fangled mines, such a depth, and all machinery to work them. Some of them simply dreads those iron men, as they call them, those machines for hewing the coal, where men always did it before. And they say it's wasteful as well. But what goes in waste is saved in wages, and a lot more. It seems soon there'll be no use for men on the face of the earth, it'll be all machines. But they say that's what folks said when they had to give up the old stocking frames. I can remember one or two. But my word, the more machines the more people, that's what it looks like. They say you can't get the same chemicals out of Tevershall coal as you can out of Stacks Gate, and that's funny, they're not three miles apart. But they say so. But everybody says it's a shame something can't be started, to keep the men going a bit better, and employ the girls. All the girls traipsing off to Sheffield every day! My word, it would be something to talk about if Tevershall Collieries took a new lease on life, after everybody saying they're finished, and a sinking ship, and the men ought to leave them like rats leave a sinking ship. But folks talk so much. Of course there was a boom during the war. When Sir Geoffrey made a trust of himself and got the money safe for ever, somehow. So they say! But they say even the masters and the owners don't get much out of it now. You can hardly believe it, can you! Why, I always thought the Pits would go on for ever and ever. Who'd have thought, when I was a girl! But New England's shut down, so is Colwick Wood: yes, it's fair haunting to go through that coppy and see Colwick Wood standing there deserted among the trees, and bushes growing up all over the pit-head, and the lines red rusty. It's like death itself, a dead colliery. Why, whatever we should do if Tevershall shut down—? it doesn't bear thinking of. Always that throng it's been, except at strikes, and even then the fan-wheels didn't stand, except when they fetched the ponies up. I'm sure it's a funny world, you don't know where you are from year to year, you really don't."

It was Mrs. Bolton's talk that really put a new fight into Clifford. His income, as she pointed out to him, was secure, from his father's trust, even though it was not large. The pits did not really concern him. It was the other world he wanted to capture, the world of literature and fame; the popular world, not the working world.

Now he realized the distinction between popular success and working success: the populace of pleasure and the populace of work. He, as a private individual, had been catering with his stories for the populace of pleasure. And he had caught on. But beneath the populace of pleasure lay the populace of work, grim, grimey, and rather terrible. They, too, had to have their providers. And it was a much grimmer business, providing for the populace of work, than for the populace of pleasure. While he was doing his stories, and "getting on" in the world, Tevershall was going to the wall.

He realized now that the bitch-goddess of success had two main appetites: one for flattery, adulation, stroking and tickling, such as writers and artists gave her; but the other a grimmer appetite for meat and bones. And the meat and bones for the bitch-goddess were provided by the men who made money in industry.

Yes, there were two great groups of dogs wrangling for the bitch-goddess: the group of the flatterers, those who offered her amusement, stories, films, plays: and the other, much less showy, much more savage breed, those who gave her meat, the real substance of money. The well-groomed showy dogs of amusement wrangled and snarled among themselves for the favors of the bitch-goddess. But it was nothing to the silent fight-to-the-death that went on among the indispensables, the bone-bringers.

But under Mrs. Bolton's influence, Clifford was tempted to enter this other fight, to capture the bitch-goddess by brute means of industrial production. Somehow he got his pecker up. In one way, Mrs. Bolton made a man of him, as Connie never did. Connie kept him apart, and made him sensitive and conscious of himself and his own states. Mrs. Bolton made him aware only of outside things. Inwardly he began to go soft as pulp. But outwardly he began to be effective.

He even roused himself to go to the mines once more: and when he was there, he went down in a tub, and in a tub he was hauled out into the workings. Things he had learned before the war, and seemed utterly to have forgotten, now came back to him. He sat there, crippled, in a tub, with the underground manager showing him the seam with a powerful torch. And he said little. But his mind began to work.

He began to read again his technical works on the coal-mining industry, he studied the Government reports, and he read with care the latest things on mining and the chemistry of coal and of shale which were written in German. Of course the most valuable discoveries were kept secret as far as possible. But once you started a sort of research in the field of coal-mining, a study of methods and means, a study of by-products and the chemical possibilities of coal, it was astounding the ingenuity and the almost uncanny cleverness of the modern technical mind, as if really the devil himself had lent fiend's wits to the technical scientists of industry. It was far more interesting than art, than literature, poor emotional half-witted stuff, was this technical science of industry. In this field, men were like gods, or demons, inspired to discoveries, and fighting to carry them out. In this activity, men were beyond any mental age calculable. But Clifford knew that when it did come to the emotional and human life, these self-made men were of a mental age of about thirteen, feeble boys. The discrepancy was enormous and appalling.

But let that be. Let man slide down to general idiocy in the emotional and "human" mind, Clifford did not care. Let all that go hang. He was interested in the technicalities of modern coal-mining, and in pulling Tevershall out of the hole.

He went down to the pit day after day, he studied, he put the general manager, and the overhead manager, and the underground manager, and the engineers through a mill they had never dreamed of. Power! He felt a new sense of power flowing through him: power over all these men, over the hundreds and hundreds of colliers. He was finding out: and he was getting things into his grip. And he seemed verily to be re-born. *Now* life came into him! He had been gradually dying, with Connie, in the isolated private life of the artist and the conscious being. Now let all that go. Let it sleep. He simply felt life rush into him out of the coal, out of the pit. The very stale air of the colliery was better than oxygen to him. It gave him a sense of power, power. He was doing something: and he was *going* to do something. He was going to win, to win: not as he had won with his stories, mere publicity, amid a whole sapping of energy and malice. But a man's victory.

At first he thought the solution lay in electricity: convert the coal into electric power. Then a new idea came. The Germans invented a new locomotive engine with a self-feeder, that did not need a fireman. And it was to be fed with a new fuel, that burnt in small quantities at a great heat, under peculiar conditions.

The idea of a new concentrated fuel that burnt with a hard slowness at a fierce heat was what first attracted Clifford. There must be some sort of external stimulus to the burning of such fuel, not merely air supply. He began to experiment, and got a clever young fellow who had proved brilliant in chemistry, to help him.

And he felt triumphant. He had at last got out of himself. He had fulfilled his life-long secret yearning to get out of himself. Art had not done it for him. Art had only made it worse. But now, now he had done it.

He was not aware how much Mrs. Bolton was behind him. He did not know how much he depended on her. But for all that, it was evident that when he was with her his voice dropped to an easy rhythm of intimacy, almost a trifle vulgar.

With Connie, he was a little stiff. He felt he owed her everything, everything, and he showed her the utmost respect and consideration, so long as she gave him mere outward respect. But it was obvious he had a secred dread of her. The new Achilles in him had a heel, and in this heel the woman, the woman like Connie his wife, could lame him fatally. He went in a certain half-subservient dread of her, and was extremely nice to her. But his voice was a little tense when he spoke to her, and he began to be silent whenever she was present.

Only when he was alone with Mrs. Bolton did he really feel a lord and a master, and his voice ran on with her almost as easily and garrulously as her own could run. And he let her shave him or sponge all his body as if he were a child, really as if he were a child.

X

Connie was a good deal alone now, fewer people came to Wragby. Clifford no longer wanted them. He had turned against even the cronies. He was queer. He preferred the radio, which he had installed at some expense, with a good deal of success at last. He could sometimes get Madrid or Frankfort, even there in the uneasy Midlands.

And he would sit alone for hours listening to the loud-speaker bellowing forth. It amazed and stunned Connie. But there he would sit, with a blank entranced expression on his face, like a person losing his mind, and listen, or seem to listen, to the unspeakable thing.

Was he really listening? Or was it a sort of soporific he took, whilst something else worked on underneath in him? Connie did not know. She fled up to her room, or out of doors to the wood. A kind of terror filled her sometimes, a terror of the incipient insanity of the whole civilized species.

But now that Clifford was drifting off to this other weirdness of industrial activity, becoming almost a *creature,* with a hard, efficient shell of an exterior and a pulpy interior, one of the amazing crabs and lobsters of the modern, industrial and financial world, invertebrates of the crustacean order, with shells of steel, like machines, and inner bodies of soft pulp, Connie herself was really completely stranded.

She was not even free, for Clifford must have her there, he seemed to have a nervous terror that she should leave him. The curious pulpy part of him, the emotional and humanly-individual part, depended on her with terror, like a child, almost like an idiot. She must be there, there at Wragby, a Lady Chatterley, his wife. Otherwise he would be lost like an idiot on a moor.

This amazing dependence Connie realized with a sort of horror. She heard him with his pit managers, with the members of his Board, with young scientists, and she was amazed at his shrewd insight into things, his power, his uncanny material power over what is called practical men. He had become a practical man himself, and an amazingly astute and powerful one, a master. Connie attributed it to Mrs. Bolton's influence upon him, just at the crisis in his life.

But this astute and practical man was almost an idiot when left alone to his own emotional life. He worshipped Connie, she was his wife, a higher being, and he worshipped her with a queer, craven idolatry, like a savage, a worship based on enormous fear, and even hate of the power of the idol, the dread idol. All he wanted was for Connie to swear, to swear not to leave him, not to give him away.

"Clifford," she said to him—but this was after she had the key to the hut—"would you really like me to have a child one day?"

He looked at her with a furtive apprehension in his rather prominent pale eyes.

"I shouldn't mind, if it made no difference between us," he said.

"No difference to what?" she asked.

"To you and me; to our love for one another. If it's going to affect that, then I'm all against it. Why, I might even one day have a child of my own!"

She looked at him in amazement.

"I mean, it might come back to me one of these days."

She still stared in amazement, and he was uncomfortable.

"So you would not like it if I had a child?" she said.

"I tell you," he replied quickly, like a cornered dog. "I am quite willing, provided it doesn't touch your love for me. If it would touch that, I am dead against it."

Connie could only be silent in cold fear and contempt. Such talk was really the gabbling of an idiot. He no longer knew what he was talking about.

"Oh, it wouldn't make any difference to my feeling for you," she said, with a certain sarcasm.

"There!" he said. "That is the point. In that case I don't mind in the least. I mean it would be awfully nice to have a child running about the house, and feel one was building up a future for it. I should have something to strive for then, and I should know it was your child, shouldn't I, dear? And it would seem just the same as my own. Because it is you who count in these matters. You know that, don't you, dear? I don't enter, I am a cipher. You are the great I-am, as far as life goes. You know that, don't you? I mean, as far as I am concerned. I mean, but for you I am absolutely nothing. I live for your sake and your future. I am nothing to myself."

Connie heard it all with deepening dismay and repulsion. It was one of the ghastly half-truths that poison human existence. What man in his senses would say such things to a woman! But men aren't in their senses. What man with a spark of honor would put this ghastly burden of life-responsibility upon a woman, and leave her there, in the void?

Moreover, in half-an-hour's time, Connie heard Clifford talking to Mrs. Bolton, in a hot, impulsive voice, revealing himself in a sort of passionless passion to the woman, as if she were half mistress, half foster-mother to him. And Mrs. Bolton was carefully dressing him in evening clothes, for there were important business guests in the house.

Connie really sometimes felt she would die at this time. She felt she was being crushed to death by weird lies, and by the amazing cruelty of idiocy. Clifford's strange business efficiency in a way overawed her, and his declaration of private worship put her into a panic. There was nothing between them. She never even touched him nowadays, and he never touched her. He never even took her hand and held it kindly. No, and because they were so utterly out of touch, he tortured her with his declaration of idolatry. It was the cruelty of utter impotence. And she felt her reason would give way, or she would die.

She fled as much as possible to the wood. One afternoon, as she sat brooding, watching the water bubbling coldly in John's Well, the keeper had strode up to her.

"I got you a key made, my Lady!" he said, saluting, and he offered her the key.

"Thank you so much!" she said, startled.

"The hut's not very tidy, if you don't mind," he said. "I cleared it of what I could."

"But I didn't want you to trouble!" she said.

"Oh, it wasn't any trouble. I am setting the hens in about a week. But they won't be scared of you. I s'll have to see to them morning and night, but I shan't bother you any more than I can help."

"But you wouldn't bother me," she pleaded. "I'd rather not go to the hut at all, if I am going to be in the way."

He looked at her with his keen blue eyes. He seemed kindly, but distant. But at least he was sane, and wholesome, if even he looked thin and ill. A cough troubled him.

"You have a cough," she said.

"Nothing—a cold! The last pneumonia left me with a cough, but it's nothing."

He kept distant from her, and would not come any nearer.

She went fairly often to the hut, in the morning or in the afternoon, but he was never there. No doubt he avoided her on purpose. He wanted to keep his own privacy.

He had made the hut tidy, put the little table and chair near the fireplace, left a little pile of kindling and small logs, and put the tools and traps away as far as possible, effacing himself. Outside, by the clearing, he had built a low little roof of boughs and straw, a shelter for the birds, and under it stood the five coops. And, one day when she came, she found two brown hens sitting alert and fierce in the coops, sitting on pheasants' eggs, and fluffed out so proud and deep in all the heat of the pondering female blood. This almost broke Connie's heart. She, herself, was so forlorn and unused, not a female at all, just a mere thing of terrors.

Then all the five coops were occupied by hens, three brown and a grey and a black. All alike, they clustered themselves down on the eggs in the soft nestling ponderosity of the female urge, the female nature, fluffing out their feathers. And with brilliant eyes they watched Connie, as she crouched before them, and they gave short sharp clucks of anger and alarm, but chiefly of female anger at being approached.

Connie found corn in the corn-bin in the hut. She offered it to the hens in her hand. They would not eat it. Only one hen pecked at her hand with a fierce little jab, so Connie was frightened. But she was pining to give them something, the brooding mothers who neither fed themselves nor drank. She brought water in a little tin, and was delighted when one of the hens drank.

Now she came every day to the hens, they were the only things in the world that warmed her heart. Clifford's protestations made her go cold from head to foot. Mrs. Bolton's voice made her go cold, and the sound of the business men who came. An occasional letter from Michaelis affected her with the same sense of chill. She felt she would surely die if it lasted much longer.

Yet it was spring, and the bluebells were coming in the wood, and the leaf-buds on the hazels were opening like the spatter of green rain. How terrible it was that it should be spring, and everything cold-hearted, cold-hearted. Only the hens, fluffed so wonderfully on the eggs, were warm with their hot, brooding female bodies! Connie felt herself living on the brink of fainting all the time.

Then, one day, a lovely sunny day with great tufts of primroses under the hazels, and many violets dotting the paths, she came in the afternoon to the coops and there was one tiny, tiny perky chicken tinily prancing round in front of a coop, and the mother hen clucking in terror. The slim little chick was greyish-brown with dark markings, and it was the most alive little spark of a creature in seven kingdoms at that moment. Connie crouched to watch in a sort of ecstasy. Life, life! Pure, sparky, fearless new life! New life! So tiny and so utterly without fear! Even when it scampered a little scramblingly into the coop again, and disappeared under the hen's feathers in answer to the mother hen's wild alarm-cries, it was not really frightened; it took it as a game, the game of living. For in a moment a tiny sharp head was poking through the gold-brown feathers of the hen, and eyeing the Cosmos.

Connie was fascinated. And at the same time never had she felt so acutely the agony of her own female forlornness. It was becoming unbearable.

She had only one desire now, to go to the clearing in the wood. The rest was a kind of painful dream. But sometimes she was kept all day at Wragby, by her duties as hostess. And then she felt as if she, too, were going blank, just blank and insane.

One evening, guests or no guests, she escaped after tea. It was late, and she fled across the park like one who fears to be called back. The sun was setting rosy as she entered the wood, but she pressed on among the flowers. The light would last long overhead.

She arrived at the clearing, flushed and semi-conscious. The keeper was there, in his shirt-sleeves, just closing up the coops for the night, so the little occupants would be safe. But still one little trio was pattering about on tiny feet, alert drab mites, under the straw shelter, refusing to be called in by the anxious mother.

"I had to come and see the chickens!" she said, panting, glancing shyly at the keeper, almost unaware of him. "Are there any more?"

"Thirty-six so far!" he said. "Not bad!"

He, too, took a curious pleasure in watching the young things come out. Connie crouched in front of the last coop. The three chicks had run in. But still their cheeky heads came poking sharply through the yellow feathers, then withdrawing, then only one beady little head eyeing forth from the vast mother-body.

"I'd love to touch them," she said, putting her fingers gingerly through the bars of the coop. But the mother-hen pecked at her hand fiercely, and Connie drew back startled and frightened.

"How she pecks at me! She hates me!" she said in a wondering voice. "But I wouldn't hurt them!"

The man standing above her laughed, and crouched down beside her, knees apart, and put his hand with quiet confidence slowly into the coop. The old hen pecked at him, but not so savagely. And slowly, softly, with sure gentle fingers, he felt among the old bird's feathers and drew out a faintly-peeping chick in his closed hand.

"There!" he said, holding out his hand to her. She took the little drab thing between her hands, and there it stood, on its impossible little stalks of legs, its atom of balancing life trembling through its almost weightless feet into Connie's hands. But it lifted its handsome, clean-shaped little head boldly, and looked sharply round, and gave a little "peep."

"So adorable! So cheeky!" she said softly.

The keeper, squatting beside her, was also watching with an amused face the bold little bird in her hands. Suddenly he saw a tear fall on to her wrist.

And he stood up, and stood away, moving to the other coop. For suddenly he was aware of the old flame shooting and leaping up in his loins, that he had hoped was quiescent for ever. He fought against it, turning his back to her. But it leapt, and leapt downward, circling in his knees.

He turned again to look at her. She was kneeling and holding her two hands slowly forward, blindly, so that the chicken should run in to the mother-hen again. And there was something so mute and forlorn in her, compassion flamed in his bowels for her.

Without knowing, he came quickly towards her and crouched beside her again, taking the chick from her hands, because she was afraid of the hen, and putting it back in the coop. At the back of his loins the fire suddenly darted stronger.

He glanced apprehensively at her. Her face was averted, and she was crying blindly, in all the anguish of her generation's forlornness. His heart melted suddenly, like a drop of fire, and he put out his hand and laid his fingers on her knee.

"You shouldn't cry," he said softly.

But then she put her hands over her face and felt that really her heart was broken and nothing mattered any more.

He laid his hand on her shoulder, and softly, gently, it began to travel down the curve of her back, blindly, with a blind stroking motion, to the curve of her crouching loins. And there his hand softly, softly, stroked the curve of her flank, in the blind instinctive caress.

She had found her scrap of handkerchief and was blindly trying to dry her face.

"Shall you come to the hut?" he said, in a quiet, neutral voice.

And closing his hand softly on her upper arm, he drew her up and led her slowly to the hut, not letting go of her till she was inside. Then he cleared aside the chair and table, and took a brown soldier's blanket from the tool-chest, spreading it slowly. She glanced at his face, as she stood motionless.

His face was pale and without expression, like that of a man submitting to fate.

"You lie there," he said softly, and he shut the door, so that it was dark, quite dark.

With a queer obedience, she lay down on the blanket. Then she felt the soft, groping, helplessly desirous hand touching her body, feeling for her face. The hand stroked her face softly, softly, with infinite soothing and assurance, and at last there was the soft touch of a kiss on her cheek.

She lay quite still, in a sort of sleep, in a sort of dream. Then she quivered as she felt his hand groping softly, yet with queer thwarted clumsiness among her clothing. Yet the hand knew, too, how to unclothe her where it wanted. He drew down the thin silk sheath, slowly, carefully, right down and over her feet. Then with a quiver of exquisite pleasure he touched the warm soft body, and touched her navel for a moment in a kiss. And he had to come into her at once, to enter the peace on earth of her soft, quiescent body. It was the moment of pure peace for him, the entry into the body of a woman.

She lay still, in a kind of sleep, always in a kind of sleep. The activity, the orgasm was his, all his; she could strive for herself no more. Even the tightness of his arms round her, even the intense movement of his body, and the springing seed in her, was a kind of sleep, from which she did not begin to rouse till he had finished and lay softly panting against her breast.

Then she wondered, just dimly wondered, why? Why was this necessary? Why had it lifted a great cloud from her and given her peace? Was it real? Was it real?

Her tormented modern-woman's brain still had no rest. Was it real? And she knew, if she gave herself to the man, it was real. But if she kept herself for herself, it was nothing. She was old; millions of years old, she felt. And at last, she could bear the burden of herself no more. She was to be had for the taking. To be had for the taking.

The man lay in a mysterious stillness. What was he feeling? What was he thinking? She did not know. He was a strange man to her, she did not know him. She must only wait, for she did not dare to break his mysterious stillness. He lay there with his arms round her, his body on hers, his wet body touching hers, so close. And completely unknown. Yet not unpeaceful. His very silence was peaceful.

She knew that, when at last he roused and drew away from her. It was like an abandonment. He drew her dress in the darkness down over her knees and stood for a few moments, apparently adjusting his own clothing. Then he quietly opened the door and went out.

She saw a very brilliant little moon shining above the afterglow over the oaks. Quickly she got up and arranged herself; she was tidy. Then she went to the door of the hut.

All the lower wood was in shadow, almost darkness. Yet the sky overhead was crystal. But it shed hardly any light. He came through the lower shadow towards her, his face lifted like a pale blotch.

"Shall we go, then?" he said.

"Where?"

"I'll go with you to the gate."

He arranged things his own way. He locked the door of the hut and came after her.

"You aren't sorry, are you?" he asked, as he went at her side.

"No! No! Are you?" she said.

"For that! No!" he said. Then after a while he added: "But there's the rest of things."

"What rest of things?" she said.

"Sir Clifford. Other folks. All the complications."

"Why complications?" she said, disappointed.

"It's always so. For you as well as for me. There's always complications." He walked on steadily in the dark.

"And are you sorry?" she said.

"In a way!" he replied, looking up at the sky. "I thought I'd done with it all. Now I've begun again."

"Begun what?"

"Life."

"Life!" she re-echoed, with a queer thrill.

"It's life," he said. "There's no keeping clear. And if you do keep clear you might almost as well die. So if I've got to be broken open again, I have."

She did not quite see it that way, but still . . .

"It's just love," she said cheerfully.

"Whatever that may be," he replied.

They went on through the darkening wood in silence, till they were almost at the gate.

"But you don't hate me, do you?" she said wistfully.

"Nay, nay," he replied. And suddenly he held her fast against his breast again, with the old connecting passion. "Nay, for me it was good, it was good. Was it for you?"

"Yes, for me too," she answered, a little untruthfully, for she had not been conscious of much.

He kissed her softly, softly, with the kisses of warmth.

"If only there weren't so many other people in the world," he said lugubriously.

She laughed. They were at the gate to the park. He opened it for her.

"I won't come any farther," he said.

"No!" And she held out her hand, as if to shake hands. But he took it in both his.

"Shall I come again?" she asked wistfully.

"Yes! Yes!"

She left him and went across the park.

He stood back and watched her going into the dark, against the pallor of the horizon. Almost with bitterness he watched her go. She had connected him up again, when he had wanted to be alone. She had cost him that bitter privacy of a man who at last wants only to be alone.

He turned into the dark of the wood. All was still, the moon had set. But he was aware of the noises of the night, the engines at Stacks Gate, the traffic on the main road. Slowly he climbed the denuded knoll. And from the top he could see the country, bright rows of lights at Stacks Gate, smaller lights at Tevershall pit, the yellow lights of Tevershall and lights everywhere, here and there, on the dark country, with the distant blush of furnaces, faint and rosy, since the night was clear, the rosiness of the outpouring of white-hot metal. Sharp, wicked electric lights at Stacks Gate! An undefinable quick of evil in them! And all the unease, the ever-shifting dread of the industrial night in the Midlands. He could hear the winding-engines at Stacks Gate turning down the seven-o'clock miners. The pit worked three shifts.

He went down again in to the darkness and seclusion of the wood. But he knew that the seclusion of the wood was illusory. The industrial noises broke the solitude, the sharp lights, though unseen, mocked it. A man could no longer be private and withdrawn. The world allows no hermits. And now he had taken the woman, and brought on himself a new cycle of pain and doom. For he knew by experience what it meant.

It was not woman's fault, nor even love's fault, nor the fault of sex. The fault lay there, out there, in those evil electric lights and diabolical rattlings of engines. There, in the world of the mechanical greedy, greedy mechanism and mechanized greed, sparkling with lights and gushing hot metal and roaring with traffic, there lay the vast evil thing, ready to destroy whatever did not conform. Soon it would destroy the wood, and the bluebells would spring no more. All vulnerable things must perish under the rolling and running of iron.

He thought with infinite tenderness of the woman. Poor forlorn thing, she was nicer than she knew, and oh! so much too nice for the tough lot she was in contact with. Poor thing, she too had some of the vulnerability of the wild hyacinths, she wasn't all tough rubber-goods and platinum, like the modern girl. And they would do her in! As sure as life, they would do her in, as they do in all naturally tender life. Tender! Somewhere she was tender, tender with a tenderness of the growing hyacinths, something that has gone out of the celluloid women of today. But he would protect her with his heart for a little while. For a little while, before the insentient iron world and the Mammon of mechanized greed did them both in, her as well as him.

He went home with his gun and his dog, to the dark cottage, lit the lamp, started the fire, and ate his supper of bread and cheese, young onions and beer. He was alone, in a silence he loved. His room was clean and tidy, but rather stark. Yet the fire was bright, the hearth white, the petroleum lamp hung right over the table, with its white, oil-cloth. He tried to read a book about India, but tonight he could not read. He sat by the fire in his shirt-sleeves, not smoking, but with a mug of beer in reach. And he thought about Connie.

To tell the truth, he was sorry for what had happened, perhaps most for her sake. He had a sense of foreboding. No sense of wrong or sin; he was troubled by no conscience in that respect. He knew that conscience was chiefly fear of society, or fear of oneself. He was not afraid of himself. But he was quite consciously afraid of society, which he knew by instinct to be a malevolent, partly-insane beast.

The woman! If she could be there with him, and there were nobody else in the world! The desire rose again, his penis began to stir like a live bird. At the same time an oppression, a dread of exposing himself and her to that outside Thing that sparkled viciously in the electric lights, weighed down his shoulders. She, poor thing, was just a young female creature to him; but a young female creature whom he had gone into and whom he desired again.

Stretching with the curious yawn of desire, for he had been alone and apart from man or woman for four years, he rose and took his coat again, and his gun, lowered the lamp and went out into the starry night, with the dog. Driven by desire and by dread of the malevolent Thing outside, he made his round in the wood, slowly, softly. He loved the darkness and folded himself into it. It fitted the turgidity of his desire which, in spite of all, was like a riches; the stirring restlessness of his penis, the stirring fire in his loins! Oh, if only there were other men to be with, to fight that sparkling electric Thing outside there, to preserve the tenderness of life, the tenderness of women, and the natural riches of desire. If only there were men to fight side by side with! But the men were all outside there, glorying in the Thing, triumphing or being trodden down in the rush of mechanized greed or of greedy mechanism.

Constance, for her part, had hurried across the park, home, almost without thinking. As yet she had no after-thought. She would be in time for dinner.

She was annoyed to find the doors fastened, however, so that she had to ring. Mrs. Bolton opened.

"Why, there you are, your Ladyship! I was beginning to wonder if you'd gone lost!" she said a little roguishly. "Sir Clifford hasn't asked for you, though; he's got Mr. Linley in with him, talking over something. It looks as if he'd stay to dinner, doesn't it, my Lady?"

"It does rather," said Connie.

"Shall I put dinner back a quarter of an hour? That would give you time to dress in comfort."

"Perhaps you'd better."

Mr. Linley was the general manager of the collieries, an elderly man from the north, with not quite enough punch to suit Clifford; not up to post-war conditions, nor post-war colliers either, with their "ca' canny" creed. But Connie liked Mr. Linley, though she was glad to be spared the toadying of his wife.

Linley stayed to dinner, and Connie was the hostess men liked so much, so modest, yet so attentive and aware, with big, wide blue eyes and a soft repose that sufficiently hid what she was really thinking. Connie had played this woman so much, it was almost second nature to her; but still, decidedly second. Yet it was curious how everything disappeared from her consciousness while she played it.

She waited patiently till she could go upstairs and think her own thoughts. She was always waiting, it seemed to be her *forte*.

Once in her room, however, she felt still vague and confused. She didn't know what to think. What sort of a man was he, really? Did he really like her? Not much, she felt. Yet he was kind. There was something, a sort of warm naïve kindness, curious and sudden, that almost opened her womb to him. But she felt he might be kind like that to any woman. Though even so, it was curiously soothing, comforting. And he was a passionate man, wholesome and passionate. But perhaps he wasn't quite individual enough; he might be the same with any woman as he had been with her. It really wasn't personal. She was only really a female to him.

But perhaps that was better. And after all, he was kind to the female in her,

which no man had ever been. Men were very kind to the *person* she was, but
rather cruel to the female, despising her or ignoring her altogether. Men were
awfully kind to Constance Reid or to Lady Chatterley; but not to her womb
they weren't kind. And he took no notice of Constance or of Lady Chatterley;
he just softly stroked her loins or her breasts.

She went to the wood next day. It was a grey, still afternoon, with the
dark-green dogs'-mercury spreading under the hazel copse, and all the trees
making a silent effort to open their buds. Today she could almost feel it in her
own body, the huge heave of the sap in the massive trees, upwards, up, up to the
bud-tips, there to push into little flamey oak-leaves, bronze as blood. It was like
a tide running turgid upward, and spreading on the sky.

She came to the clearing, but he was not there. She had only half expected
him. The pheasant chicks were running lightly abroad, light as insects, from the
coops where the yellow hens clucked anxiously. Connie sat and watched them,
and waited. She only waited. Even the chicks she hardly saw. She waited.

The time passed with dream-like slowness, and he did not come. She had
only half expected him. He never came in the afternoon. She must go home to
tea. But she had to force herself to leave.

As she went home, a fine drizzle of rain fell.

"Is it raining again?" said Clifford, seeing her shake her hat.

"Just drizzle."

She poured tea in silence, absorbed in a sort of obstinacy. She did want to see
the keeper today, to see if it were really real. If it were really real.

"Shall I read a little to you afterwards?" said Clifford.

She looked at him. Had he sensed something?

"The spring makes me feel queer—I thought I might rest a little," she said.

"Just as you like. Not feeling really unwell, are you?"

"No! Only rather tired—with the spring. Will you have Mrs. Bolton to play
something with you?"

"No! I think I'll listen in."

She heard the curious satisfaction in his voice. She went upstairs to her bedroom. There she heard the loudspeaker begin to bellow, in an idiotically velveteen, genteel sort of voice, something about a series of street-cries, the very
cream of genteel affectation imitating old criers. She pulled on her old violet-
colored mackintosh, and slipped out of the house at the side door.

The drizzle of rain was like a veil over the world, mysterious, hushed, not
cold. She got very warm as she hurried across the park. She had to open her light
waterproof.

The wood was silent, still and secret in the evening drizzle of rain, full of the
mystery of eggs and half-open buds, half-unsheathed flowers. In the dimness of
it all trees glistened naked and dark as if they had unclothed themselves, and the
green things on earth seemed to hum with greenness.

There was still no one at the clearing. The chicks had nearly all gone under
the mother-hens, only one or two lost adventurous ones still dibbed about in
the dryness under the straw roof-shelter. And they were doubtful of themselves.

So! He still had not been. He was staying away on purpose. Or perhaps
something was wrong. Perhaps she should go to the cottage and see.

But she was born to wait. She opened the hut with her key. It was all tidy,
the corn put in the bin, the blankets folded on the shelf, the straw neat in a
corner; a new bundle of straw. The hurricane lamp hung on a nail. The table
and chair had been put back where she had lain.

She sat down on a stool in the doorway. How still everything was! The fine
rain blew very softly, filmily, but the wind made no noise. Nothing made any
sound. The trees stood like powerful beings, dim, twilit, silent and alive. How
alive everything was!

Night was drawing near again; she would have to go. He was avoiding her.

But suddenly he came striding into the clearing, in his black oilskin jacket
like a chauffeur, shining with wet. He glanced quickly at the hut, half-saluted,
then veered aside and went on to the coops. There he crouched in silence,
looking carefully at everything, then carefully shutting the hens and chicks up
safe against the night.

At last he came slowly towards her. She still sat on her stool. He stood before
her under the porch.

"You came then," he said, using the intonation of the dialect.

"Yes," she replied, looking up at him. "You're late!"

"Ay!" he replied, looking away into the wood.

She rose slowly, drawing aside her stool.

"Did you want to come in?" she asked.

He looked down at her shrewdly.

"Won't folks be thinkin' somethink, you comin' here every night?" he said.

"Why?" She looked up at him, at a loss. "I said I'd come. Nobody knows."

"They soon will, though," he replied. "An' what then?"

She was at a loss for an answer.

"Why should they know?" she said.

"Folks always does," he said fatally.

Her lip quivered a little.

"Well, I can't help it," she faltered.

"Nay," he said. "You can help it by not comin'—if yer want to," he added,
in a lower tone.

"But I don't want to," she murmured.

He looked away into the wood, and was silent.

"But what when folks finds out?" he asked at last. "Think about it! Think
how lowered you'll feel, one of your husband's servants."

She looked up at his averted face.

"Is it," she stammered, "is it that you don't want me?"

"Think!" he said. "Think what if folks finds out—Sir Clifford an' a'—an'
everybody talkin'—"

"Well, I can go away."

"Where to?"

"Anywhere! I've got money of my own. My mother left me twenty thousand pounds in trust, and I know Clifford can't touch it. I can go away."

"But 'appen you don't want to go away."

"Yes, yes! I don't care what happens to me."

"Ah, you think that! But you'll care! You'll have to care, everybody has.
You've got to remember your ladyship is carrying on with a gamekeeper. It's
not as if I was a gentleman. Yes, you'd care. You'd care."

"I shouldn't. What do I care about my ladyship! I hate it, really. I feel people
are jeering every time they say it. And they are, they are! Even you jeer when
you say it."

"Me!"

For the first time he looked straight at her, and into her eyes.

"I don't jeer at you," he said.

As he looked into her eyes she saw his own eyes go dark, quite dark, the pupils dilating.

"Don't you care about a' the risk?" he asked in a husky voice. "You should care. Don't care when it's too late!"

There was a curious warning pleading in his voice.

"But I've nothing to lose," she said fretfully. "If you knew what it is, you'd think I'd be glad to lose it. But are you afraid for yourself?"

"Ay!" he said briefly. "I am. I'm afraid. I'm afraid. I'm afraid o' things."

"What things?" she asked.

He gave a curious backward jerk of his head, indicating the outer world.

"Things! Everybody! The lot of 'em."

Then he bent down and suddenly kissed her unhappy face.

"Nay, I don't care," he said. "Let's have it, an' damn the rest. But if you was to feel sorry you'd ever done it—!"

"Don't put me off," she pleaded.

He put his fingers to her cheek and kissed her again suddenly.

"Let me come in then," he said softly. "An' take off your mackintosh."

He hung up his gun, slipped out of his wet leather jacket, and reached for the blankets.

"I brought another blanket," he said, "so we can put one over us if we like."

"I can't stay long," she said. "Dinner is half-past seven."

He looked at her swiftly, then at his watch.

"All right," he said.

He shut the door, and lit a tiny light in the hanging hurricane lamp.

"One time we'll have a long time," he said.

He put the blankets down carefully, one folded for her head. Then he sat down for a moment on the stool, and drew her to him, holding her close with one arm, feeling for her body with his free hand. She heard the catch of his intaken breath as he found her. Under her frail petticoat she was naked.

"Eh! what it is to touch thee!" he said, as his finger caressed the delicate, warm secret skin of her waist and hips. He put his face down and rubbed his cheek against her belly and against her thighs again and again. And again she wondered a little over the sort of rapture it was to him. She did not understand the beauty he found in her, through touch upon her living secret body, almost the ecstasy of beauty. For passion alone is awake to it. And when passion is dead, or absent, then the magnificent throb of beauty is incomprehensible and even a little despicable; warm, live beauty of contact, so much deeper than the beauty of vision. She felt the glide of his cheek on her thighs and belly and buttocks, and the close brushing of his moustache and his soft thick hair, and her knees began to quiver. Far down in her she felt a new stirring, a new nakedness emerging. And she was half afraid. Half she wished he would not caress her so. He was encompassing her somehow. Yet she was waiting, waiting.

And when he came into her, with an intensification of relief and consummation that was pure peace to him, still she was waiting. She felt herself a little left out. And she knew, partly it was her own fault. She willed herself into this separateness. Now perhaps she was condemned to it. She lay still, feeling his motion within her, his deep-sunk intentness, the sudden quiver of him at the springing of his seed, then slow-subsiding thrust. That thrust of the buttocks, surely it was a little ridiculous. If you were a woman, and apart in all the business, surely that thrusting of the man's buttocks was supremely ridiculous. Surely the man was intensely ridiculous in this posture and this act!

But she lay still, without recoil. Even, when he had finished, she did not
rouse herself to get a grip on her own satisfaction, as she had done with Michaelis; she lay still, and the tears slowly filled and ran from her eyes.

He lay still, too. But he held her close and tried to cover her poor naked legs
with his legs, to keep them warm. He lay on her with a close, undoubting
warmth.

"Are ter cold?" he asked, in a soft, small voice, as if she were close, so close.
Whereas she was left out, distant.

"No! But I must go," she said gently.

He sighed, held her closer, then relaxed to rest again.

He had not guessed her tears. He thought she was there with him.

"I must go," she repeated.

He lifted himself, kneeled beside her a moment, kissed the inner side of her
thighs, then drew down her skirts, buttoning his own clothes unthinking, not
even turning aside, in the faint, faint light from the lantern.

"Tha mun come ter th' cottage one time," he said, looking down at her with
a warm, sure, easy face.

But she lay there inert, and was gazing up at him thinking. Stranger! Stranger! She even resented him a little.

He put on his coat and looked for his hat, which had fallen, then he slung on
his gun.

"Come then!" he said, looking down at her with those warm, peaceful sort
of eyes.

She rose slowly. She didn't want to go. She also rather resented staying. He
helped her with her thin waterproof, and saw she was tidy.

Then he opened the door. The outside was quite dark. The faithful dog
under the porch stood up with pleasure seeing him. The drizzle of rain drifted
greyly past upon the darkness. It was quite dark.

"Ah mun ta'e th' lantern," he said. "The'll be nob'dy."

He walked just before her in the narrow path, swinging the hurricane lamp
low, revealing the wet grass, the black shiny tree roots like snakes, wan flowers.
For the rest, all was grey rain-mist and complete darkness.

"Tha mun come to the cottage one time," he said, "shall ta? We might as
well be hung for a sheep as for a lamb."

It puzzled her, his queer, persistent wanting her, when there was nothing
between them, when he never really spoke to her, and in spite of herself she
resented the dialect. His "tha mun come" seemed not addressed to her, but
some common woman. She recognized the foxglove leaves of the riding and
knew, more or less, where they were.

"It's quarter past seven," he said, "you'll do it." He had changed his voice,
seemed to feel her distance. As they turned the last bend in the riding towards
the hazel wall and the gate, he blew out the light. "We'll see from here," he
said, taking her gently by the arm.

But it was difficult, the earth under their feet was a mystery, but he felt his
way by tread: he was used to it. At the gate he gave her his electric torch. "It's
a bit lighter in the park," he said; "but take it for fear you get off th' path."

It was true, there seemed a ghost-glimmer of greyness in the open space of
the park. He suddenly drew her to him and whipped his hand under her dress
again, feeling her warm body with his wet, chill hand.

"I could die for the touch of a woman like thee," he said in his throat. "If tha
would stop another minute."

She felt the sudden force of his wanting her again.

"No, I must run," she said, a little wildly.

"Ay," he replied, suddenly changed, letting her go.

She turned away, and on the instant she turned back to him saying: "Kiss me."

He bent over her indistinguishable and kissed her on the left eye. She held her mouth and he softly kissed it, but at once drew away. He hated mouth kisses.

"I'll come tomorrow," she said, drawing away; "if I can," she added.

"Ay! not so late," he replied out of the darkness. Already she could not see him at all. "Good night," she said.

"Good night, your Ladyship," his voice.

She stopped and looked back into the wet dark. She could just see the bulk of him. "Why did you say that?" she said

"Nay," he replied. "Good night then, run!"

She plunged on in the dark-grey tangible night. She found the side door open, and slipped into her room unseen. As she closed the door the gong sounded, but she would take her bath all the same—she must take her bath. "But I won't be late any more," she said to herself; "it's too annoying."

The next day she did not go to the wood. She went instead with Clifford to Uthwaite. He could occasionally go out now in the car, and had got a strong young man as chauffeur, who could help him out of the car if need be. He particularly wanted to see his godfather, Leslie Winter, who lived at Shipley Hall, not far from Uthwaite. Winter was an elderly gentleman now, wealthy, one of the wealthy coal-owners who had had their hey-day in King Edward's time. King Edward had stayed more than once at Shipley, for the shooting. It was a handsome old stucco hall, very elegantly appointed, for Winter was a bachelor and prided himself on his style; but the place was beset by collieries. Leslie Winter was attached to Clifford, but personally did not entertain a great respect for him, because of the photographs in illustrated papers and the literature. The old man was a buck of the King Edward school, who thought life and the scribbling fellows were something else. Towards Connie the Squire was always rather gallant; he thought her an attractive demure maiden and rather wasted on Clifford, and it was a thousand pities she stood no chance of bringing forth an heir to Wragby. He himself had no heir.

Connie wondered what he would say if he knew that Clifford's gamekeeper had been having intercourse with her, and saying to her "tha mun come to th' cottage one time." He would detest and despise her, for he had come almost to hate the shoving forward of the working classes. A man of her own class he would not mind, for Connie was gifted from nature with this appearance of demure, submissive maidenliness, and perhaps it was part of her nature. Winter called her "dear child" and gave her a rather lovely miniature of an eighteenth-century lady, rather against her will.

But Connie was preoccupied with her affair with the keeper. After all Mr. Winter, who was really a gentleman and a man of the world, treated her as a person and a discriminating individual; he did not lump her together with all the rest of his female womanhood in his "thee" and "tha."

She did not go to the wood that day nor the next, nor the day following. She did not go so long as she felt, or imagined she felt, the man waiting for her, wanting her. But the fourth day she was terribly unsettled and uneasy. She still refused to go to the wood and open her thighs once more to the man. She thought of all the things she might do—drive to Sheffield, pay visits, and the thought of all these things was repellent. At last she decided to take a walk, not towards the wood, but in the opposite direction; she would go to Marehay, through the little iron gate in the other side of the park fence. It was a quiet grey day of spring, almost warm. She walked on unheeding, absorbed in thoughts she was not even conscious of. She was not really aware of anything outside her, till she was startled by the loud barking of the dog at Marehay Farm. Marehay Farm! Its pastures ran up to Wragby park fence, so they were neighbors, but it was some time since Connie had called.

"Bell!" she said to the big white bull-terrier. "Bell! have you forgotten me? Don't you know me?"—She was afraid of dogs, and Bell stood back and bellowed, and she wanted to pass through the farmyard on to the warren path.

Mrs. Flint appeared. She was a woman of Constance's own age, had been a school-teacher, but Connie suspected her of being rather a false little thing.

"Why, it's Lady Chatterley! Why!" And Mrs. Flint's eyes glowed again, and she flushed like a young girl. "Bell, Bell. Why! barking at Lady Chatterley! Bell! Be quiet!" She darted forward and slashed at the dog with a white cloth she held in her hand, then came forward to Connie.

"She used to know me," said Connie, shaking hands. The Flints were Chatterley tenants.

"Of course she knows your ladyship! She's just showing off," said Mrs. Flint, glowing and looking up with a sort of flushed confusion, "but it's so long since she's seen you. I do hope you are better."

"Yes, thanks, I'm all right."

"We've hardly seen you all winter. Will you come in and look at the baby?"

"Well!" Connie hesitated. "Just for a minute."

Mrs. Flint flew wildly in to tidy up, and Connie came slowly after her, hesitating in the rather dark kitchen where the kettle was boiling by the fire. Back came Mrs. Flint.

"I do hope you'll excuse me," she said. "Will you come in here."

They went into the living-room, where a baby was sitting on the rag hearthrug, and the table was roughly set for tea. A young servant-girl backed down the passage, shy and awkward.

The baby was a perky little thing of about a year, with red hair like its father, and cheeky pale-blue eyes. It was a girl, and not to be daunted. It sat among cushions and was surrounded with rag dolls and other toys in modern excess.

"Why, what a dear she is!" said Connie, "and how she's grown! A big girl! A big girl."

She had given it a shawl when it was born, and celluloid ducks for Christmas.

"There, Josephine! Who's that come to see you? Who's this, Josephine? Lady Chatterley—you know Lady Chatterley, don't you?"

The queer pert little mite gazed cheekily at Connie. Ladyships were still all the same to her.

"Come! Will you come to me?" said Connie to the baby.

The baby didn't care one way or another, so Connie picked her up and held her in her lap. How warm and lovely it was to hold a child in one's lap, and the soft little arms, the unconscious cheeky little legs.

"I was just having a rough cup of tea all by myself. Luke's gone to market, so I can have it when I like. Would you care for a cup, Lady Chatterley? I don't suppose it's what you're used to, but if you would . . ."

Connie would, though she didn't want to be reminded of what she was used to. There was a great relaying of the table, and the best cups brought and the best teapot.

"If only you wouldn't take any trouble," said Connie.

But if Mrs. Flint took no trouble, where was the fun! So Connie played with the child and was amused by its little female dauntlessness, and got a deep voluptuous pleasure out of its soft young warmth. Young life. And so fearless! So fearless, because so defenseless. All the older people, so narrow with fear.

She had a cup of tea, which was rather strong, and very good bread and butter, and bottled damsons. Mrs. Flint flushed and glowed and bridled with excitement, as if Connie were some gallant knight. And they had a real female chat, and both of them enjoyed it.

"It's a poor little tea, though," said Mrs. Flint.

"It's much nicer than at home," said Connie truthfully.

"Oh-h!" said Mrs. Flint, not believing, of course.

But at last Connie rose.

"I must go," she said. "My husband has no idea where I am. He'll be wondering all kinds of things."

"He'll never think you're here," laughed Mrs. Flint excitedly. "He'll be sending the crier round."

"Good-bye, Josephine," said Connie, kissing the baby and ruffling its red, wispy hair.

Mrs. Flint insisted on opening the locked and barred front door. Connie emerged in the farm's little front garden, shut in by a privet hedge. There were two rows of auriculas by the path, very velvety and rich.

"Lovely auriculas," said Connie.

"Recklesses, as Luke calls them," laughed Mrs. Flint. "Have some."

And eagerly she picked the velvet and primrose flowers.

"Enough! Enough!" said Connie.

They came to the little garden gate.

"Which way were you going?" asked Mrs. Flint.

"By the warren."

"Let me see! Oh, yes, the cows are in the gin close. But they're not up yet. But the gate's locked, you'll have to climb."

"I can climb," said Connie.

"Perhaps I can just go down the close with you."

They went down the poor, rabbit-bitten pasture. Birds were whistling in wild evening triumph in the wood. A man was calling up the last cows, which trailed slowly over the path-worn pasture.

"They're late, milking, tonight," said Mrs. Flint severely. "They know Luke won't be back till after dark."

They came to the fence, beyond which the young firwood bristled dense. There was a little gate, but it was locked. In the grass on the inside stood a bottle, empty.

"There's the keeper's empty bottle for his milk," explained Mrs. Flint. "We bring it as far as here for him, and then he fetches it himself."

"When?" said Connie.

"Oh, any time he's around. Often in the morning. Well, good-bye, Lady Chatterley! And do come again. It was so lovely having you."

Connie climbed the fence into the narrow path between the dense, bristling young firs. Mrs. Flint went running back across the pasture, in a sun-bonnet, because she was really a school teacher. Constance didn't like this dense new part of the wood; it seemed grotesque and choking. She hurried on with her head down, thinking of the Flint's baby. It was a dear little thing, but it would be a bit bow-legged like its father. It showed already, but perhaps it would grow out of it. How warm and fulfilling somehow to have a baby, and how Mrs. Flint showed it off! She had something anyhow that Connie hadn't got, and apparently couldn't have. Yes, Mrs. Flint had flaunted her motherhood. And Connie had been just a bit, just a little bit jealous. She couldn't help it.

She started out of her muse, and gave a little cry of fear. A man was there.

It was the keeper; he stood in the path like Balaam's ass, barring her way.

"How's this?" he said in surprise.

"How did you come?" she panted.

"How did you? Have you been to the hut?"

"No! No! I went to Marehay."

He looked at her curiously, searchingly, and she hung her head a little guiltily.

"And were you going to the hut now?" he asked rather sternly.

"No! I mustn't. I stayed at Marehay. No one knows where I am. I'm late. I've got to run."

"Giving me the slip, like?" he said, with a faint ironic smile.

"No! No, not that. Only——"

"Why, what else?" he said. And he stepped up to her, and put his arm around her. She felt the front of his body terribly near to her, and alive.

"Oh, not now, not now," she cried, trying to push him away.

"Why not? It's only six o'clock. You've got half-an-hour. Nay! Nay! I want you."

He held her fast and she felt his urgency. Her old instinct was to fight for her freedom. But something else in her was strange and inert and heavy. His body was urgent against her, and she hadn't the heart any more to fight.

He looked around.

"Come—come here! Through here," he said, looking penetratingly into the dense fir-trees, that were young and not more than half-grown.

He looked back at her. She saw his eyes, tense and brilliant, fierce, not loving. But her will had left her. A strange weight was on her limbs. She was giving way. She was giving up.

He led her through the wall of prickly trees, that were difficult to come through, to a place where was a little space and a pile of dead boughs. He threw one or two dry ones down, put his coat and waistcoat over them, and she had to lie down there under the boughs of the tree, like an animal, while he waited, standing there in his shirt and breeches, watching her with haunted eyes. But still he was provident—he made her lie properly, properly. Yet he broke the band of her underclothes, for she did not help him, only lay inert.

He too had bared the front part of his body and she felt his naked flesh against her as he came into her. For a moment he was still inside her, turgid there and quivering. Then as he began to move, in the sudden helpless orgasm, there awoke in her new strange thrills rippling inside her. Rippling, rippling, rippling, like a flapping overlapping of soft flames, soft as feathers, running to points of brilliance, exquisite, exquisite and melting her all molten inside. It was like bells rippling up and up to a culmination. She lay unconscious of the wild little cries she uttered at the last. But it was over too soon, too soon, and she could no longer force her own conclusion with her own activity. This was different, different. She could do nothing. She could no longer harden and grip for her own satisfaction upon him. She could only wait, wait and moan in spirit as she felt him withdrawing, withdrawing and contracting, coming to the terrible moment when he would slip out of her and be gone. Whilst all her womb was open and soft, and softly clamoring, like a sea-anemone under the tide, clamoring for him to come in again and make a fulfillment for her. She clung to him unconscious in passion, and he never quite slipped from her, and she felt the soft bud of him within her stirring, and strange rhythms flushing up into her with a strange rhythmic growing motion, swelling and swelling till it filled all her cleaving consciousness, and then began again the unspeakable motion that was not really motion, but pure deepening whirlpools of sensation swirling deeper and deeper through all her tissue and consciousness, till she was one perfect concentric fluid of feeling, and she lay there crying in unconscious inarticulate cries. The voice out of the uttermost night, the life! The man heard it beneath him with a kind of awe, as his life sprang out into her. And as it subsided, he subsided too and lay utterly still, unknowing, while her grip on him slowly relaxed, and she lay inert. And they lay and knew nothing, not even of each other, both lost. Till at last he began to rouse and become aware of his defenseless nakedness, and she was aware that his body was loosening its clasp on her. He was coming apart; but in her breast she felt she could not bear him to leave her uncovered. He must cover her now for ever.

But he drew away at last, and kissed her and covered her over, and began to cover himself. She lay looking up to the boughs of the tree, unable as yet to move. He stood and fastened up his breeches, looking round. All was dense and silent, save for the awed dog that lay with its paws against its nose. He sat down again on the brushwood and took Connie's hand in silence.

She turned and looked at him. "We came off together that time," he said.

She did not answer.

"It's good when it's like that. Most folks lives their lives through and they never know it," he said, speaking rather dreamily.

She looked into his brooding face.

"Do they?" she said. "Are you glad?"

He looked back into her eyes. "Glad," he said. "Ay, but never mind." He did not want her to talk. And he bent over her and kissed her, and she felt, so he must kiss her for ever.

At last she sat up.

"Don't people often come off together?" she asked with naïve curiosity.

"A good many of them never. You can see by the raw look of them." He spoke unwittingly, regretting he had begun.

"Have you come off like that with other women?"

He looked at her amused.

"I don't know," he said, "I don't know."

And she knew he would never tell her anything he didn't want to tell her. She watched his face, and the passion for him moved in her bowels. She resisted it as far as she could, for it was the loss of herself to herself.

He put on his waistcoat and his coat, and pushed a way through to the path again.

The last level rays of the sun touched the wood. "I won't come with you," he said; "better not."

She looked at him wistfully before she turned. His dog was waiting so anxiously for him to go, and he seemed to have nothing whatever to say. Nothing left.

Connie went slowly home, realizing the depth of the other thing in her. Another self was alive in her, burning molten and soft in her womb and bowels, and with this self she adored him. She adored him till her knees were weak as she walked. In her womb and bowels she was flowing and alive now and vulnerable, and helpless in adoration of him as the most naïve woman.—It feels like a child, she said to herself; it feels like a child in me.—And so it did, as if her womb, that had always been shut, had opened and filled with new life, almost a burden, yet lovely.

"If I had a child!" she thought to herself; "if I had him inside me as a child!"—and her limbs turned molten at the thought, and she realized the immense difference between having a child to oneself, and having a child to a man whom one's bowels yearned towards. The former seemed in a sense ordinary: but to have a child to a man whom one adored in one's bowels and one's womb, it made her feel she was very different from her old self, and as if she was sinking deep, deep to the center of all womanhood and the sleep of creation.

It was not the passion that was new to her, it was the yearning adoration. She knew she had always feared it, for it left her helpless; she feared it still, lest if she adored him too much, then she would lose herself, become effaced, and she did not want to be effaced, a slave, like a savage woman. She must not become a slave. She feared her adoration, yet she would not at once fight against it. She knew she could fight it. She had a devil of self-will in her breast that could have fought the full soft heaving adoration of her womb and crushed it. She could even now do it, or she thought so, and she could then take up her passion with her own will.

Ah! yes, to be passionate like a Bacchante, like a Bacchanal fleeing through the woods, to call on Iacchos, the bright phallus that had no independent personality behind it, but was pure god-servant to the woman! The man, the individual, let him not dare intrude. He was but a temple-servant, the bearer and keeper of the bright phallus, her own.

So, in the flux of a new awakening, the old hard passion flamed in her for a time, and the man dwindled to a contemptible object, the mere phallus-bearer, to be torn to pieces when his service was performed. She felt the force of the Bacchae in her limbs and her body, the woman gleaming and rapid, beating down the male; but while she felt this, her heart was heavy. She did not want it, it was known and barren, birthless; the adoration was her treasure. It was so fathomless, so soft, so deep and so unknown. No, no, she would give up her hard bright female power; she was weary of it, stiffened with it; she would sink in the new bath of life, in the depths of her womb and her bowels that sang the voiceless song of adoration. It was early yet to begin to fear the man.

"I walked over by Marehay, and I had tea with Mrs. Flint," she said to Clifford. "I wanted to see the baby. It's so adorable, with hair like red cobwebs. Such a dear! Mr. Flint had gone to market, so she and I and the baby had tea together. Did you wonder where I was?"

"Well, I wondered, but I guessed you had dropped in somewhere to tea," said Clifford jealously. With a sort of second sight he sensed something new in her, something to him quite incomprehensible, but he ascribed it to the baby. He thought that all that ailed Connie was that she did not have a baby; automatically bring one forth, so to speak.

"I saw you go across the park to the iron gate, my Lady," said Mrs. Bolton; "so I thought perhaps you'd called at the Rectory."

"I nearly did, then I turned towards Marehay instead."

The eyes of the two women met: Mrs. Bolton's grey and bright and searching; Connie's blue and veiled and strangely beautiful. Mrs. Bolton was almost sure she had a lover, yet how could it be, and who could it be? Where was there a man?

"Oh, it's so good for you, if you go out and see a bit of company sometimes," said Mrs. Bolton. "I was saying to Sir Clifford, it would do her ladyship a world of good if she'd go out among people more."

"Yes, I'm glad I went, and such a quaint dear cheeky baby, Clifford," said Connie. "It's got hair just like spiderwebs, and bright orange, and the oddest, cheekiest, pale-blue china eyes. Of course, it's a girl, or it wouldn't be so bold, bolder than any little Sir Francis Drake."

"You're right, my Lady—a regular little Flint. They were always a forward, sandy-headed family," said Mrs. Bolton.

"Wouldn't you like to see it, Clifford? I've asked them to tea for you to see it."

"Who?" he asked, looking at Connie in great uneasiness.

"Mrs. Flint and the baby, next Monday."

"You can have them to tea in your room," he said.

"Why, don't you want to see the baby?" she cried.

"Oh, I'll see it, but I don't want to sit through a tea-time with them."

"Oh," said Connie, looking at him with wide veiled eyes.

She did not really see him, he was somebody else.

"You can have a nice cozy tea up in your room, my Lady, and Mrs. Flint will be more comfortable than if Sir Clifford was there," said Mrs. Bolton.

She was sure Connie had a lover, and something in her soul exulted. But who was he? Who was he? Perhaps Mrs. Flint would provide a clue.

Clifford was very uneasy. He would not let her go after dinner, and she had wanted so much to be alone. She looked at him, but was curiously submissive.

"Shall we play a game, or shall I read to you, or what shall it be?" he asked uneasily.

"You read to me," said Connie.

"What shall I read—verse or prose? Or drama?"

"Read Racine," she said.

It had been one of his stunts in the past, to read Racine in the real French grand manner, but he was rusty now, and a little self-conscious; he really preferred the loudspeaker. But Connie was sewing, sewing a little silk frock of primrose silk, cut out of one of her dresses, for Mrs. Flint's baby. Between coming home and dinner she had cut it out, and she sat in the soft quiescent rapture of herself, sewing, while the noise of the reading went on.

Inside herself she could feel the humming of passion, like the after-humming of deep bells.

Clifford said something to her about the Racine. She caught the sense after the words had gone.

"Yes! Yes!" she said, looking up at him. "It is splendid."

Again he was frightened at the deep blue haze of her eyes, and of her soft stillness, sitting there. She had never been so utterly soft and still. She fascinated him helplessly, as if some perfume about her intoxicated him. So he went on helplessly with his reading, and the throaty sound of the French was like the wind in the chimneys to her. Of the Racine she heard not one syllable.

She was gone in her own soft rapture, like a forest soughing with the dim, glad moan of spring, moving into bud. She could feel in the same world with her the man, the nameless man, moving on beautiful feet, beautiful in the phallic mystery. And in herself, in all her veins, she felt him and his child. His child was in all her veins, like a twilight.

"For hands she hath none, nor eyes, nor feet, nor golden Treasure of hair . . ."

She was like a forest, like the dark interlacing of the oak-wood, humming inaudibly with myriad unfolding buds. Meanwhile the birds of desire were asleep in the vast interlaced intricacy of her body.

But Clifford's voice went on, clapping and gurgling with unusual sounds. How extraordinary it was! How extraordinary he was, bent there over the book, queer and rapacious and civilized, with broad shoulders and no real legs! What a strange creature, with the sharp, cold, inflexible will of some bird, and no warmth, no warmth at all! One of those creatures of the afterwards, that have no soul, but an extra-alert will, cold will. She shuddered a little, afraid of him. But then, the soft warm flame of life was stronger than he, and the real things were hidden from him.

The reading finished. She was startled. She looked up, and was more startled still to see Clifford watching her with pale, uncanny eyes, like hate.

"Thank you *so* much! You do read Racine beautifully!" she said softly.

"Almost as beautifully as you listen to him," he said cruelly.

"What are you making?" he asked.

"I'm making a child's dress, for Mrs. Flint's baby."

He turned away. A child! A child! That was all her obsession.

"After all," he said, in a declamatory voice, "one gets all one wants out of Racine. Emotions that are ordered and given shape are more important than disorderly emotions."

She watched him with wide, vague, veiled eyes.

"Yes, I'm sure they are," she said.

"The modern world has only vulgarized emotion by letting it loose. What we need is classic control."

"Yes," she said slowly, thinking of him listening with vacant face to the emotional idiocy of the radio. "People pretend to have emotions, and they really feel nothing. I suppose that is being romantic."

"Exactly!" he said.

As a matter of fact, he was tired. This evening had tired him. He would rather have been with his technical books, or his pit-manager, or listening-in to the radio.

Mrs. Bolton came in with two glasses of malted milk: for Clifford, to make him sleep, and for Connie to fatten her again. It was a regular night-cap she had introduced.

Connie was glad to go, when she had drunk her glass, and thankful she needn't help Clifford to bed. She took his glass and put it on the tray, then took the tray, to leave it outside.

"Good night, Clifford! *Do* sleep well! The Racine gets into one like a dream. Good night!"

She had drifted to the door. She was going without kissing him good night. He watched her with sharp, cold eyes. So! She did not even kiss him good night, after he had spent an evening reading to her. Such depths of callousness in her! Even if the kiss was but a formality, it was on such formalities that life depends. She was a bolshevik, really. Her instincts were bolshevistic. He gazed coldly and angrily at the door whence she had gone. Anger!

And again the dread of the night came on him. He was a networks of nerves, and when he was not braced up to work, and so full of energy: or when he was not listening-in, and so utterly neuter: then he was haunted by anxiety and a sense of dangerous impending void. He was afraid. And Connie could keep the fear off him, if she would. But it was obvious she wouldn't, she wouldn't. She was callous, cold and callous to all that he did for her. He gave up his life for her, and she was callous to him. She only wanted her own way. "The lady loves her will."

Now it was a baby she was obsessed by. Just so that it should be her own, all her own, and not his!

Clifford was so healthy, considering. He looked so well and ruddy, in the face, his shoulders were broad and strong, his chest deep, he had put on flesh. And yet, at the same time, he was afraid of death. A terrible hollow seemed to menace him somewhere, somehow, a void, and into this void his energy would collapse. Energyless, he felt at times he was dead, really dead.

So his rather prominent pale eyes had a queer look, furtive, and yet a little cruel, so cold: and at the same time, almost impudent. It was a very odd look, this look of impudence: as if he were triumphing over life in spite of life. "Who knoweth the mysteries of the will—for it can triumph even against the angels—"

But his dread was the nights when he could not sleep. Then it was awful indeed, when annihilation pressed in on him on every side. Then it was ghastly, to exist without having any life: lifeless, in the night, to exist.

But now he could ring for Mrs. Bolton. And she would always come. That was a great comfort. She would come in her dressing-gown, with her hair in a plait down her back, curiously girlish and dim, though the brown plait was streaked with grey. And she would make him coffee or camomile tea, and she would play chess or piquet with him. She had a woman's queer faculty of playing even chess well enough, when she was three parts asleep, well enough to make her worth beating. So, in the silent intimacy of the night, they sat, or she sat and he lay on the bed, with the reading-lamp shedding its solitary light on them, she almost gone in sleep, he almost gone in a sort of fear, and they played, played together—then they had a cup of coffee and a biscuit together, hardly speaking, in the silence of night, but being a reassurance to one another.

And this night she was wondering who Lady Chatterley's lover was. And she was thinking of her own Ted, so long dead, yet for her never quite dead. And when she thought of him, the old, old grudge against the world rose up, but especially against the masters, that they had killed him. They had not really killed him. Yet, to her, emotionally, they had. And somewhere deep in herself, because of it, she was a nihilist, and really anarchic.

In her half-sleep, thoughts of her Ted and thoughts of Lady Chatterley's unknown lover commingled, and then she felt she shared with the other woman a great grudge against Sir Clifford and all he stood for. At the same time she was playing piquet with him, and they were gambling sixpences. And it was a source of satisfaction to be playing piquet with a baronet, and even losing sixpences to him.

When they played cards, they always gambled. It made him forget himself. And he usually won. Tonight, too, he was winning. So he would not go to sleep till the first dawn appeared. Luckily it began to appear at half-past four or thereabouts.

Connie was in bed, and fast asleep all this time. But the keeper, too, could not rest. He had closed the coops and made his round of the wood, then gone home and eaten supper. But he did not go to bed. Instead he sat by the fire and thought.

He thought of his boyhood in Tevershall, and of his five or six years of married life. He thought of his wife, and always bitterly. She had seemed so brutal. But he had not seen her now since 1915, in the spring when he joined up. Yet there she was, not three miles away, and more brutal than ever. He hoped never to see her again while he lived.

He thought of his life abroad, as a soldier. India, Egypt, then India again: the blind, thoughtless life with the horses: the colonel who had loved him and whom he had loved: the several years that he had been an officer, a lieutenant with a very fair chance of being a captain. Then the death of the colonel from pneumonia, and his own narrow escape from death: his damaged health: his deep restlessness: his leaving the army and coming back to England to be a working man again.

He was temporizing with life. He had thought he would be safe, at least for a time, in this wood. There was no shooting as yet: he had to rear the pheasants. He would have no guns to serve. He would be alone, and apart from life, which was all he wanted. He had to have some sort of a background. And this was his native place. There was even his mother, though she had never meant very much to him. And he could go on in life, existing from day to day, without connection and without hope. For he did not know what to do with himself.

He did not know what to do with himself. Since he had been an officer for some years, and had mixed among the other officers and civil servants, with their wives and families, he had lost all ambition to "get on." There was a toughness, a curious rubber-necked toughness and unlivingness about the middle and upper classes, as he had known them, which just left him feeling cold and different from them.

So, he had come back to his own class. To find there, what he had forgotten during his absence of years, a pettiness and a vulgarity of manner extremely distasteful. He admitted now at last, how important manner was. He admitted, also, how important it was even *to pretend* not to care about the halfpence and the small things of life. But among the common people there was no pretense. A penny more or less on the bacon was worse than a change in the Gospel. He could not stand it.

And again, there was the wage-squabble. Having lived among the owning classes, he knew the utter futility of expecting any solution of the wage-squabble. There was no solution, short of death. The only thing was not to care, not to care about the wages.

Yet, if you were poor and wretched you *had* to care. Anyhow, it was becoming the only thing they did care about. The *care* about money was like a great cancer, eating away individuals of all classes. He refused to care about money.

And what then? What did life offer apart from the care of money? Nothing.

Yet he could live alone, in the wan satisfaction of being alone, and raise pheasants to be shot ultimately by fat men after breakfast. It was futility, futility to the *n*th power.

But why care, why bother? And he had not cared nor bothered till now, when this woman had come into his life. He was nearly ten years older than she. And he was a thousand years older in experience, starting from the bottom. The connection between them was growing closer. He could see the day when it would clinch up and they would have to make a life together. "For the bonds of love are ill to loose!"

And what then? What then? Must he start again, with nothing to start on?

Must he entangle this woman? Must he have the horrible broil with her lame husband? And also some sort of horrible broil with his own brutal wife, who hated him? Misery! lots of misery! And he was no longer young and merely buoyant. Neither was he the insouciant sort. Every bitterness and every ugliness would hurt him: and the woman!

But even if they got clear of Sir Clifford and of his own wife, even if they got clear, what were they going to do? What was he, himself, going to do? What was he going to do with his life? For he must do something. He couldn't be a mere hanger-on, on her money and his own very small pension.

It was insoluble. He could only think of going to America, to try a new air. He disbelieved in the dollar utterly. But perhaps, perhaps there was something else.

He could not rest nor even go to bed. After sitting in a stupor of bitter thoughts until midnight, he got suddenly from his chair and reached for his coat and gun.

"Come on, lass," he said to the dog. "We're best outside."

It was a starry night, but moonless. He went on a slow, scrupulous, soft-stepping and stealthy round. The only thing he had to contend with was the colliers setting snares for rabbits, particularly the Stacks Gate colliers, on the Marehay side. But it was breeding season, and even colliers respected it a little. Nevertheless the stealthy beating of the round in search of poachers soothed his nerves and took his mind off his thoughts.

But when he had done his slow, cautious beating of his bounds—it was nearly a five-mile walk—he was tired. He went to the top of the knoll and looked out. There was no sound save the noise, the faint shuffling noise from Stacks Gate colliery, that never ceased working: and there were hardly any lights, save the brilliant electric rows at the works. The world lay darkly and fumily sleeping. It was half-past two. But even in its sleep it was an uneasy, cruel world, stirring with the noise of a train or some great lorry on the road, and flashing with some rosy lightning-flash from the furnaces. It was a world of iron and coal, the cruelty of iron and the smoke of coal, and the endless, endless greed that drove it all. Only greed, greed stirring in its sleep.

It was cold, and he was coughing. A fine cold draught blew over the knoll. He thought of the woman. Now he would have given all he had or even might have to hold her warm in his arms, both of them wrapped in one blanket, and sleep. All hopes of eternity and all gain from the past he would have given to have her there, to be wrapped warm with him in one blanket, and sleep, only sleep. It seemed the sleep with the woman in his arms was the only necessity.

He went to the hut, and wrapped himself in the blanket and lay on the floor to sleep. But he could not, he was cold. And besides, he felt cruelly his own unfinished nature. He felt his own unfinished condition of aloneness cruelly. He wanted her, to touch her, to hold her fast against him in one moment of completeness and rest.

He got up again and went out, towards the park gates this time: then slowly along the path towards the house. It was nearly four o'clock, still clear and cold, but no sign of dawn. He was so used to the dark, he could see well.

Slowly, slowly the great house drew him, as a magnet. He wanted to be near her. It was not desire, not that. It was the cruel sense of unfinished aloneness, that needed a silent woman folded in his arms. Perhaps he could find her. Perhaps he could even call her out to him: or find some way in to her. For the need was imperious.

He slowly, silently climbed the incline to the hall. Then he came round the great trees at the top of the knoll, on to the drive, which made a grand sweep round a lozenge of grass in front of the entrance. He could already see the two magnificent beeches which stood in this big level lozenge in front of the house, detaching themselves darkly in the dark air.

There was the house, low and long and obscure, with one light burning downstairs, in Sir Clifford's room. But which room she was in, the woman who held the other end of the frail thread which drew him so mercilessly, that he did not know.

He went a little nearer, gun in hand, and stood motionless on the drive, watching the house. Perhaps even now he could find her, come at her in some way. The house was not impregnable: he was as clever as burglars are. Why not come to her?

He stood motionless, waiting, while the dawn faintly and imperceptibly paled behind him. He saw the light in the house go out. But he did not see Mrs. Bolton come to the window and draw back the old curtain of dark-blue silk, and stand herself in the dark room, looking out on the half-dark of the approaching day, looking for the longed-for dawn, waiting for Clifford to be really reassured that it was daybreak. For when he was sure of daybreak, he would sleep almost at once.

She stood blind with sleep at the window, waiting. And as she stood, she started, and almost cried out. For there was a man out there on the drive, a black figure in the twilight. She woke up greyly, and watched, but without making a sound to disturb Sir Clifford.

The daylight began to rustle into the world, and the dark figure seemed to go smaller and more defined. She made out the gun and gaiters and baggy jacket— it would be Oliver Mellors, the keeper. Yes, there was the dog nosing around like a shadow, and waiting for him!

And what did the man want? Did he want to rouse the house? What was he standing there for, transfixed, looking up at the house like a love-sick male dog outside the house where the bitch is!

Goodness! The knowledge went through Mrs. Bolton like a shot. He was Lady Chatterley's lover. He! He!

To think of it! Why, she, Ivy Bolton, had once been a tiny bit in love with him herself! When he was a lad of sixteen and she a woman of twenty-six. It was when she was studying, and he had helped her a lot with the anatomy and things she had had to learn. He'd been a clever boy, had a scholarship for Sheffield Grammar School and learned French and things: and then after all had become an overhead blacksmith shoeing horses, because he was fond of horses, he said: but really because he was frightened to go out and face the world, only he'd never admit it.

But he'd been a nice lad, a nice lad, had helped her a lot, so clever at making things clear to you. He was quite as clever as Sir Clifford: and always one for the women. More with women than men, they said.

Till he'd gone and married that Bertha Coutts, as if to spite himself. Some people do marry to spite themselves, because they're disappointed or something. And no wonder it had been a failure.—For years he was gone, all the time of the war: and a lieutenant and all: quite the gentleman, really quite the gentleman!—Then to come back to Tevershall and go as a gamekeeper! Really, some people can't take their chances when they've got them! And talking broad Derbyshire again like the worst, when she, Ivy Bolton, knew he spoke like any gentleman, *really*.

Well, well! So her ladyship had fallen for him! Well, her ladyship wasn't the first: there was something about him. But fancy! A Tevershall lad born and bred, and she her ladyship in Wragby Hall! My word, that was a slap back at the high-and-mighty Chatterleys!

But he, the keeper, as the day grew, had realized: it's no good! It's no good trying to get rid of your own aloneness. You've got to stick to it all your life. Only at times, at times, the gap will be filled in. At times! But you have to wait for the times. Accept your own aloneness and stick to it, all your life. And then accept the times when the gap is filled in, when they come. But they've got to come. You can't force them.

With a sudden snap the bleeding desire that had drawn him after her broke. He had broken it, because it must be so. There must be a coming together on both sides. And if she wasn't coming to him, he wouldn't track her down. He mustn't. He must go away, till she came.

He turned slowly, ponderingly, accepting again the isolation. He knew it was better so. She must come to him: it was no use trailing after her. No use! Mrs. Bolton saw him disappear, saw his dog run after him.

"Well, well!" she said. "He's the one man I never thought of; and the one man I might have thought of. He was nice to me when he was a lad, after I lost Ted. Well, well! Whatever would *he* say if he knew!"

And she glanced triumphantly at the already sleeping Clifford, as she stepped softly from the room.

XI

Connie was sorting out one of the Wragby lumber rooms. There were several: the house was a warren, and the family never sold anything. Sir Geoffrey's father had liked pictures and Sir Geoffrey's mother had liked cinquecento furniture. Sir Geoffrey himself had liked old carved oak chests, vestry chests. So it went on through the generations. Clifford collected very modern pictures, at very moderate prices.

So in the lumber room there were bad Sir Edwin Landseers and pathetic William Henry Hunt birds' nests: and other Academy stuff, enough to frighten the daughter of an R.A. She determined to look through it one day, and clear it all. And the grotesque furniture interested her.

Wrapped up carefully to preserve it from damage and dry-rot was the old family cradle, of rosewood. She had to unwrap it, to look at it. It had a certain charm: she looked at it a long time.

"It's a thousand pities it won't be called for," sighed Mrs. Bolton, who was helping. "Though cradles like that are out-of-date nowadays."

"It might be called for. I might have a child," said Connie casually, as if saying she might have a new hat.

"You mean, if anything happened to Sir Clifford!" stammered Mrs. Bolton.

"No! I mean as things are. It's only muscular paralysis with Sir Clifford—it doesn't affect *him,*" said Connie, lying as naturally as breathing.

Clifford had put the idea into her head. He had said: "Of course, *I* may have a child yet. I'm not really mutilated at all. The potency may easily come back even if the muscles of the hips and legs are paralyzed. And then the seed may be transferred."

He really felt, when he had his periods of energy and worked so hard at the question of the mines, as if his sexual potency were returning. Connie had looked at him in terror. But she was quite quick-witted enough to use his suggestion for her own preservation. For she would have a child if she could: but not his.

Mrs. Bolton was for a moment breathless, flabbergasted. Then she didn't believe it: she saw in it a ruse. Yet doctors could do such things nowadays. They might sort of graft seed.

"Well, my Lady, I only hope and pray you may. It would be lovely for you: and for everybody. My word, a child in Wragby, what a difference it would make!"

"Wouldn't it!" said Connie.

And she chose three R.A. pictures of sixty years ago, to send to the Duchess of Shortlands for that lady's next charitable bazaar. She was called "the bazaar duchess," and she would be delighted with the three framed R.A.'s. She might even call, on the strength of them. How furious Clifford was when she called!

But oh, my dear! Mrs. Bolton was thinking to herself. Is it Oliver Mellors' child you're preparing us for? Oh, my dear, that *would* be a Tevershall baby in the Wragby cradle, my word! Wouldn't shame it, neither!

Among other monstrosities in this lumber room was a largish black japanned box, excellently and ingeniously made some sixty or seventy years ago, and fitted with every imaginable object. On top was a concentrated toilet set: brushes, bottles, mirrors, combs, boxes, even three beautiful little razors in safety sheaths, shaving-bowl and all. Underneath came a sort of escritoire outfit: blotters, pens, ink-bottles, paper, envelopes, memorandum books: and then a perfect sewing outfit, with three different-sized scissors, thimbles, needles, silks, and cottons, darning egg, all of the very best quality and perfectly finished. Then there was a little medicine store, with bottles labelled Laudanum, Tincture of Myrrh, Ess. Cloves, and so on: but empty. Everything was perfectly new, and the whole thing, when shut up, was as big as a small, but fat week-end bag. And inside, it fitted together like a puzzle. The bottles could not possibly have spilled: there wasn't room.

The thing was wonderfully made and contrived, excellent craftsmanship of the Victorian order. But somehow it was monstrous. Some Chatterley must even have felt it, for the thing had never been used. It had a peculiar soullessness.

Yet Mrs. Bolton was thrilled.

"Look what beautiful brushes, so expensive, even the shaving brushes, three perfect ones! No! and those scissors! They're the best that money could buy. Oh, I call it lovely!"

"Do you?" said Connie. "Then you have it."

"Oh, no, my Lady!"

"Of course! It will only lie here till Doomsday. If you won't have it, I'll send it to the Duchess as well as the pictures, and she doesn't deserve so much. Do have it!"

"Oh, your Ladyship! Why, I shall never be able to thank you."

"You needn't try," laughed Connie.

And Mrs. Bolton sailed down with the huge and very black box in her arms, flushing bright pink in her excitement.

Mr. Betts drove her in the trap to her house in the village, with the box. And she *had* to have a few friends in, to show it: the school-mistress, the chemist's wife, Mrs. Weedon the under-cashier's wife. They thought it marvellous. And then started the whisper of Lady Chatterley's child.

"Wonders'll never cease!" said Mrs. Weedon.

But Mrs. Bolton was *convinced,* if it did come, it would be Sir Clifford's child. So there!

Not long after, the rector said gently to Clifford:

"And may we really hope for an heir to Wragby? Ah, that would be the hand of God in mercy, indeed!"

"Well! We may *hope,"* said Clifford, with a faint irony, and, at the same time, a certain conviction. He had begun to believe it really possible it might even be *his* child.

Then one afternoon came Leslie Winter, Squire Winter, as everybody called him: lean, immaculate, and seventy: and every inch a gentleman, as Mrs. Bolton said to Mrs. Betts. Every millimeter, indeed! And with his old-fashioned, rather haw-haw! manner of speaking, he seemed more out-of-date than bag-wigs. Time, in her flight, drops these fine old feathers.

They discussed the collieries. Clifford's idea was, that his coal, even the poor sort, could be made into hard concentrated fuel that would burn at great heat if fed with certain damp, acidulated air at a fairly strong pressure. It had long been observed that in a particularly strong, wet wind the pit-bank burned very vivid, gave off hardly any fumes, and left a fine powder of ash, instead of the slow pink gravel.

"But where will you find the proper engines for burning your fuel?" asked Winter.

"I'll make them myself. And I'll use my fuel myself. And I'll sell electric power. I'm certain I could do it."

"If you can do it, then splendid, splendid, my dear boy. Haw! Splendid! If I can be of any help, I shall be delighted. I'm afraid I am a little out-of-date, and my collieries are like me. But who knows, when I'm gone, there may be men like you. Splendid! It will employ all the men again, and you won't have to sell your coal, or fail to sell it. A splendid idea, and I hope it will be a success. If I had sons of my own, no doubt they would have up-to-date ideas for Shipley: no doubt! By the way, dear boy, is there any foundation to the rumor that we may entertain hopes of an heir to Wragby?"

"Is there a rumor?" asked Clifford.

"Well, my dear boy, Marshall from Fillingwood asked *me,* that's all I can say about a rumor. Of course, I wouldn't repeat it for the world, if there were no foundation."

"Well, Sir," said Clifford uneasily, but with strange bright eyes. "There is a hope. There is a hope."

Winter came across the room and wrung Clifford's hand.

"My dear boy, my dear lad, can you believe what it means to me, to hear that! And to hear you are working in the hopes of a son: and that you may again employ every man at Tevershall. Ah my boy! to keep up the level of the race, and to have work waiting for any man who cares to work!—"

The old man was really moved.

Next day Connie was arranging tall yellow tulips in a glass vase.

"Connie," said Clifford, "did you know there was a rumor that you are going to supply Wragby with a son and heir?"

Connie felt dim with terror, yet she stood quite still, touching the flowers.

"No!" she said. "Is it a joke? Or malice?"

He paused before he answered:

"Neither, I hope. I hope it may be a prophecy."

Connie went on with her flowers.

"I had a letter from father this morning," she said. "He wants to know if I am aware he has accepted Sir Alexander Cooper's invitation for me for July and August, to the Villa Esmeralda in Venice."

"July *and* August?" said Clifford.

"Oh, I wouldn't stay all that time. Are you sure you wouldn't come?"

"I won't travel abroad," said Clifford, promptly.

She took her flowers to the window.

"Do you mind if I go?" she said. "You know it was promised, for this summer."

"For how long would you go?"

"Perhaps three weeks."

There was a silence for a time.

"Well," said Clifford slowly, and a little gloomily: "I suppose I could stand it for three weeks: if I were absolutely sure you'd want to come back."

"I should want to come back," she said, with a quiet simplicity, heavy with conviction. She was thinking of the other man.

Clifford felt her conviction, and somehow he believed her, he believed it was for him. He felt immensely relieved, joyful at once.

"In that case," he said, "I think it would be all right. Don't you?"

"I think so," she said.

"You'd enjoy the change?"

She looked up at him with strange blue eyes.

"I should like to see Venice again," she said, "and to bathe from one of the shingle islands across the lagoon. But you know I loathe Lido! And I don't fancy I shall like Sir Alexander Cooper and Lady Cooper. But if Hilda is there, and we have a gondola of our own: yes, it will be rather lovely. I *do* wish you'd come."

She said it sincerely. She would so love to make him happy, in these ways.

"Ah, but think of me, though, at the Gare du Nord: at Calais quay!"

"But why not? I see other men carried in litter-chairs, who have been wounded in the war. Besides, we'd motor all the way."

"We should need to take two men."

"Oh, no! We'd manage with Field. There would always be another man there."

But Clifford shook his head.

"Not this year, dear! Not this year! Next year, probably, I'll try."

She went away gloomily. Next year! What would next year bring? She herself did not really want to go to Venice: not now, now there was the other man. But she was going as a sort of discipline: and also because, if she had a child, Clifford would think she had a lover in Venice.

It was already May, and in June they were supposed to start. Always these arrangements! Always one's life arranged for one! Wheels that worked one and drove one, and over which one had no real control!

It was May, but cold and wet again. A cold wet May, good for corn and hay! Much the corn and hay matter nowadays! Connie had to go into Uthwaite, which was their little town, where the Chatterleys were still *the* Chatterleys. She went alone, Field driving her.

In spite of May and a new greenness, the country was dismal. It was rather chilly, and there was smoke in the rain, and a certain sense of exhaust vapor in the air. One just had to live from one's resistance. No wonder these people were ugly and tough.

The car ploughed uphill through the long squalid straggle of Tevershall, the blackened brick dwellings, the black slate roofs glistening their sharp edges, the mud black with coal-dust, the pavements wet and black. It was as if dismalness had soaked through and through everything. The utter negation of natural beauty, the utter negation of the gladness of life, the utter absence of the instinct for shapely beauty which every bird and beast has, the utter death of the human intuitive faculty was appalling. The stacks of soap in the grocers' shops, the rhubarb and lemons in the green-grocers'! the awful hats in the milliners'! all went by ugly, ugly, ugly, followed by the plaster-and-gilt horror of the cinema with its wet picture announcements, "A Woman's Love!", and the new big Primitive chapel, primitive enough in its stark brick and big panes of greenish and raspberry glass in the windows. The Wesleyan chapel, higher up, was of blackened brick and stood behind iron railings and blackened shrubs. The Congregational chapel, which thought itself superior, was built of rusticated sandstone and had a steeple, but not a very high one. Just beyond were the new school buildings, expensive pink brick, and gravelled playground inside iron railings, all very imposing, and mixing the suggestion of a chapel and a prison. Standard Five girls were having a singing lesson, just finishing the la-me-do-la exercises and beginning a "sweet children's song." Anything more unlike song, spontaneous song, would be impossible to imagine: a strange bawling yell that followed the outlines of a tune. It was not like savages: savages have subtle rhythms. It was not like animals: animals *mean* something when they yell. It was like nothing on earth, and it was called singing. Connie sat and listened with her heart in her boots, as Field was filling petrol. What could possibly become of such a people, a people in whom the living intuitive faculty was dead as nails, and only queer mechanical yells and uncanny will power remained?

A coal-cart was coming down-hill, clanking in the rain. Field started upwards, past the big but weary-looking drapers' and clothing shops, the post-office, into the little marketplace of forlorn space, where Sam Black was peering out of the door of the "Sun," that called itself an inn, not a pub, and where the commercial travellers stayed, and was bowing to Lady Chatterley's car.

The church was away to the left among black trees. The car slid on down-hill, past the Miners Arms. It had already passed the Wellington, the Nelson, the Three Tunns and the Sun, now it passed the Miners Arms, then the Mechanics Hall, then the new and almost gaudy Miners Welfare and so, past a few new "villas," out into the blackened road between dark hedges and dark green fields, towards Stacks Gate.

Tevershall! That was Tevershall! Merrie England! Shakespeare's England! No, but the England of today, as Connie had realized since she had come to live in it. It was producing a new race of mankind, over-conscious in the money and social and political side, on the spontaneous, intuitive side dead,—but dead! Half-corpses, all of them: but with a terrible insistent consciousness in the other half. There was something uncanny and underground about it all. It was an underworld. And quite incalculable. How shall we understand the reactions in half-corpses? When Connie saw the great lorries full of steel-workers from Sheffield, weird, distorted, smallish beings like men, off for an excursion to Matlock, her bowels fainted and she thought: Ah, God, what has man done to man? What have the leaders of men been doing to their fellow-men? They have reduced them to less than humanness; and now there can be no fellowship any more! It is just a nightmare.

She felt again in a wave of terror the grey, gritty hopelessness of it all. With such creatures for the industrial masses, and the upper classes as she knew them, there was no hope, no hope any more. Yet she was wanting a baby, and an heir to Wragby! An heir to Wragby! She shuddered with dread.

Yet Mellors had come out of all this!—Yes, but he was as apart from it all as she was. Even in him there was no fellowship left. It was dead. The fellowship was dead. There was only apartness and hopelessness, as far as all this was concerned. And this was England, the vast bulk of England: as Connie knew, since she had motored from the center of it.

The car was rising towards Stacks Gate. The rain was holding off, and in the air came a queer pellucid gleam of May. The country rolled away in long undulations, south towards the Peak, east towards Mansfield and Nottingham. Connie was travelling south.

As she rose on to the high country, she could see on her left, on a height above the rolling land the shadowy, powerful bulk of Warsop Castle, dark grey, with below it the reddish plastering of miners' dwellings, newish, and below those the plumes of dark smoke and white steam from the great colliery which put so many thousand pounds per annum into the pockets of the Duke and the other shareholders. The powerful old castle was a ruin, yet still it hung its bulk on the low skyline, over the black plumes and the white that waved on the damp air below.

A turn, and they ran on the high level to Stacks Gate. Stacks Gate, as seen from the highroad, was just a huge and gorgeous new hotel, the Coningsby Arms, standing red and white and gilt in barbarous isolation off the road. But if you looked, you saw on the left rows of handsome "modern" dwellings, set down like a game of dominoes, with spaces and gardens: a queer game of dominoes that some weird "masters" were playing on the surprised earth. And beyond these blocks of dwellings, at the back, rose all the astonishing and frightening overhead erections of a really modern mine, chemical works and long galleries, enormous, and of shapes not before known to man. The head-stocks and pit-bank of the mine itself were insignificant among the huge new installations. And in front of this, the game of dominoes stood forever in a sort of surprise, waiting to be played.

This was Stacks Gate, new on the face of the earth, since the war. But as a matter of fact, though even Connie did not know it, down-hill half a mile below the "hotel" was old Stacks Gate, with a little old colliery and blackish old brick dwellings, and a chapel or two and a shop or two and a little pub or two.

But that didn't count any more. The vast plumes of smoke and vapor rose from the new works up above, and this was now Stacks Gate: no chapel, no pubs, even no shops. Only the great "works," which are the modern Olympia with temples to all the gods: then the model dwellings: then the hotel. The hotel in actuality was nothing but a miners' pub, though it looked first-classy.

Even since Connie's arrival at Wragby this new place had arisen on the face of the earth, and the model dwellings had filled with riff-raff drifting in from anywhere, to poach Clifford's rabbits among other occupations.

The car ran on along the uplands, seeing the rolling county spread out. The county; it had once been a proud and lordly county. In front, looming again and hanging on the brow of the sky-line, was the huge and splendid bulk of Chadwick Hall, more window than wall, one of the most famous Elizabethan houses. Noble it stood alone above a great park, but out of date, passed over. It was still kept up, but as a show place. "Look how our ancestors lorded it!"

That was the past. The present lay below. God alone knows where the future lies. The car was already turning, between little old blackened miners' cottages, to descend to Uthwaite. And Uthwaite, on a damp day, was sending up a whole array of smoke plumes and steam, to whatever gods there be. Uthwaite down in the valley, with all the steel threads of the railways to Sheffield drawn through it, and the coal-mines and the steel-works sending up smoke and glare from long tubes, and the pathetic little corkscrew spire of the church, that is going to tumble down, still pricking the fumes, always affected Connie strangely. It was an old market-town, center of the dales. One of the chief inns was the Chatterley Arms. There, in Uthwaite, Wragby was known as Wragby, as if it were a whole place, not just a house, as it was to outsiders: Wragby Hall, near Tevershall: Wragby, a "seat."

The miners' cottages, blackened, stood flush on the pavement, with that intimacy and smallness of colliers' dwellings over a hundred years old. They lined all the way. The road had become a street, and as you sank, you forgot instantly the open, rolling country where the castles and big houses still dominated, but like ghosts. Now you were just above the tangle of naked railway-lines, and foundries and other "works" rose about you, so big you were only aware of walls. And iron clanked with a huge reverberating clank, and huge lorries shook the earth, and whistles screamed.

Yet again, once you had got right down and into the twisted and crooked heart of the town, behind the church, you were in the world of two centuries ago, in the crooked streets where the Chatterley Arms stood, and the old pharmacy, streets which used to lead out to the wild open world of the castles and stately couchant houses.

But at the corner a policeman held up his hand as three lorries loaded with iron rolled past, shaking the poor old church. And not till the lorries were past could he salute her ladyship.

So it was. Upon the old crooked burgess streets hordes of oldish, blackened miners' dwellings crowded, lining the roads out. And immediately after these came the newer, pinker rows of rather larger houses, plastering the valley: the homes of more modern workmen. And beyond that again, in the wide rolling regions of the castles, smoke waved against steam, and patch after patch of raw reddish brick showed the newer mining settlements, sometimes in the hollows, sometimes gruesomely ugly along the sky-line of the slopes. And between, in between, were the tattered remnants of the old coaching and cottage England, even the England of Robin Hood, where the miners prowled with the dismalness of suppressed sporting instincts, when they were not at work.

England, my England! But which is *my* England? The stately homes of England make good photographs, and create the illusion of a connection with the Elizabethans. The handsome old halls are here, from the days of Good Queen Anne and Tom Jones. But smuts fall and blacken on the drab stucco, that has long ceased to be golden. And one by one, like the stately homes, they are abandoned. Now they are being pulled down. As for the cottages of England—there they are—great plasterings of brick dwellings on the hopeless countryside.

Now they are pulling down the stately homes, the Georgian halls are going. Fritchley, a perfect old Georgian mansion, was even now, as Connie passed in the car, being demolished. It was in perfect repair: till the war the Weatherleys had lived in style there. But now it was too big, too expensive, and the country had become too uncongenial. The gentry were departing to pleasanter places, where they could spend their money without having to see how it was made.

This is history. One England blots out another. The mines had made the halls wealthy. Now they were blotting them out, as they had already blotted out the cottages. The industrial England blots out the agricultural England. One meaning blots out another. The new England blots out the old England. And the continuity is not organic, but mechanical.

Connie, belonging to the leisured classes, had clung to the remnants of the old England. It had taken her years to realize that it was really blotted out by this terrifying new and gruesome England, and that the blotting out would go on till it was complete. Fritchley was gone, Eastwood was gone, Shipley was going: Squire Winter's beloved Shipley.

Connie called for a moment at Shipley. The park gates, at the back, opened just near the level crossing of the colliery railway; the Shipley colliery itself stood just beyond the trees. The gates stood open, because through the park was a right-of-way that the colliers used. They hung around the park.

The car passed the ornamental ponds, in which the colliers threw their newspapers, and took the private drive to the house. It stood above, aside, a very pleasant stucco building from the middle of the eighteenth century. It had a beautiful alley of yew trees, that had approached an older house, and the hall stood serenely spread out, winking its Georgian panes as if cheerfully. Behind, there were really beautiful gardens.

Connie liked the interior much better than Wragby. It was much lighter, more alive, shapen and elegant. The rooms were panelled with creamy-painted panelling, the ceilings were touched with gilt, and everything was kept in exquisite order, all the appointments were perfect, regardless of expense. Even the corridors managed to be ample and lovely, softly curved and full of life.

Leslie Winter was alone. He had adored his house. But his park was bordered by three of his own collieries. He had been a generous man in his ideas. He had almost welcomed the colliers in his park. Had the miners not made him rich! So, when he saw the gangs of unshapely men lounging by his ornamental waters— not on the *private* part of the park; no, he drew the line there—he would say: "The miners are perhaps not so ornamental as deer, but they are far more profitable."

But that was in the golden—monetarily—latter half of Queen Victoria's reign. Miners were then "good working men."

Winter had made this speech, half apologetic, to his guest, the then Prince of Wales. And the Prince had replied, in his rather guttural English:

"You are quite right. If there were coal under Sandringham, I would open a mine on the lawns, and think it first-rate landscape gardening. Oh, I am quite willing to exchange roe-deer for colliers, at the price. Your men are good men, too, I hear."

But then, the Prince had perhaps an exaggerated idea of the beauty of money, and the blessings of industrialism.

However, the Prince had been a King, and the King had died, and now there was another King, whose chief function seemed to be to open soup-kitchens.

And the good working men were somehow hemming Shipley in. New mining villages crowded on the park, and the squire felt somehow that the population was alien. He used to feel, in a good-natured but quite grand way, lord of his own domain and of his own colliers. Now, by a subtle pervasion of the new spirit, he had somehow been pushed out. It was he who did not belong any more. There was no mistaking it. The mines, the industry had a will of its own, and this will was against the gentleman-owner. All the colliers took part in the will, and it was hard to live up against it. It either shoved you out of the place, or out of life altogether.

Squire Winter, a soldier, had stood it out. But he no longer cared to walk in the park after dinner. He almost hid, indoors. Once he had walked, bare-headed, and in his patent-leather shoes and purple silk socks, with Connie down to the gate, talking to her in his well-bred rather haw-haw fashion. But when it came to passing the little gangs of colliers who stood and stared without either salute or anything else, Connie felt how the lean, well-bred old man winced, winced as an elegant antelope stag in a cage winces from the vulgar stare. The colliers were not *personally* hostile: not at all. But their spirit was cold, and shoving him out. And deep down, there was a profound grudge. They "worked for him." And in their ugliness, they resented his elegant, well-groomed, well-bred existence. "Who's he!" It was the *difference* they resented.

And somewhere, in his secret English heart, being a good deal of a soldier, he believed they were right to resent the difference. He felt himself a little in the wrong, for having all the advantages. Nevertheless he represented a system, and he would not be shoved out.

Except by death. Which came on him soon after Connie's call, suddenly. And he remembered Clifford handsomely in his will.

The heirs at once gave out the order for the demolishing of Shipley. It cost too much to keep up. No one would live there. So it was broken up. The avenue of yews was cut down. The park was denuded of its timber, and divided into lots. It was near enough to Uthwaite. In the strange, bald desert of this still-one-more no-man's-land, new little streets of semi-detacheds were run up, very desirable! The Shipley Hall Estate!

Within a year of Connie's last call, it had happened. There stood Shipley Hall Estate, an array of red-brick semi-detached "villas" in new streets. No one would have dreamed that the stucco hall had stood there twelve months before.

But this is a later stage of King Edward's landscape gardening, the sort that has an ornamental coal-mine on the lawn.

One England blots out another. The England of the Squire Winters and the Wragby Halls was gone, dead. The blotting out was only not yet complete.

What would come after? Connie could not imagine. She could only see the new brick streets spreading into the fields, the new erections rising at the collieries, the new girls in their silk stockings, the new collier lads lounging into the Pally or the Welfare. The younger generation were utterly unconscious of the Old England. There was a gap in the continuity of consciousness, almost American: but industrial really. What next?

Connie always felt there was no next. She wanted to hide her head in the sand: or at least, in the bosom of a living man.

The world was so complicated and weird and gruesome! The common people were so many, and really, so terrible. So she thought as she was going home, and saw the colliers trailing from the pits, grey-black, distorted, one shoulder higher than the other, slurring their heavy iron-shod boots. Underground grey faces, whites of eyes rolling, necks cringing from the pit roof, shoulders out of shape. Men! Men! Alas, in some ways patient and good men. In other ways, non-existent. Something that men *should* have was bred and killed out of them. Yet they were men. They begot children. One might bear a child to them. Terrible, terrible thought! They were good and kindly. But they were only half, only the grey half of a human being. As yet, they were "good." But even that was the goodness of their halfness. Supposing the dead in them ever rose up! But no, it was too terrible to think of. Connie was absolutely afraid of the industrial masses. They seemed so *weird* to her. A life with utterly no beauty in it, no intuition, always "in the pit."

Children from such men. Oh, God! Oh, God!

Yet Mellors had come from such a father. Not quite. Forty years had made a difference, an appalling difference in manhood. The iron and the coal had eaten deep into the bodies and souls of the men.

Incarnate ugliness, and alive! What would become of them all? Perhaps with the passing of the coal they would disappear again, off the face of the earth. They had appeared out of nowhere in their thousands, when the coal had called for them. Perhaps they were only weird fauna of the coal-seams. Creatures of another reality, they were elementals, serving the elements of coal, as the metal-workers were elementals, serving the element of iron. Men not men, but animas of coal and iron and clay. Fauna of the elements, carbon, iron, silicon: elementals. They had perhaps some of the weird, inhuman beauty of minerals, the luster of coal, the weight and blueness and resistance of iron, the transparency of glass. Elemental creatures, weird and distorted, of the mineral world! They belonged to the coal, the iron, the clay, as fish belong to the sea and worms to dead wood. The anima of mineral disintegration!

Connie was glad to be home, to bury her head in the sand. She was glad even to babble to Clifford. For her fear of the mining and iron Midlands affected her with a queer feeling that went all over her, like influenza.

"Of course, I had to have tea in Miss Bentley's shop," she said.

"Really! Winter would have given you tea."

"Oh, yes, but I daren't disappoint Miss Bentley."

Miss Bentley was a sallow old maid with a rather large nose and romantic disposition, who served tea with a careful intensity worthy of a sacrament.

"Did she ask after me?" said Clifford.

"Of course!—*May* I ask your Ladyship how Sir Clifford is?—I believe she ranks you even higher than Nurse Cavell!"

"And I suppose you said I was blooming."

"Yes! And she looked as rapt as if I had said the heavens had opened to you. I said if she ever came to Tevershall she was to come to see you."

"Me! Whatever for! See me!"

"Why, yes, Clifford. You can't be so adored without making some slight return. Saint George of Cappadocia was nothing to you, in her eyes."

"And do you think she'll come?"

"Oh, she blushed! and looked quite beautiful for a moment, poor thing! Why don't men marry the women who would really adore them?"

"The women start adoring too late. But did she say she'd come?"

"Oh!" Connie imitated the breathless Miss Bentley, "your Ladyship, if ever I should dare to presume!"

"Dare to presume! how absurd! But I hope to God she won't turn up. And how was her tea?"

"Oh, Lipton's and *very* strong! But, Clifford, do you realize you are the *Roman de la rose* of Miss Bentley and lots like her?"

"I'm not flattered, even then."

"They treasure up every one of your pictures in the illustrated papers, and probably pray for you every night. It's rather wonderful."

She went upstairs to change.

That evening he said to her:

"You do think, don't you, that there is something eternal in marriage?"

She looked at him.

"But Clifford, you make eternity sound like a lid or a long, long chain that trailed after one, no matter how far one went."

He looked at her, annoyed.

"What I mean," he said, "is that if you go to Venice, you won't go in the hopes of some love affair that you can take *au grand sérieux,* will you?"

"A love affair in Venice *au grand sérieux?* No, I assure you! No, I'd never take a love affair in Venice more than *au très petit sérieux.*"

She spoke with a queer kind of contempt. He knitted his brows, looking at her.

Coming downstairs in the morning, she found the keeper's dog Flossie sitting in the corridor outside Clifford's room, and whimpering very faintly.

"Why, Flossie!" she said softly. "What are you doing here?"

And she quietly opened Clifford's door. Clifford was sitting up in bed, with the bed-table and typewriter pushed aside, and the keeper was standing attention at the foot of the bed. Flossie ran in. With a faint gesture of head and eyes, Mellors ordered her to the door again, and she slunk out.

"Oh, good morning, Clifford!" Connie said. "I didn't know you were so busy." Then she looked at the keeper, saying good morning to him. He murmured his reply, looking at her as if vaguely. But she felt a whiff of passion touch her, from his mere presence.

"Did I interrupt you, Clifford? I'm sorry."

"No, it's nothing of any importance."

She slipped out of the room again, and up to the blue boudoir on the first floor. She sat in the window, and saw him go down the drive, with his curious, silent motion, effaced. He had a natural sort of quiet distinction, an aloof pride, and also a certain look of frailty. A hireling! One of Clifford's hirelings! "The fault, dear Brutus, is not in our stars, but in ourselves, that we are underlings."

Was he an underling? Was he? What did he think of *her?*

It was a sunny day, and Connie was working in the garden, and Mrs. Bolton was helping her. For some reason, the two women had drawn together, in one of the unaccountable flows and ebbs of sympathy that exist between people. They were pegging down carnations, and putting in small plants for the summer. It was work they both liked. Connie especially felt a delight in putting the soft roots of young plants into a soft black puddle, and cradling them down. On this spring morning she felt a quiver in her womb, too, as if the sunshine had touched it and made it happy.

"It is many years since you lost your husband?" she said to Mrs. Bolton, as she took up another little plant and laid it in its hole.

"Twenty-three!" said Mrs. Bolton, as she carefully separated the young columbines into single plants. "Twenty-three years since they brought him home."

Connie's heart gave a lurch, at the terrible finality of it. "Brought him home!"

"Why did he get killed, do you think?" she asked. "He was happy with you?"

It was a woman's question to a woman. Mrs. Bolton put aside a strand of hair from her face, with the back of her hand.

"I don't know, my Lady! He sort of wouldn't give in to things: he wouldn't really go with the rest. And then he hated ducking his head for anything on earth. A sort of obstinacy, that *gets* itself killed. You see, he didn't really care. I lay it down to the pit. He ought never to have been down the pit. But his dad made him go down, as a lad; and then, when you're over twenty, it's not very easy to come out."

"Did he say he hated it?"

"Oh, no! Never! He never said he hated anything. He just made a funny face. He was one of those who wouldn't take care: like some of the first lads as went off so blithe to the war and got killed right away. He wasn't really wezzle-brained. But he wouldn't care. I used to say to him: 'You care for nought nor nobody!' But he did! The way he sat when my first baby was born, motionless, and the sort of fatal eyes he looked at me with, when it was over! I had a bad time, but I had to comfort *him*. 'It's all right, lad, it's all right!' I said to him. And he gave me a look, and that funny sort of smile. He never said anything. But I don't believe he had any right pleasure with me at nights after; he'd never really let himself go. I used to say to him: 'Oh, let thysen go, lad!'—I'd talk broad to him sometimes. And he said nothing. But he wouldn't let himself go, or he couldn't. He didn't want me to have any more children. I always blamed his mother, for letting him in th' room. He'd no right t'ave been there. Men makes so much more of things than they should, once they start brooding."

"Did he mind so much?" said Connie in wonder.

"Yes, he sort of couldn't take it for natural, all that pain. And it spoilt his pleasure in his bit of married love. I said to him: If I don't care, why should you? It's my look-out!—But all he'd ever say was: It's not right!"

"Perhaps he was too sensitive," said Connie.

"That's it! When you come to know men, that's how they are: too sensitive in the wrong place. And I believe, unbeknown to himself, he hated the pit, just hated it. He looked so quiet when he was dead, as if he'd got free. He was such a nice-looking lad. It just broke my heart to see him, so still and pure looking, as if he'd *wanted* to die. Oh, it broke my heart, that did. But it was the pit."

She wept a few bitter tears, and Connie wept more. It was a warm spring day, with a perfume of earth and of yellow flowers, many things rising to bud, and the garden still with the very sap of sunshine.

"It must have been terrible for you!" said Connie.

"Oh, my Lady! I never realized at first. I could only say: Oh, my lad, what did you want to leave me for!—That was all my cry. But somehow I felt he'd come back."

"But he *didn't* want to leave you," said Connie.

"Oh, no, my Lady! That was only my silly cry. And I kept expecting him back. Especially at nights. I kept waking up, thinking: Why, he's not here with me!—It was as if my *feelings* wouldn't believe he'd gone. I just felt he'd *have* to come back and talk to me, so I could feel him with me. That was all I wanted, to feel him there with me, warm. And it took me a thousand shocks before I knew he wouldn't come back, it took me years."

"The touch of him," said Connie.

"That's it, my Lady, the touch of him! I've never got over it to this day, and never shall. And if there's a heaven above, he'll be there, and warm up against me so I can sleep."

Connie glanced at the handsome, brooding face in fear. Another passionate one out of Tevershall! The touch of him! For the bonds of love are ill to loose!

"It's terrible, once you've got a man into your blood." she said.

"Oh, my Lady! And that's what makes you feel so bitter. You feel folks *wanted* him killed. You feel the pit fair *wanted* to kill him. Oh, I felt, if it hadn't been for the pit, an' them as runs the pit, there'd have been no leaving me. But they all *want* to separate a woman and a man, if they're together."

"If they're physically together," said Connie.

"That's right, my Lady! There's a lot of hard-hearted folks in the world. And every morning when he got up and went to th' pit, I felt it was wrong, wrong. But what else could he do? What can a man do?"

A queer hate flared in the woman.

"But can a touch last so long?" Connie asked suddenly. "That you could feel him so long?"

"Oh, my Lady, what else is there to last? Children grows away from you. But the man, well—! But even *that* they'd like to kill in you, the very thought of the touch of him. Even your own children! Ah, well! We might have drifted apart, who knows. But the feeling's something different. It's 'appen better never to care. But there, when I look at women who's never really been warmed through by a man, well, they seem to me poor dool-owls after all, no matter how they may dress up and gad. No, I'll abide by my own. I've not much respect for people."

XII

Connie went to the wood directly after lunch. It was really a lovely day, the first dandelions making suns, the first daisies so white. The hazel thicket was a lacework of half-open leaves, and the last dusty perpendicular of the catkins. Yellow celandines now were in crowds, flat open, pressed back in urgency, and the yellow glitter of themselves. It was the yellow, the powerful yellow of early summer. And primroses were broad, and full of pale abandon, thick-clustered primroses no longer shy. The lush, dark green of hyacinths was a sea, with buds rising like pale corn, while in the riding the forget-me-nots were fluffing up, and columbines were unfolding their ink-purple riches, and there were bits of blue bird's eggshell under a bush. Everywhere the bud-knots and the leap of life!

The keeper was not at the hut. Everything was serene, brown chickens running lustily. Connie walked on towards the cottage, because she wanted to find him.

The cottage stood in the sun, off the wood's edge. In the little garden the double daffodils rose in tufts, near the wide-open door, and red double daisies made a border to the path. There was the bark of a dog, and Flossie came running.

The wide-open door! so he was at home. And the sunlight falling on the red-brick floor! As she went up the path, she saw him through the window, sitting at the table in his shirt-sleeves, eating. The dog wuffed softly, slowly wagging her tail.

He rose, and came to the door, wiping his mouth with a red handkerchief, still chewing.

"May I come in?" she said.

"Come in!"

The sun shone into the bare room, which still smelled of a mutton chop, done in a dutch oven before the fire, because the dutch oven still stood on the fender, with the black potato-saucepan on a piece of paper beside it on the white hearth. The fire was red, rather low, the bar dropped, the kettle singing.

On the table was his plate, with potatoes and the remains of the chop; also bread in a basket, salt, and a blue mug with beer. The tablecloth was white oil-cloth. He stood in the shade.

"You are very late," she said. "Do go on eating!"

She sat down on a wooden chair, in the sunlight by the door.

"I had to go to Uthwaite," he said, sitting down at the table but not eating.

"Do eat," she said.

But he did not touch the food.

"Shall y'ave something?" he asked her. "Shall y'ave a cup of tea? t'kettle's on t' boil." He half rose again from his chair.

"If you'll let me make it myself," she said, rising. He seemed sad, and she felt she was bothering him.

"Well, teapot's in there,"—he pointed to a little, drab corner cupboard; "an' cups. An' tea's on th' mantel over yer 'ead."

She got the black teapot, and the tin of tea from the mantelshelf. She rinsed the teapot with hot water, and stood a moment wondering where to empty it.

"Throw it out," he said, aware of her. "It's clean."

She went to the door and threw the drop of water down the path. How lovely it was here, so still, so really woodland. The oaks were putting out ochre yellow leaves; in the garden the red daisies were like red plush buttons. She glanced at the big, hollow sandstone slab of the threshold, now crossed by so few feet.

"But it's lovely here," she said. "Such a beautiful stillness, everything alive and still."

He was eating again, rather slowly and unwillingly, and she could feel he was discouraged. She made the tea in silence, and set the teapot on the hob, as she knew the people did. He pushed his plate aside and went to the back place; she heard a latch click, then he came back with cheese on a plate, and butter.

She set the two cups on the table: there were only two.

"Will you have a cup of tea?" she said.

"If you like. Sugar's in th' cupboard, and there's a little cream-jug. Milk's in a jug in th' pantry."

"Shall I take your plate away?" she asked him. He looked up at her with a faint ironical smile.

"Why . . . if you like," he said, slowly eating bread and cheese. She went to the back, into the penthouse scullery, where the pump was. On the left was a door, no doubt the pantry door. She unlatched it, and almost smiled at the place he called a pantry; a long narrow whitewashed slip of a cupboard. But it managed to contain a little barrel of beer, as well as a few dishes and bits of food. She took a little milk from the yellow jug.

"How do you get your milk?" she asked him, when she came back to the table.

"Flints! They leave me a bottle at the warren end. You know, where I met you!"

But he was discouraged.

She poured out the tea, poising the cream-jug.

"No milk," he said; then he seemed to hear a noise, and looked keenly through the doorway.

" 'Appen we'd better shut," he said.

"It seems a pity," she replied. "Nobody will come, will they?"

"Not unless it's one time in a thousand, but you never know."

"And even then it's no matter," she said. "It's only a cup of tea. Where are the spoons?"

He reached over, and pulled open the table drawer. Connie sat at table in the sunshine of the doorway.

"Flossie!" he said to the dog, who was lying on a little mat at the stair foot. "Go an' hark, hark!"

He lifted his finger, and his "hark!" was very vivid. The dog trotted out to reconnoitre.

"Are you sad today?" she asked him.

He turned his blue eyes quickly and gazed direct on her.

"Sad! No, bored! I had to go getting summonses for two poachers I caught, and oh, well I don't like people."

He spoke cold, good English, and there was anger in his voice.

"Do you hate being a gamekeeper?" she asked.

"Being a gamekeeper, no! So long as I'm left alone. But when I have to go messing around at the police station, and various other places, and waiting for a lot of fools to attend to me . . . oh, well, I get mad . . ." and he smiled, with a certain faint humor.

"Couldn't you be really independent?" she asked.

"Me? I suppose I could, if you mean manage to exist on my pension. I could! But I've got to work, or I should die. That is, I've got to have something that keeps me occupied. And I'm not in a good enough temper to work for myself. It's got to be a sort of job for somebody else, or I should throw it up in a month, out of bad temper. So altogether I'm very well off here, especially lately. . . ."

He laughed at her again, with mocking humor.

"But why are you in a bad temper?" she asked. "Do you mean you are *always* in a bad temper?"

"Pretty well," he said, laughing. "I don't quite digest my bile."

"But what bile?" she said.

"Bile!" he said. "Don't you know what that is?" She was silent, and disappointed. He was taking no notice of her.

"I'm going away for a while next month," she said.

"You are! Where to?"

"Venice."

"Venice! With Sir Clifford? For how long?"

"For a month or so," she replied. "Clifford won't go."

"He'll stay here?" he asked.

"Yes! He hates to travel as he is."

"Ay, poor devil!" he said, with sympathy.

There was a pause.

"You won't forget me when I'm gone, will you?" she asked. Again he lifted his eyes and looked full at her.

"Forget?" he said. "You know nobody forgets. It's not a question of memory."

She wanted to say: "What, then?" but she didn't. Instead, she said in a mute kind of voice: "I told Clifford I might have a child."

Now he really looked at her, intense and searching.

"You did?" he said at last. "And what did he say?"

"Oh, he wouldn't mind. He'd be glad, really, so long as it seemed to be his." She dared not look up at him.

He was silent a long time, then he gazed again on her face.

"No mention of *me*, of course?" he said.

"No. No mention of you," she said.

"No, he'd hardly swallow me as a substitute breeder.—Then where are you supposed to be getting the child?"

"I might have a love affair in Venice," she said.

"You might," he replied slowly. "So that's why you're going?"

"Not to have the love affair," she said, looking up at him, pleading. "Just the appearance of one," he said.

There was silence. He was staring out of the window, with a faint grin, half mockery, half bitterness, on his face. She hated his grin.

"You've not taken any precautions against having a child then?" he asked her suddenly. "Because I haven't."

"No," she said faintly. "I should hate that."

He looked at her, then again with the peculiar subtle grin out of the window. There was a tense silence.

At last he turned to her and said satirically:

"That was why you wanted me, then, to get a child?"

She hung her head.

"No. Not really," she said.

"What then, *really?*" he asked, rather bitingly.

She looked up at him reproachfully, saying: "I don't know." He broke into a laugh.

"Then I'm damned if I do," he said.

There was a long pause of silence, a cold silence.

"Well," he said at last. "It's as your Ladyship likes. If you get the baby, Sir Clifford's welcome to it. I shan't have lost anything. On the contrary, I've had a very nice experience; very nice, indeed!" And he stretched in a half suppressed sort of yawn. "If you've made use of me," he said, "it's not the first time I've been made use of; and I don't suppose it's ever been as pleasant as this time; though, of course, one can't feel tremendously dignified about it." He stretched again, curiously, his muscles quivering and his jaw oddly set.

"But I didn't make use of you," she said, pleading.

"At your Ladyship's service," he replied.

"No," she said. "I liked your body."

"Did you?" he replied, and he laughed. "Well then, we're quits, because I liked yours."

He looked at her with queer darkened eyes.

"Would you like to go upstairs now?" he asked her, in a strangled sort of voice.

"No, not here. Not now!" she said heavily, though if he had used any power over her, she would have gone, for she had no strength against him.

He turned his face away again, and seemed to forget her.

"I want to touch you like you touch me," she said. "I've never really touched you."

He looked at her, and smiled again. "Now?" he said.

"No! No! Not here! At the hut. Would you mind?"

"How do I touch you?" he asked.

"When you feel me."

He looked at her, and met her heavy, anxious eyes.

"And do you like it when I touch you?" he asked, laughing at her still.

"Yes, do you?" she said.

"Oh, me!" Then he changed his tone. "Yes," he said. "You know without asking." Which was true.

She rose and picked up her hat. "I must go," she said.

"Will you go?" he replied politely.

She wanted him to touch her, to say something to her, but he said nothing, only waited politely.

"Thank you for the tea," she said.

"I haven't thanked your Ladyship for doing me the honors of my teapot," he said.

She went down the path; and he stood in the doorway, faintly grinning. Flossie came running with her tail lifted. And Connie had to plod dumbly across into the wood, knowing he was standing there watching her, with that incomprehensible grin on his face.

She walked home very much downcast and annoyed. She didn't at all like his saying he had been made use of; because, in a sense, it was true. But he oughtn't to have said it. Therefore, again, she was divided between two feelings; resentment against him, and a desire to make it up with him.

She passed a very uneasy and irritated tea-time, and at once went to her room. But when she was there it was no good; she could neither sit nor stand. She would have to do something about it. She would have to go back to the hut; if he was not there, well and good.

She slipped out of the side door, and took her way direct and a little sullen. When she came to the clearing she was terribly uneasy. But there he was again, in his shirt-sleeves, stooping, letting the hens out of the coops, among the chicks that were now growing a little gawky, but were much more trim than hen-chickens.

She went straight across to him.

"You see, I've come!" she said.

"Ay, I see it!" he said, straightening his back, and looking at her with a faint amusement.

"Do you let the hens out now?" she asked.

"Yes, they've sat themselves to skin and bone," he said. "An' now they're not all that anxious to come out an' feed. There's no self in a sitting hen; she's all in the eggs or the chicks."

The poor mother-hens; such blind devotion; even to eggs not their own! Connie looked at them in compassion. A helpless silence fell between the man and the woman.

"Shall us go i' th' 'ut?" he asked.

"Do you want me?" she asked, in a sort of mistrust.

"Ay, if you want to come."

She was silent.

"Come then!" he said.

And she went with him to the hut. It was quite dark when he had shut the door, so he made a small light in the lantern, as before.

"Have you left your underthings off?" he asked her.

"Yes!"

"Ay, well, then I'll take my things off too."

He spread the blankets, putting one at the side for a coverlet. She took off her hat, and shook her hair. He sat down, taking off his shoes and gaiters, and undoing his cord breeches.

"Lie down then!" he said, when he stood in his shirt. She obeyed in silence, and he lay beside her, and pulled the blanket over them both.

"There!" he said.

And he lifted her dress right back, till he came even to her breasts. He kissed them softly, taking the nipples in his lips in tiny caresses.

"Eh, but tha'rt nice, tha'rt nice!" he said, suddenly rubbing his face with a snuggling movement against her warm belly.

And she put her arms round him under his shirt, but she was afraid, afraid of his thin, smooth, naked body, that seemed so powerful, afraid of the violent muscles. She shrank, afraid.

And when he said, with a sort of little sigh: "Eh, tha'rt nice!" something in her quivered, and something in her spirit stiffened in resistance: stiffened from the terribly physical intimacy, and from the peculiar haste of his possession. And this time the sharp ecstasy of her own passion did not overcome her; she lay with her hands inert on his striving body, and do what she might, her spirit seemed to look on from the top of her head, and the butting of his haunches seemed ridiculous to her, and the sort of anxiety of his penis to come to its little evacuating crisis seemed farcical. Yes, this was love, this ridiculous bouncing of the buttocks, and the wilting of the poor insignificant, moist little penis. This was the divine love! After all, the moderns were right when they felt contempt for the performance; for it was a performance. It was quite true, as some poets said, that the God who created man must have had a sinister sense of humor, creating him a reasonable being, yet forcing him to take this ridiculous posture, and driving him with blind craving for this ridiculous performance. Even a Maupassant found it a humiliating anti-climax. Men despised the intercourse act, and yet did it.

Cold and derisive her queer female mind stood apart, and though she lay perfectly still, her impulse was to heave her loins, and throw the man out, escape his ugly grip, and the butting overriding of his absurd haunches. His body was a foolish, impudent, imperfect thing, a little disgusting in its unfinished clumsiness. For surely a complete evolution would eliminate this performance, this "function."

And yet when he had finished, soon over, and lay very still, receding into silence, and a strange, motionless distance, far, farther than the horizon of her awareness, her heart began to weep. She could feel him ebbing away, ebbing away, leaving her there like a stone on the shore. He was withdrawing, his spirit was leaving her. He knew.

And in real grief, tormented by her own double consciousness and reaction, she began to weep. He took no notice, or did not even know. The storm of weeping swelled and shook her, and shook him.

"Ay!" he said. "It was no good that time. You wasn't there."—So he knew! Her sobs became violent.

"But what's amiss?" he said. "It's once in a while that way."

"I . . . I can't love you," she sobbed, suddenly feeling her heart breaking.

"Canna ter? Well, dunna fret! There's no law says tha's got to. Ta'e it for what it is."

He still lay with his hand on her breast. But she had drawn both her hands from him.

His words were small comfort. She sobbed aloud.

"Nay, nay!" he said. "Ta'e the thick wi' th' thin. This wor' a bit o' thin for once."

She wept bitterly, sobbing: "But I want to love you, and I can't. It only seems horrid."

He laughed a little, half bitter, half amused.

"It isna horrid," he said, "even if tha thinks it is. An' tha canna ma'e it horrid. Dunna fret thysen about lovin' me. Tha'lt niver force thysen to 't. There's sure to be a bad nut in a basketful. Tha mun ta'e th' rough wi' th' smooth."

He took his hand away from her breast, not touching her. And now she was untouched she took an almost perverse satisfaction in it. She hated the dialect: the *thee* and the *tha* and the *thysen*. He could get up if he liked, and stand there above her buttoning down those absurd corduroy breeches, straight in front of her. After all, Michaelis had had the decency to turn away. This man was so assured in himself he didn't know what a clown other people found him, a half-bred fellow.

Yet, as he was drawing away, to rise silently and leave her, she clung to him in terror.

"Don't! Don't go! Don't leave me! Don't be cross with me! Hold me! Hold me fast!" she whispered in blind frenzy, not even knowing what she said, and clinging to him with uncanny force. It was from herself she wanted to be saved, from her own inward anger and resistance. Yet how powerful was that inward resistance that possessed her!

He took her in his arms again and drew her to him, and suddenly she became small in his arms, small and nestling. It was gone, and she began to melt in marvellous peace. And as she melted small and wonderful in his arms, she became infinitely desirable to him, all his blood vessels seemed to scald with intense yet tender desire, for her, for her softness, for the penetrating beauty of her in his arms, passing into his blood. And softly, with that marvellous swoon-like caress of his hand in pure soft desire, softly he stroked the silky slope of her loins, down, down between her soft warm buttocks, coming nearer and nearer to the very quick of her. And she felt him like a flame of desire, yet tender, and she felt herself melting in the flame. She let herself go. She felt his penis risen against her with silent amazing force and assertion, and she let herself go to him. She yielded with a quiver that was like death, she went all open to him. And oh, if he were not tender to her now, how cruel, for she was all open to him and helpless!

She quivered again at the potent inexorable entry inside her, so strange and terrible. It might come with the thrust of a sword in her softly-opened body, and that would be death. She clung in a sudden anguish of terror. But it came with a strange slow thrust of peace, the dark thrust of peace and a ponderous, primordial tenderness, such as made the world in the beginning. And her terror subsided in her breast, her breast dared to be gone in peace, she held nothing. She dared to let go everything, all herself, and be gone in the flood.

And it seemed she was like the sea, nothing but dark waves rising and heaving, heaving with a great swell, so that slowly her whole darkness was in motion, and she was ocean rolling its dark, dumb mass. Oh, and far down inside her the deeps parted and rolled asunder, in long, far-travelling billows, and ever, at the quick of her, the depths parted and rolled asunder, from the center of soft plunging, as the plunger went deeper and deeper, touching lower, and she was deeper and deeper and deeper disclosed, and heavier the billows of her rolled away to some shore, uncovering her, and closer and closer plunged the palpable unknown, and further and further rolled the waves of herself away from herself, leaving her, till suddenly, in a soft, shuddering convulsion, the quick of all her plasm was touched, she knew herself touched, the consummation was upon her, and she was gone. She was gone, she was not, and she was born: a woman.

Ah, too lovely, too lovely! In the ebbing she realized all the loveliness. Now all her body clung with tender love to the unknown man, and blindly to the wilting penis, as it so tenderly, frailly, unknowingly withdrew, after the fierce thrust of its potency. As it drew out and left her body, the secret, sensitive thing, she gave an unconscious cry of pure loss, and she tried to put it back. It had been so perfect! And she loved it so!

And only now she became aware of the small, bud-like reticence and tenderness of the penis, and a little cry of wonder and poignancy escaped her again, her woman's heart crying out over the tender frailty of that which had been the power.

"It was so lovely!" she moaned. "It was so lovely!" But he said nothing, only softly kissed her, lying still above her. And she moaned with a sort of bliss, as a sacrifice, and a new-born thing.

And now in her heart the queer wonder of him was awakened. A man! the strange potency of manhood upon her! Her hands strayed over him, still a little afraid. Afraid of that strange, hostile, slightly repulsive thing that he had been to her, a man. And now she touched him, and it was the sons of god with the daughters of men. How beautiful he felt, how pure in tissue! How lovely, how lovely, strong, and yet pure and delicate, such stillness of the sensitive body! Such utter stillness of potency and delicate flesh! How beautiful! How beautiful! Her hands came timorously down his back to the soft, smallish globes of the buttocks. Beauty! What beauty! a sudden little flame of new awareness went through her. How was it possible this beauty here, where she had previously been repelled? The unspeakable beauty to the touch, of the warm, living buttocks! The life within life, the sheer warm, potent loveliness. And the strange weight of the balls between his legs! What a mystery! What a strange heavy weight of mystery, that could lie soft and heavy in one's hand! The roots, root of all that is lovely, the primeval root of all full beauty.

She clung to him, with a hiss of wonder that was almost awe, terror. He held her close, but he said nothing. He would never say anything. She crept nearer to him, nearer, only to be near the sensual wonder of him. And out of his utter, incomprehensible stillness, she felt again the slow, momentous, surging rise of the phallus again, the other power. And her heart melted out with a kind of awe.

And this time his being within her was all soft and iridescent, purely soft and iridescent, such as no consciousness could seize. Her whole self quivered unconscious and alive, like plasm. She could not know what it was. She could not remember what it had been. Only that it had been more lovely than anything ever could be. Only that. And afterwards she was utterly still, utterly unknowing, she was not aware for how long. And he was still with her, in an unfathomable silence along with her. And of this, they would never speak.

When awareness of the outside began to come back, she clung to his breast, murmuring: "My love! my love!" And he held her silently. And she curled on his breast, perfect..

But his silence was fathomless. His hands held her like flowers, so still and strange. "Where are you?" she whispered to him. "Where are you? Speak to me! Say something to me!"

He kissed her softly, murmuring: "Ay, my lass!"

But she did not know what he meant, she did not know where he was. In his silence he seemed lost to her.

"You love me, don't you?" she murmured.

"Ay, tha knows!" he said.

"But tell me!" she pleaded.

"Ay! Ay! 'asn't ter felt it?" he said dimly, but softly and surely. And she clung close to him, closer. He was so much more peaceful in love than she was, and she wanted him to reassure her.

"You do love me!" she whispered, assertive. And his hands stroked her softly, as if she were a flower, without the quiver of desire, but with delicate nearness. And still there haunted her a restless necessity to get a grip on love.

"Say you'll always love me!" she pleaded.

"Ay!" he said, abstractedly. And she felt her questions driving him away from her.

"Mustn't we get up?" he said at last.

"No!" she said.

But she could feel his consciousness straying, listening to the noises outside.

"It'll be nearly dark," he said. And she heard the pressure of circumstance in his voice. She kissed him, with a woman's grief at yielding up her hour.

He rose, and turned up the lantern, then began to pull on his clothes, quickly disappearing inside them. Then he stood there, above her with dark, wide eyes, his face a little flushed and his hair ruffled, curiously warm and still and beautiful in the dim light of the lantern, so beautiful, she would never tell him how beautiful. It made her want to cling fast to him, to hold him, for there was a warm, half-sleepy remoteness in his beauty that made her want to cry out and clutch him, to have him. She would never have him. So she lay on the blanket with curved, soft naked haunches, and he had no idea what she was thinking, but to him she too was beautiful, the soft, marvellous thing he could go into, beyond everything.

"I love thee that I can go into thee," he said.

"Do you like me?" she said, her heart beating.

"It heals it all up, that I can go into thee. I love thee that tha opened to me. I love thee that I came into thee like that."

He bent down and kissed her soft flank, rubbed his cheek against it, then covered it up.

"And will you never leave me?" she said.

"Dunna ask them things," he said.

"But you do believe I love you?" she said.

"Tha loved me just now, wider than iver tha thout tha would. But who knows what'll 'appen, once tha starts thinkin' about it!"

"No, don't say those things!—And you don't really think that I wanted to make use of you, do you?"

"How?"

"To have a child—?"

"Now anybody can 'ave any childt i' th' world," he said, as he sat down fastening on his leggings.

"Ah no!" she cried. "You don't mean it?"

"Eh well!" he said, looking at her under his brows. "This wor t' best."

She lay still. He softly opened the door. The sky was dark blue, with crystalline, turquoise rim. He went out, to shut up the hens, speaking softly to his dog. And she lay and wondered at the wonder of life, and of being.

When he came back she was still lying there, glowing like a gipsy. He sat on the stool by her.

"Tha mun come one naight ter th' cottage, afore tha goos; sholl ter?" he asked, lifting his eyebrows as he looked at her, his hands dangling between his knees.

"Sholl ter?" she echoed, teasing.

He smiled.

"Ay, sholl ter?" he repeated.

"Ay!" she said, imitating the dialect sound.

"Yi!" he said.

"Yi!" she repeated.

"An' slaip wi' me," he said. "It needs that. When sholt come?"

"When sholl I?" she said.

"Nay," he said, "tha canna do't. When sholt come then?"

" 'Appen Sunday," she said.

" 'Appen a' Sunday! Ay!"

He laughed at her quickly.

"Nay, tha canna," he protested.

"Why canna I?" she said.

He laughed. Her attempts at the dialect were so ludicrous, somehow.

"Coom then, tha mun goo!" he said.

"Mun I?" she said.

"Maun Ah!" he corrected.

"Why should I say *maun* when you say *mun,*" she protested. "You're not playing fair."

"Arena Ah!" he said, leaning forward and softly stroking her face.

"Th'art good cunt, though, are'nt ter? Best bit o' cunt left on earth. When ter likes! When tha'rt willin'!"

"What is cunt?" she said.

"An' doesn't ter know? Cunt! It's thee down theer; an' what I get when I'm i'side thee; it's a' as it is, all on't."

"All on't," she teased. "Cunt! It's like fuck then."

"Nay, nay! Fuck's only what you do. Animals fuck. But cunt's a lot more than that. It's thee, dost see: an' tha'rt a lot besides an animal, aren't ter? even ter fuck! Cunt! Eh, that's the beauty o' thee, lass."

She got up and kissed him between the eyes that looked at her so dark and soft and unspeakably warm, so unbearably beautiful.

"Is it?" she said. "And do you care for me?"

He kissed her without answering.

"Tha mun goo, let me dust thee," he said.

His hand passed over the curves of her body, firmly, without desire, but with soft, intimate knowledge.

As she ran home in the twilight the world seemed a dream; the trees in the park seemed bulging and surging at anchor on a tide, and the heave of the slope to the house was alive.

XIII

On Sunday Clifford wanted to go into the wood. It was a lovely morning, the pear blossom and plum had suddenly appeared in the world in a wonder of white here and there.

It was cruel for Clifford, while the world bloomed, to have to be helped from chair to bath-chair. But he had forgotten, and even seemed to have a certain conceit of himself in his lameness. Connie still suffered, having to lift his inert legs into place. Mrs. Bolton did it now, or Field.

She waited for him at the top of the drive, at the edge of the screen of beeches. His chair came puffing along with a sort of valetudinarian slow importance. As he joined his wife he said:

"Sir Clifford on his foaming steed!"

"Snorting, at least!" she laughed.

He stopped and looked around at the facade of the long, low old brown house.

"Wragby doesn't wink an eyelid!" he said. "But then why should it? I ride upon the achievements of the mind of man, and that beats a horse."

"I suppose it does. And the souls in Plato riding up to heaven in a two-horse chariot would go in a Ford car now," she said.

"Or a Rolls-Royce: Plato was an aristocrat!"

"Quite! No more black horse to thrash and maltreat. Plato never thought we'd go one better than his black steed and his white steed, and have no steeds at all, only an engine!"

"Only an engine and gas!" said Clifford.

"I hope I can have some repairs done to the old place next year. I think I shall have about a thousand to spare for that: but work costs so much!" he added.

"Oh, good!" said Connie. "If only there aren't more strikes!"

"What would be the use of their striking again! Merely ruin the industry, what's left of it: and surely the owls are beginning to see it!"

"Perhaps they don't mind ruining the industry," said Connie.

"Ah, don't talk like a woman! The industry fills their bellies, even if it can't keep their pockets quite so flush," he said, using terms of speech that oddly had a twang of Mrs. Bolton.

"But didn't you say the other day that you were a conservative-anarchist?" she asked innocently.

"And did you understand what I meant?" he retorted. "All I meant is, people can be what they like and feel what they like and do what they like, strictly privately, so long as they keep the *form* of life intact, and the apparatus."

Connie walked on in silence a few paces. Then she said, obstinately:

"It sounds like saying an egg may go as addled as it likes, so long as it keeps its shell on whole. But addled eggs do break of themselves."

"I don't think people are eggs," he said. "Not even angels' eggs, my dear little evangelist."

He was in rather high feather this bright morning. The larks were trilling away over the park, the distant pit in the hollow was fuming silent steam. It was almost like old days, before the war. Connie didn't really want to argue. But then she did not really want to go to the wood with Clifford either. So she walked beside his chair in a certain obstinacy of spirit.

"No," he said. "There will be no more strikes, if the thing is properly managed."

"Why not?"

"Because strikes will be made as good as impossible."

"But will the men let you?" she asked.

"We shan't ask them. We shall do it while they aren't looking: for their own good, to save the industry."

"For your own good, too," she said.

"Naturally! For the good of everybody. But for their good even more than mine. I can live without the pits. They can't. They'll starve if there are no pits. I've got other provision."

They looked up the shallow valley at the mine, and beyond it, at the black-lidded houses of Tevershall crawling like some serpent up the hill. From the old brown church the bells were ringing: Sunday, Sunday, Sunday!

"But will the men let you dictate terms?" she said.

"My dear, they will have to: if one does it gently."

"But mightn't there be a mutual understanding?"

"Absolutely: when they realize that the industry comes before the individual."

"But must you own the industry?" she said.

"I don't. But to the extent I do own it, yes, most decidedly. The ownership of property has now become a religious question: as it has been since Jesus and St. Francis. The point is *not:* take all thou hast and give to the poor, but use all thou hast to encourage the industry and give work to the poor. It's the only way to feed all the mouths and clothe all the bodies. Giving away all we have to the poor spells starvation for the poor just as much as for us. And universal starvation is no high aim. Even general poverty is no lovely thing. Poverty is ugly."

"But the disparity?"

"That is fate. Why is the star Jupiter bigger than the star Neptune? You can't start altering the make-up of things!"

"But when this envy and jealousy and discontent has once started," she began.

"Do your best to stop it. Somebody's *got* to be boss of the show."

"But who is the boss of the show?" she asked.

"The men who own and run the industries."

There was a long silence.

"It seems to me they're a bad boss," she said.

"Then you suggest what they should do."

"They don't take their boss-ship seriously enough," she said.

"They take it far more seriously than you take your ladyship," he said.

"That's thrust upon me. I don't really want it," she blurted out. He stopped the chair and looked at her.

"Who's shirking their responsibility now!" he said. "Who is trying to get away *now* from the responsibility of their own boss-ship, as you call it?"

"But I don't want any boss-ship," she protested.

"Ah! But that is funk. You've got it: fated to it. And you should live up to it. Who has given the colliers all they have that's worth having; all their political liberty, and their education, such as it is; their sanitation, their health-conditions, their books, their music, everything? Who has given it to them? Have colliers given it to the colliers? No! All the Wragbys and Shipleys in England have given their part, and must go on giving. There's your responsibility."

Connie listened, and flushed very red.

"I'd like to give something," she said. "But I'm not allowed. Everything is to be sold and paid for now; and all the things you mention now, Wragby and Shipley *sell* them to the people, at a good profit. Everything is sold. You don't give one heart-beat of real sympathy. And besides, who has taken away from the people their natural life and manhood, and given them this industrial horror? Who has done that?"

"And what must I do?" he asked, green. "Ask them to come and pillage me?"

"Why is Tevershall so ugly, so hideous? Why are their lives so hopeless?"

"They built their own Tevershall. That's part of their display of freedom. They built themselves their pretty Tevershall, and they live their own pretty lives. I can't live their lives for them. Every beetle must live its own life."

"But you make them work for you. They live the life of your coal mine."

"Not at all. Every beetle finds its own food. Not one man is forced to work for me."

"Their lives are industrialized and hopeless, and so are ours," she cried.

"I don't think they are. That's just a romantic figure of speech, a relic of the swooning and die-away romanticism. You don't look at all a hopeless figure standing there, Connie, my dear."

Which was true. For her dark blue eyes were flashing, color was hot in her cheeks, she looked full of a rebellious passion far from the dejection of hopelessness. She noticed, in the tussocky places of the grass, cottony young cowslips standing up still bleared in their down. And she wondered with rage, why it was she felt Clifford was so *wrong,* yet she couldn't say it to him, she could not say exactly *where* he was wrong.

"No wonder the men hate you," she said.

"They don't!" he replied. "And don't fall into errors: in your sense of the word, they are *not* men. They are animals you don't understand and never could. Don't thrust your illusions on other people. The masses were always the same, and will always be the same. Nero's slaves were extremely little different from our colliers or the Ford motor-car workmen. I mean Nero's mine slaves and his field slaves. It is the masses: they are the unchangeable. An individual may emerge from the masses. But the emergence doesn't alter the mass. The masses are unalterable. It is one of the most momentous facts of social science. *Panem et circenses!* Only today education is one of the bad substitutes for a circus. What is wrong today is that we've made a profound hash of the circuses part of the program, and poisoned our masses with a little education."

When Clifford became really aroused in his feelings about the common people, Connie was frightened. There was something devastatingly true in what he said. But it was a truth that killed.

Seeing her pale and silent, Clifford started the chair again, and no more was said till he halted again at the wood gate, which she opened.

"And what we need to take up now," he said, "is whips, not swords. The masses have been ruled since time began, and, till time ends, ruled they will have to be. It is sheer hypocrisy and farce to say they can rule themselves."

"But can you rule them?" she asked.

"I? Oh, yes! Neither my mind nor my will is crippled, and I don't rule with my legs. I can do my share of ruling: absolutely, my share; and give me a son, and he will be able to rule his portion after me."

"But he wouldn't be your own son, of your own ruling class; or, perhaps not," she stammered.

"I don't care who his father may be, so long as he is a healthy man not below normal intelligence. Give me the child of any healthy, normally intelligent man, and I will make a perfectly competent Chatterley of him. It is not who begets us that matters, but where fate places us. Place any child among the ruling classes, and he will grow up, to his own extent, a ruler. Put kings' and dukes' children among the masses, and they'll be little plebians, mass products. It is the overwhelming pressure of environment."

"Then the common people aren't a race, and the aristocrats aren't blood," she said.

"No, my child! All that is romantic illusion. Aristocracy is a function, a part of fate. And the masses are a functioning of another part of fate. The individual hardly matters. It is a question of which function you are brought up to and adapted to. It is not the individuals that make an aristocracy: it is the functioning of the aristocratic whole. And it is the functioning of the whole mass that makes the common man what he is."

"Then there is no common humanity between us all!"

"Just as you like. We all need to fill our bellies. But when it comes to expressive or executive functioning, I believe there is a gulf and an absolute one, between the ruling and the serving classes. The two functions are opposed. And the function determines the individual."

Connie looked at him with dazed eyes.

"Won't you come on?" she said.

And he started his chair. He had said his say. Now he lapsed into his peculiar and rather vacant apathy, that Connie found so trying. In the wood, anyhow, she was determined not to argue.

In front of them ran the open cleft of the riding, between the hazel walls and the grey trees. The chair puffed slowly on, slowly surging into the forget-me-nots that rose up in the drive like milk froth, beyond the hazel shadows. Clifford steered the middle course, where feet passing had kept a channel through the flowers. But Connie, walking behind, had watched the wheels jolt over the woodruff and the bugle, and squash the little yellow cups of the creeping-jenny. Now they made a wake through the forget-me-nots.

All the flowers were there, the first bluebells in blue pools, like standing water.

"You are quite right about its being beautiful," said Clifford. "It is so amazingly. What is *quite* so lovely as an English spring!"

Connie thought it sounded as if even the spring bloomed by Act of Parliament. An English spring! Why not an Irish one? or Jewish? The chair moved slowly ahead, past tufts of sturdy bluebells that stood up like wheat and over grey burdock leaves. Then they came to the open place where the trees had been felled, the light flooded in rather stark. And the bluebells made sheets of bright blue color, here and there, sheering off into lilac and purple. And between, the bracken was lifting its brown curled heads, like legions of young snakes with a new secret to whisper to Eve.

Clifford kept the chair going till he came to the brow of the hill; Connie followed slowly behind. The oak buds were opening soft and brown. Everything came tenderly out of the old hardness. Even the snaggy craggy oak trees put out the softest leaves, spreading thin, brown little wings like young bat wings in the light. Why had men never any newness in them, any freshness to come forth with? Stale men!

Clifford stopped the chair at the top of the rise and looked down. The bluebells washed blue like flood-water over the broad riding, and lit up the down-hill with a warm blueness.

"It's a very fine color in itself," said Clifford, "but useless for making a painting."

"Quite!" said Connie, completely uninterested.

"Shall I venture as far as the spring?" said Clifford.

"Will the chair get up again?" she said.

"We'll try; nothing venture, nothing win!"

And the chair began to advance slowly, joltingly down the beautiful broad riding washed over with blue encroaching hyacinths. Oh last of all ships, through the hyacinthian shallows! Oh pinnace on the last wild waters, sailing on the last voyage of our civilization! Whither, Oh weird wheeled ship, your slow course steering! Quiet and complacent, Clifford sat at the wheel of adventure: in his old black hat and tweed jacket, motionless and cautious. Oh captain, my Captain, our splendid trip is done! Not yet though! Downhill in the wake, came Constance in her grey dress, watching the chair jolt downwards.

They passed the narrow track to the hut. Thank heaven it was not wide enough for the chair: hardly wide enough for one person. The chair reached the bottom of the slope, and swerved round, to disappear. And Connie heard a low whistle behind her. She glanced sharply round: the keeper was striding down-hill towards her, his dog keeping behind him.

"Is Sir Clifford going to the cottage?" he asked, looking into her eyes.

"No, only to the well."

"Ah! Good! Then I can keep out of sight. But I shall see you tonight. I shall wait for you at the park gate about ten."

He looked again direct into her eyes.

"Yes," she faltered.

They heard the Papp! Papp! of Clifford's horn, tooting for Connie. She "Coo-eed!" in reply. The keeper's face flickered with a little grimace, and with his hand he softly brushed her breast upwards, from underneath. She looked at him, frightened, and started running down the hill, calling Coo-ee! again to Clifford. The man above watched her, then turned, grinning faintly, back into his path.

She found Clifford slowly mounting to the spring, which was half-way up the slope of the dark larch-wood. He was there by the time she caught him up.

"She did that all right," he said, referring to the chair.

Connie looked at the great grey leaves of burdock that grew out ghostly from the edge of the larch-wood. The people call it Robin Hood's Rhubarb. How silent and gloomy it seemed by the well! Yet the water bubbled so bright, wonderful! And there were bits of eye-bright and strong blue bugle. And there, under the bank, the yellow earth was moving. A mole! It emerged, rowing its pink hands, and waving its blind gimlet of a face, with the tiny nose-tip uplifted.

"It seems to see with the end of its nose," said Connie.

"Better than with its eyes!" he said. "Will you drink?"

"Will you?"

She took an enamel mug from a twig on a tree, and stooped to fill it for him. He drank in sips. Then she stooped again, and drank a little herself.

"So icy!" she said, gasping.

"Good, isn't it! Did you wish?"

"Did you?"

"Yes, I wished. But I won't tell."

She was aware of the rapping of a woodpecker, then of the wind, soft and eerie through the larches. She looked up. White clouds were crossing the blue.

"Clouds!" she said.

"White lambs only," he replied.

A shadow crossed the little clearing. The mole had swum out on to the soft yellow earth.

"Unpleasant little beast, we ought to kill him," said Clifford.

"Look! he's like a parson in a pulpit," she said.

She gathered some sprigs of woodruff and brought them to him.

"New-mown hay!" he said. "Doesn't it smell like the romantic ladies of the last century, who had their heads screwed on the right way after all!"

She was looking at the white clouds.

"I wonder if it will rain," she said.

"Rain! Why! Do you want it to?"

They started on the return journey, Clifford jolting cautiously down-hill. They came to the dark bottom of the hollow, turned to the right, and after a hundred yards swerved up the foot of the long slope, where bluebells stood in the light.

"Now, old girl!" said Clifford, putting the chair to it.

It was a steep and jolty climb. The chair plugged slowly, in a struggling unwilling fashion. Still, she nosed her way up unevenly, till she came to where the hyacinths were all around her, then she balked, struggled, jerked a little way out of the flowers, then stopped.

"We'd better sound the horn and see if the keeper will come," said Connie. "He could push her a bit. For that matter, I will push. It helps."

"We'll let her breathe," said Clifford. "Do you mind putting a scotch under the wheel?"

Connie found a stone, and they waited. After a while Clifford started his motor again, then set the chair in motion. It struggled and faltered like a sick thing, with curious noises.

"Let me push!" said Connie, coming up behind.

"No! Don't push!" he said angrily. "What's the good of the damned thing, if it has to be pushed! Put the stone under!"

There was another pause, then another start; but more ineffectual than before.

"You *must* let me push," she said. "Or sound the horn for the keeper."

"Wait!"

She waited; and he had another try, doing more harm than good.

"Sound the horn, then, if you won't let me push," she said.

"Hell! Be quiet a moment!"

She was quiet a moment: he made shattering efforts with the little motor.

"You'll only break the thing down altogether, Clifford," she remonstrated: "besides wasting your nervous energy."

"If I could only get out and look at the damned thing!" he said, exasperated. And he sounded the horn stridently. "Perhaps Mellors can see what's wrong."

They waited, among the mashed flowers under a sky softly curdling with clouds. In the silence a wood-pigeon began to coo, roo-hoo hoo! roo-hoo hoo! Clifford shut her up with a blast on the horn.

The keeper appeared directly, striding inquiringly round the corner. He saluted.

"Do you know anything about motors?" asked Clifford sharply.

"I'm afraid I don't. Has she gone wrong?"

"Apparently!" snapped Clifford.

The man crouched solicitously by the wheel, and peered at the little engine.

"I'm afraid I know nothing at all about these mechanical things, Sir Clifford," he said calmly. "If she has enough petrol and oil—"

"Just look carefully and see if you can see anything broken," snapped Clifford.

The man laid his gun against a tree, took off his coat and threw it beside it. The brown dog sat guard. Then he sat down on his heels and peered under the chair, poking with his finger at the greasy little engine, and resenting the grease-marks on his clean Sunday shirt.

"Doesn't seem anything broken," he said. And he stood up, pushing back his hat from his forehead, rubbing his brow and apparently studying.

"Have you looked at the rods underneath?" asked Clifford. "See if they are all right!"

The man lay flat on his stomach on the floor, his neck pressed back, wriggling under the engine and poking with his finger. Connie thought what a pathetic sort of thing a man was, feeble and small looking, when he was lying on his belly on the big earth.

"Seems all right as far as I can see," came his muffled voice.

"I don't suppose you can do anything," said Clifford.

"Seems as if I can't!" And he scrambled up and sat on his heels, collier fashion. "There's certainly nothing obviously broken."

Clifford started his engine, then put her in gear. She would not move.

"Run her a bit hard, like," suggested the keeper.

Clifford resented the interference: but he made his engine buzz like a bluebottle. Then she coughed and snarled and seemed to go better.

"Sounds as if she'd come clear," said Mellors.

But Clifford had already jerked her into gear. She gave a sick lurch and ebbed weakly forwards.

"If I give her a push, she'll do it," said the keeper, going behind.

"Keep off!" snapped Clifford. "She'll do it by herself."

"But Clifford!" put in Connie from the bank, "you know it's too much for her. Why are you so obstinate!"

Clifford was pale with anger. He jabbed at his levers. The chair gave a sort of scurry, reeled on a few more yards, and came to her end amid a particularly promising patch of bluebells.

"She's done!" said the keeper. "Not power enough."

"She's been up here before," said Clifford coldly.

"She won't do it this time," said the keeper.

Clifford did not reply. He began doing things with his engine, running her fast and slow as if to get some sort of tune out of her. The wood re-echoed with weird noises. Then he put her in gear with a jerk, having jerked off his brake.

"You'll rip her inside out," murmured the keeper.

The chair charged in a sick lurch sideways at the ditch.

"Clifford!" cried Connie, rushing forward.

But the keeper had got the chair by the rail. Clifford, however, putting on all his pressure, managed to steer into the riding, and with a strange noise the chair was fighting the hill. Mellors pushed steadily behind, and up she went, as if to retrieve herself.

"You see, she's doing it!" said Clifford victorious, glancing over his shoulder. There he saw the keeper's face.

"Are you pushing her?"

"She won't do it without."

"Leave her alone. I asked you not."

"She won't do it."

"*Let her try!*" snarled Clifford, with all his emphasis.

The keeper stood back: then turned to fetch his coat and gun. The chair seemed to strangle immediately. She stood inert. Clifford, seated a prisoner, was white with vexation. He jerked at the levers with his hand, his feet were no good. He got queer noises out of her. In savage impatience he moved little handles and got more noises out of her. But she would not budge. No, she would not budge. He stopped the engine and sat rigid with anger.

Constance sat on the bank and looked at the wretched and trampled blue-bells. "Nothing quite so lovely as an English spring." "I can do my share of ruling." "What we need to take up now is whips, not swords." "The ruling classes!"

The keeper strode up with his coat and gun, Flossie cautiously at his heels. Clifford asked the man to do something or other to the engine. Connie, who understood nothing at all of the technicalities of motors, and who had had experience of breakdowns, sat patiently on the bank as if she were a cipher. The keeper lay on his stomach again. The ruling classes and the serving classes!

He got to his feet and said patiently:

"Try her again, then."

He spoke in a quiet voice, almost as if to a child.

Clifford tried her, and Mellors stepped quickly behind and began to push. She was going, the engine doing about half the work, the man the rest. Clifford glanced round yellow with anger.

"Will you get off there!"

The keeper dropped his hold at once, and Clifford added: "How shall I know what she is doing!"

The man put his gun down and began to pull on his coat. He'd done.

The chair began slowly to run backwards.

"Clifford, your brake!" cried Connie.

She, Mellors, and Clifford moved at once, Connie and the keeper jostling lightly. The chair stood. There was a moment of dead silence.

"It's obvious I'm at everybody's mercy!" said Clifford. He was yellow with anger.

No one answered. Mellors was slinging his gun over his shoulder, his face queer and expressionless, save for an abstracted look of patience. The dog Flossie, standing on guard almost between her master's legs, moved uneasily, eyeing the chair with great suspicion and dislike, and very much perplexed between the three human beings. The *tableau vivant* remained set among the squashed bluebells, nobody proffering a word.

"I expect she'll have to be pushed," said Clifford at last, with an affectation of *sang froid*.

No answer. Mellors' abstracted face looked as if he had heard nothing. Connie glanced anxiously at him. Clifford, too, glanced round.

"Do you mind pushing her home, Mellors!" he said in a cold, superior tone. "I hope I have said nothing to offend you," he added, in a tone of dislike.

"Nothing at all, Sir Clifford! Do you want me to push that chair?"

"If you please."

The man stepped up to it: but this time it was without effect. The brake was jammed. They poked and pulled, and the keeper took off his gun and his coat once more. And now Clifford said never a word. At last the keeper heaved the back of the chair off the ground, and with an instantaneous push of his foot, tried to loosen the wheels. He failed, the chair sank. Clifford was clutching the sides. The man gasped with the weight.

"Don't do it!" cried Connie to him.

"If you'll pull the wheel that way, so!" he said to her, showing her how.

"No! You mustn't lift it! You'll strain yourself," she said, flushed now with anger.

But he looked into her eyes and nodded. And she had to go and take hold of the wheel, ready. He heaved and she tugged, and the chair reeled.

"For God's sake!" cried Clifford in terror.

But it was all right, and the brake was off. The keeper put a stone under the wheel, and went to sit on the bank, his heart beating and his face white with the effort, semiconscious. Connie looked at him, and almost cried with anger. There was a pause and a dead silence. She saw his hands trembling on his thighs.

"Have you hurt yourself?" she asked, going to him.

"No. No!" he turned away almost angrily.

There was dead silence. The back of Clifford's fair head did not move. Even the dog stood motionless. The sky had clouded over.

At last he sighed, and blew his nose on his red handkerchief.

"That pneumonia took a lot out of me," he said.

No one answered. Connie calculated the amount of strength it must have taken to heave up that chair and the bulky Clifford: too much, far too much! If it hadn't killed him!

He rose, and again picked up his coat, slinging it through the handle of the chair.

"Are you ready, then, Sir Clifford?"

"When you are!"

He stooped and took out the scotch, then put his weight against the chair. He was paler than Connie had ever seen him: and more absent. Clifford was a heavy man: and the hill was steep. Connie stepped to the keeper's side.

"I'm going to push too!" she said.

And she began to shove with a woman's turbulent energy of anger. The chair went faster. Clifford looked round.

"Is that necessary?" he said.

"Very! Do you want to kill the man! If you'd let the motor work while it would—"

But she did not finish. She was already panting. She slackened off a little, for it was surprisingly hard work.

"Ay! slower!" said the man at her side, with a faint smile of the eyes.

"Are you sure you've not hurt yourself?" she said fiercely.

He shook his head. She looked at his smallish, short, alive hand, browned by the weather. It was the hand that caressed her. She had never even looked at it before. It seemed so still, like him, with a curious inward stillness that made her want to clutch it, as if she could not reach it. All her soul suddenly swept towards him: he was so silent, and out of reach! And he felt his limbs revive. Shoving with his left hand, he laid his right on her round white wrist, softly enfolding her wrist, with caress. And the flame of strength went down his back and his loins, reviving him. And she bent suddenly and kissed his hand. Meanwhile the back of Clifford's head was held sleek and motionless, just in front of them.

At the top of the hill they rested, and Connie was glad to let go. She had had fugitive dreams of friendship between these two men: one her husband, the other the father of her child. Now she saw the screaming absurdity of her dreams. The two males were as hostile as fire and water. They mutually exterminated one another. And she realized for the first time, what a queer subtle thing hate is. For the first time, she had consciously and definitely hated Clifford, with vivid hate: as if he ought to be obliterated from the face of the earth. And it was strange, how free and full of life it made her feel, to hate him and to admit it fully to herself.—"Now, I've hated him, I shall never be able to go on living with him," came the thought into her mind.

On the level the keeper could push the chair alone. Clifford made a little conversation with her, to show his complete composure: about Aunt Eva, who was at Dieppe, and about Sir Malcolm, who had written to ask would Connie drive with him in his small car, to Venice, or would she and Hilda go by train.

"I'd much rather go by train," said Connie. "I don't like long motor drives, especially when there's dust. But I shall see what Hilda wants."

"She will want to drive her own car, and take you with her," he said.

"Probably!—I must help up here. You've no idea how heavy this chair is."

She went to the back of his chair, and plodded side by side with the keeper, shoving up the pink path. She did not care who saw.

"Why not let me wait, and fetch Field. He is strong enough for the job," said Clifford.

"It's so near," she panted.

But both she and Mellors wiped the sweat from their faces when they came to the top. It was curious, but this bit of work together had brought them much closer than they had been before.

"Thanks so much, Mellors," said Clifford, when they were at the house door. "I must get a different sort of motor, that's all. Won't you go to the kitchen and have a meal? it must be about time."

"Thank you, Sir Clifford. I was going to my mother for dinner today, Sunday."

"As you like."

Mellors slung into his coat, looked at Connie, saluted, and was gone. Connie, furious, went upstairs.

At lunch she could not contain her feelings.

"Why are you so abominably inconsiderate, Clifford?" she said to him.

"Of whom?"

"Of the keeper! If that is what you call the ruling classes, I'm sorry for you."

"Why?"

"A man who's been ill, and isn't strong! My word, if I were the serving classes, I'd let you wait for service. I'd let you whistle."

"I quite believe it."

"If he'd been sitting in a chair with paralyzed legs, and behaved as you behaved, what would you have done for *him?*"

"My dear evangelist, this confusing of persons and personalities is in bad taste."

"And your nasty, sterile want of common sympathy is in the worst taste imaginable. *Noblesse oblige!* You and your ruling class!"

"And to what should it oblige me? To have a lot of unnecessary emotions about my gamekeeper? I refuse. I leave it all to my evangelist."

"As if he weren't a man as much as you are, my word!"

"My gamekeeper to boot, and I pay him two pounds a week and give him a house."

"Pay him! What do you think you pay him for, with two pounds a week and a house?"

"His services."

"Bah! I would tell you to keep your two pounds a week and your house."

"Probably he would like to; but can't afford the luxury!"

"You and *rule!*" she said. "You don't rule, don't flatter yourself. You have only got more than your share of the money, and make people work for you for two pounds a week, or threaten them with starvation. Rule! What do you give forth of rule? Why, you're dried up! You only bully with your money, like any Jew or any Schieber!"

"You are very elegant in your speech, Lady Chatterley!"

"I assure you, you were very elegant altogether out there in the wood. I was utterly ashamed of you. Why, my father is ten times the human being you are: you *gentleman!*"

He reached and rang the bell for Mrs. Bolton. But he was yellow at the gills.

She went up to her room, furious, saying to herself: "Him and buying people! Well, he doesn't buy me, and therefore there's no need for me to stay with him. Dead fish of a gentleman, with his celluloid soul! And how they take one in, with their manners and their mock wistfulness and gentleness. They've got about as much feeling as celluloid has."

She made her plans for the night, and determined to get Clifford off her mind. She didn't want to hate him. She didn't want to be mixed up very intimately with him in any sort of feeling. She wanted him not to know anything at all about herself: and especially, not to know anything about her feeling for the keeper. This squabble of her attitude to the servants was an old one. He found her too familiar, she found him stupidly insentient, tough and india rubbery where other people were concerned.

She went downstairs calmly, with her old demure bearing, at dinner time. He was still yellow at the gills: in for one of his liver bouts, when he was really very queer.—He was reading a French book.

"Have you ever read Proust?" he asked her.

"I've tried, but he bores me."

"He's really very extraordinary."

"Possibly! But he bores me: all that sophistication! He doesn't have feelings, he only has streams of words about feelings. I'm tired of self-important mentalities."

"Would you prefer self-important animalities?"

"Perhaps! But one might possibly get something that wasn't self-important."

"Well, I like Proust's subtlety and his well-bred anarchy."

"It makes you very dead, really."

"There speaks my evangelical little wife."

They were at it again, at it again! But she couldn't help fighting him. He seemed to sit there like a skeleton, sending out a skeleton's cold grizzly *will* against her. Almost she could feel the skeleton clutching her and pressing her to its cage of ribs. He, too, was really up in arms: and she was a little afraid of him.

She went upstairs as soon as possible, and went to bed quite early. But at half-past nine she got up, and went outside to listen. There was no sound. She slipped on a dressing-gown and went downstairs. Clifford and Mrs. Bolton were playing cards, gambling. They would probably go on until midnight.

Connie returned to her room, threw her pajamas on the tossed bed, put on a thin tennis-dress and over that a woolen day-dress, put on rubber tennis-shoes, and then a light coat. And she was ready. If she met anybody, she was just going out for a few minutes. And in the morning, when she came in again, she would just have been for a little walk in the dew, as she fairly often did before breakfast. For the rest, the only danger was that someone should go into her room during the night. But that was most unlikely: not one chance in a hundred.

Betts had not yet locked up. He fastened up the house at ten o'clock, and unfastened it again at seven in the morning. She slipped out silently and unseen. There was a half-moon shining, enough to make a little light in the world, not enough to show her up in her dark-grey coat. She walked quickly across the park, not really in the thrill of the assignation, but with a certain anger and rebellion burning in her heart. It was not the right sort of heart to take to a love-meeting. But *à la guerre comme à la guerre!*

XIV

When she got near the park gate, she heard the click of the latch. He was there, then, in the darkness of the wood, and had seen her!

"You are good and early," he said out of the dark. "Was everything all right?"

"Perfectly easy."

He shut the gate quietly after her, and made a spot of light on the dark ground, showing the pallid flowers still standing there open in the night. They went on apart, in silence.

"Are you sure you didn't hurt yourself this morning with that chair?" she asked.

"No, no!"

"When you had that pneumonia, what did it do to you?"

"Oh nothing! It left my heart not so strong and the lungs not so elastic. But it always does that."

"And you ought not to make violent physical efforts?"

"Not often."

She plodded on in an angry silence.

"Did you hate Clifford?" she said at last.

"Hate him, no! I've met too many like him to upset myself hating him. I know beforehand I don't care for his sort, and I let it go at that."

"What is his sort?"

"Nay, you know better than I do. The sort of youngish gentleman, a bit like a lady, and no balls."

"What balls?"

"Balls! A man's balls!"

She pondered this.

"But is it a question of that?" she said, a little annoyed.

"You say a man's got no brain, when he's a fool: and no heart, when he's mean; and no stomach when he's a funker. And when he's got none of that spunky wild bit of a man in him, you say he's got no balls. When he's sort of tame."

She pondered this.

"And is Clifford tame?" she asked.

"Tame, and nasty with it: like most such fellows, when you come up against 'em."

"And do you think you're not tame?"

"Maybe not quite!"

At length she saw in the distance a yellow light. She stood still.

"There is a light!" she said.

"I always leave a light in the house," he said.

She went on again at his side, but not touching him, wondering why she was going with him at all.

He unlocked, and they went in, he bolting the door behind them. As if it were a prison, she thought! The kettle was singing by the red fire, there were cups on the table.

She sat in the wooden armchair by the fire. It was warm after the chill outside.

"I'll take off my shoes, they are wet," she said.

She sat with her stockinged feet on the bright steel fender. He went to the pantry, bringing food: bread and butter and pressed tongue. She was warm: she took off her coat. He hung it on the door.

"Shall you have cocoa or tea or coffee to drink?" he asked.

"I don't think I want anything," she said, looking at the table. "But you eat."

"Nay, I don't care about it. I'll just feed the dog."

He tramped with a quiet inevitability over the brick floor, putting food for the dog in a brown bowl. The spaniel looked up at him anxiously.

"Ay, this thy supper, tha nedna look as if tha wouldna get it!" he said.

He set the bowl on the stairfoot mat, and sat himself on a chair by the wall, to take off his leggings and boots. The dog, instead of eating, came to him again, and sat looking up at him, troubled.

He slowly unbuckled his leggings. The dog edged a little nearer.

"What's amiss wi' thee then? Art upset because there's somebody else here? Tha'rt a female, tha art! Go an' eat thy supper."

He put his hand on her head, and the bitch leaned her head sideways against him. He slowly, softly pulled the long silky ear.

"There!" he said. "There! Go an' eat thy supper! Go!"

He tilted his chair towards the pot on the mat, and the dog meekly went, and fell to eating.

"Do you like dogs?" Connie asked him.

"No, not really. They're too tame and clinging."

He had taken off his leggings and was unlacing his heavy boots. Connie had turned from the fire. How bare the little room was! Yet over his head on the wall hung a hideous enlarged photograph of a young married couple, apparently him and a bold-faced young woman, no doubt his wife.

"Is that you?" Connie asked him.

He twisted and looked at the enlargement above his head.

"Ay! Taken just afore we was married, when I was twenty-one." He looked at it impassively.

"Do you like it?" Connie asked him.

"Like it? No! I never liked the thing. But she fixed it all up to have it done, like."

He returned to pulling off his boots.

"If you don't like it, why do you keep it hanging there? Perhaps your wife would like to have it," she said.

He looked up at her with a sudden grin.

"She carted off iverything as was worth taking from th'ouse," he said. "But she left *that!*"

"Then why do you keep it? For sentimental reasons?"

"Nay, I niver look at it. I hardly knowed it wor theer. It's been theer sin' we come to this place."

"Why don't you burn it?" she said.

He twisted round again and looked at the enlarged photograph. It was framed in a brown-and-gilt frame, hideous. It showed a clean shaven, alert, very young looking man in a rather high collar, and a somewhat plump, bold young woman with hair fluffed out and crimped, and wearing a dark satin blouse.

"It wouldn't be a bad idea, would it?" he said.

He pulled off his boots, and put on a pair of slippers. He stood up on the chair, and lifted down the photograph. It left a big pale place on the greenish wallpaper.

"No use dusting it now," he said, setting the thing against the wall.

He went to the scullery, and returned with hammer and pincers. Sitting where he had sat before, he started to tear off the back-paper from the big frame and to pull out the sprigs that held the backboard in position, working with the immediate quiet absorption that was characteristic of him.

He soon had the nails out: then he pulled out the backboards, then the enlargement itself, in its solid white mount. He looked at the photograph with amusement.

"Shows me for what I was, a young curate, and her for what she was, a bully," he said. "The prig and the bully!"

"Let me look!" said Connie.

He did look indeed very clean shaven and very clean altogether, one of the clean young men of twenty years ago. But even in the photograph his eyes were alert, and dauntless. And the woman was not altogether a bully, though her jowl was heavy. There was a touch of appeal in her.

"One never should keep these things," said Connie.

"That one shouldn't! One should never have them made!"

He broke the cardboard photograph and mount over his knee, and when it was small enough, put it on the fire.

"It'll spoil the fire, though," he said.

The glass and the backboards he carefully took upstairs.

The frame he knocked asunder with a few blows of the hammer, making the stucco fly. Then he took the pieces into the scullery.

"We'll burn that tomorrow," he said. "There's too much plaster-molding on it."

Having cleared away, he sat down.

"Did you love your wife?" she asked him.

"Love?" he said. "Did you love Sir Clifford?"

But she was not going to be put off.

"But you cared for her?" she insisted.

"Cared?" he grinned.

"Perhaps you care for her now," she said.

"Me!" His eyes widened. "Ah, no, I can't think of her," he said quietly.

"Why?"

But he shook his head.

"Then why don't you get a divorce? She'll come back to you one day," said Connie.

He looked up at her sharply.

"She wouldn't come within a mile of me. She hates me a lot worse than I hate her."

"You'll see, she'll come back to you."

"That she never shall. That's done. It would make me sick to see her."

"You will see her. And you're not even legally separated, are you?"

"No."

"Ah, well, then she'll come back, and you'll have to take her in."

He gazed at Connie fixedly. Then he gave the queer toss of his head.

"You may be right. I was a fool ever to come back here. But I felt stranded and had to go somewhere. A man's a poor bit of a wastrel, blown about. But you're right. I'll get a divorce and get clear. I hate those things like death, officials and courts and judges. But I've got to get through with it. I'll get a divorce."

And she saw his jaw set. Inwardly she exulted.

"I think I will have a cup of tea now," she said.

He rose to make it. But his face was set.

As they sat at the table she asked him:

"Why did you marry her? She was commoner than yourself. Mrs. Bolton told me about her. She could never understand why you married her."

He looked at her fixedly.

"I'll tell you," he said. "The first girl I had, I began with when I was sixteen. She was a schoolmaster's daughter over at Ollerton, pretty, beautiful really. I was supposed to be a clever sort of young fellow from Sheffield Grammar School, with a bit of French and German, very much up aloft. She was the romantic sort that hated commonness. She egged me on to poetry and reading: in a way, she made a man of me. I read and I thought like a house on fire, for her. And I was a clerk in Butterley Offices, a thin, white-faced fellow fuming with all the things I read. And about *everything* I talked to her: but everything. We talked ourselves into Persepolis and Timbuctoo. We were the most literary-cultured couple in ten counties. I held forth with rapture to her, positively with rapture. I simply went up in smoke. And she adored me. The serpent in the grass was sex. She somehow didn't have any; at least where it's supposed to be. I got thinner and crazier. Then I said we'd got to be lovers. I talked her into it, as usual. So she let me. I was excited, and she never wanted it. She just didn't want it. She adored me, she loved me to talk to her and kiss her: in that way she had a passion for me. But the other, she just didn't want it. And there are lots of women like her. And it was just the other that I *did* want. So there we split. I was cruel, and left her. Then I took on with another girl, a teacher, who had made a scandal by carrying on with a married man and driving him nearly out of his mind. She was a soft, white-skinned, soft sort of a woman, older than me, and played the fiddle. And she was a demon. She loved everything about love, except the sex. Clinging, caressing, creeping into you in every way: but if you forced her to sex itself, she just ground her teeth and sent out hate. I forced her to it, and she could simply numb me with hate because of it. So I was balked again. I loathed all that. I wanted a woman who wanted me, and wanted *it*.

"Then came Bertha Coutts. They'd lived next door to us when I was a little lad, so I knew 'em all right. And they were common. Well, Bertha went away to some place or other in Birmingham; she said, as a lady's companion; everybody else said, as a waitress or something in an hotel. Anyhow, just when I was more than fed up with that other girl, when I was twenty-one, back comes Bertha, with airs and grace and smart clothes and a sort of bloom on her: a sort of bloom on her: a sort of sensual bloom that you'd see sometimes on a woman, or on a trolly. Well I was in a state of murder. I chucked up my job at Butterley because I thought I was a weed, clerking there: and I got on as overhead blacksmith at Tevershall: shoeing horses mostly. It had been my dad's job, and I'd always been with him. It was a job I liked: handling horses: and it came natural to me. So I stopped talking 'fine,' as they call it, talking proper English, and went back to talking broad. I still read books, at home, but I blacksmithed and had a pony-trap of my own, and was My Lord Duckfoot. My dad left me three hundred pounds when he died. So I took on with Bertha, and I was glad she was common. I wanted her to be common. I wanted to be common myself. Well, I married her, and she wasn't bad. Those other 'pure' women had nearly taken all the balls out of me, but she was all right that way. She wanted me, and made no bones about it. And I was as pleased as punch. That was what I wanted: a woman who *wanted* me to fuck her. So I fucked her like a good un. And I think she despised me a bit, for being so pleased about it, and bringin' her her breakfast in bed sometimes. She sort of let things go, didn't get me a proper dinner when I came home from work, and if I said anything, flew out at me. And I flew back, hammer and tongs. She flung a cup at me, and I took her by the scruff of the neck and squeezed the life out of her. That sort of thing! But she treated me with insolence. And she got so's she'd never see me when I wanted her; never. Always put me off, brutal as you like. And then when she'd put me right off, and I didn't want her, she'd come all lovey-dovey, and get me. And I always went. But when I had her, she'd never come off when I did. Never! She'd just wait. If I kept back for half an hour, she'd keep back longer. And when I'd come and really finished then she'd start on her own account, and I had to stop inside her till she brought herself off, wriggling and shouting, she'd clutch clutch with herself down there, an' then she'd come off, fair in ecstasy. And then she'd say: That was lovely! Gradually, I got sick of it: and she got worse. She sort of got harder and harder to bring off, and she'd sort of tear at me down there, as if it was a beak tearing me. By God, you think a woman's soft down there, like a fig. But I tell you the old rampers have beaks between their legs, and they tear at you with it till you're sick. Self! Self! Self! all self! tearing and shouting! They talk about men's selfishness, but I doubt if it can ever touch a woman's blind beak-ishness, once she's gone that way. Like an old trull! And she couldn't help it. I told her about it, I told her how I hated it. And she'd even try. She'd try to lie still and let *me* work the business. She'd try. But it was no good. She got no feeling off it, from my working. She had to work the thing herself, grind her own coffee. And it came back on her like a raving necessity; she had to let herself go, and tear, tear, tear, as if she had no sensation in her except in the top of her beak, the very outside top tip, that rubbed and tore. That's how old whores used to be, so men used to say. It was a low kind of self-will in her, a raving sort of self-will: like in a woman who drinks. Well, in the end I couldn't stand it. We slept apart. She herself had started it, in her bouts, when she wanted to be clear of me, when she said I bossed her. She had started having a room for herself. But the time came when I wouldn't have her coming to my room. I wouldn't.

"I hated her. And she hated me. My God, how she hated me before that child was born! I often think that she conceived it out of hate. Anyhow, after the child was born I left her alone. And then came the war, and I joined up. And I didn't come back till I knew she was with that fellow at Stacks Gate."

He broke off, pale in the face.

"And what is the man at Stacks Gate like?" asked Connie.

"A big baby sort of fellow, very low-mouthed. She bullies him, and they both drink."

"My word, if she came back!"

"My God, yes! I should just go, disappear again."

There was a silence. The pasteboard in the fire had turned to grey ash.

"So when you did get a woman who wanted you," said Connie, "you got a bit too much of a good thing."

"Ay! Seems so! Yet even then I'd rather have her than the never-never ones:

the white love of my youth, and that other poison-smelling lily, and the rest."

"What about the rest?" said Connie.

"The rest? There is no rest. Only to my experience the mass of women are like this: most of them want a man, but don't want the sex, but they put up with it, as part of the bargain. The more old-fashioned sort just lie there like nothing and let you go ahead. They don't mind afterwards: then they like you. But the actual thing itself is nothing to them, a bit distasteful. And most men like it that way. I hate it. But the sly sort of women who are like that pretend they're not. They pretend they're passionate and have thrills. But it's all cockaloopy. They make it up.—Then there's the ones that love everything, every kind of feeling and cuddling and going off, every kind except the natural one. They always make you go off when you're *not* in the only place you should be, when you go off.—Then there's the hard sort, that are the devil to bring off at all, and bring themselves off, like my wife. They want to be the active party.—Then there's the sort that's just dead inside: but dead: and they know it. Then there's the sort that puts you out before you really 'come,' and go on writhing their loins till they bring themselves off against your thighs. But they're mostly the Lesbian sort. It's astonishing how Lesbian women are, consciously or unconsciously. Seems to me they're nearly all Lesbian."

"And do you mind?" asked Connie.

"I could kill them. When I'm with a woman who's really Lesbian, I fairly howl in my soul, wanting to kill her."

"And what do you do?"

"Just get away as fast as I can."

"But do you think Lesbian women any worse than homosexual men?"

"*I* do! Because I've suffered more from them. In the abstract, I've no idea. When I get with a Lesbian woman, whether she knows she's one or not, I see red. No, no! But I wanted to have nothing to do with any woman any more. I wanted to keep to myself: keep my privacy and my decency."

He looked pale, and his brows were somber.

"And were you sorry when I came along?" she said.

"I was sorry and I was glad."

"And what are you now?"

"I'm sorry, from the outside: all the complications and the ugliness and re-crimination that's bound to come, sooner or later. That's when my blood sinks, and I'm low. But when my blood comes up, I'm glad. I'm even triumphant. I was really getting bitter. I thought there was no real sex left: never a woman who'd really 'come' naturally with a man: except black women, and somehow, well, we're white men: and they're a bit like mud."

"And now, are you glad of me?" she asked.

"Yes. When I can forget the rest. When I can't forget the rest, I want to get under the table and die."

"Why under the table?"

"Why?" he laughed. "Hide, I suppose. Baby!"

"You do seem to have had awful experiences of women," she said.

"You see, I couldn't fool myself. That's where most men manage. They take an attitude, and accept a lie. I could never fool myself. I knew what I wanted with a woman, and I could never say I'd got it when I hadn't."

"But have you got it now?"

"Looks as if I might have."

"Then why are you so pale and gloomy?"

"Bellyful of remembering: and perhaps afraid of myself."

She sat in silence. It was growing late.

"And you do think it's important, a man and a woman?" she asked him.

"For me it is. For me it's the core of my life: if I have a right relation with a woman."

"And if you didn't get it?"

"Then I'd have to do without."

Again she pondered, before she asked:

"And do you think you've always been right with women?"

"God, no! I let my wife get to what she was: my fault a good deal. I spoilt her. And I'm very mistrustful. You'll have to expect it. It takes a lot to make me trust anybody, inwardly. So perhaps I'm a fraud too. I mistrust. And tenderness is not to be mistaken."

She looked at him.

"You don't mistrust with your body, when your blood comes up," she said. "You don't mistrust then, do you?"

"No, alas! That's how I've got into all the trouble. And that's why my mind mistrusts so thoroughly."

"Let your mind mistrust. What does it matter!"

The dog sighed with discomfort on the mat. The ash-clogged fire sank.

"We *are* a couple of battered warriors," said Connie.

"Are you battered too?" he laughed. "And here we are returning to the fray!"

"Yes! I feel really frightened."

"Ay!"

He got up, and put her shoes to dry, and wiped his own and set them near the fire. In the morning he would grease them. He poked the ash of pasteboard as much as possible out of the fire. "Even burnt, it's filthy," he said. Then he brought sticks and put them on the hob for the morning. Then he went out awhile with the dog.

When he came back Connie said: "I want to go out, too, for a minute."

She went alone into the darkness. There were stars overhead. She could smell flowers on the night air. And she could feel her shoes getting wetter again. But she felt like going away, right away from him and everybody.

It was chilly. She shuddered, and returned to the house. He was sitting in front of the low fire.

"Ugh! Cold!" she shuddered.

He put the sticks on the fire, and fetched more, till they had a good crackling chimneyful of blaze. The rippling running yellow flame made them both happy, warmed their faces and their souls.

"Never mind!" she said, taking his hand as he sat silent and remote. "One does one's best."

"Ay"—He sighed, with a twist of a smile.

She slipped over to him, and into his arms, as he sat there before the fire.

"Forget then!" she whispered. "Forget!"

He held her close, in the running warmth of the fire. The flame itself was like a forgetting. And her soft, warm, ripe weight! Slowly his blood turned, and began to ebb back into strength and reckless vigor again.

"And perhaps the women *really* wanted to be there and love you properly, only perhaps they couldn't. Perhaps it wasn't all their fault," she said.

"I know it. Do you think I don't know what a broken-backed snake that's been trodden on I was myself!"

She clung to him suddenly. She had not wanted to start all this again. Yet some perversity had made her.

"But you're not now," she said. "You're not that now: a broken-backed snake that's been trodden on."

"I don't know what I am. There's black days ahead," he repeated with a prophetic gloom.

"No! You're not to say it!"

He was silent. But she could feel the black void of despair inside him. That was the death of all desire, the death of all love: this despair that was like the dark cave inside the men, in which their spirit was lost.

"And you talk so coldly about sex," she said. "You talk as if you had only wanted your own pleasure and satisfaction."

She was protesting nervously against him.

"Nay!" he said. "I wanted to have my pleasure and satisfaction of a woman, and I never got it: because I could never get my pleasure and satisfaction of *her* unless she got hers of me at the same time. And it never happened. It takes two."

"But you never believed in your women. You don't even believe really in me," she said.

"I don't know what believing in a woman means."

"That's it, you see!"

She still was curled on his lap. But his spirit was grey and absent, he was not there for her. And everything she said drove him further.

"But what *do* you believe in?" she insisted.

"I don't know."

"Nothing, like all the men I've ever known," she said.

They were both silent. Then he roused himself and said:

"Yes, I do believe in something. I believe in being warm-hearted. I believe especially in being warm-hearted in love, in fucking with a warm heart. I believe if men could fuck with warm hearts, and the women take it warm-heartedly, everything would come all right. It's all this cold-hearted fucking that is death and idiocy."

"But you don't fuck me cold-heartedly," she protested.

"I don't want to fuck you at all. My heart's as cold as cold potatoes just now."

"Oh!" she said, kissing him mockingly. "Let's have them *sautées*." He laughed, and sat erect.

"It's a fact!" he said. "Anything for a bit of warm-heartedness. But the women don't like it. Even you don't really like it. You like good, sharp, piercing cold-hearted fucking, and then pretending it's all sugar. Where's your tenderness for me? You're as suspicious of me as a cat is of a dog. I tell you it takes two even to be tender and warm-hearted. You love fucking all right: but you want it to be called something grand and mysterious, just to flatter your own self-importance. Your own self-importance is more to you, fifty times more, than any man, or being together with a man."

"But that's what I'd say of you. Your own self-importance is everything to you."

"Ay! Very well then!" he said, moving as if he wanted to rise. "Let's keep apart then. I'd rather die than do any more cold-hearted fucking."

She slid away from him, and he stood up.

"And do you think *I* want it?" she said.

"I hope you don't," he replied. "But anyhow, you go to bed an' I'll sleep down here."

She looked at him. He was pale, his brows were sullen, he was as distant in recoil as the cold pole. Men were all alike.

"I can't go home till morning," she said.

"No! Go to bed. It's a quarter to one."

"I certainly won't," she said.

He went across and picked up his boots.

"Then I'll go out!" he said.

He began to put on his boots. She stared at him.

"Wait!" she faltered. "Wait! What's come between us?"

He was bent over, lacing his boot, and did not reply. The moments passed. A dimness came over her, like a swoon. All her consciousness died, and she stood there wide-eyed, looking at him from the unknown, knowing nothing any more.

He looked up, because of the silence, and saw her wide-eyed and lost. And as if a wind tossed him he got up and hobbled over to her, one shoe off and one shoe on, and took her in his arms, pressing her against his body, which somehow felt hurt right through. And there he held her, and there she remained.

Till his hands reached blindly down and felt for her, and felt under the clothing to where she was smooth and warm.

"Ma lass!" he murmured. "Ma little lass! Dunna let's fight! Dunna let's niver fight! I love thee an' th' touch on thee. Dunna argue wi' me! Dunna! Dunna! Dunna! Let's be together."

She lifted her face and looked at him.

"Don't be upset," she said steadily. "It's no good being upset. Do you really want to be together with me?"

She looked with wide, steady eyes into his face. He stopped, and went suddenly still, turning his face aside. All his body went perfectly still, but did not withdraw.

Then he lifted his head and looked into her eyes, with his odd, faintly mocking grin, saying: "Ay-ay! Let's be together on oath."

"But really?" she said, her eyes filling with tears.

"Ay really! Heart an' belly an' cock."

He still smiled faintly down at her, with the flicker of irony in his eyes, and a touch of bitterness.

She was silently weeping, and he lay with her and went into her there on the hearthrug, and so they gained a measure of equanimity. And then they went quickly to bed, for it was growing chill, and they had tired each other out. And she nestled up to him, feeling small and enfolded, and they both went to sleep at once, fast in one sleep. And so they lay and never moved, till the sun rose over the wood and day was beginning.

Then he woke up and looked at the light. The curtains were drawn. He listened to the loud wild calling of blackbirds and thrushes in the wood. It would be a brilliant morning, about half-past five, his hour for rising. He had slept so fast! It was such a new day! The woman was still curled asleep and tender. His hand moved on her, and she opened her blue wondering eyes, smiling unconsciously into his face.

"Are you awake?" she said to him.

He was looking into her eyes. He smiled, and kissed her. And suddenly she roused and sat up.

"Fancy that I am here!" she said.

She looked round the whitewashed little bedroom with its sloping ceiling and gable window where the white curtains were closed. The room was bare save for a little yellow-painted chest of drawers, and a chair: and the smallish white bed in which she lay.

"Fancy that we are here!" she said, looking down at him. He was lying watching her, stroking her breasts with his fingers, under the thin night-dress. When he was warm and smoothed out, he looked young and handsome. His eyes could look so warm. And she was fresh and young like a flower.

"I want to take this off!" he said, gathering the thin batiste night-dress and pulling it over her head. She sat there with bare shoulders and longish breasts faintly golden. He loved to make her breasts swing softly, like bells.

"You must take off your pyjamas too," she said.

"Eh nay!"

"Yes! Yes!" she commanded.

And he took off his old cotton pyjama-jacket and pushed down the trousers. Save for his hands and wrists and face and neck he was white as milk, with fine slender muscular flesh. To Connie he was suddenly piercingly beautiful again, as when she had seen him that afternoon washing himself.

Gold of sunshine touched the closed white curtains. She felt it wanted to come in.

"Oh! do let's draw the curtains! The birds are singing so! Do let the sun in," she said.

He slipped out of bed with his back to her, naked and white and thin, and went to the window, stooping a little, drawing the curtains and looking out for a moment. The back was white and fine, the small buttocks beautiful with exquisite, delicate manliness, the back of the neck ruddy and delicate and yet strong.

There was an inward, not an outward strength in the delicate and yet strong body.

"But you are beautiful!" she said. "So pure and fine! Come!" She held her arms out.

He was ashamed to turn to her, because of his aroused nakedness.

He caught his shirt off the floor, and held it to him, coming to her.

"No!" she said, still holding out her beautiful slim arms from her drooping breasts. "Let me see you!"

He dropped the shirt and stood still, looking towards her. The sun through the low window sent a beam that lit up his thighs and slim belly, and the erect phallus rising darkish and hot-looking from the little cloud of vivid gold-red hair. She was startled and afraid.

"How strange!" she said slowly. "How strange he stands there! So big! and so dark and cocksure! Is he like that?"

The man looked down the front of his slender white body, and laughed. Between the slim breasts the hair was dark, almost black. But at the root of the belly, where the phallus rose thick and arching, it was gold-red, vivid in a little cloud.

"So proud!" she murmured, uneasy. "And so lordly! Now I know why men are so overbearing. But he's lovely, *really*. Like another being! A bit terrifying! But lovely really! And he comes to *me!*—" She caught her lower lip between her teeth, in fear and excitement.

The man looked down in silence at his tense phallus, that did not change.—
"Ay!" he said at last, in a little voice. "Ay ma lad! Tha'rt theer right enough. Yi,
tha mun rear thy head! Theer on thy own, eh? an ta'es no count o' nob'dy! Tha
ma'es nowt o' me, John Thomas. Art boss? of me? Eh well, tha'rt more cocky
than me, an' tha says less. John Thomas! Dost want *her*? Dost want my lady Jane?
Tha's dipped me in again, tha hast. Ay, an' tha comes up smilin'.—Ax 'er than!
Ax lady Jane! Say: Lift up you heads o' ye gates, that the king of glory may come
in. Ay, th' cheek on thee! Cunt, that's what tha'rt after. Tell lady Jane tha wants
cunt. John Thomas, an' th' cunt o'lady Jane!—"

"Oh, don't tease him" said Connie, crawling on her knees on the bed towards him and putting her arms round his white slender loins, and drawing him
to her so that her hanging, swinging, breasts touched the tip of the stirring, erect
phallus, and caught the drop of moisture. She held the man fast.

"Lie down!" he said. "Lie down! Let me come!"

He was in a hurry now.

And afterwards, when they had been quite still, the woman had to uncover
the man again, to look at the mystery of the phallus.

"And now he's tiny, and soft like a little bud of life!" she said, taking the soft
small penis in her hand. "Isn't he somehow lovely! so on his own, so strange!
And *so* innocent! And he comes so far into me! You must *never* insult him, you
know. He's mine too. He's not only yours. He's mine! And so lovely and
innocent!" An she held the penis soft in her hand.

He laughed.

"Blest be the tie that binds our hearts in kindred love," he said.

"Of course!" she said. "Even when he's soft and little I feel my heart simply
tied to him. And how lovely your hair is here! quite quite different!"

"That's John Thomas' hair, not mine!" he said.

"John Thomas! John Thomas!" and she quickly kissed the soft penis, that
was beginning to stir again.

"Ay!" said the man, stretching his body almost painfully. "He's got his root
in my soul, has that gentleman! An' sometimes I don't know what ter do wi'
him. Ay, he's got a will of his own, an' it's hard to suit him. Yet I wouldn't have
him killed."

"No wonder men have always been afraid of him!" she said. "He's rather
terrible."

The quiver was going through the man's body, as the stream of consciousness again changed its direction, turning downwards. And he was helpless, as the
penis in slow soft undulations filled and surged and rose up, and grew hard,
standing there hard and overweening, in its curious towering fashion. The
woman too trembled a little as she watched.

"There! Take him then! He's thine," said the man.

And she quivered, and her own mind melted out. Sharp soft waves of unspeakable pleasure washed over her as he entered her, and started the curious
molten thrilling that spread and spread till she was carried away with the last,
blind flush of extremity.

He heard the distant hooters of Stacks Gate for seven o'clock. It was Monday
morning. He shivered a little, and with his face between her breasts pressed her
soft breasts up over his ears, to deafen him.

She had not even heard the hooters. She lay perfectly still, her soul washed
transparent.

"You must get up, mustn't you?" he muttered.

"What time?" came her colorless voice.

"Seven o'clock blowers a bit sin'."

"I suppose I must."

She was resenting, as she always did, the compulsion from outside.

He sat up and looked blankly out of the window.

"You do love me, don't you?" she asked calmly.

He looked down at her.

"Tha knows what tha knows. What dost ax for!" he said, a little fretfully.

"I want you to keep me, not to let me go," she said.

His eyes seemed full of a warm, soft darkness that could not think.

"When? Now?"

"Now, in your heart. Then I want to come and live with you always, soon."

He sat on the bed, with his head dropped, unable to think.

"Don't you want it?" she asked.

"Ay!" he said.

Then with the same eyes darkened with another flame of consciousness, almost like sleep, he looked at her.

"Dunna ax me nowt now," he said. "Let me be. I like thee. I luv thee when tha lies theer. A woman's a lovely thing when 'er's deep ter fuck, and cunt's good. Ah luv thee, thy legs, an' th' shape on thee, an' th' womanness on thee. Ah luv th' womanness on thee. Ah luv thee wi' my ba's an' wi' my heart. But dunna ax me nowt. Dunna ma'e me say nowt. Let me stop as I am while I can. Tha can ax me ivrything after. Now let me be, let me be!"

And softly, he laid his hand over her mound of Venus, on the soft brown maiden-hair, and himself sat still and naked on the bed, his face motionless in physical abstraction, almost like the face of Buddha. Motionless, and in the invisible flame of another consciousness, he sat with his hand on her, and waited for the turn.

After a while, he reached for his shirt and put it on, dressed himself swiftly in silence, looked at her once as she still lay naked and faintly golden like a Gloire de Dijon rose on the bed, and was gone. She heard him downstairs opening the door.

And she still lay musing, musing. It was very hard to go: to go out of his house. He called from the foot of the stairs: "Half-past seven!" She sighed, and got out of bed. The bare little room! Nothing in it at all but the small chest of drawers and the smallish bed. But the board floor was scrubbed clean. And in the corner by the window gable was a shelf with some books, and some from a circulating library. She looked. There were books about bolshevist Russia, books of travel, a volume about the atom and the electron, another about the composition of the earth's core, and the causes of earthquakes: then a few novels: then three books on India. So! He was a reader after all.

The sun fell on her naked limbs through the gable window. Outside she saw the dog Flossie roaming round. The hazel-brake was misted with green, and dark-green dogs'-mercury under. It was a clear clean morning with birds flying and triumphantly singing. If only she could stay! If only there weren't the other ghastly world of smoke and iron! If only *he* would make her a world.

She came downstairs, down the steep, narrow wooden stairs. Still, she would be content with this little house, if only it were in a world of its own.

He was washed and fresh, and the fire was burning.

"Will you eat anything?" he said.

"No! Only lend me a comb."

She followed him into the scullery, and combed her hair before the handbreath of mirror by the back door. Then she was ready to go.

She stood in the little front garden, looking at the dewy flowers, the grey bed of pinks in bud already.

"I would like to have all the rest of the world disappear," she said, "and live with you here."

"It won't disappear," he said.

They went almost in silence through the lovely dewy wood. But they were together in a world of their own.

It was bitter to her to go on to Wragby.

"I want soon to come and live with you altogether," she said as she left him.

He smiled unanswering.

She got home quietly and unremarked, and went up to her room.

<h1 style="text-align:center">XV</h1>

There was a letter from Hilda on the breakfast tray. "Father is going to London this week, and I shall call for you on Thursday week, June 17th. You must be ready so that we can go at once. I don't want to waste time at Wragby, it's an awful place. I shall probably stay the night at Retford with the Colemans, so I should be with you for lunch Thursday. Then we could start at tea-time, and sleep perhaps in Grantham. It is no use our spending an evening with Clifford. If he hates your going, it would be no pleasure to him."

So! She was being pushed around on the chessboard again.

Clifford hated her going, but it was only because he didn't feel *safe* in her absence. Her presence, for some reason, made him feel safe, and free to do the things he was occupied with. He was a great deal at the pits, and wrestling in spirit with the almost hopeless problems of getting out his coal in the most economical fashion, and then selling it when he'd got it out. He knew he ought to find some way of *using* it, or converting it, so that he needn't sell it, or needn't have the chagrin of failing to sell it. But if he made electric power, could he sell that or use it? And to convert into oil was as yet too costly and elaborate. To keep industry alive there must be more industry, like a madness.

It was a madness, and it required a madman to succeed in it. Well, he was a little mad. Connie thought so. His very intensity and acumen in the affairs of the pits seemed like a manifestation of madness to her, his very inspirations were the inspirations of insanity.

He talked to her of all his serious schemes, and she listened in a kind of wonder, and let him talk. Then his flow ceased, and he turned on the loud-speaker, and became a blank, while apparently his schemes coiled on inside him like a kind of dream.

And every night now he played pontoon, that game of the Tommies, with Mrs. Bolton, gambling with sixpences. And again, in the gambling he was gone in a kind of unconscious, or blank intoxication, or intoxication of blankness, whatever it was. Connie could not bear to see him. But when she had gone to bed, he and Mrs. Bolton would gamble on till two and three in the morning, safely, and with strange lust. Mrs. Bolton was caught in the lust as much as Clifford: the more so, as she nearly always lost.

She told Connie one day: "I lost twenty-three shillings to Sir Clifford last night."

"And did he take the money from you?" asked Connie aghast.

"Why, of course, my Lady! Debt of honor!"

Connie expostulated roundly and was angry with both of them. The upshot was, Sir Clifford raised Mrs. Bolton's wages a hundred a year, and she could gamble on that. Meanwhile it seemed to Connie, Clifford was really going deader.

She told him at length she was leaving on the seventeenth.

"Seventeenth!" he said. "And when will you be back?"

"By the twentieth of July at the latest."

"Yes! the twentieth of July."

Strangely and blankly he looked at her, with the vagueness of a child, but with the queer blank cunning of an old man.

"You won't let me down, will you?" he said.

"How?"

"While you're away. I mean, you're sure to come back?"

"I'm as sure as I can be of anything, that I shall come back."

"Yes! Well! Twentieth of July."

Yet he really wanted her to go. That was so curious. He wanted her to go, positively, to have her little adventures and perhaps become pregnant, and all that. At the same time, he was afraid of her going.

She was quivering, watching her real opportunity for leaving him altogether, waiting till the time, herself, himself, should be ripe.

She sat and talked to the keeper of her going abroad.

"And then when I come back," she said, "I can tell Clifford I must leave him. And you and I can go away. They never need even know it is you. We can go to another country. Shall we? To Africa or Australia. Shall we?"

She was quite thrilled by her plan.

"You've never been to the Colonies, have you?" he asked her.

"No! Have you?"

"I've been in India, and South Africa, and Egypt."

"Why shouldn't we go to South Africa?"

"We might!" he said slowly.

"Or don't you want to?" she asked.

"I don't care. I don't much care what I do."

"Doesn't it make you happy? Why not? We shan't be poor. I have about six hundred a year. I wrote and asked. It's not much, but it's enough, isn't it?"

"It's riches to me."

"Oh, how lovely it will be!"

"But I ought to get divorced, and so ought you, unless we're going to have complications."

There was plenty to think about.

Another day she asked him about himself. They were in the hut, and there was a thunderstorm.

"And weren't you happy, when you were a lieutenant and an officer and a gentleman?"

"Happy? All right. I liked my Colonel."

"Did you love him?"

"Yes! I loved him."

"And did he love you?"

"Yes! In a way, he loved me."

"Tell me about him."

"What is there to tell? He had risen from the ranks. He loved the army. And he had never married. He was twenty years older than me. He was a very intelligent man: and alone in the army, as such a man is: a passionate man in his way: and a very clever officer. I lived under his spell while I was with him. I sort of let him run my life. And I never regret it."

"And did you mind very much when he died?"

"I was as near death myself. But when I came to, I knew another part of me was finished. But then I had always known it would finish in death. All things do, as far as that goes."

She sat and ruminated. The thunder crashed outside. It was like being in a little ark in the Flood.

"You seem to have such a lot *behind* you," she said.

"Do I? It seems to me I've died once or twice already. Yet here I am, pegging on, and in for more trouble."

She was thinking hard, yet listening to the storm.

"And weren't you happy as an officer and a gentleman, when your Colonel was dead?"

"No! They were a mingy lot." He laughed suddenly. "The Colonel used to say: Lad, the English middle classes have to chew every mouthful thirty times because their guts are so narrow, a bit as big as a pea would give them a stoppage. They're the mingiest set of ladylike snipe ever invented: full of conceit of themselves, frightened even if their boot-laces aren't correct, rotten as high game, and always in the right. That's what finishes me up. Kow-tow, kow-tow, arse-licking till their tongues are tough: yet they're always in the right. Prigs on top of everything. Prigs! A generation of ladylike prigs with half a ball each.—"

Connie laughed. The rain was rushing down.

"He hated them!"

"No," said he. "He didn't bother. He just disliked them. There's a difference. Because, as he said, the Tommies are getting just as priggish and half-balled and narrow-gutted. It's the fate of mankind, to go that way."

"The common people, too, the working people?"

"All the lot. Their spunk is gone dead. Motor cars and cinemas and aeroplanes suck that last bit out of them. I tell you, every generation breeds a more rabbity generation, with india rubber tubing for guts and tin legs and tin faces. Tin people! It's all a steady sort of bolshevism just killing off the human thing, and worshipping the mechanical thing. Money, money, money! All the modern lot get their real kick out of killing the old human feeling out of man, making mincemeat of the old Adam and the old Eve. They're all alike. The world is all alike: kill off the human reality, a quid for every foreskin, two quid for each pair of balls. What is cunt but machine-fucking!—It's all alike. Pay 'em money to cut off the world's cock. Pay money, money, money to them that will take spunk out of mankind, and leave 'em all little twiddling machines."

He sat there in the hut, his face pulled to mocking irony. Yet even then, he had one ear set backwards, listening to the storm over the wood. It made him feel so alone.

"But won't it ever come to an end?" she said.

"Ay, it will. It'll achieve its own salvation. When the last real man is killed, and they're *all* tame: white, black, yellow, all colors of tame ones: then they'll *all* be insane. Because the root of sanity is in the balls. Then they'll all be *insane*, and they'll make their grand *auto de fé*. You know *auto de fé* means act of faith? Ay, well, they'll make their own grand little act of faith. They'll offer one another up."

"You mean kill one another?"

"I do, duckie! If we go on at our present rate then in a hundred years' time there won't be ten thousand people in this island: there may not be ten. They'll have lovingly wiped each other out." The thunder was rolling further away.

"How nice!" she said.

"Quite nice! To contemplate the extermination of the human species and the long pause that follows before some other species crops up, it calms you more than anything else. And if we go on in that way, with everybody, intellectuals, artists, government, industrialists and workers all frantically killing off the last human feeling, the last bit of their intuition, the last healthy instinct; if it goes on in algebraical progression, as it is going on: then ta-tah! to the human species! Good-bye! darling! the serpent swallows itself and leaves a void, considerably messed up, but not hopeless. Very nice! When savage wild dogs bark in Wragby, and savage wild pit-ponies stamp on Tevershall pit-bank! *te deum laudamus!*"

Connie laughed, but not very happily.

"Then you ought to be pleased that they are all bolshevists," she said. "You ought to be pleased that they hurry on towards the end."

"So I am. I don't stop 'em. Because I couldn't if I would."

"Then why are you so bitter?"

"I'm not! If my cock gives its last crow, I don't mind."

"But if you have a child?" she said.

He dropped his head.

"Why," he said at last. "It seems to me a wrong and bitter thing to do, to bring a child into this world."

"No! Don't say it! Don't say it!" she pleaded. "I think I'm going to have one. Say you'll be pleased." She laid her hand on his.

"I'm pleased for you to be pleased," he said. "But for me it seems a ghastly treachery to the unborn creature."

"Ah, no!" she said, shocked. "Then you can't ever really want me! You *can't* want me, if you feel that!"

Again he was silent, his face sullen. Outside there was only the threshing of the rain.

"It's not quite true!" she whispered. "It's not quite true! There's another truth." She felt he was bitter now partly because she was leaving him, deliberately going away to Venice. And this half pleased her.

She pulled open his clothing and uncovered his belly, and kissed his navel. Then she laid her cheek on his belly, and pressed her arm around his warm, silent, loins. They were alone in the flood.

"Tell me you want a child, in hope!" she murmured, pressing her face against his belly. "Tell me you do!"

"Why!" he said at last: and she felt the curious quiver of changing consciousness and relaxation going through his body. "Why, I've thought sometimes if one but tried, here among th' colliers even! They workin' bad now, an' not earnin' much. If a man could say to 'em: Dunna think o' nowt but th' money. When it comes ter *wants,* we want but little. Let's not live for money—"

She softly rubbed her cheek on his belly, and gathered his balls in her hand. The penis stirred softly, with strange life, but did not rise up. The rain beat bruisingly outside.

"Let's live for summat else. Let's not live ter make money, neither for usselves nor for anybody else. Now we're forced to. We're forced to make a bit for us-selves, an' a fair lot for th' bosses. Let's stop it! Bit by bit, let's stop it. We needn't rant an' rave. Bit by bit, let's drop the whole industrial life, an' go back. The least little bit o' money'll do. For everybody, me an' you, bosses an' masters, even th' king. The least little bit o' money'll really do. Just make up your mind to it, an' you've got out o' th' mess." He paused, then went on:

"An' I'd tell 'em: Look! Look at Joe! He moves lovely! Look how he moves, alive and aware. He's beautiful! An' look at Jonah! He's clumsy, he's ugly, because he's niver willin' to rouse himself. I'd tell 'em: Look! look at yourselves! one shoulder higher than t'other, legs twisted, feet all lumps! What have yer done ter yerselves, wi' the blasted work? Spoilt yerselves. No need to work that much. Take yer clothes off an' look at yourselves. Yer ought ter be alive an' beautiful, an' yer ugly an' half dead. So I'd tell 'em. An' I'd get my men to wear different clothes: 'appen close red trousers, bright red, an' little short white jackets. Why, if men had red, fine legs, that alone would change them in a month. They'd begin to be men again, to be men! An' the women could dress as they liked. Because if once the men walked with legs close bright scarlet, and buttocks nice and showing scarlet under a little white jacket: then the women 'ud begin to be women. It's because th' men *aren't* men, that th' women have to be.—An' in time pull down Tevershall and build a few beautiful buildings, that would hold us all. An' clean the country up again. An' not have many children, because the world is overcrowded.

"But I wouldn't preach to the men: only strip 'em an' say: Look at yourselves! That's workin' for money!—Hark at yourselves! That's working for money. You've been working for money! Look at Tevershall! It's horrible. That's because it was built while you was working for money. Look at your girls! They don't care about you, you don't care about them. It's because you've spent your time working an' caring for money. You can't talk nor move nor live, you can't properly be with a woman. You're not alive. Look at yourselves!"

There fell a complete silence. Connie was half listening, and threading in the hair at the root of his belly a few forget-me-nots that she had gathered on the way to the hut. Outside the world had gone still, and a little icy.

"You've got four kinds of hair," she said to him. "On your chest it's nearly black, and your hair isn't dark on your head: but your moustache is hard and dark red, and your hair here, your love-hair, is like a little bush of bright red-gold mistletoe. It's the loveliest of all!"

He looked down and saw the milky bits of forget-me-nots in the hair on his groin.

"Ay! That's where to put forget-me-nots, in the man-hair, or the maiden-hair. But don't you care about the future?"

She looked up at him.

"Oh, I do, terribly!" she said.

"Because when I feel the human world is doomed, has doomed itself by its own mingy beastliness, then I feel the Colonies aren't far enough. The moon wouldn't be far enough, because even there you could look back and see the earth, dirty, beastly, unsavory among all the stars: made foul by men. Then I feel I've swallowed gall, and it's eating my inside out, and nowhere's far enough away to get away. But when I get a turn, I forget it all again. Though it's a shame, what's been done to people these last hundred years: men turned into nothing but labor-insects, and all their manhood taken away, and all their real life. I'd wipe the machines off the face of the earth again, and end the industrial epoch absolutely, like a black mistake. But since I can't, an' nobody can, I'd better hold my peace, an' try an' live my own life: if I've got one to live, which I rather doubt."

The thunder had ceased outside, but the rain which had abated, suddenly came striking down, with a last blench of lightning and mutter of departing storm. Connie was uneasy. He had talked so long now, and he was really talking to himself, not to her. Despair seemed to come down on him completely, and she was feeling happy, she hated despair. She knew her leaving him, which he had only just realized inside himself, had plunged him back into this mood. And she triumphed a little.

She opened the door and looked at the straight, heavy rain, like a steel curtain, and had a sudden desire to rush out into it, to rush away. She got up, and began swiftly pulling off her stockings, then her dress and underclothing, and he held his breath. Her pointed keen animal breasts tipped and stirred as she moved. She was ivory-colored in the greenish light. She slipped on her rubber shoes again and ran out with a wild little laugh, holding up her breasts to the heavy rain and spreading her arms, and running blurred in the rain with the eurythmic dance-movements she had learned so long ago in Dresden. It was a strange pallid figure lifting and falling, bending so the rain beat and glistened on the full haunches, swaying up again and coming belly-forward through the rain, then stooping again so that only the full loins and buttocks were offered in a kind of homage towards him, repeating a wild obeisance.

He laughed wryly, and threw off his clothes. It was too much. He jumped out, naked and white, with a little shiver, into the hard slanting rain. Flossie sprang before him with a frantic little bark. Connie, her hair all wet and sticking to her head, turned her hot face and saw him. Her blue eyes blazed with excitement as she turned and ran fast, with a strange charging movement, out of the clearing and down the path, the wet boughs whipping her. She ran, and he saw nothing but the round wet head, the wet back leaning forward in flight, the round buttocks twinkling: a wonderful cowering female nakedness in flight.

She was nearly at the wide riding when he came up and flung his naked arm round her soft naked-wet middle. She gave a shriek and straightened herself, and the heap of her soft, chill flesh came up against his body. He pressed it all up against him, madly, the heap of soft, chilled female flesh that became quickly warm as flame, in contact. The rain streamed on them till they smoked. He gathered her lovely, heavy posteriors one in each hand and pressed them in towards him in a frenzy, quivering motionless in the rain. Then suddenly he tipped her up and fell with her on the path, in the roaring silence of the rain, and short and sharp, he took her, short and sharp and finished, like an animal.

He got up in an instant, wiping the rain from his eyes.

"Come in," he said, and they started running back to the hut. He ran straight and swift: he didn't like the rain. But she came slower, gathering forget-me-nots and campion and bluebells, running a few steps and watching him fleeting away from her.

When she came with her flowers, panting to the hut, he had already started a fire, and the twigs were crackling. Her sharp breasts rose and fell, her hair was plastered down with rain, her face was flushed ruddy and her body glistened and trickled. Wide-eyed and breathless, with a small wet head and full, trickling, naïve haunches, she looked another creature.

He took the old sheet and rubbed her down, she standing like a child. Then he rubbed himself, having shut the door of the hut. The fire was blazing up. She ducked her head in the other end of the sheet, and rubbed her wet hair.

"We're drying ourselves together on the same towel, we shall quarrel!" he said.

She looked up for a moment, her hair all odds and ends.

"No!" she said, her eyes wide. "It's not a towel, it's a sheet."

And she went on busily rubbing her head, while he busily rubbed his.

Still panting with their exertions, each wrapped in an army blanket, but the front of the body open to the fire, they sat on a log side by side before the blaze, to get quiet. Connie hated the feel of the blanket against her skin. But now the sheet was all wet.

She dropped her blanket and kneeled on the clay hearth, holding her head to the fire, and shaking her hair to dry it. He watched the beautiful curving drop of her haunches. That fascinated him today. How it sloped with a rich downslope to the heavy roundness of her buttocks! And in between, folded in the secret warmth, the secret entrances!

He stroked her tail with his hand, long and subtly taking in the curves and the globefulness.

"Tha's got such a nice tail on thee," he said, in the throaty caressive dialect. "Tha's got the nicest arse of anybody. It's the nicest, nicest woman's arse as is! An' ivry bit of it is woman, woman sure as nuts. Tha'rt not one o' them button-arsed lasses as should be lads, are ter! Tha's got a real soft sloping bottom on thee, as a man loves in 'is guts. It's a bottom as could hold the world up, it is."

All the while he spoke he exquisitely stroked the rounded tail, till it seemed as if a slippery sort of fire came from it into his hands. And his finger-tips touched the two secret openings to her body, time after time, with a soft little brush of fire.

"An' if tha shits an' if tha pisses, I'm glad. I don't want a woman as couldna shit nor piss."

Connie couldn't help a sudden snort of astonished laughter, but he went on unmoved.

"Tha'rt real, tha art! Tha'rt real, even a bit of a bitch. Here tha shits an' here tha pisses: an' I lay my hand on 'em both an' like thee for it. I like thee for it. Tha's got a proper, woman's arse, proud of itself. It's none ashamed of itself, this isna."

He laid his hand close and firm over her secret places, in a kind of close greeting.

"I like it," he said. "I like it! An' if I only lived ten minutes, an' stroked thy arse an' got to know it, I should reckon I'd lived one life, sees ter! Industrial system or not! Here's one o' my lifetimes."

She turned round and climbed into his lap, clinging to him. "Kiss me!" she whispered.

And she knew the thought of their separation was latent in both their minds, and at last she was sad.

She sat on his thighs, her head against his breast, and her ivory-gleaming legs loosely apart, the fire glowing unequally upon them. Sitting with his head dropped, he looked at the folds of her body in the fire-glow, and at the fleece of soft brown hair that hung down to a point between her open thighs. He reached to the table behind, and took up a bunch of flowers, still so wet that drops of rain fell on the floor.

"Flowers stops out of doors all weathers," he said. "They have no houses."

"Not even a hut!" she murmured.

With quiet fingers he threaded a few forget-me-not flowers in the fine brown fleece of the mount of Venus.

"There!" he said. "There's forget-me-nots in the right place!"

She looked down at the milky odd little flowers among the brown maiden-hair at the lower tip of her body.

"Doesn't it look pretty!" she said.

"Pretty as life," he replied.

And he stuck a pink campion-bud among the hair.

"There! That's me where you won't forget me! That's Moses in the bul-rushes."

"You don't mind, do you, that I'm going away?" she asked wistfully, look-ing up into his face.

But his face was inscrutable, under the heavy brows. He kept it quite blank.

"You do as you wish," he said.

And he spoke in good English.

"But I won't go if you don't wish it," she said, clinging to him.

There was silence. He leaned and put another piece of wood on the fire. The flame glowed on his silent, abstracted face. She waited, but he said nothing.

"Only I thought it would be a good way to begin a break with Clifford. I do want a child. And it would give me a chance to, to—" she resumed.

"To let them think a few lies," he said.

"Yes, that among other things. Do you want them to think the truth?"

"I don't care what they think."

"I do! I don't want them handling me with their unpleasant cold minds, not while I'm still at Wragby. They can think what they like when I'm finally gone."

He was silent.

"But Sir Clifford expects you to come back to him?"

"Oh, I must come back," she said: and there was silence.

"And would you have a child in Wragby?" he asked.

She closed her arm round his neck.

"If you wouldn't take me away, I should have to," she said.

"Take you where to?"

"Anywhere! away! But right away from Wragby."

"When?"

"Why, when I come back."

"But what's the good of coming back, doing the thing twice, if you're once gone?" he said.

"Oh, I must come back. I've promised! I've promised so faithfully. Besides, I come back to you, really."

"To your husband's gamekeeper?"

"I don't see that that matters," she said.

"No?" He mused a while. "And when would you think of going away again, then; finally? When exactly?"

"Oh, I don't know. I'd come back from Venice. And then we'd prepare everything."

"How prepare?"

"Oh, I'd tell Clifford. I'd have to tell him."

"Would you!"

He remained silent. She put her arms fast round his neck.

"Don't make it difficult for me," she pleaded.

"Make what difficult?"

"For me to go to Venice and arrange things."

A little smile, half a grin, flickered on his face.

"I don't make it difficult," he said. "I only want to find out just what you are after. But you don't really know yourself. You want to take time: get away and look at it. I don't blame you. I think you're wise. You may prefer to stay mistress of Wragby. I don't blame you. I've no Wragbys to offer. In fact, you know what you'll get out of me. No, no, I think you're right! I really do! And I'm not keen on coming to live on you, being kept by you. There's that too."

She felt, somehow, as if he were giving her tit for tat.

"But you want me, don't you?" she asked.

"Do you want me?"

"You know I do. *That's* evident."

"Quite! And *when* do you want me?"

"You know we can arrange it all when I come back. Now I'm out of breath with you. I must get calm and clear."

"Quite! Get calm and clear!"

She was a little offended.

"But you trust me, don't you?" she said.

"Oh, absolutely!"

She heard the mockery in his tone.

"Tell me, then," she said flatly, "do you think it would be better if I *don't* go to Venice?"

"I'm sure it's better if you *do* go to Venice," he replied in the cool, slightly mocking voice.

"You know it's next Thursday?" she said.

"Yes!"

She now began to muse. At last she said:

"And we *shall* know better where we are when I come back, shan't we?"

"Oh, surely!"

The curious gulf of silence between them!

"I've been to the lawyer about my divorce," he said, a little constrainedly.

She gave a slight shudder.

"Have you!" she said. "And what did he say?"

"He said I ought to have done it before; that may be a difficulty. But since I was in the army, he thinks it will go through all right. If only it doesn't bring *her* down on my head!"

"Will she have to know?"

"Yes! she is served with a notice: so is the man she lives with, the co-respondent."

"Isn't it hateful, all the performances! I suppose I'd have to go through it with Clifford."

There was a silence.

"And of course," he said, "I have to live an exemplary life for the next six or eight months. So if you go to Venice, there's temptation removed for a week or two, at least."

"Am I temptation!" she said, stroking his face. "I'm so glad I'm temptation to you! Don't let's think about it! You frighten me when you start thinking: you roll me out flat. Don't let's think about it. We can think so much when we are apart. That's the whole point! I've been thinking, I *must* come to you for another night before I go. I must come once more to the cottage. Shall I come on Thursday night?"

"Isn't that when your sister will be there?"

"Yes! But she said we would start at tea-time. So we could start at tea-time. But she could sleep somewhere else and I could sleep with you."

"But then she'd have to know."

"Oh, I shall tell her. I've more or less told her already. I must talk it all over with Hilda. She's a great help, so sensible."

He was thinking of her plan.

"So you'd start off from Wragby at tea-time, as if you were going to London? Which way were you going?"

"By Nottingham and Grantham."

"And then your sister would drop you somewhere and you'd walk or drive back here? Sounds very risky, to me."

"Does it? Well then, Hilda could bring me back. She could sleep at Mansfield, and bring me back here in the evening, and fetch me again in the morning. It's quite easy."

"And the people who see you?"

"I'll wear goggles and a veil."

He pondered for some time.

"Well," he said. "You please yourself, as usual."

"But wouldn't it please you?"

"Oh, yes! It'd please me all right," he said a little grimly. "I might as well smite while the iron's hot."

"Do you know what I thought?" she said suddenly. "It suddenly came to me. You are the 'Knight of the Burning Pestle!'"

"Ay! And you? Are you the Lady of the Red-Hot Mortar?"

"Yes!" she said. "Yes! You're Sir Pestle and I'm Lady Mortar."

"All right, then I'm knighted. John Thomas is Sir John, to your Lady Jane."

"Yes! John Thomas is knighted! I'm my-lady-maiden-hair, and you must have flowers too. Yes!"

She threaded two pink campions in the bush of red-gold hair above his penis. "There!" she said. "Charming! Charming! Sir John!"

And she pushed a bit of forget-me-not in the dark hair of his breast.

"And you won't forget me *there*, will you?" she kissed him on the breast, and made two bits of forget-me-not lodge one over each nipple, kissing him again.

"Make a calendar of me!" he said. He laughed and the flowers shook from his breast.

"Wait a bit!" he said.

He rose, and opened the door of the hut. Flossie, lying in the porch, got up and looked at him.

"Ay, it's me!" he said.

The rain had ceased. There was a wet, heavy perfumed stillness. Evening was approaching.

He went out and down the little path in the opposite direction from the riding. Connie watched his thin, white figure, and it looked to her like a ghost, an apparition moving away from her.

When she could see it no more, her heart sank. She stood in the door of the hut, with a blanket round her, looking into the drenched motionless silence.

But he was coming back, trotting strangely, and carrying flowers. She was a little afraid of him, as if he were not quite human. And when he came near, his eyes looked into hers, but she could not understand the meaning.

He had brought columbines and campions, and new-mown-hay, and oak-tufts and honeysuckle in small bud. He fastened fluffy young oak-sprays round her breasts, sticking in tufts of bluebells and campion: and in her navel he poised a pink campion flower, and in her maiden-hair were forget-me-nots and wood-ruff.

"That's you in all your glory!" he said. "Lady Jane, at her wedding with John Thomas."

And he stuck flowers in the hair of his own body, and wound a bit of creep-ing-jenny round his penis, and stuck a single bell of a hyacinth in his navel. She watched him with amusement, his odd intentness. And she pushed a campion flower in his moustache, where it stuck dangling under his nose.

"This is John Thomas marryin' Lady Jane," he said. "An' we mun let Con-stance an' Oliver go their ways. Maybe—"

He spread out his hand with a gesture, and then he sneezed, sneezing away the flowers from his nose and his navel. He sneezed again.

"Maybe what?" she said, waiting for him to go on.

"Eh?" he said.

"Maybe what? Go on with what you were going to say," she insisted.

"Ay, what *was* I going to say?"

He had forgotten. And it was one of the disappointments of her life, that he never finished.

A yellow ray of sun shone over the trees.

"Sun!" he said. "And time you went. Time, my lady, time! What's that as flies without wings, your ladyship? Time! Time!"

He reached for his shirt.

"Say good night! to John Thomas," he said, looking down at his penis. "He's safe in the arms of creeping-jenny! Not much burning pestle about him just now."

And he put his flannel shirt over his head.

"A man's most dangerous moment," he said, when his head emerged, "is when he's getting into his shirt. Then he puts his head in a bag. That's why I prefer those American shirts, that you put on like a jacket." She still stood watching him. He stepped into his short drawers, and buttoned them round his waist.

"Look at Jane!" he said. "In all her blossoms! Who'll put blossoms on you next year, Jinny? Me, or somebody else? 'Good-bye my bluebell, farewell to you!' I hate that song, it's early war days." He had sat down, and was pulling on his stockings. She still stood unmoving. He laid his hand on the slope of her buttocks. "Pretty little lady Jane!" he said. "Perhaps in Venice you'll find a man who'll put jasmine in your maiden-hair, and a pomegranate flower in your navel. Poor little lady Jane!"

"Don't say those things!" she said. "You only say them to hurt me."

He dropped his head. Then he said, in dialect:

"Ay, maybe I do, maybe I do! Well then, I'll say nowt, an' ha' done wi't. But tha mun dress thysen, an' go back to thy stately homes of England, how beauti-ful they stand. Time's up. Time's up for Sir John, an' for little lady Jane! Put thy shimmy on, Lady Chatterley! Tha might be anybody, standin' there be-out even a shimmy, an' a few rags o' flowers. There then, there then, I'll undress thee, tha bob-tailed young throstle." And he took the leaves from her hair, kissing her damp hair, and the flowers from her breasts, and kissed her breasts, and kissed her navel, and kissed her maiden-hair, where he left the flowers threaded. "They mun stop while they will," he said. "So! There tha'rt bare again, nowt but a bare-arsed lass an' a bit of a lady Jane! Now put thy shimmy

on, for tha mun go, or else Lady Chatterley's goin' to be late for dinner, an'
where 'ave yer been to my pretty maid!"

She never knew how to answer him when he was in this condition of the
vernacular. So she dressed herself and prepared to go a little ignominiously
home to Wragby. Or so she felt it: a little ignominiously home.

He would accompany her to the broad riding. His young pheasants were all
right under the shelter.

When he and she came out on to the riding, there was Mrs. Bolton faltering
palely towards them.

"Oh, my Lady, we wondered if anything had happened!"

"No! Nothing has happened."

Mrs. Bolton looked into the man's face, that was smooth and new-looking
with love. She met his half-laughing, half-mocking eyes. He always laughed at
mischance. But he looked at her kindly.

"Evening, Mrs. Bolton! Your Ladyship will be all right now, so I can leave
you. Good night to your Ladyship! Good night, Mrs. Bolton!"

He saluted and turned away.

XVI

C onnie arrived home to an ordeal of cross-questioning. Clifford had been
out at tea-time, had come in just before the storm, and where was her
ladyship? Nobody knew, only Mrs. Bolton suggested she had gone for a walk
into the wood. Into the wood, in such a storm!—Clifford for once let himself
get into a state of nervous frenzy. He started at every flash of lightning, and
blenched at every roll of thunder. He looked at the icy thunder-rain as if it were
the end of the world. He got more and more worked up.

Mrs. Bolton tried to soothe him.

"She'll be sheltering in the hut, till it's over. Don't worry, her ladyship is all
right."

"I don't like her being in the wood in a storm like this! I don't like her being
in the wood at all! She's been gone now more than two hours. When did she go
out?"

"A little while before you came in."

"I didn't see her in the park. God knows where she is and what has happened
to her."

"Oh, nothing's happened to her. You'll see, she'll be home directly after the
rain stops. It's just the rain that's keeping her."

But her ladyship did not come home directly the rain stopped. In fact time
went by, the sun came out for his last yellow glimpse, and there was still no sign
of her. The sun was set, it was growing dark, and the first dinner-gong had rung.

"It's no good!" said Clifford in a frenzy. "I'm going to send out Field and
Betts to find her."

"Oh, don't do that!" cried Mrs. Bolton. "They'll think there's a suicide or
something. Oh, don't start a lot of talk going—Let me slip over to the hut and
see if she's not there. I'll find her all right."

So, after some persuasion, Clifford allowed her to go.

And so Connie had come upon her in the drive, alone and palely loitering.

"You mustn't mind me coming to look for you, my Lady! But Sir Clifford
worked himself up into such a state. He made sure you were struck by lightning,

or killed by a falling tree. And he was determined to send Field and Betts to the wood to find the body. So I thought I'd better come, rather than set all the servants agog."

She spoke nervously. She could still see on Connie's face the smoothness and the half-dream of passion, and she could feel the irritation against herself.

"Quite!" said Connie. And she could say no more.

The two women plodded on through the wet world, in silence, while great drops splashed like explosions in the wood. When they came to the park, Connie strode ahead, and Mrs. Bolton panted a little. She was getting plumper.

"How foolish of Clifford to make a fuss!" said Connie at length, angrily, really speaking to herself.

"Oh, you know what men are! They like working themselves up. But he'll be all right as soon as he sees your ladyship."

Connie was very angry that Mrs. Bolton knew her secret: for certainly she knew it.

Suddenly Constance stood still on the path.

"It's monstrous that I should have to be followed!" she said, her eyes flashing.

"Oh, your Ladyship, don't say that! He'd certainly have sent the two men, and they'd have come straight to the hut. I didn't know where it was, really."

Connie flushed darker with rage, at the suggestion. Yet, while her passion was on her, she could not lie. She could not even pretend there was nothing between herself and the keeper. She looked at the other woman, who stood so sly, with her head dropped: yet somehow, in her femaleness, an ally.

"Oh well!" she said. "If it is so, it is so. I don't mind!"

"Why, you're all right, my Lady! You've only been sheltering in the hut. It's absolutely nothing."

They went on to the house. Connie marched into Clifford's room, furious with him, furious with his pale, overwrought face and prominent eyes.

"I must say, I don't think you need send the servants after me!" she burst out.

"My God!" he exploded. "Where have you been, woman? You've been gone hours, hours, and in a storm like this! What the hell do you go to that bloody wood for? What have you been up to? It's hours even since the rain stopped, hours! Do you know what time it is? You're enough to drive anybody mad. Where have you been? What in the name of hell have you been doing?"

"And what if I don't choose to tell you?" She pulled her hat from her head and shook her hair.

He looked at her with his eyes bulging, and yellow coming into the whites. It was very bad for him to get into these rages: Mrs. Bolton had a weary time with him, for days after. Connie felt a sudden qualm.

"But, really!" she said, milder. "Anyone would think I'd been I don't know where! I just sat in the hut during all the storm, and made myself a little fire, and was happy."

She spoke now easily. After all, why work him up any more! He looked at her suspiciously.

"And look at your hair!" he said; "look at yourself!"

"Yes!" she replied calmly. "I ran out into the rain with no clothes on."

He stared at her speechless.

"You must be mad!" he said.

"Why? To like a shower bath from the rain?"

"And how did you dry yourself?"

0.00000000001

"On an old towel and at the fire."

He still stared at her in a dumbfounded way.

"And supposing anybody came," he said.

"Who would come?"

"Who? Why, anybody! And Mellors. Does he come? He must come in the evenings."

"Yes, he came later, when it had cleared up, to feed the pheasants with corn."

She spoke with amazing nonchalance. Mrs. Bolton, who was listening in the next room, heard in sheer admiration. To think a woman would carry it off so naturally!

"And suppose he'd come while you were running about in the rain with nothing on, like a maniac?"

"I suppose he'd have had the fright of his life, and cleared out as fast as he could."

Clifford still stared at her transfixed. What he thought in his under-consciousness he would never know. And he was too much taken aback to form one clear thought in his upper consciousness. He just simply accepted what she said, in a sort of blank. And he admired her. He could not help admiring her. She looked flushed and handsome and smooth: love-smooth.

"At least," he said, subsiding, "you'll be lucky if you've got off without a severe cold."

"Oh, I haven't got a cold," she replied. She was thinking to herself of the other man's words: Tha's got the nicest woman's arse of anybody! She wished, she dearly wished she could tell Clifford that this had been said to her, during the famous thunderstorm. However! She bore herself rather like an offended queen and went upstairs to change.

That evening, Clifford wanted to be nice to her. He was reading one of the latest scientific-religious books: he had a streak of a spurious sort of religion in him, and was egocentrically concerned with the future of his own ego. It was like his habit to make conversation to Connie about some book, since the conversation between them had to be made, almost chemically. They had almost chemically to concoct it in their heads.

"What do you think of this, by the way?" he said, reaching for his book. "You'd have no need to cool your ardent body by running out in the rain, if only we had a few more aeons of evolution behind us. Ah, here it is!—'The universe shows us two aspects: on one side it is physically wasting, on the other it is spiritually ascending.'"

Connie listened, expecting more. But Clifford was waiting. She looked at him in surprise.

"And if it spiritually ascends," she said, "what does it leave down below, in the place where its tail used to be?"

"Ah!" he said. "Take the man for what he means. Ascending is the opposite of his wasting, I presume."

"Spiritually blown out, so to speak!"

"No. But seriously, without joking: do you think there is anything in it?" She looked at him again.

"Physically wasting?" she said. "I see you getting fatter, and I'm not wasting myself. Do you think the sun is smaller than he used to be? He's not, to me. And I suppose the apple Adam offered Eve wasn't really much bigger, if any, than one of our orange pippins. Do you think it was?"

"Well, hear how he goes on: 'It is thus slowly passing, with a slowness inconceivable in our measures of time, to new creative conditions, amid which the physical world, as we at present know it, will be represented by a ripple barely to be distinguished from nonentity.' "

She listened with a glisten of amusement. All sorts of improper things suggested themselves. But she only said:

"What silly hocus-pocus! As if his little conceited consciousness could know what was happening as slowly as all that! It only means *he's* a physical failure on earth, so he wants to make the whole universe a physical failure. Priggish little impertinence!"

"Oh, but listen! Don't interrupt the great man's solemn words!—The present type of order in the world has risen from an unimaginable past, and will find its grave in an unimaginable future. There remains the inexhaustive realm of abstract forms, and creativity with its shifting character ever determined afresh by its own creatures, and God, upon whose wisdom all forms of order depend.—There, that's how he winds up!"

Connie sat listening contemptuously.

"He's spiritually blown out," she said. "What a lot of stuff! Unimaginables, and types of order in graves, and realms of abstract forms, and creativity with a shifty character, and God mixed up with forms of order! Why, it's idiotic!"

"I must say, it is a little vaguely conglomerate, a mixture of gases, so to speak," said Clifford. "Still, I think there is something in the idea that the universe is physically wasting and spiritually ascending."

"Do you? Then let it ascend, so long as it leaves me safely and solidly physically here below."

"Do you like your physique?" he asked.

"I love it!" And through her mind went the words: It's the nicest, nicest woman's arse as is!

"But that is really rather extraordinary, because there's no denying it's an encumbrance. But then, I suppose a woman doesn't take a supreme pleasure in the life of the mind."

"Supreme pleasure?" she said, looking up at him. "Is that sort of idiocy the supreme pleasure of the life of the mind? No, thank you! Give me the body. I believe the life of the body is a greater reality than the life of the mind: when the body is really awakened to life. But so many people, like your famous windmachine, have only got minds tacked on to their physical corpses."

He looked at her in wonder.

"The life of the body," he said, "is just the life of the animals."

"And that's better than the life of professional corpses. But it's not true! The human body is only just coming to real life. With the Greeks it gave a lovely flicker, then Plato and Aristotle killed it, and Jesus finished it off. But now the body is coming really to life, it is really rising from the tomb. And it will be a lovely, lovely life in the lovely universe, the life of the human body."

"My dear, you speak as if you were ushering it all in! True, you are going away on a holiday: but don't please be quite so indecently elated about it. Believe me, whatever God there is is slowly eliminating the guts and alimentary system from the human being, to evolve a higher, more spiritual being."

"Why should I believe you, Clifford, when I feel that whatever God there is has at last wakened up in my guts, as you call them, and is rippling so happily there, like dawn? Why should I believe you, when I feel so very much the contrary?"

"Oh, exactly! And what has caused this extraordinary change in you? running out stark naked in the rain, and playing Bacchante? Desire for sensation, or the anticipation of going to Venice?"

"Both! Do you think it is horrid of me to be so thrilled at going off?" she said.

"Rather horrid to show it so plainly."

"Then I'll hide it."

"Oh, don't trouble! You almost communicate a thrill to me. I almost feel that it is *I* who am going off."

"Well, why don't you come?"

"We've gone over all that. And, as a matter of fact, I suppose your greatest thrill comes from being able to say a temporary farewell to all this. Nothing so thrilling, for the moment, as Good-bye-to-it-all!—But every parting means a meeting elsewhere. And every meeting is a new bondage."

"I am not going to enter any new bondages."

"Don't boast, while the gods are listening," he said.

She pulled up short.

"No! I won't boast!" she said.

But she was thrilled, none the less, to be going off; to feel bonds snap. She couldn't help it.

Clifford, who couldn't sleep, gambled all night with Mrs. Bolton, till she was too sleepy almost to live.

And the day came around for Hilda to arrive. Connie had arranged with Mellors that if everything promised well for their night together, she would hang a green shawl out of the window. If there were frustration, a red one.

Mrs. Bolton helped Connie to pack.

"It will be so good for your ladyship to have a change."

"I think it will. You don't mind having Sir Clifford on your hands alone for a time, do you?"

"Oh, no! I can manage him quite all right. I mean, I can do all he needs me to do. Don't you think he's better than he used to be?"

"Oh, much! You do wonders with him."

"Do I though! But men are all alike: just babies and you have to flatter them and wheedle them and let them think they're having their own way. Don't you find it so, my Lady?"

"I'm afraid I haven't much experience."

Connie paused in her occupation.

"Even your husband, did you have to manage him, and wheedle him like a baby?" she asked, looking at the other woman.

Mrs. Bolton paused too.

"Well!" she said. "I had to do a good bit of coaxing with him too. But he always knew what I was after, I must say that. But he generally gave in to me."

"He was never the lord and master thing?"

"No! At least, there'd be a look in his eyes sometimes, and then I knew I'd got to give in. But usually he gave in to me. No, he was never lord and master. But neither was I. I knew when I could go no further with him, and then I gave in: though it cost me a good bit, sometimes."

"And what if you had held out against him?"

"Oh, I don't know. I never did. Even when he was in the wrong, if he was fixed, I gave in. You see, I never wanted to break what was between us. And if you really set your will against a man, that finishes it. If you care for a man, you have to give in to him once he's really determined; whether you're in the right or not, you have to give in. Else you break something. But I must say, Ted 'ud give in to me sometimes, when I was set on a thing, and in the wrong. So I suppose it cuts both ways."

"And that's how you are with all your patients?" asked Connie.

"Oh, that's different. I don't care at all, in the same way. I know what's good for them, or I try to, and then I just contrive to manage them for their own good. It's not like anybody as you're really fond of. It's quite different. Once you've been really fond of a man, you can be affectionate to almost any man, if he needs you at all. But it's not the same thing. You don't really *care*. I doubt, once you've *really* cared, if you can ever really care again."

These words frightened Connie.

"Do you think one can only care once?" she asked.

"Or never. Most women never care, never begin to. They don't know what it means. Nor men either. But when I see a woman as cares, my heart stands still for her."

"And do you think men easily take offense?"

"Yes! If you wound them on their pride. But aren't women the same? Only, our two prides are a bit different."

Connie pondered this. She began again to have some misgiving about her going away. After all, was she not giving her man the go-by, if only for a short time? And he knew it. That's why he was so queer and sarcastic.

Still! the human existence is a good deal controlled by the machine of external circumstance. She was in the power of this machine. She couldn't extricate herself all in five minutes. She didn't even want to.

Hilda arrived in good time on Thursday morning, in a nimble two-seater car, with her suitcase strapped firmly behind. She looked as demure and maidenly as ever, but she had the same will of her own. She had the very hell of a will of her own, as her husband had found out. But her husband was now divorcing her. Yes, she even made it easy for him to do that, though she had no lover. For the time being, she was "off" men. She was very well content to be quite her own mistress: and mistress of her two children, whom she was going to bring up "properly," whatever that may mean.

Connie was only allowed a suitcase, also. But she had sent on a trunk to her father, who was going by train. No use taking a car to Venice. And Italy was much too hot to motor in, in July. He was going comfortably by train. He had just come down from Scotland.

So, like a demure arcadian field-marshal, Hilda arranged the material part of the journey. She and Connie sat in the upstairs room, chatting.

"But, Hilda!" said Connie, a little frightened. "I want to stay near here tonight. Not here: near here!"

Hilda fixed her sister with grey, inscrutable eyes. She seemed so calm: and she was so often furious.

"Where, near here?" she asked softly.

"Well, you know I love somebody, don't you?"

"I gathered there was something."

"Well, he lives near here, and I want to spend this last night with him. I must! I've promised."

Connie became insistent.

Hilda bent her Minerva-like head in silence. Then she looked up.

"Do you want to tell me who he is," she said.

"He's our gamekeeper," faltered Connie, and she flushed vividly, like a shamed child.

"Connie!" said Hilda, lifting her nose slightly with disgust: a motion she had from her mother.

"I know: but he's lovely, really. He really understands tenderness," said Connie, trying to apologize for him.

Hilda, like a ruddy, rich-colored Athena, bowed her head and pondered. She was really violently angry. But she dared not show it, because Connie, taking after her father, would straightway become obstreperous and unmanageable.

It was true, Hilda did not like Clifford: his cool assurance that he was somebody! She thought he made use of Connie shamefully and impudently. She had hoped her sister *would* leave him. But, being solid Scotch middle class, she loathed any "lowering" of oneself, or the family. She looked up at last.

"You'll regret it," she said.

"I shan't," cried Connie, flushing red. "He's quite the exception. I *really* love him. He's lovely as a lover."

Hilda still pondered.

"You'll get over him quite soon," she said, "and live to be ashamed of yourself because of him."

"I shan't! I hope I'm going to have a child of his."

"*Connie!*" said Hilda, hard as a hammer-stroke, and pale with anger.

"I shall, if I possibly can. I should be fearfully proud if I had a child by him."

It was no use talking to her. Hilda pondered.

"And doesn't Clifford suspect?" she said.

"Oh, no! Why should he?"

"I've no doubt you've given him plenty of occasion for suspicion," said Hilda.

"Not at all."

"And tonight's business seems quite gratuitous folly. Where does the man live?"

"In the cottage at the other end of the wood."

"Is he a bachelor?"

"No! His wife left him."

"How old?"

"I don't know. Older than me."

Hilda became more angry at every reply, angry as her mother used to be, in a kind of paroxysm. But she still hid it.

"I would give up tonight's escapade if I were you," she advised calmly.

"I can't! I *must* stay with him tonight, or I can't go to Venice at all. I just can't."

Hilda heard her father over again, and she gave way, out of mere diplomacy. And she consented to drive to Mansfield, both of them, to dinner, to bring Connie back to the lane-end after dark, and to fetch her from the lane-end the next morning, herself sleeping in Mansfield, only half-an-hour away, good going. But she was furious. She stored it up against her sister, this balk in her plans.

Connie flung an emerald-green shawl over her windowsill.

On the strength of her anger, Hilda warmed towards Clifford. After all, he had a mind. And if he had no sex, functionally, all the better; so much the less to quarrel about. Hilda wanted no more of that sex business, where men became nasty, selfish little horrors. Connie really had less to put up with than many women, if she did but know it.

And Clifford decided that Hilda, after all, was a decidedly intelligent woman, and would make a man a first-rate help-meet, if he were going in for politics, for example. Yes, she had none of Connie's silliness, Connie was more a child: you had to make excuses for her, because she was not altogether dependable.

There was an early cup of tea in the hall, where doors were open to let in the sun. Everybody seemed to be panting a little.

"Goodbye, Connie girl! Come back to me safely."

"Goodbye, Clifford! Yes, I shan't be long." Connie was almost tender.

"Goodbye, Hilda! You will keep an eye on her, won't you?"

"I'll even keep two!" said Hilda. "She shan't go very far astray."

"It's a promise!"

"Goodbye, Mrs. Bolton. I know you'll look after Sir Clifford nobly."

"I'll do what I can, your Ladyship."

"And write to me if there is any news, and tell me about Sir Clifford, how he is."

"Very good, your Ladyship, I will. And have a good time, and come back and cheer us up."

Everybody waved. The car went off. Connie looked back and saw Clifford sitting at the top of the steps in his house-chair. After all, he was her husband: Wragby was her home: circumstance had done it.

Mrs. Chambers held the gate and wished her ladyship a happy holiday. The car slipped out of the dark spinney that masked the park, on to the highroad where the colliers were trailing home. Hilda turned to the Crosshill Road, that was not a main road, but ran to Mansfield. Connie put on goggles. They ran beside the railway, which was in a cutting below them. Then they crossed the cutting on a bridge.

"That's the lane to the cottage!" said Connie.

Hilda glanced at it impatiently.

"It's a frightful pity we can't go straight off!" she said. "We could have been in Pall Mall by nine o'clock."

"I'm sorry for your sake," said Connie, from behind her goggles.

They were soon at Mansfield, that once-romantic, now utterly disheartening colliery town. Hilda stopped at the hotel named in the motor-car book, and took a room. The whole thing was utterly uninteresting, and she was almost too angry to talk. However, Connie *had* to tell her something of the man's history.

"*He! He!* What name do you call him by? You only say *he,*" said Hilda.

"I've never called him by any name: nor he me: which is curious, when you come to think of it. Unless we say Lady Jane and John Thomas. But his name is Oliver Mellors."

"And how would you like to be Mrs. Oliver Mellors, instead of Lady Chatterley?"

"I'd love it."

There was nothing to be done with Connie. And anyhow, if the man had been a lieutenant in the army in India for four or five years, he must be more or less presentable. Apparently he had character. Hilda began to relent a little.

"But you'll be through with him in a while," she said, "and then you'll be ashamed of having been connected with him. One *can't* mix up with the working people."

"But you are such a socialist! you're always on the side of the working classes."

"I may be on their side in a political crisis, but being on their side makes me know how impossible it is to mix one's life with theirs. Not out of snobbery, but just because the whole rhythm is different."

Hilda had lived among the real political intellectuals, so she was disastrously unanswerable.

The nondescript evening in the hotel dragged out, and at last they had a nondescript dinner. Then Connie slipped a few things into a little silk bag, and combed her hair once more.

"After all, Hilda," she said, "love can be wonderful; when you feel you *live*, and are in the very middle of creation." It was almost like bragging on her part.

"I suppose every mosquito feels the same," said Hilda.

"Do you think it does? How nice for it!"

The evening was wonderfully clear and long-lingering even in the small town. It would be half-light all night. With a face like a mask, from resentment, Hilda started her car again, and the two sped back on their tracks, taking the other road, through Bolsover.

Connie wore her goggles and disguising cap, and she sat in silence. Because of Hilda's opposition, she was fiercely on the side of the man, she would stand by him through thick and thin.

They had their headlights on, by the time they passed Crosshill, and the small lit-up train that chuffed past in the cutting made it seem like real night. Hilda had calculated the turn into the lane at the bridge-end. She slowed up rather suddenly and swerved off the road, the lights glaring white into the grassy, overgrown lane. Connie looked out. She saw a shadowy figure, and she opened the door.

"Here we are!" she said softly.

But Hilda had switched off the lights, and was absorbed backing, making the turn.

"Nothing on the bridge?" she asked shortly.

"You're all right," said the man's voice.

She backed on to the bridge, reversed, let the car run forward a few yards along the road, then backed into the lane, under a wych-elm tree, crushing the grass and bracken. Then all the lights went out. Connie stepped down. The man stood under the trees.

"Did you wait long?" Connie asked.

"Not so very," he replied.

They both waited for Hilda to get out. But Hilda shut the door of the car and sat tight.

"This is my sister Hilda. Won't you come and speak to her? Hilda! This is Mr. Mellors."

The keeper lifted his hat, but went no nearer.

"Do walk down to the cottage with us, Hilda," Connie pleaded. "It's not far."

"What about the car?"

"People do leave them in the lanes. You have the key."

Hilda was silent, deliberating. Then she looked backwards down the lane.

"Can I back round that bush?" she said.

"Oh, yes!" said the keeper.

She backed slowly round the curve, out of sight of the road, locked the car, and got down. It was night, but luminous dark. The hedges rose high and wild, by the unused lane, and very dark seeming. There was a fresh sweet scent on the air. The keeper went ahead, then came Connie, then Hilda, and in silence. He lit up the difficult places with a flashlight torch, and they went on again, while an owl softly hooted over the oaks, and Flossie padded silently around. Nobody could speak. There was nothing to say.

At length Connie saw the yellow light of the house, and her heart beat fast. She was a little frightened. They trailed on, still in Indian file.

He unlocked the door and preceded them into the warm but bare little room. The fire burned low and red in the grate. The table was set with two plates and two glasses, on a proper white tablecloth for once. Hilda shook her hair and looked round the bare, cheerless room. Then she summoned her courage and looked at the man.

He was moderately tall, and thin, and she thought him good-looking. He kept a quiet distance of his own, and seemed absolutely unwilling to speak.

"Do sit down, Hilda," said Connie.

"Do!" he said. "Can I make you tea or anything, or will you drink a glass of beer? It's moderately cool."

"Beer!" said Connie.

"Beer for me, please!" said Hilda, with a mock sort of shyness. He looked at her and blinked.

He took a blue jug and tramped to the scullery. When he came back with the beer, his face had changed again.

Connie sat down by the door, and Hilda sat in his seat, with the back to the wall, against the window corner.

"That is his chair," said Connie softly. And Hilda rose as if it had burnt her.

"Sit yer still, sit yer still! Ta'e ony cheer as yo'n a mind to, none of us is th' big bear," he said, with complete equanimity.

And he brought Hilda a glass, and poured her beer first from the blue jug.

"As for cigarettes," he said, "I've got none, but 'appen you've got your own. I dunna smoke, mysen. Shall y' eat summat?"—He turned direct to Connie: "Shall t'eat a smite o' summat, if I bring it thee? Tha can usually do wi' a bite." He spoke the vernacular with a curious calm assurance, as if he were the landlord of the inn.

"What is there?" asked Connie, flushing.

"Boiled ham, cheese, pickled wa'nuts, if yer like.—Nowt much."

"Yes," said Connie. "Won't you, Hilda?"

Hilda looked up at him.

"Why do you speak Yorkshire?" she said softly.

"That! That's non Yorkshire, that's Derby."

He looked back at her with that faint, distant grin.

"Derby, then! Why do you speak Derby? You spoke natural English at first."

"Did Ah though? An' canna Ah change if Ah'n a mind to it? Nay, nay, let me talk Derby if it suits me. If yo'n nowt against it."

"It sounds a little affected," said Hilda.

"Ay, 'appen so! An' up i' Tevershall yo'd sound affected." He looked again at her, with a queer calculating distance, along his cheekbones, as if to say: Yi, an' who are you?

He tramped away to the pantry for the food.

The sisters sat in silence. He brought another plate, and knife and fork. Then he said:

"An' if it's the same to you, I s'll ta'e my coat off, like I allers do."

And he took off his coat, and hung it on the peg, then sat down to the table, in his shirtsleeves: a shirt of thin, cream-colored flannel.

" 'Elp yerselves!" he said. " 'Elp yerselves! Dunna wait f'r axin'!"

He cut the bread, then sat motionless. Hilda felt, as Connie once used to, his power of silence and distance. She saw his smallish, sensitive, loose hand on the table. He was no simple working man, not he: he was acting! Acting!

"Still!" she said, as she took a little cheese. "It would be more natural if you spoke to us in normal English, not in vernacular."

He looked at her, feeling her devil of a will.

"Would it?" he said in the normal English. "Would it? Would anything that was said between you and me be quite natural, unless you said you wished me to hell before your sister ever saw me again: and unless I said something almost as unpleasant back again? Would anything else be natural?"

"Oh, yes!" said Hilda. "Just good manners would be quite natural."

"Second nature, so to speak!" he said: then he began to laugh. "Nay," he said. "I'm weary o' manners. Let me be!"

Hilda was frankly baffled and furiously annoyed. After all, he might show that he realized he was being honored. Instead of which, with his play-acting and lordly airs, he seemed to think it was he who was conferring the honor. Just impudence! Poor misguided Connie, in the man's clutches!

The three ate in silence. Hilda looked to see what his table manners were like. She could not help realizing that he was instinctively much more delicate and well-bred than herself. She had a certain Scottish clumsiness. And moreover, he had all the quiet self-contained assurance of the English, no loose edges. It would be very difficult to get the better of him.

"And do you really think," she said, a little more humanly, "it's worth the risk?"

"Is what worth what risk?"

"This escapade with my sister."

He flickered his irritating grin.

"Yo' maun ax 'er!"

Then he looked at Connie.

"Tha comes o' thine own accord, lass, doesn't yer? It's non me as forces thee?"

Connie looked at Hilda.

"I wish you wouldn't cavil, Hilda."

"Naturally, I don't want to. But someone has to think about things. You've got to have some continuity in your life. You can't just go making a mess."

There was a moment's pause.

"Eh, continuity!" he said. "An' what by that? What continuity 'ave yer got i' *your* life? I thought you was gettin' divorced. What continuity's that? Continuity o' yer own stubbornness. I can see that much. An' what good's it goin' to do yer? Yo'll be sick o' yer continuity afore yer a fat sight older. A stubborn woman an' 'er own self-will: ay, they make a fast continuity, they do. Thank heaven, it isn't me as 'as got th' 'andlin' of yer!"

"What right have you to speak like that to me?" said Hilda.

"Right! What right ha' yo' ter start harnessin' other folks i' your Continuity? Leave folks to their own continuities."

"My dear man, do you think I am concerned with you?" said Hilda softly.

"Ay," he said. "Yo' are. For it's a force-put. Yo' more or less my sister-in-law."

"Still far from it, I assure you."

"Not a' that far, I assure *you*. I've got my own sort o' continuity, back your life! Good as yours, any day. An' if your sister there comes ter me for a bit o' cunt an' tenderness, she knows what she's after. She's been in my bed afore: which you 'aven't, thank the Lord, with your continuity." There was a dead pause, before he added: "—Eh, I don't wear me breeches arse-forrards. An' if I get a windfall, I thank my stars. A man gets a lot of enjoyment out o' that lass theer, which is more than anybody gets out o' th' likes o' you. Which is a pity, for you might 'appen a' bin a good apple, 'stead of a handsome crab. Women like you needs proper graftin'."

He was looking at her with an odd, flickering smile, faintly sensual and appreciative.

"And men like you," she said, "ought to be segregated: justifying their own vulgarity and selfish lust."

"Ay, ma'am. It's a mercy there's a few men left like me. But you deserve what you get: to be left severely alone."

Hilda had risen and gone to the door. He rose and took his coat from the peg.

"I can find my way quite well alone," she said.

"I doubt you can't," he replied easily.

They tramped in ridiculous file down the lane again, in silence. An owl still hooted. He knew he ought to shoot it.

The car stood untouched, a little dewy. Hilda got in and started the engine. The other two waited.

"All I mean," she said from her entrenchment, "is that I doubt if you'll find it's been worth it, either of you!"

"One man's meat is another man's poison," he said, out of the darkness. "But it's meat an' drink to me."

The lights flared out.

"Don't make me wait in the morning, Connie."

"No, I won't. Good night!"

The car rose slowly on to the highroad, then slid swiftly away, leaving the night silent.

Connie timidly took his arm, and they went down the lane. He did not speak. At length she drew him to a standstill.

"Kiss me!" she murmured.

"Nay, wait a bit! Let me simmer down," he said.

That amused her. She still kept hold of his arm, and they went quickly down the lane, in silence. She was so glad to be with him, just now. She shivered, knowing that Hilda might have snatched her away. He was inscrutably silent.

When they were in the cottage again, she almost jumped with pleasure, that she should be free of her sister.

"But you were horrid to Hilda," she said to him.

"She should ha' been slapped in time."

"But why? and she's *so* nice."

He didn't answer, went round doing the evening chores, with a quiet, inevitable sort of motion. He was outwardly angry, but not with her. So Connie felt. And his anger gave him a peculiar handsomeness, an inwardness and glisten that thrilled her and made her limbs go molten.

Still he took no notice of her.

Till he sat down and began to unlace his boots. Then he looked up at her from under his brows, on which the anger still sat firm.

"Shan't you go up?" he said. "There's a candle!"

He jerked his head swiftly to indicate the candle burning on the table. She took it obediently, and he watched the full curve of her hips as she went up the first stairs.

It was a night of sensual passion, in which she was a little startled and almost unwilling: yet pierced again with piercing thrills of sensuality, different, sharper, more terrible than the thrills of tenderness, but, at the moment, more desirable. Though a little frightened, she let him have his way, and the reckless, shameless sensuality shook her to her foundations, stripped her to the very last, and made a different woman of her. It was not really love. It was not voluptuousness. It was sensuality sharp and searing as fire, burning the soul to tinder.

Burning out the shames, the deepest, oldest shames, in the most secret places. It cost her an effort to let him have his way and his will of her. She had to be a passive, consenting thing, like a slave, a physical slave. Yet the passion licked round her, consuming, and when the sensual flame of it pressed through her bowels and breast, she really thought she was dying: yet a poignant, marvellous death.

She had often wondered what Abélard meant, when he said that in their year of love he and Heloïse had passed through all the stages and refinements of passion. The same thing, a thousand years ago: ten thousand years ago! The same on the Greek vases, everywhere! The refinements of passion, the extravagances of sensuality! And necessary, forever necessary, to burn out false shames and smelt out the heaviest ore of the body into purity. With the fire of sheer sensuality.

In the short summer night she learnt so much. She would have thought a woman would have died of shame. Instead of which, the shame died. Shame, which is fear: the deep organic shame, the old, old physical fear which crouches in the bodily roots of us, and can only be chased away by the sensual fire, at last it was roused up and routed by the phallic hunt of the man, and she came to the very heart of the jungle of herself. She felt, now, she had come to the real bedrock of her nature, and was essentially shameless. She was her sensual self, naked and unashamed. She felt a triumph, almost a vainglory. So! That was how it was! That was life! That was how oneself really was! There was nothing left to disguise or be ashamed of. She shared her ultimate nakedness with a man, another being.

And what a reckless devil the man was! really like a devil! One had to be strong to bear him. But it took some getting at, the core of the physical jungle, the last and deepest recess of organic shame. The phallus alone could explore it. And how he had pressed in on her!

And how, in fear, she had hated it. But how she had really wanted it! She knew now. At the bottom of her soul, fundamentally, she had needed this phallic hunting out, she had secretly wanted it, and she had believed that she would never get it. Now suddenly there it was, and a man was sharing her last and final nakedness, she was shameless.

What liars poets and everybody were! They made one think one wanted sentiment. When what one supremely wanted was this piercing, consuming, rather awful sensuality. To find a man who dared do it, without shame or sin or final misgiving! If he had been ashamed afterwards, and made one feel ashamed, how awful! What a pity most men are so doggy, a bit shameful, like Clifford! Like Michaelis even! Both sensually a bit doggy and humiliating. The supreme pleasure of the mind! And what is that to a woman? What is it, really, to the man

either? He becomes merely messy and doggy, even in his mind. It needs sheer
sensuality even to purify and quicken the mind. Sheer fiery sensuality, not mess-
iness.

Ah God, how rare a thing a man is! They are all dogs that trot and sniff and
copulate. To have found a man who was not afraid and not ashamed! She
looked at him now, sleeping so like a wild animal asleep, gone, gone in the
remoteness of it. She nestled down, not to be away from him.

Till his rousing waked her completely. He was sitting up in bed, looking
down at her. She saw her own nakedness in his eyes, immediate knowledge of
her. And the fluid, male knowledge of herself seemed to flow to her from his
eyes and wrap her voluptuously. Oh, how voluptuous and lovely it was to have
limbs and body half-asleep, heavy and suffused with passion!

"Is it time to wake up?" she said.

"Half-past six."

She had to be at the lane-end at eight. Always, always, always this compulsion on one!

"I might make the breakfast and bring it up here: should I?" he said.

"Oh, yes!"

Flossie whimpered gently below. He got up and threw off his pyjamas, and
rubbed himself with a towel. When the human being is full of courage and full
of life, how beautiful it is! So she thought, as she watched him in silence.

"Draw the curtain, will you?"

The sun was shining already on the tender green leaves of morning, and the
wood stood bluey-fresh, in the nearness. She sat up in bed, looking dreamily out
through the dormer window, her naked arms pushing her naked breasts together. He was dressing himself. She was half-dreaming of life, a life together
with him: just a life.

He was going, fleeing from her dangerous, crouching nakedness.

"Have I lost my nightie altogether?" she said.

He pushed his hand down in the bed, and pulled out the bit of flimsy silk.

"I knowed I felt silk at my ankles," he said.

But the night-dress was slit almost in two.

"Never mind!" she said. "It belongs here, really. I'll leave it."

"Ay, leave it, I can put it between my legs at night, for company. There's no
name or mark on it, is there?"

She slipped on the torn thing, and sat dreamily looking out of the window.
The window was open, the air of morning drifted in, and the sound of birds.
Birds flew continuously past. Then she saw Flossie roaming out. It was morn-
ing.

Downstairs she heard him making the fire, pumping water, going out at the
back door. By and by came the smell of bacon, and at length he came upstairs
with a huge black tray that would only just go through the door. He set the tray
on the bed, and poured out the tea. Connie squatted in her night-dress, and fell
on her food hungrily. He sat on the one chair, with his plate on his knees.

"How good it is!" she said. "How nice to have breakfast together."

He ate in silence, his mind on the time that was quickly passing. That made
her remember.

"Oh, how I wish I could stay here with you, and Wragby were a million
miles away! It's Wragby I'm going away from really. You know that, don't
you?"

"Ay!"

"And you promise we will live together and have a life together, you and me! You promise me, don't you?"

"Ay! When we can."

"Yes! And we *will!* We *will,* won't we?" She leaned over, making the tea spill, catching his wrist.

"Ay!" he said, tidying up the tea.

"We can't possibly *not* live together now, can we?" she said appealingly.

He looked up at her with his flickering grin.

"No!" he said. "Only, you've got to start in twenty-five minutes."

"Have I?" she cried. Suddenly he held up a warning finger, and rose to his feet.

Flossie had given a short bark, then three loud sharp yaps of warning.

Silent, he put his plate on the tray and went downstairs. Constance heard him go down the garden path. A bicycle bell tinkled outside there.

"Morning, Mr. Mellors! Registered letter!"

"Oh, ay! Got a pencil?"

"Here y'are!"

There was a pause.

"Canada!" said the stranger's voice.

"Ay! That's a mate o' mine out there in British Columbia. Dunno what he's got to register."

" 'Appen sent y'a fortune, like."

"More like wants summat."

Pause.

"Well! Lovely day again!"

"Ay!"

"Morning!"

"Morning!"

After a time he came upstairs again, looking a little angry.

"Postman," he said.

"Very early!" she replied.

"Rural round; he's mostly here by seven, when he does come."

"Did your mate send you a fortune?"

"No! Only some photographs and papers about a place out there in British Columbia."

"Would you go there?"

"I thought perhaps we might."

"Oh, yes! I believe it's lovely!"

But he was put out by the postman's coming.

"Them damned bikes, they're on you afore you know where you are. I hope he twigged nothing."

"After all, what could he twig?"

"You must get up now, and get ready. I'm just goin' ter look round outside."

She saw him go reconnoitering into the lane, with dog and gun. She went downstairs and washed, and was ready by the time he came back, with the few things in the little silk bag.

He locked up, and they set off, but through the wood, not down the lane. He was being wary.

"Don't you think one lives for times like last night?" she said to him.

"Ay! But there's the rest o' times to think on," he replied, rather short.

They plodded on down the overgrown path, he in front, in silence.

"And we *will* live together and make a life together, won't we?" she pleaded.

"Ay!" he replied, striding on without looking round. "When t' time comes! Just now you're off to Venice or somewhere."

She followed him dumbly, with sinking heart. Oh, now she *was* to go!

At last he stopped.

"I'll just strike across here," he said, pointing to the right.

But she flung her arms round his neck, and clung to him.

"But you'll keep the tenderness for me, won't you?" she whispered. "I loved last night. But you'll keep the tenderness for me, won't you?"

He kissed her and held her close for a moment. Then he sighed, and kissed her again.

"I must go an' look if th' car's there."

He strode over the low brambles and bracken, leaving a trail through the fern. For a minute or two he was gone. Then he came striding back.

"Car's not there yet," he said. "But there's the baker's cart on t' road."

He seemed anxious and troubled.

"Hark!"

They heard a car softly hoot as it came nearer. It slowed up on the bridge.

She plunged with utter mournfulness in his track through the fern, and came to a huge holly hedge. He was just behind her.

"Here! Go through there!" he said, pointing to a gap. "I shan't come out."

She looked at him in despair. But he kissed her and made her go. She crept in sheer misery through the holly and through the wooden fence, stumbled down the little ditch and up into the lane, where Hilda was just getting out of the car in vexation.

"Why, you're there!" said Hilda. "Where's *he?*"

"He's not coming."

Connie's face was running with tears as she got into the car with her little bag. Hilda snatched up the motoring helmet with the disfiguring goggles.

"Put it on!" she said. And Connie pulled on the disguise, then the long motoring coat, and she sat down, a goggling, inhuman, unrecognizable creature. Hilda started the car with a business-like motion. They heaved out of the lane, and were away down the road. Connie had looked round, but there was no sight of him. Away! Away! She sat in bitter tears. The parting had come so suddenly, so unexpectedly. It was like death.

"Thank goodness you'll be away from him for some time!" said Hilda, turning to avoid Crosshill village.

XVII

"You see, Hilda," said Connie after lunch, when they were nearing London, "you have never known either real tenderness or real sensuality: and if you do know them, with the same person, it makes a great difference."

"For mercy's sake, don't brag about your experiences!" said Hilda. "I've never met the man yet who was capable of intimacy with a woman, giving himself up to her. That was what I wanted. I'm not keen on their self-satisfied tenderness, and their sensuality. I'm not content to be any man's little petsywetsy, nor his *chair à plaisir* either. I wanted a complete intimacy, and I didn't get it. That's enough for me."

Connie pondered this. Complete intimacy! She supposed that meant reveal-ing everything concerning yourself to the other person, and his revealing every-thing concerning himself. But that was a bore. And all that weary self-con-sciousness between a man and a woman! a disease!

"I think you're too conscious of yourself all the time, with everybody," she said to her sister.

"I hope at least I haven't a slave nature," said Hilda.

"But perhaps you have! Perhaps you are a slave to your own idea of your-self."

Hilda drove in silence for some time after this piece of unheard-of insolence from that chit Connie.

"At least I'm not a slave to somebody else's idea of me: and the somebody else a servant of my husband's," she retorted at last, in crude anger.

"You see, it's not so," said Connie calmly.

She had always let herself be dominated by her elder sister. Now, though somewhere inside herself she was weeping, she was free of the dominion of *other women*. Ah! that in itself was a relief, like being given another life: to be free of the strange dominion and obsession of *other women*. How awful they were, women!

She was glad to be with her father, whose favorite she had always been. She and Hilda stayed in a little hotel off Pall Mall, and Sir Malcolm was in his club. But he took his daughters out in the evening, and they liked going with him.

He was still handsome and robust, though just a little afraid of the new world that had sprung up around him. He had got a second wife in Scotland, younger than himself, and richer. But he had as many holidays away from her as possible: just as with his first wife.

Connie sat next to him at the opera. He was moderately stout, and had stout thighs, but they were still strong and well-knit, the thighs of a healthy man who had taken his pleasure in life. His good-humored selfishness, his dogged sort of independence, his unrepenting sensuality, it seemed to Connie she could see them all in his well-knit, straight thighs. Just a man! And now becoming an old man, which is sad. Because in his strong, thick male legs there was none of the alert sensitiveness and power of tenderness which is the very essence of youth, that which never dies, once it is there.

Connie woke up to the existence of legs. They became more important to her than faces, which are no longer very real. How few people had live, alert legs. She looked at the men in the stalls. Great puddingy thighs in black pud-ding-cloth, or lean wooden sticks in black funeral stuff, or well-shaped young legs without any meaning whatever, either sensuality or tenderness or sensitive-ness, just mere leggy ordinariness that pranced around. Not even any sensuality like her father's. They were all daunted, daunted out of existence.

But the women were not daunted. The awful mill-posts of most females! really shocking, really enough to justify murder! Or the poor thin legs! or the trim neat things in silk stockings, without the slightest look of life! Awful, the millions of meaningless legs prancing meaninglessly around!

But she was not happy in London. The people seemed so spectral and blank. They had no alive happiness, no matter how brisk and good-looking they were. It was all barren. And Connie had a woman's blind craving for happiness, to be assured of happiness.

In Paris at any rate she felt a bit of sensuality still. But what a weary, tired worn-out sensuality. Worn-out for lack of tenderness. Oh! Paris was sad. One of the saddest towns: weary of its now-mechanical sensuality, weary of the tension of money, money, money, weary even of resentment and conceit, just weary to death, and still not sufficiently Americanized or Londonized to hide the weariness under a mechanical jig-jig-jig! Ah, these manly he-men, these flaneurs, these oglers, these eaters of good dinners! How weary they were! Weary, worn-out for lack of a little tenderness given and taken. The efficient, sometimes charming women knew a thing or two about the sensual realities: they had that pull over their jigging English sisters. But they knew even less of tenderness. Dry, with the endless dry tension of will, they too were wearing out. The human world was just getting worn out. Perhaps it would turn fiercely destructive. A sort of anarchy! Clifford and his conservative anarchy! Perhaps it wouldn't be conservative much longer. Perhaps it would develop into a very radical anarchy.

Connie found herself shrinking and afraid of the world. Sometimes she was happy for a little while in the Boulevards or in the Bois or the Luxembourg Gardens. But already Paris was full of Americans and English, strange Americans in the oddest uniforms, and the usual dreary English that are so hopeless abroad.

She was glad to drive on. It was suddenly hot weather, so Hilda was going through Switzerland and over the Brenner, then through the Dolomites down to Venice. Hilda loved all the managing and the driving and being mistress of the show. Connie was quite content to keep quiet.

And the trip was really quite nice. Only, Connie kept saying to herself: Why don't I really care? Why am I never really thrilled? How awful, that I don't really care about the landscape any more! But I don't. It's rather awful. I'm like Saint Bernard, who could sail down the lake of Lucerne without ever noticing that there were even mountains and green water. I just don't care for landscape any more. Why should one stare at it? Why should one? I refuse to.

No, she found nothing vital in France or Switzerland or the Tyrol or Italy. She just was carted through it all. And it was all less real than Wragby. Less real than the awful Wragby! She felt she didn't care if she never saw France or Switzerland or Italy again. They'd keep. Wragby was more real.

As for people! people were all alike, with very little differences. They all wanted to get money out of you: or, if they were travellers, they wanted to get enjoyment, perforce, like squeezing blood out of a stone. Poor mountains! poor landscape! it all had to be squeezed and squeezed and squeezed again, to provide a thrill, to provide enjoyment. What did people mean, with their simply *determined* enjoying of themselves?

No! said Connie to herself. I'd rather be at Wragby, where I can go about and be still, and not stare at anything or do any performing of any sort. This tourist performance of enjoying oneself is too hopelessly humiliating: it's such a failure.

She wanted to go back to Wragby, even to Clifford, even to poor crippled Clifford. He wasn't such a fool as this swarming holiday lot, anyhow.

But in her inner consciousness she was keeping touch with the other man. She mustn't let her connection with him go: oh, she mustn't let it go, or she was lost, lost utterly in this world of riff-raffy expensive people and joy-hogs. Oh, the joy-hogs! Oh, "enjoying oneself!" Another modern form of sickness.

They left the car in Mestre, in a garage, and took the regular steamer over to Venice. It was a lovely summer afternoon, the shallow lagoon rippled, the full sunshine made Venice, turning its back to them across the water, look dim.

At the station quay they changed to a gondola, giving the man the address.

He was a regular gondolier in white-and-blue blouse, not very good-looking, not at all impressive.

"Yes! The Villa Esmeralda! Yes! I know it! I have been the gondolier for a gentleman there. But a fair distance out!"

He seemed a rather childish, impetuous fellow. He rowed with a certain exaggerated impetuosity, through the dark side-canals with the horrible, slimy green walls, the canals that go through the poorer quarters, where the washing hangs high up on ropes, and there is a slight, or strong odor of sewage.

But at last he came to one of the open canals with pavement on either side, and looping bridges, that run straight, at right angles to the Grand Canal. The two women stayed under a little awning, the man was perched above, behind them.

"Are the signorine staying long at the Villa Esmeralda?" he asked, rowing easy, and wiping his perspiring face with a white-and-blue handkerchief.

"Some twenty days: we are both married ladies," said Hilda, in her curious hushed voice, that made her Italian sound so foreign.

"Ah! Twenty days!" said the man. There was a pause. After which he asked: "Do the signore want a gondolier for the twenty days or so that they will stay at the Villa Esmeralda? Or by the day, or by the week?"

Connie and Hilda considered. In Venice, it is always preferable to have one's own gondola, as it is preferable to have one's own car on land.

"What is there at the Villa? what boats?"

"There is a motor-launch, also a gondola. But—" The but meant: they won't be your property.

"How much do you charge?"

It was about thirty shillings a day, or ten pounds a week.

"Is that the regular price?" asked Hilda.

"Less, Signora, less. The regular price—"

The sisters considered.

"Well," said Hilda, "come tomorrow morning, and we will arrange it. What is your name?"

His name was Giovanni, and he wanted to know at what time he should come, and then for whom should he say he was waiting. Hilda had no card. Connie gave him one of hers. He glanced at it swiftly, with his hot, southern blue eyes, then glanced again.

"Ah!" he said, lighting up, "Milady! Milady! isn't it?"

"Milady Constanza!" said Connie.

He nodded, repeating: "Milady Constanza!" and putting the card carefully away in his blouse.

The Villa Esmeralda was quite a long way out, on the edge of the lagoon looking towards Chioggia. It was not a very old house, and pleasant, with the terraces looking seawards, and below, quite a big garden with dark trees, walled in from the lagoon.

Their host was a heavy, rather coarse Scotchman who had made a good fortune in Italy before the war, and had been knighted for his ultrapatriotism during the war. His wife was a thin, pale, sharp kind of person with no fortune of her own, and the misfortune of having to regulate her husband's rather sordid amorous exploits. He was terribly tiresome with the servants. But having had a slight stroke during the winter, he was now more manageable.

The house was pretty full. Besides Sir Malcolm and his two daughters, there were seven more people, a Scotch couple, again with two daughters; a young

Italian Contessa, a widow; a young Georgian prince, and a youngish English clergyman who had had pneumonia and was being chaplain to Sir Alexander for his health's sake. The prince was penniless, good looking, would make an excellent chauffeur, with the necessary impudence, and basta! The contessa was a quiet little puss with a game on somewhere. The clergyman was a raw simple fellow from a Bucks vicarage: luckily he had left his wife and two children at home. And the Guthries, the family of four, were good solid Edinburgh middle-class, enjoying everything in a solid fashion, and daring everything while risking nothing.

Connie and Hilda ruled out the prince at once. The Guthries were more or less their own sort, substantial, but boring: and the girls wanted husbands. The chaplain was not a bad fellow, but too deferential. Sir Alexander, after his slight stroke, had a terrible heaviness in his joviality, but he was still thrilled at the presence of so many handsome young women. Lady Cooper was a quiet, catty person who had a thin time of it, poor thing, and who watched every other woman with a cold watchfulness that had become her second nature, and who said cold, nasty little things which showed what an utterly low opinion she had of all human nature. She was also quite venomously overbearing with the servants, Connie found: but in a quiet way. And she skilfully behaved so that Sir Alexander should think that *he* was lord and monarch of the whole caboosh, with his stout, would-be-genial paunch, and his utterly boring jokes, his humorosity, as Hilda called it.

Sir Malcolm was painting. Yes, he still would do a Venetian lagoonscape, now and then, in contrast to his Scottish landscapes. So in the morning he was rowed off with a huge canvas, to his "site." A little later, Lady Cooper would be rowed off into the heart of the city, with sketching-block and colors. She was an inveterate water-color painter, and the house was full of rose-colored palaces, dark canals, swaying bridges, medieval façades, and so on. A little later the Guthries, the prince, the countess, Sir Alexander and sometimes Mr. Lind, the chaplain, would go off to the Lido where they would bathe; coming home to a late lunch at half-past one.

The house-party, as a house-party, was distinctly boring. But this did not trouble the sisters. They were out all the time. Their father took them to the exhibition, miles and miles of weary paintings. He took them to all the cronies of his in the Villa Lucchese, he sat with them on warm evenings in Piazza, having got a table at Florian's: he took them to the theater, to the Goldoni plays. There were illuminated water-fêtes, there were dances. This was a holiday-place of all holiday-places. The Lido with its acres of sun-pinked or pyjamaed bodies, was like a strand with an endless heap of seals come up for mating. Too many people in Piazza, too many limbs and trunks of humanity on the Lido, too many gondolas, too many motor launches, too many steamers, too many pigeons, too many ices, too many cocktails, too many men servants wanting tips, too many languages rattling, too much, too much sun, too much smell of Venice, too many cargoes of strawberries, too many silk shawls, too many huge, raw-beef slices of watermelon on stalls: too much enjoyment, altogether far too much enjoyment!

Connie and Hilda went around in their sunny frocks. There were dozens of people they knew, dozens of people knew them. Michaelis turned up like a bad penny. "Hullo! Where you staying? Come and have an ice cream or something! Come with me somewhere in my gondola." Even Michaelis *almost* sunburned: though sun-cooked is more appropriate to the look of the mass of human flesh.

It was pleasant in a way. It was *almost* enjoyment. But anyhow, with all the cocktails, all the lying in warmish water and sunbathing on hot sand in hot sun, jazzing with your stomach up against some fellow in the warm nights, cooling off with ices, it was a complete narcotic. And that was what they all wanted, a drug: the slow water, a drug; the sun, a drug; jazz, a drug; cigarettes, cocktails, ices, vermouth. To be drugged! Enjoyment! Enjoyment!

Hilda half liked being drugged. She liked looking at all the women, speculating about them. The women were absorbingly interested in the women. How does she look? What man has she captured? what fun is she getting out of it?—The men were like great dogs in white flannel trousers, waiting to be patted, waiting to wallow, waiting to plaster some woman's stomach against their own, in jazz.

Hilda liked jazz, because she could plaster her stomach against the stomach of some so-called man, and let him control her movements from the visceral center, here and there across the floor, and then she could break loose and ignore "the creature." He had been merely made use of. Poor Connie was rather unhappy. She wouldn't jazz, because she simply couldn't plaster her stomach against some "creature's" stomach. She hated the conglomerate mass of nearly nude flesh on the Lido: there was hardly enough water to wet them all. She disliked Sir Alexander and Lady Cooper. She did not want Michaelis or anybody else trailing her.

The happiest times were when she got Hilda to go with her away across the Lagoon, far across to some lonely shingle-bank, where they could bathe quite alone, the gondola remaining on the inner side of the reef.

Then Giovanni got another gondolier to help him, because it was a long way and he sweated terrifically in the sun. Giovanni was very nice: affectionate, as the Italians are, and quite passionless. The Italians are not passionate: passion has deep reserves. They are easily moved, and often affectionate, but they rarely have any abiding passion of any sort.

So Giovanni was already devoted to his ladies, as he had been devoted to cargoes of ladies in the past. He was perfectly ready to prostitute himself to them, if they wanted him: he secretly hoped they would want him. They would give him a handsome present, and it would come in very handy, as he was just going to be married. He told them about his marriage, and they were suitably interested.

He thought this trip to some lonely bank across the lagoon probably meant business: business being *l'amore,* love. So he got a mate to help him, for it *was* a long way; and after all, they were two ladies. Two ladies, two mackerels! Good arithmetic! Beautiful ladies too! He was justly proud of them. And though it was the Signora who paid him and gave him orders, he rather hoped it would be the young milady who would select him for *l'amore.* She would give more money too.

The mate he brought was called Daniele. He was not a regular gondolier, so he had none of the cadger and prostitute about him. He was a sandola man, a sandola being a big boat that brings in fruit and produce from the islands.

Daniele was beautiful, tall and well-shapen, with a light round head of little, close, pale-blond curls, and a good-looking man's face, a little like a lion, and long-distance blue eyes. He was not effusive, loquacious, and bibulous like Giovanni. He was silent and he rowed with a strength and ease as if he were alone on the water. The ladies were ladies, remote from him. He did not even look at them. He looked ahead.

He was a real man, a little angry when Giovanni drank too much wine and
rowed awkwardly, with effusive shoves of the great oar. He was a man as Mellors was a man, unprostituted. Connie pitied the wife of the easily-overflowing
Giovanni. But Daniele's wife could be one of those sweet Venetian women of
the people whom one still sees, modest and flower-like, in the back of that
labyrinth of a town.

Ah, how sad that man first prostitutes woman, then woman prostitutes man.
Giovanni was pining to prostitute himself, dribbling like a dog, wanting to give
himself to a woman. And for money!

Connie looked at Venice far off, low and rose-colored upon the water. Built
of money, blossomed of money, and dead with money. The money-deadness!
Money, money, money, prostitution and deadness.

Yet Daniele was still a man capable of a man's free allegiance. He did not
wear the gondolier's blouse: only the knitted blue jersey. He was a little wild,
uncouth and proud. So he was hireling to the rather doggy Giovanni, who was
hireling again of two women. So it is! When Jesus refused the devil's money, he
left the devil like a Jewish banker, master of the whole situation.

Connie would come home from the blazing light of the lagoon in a kind of
stupor, to find letters from home. Clifford wrote regularly. He wrote very good
letters: they might all have been printed in a book. And for this reason Connie
found them not very interesting.

She lived in the stupor of the light of the lagoon, the lapping saltiness of the
water, the space, the emptiness, the nothingness: but health, health, complete
stupor of health. It was gratifying, and she was lulled away in it, not caring for
anything. Besides, she was pregnant. She knew now. So the stupor of sunlight
and the lagoon salt and sea-bathing and lying on shingle and finding shells and
drifting away, away in a gondola was completed by the pregnancy inside her,
another fulness of health, satisfying and stupefying.

She had been at Venice a fortnight, and she was to stay another ten days or a
fortnight. The sunshine blazed over any count of time, and the fulness of physical health made forgetfulness complete. She was in a sort of stupor of well-
being.

From which a letter of Clifford roused her.

"We, too, have had our mild local excitement. It appears the truant wife of
Mellors, the keeper, turned up at the cottage, and found herself unwelcome. He
packed her off and locked the door. Report has it, however, that when he
returned from the wood he found the no longer fair lady firmly established in
his bed, in *puris naturalibus;* or one should say, in *impuris naturalibus.* She had
broken a window and got in that way. Unable to evict the somewhat manhan-
dled Venus from his couch, he beat a retreat and retired, it is said, to his mother's
house in Tevershall. Meanwhile, the Venus of Stacks Gate is established in the
cottage, which she claims is her home, and Apollo, apparently, is domiciled in
Tevershall.

"I repeat this from hearsay, as Mellors has not come to me personally. I had
the particular bit of local garbage from our garbage bird, our ibis, our scavenging
turkey-buzzard, Mrs. Bolton. I would not have repeated it had she not exclaimed: her Ladyship will go no more to the wood if *that* woman's going to be
about!

"I like your picture of Sir Malcolm striding into the sea with white hair
blowing and pink flesh glowing. I envy you that sun. Here it rains. But I don't
envy Sir Malcolm his inveterate mortal carnality. However, it suits his age.

Apparently one grows more carnal and more mortal as one grows older. Only youth has a taste of immortality—"

This news affected Connie in her state of semi-stupified well-being with vexation amounting to exasperation. Now she had got to be bothered by that beast of a woman! Now she must start and fret! She had no letter from Mellors. They had agreed not to write at all, but now she wanted to hear from him personally. After all, he was the father of the child that was coming. Let him write!

But how hateful! How everything was messed up. How foul those low people were! How nice it was here, in the sunshine and the indolence, compared to that dismal mess of that English midlands! After all, a clear sky was almost the most important thing in life.

She did not mention the fact of her pregnancy, even to Hilda. She wrote to Mrs. Bolton for exact information.

Duncan Forbes, an artist, friend of theirs, had arrived at the Villa Esmeralda, coming north from Rome. Now he made a third in the gondola, and he bathed with them across the lagoon, and was their escort: a quiet, almost taciturn young man, very advanced in his art.

She had a letter from Mrs. Bolton: "You will be pleased, I am sure, my Lady, when you see Sir Clifford. He's looking quite blooming and working very hard, and very hopeful. Of course, he is looking forward to seeing you among us again. It is a dull house without my Lady, and we shall all welcome her presence among us once more.

"About Mr. Mellors, I don't know how much Sir Clifford told you. It seems his wife came back all of a sudden one afternoon, and he found her sitting on the doorstep when he came in from the wood. She said she was come back to him and wanted to live with him again, as she was his legal wife, and he wasn't going to divorce her. Because it seems Mr. Mellors was trying for a divorce. But he wouldn't have anything to do with her, and wouldn't let her in the house, and did not go in himself; he went back into the wood without even opening the door.

"But when he came back after dark, he found the house broken into, so he went upstairs to see what she'd done, and he found her in bed without a rag on her. He offered her money, but she said she was his wife and he must take her back. I don't know what sort of a scene they had. His mother told me about it, she's terribly upset. Well, he told her he'd rot rather than ever live with her again, so he took his things and went straight to his mother's on Tevershall hill. He stopped the night and went to the wood next day through the park, never going near the cottage. It seems he never saw his wife that day. But the day after she was at her brother Dan's at Beggarlee, swearing and carrying on, saying she was his legal wife, and that he'd been having women at the cottage, because she'd found a scent-bottle in his drawer, and gold-tipped cigarette-ends on the ashheap, and I don't know what all. Then it seems the postman, Fred Kirk, says he heard somebody talking in Mr. Mellors' bedroom early one morning, and a motor car had been in the lane.

"Mr. Mellors stayed on with his mother, and went to the wood through the park, and it seems she stayed on at the cottage. Well, there was no end of talk. So at last Mr. Mellors and Tom Phillips went to the cottage and fetched away most of the furniture and bedding, and unscrewed the handle of the pump, so she was forced to go. But instead of going back to Stacks Gate she went and lodged with that Mrs. Swain at Beggarlee, because her brother Dan's wife wouldn't have her. And she kept going to old Mrs. Mellors' house, to catch him, and she began swearing he'd got in bed with her in the cottage, and she went to a lawyer to make him pay her an allowance. She's grown heavy, and more common than ever, and as strong as a bull. And she goes about saying the most awful things about him, how he has women at the cottage, and how he behaved to her when they were married, the low, beastly things he did to her, and I don't know what all. I'm sure it's awful, the mischief a woman can do, once she starts talking. And no matter how low she may be, there'll be some as will believe her, and some of the dirt will stick. I'm sure the way she makes out that Mr. Mellors was one of those low, beastly men with women, is simply shocking. And people are only too ready to believe things against anybody, especially things like that. She declares she'll never leave him alone while he lives. Though what I say is, if he was so beastly to her, why is she so anxious to go back to him? But, of course, she's coming near her change of life, for she's years older than he is. And these common, violent women always go partly insane when the change of life comes upon them.''—

This was a nasty blow to Connie. Here she was, sure as life, coming in for her share of the lowness and dirt. She felt angry with him for not having got clear of a Bertha Coutts: nay, for ever having married her. Perhaps he had a certain hankering after lowness. Connie remembered the last night she had spent with him, and shivered. He had known all that sensuality, even with a Bertha Coutts! It was really rather disgusting. It would be well to be rid of him, clear of him altogether. He was perhaps really common, really low.

She had a revulsion against the whole affair, and almost envied the Guthrie girls their gawky inexperience and crude maidenliness. And she now dreaded the thought that anybody would know about herself and the keeper. How unspeakably humiliating! She was weary, afraid, and felt a craving for utter respectability, even for the vulgar and deadening respectability of the Guthrie girls. If Clifford knew about her affair, how unspeakably humiliating! She was afraid, terrified of society and its unclean bite. She almost wished she could get rid of the child again, and be quite clear. In short, she fell into a state of funk.

As for the scent-bottle, that was her own folly. She had not been able to refrain from perfuming his one or two handkerchiefs and his shirts in the drawer, just out of childishness, and she had left a little bottle of Coty's Wood-violet perfume, half empty, among his things. She wanted him to remember her in the perfume. As for the cigarette-ends, they were Hilda's.

She could not help confiding a little in Duncan Forbes. She didn't say she had been the keeper's lover, she only said she liked him, and told Forbes the history of the man.

"Oh," said Forbes, "you'll see, they'll never rest till they've pulled the man down and done him in. If he has refused to creep up into the middle classes, when he had a chance; and if he's a man who stands up for his own sex, then they'll do him in. It's the one thing they won't let you be, straight and open in your sex. You can be as dirty as you like. In fact the more dirt you do on sex, the better they like it. But if you believe in your own sex, and won't have it done dirt to: they'll down you. It's the one insane taboo left: sex as a natural and vital thing. They won't have it, and they'll kill you before they'll let you have it. You'll see, they'll hound that man down. And what's he done, after all? If he's made love to his wife all ends on, hasn't he a right to? She ought to be proud of it. But you see, even a low bitch like that turns on him, and uses the hyena instinct of the mob against sex, to pull him down. You have to snivel and feel sinful or awful about your sex, before you're allowed to have any. Oh, they'll hound the poor devil down."

Connie had a revulsion in the opposite direction now. What had he done, after all? What had he done to herself, Connie, but give her an exquisite pleasure, and a sense of freedom and life? He had released her warm, natural sexual flow. And for that they would hound him down.

No, no, it should not be. She saw the image of him, naked white with tanned face and hands, looking down and addressing his erect penis as if it were another being, the odd grin flickering on his face. And she heard his voice again: Tha's got the nicest woman's arse of anybody! And she felt his hand warmly and softly closing over her tail again, over her secret places, like a benediction. And the warmth ran through her womb, and the little flames flickered in her knees, and she said: Oh no! I mustn't go back on it! I must not go back on him. I must stick to him and to what I had of him, through everything. I had no warm, flamy life till he gave it me. And I won't go back on it.

She did a rash thing. She sent a letter to Ivy Bolton, enclosing a note to the keeper, and asking Mrs. Bolton to give it to him. And she wrote to him: "I am very much distressed to hear of all the trouble your wife is making for you, but don't mind it, it is only a sort of hysteria. It will all blow over as suddenly as it came. But I'm awfully sorry about it, and I do hope you are not minding very much. After all, it isn't worth it. She is only a hysterical woman who wants to hurt you. I shall be home in ten days' time, and I·hope everything will be all right."

A few days later came a letter from Clifford. He was evidently upset.

"I am delighted to hear you are prepared to leave Venice on the sixteenth. But if you are enjoying it, don't hurry home. We miss you, Wragby misses you. But it is essential that you should get your full amount of sunshine, sunshine and pyjamas, as the advertisements of the Lido say. So please do stay on a little longer, if it is cheering you up and preparing you for our sufficiently awful winter. Even today, it rains.

"I am assiduously, admirably looked after by Mrs. Bolton. She is a queer specimen. The more I live, the more I realize what strange creatures human beings are. Some of them might just as well have a hundred legs, like a centipede, or six, like a lobster. The human consistency and dignity one has been led to expect from one's fellowmen seem actually non-existent. One doubts if they exist to any startling degree even in oneself.

"The scandal of the keeper continues and gets bigger like a snowball. Mrs. Bolton keeps me informed. She reminds me of a fish which, though dumb, seems to be breathing silent gossip through its gills, while ever it lives. All goes through the sieve of her gills, and nothing surprises her. It is as if the events of other people's lives were the necessary oxygen of her own.

"She is preoccupied with the Mellors scandal, and if I will let her begin, she takes me down to the depths. Her great indignation, which even then is like the indignation of an actress playing a role, is against the wife of Mellors, whom she persists in calling Bertha Coutts. I have been to the depths of the muddy lives of the Bertha Couttses of this world, and when, released from the current of gossip, I slowly rise to the surface again, I look at the daylight in wonder that it ever should be.

"It seems to me absolutely true, that our world, which appears to us the surface of all things, is really the *bottom* of a deep ocean: all our trees are submarine growths, and we are weird, scaly-clad submarine fauna, feeding ourselves on offal like shrimps. Only occasionally the soul rises gasping through the fathomless fathoms under which we live, far up to the surface of the ether, where there is true air. I am convinced that the air we normally breathe is a kind of water, and men and women are a species of fish.

"But sometimes the soul does come up, shoots like a kittiwake into the light, with ecstasy, after having preyed on the submarine depths. It is our mortal destiny, I suppose, to prey upon the ghastly subaqueous life of our fellow men, in the submarine jungle of mankind. But our immortal destiny is to escape, once we have swallowed our swimmy catch, up again into the bright ether, bursting out from the surface of Old Ocean into real light. Then one realizes one's eternal nature.

"When I hear Mrs. Bolton talk, I feel myself plunging down, down, to the depths where the fish of human secrets wriggle and swim. Carnal appetite makes one seize a beakful of prey: then up, up again, out of the dense into the ethereal, from the wet into the dry. To you I can tell the whole process. But with Mrs. Bolton I only feel the downward plunge, down, horribly, among the seaweeds and the pallid monsters of the very bottom.

"I am afraid we are going to lose our gamekeeper. The scandal of the truant wife, instead of dying down, has reverberated to greater and greater dimensions. He is accused of all unspeakable things, and curiously enough, the woman has managed to get the bulk of the colliers' wives behind her, gruesome fish, and the village is putrescent with talk.

"I hear this Bertha Coutts besieges Mellors in his mother's house, having ransacked the cottage and the hut. She seized one day upon her own daughter, as that chip of the female block was returning from school; but the little one, instead of kissing the loving mother's hand, bit it firmly, and so received from the other hand a smack in the face which sent her reeling into the gutter: whence she was rescued by an indignant and harassed grandmother.

"The woman has blown off an amazing quantity of poison-gas. She has aired in detail all those incidents of her conjugal life which are usually buried down in the deepest grave of matrimonial silence, between married couples. Having chosen to exhume them, after ten years of burial, she has a weird array. I hear these details from Linley and the doctor: the latter being amused. Of course, there is really nothing in it. Humanity has always had a strange avidity for unusual sexual postures, and if a man likes to use his wife, as Benvenuto Cellini says, 'in the Italian way,' well that is a matter of taste. But I had hardly expected our gamekeeper to be up to so many tricks. No doubt Bertha Coutts herself first put him up to them. In any case, it is a matter of their own personal squalor, and nothing to do with anybody else.

"However, everybody listens: as I do myself. A dozen years ago, common decency would have hushed the thing. But common decency no longer exists, and the colliers' wives are all up in arms and unabashed in voice. One would think every child in Tevershall, for the past fifty years, had been an immaculate conception, and every one of our nonconformist females was a shining Joan of Arc. That our estimable gamekeeper should have about him a touch of Rabelais seems to make him more monstrous and shocking than a murderer like Crippen. Yet these people in Tevershall are a loose lot, if one is to believe all accounts.

"The trouble is, however, the execrable Bertha Coutts has not confined herself to her own experiences and sufferings. She has discovered, at the top of her voice, that her husband has been 'keeping' women down at the cottage, and has made a few random shots at naming the women. This has brought a few decent names trailing through the mud, and the thing has gone quite considerably too far. An injunction has been taken out against the woman.

"I have had to interview Mellors about the business, as it was impossible to keep the woman away from the wood. He goes about as usual, with his Miller-of-the-Dee air, I care for nobody, no, not I, if nobody care for me! Nevertheless, I shrewdly suspect he feels like a dog with a tin can tied to its tail: though he makes a very good show of pretending the tin can isn't there. But I hear that in the village the women call away their children if he is passing, as if he were the Marquis de Sade in person. He goes on with a certain impudence, but I am afraid the tin can is firmly tied to his tail, and that inwardly he repeats, like Don Rodrigo in the Spanish ballad: 'Ah, now it bites me where I most have sinned!'"

"I asked him if he thought he would be able to attend to his duty in the wood, and he said he did not think he had neglected it. I told him it was a nuisance to have the woman trespassing: to which he replied that he had no power to arrest her. Then I hinted at the scandal and its unpleasant course. 'Ay,' he said. 'Folks should do their own fuckin', then they wouldn't want to listen to a lot of clatfart about another man's.'

"He said it with some bitterness, and no doubt it contains the real germ of truth. The mode of putting it, however, is neither delicate nor respectful. I hinted as much, and then I heard the tin can rattle again. ''It's not for a man i' the shape you're in, Sir Clifford, to twit me for havin' a cod atween my legs.'

"These things, said indiscriminately to all and sundry, of course do not help him at all, and the rector, and Linley, and Burroughs all think it would be as well if the man left the place.

"I asked him if it was true that he entertained ladies down at the cottage, and all he said was: "Why what's that to you, Sir Clifford?" I told him I intended to have decency observed on my estate, to which he replied: 'Then you mun button the mouths o' a' th' women.'—When I pressed him about his manner of life at the cottage, he said: 'Surely you might ma'e a scandal out o' me an' my bitch Flossie. You've missed summat there.' As a matter of fact, for an example of impertinence he'd be hard to beat.

"I asked him if it would be easy for him to find another job. He said: 'If you're hintin' that you'd like to shunt me out of this job, it'd be as easy as wink.' So he made no trouble at all about leaving at the end of next week, and apparently is willing to initiate a young fellow, Joe Chambers, into as many mysteries of the craft as possible. I told him I would give him a month's wages extra, when he left. He said he'd rather I kept my money, as I'd no occasion to ease my conscience. I asked him what he meant, and he said: 'You don't owe me nothing extra, Sir Clifford, so don't pay me nothing extra. If you think you see my shirt hanging out, just tell me.'

"Well, there is the end of it for the time being. The woman has gone away: we don't know where to: but she is liable to arrest if she shows her face in Tevershall. And I hear she is mortally afraid of gaol, because she merits it so well. Mellors will depart on Saturday week, and the place will soon become normal again.

"Meanwhile, my dear Connie, if you would enjoy the stay in Venice or in Switzerland till the beginning of August, I should be glad to think you were out of all this buzz of nastiness, which will have died quite away by the end of the month.

"So you see, we are deep-sea monsters, and when the lobster walks on mud, he stirs it up for everybody. We must perforce take it philosophically."—The irritation, and the lack of any sympathy in any direction, of Clifford's letter, had a bad effect on Connie. But she understood it better when she received the following from Mellors: "The cat is out of the bag, along with various other pussies. You have heard that my wife Bertha came back to my unloving arms, and took up her abode in the cottage: where, to speak disrespectfully, she smelled a rat in the shape of a little bottle of Coty. Other evidence she did not find, at least for some days, when she began to howl about the burnt photograph. She noticed the glass and the backboard in the spare bedroom. Unfortunately, on the backboard somebody had scribbled little sketches, and the initials, several times repeated: C. S. R. This, however, afforded no clue until she broke into the hut, and found one of your books, an autobiography of the actress Judith, with your name, Constance Stewart Reid, on the front page. After this, for some days she went round loudly saying that my paramour was no less a person than Lady Chatterley herself. The news came at last to the rector, Mr. Burroughs, and to Sir Clifford. They then proceeded to take legal steps against my liege lady, who for her part disappeared, having always had a mortal fear of the police.

"Sir Clifford asked to see me, so I went to him. He talked around things and seemed annoyed with me. Then he asked if I knew that even her ladyship's name had been mentioned. I said I never listened to scandal, and was surprised to hear this bit from Sir Clifford himself. He said, of course, it was a great insult, and I told him there was Queen Mary on a calendar in the scullery, no doubt because Her Majesty formed part of my harm. But he didn't appreciate the sarcasm. He as good as told me I was a disreputable character who walked about with all of my breeches' buttons undone, and I as good as told him he'd nothing to unbutton anyhow, so he gave me the sack, and I leave on Saturday week, and the place thereof shall know me no more.

"I shall go to London, and my old landlady, Mrs. Inger, 17 Coburg Square, will either give me a room or will find one for me.

"Be sure your sins will find you out, especially if you're married and her name's Bertha.—"

There was not a word about herself, or to her. Connie resented this. He might have said some few words of consolation or reassurance. But she knew he was leaving her free, free to go back to Wragby and to Clifford. She resented that too. He need not be so falsely chivalrous. She wished he had said to Clifford: "Yes, she is my lover and mistress and I am proud of it!" But his courage wouldn't carry him so far.

So her name was coupled with his in Tevershall! It was a mess. But that would soon die down.

She was angry, with the complicated and confused anger that made her inert. She did not know what to do nor what to say, so she said and did nothing. She went on at Venice just the same, rowing out in the gondola with Duncan Forbes, bathing, letting the days slip by. Duncan, who had been rather depressingly in love with her ten years ago, was in love with her again. But she said to him: "I only want one thing of men, and that is, that they should leave me alone."

So Duncan left her alone: really quite pleased to be able to. All the same, he offered her a soft stream of a queer, inverted sort of love. He wanted to be *with* her.

"Have you ever thought," he said to her one day, "how very little people are connected with one another. Look at Daniele! He is handsome as a son of the sun. But see how alone he looks in his handsomeness. Yet I bet he has a wife and family, and couldn't possibly go away from them."

"Ask him," said Connie.

Duncan did so. Daniele said he was married, and had two children, both male, aged seven and nine. But he betrayed no emotion over the fact.

"Perhaps only people who are capable of real togetherness have that look of being alone in the universe," said Connie. "The others have a certain stickiness, they stick to the mass, like Giovanni."—"And," she thought to herself, "like you, Duncan."

XVIII

She had to make up her mind what to do. She would leave Venice on the Saturday that he was leaving Wragby: in six days' time. This would bring her to London on the Monday following, and she would then see him. She wrote to him to the London address, asking him to send her a letter to Hartland's hotel, and to call for her on the Monday evening at seven.

Inside herself, she was curiously and complicatedly angry, and all her responses were numb. She refused to confide even in Hilda, and Hilda, offended by her steady silence, had become rather intimate with a Dutch woman. Connie hated those rather stifling intimacies between women, intimacies into which Hilda always entered ponderously.

Sir Malcolm decided to travel with Connie, and Duncan could come on with Hilda. The old artist always did himself well: he took berths on the Orient Express, in spite of Connie's dislike of *trains de luxe,* the atmosphere of vulgar depravity there is aboard them nowadays. However, it would make the journey to Paris shorter.

Sir Malcolm was always uneasy going back to his wife. It was a habit carried over from the first wife. But there would be a house-party for the grouse, and he wanted to be well ahead. Connie, sunburnt and handsome, sat in silence, forgetting all about the landscape.

"A little dull for you, going back to Wragby," said her father, noticing her glumness.

"I'm not sure I shall go back to Wragby," she said, with startling abruptness, looking into his eyes with her big blue eyes. His big blue eyes took on the frightened look of a man whose social conscience is not quite clear.

"You mean you'll stay on in Paris a while?"

"No! I mean never go back to Wragby."

He was bothered by his own little problems, and sincerely hoped he was getting none of hers to shoulder.

"How's that, all at once?" he asked.

"I'm going to have a child."

It was the first time she had uttered the words to any living soul, and it seemed to mark a cleavage in her life.

"How do you know?" said her father.

She smiled.

"How *should* I know?"

"But not Clifford's child, of course?"

"No! Another man's."

She rather enjoyed tormenting him.

"Do I know the man?" asked Sir Malcolm.

"No! You've never seen him."

There was a long pause.

"And what are your plans?"

"I don't know. That's the point."

"No patching it up with Clifford?"

"I suppose Clifford would take it," said Connie. "He told me, after last time you talked to him, he wouldn't mind if I had a child, so long as I went about it discreetly."

"Only sensible thing he could say, under the circumstances. Then I suppose it'll be all right."

"In what way?" said Connie, looking into her father's eyes. They were big blue eyes rather like her own, but with a certain uneasiness in them, a look sometimes of an uneasy little boy, sometimes a look of sullen selfishness, usually goodhumored and wary.

"You can present Clifford with an heir to all the Chatterleys, and put another baronet in Wragby."

Sir Malcolm's face smiled with a half-sensual smile.

"But I don't think I want to," she said.

"Why not? Feeling entangled with the other man? Well! If you want the truth from me, my child, it's this. The world goes on. Wragby stands and will go on standing. The world is more or less a fixed thing, and, externally, we have to adapt ourselves to it. Privately, in my private opinion, we can please ourselves. Emotions change. You may like one man this year and another next. But Wragby still stands. Stick to Wragby as far as Wragby sticks to you. Then please yourself. But you'll get very little out of making a break. You can make a break if you wish. You have an independent income, the only thing that never lets you down. But you won't get much out of it. Put a little baronet in Wragby. It's an amusing thing to do."

And Sir Malcolm sat back and smiled again. Connie did not answer.

"I hope you had a real man at last," he said to her after a while, sensually alert.

"I did. That's the trouble. There aren't many of them about," she said.

"No, by God!" he mused. "There aren't! Well, my dear, to look at you, he was a lucky man. Surely he wouldn't make trouble for you?"

"Oh, no! He leaves me my own mistress entirely."

"Quite! Quite! A genuine man would."

Sir Malcolm was pleased. Connie was his favorite daughter, he had always liked the female in her. Not so much of her mother in her as in Hilda. And he had always disliked Clifford. So he was pleased, and very tender with his daughter, as if the unborn child were his child.

He drove with her to Hartland's hotel, and saw her installed: then went round to his club. She had refused his company for the evening.

She found a letter from Mellors. "I won't come round to your hotel, but I'll wait for you outside the Golden Cock in Adam Street at seven."

There he stood, tall and slender, and so different, in a formal suit of thin dark cloth. He had a natural distinction, but he had not the cut-to-pattern look of her class. Yet, she saw at once, he could go anywhere. He had a native breeding which was really much nicer than the cut-to-pattern class thing.

"Ah, there you are! How well you look!"

"Yes! But not you."

She looked in his face anxiously. It was thin, and the cheekbones showed. But his eyes smiled at her, and she felt at home with him. There it was: suddenly, the tension of keeping up her appearances fell from her. Something flowed out of him physically, that made her feel inwardly at ease and happy, at home. With a woman's now alert instinct for happiness, she registered it at once. "I'm happy when he's there!" Not all the sunshine of Venice had given her this inward expansion and warmth.

"Was it horrid for you?" she asked as she sat opposite him at table. He was too thin; she saw it now. His hand lay as she knew it, with that curious loose forgottenness of a sleeping animal. She wanted so much to take it and kiss it. But she did not quite dare.

"People are always horrid," he said.

"And did you mind very much?"

"I minded, as I always shall mind. And I knew I was a fool to mind."

"Did you feel like a dog with a tin can tied to its tail? Clifford said you felt like that."

He looked at her. It was cruel of her at that moment: for his pride had suffered bitterly.

"I suppose I did," he said.

She never knew the fierce bitterness with which he resented insult.

There was a long pause.

"And did you miss me?" she asked.

"I was glad you were out of it."

Again there was a pause.

"But did people *believe* about you and me?" she asked.

"No! I don't think so for a moment."

"Did Clifford?"

"I should say not. He put it off without thinking about it. But naturally it made him want to see the last of me."

"I'm going to have a child."

The expression died utterly out of his face, out of his whole body. He looked at her with darkened eyes, whose look she could not understand at all: like some dark-flamed spirit looking at her.

"Say you're glad!" she pleaded, groping for his hand. And she saw a certain exultance spring up in him. But it was netted down by things she could not understand.

"It's the future," he said.

"But aren't you glad?" she persisted.

"I have such a terrible mistrust of the future."

"But you needn't be troubled by any responsibility. Clifford would have it as his own, he'd be glad."

She saw him go pale, and recoil under this. He did not answer.

"Shall I go back to Clifford and put a little baronet into Wragby?" she asked.

He looked at her, pale and very remote. The ugly little grin flickered on his face.

"You wouldn't have to tell him who the father was."

"Oh!" she said; "he'd take it even then, if I wanted him to."

He thought for a time.

"Ay!" he said at last, to himself. "I suppose he would."

There was silence. A big gulf was between them.

"But you don't want me to go back to Clifford, do you?" she asked him.

"What do you want yourself?" he replied.

"I want to live with you," she said simply.

In spite of himself, little flames ran over his belly as he heard her say it, and he dropped his head. Then he looked up at her again, with those haunted eyes.

"If it's worth it to you," he said. "I've got nothing."

"You've got more than most men. Come, you know it," she said.

"In one way, I know it." He was silent for a time, thinking. Then he resumed: "They used to say I had too much of the woman in me. But it's not that. I'm not a woman because I don't want to shoot birds, neither because I don't want to make money, or get on. I could have got on in the army, easily, but I didn't like the army. Though I could manage the men all right: they liked me and they had a bit of a holy fear of me when I got mad. No, it was stupid, dead-handed higher authority that made the army dead: absolutely fool-dead. I like men, and men like me. But I can't stand the twaddling bossy impudence of the people who run this world. That's why I can't get on. I hate the impudence of money, and I hate the impudence of class. So in the world as it is, what have I to offer a woman?"

"But why offer anything? It's not a bargain. It's just that we love one another," she said.

"Nay, nay! It's more than that. Living is moving and moving on. My life won't get down the proper gutters, it just won't. So I'm a bit of a waste ticket by myself. And I've no business to take a woman into my life, unless my life does something and gets somewhere, inwardly at least, to keep us both fresh. A man must offer a woman *some* meaning in his life, if it's going to be an isolated life, and if she's a genuine woman. I can't be just your male concubine."

"Why not?" she said.

"Why, because I can't. And you would soon hate it."

"As if you couldn't trust me," she said.

The grin flickered on his face.

"The money is yours, the position is yours, the decisions will lie with you. I'm not just my lady's fucker, after all."

"What else are you?"

"You may well ask. It no doubt is invisible. Yet I'm something to myself at least. I can see the point of my own existence, though I can quite understand nobody else's seeing it."

"And will your existence have less point, if you live with me?"

He paused a long time before replying:

"It might."

She, too, stayed to think about it.

"And what is the point of your existence?"

"I tell you, it's invisible. I don't believe in the world, not in money, nor in advancement, nor in the future of our civilization. If there's got to be a future for humanity, there'll have to be a very big change from what now is."

"And what will the real future have to be like?"

"God knows! I can feel something inside me, all mixed up with a lot of rage. But what it really amounts to, I don't know."

"Shall I tell you?" she said, looking into his face. "Shall I tell you what you have that other men don't have, and that will make the future? Shall I tell you?"

"Tell me, then," he replied.

"It's the courage of your own tenderness, that's what it is, like when you put your hand on my tail and say I've got a pretty tail."

The grin came flickering on his face.

"That!" he said.

Then he sat thinking.

"Ay!" he said. "You're right. It's that really. It's that all the way through. I knew it with the men. I had to be in touch with them, physically, and not go back on it. I had to be bodily aware of them and a bit tender to them, even if I put 'em through hell. It's a question of awareness, as Buddha said. But even he fought shy of the bodily awareness, and that natural physical tenderness which is the best, even between men; in a proper manly way. Makes 'em really manly, not so monkeyish. Ay! it's tenderness, really; it's cunt-awareness. Sex is really only touch, the closest of all touch. And it's touch we're afraid of. We're only half-conscious, and half alive. We've got to come alive and aware. Especially the English have got to get into touch with one another, a bit delicate and a bit tender. It's our crying need."

She looked at him.

"Then why are you afraid of me?" she said.

He looked at her a long time before he answered.

"It's the money, really, and the position. It's the world in you."

"But isn't there tenderness in me?" she said wistfully.

He looked down at her, with darkened, abstract eyes.

"Ay! It come an' goes, like in me."

"But can't you trust it between you and me?" she asked, gazing anxiously at him.

She saw his face all softening down, losing its armor.

"Maybe!" he said.

They were both silent.

"I want you to hold me in your arms," she said. "I want you to tell me you are glad we are having a child."

She looked so lovely and warm and wistful, his bowels stirred towards her.

"I suppose we can go to my room," he said. "Though it's scandalous again."

But she saw the forgetfulness of the world coming over him again, his face taking the soft, pure look of tender passion.

They walked by the remoter streets to Coburg Square, where he had a room at the top of the house, an attic room where he cooked for himself on a gas range. It was small, but decent and tidy.

She took off her things, and made him do the same. She was lovely in the soft first flush of her pregnancy.

"I ought to leave you alone," he said.

"No!" she said. "Love me! Love me, and say you'll keep me. Say you'll keep me! Say you'll never let me go, to the world nor to anybody!"

She crept close against him, clinging fast to his thin, strong naked body, the only home she had ever known.

"Then I'll keep thee," he said. "If tha wants it, then I'll keep thee."

He held her round and fast.

"And say you're glad about the child," she repeated. "Kiss it! Kiss my womb and say you're glad it's there."

But that was more difficult for him.

"I've a dread of puttin' children i' th' world," he said. "I've such a dread o' th' future for 'em."

"But you've put it into me. Be tender to it, and that will be its future already. Kiss it!"

He quivered, because it was true. "Be tender to it, and that will be its future."—At that moment he felt a sheer love for the woman. He kissed her belly and her mount of Venus, to kiss close to the womb and the fetus within the womb.

"Oh, you love me! You love me!" she said, in a little cry like one of her blind, inarticulate love cries. And he went in to her softly, feeling the stream of tenderness flowing in release from his bowels to hers, the bowels of compassion kindled between them.

And he realized as he went in to her that this was the thing he had to do, to come into tender touch, without losing his pride or his dignity or his integrity as a man. After all, if she had money and means, and he had none, he should be too proud and honorable to hold back his tenderness from her on that account. "I stand for the touch of bodily awareness between human beings," he said to himself, "and the touch of tenderness. And she is my mate. And it is a battle against the money, and the machine, and the insentient ideal monkeyishness of the world. And she will stand behind me there. Thank God I've got a woman! Thank God I've got a woman who is with me, and tender and aware of me. Thank God she's not a bully, nor a fool. Thank God she's a tender, aware woman." And as his seed sprang in her, his soul sprang towards her too, in the creative act that is far more than procreative.

She was quite determined now that there should be no parting between him and her. But the ways and means were still to settle.

"Did you hate Bertha Coutts?" she asked him.

"Don't talk to me about her."

"Yes! You must let me. Because once you liked her. And once you were as intimate with her as you are with me. So you have to tell me. Isn't it rather terrible, when you've been intimate with her, to hate her so? Why is it?"

"I don't know. She sort of kept her will ready against me, always, always: her ghastly female will: her freedom! A woman's ghastly freedom that ends in the most beastly bullying! Oh, she always kept her freedom against me, like vitriol in my face."

"But she's not free of you even now. Does she still love you?"

"No, no! If she's not free of me, it's because she's got that mad rage, she must try to bully me."

"But she must have loved you."

"No! Well, in specks, she did. She was drawn to me. And I think even that she hated. She loved me in moments. But she always took it back, and started bullying. Her deepest desire was to bully me, and there was no altering her. Her *will* was wrong, from the first."

"But perhaps she felt you didn't really love her, and she wanted to make you."

"My God, it was bloody making."

"But you didn't really love her, did you? You did her that wrong."

"How could I? I began to. I began to love her. But somehow, she always ripped me up. No, don't let's talk of it. It was a doom, that was. And she was a doomed woman. This last time, I'd have shot her like I shoot a stoat, if I'd but been allowed: a raving, doomed thing in the shape of a woman! If only I could have shot her, and ended the whole misery! It ought to be allowed. When a woman gets absolutely possessed by her own will, her own will set against everything, then it's fearful, and she should be shot at last."

"And shouldn't men be shot at last, if they get possessed by their own will."

"Ay!—the same! But I must get free of her, or she'll be at me again. I wanted to tell you. I must get a divorce if I possibly can. So we must be careful. We mustn't really be seen together, you and I. I never, *never* could stand it if she came down on me and you."

Connie pondered this.

"Then we can't be together?" she said.

"Not for six months or so. But I think my divorce will go through in September, then till March."

"But the baby will probably be born at the end of February," she said.

He was silent.

"I could wish the Cliffords and Berthas all dead," she said.

"It's not being very tender to them," she said.

"Tender to them? Yea, even then the tenderest thing you could do for them, perhaps, would be to give them death. They can't live. They only frustrate life. Their souls are awful inside them. Death ought to be sweet to them. And I ought to be allowed to shoot them."

"But you wouldn't do it," she said.

"I would though! and with less qualms than I shoot a weasel. It anyhow has a prettiness and a loneliness. But they are legion. Oh, I'd shoot them."

"Then perhaps it is just as well you daren't."

"Well."

Connie had now plenty to think of. It was evident he wanted absolutely to be free of Bertha Coutts. And she felt he was right. The last attack had been too grim.—This meant her living alone, till spring. Perhaps she could get divorced from Clifford. But how? If Mellors were named, then there was an end to *his* divorce. How loathsome! Couldn't one go right away, to the far ends of the earth, and be free from it all?

One could not. The far ends of the world are not five minutes from Charing Cross, nowadays. While the wireless is active, there are no far ends of the earth. Kings of Dahomey and Lamas of Tibet listen in to London and New York.

Patience! Patience! The world is a vast and ghastly intricacy of mechanism, and one has to be very wary, not to get mangled by it.

Connie confided in her father.

"You see, father, he was Clifford's gamekeeper: but he was an officer in the army in India. Only he is like Colonel C. E. Florence, who preferred to become a private soldier again."

Sir Malcolm, however, had no sympathy with the unsatisfactory mysticism of the famous C. E. Florence. He saw too much advertisement behind all the humility. It looked just the sort of conceit the knight most loathed, the conceit of self-abasement.

"Where did your gamekeeper spring from?" asked Sir Malcolm irritably.

"He was a collier's son in Tevershall. But he's absolutely presentable."

The knight artist became more angry.

"Looks to me like a gold-digger," he said. "And you're a pretty easy gold-mine, apparently."

"No, father, it's not like that. You'd know if you saw him. He's a man. Clifford always detested him for not being humble."

"Apparently he had a good instinct, for once."

What Sir Malcolm could not bear, was the scandal of his daughter's having an intrigue with a gamekeeper. He did not mind the intrigue: he minded the scandal.

"I care nothing about the fellow. He's evidently been able to get around you all right. But by God, think of all the talk. Think of your stepmother, how she'll take it!"

"I know," said Connie. "Talk is beastly: especially if you live in society. And he wants so much to get his own divorce. I thought we might perhaps say it was another man's child, and not mention Mellors' name at all."

"Another man's! What other man's?"

"Perhaps Duncan Forbes. He has been our friend all his life. And he's a fairly well-known artist. And he's fond of me."

"Well I'm damned! Poor Duncan. And what's he going to get out of it?"

"I don't know. But he might rather like it, even."

"He might, might he? Well, he's a funny man, if he does. Why, you've never had an affair with him, have you?"

"No! But he doesn't really want it. He only loves me to be near him, but not to touch him."

"My God, what a generation!"

"He would like me most of all to be a model for him to paint from. Only I never wanted to."

"God help him! But he looks down-trodden enough for anything."

"Still, you wouldn't mind so much the talk about him?"

"My God, Connie, all the bloody contriving!"

"I know! It's sickening! But what can I do?"

"Contriving, conniving; conniving, contriving! Makes a man think he's lived too long."

"Come, father, if you haven't done a good deal of contriving and conniving in your time, you may talk."

"But it was different, I assure you."

"It's *always* different."

Hilda arrived, also furious when she heard of the new developments. And she also simply could not stand the thought of a public scandal about her sister and a gamekeeper. Too, too humiliating!

"Why should we not just disappear, separately, to British Columbia, and have no scandal?" said Connie.

But that was no good. The scandal would come out just the same. And if Connie was going with the man, she'd better be able to marry him. This was Hilda's opinion. Sir Malcolm wasn't sure. The affair might still blow over.

"But will you see him, father?"

Poor Sir Malcolm! he was by no means keen on it. And poor Mellors, he was still less keen. Yet the meeting took place: lunch in a private room at the club, the two men alone, looking one another up and down.

Sir Malcolm drank a fair amount of whiskey, Mellors also drank. And they talked all the while about India, on which the younger man was well informed.

. This lasted during the meal. Only when coffee was served, and the waiter had gone, Sir Malcolm lit a cigar and said, heartily:

"Well, young man, and what about my daughter?"

The grin flickered on Mellors' face.

"Well, Sir, and what about her?"

"She's to have a child of yours, I understand."

"I have that honor!" grinned Mellors.

"Honor by God!" Sir Malcolm gave a little squirting laugh, and became Scotch and lewd. "Honor! How was the going, eh? Good, my boy, what?"

"Good!"

"I'll bet it was! Ha-ha! My daughter, chip of the old block, what! I never went back on a good bit of fucking, myself. Though her mother, oh, holy saints!" he rolled his eyes to heaven. "But you warmed her up, oh, you warmed her up, I can see that. Ha-ha! My blood in her! You set fire to her haystack all right. Ha-ha-ha! I was jolly glad of it, I can tell you. She needed it. Oh, she's a nice girl, she's a nice girl, and I knew she'd be good going, if only some damned man would set her stack on fire! Ha-ha-ha! A gamekeeper, oh, my boy! Bloody good poacher, if you ask me. Ha-ha! But now, look here, speaking seriously, what are we going to do about it? Speaking seriously, you know!"

Speaking seriously, they didn't get very far. Mellors, though a little tipsy, was much the soberer of the two. He kept the conversation as intelligent as possible: which isn't saying much.

"So you're a gamekeeper! Oh, you're quite right! That sort of game is worth a man's while, eh, what? The test of a woman is when you pinch her bottom. You can tell just by the feel of her bottom if she's going to come up all right. Ha-ha! I envy you, my boy. How old are you?"

"Thirty-nine."

The knight lifted his eyebrows.

"As much as that! Well, you've another good twenty years, by the look of you. Oh, gamekeeper or not, you're a good cock. I can see that with one eye shut. Not like that blasted Clifford! A lily-livered hound with never a fuck in him, never had. I like you, my boy. I'll bet you've a good cod on you: oh, you're a bantam, I can see that. You're a fighter. Gamekeeper! ha-ha, by crickey, I wouldn't trust my game to you! But look here, seriously, what are we going to do about it? The world's full of blasted old women."

Seriously, they didn't do anything about it, except establish the old freemasonry of male sensuality between them.

"And look here, my boy, if ever I can do anything for you, you can rely on me. Gamekeeper? Christ, but it's rich! I like it! Oh, I like it! Shows the girl's got spunk. What? After all, you know, she has her own income: moderate, moderate, but above starvation. And I'll leave her what I've got. By God, I will. She deserves it, for showing spunk, in a world of old women. I've been struggling to get myself clear of the skirts of old women for seventy years, and haven't managed it yet. But you're the man, I can see that."

"I'm glad you think so. They usually tell me, in a sideways fashion, that I'm the monkey."

"Oh, they would! My dear fellow, what could you be but a monkey, to all the old women."

They parted most genially, and Mellors laughed inwardly all the time for the rest of the day.

The following day he had lunch with Connie and Hilda at some discreet place.

"It's a very great pity it's such an ugly situation all round," said Hilda.

"I had a lot o' fun out of it," said he.

"I think you might have avoided putting children into the world until you were both free to marry and have children."

"The Lord blew a bit too soon on the spark," said he.

"I think the Lord had nothing to do with it. Of course, Connie has enough money to keep you both, but the situation is unbearable."

"But then, you don't have to bear more than a small corner of it, do you?" said he.

"If you'd been in her own class."

"Or if I'd been in a cage at the Zoo."

There was silence.

"I think," said Hilda, "it will be best if she names quite another man as co-respondent, and you stay out of it altogether."

"But I thought I'd put my foot right in."

"I mean, in the divorce proceedings."

He gazed at her in wonder. Connie had not dared mention the Duncan scheme to him.

"I don't follow," he said.

"We have a friend who would probably agree to be named as co-respondent, so that your name need not appear," said Hilda.

"You mean a man?"

"Of course!"

"But she's got no other?"

He looked in wonder at Connie.

"No, no!" she said hastily. "Only that old friendship, quite simple, no love."

"Then why should the fellow take the blame? If he's had nothing out of you?"

"Some men are chivalrous and don't only count what they get out of a woman," said Hilda.

"One for me, eh? But who's the johnny?"

"A friend whom we've known since we were children in Scotland, an artist."

"Duncan Forbes!" he said at once, for Connie had talked of him. "And how would you shift the blame on to him?"

"They could stay together in some hotel, or she could even stay in his apartment."

"Seems to me like a lot of fuss for nothing," he said.

"What else do you suggest?" said Hilda. "If your name appears, you will get no divorce from your wife, who is apparently quite an impossible person to be mixed up with."

"All that!" he said grimly.

There was a long silence.

"We could go right away," he said.

"There is no right away for Connie," said Hilda. "Clifford is too well known."

Again the silence of pure frustration.

"The world is what it is. If you want to live together without being persecuted, you will have to marry. To marry, you both have to be divorced. So how are you both going about it?"

He was silent for a long time.

"How are *you* going about it for us?" he said.

"We will see if Duncan will consent to figure as co-respondent: then we must get Clifford to divorce Connie: and you must go on with your divorce, and you must both keep apart till you are free."

"Sounds like a lunatic asylum."

"Possibly! And the world would look on you as lunatics: or worse."

"What is worse?"

"Criminals, I suppose."

"Hope I can plunge in the dagger a few more times yet," he said grinning. Then he was silent, and angry.

"Well!" he said at last. "I agree to anything. The world is a raving idiot, and no man can kill it: though I'll do my best. But you're right. We must rescue ourselves as best we can."

He looked in humiliation, anger, wariness and misery at Connie.

"Ma lass!" he said. "The world's goin' to put salt on thy tail."

"Not if we don't let it," she said.

She minded this conniving against the world less than he did.

Duncan, when approached, also insisted on seeing the delinquent game-keeper, so there was a dinner, this time in his flat: the four of them. Duncan was a rather short, broad, dark-skinned, taciturn Hamlet of a fellow with straight black hair and a weird Celtic conceit of himself. His art was all tubes and valves and spirals and strange colors, ultra modern, yet with a certain power, even a certain purity of form and tone: only Mellors thought it cruel and repellent. He did not venture to say so, for Duncan was almost insane on the point of his art; it was a personal cult, a personal religion with him.

They were looking at the pictures in the studio, and Duncan kept his small-ish brown eyes on the other man. He wanted to hear what the gamekeeper would say. He knew already Connie's and Hilda's opinions.

"It is like a pure bit of murder," said Mellors at last; a speech Duncan by no means expected from a gamekeeper.

"And who is murdered?" asked Hilda, rather coldly and sneeringly.

"Me! It murders all the bowels of compassion in a man."

A wave of pure hate came out of the artist. He heard the note of dislike in the other man's voice, and the note of contempt. And he himself loathed the men-tion of bowels of compassion. Sickly sentiment!

Mellors stood rather tall and thin, worn-looking, gazing with flickering de-tachment that was something like the dancing of a moth on the wing, at the pictures.

"Perhaps stupidity is murdered; sentimental stupidity," sneered the artist.

"Do you think so? I think all these tubes and corrugated vibrations are stupid enough for anything and pretty sentimental. They show a lot of self-pity and an awful lot of nervous self-opinion, seems to me."

In another wave of hate, the artist's face looked yellow. But with a sort of silent hauteur he turned the pictures to the wall.

"I think we may go to the dining-room," he said.

And they trailed off, dismally.

After coffee, Duncan said:

"I don't at all mind posing as the father of Connie's child. But only on the condition that she'll come and pose as a model for me. I've wanted her for years, and she's always refused." He uttered it with the dark finality of an inquisitor announcing an *auto da fé*.

"Ah!" said Mellors. "You only do it on condition, then?"

"Quite! I only do it on that condition." The artist tried to put the utmost contempt of the other person into his speech. He put a little too much.

"Better have me as a model at the same time," said Mellors. "Better do us in a group, Vulcan and Venus under the net of art. I used to be a blacksmith, before I was a gamekeeper."

"Thank you," said the artist. "I don't think Vulcan has a figure that inter-ests me."

"Not even if it was tubified and tittivated up?"

There was no answer. The artist was too haughty for further words.

It was a dismal party, in which the artist henceforth steadily ignored the presence of the other man, and talked only briefly, as if the words were wrung out of the depths of his gloomy portentousness, to the women.

"You didn't like him, but he's better than that, really. He's really kind," Connie explained as they left.

"He's a little black pup with a corrugated distemper," said Mellors.

"No, he wasn't nice today."

"And will you go and be a model to him?"

"Oh, I don't really mind any more. He won't touch me. And I don't mind anything, if it paves the way to a life together for you and me."

"But he'll only shit on you on canvas."

"I don't care. He'll only be painting his own feelings for me, and I don't mind if he does that. I wouldn't have him touch me, not for anything. But if he thinks he can do anything with his owlish arty staring, let him stare. He can make as many empty tubes and corrugations out of me as he likes. It's his funeral. He hated you for what you said: that his tubified art is sentimental and self-important. But of course it's true."

XIX

Dear Clifford, I am afraid what you foresaw has happened. I am really in love with another man, and I do hope you will divorce me. I am staying at present with Duncan in his flat. I told you he was at Venice with us. I'm awfully unhappy for your sake: but do try to take it quietly. You don't really need me any more, and I can't bear to come back to Wragby. I'm most awfully sorry. But do try to forgive me, and divorce me and find someone better. I'm not really the right person for you, I am too impatient and selfish, I suppose. But I can't ever come back to live with you again. And I feel so frightfully sorry about it all, for your sake. But if you don't let yourself get worked up, you'll see you won't mind so frightfully. You didn't really care about me personally. So do forgive me and get rid of me."

Clifford was not *inwardly* surprised to get this letter. Inwardly, he had known for a long time she was leaving him. But he had absolutely refused any outward admission of it. Therefore, outwardly, it came as the most terrible blow and shock to him. He had kept the surface of his confidence in her quite serene.

And that is how we are. By strength of will we cut off our inner intuitive knowledge from admitted consciousness. This causes a state of dread, or apprehension, which makes the blow ten times worse when it does fall.

Clifford was like a hysterical child. He gave Mrs. Bolton a terrible shock, sitting up in bed ghastly and blank.

"Why, Sir Clifford, whatever's the matter?"

No answer! She was terrified lest he had had a stroke. She hurried and felt his face, took his pulse.

"Is there a pain? Do try and tell me where it hurts you. Do tell me!"

No answer!

"Oh, dear! Oh, dear! Then I'll telephone to Sheffield for Dr. Carrington, and Dr. Lecky may as well run round straight away."

She was moving to the door, when he said in a hollow tone:

"No!"

She stopped and gazed at him. His face was yellow, blank, and like the face of an idiot.

"Do you mean you'd rather I didn't fetch the doctor?"

"Yes! I don't want him," came the sepulchral voice.

"Oh, but, Sir Clifford, you're ill, and I daren't take the responsibility. I *must* send for the doctor, or *I* shall be blamed."

A pause; then the hollow voice said:

"I'm not ill. My wife isn't coming back."—It was as if an image spoke.

"Not coming back? You mean her ladyship?" Mrs. Bolton moved a little nearer to the bed. "Oh, don't you believe it. You can trust her ladyship to come back."

The image in the bed did not change, but it pushed a letter over the counterpane.

"Read it!" said the sepulchral voice.

"Why, if it's a letter from her ladyship, I'm sure her ladyship wouldn't want me to read her letter to you, Sir Clifford. You can tell me what she says, if you wish."

But the face with the fixed blue eyes sticking out did not change.

"Read it!" repeated the voice.

"Why, if I must, I do it to obey you, Sir Clifford," she said.

And she read the letter.

"Well I *am* surprised at her ladyship," she said. "She promised so faithfully she'd come back!"

The face in the bed seemed to deepen its expression of wild, but motionless distraction. Mrs. Bolton looked at it and was worried. She knew what she was up against: male hysteria. She had not nursed soldiers without learning something about that very unpleasant disease.

She was a little impatient of Sir Clifford. Any man in his senses must have *known* his wife was in love with somebody else, and was going to leave him. Even, she was sure, Sir Clifford was inwardly absolutely aware of it, only he wouldn't admit it to himself. If he would have admitted it, and prepared himself for it! or if he would have admitted it, and actively struggled with his wife against it: that would have been acting like a man. But no! he knew it, and all the time tried to kid himself it wasn't so. He felt the devil twisting his tail, and pretended it was the angels smiling on him. This state of falsity had now brought on that crisis of falsity and dislocation, hysteria, which is a form of insanity. "It comes," she thought to herself, hating him a little, "because he always thinks of himself. He's so wrapped up in his own immortal self, that when he does get a shock he's like a mummy tangled in its own bandages. Look at him!"

But hysteria is dangerous: and she was a nurse, it was her duty to pull him out. Any attempt to rouse his manhood and his pride would only make him worse: for his manhood was dead, temporarily if not finally. He would only squirm softer and softer, like a worm, and become more dislocated.

The only thing was to release his self-pity. Like the lady in Tennyson, he must weep or he must die.

So Mrs. Bolton began to weep first. She covered her face with her hands and burst into little wild sobs. "I would never have believed it of her ladyship, I wouldn't!" She wept, suddenly summoning up all her old grief and sense of woe, and weeping the tears of her own bitter chagrin. Once she started her weeping was genuine enough, for she had had something to weep for.

Clifford thought of the way he had been betrayed by the woman Connie, and in a contagion of grief, tears filled his eyes and began to run down his cheeks. He was weeping for himself. Mrs. Bolton, as soon as she saw the tears running over his blank face, hastily wiped her own wet cheeks on her ltitle handkerchief, and leaned towards him.

"Now don't you fret, Sir Clifford!" she said, in a luxury of emotion. "Now, don't you fret; don't, you'll only do yourself an injury!"

His body shivered suddenly in an indrawn breath of silent sobbing, and the tears ran quicker down his face. She laid her hand on his arm, and her own tears fell again. Again the shiver went through him, like a convulsion, and she laid her arm round his shoulder. "There, there! There, there! Don't you fret, then, don't you! Don't you fret!" she moaned to him, while her own tears fell. And she drew him to her, and held her arms round his great shoulders, while he laid his face on her bosom and sobbed, shaking and hulking his huge shoulders, whilst she softly stroked his dusky-blond hair and said: "There! There! There! There, then! There, then! Never you mind! Never you mind, then!"

And he put his arms round her and clung to her like a child, wetting the bib of her starched white apron, and the bosom of her pale-blue cotton dress, with his tears. He had let himself go altogether, at last.

So at length she kissed him, and rocked him on her bosom, and in her heart she said to herself: "Oh, Sir Clifford! Oh, high and mighty Chatterleys! Is this what you've come down to!" And finally he even went to sleep, like a child. And she felt worn out, and went to her own room, where she laughed and cried at once with a hysteria of her own. It was so ridiculous! It was so awful! such a come-down! so shameful! And it *was* so upsetting as well.

After this, Clifford became like a child with Mrs. Bolton. He would hold her hand, and rest his head on her breast, and when she once lightly kissed him, he said: "Yes! Do kiss me! Do kiss me!" And when she sponged his great blond body, he would say the same: "Do kiss me!" and she would lightly kiss his body, anywhere, half in mockery.

And he lay with a queer, blank face like a child, with a bit of the wonderment of a child. And he would gaze on her with wide, childish eyes, in a relaxation of madonna-worship. It was sheer relaxation on his part, letting go all his manhood, and sinking back to a childish position that was really perverse. And then he would put his hand into her bosom and feel her breasts, and kiss them in exalttion, the exaltation of perversity of being a child when he was a man.

Mrs. Bolton was both thrilled and ashamed, she both loved and hated it. Yet she never rebuffed nor rebuked him. And they drew into a closer physical intimacy, an intimacy of perversity, when he was a child stricken with an apparent candor and an apparent wonderment, that looked almost like a religious exaltation: the perverse and literal rendering of "except ye become again as a little child."—While she was the Magna Mater, full of power and potency, having the great blond child-man under her will and her stroke entirely.

The curious thing was that when this child-man, which Clifford was now and which he had been becoming for years, emerged into the world, he was much sharper and keener than the real man he used to be. This perverted child-man was now a *real* business man; when it was a question of affairs, he was an absolute he-man, sharp as a needle, and impervious as a bit of steel. When he was out among men, seeking his own ends, and "making good" his colliery workings, he had an almost uncanny shrewdness, hardness, and a straight sharp punch. It was as if his very passivity and prostitution to the Magna Mater gave him insight into material business affairs, and lent him a certain remarkable inhuman force. The wallowing in private emotion, the utter abasement of his manly self, seemed to lend him a second nature, cold, almost visionary, business-clever. In business he was quite inhuman.

And in this Mrs. Bolton triumphed. "How he's getting on!" she would say to herself in pride. "And that's my doing! My word, he'd never have got on like this with Lady Chatterley. She was not the one to put a man forward. She wanted too much for herself."

At the same time, in some corner of her weird female soul, how she despised him and hated him! He was to her the fallen beast, the squirming monster. And while she aided and abetted him all she could, away in the remotest corner of her ancient healthy womanhood she despised him with a savage contempt that knew no bounds. The merest tramp was better than he.

His behavior with regard to Connie was curious. He insisted on seeing her again. He insisted, moreover, on her coming to Wragby. On this point he was finally and absolutely fixed. Connie had promised to come back to Wragby, faithfully.

"But is it any use?" said Mrs. Bolton. "Can't you let her go, and be rid of her?"

"No! She said she was coming back, and she's got to come."

Mrs. Bolton opposed him no more. She knew what she was dealing with.

"I needn't tell you what effect your letter has had on me," he wrote to Connie to London. "Perhaps you can imagine it if you try, though no doubt you won't trouble to use your imagination on my behalf.

"I can only say one thing in answer: I must see you personally, here at Wragby, before I can do anything. You promised faithfully to come back to Wragby, and I hold you to the promise. I don't believe anything nor understand anything until I see you personally, here under normal circumstances. I needn't tell you that nobody here suspects anything, so your return would be quite normal. Then if you feel, after we have talked things over, that you still remain in the same mind, no doubt we can come to terms."

Connie showed this letter to Mellors.

"He wants to begin his revenge on you," said he, handing the letter back.

Connie was silent. She was somewhat surprised to find that she was afraid of Clifford. She was afraid to go near him. She was afraid of him as if he were evil and dangerous.

"What shall I do?" she said.

"Nothing, if you don't want to do anything."

She replied, trying to put Clifford off. He answered: "If you don't come back to Wragby now, I shall consider that you are coming back one day, and act accordingly. I shall just go on the same, and wait for you here, if I wait for fifty years."

She was frightened. This was bullying of an insidious sort. She had no doubt he meant what he said. He would not divorce her, and the child would be his, unless she could find some means of establishing its illegitimacy.

After a time of worry and harassment, she decided to go to Wragby. Hilda would go with her. She wrote this to Clifford. He replied: "I shall not welcome your sister, but I shall not deny her the door. I have no doubt she has connived at your desertion of your duties and responsibilities, so do not expect me to show pleasure in seeing her."

They went to Wragby. Clifford was away when they arrived. Mrs. Bolton received them.

"Oh, your Ladyship, it isn't the happy home-coming we hoped for, is it?" she said.

"Isn't it!" said Connie.

So this woman knew! How much did the rest of the servants know or suspect?

She entered the house which now she hated with every fiber in her body. The great, rambling mass of a place seemed evil to her, just a menace over her. She was no longer its mistress, she was its victim.

"I can't stay long here," she whispered to Hilda, terrified.

And she suffered going into her own bedroom, re-entering into possession as if nothing had happened. She hated every minute inside the Wragby walls.

They did not meet Clifford till they went down to dinner. He was dressed, and with a black tie: rather reserved, and very much the superior gentleman. He behaved perfectly politely during the meal, and kept a polite sort of conversation going: but it seemed all touched with insanity.

"How much do the servants know?" asked Connie when the woman was out of the room.

"Of your intentions? Nothing whatsoever."

"Mrs. Bolton knows."

He changed color.

"Mrs. Bolton is not exactly one of the servants," he said.

"Oh, I don't mind."

There was tension till after coffee, when Hilda said she would go up to her room.

Clifford and Connie sat in silence when she had gone. Neither would begin to speak. Connie was so glad that he wasn't taking the pathetic line, she kept him up to as much haughtiness as possible. She just sat silent and looked down at her hands.

"I suppose you don't at all mind having gone back on your word?" he said at last.

"I can't help it," she murmured.

"But if you can't, who can?"

"I suppose nobody."

He looked at her with curious cold rage. He was used to her. She was as it were embedded in his will. How dared she now go back on him, and destroy the fabric of his daily existence? How dared she try to cause this derangement of his personality!

"And for *what* do you want to go back on everything?" he insisted.

"Love!" she said. It was best to be hackneyed.

"Love of Duncan Forbes? But you didn't think that worth having, when you met me. Do you mean to say you now love him better than anything else in life?"

"One changes," she said.

"Possibly! Possibly you may have whims. But you still have to convince me of the importance of the change. I merely don't believe in your love of Duncan Forbes."

"But why *should* you believe in it? You have only to divorce me, not to believe in my feelings."

"And why should I divorce you?"

"Because I don't want to live here any more. And you really don't want me."

"Pardon me! I don't change. For my part, since you are my wife, I should prefer that you should stay under my roof in dignity and quiet. Leaving aside personal feelings, and I assure you, on my part it is leaving aside a great deal, it is bitter as death to me to have this order of life broken up, here in Wragby, and the decent round of daily life smashed, just for some whim of yours."

After a time of silence she said:

"I can't help it. I've got to go. I expect I shall have a child." He, too, was silent for a time.

"And is it for the child's sake you must go?" he asked at length.

She nodded.

"And why? Is Duncan Forbes so keen on his spawn?"

"Surely keener than you would be," she said.

"But really? I want my wife, and I see no reason for letting her go. If she likes to bear a child under my roof, she is welcome, and the child is welcome, provided that the decency and order of life is preserved. Do you mean to tell me that Duncan Forbes has a greater hold over you? I don't believe it."

There was a pause.

"But don't you see," said Connie. "I *must* go away from you, and I *must* live with the man I love."

"No, I don't see it! I don't give tuppence for your love, nor for the man you love. I don't believe in that sort of cant."

"But, you see, I do."

"Do you? My dear Madam, you are too intelligent, I assure you, to believe in your own love for Duncan Forbes. Believe me, even now you really care more for me. So why should I give in to such nonsense!"

She felt he was right there. And she felt she could keep silent no longer.

"Because it isn't Duncan that I *do* love," she said, looking up at him. "We only said it was Duncan, to spare your feelings."

"To spare my feelings?"

"Yes! Because who I really love, and it'll make you hate me, is Mr. Mellors, who was our gamekeeper here."

If he could have sprung out of his chair, he would have done so. His face went yellow, and his eyes bulged with disaster as he glared at her.

Then he dropped back in the chair, gasping and looking up at the ceiling.

At length he sat up.

"Do you mean to say you're telling me the truth?" he asked, looking gruesome.

"Yes! You know I am."

"And when did you begin with him?"

"In the spring."

He was silent like some beast in a trap.

"And it *was* you, then, in the bedroom at the cottage?"

So he had really inwardly known all the time.

"Yes!"

He still leaned forward in his chair, gazing at her like a cornered beast.

"My God, you ought to be wiped off the face of the earth!"

"Why?" she ejaculated faintly.

But he seemed not to hear her.

"That scum! That bumptious lout! That miserable cad! And carrying on with him all the time, while you were here and he was one of my servants! My God, my God, is there any limit to the beastly lowness of women!"

He was beside himself with rage, as she knew he would be.

"And you mean to say you want to have a child to a cad like that?"

"Yes! I'm going to."

"You're going to! You mean you're sure! How long have you been sure?"

"Since June."

He was speechless, and the queer blank look of a child came over him again.

"You'd wonder," he said at last, "that such beings were ever allowed to be born."

"What beings?" she asked.

He looked at her weirdly, without an answer. It was obvious he couldn't even accept the fact of the existence of Mellors, in any connection with his own life. It was sheer, unspeakable, impotent hate.

"And do you mean to say you'd marry him?—and bear his foul name?" he asked at length.

"Yes, that's what I want."

He was again as if dumbfounded.

"Yes!" he said at last. "That proves what I've always thought about you is correct: you're not normal, you're not in your right senses. You're one of those half-insane, perverted women who must run after depravity, the *nostalgie de la boue.*"

Suddenly he had become almost wistfully moral, seeing himself the incarnation of good, and people like Mellors and Connie the incarnation of mud, of evil. He seemed to be growing vague, inside a nimbus.

"So don't you think you'd better divorce me and have done with it?" she said.

"No! You can go where you like, but I shan't divorce you," he said idiotically.

"Why not?"

He was silent, in the silence of imbecile obstinacy.

"Would you even let the child be legally yours, and your heir?" she said.

"I care nothing about the child."

"But if it's a boy it will be legally your son, and it will inherit your title, and have Wragby."

"I care nothing about that," he said.

"But you *must!* I shall prevent the child from being legally yours, if I can. I'd so much rather it were illegitimate and mine: if it can't be Mellors'."

"Do as you like about that."

He was immovable.

"And won't you divorce me?" she said. "You can use Duncan as a pretext! There'd be no need to bring in the real name. Duncan doesn't mind."

"*I* shall never divorce you," he said, as if a nail had been driven in.

"But why? Because I want you to?"

"Because I follow my own inclination, and I'm not inclined to."

It was useless. She went upstairs, and told Hilda the upshot.

"Better get away tomorrow," said Hilda, "and let him come to his senses."

So Connie spent half the night packing her really private and personal effects. In the morning she had her trunks sent to the station, without telling Clifford. She decided to see him only to say good-bye, before lunch.

But she spoke to Mrs. Bolton.

"I must say good-bye to you, Mrs. Bolton. You know why, but I can trust you not to talk."

"Oh, you can trust me, your Ladyship, though it's a sad blow for us here, indeed. But I hope you'll be happy with the other gentleman."

"The other gentleman! It's Mr. Mellors, and I care for him. Sir Clifford knows. But don't say anything to anybody. And if one day you think Sir Clifford may be willing to divorce me, let me know, will you? I should like to be properly married to the man I care for."

"I'm sure you would, my Lady. Oh, you can trust me. I'll be faithful to Sir Clifford, and I'll be faithful to you, for I can see you're both right in your own ways."

"Thank you! And look! I want to give you this—may I?—" So Connie left Wragby once more, and went on with Hilda to Scotland. Mellors went into the country and got work on a farm. The idea was, he should get his divorce, if possible, whether Connie got hers or not. And for six months he should work at farming, so that eventually he and Connie could have some small farm of their own, into which he could put his energy. For he would have to have some work, even hard work, to do, and he would have to make his own living, even if her capital started him.

So they would have to wait till spring was in, till the baby was born, till the early summer came round again.

The Grange Farm,
Old Heanor, 29 September.

"*I got on here with a bit of contriving, because I knew Richards, the company engineer, in the army. It is a farm belonging to Butler & Smitham Colliery Company, they use it for raising hay and oats for the pit-ponies; not a private concern. But they've got cows and pigs and all the rest of it, and I get thirty shillings a week as laborer. Rowley, the farmer, puts me on to as many jobs as he can, so that I can learn as much as possible between now and next Easter. I've not heard a thing about Bertha. I've no idea why she didn't show up at the divorce, nor where she is nor what she's up to. But if I keep quiet till March I suppose I shall be free. And don't you bother about Sir Clifford. He'll want to get rid of you one of these days. If he leaves you alone, it's a lot.*

"*I've got lodgings in a bit of an old cottage in Engine Row, very decent. The man is engine-driver at High Park, tall, with a beard, and very chapel. The woman is a birdy bit of a thing who loves anything superior, King's English and allow-me! all the time. But they lost their only son in the war, and it's sort of knocked a hole in them. There's a long gawky lass of a daughter training for a school teacher, and I help her with her lessons sometimes, so we're quite the family. But they're very decent people, and only too kind to me. I expect I'm more coddled than you are.*

"*I like farming all right. It's not inspiring, but then I don't ask to be inspired. I'm used to horses, and cows, though they are very female, have a soothing effect on me. When I sit with my head in her side, milking, I feel very solaced. They have six rather fine Herefords. Oat-harvest is just over and I enjoyed it, in spite of sore hands and a lot of rain. I don't take much notice of people, but get on with them all right. Most things one just ignores.*

"*The pits are working badly; this is a colliery district like Tevershall, only prettier. I sometimes sit in the Wellington and talk to the men. They grumble a lot, but they're not going to alter anything. As everybody says, the Notts-Derby miners have got their hearts in the right place. But the rest of their anatomy must be in*

*the wrong place, in a world that has no use for them. I like them, but they don't
cheer me much: not enough of the old fighting-cock in them. They talk a lot about
nationalism, nationalization of royalties, nationalization of the whole industry.
But you can't nationalize coal and leave all the other industries as they are. They
talk about putting coal to new uses, like Sir Clifford is trying to do. It may work
here and there, but not as a general thing, I doubt. Whatever you make you've got
to sell it. The men are very apathetic. They feel the whole damned thing is doomed,
and I believe it is. And they are doomed along with it. Some of the young ones
spout about a Soviet, but there's not much conviction in them. There's no sort of
conviction about anything, except that it's all a muddle and a hole. Even under a
Soviet you've still got to sell coal: and that's the difficulty.*

*"We've got this great industrial population, and they've got to be fed, so the
damn show has to be kept going somehow. The women talk a lot more than the
men nowadays, and they are a sight more cocksure. The men are limp, they feel a
doom somewhere, and they go about as if there was nothing to be done. Anyhow
nobody knows what should be done, in spite of all the talk. The young ones get
mad because they've no money to spend. Their whole life depends on spending
money, and now they've got none to spend. That's our civilization and our education: bring up the masses to depend entirely on spending money, and then the
money gives out. The pits are working two days, two-and-a-half days a week, and
there's no sign of betterment even for the winter. It means a man bringing up a
family on twenty-five and thirty shillings. The women are the maddest of all. But
then they're the maddest for spending, nowadays.*

*"If you could only tell them that living and spending isn't the same thing! But
it's no good. If only they were educated to live instead of earn and spend, they
could manage very happily on twenty-five shillings. If the men wore scarlet trousers, as I said, they wouldn't think so much of money: if they could dance and hop
and skip, and sing and swagger and be handsome, they could do with very little
cash. And amuse the women themselves, and be amused by the women. They
ought to learn to be naked and handsome, and to sing in a mass and dance the old
group dances, and carve the stools they sit on, and embroider their own emblems.
Then they wouldn't need money. And that's the only way to solve the industrial
problem: train the people to be able to live, and live in handsomeness, without
needing to spend. But you can't do it. They're all one-track minds nowadays.
Whereas the mass of people oughtn't even to try to think, because they can't! They
should be alive and frisky, and acknowledge the great god Pan. He's the only god
for the masses, forever. The few can go in for higher cults if they like. But let the
mass be forever pagan.*

*"But the colliers aren't pagan, far from it. They're a sad lot, a deadened lot of
men: dead to their women, dead to life. The young ones scoot about on motorbikes
with girls, and jazz when they get a chance. But they're very dead. And it needs
money. Money poisons you when you've got it, and starves you when you
haven't.*

*"I'm sure you're sick of all this. But I don't want to harp on myself, and I've
nothing happening to me. I don't like to think too much about you, in my head,
that only makes a mess of us both. But of course what I live for now is for you and
me to live together. I'm frightened, really. I feel the devil in the air, and he'll try to
get us. Or not the devil, Mammon: which I think, after all, is only the mass-will
of people, wanting money and hating life. Anyhow I feel great grasping white
hands in the air, wanting to get hold of the throat of anybody who tries to live, to
live beyond money, and squeeze the life out. There's a bad time coming. There's*

a bad time coming, boys, there's a bad time coming! If things go on as they are, there's nothing lies in the future but death and destruction, for these industrial masses. I feel my inside turn to water sometimes, and there you are, going to have a child by me. But never mind. All the bad times that ever have been, haven't been able to blow the crocus out: not even the love of women. So they won't be able to blow out my wanting you, nor the little glow there is between you and me. We'll be together next year. And though I'm frightened, I believe in your being with me. A man has to fend and fettle for the best, and then trust in something beyond himself. You can't insure against the future, except by really believing in the best bit of you, and in the power beyond it. So I believe in the little flame between us. For me now, it's the only thing in the world. I've got no friends, not inward friends. Only you. And now the little flame is all I care about in my life. There's the baby, but that is a side issue. It's my Pentecost, the forked flame between me and you. The old Pentecost isn't quite right. Me and God is a bit uppish, somehow. But the little forked flame between me and you: there you are! That's what I abide by, and will abide by, Cliffords and Berthas, colliery companies and governments and the money-mass of people all notwithstanding.

"That's why I don't like to start thinking about you actually. It only tortures me, and does you no good. I don't want you to be away from me. But if I start fretting it wastes something. Patience, always patience. This is my fortieth winter. And I can't help all the winters that have been. But this winter I'll stick to my little pentecost flame, and have some peace. And I won't let the breath of people blow it out. I believe in a higher mystery, that doesn't let even the crocus be blown out. And if you're in Scotland and I'm in the Midlands, and I can't put my arms round you, and wrap my legs round you, yet I've got something of you. My soul softly flaps in the little pentecost flame with you, like the peace of fucking. We fucked a flame into being. Even the flowers are fucked into being between the sun and the earth. But it's a delicate thing, and takes patience and the long pause.

"So I love chastity now, because it is the peace that comes of fucking. I love being chaste now. I love it as snowdrops love the snow. I love this chastity, which is the pause of peace of our fucking, between us now like a snowdrop of forked white fire. And when the real spring comes, when the drawing together comes, then we can fuck the little flame brilliant and yellow, brilliant. But not now, not yet! Now is the time to be chaste, it is so good to be chaste, like a river of cool water in my soul. I love the chastity now that it flows between us. It is like fresh water and rain. How can men want wearisomely to philander! What a misery to be like Don Juan, and impotent ever to fuck oneself into peace, and the little flame alight, impotent and unable to be chaste in the cool between-whiles, as by a river.

"Well, so many words, because I can't touch you. If I could sleep with my arms round you, the ink could stay in the bottle. We could be chaste together just as we can fuck together. But we have to be separate for a while, and I suppose it is really the wiser way. If only one were sure.

"Never mind, never mind, we won't get worked up. We really trust in the little flame, in the unnamed god that shields it from being blown out. There's so much of you here with me, really, that it's a pity you aren't all here.

"Never mind about Sir Clifford. If you don't hear anything from him, never mind. He can't really do anything to you. Wait, he will want to get rid of you at last, to cast you out. And if he doesn't, we'll manage to keep clear of him. But he will. In the end he will want to spew you out as the abominable thing.

"*Now I can't even leave off writing to you.*

"*But a great deal of us is together, and we can but abide by it, and steer our courses to meet soon. John Thomas says good night to lady Jane, a little droopingly, but with a hopeful heart.*"

The
Rainbow

Contents

I

Chapter I
How Tom Brangwen Married
a Polish Lady

The Brangwens had lived for generations on the Marsh Farm, in the meadows where the Erewash twisted sluggishly through alder trees, separating Derbyshire from Nottinghamshire. Two miles away, a church-tower stood on a hill, the houses of the little country town climbing assiduously up to it. Whenever one of the Brangwens in the fields lifted his head from his work, he saw the church-tower at Ilkeston in the empty sky. So that as he turned again to the horizontal land, he was aware of something standing above him and beyond him in the distance.

There was a look in the eyes of the Brangwens as if they were expecting something unknown, about which they were eager. They had that air of readiness for what would come to them, a kind of surety, an expectancy, the look of an inheritor.

They were fresh, blond, slow-speaking people, revealing themselves plainly, but slowly, so that one could watch the change in their eyes from laughter to anger, blue, lit-up laughter, to a hard blue-staring anger; through all the irresolute stages of the sky when the weather is changing.

Living on rich land, on their own land, near to a growing town, they had forgotten what it was to be in straitened circumstances. They had never become rich, because there were always children, and the patrimony was divided every time. But always, at the Marsh, there was ample.

So the Brangwens came and went without fear of necessity, working hard because of the life that was in them, not for want of the money. Neither were they thriftless. They were aware of the last halfpenny, and instinct made them not waste the peeling of their apple, for it would help to feed the cattle. But heaven and earth was teeming around them, and how should this cease? They felt the rush of the sap in spring, they knew the wave which cannot halt, but every year throws forward the seed to begetting, and, falling back, leaves the young-born on the earth. They knew the intercourse between heaven and earth, sunshine drawn into the breast and bowels, the rain sucked up in the daytime, nakedness that comes under the wind in autumn, showing the birds' nests no longer worth hiding. Their life and interrelations were such; feeling the pulse and body of the soil, that opened to their furrow for the grain, and became smooth and supple after their ploughing, and clung to their feet with a weight that pulled like desire, lying hard and unresponsive when the crops were to be shorn away. The young corn waved and was silken, and the lustre slid along the limbs of the men who saw it. They took the udder of the cows, the cows yielded milk and pulse against the hands of the men, the pulse of the blood of the teats of the cows beat into the pulse of the hands of the men. They mounted their horses, and held life between the grip of their knees, they harnessed their horses at the wagon, and, with hand on the bridle-rings, drew the heaving of the horses after their will.

In autumn the partridges whirred up, birds in flocks blew like spray across the fallow, rooks appeared on the grey, watery heavens, and flew cawing into the winter. Then the men sat by the fire in the house where the women moved about with surety, and the limbs and the body of the men were impregnated with the day, cattle and earth and vegetation and the sky, the men sat by the fire and their brains were inert, as their blood flowed heavy with the accumulation from the living day.

The women were different. On them too was the drowse of blood-intimacy, calves sucking and hens running together in droves, and young geese palpitating in the hand while the food was pushed down their throttle. But the women looked out from the heated, blind intercourse of farm-life, to the spoken world beyond. They were aware of the lips and the mind of the world speaking and giving utterance, they heard the sound in the distance, and they strained to listen.

It was enough for the men, that the earth heaved and opened its furrow to them, that the wind blew to dry the wet wheat, and set the young ears of corn wheeling freshly round about; it was enough that they helped the cow in labour, or ferreted the rats from under the barn, or broke the back of a rabbit with a sharp knock of the hand. So much warmth and generating and pain and death did they know in their blood, earth and sky and beast and green plants, so much exchange and interchange they had with these, that they lived full and surcharged, their senses full fed, their faces always turned to the heat of the blood, staring into the sun, dazed with looking towards the source of generation, unable to turn round.

But the woman wanted another form of life than this, something that was not blood-intimacy. Her house faced out from the farm-buildings and fields, looked out to the road and the village with church and Hall and the world beyond. She stood to see the far-off world of cities and governments and the active scope of man, the magic land to her, where secrets were made known and desires fulfilled. She faced outwards to where men moved dominant and creative, having turned their back on the pulsing heat of creation, and with this behind them, were set out to discover what was beyond, to enlarge their own scope and range and freedom; whereas the Brangwen men faced inwards to the teeming life of creation, which poured unresolved into their veins.

Looking out, as she must, from the front of her house towards the activity of man in the world at large, whilst her husband looked out to the back at sky and harvest and beast and land, she strained her eyes to see what man had done in fighting outwards to knowledge, she strained to hear how he uttered himself in his conquest, her deepest desire hung on the battle that she heard, far off, being waged on the edge of the unknown. She also wanted to know, and to be of the fighting host.

At home, even so near as Cossethay, was the vicar, who spoke the other, magic language, and had the other, finer bearing, both of which she could perceive, but could never attain to. The vicar moved in worlds beyond where her own menfolk existed. Did she not know her own menfolk: fresh, slow, full-built men, masterful enough, but easy, native to the earth, lacking outwardness and range of motion. Whereas the vicar, dark and dry and small beside her husband, had yet a quickness and a range of being that made Brangwen, in his large geniality, seem dull and local. She knew her husband. But in the vicar's nature was that which passed beyond her knowledge. As Brangwen had power over the cattle so the vicar had power over her husband. What was it in the vicar, that raised him above the common men as man is raised above the beast? She craved to know. She craved to achieve this higher being, if not in herself, then in her children. That which makes a man strong even if he be little and frail in body, just as any man is little and frail beside a bull, and yet stronger than the bull, what was it? It was not money nor power nor position. What power had the vicar over Tom Brangwen—none. Yet strip them and set them on a desert island, and the vicar was the master. His soul was master of the other man's. And why—why? She decided it was a question of knowledge.

The curate was poor enough, and not very efficacious as a man, either, yet he took rank with those others, the superior. She watched his children being born, she saw them running as tiny things beside their mother. And already they were separate from her own children, distinct. Why were her own children marked below the others? Why should the curate's children inevitably take precedence over her children, why should dominance be given them from the start? It was not money, nor even class. It was education and experience, she decided.

It was this, this education, this higher form of being, that the mother wished to give to her children, so that they too could live the supreme life on earth. For her children, at least the children of her heart, had the complete nature that should take place in equality with the living, vital people in the land, not be left behind obscure among the labourers. Why must they remain obscured and stifled all their lives, why should they suffer from lack of freedom to move? How should they learn the entry into the finer, more vivid circle of life?

Her imagination was fired by the squire's lady at Shelly Hall, who came to church at Cossethay with her little children, girls in tidy capes of beaver fur, and smart little hats, herself like a winter rose, so fair and delicate. So fair, so fine in mould, so luminous, what was it that Mrs. Hardy felt which she, Mrs. Brangwen, did not feel? How was Mrs. Hardy's nature different from that of the common women of Cossethay, in what was it beyond them? All the women of Cossethay talked eagerly about Mrs. Hardy, of her husband, her children, her guests, her dress, of her servants and her housekeeping. The lady of the Hall was the living dream of their lives, her life was the epic that inspired their lives. In her they lived imaginatively, and in gossiping of her husband who drank, of her scandalous brother, of Lord William Bentley her friend, member of Parliament for the division, they had their own Odyssey enacting itself, Penelope and Ulysses before them, and Circe and the swine and the endless web.

So the women of the village were fortunate. They saw themselves in the lady of the manor, each of them lived her own fulfilment of the life of Mrs. Hardy. And the Brangwen wife of the Marsh aspired beyond herself, towards the further life of the finer woman, towards the extended being she revealed, as a traveller in his self-contained manner reveals far-off countries present in himself. But why should a knowledge of far-off countries make a man's life a different thing, finer, bigger? And why is a man more than the beast and the cattle that serve him? It is the same thing.

The male part of the poem was filled in by such men as the vicar and Lord William, lean, eager men with strange movements, men who had command of the further fields, whose lives ranged over a great extent. Ah, it was something very desirable to know, this touch of the wonderful men who had the power of thought and comprehension. The women of the village might be much fonder of Tom Brangwen, and more at their ease with him, yet if their lives had been robbed of the vicar, and of Lord William, the leading shoot would have been cut away from them, they would have been heavy and uninspired and inclined to hate. So long as the wonder of the beyond was before them, they could get along, whatever their lot. And Mrs. Hardy, and the vicar, and Lord William, these moved in the wonder of the beyond, and were visible to the eyes of Cossethay in their motion.

Chapter II

About 1840, a canal was constructed across the meadows of the Marsh Farm, connect᠎ ᠎g the newly-opened collieries of the Erewash Valley. A high embankment tra᠎.᠎lled along the fields to carry the canal, which passed close to the homestead, and, reaching the road, went over in a heavy bridge.

So the Marsh was shut off from Ilkeston, and enclosed in the small valley bed, which ended in a bushy hill and the village spire of Cossethay.

The Brangwens received a fair sum of money from this trespass across their land. Then, a short time afterwards, a colliery was sunk on the other side of the canal, and in a while the Midland Railway came down the valley at the foot of the Ilkeston hill, and the invasion was complete. The town grew rapidly, the Brangwens were kept busy producing supplies, they became richer, they were almost tradesmen.

Still the Marsh remained remote and original, on the old, quiet side of the canal embankment, in the sunny valley where slow water wound along in company of stiff alders, and the road went under ash-trees past the Brangwens' garden gate.

But, looking from the garden gate down the road to the right, there, through the dark archway of the canal's square aqueduct, was a colliery spinning away in the near distance, and further, red, crude houses plastered on the valley in masses, and beyond all, the dim smoking hill of the town.

The homestead was just on the safe side of civilisation, outside the gate. The house stood bare from the road, approached by a straight garden path, along which at spring the daffodils were thick in green and yellow. At the sides of the house were bushes of lilac and guelder-rose and privet, entirely hiding the farm buildings behind.

At the back a confusion of sheds spread into the home-close from out of two or three indistinct yards. The duckpond lay beyond the furthest wall, littering its white feathers on the padded earthen banks, blowing its stray soiled feathers into the grass and the gorse bushes below the canal embankment, which rose like a high rampart near at hand, so that occasionally a man's figure passed in silhouette, or a man and a towing horse traversed the sky.

At first the Brangwens were astonished by all this commotion around them. The building of a canal across their land made them strangers in their own place, this raw bank of earth shutting them off disconcerted them. As they worked in the fields, from beyond the now familiar embankment came the rhythmic run of the winding engines, startling at first, but afterwards a narcotic to the brain. Then the shrill whistle of the trains re-echoed through the heart, with fearsome pleasure, announcing the far-off come near and imminent.

As they drove home from town, the farmers of the land met the blackened colliers trooping from the pit-mouth. As they gathered the harvest, the west wind brought a faint, sulphurous smell of pit-refuse burning. As they pulled the turnips in November, the sharp clink-clink-clink-clink-clink of empty trucks shunting on the line, vibrated in their hearts with the fact of other activity going on beyond them.

The Alfred Brangwen of this period had married a woman from Heanor, a daughter of the "Black Horse". She was a slim, pretty, dark woman, quaint in her speech, whimsical, so that the sharp things she said did not hurt. She was oddly a thing to herself, rather querulous in her manner, but intrinsically separate and indifferent, so that her long lamentable complaints, when she raised her voice against her husband in particular and against everybody else after him, only made those who heard her wonder and feel affectionately towards her, even while they were irritated and impatient with her. She railed long and loud about her husband, but always with a balanced, easy-flying voice and a quaint manner of speech that warmed his belly with pride and male triumph while he scowled with mortification at the things she said.

Consequently Brangwen himself had a humorous puckering at the eyes, a sort of fat laugh, very quiet and full, and he was spoilt like a lord of creation. He calmly did as he liked, laughed at their railing, excused himself in a teasing tone that she loved, followed his natural inclinations, and sometimes, pricked too near the quick, frightened and broke her by a deep, tense fury which seemed to fix on him and hold him for days, and which she would give anything to placate in him. They were two very separate beings, vitally connected, knowing nothing of each other, yet living in their separate ways from one root.

There were four sons and two daughters. The eldest boy ran away early to sea, and did not come back. After this the mother was more the node and centre of attraction in the home. The second boy, Alfred, whom the mother admired most, was the most reserved. He was sent to school in Ilkeston and made some progress. But in spite of his dogged, yearning effort, he could not get beyond the rudiments of anything, save of drawing. At this, in which he had some power, he worked, as if it were his hope. After much grumbling and savage rebellion against everything, after much trying and shifting about, when his father was incensed against him and his mother almost despairing, he became a draughtsman in a lace-factory in Nottingham.

He remained heavy and somewhat uncouth, speaking with broad Derbyshire accent, adhering with all his tenacity to his work and to his town position, making good designs, and becoming fairly well-off. But at drawing, his hand swung naturally in big, bold lines, rather lax, so that it was cruel for him to pedgill away at the lace designing, working from the tiny squares of his paper, counting and plotting and niggling. He did it stubbornly, with anguish, crushing the bowels within him, adhering to his chosen lot whatever it should cost. And he came back into life set and rigid, a rare-spoken, almost surly man.

He married the daughter of a chemist, who affected some social superiority, and he became something of a snob, in his dogged fashion, with a passion for outward refinement in the household, mad when anything clumsy or gross occurred. Later, when his three children were growing up, and he seemed a staid, almost middle-aged man, he turned after strange women, and became a silent, inscrutable follower of forbidden pleasure, neglecting his indignant bourgeois wife without a qualm.

Frank, the third son, refused from the first to have anything to do with learning. From the first he hung round the slaughter-house which stood away in the third yard at the back of the farm. The Brangwens had always killed their own meat, and supplied the neighbourhood. Out of this grew a regular butcher's business in connection with the farm.

As a child Frank had been drawn by the trickle of dark blood that ran across the pavement from the slaughter-house to the crew-yard, by the sight of the man carrying across to the meat-shed a huge side of beef, with the kidneys showing, embedded in their heavy laps of fat.

He was a handsome lad with soft brown hair and regular features something like a later Roman youth. He was more easily excitable, more readily carried away than the rest, weaker in character. At eighteen he married a little factory girl, a pale, plump, quiet thing with sly eyes and a wheedling voice, who insinuated herself into him and bore him a child every year and made a fool of him. When he had taken over the butchery business, already a growing callousness to it, and a sort of contempt made him neglectful of it. He drank, and was often to be found in his public house blathering away as if he knew everything, when in reality he was a noisy fool.

Of the daughters, Alice, the elder, married a collier and lived for a time stormily in Ilkeston, before moving away to Yorkshire with her numerous young family. Effie, the younger, remained at home.

The last child, Tom, was considerably younger than his brothers, so had belonged rather to the company of his sisters. He was his mother's favourite. She roused herself to determination, and sent him forcibly away to a grammar-school in Derby when he was twelve years old. He did not want to go, and his father would have given way, but Mrs. Brangwen had set her heart on it. Her slender, pretty, tightly-covered body, with full skirts, was now the centre of resolution in the house, and when she had once set upon anything, which was not often, the family failed before her.

So Tom went to school, an unwilling failure from the first. He believed his mother was right in decreeing school for him, but he knew she was only right because she would not acknowledge his constitution. He knew, with a child's deep, instinctive foreknowledge of what is going to happen to him, that he would cut a sorry figure at school. But he took the infliction as inevitable, as if he were guilty of his own nature, as if his being were wrong, and his mother's conception right. If he could have been what he liked, he would have been that which his mother fondly but deludedly hoped he was. He would have been clever, and capable of becoming a gentleman. It was her aspiration for him, therefore he knew it as the true aspiration for any boy. But you can't make a silk purse out of a sow's ear, as he told his mother very early, with regard to himself; much to her mortification and chagrin.

When he got to school, he made a violent struggle against his physical inability to study. He sat gripped, making himself pale and ghastly in his effort to concentrate on the book, to take in what he had to learn. But it was no good. If he beat down his first repulsion, and got like a suicide to the stuff, he went very little further. He could not learn deliberately. His mind simply did not work.

In feeling he was developed, sensitive to the atmosphere around him, brutal perhaps, but at the same time delicate, very delicate. So he had a low opinion of himself. He knew his own limitation. He knew that his brain was a slow hopeless good-for-nothing. So he was humble.

But at the same time his feelings were more discriminating than those of most of the boys, and he was confused. He was more sensuously developed, more refined in instinct than they. For their mechanical stupidity he hated them, and suffered cruel contempt for them. But when it came to mental things, then he was at a disadvantage. He was at their mercy. He was a fool. He had not the power to controvert even the most stupid argument, so that he was forced to admit things he did not in the least believe. And having admitted them, he did not know whether he believed them or not; he rather thought he did.

But he loved anyone who could convey enlightenment to him through feeling. He sat betrayed with emotion when the teacher of literature read, in a moving fashion, Tennyson's "Ulysses", or Shelley's "Ode to the West Wind." His lips parted, his eyes filled with a strained, almost suffering light. And the teacher read on, fired by his power over the boy. Tom Brangwen was moved by this experience beyond all calculation, he almost dreaded it, it was so deep. But when, almost secretly and shamefully, he came to take the book himself, and began the words "Oh wild west wind, thou breath of autumn's being," the very fact of the print caused a prickly sensation of repulsion to go over his skin, the blood came to his face, his heart filled with a bursting passion of rage and incompetence. He threw the book down and walked over it and went out to the cricket field. And he hated books as if they were his enemies. He hated them worse than ever he hated any person.

He could not voluntarily control his attention. His mind had no fixed habits to go by, he had nothing to get hold of, nowhere to start from. For him there was nothing palpable, nothing known in himself, that he could apply to learning. He did not know how to begin. Therefore he was helpless when it came to deliberate understanding or deliberate learning.

He had an instinct for mathematics, but if this failed him, he was helpless as an idiot. So that he felt that the ground was never sure under his feet, he was nowhere. His final downfall was his complete inability to attend to a question put without suggestion. If he had to write a formal composition on the Army, he did at last learn to repeat the few facts he knew: "You can join the army at eighteen. You have to be over five foot eight." But he had all the time a living conviction that this was a dodge and that his commonplaces were beneath contempt. Then he reddened furiously, felt his bowels sink with shame, scratched out what he had written, made an agonised effort to think of something in the real composition style, failed, became sullen with rage and humiliation, put the pen down and would have been torn to pieces rather than attempt to write another word.

He soon got used to the Grammar School, and the Grammar School got used to him, setting him down as a hopeless duffer at learning, but respecting him for a generous, honest nature. Only one narrow, domineering fellow, the Latin master, bullied him and made the blue eyes mad with shame and rage. There was a horrid scene, when the boy laid open the master's head with a slate, and then things went on as before. The teacher got little sympathy. But Brangwen winced and could not bear to think of the deed, not even long after, when he was a grown man.

He was glad to leave school. It had not been unpleasant, he had enjoyed the companionship of the other youths, or had thought he enjoyed it, the time had passed very quickly, in endless activity. But he knew all the time that he was in an ignominious position, in this place of learning. He was aware of failure all the while, of incapacity. But he was too healthy and sanguine to be wretched, he was too much alive. Yet his soul was wretched almost to hopelessness.

He had loved one warm, clever boy who was frail in body, a consumptive type. The two had had an almost classic friendship, David and Jonathan, wherein Brangwen was the Jonathan, the server. But he had never felt equal with his friend, because the other's mind outpaced his, and left him ashamed, far in the rear. So the two boys went at once apart on leaving school. But Brangwen always remembered his friend that had been, kept him as a sort of light, a fine experience to remember.

Tom Brangwen was glad to get back to the farm, where he was in his own again. "I have got a turnip on my shoulders, let me stick to th' fallow," he said to his exasperated mother. He had too low an opinion of himself. But he went about at his work on the farm gladly enough, glad of the active labour and the smell of the land again, having youth and vigour and humour, and a comic wit, having the will and the power to forget his own shortcomings, finding himself violent with occasional rages, but usually on good terms with everybody and everything.

When he was seventeen, his father fell from a stack and broke his neck. Then the mother and son and daughter lived on at the farm, interrupted by occasional loud-mouthed lamenting, jealous-spirited visitations from the butcher Frank, who had a grievance against the world, which he felt was always giving him less than his dues. Frank was particularly against the young Tom, whom he called a mardy baby, and Tom returned the hatred violently, his face growing red and his blue eyes staring. Effie sided with Tom against Frank. But when Alfred came, from Nottingham, heavy jowled and lowering, speaking very little, but treating those at home with some contempt, Effie and the mother sided with him and put Tom into the shade. It irritated the youth that his elder brother should be made something of a hero by the women, just because he didn't live at home and was a lace-designer and almost a gentleman. But Alfred was something of a Prometheus Bound, so the women loved him. Tom came later to understand his brother better.

As youngest son, Tom felt some importance when the care of the farm devolved on to him. He was only eighteen, but he was quite capable of doing everything his father had done. And of course, his mother remained as centre to the house.

The young man grew up very fresh and alert, with zest for every moment of life. He worked and rode and drove to market, he went out with companions and got tipsy occasionally and played skittles and went to the little travelling theatres. Once, when he was drunk at a public house, he went upstairs with a prostitute who seduced him. He was then nineteen.

The thing was something of a shock to him. In the close intimacy of the farm kitchen, the woman occupied the supreme position. The men deferred to her in the house, on all household points, on all points of morality and behaviour. The woman was the symbol for that further life which comprised religion and love and morality. The men placed in her hands their own conscience, they said to her "Be my conscience-keeper, be the angel at the doorway guarding my outgoing and my incoming." And the woman fulfilled her trust, the men rested implicitly in her, receiving her praise or her blame with pleasure or with anger, rebelling and storming, but never for a moment really escaping in their own souls from her prerogative. They depended on her for their stability. Without her, they would have felt like straws in the wind, to be blown hither and thither at random. She was the anchor and the security, she was the restraining hand of God, at times highly to be execrated.

Now when Tom Brangwen, at nineteen, a youth fresh like a plant, rooted in his mother and his sister, found that he had lain with a prostitute woman in a common public house, he was very much startled. For him there was until that time only one kind of woman—his mother and sister.

But now? He did not know what to feel. There was a slight wonder, a pang of anger, of disappointment, a first taste of ash and of cold fear lest this was all that would happen, lest his relations with woman were going to be no more than this nothingness; there was a slight sense of shame before the prostitute, fear that she would despise him for his inefficiency; there was a cold distaste for her, and a fear of her; there was a moment of paralysed horror when he felt he might have taken a disease from her; and upon all this startled tumult of emotion, was laid the steadying hand of common sense, which said it did not matter very much, so long as he had no disease. He soon recovered balance, and really it did not matter so very much.

But it had shocked him, and put a mistrust into his heart, and emphasised his fear of what was within himself. He was, however, in a few days going about again in his own careless, happy-go-lucky fashion, his blue eyes just as clear and honest as ever, his face just as fresh, his appetite just as keen.

Or apparently so. He had, in fact, lost some of his buoyant confidence, and doubt hindered his outgoing.

For some time after this, he was quieter, more conscious when he drank, more backward from companionship. The disillusion of his first carnal contact with woman, strengthened by his innate desire to find in a woman the embodiment of all his inarticulate, powerful religious impulses, put a bit in his mouth. He had something to lose which he was afraid of losing, which he was not sure even of possessing. This first affair did not matter much: but the business of love was, at the bottom of his soul, the most serious and terrifying of all to him.

He was tormented now with sex desire, his imagination reverted always to lustful scenes. But what really prevented his returning to a loose woman, over and above the natural squeamishness, was the recollection of the paucity of the last experience. It had been so nothing, so dribbling and functional, that he was ashamed to expose himself to the risk of a repetition of it.

He made a strong, instinctive fight to retain his native cheerfulness unimpaired. He had naturally a plentiful stream of life and humour, a sense of sufficiency and exuberance, giving ease. But now it tended to cause tension. A strained light came into his eyes, he had a slight knitting of the brows. His boisterous humour gave place to lowering silences, and days passed by in a sort of suspense.

He did not know there was any difference in him, exactly; for the most part he was filled with slow anger and resentment. But he knew he was always thinking of women, or a woman, day in, day out, and that infuriated him. He could not get free: and he was ashamed. He had one or two sweethearts, starting with them in the hope of speedy development. But when he had a nice girl, he found that he was incapable of pushing the desired development. The very presence of the girl beside him made it impossible. He could not think of her like that, he could not think of her *actual* nakedness. She was a girl and he liked her, and dreaded violently even the thought of uncovering her. He knew that, in these last issues of nakedness, he did not exist to her nor she to him. Again, if he had a loose girl, and things began to develop, she offended him so deeply all the time, that he never knew whether he was going to get away from her as quickly as possible, or whether he were going to take her out of inflamed necessity. Again he learnt his lesson: if he took her it was a paucity which he was forced to despise. He did not despise himself nor the girl. But he despised the net result in him of the experience—he despised it deeply and bitterly.

Then, when he was twenty-three, his mother died, and he was left at home with Effie. His mother's death was another blow out of the dark. He could not understand it, he knew it was no good his trying. One had to submit to these unforeseen blows that come unawares and leave a bruise that remains and hurts whenever it is touched. He began to be afraid of all that which was up against him. He had loved his mother.

After this, Effie and he quarrelled fiercely. They meant a very great deal to each other, but they were both under a strange, unnatural tension. He stayed out of the house as much as possible. He got a special corner for himself at the "Red Lion" at Cossethay, and became a usual figure by the fire, a fresh, fair young fellow with heavy limbs and head held back, mostly silent, though alert and attentive, very hearty in his greeting of everybody he knew, shy of strangers. He teased all the women, who liked him extremely, and he was very attentive to the talk of the men, very respectful.

To drink made him quickly flush very red in the face, and brought out the look of self-consciousness and unsureness, almost bewilderment, in his blue eyes. When he came home in this state of tipsy confusion his sister hated him and abused him, and he went off his head, like a mad bull with rage.

He had still another turn with a light-o'-love. One Whitsuntide he went a jaunt with two other young fellows, on horseback, to Matlock and thence to Bakewell. Matlock was at that time just becoming a famous beauty-spot, visited from Manchester and from the Staffordshire towns. In the hotel where the young men took lunch, were two girls, and the parties struck up a friendship.

The Miss who made up to Tom Brangwen, then twenty-four years old, was a handsome, reckless girl neglected for an afternoon by the man who had brought her out. She saw Brangwen and liked him, as all women did, for his warmth and his generous nature, and for the innate delicacy in him. But she saw he was one who would have to be brought to the scratch. However, she was roused and unsatisfied and made mischievous, so she dared anything. It would be an easy interlude, restoring her pride.

She was a handsome girl with a bosom, and dark hair and blue eyes, a girl full of easy laughter, flushed from the sun, inclined to wipe her laughing face in a very natural and taking manner.

Brangwen was in a state of wonder. He treated her with his chaffing deference, roused, but very unsure of himself, afraid to death of being too forward, ashamed lest he might be thought backward, mad with desire yet restrained by instinctive regard for women from making any definite approach, feeling all the while that his attitude was ridiculous, and flushing deep with confusion. She, however, became hard and daring as he became confused, it amused her to see him come on.

"When must you get back?" she asked.

"I'm not particular," he said.

There the conversation again broke down.

Brangwen's companions were ready to go on.

"Art commin', Tom," they called, "or art for stoppin'?"

"Ay, I'm commin'," he replied, rising reluctantly, an angry sense of futility and disappointment spreading over him.

He met the full, almost taunting look of the girl, and he trembled with unusedness.

"Shall you come an' have a look at my mare," he said to her, with his hearty kindliness that was now shaken with trepidation.

"Oh, I should like to," she said, rising.

And she followed him, his rather sloping shoulders and his cloth riding-gaiters, out of the room. The young men got their own horses out of the stable.

"Can you ride?" Brangwen asked her.

"I should like to if I could—I have never tried," she said.

"Come then, an' have a try," he said.

And he lifted her, he blushing, she laughing, into the saddle.

"I s'll slip off—it's not a lady's saddle," she cried.

"Hold yer tight," he said, and he led her out of the hotel gate.

The girl sat very insecurely, clinging fast. He put a hand on her waist, to support her. And he held her closely, he clasped her as in an embrace, he was weak with desire as he strode beside her.

The horse walked by the river.

"You want to sit straddle-leg," he said to her.

"I know I do," she said.

It was the time of very full skirts. She managed to get astride the horse, quite decently, showing an intent concern for covering her pretty leg.

"It's a lot better this road," she said, looking down at him.

"Ay, it is," he said, feeling the marrow melt in his bones from the look in her eyes. "I dunno why they have that side-saddle business, twistin' a woman in two."

"Should us leave you then—you seem to be fixed up there?" called Brangwen's companions from the road.

He went red with anger.

"Ay—don't worry," he called back.

"How long are yer stoppin'?" they asked.

"Not after Christmas," he said.

And the girl gave a tinkling peal of laughter.

"All right—by-bye!" called his friends.

And they cantered off, leaving him very flushed, trying to be quite normal with the girl. But presently he had gone back to the hotel and given his horse into the charge of an ostler and had gone off with the girl into the woods, not quite knowing where he was or what he was doing. His heart thumped and he thought it the most glorious adventure, and was mad with desire for the girl.

Afterwards he glowed with pleasure. That was a different experience. He wanted to see more of the girl. She, however, told him this was impossible: her own man would be back by dark, and she must be with him. He, Brangwen, must not let on that there had been anything between them.

She gave him an intimate smile, which made him feel confused and gratified.

He could not tear himself away, though he had promised not to interfere with the girl. He stayed on at the hotel over night. He saw the other fellow at the evening meal: a small, middle-aged man with iron-grey hair and a curious face, like a monkey's, but interesting, in its way almost beautiful. Brangwen guessed that he was a foreigner. He was in company with another, an Englishman, dry and hard. The four sat at table, two men and two women. Brangwen watched with all his eyes.

He saw how the foreigner treated the women with courteous contempt, as if they were pleasing animals. Brangwen's girl had put on a ladylike manner, but her voice betrayed her. She wanted to win back her man. When dessert came on, however, the little foreigner turned round from his table and calmly surveyed the room, like one unoccupied. Brangwen marvelled over the cold, animal intelligence of the face. The brown eyes were round, showing all the brown pupil, like a monkey's, and just calmly looking, perceiving the other person without referring to him at all. They rested on Brangwen. The latter marvelled at the old face turned round on him, looking at him without considering it necessary to know him at all. The eyebrows of the round, perceiving, but unconcerned eyes were rather high up, with slight wrinkles above them, just as a monkey's had. It was an old, ageless face.

The man was most amazingly a gentleman all the time, an aristocrat. Brangwen stared fascinated. The girl was pushing her crumbs about on the cloth, uneasily, flushed and angry.

As Brangwen sat motionless in the hall afterwards, too much moved and lost to know what to do, the little stranger came up to him with a beautiful smile and manner, offering a cigarette and saying:

"Will you smoke?"

Brangwen never smoked cigarettes, yet he took the one offered, fumbling painfully with thick fingers, blushing to the roots of his hair. Then he looked with his warm blue eyes at the almost sardonic, lidded eyes of the foreigner. The latter sat down beside him, and they began to talk, chiefly of horses.

Brangwen loved the other man for is exquisite graciousness, for his tact and reserve, and for his ageless, monkey-like self-surety. They talked of horses, and of Derbyshire, and of farming. The stranger warmed to the young fellow with real warmth, and Brangwen was excited. He was transported at meeting this odd, middle-aged, dry-skinned man, personally. The talk was pleasant, but that did not matter so much. It was the gracious manner, the fine contact that was all.

They talked a long while together, Brangwen flushing like a girl when the other did not understand his idiom. Then they said good night, and shook hands. Again the foreigner bowed and repeated his good night.

"Good night, and *bon voyage.*"

Then he turned to the stairs.

Brangwen went up to his room and lay staring out at the stars of the summer night, his whole being in a whirl. What was it all? There was a life so different from what he knew it. What was there outside his knowledge, how much? What was this that he had touched? What was he in this new influence? What did everything mean? Where was life, in that which he knew or all outside him?

He fell asleep, and in the morning had ridden away before any other visitors were awake. He shrank from seeing any of them again, in the morning.

His mind was one big excitement. The girl and the foreigner: he knew neither of their names. Yet they had set fire to the homestead of his nature, and he would be burned out of cover. Of the two experiences, perhaps the meeting with the foreigner was the more significant. But the girl—he had not settled about the girl.

He did not know. He had to leave it there, as it was. He could not sum up his experiences.

The result of these encounters was, that he dreamed day and night, absorbedly, of a voluptuous woman and of the meeting with a small, withered foreigner of ancient breeding. No sooner was his mind free, no sooner had he left his own companions, than he began to imagine an intimacy with fine-textured, subtle-mannered people such as the foreigner at Matlock, and amidst this subtle intimacy was always the satisfaction of a voluptuous woman.

He went about absorbed in the interest and the actuality of this dream. His eyes glowed, he walked with his head up, full of the exquisite pleasure of aristocratic subtlety and grace, tormented with the desire for the girl.

Then gradually the glow began to fade, and the cold material of his customary life to show through. He resented it. Was he cheated in his illusion? He
balked the mean enclosure of reality, stood stubbornly like a bull at a gate,
refusing to re-enter the well-known round of his own life.

He drank more than usual to keep up the glow. But it faded more and more
for all that. He set his teeth at the commonplace, to which he would not submit.
It resolved itself starkly before him, for all that.

He wanted to marry, to get settled somehow, to get out of the quandary he
found himself in. But how? He felt unable to move his limbs. He had seen a
little creature caught in bird-lime, and the sight was a nightmare to him. He
began to feel mad with the rage of impotency.

He wanted something to get hold of, to pull himself out. But there was
nothing. Steadfastly he looked at the young women, to find a one he could
marry. But not one of them did he want. And he knew that the idea of a life
among such people as the foreigner was ridiculous.

Yet he dreamed of it, and stuck to his dreams, and would not have the reality
of Cossethay and Ilkeston. There he sat stubbornly in his corner at the "Red
Lion", smoking and musing and occasionally lifting his beer-pot, and saying
nothing, for all the world like a gorping farm-labourer, as he said himself.

Then a fever of restless anger came upon him. He wanted to go away—right
away. He dreamed of foreign parts. But somehow he had no contact with them.
And it was a very strong root which held him to the Marsh, to his own house
and land.

Then Effie got married, and he was left in the house with only Tilly, the
cross-eyed woman-servant who had been with them for fifteen years. He felt
things coming to a close. All the time, he had held himself stubbornly resistant
to the action of the commonplace unreality which wanted to absorb him. But
now he had to do something.

He was by nature temperate. Being sensitive and emotional, his nausea prevented him from drinking too much.

But, in futile anger, with the greatest of determination and apparent good
humour, he began to drink in order to get drunk. "Damn it," he said to himself,
"you must have it one road or another—you can't hitch your horse to the
shadow of a gate-post—if you've got legs you've got to rise off your backside
some time or other."

So he rose and went down to Ilkeston, rather awkwardly took his place
among a gang of young bloods, stood drinks to the company, and discovered he
could carry it off quite well. He had an idea that everybody in the room was a
man after his own heart, that everything was glorious, everything was perfect.
When somebody in alarm told him his coat pocket was on fire, he could only
beam from a red, blissful face and say "Iss-all-ri-ight—iss-al'-ri-ight—it's a'
right—let it be, let it be——" and he laughed with pleasure, and was rather
indignant that the others should think it unnatural for his coat pocket to burn:—
it was the happiest and most natural thing in the world—what?

He went home talking to himself and to the moon, that was very high and
small, stumbling at the flashes of moonlight from the puddles at his feet, wondering What the Hanover! then laughing confidently to the moon, assuring her
this was first class, this was.

In the morning he woke up and thought about it, and for the first time in his
life, knew what it was to feel really acutely irritable, in a misery of real bad
temper. After bawling and snarling at Tilly, he took himself off for very shame,

to be alone. And looking at the ashen fields and the putty roads, he wondered what in the name of Hell he could do to get out of this prickly sense of disgust and physical repulsion. And he knew that this was the result of his glorious evening.

And his stomach did not want any more brandy. He went doggedly across the fields with his terrier, and looked at everything with a jaundiced eye.

The next evening found him back again in his place at the "Red Lion", moderate and decent. There he sat and stubbornly waited for what would happen next.

Did he, or did he not believe that he belonged to this world of Cossethay and Ilkeston? There was nothing in it he wanted. Yet could he ever get out of it? Was there anything in himself that would carry him out of it? Or was he a dunderheaded baby, not man enough to be like the other young fellows who drank a good deal and wenched a little without any question, and were satisfied.

He went on stubbornly for a time. Then the strain became too great for him. A hot, accumulated consciousness was always awake in his chest, his wrists felt swelled and quivering, his mind became full of lustful images, his eyes seemed blood-flushed. He fought with himself furiously, to remain normal. He did not seek any woman. He just went on as if he were normal. Till he must either take some action or beat his head against the wall.

Then he went deliberately to Ilkeston, in silence, intent and beaten. He drank to get drunk. He gulped down the brandy, and more brandy, till his face became pale, his eyes burning. And still he could not get free. He went to sleep in drunken unconsciousness, woke up at four o'clock in the morning and continued drinking. He *would* get free. Gradually the tension in him began to relax. He began to feel happy. His riveted silence was unfastened, he began to talk and babble. He was happy and at one with all the world, he was united with all flesh in a hot blood-relationship. So, after three days of incessant brandy-drinking, he had burned out the youth from his blood, he had achieved this kindled state of oneness with all the world, which is the end of youth's most passionate desire. But he had achieved his satisfaction by obliterating his own individuality, that which it depended on his manhood to preserve and develop.

So he became a bout-drinker, having at intervals these bouts of three or four days of brandy-drinking, when he was drunk for the whole time. He did not think about it. A deep resentment burned in him. He kept aloof from any women, antagonistic.

When he was twenty-eight, a thick-limbed, stiff, fair man with fresh complexion, and blue eyes staring very straight ahead, he was coming one day down from Cossethay with a load of seed out of Nottingham. It was a time when he was getting ready for another bout of drinking, so he stared fixedly before him, watchful yet absorbed, seeing everything and aware of nothing, coiled in himself. It was early in the year.

He walked steadily beside the horse, the load clanked behind as the hill descended steeper. The road curved downhill before him, under banks and hedges, seen only for a few yards ahead.

Slowly turning the curve at the steepest part of the slope, his horse britching between the shafts, he saw a woman approaching. But he was thinking for the moment of the horse.

Then he turned to look at her. She was dressed in black, was apparently rather small and slight, beneath her long black cloak, and she wore a black bonnet. She walked hastily, as if unseeing, her head rather forward. It was her curious, absorbed, flitting motion, as if she were passing unseen by everybody, that first arrested him.

She had heard the cart, and looked up. Her face was pale and clear, she had thick dark eyebrows and a wide mouth, curiously held. He saw her face clearly, as if by a light in the air. He saw her face so distinctly, that he ceased to coil on himself, and was suspended.

"That's her," he said involuntarily. As the cart passed by, splashing through the thin mud, she stood back against the bank. Then, as he walked still beside his britching horse, his eyes met hers. He looked quickly away, pressing back his head, a pain of joy running through him. He could not bear to think of anything.

He turned round at the last moment. He saw her bonnet, her shape in the black cloak, the movement as she walked. Then she was gone round the bend.

She had passed by. He felt as if he were walking again in a far world, not Cossethay, a far world, the fragile reality. He went on, quiet, suspended, rarefied. He could not bear to think or to speak, nor make any sound or sign, nor change his fixed motion. He could scarcely bear to think of her face. He moved within the knowledge of her, in the world that was beyond reality.

The feeling that they had exchanged recognition possessed him like a madness, like a torment. How could he be sure, what confirmation had he? The doubt was like a sense of infinite space, a nothingness, annihilating. He kept within his breast the will to surety. They had exchanged recognition.

He walked about in this state for the next few days. And then again like a mist it began to break to let through the common, barren world. He was very gentle with man and beast, but he dreaded the starkness of disillusion cropping through again.

As he was standing with his back to the fire after dinner a few days later, he saw the woman passing. He wanted to know that she knew him, that she was aware. He wanted it said that there was something between them. So he stood anxiously watching, looking at her as she went down the road. He called to Tilly.

"Who might that be?" he asked.

Tilly, the cross-eyed woman of forty, who adored him, ran gladly to the window to look. She was glad when he asked her for anything. She craned her head over the short curtain, the little tight knob of her black hair sticking out pathetically as she bobbed about.

"Oh why"—she lifted her head and peered with her twisted, keen brown eyes—"why, you know who it is—it's her from th' vicarage—you know——"

"*How* do I know, you hen-bird," he shouted.

Tilly blushed and drew her neck in and looked at him with her squinting, sharp, almost reproachful look.

"Why you do—it's the new housekeeper."

"Ay—an' what by that?"

"Well, an' *what* by that?" rejoined the indignant Tilly.

"She's a woman, isn't she, housekeeper or no housekeeper? She's got more to her than that! Who is she—she's got a name?"

"Well, if she has, *I* don't know," retorted Tilly, not to be badgered by this lad who had grown up into a man.

"What's her name?" he asked, more gently.

"I'm sure I couldn't tell you," replied Tilly, on her dignity.

"An' is that all as you've gathered, as she's housekeeping at the vicarage?"

"I've 'eered mention of 'er name, but I couldn't remember it for my life."

"Why yer riddle-skulled woman o' nonsense, what have you got a head for?"

"For what other folks 'as got theirs for," retorted Tilly, who loved nothing more than these tilts when he would call her names.

There was a lull.

"I don't believe as anybody could keep it in their head," the woman-servant continued, tentatively.

"What?" he asked.

"Why, 'er name."

"How's that?"

"She's fra some foreign parts or other."

"Who told you that?"

"That's all I do know, as she is."

"An' wheer do you reckon she's from, then?"

"I don't know. They do say as she hails fra th' Pole. I don't know," Tilly hastened to add, knowing he would attack her.

"Fra th' Pole, why do *you* hail fra th' Pole? Who set up that menagerie confabulation?"

"That's what they say—I don't know——"

"Who says?"

"Mrs. Bentley says as she's fra th' Pole—else she *is* a Pole, or summat."

Tilly was only afraid she was landing herself deeper now.

"Who says she's a Pole?"

"They all say so."

"Then what's brought her to these parts?"

"I couldn't tell you. She's got a little girl with her."

"Got a little girl with her?"

"Of three or four, with a head like a fuzz-ball."

"Black?"

"White—fair as can be, an' all of a fuzz."

"Is there a father, then?"

"Not to my knowledge. I don't know."

"What brought her here?"

"I couldn't say, without th' vicar axed her."

"Is the child her child?"

"I s'd think so—they say so."

"Who told you about her?"

"Why, Lizzie—a-Monday—we seed her goin' past."

"You'd have to be rattling your tongues if anything went past."

Brangwen stood musing. That evening he went up to Cossethay to the "Red Lion", half with the intention of hearing more.

She was the widow of a Polish doctor, he gathered. Her husband had died, a refugee, in London. She spoke a bit foreign-like, but you could easily make out what she said. She had one little girl named Anna. Lensky was the woman's name, Mrs. Lensky.

Brangwen felt that here was the unreality established at last. He felt also a curious certainty about her, as if she were destined to him. It was to him a profound satisfaction that she was a foreigner.

A swift change had taken place on the earth for him, as if a new creation were fulfilled, in which he had real existence. Things had all been stark, unreal, barren, mere nullities before. Now they were actualities that he could handle.

He dared scarcely think of the woman. He was afraid. Only all the time he was aware of her presence not far off, he lived in her. But he dared not know her, even acquaint himself with her by thinking of her.

One day he met her walking along the road with her little girl. It was a child with a face like a bud of apple-blossom, and glistening fair hair like thistle-down sticking out in straight, wild, flamy pieces, and very dark eyes. The child clung jealously to her mother's side when he looked at her, staring with resentful black eyes. But the mother glanced at him again, almost vacantly. And the very vacancy of her look inflamed him. She had wide grey-brown eyes with very dark, fathomless pupils. He felt the fine flame running under his skin, as if all his veins had caught fire on the surface. And he went on walking without knowledge.

It was coming, he knew, his fate. The world was submitting to its transformation. He made no move: it would come, what would come.

When his sister Effie came to the Marsh for a week, he went with her for once to church. In the tiny place, with its mere dozen pews, he sat not far from the stranger. There was a fineness about her, a poignancy about the way she sat and held her head lifted. She was strange, from far off, yet so intimate. She was from far away, a presence, so close to his soul. She was not really there, sitting in Cossethay church beside her little girl. She was not living the apparent life of her days. She belonged to somewhere else. He felt it poignantly, as something real and natural. But a pang of fear for his own concrete life, that was only Cossethay, hurt him, and gave him misgiving.

Her thick dark brows almost met above her irregular nose, she had a wide, rather thick mouth. But her face was lifted to another world of life: not to heaven or death: but to some place where she still lived, in spite of her body's absence.

The child beside her watched everything with wide, black eyes. She had an odd little defiant look, her little red mouth was pinched shut. She seemed to be jealously guarding something, to be always on the alert for defence. She met Brangwen's near, vacant, intimate gaze, and a palpitating hostility, almost like a flame of pain, came into the wide, over-conscious dark eyes.

The old clergyman droned on, Cossethay sat unmoved as usual. And there was the foreign woman with a foreign air about her, inviolate, and the strange child, also foreign, jealously guarding something.

When the service was over, he walked in the way of another existence out of the church. As he went down the churchpath with his sister, behind the woman and child, the little girl suddenly broke from her mother's hand, and slipped back with quick, almost invisible movement, and was picking at something almost under Brangwen's feet. Her tiny fingers were fine and quick, but they missed the red button.

"Have you found something?" said Brangwen to her.

And he also stooped for the button. But she had got it, and she stood back with it pressed against her little coat, her black eyes flaring at him, as if to forbid him to notice her. Then, having silenced him, she turned with a swift "Mother—," and was gone down the path.

The mother had stood watching impassive, looking not at the child, but at Brangwen. He became aware of the woman looking at him, standing there isolated yet for him dominant in her foreign existence.

He did not know what to do, and turned to his sister. But the wide grey eyes, almost vacant yet so moving, held him beyond himself.

"Mother, I may have it, mayn't I?" came the child's proud, silvery tones. "Mother"—she seemed always to be calling her mother to remember her— "mother"—and she had nothing to continue now her mother had replied "Yes, my child." But, with ready invention, the child stumbled and ran on, "What are those people's names?"

Brangwen heard the abstract:

"I don't know, dear."

He went on down the road as if he were not living inside himself, but somewhere outside.

"Who *was* that person?" his sister Effie asked.

"I couldn't tell you," he answered unknowing.

"She's *somebody* very funny," said Effie, almost in condemnation. "That child's like one bewitched."

"Bewitched—how bewitched?" he repeated.

"You can see for yourself. The mother's plain, I must say—but the child is like a changeling. She'd be about thirty-five."

But he took no notice. His sister talked on.

"There's your woman for you," she continued. "You'd better marry *her*." But still he took no notice. Things were as they were.

Another day, at tea-time, as he sat alone at table, there came a knock at the front door. It startled him like a portent. No one ever knocked at the front door. He rose and began slotting back the bolts, turning the big key. When he had opened the door, the strange woman stood on the threshold.

"Can you give me a pound of butter?" she asked, in a curious detached way of one speaking a foreign language.

He tried to attend to her question. She was looking at him questioningly. But underneath the question, what was there, in her very standing motionless, which affected him?

He stepped aside and she at once entered the house, as if the door had been opened to admit her. That startled him. It was the custom for everybody to wait on the doorstep till asked inside. He went into the kitchen and she followed.

His tea-things were spread on the scrubbed deal table, a big fire was burning, a dog rose from the hearth and went to her. She stood motionless just inside the kitchen.

"Tilly," he called loudly, "have we got any butter?"

The stranger stood there like a silence in her black cloak.

"Eh?" came the shrill cry from the distance.

He shouted his question again.

"We've got what's on t' table," answered Tilly's shrill voice out of the dairy.

Brangwen looked at the table. There was a large pat of butter on a plate, almost a pound. It was round, and stamped with acorns and oak-leaves.

"Can't you come when you're wanted?" he shouted.

"Why, what d'you want?" Tilly protested, as she came peeking inquisitively through the other door.

She saw the strange woman, stared at her with cross-eyes, but said nothing.

"Haven't we any butter?" asked Brangwen again, impatiently, as if he could command some by his question.

"I tell you there's what's on t' table," said Tilly, impatient that she was unable to create any to his demand. "We haven't a morsel besides."

There was a moment's silence.

The stranger spoke, in her curiously distinct, detached manner of one who must think her speech first.

"Oh, then thank you very much. I am sorry that I have come to trouble you."

She could not understand the entire lack of manners, was slightly puzzled. Any politeness would have made the situation quite impersonal. But here it was a case of wills in confusion. Brangwen flushed at her polite speech. Still he did not let her go.

"Get summat an' wrap *that* up for her," he said to Tilly, looking at the butter on the table.

And taking a clean knife, he cut off that side of the butter where it was touched.

His speech, the "for her", penetrated slowly into the foreign woman and angered Tilly.

"Vicar has his butter fra Brown's by rights," said the insuppressible servant-woman. "We s'll be churnin' to-morrow mornin' first thing."

"Yes"—the long-drawn foreign yes—"yes," said the Polish woman, "I went to Mrs. Brown's. She hasn't any more."

Tilly bridled her head, bursting to say that, according to the etiquette of people who bought butter, it was no sort of manners whatever coming to a place cool as you like and knocking at the front door asking for a pound as a stop-gap while your other people were short. If you go to Brown's you go to Brown's, an' my butter isn't just to make shift when Brown's has got none.

Brangwen understood perfectly this unspoken speech of Tilly's. The Polish lady did not. And as she wanted butter for the vicar, and as Tilly was churning in the morning, she waited.

"Sluther up now," said Brangwen loudly after this silence had resolved itself out; and Tilly disappeared through the inner door.

"I am afraid that I should not come, so," said the stranger, looking at him enquiringly, as if referring to him for what it was usual to do.

He felt confused.

"How's that?" he said, trying to be genial and being only protective.

"Do you——?" she began deliberately. But she was not sure of her ground, and the conversation came to an end. Her eyes looked at him all the while, because she could not speak the language.

They stood facing each other. The dog walked away from her to him. He bent down to it.

"And how's your little girl?" he asked.

"Yes, thank you, she is very well," was the reply, a phrase of polite speech in a foreign language merely.

"Sit you down," he said.

And she sat in a chair, her slim arms, coming through the slits of her cloak, resting on her lap.

"You're not used to these parts," he said, still standing on the hearthrug with his back to the fire, coatless, looking with curious directness at the woman. Her self-possession pleased him and inspired him, set him curiously free. It seemed to him almost brutal to feel so master of himself and of the situation.

Her eyes rested on him for a moment, questioning, as she thought of the meaning of his speech.

"No," she said, understanding. "No—it is strange."

"You find it middlin' rough?" he said.

Her eyes waited on him, so that he should say it again.

"Our ways are rough to you," he repeated.

"Yes—yes, I understand. Yes, it is different, it is strange. But I was in York-shire—"

"Oh, well then," he said, "it's no worse here than what they are up there."

She did not quite understand. His protective manner, and his sureness, and his intimacy, puzzled her. What did he mean? If he was her equal, why did he behave so without formality?

"No——" she said, vaguely, her eyes resting on him.

She saw him fresh and naïve, uncouth, almost entirely beyond relationship with her. Yet he was good-looking, with his fair hair and blue eyes full of energy, and with his healthy body that seemed to take equality with her. She watched him steadily. He was difficult for her to understand, warm, uncouth, and confident as he was, sure on his feet as if he did not know what it was to be unsure. What then was it that gave him this curious stability?

She did not know. She wondered. She looked round the room he lived in. It had a close intimacy that fascinated and almost frightened her. The furniture was old and familiar as old people, the whole place seemed so kin to him, as if it partook of his being, that she was uneasy.

"It is already a long time that you have lived in this house—yes?" she asked.

"I've always lived here," he said.

"Yes—but your people—your family?"

"We've been here above *two* hundred years," he said. Her eyes were on him all the time, wide-open and trying to grasp him. He felt that he was there for her.

"It is your own place, the house, the farm——?"

"Yes," he said. He looked down at her and met her look. It disturbed her. She did not know him. He was a foreigner, they had nothing to do with each other. Yet his look disturbed her to knowledge of him. He was so strangely confident and direct.

"You live quite alone?"

"Yes—if you call it alone?"

She did not understand. It seemed unusual to her. What was the meaning of it?

And whenever her eyes, after watching him for some time, inevitably met his, she was aware of a heat beating up over her consciousness. She sat motion-less and in conflict. Who was this strange man who was at once so near to her? What was happening to her? Something in his young, warm-twinkling eyes seemed to assume a right to her, to speak to her, to extend her his protection. But how? Why did he speak to her? Why were his eyes so certain, so full of light and confident, waiting for no permission nor signal?

Tilly returned with a large leaf and found the two silent. At once he felt it incumbent on him to speak, now the serving-woman had come back.

"How old is your little girl?" he asked.

"Four years," she replied.

"Her father hasn't been dead long, then?" he asked.

"She was one year when he died."

"Three years?"

"Yes, three years that he is dead—yes."

Curiously quiet she was, almost abstracted, answering these questions. She looked at him again, with some maidenhood opening in her eyes. He felt he could not move, neither towards her nor away from her. Something about her presence hurt him, till he was almost rigid before her. He saw the girl's wonder-ing look rise in her eyes.

Tilly handed her the butter and she rose.

"Thank you very much," she said. "How much is it?"

"We'll make th' vicar a present of it," he said. "It'll do for me goin' to church."

"It 'ud look better of you if you went to church and took th' money for your butter," said Tilly, persistent in her claim to him.

"You'd have to put in, shouldn't you?" he said.

"How much, please?" said the Polish woman to Tilly. Brangwen stood by and let be.

"Then, thank you very much," she said.

"Bring your little girl down sometime to look at th' fowls and horses," he said,—"if she'd like it."

"Yes, she would like it," said the stranger.

And she went. Brangwen stood dimmed by her departure. He could not notice Tilly, who was looking at him uneasily, wanting to be reassured. He could not think of anything. He felt that he had made some invisible connection with the strange woman.

A daze had come over his mind, he had another centre of consciousness. In his breast, or in his bowels, somewhere in his body, there had started another activity. It was as if a strong light were burning there, and he was blind within it, unable to know anything, except that this transfiguration burned between him and her, connecting them, like a secret power.

Since she had come to the house he went about in a daze, scarcely seeing even the things he handled, drifting, quiescent, in a state of metamorphosis. He submitted to that which was happening to him, letting go his will, suffering the loss of himself, dormant always on the brink of ecstasy, like a creature evolving to a new birth.

She came twice with her child to the farm, but there was this lull between them, an intense calm and passivity like a torpor upon them, so that there was no active change took place. He was almost unaware of the child, yet by his native good humour he gained her confidence, even her affection, setting her on a horse to ride, giving her corn for the fowls.

Once he drove the mother and child from Ilkeston, picking them up on the road. The child huddled close to him as if for love, the mother sat very still. There w-.; a vagueness, like a soft mist over all of them, and a silence as if their wills were suspended. Only he saw her hands, ungloved, folded in her lap, and he noticed the wedding-ring on her finger. It excluded him: it was a closed circle. It bound her life, the wedding-ring, it stood for her life in which he could have no part. Nevertheless, beyond all this, there was herself and himself which should meet.

As he helped her down from the trap, almost lifting her, he felt he had some right to take her thus between his hands. She belonged as yet to that other, to that which was behind. But he must care for her also. She was too living to be neglected.

Sometimes her vagueness, in which he was lost, made him angry, made him rage. But he held himself still as yet. She had no response, no being towards him. It puzzled and enraged him, but he submitted for a long time. Then, from the accumulated troubling of her ignoring him, gradually a fury broke out, destructive, and he wanted to go away, to escape her.

It happened she came down to the Marsh with the child whilst he was in this state. Then he stood over against her, strong and heavy in his revolt, and though he said nothing, still she felt his anger and heavy impatience grip hold of her, she was shaken again as out of a torpor. Again her heart stirred with a quick, out-running impulse, she looked at him, at the stranger who was not a gentleman yet who insisted on coming into her life, and the pain of a new birth in herself strung all her veins to a new form. She would have to begin again, to find a new being, a new form, to respond to that blind, insistent figure standing over against her.

A shiver, a sickness of new birth passed over her, the flame leaped up him, under his skin. She wanted it, this new life from him, with him, yet she must defend herself against it, for it was a destruction.

As he worked alone on the land, or sat up with his ewes at lambing time, the facts and material of his daily life fell away, leaving the kernel of his purpose clean. And then it came upon him that he would marry her and she would be his life.

Gradually, even without seeing her, he came to know her. He would have liked to think of her as of something given into his protection, like a child without parents. But it was forbidden him. He had to come down from this pleasant view of the case. She might refuse him. And besides, he was afraid of her.

But during the long February nights with the ewes in labour, looking out from the shelter into the flashing stars, he knew he did not belong to himself. He must admit that he was only fragmentary, something incomplete and subject. There were the stars in the dark heaven travelling, the whole host passing by on some eternal voyage. So he sat small and submissive to the greater ordering.

Unless she would come to him, he must remain as a nothingness. It was a hard experience. But, after her repeated obliviousness to him, after he had seen so often that he did not exist for her, after he had raged and tried to escape, and said he was good enough by himself, he was a man, and could stand alone, he must, in the starry multiplicity of the night humble himself, and admit and know that without her he was nothing.

He was nothing. But with her, he would be real. If she were now walking across the frosty grass near the sheep-shelter, through the fretful bleating of the ewes and lambs, she would bring him completeness and perfection. And if it should be so, that she should come to him! It should be so—it was ordained so.

He was a long time resolving definitely to ask her to marry him. And he knew, if he asked her, she must really acquiesce. She must, it could not be otherwise.

He had learned a little of her. She was poor, quite alone, and had had a hard time in London, both before and after her husband died. But in Poland she was a lady well born, a landowner's daughter.

All these things were only words to him, the fact of her superior birth, the fact that her husband had been a brilliant doctor, the fact that he himself was her inferior in almost every way of distinction. There was an inner reality, a logic of the soul, which connected her with him.

One evening in March, when the wind was roaring outside, came the moment to ask her. He had sat with his hands before him, leaning to the fire. And as he watched the fire, he knew almost without thinking that he was going this evening.

"Have you got a clean shirt?" he asked Tilly.

"You know you've got clean shirts," she said.

"Ay,—bring me a white one."

Tilly brought down one of the linen shirts he had inherited from his father, putting it before him to air at the fire. She loved him with a dumb, aching love as he sat leaning with his arms on his knees, still and absorbed, unaware of her. Lately, a quivering inclination to cry had come over her, when she did anything for him in his presence. Now her hands trembled as she spread the shirt. He was never shouting and teasing now. The deep stillness there was in the house made her tremble.

He went to wash himself. Queer little breaks of consciousness seemed to rise and burst like bubbles out of the depths of his stillness.

"It's got to be done," he said as he stooped to take the shirt out of the fender, "it's got to be done, so why balk it?" And as he combed his hair before the mirror on the wall, he retorted to himself, superficially: "The woman's not speechless dumb. She's not clutterin' at the nipple. She's got the right to please herself, and displease whosoever she likes."

This streak of common sense carried him a little further.

"Did you want anythink?" asked Tilly, suddenly appearing, having heard him speak. She stood watching him comb his fair beard. His eyes were calm and uninterrupted.

"Ay," he said, "where have you put the scissors?"

She brought them to him, and stood watching as, chin forward, he trimmed his beard.

"Don't go an' crop yourself as if you was at a shearin' contest," she said, anxiously. He blew the fine-curled hair quickly off his lips.

He put on all clean clothes, folded his stock carefully, and donned his best coat. Then, being ready, as grey twilight was falling, he went across to the orchard to gather the daffodils. The wind was roaring in the apple trees, the yellow flowers swayed violently up and down, he heard even the fine whisper of their spears as he stooped to break the flattened, brittle stems of the flowers.

"What's to-do?" shouted a friend who met him as he left the garden gate.

"Bit of courtin', like," said Brangwen.

And Tilly, in a great state of trepidation and excitement, let the wind whisk her over the field to the big gate, whence she could watch him go.

He went up the hill and on towards the vicarage, the wind roaring through the hedges, whilst he tried to shelter his bunch of daffodils by his side. He did not think of anything, only knew that the wind was blowing.

Night was falling, the bare trees drummed and whistled. The vicar, he knew, would be in his study, the Polish woman in the kitchen, a comfortable room, with her child. In the darkest of twilight, he went through the gate and down the path where a few daffodils stooped in the wind, and shattered crocuses made a pale, colourless ravel.

There was a light streaming on to the bushes at the back from the kitchen window. He began to hesitate. How could he do this? Looking through the window, he saw her seated in the rocking-chair with the child, already in its nightdress, sitting on her knee. The fair head with its wild, fierce hair was drooping towards the fire-warmth, which reflected on the bright cheeks and clear skin of the child, who seemed to be musing, almost like a grown-up person. The mother's face was dark and still, and he saw, with a pang, that she was away back in the life that had been. The child's hair gleamed like spun glass, her face was illuminated till it seemed like wax lit up from the inside. The wind boomed strongly. Mother and child sat motionless, silent, the child staring with vacant dark eyes into the fire, the mother looking into space. The little girl was almost asleep. It was her will which kept her eyes so wide.

Suddenly she looked round, troubled, as the wind shook the house, and Brangwen saw the small lips move. The mother began to rock, he heard the slight crunch of the rockers of the chair. Then he heard the low, monotonous murmur of a song in a foreign language. Then a great burst of wind, the mother seemed to have drifted away, the child's eyes were black and dilated. Brangwen looked up at the clouds which packed in great, alarming haste across the dark sky.

Then there came the child's high, complaining, yet imperative voice: "Don't sing that stuff, mother; I don't want to hear it."

The singing died away.

"You will go to bed," said the mother.

He saw the clinging protest of the child, the unmoved far-awayness of the mother, the clinging, grasping effort of the child. Then suddenly the clear childish challenge:

"I want you to tell me a story."

The wind blew, the story began, the child nestled against the mother, Brangwen waited outside, suspended, looking at the wild waving of the trees in the wind and the gathering darkness. He had his fate to follow, he lingered there at the threshold.

The child crouched distinct and motionless, curled in against her mother, the eyes dark and unblinking among the keen wisps of hair, like a curled-up animal asleep but for the eyes. The mother sat as if in shadow, the story went on as if by itself. Brangwen stood outside seeing the night fall. He did not notice the passage of time. The hand that held the daffodils was fixed and cold.

The story came to an end, the mother rose at last, with the child clinging round her neck. She must be strong, to carry so large a child so easily. The little Anna clung round her mother's neck. The fair, strange face of the child looked over the shoulder of the mother, all asleep but the eyes, and these, wide and dark, kept up the resistance and the fight with something unseen.

When they were gone, Brangwen stirred for the first time from the place where he stood, and looked round at the night. He wished it were really as beautiful and familiar as it seemed in these few moments of release. Along with the child, he felt a curious strain on him, a suffering, like a fate.

The mother came down again, and began folding the child's clothes. He knocked. She opened wondering, a little bit at bay, like a foreigner, uneasy.

"Good evening," he said. "I'll just come in a minute."

A change went quickly over her face; she was unprepared. She looked down at him as he stood in the light from the window, holding the daffodils, the darkness behind. In his black clothes she again did not know him. She was almost afraid.

But he was already stepping on to the threshold, and closing the door behind him. She turned into the kitchen, startled out of herself by this invasion from the night. He took off his hat, and came towards her. Then he stood in the light, in his black clothes and his black stock, hat in one hand and yellow flowers in the other. She stood away, at his mercy, snatched out of herself. She did not know him, only she knew he was a man come for her. She could only see the dark-clad man's figure standing there upon her, and the gripped fist of flowers. She could not see the face and the living eyes.

He was watching her, without knowing her, only aware underneath of her presence.

"I come to have a word with you," he said, striding forward to the table, laying down his hat and the flowers, which tumbled apart and lay in a loose heap. She had flinched from his advance. She had no will, no being. The wind boomed in the chimney, and he waited. He had disembarrassed his hands. Now he shut his fists.

He was aware of her standing there unknown, dread, yet related to him.

"I came up," he said, speaking curiously matter-of-fact and level, "to ask if you'd marry me. You are free, aren't you?"

There was a long silence, whilst his blue eyes, strangely impersonal, looked into her eyes to seek an answer to the truth. He was looking for the truth out of her. And she, as if hypnotised, must answer at length.

"Yes, I am free to marry."

The expression of his eyes changed, became less impersonal, as if he were looking almost at her, for the truth of her. Steady and intent and eternal they were, as if they would never change. They seemed to fix and to resolve her. She quivered, feeling herself created, will-less, lapsing into him, into a common will with him.

"You want me?" she said.

A pallor came over his face.

"Yes," he said.

Still there was no response and silence.

"No," she said, not of herself. "No, I don't know."

He felt the tension breaking up in him, his fists slackened, he was unable to move. He stood there looking at her, helpless in his vague collapse. For the moment she had become unreal to him. Then he saw her come to him, curiously direct and as if without movement, in a sudden flow. She put her hand to his coat.

"Yes I want to," she said, impersonally, looking at him with wide, candid, newly-opened eyes, opened now with supreme truth. He went very white as he stood, and did not move, only his eyes were held by hers, and he suffered. She seemed to see him with her newly-opened, wide eyes, almost of a child, and with a strange movement, that was agony to him, she reached slowly forward her dark face and her breast to him, with a slow insinuation of a kiss that made something break in his brain, and it was darkness over him for a few moments.

He had her in his arms, and, obliterated, was kissing her. And it was sheer, bleached agony to him, to break away from himself. She was there so small and light and accepting in his arms, like a child, and yet with such an insinuation of embrace, of infinite embrace, that he could not bear it, he could not stand.

He turned and looked for a chair, and keeping her still in his arms, sat down with her close to him, to his breast. Then, for a few seconds, he went utterly to sleep, asleep and sealed in the darkest sleep, utter, extreme oblivion.

From which he came to gradually, always holding her warm and close upon him, and she as utterly silent as he, involved in the same oblivion, the fecund darkness.

He returned gradually, but newly created, as after a gestation, a new birth, in the womb of darkness. Aerial and light everything was, new as a morning, fresh and newly-begun. Like a dawn the newness and the bliss filled in. And she sat utterly still with him, as if in the same.

Then she looked up at him, the wide, young eyes blazing with light. And he bent down and kissed her on the lips. And the dawn blazed in them, their new life came to pass, it was beyond all conceiving good, it was so good, that it was almost like a passing-away, a trespass. He drew her suddenly closer to him.

For soon the light began to fade in her, gradually, and as she was in his arms, her head sank, she leaned it against him, and lay still, with sunk head, a little tired, effaced because she was tired. And in her tiredness was a certain negation of him.

"There is the child," she said, out of the long silence.

He did not understand. It was a long time since he had heard a voice. Now also he heard the wind roaring, as if it had just begun again.

"Yes," he said, not understanding. There was a slight contraction of pain at his heart, a slight tension on his brows. Something he wanted to grasp and could not.

"You will love her?" she said.

The quick contraction, like pain, went over him again.

"I love her now," he said.

She lay still against him, taking his physical warmth without heed. It was great confirmation for him to feel her there, absorbing the warmth from him, giving him back her weight and her strange confidence. But where was she, that she seemed so absent? His mind was open with wonder. He did not know her.

"But I am much older than you," she said.

"How old?" he asked.

"I am thirty-four," she said.

"I am twenty-eight," he said.

"Six years."

She was oddly concerned, even as if it pleased her a little. He sat and listened and wondered. It was rather splendid, to be so ignored by her, whilst she lay against him, and he lifted her with his breathing, and felt her weight upon his living, so he had a completeness and an inviolable power. He did not interfere with her. He did not even know her. It was so strange that she lay there with her weight abandoned upon him. He was silent with delight. He felt strong, physically, carrying her on his breathing. The strange, inviolable completeness of the two of them made him feel as sure and as stable as God. Amused, he wondered what the vicar would say if he knew.

"You needn't stop here much longer, housekeeping," he said.

"I like it also, here," she said. "When one has been in many places, it is very nice here."

He was silent again at this. So close on him she lay, and yet she answered him from so far away. But he did not mind.

"What was your own home like, when you were little?" he asked.

"My father was a landowner," she replied. "It was near a river."

This did not convey much to him. All was as vague as before. But he did not care, whilst she was so close.

"I am a landowner—a little one," he said.

"Yes," she said.

He had not dared to move. He sat there with his arms round her, her lying motionless on his breathing, and for a long time he did not stir. Then softly, timidly, his hand settled on the roundness of her arm, on the unknown. She seemed to lie a little closer. A hot flame licked up from his belly to his chest.

But it was too soon. She rose, and went across the room to a drawer, taking out a little tray-cloth. There was something quiet and professional about her. She had been a nurse beside her husband, both in Warsaw and in the rebellion afterwards. She proceeded to set a tray. It was as if she ignored Brangwen. He sat up, unable to bear a contradiction in her. She moved about inscrutably.

Then, as he sat there, all mused and wondering, she came near to him, looking at him with wide, grey eyes that almost smiled with a low light. But her ugly-beautiful mouth was still unmoved and sad. He was afraid.

His eyes, strained and roused with unusedness, quailed a little before her, he felt himself quailing and yet he rose, as if obedient to her, he bent and kissed her heavy, sad, wide mouth, that was kissed, and did not alter. Fear was too strong in him. Again he had not got her.

She turned away. The vicarage kitchen was untidy, and yet to him beautiful with the untidiness of her and her child. Such a wonderful remoteness there was about her, and then something in touch with him, that made his heart knock in his chest. He stood there and waited, suspended.

Again she came to him, as he stood in his black clothes, with blue eyes very bright and puzzled for her, his face tensely alive, his hair dishevelled. She came close up to him, to his intent, black-clothed body, and laid her hand on his arm. He remained unmoved. Her eyes, with a blackness of memory struggling with passion, primitive and electric away at the back of them, rejected him and absorbed him at once. But he remained himself. He breathed with difficulty, and sweat came out at the roots of his hair, on his forehead.

"Do you want to marry me?" she asked slowly, always uncertain.

He was afraid lest he could not speak. He drew breath hard, saying:
"I do."

Then again, what was agony to him, with one hand lightly resting on his arm, she leaned forward a little, and with a strange, primeval suggestion of embrace, held him her mouth. It was ugly-beautiful, and he could not bear it. He put his mouth on hers, and slowly, slowly the response came, gathering force and passion, till it seemed to him she was thundering at him till he could bear no more. He drew away, white, unbreathing. Only, in his blue eyes, was something of himself concentrated. And in her eyes was a little smile upon a black void.

She was drifting away from him again. And he wanted to go away. It was intolerable. He could bear no more. He must go. Yet he was irresolute. But she turned away from him.

With a little pang of anguish, of denial, it was decided.

"I'll come an' speak to the vicar to-morrow," he said, taking his hat.

She looked at him, her eyes expressionless and full of darkness. He could see no answer.

"That'll do, won't it?" he said.

"Yes," she answered, mere echo without body or meaning.

"Good night," he said.

"Good night."

He left her standing there, expressionless and void as she was. Then she went on laying the tray for the vicar. Needing the table, she put the daffodils aside on the dresser without noticing them. Only their coolness, touching her hand, remained echoing there a long while.

They were such strangers, they must for ever be such strangers, that his passion was a clanging torment to him. Such intimacy of embrace, and such utter foreignness of contact! It was unbearable. He could not bear to be near her, and know the utter foreignness between them, know how entirely they were strangers to each other. He went out into the wind. Big holes were blown into the sky, the moonlight blew about. Sometimes a high moon, liquid-brilliant, scudded across a hollow space and took cover under electric, brown-iridescent cloud-edges. Then there was a blot of cloud, and shadow. Then somewhere in the night a radiance again, like a vapour. And all the sky was teeming and tearing along, a vast disorder of flying shapes and darkness and ragged fumes of light and a great brown circling halo, then the terror of a moon running liquid-brilliant into the open for a moment, hurting the eyes before she plunged under cover of cloud again.

II

THEY LIVE AT THE MARSH

She was the daughter of a Polish landowner who, deeply in debt to the Jews, had married a German wife with money, and who had died just before the rebellion. Quite young, she had married Paul Lensky, an intellectual who had studied at Berlin, and had returned to Warsaw a patriot. Her mother had married a German merchant and gone away.

Lydia Lensky, married to the young doctor, became with him a patriot and an émancipée. They were poor, but they were very conceited. She learned nursing as a mark of her emancipation. They represented in Poland the new movement just begun in Russia. But they were very patriotic: and, at the same time, very "European."

They had two children. Then came the great rebellion. Lensky, very ardent and full of words, went about inciting his countrymen. Little Poles flamed down the streets of Warsaw, on the way to shoot every Muscovite. So they crossed into the south of Russia, and it was common for six little insurgents to ride into a Jewish village, brandishing swords and words, emphasising the fact that they were going to shoot every living Muscovite.

Lensky was something of a fire-eater also. Lydia, tempered by her German blood, coming of a different family, was obliterated, carried along in her husband's emphasis of declaration, and his whirl of patriotism. He was indeed a brave man, but no bravery could quite have equalled the vividness of his talk. He worked very hard, till nothing lived in him but his eyes. And Lydia, as if drugged, followed him like a shadow, serving, echoing. Sometimes she had her two children, sometimes they were left behind.

She returned once to find them both dead of diphtheria. Her husband wept aloud, unaware of everybody. But the war went on, and soon he was back at his work. A darkness had come over Lydia's mind. She walked always in a shadow, silenced, with a strange, deep terror having hold of her, her desire was to seek satisfaction in dread, to enter a nunnery, to satisfy the instincts of dread in her, through service of a dark religion. But she could not.

Then came the flight to London. Lensky, the little, thin man, had got all his life locked into a resistance and could not relax again. He lived in a sort of insane irritability, touchy, haughty to the last degree, fractious, so that as assistant doctor in one of the hospitals he soon became impossible. They were almost beggars. But he kept still his great ideas of himself, he seemed to live in a complete hallucination, where he himself figured vivid and lordly. He guarded his wife jealously against the ignominy of her position, rushed round her like a brandished weapon, an amazing sight to the English eye, had her in his power, as if he hypnotised her. She was passive, dark, always in shadow.

He was wasting away. Already when the child was born he seemed nothing but skin and bone and fixed idea. She watched him dying, nursed him, nursed the baby, but really took no notice of anything. A darkness was on her, like remorse, or like a remembering of the dark, savage, mystic ride of dread, of death, of the shadow of revenge. When her husband died, she was relieved. He would no longer dart about her.

England fitted her mood, its aloofness and foreignness. She had known a little of the language before coming, and a sort of parrot-mind made her pick it up fairly easily. But she knew nothing of the English, nor of English life. Indeed, these did not exist for her. She was like one walking in the Underworld, where the shades throng intelligibly but have no connection with one. She felt the English people as a potent, cold, slightly hostile host amongst whom she walked isolated.

The English people themselves were almost deferential to her, the Church saw that she did not want. She walked without passion, like a shade, tormented into moments of love by the child. Her dying husband with his tortured eyes and the skin drawn tight over his face, he was as a vision to her, not a reality. In a vision he was buried and put away. Then the vision ceased, she was untroubled, time went on grey, uncoloured, like a long journey where she sat unconscious as the landscape unrolled beside her. When she rocked her baby at evening, maybe she fell into a Polish slumber song, or she talked sometimes to herself in Polish. Otherwise she did not think of Poland, nor of that life to which she had belonged. It was a great blot looming blank in its darkness. In the superficial activity of her life, she was all English. She even thought in English. But her long blanks and darkness of abstraction were Polish.

So she lived for some time. Then, with slight uneasiness, she used half to awake to the streets of London. She realised that there was something around her, very foreign, she realised she was in a strange place. And then, she was sent away into the country. There came into her mind now the memory of her home where she had been a child, the big house among the land, the peasants of the village.

She was sent to Yorkshire, to nurse an old rector in his rectory by the sea. This was the first shake of the kaleidoscope that brought in front of her eyes something she must see. It hurt her brain, the open country and the moors. It hurt her and hurt her. Yet it forced itself upon her as something living, it roused some potency of her childhood in her, it had some relation to her.

There was green and silver and blue in the air about her now. And there was a strange insistence of light from the sea, to which she must attend. Primroses glimmered around, many of them, and she stooped to the disturbing influence near her feet, she even picked one or two flowers, faintly remembering in the new colour of life, what had been. All the day long, as she sat at the upper window, the light came off the sea, constantly, constantly, without refusal, till it seemed to bear her away, and the noise of the sea created a drowsiness in her, a relaxation like sleep. Her automatic consciousness gave way a little, she stumbled sometimes, she had a poignant, momentary vision of her living child, that hurt her unspeakably. Her soul roused to attention.

Very strange was the constant glitter of the sea unsheathed in heaven, very swarm and sweet the graveyard, in a nook of the hill catching the sunshine and holding it as one holds a bee between the palms of the hands, when it is benumbed. Grey grass and lichens and a little church, and snowdrops among coarse grass, and a cupful of incredibly warm sunshine. She was troubled in spirit. Hearing the rushing of the beck away down under the trees, she was startled, and wondered what it was. Walking down, she found the bluebells around her glowing like a presence, among the trees.

Summer came, the moors were tangled with harebells like water in the ruts of the roads, the heather came rosy under the skies, setting the whole world awake. And she was uneasy. She went past the gorse bushes shrinking from their presence, she stepped into the heather as into a quickening bath that almost hurt. Her fingers moved over the clasped fingers of the child, she heard the anxious voice of the baby, as it tried to make her talk, distraught.

And she shrank away again, back into her darkness, and for a long while remained blotted safely away from living. But autumn came with the faint red glimmer of robins singing, winter darkened the moors, and almost savagely she turned again to life, demanding her life back again, demanding that it should be as it had been when she was a girl, on the land at home, under the sky. Snow lay in great expanses, the telegraph posts strode over the white earth, away under the gloom of the sky. And savagely her desire rose in her again, demanding that this was Poland, her youth, that all was her own again.

But there were no sledges nor bells, she did not see the peasants coming out like new people, in their sheepskins and their fresh, ruddy, bright faces, that seemed to become new and vivid when the snow lit up the ground. It did not come to her, the life of her youth, it did not come back. There was a little agony of struggle, then a relapse into the darkness of the convent, where Satan and the devils raged round the walls, and Christ was white on the cross of victory.

She watched from the sick-room the snow whirl past, like flocks of shadows in haste, flying on some final mission out to a leaden inalterable sea, beyond the final whiteness of the curving shore, and the snow-speckled blackness of the rocks half submerged. But near at hand on the trees the snow was soft in bloom. Only the voice of the dying vicar spoke grey and querulous from behind.

By the time the snowdrops were out, however, he was dead. He was dead. But with curious equanimity the returning woman watched the snowdrops on the edge of the grass below, blown white in the wind, but not to be blown away. She watched them fluttering and bobbing, the white, shut flowers, anchored by a thread to the grey-green grass, yet never blown away, not drifting with the wind.

As she rose in the morning, the dawn was beating up white, gusts of light blown like a thin snowstorm from the east, blown stronger and fiercer, till the rose appeared, and the gold, and the sea lit up below. She was impassive and indifferent. Yet she was outside the enclosure of darkness.

There passed a space of shadow again, the familiarity of dread-worship, during which she was moved, oblivious, to Cossethay. There, at first, there was nothing—just grey nothing. But then one morning there was a light from the yellow jasmine caught her, and after that, morning and evening, the persistent ringing of thrushes from the shrubbery, till her heart, beaten upon, was forced to lift up its voice in rivalry and answer. Little tunes came into her mind. She was full of trouble almost like anguish. Resistant, she knew she was beaten, and from fear of darkness turned to fear of light. She would have hidden herself indoors, if she could. Above all, she craved for the peace and heavy oblivion of her old state. She could not bear to come to, to realise. The first pangs of this new parturition were so acute, she knew she could not bear it. She would rather remain out of life, than be torn, mutilated into this birth, which she could not survive. She had not the strength to come to life now, in England, so foreign, skies so hostile. She knew she would die like an early, colourless, scentless flower that the end of the winter puts forth mercilessly. And she wanted to harbour her modicum of twinkling life.

But a sunshiny day came full of the scent of a mezereon tree, when bees were tumbling into the yellow crocuses, and she forgot, she felt like somebody else, not herself, a new person, quite glad. But she knew it was fragile, and she dreaded it. The vicar put pea-flower into the crocuses, for his bees to roll in, and she laughed. Then night came, with brilliant stars that she knew of old, from her girlhood. And they flashed so bright, she knew they were victors.

She could neither wake nor sleep. As if crushed between the past and the future, like a flower that comes above-ground to find a great stone lying above it, she was helpless.

The bewilderment and helplessness continued, she was surrounded by great moving masses that must crush her. And there was no escape. Save in the old obliviousness, the cold darkness she strove to retain. But the vicar showed her eggs in the thrush's nest near the back door. She saw herself the mother-thrush upon the nest, and the way her wings were spread, so eager down upon her secret. The tense, eager, nesting wings moved her beyond endurance. She thought of them in the morning, when she heard the thrush whistling as he got up, and she thought, "Why didn't I die out there, why am I brought here?"

She was aware of people who passed around her, not as persons, but as looming presences. It was very difficult for her to adjust herself. In Poland, the peasantry, the people, had been cattle to her, they had been her cattle that she owned and used. What were these people? Now she was coming awake, she was lost.

But she had felt Brangwen go by almost as if he had brushed her. She had tingled in body as she had gone on up the road. After she had been with him in the Marsh kitchen, the voice of her body had risen strong and insistent. Soon, she wanted him. He was the man who had come nearest to her for her awakening.

Always, however, between-whiles she lapsed into the old unconsciousness, indifference and there was a will in her to save herself from living any more. But she would wake in the morning one day and feel her blood running, feel herself lying open like a flower unsheathed in the sun, insistent and potent with demand.

She got to know him better, and her instinct fixed on him—just on him. Her impulse was strong against him, because he was not of her own sort. But one blind instinct led her, to take him, to leave him, and then to relinquish herself to him. It would be safety. She felt the rooted safety of him, and the life in him. Also he was young and very fresh. The blue, steady livingness of his eyes she enjoyed like morning. He was very young.

Then she lapsed again to stupor and indifference. This, however, was bound to pass. The warmth flowed through her, she felt herself opening, unfolding, asking, as a flower opens in full request under the sun, as the beaks of tiny birds open flat, to receive, to receive. And unfolded she turned to him, straight to him. And he came, slowly, afraid, held back by uncouth fear, and driven by a desire bigger than himself.

When she opened and turned to him, then all that had been and all that was, was gone from her, she was as new as a flower that unsheathes itself and stands always ready, waiting, receptive. He could not understand this. He forced himself, through lack of understanding, to the adherence to the line of honourable courtship and sanctioned, licensed marriage. Therefore, after he had gone to the vicarage and asked for her, she remained for some days held in this one spell, open, receptive to him, before him. He was roused to chaos. He spoke to the vicar and gave in the banns. Then he stood to wait.

She remained attentive and instinctively expectant before him, unfolded, ready to receive him. He could not act, because of self-fear and because of his conception of honour towards her. So he remained in a state of chaos.

And after a few days, gradually she closed again, away from him, was sheathed over, impervious to him, oblivious. Then a black, bottomless despair became real to him, he knew what he had lost. He felt he had lost it for good, he knew what it was to have been in communication with her, and to be cast off again. In misery, his heart like a heavy stone, he went about unliving.

Till gradually he became desperate, lost his understanding, was plunged in a revolt that knew no bounds. Inarticulate, he moved with her at the Marsh in violent, gloomy, wordless passion, almost in hatred of her. Till gradually she became aware of him, aware of herself with regard to him, her blood stirred to life, she began to open towards him, to flow towards him again. He waited till the spell was between them again, till they were together within one rushing, hastening flame. And then again he was bewildered, he was tied up as with cords, and could not move to her. So she came to him, and unfastened the breast of his waistcoat and his shirt, and put her hand on him, needing to know him. For it was cruel to her, to be opened and offered to him, yet not to know what he was, not even that he was there. She gave herself to the hour, but he could not, and he bungled in taking her.

So that he lived in suspense, as if only half his faculties worked, until the wedding. She did not understand. But the vagueness came over her again, and the days lapsed by. He could not get definitely into touch with her. For the time being, she let him go again.

He suffered very much from the thought of actual marriage, the intimacy and nakedness of marriage. He knew her so little. They were so foreign to each other, they were such strangers. And they could not talk to each other. When she talked, of Poland or of what had been, it was all so foreign, she scarcely communicated anything to him. And when he looked at her, an over-much reverence and fear of the unknown changed the nature of his desire into a sort of worship, holding her aloof from his physical desire, self-thwarting.

She did not know this, she did not understand. They had looked at each other, and had accepted each other. It was so, then there was nothing to balk at, it was complete between them.

At the wedding, his face was stiff and expressionless. He wanted to drink, to get rid of his forethought and afterthought, to set the moment free. But he could not. The suspense only tightened at his heart. The jesting and joviality and jolly, broad insinuation of the guests only coiled him more. He could not hear. That which was impending obsessed him, he could not get free.

She sat quiet, with a strange, still smile. She was not afraid. Having accepted him, she wanted to take him, she belonged altogether to the hour, now. No future, no past, only this, her hour. She did not even notice him, as she sat beside him at the head of the table. He was very near, their coming together was close at hand. What more!

As the time came for all the guests to go, her dark face was softly lighted, the bend of her head was proud, her grey eyes clear and dilated, so that the men could not look at her, and the women were elated by her, they served her. Very wonderful she was, as she bade farewell, her ugly wide mouth smiling with pride and recognition, her voice speaking softly and richly in the foreign accent, her dilated eyes ignoring one and all the departing guests. Her manner was gracious and fascinating, but she ignored the being of him or her to whom she gave her hand.

And Brangwen stood beside her, giving his hearty handshake to his friends, receiving their regard gratefully, glad of their attention. His heart was tormented within him, he did not try to smile. The time of his trial and his admittance, his Gethsemane and his Triumphal Entry in one, had come now.

Behind her, there was so much unknown to him. When he approached her, he came to such a terrible painful unknown. How could he embrace it and fathom it? How could he close his arms round all this darkness and hold it to his breast and give himself to it? What might not happen to him? If he stretched and strained for ever he would never be able to grasp it all, and to yield himself naked out of his own hands into the unknown power! How could a man be strong enough to take her, put his arms round her and have her, and be sure he could conquer this awful unknown next his heart? What was it then that she was, to which he must also deliver himself up, and which at the same time he must embrace, contain?

He was to be her husband. It was established so. And he wanted it more than he wanted life, or anything. She stood beside him in her silk dress, looking at him strangely, so that a certain terror, horror took possession of him, because she was strange and impending and he had no choice. He could not bear to meet her look from under her strange, thick brows.

"Is it late?" she said.

He looked at his watch.

"No—half-past eleven," he said. And he made an excuse to go into the kitchen, leaving her standing in the room among the disorder and the drinking-glasses.

Tilly was seated beside the fire in the kitchen, her head in her hands. She started up when he entered.

"Why haven't you gone to bed?" he said.

"I thought I'd better stop an' lock up an' do," she said. Her agitation quietened him. He gave her some little order, then returned, steadied now, almost ashamed, to his wife. She stood a moment watching him, as he moved with averted face. Then she said:

"You will be good to me, won't you?"

She was small and girlish and terrible, with a queer, wide look in her eyes. His heart leaped in him, in anguish of love and desire, he went blindly to her and took her in his arms.

"I want to," he said as he drew her closer and closer in. She was soothed by the stress of his embrace, and remained quite still, relaxed against him, mingling in to him. And he let himself go from past and future, was reduced to the moment with her. In which he took her and was with her and there was nothing beyond, they were together in an elemental embrace beyond their superficial foreignness. But in the morning he was uneasy again. She was still foreign and unknown to him. Only, within the fear was pride, belief in himself as mate for her. And she, everything forgotten in her new hour of coming to life, radiated vigour and joy, so that he quivered to touch her.

It made a great difference to him, marriage. Things became so remote and of so little significance, as he knew the powerful source of his life, his eyes opened on a new universe, and he wondered in thinking of his triviality before. A new, calm relationship showed to him in the things he saw, in the cattle he used, the young wheat as it eddied in a wind.

And each time he returned home, he went steadily, expectantly, like a man who goes to a profound, unknown satisfaction. At dinner-time, he appeared in the doorway, hanging back a moment from entering, to see if she was there. He saw her setting the plates on the white-scrubbed table. Her arms were slim, she had a slim body and full skirts, she had a dark, shapely head with close-banded hair. Somehow it was her head, so shapely and poignant, that revealed her his woman to him. As she moved about clothed closely, full-skirted and wearing her little silk apron, her dark hair smoothly parted, her head revealed itself to him in all its subtle, intrinsic beauty, and he knew she was his woman, he knew her essence, that it was his to possess. And he seemed to live thus in contact with her, in contact with the unknown, the unaccountable and incalculable.

They did not take much notice of each other, consciously.

"I'm betimes," he said.

"Yes," she answered.

He turned to the dogs, or to the child if she was there. The little Anna played about the farm, flitting constantly in to call something to her mother, to fling her arms round her mother's skirts, to be noticed, perhaps caressed, then, forgetting, to slip out again.

Then Brangwen, talking to the child, or to the dog between his knees, would be aware of his wife, as, in her tight, dark bodice and her lace fichu, she was reaching up to the corner cupboard. He realised with a sharp pang that she belonged to him, and he to her. He realised that he lived by her. Did he own her? Was she here for ever? Or might she go away? She was not really his, it was not a real marriage, this marriage between them. She might go away. He did not feel like a master, husband, father of her children. She belonged elsewhere. Any moment, she might be gone. And he was ever drawn to her, drawn after her, with ever-raging, ever-unsatisfied desire. He must always turn home, wherever his steps were taking him, always to her, and he could never quite reach her, he could never quite be satisfied, never be at peace, because she might go away.

At evening, he was glad. Then, when he had finished in the yard, and come in and washed himself, when the child was put to bed, he could sit on the other side of the fire with his beer on the hob and his long white pipe in his fingers, conscious of her there opposite him, as she worked at her embroidery, or as she talked to him, and he was safe with her now, till morning. She was curiously self-sufficient and did not say very much. Occasionally she lifted her head, her grey eyes shining with a strange light, that had nothing to do with him or with this place, and would tell him about herself. She seemed to be back again in the past, chiefly in her childhood or her girlhood, with her father. She very rarely talked of her first husband. But sometimes, all shining-eyed, she was back at her own home, telling him about the riotous times, the trip to Paris with her father, tales of the mad acts of the peasants when a burst of religious, self-hurting fervour had passed over the country.

She would lift her head and say:

"When they brought the railway across the country, they made afterwards smaller railways, of shorter width, to come down to our town—a hundred miles. When I was a girl, Gisla, my German gouvernante, was very shocked and she would not tell me. But I heard the servants talking. I remember, it was Pierre, the coachman. And my father, and some of his friends, landowners, they had taken a wagon, a whole railway wagon—that you travel in——"

"A railway-carriage," said Brangwen.

She laughed to herself.

"I know it was a great scandal: yes—a whole wagon, and they had girls, you know, *filles*, naked, all the wagon-full, and so they came down to our village. They came through villages of the Jews, and it was a great scandal. Can you imagine? All the countryside! And my mother, she did not like it. Gisla said to me, 'Madame, she must not know that you have heard such things.'

"My mother, she used to cry, and she wished to beat my father, plainly beat him. He would say, when she cried because he sold the forest, the wood, to jingle money in his pocket, and go to Warsaw or Paris or Kiev, when she said he must take back his word, he must not sell the forest, he would stand and say, 'I know, I know, I have heard it all, I have heard it all before. Tell me some new thing. I know, I know, I know.' Oh, but can you understand, I loved him when he stood there under the door, saying only, 'I know, I know, I know it all already.' She could not change him, no, not if she killed herself for it. And she could change everybody else, but him, she could not change him——"

Brangwen could not understand. He had pictures of a cattle-truck full of naked girls riding from nowhere to nowhere, of Lydia laughing because her father made great debts and said, "I know, I know"; of Jews running down the street shouting in Yiddish, "Don't do it, don't do it," and being cut down by demented peasants—she called them "cattle"—whilst she looked on interested and even amused; of tutors and governesses and Paris and a convent. It was too much for him. And there she sat, telling the tales to the open space, not to him, arrogating a curious superiority to him, a distance between them, something strange and foreign and outside his life, talking, rattling, without rhyme or reason, laughing when he was shocked or astounded, condemning nothing, confounding his mind and making the whole world a chaos, without order or stability of any kind. Then, when they went to bed, he knew that he had nothing to do with her. She was back in her childhood, he was a peasant, a serf, a servant, a lover, a paramour, a shadow, a nothing. He lay still in amazement, staring at the room he knew so well, and wondering whether it was really there, the window, the chest of drawers, or whether it was merely a figment in the atmosphere. And gradually he grew into a raging fury against her. But because he was so much amazed, and there was as yet such a distance between them, and she was such an amazing thing to him, with all wonder opening out behind her, he made no retaliation on her. Only he lay still and wide-eyed with rage, inarticulate, not understanding, but solid with hostility.

And he remained wrathful and distinct from her, unchanged outwardly to her, but underneath a solid power of antagonism to her. Of which she became gradually aware. And it ii :ated her to be made aware of him as a separate power. She lapsed into a sort of sombre exclusion, a curious communion with mysterious powers, a sort of mystic, dark state which drove him and the child nearly mad. He walked about for days stiffened with resistance to her, stiff with a will to destroy her as she was. Then suddenly, out of nowhere, there was connection between them again. It came on him as he was working in the fields. The tension, the bond, burst, and the passionate flood broke forward into a tremendous, magnificent rush, so that he felt he could snap off the trees as he passed, and create the world afresh.

And when he arrived home, there was no sign between them. He waited and waited till she came. And as he waited, his limbs seemed strong and splendid to him, his hands seemed like passionate servants to him, goodly, he felt a stupendous power in himself, of life, and of urgent, strong blood.

She was sure to come at last, and touch him. Then he burst into flame for her, and lost himself. They looked at each other, a deep laugh at the bottom of their eyes, and he went to take of her again, wholesale, mad to revel in the inexhaustible wealth of her, to bury himself in the depths of her in an inexhaustible exploration, she all the while revelling in that he revelled in her, tossed all her secrets aside and plunged to that which was secret to her as well, whilst she quivered with fear and the last anguish of delight.

What did it matter who they were, whether they knew each other or not?

The hour passed away again, there was severance between them, and rage and misery and bereavement for her, and deposition and toiling at the mill with slaves for him. But no matter. They had had their hour, and should it chime again, they were ready for it, ready to renew the game at the point where it was left off, on the edge of the outer darkness, when the secrets within the woman are game for the man, hunted doggedly, when the secrets of the woman are the man's adventure, and they both give themselves to the adventure.

She was with child, and there was again the silence and distance between them. She did not want him nor his secrets nor his game, he was deposed, he was cast out. He seethed with fury at the small, ugly-mouthed woman who had nothing to do with him. Sometimes his anger broke on her, but she did not cry. She turned on him like a tiger, and there was battle.

He had to learn to contain himself again, and he hated it. He hated her that she was not there for him. And he took himself off, anywhere.

But an instinct of gratitude and a knowledge that she would receive him back again, that later on she would be there for him again, prevented his straying very far. He cautiously did not go too far. He knew she might lapse into ignorance of him, lapse away from him, farther, farther, farther, till she was lost to him. He had sense enough, premonition enough in himself, to be aware of this and to measure himself accordingly. For he did not want to lose her: he did not want her to lapse away.

Cold, he called her, selfish, only caring about herself, a foreigner with a bad nature, caring really about nothing, having no proper feelings at the bottom of her, and no proper niceness. He raged, and piled up accusations that had some measure of truth in them all. But a certain grace in him forbade him from going too far. He knew, and he quivered with rage and hatred, that she was all these vile things, that she was everything vile and detestable. But he had grace at the bottom of him, which told him that, above all things, he did not want to lose her, he was not going to lose her.

So he kept some consideration for her, he preserved some relationship. He went out more often, to the "Red Lion" again, to escape the madness of sitting next to her when she did not belong to him, when she was as absent as any woman in difference could be. He could not stay at home. So he went to the "Red Lion". And sometimes he got drunk. But he preserved his measure, some things between them he never forfeited.

A tormented look came into his eyes, as if something were always dogging him. He glanced sharp and quick, he could not bear to sit still doing nothing. He had to go out, to find company, to give himself away there. For he had no other outlet, he could not work to give himself out, he had not the knowledge.

As the months of her pregnancy went on, she left him more and more alone, she was more and more unaware of him, his existence was annulled. And he felt bound down, bound, unable to stir, beginning to go mad, ready to rave. For she was quiet and polite, as if he did not exist, as one is quiet and polite to a servant.

Nevertheless she was great with his child, it was his turn to submit. She sat opposite him, sewing, her foreign face inscrutable and indifferent. He felt he wanted to break her into acknowledgement of him, into awareness of him. It was insufferable that she had so obliterated him. He would smash her into regarding him. He had a raging agony of desire to do so.

But something bigger in him withheld him, kept him motionless. So he went out of the house for relief. Or he turned to the little girl for her sympathy and her love, he appealed with all his power to the small Anna. So soon they were like lovers, father and child.

For he was afraid of his wife. As she sat there with bent head, silent, working or reading, but so unutterably silent that his heart seemed under the millstone of it, she became herself like the upper millstone lying on him, crushing him, as sometimes a heavy sky lies on the earth.

Yet he knew he could not tear her away from the heavy obscurity into which she was merged. He must not try to tear her into recognition of himself, and agreement with himself. It were disastrous, impious. So, let him rage as he might, he must withhold himself. But his wrists trembled and seemed mad, seemed as if they would burst.

When, in November, the leaves came beating against the window shutters, with a lashing sound, he started, and his eyes flickered with flame. The dog looked up at him, he sunk his head to the fire. But his wife was startled. He was aware of her listening.

"They blow up with a rattle," he said.

"What?" she asked.

"The leaves."

She sank away again. The strange leaves beating in the wind on the wood had come nearer than she. The tension in the room was overpowering, it was difficult for him to move his head. He sat with every nerve, every vein, every fibre of muscle in his body stretched on a tension. He felt like a broken arch thrust sickeningly out from support. For her response was gone, he thrust at nothing. And he remained himself, he saved himself from crashing down into nothingness, from being squandered into fragments, by sheer tension, sheer backward resistance.

During the last months of her pregnancy, he went about in a surcharged, imminent state that did not exhaust itself. She was also depressed, and sometimes she cried. It needed so much life to begin afresh, after she had lost so lavishly. Sometimes she cried. Then he stood stiff, feeling his heart would burst. For she did not want him, she did not want even to be made aware of him. By the very puckering of her face he knew that he must stand back, leave her intact, alone. For it was the old grief come back in her, the old loss, the pain of the old life, the dead husband, the dead children. This was sacred to her, and he must not violate her with his comfort. For what she wanted she would come to him. He stood aloof with turgid heart.

He had to see her tears come, fall over her scarcely moving face, that only puckered sometimes, down on to her breast, that was so still, scarcely moving. And there was no noise, save now and again, when, with a strange, somnambulant movement, she took her handkerchief and wiped her face and blew her nose, and went on with the noiseless weeping. He knew that any offer of comfort from himself would be worse than useless, hateful to her, jangling her. She must cry. But it drove him insane. His heart was scalded, his brain hurt in his head, he went away, out of the house.

His great and chiefest source of solace was the child. She had been at first aloof from him, reserved. However friendly she might seem one day, the next she would have lapsed to her original disregard of him, cold, detached, at her distance.

The first morning after his marriage he had discovered it would not be so easy with the child. At the break of dawn he had started awake hearing a small voice outside the door saying plaintively:

"Mother!"

He rose and opened the door. She stood on the threshold in her night-dress, as she had climbed out of bed, black eyes staring round and hostile, her fair hair sticking out in a wild fleece. The man and child confronted each other.

"I want my mother," she said, jealously accenting the "my".

"Come on then," he said gently.

"Where's my mother?"

"She's here—come on."

The child's eyes, staring at the man with ruffled hair and beard, did not change. The mother's voice called softly. The little bare feet entered the room with trepidation.

"Mother!"

"Come, my dear."

The small bare feet approached swiftly.

"I wondered where you were," came the plaintive voice. The mother stretched out her arms. The child stood beside the high bed. Brangwen lightly lifted the tiny girl, with an "up-a-daisy", then took his own place in the bed again.

"Mother!" cried the child, as in anguish.

"What, my pet?"

Anna wriggled close into her mother's arms, clinging tight, hiding from the fact of the man. Brangwen lay still, and waited. There was a long silence.

Then suddenly, Anna looked round, as if she thought he would be gone. She saw the face of the man lying upturned to the ceiling. Her black eyes stared antagonistic from her exquisite face, her arms clung tightly to her mother, afraid. He did not move for some time, not knowing what to say. His face was smooth and soft-skinned with love, his eyes full of soft light. He looked at her, scarcely moving his head, his eyes smiling.

"Have you just wakened up?" he said.

"Go away," she retorted, with a little darting forward of the head, something like a viper.

"Nay," he answered, *"I'm* not going. You can go."

"Go away," came the sharp little command.

"There's room for you," he said.

"You can't send your father from his own bed, my little bird," said her mother, pleasantly.

The child glowered at him, miserable in her impotence.

"There's room for you as well," he said. "It's a big bed enough."

She glowered without answering, then turned and clung to her mother. She would not allow it.

During the day she asked her mother several times:

"When are we going home, mother?"

"We are at home, darling, we live here now. This is our house, we live here with your father."

The child was forced to accept it. But she remained against the man. As night came on, she asked:

"Where are you going to sleep, mother?"

"I sleep with the father now."

And when Brangwen came in, the child asked fiercely:

"Why do you sleep with *my* mother? My mother sleeps with me," her voice quivering.

"You come as well, an' sleep with both of us," he coaxed.

"Mother!" she cried, turning, appealing against him.

"But I must have a husband, darling. All women must have a husband."

"And you like to have a father with your mother, don't you?" said Brangwen.

Anna glowered at him. She seemed to cogitate.

"No," she cried fiercely at length, "no, I don't *want.*" And slowly her face puckered, she sobbed bitterly. He stood and watched her, sorry. But there could be no altering it.

Which, when she knew, she became quiet. He was easy with her, talking to her, taking her to see the live creatures, bringing her the first chickens in his cap, taking her to gather the eggs, letting her throw crusts to the horse. She would easily accompany him, and take all he had to give, but she remained neutral still.

She was curiously, incomprehensibly jealous of her mother, always anxiously concerned about her. If Brangwen drove with his wife to Nottingham, Anna ran about happily enough, or unconcerned, for a long time. Then, as afternoon came on, there was only one cry—"I want my mother, I want my mother——" and a bitter, pathetic sobbing that soon had the soft-hearted Tilly sobbing too. The child's anguish was that her mother was gone, gone.

Yet as a rule, Anna seemed cold, resenting her mother, critical of her. It was: "I don't like you to do that, mother," or, "I don't like you to say that." She was a sore problem to Brangwen and to all the people at the Marsh. As a rule, however, she was active, lightly flitting about the farmyard, only appearing now and again to assure herself of her mother. Happy she never seemed, but quick, sharp, absorbed, full of imagination and changeability. Tilly said she was bewitched. But it did not matter so long as she did not cry. There was something heartrending about Anna's crying, her childish anguish seemed so utter and so timeless, as if it were a thing of all the ages.

She made playmates of the creatures of the farmyard, talking to them, telling them the stories she had from her mother, counselling them and correcting them. Brangwen found her at the gate leading to the paddock and to the duck-pond. She was peering through the bars and shouting to the stately white geese, that stood in a curving line:

"You're not to call at people when they want to come. You must not do it."

The heavy, balanced birds looked at the fierce little face and the fleece of keen hair thrust between the bars, and they raised their heads and swayed off, producing the long, cancanking, protesting noise of geese, rocking their ship-like, beautiful white bodies in a line beyond the gate.

"You're naughty, you're naughty," cried Anna, tears of dismay and vexation in her eyes. And she stamped her slipper.

"Why, what are they doing?" said Brangwen.

"They won't let me come in," she said, turning her flushed little face to him.

"Yi, they will. You can go in if you want to," and he pushed open the gate for her.

She stood irresolute, looking at the group of bluey-white geese standing monumental under the grey, cold day.

"Go on," he said.

She marched valiantly a few steps in. Her little body started convulsively at the sudden, derisive can-cank-ank of the geese. A blankness spread over her. The geese trailed away with uplifted heads under the low grey sky.

"They don't know you," said Brangwen. "You should tell 'em what your name is."

"They're *naughty* to shout at me," she flashed.

"They think you don't live here," he said.

Later he found her at the gate calling shrilly and imperiously:

"My name is Anna, Anna Lensky, and I live here, because Mr. Brangwen's my father now. He *is*, yes he *is*. And I live here."

This pleased Brangwen very much. And gradually, without knowing it herself, she clung to him, in her lost, childish, desolate moments, when it was good to creep up to something big and warm, and bury her little self in his big, unlimited being. Instinctively he was careful of her, careful to recognize her and to give himself to her disposal.

She was difficult of her affections. For Tilly, she had a childish, essential contempt, almost dislike, because the poor woman was such a servant. The child would not let the serving-woman attend to her, do intimate things for her, not for a long time. She treated her as one of an inferior race. Brangwen did not like it.

"Why aren't you fond of Tilly?" he asked.

"Because—because—because she looks at me with her eyes bent."

Then gradually she accepted Tilly as belonging to the household, never as a person.

For the first weeks, the black eyes of the child were for ever on the watch. Brangwen, good-humoured but impatient, spoiled by Tilly, was an easy blusterer. If for a few minutes he upset the household with his noisy impatience, he found at the end the child glowering at him with intense black eyes, and she was sure to dart forward her little head, like a serpent, with her biting:

"Go away."

"I'm *not* going away," he shouted, irritated at last. "Go yourself—hustle-stir thysen—hop." And he pointed to the door. The child backed away from him, pale with fear. Then she gathered up courage, seeing him become patient.

"We don't live with *you*," she said, thrusting forward her little head at him. "You—you're—you're a bomakle."

"A what?" he shouted.

Her voice wavered—but it came.

"A bomakle."

"Ay, an' you're a comakle."

She meditated. Then she hissed forwards her head.

"I'm not."

"Not what?"

"A comakle."

"No more am I a bomakle."

He was really cross.

Other times she would say:

"My mother *doesn't* live here."

"Oh, ay?"

"I want her to go away."

"Then want's your portion," he replied laconically.

So they drew nearer together. He would take her with him when he went out in the trap. The horse ready at the gate, he came noisily into the house, which seemed quiet and peaceful till he appeared to set everything awake.

"Now then, Topsy, pop into thy bonnet."

The child drew herself up, resenting the indignity of the address.

"I can't fasten my bonnet myself," she said haughtily.

"Not man enough yet," he said, tying the ribbons under her chin with clumsy fingers.

She held up her face to him. Her little bright-red lips moved as he fumbled under her chin.

"You talk—nonsents," she said, re-echoing one of his phrases.

"*That* face shouts for th' pump," he said, and taking out a big red handkerchief, that smelled of strong tobacco, began wiping round her mouth.

"Is Kitty waiting for me?" she asked.

"Ay," he said. "Let's finish wiping your face—it'll pass wi' a cat-lick."

She submitted prettily. Then, when he let her go, she began to skip, with a curious flicking up of one leg behind her.

"Now my young buck-rabbit," he said. "Slippy!"

She came and was shaken into her coat, and the two set off. She sat very close beside him in the gig, tucked tightly, feeling his big body sway, against her, very splendid. She loved the rocking of the gig, when his big, live body swayed upon her, against her. She laughed, a poignant little shrill laugh, and her black eyes glowed.

She was curiously hard, and then passionately tender-hearted. Her mother was ill, the child stole about on tip-toe in the bedroom for hours, being nurse, and doing the thing thoughtfully and diligently. Another day, her mother was unhappy. Anna would stand with her legs apart, glowering, balancing on the sides of her slippers. She laughed when the goslings wriggled in Tilly's hand, as the pellets of food were rammed down their throats with a skewer, she laughed nervously. She was hard and imperious with the animals, squandering no love, running about amongst them like a cruel mistress.

Summer came, and hay-harvest, Anna was a brown elfish mite dancing about. Tilly always marvelled over her, more than she loved her.

But always in the child was some anxious connection with the mother. So long as Mrs. Brangwen was all right, the little girl played about and took very little notice of her. But corn-harvest went by, the autumn drew on, and the mother, the later months of her pregnancy beginning, was strange and detached, Brangwen began to knit his brows, the old, unhealthy uneasiness, the unskinned susceptibility came on the child again. If she went to the fields with her father, then, instead of playing about carelessly, it was:

"I want to go home."

"Home, why tha's nobbut this minute come."

"I want to go home."

"What for? What ails thee?"

"I want my mother."

"Thy mother! Thy mother none wants thee."

"I want to go home."

There would be tears in a moment.

"Can ter find t'road, then?"

And he watched her scudding, silent and intent, along the hedge-bottom, at a steady, anxious pace, till she turned and was gone through the gateway. Then he saw her two fields off, still pressing forward, small and urgent. His face was clouded as he turned to plough up the stubble.

The year drew on, in the hedges the berries shone red and twinkling above bare twigs, robins were seen, great droves of birds dashed like spray from the fallow, rooks appeared, black and flapping down to earth, the ground was cold as he pulled the turnips, the roads were churned deep in mud. Then the turnips were pitted and work was slack.

Inside the house it was dark, and quiet. The child flitted uneasily round, and now and again came her plaintive, startled cry:

"Mother!"

Mrs. Brangwen was heavy and unresponsive, tired, lapsed back. Brangwen went on working out of doors.

At evening, when he came in to milk, the child would run behind him. Then, in the cosy cow-sheds, with the doors shut and the air looking warm by the light of the hanging lantern, above the branching horns of the cows, she would stand watching his hands squeezing rhythmically the teats of the placid beast, watch the froth and the leaping squirt of milk, watch his hand sometimes rubbing slowly, understandingly, upon a hanging udder. So they kept each other company, but at a distance, rarely speaking.

The darkest days of the year came on, the child was fretful, sighing as if some oppression were on her, running hither and thither without relief. And Brangwen went about at his work, heavy, his heart heavy as the sodden earth.

The winter nights fell early, the lamp was lighted before tea-time, the shutters were closed, they were all shut into the room with the tension and stress. Mrs. Brangwen went early to bed, Anna playing on the floor beside her. Brangwen sat in the emptiness of the downstairs room, smoking, scarcely conscious even of his own misery. And very often he went out to escape it.

Christmas passed, the wet, drenched, cold days of January recurred monotonously, with now and then a brilliance of blue flashing in, when Brangwen went out into a morning like crystal, when every sound rang again, and the birds were many and sudden and brusque in the hedges. Then an elation came over him in spite of everything, whether his wife were strange or sad, or whether he craved for her to be with him, it did not matter, the air rang with clear noises, the sky was like crystal, like a bell, and the earth was hard. Then he worked and was happy, his eyes shining, his cheeks flushed. And the zest of life was strong in him.

The birds pecked busily round him, the horses were fresh and ready, the bare branches of the trees flung themselves up like a man yawning, taut with energy, the twigs radiated off into the clear light. He was alive and full of zest for it all. And if his wife were heavy, separated from him, extinguished, then, let her be, let him remain himself. Things would be as they would be. Meanwhile he heard the ringing crow of a cockerel in the distance, he saw the pale shell of the moon effaced on a blue sky.

So he shouted to the horses, and was happy. If, driving into Ilkeston, a fresh young woman were going in to do her shopping, he hailed her, and reined in his horse, and picked her up. Then he was glad to have her near him, his eyes shone, his voice, laughing, teasing in a warm fashion, made the poise of her head more beautiful, her blood ran quicker. They were both stimulated, the morning was fine.

What did it matter that, at the bottom of his heart, was care and pain? It was at the bottom, let it stop at the bottom. His wife, her suffering, her coming pain—well, it must be so. She suffered, but he was out of doors, full in life, and it would be ridiculous, indecent, to pull a long face and to insist on being miserable. He was happy, this morning, driving to town, with the hoofs of the horse spanking the hard earth. Well he was happy, if half the world were weeping at the funeral of the other half. And it was a jolly girl sitting beside him. And Woman was immortal, whatever happened, whoever turned towards death. Let the misery come when it could not be resisted.

The evening arrived later very beautiful, with a rosy flush hovering above the sunset, and passing away into violet and lavender, with turquoise green north and south in the sky, and in the east, a great, yellow moon hanging heavy and radiant. It was magnificent to walk between the sunset and the moon, on a road where little holly trees thrust black into the rose and lavender, and starlings flickered in droves across the light. But what was the end of the journey? The pain came right enough, later on, when his heart and his feet were heavy, his brain dead, his life stopped.

One afternoon, the pains began, Mrs. Brangwen was put to bed, the midwife came. Night fell, the shutters were closed, Brangwen came in to tea, to the loaf and the pewter teapot, the child, silent and quivering, playing with glass beads, the house, empty, it seemed, or exposed to the winter night, as if it had no walls.

Sometimes there sounded, long and remote in the house, vibrating through everything, the moaning cry of a woman in labour. Brangwen, sitting downstairs, was divided. His lower, deeper self was with her, bound to her, suffering. But the big shell of his body remembered the sound of owls that used to fly round the farmstead when he was a boy. He was back in his youth, a boy, haunted by the sound of the owls, waking up his brother to speak to him. And his mind drifted away to the birds, their solemn, dignified faces, their flight so soft and broad-winged. And then to the birds his brother had shot, fluffy, dust-coloured, dead heaps of softness with faces absurdly asleep. It was a queer thing, a dead owl.

He lifted his cup to his lips, he watched the child with the beads. But his mind was occupied with owls, and the atmosphere of his boyhood, with his brothers and sisters. Elsewhere, fundamental, he was with his wife in labour, the child was being brought forth out of their one flesh. He and she, one flesh, out of which life must be put forth. The rent was not in his body, but it was of his body. On her the blows fell, but the quiver ran through to him, to his last fibre. She must be torn asunder for life to come forth, yet still they were one flesh, and still, from further back, the life came out of him to her, and still he was the unbroken that has the broken rock in its arms, their flesh was one rock from which the life gushed, out of her who was smitten and rent, from him who quivered and yielded.

He went upstairs to her. As he came to the bedside she spoke to him in Polish.

"Is it very bad?" he asked.

She looked at him, anc oh, the weariness to her, of the effort to understand another language, the weariness of hearing him, attending to him, making out who he was, as he stood there fair-bearded and alien, looking at her. She knew something of him, of his eyes. But she could not grasp him. She closed her eyes.

He turned away, white to the gills.

"It's not so very bad," said the midwife.

He knew he was a strain on his wife. He went downstairs.

The child glanced up at him, frightened.

"I want my mother," she quavered.

"Ay, but she's badly," he said mildly, unheeding.

She looked at him with lost, frightened eyes.

"Has she got a headache?"

"No—she's going to have a baby."

The child looked round. He was unaware of her. She was alone again in terror.

"I want my mother," came the cry of panic.

"Let Tilly undress you," he said. "You're tired."

There was another silence. Again came the cry of labour.

"I want my mother," rang automatically from the wincing, panic-stricken child, that felt cut off and lost in a horror of desolation.

Tilly came forward, her heart wrung.

"Come an' let me undress her then, pet-lamb," she crooned. "You s'll have your mother in th' mornin', don't you fret, my duckie; never mind, angel."

But Anna stood upon the sofa, her back to the wall.

"I want my mother," she cried, her little face quivering, and the great tears of childish, utter anguish falling.

"She's poorly, my lamb, she's poorly to-night, but she'll be better by mornin'. Oh, don't cry, don't cry, love, she doesn't want you to cry, precious little heart, no, she doesn't."

Tilly took gently hold of the child's skirts. Anna snatched back her dress, and cried, in a little hysteria:

"No, you're not to undress me—I want my mother,"—and her child's face was running with grief and tears, her body shaken.

"Oh, but let Tilly undress you. Let Tilly undress you, who loves you, don't be wilful to-night. Mother's poorly, she doesn't want you to cry."

The child sobbed distractedly, she could not hear.

"I want my mother," she wept.

"When you're undressed, you s'll go up to see your mother—when you're undressed, pet, when you've let Tilly undress you, when you're a little jewel in your nightie, love. Oh, don't you cry, don't you——"

Brangwen sat stiff in his chair. He felt his brain going tighter. He crossed over the room, aware only of the maddening sobbing.

"Don't make a noise," he said.

And a new fear shook the child from the sound of his voice. She cried mechanically, her eyes looking watchful through her tears, in terror, alert to what might happen.

"I want—my—mother," quavered the sobbing, blind voice.

A shiver of irritation went over the man's limbs. It was the utter, persistent unreason, the maddening blindness of the voice and the crying.

"You must come and be undressed," he said, in a quiet voice that was thin with anger.

And he reached his hand and grasped her. He felt her body catch in a convulsive sob. But he too was blind, and intent, irritated into mechanical action. He began to unfasten her little apron. She would have shrunk from him, but could not. So her small body remained in his grasp, while he fumbled at the little buttons and tapes, unthinking, intent, unaware of anything but the irritation of her. Her body was held taut and resistant, he pushed off the little dress and the petticoats, revealing the white arms. She kept stiff, overpowered, violated, he went on with his task. And all the while she sobbed, choking:

"I want my mother."

He was unheedingly silent, his face stiff. The child was now incapable of understanding, she had become a little, mechanical thing of fixed will. She wept, her body convulsed, her voice repeating the same cry.

"Eh, dear o' me!" cried Tilly, becoming distracted herself. Brangwen, slow, clumsy, blind, intent, got off all the little garments, and stood the child naked in its shift upon the sofa.

"Where's her nightie?" he asked.

Tilly brought it, and he put it on her. Anna did not move her limbs to his desire. He had to push them into place. She stood, with fixed, blind will, resistant, a small, convulsed, unchangeable thing weeping ever and repeating the same phrase. He lifted one foot after the other, pulled off slippers and socks. She was ready.

"Do you want a drink?" he asked.

She did not change. Unheeding, uncaring, she stood on the sofa, standing back, alone, her hands shut and half lifted, her face, all tears, raised and blind. And through the sobbing and choking came the broken:

"I—want—my—mother."

"Do you want a drink?" he said again.

There was no answer. He lifted the stiff, denying body between his hands. Its stiff blindness made a flash of rage go through him. He would like to break it.

He set the child on his knee, and sat again in his chair beside the fire, the wet, sobbing, inarticulate noise going on near his ear, the child sitting stiff, not yielding to him or anything, not aware.

A new degree of anger came over him. What did it all matter? What did it matter if the mother talked Polish and cried in labour, if this child were stiff with resistance, and crying? Why take it to heart? Let the mother cry in labour, let the child cry in resistance, since they would do so. Why should he fight against it, why resist? Let it be, if it were so. Let them be as they were, if they insisted.

And in a daze he sat, offering no fight. The child cried on, the minutes ticked away, a sort of torpor was on him.

It was some little time before he came to, and turned to attend to the child. He was shocked by her little wet, blinded face. A bit dazed, he pushed back the wet hair. Like a living statue of grief, her blind face cried on.

"Nay," he said, "not as bad as that. It's not as bad as that, Anna, my child. Come, what are you crying for so much? Come, stop now, it'll make you sick. I wipe you dry, don't wet your face any more. Don't cry any more wet tears, don't, it's better not to. Don't cry—it's not so bad as all that. Hush now, hush—let it be enough."

His voice was queer and distant and calm. He looked at the child. She was beside herself now. He wanted her to stop, he wanted it all to stop, to become natural.

"Come," he said, rising to turn away, "we'll go an' supper-up the beast."

He took a big shawl, folded her round, and went out into the kitchen for a lantern.

"You're never taking the child out, of a night like this," said Tilly.

"Ay, it'll quieten her," he answered.

It was raining. The child was suddenly still, shocked, finding the rain on its face, the darkness.

"We'll just give the cows their something-to-eat, afore they go to bed," Brangwen was saying to her, holding her close and sure.

There was a trickling of water into the butt, a burst of rain-drops sputtering on to her shawl, and the light of the lantern swinging, flashing on a wet pavement and the base of a wet wall. Otherwise it was black darkness: one breathed darkness.

He opened the doors, upper and lower, and they entered into the high, dry barn, that smelled warm even if it were not warm. He hung the lantern on the nail and shut the door. They were in another world now. The light shed softly on the timbered barn, on the whitewashed walls, and the great heap of hay; instruments cast their shadows largely, a ladder rose to the dark arch of a loft. Outside there was the driving rain, inside, the softly-illuminated stillness and calmness of the barn.

Holding the child on one arm, he set about preparing the food for the cows, filling a pan with chopped hay and brewer's grains and a little meal. The child, all wonder, watched what he did. A new being was created in her for the new conditions. Sometimes, a little spasm, eddying from the bygone storm of sobbing, shook her small body. Her eyes were wide and wondering, pathetic. She was silent, quite still.

In a sort of dream, his heart sunk to the bottom, leaving the surface of him still, quite still, he rose with the panful of food, carefully balancing the child on one arm, the pan in the other hand. The silky fringe of the shawl swayed softly, grains and hay trickled to the floor; he went along a dimly-lit passage behind the mangers, where the horns of the cows pricked out of the obscurity. The child shrank, he balanced stiffly, rested the pan on the manger wall, and tipped out the food, half to this cow, half to the next. There was a noise of chains running, as the cows lifted or dropped their heads sharply; then a contented, soothing sound, a long snuffing as the beasts ate in silence.

The journey had to be performed several times. There was the rhythmic sound of the shovel in the barn, then the man returned walking stiffly between the two weights, the face of the child peering out from the shawl. Then the next time, as he stooped, she freed her arm and put it round his neck, clinging soft and warm, making all easier.

The beasts fed, he dropped the pan and sat down on a box, to arrange the child.

"Will the cows go to sleep now?" she said, catching her breath as she spoke.

"Yes."

"Will they eat all their stuff up first?"

"Yes. Hark at them."

And the two sat still listening to the snuffing and breathing of cows feeding in the sheds communicating with this small barn. The lantern shed a soft, steady light from one wall. All outside was still in the rain. He looked down at the silky folds of the paisley shawl. It reminded him of his mother. She used to go to church in it. He was back again in the old irresponsibility and security, a boy at home.

The two sat very quiet. His mind, in a sort of trance, seemed to become more and more vague. He held the child close to him. A quivering little shudder, re-echoing from her sobbing, went down her limbs. He held her closer. Gradually she relaxed, the eyelids began to sink over her dark, watchful eyes. As she sank to sleep, his mind became blank.

When he came to, as if from sleep, he seemed to be sitting in a timeless stillness. What was he listening for? He seemed to be listening for some sound a long way off, from beyond life. He remembered his wife. He must go back to her. The child was asleep, the eyelids not quite shut, showing a slight film of black pupil between. Why did she not shut her eyes? Her mouth was also a little open.

He rose quickly and went back to the house.

"Is she asleep?" whispered Tilly.

He nodded. The servant-woman came to look at the child who slept in the shawl, with cheeks flushed hot and red, and a whiteness, a wanness round the eyes.

"God-a-mercy!" whispered Tilly, shaking her head.

He pushed off his boots and went upstairs with the child. He became aware of the anxiety grasped tight at his heart, because of his wife. But he remained still. The house was silent save for the wind outside, and the noisy trickling and splattering of water in the water-butts. There was a slit of light under his wife's door.

He put the child into bed wrapped as she was in the shawl, for the sheets would be cold. Then he was afraid that she might not be able to move her arms, so he loosened her. The black eyes opened, rested on him vacantly, sank shut again. He covered her up. The last little quiver from the sobbing shook her breathing.

This was his room, the room he had had before he married. It was familiar. He remembered what it was to be a young man, untouched.

He remained suspended. The child slept, pushing her small fists from the shawl. He could tell the woman her child was asleep. But he must go to the other landing. He started. There was the sound of the owls—the moaning of the woman. What an uncanny sound! It was not human—at least to a man.

He went down to her room, entering softly. She was lying still, with eyes shut, pale, tired. His heart leapt, fearing she was dead. Yet he knew perfectly well she was not. He saw the way her hair went loose over her temples, her mouth was shut with suffering in a sort of grin. She was beautiful to him—but it was not human. He had a dread of her as she lay there. What had she to do with him? She was other than himself.

Something made him go and touch her fingers that were still grasped on the sheet. Her brown-grey eyes opened and looked at him. She did not know him as himself. But she knew him as the man. She looked at him as a woman in childbirth looks at the man who begot the child in her: an impersonal look, in the extreme hour, female to male. Her eyes closed again. A great, scalding peace went over him, burning his heart and his entrails, passing off into the infinite.

When her pains began afresh, tearing her, he turned aside, and could not look. But his heart in torture was at peace, his bowels were glad. He went downstairs, and to the door, outside, lifted his face to the rain, and felt the darkness striking unseen and steadily upon him.

The swift, unseen threshing of the night upon him silenced him and he was overcome. He turned away indoors, humbly. There was the infinite world, eternal, unchanging, as well as the world of life.

III

Childhood of Anna Lensky

Tom Brangwen never loved his own son as he loved his step-child Anna. When they told him it was a boy, he had a thrill of pleasure. He liked the confirmation of fatherhood. It gave him satisfaction to know he had a son. But he felt not very much outgoing to the baby itself. He was its father, that was enough.

He was glad that his wife was mother of his child. She was serene, a little bit shadowy, as if she were transplanted. In the birth of the child she seemed to lose connection with her former self. She became now really English, really Mrs. Brangwen. Her vitality, however, seemed lowered.

She was still, to Brangwen, immeasurably beautiful. She was still passionate, with a flame of being. But the flame was not robust and present. Her eyes shone, her face glowed for him, but like some flower opened in the shade, that could not bear the full light. She loved the baby. But even this, with a sort of dimness, a faint absence about her, a shadowiness even in her mother-love. When Brangwen saw her nursing his child, happy, absorbed in it, a pain went over him like a thin flame. For he perceived how he must subdue himself in his approach to her. And he wanted again the robust, moral exchange of love and passion such as he had had at first with her, at one time and another, when they were matched at their highest intensity. This was the one experience for him now. And he wanted it, always, with remorseless craving.

She came to him again, with the same lifting of her mouth as had driven him almost mad with trammelled passion at first. She came to him again, and, his heart delirious in delight and readiness, he took her. And it was almost as before.

Perhaps it was quite as before. At any rate, it made him know perfection, it established in him a constant eternal knowledge.

But it died down before he wanted it to die down. She was finished, she could take no more. And he was not exhausted, he wanted to go on. But it could not be.

So he had to begin the bitter lesson, to abate himself, to take less than he wanted. For she was Woman to him, all other women were her shadows. For she had satisfied him. And he wanted it to go on. And it could not. However he raged, and, filled with suppression that became hot and bitter, hated her in his soul that she did not want him, however he had mad outbursts, and drank and made ugly scenes, still he knew, he was only kicking against the pricks. It was not, he had to learn, that she *would* not want him enough, as much as he demanded that she should want him. It was that she could not. She could only want him in her own way, and to her own measure. And she had spent much life before he found her as she was, the woman who could take him and give him fulfilment. She had taken him and given him fulfilment. She still could do so, in her own times and ways. But he must control himself, measure himself to her.

He wanted to give her all his love, all his passion, all his essential energy. But it could not be. He must find other things than her, other centres of living. She sat close and impregnable with the child. And he was jealous of the child.

But he loved her, and time came to give some sort of course to his troublesome current of life, so that it did not foam and flood and make misery. He formed another centre of love in her child, Anna. Gradually a part of his stream of life was diverted to the child, relieving the main flood to his wife. Also he sought the company of men, he drank heavily now and again.

The child ceased to have so much anxiety for her mother after the baby came. Seeing the mother with the baby boy, delighted and serene and secure, Anna was at first puzzled, then gradually she became indignant, and at last her little life settled on its own swivel, she was no more strained and distorted to support her mother. She became more childish, not so abnormal, not charged with cares she could not understand. The charge of the mother, the satisfying of the mother, had devolved elsewhere than on her. Gradually the child was freed. She became an independent, forgetful little soul, loving from her own centre.

Of her own choice, she then loved Brangwen most, or most obviously. For these two made a little life together, they had a joint activity. It amused him, at evening, to teach her to count, or to say her letters. He remembered for her all the little nursery rhymes and childish songs that lay forgotten at the bottom of his brain.

At first she thought them rubbish. But he laughed, and she laughed. They became to her a huge joke. Old King Cole she thought was Brangwen. Mother Hubbard was Tilly, her mother was the old woman who lived in a shoe. It was a huge, it was a frantic delight to the child, this nonsense, after her years with her mother, after the poignant folk-tales she had had from her mother, which always troubled and mystified her soul.

She shared a sort of recklessness with her father, a complete, chosen carelessness that had the laugh of ridicule in it. He loved to make her voice go high and shouting and defiant with laughter. The baby was dark-skinned and dark-haired, like the mother, and had hazel eyes. Brangwen called him the blackbird.

"Hallo," Brangwen would cry, starting as he heard the wail of the child announcing it wanted to be taken out of the cradle, "there's the blackbird tuning up."

"The blackbird's singing," Anna would shout with delight, "the blackbird's singing."

"When the pie was opened," Brangwen shouted in his bawling bass voice, going over to the cradle, "the bird began to sing."

"Wasn't it a dainty dish to set before a king?" cried Anna, her eyes flashing with joy as she uttered the cryptic words, looking at Brangwen for confirmation. He sat down with the baby, saying loudly:

"Sing up, my lad, sing up."

And the baby cried loudly, and Anna shouted lustily, dancing in wild bliss:

"Sing a song of sixpence
Pocketful of posies,
Ascha! Ascha!——"

Then she stopped suddenly in silence and looked at Brangwen again, her eyes flashing, as she shouted loudly and delightedly:

"I've got it wrong, I've got it wrong."

"Oh, my sirs," said Tilly entering, "what a racket!"

Brangwen hushed the child and Anna flipped and danced on. She loved her wild bursts of rowdiness with her father. Tilly hated it, Mrs. Brangwen did not mind.

Anna did not care much for other children. She domineered them, she treated them as if they were extremely young and incapable, to her they were little people, they were not her equals. So she was mostly alone, flying round the farm, entertaining the farm-hands and Tilly and the servant-girl, whirring on and never ceasing.

She loved driving with Brangwen in the trap. Then, sitting high up and bowling along, her passion for eminence and dominance was satisfied. She was like a little savage in her arrogance. She thought her father important, she was installed beside him on high. And they spanked along, beside the high, flourishing hedge-tops, surveying the activity of the countryside. When people shouted a greeting to him from the road below, and Brangwen shouted jovially back, her little voice was soon heard shrilling along with his, followed by her chuckling laugh, when she looked up at her father with bright eyes, and they laughed at each other. And soon it was the custom for the passerby to sing out: "How are ter, Tom? Well, my lady!" or else, "Mornin', Tom, mornin', my Lass!" or else, "You're off together then?" or else, "You're lookin' rarely, you two."

Anna would respond, with her father: "How are you, John! *Good* mornin', William! Ay, makin' for Derby," shrilling as loudly as she could. Though often, in response to "You're off out a bit then," she would reply, "Yes, we are," to the great joy of all. She did not like the people who saluted him and did not salute her.

She went into the public-house with him, if he had to call, and often sat beside him in the bar-parlour as he drank his beer or brandy. The landladies paid court to her, in the obsequious way landladies have.

"Well, little lady, an' what's your name?"

"Anna Brangwen," came the immediate, haughty answer.

"Indeed it is! An' do you like driving in a trap with your father?"

"Yes," said Anna, shy, but bored by these inanities. She had a touch-me-not way of blighting the inane inquiries of grown-up people.

"My word, she's a fawce little thing," the landlady would say to Brangwen.

"Ay," he answered, not encouraging comments on the child. Then there followed the present of a biscuit, or of cake, which Anna accepted as her dues.

"What does she say, that I'm a fawce little thing?" the small girl asked afterwards.

"She means you're a sharp-shins."

Anna hesitated. She did not understand. Then she laughed at some absurdity she found.

Soon he took her every week to market with him. "I can come, can't I?" she asked every Saturday, or Thursday morning, when he made himself look fine in his dress of a gentleman farmer. And his face clouded at having to refuse her.

So at last, he overcame his own shyness, and tucked her beside him. They drove into Nottingham and put up at the "Black Swan". So far all right. Then he wanted to leave her at the inn. But he saw her face, and knew it was impossible. So he mustered his courage, and set off with her, holding her hand, to the cattle-market.

She stared in bewilderment, flitting silent at his side. But in the cattle-market she shrank from the press of men, all men, all in heavy, filthy boots, and leathern leggins. And the road underfoot was all nasty with cow-muck. And it frightened her to see the cattle in the square pens, so many horns, and so little enclosure, and such a madness of men and a yelling of drovers. Also she felt her father was embarrassed by her, and ill-at-ease.

He bought her a cake at the refreshment-booth, and set her on a seat. A man hailed him.

"*Good* morning, Tom. That thine, then?"—and the bearded farmer jerked his head at Anna.

"Ay," said Brangwen, deprecating.

"I did-na know tha'd one that old."

"No, it's my missis's."

"Oh, that's it!" And the man looked at Anna as if she were some odd little cattle. She glowered with black eyes.

Brangwen left her there, in charge of the barman, whilst he went to see about the selling of some young stirks. Farmers, butchers, drovers, dirty, uncouth men from whom she shrank instinctively stared down at her as she sat on her seat, then went to get their drink, talking in unabated tones. All was big and violent about her.

"Whose child met that be?" they asked of the barman.

"It belongs to Tom Brangwen."

The child sat on in neglect, watching the door for her father. He never came; many, many men came, but not he, and she sat like a shadow. She knew one did not cry in such a place. And every man looked at her inquisitively, she shut herself away from them.

A deep, gathering coldness of isolation took hold on her. He was never coming back. She sat on, frozen, unmoving.

When she had become blank and timeless he came, and she slipped off her seat to him, like one come back from the dead. He had sold his beast as quickly as he could. But all the business was not finished. He took her again through the hurtling welter of the cattle-market.

Then at last they turned and went out through the gate. He was always hailing one man or another, always stopping to gossip about land and cattle and horses and other things she did not understand, standing in the filth and the smell, among the legs and great boots of men. And always she heard the questions:

"What lass is that, then? I didn't know tha'd one o' that age."

"It belongs to my missis."

Anna was very conscious of her derivation from her mother, in the end, and of her alienation.

But at last they were away, and Brangwen went with her into a little dark, ancient eating-house in the Bridlesmith-Gate. They had cow's-tail soup, and meat and cabbage and potatoes. Other men, other people, came into the dark, vaulted place, to eat. Anna was wide-eyed and silent with wonder.

Then they went into the big market, into the corn exchange, then to shops. He bought her a little book off a stall. He loved buying things, odd things that he thought would be useful. Then they went to the "Black Swan", and she drank milk and he brandy, and they harnessed the horse and drove off, up the Derby Road.

She was tired out with wonder and marvelling. But the next day, when she thought of it, she skipped, flipping her leg in the odd dance she did, and talked the whole time of what had happened to her, of what she had seen. It lasted her all the week. And the next Saturday she was eager to go again.

She became a familiar figure in the cattle-market, sitting waiting in the little booth. But she liked best to go to Derby. There her father had more friends. And she liked the familiarity of the smaller town, the nearness of the river, the strangeness that did not frighten her, it was so much smaller. She liked the covered-in market, and the old women. She liked the "George Inn", where her father put up. The landlord was Brangwen's old friend, and Anna was made much of. She sat many a day in the cosy parlour talking to Mr. Wigginton, a fat man with red hair, the landlord. And when the farmers all gathered at twelve o'clock for dinner, she was a little heroine.

At first she would only glower or hiss at these strange men with their uncouth accent. But they were good-humoured. She was a little oddity, with her fierce, fair hair like spun glass sticking out in a flamy halo round the apple-blossom face and the black eyes, and the men liked an oddity. She kindled their attention.

She was very angry because Marriott, a gentleman-farmer from Ambergate, called her the little pole-cat.

"Why, you're a pole-cat," he said to her.

"I'm not," she flashed.

"You are. That's just how a pole-cat goes."

She thought about it.

"Well, you're—you're——" she began.

"I'm what?"

She looked him up and down.

"You're a bow-leg man."

Which he was. There was a roar of laughter. They loved her that she was indomitable.

"Ah," said Marriott. "Only a pole-cat says that."

"Well, I *am* a pole-cat," she flamed.

There was another roar of laughter from the men.

They loved to tease her.

"Well, me little maid," Braithwaite would say to her, "an' how's th' lamb's wool?"

He gave a tug at a glistening, pale piece of her hair.

"It's not lamb's wool," said Anna, indignantly putting back her offended lock.

"Why, what'st ca' it then?"

"It's hair."

"Hair! Wheriver dun they rear that sort?"

"Wheriver dun they?" she asked, in dialect, her curiosity overcoming her.

Instead of answering he shouted with joy. It was the triumph, to make her speak dialect.

She had one enemy, the man they called Nut-Nat, or Nat-Nut, a cretin, with inturned feet, who came flap-lapping along, shoulder jerking up at every step. This poor creature sold nuts in the public-houses where he was known. He had no roof to his mouth, and the men used to mock his speech.

The first time he came into the "George" when Anna was there, she asked, after he had gone, her eyes very round:

"Why does he do that when he walks?"

" 'E canna 'elp 'isself, Duckie, it's th' make o' th' fellow."

She thought about it, then she laughed nervously. And then she bethought herself, her cheeks flushed, and she cried:

"He's a *horrid* man."

"Nay, he's non horrid; he canna help it if he wor struck that road."

But when poor Nat came wambling in again, she slid away. And she would not eat his nuts, if the men bought them for her. And when the farmers gambled at dominoes for them, she was angry.

"They are dirty-man's nuts," she cried.

So a revulsion started against Nat, who had not long after to go to the work-house.

There grew in Brangwen's heart now a secret desire to make her a lady. His brother Alfred, in Nottingham, had caused a great scandal by becoming the lover of an educated woman, a lady, widow of a doctor. Very often, Alfred Brangwen went down as a friend to her cottage, which was in Derbyshire, leaving his wife and family for a day or two, then returning to them. And no-one dared gainsay him, for he was a strong-willed, direct man, and he said he was a friend of this widow.

One day Brangwen met his brother on the station.

"Where are *you* going to, then?" asked the younger brother.

"I'm going down to Wirksworth."

"You've got friends down there, I'm told."

"Yes."

"I s'll have to be lookin' in when I'm down that road."

"You please yourself."

Tom Brangwen was so curious about the woman that the next time he was in Wirksworth he asked for her house.

He found a beautiful cottage on the steep side of a hill, looking clean over the town, that lay in the bottom of the basin, and away at the old quarries on the opposite side of the space. Mrs. Forbes was in the garden. She was a tall woman with white hair. She came up the path taking off her thick gloves, laying down her shears. It was autumn. She wore a wide-brimmed hat.

Brangwen blushed to the roots of his hair, and did not know what to say.

"I thought I might look in," he said, "knowing you were friends of my brother's. I had to come to Wirksworth."

She saw at once that he was a Brangwen.

"Will you come in?" she said. "My father is lying down."

She took him into a drawing-room, full of books, with a piano and a violin-stand. And they talked, she simply and easily. She was full of dignity. The room was of a kind Brangwen had never known; the atmosphere seemed open and spacious, like a mountain-top to him.

"Does my brother like reading?" he asked.

"Some things. He has been reading Herbert Spencer. And we read Browning sometimes."

Brangwen was full of admiration, deep thrilling, almost reverential admiration. He looked at her with lit-up eyes when she said, "we read". At last he burst out, looking round the room:

"I didn't know our Alfred was this way inclined."

"He is quite an unusual man."

He looked at her in amazement. She evidently had a new idea of his brother: she evidently appreciated him. He looked again at the woman. She was about forty, straight, rather hard, a curious, separate creature. Himself, he was not in love with her, there was something chilling about her. But he was filled with boundless admiration.

At tea-time he was introduced to her father, an invalid who had to be helped about, but who was ruddy and well-favoured, with snowy hair and watery blue eyes, and a courtly naïve manner that again was new and strange to Brangwen, so suave, so merry, so innocent.

His brother was this woman's lover! It was too amazing. Brangwen went home despising himself for his own poor way of life. He was a clod-hopper and a boor, dull, stuck in the mud. More than ever he wanted to clamber out, to this visionary polite world.

He was well off. He was as well off as Alfred, who could not have above six hundred a year, all told. He himself made about four hundred, and could make more. His investments got better every day. Why did he not do something? His wife was a lady also.

But when he got to the Marsh, he realised how fixed everything was, how the other form of life was beyond him, and he regretted for the first time that he had succeeded to the farm. He felt a prisoner, sitting safe and easy and unadventurous. He might, with risk, have done more with himself. He could neither

.H. LAWRENCE

read Browning nor Herbert Spencer, nor have access to such a room as Mrs. Forbes's. All that form of life was outside him.

But then, he said he did not want it. The excitement of the visit began to pass off. The next day he was himself, and if he thought of the other woman, there was something about her and her place that he did not like, something cold something alien, as if she were not a woman, but an inhuman being who used up human life for cold, unliving purposes.

The evening came on, he played with Anna, and then sat alone with his own wife. She was sewing. He sat very still, smoking, perturbed. He was aware of his wife's quiet figure, and quiet dark head bent over her needle. It was too quiet for him. It was too peaceful. He wanted to smash the walls down, and let the night in, so that his wife should not be so secure and quiet, sitting there. He wished the air were not so close and narrow. His wife was obliterated from him, she was in her own world, quiet, secure, unnoticed, unnoticing. He was shut down by her.

He rose to go out. He could not sit still any longer. He must get out of this oppressive, shut-down, woman-haunt.

His wife lifted her head and looked at him.

"Are you going out?" she asked.

He looked down and met her eyes. They were darker than darkness, and gave deeper space. He felt himself retreating before her, defensive, whilst her eyes followed and tracked him down.

"I was just going up to Cossethay," he said.

She remained watching him.

"Why do you go?" she said.

His heart beat fast, and he sat down, slowly.

"No reason particular," he said, beginning to fill his pipe again, mechanically.

"Why do you go away so often?" she said.

"But you don't want me," he replied.

She was silent for a while.

"You do not want to be with me any more," she said.

It startled him. How did she know this truth? He thought it was his secret.

"Yi," he said.

"You want to find something else," she said.

He did not answer. "Did he?" he asked himself.

"You should not want so much attention," she said. "You are not a baby."

"I'm not grumbling," he said. Yet he knew he was.

"You think you have not enough," she said.

"How enough?"

"You think you have not enough in me. But how do you know me? What do you do to make me love you?"

He was flabbergasted.

"I never said I hadn't enough in you," he replied. "I didn't know you wanted making to love me. What do you want?"

"You don't make it good between us any more, you are not interested. You do not make me want you."

"And you don't make me want you, do you now?" There was a silence. They were such strangers.

"Would you like to have another woman?" she asked.

His eyes grew round, he did not know where he was. How could she, his own wife, say such a thing? But she sat there, small and foreign and separate. It dawned upon him she did not consider herself his wife, except in so far as they agreed. She did not feel she had married him. At any rate, she was willing to allow he might want another woman. A gap, a space opened before him.

"No," he said slowly. "What other woman should I want?"

"Like your brother," she said.

He was silent for some time, ashamed also.

"What of her?" he said. "I didn't like the woman."

"Yes, you liked her," she answered persistently.

He stared in wonder at his own wife as she told him his own heart so callously. And he was indignant. What right had she to sit there telling him these things? She was his wife, what right had she to speak to him like this, as if she were a stranger.

"I didn't," he said. "I want no woman."

"Yes, you would like to be like Alfred."

His silence was one of angry frustration. He was astonished. He had told her of his visit to Wirksworth, but briefly, without interest, he thought.

As she sat with her strange dark face turned towards him, her eyes watched him, inscrutable, casting him up. He began to oppose her. She was again the active unknown facing him. Must he admit her? He resisted involuntarily.

"Why should you want to find a woman who is more to you than me?" she said.

The turbulence raged in his breast.

"I don't," he said.

"Why do you?" she repeated. "Why do you want to deny me?"

Suddenly, in a flash, he saw she might be lonely, isolated, unsure. She had seemed to him the utterly certain, satisfied, absolute, excluding him. Could she need anything?

"Why aren't you satisfied with me?—I'm not satisfied with you. Paul used to come to me and take me like a man does. You only leave me alone or take me like your cattle, quickly, to forget me again—so that you can forget me again."

"What am I to remember about you?" said Brangwen.

"I want you to know there is somebody there besides yourself."

"Well, don't I know it?"

"You come to me as if it was for nothing, as if I was nothing there. When Paul came to me, I *was* something to him—a woman, I was. To you I am nothing—it is like cattle—or nothing——"

"You make me feel as if *I* was nothing," he said.

They were silent. She sat watching him. He could not move, his soul was seething and chaotic. She turned to her sewing again. But the sight of her bent before him held him and would not let him be. She was a strange, hostile, dominant thing. Yet not quite hostile. As he sat he felt his limbs were strong and hard, he sat in strength.

She was silent for a long time, stitching. He was aware, poignantly, of the round shape of her head, very intimate, compelling. She lifted her head and sighed. The blood burned in him, her voice ran to him like fire.

"Come here," she said, unsure.

For some moments he did not move. Then he rose slowly and went across the hearth. It required an almost deathly effort of volition, or of acquiescence. He stood before her and looked down at her. Her face was shining again, her eyes were shining again like terrible laughter. It was to him terrible, how she could be transfigured. He could not look at her, it burnt his heart.

"My love!" she said.

And she put her arms round him as he stood before her, round his thighs, pressing him against her breast. And her hands on him seemed to reveal to him the mould of his own nakedness, he was passionately lovely to himself. He could not bear to look at her.

"My dear!" she said. He knew she spoke a foreign language. The fear was like bliss in his heart. He looked down. Her face was shining, her eyes were full of light, she was awful. He suffered from the compulsion to her. She was the awful unknown. He bent down to her, suffering, unable to let go, unable to let himself go, yet drawn, driven. She was now the transfigured, she was wonderful, beyond him. He wanted to go. But he could not as yet kiss her. He was himself apart. Easiest he could kiss her feet. But he was too ashamed for the actual deed, which were like an affront. She waited for him to meet her, not to bow before her and serve her. She wanted his active participation, not his submission. She put her fingers on him. And it was torture to him, that he must give himself to her actively, participate in her, that he must meet and embrace and know her, who was other than himself. There was that in him which shrank from yielding to her, resisted the relaxing towards her, opposed the mingling with her, even while he most desired it. He was afraid, he wanted to save himself.

There were a few moments of stillness. Then gradually, the tension, the withholding relaxed in him, and he began to flow towards her. She was beyond him, the unattainable. But he let go his hold on himself, he relinquished himself, and knew the subterranean force of his desire to come to her, to be with her, to mingle with her, losing himself to find her, to find himself in her. He began to approach her, to draw near.

His blood beat up in waves of desire. He wanted to come to her, to meet her. She was there, if he could reach her. The reality of her who was just beyond him absorbed him. Blind and destroyed, he pressed forward, nearer, nearer, to receive the consummation of himself, he received within the darkness which should swallow him and yield him up to himself. If he could come really within the blazing kernel of darkness, if really he could be destroyed, burnt away till he lit with her in one consummation, that were supreme, supreme.

Their coming together now, after two years of married life, was much more wonderful to them than it had been before. It was the entry into another circle of existence, it was the baptism to another life, it was the complete confirmation. Their feet trod strange ground of knowledge, their footsteps were lit-up with discovery. Wherever they walked, it was well, the world re-echoed round them in discovery. They went gladly and forgetful. Everything was lost, and everything was found. The new world was discovered, it remained only to be explored.

They had passed through the doorway into the further space, where movement was so big, that it contained bonds and constraints and labours, and still was complete liberty. She was the doorway to him, he to her. At last they had thrown open the doors, each to the other, and had stood in the doorways facing each other, whilst the light flooded out from behind on to each of their faces, it was the transfiguration, glorification, the admission.

And always the light of the transfiguration burned on in their hearts. He went his way, as before, she went her way, to the rest of the world there seemed no change. But to the two of them, there was the perpetual wonder of the transfiguration.

```
            J-R TOBACCO
         I-77 Statesville, N.C.
            (704) 872-5300
           7/05/96  12:13:44

960231860  VISA PAYMENT              R2

 $6.00 APPAREL ITEM     SAVE UP TO 50%
AP6      1 BOX   @ 6.00        6.00
 39 CENT MISC BATH/COSMET
660039   7 BOXES @  .39        2.73
 CASWELL-MASSEY         ASST LOTIONS
66CML    5 BOXES @ 2.00       10.00
 CASWELL-MASSEY         ASST BATH SALTS
66CMBS   3 BOXES @ 2.00        6.00
 RE $6.00 CERAMIC       AT 50% OFF
C3       1 BOX   @ 3.00        3.00
 REG $2.00 MISC         AT 50% OFF
M1       1 BOX   @ 1.00        1.00
 REG $2.00 JEWELRY      AT 50% OFF
J1       1 BOX   @ 1.00        1.00
 $3.00 WORLD BOOK-ADULTS VALUES TO $20
WBA3     1 BOX   @ 3.00        3.00
 $2.50 MILTON BRADLEY
TM250    1 BOX   @ 2.50        2.50
 REG $4.00 MISC         AT 50% OFF
M2       2 BOXES @ 2.00        4.00
 TOWELS BATH          REG $12 TO $19
NCBT     1 BOX   @ 5.00        5.00
 APPAREL AT $12.95      SAVE UP TO 50%
AP1295   1 BOX   @ 12.95      12.95

        SUB-TOTAL             57.18

  6.00% SALES TAX              3.43

        TOTAL SALE            60.61

NORTH CAROLINA OTHER TOB. PROD. TAX PAID

        UNIT COUNT              25
```

He did not know her any better, any more precisely, now that he knew her altogether. Poland, her husband, the war—he understood no more of this in her. He did not understand her foreign nature, half German, half Polish, nor her foreign speech. But he knew her, he knew her meaning, without understanding. What she said, what she spoke, this was a blind gesture on her part. In herself she walked strong and clear, he knew her, he saluted her, was with her. What was memory after all, but the recording of a number of possibilities which had never been fulfilled? What was Paul Lensky to her, but an unfulfilled possibility to which he, Brangwen, was the reality and the fulfilment? What did it matter, that Anna Lensky was born of Lydia and Paul? God was her father and her mother. He had passed through the married pair without fully making Himself known to them.

Now he was declared to Brangwen and to Lydia Brangwen, as they stood together. When at last they had joined hands, the house was finished, and the Lord took up his abode. And they were glad.

The days went on as before, Brangwen went out to his work, his wife nursed her child and attended in some measure to the farm. They did not think of each other—why should they? Only when she touched him, he knew her instantly, that she was with him, near him, that she was the gateway and the way out, that she was beyond, and that he was travelling in her through the beyond. Whither?—What does it matter? He responded always. When she called, he answered, when he asked, her response came at once, or at length.

Anna's soul was put at peace between them. She looked from one to the other, and she saw them established to her safety, and she was free. She played between the pillar of fire and the pillar of cloud in confidence, having the assurance on her right hand and the assurance on her left. She was no longer called upon to uphold with her childish might the broken end of the arch. Her father and her mother now met to the span of the heavens, and she, the child, was free to play in the space beneath, between.

IV

GIRLHOOD OF ANNA BRANGWEN

When Anna was nine years old, Brangwen sent her to the dames' school in Cossethay. There she went, flipping and dancing in her inconsequential fashion, doing very much as she liked, disconcerting old Miss Coates by her indifference to respectability and by her lack of reverence. Anna only laughed at Miss Coates, liked her, and patronised her in superb, childish fashion.

The girl was at once shy and wild. She had a curious contempt for ordinary people, a benevolent superiority. She was very shy, and tortured with misery when people did not like her. On the other hand, she cared very little for anybody save her mother, whom she still rather resentfully worshipped, and her father, whom she loved and patronised, but upon whom she depended. These two, her mother and father, held her still in fee. But she was free of other people, towards whom, on the whole, she took the benevolent attitude. She deeply hated ugliness or intrusion or arrogance, however. As a child, she was as proud and shadowy as a tiger, and as aloof. She could confer favours, but, save from her mother and father, she could receive none. She hated people who came too near to her. Like a wild thing, she wanted her distance. She mistrusted intimacy.

In Cossethay and Ilkeston she was always an alien. She had plenty of acquaintances, but no friends. Very few people whom she met were significant to her. They seemed part of a herd, undistinguished. She did not take people very seriously.

She had two brothers, Tom, dark-haired, small, volatile, whom she was intimately related to but whom she never mingled with, and Fred, fair and responsive, whom she adored but did not consider as a real, separate thing. She was too much the centre of her own universe, too little aware of anything outside.

The first *person* she met, who affected her as a real, living person, whom she regarded as having definite existence, was Baron Skrebensky, her mother's friend. He also was a Polish exile, who had taken orders, and had received from Mr. Gladstone a small country living in Yorkshire.

When Anna was about ten years old, she went with her mother to spend a few days with the Baron Skrebensky. He was very unhappy in his red-brick vicarage. He was vicar of a country church, a living worth a little over two hundred pounds a year, but he had a large parish containing several collieries, with a new, raw, heathen population. He went to the north of England expecting homage from the common people, for he was an aristocrat. He was roughly, even cruelly received. But he never understood it. He remained a fiery aristocrat. Only he had to learn to avoid his parishioners.

Anna was very much impressed by him. He was a smallish man with a rugged, rather crumpled face and blue eyes set very deep and glowing. His wife was a tall thin woman, of noble Polish family, mad with pride. He still spoke broken English, for he had kept very close to his wife, both of them forlorn in this strange, inhospitable country, and they always spoke in Polish together. He was disappointed with Mrs. Brangwen's soft, natural English, very disappointed that her child spoke no Polish.

Anna loved to watch him. She liked the big, new, rambling vicarage, desolate and stark on its hill. It was so exposed, so bleak and bold after the Marsh. The Baron talked endlessly in Polish to Mrs. Brangwen; he made furious gestures with his hands, his blue eyes were full of fire. And to Anna, there was a significance about his sharp, flinging movements. Something in her responded to his extravagance and his exuberant manner. She thought him a very wonderful person. She was shy of him, she liked him to talk to her. She felt a sense of freedom near him.

She never could tell how she knew it, but she did know that he was a knight of Malta. She could never remember whether she had seen his star, or cross, of his order or not, but it flashed in her mind, like a symbol. He at any rate represented to the child the real world, where kings and lords and princes moved and fulfilled their shining lives, whilst queens and ladies and princesses upheld the noble order.

She had recognized the Baron Skrebensky as a real person, he had had some regard for her. But when she did not see him any more, he faded and became a memory. But as a memory he was always alive to her.

Anna became a tall, awkward girl. Her eyes were still very dark and quick, but they had grown careless, they had lost their watchful, hostile look. Her fierce, spun hair turned brown, it grew heavier and was tied back. She was sent to a young ladies' school in Nottingham.

And at this period she was absorbed in becoming a young lady. She was intelligent enough, but not interested in learning. At first, she thought all the girls at school very ladylike and wonderful, and she wanted to be like them. She

came to a speedy disillusion: they galled and maddened her, they were petty and
mean. After the loose, generous atmosphere of her home, where little things did
not count, she was always uneasy in the world, that would snap and bite at every
trifle.

A quick change came over her. She mistrusted herself, she mistrusted the
outer world. She did not want to go on, she did not want to go out into it, she
wanted to go no further.

"What do *I* care about that lot of girls?" she would say to her father, contemptuously; "they are nobody."

The trouble was that the girls would not accept Anna at her measure. They
would have her according to themselves or not at all. So she was confused,
seduced, she became as they were for a time, and then, in revulsion, she hated
them furiously.

"Why don't you ask some of your girls here?" her father would say.

"They're not coming here," she cried.

"And why not?"

"They're bagatelle," she said, using one of her mother's rare phrases.

"Bagatelles or billiards, it makes no matter, they're nice young lasses
enough."

But Anna was not to be won over. She had a curious shrinking from commonplace people, and particularly from the young lady of her day. She would
not go into company because of the ill-at-ease feeling other people brought
upon her. And she never could decide whether it were her fault or theirs. She
half respected these other people, and continuous disillusion maddened her. She
wanted to respect them. Still she thought the people she did not *know* were
wonderful. Those she knew seemed always to be limiting her, tying her up in
little falsities that irritated her beyond bearing. She would rather stay at home
and avoid the rest of the world, leaving it illusory.

For at the Marsh life had indeed a certain freedom and largeness. There was
no fret about money, no mean little precedence, nor care for what other people
thought, because neither Mrs. Brangwen nor Brangwen could be sensible of
any judgment passed on them from outside. Their lives were too separate.

So Anna was only easy at home, where the common sense and the supreme
relation between her parents produced a freer standard of being than she could
find outside. Where, outside the Marsh, could she find the tolerant dignity she
had been brought up in? Her parents stood undiminished and unaware of criticism. The people she met outside seemed to begrudge her her very existence.
They seemed to want to belittle her also. She was exceedingly reluctant to go
amongst them. She depended upon her mother and her father. And yet she
wanted to go out.

At school, or in the world, she was usually at fault, she felt usually that she
ought to be slinking in disgrace. She never felt quite sure, in herself, whether
she were wrong, or whether the others were wrong. She had not done her
lessons: well, she did not see any reason why she *should* do her lessons, if she did
not want to. Was there some occult reason why she should? Were these people,
schoolmistresses, representatives of some mystic Right, some Higher Good?
They seemed to think so themselves. But she could not for her life see why a
woman should bully and insult her because she did not know thirty lines of *As
You Like It*. After all, *what* did it matter if she knew them or not? Nothing could
persuade her that it was of the slightest importance. Because she despised inwardly the coarsely working nature of the mistress. Therefore she was always at

outs with authority. From constant telling, she came almost to believe in her own badness, her own intrinsic inferiority. She felt that she ought always to be in a state of slinking disgrace, if she fulfilled what was expected of her. But she rebelled. She never really believed in her own badness. At the bottom of her heart she despised the other people, who carped and were loud over trifles. She despised them, and wanted revenge on them. She hated them whilst they had power over her.

Still she kept an ideal: a free, proud lady absolved from the petty ties, existing beyond petty considerations. She would see such ladies in pictures: Alexandra, Princess of Wales, was one of her models. This lady was proud and royal, and stepped indifferently over all small, mean desires: so thought Anna, in her heart. And the girl did up her hair high under a little slanting hat, her skirts were fashionably bunched up, she wore an elegant, skin-fitting coat.

Her father was delighted. Anna was very proud in her bearing, too naturally indifferent to smaller bonds to satisfy Ilkeston, which would have liked to put her down. But Brangwen was having no such thing. If she chose to be royal, royal she should be. He stood like a rock between her and the world.

After the fashion of his family, he grew stout and handsome. His blue eyes were full of light, twinkling and sensitive, his manner was deliberate, but hearty, warm. His capacity for living his own life without attention from his neighbours made them respect him. They would run to do anything for him. He did not consider them, but was open-handed towards them, so they made profit of their willingness. He liked people, so long as they remained in the background.

Mrs. Brangwen went on in her own way, following her own devices. She had her husband, her two sons and Anna. These staked out and marked her horizon. The other people were outsiders. Inside her own world, her life passed along like a dream for her, it lapsed, and she lived within its lapse, active and always pleased, intent. She scarcely noticed the outer things at all. What was outside was outside, non-existent. She did not mind if the boys fought, so long as it was out of her presence. But if they fought when she was by, she was angry, and they were afraid of her. She did not care if they broke a window of a railway carriage or sold their watches to have a revel at the Goose Fair. Brangwen was perhaps angry over these things. To the mother they were insignificant. It was odd little things that offended her. She was furious if the boys hung around the slaughter-house, she was displeased when the school reports were bad. It did not matter how many sins her boys were accused of, so long as they were not stupid, or inferior. If they seemed to brook insult, she hated them. And it was only a certain *gaucherie*, a gawkiness on Anna's part that irritated her against the girl. Certain forms of clumsiness, grossness, made the mother's eyes glow with curious rage. Otherwise she was pleased, indifferent.

Pursuing her splendid-lady ideal, Anna became a lofty demoiselle of sixteen, plagued by family shortcomings. She was very sensitive to her father. She knew if he had been drinking, were he ever so little affected, and she could not bear it. He flushed when he drank, the veins stood out on his temples, there was a twinkling, cavalier boisterousness in his eye, his manner was jovially overbearing and mocking. And it angered her. When she heard his loud, roaring, boisterous mockery, an anger of resentment filled her. She was quick to forestall him, the moment he came in.

"You look a sight, you do, red in the face," she cried.

"I might look worse if I was green," he answered.

"Boozing in Ilkeston."

"And what's wrong wi' Il'son?"

She flounced away. He watched her with amused, twinkling eyes, yet in spite of himself said that she flouted him.

They were a curious family, a law to themselves, separate from the world, isolated, a small republic set in invisible bounds. The mother was quite indifferent to Ilkeston and Cossethay, to any claims made on her from outside, she was very shy of any outsider, exceedingly courteous, winning even. But the moment the visitor had gone, she laughed and dismissed him, he did not exist. It had been all a game to her. She was still a foreigner, unsure of her ground. But alone with her own children and husband at the Marsh, she was mistress of a little native land that lacked nothing.

She had some beliefs somewhere, never defined. She had been brought up a Roman Catholic. She had gone to the Church of England for protection. The outward form was a matter of indifference to her. Yet she had some fundamental religion. It was as if she worshipped God as a mystery, never seeking in the least to define what He was.

And inside her, the subtle sense of the Great Absolute wherein she had her being was very strong. The English dogma never reached her: the language was too foreign. Through it all she felt the great Separator who held life in His hands, gleaming, imminent, terrible, the Great Mystery, immediate beyond all telling.

She shone and gleamed to the Mystery, Whom she knew through all her senses, she glanced with strange, mystic superstitions that never found expression in the English language, never mounted to thought in English. But so she lived, within a potent, sensuous belief that included her family and contained her destiny.

To this she had reduced her husband. He existed with her entirely indifferent to the general values of the world. Her very ways, the very mark of her eyebrows were symbols and indication to him. There, on the farm with her, he lived through a mystery of life and death and creation, strange, profound ecstasies and incommunicable satisfactions, of which the rest of the world knew nothing; which made the pair of them apart and respected in the English village, for they were also well-to-do.

But Anna was only half safe within her mother's unthinking knowledge. She had a mother-of-pearl rosary that had been her own father's. What it meant to her she could never say. But the string of moonlight and silver, when she had it between her fingers, filled her with strange passion. She learned at school a little Latin, she learned an Ave Maria and a Pater Noster, she learned how to say her rosary. But that was no good. "Ave Maria, gratia plena, Dominus tecum, Benedicta tu in mulieribus et benedictus fructus ventris tui Jesus. Ave Maria, Sancta Maria, ora pro nobis peccatoribus, nunc et in hora mortis nostrae, Amen."

It was not right, somehow. What these words meant when translated was not the same as the pale rosary meant. There was a discrepancy, a falsehood. It irritated her to say, "Dominus tecum," or, "benedicta tu in mulieribus." She loved the mystic words, "Ave Maria, Sancta Maria;" she was moved by "benedictus fructus ventris tui Jesus," and by "nunc et in hora mortis nostrae." But none of it was quite real. It was not satisfactory, somehow.

She avoided her rosary, because, moving her with curious passion as it did, it *meant* only these not very significant things. She put it away. It was her instinct to put all these things away. It was her instinct to avoid thinking, to avoid it, to save herself.

She was seventeen, touchy, full of spirits, and very moody: quick to flush, and always uneasy, uncertain. For some reason or other, she turned more to her father, she felt almost flashes of hatred for her mother. Her mother's dark muzzle and curiously insidious ways, her mother's utter surety and confidence, her strange satisfaction, even triumph, her mother's way of laughing at things and her mother's silent overriding of vexatious propositions, most of all her mother's triumphant power maddened the girl.

She became sudden and incalculable. Often she stood at the window, looking out, as if she wanted to go. Sometimes she went, she mixed with people. But always she came home in anger, as if she were diminished, belittled, almost degraded.

There was over the house a kind of dark silence and intensity, in which passion worked its inevitable conclusions. There was in the house a sort of richness, a deep, inarticulate interchange which made other places seem thin and unsatisfying. Brangwen could sit silent, smoking in his chair, the mother could move about in her quiet, insidious way, and the sense of the two presences was powerful, sustaining. The whole intercourse was wordless, intense and close.

But Anna was uneasy. She wanted to get away. Yet wherever she went, there came upon her that feeling of thinness, as if she were made smaller, belittled. She hastened home.

There she raged and interrupted the strong, settled interchange. Sometimes her mother turned on her with a fierce, destructive anger, in which was no pity or consideration. And Anna shrank, afraid. She went to her father.

He would still listen to the spoken word, which fell sterile on the unheeding mother. Sometimes Anna talked to her father. She tried to discuss people, she wanted to know what was meant. But her father became uneasy. He did not want to have things dragged into consciousness. Only out of consideration for her he listened. And there was a kind of bristling rousedness in the room. The cat got up and stretching itself, went uneasily to the door. Mrs. Brangwen was silent, she seemed ominous. Anna could not go on with her fault-finding, her criticism, her expression of dissatisfactions. She felt even her father against her. He had a strong, dark bond with her mother, a potent intimacy that existed inarticulate and wild, following its own course, and savage if interrupted, uncovered.

Nevertheless Brangwen was uneasy about the girl, the whole house continued to be disturbed. She had a pathetic, baffled appeal. She was hostile to her parents, even whilst she lived entirely with them, within their spell.

Many ways she tried, of escape. She became an assiduous church-goer. But the *language* meant nothing to her: it seemed false. She hated to hear things expressed, put into words. Whilst the religious feelings were inside her they were passionately moving. In the mouth of the clergyman, they were false, indecent. She tried to read. But again the tedium and the sense of the falsity of the spoken word put her off. She went to stay with girl friends. At first she thought it splendid. But then the inner boredom came on, it seemed to her all nothingness. And she felt always belittled, as if never, never could she stretch her length and stride her stride.

Her mind reverted often to the torture cell of a certain Bishop of France, in which the victim could neither stand nor lie stretched out, never. Not that she thought of herself in any connection with this. But often there came into her mind the wonder, how the cell was built, and she could feel the horror of the crampedness, as something very real.

She was, however, only eighteen when a letter came from Mrs. Alfred Brangwen, in Nottingham, saying that her son William was coming to Ilkeston to take a place as junior draughtsman, scarcely more than apprentice, in a lace factory. He was twenty years old, and would the Marsh Brangwens be friendly with him.

Tom Brangwen at once wrote offering the young man a home at the Marsh. This was not accepted, but the Nottingham Brangwens expressed gratitude.

There had never been much love lost between the Nottingham Brangwens and the Marsh. Indeed, Mrs. Alfred, having inherited three thousand pounds, and having occasion to be dissatisfied with her husband, held aloof from all the Brangwens whatsoever. She affected, however, some esteem of Mrs. Tom, as she called the Polish woman, saying that at any rate she was a lady.

Anna Brangwen was faintly excited at the news of her Cousin Will's coming to Ilkeston. She knew plenty of young men, but they had never become real to her. She had seen in this young gallant a nose she liked, in that a pleasant moustache, in the other a nice way of wearing clothes, in one a ridiculous fringe of hair, in another a comical way of talking. They were objects of amusement and faint wonder to her, rather than real beings, the young men.

The only man she knew was her father; and, as he was something large, looming, a kind of Godhead, he embraced all manhood for her, and other men were just incidental.

She remembered her cousin Will. He had town clothes and was thin, with a very curious head, black as jet, with hair like sleek, thin fur. It was a curious head: it reminded her she knew not of what: of some animal, some mysterious animal that lived in the darkness under the leaves and never came out, but which lived vividly, swift and intense. She always thought of him with that black, keen, blind head. And she considered him odd.

He appeared at the Marsh one Sunday morning: a rather long, thin youth with a bright face and a curious self-possession among his shyness, a native unawareness of what other people might be, since he was himself.

When Anna came downstairs in her Sunday clothes, ready for church, he rose and greeted her conventionally, shaking hands. His manners were better than hers. She flushed. She noticed that he now had a thick fledge on his upper lip, a black, finely-shapen line marking his wide mouth. It rather repelled her. It reminded her of the thin, fine fur of his hair. She was aware of something strange in him.

His voice had rather high upper notes, and very resonant middle notes. It was queer. She wondered why he did it. But he sat very naturally in the Marsh living-room. He had some uncouthness, some natural self-possession of the Brangwens, that made him at home there.

Anna was rather troubled by the strangely intimate, affectionate way her father had towards this young man. He seemed gentle towards him, he put himself aside in order to fill out the young man. This irritated Anna.

"Father," she said abruptly, "give me some collection."

"What collection?" asked Brangwen.

"Don't be ridiculous," she cried, flushing.

"Nay," he said, "what collection's this?"

"You know it's the first Sunday of the month."

Anna stood confused. Why was he doing this, why was he making her conspicuous before this stranger?

"I want some collection," she reasserted.

"So tha says," he replied indifferently, looking at her, then turning again to this nephew.

She went forward, and thrust her hand into his breeches pocket. He smoked steadily, making no resistance, talking to his nephew. Her hand groped about in his pocket, and then drew out his leathern purse. Her colour was bright in her clear cheeks, her eyes shone. Brangwen's eyes were twinkling. The nephew sat sheepishly. Anna, in her finery, sat down and slid all the money into her lap. There was silver and gold. The youth could not help watching her. She was bent over the heap of money, fingering the different coins.

"I've a good mind to take half a sovereign," she said, and she looked up with glowing dark eyes. She met the light-brown eyes of her cousin, close and intent upon her. She was startled. She laughed quickly, and turned to her father.

"I've a good mind to take half a sovereign, our Dad," she said.

"Yes, nimble fingers," said her father. "You take what's your own."

"Are you coming, our Anna?" asked her brother from the door.

She suddenly chilled to normal, forgetting both her father and her cousin.

"Yes, I'm ready," she said, taking sixpence from the heap of money and sliding the rest back into the purse, which she laid on the table.

"Give it here," said her father.

Hastily she thrust the purse into his pocket and was going out.

"You'd better go wi' 'em, lad, hadn't you?" said the father to the nephew.

Will Brangwen rose uncertainly. He had golden-brown, quick, steady eyes, like a bird's, like a hawk's, which cannot look afraid.

"Your Cousin Will'll come with you," said the father.

Anna glanced at the strange youth again. She felt him waiting there for her to notice him. He was hovering on the edge of her consciousness, ready to come in. She did not want to look at him. She was antagonistic to him.

She waited without speaking. Her cousin took his hat and joined her. It was summer outside. Her brother Fred was plucking a sprig of flowery currant to put in his coat, from the bush at the angle of the house. She took no notice. Her cousin followed just behind her.

They were on the high road. She was aware of a strangeness in her being. It made her uncertain. She caught sight of the flowering currant in her brother's buttonhole.

"Oh, our Fred," she cried. "Don't wear that stuff to go to church."

Fred looked down protectively at the pink adornment on his breast.

"Why, I like it," he said.

"Then you're the only one who does, I'm sure," she said.

And she turned to her cousin.

"Do *you* like the smell of it?" she asked.

He was there beside her, tall and uncouth and yet self-possessed. It excited her.

"I can't say whether I do or not," he replied.

"Give it here, Fred, don't have it smelling in church," she said to the little boy, her page.

Her fair, small brother handed her the flower dutifully. She sniffed it and gave it without a word to her cousin, for his judgment. He smelled the dangling flower curiously.

"It's a funny smell," he said.

And suddenly she laughed, and a quick light came on all their faces, there was a blithe trip in the small boy's walk.

The bells were ringing, they were going up the summery hill in their Sunday clothes. Anna was very fine in a silk frock of brown and white stripes, tight along the arms and the body, bunched up very elegantly behind the skirt. There was something of the cavalier about Will Brangwen, and he was well dressed.

He walked along with the sprig of currant-blossom dangling between his fingers, and none of them spoke. The sun shone brightly on little showers of buttercup down the bank, in the fields the fool's-parsley was foamy, held very high and proud above a number of flowers that flitted in the greenish twilight of the mowing-grass below.

They reached the church. Fred led the way to the pew, followed by the cousin, then Anna. She felt very conspicuous and important. Somehow, this young man gave her away to other people. He stood aside and let her pass to her place, then sat next to her. It was a curious sensation, to sit next to him.

The colour came streaming from the painted window above her. It lit on the dark wood of the pew, on the stone, worn aisle, on the pillar behind her cousin, and on her cousin's hands, as they lay on his knees. She sat amid illumination, illumination and luminous shadow all around her, her soul very bright. She sat, without knowing it, conscious of the hands and motionless knees of her cousin. Something strange had entered into her world, something entirely strange and unlike what she knew.

She was curiously elated. She sat in a glowing world of unreality, very delightful. A brooding light, like laughter, was in her eyes. She was aware of a strange influence entering in to her, which she enjoyed. It was a dark enrichening influence she had not known before. She did not think of her cousin. But she was startled when his hands moved.

She wished he would not say the responses so plainly. It diverted her from her vague enjoyment. Why would he obtrude, and draw notice to himself? It was bad taste. But she went on all right till the hymn came. He stood up beside her to sing, and that pleased her. Then suddenly, at the very first word, his voice came strong and over-riding, filling the church. He was singing the tenor. Her soul opened in amazement. His voice filled the church! It rang out like a trumpet, and rang out again. She started to giggle over her hymn-book. But he went on, perfectly steady. Up and down rang his voice, going its own way. She was helplessly shocked into laughter. Between moments of dead silence in herself she shook with laughter. On came the laughter, seized her and shook her till the tears were in her eyes. She was amazed, and rather enjoyed it. And still the hymn rolled on, and still she laughed. She bent over her hymn-book crimson with confusion, but still her sides shook with laughter. She pretended to cough, she pretended to have a crumb in her throat. Fred was gazing up at her with clear blue eyes. She was recovering herself. And then a slur in the strong, blind voice at her side brought it all on again, in a gust of mad laughter.

She bent down to prayer in cold reproof of herself. And yet, as she knelt, little eddies of giggling went over her. The very sight of his knees on the praying cushion sent the little shock of laughter over her.

She gathered herself together and sat with prim, pure face, white and pink and cold as a Christmas rose, her hands in her silk gloves folded on her lap, her dark eyes all vague, abstracted in a sort of dream, oblivious of everything.

The sermon rolled on vaguely, in a tide of pregnant peace.

Her cousin took out his pocket-handkerchief. He seemed to be drifted absorbed into the sermon. He put his handkerchief to his face. Then something dropped on to his knee. There lay the bit of flowering currant! He was looking down at it in real astonishment. A wild snirt of laughter came from Anna. Everybody heard: it was torture. He had shut the crumpled flower in his hand and was looking up again with the same absorbed attention to the sermon. Another snirt of laughter from Anna. Fred nudged her remindingly. Her cousin sat motionless. Somehow he was aware that his face was red. She could feel him. His hand, closed over the flower, remained quite still, pretending to be normal. Another wild struggle in Anna's breast, and the snirt of laughter. She bent forward shaking with laughter. It was now no joke. Fred was nudge-nudging at her. She nudged him back fiercely. Then another vicious spasm of laughter seized her. She tried to ward it off in a little cough. The cough ended in a suppressed whoop. She wanted to die. And the closed hand crept away to the pocket. Whilst she sat in taut suspense, the laughter rushed back at her, knowing he was fumbling in his pocket to shove the flower away.

In the end, she felt weak, exhausted and thoroughly depressed. A blankness of wincing depression came over her. She hated the presence of the other people. Her face became quite haughty. She was unaware of her cousin any more.

When the collection arrived with the last hymn, her cousin was again singing resoundingly. And still it amused her. In spite of the shameful exhibition she had made of herself, it amused her still. She listened to it in a spell of amusement. And the bag was thrust in front of her, and her sixpence was mingled in the folds of her glove. In her haste to get it out, it flipped away and went twinkling in the next pew. She stood and giggled. She could not help it: she laughed outright, a figure of shame.

"What were you laughing about, our Anna?" asked Fred, the moment they were out of the church.

"Oh, I couldn't help it," she said, in her careless, half-mocking fashion. "I don't know *why* Cousin Will's singing set me off."

"What was there in my singing to make you laugh?" he asked.

"It was so loud," she said.

They did not look at each other, but they both laughed again, both reddening.

"What were you snorting and laughing for, our Anna?" asked Tom, the elder brother, at the dinner table, his hazel eyes bright with joy. "Everybody stopped to look at you." Tom was in the choir.

She was aware of Will's eyes shining steadily upon her, waiting for her to speak.

"It was Cousin Will's singing," she said.

At which her cousin burst into a suppressed, chuckling laugh, suddenly showing all his small, regular, rather sharp teeth, and just as quickly closing his mouth again.

"Has he got such a remarkable voice on him then?" asked Brangwen.

"No, it's not that," said Anna. "Only it tickled me—I couldn't tell you why."

And again a ripple of laughter went down the table.

Will Brangwen thrust forward his dark face, his eyes dancing, and said:

"I'm in the choir of St. Nicholas."

"Oh, you go to church then!" said Brangwen.

"Mother does—father doesn't," replied the youth.

It was the little things, his movement, the funny tones of his voice, that showed up big to Anna. The matter-of-fact things he said were absurd in contrast. The things her father said seemed meaningless and neutral.

During the afternoon they sat in the parlour, that smelled of geranium, and they ate cherries, and talked. Will Brangwen was called on to give himself forth. And soon he was drawn out.

He was interested in churches, in church architecture. The influence of Ruskin had stimulated him to a pleasure in the medieval forms. His talk was fragmentary, he was only half articulate. But listening to him, as he spoke of church after church, of nave and chancel and transept, of rood-screen and font, of hatchet-carving and moulding and tracery, speaking always with close passion of particular things, particular places, there gathered in her heart a pregnant hush of churches, a mystery, a ponderous significance of bowed stone, a dim-coloured light through which something took place obscurely, passing into darkness: a high, delighted framework of the mystic screen, and beyond, in the furthest beyond, the altar. It was a very real experience. She was carried away. And the land seemed to be covered with a vast, mystic church, reserved in gloom, thrilled with an unknown Presence.

Almost it hurt her, to look out of the window and see the lilacs towering in the vivid sunshine. Or was this the jewelled glass?

He talked of Gothic and Renaissance and Perpendicular, and Early English and Norman. The words thrilled her.

"Have you been to Southwell?" he said. "I was there at twelve o'clock at midday, eating my lunch in the churchyard. And the bells played a hymn.

"Ay, it's a fine Minster, Southwell, heavy. It's got heavy, round arches, rather low, on thick pillars. It's grand, the way those arches travel forward.

"There's a sedilia as well—pretty. But I like the main body of the church—and that north porch——"

He was very much excited and filled with himself that afternoon. A flame kindled round him, making his experience passionate and glowing, burningly real.

His uncle listened with twinkling eyes, half-moved. His aunt bent forward her dark face, half-moved, but held by other knowledge. Anna went with him.

He returned to his lodging at night treading quick, his eyes glittering, and his face shining darkly as if he came from some passionate, vital tryst.

The glow remained in him, the fire burned, his heart was fierce like a sun. He enjoyed his unknown life and his own self. And he was ready to go back to the Marsh.

Without knowing it, Anna was wanting him to come. In him she had escaped. In him the bounds of her experience were transgressed: he was the hole in the wall, beyond which the sunshine blazed on an outside world.

He came. Sometimes, not often, but sometimes, talking again, there recurred the strange, remote reality which carried everything before it. Sometimes, he talked of his father, whom he hated with a hatred that was burningly close to love, of his mother, whom he loved, with a love that was keenly close to hatred, or to revolt. His sentences were clumsy, he was only half articulate. But he had the wonderful voice, that could ring its vibration through the girl's soul, transport her into his feeling. Sometimes his voice was hot and declamatory, sometimes it had a strange, twanging, almost cat-like sound, sometimes it hesitated, puzzled, sometimes there was the break of a little laugh. Anna was taken by him. She loved the running flame that coursed through her as she listened to him. And his mother and his father became to her two separate people in her life.

For some weeks the youth came frequently, and was received gladly by them all. He sat amongst them, his dark face glowing, an eagerness and a touch of derisiveness on his wide mouth, something grinning and twisted, his eyes always shining like a bird's, utterly without depth. There was no getting hold of the fellow, Brangwen irritably thought. He was like a grinning young tom-cat, that came when he thought he would, and without cognisance of the other person.

At first the youth had looked towards Tom Brangwen when he talked; and then he looked towards his aunt, for her appreciation, valuing it more than his uncle's; and then he turned to Anna, because from her he got what he wanted, which was not in the elder people.

So that the two young people, from being always attendant on the elder, began to draw apart and establish a separate kingdom. Sometimes Tom Brangwen was irritated. His nephew irritated him. The lad seemed to him too special, self-contained. His nature was fierce enough, but too much abstracted, like a separate thing, like a cat's nature. A cat could lie perfectly peacefully on the hearthrug whilst its master or mistress writhed in agony a yard away. It had nothing to do with other people's affairs. What did the lad really care about anything, save his own instinctive affairs?

Brangwen was irritated. Nevertheless he liked and respected his nephew. Mrs. Brangwen was irritated by Anna, who was suddenly changed, under the influence of the youth. The mother liked the boy: he was not quite an outsider. But she did not like her daughter to be so much under the spell.

So that gradually the two young people drew apart, escaped from the elders, to create a new thing by themselves. He worked in the garden to propitiate his uncle. He talked churches to propitiate his aunt. He followed Anna like a shadow: like a long, persistent, unswerving black shadow he went after the girl. It irritated Brangwen exceedingly. It exasperated him beyond bearing, to see the lit-up grin, the cat-grin as he called it, on his nephew's face.

And Anna had a new reserve, a new independence. Suddenly she began to act independently of her parents, to live beyond them. Her mother had flashes of anger.

But the courtship went on. Anna would find occasion to go shopping in Ilkeston at evening. She always returned with her cousin; he walking with his head over her shoulder, a little bit behind her, like the Devil looking over Lincoln, as Brangwen noted angrily and yet with satisfaction.

To his own wonder, Will Brangwen found himself in an electric state of passion. To his wonder, he had stopped her at the gate as they came home from Ilkeston one night, and had kissed her, blocking her way and kissing her whilst he felt as if some blow were struck at him in the dark. And when they went indoors, he was acutely angry that her parents looked up scrutinisingly at him and her. What right had they there: why should they look up! Let them remove themselves, or look elsewhere.

And the youth went home with the stars in heaven whirling fiercely about the blackness of his head, and his heart fierce, insistent, but fierce as if he felt something baulking him. He wanted to smash through something.

A spell was cast over her. And how uneasy her parents were, as she went about the house unnoticing, not noticing them, moving in a spell as if she were invisible to them. She *was* invisible to them. It made them angry. Yet they had to submit. She went about absorbed, obscured for a while.

Over him too the darkness of obscurity settled. He seemed to be hidden in a tense, electric darkness, in which his soul, his life was intensely active, but without his aid or attention. His mind was obscured. He worked swiftly and mechanically, and he produced some beautiful things.

His favourite work was wood-carving. The first thing he made for her was a butter-stamper. In it he carved a mythological bird, a phœnix, something like an eagle, rising on symmetrical wings, from a circle of very beautiful flickering flames that rose upwards from the rim of the cup.

Anna thought nothing of the gift on the evening when he gave it to her. In the morning, however, when the butter was made, she fetched his seal in place of the old wooden stamper of oak-leaves and acorns. She was curiously excited to see how it would turn out. Strange, the uncouth bird moulded there, in the cup-like hollow, with curious, thick waverings running inwards from a smooth rim. She pressed another mould. Strange, to lift the stamp and see that eagle-beaked bird raising its breast to her. She loved creating it over and over again. And every time she looked, it seemed a new thing come to life. Every piece of butter became this strange, vital emblem.

She showed it to her mother and father.

"That is beautiful," said her mother, a little light coming on to her face.

"Beautiful!" exclaimed the father, puzzled, fretted. "Why, what sort of a bird does he call it?"

And this was the question put by the customers during the next weeks. "What sort of a bird do you call *that,* as you've got on th' butter?"

When he came in the evening, she took him into the dairy to show him.

"Do you like it?" he asked, in his loud, vibrating voice that always sounded strange, re-echoing in the dark places of her being.

They very rarely touched each other. They liked to be alone together, near to each other, but there was still a distance between them.

In the cool dairy the candle-light lit on the large, white surfaces of the cream pans. He turned his head sharply. It was so cool and remote in there, so remote. His mouth was open in a little, strained laugh. She stood with her head bent, turned aside. He wanted to go near to her. He had kissed her once. Again his eye rested on the round blocks of butter, where the emblematic bird lifted its breast from the shadow cast by the candle flame. What was restraining him? Her breast was near him; his head lifted like an eagle's. She did not move. Suddenly, with an incredibly quick, delicate movement, he put his arms round her and drew her to him. It was quick, cleanly done, like a bird that swoops and sinks close, closer.

He was kissing her throat. She turned and looked at him. Her eyes were dark and flowing with fire. His eyes were hard and bright with a fierce purpose and gladness, like a hawk's. She felt him flying into the dark space of her flames, like a brand, like a gleaming hawk.

They had looked at each other, and seen each other strange, yet near, very near, like a hawk stooping, swooping, dropping into a flame of darkness. So she took the candle and they went back to the kitchen.

They went on in this way for some time, always coming together, but rarely touching, very seldom did they kiss. And then, often, it was merely a touch of the lips, a sign. But her eyes began to waken with a constant fire, she paused often in the midst of her transit, as if to recollect something, or to discover something.

And his face became sombre, intent, he did not really hear what was said to him.

One evening in August he came when it was raining. He came in with his jacket collar turned up, his jacket buttoned close, his face wet. And he looked so slim and definite, coming out of the chill rain, she was suddenly blinded with love for him. Yet he sat and talked with her father and mother, meaninglessly, whilst her blood seethed to anguish in her. She wanted to touch him now, only to touch him.

There was the queer, abstract look on her silvery radiant face that maddened her father, her dark eyes were hidden. But she raised them to the youth. And they were dark with a flare that made him quail for a moment.

She went into the second kitchen and took a lantern. Her father watched her as she returned.

"Come with me, Will," she said to her cousin. "I want to see if I put the brick over where that rat comes in."

"You've no need to do that," retorted her father. She took no notice. The youth was between the two wills. The colour mounted into the father's face, his blue eyes stared. The girl stood near the door, her head held slightly back, like an indication that the youth must come. He rose, in his silent, intent way, and was gone with her. The blood swelled in Brangwen's forehead veins.

It was raining. The light of the lantern flashed on the cobbled path and the bottom of the wall. She came to a small ladder, and climbed up. He reached her the lantern, and followed. Up there in the fowl-loft, the birds sat in fat bunches on the perches, the red combs shining like fire. Bright, sharp eyes opened. There was a sharp crawk of expostulation as one of the hens shifted over. The cock sat watching, his yellow neck-feathers bright as glass. Anna went across the dirty floor. Brangwen crouched in the loft watching. The light was soft under the red, naked tiles. The girl crouched in a corner. There was another explosive bustle of a hen springing from her perch.

Anna came back, stooping under the perches. He was waiting for her near the door. Suddenly she had her arms round him, was clinging close to him, cleaving her body against his, and crying, in a whispering, whimpering sound.

"Will, I love you, I love you, Will, I love you." It sounded as if it were tearing her.

He was not even very much surprised. He held her in his arms, and his bones melted. He leaned back against the wall. The door of the loft was open. Outside, the rain slanted by in fine, steely, mysterious haste, emerging out of the gulf of darkness. He held her in his arms, and he and she together seemed to be swinging in big, swooping oscillations, the two of them clasped together up in the darkness. Outside the open door of the loft in which they stood, beyond them and below them, was darkness, with a travelling veil of rain.

"I love you, Will, I love you," she moaned, "I love you, Will."

He held her as though they were one, and was silent.

In the house, Tom Brangwen waited a while. Then he got up and went out. He went down the yard. He saw the curious misty shaft coming from the loft door. He scarcely knew it was the light in the rain. He went on till the illumination fell on him dimly. Then looking up, through the blurr, he saw the youth and the girl together, the youth with his back against the wall, his head sunk over the head of the girl. The elder man saw them, blurred through the rain, but lit up. They thought themselves so buried in the night. He even saw the lighted dryness of the loft behind, and shadows and bunches of roosting fowls, up in the night, strange shadows cast from the lantern on the floor.

And a black gloom of anger, and a tenderness of self-effacement, fought in his heart. She did not understand what she was doing. She betrayed herself. She was a child, a mere child. She did not know how much of herself she was squandering. And he was blackly and furiously miserable. Was he then an old man, that he should be giving her away in marriage? Was he old? He was not old. He was younger than that young thoughtless fellow in whose arms she lay. Who knew her—he or that blind-headed youth? To whom did she belong, if not to himself?

He thought again of the child he had carried out at night into the barn, whilst his wife was in labour with the young Tom. He remembered the soft, warm weight of the little girl on his arm, round his neck. Now she would say he was finished. She was going away, to deny him, to leave an unendurable emptiness in him, a void that he could not bear. Almost he hated her. How dared she say he was old. He walked on in the rain, sweating with pain, with the horror of being old, with the agony of having to relinquish what was life to him.

Will Brangwen went home without having seen his uncle. He held his hot face to the rain, and walked on in a trance. "I love you, Will, I love you." The words repeated themselves endlessly. The veils had ripped and issued him naked into the endless space, and he shuddered. The walls had thrust him out and given him a vast space to walk in. Whither, through this darkness of infinite space, was he walking blindly? Where, at the end of all the darkness, was God the Almighty still darkly, seated, thrusting him on? "I love you, Will, I love you." He trembled with fear as the words beat in his heart again. And he dared not think of her face, of her eyes which shone, and of her strange, transfigured face. The hand of the Hidden Almighty, burning bright, had thrust out of the darkness and gripped him. He went on subject and in fear, his heart gripped and burning from the touch.

The days went by, they ran on dark-padded feet in silence. He went to see Anna, but again there had come a reserve between them. Tom Brangwen was gloomy, his blue eyes sombre. Anna was strange and delivered up. Her face in its delicate colouring was mute, touched dumb and poignant. The mother bowed her head and moved in her own dark world, that was pregnant again with fulfilment.

Will Brangwen worked at his wood-carving. It was a passion, a passion for him to have the chisel under his grip. Verily the passion of his heart lifted the fine bite of steel. He was carving, as he had always wanted, the Creation of Eve. It was a panel in low relief, for a church. Adam lay asleep as if suffering, and God, a dim, large figure, stooped towards him, stretching forward His unveiled hand; and Eve, a small vivid, naked female shape, was issuing like a flame towards the hand of God, from the torn side of Adam.

Now, Will Brangwen was working at the Eve. She was thin, a keen, unripe thing. With trembling passion, fine as a breath of air, he sent the chisel over her belly, her hard, unripe, small belly. She was a stiff little figure, with sharp lines, in the throes and torture and ecstasy of her creation. But he trembled as he touched her. He had not finished any of his figures. There was a bird on a bough overhead, lifting its wings for flight, and a serpent wreathing up to it. It was not finished yet. He trembled with passion, at last able to create the new, sharp body of his Eve.

At the sides, at the far sides, at either end, were two Angels covering their faces with their wings. They were like trees. As he went to the Marsh, in the twilight, he felt that the Angels, with covered faces, were standing back as he went by. The darkness was of their shadows and the covering of their faces. When he went through the Canal bridge, the evening glowed in its last deep colours, the sky was dark blue, the stars glittered from afar, very remote and approaching above the darkening cluster of the farm, above the paths of crystal along the edge of the heavens.

She waited for him like the glow of light, and as if his face were covered. And he dared not lift his face to look at her.

Corn harvest came on. One evening they walked out through the farm buildings at nightfall. A large gold moon hung heavily to the grey horizon, trees hovered tall, standing back in the dusk, waiting. Anna and the young man went on noiselessly by the hedge, along where the farm-carts had made dark ruts in the grass. They came through a gate into a wide open field where still much light seemed to spread against their faces. In the under-shadow the sheaves lay on the ground where the reapers had left them, many sheaves like bodies prostrate in shadowy bulk; others were riding hazily in shocks, like ships in the haze of moonlight and of dusk, farther off.

They did not want to turn back, yet whither were they to go, towards the moon? For they were separate, single.

"We will put up some sheaves," said Anna. So they could remain there in the broad, open place.

They went across the stubble to where the long rows of upreared shocks ended. Curiously populous that part of the field looked, where the shocks rode erect; the rest was open and prostrate.

The air was all hoary silver. She looked around her. Trees stood vaguely at their distance, as if waiting like heralds, for the signal to approach. In this space of vague crystal her heart seemed like a bell ringing. She was afraid lest the sound should be heard.

"You take this row," she said to the youth, and passing on, she stooped in the next row of lying sheaves, grasping her hands in the tresses of the oats, lifting the heavy corn in either hand, carrying it, as it hung heavily against her, to the cleared space, where she set the two sheaves sharply down, bringing them together with a faint, keen clash. Her two bulks stood leaning together. He was coming, walking shadowily with the gossamer dusk, carrying his two sheaves. She waited near-by. He set his sheaves with a keen, faint clash, next to her sheaves. They rode unsteadily. He tangled the tresses of corn. It hissed like a fountain. He looked up and laughed.

Then she turned away towards the moon, which seemed glowingly to uncover her bosom every time she faced it. He went to the vague emptiness of the field opposite, dutifully.

They stooped, grasped the wet, soft hair of the corn, lifted the heavy bundles, and returned. She was always first. She set down her sheaves, making a penthouse with those others. He was coming shadowy across the stubble, carrying his bundles. She turned away, hearing only the sharp hiss of his mingling corn. She walked between the moon and his shadowy figure.

She took her two new sheaves and walked towards him, as he rose from stooping over the earth. He was coming out of the near distance. She set down her sheaves to make a new stook. They were unsure. Her hands fluttered. Yet she broke away, and turned to the moon, which laid bare her bosom, so she felt as if her bosom were heaving and panting with moonlight. And he had to put up her two sheaves, which had fallen down. He worked in silence. The rhythm of the work carried him away again, as she was coming near.

They worked together, coming and going, in a rhythm, which carried their feet and their bodies in tune. She stooped, she lifted the burden of sheaves, she turned her face to the dimness where he was, and went with her burden over the stubble. She hesitated, set down her sheaves, there was a swish and hiss of mingling oats, he was drawing near, and she must turn again. And there was the flaring moon laying bare her bosom again, making her drift and ebb like a wave.

He worked steadily, engrossed, threading backwards and forwards like a shuttle across the strip of cleared stubble, weaving the long line of riding shocks, nearer and nearer to the shadowy trees, threading his sheaves with hers.

And always, she was gone before he came. As he came, she drew away, as he drew away, she came. Were they never to meet? Gradually a low, deep-sounding will in him vibrated to her, tried to set her in accord, tried to bring her gradually to him, to a meeting, till they should be together, till they should meet as the sheaves that swished together.

And the work went on. The moon grew brighter, clearer, the corn glistened. He bent over the prostrate bundles, there was a hiss as the sheaves left the ground, a trailing of heavy bodies against him, a dazzle of moonlight on his eyes. And then he was setting the corn together at the stook. And she was coming near.

He waited for her, he fumbled at the stook. She came. But she stood back till he drew away. He saw her in shadow, a dark column, and spoke to her, and she answered. She saw the moonlight flash question on his face. But there was a space between them, and he went away, the work carried them, rhythmic.

Why was there always a space between them, why were they apart? Why, as she came up from under the moon, would she halt and stand off from him? Why was he held away from her? His will drummed persistently, darkly, it drowned everything else.

Into the rhythm of his work there came a pulse and a steadied purpose. He stooped, he lifted the weight, he heaved it towards her, setting it as in her, under the moonlit space. And he went back for more. Ever with increasing closeness he lifted the sheaves and swung striding to the centre with them, ever he drove her more nearly to the meeting, ever he did his share, and drew towards her, overtaking her. There was only the moving to and fro in the moonlight, engrossed, the swinging in the silence, that was marked only by the splash of sheaves, and silence, and a splash of sheaves. And ever the splash of his sheaves broke swifter, beating up to hers, and ever the splash of her sheaves recurred monotonously, unchanging, and ever the splash of his sheaves beat nearer.

Till at last, they met at the shock, facing each other, sheaves in hand. And he was silvery with moonlight, with a moonlit, shadowy face that frightened her. She waited for him.

"Put yours down," she said.

"No, it's your turn." His voice was twanging and insistent.

She set her sheaves against the shock. He saw her hands glisten among the spray of grain. And he dropped his sheaves and he trembled as he took her in his arms. He had overtaken her, and it was his privilege to kiss her. She was sweet and fresh with the night air, and sweet with the scent of grain. And the whole rhythm of him beat into his kisses, and still he pursued her, in his kisses, and still she was not quite overcome. He wondered over the moonlight on her nose! All the moonlight upon her, all the darkness within her! All the night in his arms, darkness and shine, he possessed of it all! All the night for him now, to unfold, to venture within, all the mystery to be entered, all the discovery to be made.

Trembling with keen triumph, his heart was white as a star as he drove his kisses nearer.

"My love!" she called, in a low voice, from afar. The low sound seemed to call to him from far off, under the moon, to him who was unaware. He stopped, quivered, and listened.

"My love," came again the low, plaintive call, like a bird unseen in the night. He was afraid. His heart quivered and broke. He was stopped.

"Anna," he said, as if he answered her from a distance, unsure.

"My love."

And he drew near, and she drew near.

"Anna," he said, in wonder and the birthpain of love.

"My love," she said, her voice growing rapturous. And they kissed on the mouth, in rapture and surprise, long, real kisses. The kiss lasted, there among the moonlight. He kissed her again, and she kissed him. And again they were kissing together. Till something happened in him, he was strange. He wanted her. He wanted her exceedingly. She was something new. They stood there folded, suspended in the night. And his whole being quivered with surprise, as from a blow. He wanted her, and he wanted to tell her so. But the shock was too great to him. He had never realised before. He trembled with irritation and unusedness, he did not know what to do. He held her more gently, gently, much more gently. The conflict was gone by. And he was glad, and breathless, and almost in tears. But he knew he wanted her. Something fixed in him for ever. He was hers. And he was very glad and afraid. He did not know what to do, as they stood there in the open, moonlit field. He looked through her hair at the moon, which seemed to swim liquid-bright.

She sighed, and seemed to wake up, then she kissed him again. Then she loosened herself away from him and took his hand. It hurt him when she drew away from his breast. It hurt him with a chagrin. Why did she draw away from him? But she held his hand.

"I want to go home," she said, looking at him in a way he could not understand.

He held close to her hand. He was dazed and he could not move, he did not know how to move. She drew him away.

He walked helplessly beside her, holding her hand. She went with bent head. Suddenly he said, as the simple solution stated itself to him:

"We'll get married, Anna."

She was silent.

"We'll get married, Anna, shall we?"

She stopped in the field again and kissed him, clinging to him passionately, in a way he could not understand. He could not understand. But he left it all now, to marriage. That was the solution now, fixed ahead. He wanted her, he wanted to be married to her, he wanted to have her altogether, as his own for ever. And he waited, intent, for the accomplishment. But there was all the while a slight tension of irritation.

He spoke to his uncle and aunt that night.

"Uncle," he said, "Anna and me think of getting married."

"Oh ay!" said Brangwen.

"But how, you have no money?" said the mother.

The youth went pale. He hated these words. But he was like a gleaming, bright pebble, something bright and inalterable. He did not think. He sat there in his hard brightness, and did not speak.

"Have you mentioned it to your own mother?" asked Brangwen.

"No—I'll tell her on Saturday."

"You'll go and see her?"

"Yes."

There was a long pause.

"And what are you going to marry on—your pound a week?"

Again the youth went pale, as if the spirit were being injured in him.

"I don't know," he said, looking at his uncle with his bright inhuman eyes, like a hawk's.

Brangwen stirred in hatred.

"It needs knowing," he said.

"I shall have the money later on," said the nephew. "I will raise some now, and pay it back then."

"Oh ay!—And why this desperate hurry? She's a child of eighteen, and you're a boy of twenty. You're neither of you of age to do as you like yet."

Will Brangwen ducked his head and looked at his uncle with swift, mistrustful eyes, like a caged hawk.

"What does it matter how old she is, and how old I am?" he said. "What's the difference between me now and when I'm thirty?"

"A big difference, let us hope."

"But you have no experience—you have no experience, and no money. Why do you want to marry, without experience or money?" asked the aunt.

"What experience do I want, Aunt?" asked the boy.

And if Brangwen's heart had not been hard and intact with anger, like a precious stone, he would have agreed.

Will Brangwen went home strange and untouched. He felt he could not alter from what he was fixed upon, his will was set. To alter it he must be destroyed. And he would not be destroyed. He had no money. But he would get some from somewhere, it did not matter. He lay awake for many hours, hard and clear and unthinking, his soul crystallising more inalterably. Then he went fast asleep.

It was as if his soul had turned into a hard crystal. He might tremble and quiver and suffer, it did not alter.

The next morning Tom Brangwen, inhuman with anger spoke to Anna.

"What's this about wanting to get married?" he said.

She stood, paling a little, her dark eyes springing to the hostile, startled look of a savage thing that will defend itself, but trembles with sensitiveness.

"I do," she said, out of her unconsciousness.

His anger rose, and he would have liked to break her.

"You do—you do—and what for?" he sneered with contempt. The old, childish agony, the blindness that could recognize nobody, the palpitating antagonism as of a raw, helpless, undefended thing came back on her.

"I do because I do," she cried, in the shrill, hysterical way of her childhood. "*You* are not my father—my father is dead—*you* are not my father."

She was still a stranger. She did not recognize him. The cold blade cut down, deep into Brangwen's soul. It cut him off from her.

"And what if I'm not?" he said.

But he could not bear it. It had been so passionately dear to him, her "Father—Daddie."

He went about for some days as if stunned. His wife was bemused. She did not understand. She only thought the marriage was impeded for want of money and position.

There was a horrible silence in the house. Anna kept out of sight as much as possible. She could be for hours alone.

Will Brangwen came back, after stupid scenes at Nottingham. He too was pale and blank, but unchanging. His uncle hated him. He hated this youth, who was so inhuman and obstinate. Nevertheless, it was to Will Brangwen that the uncle, one evening, handed over the shares which he had transferred to Anna Lensky. They were for two thousand five hundred pounds. Will Brangwen looked at his uncle. It was a great deal of the Marsh capital here given away. The youth, however, was only colder and more fixed. He was abstract, purely a fixed will. He gave the shares to Anna.

After which she cried for a whole day, sobbing her eyes out. And at night, when she had heard her mother go to bed, she slipped down and hung in the doorway. Her father sat in his heavy silence, like a monument. He turned his head slowly.

"Daddy," she cried from the doorway, and she ran to him sobbing as if her heart would break. "Daddy—daddy—daddy."

She crouched on the hearthrug with her arms round him and her face against him. His body was so big and comfortable. But something hurt her head intolerably. She sobbed almost with hysteria.

He was silent, with his hand on her shoulder. His heart was bleak. He was not her father. That beloved image she had broken. Who was he then? A man put apart with those whose life has no more developments. He was isolated from her. There was a generation between them, he was old, he had died out from hot life. A great deal of ash was in his fire, cold ash. He felt the inevitable coldness, and in bitterness forgot the fire. He sat in his coldness of age and isolation. He had his own wife. And he blamed himself, he sneered at himself, for this clinging to the young, wanting the young to belong to him.

The child who clung to him wanted her child-husband. As was natural. And from him, Brangwen, she wanted help, so that her life might be properly fitted out. But love she did not want. Why should there be love between them, between the stout, middle-aged man and this child? How could there be anything between them, but mere human willingness to help each other? He was her guardian, no more. His heart was like ice, his face cold and expressionless. She could not move him any more than a statue.

She crept to bed, and cried. But she was going to be married to Will Brangwen, and then she need not bother any more. Brangwen went to bed with a hard, cold heart, and cursed himself. He looked at his wife. She was still his wife. Her dark hair was threaded with grey, her face was beautiful in its gathering age. She was just fifty. How poignantly he saw her! And he wanted to cut out some of his own heart, which was incontinent, and demanded still to share the rapid life of youth. How he hated himself.

His wife was so poignant and timely. She was still young and naïve, with some girl's freshness. But she did not want any more the fight, the battle, the control, as he, in his incontinence, still did. She was so natural, and he was ugly, unnatural, in his inability to yield place. How hideous, this greedy middle-age, which must stand in the way of life, like a large demon.

What was missing in his life, that, in his ravening soul, he was not satisfied? He had had that friend at school, his mother, his wife, and Anna? What had he done? He had failed with his friend, he had been a poor son; but he had known satisfaction with his wife, let it be enough; he loathed himself for the state he was in over Anna. Yet he was *not* satisfied. It was agony to know it.

Was his life nothing? Had he nothing to show, no work? He did not count his work, anybody could have done it. What had he known, but the long, marital embrace with his wife! Curious, that this was what his life amounted to!

At any rate, it was something, it was eternal. He would say so to anybody, and be proud of it. He lay with his wife in his arms, and she was still his fulfilment, just the same as ever. And that was the be-all and the end-all. Yes, and he was proud of it.

But the bitterness, underneath, that there still remained an unsatisfied Tom Brangwen, who suffered agony because a girl cared nothing for him. He loved his sons—he had them also. But it was the further, the creative life with the girl, he wanted as well. Oh, and he was ashamed. He trampled himself to extinguish himself.

What weariness! There was no peace, however old one grew! One was never right, never decent, never master of oneself. It was as if his hope had been in the girl.

Anna quickly lapsed again into her love for the youth. Will Brangwen had fixed his marriage for the Saturday before Christmas. And he waited for her, in his bright, unquestioning fashion, until then. He wanted her, she was his, he suspended his being till the day should come. The wedding day, December the twenty-third, had come into being for him as an absolute thing. He lived in it.

He did not count the days. But like a man who journeys in a ship, he was suspended till the coming to port.

He worked at his carving, he worked in his office, he came to see her; all was but a form of waiting, without thought or question.

She was much more alive. She wanted to enjoy courtship. He seemed to come and got like the wind, without asking why or whither. But she wanted to enjoy his presence. For her, he was the kernal of life, to touch him alone was bliss. But for him, she was the essence of life. She existed as much when he was at his carving in his lodging in Ilkeston, as when she sat looking at him in the Marsh kitchen. In himself, he knew her. But his outward faculties seemed suspended. He did not see her with his eyes, nor hear her with his voice.

And yet he trembled, sometimes into a kind of swoon, holding her in his arms. They would stand sometimes folded together in the barn, in silence. Then to her, as she felt his young, tense figure with her hands, the bliss was intolerable, intolerable the sense that she possessed him. For his body was so keen and wonderful, it was the only reality in her world. In her world, there was this one tense, vivid body of a man, and then many other shadowy men, all unreal. In him, she touched the centre of reality. And they were together, he and she, at the heart of the secret. How she clutched him to her, his body the central body of all life. Out of the rock of his form the very fountain of life flowed.

But to him, she was a flame that consumed him. The flame flowed up his limbs, flowed through him, till he was consumed, till he existed only as an unconscious, dark transit of flame, deriving from her.

Sometimes, in the darkness, a cow coughed. There was, in the darkness, a slow sound of cud chewing. And it all seemed to flow round them and upon them as the hot blood flows through the womb, laving the unborn young.

Sometimes, when it was cold, they stood to be lovers in the stables, where the air was warm and sharp with ammonia. And during these dark vigils, he learned to know her, her body against his, they drew nearer and nearer together, the kisses came more subtly close and fitting. So when in the thick darkness a horse suddenly scrambled to its feet, with a dull, thunderous sound, they listened as one person listening, they knew as one person, they were conscious of the horse.

Tom Brangwen had taken them a cottage at Cossethay, on a twenty-one years' lease. Will Brangwen's eyes lit up as he saw it. It was the cottage next the church, with dark yew-trees, very black old trees, along the side of the house and the grassy front garden; a red, squarish cottage with a low slate roof, and low windows. It had a long dairy-scullery, a big flagged kitchen, and a low parlour, that went up one step from the kitchen. There were whitewashed beams across the ceilings, and odd corners with cupboards. Looking out through the windows, there was the grassy garden, the procession of black yew trees down one side, and along the other sides, a red wall with ivy separating the place from the high-road and the churchyard. The old, little church, with its small spire on a square tower, seemed to be looking back at the cottage windows.

"There'll be no need to have a clock," said Will Brangwen, peeping out at the white clock-face on the tower, his neighbour.

At the back of the house was a garden adjoining the paddock, a cowshed with standing for two cows, pig-cotes and fowl-houses. Will Brangwen was very happy. Anna was glad to think of being mistress of her own place.

Tom Brangwen was now the fairy godfather. He was never happy unless he was buying something. Will Brangwen, with his interest in all wood-work, was getting the furniture. He was left to buy tables and round-staved chairs and the dressers, quite ordinary stuff, but such as was identified with his cottage.

Tom Brangwen, with more particular thought, spied out what he called handy little things for her. He appeared with a set of new-fangled cooking-pans, with a special sort of hanging lamp, though the rooms were so low, with canny little machines for grinding meat or mashing potatoes or whisking eggs.

Anna took a sharp interest in what he bought, though she was not always pleased. Some of the little contrivances, which he thought so canny, left her doubtful. Nevertheless she was always expectant, on market days there was always a long thrill of anticipation. He arrived with the first darkness, the copper lamps of his cart glowing. And she ran to the gate, as he, a dark, burly figure up in the cart, was bending over his parcels.

"It's cupboard love as brings you out so sharp," he said, his voice resounding in the cold darkness. Nevertheless he was excited. And she, taking one of the cart lamps, poked and peered among the jumble of things he had brought, pushing aside the oil or implements he had got for himself.

She dragged out a pair of small, strong bellows, registered them in her mind, and then pulled uncertainly at something else. It had a long handle, and a piece of brown paper round the middle of it, like a waistcoat.

"What's this?" she said, poking.

He stopped to look at her. She went to the lamp-light by the horse, and stood there bent over the new thing, while her hair was like bronze, her apron white and cheerful. Her fingers plucked busily at the paper. She dragged forth a little wringer, with clean indiarubber rollers. She examined it critically, not knowing quite how it worked.

She looked up at him. He stood a shadowy presence beyond the light.

"How does it go?" she asked.

"Why, it's for pulpin' turnips," he replied.

She looked at him. His voice disturbed her.

"Don't be silly. It's a little mangle," she said. "How do you stand it, though?"

"You screw it on th' side o' your wash-tub." He came and held it out to her.

"Oh, yes!" she cried, with one of her little skipping movements, which still came when she was suddenly glad.

And without another thought she ran off into the house, leaving him to untackle the horse. And when he came into the scullery, he found her there, with the little wringer fixed on the dolly-tub, turning blissfully at the handle, and Tilly beside her, exclaiming:

"My word, that's a natty little thing! That'll save you luggin' your inside out. That's the latest contraption, that is."

And Anna turned away at the handle, with great gusto of possession. Then she let Tilly have a turn.

"It fair runs by itself," said Tilly, turning on and on. "Your clothes'll nip out on to th' line."

V

WEDDING AT THE MARSH

It was a beautiful sunny day for the wedding, a muddy earth but a bright sky. They had three cabs and two big closed-in vehicles. Everybody crowded in the parlour in excitement. Anna was still upstairs. Her father kept taking a nip of brandy. He was handsome in his black coat and grey trousers. His voice was hearty but troubled. His wife came down in dark grey silk with lace, and a touch of peacock-blue in her bonnet. Her little body was very sure and definite. Brangwen was thankful she was there, to sustain him among all these people.

The carriages! The Nottingham Mrs. Brangwen, in silk brocade, stands in the doorway saying who must go with whom. There is a great bustle. The front door is opened, and the wedding guests are walking down the garden path, whilst those still waiting peer through the window, and the little crowd at the gate gorps and stretches. How funny such dressed-up people look in the winter sunshine!

They are gone—another lot! There begins to be more room. Anna comes down blushing and very shy, to be viewed in her white silk and her veil. Her mother-in-law surveys her objectively, twitches the white train, arranges the folds of the veil and asserts herself.

Loud exclamations from the window that the bridegroom's carriage has just passed.

"Where's your hat, father, and your gloves?" cries the bride, stamping her white slipper, her eyes flashing through her veil. He hunts round—his hair is ruffled. Everybody has gone but the bride and her father. He is ready—his face very red and daunted. Tilly dithers in the little porch, waiting to open the door. A waiting woman walks round Anna, who asks:

"Am I all right?"

She is ready. She bridles herself and looks queenly. She waves her hand sharply to her father:

"Come here!"

He goes. She puts her hand very lightly on his arm, and holding her bouquet like a shower, stepping, oh, very graciously, just a little impatient with her father for being so red in the face, she sweeps slowly past the fluttering Tilly, and down the path. There are hoarse shouts at the gate, and all her floating foamy whiteness passes slowly into the cab.

Her father notices her slim ankle and foot as she steps up: a child's foot. His heart is hard with tenderness. But she is in ecstasies with herself for making such a lovely spectacle. All the way she sat flamboyant with bliss because it was all so lovely. She looked down solicitiously at her bouquet: white roses and lilies-of-the-valley and tube-roses and maidenhair fern—very rich and cascade-like.

Her father sat bewildered with all this strangeness, his heart was so full it felt hard, and he couldn't think of anything.

The church was decorated for Christmas, dark with evergreens, cold and snowy with white flowers. He went vaguely down to the altar. How long was it since he had gone to be married himself? He was not sure whether he was going to be married now, or what he had come for. He had a troubled notion that he had to do something or other. He saw his wife's bonnet, and wondered why she wasn't there with him.

They stood before the altar. He was staring up at the east window, that glowed intensely, a sort of blue purple: it was deep blue glowing, and some crimson, and little yellow flowers held fast in veins of shadow, in a heavy web of darkness. How it burned alive in radiance among its black web.

"Who giveth this woman to be married to this man?" He felt somebody touch him. He started. The words still re-echoed in his memory, but were drawing off.

"Me," he said hastily.

Ann bent her head and smiled in her veil. How absurd he was.

Brangwen was staring away at the burning blue window at the back of the altar, and wondering vaguely, with pain, if he ever should get old, if he ever should feel arrived and established. He was here at Anna's wedding. Well, what right had he to feel responsible, like a father? He was still as unsure and unfixed as when he had married himself. His wife and he! With a pang of anguish he realised what uncertainties they both were. He was a man of forty-five. Forty-five! In five more years fifty. Then sixty—then seventy—then it was finished. My God—and one still was so unestablished!

How did one grow old—how could one become confident? He wished he felt older. Why, what difference was there, as far as he felt matured or completed, between him now and him at his own wedding? He might be getting married over again—he and his wife. He felt himself tiny, a little, upright figure on a plain circled round with the immense, roaring sky: he and his wife, two little, upright figures walking across this plain, whilst the heavens shimmered and roared about them. When did it come to an end? In which direction was it finished? There was no end, no finish, only this roaring vast space. Did one never get old, never die? That was the clue. He exulted strangely, with torture. He would go on with his wife, he and she like two children camping in the plains. What was sure but the endless sky? But that was so sure, so boundless.

Still the royal blue colour burned and blazed and sported itself in the web of darkness before him, unwearingly rich and splendid. How rich and splendid his own life was, red and burning and blazing and sporting itself in the dark meshes of his body: and his wife, how she glowed and burned dark within her meshes! Always it was so unfinished and unformed!

There was a loud noise of the organ. The whole party was trooping to the vestry. There was a blotted, scrawled book—and that young girl putting back her veil in her vanity, and laying her hand with the wedding-ring self-consciously conspicuous, and signing her name proudly because of the vain spectacle she made:

"Anna Theresa Lensky."

"Anna Theresa Lensky"—what a vain, independent minx she was! The bridegroom, slender in his black swallow-tail and grey trousers, solemn as a young solemn cat, was writing seriously:

"William Brangwen."

That looked more like it.

"Come and sign, father," cried the imperious young hussy.

"Thomas Brangwen—clumsy-fist," he said to himself as he signed.

Then his brother, a big, sallow fellow with black side-whiskers wrote:

"Alfred Brangwen."

"How many more Brangwens?" said Tom Brangwen, ashamed of the too-frequent recurrence of his family name.

When they were out again in the sunshine, and he saw the frost hoary and blue among the long grass under the tombstones, the holly-berries overhead twinkling scarlet as the bells rang, the yew trees hanging their black, motionless, ragged boughs, everything seemed like a vision.

The marriage party went across the graveyard to the wall, mounted it by the little steps, and descended. Oh, a vain white peacock of a bride perching herself on the top of the wall and giving her hand to the bridegroom on the other side, to be helped down! The vanity of her white, slim, daintily-stepping feet, and her arched neck. And the regal impudence with which she seemed to dismiss them all, the others, parents and wedding guests, as she went with her young husband.

In the cottage big fires were burning, there were dozens of glasses on the table, and holly and mistletoe hanging up. The wedding party crowded in, and Tom Brangwen, becoming roisterous, poured out drinks. Everybody must drink. The bells were ringing away against the windows.

"Lift your glasses up," shouted Tom Brangwen from the parlour, "lift your glasses up, an' drink to the hearth an' home—hearth an' home, an' may they enjoy it."

"Night an' day, an' may they enjoy it," shouted Frank Brangwen, in addition.

"Hammer an' tongs, and may they enjoy it," shouted Alfred Brangwen, the saturnine.

"Fill your glasses up, an' let's have it all over again," shouted Tom Brangwen.

"Hearth an' home, an' may ye enjoy it."

There was a ragged shout of the company in response.

"Bed an' blessin', an' may ye enjoy it," shouted Frank Brangwen.

There was a swelling chorus in answer.

"Comin' and goin', an' may ye enjoy it," shouted the saturnine Alfred Brangwen, and the men roared by now boldly, and the women said, "Just hark, now!"

There was a touch of scandal in the air.

Then the party rolled off in the carriages, full speed back to the Marsh, to a large meal of the high-tea order, which lasted for an hour and a half. The bride and bridegroom sat at the head of the table, very prim and shining both of them, wordless, whilst the company raged down the table.

The Brangwen men had brandy in their tea, and were becoming unmanageable. The saturnine Alfred had glittering, unseeing eyes, and a strange, fierce way of laughing that showed his teeth. His wife glowered at him and jerked her head at him like a snake. He was oblivious. Frank Brangwen, the butcher, flushed and florid and handsome, roared echoes to his two brothers. Tom

Brangwen, in his solid fashion, was letting himself go at last.

These three brothers dominated the whole company. Tom Brangwen wanted to make a speech. For the first time in his life, he must spread himself wordily.

"Marriage," he began, his eyes twinkling and yet quite profound, for he was deeply serious and hugely amused at the same time, "Marriage," he said, speaking in the slow, full-mouthed way of the Brangwens, "is what we're made for——"

"Let him talk," said Alfred Brangwen, slowly and inscrutably, "let him talk." Mrs. Alfred darted indignant eyes at her husband.

"A man," continued Tom Brangwen, "enjoys being a man: for what purpose was he made a man, if not to enjoy it?"

"That a true word," said Frank, floridly.

"And likewise," continued Tom Brangwen, "a woman enjoys being a woman: at least we surmise she does——"

"Oh, don't you bother——" called a farmer's wife.

"You may back your life they'd be summisin'," said Frank's wife.

"Now," continued Tom Brangwen, "for a man to be a man, it takes a woman——"

"It does that," said a woman grimly.

"And for a woman to be a woman, it takes a man——" continued Tom Brangwen.

"All speak up, men," chimed in a feminine voice.

"Therefore we have marriage," continued Tom Brangwen.

"Hold, hold," said Alfred Brangwen. "Don't run us off our legs."

And in dead silence the glasses were filled. The bride and bridegroom, two children, sat with intent, shining faces at the head of the table, abstracted.

"There's no marriage in heaven," went on Tom Brangwen; "but on earth there is marriage."

"That's the difference between 'em," said Alfred Brangwen, mocking.

"Alfred," said Tom Brangwen, "keep your remarks till afterwards, and then we'll thank you for them.—There's very little else, on earth, but marriage. You can talk about making money, or saving souls. You can save your own soul seven times over, and you may have a mint of money, but your soul goes gnawin', gnawin', gnawin', and it says there's something it must have. In heaven there is no marriage. But on earth there is marriage, else heaven drops out, and there's no bottom to it."

"Just hark you now," said Frank's wife.

"Go on, Thomas," said Alfred sardonically.

"If we've got to be Angels," went on Tom Brangwen, haranguing the company at large, "and if there is no such thing as a man nor a woman amongst them, then it seems to me as a married couple makes one Angel."

"It's the brandy," said Alfred Brangwen wearily.

"For," said Tom Brangwen, and the company was listening to the conundrum, "an Angel can't be less than a human being. And if it was only the soul of a man minus the man, then it would be less than a human being."

"Decidedly," said Alfred.

And a laugh went round the table. But Tom Brangwen was inspired.

"An Angel's got to be more than a human being," he continued. "So I say, an Angel is the soul of man and woman in one: they rise united at the Judgment Day, as one Angel——"

"Praising the Lord," said Frank.

"Praising the Lord," repeated Tom.

"And what about the women left over?" asked Alfred, jeering. The company was getting uneasy.

"That I can't tell. How do I know as there *is* anybody left over at the Judgment Day? Let that be. What I say is, that when a man's soul and a woman's soul unites together—that makes an Angel——"

"I dunno about souls. I know as one plus one makes three, sometimes," said Frank. But he had the laugh to himself.

"Bodies and souls, it's the same," said Tom.

"And what about your missis, who was married afore you knew her?" asked Alfred, set on edge by this discourse.

"That I can't tell you. If I am to become an Angel, it'll be my married soul, and not my single soul. It'll not be the soul of me when I was a lad: for I hadn't a soul as would *make* an Angel then."

"I can always remember," said Frank's wife, "when our Harold was bad, he did nothink but see an angel at th' back o' th' lookin'-glass. 'Look, mother,' 'e said, 'at that angel!' 'Theer isn't no angel, my duck,' I said, but he wouldn't have it. I took th' lookin'-glass off'n th' dressin'-table, but it made no difference. He kep' on sayin' it was there. My word, it did give me a turn. I thought for sure as I'd lost him."

"I can remember," said another man, Tom's sister's husband, "my mother gave me a good hidin' once, for sayin' I'd got an angel up my nose. She seed me pokin', an' she said: 'What are you pokin' at your nose for—give over.' 'There's an angel up it,' I said, an' she fetched me such a wipe. But there was. We used to call them thistle things 'angels' as wafts about. An' I'd pushed one o' these up my nose, for some reason or other."

"It's wonderful what children will get up their noses," said Frank's wife. "I c'n remember our Hemmie, she shoved one o' them bluebell things out o' th' middle of a bluebell, what they call 'candles', up her nose, and oh, we had some work! I'd seen her stickin' 'em on the end of her nose, like, but I never thought she'd be so soft as to shove it right up. She was a gel of eight or more. Oh, my word, we got a crochet-hook an' I don't know what . . ."

Tom Brangwen's mood of inspiration began to pass away. He forgot all about it, and was soon roaring and shouting with the rest. Outside the wake came, singing the carols. They were invited into the bursting house. They had two fiddles and a piccolo. There in the parlour they played carols, and the whole company sang them at the top of its voice. Only the bride and bridegroom sat with shining eyes and strange, bright faces, and scarcely sang, or only with just moving lips.

The wake departed, and the guysers came. There was loud applause, and shouting and excitement as the old mystery play of St. George, in which every man present had acted as a boy, proceeded, with banging and thumping of club and dripping pan.

"By Jove, I got a crack once, when I was playin' Beelzebub," said Tom Brangwen, his eyes full of water with laughing. "It knocked all th' sense out of me as you'd crack an egg. But I tell you, when I come to, I played Old Johnny Roger with St. George, I did that."

He was shaking with laughter. Another knock came at the door. There was a hush.

"It's th' cab," said somebody from the door.

"Walk in," shouted Tom Brangwen, and a red-faced grinning man entered. "Now, you two, get yourselves ready an' off to blanket fair," shouted Tom Brangwen. "Strike a daisy, but if you're not off like a blink o' lightnin', you shanna go, you s'll sleep separate."

Anna rose silently and went to change her dress. Will Brangwen would have gone out, but Tilly came with his hat and coat. The youth was helped on.

"Well, here's luck, my boy," shouted his father.

"When th' fat's in th' fire, let it frizzle," admonished his uncle Frank.

"Fair and *softly* does it, fair an' *softly* does it," cried his aunt, Frank's wife, contrary.

"You don't want to fall over yourself," said his uncle by marriage. "You're not a bull at a gate."

"Let a man have his own road," said Tom Brangwen testily. "Don't be so free of your advice—it's his wedding this time, not yours."

" 'E don't want many sign-posts," said his father. "There's some roads a man has to be led, an' there's some roads a boss-eyed man can only follow wi' one eye shut. But this road can't be lost by a blind man nor a boss-eyed man nor a cripple—and he's neither, thank God."

"Don't you be so sure o' your walkin' powers," cried Frank's wife. "There's many a man gets no further than half-way, nor can't to save his life, let him live for ever."

"Why, how do you know?" said Alfred.

"It's plain enough in th' looks o' some," retorted Lizzie, his sister-in-law.

The youth stood with a faint, half-hearing smile on his face. He was tense and abstracted. These things, or anything, scarcely touched him.

Anna came down, in her day dress, very elusive. She kissed everybody, men and women, Will Brangwen shook hands with everybody, kissed his mother, who began to cry, and the whole party went surging out to the cab.

The young couple were shut up, last injunctions shouted at them.

"Drive on," shouted Tom Brangwen.

The cab rolled off. They saw the light diminish under the ash trees. Then the whole party, quietened, went indoors.

"They'll have three good fires burning," said Tom Brangwen, looking at his watch. "I told Emma to make 'em up at nine, an' then leave the door on th' latch. It's only half-past. They'll have three fires burning, an' lamps lighted, an' Emma will ha' warmed th' bed wi' th' warmin' pan. So I s'd think they'll be all right."

The party was much quieter. They talked of the young couple.

"She said she didn't want a servant in," said Tom Brangwen. "The house isn't big enough, she'd always have the creature under her nose. Emma'll do what is wanted of her, an' they'll be to themselves."

"It's best," said Lizzie, "you're more free."

The party talked on slowly. Brangwen looked at his watch.

"Let's go an' give 'em a carol," he said. "We s'll find th' fiddles at the 'Cock an' Robin'."

"Ay, come on," said Frank.

Alfred rose in silence. The brother-in-law and one of Will's brothers rose also.

The five men went out. The night was flashing with stars. Sirius blazed like a signal at the side of the hill, Orion, stately and magnificent, was sloping along.

Tom walked with his brother, Alfred. The men's heels rang on the ground.

"It's a fine night," said Tom.

"Ay," said Alfred.

"Nice to get out."

"Ay."

The brothers walked close together, the bond of blood strong between them. Tom always felt very much the junior to Alfred.

"It's a long while since *you* left home," he said.

"Ay," said Alfred. "I thought I was getting a bit oldish—but I'm not. It's the things you've got as gets worn out, it's not you yourself."

"Why, what's worn out?"

"Most folks as I've anything to do with—as has anything to do with me. They all break down. You've got to go on by yourself, if it's only to perdition. There's nobody going alongside even there."

Tom Brangwen meditated this.

"Maybe you was never broken in," he said.

"No, I never was," said Alfred proudly.

And Tom felt his elder brother despised him a little. He winced under it.

"Everybody's got a way of their own," he said, stubbornly. "It's only a dog as hasn't. An' them as can't take what they give an' give what they take, they must go by themselves, or get a dog as'll follow 'em."

"They can do without the dog," said his brother. And again Tom Brangwen was humble, thinking his brother was bigger than himself. But if he was, he was. And if it were finer to go alone, it was: he did not want to go for all that.

They went over the field, where a thin, keen wind blew round the ball of the hill, in the starlight. They came to the stile, and to the side of Anna's house. The lights were out, only on the blinds of the rooms downstairs, and of a bedroom upstairs, firelight flickered.

"We'd better leave 'em alone," said Alfred Brangwen.

"Nay, nay," said Tom. "We'll carol 'em, for th' last time."

And in a quarter of an hour's time, eleven silent, rather tipsy men scrambled over the wall, and into the garden by the yew trees, outside the windows where faint firelight glowered on the blinds. There came a shrill sound, two violins and a piccolo shrilling on the frosty air.

"In the fields with their flocks abiding." A commotion of men's voices broke out singing in ragged unison.

Anna Brangwen had started up, listening, when the music began. She was afraid.

"It's the wake," he whispered.

She remained tense, her heart beating heavily, possessed with strange, strong fear. Then there came the burst of men's singing, rather uneven. She strained still, listening.

"It's Dad," she said, in a low voice. They were silent, listening.

"And my father," he said.

She listened still. But she was sure. She sank down again into bed, into his arms. He held her very close, kissing her. The hymn rambled on outside, all the men singing their best, having forgotten everything else under the spell of the fiddles and the tune. The firelight glowed against the darkness in the room. Anna could hear her father singing with gusto.

"Aren't they silly," she whispered.

And they crept closer, closer together, hearts beating to one another. And even as the hymn rolled on, they ceased to hear it.

VI

Anna Victrix

Will Brangwen had some weeks of holiday after his marriage, so the two took their honeymoon in full hands, alone in their cottage together.

And to him, as the days went by, it was as if the heavens had fallen, and he were sitting with her among the ruins, in a new world, everybody else buried, themselves two blissful survivors, with everything to squander as they would. At first, he could not get rid of a culpable sense of licence on his part. Wasn't there some duty outside, calling him and he did not come?

It was all very well at night, when the doors were locked and the darkness drawn round the two of them. Then they were the only inhabitants of the visible earth, the rest were under the flood. And being alone in the world, they were a law unto themselves, they could enjoy and squander and waste like conscienceless gods.

But in the morning, as the carts clanked by, and children shouted down the lane; as the hucksters came calling their wares, and the church clock struck eleven, and he and she had not got up yet, even to breakfast, he could not help feeling guilty, as if he were committing a breach of the law—ashamed that he was not up and doing.

"Doing what?" she asked. "What is there to do? You will only lounge about."

Still, even lounging about was respectable. One was at least in connection with the world, then. Whereas now, lying so still and peacefully, while the daylight came obscurely through the drawn blind, one was severed from the world, one shut oneself off in tacit denial of the world. And he was troubled.

But it was so sweet and satisfying lying there talking desultorily with her. It was sweeter than sunshine, and not so evanescent. It was even irritating the way the church-clock kept on chiming: there seemed no space between the hours, just a moment, golden and still, whilst she traced his features with her finger-tips, utterly careless and happy, and he loved her to do it.

But he was strange and unused. So suddenly, everything that had been before was shed away and gone. One day, he was a bachelor, living with the world. The next day, he was with her, as remote from the world as if the two of them were buried like a seed in darkness. Suddenly, like a chestnut falling out of a burr, he was shed naked and glistening on to a soft, fecund earth, leaving behind him the hard rind of worldly knowledge and experience. He heard it in the huckster's cries, the noise of carts, the calling of children. And it was all like the hard, shed rind, discarded. Inside, in the softness and stillness of the room, was the naked kernel, that palpitated in silent activity, absorbed in reality.

Inside the room was a great steadiness, a core of living eternity. Only far outside, at the rim, went on the noise and the destruction. Here at the centre the great wheel was motionless, centred upon itself. Here was a poised, unflawed stillness that was beyond time, because it remained the same, inexhaustible, unchanging, unexhausted.

As they lay close together, complete and beyond the touch of time or change, it was as if they were at the very centre of all the slow wheeling of space and the rapid agitation of life, deep, deep inside them all, at the centre where there is utter radiance, and eternal being, and the silence absorbed in praise: the steady core of all movements, the unawakened sleep of all wakefulness. They found themselves there, and they lay still, in each other's arms; for their moment they were at the heart of eternity, whilst time roared far off, for ever far off, towards the rim.

Then gradually they were passed away from the supreme centre, down the circles of praise and joy and gladness, further and further out, towards the noise and the friction. But their hearts had burned and were tempered by the inner reality, they were unalterably glad.

Gradually they began to wake up, the noises outside became more real. They understood and answered the call outside. They counted the strokes of the bell. And when they counted midday, they understood that it was midday, in the world, and for themselves also.

It dawned upon her that she was hungry. She had been getting hungrier for a lifetime. But even yet it was not sufficiently real to rouse her. A long way off she could hear the words, "I am dying of hunger." Yet she lay still, separate, at peace, and the words were unuttered. There was still another lapse.

And then, quite calmly, even a little surprised, she was in the present, and was saying:

"I am dying with hunger."

"So am I," he said calmly, as if it were of not the slightest significance. And they relapsed into the warm, golden stillness. And the minutes flowed unheeded past the window outside.

Then suddenly she stirred against him.

"My dear, I am dying of hunger," she said.

It was a slight pain to him to be brought to.

"We'll get up," he said, unmoving.

And she sank her head on to him again, and they lay still, lapsing. Half consciously, he heard the clock chime the hour. She did not hear.

"Do get up," she murmured at length, "and give me something to eat."

"Yes," he said, and he put his arms round her, and she lay with her face on him. They were faintly astonished that they did not move. The minutes rustled louder at the window.

"Let me go then," he said.

She lifted her head from him, relinquishingly. With a little breaking away, she moved out of bed, and was taking his clothes. She stretched out her hand to him.

"You are so nice," she said, and he went back for a moment or two.

Then actually he did slip into some clothes, and, looking round quickly at her, was gone out of the room. She lay translated again into a pale, clearer peace. As if she were a spirit, she listened to the noise of him downstairs, as if she were no longer of the material world.

It was half-past one. He looked at the silent kitchen, untouched from last night, dim with the drawn blind. And he hastened to draw up the blind, so people should know they were not in bed any later. Well, it was his own house, it did not matter. Hastily he put wood in the grate and made a fire. He exulted in himself, like an adventurer on an undiscovered island. The fire blazed up, he put on the kettle. How happy he felt! How still and secluded the house was! There were only he and she in the world.

But when he unbolted the door, and, half-dressed, looked out, he felt furtive and guilty. The world *was* there, after all. And he had felt so secure, as though this house were the Ark in the flood, and all the rest was drowned. The world was there: and it was afternoon. The morning had vanished and gone by, the day was growing old. Where was the bright, fresh morning? He was accused. Was the morning gone, and he had lain with blinds drawn, let it pass by unnoticed?

He looked again round the chill, grey afternoon. And he himself so soft and warm and glowing! There were two sprigs of yellow jasmine in the saucer that covered the milk-jug. He wondered who had been and left the sign. Taking the jug, he hastily shut the door. Let the day and the daylight drop out, let it go by unseen. He did not care. What did one day more or less matter to him. It could fall into oblivion unspent if it liked, this one course of daylight.

"Somebody has been and found the door locked," he said when he went upstairs with the tray. He gave her the two sprigs of jasmine. She laughed as she sat up in bed, childishly threading the flowers in the breast of her nightdress. Her brown hair stuck out like a nimbus, all fierce, round her softly glowing face. Her dark eyes watched the tray eagerly.

"How good!" she cried, sniffing the cold air. "I'm glad you did a lot." And she stretched out her hands eagerly for her plate—"Come back to bed, quick— it's cold." She rubbed her hands together sharply.

He sat beside her in the bed.

"You look like a lion, with your mane sticking out, and your nose pushed over your food," he said.

She tinkled with laughter, and gladly ate her breakfast.

The morning was sunk away unseen, the afternoon was steadily going too, and he was letting it go. One bright transit of daylight gone by unacknowledged! There was something unmanly, recusant in it. He could not quite reconcile himself to the fact. He felt he ought to get up, go out quickly into the daylight, and work or spend himself energetically in the open air of the afternoon, retrieving what was left to him of the day.

But he did not go. Well, one might as well be hung for a sheep as for a lamb. If he had lost this day of his life, he had lost it. He gave it up. He was not going to count his losses. *She* didn't care. *She* didn't care in the least. Then why should he? Should he be behind her in recklessness and independence? She was superb in her indifference. He wanted to be like her.

She took her responsibilities lightly. When she spilled her tea on the pillow, she rubbed it carelessly with a handkerchief, and turned over the pillow. He would have felt guilty. She did not. And it pleased him. It pleased him very much to see how these things did not matter to her.

When the meal was over, she wiped her mouth on her handkerchief quickly, satisfied and happy, and settled down on the pillow again, with her fingers in his close, strange, fur-like hair.

The evening began to fall, the light was half alive, livid. He hid his face against her.

"I don't like the twilight," he said.

"I love it," she answered.

He hid his face against her, who was warm and like sunlight. She seemed to have sunlight inside her. Her heart beating seemed like sunlight upon him. In her was a more real day than the day could give: so warm and steady and restoring. He hid his face against her whilst the twilight fell, whilst she lay staring out with her unseeing dark eyes, as if she wandered forth untrammelled in the vagueness. The vagueness gave her scope and set her free.

To him, turned towards her heart-pulse, all was very still and very warm and very close, like noon-tide. He was glad to know this warm, full noon. It ripened him and took away his responsibility, some of his conscience.

They got up when it was quite dark. She hastily twisted her hair into a knot, and was dressed in a twinkling. Then they went downstairs, drew to the fire, and sat in silence, saying a few words now and then.

Her father was coming. She bundled the dishes away, flew round and tidied the room, assumed another character, and again seated herself. He sat thinking of his carving of Eve. He loved to go over his carving in his mind, dwelling on every stroke, every line. How he loved it now! When he went back to his Creation-panel again, he would finish his Eve, tender and sparkling. It did not satisfy him yet. The Lord should labour over her in a silent passion of Creation, and Adam should be tense as if in a dream of immortality, and Eve should take form glimmeringly, shadowily, as if the Lord must wrestle with His own soul for her, yet she was a radiance.

"What are you thinking about?" she asked.

He found it difficult to say. His soul became shy when he tried to communicate it.

"I was thinking my Eve was too hard and lively."

"Why?"

"I don't know. She should be more——," he made a gesture of infinite tenderness.

There was a stillness with a little joy. He could not tell her any more. Why could he not tell her any more? She felt a pang of disconsolate sadness. But it was nothing. She went to him.

Her father came, and found them both very glowing, like an open flower. He loved to sit with them. Where there was a perfume of love, anyone who came must breathe it. They were both very quick and alive, lit up from the other-world, so that it was quite an experience for them, that anyone else could exist.

But still it troubled Will Brangwen a little, in his orderly, conventional mind, that the established rule of things had gone so utterly. One ought to get up in the morning and wash oneself and be a decent social being. Instead, the two of them stayed in bed till nightfall, and then got up, she never washed her face, but sat there talking to her father as bright and shameless as a daisy opened out of the dew. Or she got up at ten o'clock, and quite blithely went to bed again at three, or at half-past four, stripping him naked in the daylight, and all so gladly and perfectly, oblivious quite of his qualms. He let her do as she liked with him, and shone with strange pleasure. She was to dispose of him as she would. He was translated with gladness to be in her hands. And down went his qualms, his maxims, his rules, his smaller beliefs, she scattered them like an expert skittle-player. He was very much astonished and delighted to see them scatter.

He stood and gazed and grinned with wonder whilst his Tablets of Stone went bounding and bumping and splintering down the hill, dislodged for ever. Indeed, it was true as they said, that a man wasn't born before he was married. What a change indeed!

He surveyed the rind of the world: houses, factories, trams, the discarded rind; people scurrying about, work going on, all on the discarded surface. An earthquake had burst it all from inside. It was as if the surface of the world had been broken away entire: Ilkeston, streets, church, people, work, rule-of-the-day, all intact; and yet peeled away into unreality, leaving here exposed the inside, the reality: one's own being, strange feelings and passions and yearnings and beliefs and aspirations, suddenly become present, revealed, the permanent bedrock, knitted one rock with the woman one loved. It was confounding. Things are not what they seem! When he was a child, he had thought a woman was a woman merely by virtue of her skirts and petticoats. And now, lo, the whole world could be divested of its garment, the garment could lie there shed away intact, and one could stand in a new world, a new earth, naked in a new, naked universe. It was too astounding and miraculous.

This then was marriage! The old things didn't matter any more. One got up at four o'clock, and had broth at tea-time and made toffee in the middle of the night. One didn't put on one's clothes or one did put on one's clothes. He still was not quite sure it was not criminal. But it was a discovery to find one might be so supremely absolved. All that mattered was that he should love her and she should love him and they should live kindled to one another, like the Lord in two burning bushes that were not consumed. And so they lived for the time.

She was less hampered than he, so she came more quickly to her fulness, and was sooner ready to enjoy again a return to the outside world. She was going to give a tea-party. His heart sank. He wanted to go on, to go on as they were. He wanted to have done with the outside world, to declare it finished for ever. He was anxious with a deep desire and anxiety that she should stay with him where they were in the timeless universe of free, perfect limbs and immortal breast, affirming that the old outward order was finished. The new order was begun to last for ever, the living life, palpitating from the gleaming core, to action, without crust or cover or outward lie. But no, he could not keep her. She wanted the dead world again—she wanted to walk on the outside once more. She was going to give a tea-party. It made him frightened and furious and miserable. He was afraid all would be lost that he had so newly come into: like the youth in the fairy tale, who was king for one day in the year, and for the rest a beaten herd: like Cinderella also, at the feast. He was sullen. But she blithely began to make preparations for her tea-party. His fear was too strong, he was troubled, he hated her shallow anticipation and joy. Was she not forfeiting the reality, the one reality, for all that was shallow and worthless? Wasn't she carelessly taking off her crown to be an artificial figure having other artificial women to tea: when she might have been perfect with him, and kept him perfect, in the land of intimate connection? Now he must be deposed, his joy must be destroyed, he must put on the vulgar, shallow death of an outward existence.

He ground his soul in uneasiness and fear. But she rose to a real outburst of house-work, turning him away as she shoved the furniture aside to her broom. He stood hanging miserable near. He wanted her back. Dread, and desire for her to stay with him, and shame at his own dependence on her drove him to anger. He began to lose his head. The wonder was going to pass away again. All the love, the magnificent new order was going to be lost, she would forfeit it all for the outside things. She would admit the outside world again, she would throw away the living fruit for the ostensible rind. He began to hate this in her. Driven by fear of her departure into a state of helplessness, almost of imbecility, he wandered about the house.

And she, with her skirts kilted up, flew round at her work, absorbed.

"Shake the rug then, if you must hang round," she said.

And fretting with resentment, he went to shake the rug. She was blithely unconscious of him. He came back, hanging near to her.

"Can't you do anything?" she said, as if to a child, impatiently. "Can't you do your wood-work?"

"Where shall I do it?" he asked, harsh with pain.

"Anywhere."

How furious that made him.

"Or go for a walk," she continued. "Go down to the Marsh. Don't hang about as if you were only half there."

He winced and hated it. He went away to read. Never had his soul felt so flayed and uncreated.

And soon he must come down again to her. His hovering near her, wanting her to be with him, the futility of him, the way his hands hung, irritated her beyond bearing. She turned on him blindly and destructively, he became a mad creature, black and electric with fury. The dark storms rose in him, his eyes glowed black and evil, he was fiendish in his thwarted soul.

There followed two black and ghastly days, when she was set in anguish against him, and he felt as if he were in a black, violent underworld, and his wrists quivered murderously. And she resisted him. He seemed a dark, almost evil thing, pursuing her, hanging on to her, burdening her. She would give anything to have him removed.

"You need some work to do," she said. "You ought to be at work. Can't you *do* something?"

His soul only grew the blacker. His condition now became complete, the darkness of his soul was thorough. Everything had gone: he remained complete in his own tense, black will. He was now unaware of her. She did not exist. His dark, passionate soul had recoiled upon itself, and now, clinched and coiled round a centre of hatred, existed in its own power. There was a curiously ugly pallor, an expressionlessness in his face. She shuddered from him. She was afraid of him. His will seemed grappled upon her.

She retreated before him. She went down to the Marsh, she entered again the immunity of her parents' love for her. He remained at Yew Cottage, black and clinched, his mind dead. He was unable to work at his wood-carving. He went on working monotonously at the garden, blindly, like a mole.

As she came home, up the hill, looking away at the town dim and blue on the hill, her heart relaxed and became yearning. She did not want to fight him any more. She wanted love—oh, love. Her feet began to hurry. She wanted to get back to him. Her heart became tight with yearning for him.

He had been making the garden in order, cutting the edges of the turf, laying the path with stones. He was a good, capable workman.

"How nice you've made it," she said, approaching tentatively down the path.

But he did not heed, he did not hear. His brain was solid and dead.

"Haven't you made it nice?" she repeated, rather plaintively.

He looked up at her, with that fixed, expressionless face and unseeing eyes which shocked her, made her go dazed and blind. Then he turned away. She saw his slender, stooping figure groping. A revulsion came over her. She went indoors.

As she took off her hat in the bedroom, she found herself weeping bitterly, with some of the old, anguished, childish desolation. She sat still and cried on. She did not want him to know. She was afraid of his hard, evil moments, the head dropped a little, rigidly, in a crouching, cruel way. She was afraid of him. He seemed to lacerate her sensitive femaleness. He seemed to hurt her womb, to take pleasure in torturing her.

He came into the house. The sound of his footsteps in his heavy boots filled her with horror: a hard, cruel, malignant sound. She was afraid he would come upstairs. But he did not. She waited apprehensively. He went out.

Where she was most vulnerable, he hurt her. Oh, where she was delivered over to him, in her very soft femaleness, he seemed to lacerate her and desecrate her. She pressed her hands over her womb in anguish, whilst the tears ran down her face. And why, and why? Why was he like this?

Suddenly she dried her tears. She must get the tea ready. She went downstairs and set the table. When the meal was ready, she called to him.

"I've mashed the tea, Will, are you coming?"

She herself could hear the sound of tears in her own voice, and she began to cry again. He did not answer, but went on with his work. She waited a few minutes, in anguish. Fear came over her, she was panic-stricken with terror, like a child; and she could not go home again to her father; she was held by the power in this man who had taken her.

She turned indoors so that he should not see her tears. She sat down to table. Presently he came into the scullery. His movements jarred on her, as she heard them. How horrible was the way he pumped, exacerbating, so cruel! How she hated to hear him! How he hated her! How his hatred was like blows upon her! The tears were coming again.

He came in, his face wooden and lifeless, fixed, persistent. He sat down to tea, his head dropped over his cup, uglily. His hands were red from the cold water, and there were rims of earth in his nails. He went on with his tea.

It was his negative insensitiveness to her that she could not bear, something clayey and ugly. His intelligence was self-absorbed. How unnatural it was to sit with a self-absorbed creature, like something negative ensconced opposite one. Nothing could touch him—he could only absorb things into his own self.

The tears were running down her face. Something startled him, and he was looking up at her with his hateful, hard, bright eyes, hard and unchanging as a bird of prey.

"What are you crying for?" came the grating voice.

She winced through her womb. She could not stop crying.

"What are you crying for?" came the question again, in just the same tone. And still there was silence, with only the sniff of her tears.

His eyes glittered, and as if with malignant desire. She shrank and became blind. She was like a bird being beaten down. A sort of swoon of helplessness came over her. She was of another order than he, she had no defence against him. Against such an influence, she was only vulnerable, she was given up.

He rose and went out of the house, possessed by the evil spirit. It tortured him and wracked him, and fought in him. And whilst he worked, in the deepening twilight, it left him. Suddenly he saw that she was hurt. He had only seen her triumphant before. Suddenly his heart was torn with compassion for her. He became alive again, in an anguish of compassion. He could not bear to think of her tears—he could not bear it. He wanted to go to her and pour out his heart's blood to her. He wanted to give everything to her, all his blood, his life, to the last dregs, pour everything away to her. He yearned with passionate desire to offer himself to her, utterly.

The evening star came, and the night. She had not lighted the lamp. His heart burned with pain and with grief. He trembled to go to her.

And at last he went, hesitating, burdened with a great offering. The hardness had gone out of him, his body was sensitive, slightly trembling. His hand was curiously sensitive, shrinking, as he shut the door. He fixed the latch almost tenderly.

In the kitchen was only the fireglow, he could not see her. He quivered with dread lest she had gone—he knew not where. In shrinking dread, he went through to the parlour, to the foot of the stairs.

"Anna," he called.

There was no answer. He went up the stairs, in dread of the empty house—the horrible emptiness that made his heart sing with insanity. He opened the bedroom door, and his heart flashed with certainty that she had gone, that he was alone.

But he saw her on the bed, lying very still and scarcely noticeable, with her back to him. He went and put his hand on her shoulder, very gently, hesitating, in a great fear and self-offering. She did not move. He waited. The hand that touched her shoulder hurt him, as if she were sending it away. He stood dim with pain.

"Anna," he said.

But still she was motionless, like a curled up, oblivious creature. His heart beat with strange throes of pain. Then, by a motion under his hand, he knew she was crying, holding herself hard so that her tears should not be known. He waited. The tension continued—perhaps she was not crying—then suddenly relapsed with a sharp catch of a sob. His heart flamed with love and suffering for her. Kneeling carefully on the bed, so that his earthy boots should not touch it, he took her in his arms to comfort her. The sobs gathered in her, she was sobbing bitterly. But not to him. She was still away from him.

He held her against his breast, whilst she sobbed, withheld from him, and all his body vibrated against her.

"Don't cry—don't cry," he said, with an odd simplicity. His heart was calm and numb with a sort of innocence of love, now.

She still sobbed, ignoring him, ignoring that he held her. His lips were dry.

"Don't cry, my love," he said, in the same abstract way. In his breast his heart burned like a torch, with suffering. He could not bear the desolateness of her crying. He would have soothed her with his blood. He heard the church clock chime, as if it touched him, and he waited in suspense for it to have gone by. It was quiet again.

"My love," he said to her, bending to touch her wet face with his mouth. He was afraid to touch her. How wet her face was! His body trembled as he held her. He loved her till he felt his heart and all his veins would burst and flood her with his hot, healing blood. He knew his blood would heal and restore her.

She was becoming quieter. He thanked the God of mercy that at last she was becoming quieter. His head felt so strange and blazed. Still he held her close, with trembling arms. His blood seemed very strong, enveloping her.

And at last she began to draw near to him, she nestled to him. His limbs, his body, took fire and beat up in flames. She clung to him, she cleaved to his body. The flames swept him, he held her in sinews of fire. If she would kiss him! He bent his mouth down. And her mouth, soft and moist, received him. He felt his veins would burst with anguish of thankfulness, his heart was mad with gratefulness, he could pour himself out upon her for ever.

When they came to themselves, the night was very dark. Two hours had gone by. They lay still and warm and weak, like the new-born, together. And there was a silence almost of the unborn. Only his heart was weeping happily, after the pain. He did not understand, he had yielded, given way. There *was* no understanding. There could be only acquiescence and submission, and tremulous wonder of consummation.

The next morning, when they woke up, it had snowed. He wondered what was the strange pallor in the air, and the unusual tang. Snow was on the grass and the window-sill, it weighed down the black, ragged branches of the yews, and smoothed the graves in the churchyard.

Soon, it began to snow again, and they were shut in. He was glad, for then they were immune in a shadowy silence, there was n   world, no time.

The snow lasted for some days. On the Sunday they went to church. They made a line of footprints across the garden, he left a flat snowprint of his hand on the wall as he vaulted over, they traced the snow across the churchyard. For three days they had been immune in a perfect love.

There were very few people in church, and she was glad. She did not care much for church. She had never questioned any beliefs, and she was, from habit and custom, a regular attendant at morning service. But she had ceased to come with any anticipation. To-day, however, in the strangeness of snow, after such consummation of love, she felt expectant again, and delighted. She was still in the eternal world.

She used, after she went to the High School, and wanted to be a lady, wanted to fulfil some mysterious ideal, always to listen to the sermon and to try to gather suggestions. That was all very well for a while. The vicar told her to be good in this way and in that. She went away feeling it was her highest aim to fulfil these injunctions.

But quickly this palled. After a short time, she was not very much interested in being good. Her soul was in quest of something, which was not just being good, and doing one's best. No, she wanted something else: something that was not her ready-made duty. Everything seemed to be merely a matter of social duty, and never of her *self*. They talked about her soul, but somehow never managed to rouse or to implicate her soul. As yet her soul was not brought in at all.

So that whilst she had an affection for Mr. Loverseed, the vicar, and a protective sort of feeling for Cossethay church, wanting always to help it and defend it, it counted very small in her life.

Not but that she was conscious of some unsatisfaction. When her husband was roused by the thought of the churches, then she became hostile to the ostensible church, she hated it for not fulfilling anything in her. The Church told her to be good: very well, she had no idea of contradicting what it said. The Church talked about her soul, about the welfare of mankind, as if the saving of her soul lay in her performing certain acts conducive to the welfare of mankind. Well and good—it was so, then.

Nevertheless, as she sat in church her face had a pathos and poignancy. Was this what she had come to hear: how by doing this thing and by not doing that, she could save her soul? She did not contradict it. But the pathos of her face gave the lie. There was something else she wanted to hear, it was something else she asked for from the Church.

But who was *she* to affirm it? And what was *she* doing with unsatisfied desires? She was ashamed. She ignored them and left them out of count as much as possible, her underneath yearnings. They angered her. She wanted to be like other people, decently satisfied.

He angered her more than ever. Church had an irresistible attraction for him. And he paid no more attention to that part of the service which was Church to her, than if he had been an angel or a fabulous beast sitting there. He simply paid no heed to the sermon or to the meaning of the service. There was something thick, dark, dense, powerful about him that irritated her too deeply for her to speak of it. The Church teaching in itself meant nothing to him. "And forgive us our trespasses as we forgive them that trespass against us"—it simply did not touch him. It might have been mere sounds, and it would have acted upon him in the same way. He did not want things to be intelligible. And he did not care about his trespasses, neither about the trespasses of his neighbour, when he was in church. Leave that care for weekdays. When he was in church, he took no more notice of his daily life. It was weekday stuff. As for the welfare of mankind—he merely did not realise that there was any such thing: except on weekdays, when he was good-natured enough. In church, he wanted a dark, nameless emotion, the emotion of all the great mysteries of passion.

He was not interested in the *thought* of himself or of her: oh, and how that irritated her! He ignored the sermon, he ignored the greatness of mankind, he did not admit the immediate importance of mankind. He did not care about himself as a human being. He did not attach any vital importance to his life in the drafting office, or his life among men. That was just merely the margin to the text. The verity was his connection with Anna and his connection with the Church, his real being lay in his dark emotional experience of the Infinite, of the Absolute. And the great mysterious, illuminated capitals to the text, were his feelings with the Church.

It exasperated her beyond measure. She could not get out of the Church the satisfaction he got. The thought of her soul was intimately mixed up with the thought of her own self. Indeed, her soul and her own self were one and the same in her. Whereas he seemed simply to ignore the fact of his own self, almost to refute it. He had a soul—a dark, inhuman thing caring nothing for humanity. So she conceived it. And in the gloom and the mystery of the Church his soul lived and ran free, like some strange, underground thing, abstract.

He was very strange to her, and, in this church spirit, in conceiving himself as a soul, he seemed to escape and run free of her. In a way, she envied it him, this dark freedom and jubilation of the soul, some strange entity in him. It fascinated her. Again she hated it. And again, she despised him, wanted to destroy it in him.

This snowy morning, he sat with a dark-bright face beside her, not aware of her, and somehow, she felt he was conveying to strange, secret places the love that sprang in him for her. He sat with a dark-rapt, half-delighted face, looking at a little stained window. She saw the ruby-coloured glass, with the shadow heaped along the bottom from the snow outside, and the familiar yellow figure of the lamb holding the banner, a little darkened now, but in the murky interior strangely luminous, pregnant.

She had always liked the little red and yellow window. The lamb, looking very silly and self-conscious, was holding up a forepaw, in the cleft of which was dangerously perched a little flag with a red cross. Very pale yellow, the lamb, with greenish shadows. Since she was a child she had liked this creature, with the same feeling she felt for the little woolly lambs on green legs that children carried home from the fair every year. She had always liked these these toys, and she had the same amused, childish liking for this church lamb. Yet she had always been uneasy about it. She was never sure that this lamb with a flag did not want to be more than it appeared. So she half mistrusted it, there was a mixture of dislike in her attitude to it.

Now, by a curious gathering, knitting of his eyes, the faintest tension of ecstasy on his face, he gave her the uncomfortable feeling that he was in correspondence with the creature, the lamb in the window. A cold wonder came over her—her soul was perplexed. There he sat, motionless, timeless, with the faint, bright tension on his face. What was he doing? What connection was there between him and the lamb in the glass?

Suddenly it gleamed to her dominant, this lamb with the flag. Suddenly she had a powerful mystic experience, the power of the tradition seized on her, she was transported to another world. And she hated it, resisted it.

Instantly, it was only a silly lamb in the glass again. And dark, violent hatred of her husband swept up in her. What was he doing, sitting there gleaming, carried away, soulful?

She shifted sharply, she knocked him as she pretended to pick up her glove, she groped among his feet.

He came to, rather bewildered, exposed. Anybody but her would have pitied him. She wanted to rend him. He did not know what was amiss, what he had been doing.

As they sat at dinner, in their cottage, he was dazed by the chill of antagonism from her. She did not know why she was so angry. But she was incensed.

"Why do you never listen to the sermon?" she asked, seething with hostility and violation.

"I do," he said.

"You don't—you don't hear a single word."

He retired into himself, to enjoy his own sensation. There was something subterranean about him, as if he had an underworld refuge. The young girl hated to be in the house with him when he was like this.

After dinner, he retired into the parlour, continuing in the same state of abstraction, which was a burden intolerable to her. Then he went to the bookshelf and took down books to look at, that she had scarcely glanced over.

He sat absorbed over a book on the illuminations in old missals, and then over a book on paintings in churches: Italian, English, French and German. He had, when he was sixteen, discovered a Roman Catholic bookshop where he could find such things.

He turned the leaves in absorption, absorbed in looking, not thinking. He was like a man whose eyes were in his chest, she said of him later.

She came to look at the things with him. Half they fascinated her. She was puzzled, interested, and antagonistic.

It was when she came to pictures of the Pietà that she burst out.

"I do think they're loathsome," she cried.

"What?" he said, surprised, abstracted.

"Those bodies with slits in them, posing to be worshipped."

"You see, it means the Sacraments, the Bread," he said slowly.

"Does it," she cried. "Then it's worse. I don't want to see your chest slit, nor to eat your dead body, even if you offer it to me. Can't you see it's horrible?"

"It isn't me, it's Christ."

"What if it is, it's you! And it's horrible, you wallowing in your own dead body, and thinking of eating it in the Sacrament."

"You've to take it for what it means."

"It means your human body put up to be slit and killed and then worshipped—what else?"

They lapsed into silence. His soul grew angry and aloof.

"And I think that lamb in Church," she said, "is the biggest joke in the parish——"

She burst into a "Pouf" of ridiculing laughter.

"It might be, to those that see nothing in it," he said. "You know it's the symbol of Christ, of His innocence and sacrifice."

"Whatever it means, it's a *lamb,*" she said. "And I like lambs too much to treat them as if they had to mean something. As for the Christmas-tree flag—no——"

And again she poufèd with mockery.

"It's because you don't know anything," he said violently, harshly. "Laugh at what you know, not at what you don't know."

"What don't I know?"

"What things mean."

"And what does it mean?"

He was reluctant to answer her. He found it difficult.

"What does it mean?" she insisted.

"It means the triumph of the Resurrection."

She hesitated, baffled, a fear came upon her. What were these things? Something dark and powerful seemed to extend before her. Was it wonderful after all?

But no—she refused it.

"Whatever it may pretend to mean, what it *is* is a silly absurd toy-lamb with a Christmas-tree flag ledged on its paw—and if it wants to mean anything else, it must look different from that."

He was in a state of violent irritation against her. Partly he was ashamed of his love for these things; he hid his passion for them. He was ashamed of the ecstasy into which he could throw himself with these symbols. And for a few moments he hated the lamb and the mystic pictures of the Eucharist, with a violent, ashy hatred. His fire was put out, she had thrown cold water on it. The whole thing was distasteful to him, his mouth was full of ashes. He went out cold with corpse-like anger, leaving her alone. He hated her. He walked through the white snow, under a sky of lead.

And she wept again, in bitter recurrence of the previous gloom. But her heart was easy—oh, much more easy.

She was quite willing to make it up with him when he came home again. He was black and surly, but abated. She had broken a little of something in him. And at length he was glad to forfeit from his soul all his symbols, to have her making love to him. He loved it when she put her head on his knee, and he had not asked her to or wanted her to, he loved her when she put her arms round him and made bold love to him, and he did not make love to her. He felt a strong blood in his limbs again.

And she loved the intent, far look of his eyes when they rested on her: intent, yet far, not near, not with her. And she wanted to bring them near. She wanted his eyes to come to hers, to know her. And they would not. They remained intent, and far, and proud, like a hawk's, naïve and inhuman as a hawk's. So she loved him and caressed him and roused him like a hawk, till he was keen and instant, but without tenderness. He came to her fierce and hard, like a hawk striking and taking her. He was no mystic any more, she was his aim and object, his prey. And she was carried off, and he was satisfied, or satiated at last.

Then immediately she began to retaliate on him. She too was a hawk. If she imitated the pathetic plover running plaintive to him, that was part of the game. When he, satisfied, moved with a proud, insolent slouch of the body and a half-contemptuous drop of the head, unaware of her, ignoring her very existence, after taking his fill of her and getting his satisfaction of her, her soul roused, its pinions became like steel, and she struck at him. When he sat on his perch glancing sharply round with solitary pride, pride eminent and fierce, she dashed at him and threw him from his station savagely, she goaded him from his keen dignity of a male, she harassed him from his unperturbed pride, till he was mad with rage, his light brown eyes burned with fury, they saw her now, like flames of anger they flared at her and recognized her as the enemy.

Very good, she was the enemy, very good. As he prowled round her, she watched him. As he struck at her, she struck back.

He was angry because she had carelessly pushed away his tools so that they got rusty.

"Don't leave them littering in my way, then," she said.

"I shall leave them where I like," he cried.

"Then I shall throw them where I like."

They glowered at each other, he with rage in his hands, she with her soul fierce with victory. They were very well matched. They would fight it out.

She turned to her sewing. Immediately the tea-things were cleared away, she fetched out the stuff, and his soul rose in rage. He hated beyond measure to hear the shriek of calico as she tore the web sharply, as if with pleasure. And the run of the sewing-machine gathered a frenzy in him at last.

"Aren't you going to stop that row?" he shouted. "Can't you do it in the daytime?"

She looked up sharply, hostile from her work.

"No, I can't do it in the daytime. I have other things to do. Besides, I like sewing, and you're not going to stop me doing it."

Whereupon she turned back to her arranging, fixing, stitching, his nerves jumped with anger as the sewing-machine started and stuttered and buzzed.

But she was enjoying herself, she was triumphant and happy as the darting needle danced ecstatically down a hem, drawing the stuff along under its vivid stabbing, irresistibly. She made the machine hum. She stopped it imperiously, her fingers were deft and swift and mistress.

If he sat behind her stiff with impotent rage it only made a trembling vividness come into her energy. On she worked. At last he went to bed in a rage, and lay stiff, away from her. And she turned her back on him. And in the morning they did not speak, except in mere cold civilities.

And when he came home at night, his heart relenting and growing hot for love of her, when he was just ready to feel he had been wrong, and when he was expecting her to feel the same, there she sat at the sewing-machine, the whole house was covered with clipped calico, the kettle was not even on the fire.

She started up, affecting concern.

"Is it so late?" she cried.

But his face had gone stiff with rage. He walked through to the parlour, then he walked back and out of the house again. Her heart sank. Very swiftly she began to make his tea.

He went black-hearted down the road to Ilkeston. When he was in this state he never thought. A bolt shot across the doors of his mind and shut him in, a prisoner. He went back to Ilkeston, and drank a glass of beer. What was he going to do? He did not want to see anybody.

He would go to Nottingham, to his own town. He went to the station and took a train. When he got to Nottingham, still he had nowhere to go. However, it was more agreeable to walk familiar streets. He paced them with a mad restlessness, as if he were running amok. Then he turned to a book-shop and found a book on Bamberg Cathedral. Here was a discovery! here was something for him! He went into a quiet restaurant to look at his treasure. He lit up with thrills of bliss as he turned from picture to picture. He had found something at last, in these carvings. His soul had great satisfaction. Had he not come out to seek, and had he not found! He was in a passion of fulfilment. These were the finest carvings, statues, he had ever seen. The book lay in his hands like a doorway. The world around was only an enclosure, a room. But he was going away. He lingered over the lovely statues of women. A marvellous, finely-wrought universe crystallised out around him as he looked again, at the crowns, the twining hair, the woman-faces. He liked all the better the unintelligible text of the German. He preferred things he could not understand with the mind. He loved the undiscovered and the undiscoverable. He pored over the pictures intensely. And these were wooden statues, "Holz"—he believed that meant wood. Wooden statues so shapen to his soul! He was a million times gladdened. How undiscovered the world was, how it revealed itself to his soul! What a fine, exciting thing his life was, at his hand! Did not Bamberg Cathedral make the world his own? He celebrated his triumphant strength and life and verity, and embraced the vast riches he was inheriting.

But it was about time to go home. He had better catch a train. All the time there was a steady bruise at the bottom of his soul, but so steady as to be forgettable. He caught a train for Ilkeston.

It was ten o'clock as he was mounting the hill to Cossethay, carrying his limp book on Bamberg Cathedral. He had not yet thought of Anna, not definitely. The dark finger pressing a bruise controlled him thoughtlessly.

Anna had started guiltily when he left the house. She had hastened preparing the tea, hoping he would come back. She had made some toast, and got all ready. Then he didn't come. She cried with vexation and disappointment. Why had he gone? Why couldn't he come back now? Why was it such a battle between them? She loved him—she did love him—why couldn't he be kinder to her, nicer to her?

She waited in distress—then her mood grew harder. He passed out of her thoughts. She had considered indignantly, what right he had to interfere with her sewing? She had indignantly refuted his right to interfere with her at all. She was not to be interfered with. Was she not herself, and he the outsider.

Yet a quiver of fear went through her. If he should leave her? She sat conjuring fears and sufferings, till she wept with very self-pity. She did not know what she would do if he left her, or if he turned against her. The thought of it chilled her, made her desolate and hard. And against him, the stranger, the outsider, the being who wanted to arrogate authority, she remained steadily fortified. Was she not herself? How could one who was not of her own kind presume with authority? She knew she was immutable, unchangeable, she was not afraid for her own being. She was only afraid of all that was not herself. It pressed round her, it came to her and took part in her, in form of her man, this vast, resounding, alien world which was not herself. And he had so many weapons, he might strike from so many sides.

When he came in at the door, his heart was blazed with pity and tenderness, she looked so lost and forlorn and young. She glanced up, afraid. And she was surprised to see him, shining-faced, clear and beautiful in his movements, as if he were clarified. And a startled pang of fear, and shame of herself went through her.

They waited for each other to speak.

"Do you want to eat anything?" she said.

"I'll get it myself," he answered, not wanting her to serve him. But she brought out food. And it pleased him she did it for him. He was again a bright lord.

"I went to Nottingham," he said mildly.

"To your mother?" she asked, in a flash of contempt.

"No—I didn't go home."

"Who did you go to see?"

"I went to see nobody."

"Then why did you go to Nottingham?"

"I went because I wanted to go."

He was getting angry that she again rebuffed him when he was so clear and shining.

"And who did you see?"

"I saw nobody."

"Nobody?"

"No—who should I see?"

"You saw nobody you knew?"

"No, I didn't," he replied irritably.

She believed him, and her mood became cold.

"I bought a book," he said, handing her the propitiatory volume.

She idly looked at the pictures. Beautiful, the pure women, with their clear-dropping gowns. Her heart became colder. What did they mean to *him?*

He sat and waited for her. She bent over the book.

"Aren't they nice?" he said, his voice roused and glad. Her blood flushed, but she did not lift her head.

"Yes," she said. In spite of herself, she was compelled by him. He was strange, attractive, exerting some power over her.

He came over to her, and touched her delicately. Her heart beat with wild passion, wild raging passion. But she resisted as yet. It was always the unknown, always the unknown, and she clung fiercely to her known self. But the rising flood carried her away.

They loved each other to transport again, passionately and fully.

"Isn't it more wonderful than ever?" she asked him, radiant like a newly opened flower, with tears like dew.

He held her closer. He was strange and abstracted.

"It is always more wonderful," she asseverated, in a glad, child's voice, remembering her fear, and not quite cleared of it yet.

So it went on continually, the recurrence of love and conflict between them. One day it seemed as if everything was shattered, all life spoiled, ruined, desolate and laid waste. The next day it was all marvellous again, just marvellous. One day she thought she would go mad from his very presence, the sound of his drinking was detestable to her. The next day she loved and rejoiced in the way he crossed the floor, he was sun, moon and stars in one.

She fretted, however, at last, over the lack of stability. When the perfect hours came back, her heart did not forget that they would pass away again. She was uneasy. The surety, the surety, the inner surety, the confidence in the abidingness of love: that was what she wanted. And that she did not get. She knew also that he had not got it.

Nevertheless it was a marvellous world, she was for the most part lost in the marvellousness of it. Even her great woes were marvellous to her.

She could be very happy. And she wanted to be happy. She resented it when he made her unhappy. Then she could kill him, cast him out. Many days, she waited for the hour when he would be gone to work. Then the flow of her life, which he seemed to damn up, was let loose, and she was free. She was free, she was full of delight. Everything delighted her. She took up the rug and went to shake it in the garden. Patches of snow were on the fields, the air was light. She heard the ducks shouting on the pond, she saw them charge and sail across the water as if they were setting off on an invasion of the world. She watched the rough horses, one of which was clipped smooth on the belly, so that he wore a jacket and long stockings of brown fur, stand kissing each other in the wintry morning by the church-yard wall. Everything delighted her, now he was gone, the insulator, the obstruction removed, the world was all hers, in connection with her.

She was joyfully active. Nothing pleased her more than to hang out the washing in a high wind that came full-butt over the round of the hill, tearing the wet garments out of her hands, making flap-flap-flap of the waving stuff. She laughed and struggled and grew angry. But she loved her solitary days.

Then he came home at night, and she knitted her brows because of some endless contest between them. As he stood in the doorway her heart changed. It steeled itself. The laughter and zest of the day disappeared from her. She was stiffened.

They fought an unknown battle, unconsciously. Still they were in love with each other, the passion was there. But the passion was consumed in a battle. And the deep, fierce unnamed battle went on. Everything glowed intensely about them, the world had put off its clothes and was awful, with new, primal nakedness.

Sunday came when the strange spell was cast over her by him. Half she loved it. She was becoming more like him. All the week-days, there was a glint of sky and fields, the little church seemed to babble away to the cottages the morning through. But on Sundays, when he stayed at home, a deeply-coloured, intense gloom seemed to gather on the face of the earth, the church seemed to fill itself with shadow, to become big, a universe to her, there was a burning of blue and ruby, a sound of worship about her. And when the doors were opened, and she came out into the world, it was a world new-created, she stepped into the resurrection of the world, her heart beating to the memory of the darkness and the Passion.

If, as very often, they went to the Marsh for tea on Sundays, then she regained another, lighter world, that had never known the gloom and the stained glass and the ecstasy of chanting. Her husband was obliterated, she was with her father again, who was so fresh and free and all daylight. Her husband, with his intensity and his darkness, was obliterated. She left him, she forgot him, she accepted her father.

Yet, as she went home again with the young man, she put her hand on his arm tentatively, a little bit ashamed, her hand pleaded that he would not hold it against her, her recusancy. But he was obscured. He seemed to become blind, as if he were not there with her.

Then she was afraid. She wanted him. When he was oblivious of her, she almost went mad with fear. For she had become so vulnerable, so exposed. She was in touch so intimately. All things about her had become intimate, she had known them near and lovely, like presences hovering upon her. What if they should all go hard and separate again, standing back from her terrible and distinct, and she, having known them, should be at their mercy?

This frightened her. Always, her husband was to her the unknown to which she was delivered up. She was a flower that has been tempted forth into blossom, and has no retreat. He had her nakedness in his power. And who was he, what was he? A blind thing, a dark force, without knowledge. She wanted to preserve herself.

Then she gathered him to herself again and was satisfied for a moment. But as time went on, she began to realise more and more that he did not alter, that he was something dark, alien to herself. She had thought him just the bright reflex of herself. As the weeks and months went by she realised that he was a dark opposite to her, that they were opposites, not complements.

He did not alter, he remained separately himself, and he seemed to expect her to be part of himself, the extension of his will. She felt him trying to gain power over her, without knowing her. What did he want? Was he going to bully her?

What did she want herself? She answered herself, that she wanted to be happy, to be natural, like the sunlight and the busy day-time. And, at the bottom of her soul, she felt he wanted her to be dark, unnatural. Sometimes, when he seemed like the darkness covering and smothering her, she revolted almost in horror, and struck at him. She struck at him, and made him bleed, and he became wicked. Because she dreaded him and held him in horror, he became wicked, he wanted to destroy. And then the fight between them was cruel.

She began to tremble. He wanted to impose himself on her. And he began to shudder. She wanted to desert him, to leave him a prey to the open, with the unclean dogs of the darkness setting on to devour him. He must beat her, and make her stay with him. Whereas she fought to keep herself free of him.

They went their ways now shadowed and stained with blood, feeling the world far off, unable to give help. Till she began to get tired. After a certain point, she became impassive, detached utterly from him. He was always ready to burst out murderously against her. Her soul got up and left him, she went her way. Nevertheless in her apparent blitheness, that made his soul black with opposition, she trembled as if she bled.

And ever and again, the pure love came in sunbeams between them, when she was like a flower in the sun to him, so beautiful, so shining, so intensely dear that he could scarcely bear it. Then as if his soul had six wings of bliss he stood absorbed in praise, feeling the radiance from the Almighty beat through him like a pulse, as he stood in the upright flame of praise, transmitting the pulse of Creation.

And ever and again he appeared to her as the dread flame of power. Sometimes, when he stood in the doorway, his face lit up, he seemed like an Annunciation to her, her heart beat fast. And she watched him, suspended. He had a dark, burning being that she dreaded and resisted. She was subject to him as to the Angel of the Presence. She waited upon him and heard his will, and she trembled in his service.

Then all this passed away. Then he loved her for her childishness and for her strangeness to him, for the wonder of her soul which was different from his soul, and which made him genuine when he would be false. And she loved him for the way he sat loosely in a chair, or for the way he came through a door with his face open and eager. She loved his ringing, eager voice, and the touch of the unknown about him, his absolute simplicity.

Yet neither of them was quite satisfied. He felt, somewhere, that she did not respect him. She only respected him as far as he was related to herself. For what he was, beyond her, she had no care. She did not care for what he represented in himself. It is true, he did not know himself what he represented. But whatever it was she did not really honour it. She did no service to his work as a lace-designer, nor to himself as bread-winner. Because he went down to the office and worked every day—that entitled him to no respect or regard from her, he knew. Rather she despised him for it. And he almost loved her for this, though at first it maddened him like an insult.

What was much deeper, she soon came to combat his deepest feelings. What he thought about life and about society and mankind did not matter very much to her: he was right enough to be insignificant. This was again galling to him. She would judge beyond him on these things. But at length he came to accept her judgments, discovering them as if they were his own. It was not here the deep trouble lay. The deep root of his enmity lay in the fact that she jeered at his soul. He was inarticulate and stupid in thought. But to some things he clung passionately. He loved the Church. If she tried to get out of him, what he *believed*, then they were both soon in a white rage.

Did he believe the water turned to wine at Cana? She would drive him to the thing as a historical fact: so much rain-water—look at it—can it become grape-juice, wine? For an instant, he saw with the clear eyes of the mind and said no, his clear mind, answering her for a moment, rejected the idea. And immediately his whole soul was crying in a mad, inchoate hatred against his violation of himself. It *was* true for him. His mind was extinguished again at once, his blood was up. In his blood and bones, he wanted the scene, the wedding, the water brought forward from the firkins as red wine: and Christ saying to His mother: "Woman, what have I to do with thee?—mine hour is not yet come."

And then:

"His mother saith unto the servants, 'Whatsoever he saith unto you, do it.' "

Brangwen loved it, with his bones and blood he loved it, he could not let it go. Yet she forced him to let it go..She hated his blind attachments.

Water, natural water, could it suddenly and unnaturally turn into wine, depart from its being and at haphazard take on another being? Ah no, he knew it was wrong.

She became again the palpitating, hostile child, hateful, putting things to destruction. He became mute and dead. His own being gave him the lie. He knew it was so: wine was wine, water was water, for ever: the water had not become wine. The miracle was not a real fact. She seemed to be destroying him. He went out, dark and destroyed, his soul running its blood. And he tasted of death. Because his life was formed in these unquestioned concepts.

She, desolate again as she had been when she was a child, went away and sobbed. She did not care, she did not care whether the water had turned to wine or not. Let him believe it if he wanted to. But she knew she had won. And an ashy desolation came over her.

They were ashenly miserable for some time. Then the life began to come back. He was nothing if not dogged. He thought again of the chapter of St. John. There was a great biting pang. "But thou hast kept the good wine until now." "The best wine!" The young man's heart responded in a craving, in a triumph, although the knowledge that it was not true in fact bit at him like a weasel in his heart. Which was stronger, the pain of the denial, or the desire for affirmation? He was stubborn in spirit, and abode by his desire. But he would not any more affirm the miracles as true.

Very well, it was not true, the water had not turned into wine. The water had not turned into wine. But for all that he would live in his soul as if the water *had* turned into wine. For truth of fact, it had not. But for his soul, it had.

"Whether it turned into wine or whether it didn't," he said, "it doesn't bother me. I take it for what it is."

"And *what* is it?" she asked, quickly, hopefully.

"It's the Bible," he said.

That answer enraged her, and she despised him. She did not actively question the Bible herself. But he drove her to contempt.

And yet he did not care about the Bible, the written letter. Although he could not satisfy her, yet she knew of herself that he had something real. He was not a dogmatist. He did not believe in *fact* that the water turned into wine. He did not want to make a fact out of it. Indeed, his attitude was without criticism. It was purely individual. He took that which was of value to him from the Written Word, he added to his spirit. His mind he let sleep.

And she was bitter against him, that he let his mind sleep. That which was human, belonged to mankind, he would not exert. He cared only for himself. He was no Christian. Above all, Christ had asserted the brotherhood of man.

She, almost against herself, clung to the worship of the human knowledge. Man must die in the body, but in his knowledge he was immortal. Such, somewhere, was her belief, quite obscure and unformulated. She believed in the omnipotence of the human mind.

He, on the other hand, blind as a subterranean thing, just ignored the human mind and ran after his own dark-souled desires, following his own tunnelling nose. She felt often she must suffocate. And she fought him off.

Then he, knowing he was blind, fought madly back again, frantic in sensual fear. He did foolish things. He asserted himself on his rights, he arrogated the old position of master of the house.

"You've a right to do as I want," he cried.

"Fool!" she answered. "Fool!"

"I'll let you know who's master," he cried.

"Fool!" she answered. "Fool! I've known my own father, who could put a dozen of you in his pipe and push them down with his finger-end. Don't I know what a fool you are!"

He knew himself what a fool he was, and was flayed by the knowledge. Yet he went on trying to steer the ship of their dual life. He asserted his position as the captain of the ship. And captain and ship bored her. He wanted to loom important as master of one of the innumerable domestic craft that make up the great fleet of society. It seemed to her a ridiculous armada of tubs jostling in futility. She felt no belief in it. She jeered at him as master of the house, master of their dual life. And he was black with shame and rage. He knew, with shame, how her father had been a man without arrogating any authority.

He had gone on the wrong tack, and he felt it hard to give up the expedition. There was great surging and shame. Then he yielded. He had given up the master-of-the-house idea.

There was something he wanted, nevertheless, some form of mastery. Ever and anon, after his collapses into the petty and the shameful, he rose up again, and, stubborn in spirit, strong in his power to start afresh, set out once more in his male pride of being to fulfil the hidden passion of his spirit.

It began well, but it ended always in war between them, till they were both driven almost to madness. He said, she did not respect him. She laughed in hollow scorn of this. For her it was enough that she loved him.

"Respect what?" she asked.

But he always answered the wrong thing. And though she cudgelled her brains, she could not come at it.

"Why don't you go on with your wood-carving?" she said. "Why don't you finish your Adam and Eve?"

But she did not care for the Adam and Eve, and he never put another stroke to it. She jeered at the Eve, saying, "She is like a little marionette. Why is she so small? You've made Adam as big as God, and Eve like a doll."

"It is impudence to say that Woman was made out of Man's body," she continued, "when every man is born of woman. What impudence men have, what arrogance!"

In a rage one day, after trying to work on the board, and failing, so that his belly was a flame of nausea, he chopped up the whole panel and put it on the fire. She did not know. He went about for some days very quiet and subdued after it.

"Where is the Adam and Eve board?" she asked him.

"Burnt."

She looked at him.

"But your carving?"

"I burned it."

"When?"

She did not believe him.

"On Friday night."

"When I was at the Marsh?"

"Yes."

She said no more.

Then, when he had gone to work, she wept for a whole day, and was much chastened in spirit. So that a new, fragile flame of love came out of the ashes of this last pain.

Directly, it occurred to her that she was with child. There was a great trembling of wonder and anticipation through her soul. She wanted a child. Not that she loved babies so much, though she was touched by all young things. But she wanted to bear children. And a certain hunger in her heart wanted to unite her husband with herself, in a child.

She wanted a son. She felt, a son would be everything. She wanted to tell her husband. But it was such a trembling, intimate thing to tell him, and he was at this time hard and unresponsive. So that she went away and wept. It was such a waste of a beautiful opportunity, such a frost that nipped in the bud one of the beautiful moments of her life. She went about heavy and tremulous with her secret, wanting to touch him, oh, most delicately, and see his face, dark and sensitive, attend to her news. She waited and waited for him to become gentle and still towards her. But he was always harsh and he bullied her.

So that the buds shrivelled from her confidence, she was chilled. She went down to the Marsh.

"Well," said her father, looking at her and seeing her at the first glance, "what's amiss wi' you now?"

The tears came at the touch of his careful love.

"Nothing," she said.

"Can't you hit it off, you two?" he said.

"He's so obstinate," she quivered; but her soul was obdurate itself.

"Ay, an' I know another who's all that," said her father.

She was silent.

"You don't want to make yourselves miserable," said her father; "all about nowt."

"He isn't miserable," she said.

"I'll back my life, if you can do nowt else, you can make him as miserable as a dog. You'd be a dab hand at that, my lass."

"I do nothing to make him miserable," she retorted.

"Oh no—oh no! A packet o' butterscotch, you are."

She laughed a little.

"You mustn't think I *want* to be miserable," she cried. "I don't."

"We quite readily believe it," retorted Brangwen. "Neither do you intend him to be hopping for joy like a fish in a pond."

This made her think. She was rather surprised to find that she did *not* intend her husband to be hopping for joy like a fish in a pond.

Her mother came, and they all sat down to tea, talking casually.

"Remember, child," said her mother, "that everything is not waiting for *your* hand just to take or leave. You mustn't expect it. Between two people, the love itself is the important thing, and that is neither you nor him. It is a third thing you must create. You mustn't expect it to be just your way."

"Ha—nor do I. If I did I should soon find my mistake out. If I put my hand out to take anything, my hand is very soon bitten, I can tell you."

"Then you must mind where you put your hand," said her father.

Anna was rather indignant that they took the tragedy of her young married life with such equanimity.

"You love the man right enough," said her father, wrinkling his forehead in distress. "That's all as counts."

"I *do* love him, more shame to him," she cried. "I want to tell him—I've been waiting for four days now to tell him——" her face began to quiver, the tears came. Her parents watched her in silence. She did not go on.

"Tell him what?" said her father.

"That we're going to have an infant," she sobbed, "and he's never, never let me, not once, every time I've come to him, he's been horrid to me, and I wanted to tell him, I did. And he won't let me—he's cruel to me."

She sobbed as if her heart would break. Her mother went and comforted her, put her arms round her, and held her close. Her father sat with a queer, wrinkled brow, and was rather paler than usual. His heart went tense with hatred of his son-in-law.

So that, when the tale was sobbed out, and comfort administered and tea sipped, and something like calm restored to the little circle, the thought of Will Brangwen's entry was not pleasantly entertained.

Tilly was set to watch out for him as he passed by on his way home. The little party at table heard the woman-servant's shrill call:

"You've got to come in, Will. Anna's here."

After a few moments, the youth entered.

"Are you stopping?" he asked in his hard, harsh voice.

He seemed like a blade of destruction standing there. She quivered to tears.

"Sit you down," said Tom Brangwen, "an' take a bit off your length."

Will Brangwen sat down. He felt something strange in the atmosphere. He was dark browed, but his eyes had the keen, intent, sharp look, as if he could only see in the distance; which was a beauty in him, and which made Anna so angry.

"Why does he always deny me?" she said to herself. "Why is it nothing to him, what I am?"

And Tom Brangwen, blue-eyed and warm, sat in opposition to the youth. "How long are you stopping?" the young husband asked his wife.

"Not very long," she said.

"Get your tea, lad," said Tom Brangwen. "Are you itchin' to be off the moment you enter?"

They talked of trivial things. Through the open door the level rays of sunset poured in, shining on the floor. A grey hen appeared stepping swiftly in the doorway, pecking, and the light through her comb and her wattles made an oriflamme tossed here and there, as she went, her grey body was like a ghost.

Anna, watching, threw scraps of bread, and she felt the child flame within her. She seemed to remember again forgotten, burning, far-off things.

"Where was I born, mother?" she asked.

"In London."

"And was my father"—she spoke of him as if he were merely a strange name: she could never connect herself with him—"was he dark?"

"He had dark-brown hair and dark eyes and a fresh colouring. He went bald, rather bald, when he was quite young," replied her mother, also as if telling a tale which was just old imagination.

"Was he good-looking?"

"Yes—he was very good-looking—rather small. I have never seen an Englishman who looked like him."

"Why?"

"He was"—the mother made a quick, running movement with her hands—"his figure was alive and changing—it was never fixed. He was not in the least steady—like a running stream."

It flashed over the youth—Anna too was like a running stream. Instantly he was in love with her again.

Tom Brangwen was frightened. His heart always filled with fear, fear of the unknown, when he heard his women speak of their bygone men as of strangers they had known in passing and had taken leave of again.

In the room, there came a silence and a singleness over all their hearts. They were separate people with separate destinies. Why should they seek each to lay violent hands of claim on the other?

The young people went home as a sharp little moon was setting in the dusk of spring. Tufts of trees hovered in the upper air, the little church pricked up shadowily at the top of the hill, the earth was a dark blue shadow.

She put her hand lightly on his arm, out of her far distance. And out of the distance, he felt her touch him. They walked on, hand in hand, along opposite horizons, touching across the dusk. There was a sound of thrushes calling in the dark blue twilight.

"I think we are going to have an infant, Bill," she said from far off.

He trembled, and his fingers tightened on hers.

"Why?" he asked, his heart beating. "You don't know?"

"I do," she said.

They continued without saying any more, walking along opposite horizons, hand in hand across the intervening space, two separate people. And he trembled as if a wind blew on to him in strong gusts, out of the unseen. He was afraid. He was afraid to know he was alone. For she seemed fulfilled and separate and sufficient in her half of the world. He could not bear to know that he was cut off. Why could he not be always one with her? It was he who had given her the child. Why could she not be with him, one with him? Why must he be set in this separateness, why could she not be with him, close, close as one with him? She must be one with him.

He held her fingers tightly in his own. She did not know what he was thinking. The blaze of light on her heart was too beautiful and dazzling, from the conception in her womb. She walked glorified, and the sound of the thrushes, of the trains in the valley, of the far-off, faint noises of the town, were her "Magnificat".

But he was struggling in silence. It seemed as though there were before him a solid wall of darkness that impeded him and suffocated him and made him mad. He wanted her to come to him, to complete him, to stand before him so that his eyes did not, should not meet the naked darkness. Nothing mattered to him but that she should come and complete him. For he was ridden by the awful sense of his own limitation. It was as if he ended uncompleted, as yet uncreated on the darkness, and he wanted her to come and liberate him into the whole.

But she was complete in herself, and he was ashamed of his need, his helpless need of her. His need, and his shame of need, weighed on him like a madness. Yet still he was quiet and gentle, in reverence of her conception, and because she was with child by him.

And she was happy in showers of sunshine. She loved her husband, as a presence, as a grateful condition. But for the moment her need was fulfilled, and now she wanted only to hold her husband by the hand in sheer happiness, without taking thought, only being glad.

He had various folios of reproductions, and among them a cheap print from Fra Angelico's "Entry of the Blessed into Paradise". This filled Anna with bliss. The beautiful, innocent way in which the Blessed held each other by the hand as they moved towards the radiance, the real, real, angelic melody, made her weep with happiness. The floweriness, the beams of light, the linking of hands, was almost too much for her, too innocent.

Day after day came shining through the door of Paradise, day after day she entered into the brightness. The child in her shone till she herself was a beam of sunshine; and how lovely was the sunshine that loitered and wandered out of doors, where the catkins on the big hazel bushes at the end of the garden hung in their shaken, floating aureole, where little fumes like fire burst out from the black yew trees as a bird settled clinging to the branches. One day bluebells were along the hedge-bottoms, then cowslips twinkled like manna, golden and eva-nescent on the meadows. She was full of a rich drowsiness and loneliness. How happy she was, how gorgeous it was to live: to have known herself, her hus-band, the passion of love and begetting; and to know that all this lived and waited and burned on around her, a terrible purifying fire, through which she had passed for once to come to this peace of golden radiance, when she was with child, and innocent, and in love with her husband and with all the many angels hand in hand. She lifted her throat to the breeze that came across the fields, and she felt it handling her like sisters fondling her, she drank it in per-fume of cowslips and of apple-blossoms.

And in all the happiness a black shadow, shy, wild, a beast of prey, roamed and vanished from sight, and like strands of gossamer blown across her eyes, there was a dread for her.

She was afraid when he came home at night. As yet, her fear never spoke, the shadow never rushed upon her. He was gentle, humble, he kept himself withheld. His hands were delicate upon her, and she loved them. But there ran through her the thrill, crisp as pain, for she felt the darkness and other-world still in his soft, sheathed hands.

But the summer drifted in with the silence of a miracle, she was almost always alone. All the while, went on the long, lovely drowsiness, the maiden-blush roses in the garden were all shed, washed away in a pouring rain, summer drifted into autumn, and the long, vague, golden days began to close. Crimson clouds fumed about the west, and as night came on, all the sky was fuming and steaming, and the moon, far above the swiftness of vapours, was white, bleared, the night was uneasy. Suddenly the moon would appear at a clear window in the sky, looking down from far above, like a captive. And Anna did not sleep. There was a strange, dark tension about her husband.

She became aware that he was trying to force his will upon her, something, there was something he wanted, as he lay there dark and tense. And her soul sighed in weariness.

Everything was so vague and lovely, and he wanted to wake her up to the hard, hostile reality. She drew back in resistance. Still he said nothing. But she felt his power persisting on her, till she became aware of the strain, she cried out against the exhaustion. He was forcing her, he was forcing her. And she wanted so much the joy and the vagueness and the innocence of her pregnancy. She did not want his bitter-corrosive love, she did not want it poured into her, to burn her. Why must she have it? Why, oh, why was he not content, contained?

She sat many hours by the window, in those days when he drove her most with the black constraint of his will, and she watched the rain falling on the yew trees. She was not sad, only wistful, blanched. The child under her heart was a perpetual warmth. And she was sure. The pressure was only upon her from the outside, her soul had no stripes.

Yet in her heart itself was always this same strain, tense, anxious. She was not safe, she was always exposed, she was always attacked. There was a yearning in her for a fulness of peace and blessedness. What a heavy yearning it was—so heavy.

She knew, vaguely, that all the time he was not satisfied, all the time he was trying to force something from her. Ah, how she wished she could succeed with him, in her own way! He was there, so inevitable. She lived in him also. And how she wanted to be at peace with him, at peace. She loved him. She would give him love, pure love. With a strange, rapt look in her face, she awaited his homecoming that night.

Then, when he came, she rose with her hands full of love, as of flowers, radiant, innocent. A dark spasm crossed his face. As she watched, her face shining and flower-like with innocent love, his face grew dark and tense, the cruelty gathered in his brows, his eyes turned aside, she saw the whites of his eyes as he looked aside from her. She waited, touching him with her hands. But from his body through her hands came the bitter-corrosive shock of his passion upon her, destroying her in blossom. She shrank. She rose from her knees and went away from him, to preserve herself. And it was great pain to her.

To him also it was agony. He saw the glistening, flower-like love in her face, and his heart was black because he did not want it. Not this—not this. He did not want flowery innocence. He was unsatisfied. The rage and storm of unsatisfaction tormented him ceaselessly. Why had she not satisfied him? He had satisfied her. She was satisfied, at peace, innocent round the doors of her own paradise.

And he was unsatisfied, unfulfilled, he raged in torment, wanting, wanting.

It was for her to satisfy him: then let her do it. Let her not come with flowery handfuls of innocent love. He would throw these aside and trample the flowers to nothing. He would destroy her flowery, innocent bliss. Was he not entitled to satisfaction from her, and was not his heart all raging desire, his soul a black torment of unfulfilment. Let it be fulfilled in him, then, as it was fulfilled in her. He had given her her fulfilment. Let her rise up and do her part.

He was cruel to her. But all the time he was ashamed. And being ashamed, he was more cruel. For he was ashamed that he could not come to fulfilment without her. And he could not. And she would not heed him. He was shackled and in darkness of torment.

She beseeched him to work again, to do his wood-carving. But his soul was too black. He had destroyed his panel of Adam and Eve. He could not begin again, least of all now, whilst he was in this condition.

For her there was no final release, since he could not be liberated from himself. Strange and amorphous, she must go yearning on through the trouble, like a warm, glowing cloud blown in the middle of a storm. She felt so rich, in her warm vagueness, that her soul cried out on him, because he harried her and wanted to destroy her.

She had her moments of exaltation still, re-births of old exaltations. As she sat by her bedroom window, watching the steady rain, her spirit was somewhere far off.

She sat in pride and curious pleasure. When there was no one to exult with, and the unsatisfied soul must dance and play, then one danced before the Unknown.

Suddenly she realised that this was what she wanted to do. Big with child as she was, she danced there in the bedroom by herself, lifting her hands and her body to the Unseen, to the unseen Creator who had chosen her, to Whom she belonged.

She would not have had anyone know. She danced in secret, and her soul rose in bliss. She danced in secret before the Creator, she took off her clothes and danced in the pride of her bigness.

It surprised her, when it was over. She was shrinking and afraid. To what was she now exposed? She half wanted to tell her husband. Yet she shrank from him.

All the time she ran on by herself. She liked the story of David, who danced before the Lord, and uncovered himself exultingly. Why should he uncover himself to Michal, a common woman? He uncovered himself to the Lord.

"Thou comest to me with a sword and a spear and a shield, but I come to thee in the name of the Lord:—for the battle is the Lord's, and he will give you into our hands."

Her heart rang to the words. She walked in her pride. And her battle was her own Lord's, her husband was delivered over.

In these days she was oblivious of him. Who was he, to come against her? No, he was not even the Philistine, the Giant. He was like Saul proclaiming his own kingship. She laughed in her heart. Who was he, proclaiming his kingship? She laughed in her heart with pride.

And she had to dance in exultation beyond him. Because he was in the house, she had to dance before her Creator in exemption from the man. On a Saturday afternoon, when she had a fire in the bedroom, again she took off her things and danced, lifting her knees and her hands in a slow, rhythmic exulting. He was in the house, so her pride was fiercer. She would dance in nullification, she would dance to her unseen Lord. She was exalted over him, before the Lord.

She heard him coming up the stairs, and she flinched. She stood with the firelight on her ankles and feet, naked in the shadowy, late afternoon, fastening up her hair. He was startled. He stood in the doorway, his brows black and lowering.

"What are you doing?" he said, gratingly. "You'll catch a cold."

And she lifted her hands and danced again, to annul him, the light glanced on her knees as she made her slow, fine movements down the far side of the room, across the firelight. He stood away near the door in blackness of shadow, watching, transfixed. And with slow, heavy movements she swayed backwards and forwards, like a full ear of corn, pale in the dusky afternoon, threading before the firelight, dancing his non-existence, dancing herself to the Lord, to exultation.

He watched, and his soul burned in him. He turned aside, he could not look, it hurt his eyes. Her fine limbs lifted and lifted, her hair was sticking out all fierce, and her belly, big, strange, terrifying, uplifted to the Lord. Her face was rapt and beautiful, she danced exulting before her Lord, and knew no man.

It hurt him as he watched as if he were at the stake. He felt he was being burned alive. The strangeness, the power of her in her dancing consumed him, he was burned, he could not grasp, he could not understand. He waited obliterated. Then his eyes became blind to her, he saw her no more. And through the unseeing veil between them he called to her, in his jarring voice:

"What are you doing that for?"

"Go away," she said. "Let me dance by myself."

"That isn't dancing," he said harshly. "What do you want to do that for?"

"I don't do it for you," she said. "You go away."

Her strange, lifted belly, big with his child! Had he no right to be there? He felt his presence a violation. Yet he had his right to be there. He went and sat on the bed.

She stopped dancing, and confronted him, again lifting her slim arms and twisting at her hair. Her nakedness hurt her, opposed to him.

"I can do as I like in my bedroom," she cried. "Why do you interfere with me?"

And she slipped on a dressing-gown and crouched before the fire. He was more at ease now she was covered up. The vision of her tormented him all the days of his life, as she had been then, a strange, exalted thing having no relation to himself.

After this day, the door seemed to shut on his mind. His brow shut and became impervious. His eyes ceased to see, his hands were suspended. Within himself his will was coiled like a beast, hidden under the darkness, but always potent, working.

At first she went on blithely enough with him shut down beside her. But then his spell began to take hold of her. The dark, seething potency of him, the power of a creature that lies hidden and exerts its will to the destruction of the free-running creature, as the tiger lying in the darkness of the leaves steadily enforces the fall and death of the light creatures that drink by the waterside in the morning, gradually began to take effect on her. Though he lay there in his darkness and did not move, yet she knew he lay waiting for her. She felt his will fastening on her and pulling her down, even whilst he was silent and obscure.

She found that, in all her outgoings and her incomings, he prevented her.

Gradually she realised that she was being borne down by him, borne down by the clinging, heavy weight of him, that he was pulling her down as a leopard clings to a wild cow and exhausts her and pulls her down.

Gradually she realised that her life, her freedom, was sinking under the silent grip of his physical will. He wanted her in his power. He wanted to devour her at leisure, to have her. At length she realised that her sleep was a long ache and a weariness and exhaustion, because of his will fastened upon her, as he lay there beside her, during the night.

She realised it all, and there came a momentous pause, a pause in her swift running, a moment's suspension in her life, when she was lost.

Then she turned fiercely on him, and fought him. He was not to do this to her, it was monstrous. What horrible hold did he want to have over her body? Why did he want to drag her down, and kill her spirit? Why did he want to deny her spirit? Why did he deny her spirituality, hold her for a body only? And was he to claim her carcase?

Some vast, hideous darkness he seemed to represent to her.

"What do you do to me?" she cried. "What beastly thing do you do to me? You put a horrible pressure on my head, you don't let me sleep, you don't let me *live*. Every moment of your life you are doing something to me, something horrible, that destroys me. There is something horrible in you, something dark and beastly in your will. What do you want of me? What do you want to do to me?"

All the blood in his body went black and powerful and corrosive as he heard her. Black and blind with hatred of her he was. He was in a very black hell, and could not escape.

He hated her for what she said. Did he not give her everything, was she not everything to him? And the shame was a bitter fire in him, that she was everything to him, that he had nothing but her. And then that she should taunt him with it, that he could not escape! The fire went black in his veins. For try as he might, he could not escape. She was everything to him, she was his life and his derivation. He depended on her. If she were taken away, he would collapse as a house from which the central pillar is removed.

And she hated him, because he depended on her so utterly. He was horrible to her. She wanted to thrust him off, to set him apart. It was horrible that he should cleave to her, so close, so close, like a leopard that had leapt on her, and fastened.

He went on from day to day in a blackness of rage and shame and frustration. How he tortured himself, to be able to get away from her. But he could not. She was as the rock on which he stood, with deep, heaving water all round, and he was unable to swim. He *must* take his stand on her, he must depend on her.

What had he in life, save her? Nothing. The rest was a great heaving flood. The terror of the night of heaving, overwhelming flood, which was his vision of life without her, was too much for him. He clung to her fiercely and abjectly.

And she beat him off, she beat him off. Where could he turn, like a swimmer in a dark sea, beaten off from his hold, whither could he turn? He wanted to leave her, he wanted to be able to leave her. For his soul's sake, for his manhood's sake, he must be able to leave her.

But for what? She was the ark, and the rest of the world was flood. The only tangible, secure thing was the woman. He could leave her only for another woman. And where was the other woman, and who was the other woman? Besides, he would be just in the same state. Another woman would be woman, the case would be the same.

Why was she the all, the everything, why must he live only through her, why must he sink if he were detached from her? Why must he cleave to her in a frenzy as for his very life?

The only other way to leave her was to die. The only straight way to leave her was to die. His dark, raging soul knew that. But he had no desire for death.

Why could he not leave her? Why could he not throw himself into the hidden water to live or die, as might be? He could not, he could not. But supposing he went away, right away, and found work, and had a lodging again. He could be again as he had been before.

But he knew he could not. A woman, he must have a woman. And having a woman, he must be free of her. It would be the same position. For he could not be free of her.

For how can a man stand, unless he have something sure under his feet. Can a man tread the unstable water all his life, and call that standing? Better give in and drown at once.

And upon what could he stand, save upon a woman? Was he then like the old man of the seas, impotent to move save upon the back of another life? Was he impotent, or a cripple, or a defective, or a fragment?

It was black, mad, shameful torture, the frenzy of fear, the frenzy of desire, and the horrible, grasping back-wash of shame.

What was he afraid of? Why did life, without Anna, seem to him just a horrible welter, everything jostling in a meaningless, dark, fathomless flood? Why, if Anna left him even for a week, did he seem to be clinging like a madman to the edge of reality, and slipping surely, surely into the flood of unreality that would drown him. This horrible slipping into unreality drove him mad, his soul screamed with fear and agony.

Yet she was pushing him off from her, pushing him away, breaking his fingers from their hold on her, persistently, ruthlessly. He wanted her to have pity. And sometimes for a moment she had pity. But she always began again, thrusting him off, into the deep water, into the frenzy and agony of uncertainty.

She became like a fury to him, without any sense of him. Her eyes were bright with a cold, unmoving hatred. Then his heart seemed to die in its last fear. She might push him off into the deeps.

She would not sleep with him any more. She said he destroyed her sleep. Up started all his frenzy and madness of fear and suffering. She drove him away. Like a cowed, lurking devil he was driven off, his mind working cunningly against her, devising evil for her. But she drove him off. In his moments of intense suffering, she seemed to him inconceivable, a monster, the principle of cruelty.

However her pity might give way for moments, she was hard and cold as a jewel. He must be put off from her, she must sleep alone. She made him a bed in the small room.

And he lay there whipped, his soul whipped almost to death, yet unchanged. He lay in agony of suffering, thrown back into unreality, like a man thrown overboard into a sea, to swim till he sinks, because there is no hold, only a wide, weltering sea.

He did not sleep, save for the white sleep when a thin veil is drawn over the mind. It was not sleep. He was awake, and he was not awake. He could not be alone. He needed to be able to put his arms round her. He could not bear the empty space against his breast, where she used to be. He could not bear it. He felt as if he were suspended in space, held there by the grip of his will. If he relaxed his will would fall, fall through endless space, into the bottomless pit, always falling, will-less, helpless, non-existent, just dropping to extinction, falling till the fire of friction had burned out, like a falling star, then nothing, nothing, complete nothing.

He rose in the morning grey and unreal. And she seemed fond of him again, she seemed to make up to him a little.

"I slept well," she said, with her slightly false brightness. "Did you?"

"All right," he answered.

He would never tell her.

For three or four nights he lay alone through the white sleep, his will unchanged, unchanged, still tense, fixed in its grip. Then, as if she were revived and free to be fond of him again, deluded by his silence and seeming acquiescence, moved also by pity, she took him back again.

Each night, in spite of all the shame, he had waited with agony for bedtime, to see if she would shut him out. And each night, as in her false brightness, she said Good night, he felt he must kill her or himself. But she asked for her kiss, so pathetically, so prettily. So he kissed her, whilst his heart was ice.

And sometimes he went out. Once he sat for a long time in the church porch, before going in to bed. It was dark with a wind blowing. He sat in the church porch and felt some shelter, some security. But it grew cold, and he must go in to bed.

Then came the night when she said, putting her arms round him and kissing him fondly:

"Stay with me to-night, will you?"

And he had stayed without demur. But his will had not altered. He would have her fixed to him.

So that soon she told him again she must be alone.

"I don't *want* to send you away. I *want* to sleep with you. But I can't sleep, you don't let me sleep."

His blood turned black in his veins.

"What do you mean by such a thing? It's an arrant lie. *I* don't let you sleep———"

"But you don't. I sleep so well when I'm alone. And I can't sleep when you're there. You do something to me, you put a pressure on my head. And I *must* sleep, now the child is coming."

"It's something in yourself," he replied, "something wrong in you."

Horrible in the extreme were these nocturnal combats, when, all the world was asleep, and they two were alone, alone in the world, and repelling each other. It was hardly to be borne.

He went and lay down alone. And at length, after a grey and livid and ghastly period, he relaxed, something gave way in him. He let go, he did not care what became of him. Strange and dim he became to himself, to her, to everybody. A vagueness had come over everything, like a drowning. And it was an infinite relief to drown, a relief, a great, great relief.

He would insist no more, he would force her no more. He would force himself upon her no more. He would let go, relax, lapse, and what would be, should be.

Yet he wanted her still, he always, always wanted her. In his soul, he was desolate as a child, he was so helpless. Like a child on its mother, he depended on her for his living. He knew it, and he knew he could hardly help it.

Yet he must be able to be alone. He must be able to lie down alongside the empty space, and let be. He must be able to leave himself to the flood, to sink or live as might be. For he recognised at length his own limitation, and the limitation of his power. He had to give in.

There was a stillness, a wanness between them. Half at least of the battle was over. Sometimes she wept as she went about, her heart was very heavy. But the child was always warm in her womb.

They were friends again, new, subdued friends. But there was a wanness between them. They slept together once more, very quietly, and distinct, not one together as before. And she was intimate with him as at first. But he was very quiet, and not intimate. He was glad in his soul, but for the time being he was not alive.

He could sleep with her, and let her be. He could be alone now. He had just learned what it was to be able to be alone. It was right and peaceful. She had given him a new, deeper freedom. The world might be a welter of uncertainty, but he was himself now. He had come into his own existence. He was born for a second time, born at last unto himself, out of the vast body of humanity. Now at last he had a separate identity, he existed alone, even if he were not quite alone. Before he had only existed in so far as he had relations with another being. Now he had an absolute self—as well as a relative self.

But it was a very dumb, weak, helpless self, a crawling nursling. He went about very quiet, and in a way, submissive. He had an unalterable self at last, free, separate, independent.

She was relieved, she was free of him. She had given him to himself. She wept sometimes with tiredness and helplessness. But he was a husband. And she seemed, in the child that was coming, to forget. It seemed to make her warm and drowsy. She lapsed into a long muse, indistinct, warm, vague, unwilling to be taken out of her vagueness. And she rested on him also.

Sometimes she came to him with a strange light in her eyes, poignant, pathetic, as if she were asking for something. He looked and he could not understand. She was so beautiful, so visionary, the rays seemed to go out of his breast to her, like a shining. He was there for her, all for her. And she would hold his breast, and kiss it, and kiss it, kneeling beside him, she who was waiting for the hour of her delivery. And he would lie looking down at his breast, till it seemed that his breast was not himself, that he had left it lying there. Yet it was himself also, and beautiful and bright with her kisses. He was glad with a strange, radiant pain. Whilst she kneeled beside him, and kissed his breast with a slow, rapt, half-devotional movement.

He knew she wanted something, his heart yearned to give it her. His heart yearned over her. And as she lifted her face, that was radiant and rosy as a little cloud, his heart still yearned over her, and, now from the distance, adored her. She had a flower-like presence which he adored as he stood far off, a stranger.

The weeks passed on, the time drew near, they were very gentle, and delicately happy. The insistent, passionate, dark soul, the powerful unsatisfaction in him seemed stilled and tamed, the lion lay down with the lamb in him.

She loved him very much indeed, and he waited near her. She was a precious, remote thing to him at this time, as she waited for her child. Her soul was glad with an ecstasy because of the coming infant. She wanted a boy: oh, very much she wanted a boy.

But she seemed so young and so frail. She was indeed only a girl. As she stood by the fire washing herself—she was proud to wash herself at this time—and he looked at her, his heart was full of extreme tenderness for her. Such fine, fine limbs, her slim, round arms like chasing lights, and her legs so simple and childish, yet so very proud. Oh, she stood on proud legs, with a lovely reckless balance of her full belly, and the adorable little roundnesses, and the breasts becoming important. Above it all, her face was like a rosy cloud shining.

How proud she was, what a lovely proud thing her young body! And she loved him to put his hand on her ripe fullness, so that he should thrill also with the stir and the quickening there. He was afraid and silent, but she flung her arms round his neck with proud, impudent joy.

The pains came on, and Oh—how she cried! She would have him stay with her. And after her long cries she would look at him, with tears in her eyes and a sobbing laugh on her face, saying:

"I don't mind it really."

It was bad enough. But to her it was never deathly. Even the fierce, tearing pain was exhilarating. She screamed and suffered, but was all the time curiously alive and vital. She felt so powerfully alive and in the hands of such a masterly force of life, that her bottom-most feeling was one of exhilaration. She knew she was winning, winning, she was always winning, with each onset of pain she was nearer to victory.

Probably he suffered more than she did. He was not shocked or horrified. But he was screwed very tight in the vise of suffering.

It was a girl. The second of silence on her face when they said so showed him she was disappointed. And a great blazing passion of resentment and protest sprang up in his heart. In that moment he claimed the child.

But when the milk came, and the infant sucked her breast, she seemed to be leaping with extravagant bliss.

"It sucks me, it sucks me, it likes me—oh, it loves it!" she cried, holding the child to her breast with her two hands covering it, passionately.

And in a few moments, as she became used to her bliss, she looked at the youth with glowing, unseeing eyes, and said:

"Anna Victrix."

He went away, trembling, and slept. To her, her pains were the wound-smart of a victor, she was the prouder.

When she was well again she was very happy. She called the baby Ursula. Both Anna and her husband felt they must have a name that gave them private satisfaction. The baby was tawny skinned, it had a curious downy skin, and wisps of bronze hair, and the yellow grey eyes that wavered, and then became golden-brown like the father's. So they called her Ursula because of the picture of the saint.

It was a rather delicate baby at first, but soon it became stronger, and was restless as a young eel. Anna was worn out with the day-long wrestling with its young vigour.

As a little animal, she loved and adored it and was happy. She loved her husband, she kissed his eyes and nose and mouth, and made much of him, she said his limbs were beautiful, she was fascinated by the physical form of him.

And she was indeed Anna Victrix. He could not combat her any more. He was out in the wilderness, alone with her. Having occasion to go to London, he marvelled, as he returned, thinking of naked, lurking savages on an island, how these had built up and created the great mass of Oxford Street or Piccadilly. How had helpless savages, running with their spears on the riverside, after fish, how had they come to rear up this great London, the ponderous, massive, ugly superstructure of a world of man upon a world of nature! It frightened and awed him. Man was terrible, awful in his works. The works of man were more terrible than man himself, almost monstrous.

And yet, for his own part, for his private being, Brangwen felt that the whole of the man's world was exterior and extraneous to his own real life with Anna. Sweep away the whole monstrous superstructure of the world of to-day, cities and industries and civilisation, leave only the bare earth with plants growing and waters running, and he would not mind, so long as he were whole, had Anna and the child and the new, strange certainty in his soul. Then, if he were naked, he would find clothing somewhere, he would make a shelter and bring food to his wife.

And what more? What more would be necessary? The great mass of activity in which mankind was engaged meant nothing to him. By nature, he had no part in it. What did he live for, then? For Anna only, and for the sake of living? What did he want on this earth? Anna only, and his children, and his life with his children and her? Was there no more?

He was attended by a sense of something more, something further, which gave him absolute being. It was as if now he existed in Eternity, let Time be what it might. What was there outside? The fabricated world, that he did not believe in? What should he bring to her, from outside? Nothing? Was it enough, as it was? He was troubled in his acquiescence. She was not with him. Yet he scarcely believed in himself, apart from her, though the whole Infinite was with him. Let the whole world slide down and over the edge of oblivion, he would stand alone. But he was unsure of her. And he existed also in her. So he was unsure.

He hovered near to hear, never quite able to forget the vague, haunting uncertainty, that seemed to challenge him, and which he would not hear. A pang of dread, almost guilt, as of insufficiency, would go over him as he heard her talking to the baby. She stood before the window, with the month-old child in her arms, talking in a musical, young sing-song that he had not heard before, and which rang on his heart like a claim from the distance, or the voice of another world sounding its claim on him. He stood near, listening, and his heart surged, surged to rise and submit. Then it shrank back and stayed aloof. He could not move, a denial was upon him, as if he could not deny himself. He must, he must be himself.

"Look at the silly blue-caps, my beauty," she crooned, holding up the infant to the window, where shone the white garden, and the blue-tits scuffling in the snow: "Look at the silly blue-caps, my darling, having a fight in the snow! Look at them, my bird—beating the snow about with their wings, and shaking their heads. Oh, aren't they wicked things, wicked things! Look at their yellow feathers on the snow there! They'll miss them, won't they, when they're cold later on.

"Must we tell them to stop, must we say 'stop it' to them, my bird? But they are naughty, naughty! Look at them!" Suddenly her voice broke loud and fierce, she rapped the pane sharply.

"Stop it," she cried, "stop it, you little nuisances. Stop it!" She called louder, and rapped the pane more sharply. Her voice was fierce and imperative.

"Have more sense," she cried.

"There, now they're gone. Where have they gone, the silly things? What will they say to each other? What will they say, my lambkin? They'll forget, won't they, they'll forget all about it, out of their silly little heads, and their blue caps."

After a moment, she turned her bright face to her husband.

"They were *really* fighting, they were really fierce with each other!" she said, her voice keen with excitement and wonder, as if she belonged to the birds' world, were identified with the race of birds.

"Ay, they'll fight, will blue-caps," he said, glad when she turned to him with her glow from elsewhere. He came and stood beside her and looked out at the marks on the snow where the birds had scuffled, and at the yew trees' burdened, white and black branches. What was the appeal it made to him, what was the question of her bright face, what was the challenge he was called to answer? He did not know. But as he stood there he felt some responsibility which made him glad, but uneasy, as if he must put out his own light. And he could not move as yet.

Anna loved the child very much, oh, very much. Yet still she was not quite fulfilled. She had a slight expectant feeling, as of a door half opened. Here she was, safe and still in Cossethay. But she felt as if she were not in Cossethay at all. She was straining her eyes to something beyond. And from her Pisgah mount, which she had attained, what could she see? A faint, gleaming horizon, a long way off, and a rainbow like an archway, a shadow-door with faintly coloured coping above it. Must she be moving thither?

Something she had not, something she did not grasp, could not arrive at. There was something beyond her. But why must she start on the journey? She stood so safely on the Pisgah mountain.

In the winter, when she rose with the sunrise, and out of the back windows saw the east flaming yellow and orange above the green, glowing grass, while the great pear tree in between stood dark and magnificent as an idol, and under the dark pear tree, the little sheet of water spread smooth in burnished, yellow light, she said, "It is here". And when, at evening, the sunset came in a red glare through the big opening in the clouds, she said again, "It is beyond".

Dawn and sunset were the feet of the rainbow that spanned the day, and she saw the hope, the promise. Why should she travel any further?

Yet she always asked the question. As the sun went down in his fiery winter haste, she faced the blazing close of the affair, in which she had not played her fullest part, and she made her demand still: "What are you doing, making this big shining commotion? What is it that you keep so busy about, that you will not let us alone?"

She did not turn to her husband, for him to lead her. He was apart from her, with her, according to her different conceptions of him. The child she might hold up, she might toss the child forward into the furnace, the child might walk there, amid the burning coals and the incandescent roar of heat, as the three witnesses walked with the angel in the fire.

Soon, she felt sure of her husband. She knew his dark face and the extent of its passion. She knew his slim, vigorous body, she said it was hers. Then there was no denying her. She was a rich woman enjoying her riches.

And soon again she was with child. Which made her satisfied and took away her discontent. She forgot that she had watched the sun climb up and pass his way, a magnificent traveller surging forward. She forgot that the moon had looked through a window of the high, dark night, and nodded like a magic recognition, signalled to her to follow. Sun and moon travelled on, and left her, passed her by, a rich woman enjoying her riches. She should go also. But she could not go, when they called, because she must stay at home now. With satisfaction she relinquished the adventure to the unknown. She was bearing her children.

There was another child coming, and Anna lapsed into vague content. If she were not the wayfarer to the unknown, if she were arrived now, settled in her builded house, a rich woman, still her doors opened under the arch of the rainbow, her threshold reflected the passing of the sun and moon, the great travellers, her house was full of the echo of journeying.

She was a door and a threshold, she herself. Through her another soul was coming, to stand upon her as upon the threshold, looking out, shading its eyes for the direction to take.

VII

THE CATHEDRAL

During the first year of her marriage, before Ursula was born, Anna Brangwen and her husband went to visit her mother's friend, the Baron Skrebensky. The latter had kept a slight connection with Anna's mother, and had always preserved some officious interest in the young girl, because she was a pure Pole.

When Baron Skrebensky was about forty years old, his wife died, and left him raving, disconsolate. Lydia had visited him then, taking Anna with her. It was when the girl was fourteen years old. Since then she had not seen him. She remembered him as a small sharp clergyman who cried and talked and terrified her, whilst her mother was most strangely consoling, in a foreign language.

The little Baron never quite approved of Anna, because she spoke no Polish. Still, he considered himself in some way her guardian, on Lensky's behalf, and he presented her with some old, heavy Russian jewellery, the least valuable of his wife's relics. Then he lapsed out of the Brangwen's life again, though he lived only about thirty miles away.

Three years later came the startling news that he had married a young English girl of good family. Everybody marvelled. Then came a copy of "The History of the Parish of Briswell, by Rudolph, Baron Skrebensky, Vicar of Briswell." It was a curious book, incoherent, full of interesting exhumations. It was dedicated: "To my wife, Millicent Maud Pearse, in whom I embrace the generous spirit of England."

"If he embraces no more than the spirit of England," said Tom Brangwen, "it's a bad look-out for him."

But paying a formal visit with his wife, he found the new Baroness a little, creamy-skinned, insidious thing with red-brown hair and a mouth that one must always watch, because it curved back continually in an incomprehensible, strange laugh that exposed her rather prominent teeth. She was not beautiful, yet Tom Brangwen was immediately under her spell. She seemed to snuggle like a kitten within his warmth, whilst she was at the same time elusive and ironical, suggesting the fine steel of her claws.

The Baron was almost dotingly courteous and attentive to her. She, almost mockingly, yet quite happy, let him dote. Curious little thing she was, she had the soft, creamy, elusive beauty of a ferret. Tom Brangwen was quite at a loss, at her mercy, and she laughed, a little breathlessly, as if tempted to cruelty. She did put fine torments on the elderly Baron.

When some months later she bore a son, the Baron Skrebensky was loud with delight.

Gradually she gathered a circle of acquaintances in the county. For she was of good family, half Venetian, educated in Dresden. The little foreign vicar attained to a social status which almost satisfied his maddened pride.

Therefore the Brangwens were surprised when the invitation came for Anna and her young husband to pay a visit to Briswell vicarage. For the Skrebenskys were now moderately well off, Millicent Skrebensky having some fortune of her own.

Anna took her best clothes, recovered her best high-school manner, and arrived with her husband. Will Brangwen, ruddy, bright, with long limbs and a small head, like some uncouth bird, was not changed in the least. The little Baroness was smiling, showing her teeth. She had a real charm, a kind of joyous coldness, laughing, delighted, like some weasel. Anna at once respected her, and was on her guard before her, instinctively attracted by the strange, childlike surety of the Baroness, yet mistrusting it, fascinated. The little baron was now quite white-haired, very brittle. He was wizened and wrinkled, yet fiery, unsubdued. Anna looked at his lean body, at his small, fine lean legs and lean hands as he sat talking, and she flushed. She recognized the quality of the male in him, his lean, concentrated age, his informed fire, his faculty for sharp, deliberate response. He was so detached, so purely objective. A woman was thoroughly outside him. There was no confusion. So he could give that fine, deliberate response.

He was something separate and interesting; his hard, intrinsic being, whittled down by age to an essentiality and a directness almost death-like, cruel, was yet so unswervingly sure in its action, so distinct in its surety, that she was attracted to him. She watched his cool, hard, separate fire, fascinated by it. Would she rather have it than her husband's diffuse heat, than his blind, hot youth?

She seemed to be breathing high, sharp air, as if she had just come out of a hot room. These strange Skrebenskys made her aware of another, freer element, in which each person was detached and isolated. Was not this her natural element? Was not the close Brangwen life stifling her?

Meanwhile the little baroness, with always a subtle light stirring of her full, lustrous, hazel eyes, was playing with Will Brangwen. He was not quick enough to see all her movements. Yet he watched her steadily, with unchanging, lit-up eyes. She was a strange creature to him. But she had no power over him. She flushed, and was irritated. Yet she glanced again and again at his dark, living face, curiously, as if she despised him. She despised his uncritical, unironical nature, it had nothing for her. Yet it angered her as if she were jealous. He watched her with deferential interest as he would watch a stoat playing. But he himself was not implicated. He was different in kind. She was all lambent, biting flames, he was a red fire glowing steadily. She could get nothing out of him. So she made him flush darkly by assuming a biting, subtle class-superiority. He flushed, but still he did not object. He was too different.

Her little boy came in with the nurse. He was a quick, slight child, with fine preceptiveness, and a cool transitoriness in his interest. At once he treated Will Brangwen as an outsider. He stayed by Anna for a moment, acknowledged her, then was gone again, quick, observant, restless, with a glance of interest at everything.

The father adored him, and spoke to him in Polish. It was queer, the stiff, aristocratic manner of the father with the child, the distance in the relationship, the classic fatherhood on the one hand, the filial subordination on the other. They played together, in their different degrees very separate, two different beings, differing as it were in rank rather than in relationship. And the baroness

smiled, smiled, smiled, always smiled, showing her rather protruding teeth, having always a mysterious attraction and charm.

Anna realised how different her own life might have been, how different her
own living. Her soul stirred, she became as another person. Her intimacy with
her husband passed away, the curious enveloping Brangwen intimacy, so warm,
so close, so stifling, when one seemed always to be in contact with the other
person, like a blood-relation, was annulled. She denied it, this close relationship
with her young husband. He and she were not one. His heat was not always to
suffuse her, suffuse her, through her mind and her individuality, till she was of
one heat with him, till she had not her own self apart. She wanted her own life.
He seemed to lap her and suffuse her with his being, his hot life, till she did not
know whether she were herself, or whether she were another creature, united
with him in a world of close blood-intimacy that closed over her and excluded
her from all the cool outside.

She wanted her own, old sharp self, detached, detached, active but not absorbed, active for her own part, taking and giving, but never absorbed. Whereas
he wanted this strange absorption with her, which still she resisted. But she was
partly helpless against it. She had lived so long in Tom Brangwen's love, beforehand.

From the Skrebensky's, they went to Will Brangwen's beloved Lincoln Cathedral, because it was not far off. He had promised her, that one by one, they
should visit all the cathedrals of England. They began with Lincoln, which he
knew well.

He began to get excited as the time drew near to set off. What was it that
changed him so much? She was almost angry, coming as she did from the Skrebensky's. But now he ran on alone. His very breast seemed to open its doors to
watch for the great church brooding over the town. His soul ran ahead.

When he saw the cathedral in the distance, dark blue lifted watchful in the
sky, his heart leapt. It was the sign in heaven, it was the Spirit hovering like a
dove, like an eagle over the earth. He turned his glowing, ecstatic face to her,
his mouth opened with a strange, ecstatic grin.

"There she is," he said.

The "she" irritated her. Why "she"? It was "it". What was the cathedral, a
big building, a thing of the past, obsolete, to excite him to such a pitch? She
began to stir herself to readiness.

They passed up the steep hill, he eager as a pilgrim arriving at the shrine. As
they came near the precincts, with castle on one side and cathedral on the other,
his veins seemed to break into fiery blossom, he was transported.

They had passed through the gate, and the great west front was before them,
with all its breadth and ornament.

"It is a false front," he said, looking at the golden stone and the twin towers,
and loving them just the same. In a little ecstasy he found himself in the porch,
on the brink of the unrevealed. He looked up to the lovely unfolding of the
stone. He was to pass within to the perfect womb.

Then he pushed open the door, and the great, pillared gloom was before
him, in which his soul shuddered and rose from her nest. His soul leapt, soared
up into the great church. His body stood still, absorbed by the height. His soul
leapt up into the gloom, into possession, it reeled, it swooned with a great
escape, it quivered in the womb, in the hush and the gloom of fecundity, like
seed of procreation in ecstasy.

She too was overcome with wonder and awe. She followed him in his progress. Here, the twilight was the very essence of life, the coloured darkness was the embryo of all light, and the day. Here, the very first dawn was breaking, the very last sunset sinking, and the immemorial darkness, whereof life's day would blossom and fall away again, re-echoed peace and profound immemorial silence.

Away from time, always outside of time! Between east and west, between dawn and sunset, the church lay like a seed in silence, dark before germination, silenced after death. Containing birth and death, potential with all the noise and transition of life, the cathedral remained hushed, a great, involved seed, whereof the flower would be radiant life inconceivable, but whose beginning and whose end were the circle of silence. Spanned round with the rainbow, the jewelled gloom folded music upon silence, light upon darkness, fecundity upon death, as a seed folds leaf upon leaf and silence upon the root and the flower, hushing up the secret of all between its parts, the death out of which it fell, the life into which it has dropped, the immortality it involves, and the death it will embrace again.

Here in the church, "before" and "after" were folded together, all was contained in oneness. Brangwen came to his consummation. Out of the doors of the womb he had come, putting aside the wings of the womb, and proceeding into the light. Through daylight and day-after-day he had come, knowledge after knowledge, and experience after experience, remembering the darkness of the womb, having prescience of the darkness after death. Then between-while he had pushed open the doors of the cathedral, and entered the twilight of both darkness, the hush of the two-fold silence where dawn was sunset, and the beginning and the end were one.

Here the stone leapt up from the plain of earth, leapt up in a manifold, clustered desire each time, up, away from the horizontal earth, through twilight and dusk and the whole range of desire, through the swerving, the declination, ah, to the ecstasy, the touch, to the meeting and the consummation, the meeting, the clasp, the close embrace, the neutrality, the perfect, swooning consummation, the timeless ecstasy. There his soul remained, at the apex of the arch, clinched in the timeless ecstasy, consummated.

And there was no time nor life nor death, but only this, this timeless consummation, where the thrust from earth met the thrust from earth and the arch was locked on the keystone of ecstasy. This was all, this was everything. Till he came to himself in the world below. Then again he gathered himself together, in transit, every jet of him strained and leaped, leaped clear into the darkness above, to the fecundity and the unique mystery, to the touch, the clasp, the consummation, the climax of eternity, the apex of the arch.

She too was overcome, but silenced rather than tuned to the place. She loved it as a world not quite her own, she resented his transports and ecstasies. His passion in the cathedral at first awed her, then made her angry. After all, there was the sky outside, and in here, in this mysterious half-night, when his soul leapt with the pillars upwards, it was not to the stars and the crystalline dark space, but to meet and clasp with the answering impulse of leaping stone, there in the dusk and secrecy of the roof. The far-off clinching and mating of the arches, the leap and thrust of the stone, carrying a great roof overhead, awed and silenced her.

But yet—yet she remembered that the open sky was no blue vault, no dark dome hung with many twinkling lamps, but a space where stars were wheeling in freedom, with freedom above them always higher.

The cathedral roused her too. But she would never consent to the knitting of all the leaping stone in a great roof that closed her in, and beyond which was nothing, nothing, it was the ultimate confine. His soul would have liked it to be so: here, here is all, complete, eternal: motion, meeting, ecstasy, and no illusion of time, of night and day passing by, but only perfectly proportioned space and movement clinching and renewing, and passion surging its way into great waves to the altar, recurrence of ecstasy.

Her soul too was carried forward to the altar, to the threshold of Eternity, in reverence and fear and joy. But ever she hung back in the transit, mistrusting the culmination of the altar. She was not to be flung forward on the lift and lift of passionate flights, to be cast at last upon the altar steps as upon the shore of the unknown. There was a great joy and a verity in it. But even in the dazed swoon of the cathedral, she claimed another right. The altar was barren, its lights gone out. God burned no more in that bush. It was dead matter lying there. She claimed the right to freedom above her, higher than the roof. She had always a sense of being roofed in.

So that she caught at little things, which saved her from being swept forward headlong in the tide of passion that leaps on into the Infinite in a great mass, triumphant and flinging its own course. She wanted to get out of this fixed, leaping, forward-travelling movement, to rise from it as a bird rises with wet, limp feet from the sea, to lift herself as a bird lifts its breast and thrusts its body from the pulse and heave of a sea that bears it forward to an unwilling conclusion, tear herself away like a bird on wings, and in open space where there is clarity, rise up above the fixed, surcharged motion, a separate speck that hangs suspended, moves this way and that, seeing and answering before it sinks again, having chosen or found the direction in which it shall be carried forward.

And it was as if she must grasp at something, as if her wings were too weak to lift her straight off the heaving motion. So she caught sight of the wicked, odd little faces carved in stone, and she stood before them arrested.

These sly little faces peeped out of the grand tide of the cathedral like something that knew better. They knew quite well, these little imps that retorted on man's own illusion, that the cathedral was not absolute. They winked and leered, giving suggestion of the many things that had been left out of the great concept of the church. "However much there is inside here, there's a good deal they haven't got in," the little faces mocked.

Apart from the lift and spring of the great impulse towards the altar, these little faces had separate wills, separate motions, separate knowledge, which rippled back in defiance of the tide, and laughed in triumph of their own very littleness.

"Oh, look!" cried Anna. "Oh, look how adorable, the faces! Look at her."

Brangwen looked unwillingly. This was the voice of the serpent in his Eden. She pointed him to a plump, sly, malicious little face carved in stone.

"He knew her, the man who carved her," said Anna. "I'm sure she was his wife."

"It isn't a woman at all, it's a man," said Brangwen curtly.

"Do you think so?—No! That isn't a man. That is no man's face."

Her voice sounded rather jeering. He laughed shortly, and went on. But she would not go forward with him. She loitered about the carvings. And he could not go forward without her. He waited impatient of this counteraction. She was spoiling his passionate intercourse with the cathedral. His brows began to gather.

"Oh, this is good!" she cried again. "Here is the same woman—look!—only he's made her cross! Isn't it lovely! Hasn't he made her hideous to a degree?" She laughed with pleasure. "Didn't he hate her? He must have been a nice man! Look at her—isn't it awfully good—just like a shrewish woman. He must have enjoyed putting her in like that. He got his own back on her, didn't he?"

"It's a man's face, no woman's at all—a monk's—clean shaven," he said.

She laughed with a pouf! of laughter.

"You hate to think he put his wife in your cathedral, don't you?" she mocked, with a tinkle of profane laughter. And she laughed with malicious triumph.

She had got free from the cathedral, she had even destroyed the passion he had. She was glad. He was bitterly angry. Strive as he would, he could not keep the cathedral wonderful to him. He was disillusioned. That which had been his absolute, containing all heaven and earth, was become to him as to her, a shapely heap of dead matter—but dead, dead.

His mouth was full of ash, his soul was furious. He hated her for having destroyed another of his vital illusions. Soon he would be stark, stark, without one place wherein to stand, without one belief in which to rest.

Yet somewhere in him he responded more deeply to the sly little face that knew better, than he had done before to the perfect surge of his cathedral.

Nevertheless for the time being his soul was wretched and homeless, and he could not bear to think of Anna's ousting him from his beloved realities. He wanted his cathedral; he wanted to satisfy his blind passion. And he could not any more. Something intervened.

They went home again, both of them altered. She had some new reverence for that which he wanted, he felt that his cathedrals would never again be to him as they had been. Before, he had thought them absolute. But now he saw them crouching under the sky, with still the dark, mysterious world of reality inside, but as a world within a world, a sort of side show, whereas before they had been as a world to him within a chaos: a reality, an order, an absolute, within a meaningless confusion.

He had felt, before, that could he but go through the great door and look down the gloom towards the far-off, concluding wonder of the altar, that then, with the windows suspended around like tablets of jewels, emanating their own glory, then he had arrived. Here the satisfaction he had yearned after came near, towards this, the porch of the great Unknown, all reality gathered, and there, the altar was the mystic door, through which all and everything must move on to eternity.

But now, somehow, sadly and disillusioned, he realised that the doorway was no doorway. It was too narrow, it was false. Outside the cathedral were many flying spirits that could never be sifted through the jewelled gloom. He had lost his absolute.

He listened to the thrushes in the gardens and heard a note which the cathedrals did not include: something free and careless and joyous. He crossed a field that was all yellow with dandelions, on his way to work, and the bath of yellow glowing was something at once so sumptuous and so fresh, that he was glad he was away from his shadowy cathedral.

There was life outside the Church. There was much that the Church did not include. He thought of God, and of the whole blue rotunda of the day. That was something great and free. He thought of the ruins of the Grecian worship, and it seemed, a temple was never perfectly a temple, till it was ruined and mixed up with the winds and the sky and the herbs.

Still he loved the Church. As a symbol, he loved it. He tended it for what it tried to represent, rather than for that which it did represent. Still he loved it. The little church across his garden-wall drew him, he gave it loving attention. But he went to take charge of it, to preserve it. It was as an old, sacred thing to him. He looked after the stone and woodwork, mending the organ and restoring a piece of broken carving, repairing the church furniture. Later, he became choirmaster also.

His life was shifting its centre, becoming more superficial. He had failed to become really articulate, failed to find real expression. He had to continue in the old form. But in spirit, he was uncreated.

Anna was absorbed in the child now, she left her husband to take his own way. She was willing now to postpone all adventure into unknown realities. She had the child, her palpable and immediate future was the child. If her soul had found no utterance, her womb had.

The church that neighboured with his house became very intimate and dear to him. He cherished it, he had it entirely in his charge. If he could find no new activity, he would be happy cherishing the old, dear form of worship. He knew this little, whitewashed church. In its shadowy atmosphere he sank back into being. He liked to sink himself in its hush as a stone sinks into water.

He went across his garden, mounted the wall by the little steps, and entered the hush and peace of the church. As the heavy door clanged to behind him, his feet re-echoed in the aisle, his heart re-echoed with a little passion of tenderness and mystic peace. He was also slightly ashamed, like a man who has failed, who lapses back for his fulfilment.

He loved to light the candles at the organ, and sitting there alone in the little glow, practise the hymns and chants for the service. The whitewashed arches retreated into darkness, the sound of the organ and the organ-pedals died away upon the unalterable stillness of the church, there were faint, ghostly noises in the tower, and then the music swelled out again, loudly, triumphantly.

He ceased to fret about his life. He relaxed his will, and let everything go. What was between him and his wife was a great thing, if it was not everything. She had conquered, really. Let him wait and abide, wait and abide. She and the baby and himself, they were one. The organ rang out his protestation. His soul lay in the darkness as he pressed the keys of the organ.

To Anna, the baby was a complete bliss and fulfilment. Her desires sank into abeyance, her soul was in bliss over the baby. It was rather a delicate child, she had trouble to rear it. She never for a moment thought it would die. It was a delicate infant, therefore it behoved her to make it strong. She threw herself into the labour, the child was everything. Her imagination was all occupied here. She was a mother. It was enough to handle the new little limbs, the new little body, hear the new little voice crying in the stillness. All the future rang to her out of the sound of the baby's crying and cooing, she balanced the coming years of life in her hands, as she nursed the child. The passionate sense of fulfilment, of the future germinated in her, made her vivid and powerful. All the future was in her hands, in the hands of the woman. And before this baby was ten months old, she was again with child. She seemed to be in the fecund of storm life, every moment was full and busy with productiveness to her. She felt like the earth, the mother of everything.

Brangwen occupied himself with the church, he played the organ, he trained the choir-boys, he taught a Sunday-school class of youths. He was happy enough. There was an eager, yearning kind of happiness in him as he taught the boys on Sundays. He was all the time exciting himself with the proximity of some secret that he had not yet fathomed.

In the house, he served his wife and the little matriarchy. She loved him because he was the father of her children. And she always had a physical passion for him. So he gave up trying to have the spiritual superiority and control, or even her respect for his conscious or public life. He lived simply by her physical love for him. And he served the little matriarchy, nursing the child and helping with the housework, indifferent any more of his own dignity and importance. But his abandoning of claims, his living isolated upon his own interest, made him seem unreal, unimportant.

Anna was not publicly proud of him. But very soon she learned to be indifferent to public life. He was not what is called a manly man: he did not drink or smoke or arrogate importance. But he was her man, and his very indifference to all claims of manliness set her supreme in her own world with him. Physically, she loved him and he satisfied her. He went alone and subsidiary always. At first it had irritated her, the outer world existed so little to him. Looking at him with outside eyes, she was inclined to sneer at him. But her sneer changed to a sort of respect. She respected him, that he could serve her so simply and completely. Above all, she loved to bear his children. She loved to be the source of children.

She could not understand him, his strange, dark rages and his devotion to the church. It was the church *building* he cared for; and yet his soul was passionate for something. He laboured cleaning the stonework, repairing the woodwork, restoring the organ, and making the singing as perfect as possible. To keep the church fabric and the church-ritual intact was his business; to have the intimate sacred building utterly in his own hands, and to make the form of service complete. There was a little bright anguish and tension on his face, and in his intent movements. He was like a lover who knows he is betrayed, but who still loves, whose love is only the more intense. The church was false, but he served it the more attentively.

During the day, at his work in the office, he kept himself suspended. He did not exist. He worked automatically till it was time to go home.

He loved with a hot heart the dark-haired little Ursula, and he waited for the child to come to consciousness. Now the mother monopolised the baby. But his heart waited in its darkness. His hour would come.

In the long run, he learned to submit to Anna. She forced him to the spirit of her laws, whilst leaving him the letter of his own. She combated in him his devils. She suffered very much from his inexplicable and incalculable dark rages, when a blackness filled him, and a black wind seemed to sweep out of existence everything that had to do with him. She could feel herself, everything, being annihilated by him.

At first she fought him. At night, in this state, he would kneel down to say his prayers. She looked at his crouching figure.

"Why are you kneeling there, pretending to pray?" she said, harshly. "Do you think anybody can pray, when they are in the vile temper you are in?"

He remained crouching by the bedside, motionless.

"It's horrible," she continued, "and such a pretence! What do you pretend you are saying? Who do you pretend you are praying to?"

He still remained motionless, seething with inchoate rage, when his whole nature seemed to disintegrate. He seemed to live with a strain upon himself, and occasionally came these dark, chaotic rages, the lust for destruction. She then fought with him, and their fights were horrible, murderous. And then the passion between them came just as black and awful.

But little by little, as she learned to love him better, she would put herself aside, and when she felt one of his fits upon him, would ignore him, successfully leave him in his world, whilst she remained in her own. He had a black struggle with himself, to come back to her. For at last he learned that he would be in hell until he came back to her. So he struggled to submit to her, and she was afraid of the ugly strain in his eyes. She made love to him, and took him. Then he was grateful to her love, humble.

He made himself a woodwork shed, in which to restore things which were destroyed in the church. So he had plenty to do: his wife, his child, the church, the woodwork, and his wage-earning, all occupying him. If only there were not some limit to him, some darkness across his eyes! He had to give in to it at last himself. He must submit to his own inadequacy, the limitation of his being. He even had to know of his own black, violent temper, and to reckon with it. But as she was more gentle with him, it became quieter.

As he sat sometimes very still, with a bright, vacant face, Anna could see the suffering among the brightness. He was aware of some limit to himself, of something unformed in his very being, of some buds which were not ripe in him, some folded centres of darkness which would never develop and unfold whilst he was alive in the body. He was unready for fulfilment. Something undeveloped in him limited him, there was a darkness in him which he *could* not unfold, which would never unfold in him.

VIII
The Child

From the first, the baby stirred in the young father a deep, strong emotion he dared scarcely acknowledge, it was so strong and came out of the dark of him. When he heard the child cry, a terror possessed him, because of the answering echo from the unfathomed distances in himself. Must he know in himself such distances, perilous and imminent?

He had the infant in his arms, he walked backwards and forwards troubled by the crying of his own flesh and blood. This was his own flesh and blood crying! His soul rose against the voice suddenly breaking out from him, from the distances in him.

Sometimes in the night, the child cried and cried, when the night was heavy and sleep oppressed him. And half asleep, he stretched out his hand to put it over the baby's face to stop the crying. But something arrested his hand: the very inhumanness of the intolerable, continuous crying arrested him. It was so impersonal, without cause or object. Yet he echoed to it directly, his soul answered its madness. It filled him with terror, almost with frenzy.

He learned to acquiesce to this, to submit to the awful, obliterated sources which were the origin of his living tissue. He was not what he conceived himself to be! Then he was what he was, unknown, potent, dark.

He became accustomed to the child, he knew how to lift and balance the little body. The baby had a beautiful, rounded head that moved him passionately. He would have fought to the last drop to defend that exquisite, perfect round head.

He learned to know the little hands and feet, the strange, unseeing, golden-brown eyes, the mouth that opened only to cry, or to suck, or to show a queer, toothless laugh. He could almost understand even the dangling legs, which at first had created in him a feeling of aversion. They could kick in their queer little way, they had their own softness.

One evening, suddenly, he saw the tiny, living thing rolling naked in the mother's lap, and he was sick, it was so utterly helpless and vulnerable and extraneous; in a world of hard surfaces and varying altitudes, it lay vulnerable and naked at every point. Yet it was quite blithe. And yet, in its blind, awful crying, was there not the blind, far-off terror of its own vulnerable nakedness, the terror of being so utterly delivered over, helpless at every point. He could not bear to hear it crying. His heart strained and stood on guard against the whole universe.

But he waited for the dread of these days to pass; he saw the joy coming. He saw the lovely, creamy, cool little ear of the baby, a bit of dark hair rubbed to a bronze floss, like bronze-dust. And he waited, for the child to become his, to look at him and answer him.

It had a separate being, but it was his own child. His flesh and blood vibrated to it. He caught the baby to his breast with his passionate, clapping laugh. And the infant knew him.

As the newly-opened, newly-dawned eyes looked at him, he wanted them to perceive him, to recognize him. Then he was verified. The child knew him, a queer contortion of laughter came on its face for him. He caught it to his breast, clapping with a triumphant laugh.

The golden-brown eyes of the child gradually lit up and dilated at the sight of the dark-glowing face of the youth. It knew its mother better, it wanted its mother more. But the brightest, sharpest little ecstasy was for the father.

It began to be strong, to move vigorously and freely, to make sounds like words. It was a baby girl now. Already it knew his strong hands, it exulted in his strong clasp, it laughed and crowed when he played with it.

And his heart grew red-hot with passionate feeling for the child. She was not much more than a year old when the second baby was born. Then he took Ursula for his own. She his first little girl. He had set his heart on her.

The second had dark blue eyes and a fair skin: it was more a Brangwen, people said. The hair was fair. But they forgot Anna's stiff blonde fleece of childhood. They called the newcomer Gudrun.

This time, Anna was stronger, and not so eager. She did not mind that the baby was not a boy. It was enough that she had milk and could suckle her child: Oh, oh, the bliss of the little life sucking the milk of her body! Oh, oh, oh the bliss, as the infant grew stronger, of the two tiny hands clutching, catching blindly yet passionately at her breast, of the tiny mouth seeking her in blind, sure, vital knowledge, of the sudden consummate peace as the little body sank, the mouth and throat sucking, sucking, sucking, drinking life from her to make a new life, almost sobbing with passionate joy of receiving its own existence, the tiny hands clutching frantically as the nipple was drawn back, not to be gainsaid. This was enough for Anna. She seemed to pass off into a kind of rapture of motherhood, her rapture of motherhood was everything.

So that the father had the elder baby, the weaned child, the golden-brown, wondering vivid eyes of the little Ursula were for him, who had waited behind the mother till the need was for him. The mother felt a sharp stab of jealousy. But she was still more absorbed in the tiny baby. It was entirely hers, its need was direct upon her.

So Ursula became the child of her father's heart. She was the little blossom, he was the sun. He was patient, energetic, inventive for her. He taught her all the funny little things, he filled her and roused her to her fullest tiny measure. She answered him with her extravagant infant's laughter and her call of delight.

Now there were two babies, a woman came in to do the housework. Anna was wholly nurse. Two babies were not too much for her. But she hated any form of work, now her children had come, except the charge of them.

When Ursula toddled about, she was an absorbed, busy child, always amusing herself, needing not much attention from other people. At evening, towards six o'clock, Anna very often went across the lane to the stile, lifted Ursula over into the field with a: "Go and meet Daddy." Then Brangwen, coming up the steep round of the hill, would see before him on the brow of the path a tiny, tottering, windblown little mite with a dark head, who, as soon as she saw him, would come running in tiny, wild, windmill fashion, lifting her arms up and down to him, down the steep hill. His heart leapt up, he ran his fastest to her, to catch her, because he knew she would fall. She came fluttering on, wildly, with her little limbs flying. And he was glad when he caught her up in his arms. Once she fell as she came flying to him, he saw her pitch forward suddenly as she was running with her hands lifted to him; and when he picked her up, her mouth was bleeding. He could never bear to think of it, he always wanted to cry, even when he was an old man and she had become a stranger to him. How he loved that little Ursula!—his heart had been sharply seared for her, when he was a youth, first married.

When she was a little older, he would see her recklessly climbing over the bars of the stile, in her red pinafore, swinging in peril and tumbling over, picking herself up and flitting towards him. Sometimes she liked to ride on his shoulder, sometimes she preferred to walk with his hand, sometimes she would fling her arms round his legs for a moment, then race free again, whilst he went shouting and calling to her, a child along with her. He was still only a tall, thin, unsettled lad of twenty-two.

It was he who had made her her cradle, her little chair, her little stool, her high chair. It was he who would swing her up to table or who would make for her a doll out of an old table-leg, whilst she watched him, saying:

"Make her eyes, Daddy, make her eyes!"

And he made her eyes with his knife.

She was very fond of adorning herself, so he would tie a piece of cotton round her ear, and hang a blue bead on it underneath for an ear-ring. The ear-rings varied with a red bead, and a golden bead, and a little pearl bead. And as he came home at night, seeing her bridling and looking very self-conscious, he took notice and said:

"So you're wearing your best golden and pearl ear-rings, to-day?"

"Yes."

"I suppose you've been to see the queen?"

"Yes, I have."

"Oh, and what had she to say?"

"She said—she said—'You won't dirty your nice white frock.' "

He gave her the nicest bits from his plate, putting them into her red, moist mouth. And he would make on a piece of bread-and-butter a bird, out of jam: which she ate with extraordinary relish.

After the tea-things were washed up, the woman went away, leaving the family free. Usually Brangwen helped in the bathing of the children. He held long discussions with his child as she sat on his knee and he unfastened her clothes. And he seemed to be talking really of momentous things, deep moralities. Then suddenly she ceased to hear, having caught sight of a glassie rolled into a corner. She slipped away, and was in no hurry to return.

"Come back here," he said, waiting. She became absorbed, taking no notice.

"Come on," he repeated, with a touch of command.

An excited little chuckle came from her, but she pretended to be absorbed.

"Do you hear, Milady?"

She turned with a fleeting, exulting laugh. He rushed on her, and swept her up.

"Who was it that didn't come!" he said, rolling her between his strong hands, tickling her. And she laughed heartily, heartily. She loved him that he compelled her with his strength and decision. He was all-powerful, the tower of strength which rose out of her sight.

When the children were in bed, sometimes Anna and he sat and talked, desultorily, both of them idle. He read very little. Anything he was drawn to read became a burning reality to him, another scene outside his window. Whereas Anna skimmed through a book to see what happened, then she had enough.

Therefore they would often sit together, talking desultorily. What was really between them they could not utter. Their words were only accidents in the mutual silence. When they talked, they gossiped. She did not care for sewing.

She had a beautiful way of sitting musing, gratefully, as if her heart were lit up. Sometimes she would turn to him, laughing, to tell him some little thing that had happened during the day. Then he would laugh, they would talk awhile, before the vital, physical silence was between them again.

She was thin but full of colour and life. She was perfectly happy to do just nothing, only to sit with a curious, languid dignity, so careless as to be almost regal, so utterly indifferent, so confident. The bond between them was undefinable, but very strong. It kept everyone else at a distance.

His face never changed whilst she knew him, it only became more intense. It was ruddy and dark in its abstraction, not very human, it had a strong, intent brightness. Sometimes, when his eyes met hers, a yellow flash from them caused a darkness to swoon over her consciousness, electric, and a slight strange laugh came on his face. Her eyes would turn languidly, then close, as if hypnotised. And they lapsed into the same potent darkness. He had the quality of a young black cat, intent, unnoticeable, and yet his presence gradually made itself felt, stealthily and powerfully took hold of her. He called, not to her, but to something in her, which responded subtly, out of her unconscious darkness.

So they were together in a darkness, passionate, electric, for ever haunting the back of the ꭎmmon day, never in the light. In the light, he seemed to sleep, unknowing. Only she knew him when the darkness set him free, and he could see with his gold-glowing eyes his intention and his desires in the dark. Then she was in a spell, then she answered his harsh, penetrating call with a soft leap of her soul, the darkness woke up, electric, bristling with an unknown, overwhelming insinuation.

By now they knew each other; she was the daytime, the daylight, he was the shadow, put aside, but in the darkness potent with an overwhelming voluptuousness.

She learned not to dread and to hate him, but to fill herself with him, to give herself to his black, sensual power, that was hidden all the daytime. And the curious rolling of the eyes, as if she were lapsing in a trance away from her ordinary consciousness became habitual with her, when something threatened and opposed her in life, the conscious life.

So they remained as separate in the light, and in the thick darkness, married. He supported her daytime authority, kept it inviolable at last. And she, in all the darkness, belonged to him, to his close, insinuating, hypnotic familiarity.

All his daytime activity, all his public life, was a kind of sleep. She wanted to be free, to belong to the day. And he ran avoiding the day in work. After tea, he went to the shed to his carpentry or his wood-carving. He was restoring the patched, degraded pulpit to its original form.

But he loved to have the child near him, playing by his feet. She was a piece of light that really belonged to him, that played within his darkness. He left the shed door on the latch. And when, with his second sense of another presence, he knew she was coming, he was satisfied, he was at rest. When he was alone with her, he did not want to take notice, to talk. He wanted to live unthinking, with her presence flickering upon him.

He always went in silence. The child would push open the shed door, and see him working by lamplight, his sleeves rolled back. His clothes hung about him, carelessly, like mere wrapping. Inside, his body was concentrated with a flexible, charged power all of its own, isolated. From when she was a tiny child Ursula could remember his forearm, with its fine black hairs and its electric flexibility, working at the bench through swift, unnoticeable movements, always ambushed in a sort of silence.

She hung a moment in the door of the shed, waiting for him to notice her. He turned, his black, curved eyebrows arching slightly.

"Hullo, Twittermiss!"

And he closed the door behind her. Then the child was happy in the shed that smelled of sweet wood and resounded to the noise of the plane or the hammer or the saw, yet was charged with the silence of the worker. She played on, intent and absorbed, among the shavings and the little nogs of wood. She never touched him: his feet and legs were near, she did not approach them.

She liked to flit out after him when he was going to church at night. If he were going to be alone, he swung her over the wall, and let her come.

Again she was transported when the door was shut behind them, and they two inherited the big, pale, void place. She would watch him as he lit the organ candles, wait whilst he began his practising his tunes, then she ran foraging here and there, like a kitten playing by herself in the darkness with eyes dilated. The ropes hung vaguely, twining on the floor, from the bells in the tower, and Ursula always wanted the fluffy, red-and-white, or blue-and-white rope-grips. But they were above her.

Sometimes her mother came to claim her. Then the child was seized with resentment. She passionately resented her mother's superficial authority. She wanted to assert her own detachment.

He, however, also gave her occasional cruel shocks. He let her play about in the church, she rifled foot-stools and hymn-books and cushions, like a bee among flowers, whilst the organ echoed away. This continued for some weeks. Then the charwoman worked herself up into a frenzy of rage, to dare to attack Brangwen, and one day descended on him like a harpy. He wilted away, and wanted to break the old beast's neck.

Instead he came glowering in fury to the house, and turned on Ursula.

"Why, you tiresome little monkey, can't you even come to church without pulling the place to bits?"

His voice was harsh and cat-like, he was blind to the child. She shrank away in childish anguish and dread. What was it, what awful thing was it?

The mother turned with her calm, almost superb manner.

"What has she done, then?"

"Done? She shall go in the church no more, pulling and littering and destroying."

The wife slowly rolled her eyes and lowered her eyelids.

"What has she destroyed, then?"

He did not know.

"I've just had Mrs. Wilkinson at me," he cried, "with a list of things she's done."

Ursula withered under the contempt and anger of the "she," as he spoke of her.

"Send Mrs. Wilkinson here to me with a list of the things she's done," said Anna. "*I* am the one to hear that."

"It's not the things the child has done," continued the mother, "that have put you out so much, it's because you can't bear being spoken to by that old woman. But you haven't the courage to turn on *her* when she attacks you, you bring your rage here."

He relapsed into silence. Ursula knew that he was wrong. In the outside, upper world, he was wrong. Already came over the child the cold sense of the impersonal world. There she knew her mother was right. But still her heart clamoured after her father, for him to be right, in his dark, sensuous underworld. But he was angry, and went his way in blackness and brutal silence again.

The child ran about absorbed in life, quiet, full of amusement. She did not notice things, nor changes nor alterations. One day she would find daisies in the grass, another day, apple-blossoms would be sprinkled white on the ground, and she would run among it, for pleasure because it was there. Yet again birds would be pecking at the cherries, her father would throw cherries down from the tree all round her on the garden. Then the fields were full of hay.

She did not remember what had been nor what would be, the outside things were there each day. She was always herself, the world outside was accidental. Even her mother was accidental to her: a condition that happened to endure.

Only her father occupied any permanent position in the childish consciousness. When he came back she remembered vaguely how he had gone away, when he went away she knew vaguely that she must wait for his coming back. Whereas her mother, returning from an outing, merely became present, there was no reason for connecting her with some previous departure.

The return or the departure of the father was the one event which the child remembered. When he came, something woke up in her, some yearning. She knew when he was out of joint or irritable or tired: then she was uneasy, she could not rest.

When he was in the house, the child felt full and warm, rich like a creature in the sunshine. When he was gone, she was vague, forgetful. When he scolded her even, she was often more aware of him than of herself. He was her strength and her greater self.

Ursula was three years old when another baby girl was born. Then the two small sisters were much together, Gudrun and Ursula. Gudrun was a quiet child who played for hours alone, absorbed in her fancies. She was brown-haired, fair-skinned, strangely placid, almost passive. Yet her will was indomitable, once set. From the first she followed Ursula's lead. Yet she was a thing to herself, so that to watch the two together was strange. They were like two young animals playing together but not taking real notice of each other. Gudrun was the mother's favourite—except that Anna always lived in her latest baby.

The burden of so many lives depending on him wore the youth down. He had his work in the office, which was done purely by effort of will: he had his barren passion for the church; he had three young children. Also at this time his health was not good. So he was haggard and irritable, often a pest in the house. Then he was told to go to his woodwork, or to the church.

Between him and the little Ursula there came into being a strange alliance. They were aware of each other. He knew the child was always on his side. But in his consciousness he counted it for nothing. She was always for him. He took it for granted. Yet his life was based on her, even whilst she was a tiny child, on her support and her accord.

Anna continued in her violent trance of motherhood, always busy, often harassed, but always contained in her trance of motherhood. She seemed to exist in her own violent fruitfulness, and it was as if the sun shone tropically on her. Her colour was bright, her eyes full of a fecund gloom, her brown hair tumbled loosely over her ears. She had a look of richness. No responsibility, no sense of duty troubled her. The outside, public life was less than nothing to her, really.

Whereas when, at twenty-six, he found himself father of four children, with a wife who lived intrinsically like the ruddiest lilies of the field, he let the weight of responsibility press on him and drag him. It was then that his child Ursula strove to be with him. She was with him, even as a baby of four, when he was irritable and shouted and made the household unhappy. She suffered from his shouting, but somehow it was not really him. She wanted it to be over, she wanted to resume her normal connection with him. When he was disagreeable, the child echoed to the crying of some need in him, and she responded blindly. Her heart followed him as if he had some tie with her, and some love which he could not deliver. Her heart followed him persistently, in its love.

But there was the dim, childish sense of her own smallness and inadequacy, a fatal sense of worthlessness. She could not do anything, she was not enough. She could not be important to him. This knowledge deadened her from the first.

Still she set towards him like a quivering needle. All her life was directed by her awareness of him, her wakefulness to his being. And she was against her mother.

Her father was the dawn wherein her consciousness woke up. But for him, she might have gone on like the other children, Gudrun and Theresa and Catherine, one with the flowers and insects and playthings, having no existence apart from the concrete object of her attention. But her father came too near to her. The clasp of his hands and the power of his breast woke her up almost in pain from the transient unconsciousness of childhood. Wide-eyed, unseeing, she was awake before she knew how to see. She was wakened too soon. Too soon the call had come to her, when she was a small baby, and her father held her close to his breast, her sleep-living heart was beaten into wakefulness by the striving of his bigger heart, by his clasping her to his body for love and for fulfilment, asking as a magnet must always ask. From her the response had struggled dimly, vaguely into being.

The children were dressed roughly for the country. When she was little, Ursula pattered about in little wooden clogs, a blue overall over her thick red dress, a red shawl crossed on her breast and tied behind again. So she ran with her father to the garden.

The household rose early. He was out digging by six o'clock in the morning,

he went to his work at half-past eight. And Ursula was usually in the garden
with him, though not near at hand.

At Eastertime one year, she helped him to set potatoes. It was the first time
she had ever helped him. The occasion remained as a picture, one of her earliest
memories. They had gone out soon after dawn. A cold wind was blowing. He
had his old trousers tucked into his boots, he wore no coat nor waistcoat, his
shirt-sleeves fluttered in the wind, his face was ruddy and intent, in a kind of
sleep. When he was at work he neither heard nor saw. A long, thin man, looking still a youth, with a line of black moustache above his thick mouth, and his
fine hair blown on his forehead, he worked away at the earth in the grey first
light, alone. His solitariness drew the child like a spell.

The wind came chill over the dark-green fields. Ursula ran up and watched
him push the setting-peg in at one side of his ready earth, stride across, and push
it in the other side, pulling the line taut and clear upon the clods intervening.
Then with a sharp cutting noise the bright spade came towards her, cutting a
grip into the new, soft earth.

He struck his spade upright and straightened himself.

"Do you want to help me?" he said.

She looked up at him from out of her little woollen bonnet.

"Ay," he said, "you can put some taters in for me. Look—like that—these
little sprits standing up—so much apart, you see."

And stooping down he quickly, surely placed the spritted potatoes in the soft
grip, where they rested separate and pathetic on the heavy cold earth.

He gave her a little basket of potatoes, and strode himself to the other end of
the line. She saw him stooping, working towards her. She was excited, and
unused. She put in one potato, then rearranged it, to make it sit nicely. Some of
the sprits were broken, and she was afraid. The responsibility excited her like a
string tying her up. She could not help looking with dread at the string buried
under the heaped-back soil. Her father was working nearer, stooping, working
nearer. She was overcome by her responsibility. She put potatoes quickly into
the cold earth.

He came near.

"Not so close," he said, stooping over her potatoes, taking some out and
rearranging the others. She stood by with the painful terrified helplessness of
childhood. He was so unseeing and confident, she wanted to do the thing and
yet she could not. She stood by looking on, her little blue overall fluttering in
the wind, the red woollen ends of her shawl blowing gustily. Then he went
down the row, relentlessly, turning the potatoes in with his sharp spade-cuts.
He took no notice of her, only worked on. He had another world from hers.

She stood helplessly stranded on his world. He continued his work. She
knew she could not help him. A little bit forlorn, at last she turned away, and ran
down the garden, away from him, as fast as she could go away from him, to
forget him and his work.

He missed her presence, her face in her red woollen bonnet, her blue overall
fluttering. She ran to where a little water ran trickling between grass and stones.
That she loved.

When he came by he said to her:

"You didn't help me much."

The child looked at him dumbly. Already her heart was heavy because of her
own disappointment. Her mouth was dumb and pathetic. But he did not notice, he went his way.

And she played on, because of her disappointment persisting even the more in her play. She dreaded work, because she could not do it as he did it. She was conscious of the great breach between them. She knew she had no power. The grown-up power to work deliberately was a mystery to her.

He would smash into her sensitive child's world destructively. Her mother was lenient, careless. The children played about as they would all day. Ursula was thoughtless—why should she remember things? If across the garden she saw the hedge had budded, and if she wanted these greeny-pink, tiny buds for bread-and-cheese, to play at tea-party with, over she went for them.

Then suddenly, perhaps the next day, her soul would almost start out of her body as her father turned on her, shouting:

"Who's been tramplin' an' dancin' across where I've just sowed seed? I know it's you, nuisance! Can you find nowhere else to walk, but just over my seed beds? But it's like you, that is—no heed but to follow your own greedy nose."

It had shocked him in his intent world to see the zigzagging lines of deep little footprints across his work. The child was infinitely more shocked. Her vulnerable little soul was flayed and trampled. *Why* were the footprints there? She had not wanted to make them. She stood dazzled with pain and shame and unreality.

Her soul, her consciousness seemed to die away. She became shut off and senseless, a little fixed creature whose soul had gone hard and unresponsive. The sense of her own unreality hardened her like a frost. She cared no longer.

And the sight of her face, shut and superior with self-asserting indifference, made a flame of rage go over him. He wanted to break her.

"I'll break your obstinate little face," he said, through shut teeth, lifting his hand.

The child did not alter in the least. The look of indifference, complete glancing indifference, as if nothing but herself existed to her, remained fixed.

Yet far away in her, the sobs were tearing her soul. And when he had gone, she would go and creep under the parlour sofa, and lie clinched in the silent, hidden misery of childhood.

When she crawled out, after an hour or so, she went rather stiffly to play. She willed to forget. She cut off her childish soul from memory, so that the pain, and the insult should not be real. She asserted herself only. There was now nothing in the world but her own self. So very soon, she came to believe in the outward malevolence that was against her. And very early, she learned that even her adored father was part of this malevolence. And very early she learned to harden her soul in resistance and denial of all that was outside her, harden herself upon her own being.

She never felt sorry for what she had done, she never forgave those who had made her guilty. If he had said to her, "Why, Ursula, did you trample my carefully-made bed?" that would have hurt her to the quick, and she would have done anything for him. But she was always tormented by the unreality of outside things. The earth was to walk on. Why must she avoid a certain patch, just because it was called a seed-bed? It was the earth to walk on. This was her instinctive assumption. And when he bullied her, she became hard, cut herself off from all connection, lived in the little separate world of her own violent will.

As she grew older, five, six, seven, the connection between her and her father was even stronger. Yet it was always straining to break. She was always relapsing on her own violent will into her own separate world of herself. This made him grind his teeth with bitterness, for he still wanted her. But she could harden herself into her own self's universe, impregnable.

He was very fond of swimming, and in warm weather would take her down to the canal, to a silent place, or to a big pond or reservoir, to bathe. He would take her on his back as he went swimming, and she clung close, feeling his strong movement under her, so strong, as if it would uphold all the world. Then he taught her to swim.

She was a fearless little thing, when he dared her. And he had a curious craving to frighten her, to see what she would do with him. He said, would she ride on his back whilst he jumped off the canal bridge down into the water beneath.

She would. He loved to feel the naked child clinging on to his shoulders. There was a curious fight between their two wills. He mounted the parapet of the canal bridge. The water was a long way down. But the child had a deliberate will set upon his. She held herself fixed to him.

He leapt, and down they went. The crash of the water as they went under struck through the child's small body, with a sort of unconsciousness. But she remained fixed. And when they came up again, and when they went to the bank, and when they sat on the grass side by side, he laughed, and said it was fine. And the dark-dilated eyes of the child looked at him wonderingly, darkly, wondering from the shock, yet reserved and unfathomable, so he laughed almost with a sob.

In a moment she was clinging safely on his back again, and he was swimming in deep water. She was used to his nakedness, and to her mother's nakedness, ever since she was born. They were clinging to each other, and making up to each other for the strange blow that had been struck at them. Yet still, on other days, he would leap again with her from the bridge, daringly, almost wickedly. Till at length, as he leapt, once, she dropped forward on to his head, and nearly broke his neck, so that they fell into the water in a heap, and fought for a few moments with death. He saved her, and sat on the bank, quivering. But his eyes were full of the blackness of death. It was as if death had cut between their two lives, and separated them.

Still they were not separate. There was this curious taunting intimacy between them. When the fair came, she wanted to go in the swing-boats. He took her, and, standing up in the boat, holding on to the irons, began to drive higher, perilously higher. The child clung fast on her seat.

"Do you want to go any higher?" he said to her, and she laughed with her mouth, her eyes wide and dilated. They were rushing through the air.

· "Yes," she said, feeling as if she would turn into vapour, lose hold of everything, and melt away. The boat swung far up, then down like a stone, only to be caught sickeningly up again.

"Any higher?" he called, looking at her over his shoulder, his face evil and beautiful to her.

She laughed with white lips.

He sent the swingboat sweeping through the air in a great semi-circle, till it jerked and swayed at the high horizontal. The child clung on, pale, her eyes fixed on him. People below were calling. The jerk at the top had almost shaken them both out. He had done what he could—and he was attracting censure. He sat down, and let the swingboat swing itself out.

People in the crowd cried shame on him as he came out of the swingboat. He laughed. The child clung to his hand, pale and mute. In a while she was violently sick. He gave her lemonade, and she gulped a little.

"Don't tell your mother you've been sick," he said. There was no need to ask that. When she got home, the child crept away under the parlour sofa, like a sick little animal, and was a long time before she crawled out.

But Anna got to know of this escapade, and was passionately angry and contemptuous of him. His golden-brown eyes glittered, he had a strange, cruel little smile. And as the child watched him, for the first time in her life a disillusion came over her, something cold and isolating. She went over to her mother. Her soul was dead towards him. It made her sick.

Still she forgot and continued to love him, but ever more coldly. He was at this time, when he was about twenty-eight years old, strange and violent in his being, sensual. He acquired some power over Anna, over everybody he came into contact with.

After a long bout of hostility, Anna at last closed with him. She had now four children, all girls. For seven years she had been absorbed in wifehood and motherhood. For years he had gone on beside her, never really encroaching upon her. Then gradually another self seemed to assert its being within him. He was still silent and separate. But she could feel him all the while coming near upon her, as if his breast and his body were threatening her, and he was always coming closer. Gradually he became indifferent of responsibility. He would do what pleased him, and no more.

He began to go away from home. He went to Nottingham on Saturdays, always alone, to the football match and to the music-hall, and all the time he was watching, in readiness. He never cared to drink. But with his hard, golden-brown eyes, so keen seeing with their tiny black pupils, he watched all the people, everything that happened, and he waited.

In the Empire one evening he sat next to two girls. He was aware of the one beside him. She was rather small, common, with a fresh complexion and an upper lip that lifted from her teeth, so that, when she was not conscious, her mouth was slightly open and her lips pressed outwards in a kind of blind appeal. She was strongly aware of the man next to her, so that all her body was still, very still. Her face watched the stage. Her arms went down into her lap, very self-conscious and still.

A gleam lit up in him: should he begin with her? Should he begin with her to live the other, the unadmitted life of his desire? Why not? He had always been so good. Save for his wife, he was a virgin. And why, when all women were different? Why, when he would only live once? He wanted the other life. His own life was barren, not enough. He wanted the other.

Her open mouth, showing the small, irregular, white teeth, appealed to him. It was open and ready. It was so vulnerable. Why should he not go in and enjoy what was there? The slim arm that went down so still and motionless to the lap, it was pretty. She would be small, he would be able almost to hold her in his two hands. She would be small, almost like a child, and pretty. Her childishness whetted him keenly. She would be helpless between his hands.

"That was the best turn we've had," he said to her, leaning over as he clapped his hands. He felt strong and unshakeable in himself, set over against all the world. His soul was keen and watchful, glittering with a kind of amusement. He was perfectly self-contained. He was himself, the absolute, the rest of the world was the object that should contribute to his being.

The girl started, turned round, her eyes lit up with an almost painful flash of a smile, the colour came deeply in her cheeks.

"Yes, it was," she said, quite meaninglessly, and she covered her rather prominent teeth with her lips. Then she sat looking straight before her, seeing nothing, only conscious of the colour burning in her cheeks.

It pricked him with a pleasant sensation. His veins and his nerves attended to her, she was so young and palpitating.

"It's not such a good programme as last week's," he said.

Again she half turned her face to him, and her clear, bright eyes, bright like shallow water, filled with light, frightened, yet involuntarily lighting and shaking with response.

"Oh, isn't it! I wasn't able to come last week."

He noted the common accent. It pleased him. He knew what class she came of. Probably she was a warehouse-lass. He was glad she was a common girl.

He proceeded to tell her about the last week's programme. She answered at random, very confusedly. The colour burned in her cheek. Yet she always answered him. The girl on the other side sat remotely, obviously silent. He ignored her. All his address was for his own girl, with her bright, shallow eyes and her vulnerably opened mouth.

The talk went on, meaningless and random on her part, quite deliberate and purposive on his. It was a pleasure to him to make this conversation, an activity pleasant as a fine game of chance and skill. He was very quiet and pleasant-humoured, but so full of strength. She fluttered beside his steady pressure of warmth and his surety.

He saw the performance drawing to a close. His senses were alert and wilful. He would press his advantages. He followed her and her plain friend down the stairs to the street. It was raining.

"It's a nasty night," he said. "Shall you come and have a drink of something—a cup of coffee—it's early yet."

"Oh, I don't think so," she said, looking away into the night.

"I wish you would," he said, putting himself as it were at her mercy. There was a moment's pause.

"Come to Rollins?" he said.

"No—not there."

"To Carson's, then?"

There was a silence. The other girl hung on. The man was the centre of positive force.

"Will your friend come as well?"

There was another moment of silence, while the other girl felt her ground.

"No, thanks," she said. "I've promised to meet a friend."

"Another time, then?" he said.

"Oh, thanks," she replied, very awkward.

"Good night," he said.

"See you later," said his girl to her friend.

"Where?" said the friend.

"You know, Gertie," replied his girl.

"All right, Jennie."

The friend was gone into the darkness. He turned with his girl to the tea-shop. They talked all the time. He made his sentences in sheer, almost muscular pleasure of exercising himself with her. He was looking at her all the time, perceiving her, appreciating her, finding her out, gratifying himself with her. He could see distinct attractions in her; her eyebrows, with their particular curve, gave him keen aesthetic pleasure. Later on he would see her bright, pellucid eyes, like shallow water, and know those. And there remained the open, exposed mouth, red and vulnerable. That he reserved as yet. And all the while his eyes were on the girl, estimating and handling with pleasure her young softness. About the girl herself, who or what she was, he cared nothing, he was quite unaware that she was anybody. She was just the sensual object of his attention.

"Shall we go, then?" he said.

She rose in silence, as if acting without a mind, merely physically. He seemed to hold her in his will. Outside it was still raining.

"Let's have a walk," he said. "I don't mind the rain, do you?"

"No, I don't mind it," she said.

He was alert in every sense and fibre, and yet quite sure and steady, and lit up, as if transfused. He had a free sensation of walking in his own darkness, not in anybody else's world at all. He was purely a world to himself, he had nothing to do with any general consciousness. Just his own senses were supreme. All the rest was external, insignificant, leaving him alone with this girl whom he wanted to absorb, whose properties he wanted to absorb into his own senses. He did not care about her, except that he wanted to overcome her resistance, to have her in his power, fully and exhaustively to enjoy her.

They turned into the dark streets. He held her umbrella over her, and put his arm round her. She walked as if she were unaware. But gradually, as he walked, he drew her a little closer, into the movement of his side and hip. She fitted in there very well. It was a real good fit, to walk with her like this. It made him exquisitely aware of his own muscular self. And his hand that grasped her side felt one curve of her, and it seemed like a new creation to him, a reality, an absolute, an existing tangible beauty of the absolute. It was like a star. Everything in him was absorbed in the sensual delight of this one small, firm curve in her body, that his hand, and his whole being, had lighted upon.

He led her into the Park, where it was almost dark. He noticed a corner between two walls, under a great overhanging bush of ivy.

"Let us stand here a minute," he said.

He put down the umbrella, and followed her into the corner, retreating out of the rain. He needed no eyes to see. All he wanted was to know through touch. She was like a piece of palpable darkness. He found her in the darkness, put his arms round her and his hands upon her. She was silent and inscrutable. But he did not want to know anything about her, he only wanted to discover her. And through her clothing, what absolute beauty he touched.

"Take your hat off," he said.

Silently, obediently, she shook off her hat and gave herself to his arms again. He liked her—he liked the feel of her—he wanted to know her more closely. He let his fingers subtly seek out her cheek and neck. What amazing beauty and pleasure, in the dark! His fingers had often touched Anna on the face and neck like that. What matter! It was one man who touched Anna, another who now touched this girl. He liked best his new self. He was given over altogether to the sensuous knowledge of this woman, and every moment he seemed to be touching absolute beauty, something beyond knowledge.

Very close, marvelling and exceedingly joyful in their discoveries, his hands pressed upon her, so subtly, so seekingly, so finely and desirously searching her out, that she too was almost swooning in the absolute of sensual knowledge. In utter sensual delight she clenched her knees, her thighs, her loins together! It was an added beauty to him.

But he was patiently working for her relaxation, patiently, his whole being fixed in the smile of latent gratification, his whole body electric with a subtle, powerful, reducing force upon her. So he came at length to kiss her, and she was almost betrayed by his insidious kiss. Her open mouth was too helpless and unguarded. He knew this, and his first kiss was very gentle, and soft, and assuring, so assuring. So that her soft, defenceless mouth became assured, even bold, seeking upon his mouth. And he answered her gradually, gradually, his soft kiss sinking in softly, softly, but ever more heavily, more heavily yet, till it was too heavy for her to meet, and she began to sink under it. She was sinking, sinking, his smile of latent gratification was becoming more tense, he was sure of her. He let the whole force of his will sink upon her to sweep her away. But it was too great a shock for her. With a sudden horrible movement she ruptured the state that contained them both.

"Don't—don't!"

It was a rather horrible cry that seemed to come out of her, not to belong to her. It was some strange agony of terror crying out the words. There was something vibrating and beside herself in the noise. His nerves ripped like silk.

"What's the matter?" he said, as if calmly. "What's the matter?"

She came back to him, but trembling, reservedly this time.

Her cry had given him gratification. But he knew he had been too sudden for her. He was now careful. For a while he merely sheltered her. Also there had broken a flaw into his perfect will. He wanted to persist, to begin again, to lead up to the point where he had let himself go on her, and then manage more carefully, successfully. So far she had won. And the battle was not over yet. But another voice woke in him and prompted him to let her go—let her go in contempt.

He sheltered her, and soothed her, and caressed her, and kissed her, and again began to come nearer, nearer. He gathered himself together. Even if he did not take her, he would make her relax, he would fuse away her resistance. So softly, softly, with infinite caressiveness he kissed her, and the whole of his being seemed to fondle her. Till, at the verge, swooning at the breaking point, there came from her a beaten, inarticulate, moaning cry:

"Don't—oh, don't!"

His veins fused with extreme voluptuousness. For a moment he almost lost control of himself, and continued automatically. But there was a moment of inaction, of cold suspension. He was not going to take her. He drew her to him and soothed her, and caressed her. But the pure zest had gone. She struggled to herself and realised he was not going to take her. And then, at the very last moment, when his fondling had come near again, his hot living desire despising her, against his cold sensual desire, she broke violently away from him.

"Don't," she cried, harsh now with hatred, and she flung her hand across and hit him violently. "Keep off of me."

His blood stood still for a moment. Then the smile came again within him, steady, cruel.

"Why, what's the matter?" he said, with suave irony. "Nobody's going to hurt you."

"I know what *you* want," she said.

"*I* know what I want," he said. "What's the odds?"

"Well, you're not going to have it off *me*."

"Aren't I? Well, then I'm not. It's no use crying about it, is it?"

"No, it isn't," said the girl, rather disconcerted by his irony.

"But there's no need to have a row about it. We can kiss good night just the same, can't we?"

She was silent in the darkness.

"Or do you want your hat and umbrella to go home this minute?"

Still she was silent. He watched her dark figure as she stood there on the edge of the faint darkness, and he waited.

"Come and say good night nicely, if we're going to say it," he said.

Still she did not stir. He put his hand out and drew her into the darkness again.

"It's warmer in here," he said; "a lot cosier."

His will had not yet relaxed from her. The moment of hatred exhilarated him.

"I'm going now," she muttered, as he closed his hand over her.

"See how well you fit your place," he said, as he drew her to her previous position, close upon him. "What do you want to leave it for?"

And gradually the intoxication invaded him again, the zest came back. After all, why should he not take her?

But she did not yield to him entirely.

"Are you a married man?" she asked at length.

"What if I am?" he said.

She did not answer.

"I don't ask you whether *you're* married or not," he said.

"You know jolly well I'm *not*," she answered hotly. Oh, if she could only break away from him, if only she need not yield to him.

At length her will became cold against him. She had escaped. But she hated him for her escape more than for her danger. Did he despise her so coldly? And she was in torture of adherence to him still.

"Shall I see you next week—next Saturday?" he said, as they returned to the town. She did not answer.

"Come to the Empire with me—you and Gertie," he said.

"I should look well, going with a married man," she said.

"I'm no less of a man for being married, am I?" he said.

"Oh, it's a different matter altogether with a married man," she said, in a ready-made speech that showed her chagrin.

"How's that?" he asked.

But she would not enlighten him. Yet she promised, without promising, to be at the meeting-place next Saturday evening.

So he left her. He did not know her name. He caught a train and went home.

It was the last train, he was very late. He was not home till midnight. But he was quite indifferent. He had no real relation with his home, not this man which he now was. Anna was sitting up for him. She saw the queer, absolved look on his face, a sort of latent, almost sinister smile, as if he were absolved from his "good" ties.

"Where have you been?" she asked, puzzled, interested.

"To the Empire."

"Who with?"

"By myself. I came home with Tom Cooper."

She looked at him, and wondered what he had been doing. She was indifferent as to whether he lied or not.

"You have come home very strange," she said. And there was an appreciative inflexion in the speech.

He was not affected. As for his humble, good self, he was absolved from it. He sat down and ate heartily. He was not tired. He seemed to take no notice of her.

For Anna the moment was critical. She kept herself aloof, and watched him. He talked to her, but with a little indifference, since he was scarcely aware of her. So, then she did not affect him. Here was a new turn of affairs! He was better attractive, nevertheless. She liked him better than the ordinary mute, half-effaced, half-subdued man she usually knew him to be. So, he was blossoming out into his real self! It piqued her. Very good, let him blossom! She liked a new turn of affairs. He was a strange man come home to her. Glancing at him, she saw she could not reduce him to what he had been before. In an instant she gave it up. Yet not without a pang of rage, which would insist on their old, beloved love, their old, accustomed intimacy and her old, established supremacy. She almost rose up to fight for them. And looking at him, and remembering his father, she was wary. This was the new turn of affairs!

Very good, if she could not influence him in the old way, she would be level with him in the new. Her old defiant hostility came up. Very good, she too was out on her own adventure. Her voice, her manner changed, she was ready for the game. Something was liberated in her. She liked him. She liked this strange man come home to her. He was very welcome, indeed! She was very glad to welcome a stranger. She had been bored by the old husband. To his latent, cruel smile she replied with brilliant challenge. He expected her to keep the moral fortress. Not she! It was much too dull a part. She challenged him back with a sort of radiance, very bright and free, opposite to him. He looked at her, and his eyes glinted. She too was out in the field.

His senses pricked up and keenly attended to her. She laughed, perfectly indifferent and loose as he was. He came towards her. She neither rejected him nor responded to him. In a kind of radiance, superb in her inscrutability, she laughed before him. She too could throw everything overboard, love, intimacy, responsibility. What were her four children to her now? What did it matter that this man was the father of her four children?

He was the sensual male seeking his pleasure, she was the female ready to take hers: but in her own way. A man could turn into a free lance: so then could a woman. She adhered as little as he to the moral world. All that had gone before was nothing to her. She was another woman, under the instance of a strange man. He was a stranger to her, seeking his own ends. Very good. She wanted to see what this stranger would do now, what he was.

She laughed, and kept him at arm's length, whilst apparently ignoring him. She watched him undress as if he were a stranger. Indeed he was a stranger to her.

And she roused him profoundly, violently, even before he touched her. The little creature in Nottingham had but been leading up to this. They abandoned in one motion the moral position, each was seeking gratification pure and simple.

Strange his wife was to him. It was as if he were a perfect stranger, as if she were infinitely and essentially strange to him, the other half of the world, the dark half of the moon. She waited for his touch as if he were a marauder who had come in, infinitely unknown and desirable to her. And he began to discover her. He had an inkling of the vastness of the unknown sensual store of delights she was. With a passion of voluptuousness that made him dwell on each tiny beauty, in a kind of frenzy of enjoyment, he lit upon her: her beauty, the beauties, the separate, several beauties of her body.

He was quite ousted from himself, and sensually transported by that which he discovered in her. He was another man revelling over her. There was no tenderness, no love between them any more, only the maddening, sensuous lust for discovery and the insatiable, exorbitant gratification in the sensual beauties of her body. And she was a store, a store of absolute beauties that it drove him to contemplate. There was such a feast to enjoy, and he with only one man's capacity.

He lived in a passion of sensual discovery with her for some time—it was a duel: no love, no words, no kisses even, only the maddening perception of beauty consummate, absolute through touch. He wanted to touch her, to discover her, maddeningly he wanted to know her. Yet he must not hurry, or he missed everything. He must enjoy one beauty at a time. And the multitudinous beauties of her body, the many little rapturous places, sent him mad with delight, and with desire to be able to know more, to have strength to know more. For all was there.

He would say during the daytime:

"To-night I shall know the little hollow under her ankle, where the blue vein crosses." And the thought of it, and the desire for it, made a thick darkness of anticipation.

He would go all the day waiting for the night to come, when he could give himself to the enjoyment of some luxurious absolute of beauty in her. The thought of the hidden resources of her, the undiscovered beauties and ecstatic places of delight in her body, waiting, only waiting for him to discover them, sent him slightly insane. He was obsessed. If he did not discover and make known to himself these delights, they might be lost for ever. He wished he had a hundred men's energies, with which to enjoy her.

And she, separate, with a strange, dangerous, glistening look in her eyes received all his activities upon her as if they were expected by her, and provoked him when he was quiet to more, till sometimes he was ready to perish for sheer inability to be satisfied of her, inability to have had enough of her.

Their children became mere offspring to them, they lived in the darkness and death of their own sensual activities. Sometimes he felt he was going mad with a sense of Absolute Beauty, perceived by him in her through his senses. It was something too much for him. And in everything, was this same, almost sinister, terrifying beauty. But in the revelations of her body through contact with his body, was the ultimate beauty, to know which was almost death in itself, and yet for the knowledge of which he would have undergone endless torture. He would have forfeited anything, anything, rather than forego his right even to the instep of her foot, and the place from which the toes radiated out, the little, miraculous white plain from which ran the little hillocks of the toes, and the folded, dimpling hollows between the toes. He felt he would have died rather than forfeit this.

This was what their love had become, a sensuality violent and extreme as death. They had no conscious intimacy, no tenderness of love. It was all the lust and the infinite, maddening intoxication of the sense, a passion of death.

He had always, all his life, had a secret dread of Absolute Beauty. It had always been like a fetish to him, something to fear, really. For it was immoral and against mankind. So he had turned to the Gothic form, which always asserted the broken desire of mankind in its pointed arches, escaping the rolling, absolute beauty of the round arch.

But now he had given way, and with infinite sensual violence gave himself to the realisation of this supreme, immoral, Absolute Beauty, in the body of woman. It seemed to him, that it came to being in the body of woman, under his touch. Under his touch, even under his sight, it was there. But when he neither saw nor touched the perfect place, it was not perfect, it was not there. And he must make it exist.

But still the thing terrified him. Awful and threatening it was, dangerous to a degree, even whilst he gave himself to it. It was pure darkness, also. All the shameful things of the body revealed themselves to him now with a sort of sinister, tropical beauty. All the shameful, natural and unnatural acts of sensual voluptuousness which he and the woman partook of together, created together, they had their heavy beauty and their delight. Shame, what was it? It was part of extreme delight. It was that part of delight of which man is usually afraid. Why afraid? The secret, shameful things are most terribly beautiful.

They accepted shame, and were one with it in their most unlicensed pleasures. It was incorporated. It was a bud that blossomed into beauty and heavy, fundamental gratification.

Their outward life went on much the same, but the inward life was revolutionised. The children became less important, the parents were absorbed in their own living.

And gradually, Brangwen began to find himself free to attend to the outside life as well. His intimate life was so violently active, that it set another man in him free. And this new man turned with interest to public life, to see what part he could take in it. This would give him scope for new activity, activity of a kind for which he was now created and released. He wanted to be unanimous with the whole of purposive mankind.

At this time Education was in the forefront as a subject of interest. There was the talk of new Swedish methods, of handwork instruction, and so on. Brangwen embraced sincerely the idea of handwork in schools. For the first time, he began to take real interest in a public affair. He had at length, from his profound sensual activity, developed a real purposive self.

There was talk of night-schools, and of handicraft classes. He wanted to start a woodwork class in Cossethay, to teach carpentry and joinery and wood-carving to the village boys, two nights a week. This seemed to him a supremely desirable thing to be doing. His pay would be very little—and when he had it, he spent it all on extra wood and tools. But he was very happy and keen in his new public spirit.

He started his night-classes in woodwork when he was thirty years old. By this time he had five children, the last a boy. But boy or girl mattered very little to him. He had a natural blood-affection for his children, and he liked them as they turned up: boys or girls. Only he was fondest of Ursula. Somehow, she seemed to be at the back of his new night-school venture.

The house by the yew trees was in connection with the great human endeavour at last. It gained a new vigour thereby.

To Ursula, a child of eight, the increase in magic was considerable. She heard all the talk, she saw the parish room fitted up as a workshop. The parish room was a high, stone, barn-like, ecclesiastical building standing away by itself in the Brangwens' second garden, across the lane. She was always attracted by its age and its stranded obsoleteness. Now she watched preparations made, she sat on the flight of stone steps that came down from the porch to the garden, and heard her father and the vicar talking and planning and working. Then an inspector came, a very strange man, and stayed talking with her father all one evening. Everything was settled, and twelve boys enrolled their names. It was very exciting.

But to Ursula, everything her father did was magic. Whether he came from Ilkeston with news of the town, whether he went across to the church with his music or his tools on a sunny evening, whether he sat in his white surplice at the organ on Sundays, leading the singing with his strong tenor voice, or whether he were in the workshop with the boys, he was always a centre of magic and fascination to her, his voice, sounding out in command, cheerful, laconic, had always a twang in it that sent a thrill over her blood, and hypnotised her. She seemed to run in the shadow of some dark, potent secret of which she would not, of whose existence even she dared not become conscious, it cast such a spell over her, and so darkened her mind.

IX

The Marsh and the Flood

There was always regular connection between the Yew Cottage and the Marsh, yet the two households remained separate, distinct.

After Anna's marriage, the Marsh became the home of the two boys, Tom and Fred. Tom was a rather short, goodlooking youth, with crisp black hair and long black eyelashes and soft, dark, possessed eyes. He had a quick intelligence. From the High School he went to London to study. He had an instinct for attracting people of character and energy. He gave place entirely to the other person, and at the same time kept himself independent. He scarcely existed except through other people. When he was alone he was unresolved. When he was with another man, he seemed to add himself to the other, make the other bigger than life size. So that a few people loved him and attained a sort of fulfilment in him. He carefully chose these few.

He had a subtle, quick, critical intelligence, a mind that was like a scale or balance. There was something of a woman in all this.

In London he had been the favourite pupil of an engineer, a clever man, who became well-known at the time when Tom Brangwen had just finished his studies. Through this master the youth kept acquaintance with various individual, outstanding characters. He never asserted himself. He seemed to be there to estimate and establish the rest. He was like a presence that makes us aware of our own being. So that he was while still young connected with some of the most energetic scientific and mathematical people in London. They took him as an equal. Quiet and perceptive and impersonal as he was, he kept his place and learned how to value others in just degree. He was there like a judgment. Besides, he was very good-looking, of medium stature, but beautifully proportioned, dark, with fine colouring, always perfectly healthy.

His father allowed him a liberal pocket-money, besides which he had a sort of post as assistant to his chief. Then from time to time the young man appeared at the Marsh, curiously attractive, well-dressed, reserved, having by nature a subtle, refined manner. And he set the change in the farm.

Fred, the younger brother, was a Brangwen, large-boned, blue-eyed, English. He was his father's very son, the two men, father and son, were supremely at ease with one another. Fred was succeeding to the farm.

Between the elder brother and the younger existed an almost passionate love. Tom watched over Fred with a woman's poignant attention and self-less care. Fred looked up to Tom as to something miraculous, that which he himself would aspire to be, were he great also.

So that after Anna's departure, the Marsh began to take on a new tone. The boys were gentlemen; Tom had a rare nature and had risen high. Fred was sensitive and fond of reading, he pondered Ruskin and then the Agnostic writings. Like all the Brangwens, he was very much a thing to himself, though fond of people, and indulgent to them, having an exaggerated respect for them.

There was a rather uneasy friendship between him and one of the young Hardys at the Hall. The two households were different, yet the young men met on shy terms of equality.

It was young Tom Brangwen, with his dark lashes and beautiful colouring, his soft, inscrutable nature, his strange repose and his informed air, added to his position in London, who seemed to emphasise the superior foreign element in the Marsh. When he appeared, perfectly dressed, as if soft and affable, and yet quite removed from everybody, he created an uneasiness in people, he was reserved in the minds of the Cossethay and Ilkeston acquaintances to a different, remote world.

He and his mother had a kind of affinity. The affection between them was of a mute, distant character, but radical. His father was always uneasy and slightly deferential to his eldest son. Tom also formed the link that kept the Marsh in real connection with the Skrebenskys, now quite important people in their own district.

So a change in tone came over the Marsh. Tom Brangwen the father, as he grew older, seemed to mature into a gentleman-farmer. His figure lent itself: burly and handsome. His face remained fresh and his blue eyes as full of light, his thick hair and beard had turned gradually to a silky whiteness. It was his custom to laugh a great deal, in his acquiescent, wilful manner. Things had puzzled him very much, so he had taken the line of easy, good-humoured acceptance. He was not responsible for the frame of things. Yet he was afraid of the unknown in life.

He was fairly well-off. His wife was there with him, a different being from himself, yet somewhere vitally connected with him:—who was he to understand where and how? His two sons were gentlemen. They were men distinct from himself, they had separate beings of their own, yet they were connected with himself. It was all adventurous and puzzling. Yet one remained vital within one's own existence, whatever the off-shoots.

So, handsome and puzzled, he laughed and stuck to himself as the only thing he could stick to. His youngness and the wonder remained almost the same in him. He became indolent, he developed a luxuriant ease. Fred did most of the farm-work, the father saw to the more important transactions. He drove a good mare, and sometimes he rode his cob. He drank in the hotels and the inns with better-class farmers and proprietors, he had well-to-do acquaintances among men. But one class suited him no better than another.

His wife, as ever, had no acquaintances. Her hair was threaded now with grey, her face grew older in form without changing in expression. She seemed the same as when she had come to the Marsh twenty-five years ago, save that her health was more fragile. She seemed always to haunt the Marsh rather than to live there. She was never part of the life. Something she represented was alien there, she remained a stranger within the gates, in some ways fixed and impervious, in some ways curiously refining. She caused the separateness and individuality of all the Marsh inmates, the friability of the household.

When young Tom Brangwen was twenty-three years old there was some breach between him and his chief which was never explained, and he went away to Italy, then to America. He came home for a while, then went to Germany; always the same good-looking, carefully-dressed, attractive young man, in perfect health, yet somehow outside of everything. In his dark eyes was a deep misery which he wore with the same ease and pleasantness as he wore his close-sitting clothes.

To Ursula he was a romantic, alluring figure. He had a grace of bringing beautiful presents: a box of expensive sweets, such as Cossethay had never seen; or he gave her a hair-brush and a long slim mirror of mother-of-pearl, all pale and glimmering and exquisite; or he sent her a little necklace of rough stones, amethyst and opal and brilliants and garnet. He spoke other languages easily and fluently, his nature was curiously gracious and insinuating. With all that, he was undefinably an outsider. He belonged to nowhere, to no society.

Anna Brangwen had left her intimacy with her father undeveloped since the time of her marriage. At her marriage it had been abandoned. He and she had drawn a reserve between them. Anna went more to her mother.

Then suddenly the father died.

It happened one springtime when Ursula was about eight years old, he, Tom Brangwen, drove off on a Saturday morning to the market in Nottingham, saying he might not be back till late, as there was a special show and then a meeting he had to attend. His family understood that he would enjoy himself.

The season had been rainy and dreary. In the evening it was pouring with rain. Fred Brangwen, unsettled, uneasy, did not go out, as was his wont. He smoked and read and fidgeted, hearing always the trickling of water outside. This wet, black night seemed to cut him off and make him unsettled, aware of himself, aware that he wanted something else, aware that he was scarcely living. There seemed to him to be no root to his life, no place for him to get satisfied in. He dreamed of going abroad. But his instinct knew that change of place would not solve his problem. He wanted change, deep, vital change of living. And he did not know how to get it.

Tilly, an old woman now, came in saying that the labourers who had been suppering up said the yard and everywhere was just a slew of water. He heard in indifference. But he hated a desolate, raw wetness in the world. He would leave the Marsh.

His mother was in bed. At last he shut his book, his mind was blank, he walked upstairs intoxicated with depression and anger, and, intoxicated with depression and anger, locked himself into sleep.

Tilly set slippers before the kitchen fire, and she also went to bed, leaving the door unlocked. Then the farm was in darkness, in the rain.

At eleven o'clock it was still raining. Tom Brangwen stood in the yard of the "Angel", Nottingham, and buttoned his coat.

"Oh, well," he said cheerfully, "it's rained on me before. Put 'er in, Jack, my lad, put her in—Tha'rt a rare old cock, Jacky-boy, wi' a belly on thee as does credit to thy drink, if not to thy corn. Co' up lass, let's get off ter th' old homestead. Oh, my heart, what a wetness in the night! There'll be no volcanoes after this. Hey, Jack, my beautiful young slender feller, which of us is Noah? It seems as though the water-works is bursted. Ducks and ayquatic fowl 'll be king o' the castle at this rate—dove an' olive branch an' all. Stand up then, gel, stand up, we're not stoppin' here all night, even if you thought we was. I'm dashed if the jumping rain wouldn't make anybody think they was drunk. Hey, Jack— does rain-water wash the sense in, or does it wash it out?" And he laughed to himself at the joke.

He was always ashamed when he had to drive after he had been drinking, always apologetic to the horse. His apologetic frame made him facetious. He was aware of his inability to walk quite straight. Nevertheless his will kept stiff and attentive, in all his fuddleness.

He mounted and bowled off through the gates of the innyard. The mare went well, he sat fixed, the rain beating on his face. His heavy body rode motionless in a kind of sleep, one centre of attention was kept fitfully burning, the rest was dark. He concentrated his last attention on the fact of driving along the road he knew so well. He knew it so well, he watched for it attentively, with an effort of will.

He talked aloud to himself, sententious in his anxiety, as if he were perfectly sober, whilst the mare bowled along and the rain beat on him. He watched the rain before the giglamps, the faint gleaming of the shadowy horse's body, the passing of the dark hedges.

"It's not a fit night to turn a dog out," he said to himself, aloud. "It's high time as it did a bit of clearing up, I'll be damned if it isn't. It was a lot of use putting those ten loads of cinders on th' road. They'll be washed to kingdom-come if it doesn't alter. Well, it's our Fred's look-out, if they are. He's top-sawyer as far as those things go. I don't see why I should concern myself. They can wash to kingdom-come and back again for what I care. I suppose they would be washed back again some day. That's how things are. Th' rain tumbles down just to mount up in clouds again. So they say. There's no more water on the earth than there was in the year naught. That's the story, my boy, if you understand it. There's no more to-day than there was a thousand years ago— nor no less either. You can't wear water out. No, my boy: it'll give you the go-by. Try to wear it out, and it takes its hook into vapour, it has its fingers at its nose to you. It turns into cloud and falleth as rain on the just and unjust. I wonder if I'm the just or the unjust."

He started awake as the trap lurched deep into a rut. And he wakened to the point in his journey. He had travelled some distance since he was last conscious.

But at length he reached the gate, and stumbled heavily down, reeling, gripping fast to the trap. He descended into several inches of water.

"Be damned!" he said angrily. "Be damned to the miserable slop."

And he led the horse washing through the gate. He was quite drunk now, moving blindly, in habit. Everywhere there was water underfoot.

The raised causeway of the house and the farm-stead was dry, however. But there was a curious roar in the night which seemed to be made in the darkness of his own intoxication. Reeling, blinded, almost without consciousness he carried his parcels and the rug and cushions into the house, dropped them, and went out to put up the horse.

Now he was at home, he was a sleep-walker, waiting only for the moment of activity to stop. Very deliberately and carefully, he led the horse down the slope to the cart-shed. She shied and backed.

"Why, wha's amiss?" he hiccupped, plodding steadily on. And he was again in a wash of water, the horse splashed up water as he went. It was thickly dark, save for the gig-lamps, and they lit on a rippling surface of water.

"Well, that's a knock-out," he said, as he came to the cart-shed, and was wading in six inches of water. But everything seemed to him amusing. He laughed to think of six inches of water being in the cart-shed.

He backed in the mare. She was restive. He laughed at the fun of untackling the mare with a lot of water washing round his feet. He laughed because it upset her. "What's amiss, what's amiss, a drop o' water won't hurt you!" As soon as he had undone the traces, she walked quickly away.

He hung up the shafts and took the gig-lamp. As he came out of the familiar jumble of shafts and wheels in the shed, the water, in little waves, came washing strongly against his legs. He staggered and almost fell.

"Well, what the deuce!" he said, staring round at the running water in the black, watery night.

He went to meet the running flood, sinking deeper and deeper. His soul was full of great astonishment. He *had* to go and look where it came from, though the ground was going from under his feet. He went on, down towards the pond, shakily. He rather enjoyed it. He was knee-deep, and the water was pulling heavily. He stumbled, reeled sickeningly.

Fear took hold of him. Gripping tightly to the lamp, he reeled, and looked round. The water was carrying his feet away, he was dizzy. He did not know which way to turn. The water was whirling, whirling, the whole black night was swooping in rings. He swayed uncertainly at the centre of all the attack, reeling in dismay. In his soul, he knew he would fall.

As he staggered something in the water struck his legs, and he fell. Instantly he was in the turmoil of suffocation. He fought in a black horror of suffocation, fighting, wrestling, but always borne down, borne inevitably down. Still he wrestled and fought to get himself free, in the unutterable struggle of suffocation, but he always fell again deeper. Something struck his head, a great wonder of anguish went over him, then the blackness covered him entirely.

In the utter darkness, the unconscious, drowning body was rolled along, the waters pouring, washing, filling in the place. The cattle woke up and rose to their feet, the dog began to yelp. And the unconscious, drowning body was washed along in the black, swirling darkness, passively.

Mrs. Brangwen woke up and listened. With preternaturally sharp senses she heard the movement of all the darkness that swirled outside. For a moment she lay still. Then she went to the window. She heard the sharp rain, and the deep running of water. She knew her husband was outside.

"Fred," she called, "Fred!"

Away in the night was a hoarse, brutal roar of a mass of water rushing downwards.

She went downstairs. She could not understand the multiplied running of water. Stepping down the step into the kitchen, she put her foot into water. The kitchen was flooded. Where did it come from? She could not understand.

Water was running in out of the scullery. She paddled through barefoot, to see. Water was bubbling fiercely under the outer door. She was afraid. Then something washed against her, something twined under her foot. It was the riding whip. On the table were the rug and the cushion and the parcel from the gig.

He had come home.

"Tom!" she called, afraid of her own voice.

She opened the door. Water ran in with a horrid sound. Everywhere was moving water, a sound of waters.

"Tom!" she cried, standing in her nightdress with the candle, calling into the darkness and the flood out of the doorway.

"Tom! Tom!"

And she listened. Fred appeared behind her, in trousers and shirt.

"Where is he?" he asked.

He looked at the flood, then at his mother. She seemed small and uncanny, elvish, in her nightdress.

"Go upstairs," he said. "He'll be in th' stable."

"To-om! To-om!" cried the elderly woman, with a long, unnatural, penetrating call that chilled her son to the marrow. He quickly pulled on his boots and his coat.

"Go upstairs, mother," he said; "I'll go an' see where he is."

"To—om! To—o—om!" rang out the shrill, unearthly cry of the small woman. There was only the noise of water and the mooing of uneasy cattle, and the long yelping of the dog, clamouring in the darkness.

Fred Brangwen splashed out into the flood with a lantern. His mother stood on a chair in the doorway, watching him go. It was all water, water, running, flashing under the lantern.

"Tom! Tom! To—o—om!" came her long, unnatural cry, ringing over the night. It made her son feel cold in his soul.

And the unconscious, drowning body of the father rolled on below the house, driven by the black water towards the high-road.

Tilly appeared, a skirt over her nightdress. She saw her mistress clinging on the top of a chair in the open doorway, a candle burning on the table.

"God's sake!" cried the old serving-woman. "The cut's burst. That embankment's broke down. Whativer are we goin' to do!"

Mrs. Brangwen watched her son, and the lantern, go along the upper causeway to the stable. Then she saw the dark figure of a horse: then her son hung the lamp in the stable, and the light shone out faintly on him as he untackled the mare. The mother saw the soft blazed face of the horse thrust forward into the stable-door. The stables were still above the flood. But the water flowed strongly into the house.

"It's getting higher," said Tilly. "Hasn't master come in?"

Mrs. Brangwen did not hear.

"Isn't he the—ere?" she called, in her far-reaching, terrifying voice.

"No," came the short answer out of the night.

"Go and loo-ok for him."

His mother's voice nearly drove the youth mad.

He put the halter on the horse and shut the stable door. He came splashing back through the water, the lantern swinging.

The unconscious, drowning body was pushed past the house in the deepest current. Fred Brangwen came to his mother.

"I'll go to th' cart-shed," he said.

"To-om, To-o-om!" rang out the strong, inhuman cry. Fred Brangwen's blood froze, his heart was very angry. He gripped his veins in a frenzy. Why was she yelling like this? He could not bear the sight of her, perched on a chair in her white nightdress in the doorway, elvish and horrible.

"He's taken the mare out of the trap, so he's all right," he said, growling, pretending to be normal.

But as he descended to the cart-shed, he sank into a foot of water. He heard the rushing in the distance, he knew the canal had broken down. The water was running deeper.

The trap was there all right, but no signs of his father. The young man waded down to the pond. The water rose above his knees, it swirled and forced him. He drew back.

"Is he the-e-ere?" came the maddening cry of the mother.

"No," was the sharp answer.

"To-om—To-o-om!" came the piercing, free, unearthly call. It seemed high and supernatural, almost pure. Fred Brangwen hated it. It nearly drove him mad. So awfully it sang out, almost like a song.

The water was flowing fuller into the house.

"You'd better go up to Beeby's and bring him and Arthur down, and tell Mrs. Beeby to fetch Wilkinson," said Fred to Tilly. He forced his mother to go upstairs.

"I know your father is drowned," she said, in a curious dismay.

The flood rose through the night, till it washed the kettle off the hob in the kitchen. Mrs. Brangwen sat alone at a window upstairs. She called no more. The men were busy with the pigs and the cattle. They were coming with a boat for her.

Towards morning the rain ceased, the stars came out over the noise and the terrifying clucking and trickling of the water. Then there was a pallor in the east, the light began to come. In the ruddy light of the dawn she saw the waters spreading out, moving sluggishly, the buildings rising out of a waste of water. Birds began to sing, drowsily, and as if slightly hoarse with the dawn. It grew brighter. Up the second field was the great, raw gap in the canal embankment.

Mrs. Brangwen went from window to window, watching the flood. Somebody had brought a little boat. The light grew stronger, the red gleam was gone off the flood-waters, day took place. Mrs. Brangwen went from the front of the house to the back, looking out, intent and unrelaxing, on the pallid morning of spring.

She saw a glimpse of her husband's buff coat in the floods, as the water rolled the body against the garden hedge. She called to the men in the boat. She was glad he was found. They dragged him out of the hedge. They could not lift him into the boat. Fred Brangwen jumped into the water, up to his waist, and half carried the body of his father through the flood to the road. Hay and twigs and dirt were in the beard and hair. The youth pushed through the water crying loudly without tears, like a stricken animal. The mother at the window cried, making no trouble.

The doctor came. But the body was dead. They carried it up to Cossethay, to Anna's house.

When Anna Brangwen heard the news, she pressed back her head and rolled her eyes, as if something were reaching forward to bite at her throat. She pressed back her head, her mind was driven back to sleep. Since she had married and become a mother, the girl she had been was forgotten. Now, the shock threatened to break in upon her and sweep away all her intervening life, make her as a girl of eighteen again, loving her father. So she pressed back, away from the shock, she clung to her present life.

It was when they brought him to her house dead and in his wet clothes, his wet, sodden clothes, fully dressed as he came from market, yet all sodden and inert, that the shock really broke into her, and she was terrified. A big, soaked, inert heap, he was, who had been to her the image of power and strong life.

Almost in horror, she began to take the wet things from him, to pull off him the incongruous market-clothes of a well-to-do farmer. The children were sent away to the Vicarage, the dead body lay on the parlour floor, Anna quickly began to undress him, laid his fob and seals in a wet heap on the table. Her husband and the woman helped her. They cleared and washed the body, and laid it on the bed.

There, it looked still and grand. He was perfectly calm in death, and, now he was laid in line, inviolable, unapproachable. To Anna, he was the majesty of the inaccessible male, the majesty of death. It made her still and awe-stricken, almost glad.

Lydia Brangwen, the mother, also came and saw the impressive, inviolable body of the dead man. She went pale, seeing death. He was beyond change or knowledge, absolute, laid in line with the infinite. What had she to do with him? He was a majestic Abstraction, made visible now for a moment, inviolate, absolute. And who could lay claim to him, who could speak of him, of the him who was revealed in the stripped moment of transit from life into death? Neither the living nor the dead could claim him, he was both the one and the other, inviolable, inaccessibly himself.

"I shared life with you, I belong in my own way to eternity," said Lydia Brangwen, her heart cold, knowing her own singleness.

"I did not know you in life. You are beyond me, supreme now in death," said Anna Brangwen, awe-stricken, almost glad.

It was the sons who could not bear it. Fred Brangwen went about with a set, blanched face and shut hands, his heart full of hatred and rage for what had been done to his father, bleeding also with desire to have his father again, to see him, to hear him again. He could not bear it.

Tom Brangwen only arrived on the day of the funeral. He was quiet and controlled as ever. He kissed his mother, who was still dark-faced, inscrutable, he shook hands with his brother without looking at him, he saw the great coffin with its black handles. He even read the name-plate, "Tom Brangwen, of the Marsh Farm. Born ——. Died ——."

The good-looking, still face of the young man crinkled up for a moment in a terrible grimace, then resumed its stillness. The coffin was carried round to the church, the funeral bell tanged at intervals, the mourners carried their wreaths of white flowers. The mother, the Polish woman, went with dark, abstract face, on her son's arm. He was good-looking as ever, his face perfectly motionless and somehow pleasant. Fred walked with Anna, she strange and winsome, he with a face like wood, stiff, unyielding.

Only afterwards Ursula, flitting between the currant bushes down the garden, saw her Uncle Tom standing in his black clothes, erect and fashionable, but his fists lifted, and his face distorted, his lips curled back from his teeth in a horrible grin, like an animal which grimaces with torment, whilst his body panted quick, like a panting dog's. He was facing the open distance, panting, and holding still, then panting rapidly again, but his face never changing from its almost bestial look of torture, the teeth all showing, the nose wrinkled up, the eyes, unseeing, fixed.

Terrified, Ursula slipped away. And when her Uncle Tom was in the house again, grave and very quiet, so that he seemed almost to affect gravity, to pretend grief, she watched his still, handsome face, imagining it again in its distortion. But she saw the nose was rather thick, rather Russian, under its transparent skin, she remembered the teeth under the carefully cut moustache were small and sharp and spaced. She could see him, in all his elegant demeanour, bestial, almost corrupt. And she was frightened. She never forgot to look for the bestial, frightening side of him, after this.

He said "Good-bye" to his mother and went away at once. Ursula almost shrank from his kiss, now. She wanted it, nevertheless, and the little revulsion as well.

At the funeral, and after the funeral, Will Brangwen was madly in love with his wife. The death had shaken him. But death and all seemed to gather in him into a mad, overwhelming passion for his wife. She seemed so strange and winsome. He was almost beside himself with desire for her.

And she took him, she seemed ready for him, she wanted him.

The grandmother stayed a while at the Yew Cottage, till the Marsh was restored. Then she returned to her own rooms, quiet, and it seemed, wanting nothing. Fred threw himself into the work of restoring the farm. That his father was killed there, seemed to make it only the more intimate and the more inevitably his own place.

There was a saying that the Brangwens always died a violent death. To them all, except perhaps Tom, it seemed almost natural. Yet Fred went about obstinate, his heart fixed. He could never forgive the Unknown this murder of his father.

After the death of the father, the Marsh was very quiet. Mrs. Brangwen was unsettled. She could not sit all the evening peacefully, as she could before, and during the day she was always rising to her feet and hesitating, as if she must go somewhere, and were not quite sure whither.

She was seen loitering about the garden, in her little woollen jacket. She was often driven out in the gig, sitting beside her son and watching the countryside or the streets of the town, with a childish, candid, uncanny face, as if it all were strange to her.

The children, Ursula and Gudrun and Theresa went by the garden gate on their way to school. The grandmother would have them call in each time they passed, she would have them come to the Marsh for dinner. She wanted children about her.

Of her sons, she was almost afraid. She could see the sombre passion and desire and dissatisfaction in them, and she wanted not to see it any more. Even Fred, with his blue eyes and his heavy jaw, troubled her. There was no peace. He wanted something, he wanted love, passion, and he could not find them. But why must he trouble her? Why must he come to her with his seething and suffering and dissatisfactions? She was too old.

Tom was more restrained, reserved. He kept his body very still. But he troubled her even more. She could not but see the black depths of disintegration in his eyes, the sudden glance upon her, as if she could save him, as if he would reveal himself.

And how could age save youth? Youth must go to youth. Always the storm! Could she not lie in peace, these years, in the quiet, apart from life? No, always the swell must heave upon her and break against the barriers. Always she must be embroiled in the seethe and rage and passion, endless, endless, going on for ever. And she wanted to draw away. She wanted at last her own innocence and peace. She did not want her sons to force upon her any more the old brutal story of desire and offerings and deep, deep-hidden rage of unsatisfied men against women. She wanted to be beyond it all, to know the peace and innocence of age.

She had never been a woman to work much. So that now she would stand often at the garden-gate, watching the scant world go by. And the sight of children pleased her, made her happy. She had usually an apple or a few sweets in her pocket. She liked children to smile at her.

She never went to her husband's grave. She spoke of him simply, as if he were alive. Sometimes the tears would run down her face, in helpless sadness. Then she recovered, and was herself again, happy.

On wet days, she stayed in bed. Her bedroom was her city of refuge, where she could lie down and muse and muse. Sometimes Fred would read to her. But that did not mean much. She had so many dreams to dream over, such an unsifted store. She wanted time.

Her chief friend at this period was Ursula. The little girl and the musing, fragile woman of sixty seemed to understand the same language. At Cossethay all was activity and passion, everything moved upon poles of passion. Then there were four children younger than Ursula, a throng of babies, all the time many lives beating against each other.

So that for the eldest child, the peace of the grandmother's bedroom was exquisite. Here Ursula came as to a hushed, paradisal land, here her own existence became simple and exquisite to her as if she were a flower.

Always on Saturdays she came down to the Marsh, and always clutching a little offering, either a little mat made of strips of coloured, woven paper, or a tiny basket made in the kindergarten lesson, or a little crayon drawing of a bird.

When she appeared in the doorway, Tilly, ancient but still in authority, would crane her skinny neck to see who it was.

"Oh, it's you, is it?" she said. "I thought we should be seein' you. My word, that's a bobby-dazzlin' posy you've brought!"

It was curious how Tilly preserved the spirit of Tom Brangwen, who was dead, in the Marsh. Ursula always connected her with her grandfather.

This day the child had brought a tight little nosegay of pinks, white ones, with a rim of pink ones. She was very proud of it, and very shy because of her pride.

"Your gran'mother's in her bed. Wipe your shoes well if you're goin' up, and don't go burstin' in on her like a skyrocket. My word, but that's a fine posy! Did you do it all by yourself, an' all?"

Tilly stealthily ushered her into the bedroom. The child entered with a strange, dragging hesitation characteristic of her when she was moved. Her grandmother was sitting up in bed, wearing a little grey woollen jacket.

The child hesitated in silence near the bed, clutching the nosegay in front of her. Her childish eyes were shining. The grandmother's grey eyes shone with a similar light.

"How pretty!" she said. "How pretty you have made them! What a darling little bunch."

Ursula, glowing, thrust them into her grandmother's hand, saying, "I made them you."

"That is how the peasants tied them at home," said the grandmother, pushing the pinks with her fingers, and smelling them. "Just such tight little bunches! And they make wreaths for their hair—they weave the stalks. Then they go round with wreaths in their hair, and wearing their best aprons."

Ursula immediately imagined herself in this story-land.

"Did you used to have a wreath in your hair, grandmother?"

"When I was a little girl, I had golden hair, something like Katie's. Then I used to have a wreath of little blue flowers, oh, so blue, that come when the snow is gone. Andrey, the coachman, used to bring me the very first."

They talked, and then Tilly brought the tea-tray, set for two. Ursula had a special green and gold cup kept for herself at the Marsh. There was thin bread and butter, and cress for tea. It was all special and wonderful. She ate very daintily, with little fastidious bites.

"Why do you have two wedding-rings, grandmother?—Must you?" asked the child, noticing her grandmother's ivory coloured hand with blue veins, above the tray.

"If I had two husbands, child."

Ursula pondered a moment.

"Then you must wear both rings together?"

"Yes."

"Which was my grandfather's ring?"

The woman hesitated.

"This grandfather whom you knew? This was his ring, the red one. The yellow one was your other grandfather's whom you never knew."

Ursula looked interestedly at the two rings on the proffered finger.

"Where did he buy it you?" she asked.

"This one? In Warsaw, I think."

"You didn't know my own grandfather then?"

"Not this grandfather."

Ursula pondered this fascinating intelligence.

"Did he have white whiskers as well?"

"No, his beard was dark. You have his brows, I think."

Ursula ceased and became self-conscious. She at once identified herself with her Polish grandfather.

"And did he have brown eyes?"

"Yes, dark eyes. He was a clever man, as quick as a lion. He was never still."

Lydia still resented Lensky. When she thought of him, she was always younger than he, she was always twenty, or twenty-five, and under his domination. He incorporated her in his ideas as if she were not a person herself, as if she were just his aide-de-camp, or part of his baggage, or one among his surgical appliances. She still resented it. And he was always only thirty: he had died when he was thirty-four. She did not feel sorry for him. He was older than she. Yet she still ached in the thought of those days.

"Did you like my first grandfather best?" asked Ursula.

"I liked them both," said the grandmother.

And, thinking, she became again Lensky's girl-bride. He was of good family, of better family even than her own, for she was half German. She was a young girl in a house of insecure fortune. And he, an intellectual, a clever surgeon and physician, had loved her. How she had looked up to him! She remembered her first transports when he talked to her, the important young man with the severe black beard. He had seemed so wonderful, such an authority. After her own lax household, his gravity and confident, hard authority seemed almost God-like to her. For she had never known it in her life, all her surroundings had been loose, lax, disordered, a welter.

"Miss Lydia, will you marry me?" he had said to her in German, in his grave, yet tremulous voice. She had been afraid of his dark eyes upon her. They did not see her, they were fixed upon her. And he was hard, confident. She thrilled with the excitement of it, and accepted. During the courtship, his kisses were a wonder to her. She always thought about them, and wondered over them. She never wanted to kiss him back. In her idea, the man kissed, and the woman examined in her soul the kisses she had received.

She had never quite recovered from her prostration of the first days, or nights, of marriage. He had taken her to Vienna, and she was utterly alone with him, utterly alone in another world, everything, everything foreign, even he foreign to her. Then came the real marriage, passion came to her, and she became his slave, he was her lord, her lord. She was the girl-bride, the slave, she kissed his feet, she had thought it an honour to touch his body, to unfasten his boots. For two years, she had gone on as his slave, crouching at his feet, embracing his knees.

Children had come, he had followed his ideas. She was there for him, just to keep him in condition. She was to him one of the baser or material conditions necessary for his welfare in prosecuting his ideas, of nationalism, of liberty, of science.

But gradually, at twenty-three, twenty-four, she began to realise that she too might consider these ideas. By his acceptance of her self-subordination, he exhausted the feeling in her. There were those of his associates who would discuss the ideas with her, though he did not wish to do so himself. She adventured into the minds of other men. His, then, was not the only male mind! She did not exist, then, just as his attribute! She began to perceive the attention of other men. An excitement came over her. She remembered now the men who had paid her court, when she was married, in Warsaw.

Then the rebellion broke out, and she was inspired too. She would go as a nurse at her husband's side. He worked like a lion, he wore his life out. And she followed him helplessly. But she disbelieved in him. He was so separate, he ignored so much. He counted too much on himself. His work, his ideas,—did nothing else matter?

Then the children were dead, and for her, everything became remote. He became remote. She saw him, she saw him go white when he heard the news, then frown, as if he thought, *"Why* have they died now, when I have no time to grieve?"

"He has no time to grieve," she had said, in her remote, awful soul. "He has no time. It is so important, what he does! He is then so self-important, this half-frenzied man! Nothing matters, but this work of rebellion! He has not time to grieve, nor to think of his children! He had not time even to beget them, really."

She had let him go on alone. But, in the chaos, she had worked by his side again. And out of the chaos, she had fled with him to London.

He was a broken, cold man. He had no affection for her, nor for anyone. He had failed in *his* work, so everything had failed. He stiffened, and died.

She could not subscribe. He had failed, everything had failed, yet behind the failure was the unyielding passion of life. The individual effort might fail, but not the human joy. She belonged to the human joy.

He died and went his way, but not before there was another child. And this little Ursula was his grandchild. She was glad of it. For she still honoured him, though he had been mistaken.

She, Lydia Brangwen, was sorry for him now. He was dead—he had scarcely lived. He had never known her. He had lain with her, but he had never known her. He had never received what she could give him. He had gone away from her empty. So, he had never lived. So, he had died and passed away. Yet there had been strength and power in him.

She could scarcely forgive him that he had never lived. If it were not for Anna, and for this little Ursula, who had his brows, there would be no more left of him than of a broken vessel thrown away, and just remembered.

Tom Brangwen had served her. He had come to her, and taken from her. He had died and gone his way into death. But he had made himself immortal in his knowledge with her. So she had her place here, in life, and in immortality. For he had taken his knowledge of her into death, so that she had her place in death. "In my father's house are many mansions."

She loved both her husbands. To one she had been a naked little girl-bride, running to serve him. The other she loved out of fulfilment, because he was good and had given her being, because he had served her honourably, and become her man, one with her.

She was established in this stretch of life, she had come to herself. During her first marriage, she had not existed, except through him, he was the substance and she the shadow running at his feet. She was very glad she had come to her own self. She was grateful to Brangwen. She reached out to him in gratitude, into death.

In her heart she felt a vague tenderness and pity for her first husband, who had been her lord. He was so wrong when he died. She could not bear it, that he had never lived, never really become himself. And he had been her lord! Strange, it all had been! Why had he been her lord? He seemed now so far off, so without bearing on her.

"Which did you, grandmother?"

"What?"

"Like best."

"I liked them both. I married the first when I was quite a girl. Then I loved your grandfather when I was a woman. There is a difference."

They were silent for a time.

"Did you cry when my first grandfather died?" the child asked.

Lydia Brangwen rocked herself on the bed, thinking aloud.

"When we came to England, he hardly ever spoke, he was too much concerned to take any notice of anybody. He grew thinner and thinner, till his cheeks were hollow and his mouth stuck out. He wasn't handsome any more. I knew he couldn't bear being beaten, I thought everything was lost in the world. Only I had your mother a baby, it was no use my dying.

"He looked at me with his black eyes, almost as if he hated me, when he was ill, and said, 'It only wanted this. It only wanted that I should leave you and a young child to starve in this London.' I told him we should not starve. But I was young, and foolish, and frightened, which he knew.

"He was bitter, and he never gave way. He lay beating his brains, to see what he could do. 'I don't know what you will do,' he said. 'I am no good, I am a failure from beginning to end. I cannot even provide for my wife and child!'

"But you see, it was not for him to provide for us. My life went on, though his stopped, and I married your grandfather.

"I ought to have known, I ought to have been able to say to him: 'Don't be so bitter, don't die because this has failed. You are not the beginning and the end.' But I was too young, he had never let me become myself, I thought he was truly the beginning and the end. So I let him take all upon himself. Yet all did not depend on him. Life must go on, and I must marry your grandfather, and have your Uncle Tom, and your Uncle Fred. We cannot take so much upon ourselves."

The child's heart beat fast as she listened to these things. She could not understand, but she seemed to feel far-off things. It gave her a deep, joyous thrill, to know she hailed from far off, from Poland, and that dark-bearded impressive man. Strange, her antecedents were, and she felt fate on either side of her terrible.

Almost every day, Ursula saw her grandmother, and every time, they talked together. Till the grandmother's sayings and stories, told in the complete hush of the Marsh bedroom, accumulated with mystic significance, and became a sort of Bible to the child.

And Ursula asked her deepest childish questions of her grandmother.

"Will somebody love me, grandmother?"

"Many people love you, child. We all love you."

"But when I am grown up, will somebody love me?"

"Yes, some man will love you, child, because it's your nature. And I hope it will be somebody who will love you for what you are, and not for what he wants of you. But we have a right to what we want."

Ursula was frightened, hearing these things. Her heart sank, she felt she had no ground under her feet. She clung to her grandmother. Here was peace and security. Here, from her grandmother's peaceful room, the door opened on to the greater space, the past, which was so big, that all it contained seemed tiny; loves and births and deaths, tiny units and features within a vast horizon. That was a great relief, to know the tiny importance of the individual, within the great past.

X

THE WIDENING CIRCLE

It was very burdensome to Ursula, that she was the eldest of the family. By the time she was eleven, she had to take to school Gudrun and Theresa and Catherine. The boy, William, always called Billy, so that he should not be confused with his father, was a lovable, rather delicate child of three, so he stayed at home as yet. There was another baby girl, called Cassandra.

The children went for a time to the little church school just near the Marsh. It was the only place within reach, and being so small, Mrs. Brangwen felt safe in sending her children there, though the village boys did nickname Ursula "Urtler", and Gudrun "Good-runner", and Theresa "Tea-pot".

Gudrun and Ursula were co-mates. The second child, with her long, sleepy body and her endless chain of fancies, would have nothing to do with realities. She was not for them, she was for her own fancies. Ursula was the one for realities. So Gudrun left all such to her elder sister, and trusted in her implicitly, indifferently. Ursula had a great tenderness for her co-mate sister.

It was no good trying to make Gudrun responsible. She floated along like a fish in the sea, perfect within the medium of her own difference and being. Other existence did not trouble her. Only she believed in Ursula, and trusted to Ursula.

The eldest child was very much fretted by her responsibility for the other young ones. Especially Theresa, a sturdy, bold-eyed thing, had a faculty for warfare.

"Our Ursula, Billy Pillins has lugged my hair."

"What did you say to him?"

"I said nothing."

Then the Brangwen girls were in for a feud with the Pillinses, or Phillipses.

"You won't pull my hair again, Billy Pillins," said Theresa, walking with her sisters, and looking superbly at the freckled, red-haired boy.

"Why shan't I?" retorted Billy Pillins.

"You won't because you dursn't," said the tiresome Theresa.

"You come here, then, Tea-pot, an' see if I dursna."

Up marched Tea-pot, and immediately Billy Pillins lugged her black, snaky locks. In a rage she flew at him. Immediately in rushed Ursula and Gudrun, and little Katie, in clashed the other Phillipses, Clem and Walter, and Eddie Anthony. Then there was a fray. The Brangwen girls were well-grown and stronger than many boys. But for pinafores and long hair, they would have carried easy victories. They went home, however, with hair lugged and pinafores torn. It was a joy to the Phillips boys to rip the pinafores of the Brangwen girls.

Then there was an outcry. Mrs. Brangwen *would not* have it; no, she would not. All her innate dignity and standoffishness rose up. Then there was the vicar lecturing the school. "It was a sad thing that the boys of Cossethay could not behave more like gentlemen to the girls of Cossethay. Indeed, what kind of boy was it that should set upon a girl, and kick her, and beat her, and tear her pinafore? That boy deserved severe castigation, and the name of *coward,* for no boy who was not a *coward*—etc., etc."

Meanwhile much hang-dog fury in the Pillinses' hearts, much virtue in the Brangwen girls', particularly in Theresa's. And the feud continued, with periods of extraordinary amity, when Ursula was Clem Phillips's sweetheart, and Gudrun was Walter's, and Theresa was Billy's, and even the tiny Katie had to be Eddie Ant'ny's sweetheart. There was the closest union. At every possible moment the little gang of Brangwens and Phillipses flew together. Yet neither Ursula nor Gudrun would have any real intimacy with the Phillips boys. It was a sort of fiction to them, this alliance and this dubbing of sweethearts.

Again Mrs. Brangwen rose up.

"Ursula, I will *not* have you raking the roads with lads, so I tell you. Now stop it, and the rest will stop it."

How Ursula *hated* always to represent the little Brangwen club. She could never be herself, no, she was always Ursula-Gudrun-Theresa-Catherine—and later even Billy was added on to her. Moreover, she did not want the Phillipses either. She was out of taste with them.

However, the Brangwen-Pillins coalition readily broke down, owing to the unfair superiority of the Brangwens. The Brangwens were rich. They had free access to the Marsh Farm. The school teachers were almost respectful to the girls, the vicar spoke to them on equal terms. The Brangwen girls presumed, they tossed their heads.

"*You're* not ivrybody, Urtler Brangwin, ugly-mug," said Clem Phillips, his face going very red.

"I'm better than you, for all that," retorted Urtler.

"You *think* you are—wi' a face like that—Ugly Mug,—Urtler Brangwin," he began to jeer, trying to set all the others in cry against her. Then there was hostility again. How she *hated* their jeering. She became cold against the Phillipses. Ursula was very proud in her family. The Brangwen girls had all a curious blind dignity, even a kind of nobility in their bearing. By some result of breed and upbringing, they seemed to rush along their own lives without caring that they existed to other people. Never from the start did it occur to Ursula that other people might hold a low opinion of her. She thought that whosoever knew her, knew she was enough and accepted her as such. She thought it was a world of people like herself. She suffered bitterly if she were forced to have a low opinion of any person, and she never forgave that person.

This was maddening to many little people. All their lives, the Brangwens were meeting folk who tried to pull them down to make them seem little. Curiously, the mother was aware of what would happen, and was always ready to give her children the advantage of the move.

When Ursula was twelve, and the common school and the companionship of the village children, niggardly and begrudging, was beginning to affect her, Anna sent her with Gudrun to the Grammar School in Nottingham. This was a great release for Ursula. She had a passionate craving to escape from the belittling circumstances of life, the little jealousies, the little differences, the little meannesses. It was a torture to her that the Phillipses were poorer and meaner than herself, that they used mean little reservations, took petty little advantages. She wanted to be with her equals: but not by diminishing herself. She *did* want Clem Phillips to be her equal. But by some puzzling, painful fate or other, when he was really there with her, he produced in her a tight feeling in the head. She wanted to beat her forehead, to escape.

Then she found that the way to escape was easy. One departed from the whole circumstance. One went away to the Grammar School, and left the little school, the meagre teachers, the Phillipses whom she had tried to love but who had made her fail, and whom she could not forgive. She had an instinctive fear of petty people, as a deer is afraid of dogs. Because she was blind, she could not calculate nor estimate people. She must think that everybody was just like herself.

She measured by the standard of her own people: her father and mother, her grandmother, her uncles. Her beloved father, so utterly simple in his demeanour, yet with his strong, dark soul fixed like a root in unexpressed depths that fascinated and terrified her: her mother, so strangely free of all money and convention and fear, entirely indifferent to the world, standing by herself, without connection: her grandmother, who had come from so far and was centred in so wide an horizon: people must come up to these standards before they could be Ursula's people.

So even as a girl of twelve she was glad to burst the narrow boundary of Cossethay, where only limited people lived. Outside, was all vastness, and a throng of real, proud people whom she would love.

Going to school by train, she must leave home at a quarter to eight in the morning, and she did not arrive again till halfpast five at evening. Of this she was glad, for the house was small and overful. It was a storm of movement, whence there had been no escape. She hated so much being in charge.

The house was a storm of movement. The children were healthy and turbulent, the mother only wanted their animal well-being. To Ursula, as she grew a little older, it became a nightmare. When she saw, later, a Rubens picture with storms of naked babies, and found this was called "Fecundity", she shuddered, and the world became abhorrent to her. She knew as a child what it was to live amidst storms of babies, in the heat and swelter of fecundity. And as a child, she was against her mother, passionately against her mother, she craved for some spirituality and stateliness.

In bad weather, home was a bedlam. Children dashed in and out of the rain, to the puddles under the dismal yew trees, across the wet flagstones of the kitchen, whilst the cleaning woman grumbled and scolded; children were swarming on the sofa, children were kicking the piano in the parlour, to make it sound like a beehive, children were rolling on the hearthrug, legs in air, pulling a book in two between them, children, fiendish, ubiquitous, were stealing upstairs to find out where our Ursula was, whispering at bedroom doors, hanging on the latch, calling mysteriously, "Ursula! Ursula!" to the girl who had locked herself in to read. And it was hopeless. The locked door excited their sense of mystery, she had to open to dispel the lure. These children hung on to her with round-eyed excited questions.

The mother flourished amid all this.

"Better have them noisy than ill," she said.

But the growing girls, in turn, suffered bitterly. Ursula was just coming to the stage when Andersen and Grimm were being left behind for the "Idylls of the King" and romantic love-stories.

> "Elaine the fair Elaine the lovable,
> Elaine the lily maid of Astolat,
> High in her chamber in a tower to the east
> Guarded the sacred shield of Launcelot."

How she loved it! How she leaned in her bedroom window with her black, rough hair on her shoulders, and her warm face all rapt, and gazed across at the churchyard and the little church, which was a turreted castle, whence Launcelot would ride just now, would wave to her as he rode by, his scarlet cloak passing behind the dark yew trees and between the open space: whilst she, ah, she, would remain the lonely maid high up and isolated in the tower, polishing the terrible shield, weaving it a covering with a true device, and waiting, waiting, always remote and high.

At which point there would be a faint scuffle on the stairs, a light-pitched whispering outside the door, and a creaking of the latch: then Billy, excited, whispering:

"It's locked—it's locked."

Then the knocking, kicking at the door with childish knees, and the urgent, childish:

"Ursula—our Ursula? Ursula? Eh, our Ursula?"

No reply.

"Ursula! Eh—our Ursula?" the name was shouted now. Still no answer.

"Mother, she won't answer," came the yell. "She's dead."

"Go away—I'm not dead. What do you want?" came the angry voice of the girl.

"Open the door, our Ursula," came the complaining cry. It was all over. She must open the door. She heard the screech of the bucket downstairs dragged across the flagstones as the woman washed the kitchen floor. And the children were prowling in the bedroom, asking:

"What were you doing? What had you locked the door for?" Then she discovered the key of the parish room, and betook herself there, and sat on some sacks with her books. There began another dream.

She was the only daughter of the old lord, she was gifted with magic. Day followed day of rapt silence, whilst she wandered ghost-like in the hushed, ancient mansion, or flitted along the sleeping terraces.

Here a grave grief attacked her: that her hair was dark. She *must* have fair hair and a white skin. She was rather bitter about her black mane.

Never mind, she would dye it when she grew up, or bleach it in the sun, till it was bleached fair. Meanwhile she wore a fair white coif of pure Venetian lace.

She flitted silently along the terraces, where jewelled lizards basked upon the stone, and did not move when her shadow fell upon them. In the utter stillness she heard the tinkle of the fountain, and smelled the roses whose blossoms hung rich and motionless. So she drifted, drifted on the wistful feet of beauty, past the water and the swans, to the noble park, where, underneath a great oak, a doe all dappled lay with her four fine feet together, her fawn nestling sun-coloured beside her.

Oh, and this doe was her familiar. It would talk to her, because she was a magician, it would tell her stories as if the sunshine spoke.

Then one day, she left the door of the parish room unlocked, careless and unheeding as she always was; the children found their way in, Katie cut her finger and howled, Billy hacked notches in the fine chisels, and did much damage. There was a great commotion.

The crossness of the mother was soon finished. Ursula locked up the room again, and considered all was over. Then her father came in with the notched tools, his forehead knotted.

"Who the deuce opened the door?" he cried in anger.

"It was Ursula who opened the door," said her mother. He had a duster in his hand. He turned and flapped the cloth hard across the girl's face. The cloth stung, for a moment the girl was as if stunned. Then she remained motionless, her face closed and stubborn. But her heart was blazing. In spite of herself the tears surged higher, in spite of her they surged higher.

In spite of her, her face broke, she made a curious gulping grimace, and the tears were falling. So she went away, desolate. But her blazing heart was fierce and unyielding. He watched her go, and a pleasurable pain filled him, a sense of triumph and easy power, followed immediately by acute pity.

"I'm sure that was unnecessary—to hit the girl across the face," said the mother coldly.

"A flip with the duster won't hurt her," he said.

"Nor will it do her any good."

For days, for weeks, Ursula's heart burned from this rebuff. She felt so cruelly vulnerable. Did he not know how vulnerable she was, how exposed and wincing? He, of all people, knew. And he wanted to do this to her. He wanted to hurt her right through her closest sensitiveness, he wanted to treat her with shame, to maim her with insult.

Her heart burnt in isolation, like a watchfire lighted. She did not forget, she did not forget, she never forgot. When she returned to her love for her father, the seed of mistrust and defiance burned unquenched, though covered up far from sight. She no longer belonged to him unquestioned. Slowly, slowly, the fire of mistrust and defiance burned in her, burned away her connection with him.

She ran a good deal alone, having a passion for all moving, active things. She loved the little brooks. Wherever she found a little running water, she was happy. It seemed to make her run and sing in spirit along with it. She could sit for hours by a brook or stream, on the roots of the alders, and watch the water hasten dancing over the stones, or among the twigs of a fallen branch. Sometimes, little fish vanished before they had become real, like hallucinations, sometimes wagtails ran by the water's brink, sometimes other little birds came to drink. She saw a kingfisher darting blue—and then she was very happy. The kingfisher was the key to the magic world: he was witness of the border of enchantment.

But she must move out of the intricately woven illusion of her life: the illusion of a father whose life was an Odyssey in an outer world; the illusion of her grandmother, of realities so shadowy and far-off that they became as mystic symbols:—peasant-girls with wreaths of blue flowers in their hair, the sledges and the depths of winter; the dark-bearded young grandfather, marriage and war and death; then the multitude of illusions concerning herself, how she was truly a princess of Poland, how in England she was under a spell, she was not

really this Ursula Brangwen; then the mirage of her reading: out of the mul-
ticoloured illusion of this her life, she must move on, to the Grammar School in
Nottingham.

She was shy, and she suffered. For one thing, she bit her nails, and had a cruel
consciousness in her finger-tips, a shame, an exposure. Out of all proportion,
this shame haunted her. She spent hours of torture, conjuring how she might
keep her gloves on: if she might say her hands were scalded, if she might seem
to forget to take off her gloves.

For she was going to inherit her own estate, when she went to the High
School. There, each girl was a lady. There, she was going to walk among free
souls, her co-mates and her equals, and all petty things would be put away. Ah,
if only she did not bite her nails! If only she had not this blemish! She wanted so
much to be perfect—without spot or blemish, living the high, noble life.

It was a grief to her that her father made such a poor introduction. He was
brief as ever, like a boy saying his errand, and his clothes looked ill-fitting and
casual. Whereas Ursula would have liked robes and a ceremonial of introduction to this, her new estate.

She made a new illusion of school. Miss Grey, the head-mistress, had a certain silvery, school-mistressy beauty of character. The school itself had been a
gentleman's house. Dark, sombre lawns separated it from the dark, select avenue. But its rooms were large and of good appearance, and from the back, one
looked over lawns and shrubbery, over the trees and the grassy slope of the
Arboretum, to the town which heaped the hollow with its roofs and cupolas
and its shadows.

So Ursula seated herself upon the hill of learning, looking down on the
smoke and confusion and the manufacturing, engrossed activity of the town.
She was happy. Up here, in the Grammar School, she fancied the air was finer,
beyond the factory smoke. She wanted to learn Latin and Greek and French and
mathematics. She trembled like a postulant when she wrote the Greek alphabet
for the first time.

She was upon another hill-slope, whose summit she had not scaled. There
was always the marvellous eagerness in her heart, to climb and to see beyond. A
Latin verb was virgin soil to her: she sniffed a new odour in it; it meant something, though she did not know what it meant. But she gathered it up: it was
significant. When she knew that:

$$x^2 - y^2 = (x + y)(x - y)$$

then she felt that she had grasped something, that she was liberated into an
intoxicating air, rare and unconditioned. And she was very glad as she wrote her
French exercise:

"J'ai donné le pain à mon petit frére."

In all these things there was the sound of a bugle to her heart, exhilarating,
summoning her to perfect places. She never forgot her brown "Longman's First
French Grammar", nor her "Via Latina" with its red edges, nor her little grey
Algebra book. There was always a magic in them.

At learning she was quick, intelligent, instinctive, but she was not "thorough". If a thing did not come to her instinctively, she could not learn it. And
then, her mad rage of loathing for all lessons, her bitter contempt of all teachers
and schoolmistresses, her recoil to a fierce, animal arrogance made her detestable.

She was a free, unabateable animal, she declared in her revolts: there was no law for her, nor any rule. She existed for herself alone. Then ensued a long struggle with everybody, in which she broke down at last, when she had run the full length of her resistance, and sobbed her heart out, desolate; and afterwards, in a chastened, washed-out, bodiless state, she received the understanding that would not come before, and went her way sadder and wiser.

Ursula and Gudrun went to school together. Gudrun was a shy, quiet, wild creature, a thin slip of a thing hanging back from notice or twisting past to disappear into her own world again. She seemed to avoid all contact, instinctively, and pursued her own intent way, pursuing half-formed fancies that had no relation to anyone else.

She was not clever at all. She thought Ursula clever enough for two. Ursula understood, so why should she, Gudrun, bother herself? The younger girl lived her religious, responsible life in her sister, by proxy. For herself, she was indifferent and intent as a wild animal, and as irresponsible.

When she found herself at the bottom of the class, she laughed, lazily, and was content, saying she was safe now. She did not mind her father's chagrin nor her mother's tinge of mortification.

"What do I pay for you to go to Nottingham for?" her father asked, exasperated.

"Well, Dad, you know you needn't pay for me," she replied, nonchalant. "I'm ready to stop at home."

She was happy at home, Ursula was not. Slim and unwilling abroad, Gudrun was easy in her own house as a wild thing in its lair. Whereas Ursula, attentive and keen abroad, at home was reluctant, uneasy, unwilling to be herself, or unable.

Nevertheless Sunday remained the maximum day of the week for both. Ursula turned passionately to it, to the sense of eternal security it gave. She suffered anguish of fears during the week-days, for she felt strong powers that would not recognise her. There was upon her always a fear and a dislike of authority. She felt she could always do as she wanted if she managed to avoid a battle with Authority and the authorised Powers. But if she gave herself away, she would be lost, destroyed. There was always the menace against her.

This strange sense of cruelty and ugliness always imminent, ready to seize hold upon her this feeling of the grudging power of the mob lying in wait for her, who was the exception, formed one of the deepest influences of her life. Wherever she was, at school, among friends, in the street, in the train, she instinctively abated herself, made herself smaller, feigned to be less than she was, for fear that her undiscovered self should be seen, pounced upon, attacked by brutish resentment of the commonplace, the average Self.

She was fairly safe at school, now. She knew how to take her place there, and how much of herself to reserve. But she was free only on Sundays. When she was but a girl of fourteen, she began to feel a resentment growing against her in her own home. She knew she was the disturbing influence there. But as yet, on Sundays, she was free, really free, free to be herself, without fear or misgiving.

Even at its stormiest, Sunday was a blessed day. Ursula woke to it with a feeling of immense relief. She wondered why her heart was so light. Then she remembered it was Sunday. A gladness seemed to burst out around her, a feeling of great freedom. The whole world was for twenty-four hours revoked, put back. Only the Sunday world existed.

She loved the very confusion of the household. It was lucky if the children slept till seven o'clock. Usually, soon after six, a chirp was heard, a voice, an excited chirrup began, announcing the creation of a new day, there was a thudding of quick little feet, and the children were up and about, scampering in their shirts, with pink legs and glistening, flossy hair all clean from the Saturday's night bathing, their souls excited by their bodies' cleanliness.

As the house began to teem with rushing, half-naked clean children, one of the parents rose, either the mother, easy and slatternly, with her thick, dark hair loosely coiled and slipping over one ear, or the father, warm and comfortable, with ruffled black hair and shirt unbuttoned at the neck.

Then the girls upstairs heard the continual:

"Now then, Billy, what are you up to?" in the father's strong, vibrating voice: or the mother's dignified:

"I have said, Cassie, I will not have it."

It was amazing how the father's voice could ring out like a gong, without his being in the least moved, and how the mother could speak like a queen holding an audience, though her blouse was sticking out all round and her hair was not fastened up and the children were yelling a pandemonium.

Gradually breakfast was produced, and the elder girls came down into the babel, whilst half-naked children flitted round like the wrong ends of cherubs, as Gudrun said, watching the bare little legs and the chubby tails appearing and disappearing.

Gradually the young ones were captured, and nightdresses finally removed, ready for the clean Sunday shirt. But before the Sunday shirt was slipped over the fleecy head, away darted the naked body, to wallow in the sheepskin which formed the parlour rug, whilst the mother walked after, protesting sharply, holding the shirt like a noose, and the father's bronze voice rang out, and the naked child wallowing on its back in the deep sheepskin announced gleefully:

"I'm bading in the sea, mother."

"Why should I walk after you with your shirt?" said the mother. "Get up now."

"I'm bading in the sea, mother," repeated the wallowing, naked figure.

"We say bathing, not bading," said the mother, with her strange, indifferent dignity. "I am waiting here with your shirt."

At length shirts were on, and stockings were paired, and little trousers buttoned and little petticoats tied behind. The besetting cowardice of the family was its shirking of the garter question.

"Where are your garters, Cassie?"

"I don't know."

"Well, look for them."

But not one of the elder Brangwens would really face the situation. After Cassie had grovelled under all the furniture and blacked up all her Sunday cleanliness, to the infinite grief of everybody, the garter was forgotten in the new washing of the young face and hands.

Later, Ursula would be indignant to see Miss Cassie marching into church from Sunday school with her stocking sluthered down to her ankle, and a grubby knee showing.

"It's disgraceful!" cried Ursula at dinner. "People will think we're pigs, and the children are *never* washed."

"Never mind what people think," said the mother superbly. "*I* see that the child is bathed properly, and if I satisfy myself I satisfy everybody. She can't keep her stocking up and no garter, and it isn't the child's fault she was let to go without one."

The garter trouble continued in varying degrees, but till each child wore long skirts or long trousers, it was not removed.

On this day of decorum, the Brangwen family went to church by the high-road, making a detour outside all the garden-hedge, rather than climb the wall into the churchyard. There was no law of this, from the parents. The children themselves were the wardens of the Sabbath decency, very jealous and instant with each other.

It came to be, gradually, that after church on Sundays the house was really something of a sanctuary, with peace breathing like a strange bird alighted in the rooms. Indoors, only reading and tale-telling and quiet pursuits, such as drawing, were allowed. Out of doors, all playing was to be carried on unobtrusively. If there were noise, yelling or shouting, then some fierce spirit woke up in the father and the elder children, so that the younger were subdued, afraid of being excommunicated.

The children themselves preserved the Sabbath. If Ursula in her vanity sang:

> "Il était un' bergère
> Et ron-ron-ron petit patapon,"

Theresa was sure to cry:
"That's not a Sunday song, our Ursula."
"You don't know," replied Ursula, superior. Nevertheless, she wavered. And her song faded down before she came to the end.

Because, though she did not know it, her Sunday was very precious to her. She found herself in a strange, undefined place, where her spirit could wander in dreams, unassailed.

The white-robed spirit of Christ passed between olive trees. It was a vision, not a reality. And she herself partook of the visionary being. There was the voice in the night calling, "Samuel, Samuel!" And still the voice called in the night. But not this night, nor last night, but in the unfathomed night of Sunday, of the Sabbath silence.

There was Sin, the serpent, in whom was also wisdom. There was Judas with the money and the kiss.

But there was no *actual* Sin. If Ursula slapped Theresa across the face, even on a Sunday, that was not Sin, the everlasting. It was misbehaviour. If Billy played truant from Sunday school, he was bad, he was wicked, but he was not a Sinner.

Sin was absolute and everlasting: wickedness and badness were temporary and relative. When Billy, catching up the local jargon, called Cassie a "sinner", everybody detested him. Yet when there came to the Marsh a flippetty-floppetty foxhound puppy, he was mischievously christened "Sinner."

The Brangwens shrank from applying their religion to their own immediate actions. They wanted the sense of the eternal and immortal, not a list of rules for everyday conduct. Therefore they were badly-behaved children, headstrong and arrogant, though their feelings were generous. They had, moreover—intolerable to their ordinary neighbours—a proud gesture, that did not fit with the jealous idea of the democratic Christian. So that they were always extraordinary, outside of the ordinary.

How bitterly Ursula resented her first acquaintance with evangelical teachings. She got a peculiar thrill from the application of salvation to her own personal case. "Jesus died for *me,* He suffered for me." There was a pride and a thrill in it, followed almost immediately by a sense of dreariness. Jesus with holes in His hands and feet: it was distasteful to her. The shadowy Jesus with the Stigmata: that was her own vision. But Jesus the actual man, talking with teeth and lips, telling one to put one's finger into His wounds, like a villager gloating in his sores, repelled her. She was enemy of those who insisted on the humanity of Christ. If He were just a man, living an ordinary human life, then she was indifferent.

But it was the jealousy of vulgar people which must insist on the humanity of Christ. It was the vulgar mind which would allow nothing extra-human, nothing beyond itself to exist. It was the dirty, desecrating hands of the revivalists which wanted to drag Jesus into this everyday life, to dress Jesus up in trousers and frock-coat, to compel Him to a vulgar equality of footing. It was the impudent suburban soul which would ask, "What would Jesus do, if He were in my shoes?"

Against all this, the Brangwens stood at bay. If any one, it was the mother who was caught by, or who was most careless of the vulgar clamour. She would have nothing extra-human. She never really subscribed, all her life, to Brangwen's mystical passion.

But Ursula was with her father. As she became adolescent, thirteen, fourteen, she set more and more against her mother's practical indifference. To Ursula, there was something callous, almost wicked in her mother's attitude. What did Anna Brangwen, in these years, care for God or Jesus or Angels? She was the immediate life of to-day. Children were still being born to her, she was throng with all the little activities of her family. And almost instinctively she resented her husband's slavish service to the Church, his dark, subject hankering to worship an unseen God. What did the unrevealed God matter, when a man had a young family that needed fettling for? Let him attend to the immediate concerns of his life, not go projecting himself towards the ultimate.

But Ursula was all for the ultimate. She was always in revolt against babies and muddled domesticity. To her Jesus was another world, He was not of this world. He did not thrust His hands under her face and, pointing to His wounds, say:

"Look, Ursula Brangwen, I got these for your sake. Now do as you're told."

To her, Jesus was beautifully remote, shining in the distance, like a white moon at sunset, a crescent moon beckoning as it follows the sun, out of our ken. Sometimes dark clouds standing very far off, pricking up into a clear yellow band of sunset, of a winter evening, reminded her of Calvary, sometimes the full moon rising blood-red upon the hill terrified her with the knowledge that Christ was now dead, hanging heavy and dead upon the Cross.

On Sundays, this visionary world came to pass. She heard the long hush, she knew the marriage of dark and light was taking place. In church, the Voice sounded, re-echoing not from this world, as if the Church itself were a shell that still spoke the language of creation.

"The Sons of God saw the daughters of men that they were fair: and they took them wives of all which they chose.

"And the Lord said, My spirit shall not always strive with Man, for that he also is flesh; yet his days shall be an hundred and twenty years.

"There were giants in the earth in those days; and also after that, when the Sons of God came in unto the daughters of men, and they bare children unto them, the same became mighty men which were of old, men of renown."

Over this Ursula was stirred as by a call from far off. In those days, would not the Sons of God have found her fair, would she not have been taken to wife by one of the Sons of God? It was a dream that frightened her, for she could not understand it.

Who were the Sons of God? Was not Jesus the only begotten Son? Was not Adam the only man created from God? Yet there were men not begotten by Adam. Who were these, and whence did they come? They too must derive from God. Had God many offspring, besides Adam and besides Jesus, children whose origin the children of Adam cannot recognise? And perhaps these children, these Sons of God, had known no expulsion, no ignominy of the fall.

These came on free feet to the daughters of men, and saw they were fair, and took them to wife, so that the women conceived and brought forth men of renown. This was a genuine fate. She moved about in the essential days, when the Sons of God came in unto the daughters of men.

Nor would any comparison of myths destroy her passion in the knowledge. Jove had become a bull, or a man, in order to love a mortal woman. He had begotten in her a giant, a hero.

Very good, so he had, in Greece. For herself, she was no Grecian woman. Not Jove nor Pan nor any of those gods, not even Bacchus nor Apollo, could come to her. But the Sons of God who took to wife the daughters of men, these were such as should take her to wife.

She clung to the secret hope, the aspiration. She lived a dual life, one where the facts of daily life encompassed everything, being legion, and the other wherein the facts of daily life were superseded by the eternal truth. So utterly did she desire the Sons of God should come to the daughters of men; and she believed more in her desire and its fulfilment than in the obvious facts of life. The fact that a man was a man, did not state his descent from Adam, did not exclude that he was also one of the unhistoried, unaccountable Sons of God. As yet, she was confused, but not denied.

Again she heard the Voice:

"It is easier for a camel to go through the eye of a needle, than for a rich man to enter into heaven."

But it was explained, the needle's eye was a little gateway for foot passengers, through which the great, humped camel with his load could not possibly squeeze himself: or perhaps, at a great risk, if he were a little camel, he might get through. For one could not absolutely exclude the rich man from heaven, said the Sunday school teachers.

· It pleased her also to know, that in the East one must use hyperbole, or else remain unheard; because the Eastern man must see a thing swelling to fill all heaven, or dwindled to a mere nothing, before he is suitably impressed. She immediately sympathised with this Eastern mind.

Yet the words continued to have a meaning that was untouched either by the knowledge of gateways or hyperboles. The historical, or local, or psychological interest in the words was another thing. There remained unaltered the inexplicable value of the saying. What was this relation between a needle's eye, a rich man, and heaven? What sort of a needle's eye, what sort of a rich man, what sort of heaven? Who knows? It means the Absolute World, and can never be more than half interpreted in terms of the relative world.

But must one apply the speech literally? Was her father a rich man? Couldn't he get to heaven? Or was he only a half-rich man? Or was he merely a poor man? At any rate, unless he gave everything away to the poor, he would find it much harder to get to heaven. The needle's eye would be too tight for him. She almost wished he were penniless poor. If one were coming to the base of it, any man was rich who was not as poor as the poorest.

She had her qualms, when in imagination she saw her father giving away their piano and the two cows, and the capital at the bank, to the labourers of the district, so that they, the Brangwens, should be as poor as the Wherrys. And she did not want it. She was impatient.

"Very well," she thought, "we'll forego that heaven, that's all—at any rate the needle's eye sort." And she dismissed the problem. She was *not* going to be as poor as the Wherrys, not for all the sayings on earth—the miserable squalid Wherrys.

So she reverted to the non-literal application of the scriptures. Her father very rarely read, but he had collected many books of reproductions, and he would sit and look at these, curiously intent, like a child, yet with a passion that was not childish. He loved the early Italian painters, but particularly Giotto and Fra Angelico and Filippo Lippi. The great compositions cast a spell over him. How many times had he turned to Raphael's "Dispute of the Sacrament" or Fra Angelico's "Last Judgment" or the beautiful, complicated renderings of the Adoration of the Magi, and always, each time, he received the same gradual fulfilment of delight. It had to do with the establishment of a whole mystical, architectural conception which used the human figure as a unit. Sometimes he had to hurry home, and go to the Fra Angelico "Last Judgment". The pathway of open graves, the huddled earth on either side, the seemly heaven arranged above, the singing process to paradise on the one hand, the stuttering descent to hell on the other, completed and satisfied him. He did not care whether or not he believed in devils or angels. The whole conception gave him the deepest satisfaction, and he wanted nothing more.

Ursula, accustomed to these pictures from her childhood, hunted out their detail. She adored Fra Angelico's flowers and light and angels, she liked the demons and enjoyed the hell. But the representation of the encircled God, surrounded by all the angels on high, suddenly bored her. The figure of the Most High bored her, and roused her resentment. Was this the culmination and the meaning of it all, this draped, null figure? The angels were so lovely, and the light so beautiful. And only for this, to surround such a banality for God!

She was dissatisfied, but not fit as yet to criticise. There was yet so much to wonder over. Winter came, pine branches were torn down in the snow, the green pine needles looked rich upon the ground. There was the wonderful, starry, straight track of a pheasant's footsteps across the snow imprinted so clear; there was the lobbing mark of the rabbit, two holes abreast, two holes following behind; the hare shoved deeper shafts, slanting, and his two hind feet came down together and made one large pit; the cat podded little holes, and birds made a lacy pattern.

Gradually there gathered the feeling of expectation. Christmas was coming. In the shed, at nights, a secret candle was burning, a sound of veiled voices was heard. The boys were learning the old mystery play of St. George and Beelzebub. Twice a week, by lamplight, there was choir practice in the church, for the learning of old carols Brangwen wanted to hear. The girls went to these practices. Everywhere was a sense of mystery and rousedness. Everybody was preparing for something.

The time came near, the girls were decorating the church, with cold fingers binding holly and fir and yew about the pillars, till a new spirit was in the church, the stone broke out into dark, rich leaf, the arches put forth their buds, and cold flowers rose to blossom in the dim, mystic atmosphere. Ursula must weave mistletoe over the door, and over the screen, and hang a silver dove from a sprig of yew, till dusk came down, and the church was like a grove.

In the cow-shed the boys were blacking their faces for a dress-rehearsal; the turkey hung dead, with opened, speckled wings, in the dairy. The time was come to make pies, in readiness.

The expectation grew more tense. The star was risen into the sky, the songs, the carols were ready to hail it. The star was the sign in the sky. Earth too should give a sign. As evening drew on, hearts beat fast with anticipation, hands were full of ready gifts. There were the tremulously expectant words of the church service, the night was past and the morning was come, the gifts were given and received, joy and peace made a flapping of wings in each heart, there was a great burst of carols, the Peace of the World had dawned, strife had passed away, every hand was linked in hand, every heart was singing.

It was bitter, though, that Christmas Day, as it drew on to evening, and night, became a sort of bank holiday, flat and stale. The morning was so wonderful, but in the afternoon and evening the ecstasy perished like a nipped thing, like a bud in a false spring. Alas, that Christmas was only a domestic feast, a feast of sweetmeats and toys! Why did not the grown-ups also change their everyday hearts, and give way to ecstasy? Where was the ecstasy?

How passionately the Brangwens craved for it, the ecstasy. The father was troubled, dark-faced and disconsolate, on Christmas night, because the passion was not there, because the day was become as every day, and hearts were not aflame. Upon the mother was a kind of absentness, as ever, as if she were exiled for all her life. Where was the fiery heart of joy, now the coming was fulfilled; where was the star, the Magi's transport, the thrill of new being that shook the earth?

Still it was there, even if it were faint and inadequate. The cycle of creation still wheeled in the Church year. After Christmas, the ecstasy slowly sank and changed. Sunday followed Sunday, trailing a fine movement, a finely developed transformation over the heart of the family. The heart that was big with joy, that had seen the star and had followed to the inner walls of the Nativity, that there had swooned in the great light, must now feel the light slowly withdrawing, a shadow falling, darkening. The chill crept in, silence came over the earth, and then all was darkness. The veil of the temple was rent, each heart gave up the ghost, and sank dead.

They moved quietly, a little wanness on the lips of the children, at Good Friday, feeling the shadow upon their hearts. Then, pale with a deathly scent, came the lilies of resurrection, that shone coldly till the Comforter was given.

But why the memory of the wounds and the death? Surely Christ rose with healed hands and feet, sound and strong and glad? Surely the passage of the cross and the tomb was forgotten? But no—always the memory of the wounds, always the smell of grave-clothes? A small thing was Resurrection, compared with the Cross and the death, in this cycle.

So the children lived the year of christianity, the epic of the soul of mankind. Year by year the inner, unknown drama went on in them, their hearts were born and came to fulness, suffered on the cross, gave up the ghost, and rose again to unnumbered days, untired, having at least this rhythm of eternity in a ragged, inconsequential life.

But it was becoming a mechanical action now, this drama: birth at Christmas for death at Good Friday. On Easter Sunday the life-drama was as good as finished. For the Resurrection was shadowy and overcome by the shadow of death, the Ascension was scarce noticed, a mere confirmation of death.

What was the hope and the fulfilment? Nay, was it all only a useless after-death, a wan, bodiless after-death? Alas, and alas for the passion of the human heart, that must die so long before the body was dead.

For from the grave, after the passion and the trial of anguish, the body rose torn and chill and colourless. Did not Christ say, "Mary!" and when she turned with outstretched hands to him, did he not hasten to add, "Touch me not; for I am not yet ascended to my father."

Then how could the hands rejoice, or the heart be glad, seeing themselves repulsed. Alas, for the resurrection of the dead body! Alas, for the wavering, glimmering appearance of the risen Christ. Alas, for the Ascension into heaven, which is a shadow within death, a complete passing away.

Alas, that so soon the drama is over; that life is ended at thirty-three; that the half of the year of the soul is cold and historiless! Alas, that a risen Christ has no place with us! Alas, that the memory of the passion of Sorrow and Death and the Grave holds triumph over the pale fact of Resurrection!

But why? Why shall I not rise with my body whole and perfect, shining with strong life? Why, when Mary says: Rabboni, shall I not take her in my arms and kiss her and hold her to my breast? Why is the risen body deadly, and abhorrent with wounds?

The Resurrection is to life, not to death. Shall I not see those who have risen again walk here among men perfect in body and spirit, whole and glad in the flesh, living in the flesh, loving in the flesh, begetting children in the flesh, arrived at last to wholeness, perfect without scar or blemish, healthy without fear of ill health? Is this not the period of manhood and of joy and fulfilment, after the Resurrection? Who shall be shadowed by Death and the Cross, being risen, and who shall fear the mystic, perfect flesh that belongs to heaven?

Can I not, then, walk this earth in gladness, being risen from sorrow? Can I not eat with my brother happily, and with joy kiss my beloved, after my resurrection, celebrate my marriage in the flesh with feastings, go about my business eagerly, in the joy of my fellows? Is heaven impatient for me, and bitter against this earth, that I should hurry off, or that I should linger pale and untouched? Is the flesh which was crucified become as poison to the crowds in the street, or is it as a strong gladness and hope to them, as the first flower blossoming out of the earth's humus?

XI

FIRST LOVE

As Ursula passed from girlhood towards womanhood, gradually the cloud of self-responsibility gathered upon her. She became aware of herself, that she was a separate entity in the midst of an unseparated obscurity, that she must go somewhere, she must become something. And she was afraid, troubled. Why, oh why must one grow up, why must one inherit this heavy, numbing responsibility of living an undiscovered life? Out of the nothingness and the undifferentiated mass, to make something of herself! But what? In the obscurity and pathlessness to take a direction! But whither? How take even one step? And yet, how stand still? This was torment indeed, to inherit the responsibility of one's own life.

The religion which had been another world for her, a glorious sort of play-world, where she lived, climbing the tree with the short-statured man, walking shakily on the sea like the disciple, breaking the bread into five thousand portions, like the Lord, giving a great picnic to five thousand people, now fell away from reality, and became a tale, a myth, an illusion, which, however much one might assert it to be true an historical fact, one knew was not true—at least, for this present-day life of ours. There could, within the limits of this life we know, be no Feeding of the Five Thousand. And the girl had come to the point where she held that that which one cannot experience in daily life is not true for oneself.

So, the old duality of life, wherein there had been a weekday world of people and trains and duties and reports, and besides that a Sunday world of absolute truth and living mystery, of walking upon the waters and being blinded by the face of the Lord, of following the pillar of cloud across the desert and watching the bush that crackled yet did not burn away, this old, unquestioned duality suddenly was found to be broken apart. The weekday world had triumphed over the Sunday world. The Sunday world was not real, or at least, not actual. And one lived by action.

Only the weekday world mattered. She herself, Ursula Brangwen, must know how to take the weekday life. Her body must be a weekday body, held in the world's estimate. Her soul must have a weekday value, known according to the world's knowledge.

Well, then, there was a weekday life to live, of action and deeds. And so there was a necessity to choose one's action and one's deeds. One was responsible to the world for what one did.

Nay, one was more than responsible to the world. One was responsible to oneself. There was some puzzling, tormenting residue of the Sunday world within her, some persistent Sunday self, which insisted upon a relationship with the now shed-away vision world. How could one keep up a relationship with that which one denied? Her task was now to learn the week-day life.

How to act, that was the question? Whither to go, how to become oneself? One was not oneself, one was merely a half-stated question. How to become oneself, how to know the question and the answer of oneself, when one was merely an unfixed something-nothing, blowing about like the winds of heaven, undefined, unstated.

She turned to the visions, which had spoken far-off words that ran along the blood like ripples of an unseen wind, she heard the words again, she denied the vision, for she must be a weekday person, to whom visions were not true, and she demanded only the weekday meaning of the words.

There *were* words spoken by the vision: and words must have a weekday meaning, since words were weekday stuff. Let them speak now: let them bespeak themselves in weekday terms. The vision should translate itself into weekday terms.

"Sell all thou hast, and give to the poor," she heard on Sunday morning. That was plain enough, plain enough for Monday morning too. As she went down the hill to the station, going to school, she took the saying with her.

"Sell all thou hast, and give to the poor."

Did she want to do that? Did she want to sell her pearl-backed brush and mirror, her silver candlestick, her pendant, her lovely little necklace, and go dressed in drab like the Wherrys: the unlovely uncombed Wherrys, who were the "poor" to her? She did not.

She walked this Monday morning on the verge of misery. For she *did* want to do what was right. And she *didn't* want to do what the gospels said. She didn't want to be poor—really poor. The thought was a horror to her: to live like the Wherrys, so ugly, to be at the mercy of everybody.

"Sell that thou hast, and give to the poor."

One could not do it in real life. How dreary and hopeless it made her!

Nor could one turn the other cheek. Theresa slapped Ursula on the face. Ursula, in a mood of Christian humility, silently presented the other side of her face. Which Theresa, in exasperation at the challenge, also hit. Whereupon Ursula, with boiling heart, went meekly away.

But anger, and deep, writhing shame tortured her, so she was not easy till she had again quarrelled with Theresa and had almost shaken her sister's head off.

"That'll teach *you,*" she said, grimly.

And she went away, unchristian but clean.

There was something unclean and degrading about this humble side of Christianity. Ursula suddenly revolted to the other extreme.

"I hate the Wherrys, and I wish they were dead. Why does my father leave us in the lurch like this, making us be poor and insignificant? Why is he not more? If we had a father as he ought to be, he would be Earl William Brangwen, and I should be the Lady Ursula? What right have *I* to be poor? crawling along the lane like vermin? If I had my rights I should be seated on horseback in a green riding-habit, and my groom would be behind me. And I should stop at the gates of the cottages, and enquire of the cottage woman who came out with a child in her arms, how did her husband, who had hurt his foot. And I would pat the flaxen head of the child, stooping from my horse, and I would give her a shilling from my purse, and order nourishing food to be sent from the hall to the cottage."

So she rode in her pride. And sometimes, she dashed into flames to rescue a forgotten child; or she dived into the canal locks and supported a boy who was seized with cramp; or she swept up a toddling infant from the feet of a runaway horse: always imaginatively, of course.

But in the end there returned the poignant yearning from the Sunday world. As she went down in the morning from Cossethay and saw Ilkeston smoking blue and tender upon its hill, then her heart surged with far-off words:

"Oh, Jerusalem, Jerusalem—how often would I have gathered thy children together as a hen gathereth her chickens under her wings, and ye would not——"

The passion rose in her for Christ, for the gathering under the wings of security and warmth. But how did it apply to the weekday world? What could it mean, but that Christ should clasp her to his breast, as a mother clasps her child? And oh, for Christ, for him who could hold her to his breast and lose her there. Oh, for the breast of man, where she should have refuge and bliss for ever! All her senses quivered with passionate yearning.

Vaguely she knew that Christ meant something else: that in the vision-world He spoke of Jerusalem, something that did not exist in the everyday world. It was not houses and factories He would hold in His bosom: nor householders nor factory-workers nor poor people: but something that had no part in the weekday world, nor seen nor touched with weekday hands and eyes.

Yet she *must* have it in weekday terms—she must. For all her life was a weekday life, now, this was the whole. So he must gather her body to his breast, that was strong with a broad bone, and which sounded with the beating of the heart, and which was warm with the life of which she partook, the life of the running blood.

So she craved for the breast of the Son of Man, to lie there. And she was ashamed in her soul, ashamed. For whereas Christ spoke for the Vision to answer, she answered from the weekday fact. It was a betrayal, a transference of meaning, from the vision world, to the matter-of-fact world. So she was ashamed of her religious ecstasy, and dreaded lest any one should see it.

Early in the year, when the lambs came, and shelters were built of straw, and on her uncle's farm the men sat at night with a lantern and a dog, then again there swept over her this passionate confusion between the vision world and the weekday world. Again she felt Jesus in the countryside. Ah, he would lift up the lambs in his arms! Ah, and she was the lamb. Again, in the morning, going down the lane, she heard the ewe call, and the lambs came running, shaking and twinkling with new-born bliss. And she saw them stooping, nuzzling, groping to the udder, to find the teats, whilst the mother turned her head gravely and sniffed her own. And they were sucking, vibrating with bliss on their little, long legs, their throats stretched up, their new bodies quivering to the stream of blood-warm, loving milk.

Oh, and the bliss, the bliss! She could scarcely tear herself away to go to school. The little noses nuzzling at the udder, the little bodies so glad and sure, the little black legs, crooked, the mother standing still, yielding herself to their quivering attraction—then the mother walked calmly away.

Jesus—the vision world—the everyday world—all mixed inextricably in a confusion of pain and bliss. It was almost agony, the confusion, the inextricability. Jesus, the vision, speaking to her, who was non-visionary! And she would take his words of the spirit and make them to pander to her own carnality.

This was a shame to her. The confusing of the spirit world with the material world, in her own soul, degraded her. She answered the call of the spirit in terms of immediate, everyday desire.

"Come unto me, all ye that labour and are heavy-laden, and I will give you rest."

It was the temporal answer she gave. She leapt with sensuous yearning to respond to Christ. If she could go to him really, and lay her head on his breast, to have comfort, to be made much of, caressed like a child!

All the time she walked in a confused heat of religious yearning. She wanted Jesus to love her deliciously, to take her sensuous offering, to give her sensuous response. For weeks she went in a muse of enjoyment.

And all the time she knew underneath that she was playing false, accepting the passion of Jesus for her own physical satisfaction. But she was in such a daze, such a tangle. How could she get free?

She hated herself, she wanted to trample on herself, destroy herself. How could one become free? She hated religion, because it lent itself to her confusion. She abused everything. She wanted to become hard, indifferent, brutally callous to everything but just the immediate need, the immediate satisfaction. To have a yearning towards Jesus, only that she might use him to pander to her own soft sensation, use him as a means of reacting upon herself, maddened her in the end. There was then no Jesus, no sentimentality. With all the bitter hatred of helplessness she hated sentimentality.

At this period came the young Skrebensky. She was nearly sixteen years old, a slim, smouldering girl, deeply reticent, yet lapsing into unreserved expansiveness now and then, when she seemed to give away her whole soul, but when in fact she only made another counterfeit of her soul for outward presentation. She was sensitive in the extreme, always tortured, always affecting a callous indifference to screen herself.

She was at this time a nuisance on the face of the earth, with her spasmodic passion and her slumberous torment. She seemed to go with all her soul in her hands, yearning, to the other person. Yet all the while, deep at the bottom of her was a childish antagonism of distrust. She thought she loved everybody and believed in everybody. But because she could not love herself nor believe in herself, she mistrusted everybody with the mistrust of a serpent or a captured bird. Her starts of revulsion and hatred were more inevitable than her impulses of love.

So she wrestled through her dark days of confusion, soulless, uncreated, unformed.

One evening, as she was studying in the parlour, her head buried in her hands, she heard new voices in the kitchen speaking. At once, from its apathy, her excitable spirit started and strained to listen. It seemed to crouch, to lurk under cover, tense, glaring forth unwilling to be seen.

There were two strange men's voices, one soft and candid, veiled with soft candour, the other veiled with easy mobility, running quickly. Ursula sat quite tense, shocked out of her studies, lost. She listened all the time to the sound of the voices, scarcely heeding the words.

The first speaker was her Uncle Tom. She knew the naïve candour covering the girding and savage misery of his soul. Who was the other speaker? Whose voice ran on so easy, yet with an inflamed pulse? It seemed to hasten and urge her forward, that other voice.

"I remember you," the young man's voice was saying. "I remember you from the first time I saw you, because of your dark eyes and fair face."

Mrs. Brangwen laughed, shy and pleased.

"You were a curly-headed little lad," she said.

"Was I? Yes, I know. They were very proud of my curls."

And a laugh ran to silence.

"You were a very well-mannered lad, I remember," said her father.

"Oh! did I ask you to stay the night? I always used to ask people to stay the night. I believe it was rather trying for my mother."

There was a general laugh. Ursula rose. She had to go.

At the click of the latch everybody looked round. The girl hung in the doorway, seized with a moment's fierce confusion. She was going to be good-looking. Now she had an attractive gawkiness, as she hung a moment, not knowing how to carry her shoulders. Her dark hair was tied behind, her yellow-brown eyes shone without direction. Behind her, in the parlour, was the soft light of a lamp upon open books.

A superficial readiness took her to her Uncle Tom, who kissed her, greeting her with warmth, making a show of intimate possession of her, and at the same time leaving evident his own complete detachment.

But she wanted to turn to the stranger. He was standing back a little, waiting. He was a young man with very clear greyish eyes that waited until they were called upon, before they took expression.

Something in his self-possessed waiting moved her, and she broke into a confused, rather beautiful laugh as she gave him her hand, catching her breath like an excited child. His hand closed over hers very close, very near, he bowed, and his eyes were watching her with some attention. She felt proud—her spirit leapt to life.

"You don't know Mr. Skrebensky, Ursula," came her Uncle Tom's intimate voice. She lifted her face with an impulsive flash to the stranger, as if to declare a knowledge, laughing her palpitating, excited laugh.

His eyes became confused with roused lights, his detached attention changed to a readiness for her. He was a young man of twenty-one, with a slender figure and soft brown hair brushed up on the German fashion straight from his brow.

"Are you staying long?" she asked.

"I've got a month's leave," he said, glancing at Tom Brangwen. "But I've various places I must go to—put in some time here and there."

He brought her a strong sense of the outer world. It was as if she were set on a hill and could feel vaguely the whole world lying spread before her.

"What have you a month's leave from?" she asked.

"I'm in the Engineers—in the Army."

"Oh!" she exclaimed, glad.

"We're taking *you* away from your studies," said her Uncle Tom.

"Oh, no," she replied quickly.

Skrebensky laughed, young and inflammable.

"She won't wait to be taken away," said her father. But that seemed clumsy. She wished he would leave her to say her own things.

"Don't you like study?" asked Skrebensky, turning to her, putting the question from his own case.

"I like some things," said Ursula. "I like Latin and French—and grammar."

He watched her, and all his being seemed attentive to her, then he shook his head.

"I don't," he said. "They say all the brains of the army are in the Engineers. I think that's why I joined them—to get the credit of other people's brains."

He said this quizzically and with chagrin. And she became alert to him. It interested her. Whether he had brains or not, he was interesting. His directness attracted her, his independent motion. She was aware of the movement of his life over against hers.

"I don't think brains matter," she said.

"What does matter then?" came her Uncle Tom's intimate, caressing, half-jeering voice.

She turned to him.

"It matters whether people have courage or not," she said.

"Courage for what?" asked her uncle.

"For everything."

Tom Brangwen gave a sharp little laugh. The mother and father sat silent, with listening faces. Skrebensky waited. She was speaking for him.

"Everything's nothing," laughed her uncle.

She disliked him at that moment.

"She doesn't practise what she preaches," said her father, stirring in his chair and crossing one leg over the other. "She has courage for mighty little."

But she would not answer. Skrebensky sat still, waiting. His face was irregular, almost ugly, flattish, with a rather thick nose. But his eyes were pellucid, strangely clear, his brown hair was soft and thick as silk, he had a slight moustache. His skin was fine, his figure slight, beautiful. Beside him, her Uncle Tom looked full-blown, her father seemed uncouth. Yet he reminded her of her father, only he was finer, and he seemed to be shining. And his face was almost ugly.

He seemed simply acquiescent in the fact of his own being, as if he were beyond any change or question. He was himself. There was a sense of fatality about him that fascinated her. He made no effort to prove himself to other people. Let it be accepted for what it was, his own being. In its isolation it made no excuse or explanation for itself.

So he seemed perfectly, even fatally established, he did not asked to be rendered before he could exist, before he could have relationship with another person.

This attracted Ursula very much. She was so used to unsure people who took on a new being with every new influence. Her Uncle Tom was always more or less what the other person would have him. In consequence, one never knew the real Uncle Tom, only a fluid, unsatisfactory flux with a more or less consistent appearance.

But, let Skrebensky do what he would, betray himself entirely, he betrayed himself always upon his own responsibility. He permitted no question about himself. He was irrevocable in his isolation.

So Ursula thought him wonderful, he was so finely constituted, and so distinct, self-contained, self-supporting. This, she said to herself, was a gentleman, he had a nature like fate, the nature of an aristocrat.

She laid hold of him at once for her dreams. Here was one such as those Sons of God who saw the daughters of men, that they were fair. He was no son of Adam. Adam was servile. Had not Adam been driven cringing out of his native place, had not the human race been a beggar ever since, seeking its own being? But Anton Skrebensky could not beg. He was in possession of himself, of that, and no more. Other people could not really give him anything nor take anything from him. His soul stood alone.

She knew that her mother and father acknowledged him. The house was changed. There had been a visit paid to the house. Once three angels stood in Abraham's doorway, and greeted him, and stayed and ate with him, leaving his household enriched for ever when they went.

The next day she went down to the Marsh according to invitation. The two men were not come home. Then, looking through the window, she saw the dogcart drive up, and Skrebensky leapt down. She saw him draw himself together, jump, laugh to her uncle, who was driving, then come towards her to the house. He was so spontaneous and revealed in his movements. He was isolated within his own clear, fine atmosphere, and as still as if fated.

His resting in his own fate gave him an appearance of indolence, almost of languor: he made no exuberant movement. When he sat down, he seemed to go loose, languid.

"We are a little late," he said.

"Where have you been?"

"We went to Derby to see a friend of my father's."

"Who?"

It was an adventure to her to put direct questions and get plain answers. She knew she might do it with this man.

"Why, he is a clergyman too—he is my guardian—one of them."

Ursula knew that Skrebensky was an orphan.

"Where is really your home now?" she asked.

"My home?—I wonder. I am very fond of my colonel—Colonel Hepburn: then there are my aunts: but my real home, I suppose, is the army."

"Do you like being on your own?"

His clear, greenish-grey eyes rested on her a moment, and, as he considered, he did not see her.

"I suppose so," he said. "You see my father—well, he was never acclimatised here. He wanted—I don't know what he wanted—but it was a strain. And my mother—I always knew she was too good to me. I could feel her being too good to me—my mother! Then I went away to school so early. And I must say, the outside world was always more naturally a home to me than the vicarage—I don't know why."

"Do you feel like a bird blown out of its own latitude?" she asked, using a phrase she had met.

"No, no. I find everything very much as I like it."

He seemed more and more to give her a sense of the vast world, a sense of distances and large masses of humanity. It drew her as a scent draws a bee from afar. But also it hurt her.

It was summer, and she wore cotton frocks. The third time he saw her she had on a dress with fine blue-and-white stripes, with a white collar, and a large white hat. It suited her golden, warm complexion.

"I like you best in that dress," he said, standing with his head slightly on one side, and appreciating her in a perceiving, critical fashion.

She was thrilled with a new life. For the first time she was in love with a vision of herself: she saw as it were a fine little reflection of herself in his eyes. And she must act up to this: she must be beautiful. Her thoughts turned swiftly to clothes, her passion was to make a beautiful appearance. Her family looked on in amazement at the sudden transformation of Ursula. She became elegant, really elegant, in figured cotton frocks she made for herself, and hats she bent to her fancy. An inspiration was upon her.

He sat with a sort of languor in her grandmother's rocking-chair, rocking slowly, languidly, backward and forward, as Ursula talked to him.

"You are not poor, are you?" she said.

"Poor in money? I have about a hundred and fifty a year of my own—so I am poor or rich, as you like. I am poor enough, in fact."

"But you will earn money?"

"I shall have my pay—I have my pay now. I've got my commission. That is another hundred and fifty."

"You will have more, though?"

"I shan't have more than £200 a year for ten years to come. I shall always be poor, if I have to live on my pay."

"Do you mind it?"

"Being poor? Not now—not very much. I may later. People—the officers, are good to me. Colonel Hepburn has a sort of fancy for me—he is a rich man, I suppose."

A chill went over Ursula. Was he going to sell himself in some way?

"Is Colonel Hepburn married?"

"Yes—with two daughters."

But she was too proud at once to care whether Colonel Hepburn's daughter wanted to marry him or not.

There came a silence. Gudrun entered, and Skrebensky still rocked languidly on the chair.

"You look very lazy," said Gudrun.

"I am lazy," he answered.

"You look really floppy," she said.

"I am floppy," he answered.

"Can't you stop?" asked Gudrun.

"No—it's the *perpetuum mobile.*"

"You look as if you hadn't a bone in your body."

"That's how I like to feel."

"I don't admire your taste."

"That's my misfortune."

And he rocked on.

Gudrun seated herself behind him, and as he rocked back, she caught his hair between her finger and thumb, so that it tugged him as he swung forward again. He took no notice. There was only the sound of the rockers on the floor. In silence, like a crab, Gudrun caught a strand of his hair each time he rocked back. Ursula flushed, and sat in some pain. She saw the irritation gathering on his brow.

At last he leapt up, suddenly, like a steel spring going off, and stood on the hearthrug.

"Damn it, *why* can't I rock?" he asked petulantly, fiercely.

Ursula loved him for his sudden, steel-like start out of the languor. He stood on the hearthrug fuming, his eyes gleaming with anger.

Gudrun laughed in her deep, mellow fashion.

"Men don't rock themselves," she said.

"Girls don't pull men's hair," he said.

Gudrun laughed again.

Ursula sat amused, but waiting. And he knew Ursula was waiting for him. It roused his blood. He had to go to her, to follow her call.

Once he drove her to Derby in the dog-cart. He belonged to the horsey set of the sappers. They had lunch in an inn, and went through the market, pleased with everything. He bought her a copy of *Wuthering Heights* from a bookstall. Then they found a little fair in progress and she said:

"My father used to take me in the swingboats."

"Did you like it?" he asked.

"Oh, it was fine," she said.

"Would you like to go now?"

"Love it," she said, though she was afraid. But the prospect of doing an unusual, exciting thing was attractive to her.

He went straight to the stand, paid the money, and helped her to mount. He seemed to ignore everything but just what he was doing. Other people were mere objects of indifference to him. She would have liked to hang back, but she was more ashamed to retreat from him than to expose herself to the crowd or to dare the swingboat. His eyes laughed, and standing before her with his sharp, sudden figure, he set the boat swinging. She was not afraid, she was thrilled. His colour flushed, his eyes shone with a roused light, and she looked up at him, her face like a flower in the sun, so bright and attractive. So they rushed through the bright air, up at the sky as if flung from a catapult, then falling terribly back. She loved it. The motion seemed to fan their blood to fire, they laughed, feeling the flames.

After the swingboats, they went on the roundabouts to calm down, he twisting astride on his jerky wooden steed towards her, and always seeming at his ease, enjoying himself. A zest of antagonism to the convention made him fully himself. As they sat on the whirling carousal, with the music grinding out, she was aware of the people on the earth outside, and it seemed that he and she were riding carelessly over the faces of the crowd, riding for ever buoyantly, proudly, gallantly over the upturned faces of the crowd, moving on a high level, spurning the common mass.

When they must descend and walk away, she was unhappy, feeling like a giant suddenly cut down to ordinary level, at the mercy of the mob.

They left the fair, to return for the dog-cart. Passing the large church, Ursula must look in. But the whole interior was filled with scaffolding, fallen stone and rubbish were heaped on the floor, bits of plaster crunched underfoot, and the place re-echoed to the calling of secular voices and to blows of the hammer.

She had come to plunge in the utter gloom and peace for a moment, bringing all her yearning, that had returned on her uncontrolled after the reckless riding over the face of the crowd, in the fair. After pride, she wanted comfort, solace, for pride and scorn seemed to hurt her most of all.

And she found the immemorial gloom full of bits of falling plaster, and dust of floating plaster, smelling of old lime, having scaffolding and rubbish heaped about, dust cloths over the altar.

"Let us sit down a minute," she said.

They sat unnoticed in the back pew, in the gloom, and she watched the dirty, disorderly work of bricklayers and plasterers. Workmen in heavy boots walking grinding down the aisles, calling out in a vulgar accent:

"Hi, mate, has them corner mouldin's come?"

There were shouts of coarse answer from the roof of the church. The place echoed desolate.

Skrebensky sat close to her. Everything seemed wonderful, if dreadful to her, the world tumbling into ruins, and she and he clambering unhurt, lawless over the face of it all. He sat close to her, touching her, and she was aware of his influence upon her. But she was glad. It excited her to feel the press of him upon her, as if his being were urging her to something.

As they drove home, he sat near to her. And when he swayed to the cart, he swayed in a voluptuous, lingering way, against her, lingering as he swung away to recover balance. Without speaking, he took her hand across, under the wrap, and with his unseeing face lifted to the road, his soul intent, he began with his one hand to unfasten the buttons of her glove, to push back her glove from her hand, carefully laying bare her hand. And the close-working, instinctive subtlety of his fingers upon her hand sent the young girl mad with voluptuous delight. His hand was so wonderful, intent as a living creature skilfully pushing and manipulating in the dark underworld, removing her glove and laying bare her palm, her fingers. Then his hand closed over hers, so firm, so close, as if the flesh knitted to one thing his hand and hers. Meanwhile his face watched the road and the ears of the horse, he drove with steady attention through the villages, and she sat beside him, rapt, glowing, blinded with a new light. Neither of them spoke. In outward attention they were entirely separate. But between them was the compact of his flesh with hers, in the hand-clasp.

Then, in a strange voice, affecting nonchalance and superficiality he said to her:

"Sitting in the church there reminded me of Ingram."

"Who is Ingram?" she asked.

She also affected calm superficiality. But she knew that something forbidden was coming.

"He is one of the other men with me down at Chatham—a subaltern—but a year older than I am."

"And why did the church remind you of him?"

"Well, he had a girl in Rochester, and they always sat in a particular corner in the cathedral for their love-making."

"How nice!" she cried, impulsively.

They misunderstood each other.

"It had its disadvantages though. The verger made a row about it."

"What a shame! Why shouldn't they sit in a cathedral?"

"I suppose they all think it a profanity—except you and Ingram and the girl."

"I don't think it a profanity—I think it's right, to make love in a cathedral."

She said this almost defiantly, in despite of her own soul.

He was silent.

"And was she nice?"

"Who? Emily? Yes, she was rather nice. She was a milliner, and she wouldn't be seen in the streets with Ingram. It was rather sad, really, because the verger spied on them, and got to know their names and then made a regular row. It was a common tale afterwards."

"What did she do?"

"She went to London, into a big shop. Ingram still goes up to see her."

"Does he love her?"

"It's a year and a half he's been with her now."

"What was she like?"

"Emily? Little, shy-violet sort of girl with nice eyebrows."

Ursula meditated this. It seemed like real romance of the outer world.

"Do all men have lovers?" she asked, amazed at her own temerity. But her hand was still fastened with his, and his face still had the same unchanging fixity of outward calm.

"They're always mentioning some amazing fine woman or other, and getting drunk to talk about her. Most of them dash up to London the moment they are free."

"What for?"

"To some amazing fine woman or other."

"What sort of woman?"

"Various. Her name changes pretty frequently, as a rule. One of the fellows is a perfect maniac. He keeps a suit-case always ready, and the instant he is at liberty, he bolts with it to the station, and changes in the train. No matter who is in the carriage, off he whips his tunic, and performs at least the top half of his toilet."

Ursula quivered and wondered.

"Why is he in such a hurry?" she asked.

Her throat was becoming hard and difficult.

"He's got a woman in his mind, I suppose."

She was chilled, hardened. And yet this world of passions and lawlessness was fascinating to her. It seemed to her a splendid recklessness. Her adventure in life was beginning. It seemed very splendid.

That evening she stayed at the Marsh till after dark, and Skrebensky escorted her home. For she could not go away from him. And she was waiting, waiting for something more.

In the warm of the early night, with the shadows new about them, she felt in another, harder, more beautiful, less personal world. Now a new state should come to pass.

He walked near to her, and with the same, silent, intent approach put his arm round her waist, and softly, very softly, drew her to him, till his arm was hard and pressed in upon her; she seemed to be carried along, floating, her feet scarce touching the ground, borne upon the firm, moving surface of his body, upon whose side she seemed to lie, in a delicious swoon of motion. And whilst she swooned, his face bent nearer to her, her head was leaned on his shoulder, she felt his warm breath on her face. Then softly, oh softly, so softly that she seemed to faint away, his lips touched her cheek, and she drifted through strands of heat and darkness.

Still she waited, in her swoon and her drifting, waited, like the Sleeping Beauty in the story. She waited, and again his face was bent to hers, his lips came warm to her face, their footsteps lingered and ceased, they stood still under the trees, whilst his lips waited on her face, waited like a butterfly that does not move on a flower. She pressed her breast a little nearer to him, he moved, put both his arms round her, and drew her close.

And then, in the darkness, he bent to her mouth, softly, and touched her mouth with his mouth. She was afraid, she lay still on his arm, feeling his lips on her lips. She kept still, helpless. Then his mouth drew near, pressing open her mouth, a hot, drenching surge rose within her, she opened her lips to him, in pained, poignant eddies she drew him nearer, she let him come farther, his lips came and surging, surging, soft, oh soft, yet oh, like the powerful surge of water, irresistible, till with a little blind cry, she broke away.

She heard him breathing heavily, strangely, beside her. A terrible and magnificent sense of his strangeness possessed her. But she shrank a little now, within herself. Hesitating, they continued to walk on, quivering like shadows under the ash trees of the hill, where her grandfather had walked with his daffodils to make his proposal, and where her mother had gone with her young husband, walking close upon him as Ursula was now walking upon Skrebensky.

Ursula was aware of the dark limbs of the trees stretching overhead, clothed with leaves, and of fine ash leaves tressing the summer night.

They walked with their bodies moving in complex unity, close together. He held her hand, and they went the long way round by the road, to be farther. Always she felt as if she were supported off her feet, as if her feet were light as little breezes in motion.

He would kiss her again—but not again that night with the same deep-reaching kiss. She was aware now, aware of what a kiss might be. And so, it was more difficult to come to him.

She went to bed feeling all warm with electric warmth, as if the gush of dawn were within her, upholding her. And she slept deeply, sweetly, oh, so sweetly. In the morning she felt sound as an ear of wheat, fragrant and firm and full.

They continued to be lovers, in the first wondering state of unrealisation. Ursula told nobody; she was entirely lost in her own world.

Yet some strange affectation made her seek for a spurious confidence. She had at school a quiet, meditative, serious-souled friend called Ethel, and to Ethel must Ursula confide the story. Ethel listened absorbedly, with bowed, unbetraying head, whilst Ursula told her secret. Oh, it was so lovely, his gentle, delicate way of making love! Ursula talked like a practised lover.

"Do you think," asked Ursula, "it is wicked to let a man kiss you—*real* kisses, not flirting?"

"I should think," said Ethel, "it depends."

"He kissed me under the ash trees on Cossethay hill—do you think it was wrong?"

"When?"

"On Thursday night when he was seeing me home—but real kisses—real——. He is an officer in the army."

"What time was it?" asked the deliberate Ethel.

"I don't know—about half-past nine."

There was a pause.

"*I* think it's wrong," said Ethel, lifting her head with impatience. "You don't know him."

She spoke with some contempt.

"Yes, I do. He is half a Pole, and a Baron too. In England he is equivalent to a Lord. My grandmother was his father's friend."

But the two friends were hostile. It was as if Ursula *wanted* to divide herself from her acquaintances, in asserting her connection with Anton, as she now called him.

He came a good deal to Cossethay, because her mother was fond of him. Anna Brangwen became something of a *grande dame* with Skrebensky, very calm, taking things for granted.

"Aren't the children in bed?" cried Ursula petulantly, as she came in with the young man.

"They will be in bed in half an hour," said the mother.

"There is no peace," cried Ursula.

"The children must *live,* Ursula," said her mother.

And Skrebensky was against Ursula in this. Why should she be so insistent? But then, as Ursula knew, he did not have the perpetual tyranny of young children about him. He treated her mother with great courtliness, to which Mrs. Brangwen returned an easy, friendly hospitality. Something pleased the girl in her mother's calm assumption of state. It seemed impossible to abate Mrs. Brangwen's position. She could never be beneath anyone in public relation. Between Brangwen and Skrebensky there was an unbridgeable silence. Sometimes the two men made a slight conversation, but there was no interchange. Ursula rejoiced to see her father retreating into himself against the young man.

She was proud of Skrebensky in the house. His lounging, languorous indifference irritated her and yet cast a spell over her. She knew it was the outcome of a spirit of *laissez-aller* combined with profound young vitality. Yet it irritated her deeply.

Notwithstanding, she was proud of him as he lounged in his lambent fashion in her home, he was so attentive and courteous to her mother and to herself all the time. It was wonderful to have his awareness in the room. She felt rich and augmented by it, as if she were the positive attraction and he the flow towards her. And his courtesy and his agreement might be all her mother's, but the lambent flicker of his body was for herself. She held it.

She must ever prove her power.

"I meant to show you my little wood-carving," she said.

"I'm sure it's not worth showing, that," said her father.

"Would you like to see it?" she asked, leaning towards the door.

And his body had risen from the chair, though his face seemed to want to agree with her parents.

"It is in the shed," she said.

And he followed her out of the door, whatever his feelings might be.

In the shed they played at kisses, really played at kisses. It was a delicious, exciting game. She turned to him, her face all laughing, like a challenge. And he accepted the challenge at once. He twined his hand full of her hair, and gently, with his hand wrapped round with hair behind her head, gradually brought her face nearer to his, whilst she laughed breathless with challenge, and his eyes gleamed with answer, with enjoyment of the game. And he kissed her, asserting his will over her, and she kissed him back, asserting her deliberate enjoyment of him. Daring and reckless and dangerous they knew it was, their game, each playing with fire, not with love. A sort of defiance of all the world possessed her in it—she would kiss him just because she wanted to. And a dare-devilry in him, like a cynicism, a cut at everything he pretended to serve, retaliated in him.

She was very beautiful then, so wide opened, so radiant, so palpitating, exquisitely vulnerable and poignantly, wrongly, throwing herself to risk. It roused a sort of madness in him. Like a flower shaking and wide-opened in the sun, she tempted him and challenged him, and he accepted the challenge, something went fixed in him. And under all her laughing, poignant recklessness was the quiver of tears. That almost sent him mad, mad with desire, with pain, whose only issue was through possession of her body.

So, shaken, afraid, they went back to her parents in the kitchen, and dissimulated. But something was roused in both of them that they could not now allay. It intensified and heightened their senses, they were more vivid, and powerful in their being. But under it all was a poignant sense of transience. It was a magnificent self-assertion on the part of both of them, he asserted himself before her, he felt himself infinitely male and infinitely irresistible, she asserted herself before him, she knew herself infinitely desirable, and hence infinitely strong. And after all, what could either of them get from such a passion but a sense of his or of her own maximum self, in contradistinction to all the rest of life? Wherein was something finite and sad, for the human soul at its maximum wants a sense of the infinite.

Nevertheless, it was begun now, this passion, and must go on, the passion of Ursula to know her own maximum self, limited and so defined against him. She could limit and define herself against him, the male, she could be her maximum self, female, oh female, triumphant for one moment in exquisite assertion against the male, in supreme contradistinction to the male.

The next afternoon, when he came, prowling, she went with him across to the church. Her father was gradually gathering in anger against him, her mother was hardening in anger against her. But the parents were naturally tolerant in action.

They went together across the churchyard, Ursula and Skrebensky, and ran to hiding in the church. It was dimmer in there than the sunny afternoon outside, but the mellow glow among the bowed stone was very sweet. The windows burned in ruby and in blue, they made magnificent arras to their bower of secret stone.

"What a perfect place for a *rendezvous*," he said, in a hushed voice, glancing round.

She too glanced round the familiar interior. The dimness and stillness chilled her. But her eyes lit up with daring. Here, here she would assert her indomitable gorgeous female self, here. Here she would open her female flower like a flame, in this dimness that was more passionate than light.

They hung apart a moment, then wilfully turned to each other for the desired contact. She put her arms round him, she cleaved her body to his, and with her hands pressed upon his shoulders, on his back, she seemed to feel right through him, to know his young, tense body right through. And it was so fine, so hard, yet so exquisitely subject and under her control. She reached him her mouth and drank his full kiss, drank it fuller and fuller.

And it was so good, it was very, very good. She seemed to be filled with his kiss, filled as if she had drunk strong, glowing sunshine. She glowed all inside, the sunshine seemed to beat upon her heart underneath, she had drunk so beautifully.

She drew away, and looked at him radiant, exquisitely, glowingly beautiful, and satisfied, but radiant as an illumined cloud.

To him this was bitter, that she was so radiant and satisfied. She laughed upon him, blind to him, so full of her own bliss, never doubting but that he was the same as she was. And radiant as an angel she went with him out of the church, as if her feet were beams of light that walked on flowers for footsteps.

He went beside her, his soul clenched, his body unsatisfied. Was she going to make this easy triumph over him? For him, there was now no self-bliss, only pain and confused anger.

It was high summer, and the hay-harvest was almost over. It would be finished on Saturday. On Saturday, however, Skrebensky was going away. He could not stay any longer.

Having decided to go he became very tender and loving to her, kissing her gently, with such soft, sweet, insidious closeness that they were both of them intoxicated.

The very last Friday of his stay he met her coming out of school, and took her to tea in the town. Then he had a motor-car to drive her home.

Her excitement at riding in a motor-car was greatest of all. He too was very proud of this last *coup*. He saw Ursula kindle and flare up to the romance of the situation. She raised her head like a young horse snuffing with wild delight.

The car swerved round a corner, and Ursula was swung against Skrebensky. The contact made her aware of him. With a swift, foraging impulse she sought for his hand and clasped it in her own, so close, so combined, as if they were two children.

The wind blew in on Ursula's face, the mud flew in a soft, wild rush from the wheels, the country was blackish green, with the silver of new hay here and there, and masses of trees under a silver-gleaming sky.

Her hand tightened on his with a new consciousness, troubled. They did not speak for some time, but sat, hand-fast, with averted, shining faces.

And every now and then the car swung her against him. And they waited for the motion to bring them together. Yet they stared out of the windows, mute.

She saw the familiar country racing by. But now, it was no familiar country, it was wonderland. There was the Hemlock Stone standing on its grassy hill. Strange it looked on this wet, early summer evening, remote, in a magic land. Some rooks were flying out of the trees.

Ah, if only she and Skrebensky could get out, dismount into this enchanted land where nobody had ever been before! Then they would be enchanted people, they would put off the dull, customary self. If she were wandering there, on that hill-slope under a silvery, changing sky, in which many rooks melted like hurrying showers of blots! If they could walk past the wetted hay-swaths, smelling the early evening, and pass in to the wood where the honeysuckle scent was sweet on the cold tang in the air, and showers of drops fell when one brushed a bough, cold and lovely on the face!

But she was here with him in the car, close to him, and the wind was rushing on her lifted, eager face, blowing back the hair. He turned and looked at her, at her face clean as a chiselled thing, her hair chiselled back by the wind, her fine nose keen and lifted.

It was agony to him, seeing her swift and clean-cut and virgin. He wanted to kill himself, and throw his detested carcase at her feet. His desire to turn round on himself and rend himself was an agony to him.

Suddenly she glanced at him. He seemed to be crouching towards her, reaching, he seemed to wince between the brows. But instantly, seeing her lighted eyes and radiant face, his expression changed, his old reckless laugh shone to her. She pressed his hand in utter delight, and he abided. And suddenly she stooped and kissed his hand, bent her head and caught it to her mouth, in generous homage. And the blood burned in him. Yet he remained still, he made no move.

She started. They were swinging into Cossethay. Skrebensky was going to leave her. But it was all so magic, her cup was so full of bright wine, her eyes could only shine.

He tapped and spoke to the man. The car swung up by the yew trees. She gave him her hand and said good-bye, naïve and brief as a schoolgirl. And she stood watching him go, her face shining. The fact of his driving on meant nothing to her, she was so filled by her own bright ecstacy. She did not see him go, for she was filled with light, which was of him. Bright with an amazing light as she was, how could she miss him.

In her bedroom she threw her arms in the air in clear pain of magnificence. Oh, it was her transfiguration, she was beyond herself. She wanted to fling herself into all the hidden brightness of the air. It was there, it was there, if she could but meet it.

But the next day she knew he had gone. Her glory had partly died down—but never from her memory. It was too real. Yet it was gone by, leaving a wistfulness. A deeper yearning came into her soul, a new reserve.

She shrank from touch and question. She was very proud, but very new, and very sensitive. Oh, that no one should lay hands on her!

She was happier running on by herself. Oh, it was a joy to run along the lanes without seeing things, yet being with them. It was such a joy to be alone with all one's riches.

The holidays came, when she was free. She spent most of her time running on by herself, curled up in a squirrel-place in the garden, lying in a hammock in the coppice, while the birds came near—near—so near. Oh, in rainy weather, she flitted to the Marsh, and lay hidden with her book in a hay-loft.

All the time, she dreamed of him, sometimes definitely, but when she was happiest, only vaguely. He was the warm colouring of her dreams, he was the hot blood beating within them.

When she was less happy, out of sorts, she pondered over his appearance, his clothes, the buttons with his regimental badge, which he had given her. Or she tried to imagine his life in barracks. Or she conjured up a vision of herself as she appeared in his eyes.

His birthday was in August, and she spent some pains on making him a cake. She felt that it would not be in good taste for her to give him a present.

Their correspondence was brief, mostly an exchange of post-cards, not at all frequent. But with her cake she must send him a letter.

"*Dear Anton. The sunshine has come back specially for your birthday, I think.*
"*I made the cake myself, and wish you many happy returns of the day. Don't
eat it if it is not good. Mother hopes you will come and see us when you are near
enough.*

"*I am
"*Your sincere friend,
"*Ursula Brangwen.*"

It bored her to write a letter even to him. After all, writing words on paper
had nothing to do with him and her.

The fine weather had set in, the cutting machine went on from dawn till
sunset, chattering round the fields. She heard from Skrebensky; he too was on
duty in the country, on Salisbury Plain. He was now a second lieutenant in a
Field Troop. He would have a few days off shortly, and would come to the
Marsh for the wedding.

Fred Brangwen was going to marry a schoolmistress out of Ilkeston as soon as
corn-harvest was at an end.

The dim blue-and-gold of a hot, sweet autumn saw the close of the corn-
harvest. To Ursula, it was as if the world had opened its softest purest flower, its
chicory flower, its meadow saffron. The sky was blue and sweet, the yellow
leaves down the lane seemed like free, wandering flowers as they chittered
round the feet, making a keen, poignant, almost unbearable music to her heart.
And the scents of autumn were like a summer madness to her. She fled away
from the little, purple-red button-chrysanthemums like a frightened dryad, the
bright yellow little chrysanthemums smelled so strong, her feet seemed to dither
in a drunken dance.

Then her Uncle Tom appeared, always like the cynical Bacchus in the picture. He would have a jolly wedding, a harvest supper and a wedding feast in
one: a tent in the home close, and a band for dancing, and a great feast out of
doors.

Fred demurred, but Tom must be satisfied. Also Laura, a handsome, clever
girl, the bride, she also must have a great and jolly feast. It appealed to her
educated sense. She had been to Salisbury Training College, knew folk-songs
and morris-dancing.

So the preparations were begun, directed by Tom Brangwen. A marquee
was set up on the home close, two large bonfires were prepared. Musicians were
hired, feast made ready.

Skrebensky was to come, arriving in the morning. Ursula had a new white
dress of soft crèpe, and a white hat. She liked to wear white. With her black hair
and clear golden skin, she looked southern, or rather tropical, like a Creole. She
wore no colour whatsoever.

She trembled that day as she appeared to go down to the wedding. She was
to be a bridesmaid. Skrebensky would not arrive till afternoon. The wedding
was at two o'clock.

As the wedding-party returned home, Skrebensky stood in the parlour at the
Marsh. Through the window he saw Tom Brangwen, who was best man, coming up the garden path most elegant in cut-away coat and white slip and spats,
with Ursula laughing on his arm. Tom Brangwen was handsome, with his
womanish colouring and dark eyes and black close-cut moustache. But there
was something subtly coarse and suggestive about him for all his beauty; his
strange, bestial nostrils opened so hard and wide, and his well-shaped head al-

most disquieting in its nakedness, rather bald from the front, and all its soft fulness betrayed.

Skrebensky saw the man rather than the woman. She saw only the slender, unchangeable youth waiting there inscrutable, like her fate. He was beyond her, with his loose, slightly horsey appearance, that made him seem very manly and foreign. Yet his face was smooth and soft and impressionable. She shook hands with him, and her voice was like the rousing of a bird startled by the dawn.

"Isn't it nice," she cried, "to have a wedding?"

There were bits of coloured confetti lodged on her dark hair.

Again the confusion came over him, as if he were losing himself and becoming all vague, undefined, inchoate. Yet he wanted to be hard, manly, horsey. And he followed her.

There was a light tea, and the guests scattered. The real feast was for the evening. Ursula walked out with Skrebensky through the stackyard to the fields, and up the embankment to the canal-side.

The new corn-stacks were big and golden as they went by, an army of white geese marched aside in braggart protest. Ursula was light as a white ball of down. Skrebensky drifted beside her, indefinite, his old form loosened, and another self, grey, vague, drifting out as from a bud. They talked lightly, of nothing.

The blue way of the canal wound softly between the autumn hedges, on towards the greenness of a small hill. On the left was the whole black agitation of colliery and railway and the town which rose on its hill, the church tower topping all. The round white dot of the clock on the tower was distinct in the evening light.

That way, Ursula felt, was the way to London, through the grim, alluring seethe of the town. On the other hand was the evening, mellow over the green water-meadows and the winding alder trees beside the river, and the pale stretches of stubble beyond. There the evening glowed softly, and even a pee-wit was flapping in solitude and peace.

Ursula and Anton Skrebensky walked along the ridge of the canal between. The berries on the hedges were crimson and bright red, above the leaves. The glow of evening and the wheeling of the solitary pee-wit and the faint cry of the birds came to meet the shuffling noise of the pits, the dark, fuming stress of the town opposite, and they two walked the blue strip of water-way, the ribbon of sky between.

He was looking, Ursula thought, very beautiful, because of a flush of sun-burn on his hands and face. He was telling her how he had learned to shoe horses and select cattle fit for killing.

"Do you like to be a soldier?" she asked.

"I am not exactly a soldier," he replied.

"But you only do things for wars," she said.

"Yes."

"Would you like to go to war?"

"I? Well, it would be exciting. If there were a war I would want to go."

A strange, distracted feeling came over her, a sense of potent unrealities.

"Why would you want to go?"

"I should be doing something, it would be genuine. It's a sort of toy-life as it is."

"But what would you be doing if you went to war?"

"I would be making railways or bridges, working like a nigger."

"But you'd only make them to be pulled down again when the armies had done with them. It seems just as much a game."

"If you call war a game."

"What is it?"

"It's about the most serious business there is, fighting."

A sense of hard separateness came over her.

"Why is fighting more serious than anything else?" she asked.

"You either kill or get killed—and I suppose it is serious enough, killing."

"But when you're dead you don't matter any more," she said.

He was silenced for a moment.

But the result matters," he said. "It matters whether we settle the Mahdi or not."

"Not to you—nor me—we don't care about Khartoum."

"You want to have room to live in: and somebody has to make room."

"But I don't want to live in the desert of Sahara—do you?" she replied, laughing with antagonism.

"*I* don't—but we've got to back up those who do."

"Why have we?"

"Where is the nation if we don't?"

"But we aren't the nation. There are heaps of other people who are the nation."

"They might say *they* weren't either."

"Well, if everybody said it, there wouldn't be a nation. But I should still be myself," she asserted brilliantly.

"You wouldn't be yourself if there were no nation."

"Why not?"

"Because you'd just be a prey to everybody and anybody."

"How a prey?"

"They'd come and take everything you'd got."

"Well, they couldn't take much even then. I don't care what they take. I'd rather have a robber who carried me off than a millionaire who gave me everything you can buy."

"That's because you are a romanticist."

"Yes, I am. I want to be romantic. I hate houses that never go away, and people just living in the houses. It's all so stiff and stupid. I hate soldiers, they are stiff and wooden. What do you fight for, really?"

"I would fight for the nation."

"For all that, you aren't the nation. What would you do for yourself?"

"I belong to the nation and must do my duty by the nation."

"But when it didn't need your services in particular—when there *is* no fighting? What would you do then?"

He was irritated.

"I would do what everybody else does."

"What?"

"Nothing. I would be in readiness for when I was needed."

The answer came in exasperation.

"It seems to me," she answered, "as if you weren't anybody—as if there weren't anybody there, where you are. Are you anybody, really? You seem like nothing to me."

They had walked till they had reached a wharf, just above a lock. There an empty barge, painted with a red and yellow cabin hood, but with a long, coal-black hold, was lying moored. A man, lean and grimy, was sitting on a box against the cabin-side by the door, smoking, and nursing a baby that was wrapped in a drab shawl, and looking into the glow of evening. A woman bustled out, sent a pail dashing into the canal, drew her water, and bustled in again. Children's voices were heard. A thin blue smoke ascended from the cabin chimney, there was a smell of cooking.

Ursula, white as a moth, lingered to look. Skrebensky lingered by her. The man glanced up.

"Good evening," he called, half impudent, half attracted. He had blue eyes which glanced impudently from his grimy face.

"Good evening," said Ursula, delighted. *"Isn't* it nice now?"

"Ay," said the man, "very nice."

His mouth was red under his ragged, sandy moustache. His teeth were white as he laughed.

"Oh, but——" stammered Ursula, laughing, "it *is*. Why do you say it as if it weren't?"

" 'Appen for them as is childt-nursin' it's none so rosy."

"May I look inside your barge?" asked Ursula.

"There's nobody'll stop you; you come if you like."

The barge lay at the opposite bank, at the wharf. It was the *Annabel,* belonging to J. Ruth of Loughborough. The man watched Ursula closely from his keen, twinkling eyes. His fair hair was wispy on his grimed forehead. Two dirty children appeared to see who was talking.

Ursula glanced at the great lock gates. They were shut, and the water was sounding, spurting and trickling down in the gloom beyond. On this side the bright water was almost to the top of the gate. She went boldly across, and round to the wharf.

Stooping from the bank she peeped into the cabin, where was a red glow of fire and the shadowy figure of a woman. She *did* want to go down.

"You'll mess your frock," said the man, warningly.

"I'll be careful," she answered. "May I come?"

"Ay, come if you like."

She gathered her skirts, lowered her foot to the side of the boat, and leapt down, laughing. Coal-dust flew up.

The woman came to the door. She was plump and sandy-haired, young, with an odd, stubby nose.

"Oh, you *will* make a mess of yourself," she cried, surprised and laughing with a little wonder.

"I did want to see. Isn't it lovely living on a barge?" asked Ursula.

"I don't live on one altogether," said the woman cheerfully.

"She's got her parlour an' her plush suite in Loughborough," said her husband with just pride.

Ursula peeped into the cabin, where saucepans were boiling and some dishes were on the table. It was very hot. Then she came out again. The man was talking to the baby. It was a blue-eyed, fresh-faced thing with floss of red-gold hair.

"Is it a boy or a girl?" she asked.

"It's a girl—aren't you a girl, eh?" he shouted at the infant, shaking his head. Its little face wrinkled up into the oddest, funniest smile.

"Oh!" cried Ursula. "Oh, the dear! Oh, how nice when she laughs!"

"She'll laugh hard enough," said the father.

"What is her name?" asked Ursula.

"She hasn't got a name, she's not worth one," said the man. "Are you, you fag-end o' nothing?" he shouted to the baby. The baby laughed.

"No we've been that busy, we've never took her to th' registry office," came the woman's voice. "She was born on th' boat here."

"But you know what you're going to call her?" asked Ursula.

"We did think of Gladys Em'ly," said the mother.

"We thought of nowt o' th' sort," said the father.

"Hark at him! What *do* you want?" cried the mother in exasperation.

"She'll be called Annabel after th' boat she was born on."

"She's not, so there," said the mother, viciously defiant.

The father sat in humorous malice, grinning.

"Well, you'll see," he said.

And Ursula could tell, by the woman's vibrating exasperation, that he would never give way.

"They're all nice names," she said. "Call her Gladys Annabel Emily."

"Nay, that's heavy-laden, if you like," he answered.

"You see!" cried the woman. "He's that *pig-headed!*"

"And she's so nice, and she laughs, and she hasn't even got a name," crooned Ursula to the child.

"Let me hold her," she added.

He yielded her the child, that smelt of babies. But it had such blue, wide, china blue eyes, and it laughed so oddly, with such a taking grimace, Ursula loved it. She cooed and talked to it. It was such an odd, exciting child.

"What's *your* name?" the man suddenly asked of her.

"My name is Ursula—Ursula Brangwen," she replied.

"Ursula!" he exclaimed, dumbfounded.

"There was a Saint Ursula. It's a very old name," she added hastily, in justification.

"Hey, mother!" he called.

There was no answer.

"Pem!" he called, "can't y'hear?"

"What?" came the short answer.

"What about 'Ursula'?" he grinned.

"What about *what?*" came the answer, and the woman appeared in the doorway, ready for combat.

"Ursula—it's the lass's name there," he said, gently.

The woman looked the young girl up and down. Evidently she was attracted by her slim, graceful, new beauty, her effect of white elegance, and her tender way of holding the child.

"Why, how do you write it?" the mother asked, awkward now she was touched. Ursula spelled out her name. The man looked at the woman. A bright, confused flush came over the mother's face, a sort of luminous shyness.

"It's not a *common* name, is it!" she exclaimed, excited as by an adventure.

"Are you goin' to have it then?" he asked.

"I'd rather have it than Annabel," she said, decisively.

"An' I'd rather have it than Gladys Em'ler," he replied.

There was a silence, Ursula looked up.

"Will you really call her Ursula?" she asked.

"Ursula Ruth," replied the man, laughing vainly, as pleased as if he had found something.

It was now Ursula's turn to be confused.

"It *does* sound awfully nice," she said. "I *must* give her something. And I haven't got anything at all."

She stood in her white dress, wondering, down there in the barge. The lean man sitting near to her watched her as if she were a strange being, as if she lit up his face. His eyes smiled on her, boldly, and yet with exceeding admiration underneath.

"Could I give her my necklace?" she said.

It was the little necklace made of pieces of amethyst and topaz and pearl and crystal, strung at intervals on a little golden chain, which her Uncle Tom had given her. She was very fond of it. She looked at it lovingly, when she had taken it from her neck.

"Is it valuable?" the man asked her, curiously.

"I think so," she replied.

"The stones and pearl are real; it is worth three or four hundred pounds," said Skrebensky from the wharf above. Ursula could tell he disapproved of her.

"I *must* give it to your baby—may I?" she said to the bargee.

He flushed, and looked away into the evening.

"Nay," he said, "it's not for me to say."

"What would your father and mother say?" cried the woman curiously, from the door.

"It is my own," said Ursula, and she dangled the little glittering string before the baby. The infant spread its little fingers. But it could not grasp. Ursula closed the tiny hand over the jewel. The baby waved the bright ends of the string. Ursula had given her necklace away. She felt sad. But she did not want it back.

The jewel swung from the baby's hand and fell in a little heap on the coal-dusty bottom of the barge. The man groped for it, with a kind of careful reverence. Ursula noticed the coarsened, blunted fingers groping at the little jewelled heap. The skin was red on the back of the hand, the fair hairs glistened stiffly. It was a thin, sinewy, capable hand nevertheless, and Ursula liked it. He took up the necklace carefully, and blew the coal-dust from it, as it lay in the hollow of his hand. He seemed still and attentive. He held out his hand with the necklace shining small in its hard, black hollow.

"Take it back," he said.

Ursula hardened with a kind of radiance.

"No," she said. "It belongs to little Ursula."

And she went to the infant and fastened the necklace round its warm, soft, weak little neck.

There was a moment of confusion, then the father bent over his child:

"What do you say?" he said. "Do you say thank you? Do you say thank you, Ursula?"

"Her name's Ursula *now*," said the mother, smiling a little bit ingratiatingly from the door. And she came out to examine the jewel on the child's neck.

"It *is* Ursula, isn't it?" said Ursula Brangwen.

The father looked up at her, with an intimate, half-gallant, half-impudent, but wistful look. His captive soul loved her: but his soul was captive, he knew, always.

She wanted to go. He set a little ladder for her to climb up to the wharf. She kissed the child, which was in its mother's arms, then she turned away. The mother was effusive. The man stood silent by the ladder.

Ursula joined Skrebensky. The two young figures crossed the lock, above the shining yellow water. The barge-man watched them go.

"I *loved* them," she was saying. "He was so gentle—oh, so gentle! And the baby was such a dear!"

"Was he gentle?" said Skrebensky. "The woman had been a servant, I'm sure of that."

Ursula winced.

"But I loved his impudence—it was so gentle underneath."

She went hastening on, gladdened by having met the grimy, lean man with the ragged moustache. He gave her a pleasant warm feeling. He made her feel the richness of her own life. Skrebensky, somehow, had created a deadness round her, a sterility, as if the world were ashes.

They said very little as they hastened home to the big supper. He was envying the lean father of three children, for his impudent directness and his worship of the woman in Ursula, a worship of body and soul together, the man's body and soul wistful and worshipping the body and spirit of the girl, with a desire that knew the inaccessibility of its object, but was only glad to know that the perfect thing existed, glad to have had a moment of communion.

Why could not he himself desire a woman so? Why did he never really want a woman, not with the whole of him: never loved, never worshipped, only just physically wanted her.

But he would want her with his body, let his soul do as it would. A kind of flame of physical desire was gradually beating up in the Marsh, kindled by Tom Brangwen, and by the fact of the wedding of Fred, the shy, fair, stiff-set farmer with the handsome, half-educated girl. Tom Brangwen, with all his secret power, seemed to fan the flame that was rising. The bride was strongly attracted by him, and he was exerting his influence on another beautiful, fair girl, chill and burning as the sea, who said witty things which he appreciated, making her glint with more, like phosphorescence. And her greenish eyes seemed to rock a secret, and her hands like mother-of-pearl seemed luminous, transparent, as if the secret were burning visible in them.

At the end of supper, during dessert, the music began to play, violins, and flutes. Everybody's face was lit up. A glow of excitement prevailed. When the little speeches were over, and the port remained unreached for any more, those who wished were invited out to the open for coffee. The night was warm.

Bright stars were shining, the moon was not yet up. And under the stars burned two great, red, flameless fires, and round these lights and lanterns hung, the marquee stood open before a fire, with its lights inside.

The young people flocked out into the mysterious night. There was sound of laughter and voices, and a scent of coffee. The farm-buildings loomed dark in the background. Figures, pale and dark, flitted about, intermingling. The red fire glinted on a white or a silken skirt, the lanterns gleamed on the transient heads of the wedding guests.

To Ursula it was wonderful. She felt she was a new being. The darkness seemed to breathe like the sides of some great beast, the haystacks loomed half-revealed, a crowd of them, a dark, fecund lair just behind. Waves of delirious darkness ran through her soul. She wanted to let go. She wanted to reach and be amongst the flashing stars, she wanted to race with her feet and be beyond the confines of this earth. She was mad to be gone. It was as if a hound were straining on the leash, ready to hurl itself after a nameless quarry into the dark. And she was the quarry, and she was also the hound. The darkness was passionate and breathing with immense, unperceived heaving. It was waiting to receive her in her flight. And how could she start—and how could she let go? She must leap from the known into the unknown. Her feet and hands beat like a madness, her breast strained as if in bonds.

The music began, and the bonds began to slip. Tom Brangwen was dancing with the bride, quick and fluid and as if in another element, inaccessible as the creatures that move in the water. Fred Brangwen went in with another partner. The music came in waves. One couple after another was washed and absorbed into the deep underwater of the dance.

"Come," said Ursula to Skrebensky, laying her hand on his arm.

At the touch of her hand on his arm, his consciousness melted away from him. He took her into his arms, as if into the sure, subtle power of his will, and they became one movement, one dual movement, dancing on the slippery grass. It would be endless, this movement, it would continue for ever. It was his will and her will locked in a trance of motion, two wills locked in one motion, yet never fusing, never yielding one to the other. It was a glaucous, intertwining, delicious flux and contest in flux.

They were both absorbed into a profound silence, into a deep, fluid underwater energy that gave them unlimited strength. All the dancers were waving intertwined in the flux of music. Shadowy couples passed and repassed before the fire, the dancing feet danced silently by into the darkness. It was a vision of the depths of the underworld, under the great flood.

There was a wonderful rocking of the darkness, slowly, a great, slow swinging of the whole night, with the music playing lightly on the surface, making the strange, ecstatic, rippling on the surface of the dance, but underneath only one great flood heaving slowly backwards to the verge of oblivion, slowly forward to the other verge, the heart sweeping along each time, and tightening with anguish as the limit was reached, and the movement, at crises, turned and swept back.

As the dance surged heavily on, Ursula was aware of some influence looking in upon her. Something was looking at her. Some powerful, glowing sight was looking right into her, not upon her, but right at her. Out of the great distance, and yet imminent, the powerful, overwhelming watch was kept upon her. And she danced on and on with Skrebensky, while the great, white watching continued, balancing all in its revelation.

"The moon has risen," said Anton, as the music ceased, and they found themselves suddenly stranded, like bits of jetsam on a shore. She turned, and saw a great white moon looking at her over the hill. And her breast opened to it, she was cleaved like a transparent jewel to its light. She stood filled with the full moon, offering herself. Her two breasts opened to make way for it, her body opened wide like a quivering anemone, a soft, dilated invitation touched by the moon. She wanted the moon to fill in to her, she wanted more, more communion with the moon, consummation. But Skrebensky put his arm round her, and led her away. He put a big, dark cloak round her, and sat holding her hand, whilst the moonlight streamed above the glowing fires.

She was not there. Patiently she sat, under the cloak, with Skrebensky holding her hand. But her naked self was away there beating upon the moonlight, dashing the moonlight with her breasts and her knees, in meeting, in communion. She half started, to go in actuality, to fling away her clothing and flee away, away from this dark confusion and chaos of people to the hill and the moon. But the people stood round her like stones, like magnetic stones, and she could not go, in actuality. Skrebensky, like a load-stone weighed on her, the weight of his presence detained her. She felt the burden of him, the blind, persistent, inert burden. He was inert, and he weighed upon her. She sighed in pain. Oh, for the coolness and entire liberty and brightness of the moon. Oh, for the cold liberty to be herself, to do entirely as she liked. She wanted to get right away. She felt like bright metal weighted down by dark, impure magnetism. He was the dross, people were the dross. If she could but get away to the clean free moonlight

"Don't [...] night?" said his low voice, the voice of the shadow over her s[...] in the dewy brilliance of the moon, as if she w[...]

"Don[...] the soft voice.

And s[...] ould die. A strange rage filled her, a rage to [...] destructive, like metal blades of destruction

"Let[...]

A da[...] too, in a kind of inertia. He sat inert beside [...] alked towards the moon, silver-white herself

Th[...] e. He appropriated her. There was a fierce, [...] But he held her close, and danced with her. A[...] upon her, bearing her down, was his body [...] her very close, so that she could feel his body [...] ing upon her, overcoming her life and energ[...] m, she felt his hands pressing behind her, upo[...] subdued, cold, indomitable passion. She like[...] to a sort of trance. But it was only a kind of v[...] t intervened between her and her pure bei[...] e let him exert all his power over her, to bea[...] force of his power. She even wished he mi[...] nd unmoved as a pillar of salt.

co[...] ith all its tension to encompass him and co[...] her. He seemed to be annihilated. She was th[...] ance as the moon itself, and beyond him as se[...] er to be grasped or known. If he could only [...] er!

i[...] ces, always together, always his will becom-[...] le, playing upon her. And still he had not got [...] r, intact. But he must weave himself round [...] net of shadow, of darkness, so she would be [...] net of shadows, caught. Then he would have [...] e would enjoy her, when she was caught.

[...] ver, she would not sit down, she walked away. [...] keeping her upon the movement of his walk-[...] he was bright as a piece of moonlight, as bright [...] e clasping a blade that hurt him. Yet he would

[...] yard. There he saw, with something like terror, [...] istening and gleaming transfigured, silvery and [...] sky, throwing dark, substantial shadows, but [...] present. She, like glimmering gossamer, seemed [...] ose like cold fires to the silvery-bluish air. All was [...] glimmering, whitish-steely fires. He was afraid of [...] of the cornstacks rising above him. His heart grew [...] bead. He knew he would die.

See!
I will not
forget you . . .
I have carved
you
on the palm
of my hand.
Isaiah 49:15

She stood for some moments out in the overwhelming luminosity of the moon. She seemed a beam of gleaming power. She was afraid of what she was. Looking at him, at his shadowy, unreal, wavering presence a sudden lust seized her, to lay hold of him and tear him and make him into nothing. Her hands and wrists felt immeasurably hard and strong, like blades. He waited there beside her like a shadow which she wanted to dissipate, destroy as the moonlight destroys a darkness, annihilate, have done with. She looked at him and her face gleamed bright and inspired. She tempted him.

And an obstinacy in him made him put his arm round her and draw her to the shadow. She submitted: let him try what he could do. Let him try what he could do. He leaned against the side of the stack, holding her. The stack stung him keenly with a thousand cold, sharp flames. Still obstinately he held her.

And timorously, his hands went over her, over the salt, compact brilliance of her body. If he could but have her, how he would enjoy her! If he could but net her brilliant, cold, salt-burning body in the soft iron of his own hands, net her, capture her, hold her down, how madly he would enjoy her. He strove subtly, but with all his energy, to enclose her, to have her. And always she was burning and brilliant and hard as salt, and deadly. Yet obstinately, all his flesh burning and corroding, as if he were invaded by some consuming, scathing poison, still he persisted, thinking at last he might overcome her. Even, in his frenzy, he sought for her mouth with his mouth, though it was like putting his face into some awful death. She yielded to him, and he pressed himself upon her in extremity, his soul groaning over and over.

She took him in the kiss, hard her kiss seized upon him, hard and fierce and burning corrosive as the moonlight. She seemed to be destroying him. He was reeling, summoning all his strength to keep his kiss upon her, to keep himself in the kiss.

But hard and fierce she had fastened upon him, cold as the moon and burning as a fierce salt. Till gradually his warm, soft iron yielded, yielded, and she was there fierce, corrosive, seething with his destruction, seething like some cruel, corrosive salt around the last substance of his being, destroying him, destroying him in the kiss. And her soul crystallised with triumph, and his soul was dissolved with agony and annihilation. So she held him there, the victim, consumed, annihilated. She had triumphed: he was not any more.

Gradually she began to come to herself. Gradually a sort of daytime consciousness came back to her. Suddenly the night was struck back into its old, accustomed, mild reality. Gradually she realised that the night was common and ordinary, that the great, blistering, transcendent night did not really exist. She was overcome with slow horror. Where was she? What was this nothingness she felt? The nothingness was Skrebensky. Was he really there?—who was he? He was silent, he was not there. What had happened? Had she been mad: what horrible thing had possessed her? She was filled with overpowering fear of herself, overpowering desire that it should not be, that other burning, corrosive self. She was seized with a frenzied desire that what had been should never be remembered, never be thought of, never be for one moment allowed possible. She denied it with all her might. With all her might she turned away from it. She was good, she was loving. Her heart was warm, her blood was dark and warm and soft. She laid her hand caressively on Anton's shoulder.

"Isn't it lovely?" she said, softly, coaxingly, caressingly. And she began to caress him to life again. For he was dead. And she intended that he should never know, never become aware of what had been. She would bring him back from the dead without leaving him one trace of fact to remember his annihilation by.

She exerted all her ordinary, warm self, she touched him, she did him homage of loving awareness. And gradually he came back to her, another man. She was soft and winning and caressing. She was his servant, his adoring slave. And she restored the whole shell of him. She restored the whole form and figure of him. But the core was gone. His pride was bolstered up, his blood ran once more in pride. But there was no core to him: as a distinct male he had no core. His triumphant, flaming, overweening heart of the intrinsic male would never beat again. He would be subject now, reciprocal, never the indomitable thing with a core of overweening, unabateable fire. She had abated that fire, she had broken him.

But she caressed him. She would not have him remember what had been. She would not remember herself.

"Kiss me, Anton, kiss me," she pleaded.

He kissed her, but she knew he could not touch her. His arms were round her, but they had not got her. She could feel his mouth upon her, but she was not at all compelled by it.

"Kiss me," she whispered, in acute distress, "kiss me."

And he kissed her as she bade him, but his heart was hollow. She took his kisses, outwardly. But her soul was empty and finished.

Looking away, she saw the delicate glint of oats dangling from the side of the stack, in the moonlight, something proud and royal, and quite impersonal. She had been proud with them, where they were, she had been also. But in this temporary warm world of the commonplace, she was a kind, good girl. She reached out yearningly for goodness and affection. She wanted to be kind and good.

They went home through the night that was all pale and glowing around, with shadows and glimmerings and presences. Distinctly, she saw the flowers in the hedge-bottoms, she saw the thin, raked sheaves flung white upon the thorny hedge.

How beautiful, how beautiful it was! She thought with anguish how wildly happy she was to-night, since he had kissed her. But as he walked with his arm round her waist, she turned with a great offering of herself to the night that glistened tremendous, a magnificent godly moon white and candid as a bridegroom, flowers silvery and transformed filling up the shadows.

He kissed her again, under the yew trees at home, and she left him. She ran from the intrusion of her parents at home, to her bedroom, where, looking out on the moonlit country, she stretched up her arms, hard, hard, in bliss, agony offering herself to the blond, debonair presence of the night.

But there was a wound of sorrow, she had hurt herself, as if she had bruised herself, in annihilating him. She covered up her two young breasts with her hands, covering them to herself; and covering herself with herself, she crouched in bed, to sleep.

In the morning the sun shone, she got up strong and dancing. Skrebensky was still at the Marsh. He was coming to church. How lovely, how amazing life was! On the fresh Sunday morning she went out to the garden, among the yellows and the deep-vibrating reds of autumn, she smelled the earth and felt the gossamer, the cornfields across the country were pale and unreal, everywhere was the intense silence of the Sunday morning, filled with unacquainted noises. She smelled the body of the earth, it seemed to stir its powerful flank beneath her as she stood. In the bluish air came the powerful exudation, the peace was the peace of strong, exhausted breathing, the reds and yellows and the white gleam of stubble were the quivers and motion of the last subsiding transports and clear bliss of fulfilment.

The church-bells were ringing when he came. She looked up in keen anticipation at his entry. But he was troubled and his pride was hurt. He seemed very much clothed, she was conscious of his tailored suit.

"Wasn't it lovely last night?" she whispered to him.

"Yes," he said. But his face did not open nor become free.

The service and the singing in church that morning passed unnoticed by her. She saw the coloured glow of the windows, the forms of the worshippers. Only she glanced at the book of Genesis, which was her favourite book in the Bible.

"And God blessed Noah and his sons, and said unto them, Be fruitful and multiply and replenish the earth.

"And the fear of you and the dread of you shall be upon every beast of the earth, and upon every fowl of the air, upon all that moveth upon the earth, and upon all the fishes in the sea; into your hand are they delivered.

"Every moving thing that liveth shall be meat for you; even as the green herb have I given you all things."

But Ursula was not moved by the history this morning. Multiplying and replenishing the earth bored her. Altogether it seemed merely a vulgar and stock-raising sort of business. She was left quite cold by man's stock-breeding lordship over beast and fishes.

"And you, be ye fruitful and multiply; bring forth abundantly in the earth, and multiply therein."

In her soul she mocked at this multiplication, every cow becoming two cows, every turnip ten turnips.

"And God said; This is the token of the covenant which I make between me and you and every living creature that is with you, for perpetual generations;

"I do set my bow in the cloud, and it shall be a token of a covenant between me and the earth.

"And it shall come to pass, when I bring a cloud over the earth, that a bow shall be seen in the cloud;

"And I will remember my covenant, which is between me and you and every living creature of all flesh, and the waters shall no more become a flood to destroy all flesh."

"Destroy all flesh," why "flesh" in particular? Who was this lord of flesh? After all, how big was the Flood? Perhaps a few dryads and fauns had just run into the hills and the farther valleys and woods, frightened, but most had gone on blithely unaware of any flood at all, unless the nymphs should tell them. It pleased Ursula to think of the naiads in Asia Minor meeting the nereids at the mouth of the streams, where the sea washed against the fresh, sweet tide, and calling to their sisters the news of Noah's Flood. They would tell amusing accounts of Noah in his ark. Some nymphs would relate how they had hung on the side of the ark, peeped in, and heard Noah and Shem and Ham and Japeth, sitting in their place under the rain, saying, how they four were the only men on earth now, because the Lord had drowned all the rest, so that they four would have everything to themselves, and be masters of every thing, sub-tenants under the great Proprietor.

Ursula wished she had been a nymph. She would have laughed through the window of the ark, and flicked drops of the flood at Noah, before she drifted away to people who were less important in their Proprietor and their Flood.

What was God, after all? If maggots in a dead dog be but God kissing carrion, what then is not God? She was surfeited of this God. She was weary of the Ursula Brangwen who felt troubled about God. What ever God was, He was, and there was no need for her to trouble about Him. She felt she had now all licence.

Skrebensky sat beside her, listening to the sermon, to the voice of law and order. "The very hairs of your head are all numbered." He did not believe it. He believed his own things were quite at his own disposal. You could do as you liked with your own things, so long as you left other people's alone.

Ursula caressed him and made love to him. Nevertheless he knew she wanted to react upon him and to destroy his being. She was not with him, she was against him. But her making love to him, her complete admiration of him, in open life, gratified him.

She caught him out of himself, and they were lovers, in a young, romantic, almost fantastic way. He gave her a little ring. They put it in Rhine wine, in their glass, and she drank, then he drank. They drank till the ring lay exposed at the bottom of the glass. Then she took the simple jewel, and tied it on a thread round her neck, where she wore it.

He asked her for a photograph when he was going away. She went in great excitement to the photographer, with five shillings. The result was an ugly little picture of herself with her mouth on one side. She wondered over it and admired it.

He saw only the live face of the girl. The picture hurt him. He kept it, he always remembered it, but he could scarcely bear to see it. There was a hurt to his soul in the clear, fearless face that was touched with abstraction. Its abstraction was certainly away from him.

Then war was declared with the Boers in South Africa, and everywhere was a fizz of excitement. He wrote that he might have to go. And he sent her a box of sweets.

She was slightly dazed at the thought of his going to the war, not knowing how to feel. It was a sort of romantic situation that she knew so well in fiction she hardly understood it in fact. Underneath a top elation was a sort of dreariness, deep, ashy disappointment.

However, she secreted the sweets under her bed, and ate them all herself, when she went to bed, and when she woke in the morning. All the time she felt very guilty and ashamed, but she simply did not want to share them.

That box of sweets remained stuck in her mind afterwards. Why had she secreted them and eaten them every one? Why? She did not feel guilty—she only knew she ought to feel guilty. And she could not make up her mind. Curiously monumental that box of sweets stood up, now it was empty. It was a crux for her. What was she to think of it?

The idea of war altogether made her feel uneasy, uneasy. When men began organised fighting with each other it seemed to her as if the poles of the universe were cracking, and the whole might go tumbling into the bottomless pit. A horrible bottomless feeling she had. Yet of course there was the minted superscription of romance and honour and even religion about war. She was very confused.

Skrebensky was busy, he could not come to see her. She asked for no assurance, no security. What was between them, was, and could not be altered by avowals. She knew that by instinct, she trusted to the intrinsic reality.

But she felt an agony of helplessness. She could do nothing. Vaguely she knew the huge powers of the world rolling and crashing together, darkly, clumsily, stupidly, yet colossal, so that one was brushed along almost as dust. Helpless, helpless, swirling like dust! Yet she wanted so hard to rebel, to rage, to fight. But with what?

Could she with her hands fight the face of the earth, beat the hills in their places? Yet her breast wanted to fight, to fight the whole world. And these two small hands were all she had to do it with.

The months went by, and it was Christmas—the snowdrops came. There was a little hollow in the wood near Cossethay, where snowdrops grew wild. She sent him some in a box, and he wrote her a quick little note of thanks—very grateful and wistful he seemed. Her eyes grew childlike and puzzled. Puzzled from day to day she went on, helpless, carried along by all that must happen.

He went about at his duties, giving himself up to them. At the bottom of his heart his self, the soul that aspired and had true hope of self-effectuation lay as dead, still-born, a dead weight in his womb. Who was he, to hold important his personal connection? What did a man matter personally? He was just a brick in the whole great social fabric, the nation, the modern humanity. His personal movements were small, and entirely subsidiary. The whole form must be ensured, not ruptured, for any personal reason whatsoever, since no personal reason could justify such a breaking. What did personal intimacy matter? One had to fill one's place in the whole, the great scheme of man's elaborate civilisation, that was all. The Whole mattered—but the unit, the person, had no importance, except as he represented the Whole.

So Skrebensky left the girl out and went his way, serving what he had to serve, and enduring what he had to endure, without remark. To his own intrinsic life, he was dead. And he could not rise again from the dead. His soul lay in the tomb. His life lay in the established order of things. He had his five senses too. They were to be gratified. Apart from this, he represented the great, established, extant Idea of life, and as this he was important and beyond question.

The good of the greatest number was all that mattered. That which was the greatest good for them all, collectively, was the greatest good for the individual. And so, every man must give himself to support the state, and so labour for the greatest good of all. One might make improvements in the state, perhaps, but always with a view to preserving it intact.

No highest good of the community, however, would give him the vital fulfilment of his soul. He knew this. But he did not consider the soul of the individual sufficiently important. He believed a man was important in so far as he represented all humanity.

He could not see, it was not born in him to see, that the highest good of the community as it stands is no longer the highest good of even the average individual. He thought that, because the community represents millions of people, therefore it must be millions of times more important than any individual, forgetting that the community is an abstraction from the many, and is not the many themselves. Now when the statement of the abstract good for the community has become a formula lacking in all inspiration or value to the average intelligence, then the "common good" becomes a general nuisance, representing the vulgar, conservative materialism at a low level.

And by the highest good of the greatest number is chiefly meant the material prosperity of all classes. Skrebensky did not really care about his own material prosperity. If he had been penniless—well, he would have taken his chances. Therefore, how could he find his highest good in giving up his life for the material prosperity of everybody else! What he considered an unimportant thing for himself he could not think worthy of every sacrifice on behalf of other people. And that which he would consider of the deepest importance to himself as an individual—oh, he said, you mustn't consider the community from that standpoint. No—no—we know what the community wants; it wants something solid, it wants good wages, equal opportunities, good conditions of living, that's what the community wants. It doesn't want anything subtle or difficult. Duty is very plain—keep in mind the material, the immediate welfare of every man, that's all.

So there came over Skrebensky a sort of nullity, which more and more terrified Ursula. She felt there was something hopeless which she had to submit to. She felt a great sense of disaster impending. Day after day was made inert with a sense of disaster. She became morbidly sensitive, depressed, apprehensive. It was anguish to her when she saw one rook slowly flapping in the sky. That was a sign of ill-omen. And the foreboding became so black and so powerful in her, that she was almost extinguished.

Yet what was the matter? At the worst he was only going away. Why did she mind, what was it she feared? She did not know. Only she had a black dread possessing her. When she went at night and saw the big, flashing stars they seemed terrible, by day she was always expecting some charge to be made against her.

He wrote in March to say that he was going to South Africa in a short time, but before he went, he would snatch a day at the Marsh.

As if in a painful dream, she waited suspended, unresolved. She did not know, she could not understand. Only she felt that all the threads of her fate were being held taut, in suspense. She only wept sometimes as she went about, saying blindly:

"I am so fond of him, I am so fond of him."

He came. But why did he come? She looked at him for a sign. He gave no sign. He did not even kiss her. He behaved as if he were an affable, usual acquaintance. This was superficial, but what did it hide? She waited for him, she wanted him to make some sign.

So the whole of the day they wavered and avoided contact, until evening. Then, laughing, saying he would be back in six months' time and would tell them all about it, he shook hands with her mother and took his leave.

Ursula accompanied him into the lane. The night was windy, the yew trees seethed and hissed and vibrated. The wind seemed to rush about among the chimneys and the church-tower. It was dark.

The wind blew Ursula's face, and her clothes cleaved to her limbs. But it was a surging, turgid wind, instinct with compressed vigour of life. And she seemed to have lost Skrebensky. Out there in the strong, urgent night she could not find him.

"Where are you?" she asked.

"Here," came his bodiless voice.

And groping, she touched him. A fire like lightning drenched them.

"Anton?" she said.

"What?" he answered.

She held him with her hands in the darkness, she felt his body again with hers.

"Don't leave me—come back to me," she said.

"Yes," he said, holding her in his arms.

But the male in him was scotched by the knowledge that she was not under his spell nor his influence. He wanted to go away from her. He rested in the knowledge that to-morrow he was going away, his life was really elsewhere. His life was elsewhere—his life was elsewhere—the centre of his life was not what she would have. She was different—there was a breach between them. They were hostile worlds.

"You will come back to me?" she reiterated.

"Yes," he said. And he meant it. But as one keeps an appointment, not as a man returning to his fulfilment.

So she kissed him, and went indoors, lost. He walked down to the Marsh abstracted. The contact with her hurt him, and threatened him. He shrank, he had to be free of her spirit. For she would stand before him, like the angel before Balaam, and drive him back with a sword from the way he was going, into a wilderness.

The next day she went to the station to see him go. She looked at him, she turned to him, but he was always so strange and null—so null. He was so collected. She thought it was that which made him null. Strangely nothing he was.

Ursula stood near him with a mute, pale face which he would rather not see. There seemed some shame at the very root of life, cold, dead shame for her.

The three made a noticeable group on the station; the girl in her fur cap and tippet and her olive green costume, pale, tense with youth, isolated, unyielding; the soldierly young man in a crush hat and a heavy overcoat, his face rather pale and reserved above his purple scarf, his whole figure neutral; then the elder man, a fashionable bowler hat pressed low over his dark brows, his face warm-coloured and calm, his whole figure curiously suggestive of full-blooded indifference; he was the eternal audience, the chorus, the spectator at the drama; in his own life he would have no drama.

The train was rushing up. Ursula's heart heaved, but the ice was frozen too strong upon it.

"Good-bye," she said, lifting her hand, her face laughing with her peculiar, blind, almost dazzling laugh. She wondered what he was doing, when he stooped and kissed her. He should be shaking hands and going.

"Good-bye," she said again.

He picked up his little bag and turned his back on her. There was a hurry along the train. Ah, here was his carriage. He took his seat. Tom Brangwen shut the door, and the two men shook hands as the whistle went.

"Good-bye—and good luck," said Brangwen.

"Thank you—good-bye."

The train moved off. Skrebensky stood at the carriage window, waving, but not really looking to the two figures, the girl and the warm-coloured, almost effeminately-dressed man. Ursula waved her handkerchief. The train gathered speed, it grew smaller and smaller. Still it ran in a straight line. The speck of white vanished. The rear of the train was small in the distance. Still she stood on the platform, feeling a great emptiness about her. In spite of herself her mouth was quivering: she did not want to cry: her heart was dead cold.

Her Uncle Tom had gone to an automatic machine, and was getting matches.

"Would you like some sweets?" he said, turning round.

Her face was covered with tears, she made curious, downward grimaces with her mouth, to get control. Yet her heart was not crying—it was cold and earthy.

"What kind would you like—any?" persisted her uncle.

"I should love some peppermint drops," she said, in a strange, normal voice, from her distorted face. But in a few moments she had gained control of herself, and was still, detached.

"Let us go into the town," he said, and he rushed her into a train, moving to the town station. They went to a café to drink coffee, she sat looking at people in the street, and a great wound was in her breast, a cold imperturbability in her soul.

This cold imperturbability of spirit continued in her now. It was as if some disillusion had frozen upon her, a hard disbelief. Part of her had gone cold, apathetic. She was too young, too baffled to understand, or even to know that she suffered much. And she was too deeply hurt to submit.

She had her blind agonies, when she wanted him, she wanted him. But from the moment of his departure, he had become a visionary thing of her own. All her roused torment and passion and yearning she turned to him.

She kept a diary, in which she wrote impulsive thoughts. Seeing the moon in the sky, her own heart surcharged, she went and wrote:

"If I were the moon, I know where I would fall down."

It meant so much to her, that sentence—she put into it all the anguish of her youth and her young passion and yearning. She called to him from her heart wherever she went, her limbs vibrated with anguish towards him wherever she was, the radiating force of her soul seemed to travel to him, endlessly, endlessly, and in her soul's own creation, find him.

But who was he, and where did he exist? In her own desire only.

She received a post-card from him, and she put it in her bosom. It did not mean much to her, really. The second day, she lost it, and never even remembered she had had it, till some days afterwards.

The long weeks went by. There came the constant bad news of the war. And she felt as if all, outside there in the world, were a hurt, a hurt against her. And something in her soul remained cold, apathetic, unchanging.

Her life was always only partial at this time, never did she live completely. There was the cold, unliving part of her. Yet she was madly sensitive. She could not bear herself. When a dirty, red-eyed old woman came begging of her in the street, she started away as from an unclean thing. And then, when the old woman shouted acrid insults after her, she winced, her limbs palpitated with insane torment, she could not bear herself. Whenever she thought of the red-eyed old woman, a sort of madness ran in inflammation over her flesh and her brain, she almost wanted to kill herself.

And in this state, her sexual life flamed into a kind of disease within her. She was so overwrought and sensitive, that the mere touch of coarse wool seemed to tear her nerves.

XII

SHAME

Ursula had only two more terms at school. She was studying for her matriculation examination. It was dreary work, for she had very little intelligence when she was disjointed from happiness. Stubbornness and a consciousness of impending fate kept her half-heartedly pinned to it. She knew that soon she would want to become a self-responsible person, and her dread was that she would be prevented. An all-containing will in her for complete independence, complete social independence, complete independence from any personal authority, kept her dullishly at her studies. For she knew that she had always her price of ransom—her femaleness. She was always a woman, and what she could not get because she was a human being, fellow to the rest of mankind, she would get because she was a female, other than the man. In her femaleness she felt a secret riches, a reserve, she had always the price of freedom.

However, she was sufficiently reserved about this last resource. The other things should be tried first. There was the mysterious man's world to be adventured upon, the world of daily work and duty, and existence as a working member of the community. Against this she had a subtle grudge. She wanted to make her conquest also of this man's world.

So she ground away at her work, never giving it up. Some things she liked. Her subjects were English, Latin, French, mathematics and history. Once she knew how to read French and Latin, the syntax bored her. Most tedious was the close study of English literature. Why should one remember the things one read? Something in mathematics, their cold absoluteness, fascinated her, but the actual practice was tedious. Some people in history puzzled her and made her ponder, but the political parts angered her, and she hated ministers. Only in odd streaks did she get a poignant sense of acquisition and enrichment and enlarging from her studies; one afternoon, reading *As You Like It;* once when, with her blood, she heard a passage of Latin, and she knew how the blood beat in a Roman's body; so that ever after she felt she knew the Romans by contact. She enjoyed the vagaries of English Grammar, because it gave her pleasure to detect the live movements of words and sentences; and mathematics, the very sight of the letters in Algebra, had a real lure for her.

She felt so much and so confusedly at this time, that her face got a queer, wondering, half-scared look, as if she were not sure what might seize upon her at any moment out of the unknown.

Odd little bits of information stirred unfathomable passion in her. When she knew that in the tiny brown buds of autumn were folded, minute and complete, the finished flowers of the summer nine months hence, tiny, folded up, and left there waiting, a flash of triumph and love went over her.

"I could never die while there was a tree," she said passionately, sententiously, standing before a great ash in worship.

It was the people who, somehow, walked as an upright menace to her. Her life at this time was unformed, palpitating, essentially shrinking from all touch. She gave something to other people, but she was never herself, since she *had* no self. She was not afraid nor ashamed before trees, and birds, and the sky. But she shrank violently from people, ashamed she was not as they were, fixed, emphatic, but a wavering, undefined sensibility only, without form or being.

Gudrun was at this time a great comfort and shield to her. The younger girl was a lithe, *farouche* animal, who mistrusted all approach, and would have none of the petty secrecies and jealousies of schoolgirl intimacy. She would have no truck with the tame cats, nice or not, because she believed that they were all only untamed cats with a nasty, untrustworthy habit of tameness.

This was a great stand-back for Ursula, who suffered agonies when she thought a person disliked her, no matter how much she despised that other person. How could anyone dislike *her*, Ursula Brangwen? The question terrified her and was unanswerable. She sought refuge in Gudrun's natural, proud indifference.

It had been discovered that Gudrun had a talent for drawing. This solved the problem of the girl's indifference to all study. It was said of her, "She can draw marvellously."

Suddenly Ursula found a queer awareness existed between herself and her class-mistress, Miss Inger. The latter was a rather beautiful woman of twenty-eight, a fearless-seeming, clean type of modern girl whose very independence betrays her sorrow. She was clever, and expert in what she did, accurate, quick, commanding.

To Ursula she had always given pleasure, because of her clear, decided, yet graceful appearance. She carried her head high, a little thrown back, and Ursula thought there was a look of nobility in the way she twisted her smooth brown hair upon her head. She always wore clean, attractive, well-fitting blouses, and a well-made skirt. Everything about her was so well-ordered, betraying a fine, clear spirit, that it was a pleasure to sit in her class.

Her voice was just as ringing and clear, and with unwavering, finely-touched modulation. Her eyes were blue, clear, proud, she gave one altogether the sense of a fine-mettled, scrupulously groomed person, and of an unyielding mind. Yet there was an infinite poignancy about her, a great pathos in her lonely, proudly closed mouth.

It was after Skrebensky had gone that there sprang up between the mistress and the girl that strange awareness, then the unspoken intimacy that sometimes connects two people who may never even make each other's acquaintance. Before, they had always been good friends, in the undistinguished way of the class-room, with the professional relationship of mistress and scholar always present. Now, however, another thing came to pass. When they were in the room together, they were aware of each other, almost to the exclusion of everything else. Winifred Inger felt a hot delight in the lessons when Ursula was present, Ursula felt her whole life begin when Miss Inger came into the room. Then, with the beloved, subtly-intimate teacher present, the girl sat as within the rays of some enriching sun, whose intoxicating heat poured straight into her veins.

The state of bliss, when Miss Inger was present, was supreme in the girl, but always eager, eager. As she went home, Ursula dreamed of the schoolmistress, made infinite dreams of things she could give her, of how she might make the elder woman adore her.

Miss Inger was a Bachelor of Arts, who had studied at Newnham. She was a clergyman's daughter, of good family. But what Ursula adored so much was her fine, upright, athletic bearing, and her indomitably proud nature. She was proud and free as a man, yet exquisite as a woman.

The girl's heart burned in her breast as she set off for school in the morning. So eager was her breast, so glad her feet, to travel towards the beloved. Ah, Miss Inger, how straight and fine was her back, how strong her loins, how calm and free her limbs!

Ursula craved ceaselessly to know if Miss Inger cared for her. As yet no definite sign had been passed between the two. Yet surely, surely Miss Inger loved her too, was fond of her, liked her at least more than the rest of the scholars in the class. Yet she was never certain. It might be that Miss Inger cared nothing for her. And yet, and yet, with blazing heart, Ursula felt that if only she could speak to her, touch her, she would know.

The summer term came, and with it the swimming class. Miss Inger was to take the swimming class. Then Ursula trembled and was dazed with passion.

Her hopes were soon to be realised. She would see Miss Inger in her bathing dress.

The day came. In the great bath the water was glimmering pale emerald green, a lovely, glimmering mass of colour within the whitish marble-like confines. Overhead the light fell softly and the great green body of pure water moved under it as someone dived from the side.

Ursula, trembling, hardly able to contain herself, pulled off her clothes, put on her tight bathing-suit, and opened the door of her cabin. Two girls were in the water. The mistress had not appeared. She waited. A door opened. Miss Inger came out, dressed in a rust-red tunic like a Greek girl's, tied round the waist, and a red silk handkerchief round her head. How lovely she looked! Her knees were so white and strong and proud, and she was firm-bodied as Diana. She walked simply to the side of the bath, and with a negligent movement, flung herself in. For a moment Ursula watched the white, smooth, strong shoulders, and the easy arms swimming. Then she too dived into the water.

Now, ah now, she was swimming in the same water with her dear mistress. The girl moved her limbs voluptuously, and swam by herself, deliciously, yet with a craving of unsatisfaction. She wanted to touch the other, to touch her, to feel her.

"I will race you, Ursula," came the well-modulated voice.

Ursula started violently. She turned to see the warm, unfolded face of her mistress looking at her, to her. She was acknowledged. Laughing her own beautiful, startled laugh, she began to swim. The mistress was just ahead, swimming with easy strokes. Ursula could see the head put back, the water flickering upon the white shoulders, the strong legs kicking shadowily. And she swam blinded with passion. Ah, the beauty of the firm, white, cool flesh! Ah, the wonderful firm limbs. Ah, if she did not so despise her own thin, dusky fragment of a body, if only she too were fearless and capable.

She swam on eagerly, not wanting to win, only wanting to be near her mistress, to swim in a race with her. They neared the end of the bath, the deep end. Miss Inger touched the pipe, swung herself round, and caught Ursula round the waist in the water, and held her for a moment.

"I won," said Miss Inger, laughing.

There was a moment of suspense. Ursula's heart was beating so fast, she clung to the rail, and could not move. Her dilated, warm, unfolded, glowing face turned to the mistress, as if to her very sun.

"Good-bye," said Miss Inger, and she swam away to the other pupils, taking professional interest in them.

Ursula was dazed. She could still feel the touch of the mistress's body against her own—only this, only this. The rest of the swimming time passed like a trance. When the call was given to leave the water, Miss Inger walked down the bath towards Ursula. Her rust-red, thin tunic was clinging to her, the whole body was defined, firm and magnificent, as it seemed to the girl.

"I enjoyed our race, Ursula, did you?" said Miss Inger.

The girl could only laugh with revealed, open, glowing face.

The love was now tacitly confessed. But it was some time before any further progress was made. Ursula continued in suspense, in inflamed bliss.

Then one day, when she was alone, the mistress came near to her, and touching her cheek with her fingers, said with some difficulty:

"Would you like to come to tea with me on Saturday, Ursula?"

The girl flushed all gratitude.

"We'll go to a lovely little bungalow on the Soar, shall we? I stay the week-ends there sometimes."

Ursula was beside herself. She could not endure till the Saturday came, her thoughts burned up like a fire. If only it were Saturday, if only it were Saturday.

Then Saturday came, and she set out. Miss Inger met her in Sawley, and they walked about three miles to the bungalow. It was a moist, warm cloudy day.

The bungalow was a tiny, two-roomed shanty set on a steep bank. Everything in it was exquisite. In delicious privacy, the two girls made tea, and then they talked. Ursula need not be home till about ten o'clock.

The talk was led, by a kind of spell, to love. Miss Inger was telling Ursula of a friend, how she had died in childbirth, and what she had suffered; then she told of a prostitute, and of some of her experiences with men.

As they talked thus, on the little verandah of the bungalow, the night fell, there was a little warm rain.

"It is really stifling," said Miss Inger.

They watched a train, whose lights were pale in the lingering twilight, rushing across the distance.

"It will thunder," said Ursula.

The electric suspense continued, the darkness sank, they were eclipsed.

"I think I shall go and bathe," said Miss Inger, out of the cloud-black darkness.

"At night?" said Ursula.

"It is best at night. Will you come?"

"I should like to."

"It is quite safe—the grounds are private. We had better undress in the bungalow, for fear of the rain, then run down."

Shyly, stiffly, Ursula went into the bungalow, and began to remove her clothes. The lamp was turned low, she stood in the shadow. By another chair Winifred Inger was undressing.

Soon the naked, shadowy figure of the elder girl came to the younger.

"Are you ready?" she said.

"One moment."

Ursula could hardly speak. The other naked woman stood by, stood near, silent. Ursula was ready.

They ventured out into the darkness, feeling the soft air of night upon their skins.

"I can't see the path," said Ursula.

"It is here," said the voice, and the wavering, pallid figure was beside her, a hand grasping her arm. And the elder held the younger close against her, close, as they went down, and by the side of the water, she put her arms round her, and kissed her. And she lifted her in her arms, close, saying, softly:

"I shall carry you into the water."

After awhile the rain came down on their flushed, hot limbs, startling, delicious. A sudden, ice-cold shower burst in a great weight upon them. They stood up to it with pleasure. Ursula received the stream of it upon her breasts and her limbs. It made her cold, and a deep, bottomless silence welled up in her, as if bottomless darkness were returning upon her.

So the heat vanished away, she was chilled, as if from a waking up. She ran indoors, a chill, non-existent thing, wanting to get away. She wanted the light, the presence of other people, the external connection with the many. Above all she wanted to lose herself among natural surroundings.

She took her leave of her mistress and returned home. She was glad to be on the station with a crowd of Saturday-night people, glad to sit in the lighted, crowded railway carriage. Only she did not want to meet anybody she knew. She did not want to talk. She was alone, immune.

All this stir and seethe of lights and people was but the rim, the shores of a great inner darkness and void. She wanted very much to be on the seething, partially illuminated shore, for within her was the void reality of dark space.

For a time Miss Inger, her mistress, was gone; she was only a dark void, and Ursula was free as a shade walking in an underworld of extinction, of oblivion. Ursula was glad, with a kind of motionless, lifeless gladness, that her mistress was extinct, gone out of her.

In the morning, however, the love was there again, burning, burning. She remembered yesterday, and she wanted more, always more. She wanted to be with her mistress. All separation from her mistress was a restriction from living. Why could she not go to her to-day, to-day? Why must she pace about revoked at Cossethay whilst her mistress was elsewhere? She sat down and wrote a burning, passionate love-letter: she could not help it.

The two women became intimate. Their lives seemed suddenly to fuse into one, inseparable. Ursula went to Winifred's lodging, she spent there her only living hours. Winifred was very fond of water,—of swimming, of rowing. She belonged to various athletic clubs. Many delicious afternoons the two girls spent in a light boat on the river, Winifred always rowing. Indeed, Winifred seemed to delight in having Ursula in her charge, in giving things to the girl, in filling and enrichening her life.

So that Ursula developed rapidly during the few months of her intimacy with her mistress. Winifred had had a scientific education. She had known many clever people. She wanted to bring Ursula to her own position of thought.

They took religion and rid it of its dogmas, its falsehoods. Winifred humanised it all. Gradually it dawned upon Ursula that all the religion she knew was but a particular clothing to a human aspiration. The aspiration was the real thing,—the clothing was a matter almost of national taste or need. The Greeks had a naked Apollo, the Christians a white-robed Christ, the Buddhists a royal prince, the Egyptians their Osiris. Religions were local and religion was universal. Christianity was a local branch. There was as yet no assimilation of local religions into universal religion.

In religion there were the two great motives of fear and love. The motive of fear was as great as the motive of love. Christianity accepted crucifixion to escape from fear; "Do your worst to me, that I may have no more fear of the worst." But that which was feared was not necessarily all evil, and that which was loved not necessarily all good. Fear shall become reverence, and reverence is submission in identification; love shall become triumph, and triumph is delight in identification.

So much she talked of religion, getting the gist of many writings. In philosophy she was brought to the conclusion that the human desire is the criterion of all truth and all good. Truth does not lie beyond humanity, but is one of the products of the human mind and feeling. There is really nothing to fear. The motive of fear in religion is base, and must be left to the ancient worshippers of power, worship of Moloch. We do not worship power, in our enlightened souls. Power is degenerated to money and Napoleonic stupidity.

Ursula could not help dreaming of Moloch. Her God was not mild and gentle, neither Lamb nor Dove. He was the lion and the eagle. Not because the lion and the eagle had power, but because they were proud and strong; they were themselves, they were not passive subjects of some shepherd, or pets of some loving woman, or sacrifices of some priest. She was weary to death of mild, passive lambs and monotonous doves. If the lamb might lie down with the lion, it would be a great honour to the lamb, but the lion's powerful heart would suffer no diminishing. She loved the dignity and self-possession of lions.

She did not see how lambs could love. Lambs could only be loved. They could only be afraid, and tremblingly submit to fear, and become sacrificial; or they could submit to love, and become beloveds. In both they were passive. Raging, destructive lovers, seeking the moment when fear is greatest, and triumph is greatest, the fear not greater than the triumph, the triumph not greater than the fear, these were no lambs nor doves. She stretched her own limbs like a lion or a wild horse, her heart was relentless in its desires. It would suffer a thousand deaths, but it would still be a lion's heart when it rose from death, a fiercer lion she would be, a surer, knowing herself different from and separate from the great, conflicting universe that was not herself.

Winifred Inger was also interested in the Women's Movement.

"The men will do no more,—they have lost the capacity for doing," said the elder girl. "They fuss and talk, but they are really inane. They make everything fit into an old, inert idea. Love is a dead idea to them. They don't come to one and love one, they come to an idea, and they say 'You are my idea,' so they embrace themselves. As if I were any man's idea! As if I exist because a man has an idea of me! As if I will be betrayed by him, lend him my body as an instrument for his idea, to be a mere apparatus of his dead theory. But they are too fussy to be able to act; they are all impotent, they can't take a woman. They come to their own idea every time, and take that. They are like serpents trying to swallow themselves because they are hungry."

Ursula was introduced by her friend to various women and men, educated, unsatisfied people, who still moved within the smug provincial society as if they were nearly as tame as their outward behaviour showed, but who were inwardly raging and mad.

It was a strange world the girl was swept into, like a chaos, like the end of the world. She was too young to understand it all. Yet the inoculation passed into her, through her love for her mistress.

The examination came, and then school was over. It was the long vacation. Winifred Inger went away to London. Ursula was left alone in Cossethay. A terrible, outcast, almost poisonous despair possessed her. It was no use doing anything, or being anything. She had no connection with other people. Her lot was isolated and deadly. There was nothing for her anywhere, but this black disintegration. Yet, within all the great attack of disintegration upon her, she remained herself. It was the terrible core of all her suffering, that she was always herself. Never could she escape that: she could not put off being herself.

She still adhered to Winifred Inger. But a sort of nausea was coming over her. She loved her mistress. But a heavy, clogged sense of deadness began to gather upon her, from the other woman's contact. And sometimes she thought Winifred was ugly, clayey. Her female hips seemed big and earthy, her ankles and her arms were too thick. She wanted some fine intensity, instead of this heavy cleaving of moist clay, that cleaves because it has no life of its own.

Winifred still loved Ursula. She had a passion for the fine flame of the girl, she served her endlessly, would have done anything for her.

"Come with me to London," she pleaded to the girl. "I will make it nice for you,—you shall do lots of things you will enjoy."

"No," said Ursula, stubbornly and dully. "No, I don't want to go to London, I want to be by myself."

Winifred knew what this meant. She knew that Ursula was beginning to reject her. The fine, unquenchable flame of the younger girl would consent no more to mingle with the perverted life of the elder woman. Winifred knew it would come. But she too was proud. At the bottom of her was a black pit of despair. She knew perfectly well that Ursula would cast her off.

And that seemed like the end of her life. But she was too hopeless to rage. Wisely, economising what was left of Ursula's love, she went away to London, leaving the beloved girl alone.

And after a fortnight, Ursula's letters became tender again, loving. Her Uncle Tom had invited her to go and stay with him. He was managing a big, new colliery in Yorkshire. Would Winifred come too?

For now Ursula was imagining marriage for Winifred. She wanted her to marry her Uncle Tom. Winifred knew this. She said she would come to Wiggiston. She would now let fate do as it liked with her, since there was nothing remaining to be done. Tom Brangwen also saw Ursula's intention. He too was at the end of his desires. He had done the things he had wanted to. They had all ended in a disintegrated lifelessness of soul, which he hid under an utterly tolerant good-humour. He no longer cared about anything on earth, neither man nor woman, nor God nor humanity. He had come to a stability of nullification. He did not care any more, neither about his body nor about his soul. Only he would preserve intact his own life. Only the simple, superficial fact of living persisted. He was still healthy. He lived. Therefore he would fill each moment. That had always been his creed. It was not instinctive easiness: it was the inevitable outcome of his nature. When he was in the absolute privacy of his own life, he did as he pleased, unscrupulous, without any ulterior thought. He believed neither in good nor evil. Each moment was like a separate little island, isolated from time, and blank, unconditioned by time.

He lived in a large new house of red brick, standing outside a mass of homogeneous red-brick dwellings, called Wiggiston. Wiggiston was only seven years old. It had been a hamlet of eleven houses on the edge of healthy, half-agricultural country. Then the great seam of coal had been opened. In a year Wiggiston appeared, a great mass of pinkish rows of thin, unreal dwellings of five rooms each. The streets were like visions of pure ugliness; a grey-black macadamised road, asphalt causeways, held in between a flat succession of wall, window, and door, a new-brick channel that began nowhere, and ended nowhere. Everything was amorphous, yet everything repeated itself endlessly. Only now and then, in one of the house-windows vegetables or small groceries were displayed for sale.

In the middle of the town was a large, open, shapeless space, or market-place, of black trodden earth, surrounded by the same flat material of dwellings, new red-brick becoming grimy, small oblong windows, and oblong doors, repeated endlessly, with just, at one corner, a great and gaudy public-house, and somewhere lost on one of the sides of the square, a large window opaque and darkish green, which was the post-office.

The place had the strange desolation of a ruin. Colliers hanging about in gangs and groups, or passing along the asphalt pavements heavily to work, seemed not like living people, but like spectres. The rigidity of the blank streets, the homogeneous amorphous sterility of the whole suggested death rather than life. There was no meeting place, no centre, no artery, no organic formation. There it lay, like the new foundations of a red-brick confusion rapidly spreading, like a skin-disease.

Just outside of this, on a little hill, was Tom Brangwen's big, red-brick house. It looked from the front upon the edge of the place, a meaningless squalor of ash-pits and closets and irregular rows of the backs of houses, each with its small activity made sordid by barren cohesion with the rest of the small activities. Farther off was the great colliery that went night and day. And all around was the country, green with two winding streams, ragged with gorse, and heath, the darker woods in the distance.

The whole place was just unreal, just unreal. Even now, when he had been there for two years, Tom Brangwen did not believe in the actuality of the place. It was like some gruesome dream, some ugly, dead, amorphous mood become concrete.

Ursula and Winifred were met by the motor-car at the raw little station, and drove through what seemed to them like the horrible raw beginnings of something. The place was a moment of chaos perpetuated, persisting, chaos fixed and rigid. Ursula was fascinated by the many men who were there—groups of men standing in the streets, four or five men walking in a gang together, their dogs running behind or before. They were all decently dressed, and most of them rather gaunt. The terrible gaunt repose of their bearing fascinated her. Like creatures with no more hope, but which still live and have passionate being, within some utterly unliving shell, they passed meaninglessly along, with strange, isolated dignity. It was as if a hard, horny shell enclosed them all.

Shocked and startled, Ursula was carried to her Uncle Tom's house. He was not yet at home. His house was simply, but well furnished. He had taken out a dividing wall, and made the whole front of the house into a large library, with one end devoted to his science. It was a handsome room, appointed as a laboratory and reading room, but giving the same sense of hard, mechanical activity, activity mechanical yet inchoate, and looking out on the hideous abstraction of the town, and at the green meadows and rough country beyond, and at the great, mathematical colliery on the other side.

They saw Tom Brangwen walking up the curved drive. He was getting stouter, but with his bowler hat worn well set down on his brows, he looked manly, handsome, curiously like any other man of action. His colour was as fresh, his health as perfect as ever, he walked like a man rather absorbed.

Winifred Inger was startled when he entered the library, his coat fastened and correct, his head bald to the crown, but not shiny, rather like something naked that one is accustomed to see covered, and his dark eyes liquid and formless. He seemed to stand in the shadow, like a thing ashamed. And the clasp of his hand was so soft and yet so forceful, that it chilled the heart. She was afraid of him, repelled by him, and yet attracted.

He looked at the athletic, seemingly fearless girl, and he detected in her a kinship with his own dark corruption. Immediately, he knew they were akin.

His manner was polite, almost foreign, and rather cold. He still laughed in his curious, animal fashion, suddenly wrinkling up his wide nose, and showing his sharp teeth. The fine beauty of his skin and his complexion, some almost waxen quality, hid the strange, repellent grossness of him, the slight sense of putrescence, the commonness which revealed itself in his rather fat thighs and loins.

Winifred saw at once the deferential, slightly servile, slightly cunning regard he had for Ursula, which made the girl at once so proud and so perplexed.

"But is this place as awful as it looks?" the young girl asked, a strain in her eyes.

"It is just what it looks," he said. "It hides nothing."

"Why are the men so sad?"

"Are they sad?" he replied.

"They seem unutterably, unutterably sad," said Ursula, out of a passionate throat.

"I don't think they are that. They just take it for granted."

"What do they take for granted?"

"This—the pits and the place altogether."

"Why don't they alter it?" she passionately protested.

"They believe they must alter themselves to fit the pits and the place, rather than alter the pits and the place to fit themselves. It is easier," he said.

"And you agree with them," burst out his niece, unable to bear it. "You think like they do—that living human beings must be taken and adapted to all kinds of horrors. We could easily do without the pits."

He smiled, uncomfortably, cynically. Ursula felt again the revolt of hatred from him.

"I suppose their lives are not really so bad," said Winifred Inger, superior to the Zolaesque tragedy.

He turned with his polite, distant attention.

"Yes, they are pretty bad. The pits are very deep, and hot, and in some places wet. The men die of consumption fairly often. But they earn good wages."

"How gruesome!" said Winifred Inger.

"Yes," he replied gravely. It was his grave, solid, self-contained manner which made him so much respected as a colliery manager.

The servant came in to ask where they would have tea.

"Put it in the summer-house, Mrs. Smith," he said.

The fair-haired, good-looking young woman went out.

"Is she married and in service?" asked Ursula.

"She is a widow. Her husband died of consumption a little while ago." Brangwen gave a sinister little laugh. "He lay there in the house-place at her mother's, and five or six other people in the house, and died very gradually. I asked her if his death wasn't a great trouble to her. 'Well,' she said, 'he was very fretful towards the last, never satisfied, never easy, always fret-fretting, an' never knowing what would satisfy him. So in one way it was a relief when it was over—for him and for everybody.' They had only been married two years, and she has one boy. I asked her if she hadn't been very happy. 'Oh, yes, sir, we was very comfortable at first, till he took bad—oh, we was very comfortable—oh, yes—but, you see, you get used to it. I've had my father and two brothers go off just the same. You get used to it.' "

"It's a horrible thing to get used to," said Winifred Inger, with a shudder.

"Yes," he said, still smiling. "But that's how they are. She'll be getting married again directly. One man or another—it does not matter very much. They're all colliers."

"What do you mean?" asked Ursula. "They're all colliers?"

"It is with the women as with us," he replied. "Her husband was John Smith, loader. We reckoned him as a loader, he reckoned himself as a loader, and so she knew he represented his job. Marriage and home is a little side-show. The women know it right enough, and take it for what it's worth. One man or another, it doesn't matter all the world. The pit matters. Round the pit there will always be the sideshows, plenty of 'em."

He looked round at the red chaos, the rigid, amorphous confusion of Wigg-iston.

"Every man his own little side-show, his home, but the pit owns every man. The women have what is left. What's left of this man, or what is left of that—it doesn't matter altogether. The pit takes all that really matters."

"It is the same everywhere," burst out Winifred. "It is the office, or the shop, or the business that gets the man, the woman gets the bit the shop can't digest. What is he at home, a man? He is a meaningless lump—a standing machine, a machine out of work."

"They know they are sold," said Tom Brangwen. "That's where it is. They know they are sold to their job. If a woman talks her throat out, what difference can it make? The man's sold to his job. So the women don't bother. They take what they can catch—and *vogue la galère*."

"Aren't they very strict here?" asked Miss Inger.

"Oh, no. Mrs. Smith has two sisters who have just changed husbands. They're not very particular—neither are they very interested. They go dragging along what is left from the pits. They're not interested enough to be very immoral—it all amounts to the same thing, moral or immoral—just a question of pit-wages. The most moral duke in England makes two hundred thousand a year out of these pits. He keeps the morality end up."

Ursula sat black-souled and very bitter, hearing the two of them talk. There seemed something ghoulish even in their very deploring of the state of things. They seemed to take a ghoulish satisfaction in it. The pit was the great mistress. Ursula looked out of the window and saw the proud, demon-like colliery with her wheels twinkling in the heavens, the formless, squalid mass of the town lying aside. It was the squalid heap of side-shows. The pit was the main show, the *raison d'être* of all.

How terrible it was! There *was* a horrible fascination in it—human bodies and lives subjected in slavery to that symmetric monster of the colliery. There was a swooning, perverse satisfaction in it. For a moment she was dizzy.

Then she recovered, felt herself in a great loneliness, wherein she was sad but free. She had departed. No more would she subscribe to the great colliery, to the great machine which has taken us all captives. In her soul, she was against it, she disowned even its power. It had only to be forsaken to be inane, meaningless. And she knew it was meaningless. But it needed a great, passionate effort of will on her part, seeing the colliery, still to maintain her knowledge that it was meaningless.

But her Uncle Tom and her mistress remained there among the horde, cynically reviling the monstrous state and yet adhering to it, like a man who reviles his mistress, yet who is in love with her. She knew her Uncle Tom perceived what was going on. But she knew moreover that in spite of his criticism and condemnation, he still wanted the great machine. His only happy moments, his only moments of pure freedom were when he was serving the machine. Then, and then only, when the machine caught him up, was he free from the hatred of himself, could he act wholely, without cynicism and unreality.

His real mistress was the machine, and the real mistress of Winifred was the machine. She too, Winifred, worshipped the impure abstraction, the mechanisms of matter. There, there, in the machine, in service of the machine, was she free from the clog and degradation of human feeling. There, in the monstrous mechanism that held all matter, living or dead, in its service, did she achieve her consummation and her perfect unison, her immortality.

Hatred sprang up in Ursula's heart. If she could she would smash the machine. Her soul's action should be the smashing of the great machine. If she could destroy the colliery, and make all the men of Wiggiston out of work, she would do it. Let them starve and grub in the earth for roots, rather than serve such a Moloch as this.

She hated her Uncle Tom, she hated Winifred Inger. They went down to the summer-house for tea. It was a pleasant place among a few trees, at the end of a tiny garden, on the edge of a field. Her Uncle Tom and Winifred seemed to jeer at her, to cheapen her. She was miserable and desolate. But she would never give way.

Her coldness for Winifred should never cease. She knew it was over between them. She saw gross, ugly movements in her mistress, she saw a clayey, inert, unquickened flesh, that reminded her of the great prehistoric lizards. One day her Uncle Tom came in out of the broiling sunshine heated from walking. Then the perspiration stood out upon his head and brow, his hand was wet and hot and suffocating in its clasp. He too had something marshy about him—the succulent moistness and turgidity, and the same brackish, nauseating effect of a marsh, where life and decaying are one.

He was repellent to her, who was so dry and fine in her fire. Her very bones seemed to bid him keep his distance from her.

It was in these weeks that Ursula grew up. She stayed two weeks at Wiggiston, and she hated it. All was grey, dry ash, cold and dead and ugly. But she stayed. She stayed also to get rid of Winifred. The girl's hatred and her sense of repulsiveness in her mistress and in her uncle seemed to throw the other two together. They drew together as if against her.

In hardness and bitterness of soul, Ursula knew that Winifred was become her uncle's lover. She was glad. She had loved them both. Now she wanted to be rid of them both. Their marshy, bitter-sweet corruption came sick and unwholesome in her nostrils. Anything, to get out of the foetid air. She would leave them both for ever, leave for ever their strange, soft, half-corrupt element. Anything to get away.

One night Winifred came all burning into Ursula's bed, and put her arms round the girl, holding her to herself in spite of unwillingness, and said,

"Dear, my dear—shall I marry Mr. Brangwen—shall I?"

The clinging, heavy, muddy question weighed on Ursula intolerably.

"Has he asked you?" she said, using all her might of hard resistance.

"He's asked me," said Winifred. "Do you want me to marry him, Ursula?"

"Yes," said Ursula.

The arms tightened more on her.

"I knew you did, my sweet—and I will marry him. You're *fond* of him, aren't you?"

"I've been *awfully* fond of him—ever since I was a child."

"I know—I know. I can see what you like in him. He *is* a man by himself, he has something apart from the rest."

"Yes," said Ursula.

"But he's not like you, my dear—ha, he's not as good as you. There's something even objectionable in him."

Ursula was silent.

"But I'll marry him, my dear—it will be best. Now say you love me."

A sort of profession was extorted out of the girl. Nevertheless her mistress went away sighing, to weep in her own chamber.

In two days' time Ursula left Wiggiston. Miss Inger went to Nottingham. There was an engagement between her and Tom Brangwen, which the uncle seemed to vaunt as if it were an assurance of his validity.

Brangwen and Winifred Inger continued engaged for another term. Then they married. Brangwen had reached the age when he wanted children. He wanted children. Neither marriage nor the domestic establishment meant anything to him. He wanted to propagate himself. He knew what he was doing. He had the instinct of a growing inertia, of a thing that chooses its place of rest in which to lapse into apathy, complete, profound indifference. He would let the machinery carry him; husband, father, pit-manager, warm clay lifted through the recurrent action of day after day by the great machine from which it derived its motion. As for Winifred, she was an educated woman, and of the same sort as himself. She would make a good companion. She was his mate.

XIII

THE MAN'S WORLD

Ursula came back to Cossethay to fight with her mother. Her schooldays were over. She had passed the matriculation examination. Now she came home to face that empty period between school and possible marriage.

At first she thought it would be just like holidays all the time, she would feel just free. Her soul was in chaos, blinded suffering, maimed. She had no will left to think about herself. For a time she must just lapse.

But very shortly she found herself up against her mother. Her mother had, at this time, the power to irritate and madden the girl continuously. There were already seven children, yet Mrs. Brangwen was again with child, the ninth she had borne. One had died of diphtheria in infancy.

Even this fact of her mother's pregnancy enraged the eldest girl. Mrs. Brangwen was so complacent, so utterly fulfilled in her breeding. She would not have the existence at all of anything but the immediate, physical, common things. Ursula inflamed in soul, was suffering all the anguish of youth's reaching for some unknown ordeal, that it can't grasp, can't even distinguish or conceive. Maddened, she was fighting all the darkness she was up against. And part of this darkness was her mother. To limit, as her mother did, everything to the ring of physical considerations, and complacently to reject the reality of anything else, was horrible. Not a thing did Mrs. Brangwen care about, but the children, the house, and a little local gossip. And she *would not* be touched, she would let nothing else live near her. She went about, big with child, slovenly, easy, having a certain lax dignity, taking her own time, pleasing herself, always, always doing things for the children, and feeling that she thereby fulfilled the whole of womanhood.

This long trance of complacent child-bearing had kept her young and undeveloped. She was scarcely a day older than when Gudrun was born. All these years nothing had happened save the coming of the children, nothing had mattered but the bodies of her babies. As her children came into consciousness, as they began to suffer their own fulfilment, she cast them off. But she remained dominant in the house. Brangwen continued in a kind of rich drowse of physical heat, in connection with his wife. They were neither of them quite personal, quite defined as individuals, so much were they pervaded by the physical heat of breeding and rearing their young.

How Ursula resented it, how she fought against the close, physical, limited life of herded domesticity! Calm, placid, unshakeable as ever, Mrs. Brangwen went about in her dominance of physical maternity.

There were battles. Ursula would fight for things that mattered to her. She would have the children less rude and tyrannical, she *would* have a place in the house. But her mother pulled her down, pulled her down. With all the cunning instinct of a breeding animal, Mrs. Brangwen ridiculed and held cheap Ursula's passions, her ideas, her pronunciations. Ursula would try to insist, in her own home, on the right of women to take equal place with men in the field of action and work.

"Ay," said the mother, "there's a good crop of stockings lying ripe for mending. Let that be your field of action."

Ursula disliked mending stockings, and this retort maddened her. She hated her mother bitterly. After a few weeks of enforced domestic life, she had had enough of her home. The commonness, the triviality, the immediate meaninglessness of it all drove her to frenzy. She talked and stormed ideas, she corrected and nagged at the children, she turned her back in silent contempt on her breeding mother, who treated her with supercilious indifference, as if she were a pretentious child not to be taken seriously.

Brangwen was sometimes dragged into the trouble. He loved Ursula, therefore he always had a sense of shame, almost of betrayal, when he turned on her. So he turned fiercely and scathingly, and with a wholesale brutality that made Ursula go white, mute, and numb. Her feelings seemed to be becoming deadened in her, her temper hard and cold.

Brangwen himself was in one of his states of flux. After all these years, he began to see a loophole of freedom. For twenty years he had gone on at this office as a draughtsman, doing work in which he had no interest, because it seemed his allotted work. The growing up of his daughters, their developing rejection of old forms set him also free.

He was a man of ceaseless activity. Blindly, like a mole, he pushed his way out of the earth that covered him, working always away from the physical element in which his life was captured. Slowly, blindly, gropingly, with what initiative was left to him, he made his way towards individual expression and individual form.

At last, after twenty years, he came back to his woodcarving, almost to the point where he had left off his Adam and Eve panel, when he was courting. But now he had knowledge and skill without vision. He saw the puerility of his young conceptions, he saw the unreal world in which they had been conceived. He now had a new strength in his sense of reality. He felt as if he were real, as if he handled real things. He had worked for many years at Cossethay, building the organ for the church, restoring the woodwork, gradually coming to a knowledge of beauty in the plain labours. Now he wanted again to carve things that were utterances of himself.

But he could not quite hitch on—always he was too busy, too uncertain, confused. Wavering, he began to study modelling. To his surprise he found he could do it. Modelling in clay, in plaster, he produced beautiful reproductions, really beautiful. Then he set-to to make a head of Ursula, in high relief, in the Donatello manner. In his first passion, he got a beautiful suggestion of his desire.

But the pitch of concentration would not come. With a little ash in his mouth he gave up. He continued to copy, or to make designs by selecting motives from classic stuff. He loved the Della Robbia and Donatello as he had loved Fra Angelico when he was a young man. His work had some of the freshness, the naïve alertness of the early Italians. But it was only reproduction.

Having reached his limit in modelling, he turned to painting. But he tried water-colour painting after the manner of any other amateur. He got his results but was not much interested. After one or two drawings of his beloved church, which had the same alertness as his modelling, he seemed to be incongruous with the modern atmospheric way of painting, so that his church tower stood up, really stood and asserted its standing, but was ashamed of its own lack of meaning, he turned away again.

He took up jewellery, read Benvenuto Cellini, pored over reproductions of ornament, and began to make pendants in silver and pearl and matrix. The first things he did, in his start of discovery, were really beautiful. Those later were more imitative. But, starting with his wife, he made a pendant each for all his womenfolk. Then he made rings and bracelets.

Then he took up beaten and chiselled metal work. When Ursula left school, he was making a silver bowl of lovely shape. How he delighted in it, almost lusted after it.

All this time his only connection with the real outer world was through his winter evening classes, which brought him into contact with state education. About all the rest, he was oblivious, and entirely indifferent—even about the war. The nation did not exist to him. He was in a private retreat of his own, that had neither nationality, nor any great adherent.

Ursula watched the newspapers, vaguely, concerning the war in South Africa. They made her miserable, and she tried to have as little to do with them as possible. But Skrebensky was out there. He sent her an occasional post-card. But it was as if she were a blank wall in his direction, without windows or outgoing. She adhered to the Skrebensky of her memory.

Her love for Winifred Inger wrenched her life as it seemed from the roots and native soil where Skrebensky had belonged to it, and she was aridly transplanted. He was really only a memory. She revived his memory with strange passion, after the departure of Winifred. He was to her almost the symbol of her real life. It was as if, through him, in him, she might return to her own self, which she was before she had loved Winifred, before this deadness had come upon her, this pitiless transplanting. But even her memories were the work of her imagination.

She dreamed of him and her as they had been together. She could not dream of him progressively, of what he was doing now, of what relation he would have to her now. Only sometimes she wept to think how cruelly she had suffered when he left her—ah, *how* she had suffered! She remembered what she had written in her diary:

"If I were the moon, I know where I would fall down."

Ah, it was a dull agony to her to remember what she had been then. For it was remembering a dead self. All that was dead after Winifred. She knew the corpse of her young, loving self, she knew its grave. And the young loving self she mourned for had scarcely existed, it was the creature of her imagination.

Deep within her a cold despair remained unchanging and unchanged. No one would ever love her now—she would love no one. The body of love was killed in her after Winifred, there was something of the corpse in her. She would live, she would go on, but she would have no lovers, no lover would want her any more. She herself would want no lover. The vividest little flame of desire was extinct in her for ever. The tiny, vivid germ that contained the bud of her real self, her real love, was killed, she would go on growing as a plant, she would do her best to produce her minor flowers, but her leading flower was dead before it was born, all her growth was the conveying of a corpse of hope.

The miserable weeks went on, in the poky house crammed with children. What was her life—a sordid, formless, disintegrated nothing; Ursula Brangwen a person without worth or importance, living in the mean village of Cossethay, within the sordid scope of Ilkeston. Ursula Brangwen, at seventeen, worthless and unvalued, neither wanted nor needed by anybody, and conscious herself of her own dead value. It would not bear thinking of.

But still her dogged pride held its own. She might be defiled, she might be a corpse that should never be loved, she might be a core-rotten stalk living upon the food that others provided; yet she would give in to nobody.

Gradually she became conscious that she could not go on living at home as she was doing, without place or meaning or worth. The very children that went to school held her uselessness in contempt. She must do something.

Her father said she had plenty to do to help her mother. From her parents she would never get more than a hit in the face. She was not a practical person. She thought of wild things, of running away and becoming a domestic servant, of asking some man to take her.

She wrote to the mistress of the High School for advice.

"I cannot see very clearly what you should do, Ursula," came the reply, "unless you are willing to become an elementary school teacher. You have matriculated, and that qualifies you to take a post as uncertificated teacher in any school, at a salary of about fifty pounds a year.

"I cannot tell you how deeply I sympathize with you in your desire to do something. You will learn that mankind is a great body of which you are one useful member, you will take your own place at the great task which humanity is trying to fulfil. That will give you a satisfaction and a self-respect which nothing else could give."

Ursula's heart sank. It was a cold, dreary satisfaction to think of. Yet her cold will acquiesced. This was what she wanted.

"You have an emotional nature," the letter went on, "a quick natural response. If only you could learn patience and self-discipline, I do not see why you should not make a good teacher. The least you could do is to try. You need only serve a year, or perhaps two years, as uncertificated teacher. Then you would go to one of the training colleges, where I hope you would take your degree. I most strongly urge and advise you to keep up your studies always with the intention of taking a degree. That will give you a qualification and a position in the world, and will give you more scope to choose your own way.

"I shall be proud to see one of my girls win her own economical independence, which means so much more than it seems. I shall be glad indeed to know that one more of my girls has provided for herself the means of freedom to choose for herself."

It all sounded grim and desperate. Ursula rather hated it. But her mother's contempt and her father's harshness had made her raw at the quick, she knew the ignominy of being a hanger-on, she felt the festering thorn of her mother's animal estimation.

At length she had to speak. Hard and shut down and silent within herself, she slipped out one evening to the work-shed. She heard the tap-tap-tap of the hammer upon the metal. Her father lifted his head as the door opened. His face was ruddy and bright with instinct, as when he was a youth, his black moustache was cut close over his wide mouth, his black hair was fine and close as ever. But there was about him an abstraction, a sort of instrumental detachment from human things. He was a worker. He watched his daughter's hard, expressionless face. A hot anger came over his breast and belly.

"What now?" he said.

"Can't I," she answered, looking aside, not looking at him, "can't I go out to work?"

"Go out to work, what for?"

His voice was so strong, and ready, and vibrant. It irritated her.

"I want some other life than this."

A flash of strong rage arrested all his blood for a moment.

"Some other life?" he repeated. "Why, what other life do you want?"

She hesitated.

"Something else besides housework and hanging about. And I want to earn something."

Her curious, brutal hardness of speech, and the fierce invincibility of her youth, which ignored him, made him also harden with anger.

"And how do you think *you're* going to earn anything?" he asked.

"I can become a teacher—I'm qualified by my matric."

He wished her matric. in hell.

"And how much are you qualified to earn by your matric?" he asked, jeering.

"Fifty pounds a year," she said.

He was silent, his power taken out of his hand.

He had always hugged a secret pride in the fact that his daughters need not go out to work. With his wife's money and his own they had four hundred a year. They could draw on the capital if need be later on. He was not afraid for his old age. His daughters might be ladies.

Fifty pounds a year was a pound a week—which was enough for her to live on independently.

"And what sort of a teacher do you think *you'd* make? You haven't the patience of a Jack-gnat with your own brothers and sisters, let alone with a class of children. And I thought you didn't like dirty, board-school brats."

"They're not all dirty."

"You'd find they're not all clean."

There was silence in the workshop. The lamplight fell on the burned silver bowl that lay between him, on mallet and furnace and chisel. Brangwen stood with a queer, cat-like light on his face, almost like a smile. But it was no smile.

"Can I try?" she said.

"You can do what the deuce you like, and go where you like."

Her face was fixed and expressionless and indifferent. It always sent him to a pitch of frenzy to see it like that. He kept perfectly still.

Cold, without any betrayal of feeling, she turned and left the shed. He worked on, with all his nerves jangled. Then he had to put down his tools and go into the house.

In a bitter tone of anger and contempt he told his wife. Ursula was present. There was a brief altercation, closed by Mrs. Brangwen's saying, in a tone of biting superiority and indifference:

"Let her find out what it's like. She'll soon have had enough."

The matter was left there. But Ursula considered herself free to act. For some days she made no move. She was reluctant to take the cruel step of finding work, for she shrank with extreme sensitiveness and shyness from new contact, new situations. Then at length a sort of doggedness drove her. Her soul was full of bitterness.

She went to the Free Library in Ilkeston, copied out addresses from the *Schoolmistress,* and wrote for application forms. After two days she rose early to meet the postman. As she expected, there were three long envelopes.

Her heart beat painfully as she went up with them to her bedroom. Her fingers trembled, she could hardly force herself to look at the long, official forms she had to fill in. The whole thing was so cruel, so impersonal. Yet it must be done.

"Name (surname first): .... "

In a trembling hand she wrote, "Brangwen,—Ursula."

"Age and date of birth: .... "

After a long time considering, she filled in that line.

"Qualifications, with date of Examination: .... "

With a little pride she wrote:

"London Matriculation Examination."

"Previous experience and where obtained: .... "

Her heart sank as she wrote:

"None."

Still there was much to answer. It took her two hours to fill in the three forms. Then she had to copy her testimonials from her head-mistress and from the clergyman.

At last, however, it was finished. She had sealed the three long envelopes. In the afternoon she went down to Ilkeston to post them. She said nothing of it all to her parents. As she stamped her long letters and put them into the box at the main post-office she felt as if already she was out of the reach of her father and mother, as if she had connected herself with the outer, greater world of activity, the man-made world.

As she returned home, she dreamed again in her own fashion her old, gorgeous dreams. One of her applications was to Gillingham, in Kent, one to Kingston-on-Thames, and one to Swanwick in Derbyshire.

Gillingham was such a lovely name, and Kent was the Garden of England. So that, in Gillingham, an old, old village by the hopfields, where the sun shone softly, she came out of school in the afternoon into the shadow of the plane trees by the gate, and turned down the sleepy road towards the cottage where cornflowers poked their blue heads through the old wooden fence, and phlox stood built up of blossom beside the path.

A delicate, silver-haired lady rose with delicate, ivory hands uplifted as Ursula entered the room, and:

"Oh, my dear, what do you think!"

"What is it, Mrs. Wetherall?"

Frederick had come home. Nay, his manly step was heard on the stair, she saw his strong boots, his blue trousers, his uniformed figure, and then his face, clean and keen as an eagle's, and his eyes lit up with the glamour of strange seas, ah, strange seas that had woven through his soul, as he descended into the kitchen.

This dream, with its amplifications, lasted her a mile of walking. Then she went to Kingston-on-Thames.

Kingston-on-Thames was an old historic place just south of London. There lived the well-born dignified souls who belonged to the metropolis, but who loved peace. There she met a wonderful family of girls living in a large old Queen Anne house, whose lawns sloped to the river, and in an atmosphere of stately peace she found herself among her soul's intimates. They loved her as sisters, they shared with her all noble thoughts.

She was happy again. In her musings she spread her poor, clipped wings, and flew into the pure empyrean.

Day followed day. She did not speak to her parents. Then came the return of her testimonials from Gillingham. She was not wanted, neither at Swanwick. The bitterness of rejection followed the sweets of hope. Her bright feathers were in the dust again.

Then, suddenly, after a fortnight, came an intimation from Kingston-on-Thames. She was to appear at the Education Office of that town on the following Thursday, for an interview with the Committee. Her heart stood still. She knew she would make the Committee accept her. Now she was afraid, now that her removal was imminent. Her heart quivered with fear and reluctance. But underneath her purpose was fixed.

She passed shadowily through the day, unwilling to tell her news to her mother, waiting for her father. Suspense and fear were strong upon her. She dreaded going to Kingston. Her easy dreams disappeared from the grasp of reality.

And yet, as the afternoon wore away, the sweetness of the dream returned again. Kingston-on-Thames—there was such sound of dignity to her. The shadow of history and the glamour of stately progress enveloped her. The palaces would be old and darkened, the place of kings obscured. Yet it was a place of kings for her—Richard and Henry and Wolsey and Queen Elizabeth. She divined great lawns with noble trees, and terraces whose steps the water washed softly, where the swans sometimes came to earth. Still she must see the stately, gorgeous barge of the Queen float down, the crimson carpet put upon the landing stairs, the gentlemen in their purple-velvet cloaks, bare-headed, standing in the sunshine grouped on either side waiting.

"Sweet Thames, run softly till I end my song."

Evening came, her father returned home, sanguine and alert and detached as ever. He was less real than her fancies. She waited whilst he ate his tea. He took big mouthfuls, big bites, and ate unconsciously with the same abandon an animal gives to its food.

Immediately after tea he went over to the church. It was choir-practice, and he wanted to try the tunes on his organ.

The latch of the big door clicked loudly as she came after him, but the organ rolled more loudly still. He was unaware. He was practising the anthem. She saw his small, jet-black head and alert face between the candle-flames, his slim body sagged on the music-stool. His face was so luminous and fixed, the movements of his limbs seemed strange, apart from him. The sound of the organ seemed to belong to the very stone of the pillars, like sap running in them.

Then there was a close of music and silence.

"Father!" she said.

He looked round as if at an apparition. Ursula stood shadowily within the candle-light.

"What now?" he said, not coming to earth.

It was difficult to speak to him.

"I've got a situation," she said, forcing herself to speak.

"You've got what?" he answered, unwilling to come out of his mood of organ-playing. He closed the music before him.

"I've got a situation to go to."

Then he turned to her, still abstracted, unwilling.

"Oh, where's that?" he said.

"At Kingston-on-Thames. I must go on Thursday for an interview with the Committee."

"You must go on Thursday?"

"Yes."

And she handed him the letter. He read it by the light of the candles.

"Ursula Brangwen, Yew Tree Cottage, Cossethay, Derbyshire.

"Dear Madam, You are requested to call at the above offices on Thursday next, the 10th, at 11.30 a.m., for an interview with the committee, referring to your application for the post of assistant mistress at the Wellingborough Green Schools."

It was very difficult for Brangwen to take in this remote and official information, glowing as he was within the quiet of his church and his anthem music.

"Well, you needn't bother me with it now, need you?" he said impatiently, giving her back the letter.

"I've got to go on Thursday," she said.

He sat motionless. Then he reached more music, and there was a rushing sound of air, then a long, emphatic trumpet-note of the organ, as he laid his hands on the keys. Ursula turned and went away.

He tried to give himself again to the organ. But he could not. He could not get back. All the time a sort of string was tugging, tugging him elsewhere, miserably.

So that when he came into the house after choir-practice his face was dark and his heart black. He said nothing, however, until all the younger children were in bed. Ursula, however, knew what was brewing.

At length he asked:

"Where's that letter?"

She gave it to him. He sat looking at it. "You are requested to call at the above offices on Thursday next——" It was a cold, official notice to Ursula herself and had nothing to do with him. So! She existed now as a separate social individual. It was for her to answer this note, without regard to him. He had even no right to interfere. His heart was hard and angry.

"You had to do it behind our backs, had you?" he said, with a sneer. And her heart leapt with hot pain. She knew she was free—she had broken away from him. He was beaten.

"You said, 'let her try,' " she retorted, almost apologising to him.

He did not hear. He sat looking at the letter.

"Education Office, Kingston-on-Thames"—and then the typewritten "Miss Ursula Brangwen, Yew Tree Cottage, Cossethay." It was all so complete and so final. He could not but feel the new position Ursula held, as recipient of that letter. It was an iron in his soul.

"Well," he said at length, "you're not going."

Ursula started and could find no words to clamour her revolt.

"If you think you're going dancin' off to th' other side of London, you're mistaken."

"Why not?" she cried, at once hard fixed in her will to go.

"That's why not," he said.

And there was silence till Mrs. Brangwen came downstairs.

"Look here, Anna," he said, handing her the letter.

She put back her head, seeing a typewritten letter, anticipating trouble from the outside world. There was the curious, sliding motion of her eyes, as if she shut off her sentient, maternal self, and a kind of hard trance, meaningless, took its place. Thus, meaningless, she glanced over the letter, careful not to take it in. She apprehended the contents with her callous, superficial mind. Her feeling self was shut down.

"What post is it?" she asked.

"She wants to go and be a teacher in Kingston-on-Thames, at fifty pounds a year."

"Oh, indeed."

The mother spoke as if it were a hostile fact concerning some stranger. She would have let her go, out of callousness. Mrs. Brangwen would begin to grow up again only with her youngest child. Her eldest girl was in the way now.

"She's not going all that distance," said the father.

"I have to go where they want me," cried Ursula. "And it's a good place to go to."

"What do *you* know about the place?" said her father harshly.

"And it doesn't matter whether they want you or not, if your father says you are not to go," said the mother calmly.

How Ursula hated her!

"You said I was to try," the girl cried. "Now I've got a place and I'm going to go."

"You're not going all that distance," said her father.

"Why don't you get a place at Ilkeston, where you can live at home?" asked Gudrun, who hated conflicts, who could not understand Ursula's uneasy way, yet who must stand by her sister.

"There aren't any places in Ilkeston," cried Ursula. "And I'd rather go right away."

"If you'd asked about it, a place could have been got for you in Ilkeston. But you had to play Miss High-an'-mighty, and go your own way," said her father.

"I've no doubt you'd rather go right away," said her mother, very caustic. "And I've no doubt you'd find other people didn't put up with you for very long either. You've too much opinion of yourself for your good."

Between the girl and her mother was a feeling of pure hatred. There came a stubborn silence. Ursula knew she must break it.

"Well, they've written to me, and I s'll have to go," she said.

"Where will you get the money from?" asked her father.

"Uncle Tom will give it me," she said.

Again there was silence. This time she was triumphant.

Then at length her father lifted his head. His face was abstracted, he seemed to be abstracting himself, to make a pure statement.

"Well, you're not going all that distance away," he said. "I'll ask Mr. Burt about a place here. I'm not going to have you by yourself at the other side of London."

"But I've *got* to go to Kingston," said Ursula. "They've sent for me."

"They'll do without you," he said.

There was a trembling silence when she was on the point of tears.

"Well," she said, low and tense, "you can put me off this, but I'm *going* to have a place. I'm *not* going to stop at home."

"Nobody wants you to stop at home," he suddenly shouted, going livid with rage.

She said no more. Her nature had gone hard and smiling in its own arrogance, in its own antagonistic indifference to the rest of them. This was the state in which he wanted to kill her. She went singing into the parlour.

> "C'est la mère Michel qui a perdu son chat,
> Qui cri par la fenêtre qu'est-ce qui le lui rendra——"

During the next days Ursula went about bright and hard, singing to herself, making love to the children, but her soul hard and cold with regard to her parents. Nothing more was said. The hardness and brightness lasted for four days. Then it began to break up. So at evening she said to her father:

"Have you spoken about a place for me?"

"I spoke to Mr. Burt."

"What did he say?"

"There's a committee meeting to-morrow. He'll tell me on Friday."

So she waited till Friday. Kingston-on-Thames had been an exciting dream. Here she could feel the hard, raw reality. So she knew that this would come to pass. Because nothing was ever fulfilled, she found, except in the hard limited reality. She did not want to be a teacher in Ilkeston, because she knew Ilkeston, and hated it. But she wanted to be free, so she must take her freedom where she could.

On Friday her father said there was a place vacant in Brinsley Street school. This could most probably be secured for her, at once, without the trouble of application.

Her heart halted. Brinsley Street was a school in a poor quarter, and she had had a taste of the common children of Ilkeston. They had shouted after her and thrown stones. Still, as a teacher, she would be in authority. And it was all unknown. She was excited. The very forest of dry, sterile brick had some fascination for her. It was so hard and ugly, so relentlessly ugly, it would purge her of some of her floating sentimentality.

She dreamed how she would make the little, ugly children love her. She would be so *personal*. Teachers were always so hard and impersonal. There was no vivid relationship. She would make everything personal and vivid, she would give herself, she would give, give, give all her great stores of wealth to her children, she would make them *so* happy, and they would prefer her to any teacher on the face of the earth.

At Christmas she would choose such fascinating Christmas cards for them, and she would give them such a happy party in one of the class-rooms.

The headmaster, Mr. Harby, was a short, thick-set, rather common man, she thought. But she would hold before him the light of grace and refinement, he would have her in such high esteem before long. She would be the gleaming sun of the school, the children would blossom like little weeds, the teachers like tall, hard plants would burst into rare flower.

The Monday morning came. It was the end of September, and a drizzle of fine rain like veils round her, making her seem intimate, a world to herself. She walked forward to the new land. The old was blotted out. The veil would be rent that hid the new world. She was gripped hard with suspense as she went down the hill in the rain, carrying her dinner-bag.

Through the thin rain she saw the town, a black, extensive mount. She must enter in upon it. She felt at once a feeling of repugnance and of excited fulfilment. But she shrank.

She waited at the terminus for the tram. Here it was beginning. Before her was the station to Nottingham, whence Theresa had gone to school half an hour before; behind her was the little church school she had attended when she was a child, when her grandmother was alive. Her grandmother had been dead two years now. There was a strange woman at the Marsh, with her Uncle Fred, and a small baby. Behind her was Cossethay, and blackberries were ripe on the hedges.

As she waited at the tram-terminus she reverted swiftly to her childhood; her teasing grandfather, with his fair beard and blue eyes, and his big, monumental body; he had got drowned: her grandmother, whom Ursula would sometimes say she had loved more than anyone else in the world: the little church school, the Phillips boys; one was a soldier in the Life Guards now, one was a collier. With a passion she clung to the past.

But as she dreamed of it, she heard the tram-car grinding round a bend, rumbling dully, she saw it draw into sight, and hum nearer. It sidled round the loop at the terminus, and came to a standstill, looming above her. Some shadowy grey people stepped from the far end, the conductor was walking in the puddles, swinging round the pole.

She mounted into the wet, comfortless tram, whose floor was dark with wet, whose windows were all steamed, and she sat in suspense. It had begun, her new existence.

One other passenger mounted—a sort of charwoman with a drab, wet coat. Ursula could not bear the waiting of the tram. The bell clanged, there was a lurch forward. The car moved cautiously down the wet street. She was being carried forward, into her new existence. Her heart burned with pain and suspense, as if something were cutting her living tissue.

Often, oh often the tram seemed to stop, and wet, cloaked people mounted and sat mute and grey in stiff rows opposite her, their umbrellas between their knees. The windows of the tram grew more steamy, opaque. She was shut in with these unliving, spectral people. Even yet it did not occur to her that she was one of them. The conductor came down issuing tickets. Each little ring of his clipper sent a pang of dread through her. But her ticket surely was different from the rest.

They were all going to work; she also was going to work. Her ticket was the same. She sat trying to fit in with them. But fear was at her bowels, she felt an unknown, terrible grip upon her.

At Bath Street she must dismount and change trams. She looked uphill. It seemed to lead to freedom. She remembered the many Saturday afternoons she had walked up to the shops. How free and careless she had been!

Ah, her tram was sliding gingerly downhill. She dreaded every yard of her conveyance. The car halted, she rose hastily.

She kept turning her head as the car ran on, because she was uncertain of the street. At last, her heart a flame of suspense, trembling, she rose. The conductor rang the bell brusquely.

She was walking down a small, mean, wet street, empty of people. The school squatted low within its railed, asphalt yard, that shone black with rain. The building was grimy, and horrible, dry plants were shadowily looking through the windows.

She entered the arched doorway of the porch. The whole place seemed to have a threatening expression, imitating the church's architecture, for the purpose of domineering, like a gesture of vulgar authority. She saw that one pair of feet had paddled across the flagstone floor of the porch. The place was silent, deserted, like an empty prison waiting the return of tramping feet.

Ursula went forward to the teachers' room that burrowed in a gloomy hole. She knocked timidly.

"Come in!" called a surprised man's voice, as from a prison cell. She entered the dark little room that never got any sun. The gas was lighted naked and raw. At the table a thin man in shirt-sleeves was rubbing a paper on a jelly-tray. He looked up at Ursula with his narrow, sharp face, said "Good morning," then turned away again, and stripped the paper off the tray, glancing at the violet-coloured writing transferred, before he dropped the curled sheet aside among a heap.

Ursula watched him fascinated. In the gaslight and gloom and the narrowness of the room, all seemed unreal.

"Isn't it a nasty morning," she said.

"Yes," he said, "it's not much of weather."

But in here it seemed that neither morning nor weather really existed. This place was timeless. He spoke in an occupied voice, like an echo. Ursula did not know what to say. She took off her waterproof.

"Am I early?" she asked.

The man looked first at a little clock, then at her. His eyes seemed to be sharpened to needle-points of vision.

"Twenty-five past," he said. "You're the second to come. I'm first this morning."

Ursula sat down gingerly on the edge of a chair, and watched his thin red hands rubbing away on the white surface of the paper, then pausing, pulling up a corner of the sheet, peering, and rubbing away again. There was a great heap of curled white-and-scribbled sheets on the table.

"Must you do so many?" asked Ursula.

Again the man glanced up sharply. He was about thirty or thirty-three years old, thin, greenish, with a long nose and a sharp face. His eyes were blue, and sharp as points of steel, rather beautiful, the girl thought.

"Sixty-three," he answered.

"So many!" she said, gently. Then she remembered.

"But they're not all for your class, are they?" she added.

"Why aren't they?" he replied, a fierceness in his voice.

Ursula was rather frightened by his mechanical ignoring of her, and his directness of statement. It was something new to her. She had never been treated like this before, as if she did not count, as if she were addressing a machine.

"It is too many," she said sympathetically.

"You'll get about the same," he said.

That was all she received. She sat rather blank, not knowing how to feel. Still she liked him. He seemed so cross. There was a queer, sharp, keen-edge feeling about him that attracted her and frightened her at the same time. It was so cold, and against his nature.

The door opened, and a short, neutral-tinted young woman of about twenty-eight appeared.

"Oh, Ursula!" the newcomer exclaimed. "You *are* here early! My word, I'll warrant you don't keep it up. That's Mr. Williamson's peg. *This* is yours. Standard Five teacher always has this. Aren't you going to take your hat off?"

Miss Violet Harby removed Ursula's waterproof from the peg on which it was hung, to one a little farther down the row. She had already snatched the pins from her own stuff hat, and jammed them through her coat. She turned to Ursula, as she pushed up her frizzed, flat, dun-coloured hair.

"Isn't it a beastly morning," she exclaimed, "beastly! And if there's one thing I hate above another it's a wet Monday morning;—pack of kids trailing in anyhow-nohow, and no holding 'em——"

She had taken a black pinafore from a newspaper package, and was tying it round her waist.

"You've brought an apron, haven't you?" she said jerkily, glancing at Ursula. "Oh—you'll want one. You've no idea what a sight you'll look before half-past four, what with chalk and ink and kids' dirty feet.—Well, I can send a boy down to mamma's for one."

"Oh, it doesn't matter," said Ursula.

"Oh, yes—I can send easily," cried Miss Harby.

Ursula's heart sank. Everybody seemed so cocksure and so bossy. How was she going to get on with such jolty, jerky, bossy people? And Miss Harby had not spoken a word to the man at the table. She simply ignored him. Ursula felt the callous crude rudeness between the two teachers.

The two girls went out into the passage. A few children were already clattering in the porch.

"Jim Richards," called Miss Harby, hard and authoritative. A boy came sheepishly forward.

"Shall you go down to our house for me, eh?" said Miss Harby, in a commanding, condescending, coaxing voice. She did not wait for an answer. "Go down and ask mamma to send me one of my school pinas, for Miss Brangwen—shall you?"

The boy muttered a sheepish "Yes, miss," and was moving away.

"Hey," called Miss Harby. "Come here—now what are you going for? What shall you say to mamma?"

"A school pina——" muttered the boy.

" 'Please, Mrs. Harby, Miss Harby says will you send her another school pinafore for Miss Brangwen, because she's come without one.' "

"Yes, miss," muttered the boy, head ducked, and was moving off. Miss Harby caught him back, holding him by the shoulder.

"What are you going to say?"

"Please, Mrs. Harby, Miss Harby wants a pinny for Miss Brangwin," muttered the boy very sheepishly.

"Miss *Brangwen!*" laughed Miss Harby, pushing him away. "Here, you'd better have my umbrella—wait a minute."

The unwilling boy was rigged up with Miss Harby's umbrella, and set off.

"Don't take long over it," called Miss Harby, after him. Then she turned to Ursula, and said brightly:

"Oh, he's a caution, that lad—but not bad, you know."

"No," Ursula agreed, weakly.

The latch of the door clicked, and they entered the big room. Ursula glanced down the place. Its rigid, long silence was official and chilling. Half-way down was a glass partition, the doors of which were open. A clock ticked re-echoing, and Miss Harby's voice sounded double as she said:

"This is the big room—Standard Five-Six-and-Seven.—Here's your place—Five——"

She stood in the near end of the great room. There was a small high teacher's desk facing a squadron of long benches, two high windows in the wall opposite.

It was fascinating and horrible to Ursula. The curious, unliving light in the room changed her character. She thought it was the rainy morning. Then she looked up again, because of the horrid feeling of being shut in a rigid, inflexible air, away from all feeling of the ordinary day; and she noticed that the windows were of ribbed, suffused glass.

The prison was round her now! She looked at the walls, colour washed, pale green and chocolate, at the large windows with frowsy geraniums against the pale glass, at the long rows of desks, arranged in a squadron, and dread filled her. This was a new world, a new life, with which she was threatened. But still excited, she climbed into her chair at her teacher's desk. It was high, and her feet could not reach the ground, but must rest on the step. Lifted up there, off the ground, she was in office. How queer, how queer it all was! How different it was from the mist of rain blowing over Cossethay. As she thought of her own village, a spasm of yearning crossed her, it seemed so far off, so lost to her.

She was here in this hard, stark reality—*reality*. It was queer that she should call this the reality, which she had never known till to-day, and which now so filled her with dread and dislike, that she wished she might go away. This was the reality, and Cossethay, her beloved,. beautiful, well-known Cossethay, which was as herself unto her, that was minor reality. This prison of a school was reality. Here, then, she would sit in state, the queen of scholars! Here she would realise her dream of being the beloved teacher bringing light and joy to her children! But the desks before her had an abstract angularity that bruised her sentiment and made her shrink. She winced, feeling she had been a fool in her anticipations. She had brought her feelings and her generosity to where neither generosity nor emotion were wanted. And already she felt rebuffed, troubled by the new atmosphere, out of place.

She slid down, and they returned to the teacher's room. It was queer to feel that one ought to alter one's personality. She was nobody, there was no reality in herself, the reality was all outside of her, and she must apply herself to it.

Mr. Harby was in the teachers' room, standing before a big, open cupboard, in which Ursula could see piles of pink blotting-paper, heaps of shiny new books, boxes of chalk, and bottles of coloured inks. It looked a treasure store.

The schoolmaster was a short, sturdy man, with a fine head, and a heavy jowl. Nevertheless he was good-looking, with his shapely brows and nose, and his great, hanging moustache. He seemed absorbed in his work, and took no notice of Ursula's entry. There was something insulting in the way he could be so actively unaware of another person, so occupied.

When he had a moment of absence, he looked up from the table and said good-morning to Ursula. There was a pleasant light in his brown eyes. He seemed very manly and incontrovertible, like something she wanted to push over.

"You had a wet walk," he said to Ursula.

"Oh, I don't mind, I'm used to it," she replied, with a nervous little laugh.

But already he was not listening. Her words sounded ridiculous and babbling. He was taking no notice of her.

"You will sign your name here," he said to her, as if she were some child—"and the time when you come and go."

Ursula signed her name in the time book and stood back. No one took any further notice of her. She beat her brains for something to say, but in vain.

"I'd let them in now," said Mr. Harby to the thin man, who was very hastily arranging his papers.

The assistant teacher made no sign of acquiescence, and went on with what he was doing. The atmosphere in the room grew tense. At the last moment Mr. Brunt slipped into his coat.

"You will go to the girls' lobby," said the schoolmaster to Ursula, with a fascinating, insulting geniality, purely official and domineering.

She went out and found Miss Harby, and another girl teacher, in the porch. On the asphalt yard the rain was falling. A toneless bell tang-tang-tanged drearily overhead, monotonously, insistently. It came to an end. Then Mr. Brunt was seen, bare-headed, standing at the other gate of the school yard, blowing shrill blasts on a whistle and looking down the rainy, dreary street.

Boys in gangs and streams came trotting up, running past the master and with a loud clatter of feet and voices, over the yard to the boys' porch. Girls were running and walking through the other entrance.

In the porch where Ursula stood there was a great noise of girls, who were tearing off their coats and hats, and hanging them on the racks bristling with pegs. There was a smell of wet clothing, a tossing out of wet, draggled hair, a noise of voices and feet.

The mass of girls grew greater, the rage around the pegs grew steadier, the scholars tended to fall into little noisy gangs in the porch. Then Violet Harby clapped her hands, clapped them louder, with a shrill "Quiet, girls, quiet!"

There was a pause. The hubbub died down but did not cease.

"What did I say?" cried Miss Harby, shrilly.

There was almost complete silence. Sometimes a girl, rather late, whirled into the porch and flung off her things.

"Leaders—in place," commanded Miss Harby shrilly.

Pairs of girls in pinafores and long hair stood separate in the porch.

"Standard Four, Five, and Six—fall in," cried Miss Harby.

There was a hubbub, which gradually resolved itself into three columns of girls, two and two, standing smirking in the passage. In among the peg-racks, other teachers were putting the lower classes into ranks.

Ursula stood by her own Standard Five. They were jerking their shoulders, tossing their hair, nudging, writhing, staring, grinning, whispering and twisting.

A sharp whistle was heard, and Standard Six, the biggest girls, set off, led by Miss Harby. Ursula, with her Standard Five, followed after. She stood beside a smirking, grinning row of girls, waiting in a narrow passage. What she was herself she did not know.

Suddenly the sound of a piano was heard, and Standard Six set off hollowly down the big room. The boys had entered by another door. The piano played on, a march tune, Standard Five followed to the door of the big room. Mr. Harby was seen away beyond at his desk. Mr. Brunt guarded the other door of the room. Ursula's class pushed up. She stood near them. They glanced and smirked and shoved.

"Go on," said Ursula.

They tittered.

"Go on," said Ursula, for the piano continued.

The girls broke loosely into the room. Mr. Harby, who had seemed immersed in some occupation, away at his desk, lifted his head and thundered:

"Halt!"

There was a halt, the piano stopped. The boys who were just starting through the other door, pushed back. The harsh, subdued voice of Mr. Brunt was heard, then the booming shout of Mr. Harby, from far down the room:

"Who told Standard Five girls to come in like that?"

Ursula crimsoned. Her girls were glancing up at her, smirking their accusation.

"I sent them in, Mr. Harby," she said, in a clear, struggling voice. There was a moment of silence. Then Mr. Harby roared from the distance.

"Go back to your places, Standard Five girls."

The girls glanced up at Ursula, accusing, rather jeering, fugitive. They pushed back. Ursula's heart hardened with ignominious pain.

"Forward—march," came Mr. Brunt's voice, and the girls set off, keeping time with the ranks of boys.

Ursula faced her class, some fifty-five boys and girls, who stood filling the ranks of the desks. She felt utterly non-existent. She had no place nor being there. She faced the block of children.

Down the room she heard the rapid firing of questions. She stood before her class not knowing what to do. She waited painfully. Her block of children, fifty unknown faces, watched her, hostile, ready to jeer. She felt as if she were in torture over a fire of faces. And on every side she was naked to them. Of unutterable length and torture the seconds went by.

Then she gathered courage. She heard Mr. Brunt asking questions in mental arithmetic. She stood near to her class, so that her voice need not be raised too much, and faltering, uncertain, she said:

"Seven hats at twopence ha'penny each?"

A grin went over the faces of the class, seeing her commence. She was red and suffering. Then some hands shot up like blades, and she asked for the answer.

The day passed incredibly slowly. She never knew what to do, there came horrible gaps, when she was merely exposed to the children; and when, relying on some pert little girl for information, she had started a lesson, she did not know how to go on with it properly. The children were her masters. She deferred to them. She could always hear Mr. Brunt. Like a machine, always in the same hard, high, inhuman voice he went on with his teaching, oblivious of everything. And before this inhuman number of children she was always at bay. She could not get away from it. There it was, this class of fifty collective children, depending on her for command, for command it hated and resented. It made her feel she could not breathe: she must suffocate, it was so inhuman. They were so many, that they were not children. They were a squadron. She could not speak as she would to a child, because they were not individual children, they were a collective, inhuman thing.

Dinner-time came, and stunned, bewildered, solitary, she went into the teachers' room for dinner. Never had she felt such a stranger to life before. It seemed to her she had just disembarked from some strange horrible state where everything was as in hell, a condition of hard, malevolent system. And she was not really free. The afternoon drew at her like some bondage.

The first week passed in a blind confusion. She did not know how to teach, and she felt she never would know. Mr. Harby came down every now and then to her class, to see what she was doing. She felt so incompetent as he stood by, bullying and threatening, so unreal, that she wavered, became neutral and non-existent. But he stood there watching with the listening-genial smile of the eyes, that was really threatening; he said nothing, he made her go on teaching, she felt she had no soul in her body. Then he went away, and his going was like a derision. The class was his class. She was a wavering substitute. He thrashed and bullied, he was hated. But he was master. Though she was gentle and always considerate of her class, yet they belonged to Mr. Harby, and they did not belong to her. Like some invincible source of the mechanism he kept all power to himself. And the class owned his power. And in school it was power, and power alone that mattered.

Soon Ursula came to dread him, and at the bottom of her dread was a seed of hate, for she despised him, yet he was master of her. Then she began to get on. All the other teachers hated him, and fanned their hatred among themselves. For he was master of them and the children, he stood like a wheel to make absolute his authority over the herd. That seemed to be his one reason in life, to hold blind authority over the school. His teachers were his subjects as much as the scholars. Only, because they had some authority, his instinct was to detest them.

Ursula could not make herself a favourite with him. From the first moment she set hard against him. She set against Violet Harby also. Mr. Harby was, however, too much for her, he was something she could not come to grips with, something too strong for her. She tried to approach him as a young, bright girl usually approaches a man, expecting a little chivalrous courtesy. But the fact that she was a girl, a woman, was ignored or used as a matter for contempt against her. She did not know what she was, nor what she must be. She wanted to remain her own responsive, personal self.

So she taught on. She made friends with the Standard Three teacher, Maggie Schofield. Miss Schofield was about twenty years old, a subdued girl who held aloof from the other teachers. She was rather beautiful, meditative, and seemed to live in another, lovelier world.

Ursula took her dinner to school, and during the second week ate it in Miss Schofield's room. Standard Three classroom stood by itself and had windows on two sides, looking on to the playground. It was a passionate relief to find such a retreat in the jarring school. For there were pots of chrysanthemums and co-loured leaves, and a big jar of berries: there were pretty little pictures on the wall, photogravure reproductions from Greuze, and Reynolds's "Age of Inno-cence", giving an air of intimacy; so that the room, with its window space, its smaller, tidier desks, its touch of pictures and flowers, made Ursula at once glad. Here at last was a little personal touch, to which she could respond.

It was Monday. She had been at school a week and was getting used to the surroundings, though she was still an entire foreigner in herself. She looked forward to having dinner with Maggie. That was the bright spot in the day. Maggie was so strong and remote, walking with slow, sure steps down a hard road, carrying the dream within her. Ursula went through the class teaching as through a meaningless daze.

Her class tumbled out at midday in haphazard fashion. She did not realise what host she was gathering against herself by her superior tolerance, her kind-ness and her *laisseraller*. They were gone, and she was rid of them, and that was all. She hurried away to the teachers' room.

Mr. Brunt was crouching at the small stove, putting a little rice pudding into the oven. He rose then, and attentively poked in a small saucepan on the hob with a fork. Then he replaced the saucepan lid.

"Aren't they done?" asked Ursula gaily, breaking in on his tense absorption. She always kept a bright, blithe manner, and was pleasant to all the teachers.

For she felt like the swan among the geese, of superior heritage and belonging. And her pride at being the swan in this ugly school was not yet abated.

"Not yet," replied Mr. Brunt, laconic.

"I wonder if my dish is hot," she said, bending down at the oven. She half expected him to look for her, but he took no notice. She was hungry and she poked her finger eagerly in the pot to see if her brussels sprouts and potatoes and meat were ready. They were not.

"Don't you think it's rather jolly bringing dinner?" she said to Mr. Brunt.

"I don't know as I do," he said, spreading a serviette on a corner of the table, and not looking at her.

"I suppose it is too far for you to go home?"

"Yes," he said. Then he rose and looked at her. He had the bluest, fiercest, most pointed eyes that she had ever met. He stared at her with growing fierceness.

"If I were you, Miss Brangwen," he said, menacingly, "I should get a bit tighter hand over my class."

Ursula shrank.

"Would you?" she asked, sweetly, yet in terror. "Aren't I strict enough?"

"Because," he repeated, taking no notice of her, "they'll get you down if you don't tackle 'em pretty quick. They'll pull you down, and worry you, till Harby gets you shifted—that's how it'll be. You won't be here another six weeks"—and he filled his mouth with food—"if you don't tackle 'em and tackle 'em quick."

"Oh, but——" Ursula said, resentfully, ruefully. The terror was deep in her.

"Harby'll not help you. This is what he'll do—he'll let you go on, getting worse and worse, till either you clear out or he clears you out. It doesn't matter to me, except that you'll leave a class behind you as *I* hope I shan't have to cope with."

She heard the accusation in the man's voice, and felt condemned. But still, school had not yet become a definite reality to her. She was shirking it. It was reality, but it was all outside her. And she fought against Mr. Brunt's representation. She did not want to realise.

"Will it be so terrible?" she said, quivering, rather beautiful, but with a slight touch of condescension, because she would not betray her own trepidation.

"Terrible?" said the man, turning to his potatoes again. "I dunno about terrible."

"I do feel frightened," said Ursula. "The children seem so——"

"What?" said Miss Harby, entering at that moment.

"Why," said Ursula, "Mr. Brunt says I ought to tackle my class," and she laughed uneasily.

"Oh, you have to keep order if you want to teach," said Miss Harby, hard, superior, trite.

Ursula did not answer. She felt non valid before them.

"If you want to be let to *live,* you have," said Mr. Brunt.

"Well, if you can't keep order, what good *are* you?" said Miss Harby.

"An' you've got to do it by yourself,"—his voice rose like the bitter cry of the prophets. "You'll get no *help* from anybody."

"Oh, indeed!" said Miss Harby. "Some people can't be helped." And she departed.

The air of hostility and disintegration, of wills working in antagonistic subordination, was hideous. Mr. Brunt, subordinate, afraid, acid with shame, fright-

ened her. Ursula wanted to run. She only wanted to clear out, not to understand.

Then Miss Schofield came in, and with her another, more restful note. Ursula at once turned for confirmation to the newcomer. Maggie remained personal within all this unclean system of authority.

"Is the big Anderson here?" she asked of Mr. Brunt. And they spoke of some
affair about two scholars, coldly, officially.

Miss Schofield took her brown dish, and Ursula followed with her own. The
cloth was laid in the pleasant Standard Three room, there was a jar with two or
three monthly roses on the table.

"It is so nice in here, you *have* made it different," said Ursula gaily. But she
was afraid. The atmosphere of the school was upon her.

"The big room," said Miss Schofield, "ha, it's misery to be in it!"

She too spoke with bitterness. She too lived in the ignominious position of
an upper servant hated by the master above and the class beneath. She was, she
knew, liable to attack from either side at any minute, or from both at once, for
the authorities would listen to the complaints of parents, and both would turn
round on the mongrel authority, the teacher.

So there was a hard, bitter withholding in Maggie Schofield even as she
poured out her savoury mess of big golden beans and brown gravy.

"It is vegetarian hot-pot," said Miss Schofield. "Would you like to try it?"

"I should love to," said Ursula.

Her own dinner seemed coarse and ugly beside this savoury, clean dish.

"I've never eaten vegetarian things," she said. "But I should think they can
be good."

"I'm not really a vegetarian," said Maggie, "I don't like to bring meat to
school."

"No," said Ursula, "I don't think I do either."

And again her soul rang an answer to a new refinement, a new liberty. If all
vegetarian things were as nice as this, she would be glad to escape the slight
uncleanness of meat.

"How good!" she cried.

"Yes," said Miss Schofield, and she proceeded to tell her the receipt. The
two girls passed on to talk about themselves. Ursula told all about the High
School, and about her matriculation, bragging a little. She felt so poor here, in
this ugly place. Miss Schofield listened with brooding, handsome face, rather
gloomy.

"Couldn't you have got to some better place than this?" she asked at length.

"I didn't know what it was like," said Ursula, doubtfully.

"Ah!" said Miss Schofield, and she turned aside her head with a bitter motion.

"Is it as horrid as it seems?" asked Ursula, frowning lightly, in fear.

"It *is,*" said Miss Schofield, bitterly. "Ha!—it is *hateful!*"

Ursula's heart sank, seeing even Miss Schofield in the deadly bondage.

"It is Mr. Harby," said Maggie Schofield, breaking forth. "I don't think I
could live again in the big room—Mr. Brunt's voice and Mr. Harby—ah——"

She turned aside her head with a deep hurt. Some things she could not bear.

"Is Mr. Harby really horrid?" asked Ursula, venturing into her own dread.

"He!—why, he's just a bully," said Miss Schofield, raising her shamed dark
eyes, that flamed with tortured contempt. "He's not bad as long as you keep in
with him, and refer to him, and do everything in his way—but—it's all so *mean!*

It's just a question of fighting on both sides—and those great louts——"

She spoke with difficulty and with increased bitterness. She had evidently suffered. Her soul was raw with ignominy. Ursula suffered in response.

"But why is it so horrid?" she asked, helplessly.

"You can't do *anything,"* said Miss Schofield. "He's against you on one side and he sets the children against you on the other. The children are simply awful. You've got to *make* them do everything. Everything, everything has got to come out of you. Whatever they learn, you've got to force it into them—and that's how it is."

Ursula felt her heart fail inside her. Why must she grasp all this, why must she force learning on fifty-five reluctant children, having all the time an ugly, rude jealousy behind her, ready to throw her to the mercy of the herd of children, who would like to rend her as a weaker representative of authority. A great dread of her task possessed her. She saw Mr. Brunt, Miss Harby, Miss Schofield, all the schoolteachers, drudging unwillingly at the graceless task of compelling many children into one disciplined, mechanical set, reducing the whole set to an automatic state of obedience and attention, and then of commanding their acceptance of various pieces of knowledge. The first great task was to reduce sixty children to one state of mind, or being. This state must be produced automatically, through the will of the teacher, and the will of the whole school authority, imposed upon the will of the children. The point was that the headmaster and the teachers should have one will in authority, which should bring the will of the children into accord. But the headmaster was narrow and exclusive. The will of the teachers could not agree with his, their separate wills refused to be so subordinated. So there was a state of anarchy, leaving the final judgment to the children themselves, which authority should exist.

So there existed a set of separate wills, each straining itself to the utmost to exert its own authority. Children will never naturally acquiesce to sitting in a class and submitting to knowledge. They must be compelled by a stronger, wiser will. Against which will they must always strive to revolt. So that the first great effort of every teacher of a large class must be to bring the will of the children into accordance with his own will. And this he can only do by an abnegation of his personal self, and an application of a system of laws, for the purpose of achieving a certain calculable result, the imparting of certain knowledge. Whereas Ursula thought she was going to become the first wise teacher by making the whole business personal, and using no compulsion. She believed entirely in her own personality.

So that she was in a very deep mess. In the first place she was offering to a class a relationship which only one or two of the children were sensitive enough to appreciate, so that the mass were left outsiders, therefore against her. Secondly, she was placing herself in passive antagonism to the one fixed authority of Mr. Harby, so that the scholars could more safely harry her. She did not know, but her instinct gradually warned her. She was tortured by the voice of Mr. Brunt. On it went, jarring, harsh, full of hate, but so monotonous, it nearly drove her mad: always the same set, harsh monotony. The man was become a mechanism working on and on and on. But the personal man was in subdued friction all the time. It was horrible—all hate! Must she be like this? She could feel the ghastly necessity. She must become the same—put away the personal self, become an instrument, an abstraction, working upon a certain material, the class, to achieve a set purpose of making them know so much each day. And she could not submit. Yet gradually she felt the invincible iron closing upon her.

The sun was being blocked out. Often when she went out at playtime and saw a luminous blue sky with changing clouds, it seemed just a fantasy, like a piece of painted scenery. Her heart was so black and tangled in the teaching, her personal self was shut in prison, abolished, she was subjugate to a bad, destructive will. How then could the sky be shining? There was no sky, there was no luminous atmosphere of out-of-doors. Only the inside of the school was real—hard, concrete, real and vicious.

She would not yet, however, let school quite overcome her. She always said. "It is not a permanency, it will come to an end." She could always see herself beyond the place, see the time when she had left it. On Sundays and on holidays, when she was away at Cossethay or in the woods where the beech-leaves were fallen, she could think of St. Philip's Church School, and by an effort of will put it in the picture as a dirty little low-squatting building that made a very tiny mound under the sky, while the great beech-woods spread immense about her, and the afternoon was spacious and wonderful. Moreover the children, the scholars, they were insignificant little objects far away, oh, far away. And what power had they over her free soul? A fleeting thought of them, as she kicked her way through the beech-leaves, and they were gone. But her will was tense against them all the time.

All the while, they pursued her. She had never had such a passionate love of the beautiful things about her. Sitting on top of the tram-car, at evening, sometimes school was swept away as she saw a magnificent sky settling down. And her breast, her very hands, clamoured for the lovely flare of sunset. It was poignant almost to agony, her reaching for it. She almost cried aloud seeing the sundown so lovely.

For she was held away. It was no matter how she said to herself that school existed no more once she had left it. It existed. It was within her like a dark weight, controlling her movement. It was in vain the high-spirited, proud young girl flung off the school and its association with her. She was Miss Brangwen, she was Standard Five teacher, she had her most important being in her work now.

Constantly haunting her, like a darkness hovering over her heart and threatening to swoop down over it at every moment, was the sense that somehow, somehow she was brought down. Bitterly she denied unto herself that she was really a schoolteacher. Leave that to the Violet Harbys. She herself would stand clear of the accusation. It was in vain she denied it.

Within herself some recording hand seemed to point mechanically to a negation. She was incapable of fulfilling her task. She could never for a moment escape from the fatal weight of the knowledge.

And so she felt inferior to Violet Harby. Miss Harby was a splendid teacher. She could keep order and inflict knowledge on a class with remarkable efficiency. It was no good Ursula's protesting to herself that she was infinitely, infinitely the superior of Violet Harby. She knew that Violet Harby succeeded where she failed, and this in a task which was almost a test of her. She felt something all the time wearing upon her, wearing her down. She went about in these first weeks trying to deny it, to say she was free as ever. She tried not to feel at a disadvantage before Miss Harby, tried to keep up the effect of her own superiority. But a great weight was on her, which Violet Harby could bear, and she herself could not.

Though she did not give in, she never succeeded. Her class was getting in worse condition, she knew herself less and less secure in teaching it. Ought she to withdraw and go home again? Ought she to say she had come to the wrong place, and so retire? Her very life was a test.

She went on doggedly, blindly, waiting for a crisis. Mr. Harby had now begun to persecute her. Her dread and hatred of him grew and loomed larger and larger. She was afraid he was going to bully her and destroy her. He began to persecute her because she could not keep her class in proper condition, because her class was the weak link in the chain which made up the school.

One of the offences was that her class was noisy and disturbed Mr. Harby, as he took Standard Seven at the other end of the room. She was taking composition on a certain morning, walking in among the scholars. Some of the boys had dirty ears and necks, their clothing smelled unpleasantly, but she could ignore it. She corrected the writing as she went.

"When you say 'their fur is brown', how do you write 'their'?" she asked.

There was a little pause; the boys were always jeeringly backward in answering. They had begun to jeer at her authority altogether.

"Please, miss, t-h-e-i-r", spelled a lad, loudly, with a note of mockery.

At that moment Mr. Harby was passing.

"Stand up, Hill!" he called, in a big voice.

Everybody started. Ursula watched the boy. He was evidently poor, and rather cunning. A stiff bit of hair stood straight off his forehead, the rest fitted close to his meagre head. He was pale and colourless.

"Who told you to call out?" thundered Mr. Harby.

The boy looked up and down, with a guilty air, and a cunning, cynical reserve.

"Please, sir, I was answering," he replied, with the same humble insolence.

"Go to my desk."

The boy set off down the room, the big black jacket hanging in dejected folds about him, his thin legs, rather knocked at the knees, going already with the pauper's crawl, his feet in their big boots scarcely lifted. Ursula watched him in his crawling, slinking progress down the room. He was one of *her* boys! When he got to the desk, he looked round, half furtively, with a sort of cunning grin and a pathetic leer at the big boys in Standard VII. Then, pitiable, pale, in his dejected garments, he lounged under the menace of the headmaster's desk, with one thin leg crooked at the knee and the foot stuck out sideways his hands in the low-hanging pockets of his man's jacket.

Ursula tried to get her attention back to the class. The boy gave her a little horror, and she was at the same time hot with pity for him. She felt she wanted to scream. She was responsible for the boy's punishment. Mr. Harby was looking at her handwriting on the board. He turned to the class.

"Pens down."

The children put down their pens and looked up.

"Fold arms."

They pushed back their books and folded arms.

Ursula, stuck among the back forms, could not extricate herself.

"*What* is your composition about?" asked the headmaster. Every hand shot up. "The——" stuttered some voice in its eagerness to answer.

"I wouldn't advise you to call out," said Mr. Harby. He would have a pleasant voice, full and musical, but for the detestable menace that always tailed in it. He stood unmoved, his eyes twinkling under his bushy black eyebrows, watching the class. There was something fascinating in him, as he stood, and again she wanted to scream. She was all jarred, she did not know what she felt.

"Well, Alice?" he said.

"The rabbit," piped a girl's voice.

"A very easy subject for Standard Five."

Ursula felt a slight shame of incompetence. She was exposed before the class. And she was tormented by the contradictoriness of everything. Mr. Harby stood so strong, and so male, with his black brows and clear forehead, the heavy jaw, the big, overhanging moustache: such a man, with strength and male power, and a certain blind, native beauty. She might have liked him as a man. And here he stood in some other capacity, bullying over such a trifle as a boy's speaking out without permission. Yet he was not a little, fussy man. He seemed to have some cruel, stubborn, evil spirit, he was imprisoned in a task too small and petty for him, which yet, in a servile acquiescence, he would fulfil, because he had to earn his living. He had no finer control over himself, only this blind, dogged, wholesale will. He would keep the job going, since he must. And this job was to make the children spell the word "caution" correctly, and put a capital letter after a full-stop. So at this he hammered with his suppressed hatred, always suppressing himself, till he was beside himself. Ursula suffered bitterly as he stood, short and handsome and powerful, teaching her class. It seemed such a miserable thing for him to be doing. He had a decent, powerful, rude soul. What did he care about the composition on "The Rabbit"? Yet his will kept him there before the class, threshing the trivial subject. It was habit with him now, to be so little and vulgar, out of place. She saw the shamefulness of his position, felt the fettered wickedness in him which would blaze out into evil rage in the long run, so that he was like a persistent, strong creature tethered. It was really intolerable. The jarring was torture to her. She looked over the silent, attentive class that seemed to have crystallised into order and rigid, neutral form. This he had it in his power to do, to crystallise the children into hard, mute fragments, fixed under his will: his brute will, which fixed them by sheer force. She too must learn to subdue them to her will: she must. For it was her duty, since the school was such. He had crystallised the class into order. But to see him, a strong, powerful man, using all his power for such a purpose, seemed almost horrible. There was something hideous about it. The strange, genial light in his eye was really vicious, and ugly, his smile was one of torture. He could not be impersonal. He could not have a clear, pure purpose, he could only exercise his own brute will. He did not believe in the least in the education he kept inflicting year after year upon the children. So he must bully, only bully, even while it tortured his strong, wholesome nature with shame like a spur always galling. He was so blind and ugly and out of place. Ursula could not bear it as he stood there. The whole situation was wrong and ugly.

The lesson was finished, Mr. Harby went away. At the far end of the room she heard the whistle and the thud of the cane. Her heart stood still within her. She could not bear it, no, she could not bear it when the boy was beaten. It made her sick. She felt that she must go out of this school, this torture-place. And she hated the schoolmaster, thoroughly and finally. The brute, had he no shame? He should never be allowed to continue the atrocity of this bullying cruelty. Then Hill came crawling back, blubbering piteously. There was something desolate about this blubbering that nearly broke her heart. For after all, if she had kept her class in proper discipline, this would never have happened, Hill would never have called out and been caned.

She began the arithmetic lesson. But she was distracted. The boy Hill sat away on the back desk, huddled up, blubbering and sucking his hand. It was a long time. She dared not go near, nor speak to him. She felt ashamed before him. And she felt she could not forgive the boy for being the huddled, blubbering object, all wet and snivelled, which he was.

She went on correcting the sums. But there were too many children. She could not get round the class. And Hill was on her conscience. At last he had stopped crying, and sat bunched over his hands, playing quietly. Then he looked up at her. His face was dirty with tears, his eyes had a curious washed look, like the sky after rain, a sort of wanness. He bore no malice. He had already forgotten, and was waiting to be restored to the normal position.

"Go on with your work, Hill," she said.

The children were playing over their arithmetic, and, she knew, cheating thoroughly. She wrote another sum on the blackboard. She could not get round the class. She went again to the front to watch. Some were ready. Some were not. What was she to do?

At last it was time for recreation. She gave the order to cease working, and in some way or other got her class out of the room. Then she faced the disorderly litter of blotted, uncorrected books, of broken rulers and chewed pens. And her heart sank in sickness. The misery was getting deeper.

The trouble went on and on, day after day. She had always piles of books to mark, myriads of errors to correct, a heart-wearying task that she loathed. And the work got worse and worse. When she tried to flatter herself that the composition grew more alive, more interesting, she had to see that the handwriting grew more and more slovenly, the books more filthy and disgraceful. She tried what she could, but it was of no use. But she was not going to take it seriously. Why should she? Why should she say to herself, that it mattered, if she failed to teach a class to write perfectly neatly? Why should she take the blame unto herself?

Pay day came, and she received four pounds two shillings and one penny. She was very proud that day. She had never had so much money before. And she had earned it all herself. She sat on the top of the tram-car fingering the gold and fearing she might lose it. She felt so established and strong, because of it. And when she got home she said to her mother:

"It is pay day to-day, mother."

"Ay," said her mother, coolly.

Then Ursula put down fifty shillings on the table.

"That is my board," she said.

"Ay," said her mother, letting it lie.

Ursula was hurt. Yet she had paid her scot. She was free. She paid for what she had. There remained moreover thirty-two shillings of her own. She would not spend any, she who was naturally a spendthrift, because she could not bear to damage her fine gold.

She had a standing ground now apart from her parents. She was something else besides the mere daughter of William and Anna Brangwen. She was independent. She earned her own living. She was an important member of the working community. She was sure that fifty shillings a month quite paid for her keep. If her mother received fifty shillings a month for each of the children, she would have twenty pounds a month and no clothes to provide. Very well then.

Ursula was independent of her parents. She now adhered elsewhere. Now, the "Board of Education" was a phrase that rang significant to her, and she felt Whitehall far beyond her as her ultimate home. In the government, she knew which minister had supreme control over Education, and it seemed to her that, in some way, he was connected with her, as her father was connected with her.

She had another self, another responsibility. She was no longer Ursula Brangwen, daughter of William Brangwen. She was also Standard Five teacher in St. Philip's School. And it was a case now of being Standard Five teacher, and nothing else. For she could not escape.

Neither could she succeed. That was her horror. As the weeks passed on, there was no Ursula Brangwen, free and jolly. There was only a girl of that name obsessed by the fact that she could not manage her class of children. At week-ends there came days of passionate reaction, when she went mad with the taste of liberty, when merely to be free in the morning, to sit down at her embroidery and stitch the coloured silks was a passion of delight. For the prison house was always awaiting her! This was only a respite, as her chained heart knew well. So that she seized hold of the swift hours of the week-end, and wrung the last drop of sweetness out of them, in a little, cruel frenzy.

She did not tell anybody how this state was a torture to her. She did not confide, either to Gudrun or to her parents, how horrible she found it to be a school-teacher. But when Sunday night came, and she felt the Monday morning at hand, she was strung up tight with dreadful anticipation, because the strain and the torture was near again.

She did not believe that she could ever teach that great, brutish class, in that brutal school: ever, ever. And yet, if she failed, she must in some way go under. She must admit that the man's world was too strong for her, she could not take her place in it; she must go down before Mr. Harby. And all her life henceforth, she must go on, never having freed herself of the man's world, never having achieved the freedom of the great world of responsible work. Maggie had taken her place there, she had even stood level with Mr. Harby and got free of him: and her soul was always wandering in far-off valleys and glades of poetry. Maggie was free. Yet there was something like subjection in Maggie's very freedom. Mr. Harby, the man, disliked the reserved woman, Maggie. Mr. Harby, the schoolmaster, respected his teacher, Miss Schofield.

For the present, however, Ursula only envied and admired Maggie. She herself had still to get where Maggie had got. She had still to make her footing. She had taken up a position on Mr. Harby's ground, and she must keep it. For he was now beginning a regular attack on her, to drive her away out of his school. She could not keep order. Her class was a turbulent crowd, and the weak spot in the school's work. Therefore she must go, and someone more useful must come in her place, someone who could keep discipline.

The headmaster had worked himself into an obsession of fury against her. He only wanted her gone. She had come, she had got worse as the weeks went on, she was absolutely no good. His system, which was his very life in school, the outcome of his bodily movement, was attacked and threatened at the point where Ursula was included. She was the danger that threatened his body with a blow, a fall. And blindly, thoroughly, moving from strong instinct of opposition, he set to work to expel her.

When he punished one of her children as he had punished the boy Hill, for an offence against *himself,* he made the punishment extra heavy with the significance that the extra stroke came in because of the weak teacher who allowed all these things to be. When he punished for an offence against *her,* he punished lightly, as if offences against her were not significant. Which all the children knew, and they behaved accordingly.

Every now and again Mr. Harby would swoop down to examine exercise books. For a whole hour, he would be going round the class, taking book after book, comparing page after page, whilst Ursula stood aside for all the remarks and fault-finding to be pointed at her through the scholars. It was true, since she had come, the composition books had grown more and more untidy, disorderly, filthy. Mr. Harby pointed to the pages done before her régime, and to those done after, and fell into a passion of rage. Many children he sent out to the front with their books. And after he had thoroughly gone through the silent and quivering class he caned the worst offenders well, in front of the others, thundering in real passion of anger and chagrin.

"Such a condition in a class, I can't believe it! It is simply disgraceful! I can't think how you have been let to get like it! Every Monday morning I shall come down and examine these books. So don't think that because there is nobody paying any attention to you, that you are free to unlearn everything you ever learned, and go back till you are not fit for Standard Three. I shall examine all books every Monday——"

Then in a rage, he went away with his cane, leaving Ursula to confront a pale, quivering class, whose childish faces were shut in blank resentment, fear, and bitterness, whose souls were full of anger and contempt for *her* rather than of the master, whose eyes looked at her with the cold, inhuman accusation of children. And she could hardly make mechanical words to speak to them. When she gave an order they obeyed with an insolent off-handedness, as if to say: "As for you, do you think we would obey *you*, but for the master?" She sent the blubbering, caned boys to their seats, knowing that they too jeered at her and her authority, holding her weakness responsible for what punishment had overtaken them. And she knew the whole position, so that even her horror of physical beating and suffering sank to a deeper pain, and became a moral judgment upon her, worse than any hurt.

She must, during the next week, watch over her books, and punish any fault. Her soul decided it coldly. Her personal desire was dead for that day at least. She must have nothing more of herself in school. She was to be Standard Five teacher only. That was her duty. In school, she was nothing but Standard Five teacher. Ursula Brangwen must be excluded.

So that, pale, shut, at last distant and impersonal, she saw no longer the child, how his eyes danced, or how he had a queer little soul that could not be bothered with shaping handwriting so long as he dashed down what he thought. She saw no children, only the task that was to be done. And keeping her eyes there, on the task, and not on the child, she was impersonal enough to punish where she could otherwise only have sympathised, understood, and condoned, to approve where she would have been merely uninterested before. But her interest had no place any more.

It was agony to the impulsive, bright girl of seventeen to become distant and official, having no personal relationship with the children. For a few days, after the agony of the Monday, she succeeded, and had some success with her class. But it was a state not natural to her, and she began to relax.

Then came another infliction. There were not enough pens to go round the class. She sent to Mr. Harby for more. He came in person.

"Not enough pens, Miss Brangwen?" he said, with the smile and calm of exceeding rage against her.

"No, we are six short," she said, quaking.

"Oh, how is that?" he said, menacingly. Then, looking over the class, he asked:

"How many are there here to-day?"

"Fifty-two," said Ursula, but he did not take any notice, counting for himself.

"Fifty-two," he said. "And how many pens are there, Staples?"

Ursula was now silent. He would not heed her if she answered, since he had addressed the monitor.

"That's a very curious thing," said Mr. Harby, looking over the silent class with a slight grin of fury. All the childish faces looked up at him blank and exposed.

"A few days ago there were sixty pens for this class-now there are forty-eight. What is forty-eight from sixty, Williams?" There was a sinister suspense in the question. A thin, ferret-faced boy in a sailor suit started up exaggeratedly. "Please, sir!" he said. Then a slow, sly grin came over his face. He did not know. There was a tense silence. The boy dropped his head. Then he looked up again, a little cunning triumph in his eyes. "Twelve," he said.

"I would advise you to attend," said the headmaster dangerously. The boy sat down.

"Forty-eight from sixty is twelve: so there are twelve pens to account for. Have you looked for them, Staples?"

"Yes, sir."

"Then look again."

The scene dragged on. Two pens were found: ten were missing. Then the storm burst.

"Am I to have you thieving, besides your dirt and bad work and bad behaviour?" the headmaster began. "Not content with being the worst-behaved and dirtiest class in the school, you are thieves into the bargain, are you? It is a very funny thing! Pens don't melt into the air: pens are not in the habit of mizzling away into nothing. What has become of them then? They must be somewhere. What has become of them? For they must be found, and found by Standard Five. They were lost by Standard Five, and they must be found."

Ursula stood and listened, her heart hard and cold. She was so much upset, that she felt almost mad. Something in her tempted her to turn on the headmaster and tell him to stop, about the miserable pens. But she did not. She could not.

After every session, morning and evening, she had the pens counted. Still they were missing. And pencils and india-rubbers disappeared. She kept the class staying behind, till the things were found. But as soon as Mr. Harby had gone out of the room, the boys began to jump about and shout, and at last they bolted in a body from the school.

This was drawing near a crisis. She could not tell Mr. Harby because, while he would punish the class, he would make her the cause of the punishment, and her class would pay her back with disobedience and derision. Already there was a deadly hostility grown up between her and the children. After keeping in the class, at evening, to finish some work, she would find boys dodging behind her, calling after her: "Brangwen, Brangwen—Proud-acre."

When she went into Ilkeston of a Saturday morning with Gudrun, she heard again the voices yelling after her:

"Brangwen, Brangwen."

She pretended to take no notice, but she coloured with shame at being held up to derision in the public street. She, Ursula Brangwen of Cossethay, could not escape from the Standard Five teacher which she was. In vain she went out to buy ribbon for her hat. They called after her, the boys she tried to teach.

And one evening, as she went from the edge of the town into the country, stones came flying at her. Then the passion of shame and anger surpassed her. She walked on unheeding, beside herself. Because of the darkness she could not see who were those that threw. But she did not want to know.

Only in her soul a change took place. Never more, and never more would she give herself as individual to her class. Never would she, Ursula Brangwen, the girl she was, the person she was, come into contact with those boys. She would be Standard Five teacher, as far away personally from her class as if she had never set foot in St. Philip's school. She would just obliterate them all, and keep herself apart, take them as scholars only.

So her face grew more and more shut, and over her flayed, exposed soul of a young girl who had gone open and warm to give herself to the children, there set a hard, insentient thing, that worked mechanically according to a system imposed.

It seemed she scarcely saw her class the next day. She could only feel her will, and what she would have of this class which she must grasp into subjection. It was no good, any more, to appeal, to play upon the better feelings of the class. Her swift-working soul realised this.

She, as teacher, must bring them all as scholars, into subjection. And this she was going to do. All else she would forsake. She had become hard and impersonal, almost avengeful on herself as well as on them, since the stone throwing. She did not want to be a person, to be herself any more, after such humiliation. She would assert herself for mastery, be only teacher. She was set now. She was going to fight and subdue.

She knew by now her enemies in the class. The one she hated most was Williams. He was a sort of defective, not bad enough to be so classed. He could read with fluency, and had plenty of cunning intelligence. But he could not keep still. And he had a kind of sickness very repulsive to a sensitive girl, something cunning and etiolated and degenerate. Once he had thrown an ink-well at her, in one of his mad little rages. Twice he had run home out of class. He was a well-known character.

And he grinned up his sleeve at this girl-teacher, sometimes hanging round her to fawn on her. But this made her dislike him more. He had a kind of leech-like power.

From one of the children she took a supple cane, and this she determined to use when real occasion came. One morning, at composition, she said to the boy Williams:

"Why have you made this blot?"

"Please, miss, it fell off my pen," he whined out, in the mocking voice that he was so clever in using. The boys near snorted with laughter. For Williams was an actor, he could tickle the feelings of his hearers subtly. Particularly he could tickle the children with him into ridiculing his teacher, or indeed, any authority of which he was not afraid. He had that peculiar gaol instinct.

"Then you must stay in and finish another page of composition," said the teacher.

This was against her usual sense of justice, and the boy resented it derisively. At twelve o'clock she caught him slinking out.

"Williams, sit down," she said.

And there she sat, and there he sat, alone, opposite to her, on the back desk, looking up at her with his furtive eyes every minute.

"Please, miss, I've got to go an errand," he called out insolently.

"Bring me your book," said Ursula.

The boy came out, flapping his book along the desks. He had not written a line.

"Go back and do the writing you have to do," said Ursula. And she sat at her desk, trying to correct books. She was trembling and upset. And for an hour the miserable boy writhed and grinned in his seat. At the end of that time he had done five lines.

"As it is so late now," said Ursula, "you will finish the rest this evening."

The boy kicked his way insolently down the passage.

The afternoon came again. Williams was there, glancing at her, and her heart beat thick, for she knew it was a fight between them. She watched him.

During the geography lesson, as she was pointing to the map with her cane, the boy continually ducked his whitish head under the desk, and attracted the attention of other boys.

"Williams," she said, gathering her courage, for it was critical now to speak to him, "what are you doing?"

He lifted his face, the sore-rimmed eyes half smiling. There was something intrinsically indecent about him. Ursula shrank away.

"Nothing," he replied, feeling a triumph.

"What are you doing?" she repeated, her heart-beat suffocating her.

"Nothing," replied the boy, insolently, aggrieved, comic.

"If I speak to you again, you must go down to Mr. Harby," she said.

But this boy was a match even for Mr. Harby. He was so persistent, so cringing, and flexible, he howled so when he was hurt, that the master hated more the teacher who sent him than he hated the boy himself. For of the boy he was sick of the sight. Which Williams knew. He grinned visibly.

Ursula turned to the map again, to go on with the geography lesson. But there was a little ferment in the class. Williams' spirit infected them all. She heard a scuffle, and then she trembled inwardly. If they all turned on her this time, she was beaten.

"Please, miss——" called a voice in distress.

She turned round. One of the boys she liked was ruefully holding out a torn celluloid collar. She heard the complaint, feeling futile.

"Go in front, Wright," she said.

She was trembling in every fibre. A big, sullen boy, not bad but very difficult, slouched out to the front. She went on with the lesson, aware that Williams was making faces at Wright, and that Wright was grinning behind her. She was afraid. She turned to the map again. And she was afraid.

"Please, miss, Williams——" came a sharp cry, and a boy on the back row was standing up, with drawn, pained brows, half a mocking grin on his pain, half real resentment against Williams—"Please, miss, he's nipped me,"—and he rubbed his leg ruefully.

"Come in front, Williams," she said.

The rat-like boy sat with his pale smile and did not move.

"Come in front," she repeated, definite now.

"I shan't," he cried, snarling, rat-like, grinning. Something went click in Ursula's soul. Her face and eyes set, she went through the class straight. The boy cowered before her glowering, fixed eyes. But she advanced on him, seized him by the arm, and dragged him from his seat. He clung to the form. It was the battle between him and her. Her instinct had suddenly become calm and quick.

She jerked him from his grip, and dragged him, struggling and kicking, to the front. He kicked her several times, and clung to the forms as he passed, but she went on. The class was on its feet in excitement. She saw it, and made no move.

She knew if she let go the boy he would dash to the door. Already he had run home once out of her class. So she snatched her cane from the desk, and brought it down on him. He was writhing and kicking. She saw his face beneath her, white, with eyes like the eyes of a fish, stony, yet full of hate and horrible fear. And she loathed him, the hideous writhing thing that was nearly too much for her. In horror lest he should overcome her, and yet at the heart quite calm, she brought down the cane again and again, whilst he struggled making inarticulate noises, and lunging vicious kicks at her. With one hand she managed to hold him, and now and then the cane came down on him. He writhed, like a mad thing. But the pain of the strokes cut through his writhing, vicious, coward's courage, bit deeper, till at last, with a long whimper that became a yell, he went limp. She let him go, and he rushed at her, his teeth and eyes glinting. There was a second of agonised terror in her heart: he was a beast thing. Then she caught him, and the cane came down on him. A few times, madly, in a frenzy, he lunged and writhed, to kick her. But again the cane broke him, he sank with a howling yell on the floor, and like a beaten beast lay there yelling.

Mr. Harby had rushed up towards the end of this performance.

"What's the matter?" he roared.

Ursula felt as if something were going to break in her.

"I've thrashed him," she said, her breast heaving, forcing out the words on the last breath. The headmaster stood choked with rage, helpless. She looked at the writhing, howling figure on the floor.

"Get up," she said. The thing writhed away from her. She took a step forward. She had realised the presence of the headmaster for one second, and then she was oblivious of it again.

"Get up," she said. And with a little dart the boy was on his feet. His yelling dropped to a mad blubber. He had been in a frenzy.

"Go and stand by the radiator," she said.

As if mechanically, blubbering, he went.

The headmaster stood robbed of movement or speech. His face was yellow, his hands twitched convulsively. But Ursula stood stiff not far from him. Nothing could touch her now: she was beyond Mr. Harby. She was as if violated to death.

The headmaster muttered something, turned, and went down the room, whence, from the far end, he was heard roaring in a mad rage at his own class.

The boy blubbered wildly by the radiator. Ursula looked at the class. There were fifty pale, still faces watching her, a hundred round eyes fixed on her in an attentive, expressionless stare.

"Give out the history readers," she said to the monitors.

There was dead silence. As she stood there, she could hear again the ticking of the clock, and the chock of piles of books taken out of the low cupboard. Then came the faint flap of books on the desks. The children passed in silence, their hands working in unison. They were no longer a pack, but each one separated into a silent, closed thing.

"Take page 125, and read that chapter," said Ursula.

There was a click of many books opened. The children found the page, and bent their heads obediently to read. And they read, mechanically.

Ursula, who was trembling violently, went and sat in her high chair. The blubbering of the boy continued. The strident voice of Mr. Brunt, the roar of

Mr. Harby, came muffled through the glass partition. And now and then a pair of eyes rose from the reading-book, rested on her a moment, watchful, as if calculating impersonally, then sank again.

She sat still without moving, her eyes watching the class, unseeing. She was quite still, and weak. She felt that she could not raise her hand from the desk. If she sat there for ever, she felt she could not move again, nor utter a command. It was a quarter-past four. She almost dreaded the closing of the school, when she would be alone.

The class began to recover its ease, the tension relaxed. Williams was still crying. Mr. Brunt was giving orders for the closing of the lesson. Ursula got down.

"Take your place, Williams," she said.

He dragged his feet across the room, wiping his face on his sleeve. As he sat down, he glanced at her furtively, his eyes still redder. Now he looked like some beaten rat.

At last the children were gone. Mr. Harby trod by heavily, without looking her way, or speaking. Mr. Brunt hesitated as she was locking her cupboard.

"If you settle Clarke and Letts in the same way, Miss Brangwen, you'll be all right," he said, his blue eyes glancing down in a strange fellowship, his long nose pointing at her.

"Shall I?" she laughed nervously. She did not want anybody to talk to her.

As she went along the street, clattering on the granite pavement, she was aware of boys dodging behind her. Something struck her hand that was carrying her bag, bruising her. As it rolled away she saw that it was a potato. Her hand was hurt, but she gave no sign. Soon she would take the tram.

She was afraid, and strange. It was to her quite strange and ugly, like some dream where she was degraded. She would have died rather than admit it to anybody. She could not look at her swollen hand. Something had broken in her; she had passed a crisis. Williams was beaten, but at a cost.

Feeling too much upset to go home, she rode a little farther into the town, and got down from the tram at a small tea-shop. There, in the dark little place behind the shop, she drank her tea and ate bread-and-butter. She did not taste anything. The taking of tea was just a mechanical action, to cover over her existence. There she sat in the dark, obscure little place, without knowing. Only unconsciously she nursed the back of her hand, which was bruised.

When finally she took her way home, it was sunset red across the west. She did not know why she was going home. There was nothing for her there. She had, true, only to pretend to be normal. There was nobody she could speak to, nowhere to go for escape. But she must keep on, under this red sunset, alone, knowing the horror in humanity, that would destroy her, and with which she was at war. Yet it had to be so.

In the morning again she must go to school. She got up and went without murmuring even to herself. She was in the hands of some bigger, stronger, coarser will.

School was fairly quiet. But she could feel the class watching her, ready to spring on her. Her instinct was aware of the class instinct to catch her if she were weak. But she kept cold and was guarded.

Williams was absent from school. In the middle of the morning there was a knock at the door: someone wanted the headmaster. Mr. Harby went out, heavily, angrily, nervously. He was afraid of irate parents. After a moment in the passage, he came again into school.

"Sturgess," he called to one of his larger boys. "Stand in front of the class and write down the name of anyone who speaks. Will you come this way, Miss Brangwen."

He seemed vindictively to seize upon her.

Ursula followed him, and found in the lobby a thin woman with a whitish skin, not ill-dressed in a grey costume and a purple hat.

"I called about Vernon," said the woman, speaking in a refined accent. There was about the woman altogether an appearance of refinement and of cleanliness, curiously contradicted by her half beggar's deportment, and a sense of her being unpleasant to touch, like something going bad inside. She was neither a lady nor an ordinary working man's wife, but a creature separate from society. By her dress she was not poor.

Ursula knew at once that she was Williams' mother, and that he was Vernon. She remembered that he was always clean, and well-dressed, in a sailor suit. And he had this same peculiar, half transparent unwholesomeness, rather like a corpse.

"I wasn't able to send him to school to-day," continued the woman, with a false grace of manner. "He came home last night so ill—he was violently sick—I thought I should have to send for the doctor.—You know he has a weak heart."

The woman looked at Ursula with her pale, dead eyes.

"No," replied the girl, "I did not know."

She stood still with repulsion and uncertainty. Mr. Harby, large and male, with his overhanging moustache, stood by with a slight, ugly smile at the corner of his eyes. The woman went on insidiously, not quite human:

"Oh, yes, he has had heart disease ever since he was a child. That is why he isn't very regular at school. And it is very bad to beat him. He was awfully ill this morning—I shall call on the doctor as I go back."

"Who is staying with him now, then?" put in the deep voice of the schoolmaster, cunningly.

"Oh, I left him with a woman who comes in to help me—and who understands him. But I shall call in the doctor on my way home."

Ursula stood still. She felt vague threats in all this. But the woman was so utterly strange to her, that she did not understand.

"He told me he had been beaten," continued the woman, "and when I undressed him to put him to bed, his body was covered with marks—I could show them to any doctor."

Mr. Harby looked at Ursula to answer. She began to understand. The woman was threatening to take out a charge of assault on her son against her. Perhaps she wanted money.

"I caned him," she said. "He was so much trouble."

"I'm sorry if he was troublesome," said the woman, "but he must have been shamefully beaten. I could show the marks to any doctor. I'm sure it isn't allowed, if it was known."

"I caned him while he kept kicking me," said Ursula, getting angry because she was half excusing herself, Mr. Harby standing there with the twinkle at the side of his eyes, enjoying the dilemma of the two women.

"I'm sure I'm sorry if he behaved badly," said the woman. "But I can't think he deserved beating as he has been. I can't send him to school, and really can't afford to pay the doctor.—Is it allowed for the teachers to beat the children like that, Mr. Harby?"

The headmaster refused to answer. Ursula loathed herself, and loathed Mr. Harby with his twinkling cunning and malice on the occasion. The other miserable woman watched her chance.

"It is an expense to me, and I have a great struggle to keep my boy decent."

Ursula still would not answer. She looked out at the asphalt yard, where a dirty rag of paper was blowing.

"And it isn't allowed to beat a child like that, I am sure, especially when he is delicate."

Ursula stared with a set face on the yard, as if she did not hear. She loathed all this, and had ceased to feel or to exist.

"Though I know he is troublesome sometimes—but I think it was too much. His body is covered with marks."

Mr. Harby stood sturdy and unmoved, waiting now to have done, with the twinkling, tiny wrinkles of an ironical smile at the corners of his eyes. He felt himself master of the situation.

"And he was violently sick. I couldn't possibly send him to school to-day. He couldn't keep his head up."

Yet she had no answer.

"You will understand, sir, why he is absent," she said, turning to Mr. Harby.

"Oh, yes," he said, rough and off-hand. Ursula detested him for his male triumph. And she loathed the woman. She loathed everything.

"You will try to have it remembered, sir, that he has a weak heart. He *is* so sick after these things."

"Yes," said the headmaster, "I'll see about it."

"I know he is troublesome," the woman only addressed herself to the male now—"but if you could have him punished without beating—he is really delicate."

Ursula was beginning to feel upset. Harby stood in rather superb mastery, the woman cringing to him to tickle him as one tickles trout.

"I had come to explain why he was away this morning, sir. You will understand."

She held out her hand. Harby took it and let it go, surprised and angry.

"Good morning," she said, and she gave her gloved, seedy hand to Ursula. She was not ill-looking, and had a curious insinuating way, very distasteful yet effective.

"Good morning, Mr. Harby, and thank you."

The figure in the grey costume and the purple hat was going across the school yard with a curious lingering walk. Ursula felt a strange pity for her, and revulsion from her. She shuddered. She went into the school again.

The next morning Williams turned up, looking paler than ever, very neat and nicely dressed in his sailor blouse. He glanced at Ursula with a half-smile: cunning, subdued, ready to do as she told him. There was something about him that made her shiver. She loathed the idea of having laid hands on him. His elder brother was standing outside the gate at playtime, a youth of about fifteen, tall and thin and pale. He raised his hat, almost like a gentleman. But there was something subdued, insidious about him too.

"Who is it?" said Ursula.

"It's the big Williams," said Violet Harby roughly. "*She* was here yesterday, wasn't she?"

"Yes."

"It's no good her coming—her character's not good enough for her to make any trouble."

Ursula shrank from the brutality and the scandal. But it had some vague, horrid fascination. How sordid everything seemed! She felt sorry for the queer woman with the lingering walk, and those queer, insidious boys. The Williams in her class was wrong somewhere. How nasty it was altogether.

So the battle went on till her heart was sick. She had several more boys to subjugate before she could establish herself. And Mr. Harby hated her almost as if she were a man. She knew now that nothing but a thrashing would settle some of the big louts who wanted to play cat and mouse with her. Mr. Harby would not give them the thrashing if he could help it. For he hated the teacher, the stuck-up, insolent high-school miss with her independence.

"Now, Wright, what have you done this time?" he would say genially to the boy who was sent to him from Standard Five for punishment. And he left the lad standing, lounging, wasting his time.

So that Ursula would appeal no more to the headmaster, but, when she was driven wild, she seized her cane, and slashed the boy who was insolent to her, over head and ears and hands. And at length they were afraid of her, she had them in order.

But she had paid a great price out of her own soul, to do this. It seemed as if a great flame had gone through her and burnt her sensitive tissue. She who shrank from the thought of physical suffering in any form, had been forced to fight and beat with a cane and rouse all her instincts to hurt. And afterwards she had been forced to endure the sound of their blubbering and desolation, when she had broken them to order.

Oh, and sometimes she felt as if she would go mad. What did it matter, what did it matter if their books were dirty and they did not obey? She would rather, in reality, that they disobeyed the whole rules of the school, than that they should be beaten, broken, reduced to this crying, hopeless state. She would rather bear all their insults and insolences a thousand times than reduce herself and them to this. Bitterly she repented having got beside herself, and having tackled the boy she had beaten.

Yet it had to be so. She did not want to do it. Yet she had to. Oh, why, why had she leagued herself to this evil system where she must brutalise herself to live? Why had she become a school-teacher, why, why?

The children had forced her to the beatings. No, she did not pity them. She had come to them full of kindness and love, and they would have torn her to pieces. They chose Mr. Harby. Well then, they must know her as well as Mr. Harby, they must first be subjugate to her. For she was not going to be made nought, no, neither by them, nor by Mr. Harby, nor by all the system around her. She was not going to be put down, prevented from standing free. It was not to be said of her, she could not take her place and carry out her task. She would fight and hold her place in this state also, in the world of work and man's convention.

She was isolated now from the life of her childhood, a foreigner in a new life, of work and mechanical consideration. She and Maggie, in their dinner-hours and their occasional teas at the little restaurant, discussed life and ideas. Maggie was a great suffragette, trusting in the vote. To Ursula the vote was never a reality. She had within her the strange, passionate knowledge of religion and living far transcending the limits of the automatic system that contained the vote. But her fundamental, organic knowledge had as yet to take form and rise to utterance. For her, as for Maggie, the liberty of woman meant something real and deep. She felt that somewhere, in something, she was not free. And she wanted to be. She was in revolt. For once she were free she could get somewhere. Ah, the wonderful, real somewhere that was beyond her, the somewhere that she felt deep, deep inside her.

In coming out and earning her own living she had made a strong, cruel move towards freeing herself. But having more freedom she only became more profoundly aware of the big want. She wanted so many things. She wanted to read great, beautiful books, and be rich with them; she wanted to see beautiful things, and have the joy of them for ever; she wanted to know big, free people; and there remained always the want she could put no name to.

It was so difficult. There were so many things, so much to meet and surpass. And one never knew where one was going. It was a blind fight. She had suffered bitterly in this school of St. Philip's. She was like a young filly that has been broken in to the shafts, and has lost its freedom. And now she was suffering bitterly from the agony of the shafts. The agony, the galling, the ignominy of her breaking in. This wore into her soul. But she would never submit. To shafts like these she would never submit for long. But she would know them. She would serve them that she might destroy them.

She and Maggie went to all kinds of places together, to big suffrage meetings in Nottingham, to concerts, to theatres, to exhibitions of pictures. Ursula saved her money and bought a bicycle, and the two girls rode to Lincoln, to Southwell, and into Derbyshire. They had an endless wealth of things to talk about. And it was a great joy, finding, discovering.

But Ursula never told about Winifred Inger. That was a sort of secret sideshow to her life, never to be opened. She did not even think of it. It was the closed door she had not the strength to open.

Once she was broken in to her teaching, Ursula began gradually to have a new life of her own again. She was going to college in eighteen months' time. Then she would take her degree, and she would—ah, she would perhaps be a big woman, and lead a movement. Who knows?—At any rate she would go to college in eighteen months' time. All that mattered now was work, work.

And till college, she must go on with this teaching in St. Philip's School, which was always destroying her, but which she could now manage, without spoiling all her life. She would submit to it for a time, since the time had a definite limit.

The class-teaching itself at last became almost mechanical. It was a strain on her, an exhausting wearying strain, always unnatural. But there was a certain amount of pleasure in the sheer oblivion of teaching, so much work to do, so many children to see after, so much to be done, that one's self was forgotten. When the work had become like habit to her, and her individual soul was left out, had its growth elsewhere, then she could be almost happy.

Her real, individual self drew together and became more coherent during these two years of teaching, during the struggle against the odds of class teaching. It was always a prison to her, the school. But it was a prison where her wild, chaotic soul became hard and independent. When she was well enough and not tired, then she did not hate the teaching. She enjoyed getting into the swing of work of a morning, putting forth all her strength, making the thing go. It was for her a strenuous form of exercise. And her soul was left to rest, it had the time of torpor in which to gather itself together in strength again. But the teaching hours were too long, the tasks too heavy, and the disciplinary condition of the school too unnatural for her. She was worn very thin and quivering.

She came to school in the morning seeing the hawthorn flowers wet, the little, rosy grains swimming in a bowl of dew. The larks quivered their song up into the new sunshine, and the country was so glad. It was a violation to plunge into the dust and greyness of the town.

So that she stood before her class unwilling to give herself up to the activity of teaching, to turn her energy, that longed for the country and for joy of early summer, into the dominating of fifty children and the transferring to them some morsels of arithmetic. There was a little absentness about her. She could not force herself into forgetfulness. A jar of buttercups and fool's-parsley in the window-bottom kept her away in the meadows, where in the lush grass the moon-daisies were half-submerged, and a spray of pink ragged robin. Yet before her were faces of fifty children. They were almost like big daisies in a dimness of the grass.

A brightness was on her face, a little unreality in her teaching. She could not quite see her children. She was struggling between two worlds, her own world of young summer and flowers, and this other world of work. And the glimmer of her own sunlight was between her and her class.

Then the morning passed with a strange far-awayness and quietness. Dinner-time came, when she and Maggie ate joyously, with all the windows open. And then they went out into St. Philip's churchyard, where was a shadowy corner under red hawthorn trees. And there they talked and read Shelley or Browning or some work about "Woman and Labour".

And when she went back to school, Ursula lived still in the shadowy corner of the graveyard, where pink-red petals lay scattered from the hawthorn tree, like myriad tiny shells on a beach, and a church bell sometimes rang sonorously, and sometimes a bird called out, whilst Maggie's voice went on low and sweet.

These days she was happy in her soul: oh, she was so happy, that she wished she could take her joy and scatter it in armfuls broadcast. She made her children happy, too, with a little tingling of delight. But to her, the children were not a school class this afternoon. They were flowers, birds, little bright animals, children, anything. They only were not Standard Five. She felt no responsibility for them. It was for once a game, this teaching. And if they got their sums wrong, what matter? And she would take a pleasant bit of reading. And instead of history with dates, she would tell a lovely tale. And for grammar, they could have a bit of written analysis that was not difficult, because they had done it before:

> "She shall be sportive as a fawn
> That wild with glee across the lawn
> Or up the mountain springs."

She wrote that from memory, because it pleased her.

So the golden afternoon passed away and she went home happy. She had finished her day of school, and was free to plunge into the glowing evening of Cossethay. And she loved walking home. But it had not been school. It had been playing at school beneath red hawthorn blossom.

She could not go on like this. The quarterly examination was coming, and her class was not ready. It irritated her that she must drag herself away from her happy self, and exert herself with all her strength to force, to compel this heavy class of children to work hard at arithmetic. They did not want to work, she did not want to compel them. And yet, some second conscience gnawed at her, telling her the work was not properly done. It irritated her almost to madness, and she let loose all the irritation in the class. Then followed a day of battle and hate and violence, when she went home raw, feeling the golden evening taken away from her, herself incarcerated in some dark, heavy place, and chained there with a consciousness of having done badly at work.

What good was it that it was summer, that right till evening, when the corncrakes called, the larks would mount up into the light, to sing once more before nightfall. What good was it all, when she was out of tune, when she must only remember the burden and shame of school that day.

And still, she hated school. Still she cried, she did not believe in it. Why should the children learn, and why should she teach them? It was all so much milling the wind. What folly was it that made life into this, the fulfilling of some stupid, factitious duty? It was all so made up, so unnatural. The school, the sums, the grammar, the quarterly examinations, the registers—it was all a barren nothing!

Why should she give her allegiance to this world, and let it so dominate her, that her own world of warm sun and growing, sap-filled life was turned into nothing? She was not going to do it. She was not going to be a prisoner in the dry, tyrannical man-world. She was not going to care about it. What did it matter if her class did ever so badly in the quarterly examination. Let it—what did it matter?

Nevertheless, when the time came, and the report on her class was bad, she was miserable, and the joy of the summer was taken away from her, she was shut up in gloom. She could not really escape from this world of system and work, out into her fields where she was happy. She must have her place in the working world, be a recognised member with full rights there. It was more important to her than fields and sun and poetry, at this time. But she was only the more its enemy.

It was a very difficult thing, she thought, during the long hours of intermission in the summer holidays, to be herself, her happy self that enjoyed so much to lie in the sun, to play and swim and be content, and also to be a schoolteacher getting results out of a class of children. She dreamed fondly of the time when she need not be a teacher any more. But vaguely, she knew that responsibility had taken place in her for ever, and as yet her prime business was to work.

The autumn passed away, the winter was at hand. Ursula became more and more an inhabitant of the world of work, and of what is called life. She could not see her future, but a little way off, was college, and to the thought of this she clung fixedly. She would go to college, and get her two or three years' training, free of cost. Already she had applied and had her place appointed for the coming year.

So she continued to study for her degree. She would take French, Latin, English, mathematics and botany. She went to classes in Ilkeston, she studied at evening. For there was this world to conquer, this knowledge to acquire, this qualification to attain. And she worked with intensity, because of a want inside her that drove her on. Almost everything was subordinated now to this one desire to take her place in the world. What kind of place it was to be she did not ask herself. The blind desire drove her on. She must take her place.

She knew she would never be much of a success as an elementary school teacher. But neither had she failed. She hated it, but she had managed it.

Maggie had left St. Philip's School, and had found a more congenial post. The two girls remained friends. They met at evening classes, they studied and somehow encouraged a firm hope each in the other. They did not know whither they were making, nor what they ultimately wanted. But they knew they wanted now to learn, to know and to do.

They talked of love and marriage, and the position of woman in marriage.

Maggie said that love was the flower of life, and blossomed unexpectedly and without law, and must be plucked where it was found, and enjoyed for the brief hour of its duration.

To Ursula this was unsatisfactory. She thought she still loved Anton Skrebensky. But she did not forgive him that he had not been strong enough to acknowledge her. He had denied her. How then could she love him? How then was love so absolute? She did not believe it. She believed that love was a way, a means, not an end in itself, as Maggie seemed to think. And always the way of love would be found. But whither did it lead?

"I believe there are many men in the world one might love—there is not only one man," said Ursula.

She was thinking of Skrebensky. Her heart was hollow with the knowledge of Winifred Inger.

"But you must distinguish between love and passion," said Maggie, adding, with a touch of contempt: "Men will easily have a passion for you, but they won't love you."

"Yes," said Ursula, vehemently, the look of suffering, almost of fanaticism, on her face. "Passion is only part of love. And it seems so much because it can't last. That is why passion is never happy."

She was staunch for joy, for happiness, and permanency, in contrast with Maggie, who was for sadness, and the inevitable passing-away of things. Ursula suffered bitterly at the hands of life, Maggie was always single, always withheld, so she went in a heavy brooding sadness that was almost meat to her. In Ursula's last winter at St. Philip's the friendship of the two girls came to a climax. It was during this winter that Ursula suffered and enjoyed most keenly Maggie's fundamental sadness of enclosedness. Maggie enjoyed and suffered Ursula's struggles against the confines of her life. And then the two girls began to drift apart, as Ursula broke from that form of life wherein Maggie must remain enclosed.

XIV

THE WIDENING CIRCLE

Maggie's people, the Schofields, lived in the large gardener's cottage, that was half a farm, behind Belcote Hall. The hall was too damp to live in, so the Schofields were caretakers, gamekeepers, farmers, all in one. The father was gamekeeper and stock-breeder, the eldest son was market-gardener, using the big hall gardens, the second son was farmer and gardener. There was a large family, as at Cossethay.

Ursula loved to stay at Belcote, to be treated as a grand lady by Maggie's brothers. They were good-looking men. The eldest was twenty-six years old. He was the gardener, a man not very tall, but strong and well made, with brown, sunny, easy eyes and a face handsomely hewn, brown, with a long fair moustache which he pulled as he talked to Ursula.

The girl was excited because these men attended to her when she came near. She could make their eyes light up and quiver, she could make Anthony, the eldest, twist and twist his moustache. She knew she could move them almost at will with her light laughter and chatter. They loved her ideas, watched her as she talked vehemently about politics or economics. And she, while she talked, saw the golden-brown eyes of Anthony gleam like the eyes of a satyr as they watched her. He did not listen to her words, he listened to her. It excited her.

He was like a faun pleased when she would go with him over his hothouses, to look at the green and pretty plants, at the pink primulas nodding among their leaves, and cinarrias flaunting purple and crimson and white. She asked about everything, and he told her very exactly and minutely, in a queer pedantic way that made her want to laugh. Yet she was really interested in what he did. And he had the curious light in his face, like the light in the eyes of the goat that was tethered by the farmyard gate.

She went down with him into the warmish cellar, where already in the darkness the little yellow knobs of rhubarb were coming. He held the lantern down to the dark earth. She saw the tiny knob-end of the rhubarb thrusting upwards upon the thick red stem, thrusting itself like a knob of flame through the soft soil. His face was turned up to her, the light glittered on his eyes and his teeth as he laughed, with a faint, musical neigh. He looked handsome. And she heard a new sound in her ears, the faintly-musical, neighing laugh of Anthony, whose moustache twisted up, and whose eyes were luminous with a cold, steady, arrogant-laughing glare. There seemed a little prance of triumph in his movement, she could not rid herself of a movement of acquiescence, a touch of acceptance. Yet he was so humble, his voice was so caressing. He held his hand for her to step on when she must climb a wall. And she stepped on the living firmness of him, that quivered firmly under her weight.

She was aware of him as if in a mesmeric state. In her ordinary sense, she had nothing to do with him. But the peculiar ease and unnoticeableness of his entering the house, the power of his cold, gleaming light on her when he looked at her, was like a bewitchment. In his eyes, as in the pale grey eyes of a goat, there seemed some of that steady, hard fire of moonlight which has nothing to do with the day. It made her alert, and yet her mind went out like an extinguished thing. She was all senses, all her senses were alive.

Then she saw him on Sunday, dressed up in Sunday clothes, trying to impress her. And he looked ridiculous. She clung to the ridiculous effect of his stiff, Sunday clothes.

She was always conscious of some unfaithfulness to Maggie, on Anthony's score. Poor Maggie stood apart as if betrayed. Maggie and Anthony were enemies by instinct. Ursula had to go back to her friend brimming with affection and a poignancy of pity. Which Maggie received with a little stiffness. Then poetry and books and learning took the place of Anthony, with his goats' movements and his cold, gleaming humour.

While Ursula was at Belcote, the snow fell. In the morning, a covering of snow weighed on the rhododendron bushes.

"Shall we go out?" said Maggie.

She had lost some of her leader's sureness, and was now tentative, a little in reserve from her friend.

They took the key of the gate and wandered into the park. It was a white world on which dark trees and tree masses stood under a sky keen with frost. The two girls went past the hall, that was shuttered and silent, their footprints marking the snow on the drive. Down the park, a long way off, a man was carrying armfuls of hay across the snow. He was a small, dark figure, like an animal moving in its unawareness.

Ursula and Maggie went on exploring, down to a tinkling, chilly brook, that had worn the snow away in little scoops, and ran dark between. They saw a robin glance its bright eyes and burst scarlet and grey into the hedge, then some pertly-marked blue-tits scuffled. Meanwhile the brook slid on coldly, chuckling to itself.

The girls wandered across the snowy grass to where the artificial fish-ponds lay under thin ice. There was a big tree with a thick trunk twisted with ivy, that hung almost horizontal over the ponds. Ursula climbed joyfully into this and sat amid bosses of bright ivy and dull berries. Some ivy leaves were like green spears held out, and tipped with snow. The ice was seen beneath them.

Maggie took out a book, and sitting lower down the trunk began to read Coleridge's "Christabel". Ursula half listened. She was wildly thrilled. Then she saw Anthony coming across the snow, with his confident, slightly strutting stride. His face looked brown and hard against the snow, smiling with a sort of tense confidence.

"Hello!" she called to him.

A response went over his face, his head was lifted in an answering, jerking gesture.

"Hello!" he said. "You're like a bird in there."

And Ursula's laugh rang out. She answered to the peculiar, reedy twang in his penetrating voice.

She did not think of Anthony, yet she lived in a sort of connection with him, in his world. One evening she met him as she was coming down the lane, and they walked side by side.

"I think it's so *lovely* here," she cried.

"Do you?" he said. "I'm glad you like it."

There was a curious confidence in his voice.

"Oh, I love it. What more does one want than to live in this beautiful place, and make things grow in your garden. It is like the Garden of Eden."

"Is it?" he said, with a little laugh. "Yes—well, it's not so bad——" he was hesitating. The pale gleam was strong in his eyes, he was looking at her steadily, watching her, as an animal might. Something leaped in her soul. She knew he was going to suggest to her that she should be as he was.

"Would you like to stay here with me?" he asked, tentatively.

She blenched with fear and with the intense sensation of proffered licence suggested to her.

They had come to the gate.

"How?" she asked. "You aren't alone here."

"We could marry," he answered, in the strange, coldly-gleaming insinuating tone that chilled the sunshine into moonlight. All substantial things seemed transformed. Shadows and dancing moonlight were real, and all cold, inhuman, gleaming sensations. She realised with something like terror that she was going to accept this. She was going inevitably to accept him. His hand was reaching out to the gate before them. She stood still. His flesh was hard and brown and final. She seemed to be in the grip of some insult.

"I couldn't," she answered, involuntarily.

He gave the same brief, neighing little laugh, very sad and bitter now, and slotted back the bar of the gate. Yet he did not open. For a moment they both stood looking at the fire of sunset that quivered among the purple twigs of the trees. She saw his brown, hard, well-hewn face gleaming with anger and humiliation and submission. He was an animal that knows that it is subdued. Her heart flamed with sensation of him, of the fascinating thing he offered her, and with sorrow, and with an inconsolable sense of loneliness. Her soul was an infant crying in the night. He had no soul. Oh, and why had she? He was the cleaner.

She turned away, she turned round from him, and saw the east flushed strangely rose, the moon coming yellow and lovely upon a rosy sky, above the darkening, bluish snow. All this so beautiful, all this so lovely! He did not see it. He was one with it. But she saw it, and was one with it. Her seeing separated them infinitely.

They went on in silence down the path, following their different fates. The trees grew darker and darker, the snow made only a dimness in an unreal world. And like a shadow, the day had gone into a faintly luminous, snowy evening, while she was talking aimlessly to him, to keep him at a distance, yet to keep him near her, and he walked heavily. He opened the garden gate for her quietly, and she was entering into her own pleasances, leaving him outside the gate.

Then even whilst she was escaping, or trying to escape, this feeling of pain, came Maggie the next day, saying:

"I wouldn't make Anthony love you, Ursula, if you don't want him. It is not nice."

"But, Maggie, I never made him love me," cried Ursula, dismayed and suffering, and feeling as if she had done something base.

She liked Anthony, though. All her life, at intervals, she returned to the thought of him and of that which he offered. But she was a traveller, she was a traveller on the face of the earth, and he was an isolated creature living in the fulfilment of his own senses.

She could not help it, that she was a traveller. She knew Anthony, that he was not one. But oh, ultimately and finally, she must go on and on, seeking the goal that she knew she did draw nearer to.

She was wearing away her second and last cycle at St. Philip's. As the months went she ticked them off, first October, then November, December, January. She was careful always to subtract a month from the remainder, for the summer holidays. She saw herself travelling round a circle, only an arc of which remained to complete. Then, she was in the open, like a bird tossed into mid-air, a bird that had learned in some measure to fly.

There was college ahead; that was her mid-air, unknown, spacious. Come college, and she would have broken from the confines of all the life she had known. For her father was also going to move. They were all going to leave Cossethay.

Brangwen had kept his carelessness about his circumstances.He knew his work in the lace designing meant little to him personally, he just earned his wage by it. He did not know what meant much to him. Living close to Anna Brangwen, his mind was always suffused through with physical heat, he moved from instinct to instinct, groping, always groping on.

When it was suggested to him that he might apply for one of the posts as hand-work instructor, posts about to be created by the Nottingham Education Committee, it was as if a space had been given to him, into which he could remove from his hot, dusky enclosure. He sent in his application, confidently, expectantly. He had a sort of belief in his supernatural fate. The inevitable weariness of his daily work had stiffened some of his muscles, and made a slight deadness in his ruddy, alert face. Now he might escape.

He was full of the new possibilities, and his wife was acquiescent. She was willing now to have a change. She too was tired of Cossethay. The house was too small for the growing children. And since she was nearly forty years old, she began to come awake from her sleep of motherhood, her energy moved more outwards. The din of growing lives roused her from her apathy. She too must have her hand in making life. She was quite ready to move, taking all her brood. It would be better now if she transplanted them. For she had borne her last child, it would be growing up.

So that in her easy, unused fashion she talked plans and arrangements with her husband, indifferent really as to the method of the change, since a change was coming; even if it did not come in this way it would come in another.

The house was full of ferment. Ursula was wild with excitement. At last her father was going to be something, socially. So long, he had been a social cypher, without form or standing. Now he was going to be Art and Handwork Instructor for the County of Nottingham. That was really a status. It was a position. He would be a specialist in his way. And he was an uncommon man. Ursula felt they were all getting a foothold at last. He was coming to his own. Who else that she knew could turn out from his own fingers the beautiful things her father could produce? She felt he was certain of this new job.

They would move. They would leave this cottage at Cossethay which had grown too small for them; they would leave Cossethay, where the children had all been born, and where they were always kept to the same measure. For the people who had known them as children along with the other village boys and girls would never, could never understand that they should grow up different. They had held "Urtler Brangwen" one of themselves, and had given her her place in her native village, as in a family. And the bond was strong. But now, when she was growing to something beyond what Cossethay would allow or understand, the bond between her and her old associates was becoming a bondage.

" 'Ello, Urs'ler, 'ow are yer goin' on?" they said when they met her. And it demanded of her in the old voice the old response. And something in her must respond and belong to people who knew her. But something else denied bitterly. What was true of her ten years ago was not true now. And something else which she was, and must be, they could neither see nor allow. They felt it there nevertheless, something beyond them, and they were injured. They said she was proud and conceited, that she was too big for her shoes nowadays. They said, she needn't pretend, because they knew what she was. They had known her since she was born. They quoted this and that about her. And she was ashamed because she did feel different from the people she had lived amongst. It hurt her that she could not be at her ease with them any more. And yet—and yet—one's kite will rise on the wind as far as ever one has string to let it go. It tugs and tugs and will go, and one is glad the further it goes, even if everybody else is nasty about it. So Cossethay hampered her, and she wanted to go away, to be free to fly her kite as high as she liked. She wanted to go away, to be free to stand straight up to her own height.

So that when she knew that her father had the new post, and that the family would move, she felt like skipping on the face of the earth, and making psalms of joy. The old, bound shell of Cossethay was to be cast off, and she was to dance away into the blue air. She wanted to dance and sing.

She made dreams of the new place she would live in, where stately cultured people of high feeling would be friends with her, and she would live with the noble in the land, moving to a large freedom of feeling. She dreamed of a rich, proud, simple girl-friend, who had never known Mr. Harby and his like, nor ever had a note in her voice of bondaged contempt and fear, as Maggie had.

And she gave herself to all that she loved in Cossethay, passionately, because she was going away now. She wandered about to her favourite spots. There was a place where she went trespassing to find the snowdrops that grew wild. It was evening and the winter-darkened meadows were full of mystery. When she came to the woods an oak tree had been newly chopped down in the dell. Pale drops of flowers glimmered many under the hazels, and by the sharp, golden splinters of wood that were splashed about, the grey-green blades of snowdrop leaves pricked unheeding, the drooping still little flowers were without heed.

Ursula picked some lovingly, in an ecstasy. The golden chips of wood shone yellow like sunlight, the snowdrops in the twilight were like the first stars of night. And she, alone amongst them, was wildly happy to have found her way into such a glimmering dusk, to the intimate little flowers, and the splash of wood chips like sunshine over the twilight of the ground. She sat down on the felled tree and remained awhile remote.

Going home, she left the purplish dark of the trees for the open lane, where the puddles shone long and jewel-like in the ruts, the land about her was darkened, and the sky a jewel overhead. Oh, how amazing it was to her! It was almost too much. She wanted to run, and sing, and cry out for very wildness and poignancy, but she could not run and sing and cry out in such a way as to cry out the deep things in her heart, so she was still, and almost sad with loneliness.

At Easter she went again to Maggie's home, for a few days. She was, however shy and fugitive. She saw Anthony, how suggestive he was to look on, and how his eyes had a sort of supplicating light, that was rather beautiful. She looked at him, and she looked again, for him to become real to her. But it was her own self that was occupied elsewhere. She seemed to have some other being.

And she turned to spring and the opening buds. There was a large pear tree by a wall, and it was full, thronged with tiny, grey-green buds, myriads. She stood before it arrested with delight, and a realisation went deep into her heart. There was so great a host in array behind the cloud of pale, dim green, so much to come forth—so much sunshine to pour down.

So the weeks passed on, trance-like and pregnant. The pear tree at Cossethay burst into bloom against the cottage-end, like a wave burst into foam. Then gradually the bluebells came, blue as water standing thin in the level places under the trees and bushes, flowing in more and more, till there was a flood of azure, and pale-green leaves burning, and tiny birds with fiery little song and flight. Then swiftly the flood sank and was gone, and it was summer.

There was to be no going to the seaside for a holiday. The holiday was the removal from Cossethay.

They were going to live near Willey Green, which place was most central for Brangwen. It was an old, quiet village on the edge of the thronged colliery-district. So that it served, in its quaintness of odd old cottages lingering in their sunny gardens, as a sort of bower or pleasaunce to the sprawling colliery-townlet of Beldover, a pleasant walk-round for the colliers on Sunday morning, before the public-houses opened.

In Willey Green stood the Grammar School where Brangwen was occupied for two days during the week, and where experiments in education were being carried on.

Ursula wanted to live in Willey Green on the remoter side, towards Southwell, and Sherwood Forest. There it was so lovely and romantic. But out into the world meant out into the world. Will Brangwen must become modern.

He bought, with his wife's money, a fairly large house in the new, red-brick part of Beldover. It was a villa built by the widow of the late colliery manager, and stood in a quiet, new little side-street near the large church.

Ursula was rather sad. Instead of having arrived at distinction they had come to new red-brick suburbia in a grimy, small town.

Mrs. Brangwen was happy. The rooms were splendidly large—a splendid dining-room, drawing-room and kitchen, besides a very pleasant study downstairs. Everything was admirably appointed. The widow had settled herself in lavishly. She was a native of Beldover, and had intended to reign almost queen. Her bathroom was white and silver, her stairs were of oak, her chimney-pieces were massive and oaken, with bulging, columnar supports.

"Good and substantial," was the keynote. But Ursula resented the stout, inflated prosperity implied everywhere. She made her father promise to chisel down the bulging oaken chimney-pieces, chisel them flat. That sort of important paunch was very distasteful to her. Her father was himself long and loosely built. What had he to do with so much "good and substantial" importance?

They bought a fair amount also of the widow's furniture. It was in common good taste—the great Wilton carpet, the large round table, the Chesterfield covered with glossy chintz in roses and birds. It was all really very sunny and nice, with large windows, and a view right across the shallow valley.

After all, they would be, as one of their acquaintances said, among the élite of Beldover. They would represent culture. And as there was no one of higher social importance than the doctors, the colliery-managers, and the chemists, they would shine, with their Della Robbia beautiful Madonna, their lovely reliefs from Donatello, their reproductions from Botticelli. Nay, the large photographs of the Primavera and the Aphrodite and the Nativity in the dining-room, the ordinary reception-room, would make dumb the mouth of Beldover.

And after all, it is better to be princess in Beldover than a vulgar nobody in the country.

There was great preparation made for the removal of the whole Brangwen family, ten in all. The house in Beldover was prepared, the house in Cossethay was dismantled. Come the end of the school-term the removal would begin.

Ursula left school at the end of July, when the summer holiday commenced. The morning outside was bright and sunny, and the freedom got inside the schoolroom this last day. It was as if the walls of the school were going to melt away. Already they seemed shadowy and unreal. It was breaking-up morning. Soon scholars and teachers would be outside, each going his own way. The irons were struck off, the sentence was expired, the prison was a momentary shadow halting about them. The children were carrying away books and ink-well, and rolling up maps. All their faces were bright with gladness and good-will. There was a bustle of cleaning and clearing away all marks of this last term of imprisonment. They were all breaking free. Busily, eagerly, Ursula made up her totals of attendances in the register. With pride she wrote down the thousands: to so many thousands of children had she given another session's lessons. It looked tremendous. The excited hours passed slowly in suspense. Then at last it was over. For the last time, she stood before her children whilst they said their prayers and sang a hymn. Then it was over.

"Good-bye, children," she said. "I shall not forget you, and you must not forget me."

"No, miss," cried the children in chorus, with shining faces.

She stood smiling on them, moved, as they filed out. Then she gave her monitors their term sixpences, and they too departed. Cupboards were locked, blackboards washed, inkwells and dusters removed. The place stood bare and vacated. She had triumphed over it. It was a shell now. She had fought a good fight here, and it had not been altogether unenjoyable. She owed some gratitude even to this hard, vacant place, that stood like a memorial or a trophy. So much of her life had been fought for and won and lost here. Something of this school would always belong to her, something of her to it. She acknowledged it. And now came the leave-taking.

In the teachers' room the teachers were chatting and loitering, talking excitedly of where they were going: to the Isle of Man, to Llandudno, to Yarmouth. They were eager, and attached to each other, like comrades leaving a ship.

Then it was Mr. Harby's turn to make a speech to Ursula. He looked handsome, with his silver-grey temples and black brows, and his imperturbable male solidity.

"Well," he said, "we must say good-bye to Miss Brangwen and wish her all good fortune for the future. I suppose we shall see her again some time, and hear how she is getting on."

"Oh, yes," said Ursula, stammering, blushing, laughing. "Oh, yes, I shall come and see you."

Then she realised that this sounded too personal, and she felt foolish.

"Miss Schofield suggested these two books," he said, putting a couple of volumes on the table: "I hope you will like them."

Ursula feeling very shy picked up the books. There was a volume of Swinburne's poetry, and a volume of Meredith's.

"Oh, I shall love them," she said. "Thank you very much—thank you all so much—it is so——"

She stuttered to an end, and very red, turned the leaves of the books eagerly, pretending to be taking the first pleasure, but really seeing nothing.

Mr. Harby's eyes were twinkling. He alone was at his ease, master of the situation. It was pleasing to him to make Ursula the gift, and for once extend good feeling to his teachers. As a rule, it was so difficult, each one was so strained in resentment under his rule.

"Yes," he said, "we hoped you would like the choice——"

He looked with his peculiar, challenging smile for a moment, then returned to his cupboards.

Ursula felt very confused. She hugged her books, loving them. And she felt that she loved all the teachers, and Mr. Harby. It was very confusing.

At last she was out. She cast one hasty glance over the school buildings squatting on the asphalt yard in the hot, glistening sun, one look down the well-known road, and turned her back on it all. Something strained in her heart. She was going away.

"Well, good luck," said the last of the teachers, as she shook hands at the end of the road. "We'll expect you back some day."

He spoke in irony. She laughed, and broke away. She was free. As she sat on the top of the tram in the sunlight, she looked round her with tremendous delight. She had left something which had meant much to her. She would not go to school any more, and do the familiar things. Queer! There was a little pang amid her exultation, of fear, not of regret. Yet how she exulted this morning!

She was tremulous with pride and joy. She loved the two books. They were tokens to her, representing the fruit and trophies of her two years which, thank God, were over.

"To Ursula Brangwen, with best wishes for her future, and in warm memory of the time she spent in St. Philip's School," was written in the headmaster's neat, scrupulous handwriting. She could see the careful hand holding the pen, the thick fingers with tufts of black hair on the back of each one.

He had signed, all the teachers had signed. She liked having all their signatures. She felt she loved them all. They were her fellow-workers. She carried away from the school a pride she could never lose. She had her place as comrade and sharer in the work of the school, her fellow teachers had signed to her, as one of them. And she was one of all workers, she had put in her tiny brick to the fabric man was building, she had qualified herself as co-builder.

Then the day for the home removal came. Ursula rose early, to pack up the remaining goods. The carts arrived, lent by her uncle at the Marsh, in the lull between hay and corn harvest. The goods roped in the cart, Ursula mounted her bicycle and sped away to Beldover.

The house was hers. She entered its clean-scrubbed silence. The dining-room had been covered with a thick rush matting, hard and of the beautiful, luminous, clean colour of sun-dried reeds. The walls were pale grey, the doors were darker grey. Ursula admired it very much, as the sun came through the large windows, streaming in.

She flung open doors and windows to the sunshine. Flowers were bright and shining round the small lawn, which stood above the road, looking over the raw field opposite, which would later be built upon. No one came. So she wandered down the garden at the back of the wall. The eight bells of the church rang the hour. She could hear the many sounds of the town about her.

At last, the cart was seen coming round the corner, familiar furniture piled undignified on top, Tom, her brother, and Theresa, marching on foot beside the mass, proud of having walked ten miles or more, from the tram terminus. Ursula poured out beer, and the men drank thirstily, by the door. A second cart was coming. Her father appeared on his motor bicycle. There was the staggering transport of furniture up the steps to the little lawn, where it was deposited all pellmell in the sunshine, very queer and discomforting.

Brangwen was a pleasant man to work with, cheerful and easy. Ursula loved deciding him where the heavy things should stand. She watched anxiously the struggle up the steps and through the doorways. Then the big things were in, the carts set off again. Ursula and her father worked away carrying in all the light things that remained upon the lawn, and putting them in place. Dinner time came. They ate bread and cheese in the kitchen.

"Well, we're getting on," said Brangwen, cheerfully.

Two more loads arrived. The afternoon passed away in a struggle with the furniture, upstairs. Towards five o'clock, appeared the last loads, consisting also of Mrs. Brangwen and the younger children, driven by Uncle Fred in the trap. Gudrun had walked with Margaret from the station. The whole family had come.

"There!" said Brangwen, as his wife got down from the cart: "Now we're all here."

"Ay," said his wife pleasantly.

And the very brevity, the silence of intimacy between the two made a home in the hearts of the children, who clustered round feeling strange in the new place.

Everything was at sixes and sevens. But a fire was made in the kitchen, the hearth-rug put down, the kettle set on the hob, and Mrs. Brangwen began towards sunset to prepare the first meal. Ursula and Gudrun were slaving in the bedrooms, candles were rushing about. Then from the kitchen came the smell of ham and eggs and coffee, and in the gaslight, the scrambled meal began. The family seemed to huddle together like a little camp in a strange place. Ursula felt a load of responsibility upon her, caring for the half-little ones. The smallest kept near the mother.

It was dark, and the children went sleepy but excited to bed. It was a long time before the sound of voices died out. There was a tremendous sense of adventure.

In the morning everybody was awake soon after dawn, the children crying: "When I wakened up I didn't know where I was."

There were the strange sounds of the town, and the repeated chiming of the big church bells, so much harsher and more insistent than the little bells of Cossethay. They looked through the windows past the other new red houses to the wooded hill across the valley. They had all a delightful sense of space and liberation, space and light and air.

But gradually all set to work. They were a careless, untidy family. Yet when once they set about to get the house in order, the thing went with felicity and quickness. By evening the place was roughly established.

They would not have a servant to live in the house, only a woman who could go home at night. And they would not even have the woman yet. They wanted to do as they liked in their own home, with no stranger in the midst.

XV

THE BITTERNESS OF ECSTASY

A storm of industry raged on in the house. Ursula did not go to college till October. So, with a distinct feeling of responsibility, as if she must express herself in this house, she laboured arranging, re-arranging, selecting, contriving.

She could use her father's ordinary tools, both for wood-work and metal-work, so she hammered and tinkered. Her mother was quite content to have the thing done. Brangwen was interested. He had a ready belief in his daughter. He himself was at work putting up his work-shed in the garden.

At last she had finished for the time being. The drawing-room was big and empty. It had the good Wilton carpet, of which the family was so proud, and the large couch and large chairs covered with shiny chintz, and the piano, a little sculpture in plaster that Brangwen had done, and not very much more. It was too large and empty-feeling for the family to occupy very much. Yet they liked to know it was there, large and empty.

The home was the dining-room. There the hard rush floor-covering made the ground light, reflecting light upon the bottom their hearts; in the window-bay was a broad, sunny seat, the table was so solid one could not jostle it, and the chairs so strong one could knock them over without hurting them. The familiar organ that Brangwen had made stood on one side, looking peculiarly small, the sideboard was comfortably reduced to normal proportions. This was the family living-room.

Ursula had a bedroom to herself. It was really a servants' bedroom, small and plain. Its window looked over the back garden at other back gardens, some of them old and very nice, some of them littered with packing-cases, then at the backs of the houses whose fronts were the shops in High Street, or the genteel homes of the under-manager or the chief cashier, facing the chapel.

She had six weeks still before going to college. In this time she nervously read over some Latin and some botany, and fitfully worked at some mathematics. She was going into college as a teacher, for her training. But, having already taken her matriculation examination, she was entered for a university course. At the end of a year she would sit for the Intermediate Arts, then two years after for her B.A. So her case was not that of the ordinary school-teacher. She would be working among the private students who came only for pure education, not for mere professional training. She would be of the elect.

For the next three years she would be more or less dependent on her parents again. Her training was free. All college fees were paid by the government, she had moreover a few pounds grant every year. This would just pay for her train fares and her clothing. Her parents would only have to feed her. She did not want to cost them much. They would not be well off. Her father would earn only two hundred a year, and a good deal of her mother's capital was spent in buying the house. Still, there was enough to get along with.

Gudrun was attending the Art School at Nottingham. She was working particularly at sculpture. She had a gift for this. She loved making little models in clay, of children or of animals. Already some of these had appeared in the Students' Exhibition in the Castle, and Gudrun was a distinguished person. She was chafing at the Art School and wanted to go to London. But there was not enough money. Neither would her parents let her go so far.

Theresa had left the High School. She was a great strapping, bold hussy, indifferent to all higher claims. She would stay at home. The others were at school, except the youngest. When term started, they would all be transferred to the Grammar School at Willey Green.

Ursula was excited at making acquaintances in Beldover. The excitement soon passed. She had tea at the clergyman's, at the chemist's, at the other chemist's, at the doctor's, at the under-manager's—then she knew practically everybody. She could not take people very seriously, though at the time she wanted to.

She wandered the country, on foot and on her bicycle, finding it very beautiful in the forest direction, between Mansfield and Southwell and Worksop. But she was here only skirmishing for amusement. Her real exploration would begin in college.

Term began. She went into town each day by train. The cloistered quiet of the college began to close around her.

She was not at first disappointed. The big college built of stone, standing in the quiet street, with a rim of grass and lime trees all so peaceful: she felt it remote, a magic land. Its architecture was foolish, she knew from her father. Still, it was different from that of all other buildings. Its rather pretty, plaything, Gothic form was almost a style, in the dirty industrial town.

She liked the hall, with its big stone chimney-piece and its Gothic arches supporting the balcony above. To be sure the arches were ugly, the chimney-piece of cardboard-like carved stone, with its armorial decoration, looked silly just opposite the bicycle stand and the radiator, whilst the great notice-board with its fluttering papers seemed to slam away all sense of retreat and mystery from the far wall. Nevertheless, amorphous as it might be, there was in it a reminiscence of the wondrous, cloistral origin of education. Her soul flew straight back to the medieval times, when the monks of God held the learning of men and imparted it within the shadow of religion. In this spirit she entered college.

The harshness and vulgarity of the lobbies and cloak-rooms hurt her at first. Why was it not all beautiful? But she could not openly admit her criticism. She was on holy ground.

She wanted all the students to have a high, pure spirit, she wanted them to say only the real, genuine things, she wanted their faces to be still and luminous as the nuns' and the monks' faces.

Alas, the girls chattered and giggled and were nervous, they were dressed up and frizzed, the men looked mean and clownish.

Still, it was lovely to pass along the corridor with one's books in one's hands, to push the swinging, glass-panelled door, and enter the big room where the first lecture would be given. The windows were large and lofty, the myriad brown students' desks stood waiting, the great blackboard was smooth behind the rostrum.

Ursula sat beside her window, rather far back. Looking down, she saw the lime trees turning yellow, the tradesman's boy passing silent down the still, autumn-sunny street. There was the world, remote, remote.

Here, within the great, whispering sea-shell, that whispered all the while with reminiscence of all the centuries, time faded away, and the echo of knowledge filled the timeless silence.

She listened, she scribbled her notes with joy, almost with ecstasy, never for a moment criticising what she heard. The lecturer was a mouth-piece, a priest. As he stood, black-gowned, on the rostrum, some strands of the whispering confusion of knowledge that filled the whole place seemed to be singled out and woven together by him, till they became a lecture.

At first, she preserved herself from criticism. She would not consider the professors as men, ordinary men who ate bacon, and pulled on their boots before coming to college. They were the black-gowned priests of knowledge, serving for ever in a remote, hushed temple. They were the initiated, and the beginning and the end of the mystery was in their keeping.

Curious joy she had of the lectures. It was a joy to hear the theory of education, there was such freedom and pleasure in ranging over the very stuff of knowledge, and seeing how it moved and lived and had its being. How happy Racine made her! She did not know why. But as the big lines of the drama unfolded themselves, so steady, so measured, she felt a thrill as of being in the realm of the reality. Of Latin, she was doing Livy and Horace. The curious, intimate, gossiping tone of the Latin class suited Horace. Yet she never cared for him, nor even Livy. There was an entire lack of sternness in the gossipy class-room. She tried hard to keep her old grasp of the Roman spirit. But gradually the Latin became mere gossip-stuff and artificiality to her, a question of manners and verbosities.

Her terror was the mathematics class. The lecturer went so fast, her heart beat excitedly, she seemed to be straining every nerve. And she struggled hard, during private study, to get the stuff into control.

Then came the lovely, peaceful afternoons in the botany laboratory. There were few students. How she loved to sit on her high stool before the bench, with her pith and her razor and her material, carefully mounting her slides, carefully bringing her microscope into focus, then turning with joy to record her observation, drawing joyfully in her book, if the slide were good.

She soon made a college friend, a girl who had lived in Florence, a girl who wore a wonderful purple or figured scarf draped over a plain, dark dress. She was Dorothy Russell, daughter of a south-country advocate. Dorothy lived with a maiden aunt in Nottingham, and spent her spare moments slaving for the

Women's Social and Political Union. She was quiet and intense, with an ivory face and dark hair looped plain over her ears. Ursula was very fond of her, but afraid of her. She seemed so old and so relentless towards herself. Yet she was only twenty-two. Ursula always felt her to be a creature of fate, like Cassandra.

The two girls had a close, stern friendship. Dorothy worked at all things with the same passion, never sparing herself. She came closest to Ursula during the botany hours. For she could not draw. Ursula made beautiful and wonderful drawings of the sections under the microscope, and Dorothy always came to learn the manner of the drawing.

So the first year went by, in magnificent seclusion and activity of learning. It was strenuous as a battle, her college life, yet remote as peace.

She came to Nottingham in the morning with Gudrun. The two sisters were distinguished wherever they went, slim, strong girls, eager and extremely sensitive. Gudrun was the more beautiful of the two, with her sleepy, half-languid girlishness that looked so soft, and yet was balanced and inalterable underneath. She wore soft, easy clothing, and hats which fell by themselves into a careless grace.

Ursula was much more carefully dressed, but she was self-conscious, always falling into depths of admiration of somebody else, and modelling herself upon this other, and so producing a hopeless incongruity. When she dressed for practical purposes she always looked well. In winter, wearing a tweed coat-and-skirt and a small hat of black fur pulled over her eager, palpitant face, she seemed to move down the street in a drifting motion of suspense and exceeding sensitive receptivity.

At the end of the first year Ursula got through her Intermediate Arts examination, and there came a lull in her eager activities. She slackened off, she relaxed altogether. Worn nervous and inflammable by the excitement of the preparation for the examination, and by the sort of exaltation which carried her through the crisis itself, she now fell into a quivering passivity, her will all loosened.

The family went to Scarborough for a month. Gudrun and the father were busy at the handicraft holiday school there, Ursula was left a good deal with the children. But when she could, she went off by herself.

She stood and looked out over the shining sea. It was very beautiful to her. The tears rose hot in her heart.

Out of the far, far space there drifted slowly in to her a passionate, unborn yearning. "There are so many dawns that have not yet risen." It seemed as if, from over the edge of the sea, all the unrisen dawns were appealing to her, all her unborn soul was crying for the unrisen dawns.

As she sat looking out at the tender sea, with its lovely, swift glimmer, the sob rose in her breast, till she caught her lip suddenly under her teeth, and the tears were forcing themselves from her. And in her very sob, she laughed. Why did she cry? She did not want to cry. It was so beautiful that she laughed. It was so beautiful that she cried.

She glanced apprehensively round, hoping no one would see her in this state.

Then came a time when the sea was rough. She watched the water travelling in to the coast, she watched a big wave running unnoticed, to burst in a shock of foam against a rock, enveloping all in a great white beauty, to pour away again, leaving the rock emerged black and teeming. Oh, and if, when the wave burst into whiteness, it were only set free!

Sometimes she loitered along the harbour, looking at the sea-browned sailors, who, in their close blue jerseys, lounged on the harbour-wall, and laughed at her with impudent, communicative eyes.

There was established a little relation between her and them. She never would speak to them or know any more of them. Yet as she walked by and they leaned on the sea-wall, there was something between her and them, something keen and delightful and painful. She liked best the young one whose fair, salty hair tumbled over his blue eyes. He was *so* new and fresh and salt and not of this world.

From Scarborough she went to her Uncle Tom's. Winifred had a small baby, born at the end of the summer. She had become strange and alien to Ursula. There was an unmentionable reserve between the two women. Tom Brangwen was an attentive father, a very domestic husband. But there was something spurious about his domesticity, Ursula did not like him any more. Something ugly, blatant in his nature had come out now, making him shift everything over to a sentimental basis. A materialistic unbeliever, he carried it all off by becoming full of human feeling, a warm, attentive host, a generous husband, a model citizen. And he was clever enough to rouse admiration everywhere, and to take in his wife sufficiently. She did not love him. She was glad to live in a state of complacent self-deception with him, she worked according to him.

Ursula was relieved to go home. She had still two peaceful years before her. Her future was settled for two years. She returned to college to prepare for her final examination.

But during this year the glamour began to depart from college. The professors were not priests initiated into the deep mysteries of life and knowledge. After all, they were only middle-men handling wares they had become so accustomed to that they were oblivious of them. What was Latin?—So much dry goods of knowledge. What was the Latin class altogether but a sort of second-hand curio shop, where one bought curios and learned the market-value of curios; dull curios too, on the whole. She was as bored by the Latin curiosities as she was by Chinese and Japanese curiosities in the antique shops. "Antiques"—the very word made her soul fall flat and dead.

The life went out of her studies, why, she did not know. But the whole thing seemed sham, spurious; spurious Gothic arches, spurious peace, spurious Latinity, spurious dignity of France, spurious naïveté of Chaucer. It was a second-hand dealer's shop, and one bought an equipment for an examination. This was only a little side-show to the factories of the town. Gradually the perception stole into her. This was no religious retreat, no perception of pure learning. It was a little apprentice-shop where one was further equipped for making money. The college itself was a little, slovenly laboratory for the factory.

A harsh and ugly disillusion came over her again, the same darkness and bitter gloom from which she was never safe now, the realisation of the permanent substratum of ugliness under everything. As she came to the college in the afternoon, the lawns were frothed with daisies, the lime trees hung tender and sunlit and green; and oh, the deep, white froth of the daisies was anguish to see.

For inside, inside the college, she knew she must enter the sham workshop. All the while, it was a sham store, a sham warehouse, with a single motive of material gain, and no productivity. It pretended to exist by the religious virtue of knowledge. But the religious virtue of knowledge was become a flunkey to the god of material success.

A sort of inertia came over her. Mechanically, from habit, she went on with her studies. But it was almost hopeless. She could scarcely attend to anything. At the Anglo-Saxon lecture in the afternoon, she sat looking down, out of the window, hearing no word, of Beowulf or of anything else. Down below, in the street, the sunny grey pavement went beside the palisade. A woman in a pink frock, with a scarlet sunshade, crossed the road, a little white dog running like a fleck of light about her. The woman with the scarlet sunshade came over the road, a lilt in her walk, a little shadow attending her. Ursula watched spell-bound. The woman with the scarlet sunshade and the flickering terrier was gone—and whither? Whither?

In what world of reality was the woman in the pink dress walking? To what warehouse of dead unreality was she herself confined?

What good was this place, this college? What good was Anglo-Saxon, when one only learned it in order to answer examination questions, in order that one should have a higher commercial value later on? She was sick with this long service at the inner commercial shrine. Yet what else was there? Was life all this, and this only? Everywhere, everything was debased to the same service. Everything went to produce vulgar things, to encumber material life.

Suddenly she threw over French. She would take honours in botany. This was the one study that lived for her. She had entered into the lives of the plants. She was fascinated by the strange laws of the vegetable world. She had here a glimpse of something working entirely apart from the purpose of the human world.

College was barren, cheap, a temple converted to the most vulgar, petty commerce. Had she not gone to hear the echo of learning pulsing back to the source of the mystery?—The source of mystery! And barrenly, the professors in their gowns offered commercial commodity that could be turned to good account in the examination room; ready-made stuff too, and not really worth the money it was intended to fetch; which they all knew.

All the time in the college now, save when she was labouring in her botany laboratory, for there the mystery still glimmered, she felt she was degrading herself in a kind of trade of sham jewjaws.

Angry and stiff, she went through her last term. She would rather be out again earning her own living. Even Brinsley Street and Mr. Harby seemed real in comparison. Her violent hatred of the Ilkeston School was nothing compared with the sterile degradation of college. But she was not going back to Brinsley Street either. She would take her B.A., and become a mistress in some Grammar School for a time.

The last year of her college career was wheeling slowly round. She could see ahead her examination and her departure. She had the ash of disillusion gritting under her teeth. Would the next move turn out the same? Always the shining doorway ahead; and then, upon approach, always the shining doorway was a gate into another ugly yard, dirty and active and dead. Always the crest of the hill gleaming ahead under heaven: and then, from the top of the hill only another sordid valley full of amorphous, squalid activity.

No matter! Every hill-top was a little different, every valley was somehow new. Cossethay and her childhood with her father; the Marsh and the little Church school near the Marsh, and her grandmother and her uncles; the High School at Nottingham and Anton Skrebensky; Anton Skrebensky and the dance in the moonlight between the fires; then the time she could not think of without being blasted, Winifred Inger, and the months before becoming a school-teacher; then the horrors of Brinsley Street, lapsing into comparative peacefulness, Maggie, and Maggie's brother, whose influence she could still feel in her veins, when she conjured him up; then college, and Dorothy Russell, who was now in France, then the next move into the world again!

Already it was a history. In every phase she was so different. Yet she was always Ursula Brangwen. But what did it mean, Ursula Brangwen? She did not know what she was. Only she was full of rejection, of refusal. Always, always she was spitting out of her mouth the ash and grit of disillusion, of falsity. She could only stiffen in rejection, in rejection. She seemed always negative in her action.

That which she was, positively, was dark and unrevealed, it could not come forth. It was like a seed buried in dry ash. This world in which she lived was like a circle lighted by a lamp. This lighted area, lit up by man's completest consciousness, she thought was all the world: that here all was disclosed for ever. Yet all the time, within the darkness she had been aware of points of light, like the eyes of wild beasts, gleaming, penetrating, vanishing. And her soul had acknowledged in a great heave of terror only the outer darkness. This inner circle of light in which she lived and moved, wherein the trains rushed and the factories ground out their machine-produce and the plants and the animals worked by the light of science and knowledge, suddenly it seemed like the area under an arc-lamp, wherein the moths and children played in the security of blinding light, not even knowing there was any darkness, because they stayed in the light.

But she could see the glimmer of dark movement just out of range, she saw the eyes of the wild beast gleaming from the darkness, watching the vanity of the camp fire and the sleepers; she felt the strange, foolish vanity of the camp, which said "Beyond our light and our order there is nothing," turning their faces always inward towards the sinking fire of illuminating consciousness, which comprised sun and stars, and the Creator, and the System of Righteousness, ignoring always the vast darkness that wheeled round about, with half-revealed shapes lurking on the edge.

Yea, and no man dared even throw a firebrand into the darkness. For if he did he was jeered to death by the others, who cried "Fool, anti-social knave, why would you disturb us with bogeys? There *is* no darkness. We move and live and have our being within the light, and unto us is given the eternal light of knowledge, we comprise and comprehend the innermost core and issue of knowledge. Fool and knave, how dare you belittle us with the darkness?"

Nevertheless the darkness wheeled round about, with grey shadow-shapes of wild beasts, and also with dark shadow-shapes of the angels, whom the light fenced out, as it fenced out the more familiar beasts of darkness. And some, having for a moment seen the darkness, saw it bristling with the tufts of the hyena and the wolf; and some having given up their vanity of the light, having died in their own conceit, saw the gleam in the eyes of the wolf and the hyena, that it was the flash of the sword of angels, flashing at the door to come in, that the angels in the darkness were lordly and terrible and not to be denied, like the flash of fangs.

It was a little while before Easter, in her last year of college, when Ursula was twenty-two years old, that she heard again from Skrebensky. He had written to her once or twice from South Africa, during the first months of his service out there in the war, and since had sent her a post-card every now and then, at ever longer intervals. He had become a first lieutenant, and had stayed out in Africa. She had not heard of him now for more than two years.

Often her thoughts returned to him. He seemed like the gleaming dawn, yellow, radiant, of a long, grey, ashy day. The memory of him was like the thought of the first radiant hours of morning. And here was the blank grey ashiness of later daytime. Ah, if he had only remained true to her, she might have known the sunshine, without all this toil and hurt and degradation of a spoiled day. He would have been her angel. He held the keys of the sunshine. Still he held them. He could open to her the gates of succeeding freedom and delight. Nay, if he had remained true to her, he would have been the doorway to her, into the boundless sky of happiness and plunging, inexhaustible freedom which was the paradise of her soul. Ah, the great range he would have opened to her, the illimitable endless space for self-realisation and delight for ever.

The one thing she believed in was in the love she had held for him. It remained shining and complete, a thing to hark back to. And she said to herself, when present things seemed a failure:

"Ah, I was fond of him," as if with him the leading flower of her life had died.

Now she heard from him again. The chief effect was pain. The pleasure, the spontaneous joy was not there any longer. But her *will* rejoiced. Her will had fixed itself to him. And the old excitement of her dreams stirred and woke up. He was come, the man with the wondrous lips that could send the kiss wavering to the very end of all space. Was he come back to her? She did not believe.

> *My dear Ursula, I am back in England again for a few months before going out again, this time to India. I wonder if you still keep the memory of our times together. I have still got the little photograph of you. You must be changed since then, for it is about six years ago. I am fully six years older,—I have lived through another life since I knew you at Cossethay. I wonder if you would care to see me. I shall come up to Derby next week, and I would call in Nottingham, and we might have tea together. Will you let me know? I shall look for your answer.*
> *Anton Skrebensky.*

Ursula had taken this letter from the rack in the hall at college, and torn it open as she crossed to the Women's room. The world seemed to dissolve away from around her, she stood alone in clear air.

Where could she go, to be alone? She fled away, upstairs, and through the private way to the reference library. Seizing a book, she sat down and pondered the letter. Her heart beat, her limbs trembled. As in a dream, she heard one gong sound in the college, then, strangely, another. The first lecture had gone by.

Hurriedly she took one of her note-books and began to write.

> *Dear Anton, Yes, I still have the ring. I should be very glad to see you again. You can come here to college for me, or I will meet you somewhere in the town. Will you let me know? Your sincere friend——"*

Trembling, she asked the librarian, who was her friend, if he would give her an envelope. She sealed and addressed her letter, and went out, bare-headed, to post it. When it was dropped into the pillar-box, the world became a very still, pale place, without confines. She wandered back to college, to her pale dream, like a first wan light of dawn.

Skrebensky came one afternoon the following week. Day after day, she had hurried swiftly to the letter-rack on her arrival at college in the morning, and during the intervals between lectures. Several times, swiftly, with secretive fingers, she had plucked his letter down from its public prominence, and fled across the hall holding it fast and hidden. She read her letters in the botany laboratory, where her corner was always reserved to her.

Several letters, and then he was coming. It was Friday afternoon he appointed. She worked over her microscope with feverish activity, able to give only half her attention, yet working closely and rapidly. She had on her slide some special stuff come up from London that day, and the professor was fussy and excited about it. At the same time, as she focused the light on her field, and saw the plant-animal lying shadowy in a boundless light, she was fretting over a conversation she had had a few days ago with Dr. Frankstone, who was a woman doctor of physics in the college.

"No, really," Dr. Frankstone had said, "I don't see why we should attribute some special mystery to life—do you? We don't understand it as we understand electricity, even, but that doesn't warrant our saying it is something special, something different in kind and distinct from everything else in the universe—do you think it does? May it not be that life consists in a complexity of physical and chemical activities, of the same order as the activities we already know in science? I don't see, really, why we should imagine there is a special order of life, and life alone——"

The conversation had ended on a note of uncertainty, indefinite, wistful. But the purpose, what was the purpose? Electricity had no soul, light and heat had no soul. Was she herself an impersonal force, or conjunction of forces, like one of these? She looked still at the unicellular shadow that lay within the field of light, under her microscope. It was alive. She saw it move—she saw the bright mist of its ciliary activity, she saw the gleam of its nucleus, as it slid across the plane of light. What then was its will? If it was a conjunction of forces, physical and chemical, what held these forces unified, and for what purpose were they unified?

For what purpose were the incalculable physical and chemical activities nodalised in this shadowy, moving speck under her microscope? What was the will which nodalised them and created the one thing she saw? What was its intention? To be itself? Was its purpose just mechanical and limited to itself?

It intended to be itself. But what self? Suddenly in her mind the world gleamed strangely, with an intense light, like the nucleus of the creature under the microscope. Suddenly she had passed away into an intensely-gleaming light of knowledge. She could not understand what it all was. She only knew that it was not limited mechanical energy, nor mere purpose of self-preservation and self-assertion. It was a consummation, a being infinite. Self was a oneness with the infinite. To be oneself was a supreme, gleaming triumph of infinity.

Ursula sat abstracted over her microscope, in suspense. Her soul was busy, infinitely busy, in the new world. In the new world, Skrebensky was waiting for her—he would be waiting for her. She could not go yet, because her soul was engaged. Soon she would go.

A stillness, like passing away, took hold of her. Far off, down the corridors, she heard the gong booming five o'clock. She must go. Yet she sat still.

The other students were pushing back their stools and putting their microscopes away. Everything broke into turmoil. She saw, through the window, students going down the steps, with books under their arms, talking, all talking.

A great craving to depart came upon her. She wanted also to be gone. She was in dread of the material world, and in dread of her own transfiguration. She wanted to run to meet Skrebensky—the new life, the reality.

Very rapidly she wiped her slides and put them back, cleared her place at the bench, active, active, active. She wanted to run to meet Skrebensky, hasten—hasten. She did not know what she was to meet. But it would be a new beginning. She must hurry.

She flitted down the corridor on swift feet, her razor and note-books and pencil in one hand, her pinafore over her arm. Her face was lifted and tense with eagerness. He might not be there.

Issuing from the corridor, she saw him at once. She knew him at once. Yet he was so strange. He stood with the curious self-effacing diffidence which so frightened her in well-bred young men whom she knew. He stood as if he wished to be unseen. He was very well-dressed. She would not admit to herself the chill like a sunshine of frost that came over her. This was he, the key, the nucleus to the new world.

He saw her coming swiftly across the hall, a slim girl in a white flannel blouse and dark skirt, with some of the abstraction and gleam of the unknown upon her, and he started, excited. He was very nervous. Other students were loitering about the hall.

She laughed, with a blind, dazzled face, as she gave him her hand. He too could not perceive her.

In a moment she was gone, to get her outdoor things. Then again, as when she had been at school, they walked out into the town to tea. And they went to the same tea-shop.

She knew a great difference in him. The kinship was there, the old kinship, but he had belonged to a different world from hers. It was as if they had cried a state of truce between him and her, and in this truce they had met. She knew, vaguely, in the first minute, that they were enemies come together in a truce. Every movement and word of his was alien to her being.

Yet still she loved the fine texture of his face, of his skin. He was rather browner, physically stronger. He was a man now. She thought his manliness made the strangeness in him. When he was only a youth, fluid, he was nearer to her. She thought a man must inevitably set into this strange separateness, cold otherness of being. He talked, but not to her. She tried to speak to him, but she could not reach him.

He seemed so balanced and sure, he made such a confident presence. He was a great rider, so there was about him some of a horseman's sureness and habitual definiteness of decision, also some of the horseman's animal darkness. Yet his soul was only the more wavering, vague. He seemed made up of a set of habitual actions and decisions. The vulnerable, variable quick of the man was inaccessible. She knew nothing of it. She could only feel the dark, heavy fixity of his animal desire.

This dumb desire on his part had brought him to her? She was puzzled, hurt by some hopeless fixity in him, that terrified her with a cold feeling of despair. What did he want? His desires were so underground. Why did he not admit himself? What did he want? He wanted something that should be nameless. She shrank in fear.

Yet she flashed with excitement. In his dark, subterranean male soul, he was kneeling before her, darkly exposing himself. She quivered, the dark flame ran over her. He was waiting at her feet. He was helpless, at her mercy. She could take or reject. If she rejected him, something would die in him. For him it was life or death. And yet, all must be kept so dark, the consciousness must admit nothing.

"How long," she said, "are you staying in England?"

"I am not sure—but not later than July, I believe."

Then they were both silent. He was here, in England, for six months. They had a space of six months between them. He waited. The same iron rigidity, as if the world were made of steel, possessed her again. It was no use turning with flesh and blood to this arrangement of forged metal.

Quickly, her imagination adjusted itself to the situation.

"Have you an appointment in India?" she asked.

"Yes—I have just the six months' leave."

"Will you like being out there?"

"I think so—there's a good deal of social life, and plenty going on—hunting, polo—and always a good horse—and plenty of work, any amount of work."

He was always side-tracking, always side-tracking his own soul. She would see him so well out there, in India—one of the governing class, superimposed upon an old civilisation, lord and master of a clumsier civilisation than his own. It was his choice. He would become again an aristocrat, invested with authority and responsibility, having a great helpless populace beneath him. One of the ruling class, his whole being would be given over to the fulfilling and the executing of the better idea of the state. And in India, there would be real work to do. The country did need the civilisation which he himself represented: it did need his roads and bridges, and the enlightenment of which he was part. He would go to India. But that was not her road.

Yet she loved him, the body of him, whatever his decisions might be. He seemed to want something of her. He was waiting for her to decide of him. It had been decided in her long ago, when he had kissed her first. He was her lover, though good and evil should cease. Her will never relaxed, though her heart and soul must be imprisoned and silenced. He waited upon her, and she accepted him. For he had come back to her.

A glow came into his face, into his fine, smooth skin, his eyes, gold-grey, glowed intimately to her. He burned up, he caught fire and became splendid, royal, something like a tiger. She caught his brilliant, burnished glamour. Her heart and her soul were shut away fast down below, hidden. She was free of them. She was to have her satisfaction.

She became proud and erect, like a flower, putting itself forth in its proper strength. His warmth invigorated her. His beauty of form, which seemed to glow out in contrast with the rest of people, made her proud. It was like deference to her, and made her feel as if she represented before him all the grace and flower of humanity. She was no mere Ursula Brangwen. She was Woman, she was the whole of Woman in the human order. All-containing, universal, how should she be limited to individuality?

She was exhilarated, she did not want to go away from him. She had her place by him. Who should take her away?

They came out of the café.

"Is there anything you would like to do?" he said. "Is there anything we can do?"

It was a dark, windy night in March.

"There is nothing to do," she said.

Which was the answer he wanted.

"Let us walk then—where shall we walk?" he asked.

"Shall we go to the river?" she suggested, timidly.

In a moment they were on the tram, going down to Trent Bridge. She was so glad. The thought of walking in the dark, far-reaching water-meadows, beside the full river, transported her. Dark water flowing in silence through the big, restless night made her feel wild.

They crossed the bridge, descended, and went away from the lights. In an instant, in the darkness, he took her hand and they went in silence, with subtle feet treading the darkness. The town fumed away on their left, there were strange lights and sounds, the wind rushed against the trees, and under the bridge. They walked close together, powerful in unison. He drew her very close, held her with a subtle, stealthy, powerful passion, as if they had a secret agreement which held good in the profound darkness. The profound darkness was their universe.

"It is like it was before," she said.

Yet it was not in the least as it was before. Nevertheless his heart was perfectly in accord with her. They thought one thought.

"I knew I should come back," he said at length.

She quivered.

"Did you always love me?" she asked.

The directness of the question overcame him, submerged him for a moment. The darkness travelled massively along.

"I had to come back to you," he said, as if hypnotised. "You were always at the back of everything."

She was silent with triumph, like fate.

"I loved you," she said, "always."

The dark flame leaped up in him. He must give her himself. He must give her the very foundations of himself. He drew her very close, and they went on in silence.

She started violently, hearing voices. They were near a stile across the dark meadows.

"It's only lovers," he said to her, softly.

She looked to see the dark figures against the fence, wondering that the darkness was inhabited.

"Only lovers will walk here to-night," he said.

Then in a low, vibrating voice he told her about Africa, the strange darkness, the strange, blood fear.

"I am not afraid of the darkness in England," he said. "It is soft, and natural to me, it is my medium, especially when you are here. But in Africa it seems massive and fluid with terror—not fear of anything—just fear. One breathes it, like the smell of blood. The blacks know it. They worship it, really, the darkness. One almost likes it—the fear—something sensual."

She thrilled again to him. He was to her a voice out of the darkness. He talked to her all the while, in low tones, about Africa, conveying something strange and sensual to her: the negro, with his loose, soft passion that could envelop one like a bath. Gradually he transferred to her the hot, fecund darkness that possessed his own blood. He was strangely secret. The whole world must be abolished. He maddened her with his soft, cajoling, vibrating tones. He wanted her to answer, to understand. A turgid, teeming night, heavy with fecundity in which every molecule of matter grew big with increase, secretly urgent with fecund desire, seemed to come to pass. She quivered, taut and vibrating, almost pained. And gradually, he ceased telling her of Africa, there came a silence, whilst they walked the darkness beside the massive river. Her limbs were rich and tense, she felt they must be vibrating with a low, profound vibration. She could scarcely walk. The deep vibration of the darkness could only be felt, not heard.

Suddenly, as they walked, she turned to him and held him fast, as if she were turned to steel.

"Do you love me?" she cried in anguish.

"Yes," he said, in a curious, lapping voice, unlike himself. "Yes, I love you."

He seemed like the living darkness upon her, she was in the embrace of the strong darkness. He held her enclosed, soft, unutterably soft, and with the un-relaxing softness of fate, the relentless softness of fecundity. She quivered, and quivered, like a tense thing that is struck. But he held her all the time, soft, unending, like darkness closed upon her, omnipresent as the night. He kissed her, and she quivered as if she were being destroyed, shattered. The lighted vessel vibrated, and broke in her soul, the light fell, struggled, and went dark. She was all dark, will-less, having only the receptive will.

He kissed her, with his soft, enveloping kisses, and she responded to them completely, her mind, her soul gone out. Darkness cleaving to darkness, she hung close to him, pressed herself into soft flow of his kiss, pressed herself down, down to the source and core of his kiss, herself covered and enveloped in the warm, fecund flow of his kiss, that travelled over her, flowed over her, covered her, flowed over the last fibre of her, so they were one stream, one dark fecundity, and she clung at the core of him, with her lips holding open the very bottommost source of him.

So they stood in the utter, dark kiss, that triumphed over them both, sub-jected them, knitted them into one fecund nucleus of the fluid darkness.

It was bliss, it was the nucleolating of the fecund darkness. Once the vessel had vibrated till it was shattered, the light of consciousness gone, then the dark-ness reigned, and the unutterable satisfaction.

They stood enjoying the unmitigated kiss, taking it, giving to it endlessly, and still it was not exhausted. Their veins fluttered, their blood ran together as one stream.

Till gradually a sleep, a heaviness settled on them, a drowse, and out of the drowse, a small light of consciousness woke up. Ursula became aware of the night around her, the water lapping and running full just near, the trees roaring and soughing in gusts of wind.

She kept near to him, in contact with him, but she became ever more and more herself. And she knew she must go to catch her train. But she did not want to draw away from contact with him.

At length they roused and set out. No longer they existed in the unblemished darkness. There was the glitter of a bridge, the twinkle of lights across the river, the big flare of the town in front and on their right.

But still, dark and soft and incontestable, their bodies walked untouched by the lights, darkness supreme and arrogant.

"The stupid lights," Ursula said to herself, in her dark sensual arrogance. "The stupid, artificial, exaggerated town, fuming its lights. It does not exist really. It rests upon the unlimited darkness, like a gleam of coloured oil on dark water, but what is it?—nothing, just nothing."

In the tram, in the train, she felt the same. The lights, the civic uniform was a trick played, the people as they moved or sat were only dummies exposed. She could see, beneath their pale, wooden pretence of composure and civic pur-posefulness, the dark stream that contained them all. They were like little paper ships in their motion. But in reality each one was a dark, blind, eager wave urging blindly forward, dark with the same homogeneous desire. And all their talk and all their behaviour was sham, they were dressed-up creatures. She was reminded of the Invisible Man, who was a piece of darkness made visible only by his clothes.

During the next weeks, all the time she went about in the same dark richness, her eyes dilated and shining like the eyes of a wild animal, a curious half-smile which seemed to be gibing at the civic pretence of all the human life about her.

"What are you, you pale citizens?" her face seemed to say, gleaming. "You subdued beast in sheep's clothing, you primeval darkness falsified to a social mechanism."

She went about in the sensual sub-consciousness all the time, mocking at the ready-made, artificial daylight of the rest.

"They assume selves as they assume suits of clothing," she said to herself, looking in mocking contempt at the stiffened, neutralised men. "They think it better to be clerks or professors than to be the dark, fertile beings that exist in the potential darkness. What do you think you are?" her soul asked of the professor as she sat opposite him in class. "What do you think you are, as you sit there in your gown and your spectacles? You are a lurking, blood-sniffing creature with eyes peering out of the jungle darkness, snuffing for your desires. That is what you *are,* though nobody would believe it, and you would be the very last to allow it."

Her soul mocked at all this pretence. Herself, she kept on pretending. She dressed herself and made herself fine, she attended her lectures and scribbled her notes. But all in a mood of superficial, mocking facility. She understood well enough their two-and-two-make-four tricks. She was as clever as they were. But care!—did she care about their monkey tricks of knowledge or learning or civic deportment? She did not care in the least.

There was Skrebensky, there was her dark, vital self. Outside the college, the outer darkness, Skrebensky was waiting. On the edge of the night, he was attentive. Did he care?

She was free as a leopard that sends up its raucous cry in the night. She had the potent, dark stream of her own blood, she had the glimmering core of fecundity, she had her mate, her complement, her sharer in fruition. So, she had all, everything.

Skrebensky was staying in Nottingham all the time. He too was free. He knew no one in this town, he had no civic self to maintain. He was free. Their trams and markets and theatres and public meetings were a shaken kaleidoscope to him, he watched as a lion or a tiger may lie with narrowed eyes watching the people pass before its cage, the kaleidoscopic unreality of people, or a leopard lie blinking, watching the incomprehensible feats of the keepers. He despised it all—it was all non-existent. Their good professors, their good clergymen, their good political speakers, their good, earnest women—all the time he felt his soul was grinning, grinning at the sight of them. So many performing puppets, all wood and rag for the performance!

He watched the citizen, a pillar of society, a model, saw the stiff goat's legs, which have become almost stiffened to wood in the desire to make them puppet in their action, he saw the trousers formed to the puppet-action: man's legs, but man's legs become rigid and deformed, ugly, mechanical.

He was curiously happy, being alone, now. The glimmering grin was on his face. He had no longer any necessity to take part in the performing tricks of the rest. He had discovered the clue to himself, he had escaped from the show, like a wild beast escaped straight back into its jungle. Having a room in a quiet hotel, he hired a horse and rode out into the country, staying sometimes for the night in some village, and returning the next day.

He felt rich and abundant in himself. Everything he did was a voluptuous pleasure to him—either to ride on horseback, or to walk, or to lie in the sun, or to drink in a public-house. He had no use for people, nor for words. He had an amused pleasure in everything, a great sense of voluptuous richness in himself, and of the fecundity of the universal night he inhabited. The puppet shapes of people, their wood-mechanical voices, he was remote from them.

For there were always his meetings with Ursula. Very often, she did not go to college in the afternoon, but walked with him instead. Or he took a motor-car or a dog-cart and they drove into the country, leaving the car and going away by themselves into the woods. He had not taken her yet. With subtle, instinctive economy, they went to the end of each kiss, each embrace, each pleasure in intimate contact, knowing subconsciously that the last was coming. It was to be their final entry into the source of creation.

She took him home, and he stayed a week-end at Beldover with her family. She loved having him in the house. Strange how he seemed to come into the atmosphere of her family, with his laughing, insidious grace. They all loved him, he was kin to them. His raillery, his warm, voluptuous mocking presence was meat and joy to the Brangwen household. For this house was always quivering with darkness, they put off their puppet form when they came home, to lie and drowse in the sun.

There was a sense of freedom amongst them all, of the undercurrent of darkness among them all. Yet here, at home, Ursula resented it. It became distasteful to her. And she knew that if they understood the real relationship between her and Skrebensky, her parents, her father in particular, would go mad with rage. So subtly, she seemed to be like any other girl who is more or less courted by a man. And she *was* like any other girl. But in her, the antagonism to the social imposition was for the time complete and final.

She waited, every moment of the day, for her next kiss. She admitted it to herself in shame and bliss. Almost consciously, she waited. He waited, but, until the time came, more unconsciously. When the time came that he should kiss her again, a prevention was an annihilation to him. He felt his flesh go grey, he was heavy with a corpse-like inanition, he did not exist, if the time passed unfulfilled.

He came to her finally in a superb consummation. It was very dark, and again a windy, heavy night. They had come down the lane towards Beldover, down to the valley. They were at the end of their kisses, and there was the silence between them. They stood as at the edge of a cliff, with a great darkness beneath.

Coming out of the lane along the darkness, with the dark space spreading down to the wind, and the twinkling lights of the station below, the far-off windy chuff of a shunting train, the tiny clink-clink-clink of the wagons blown between the wind, the light of Beldover-edge twinkling upon the blackness of the hill opposite, the glow of the furnaces along the railway to the right, their steps began to falter. They would soon come out of the darkness into the lights. It was like turning back. It was unfulfilment. Two quivering, unwilling creatures, they lingered on the edge of the darkness, peering out at the lights and the machine-glimmer beyond. They could not turn back to the world—they could not.

So lingering along, they came to a great oak tree by the path. In all its budding mass it roared to the wind, and its trunk vibrated in every fibre, powerful, indomitable.

"We will sit down," he said.

And in the roaring circle under the tree, that was almost invisible yet whose powerful presence received them, they lay a moment looking at the twinkling lights on the darkness opposite, saw the sweeping brand of a train past the edge of their darkened field.

Then he turned and kissed her, and she waited for him. The pain to her was the pain she wanted, the agony was the agony she wanted. She was caught up, entangled in the powerful vibration of the night. The man, what was he?—a dark, powerful vibration that encompassed her. She passed away as on a dark wind, far, far away, into the pristine darkness of paradise, into the original immortality. She entered the dark fields of immortality.

When she rose, she felt strangely free, strong. She was not ashamed,—why should she be? He was walking beside her, the man who had been with her. She had taken him, they had been together. Whither they had gone, she did not know. But it was as if she had received another nature. She belonged to the eternal, changeless place into which they had leapt together.

Her soul was sure and indifferent of the opinion of the world of artificial light. As they went up the steps of the foot-bridge over the railway, and met the train-passengers, she felt herself belonging to another world, she walked past them immune, a whole darkness dividing her from them. When she went into the lighted dining-room at home, she was impervious to the lights and the eyes of her parents. Her everyday self was just the same. She merely had another, stronger self that knew the darkness.

This curious separate strength, that existed in darkness and pride of night, never forsook her. She had never been more herself. It could not occur to her that anybody, not even the young man of the world, Skrebensky, should have anything at all to do with her permanent self. As for her temporal, social self, she let it look after itself.

Her whole soul was implicated with Skrebensky—not the young man of the world, but the undifferentiated man he was. She was perfectly sure of herself, perfectly strong, stronger than all the world. The world was not strong—she was strong. The world existed only in a secondary sense:—she existed supremely.

She continued at college, in her ordinary routine, merely as a cover to her dark, powerful under-life. The fact of herself, and with her Skrebensky, was so powerful, that she took rest in the other. She went to college in the morning, and attended her classes, flowering, and remote.

She had lunch with him in his hotel; every evening she spent with him, either in town, at his rooms, or in the country. She made the excuse at home of evening study for her degree. But she paid not the slightest attention to her study.

They were both absolute and happy and calm. The fact of their own consummate being made everything else so entirely subordinate that they were free. The only thing they wanted, as the days went by, was more time to themselves. They wanted the time to be absolutely their own.

The Easter vacation was approaching. They agreed to go right away. It would not matter if they did not come back. They were indifferent to the actual facts.

"I suppose we ought to get married," he said, rather wistfully. It *was* so magnificently free and in a deeper world, as it was. To make public their connection would be to put it in range with all the things which nullified him, and from which he was for the moment entirely dissociated. If he married he would have to assume his social self. And the thought of assuming his social self made him at once diffident and abstract. If she were his social wife, if she were part of that complication of dead reality, then what had his under-life to do with her? One's social wife was almost a material symbol. Whereas now she was something more vivid to him than anything in conventional life could be. She gave the complete lie to all conventional life, he and she stood together, dark, fluid, infinitely potent, giving the living lie to the dead whole which contained them.

He watched her pensive, puzzled face.

"I don't think I want to marry you," she said, her brow clouded.

It piqued him rather.

"Why not?" he asked.

"Let's think about it afterwards, shall we?" she said.

He was crossed, yet he loved her violently.

"You've got a *museau*, not a face," he said.

"Have I?" she cried, her face lighting up like a pure flame. She thought she had escaped. Yet he returned—he was not satisfied.

"Why?" he asked, "why don't you want to marry me?"

"I don't want to be with other people," she said. "I want to be like this. I'll tell you if ever I want to marry you."

"All right," he said.

He would rather the thing was left indefinite, and that she took the responsibility.

They talked of the Easter vacation. She thought only of complete enjoyment.

They went to an hotel in Piccadilly. She was supposed to be his wife. They bought a wedding-ring for a shilling, from a shop in a poor quarter.

They had revoked altogether the ordinary mortal world. Their confidence was like a possession upon them. They were possessed. Perfectly and supremely free they felt, proud beyond all question, and surpassing mortal conditions.

They were perfect, therefore nothing else existed. The world was a world of servants whom one civilly ignored. Wherever they went, they were the sensuous aristocrats, warm, bright, glancing with pure pride of the senses.

The effect upon other people was extraordinary. The glamour was cast from the young couple upon all they came into contact with, waiters or chance acquaintances.

"*Oui, Monsieur le baron,*" she would reply with a mocking courtesy to her husband.

So they came to be treated as titled people. He was an officer in the engineers. They were just married, going to India immediately.

Thus a tissue of romance was round them. She believed she was a young wife of a titled husband on the eve of departure for India. This, the social fact, was a delicious makebelief. The living fact was that he and she were man and woman, absolute and beyond all limitation.

The days went by—they were to have three weeks together—in perfect success. All the time, they themselves were reality, all outside was tribute to them. They were quite careless about money, but they did nothing very extravagant. He was rather surprised when he found that he had spent twenty pounds in a little under a week, but it was only the irritation of having to go to the bank. The machinery of the old system lasted for him, not the system. The money simply did not exist.

Neither did any of the old obligations. They came home from the theatre, had supper, then flitted about in their dressing-gowns. They had a large bed-room and a corner sitting-room high up, remote and very cosy. They ate all their meals in their own rooms, attended by a young German called Hans, who thought them both wonderful, and answered assiduously:

"*Gewiss, Herr Baron—bitte sehr, Frau Baronin.*"

Often, they saw the pink of dawn away across the park. The tower of West-minster Cathedral was emerging, the lamps of Piccadilly, stringing away beside the trees of the park, were becoming pale and moth-like, the morning traffic was clock-clocking down the shadowy road, which had gleamed all night like metal, down below, running far ahead into the night, beneath the lamps, and which was now vague, as in a mist, because of the dawn.

Then, as the flush of dawn became stronger, they opened the glass doors and went on to the giddy balcony, feeling triumphant as two angels in bliss, looking down at the still sleeping world, which would wake to a dutiful, rumbling, sluggish turmoil of unreality.

Soon they were fast asleep, asleep till midday, close together, sleeping one sleep. Then they awoke to the ever-changing reality of their state. They alone inhabited the world of reality. All the rest lived on a lower sphere.

Whatever they wanted to do, they did. They saw a few people—Dorothy, whose guest she was supposed to be, and a couple of friends of Skrebensky, young Oxford men, who called her Mrs. Skrebensky with entire simplicity. They treated her, indeed, with such respect, that she began to think she was really quite of the whole universe, of the old world as well as of the new. She forgot she was outside the pale of the old world. She thought she had brought it under the spell of her own, real world. And so she had.

In such ever-changing reality the weeks went by. All the time, they were an unknown world to each other. Every movement made by the one was a reality and an adventure to the other. They did not want outside excitements. They went to very few theatres, they were often in their sitting-room high up over Piccadilly, with windows open on two sides, and the door open on to the balcony, looking over the Green Park, or down upon the minute travelling of the traffic.

Then suddenly, looking at a sunset, she wanted to go. She must be gone. She must be gone at once. And in two hours' time they were at Charing Cross taking train for Paris. Paris was his suggestion. She did not care where it was. The great joy was in setting out. And for a few days she was happy in the novelty of Paris.

Then, for some reason, she must call in Rouen on the way back to London. He had an instinctive mistrust of her desire for the place. But, perversely, she wanted to go there. It was as if she wanted to try its effect upon her.

For the first time, in Rouen, he had a cold feeling of death; not afraid of any other man, but of her. She seemed to leave him. She followed after something that was not him. She did not want him. The old streets, the cathedral, the age and the monumental peace of the town took her away from him. She turned to it as if to something she had forgotten, and wanted. This was now the reality; this great stone cathedral slumbering there in its mass, which knew no tran-sience nor heard any denial. It was majestic in its stability, its splendid absolute-ness.

Her soul began to run by itself. He did not realise, nor did she. Yet in Rouen he had the first deadly anguish, the first sense of the death towards which they were wandering. And she felt the first heavy yearning, heavy, heavy hopeless

THE RAINBOW   483

warning, almost like a deep, uneasy sinking into apathy, hopelessness.

They returned to London. But still they had two days. He began to tremble, he grew feverish with the fear of her departure. She had in her some fatal prescience, that made her calm. What would be, would be.

He remained fairly easy, however, still in his state of heightened glamour, till she had gone, and he had turned away from St. Pancras, and sat on the tram-car going up Pimlico to the "Angel", to Moorgate Street on Sunday evening.

Then the cold horror gradually soaked into him. He saw the horror of the City Road, he realised the ghastly cold sordidness of the tram-car in which he sat. Cold, stark, ashen sterility had him surrounded. Where then was the luminous, wonderful world he belonged to by rights? How did he come to be thrown on this refuse-heap where he was?

He was as if mad. The horror of the brick buildings, of the tram-car, of the ashen-grey people in the street made him reeling and blind as if drunk. He went mad. He had lived with her in a close, living, pulsing world, where everything pulsed with rich being. Now he found himself struggling amid an ashen-dry, cold world of rigidity, dead walls and mechanical traffic, and creeping, spectre-like people. The life was extinct, only ash moved and stirred or stood rigid, there was a horrible, clattering activity, a rattle like the falling of dry slag, cold and sterile. It was as if the sunshine that fell were unnatural light exposing the ash of the town, as if the lights at night were the sinister gleam of decomposition.

Quite mad, beside himself, he went to his club and sat with a glass of whisky, motionless, as if turned to clay. He felt like a corpse that is inhabited with just enough life to make it appear as any other of the spectral, unliving beings which we call people in our dead language. Her absence was worse than pain to him. It destroyed his being.

Dead, he went on from lunch to tea. His face was all the time fixed and stiff and colourless, his life was a dry, mechanical movement. Yet even he wondered slightly at the awful misery that had overcome him. How could he be so ash-like and extinct? He wrote her a letter.

I have been thinking that we must get married before long. My pay will be more when I get out to India, we shall be able to get along. Or if you don't want to go to India, I could very probably stay here in England. But I think you would like India. You could ride, and you would know just everybody out there. Perhaps if you stay on to take your degree, we might marry immediately after that. I will write to your father as soon as I hear from you——

He went on, disposing of her. If only he could be with her! All he wanted now was to marry her, to be sure of her. Yet all the time he was perfectly, perfectly hopeless, cold, extinct, without emotion or connection.

He felt as if his life were dead. His soul was extinct. The whole being of him had become sterile, he was a spectre, divorced from life. He had no fullness, he was just a flat shape. Day by day the madness accumulated in him. The horror of not-being possessed him.

He went here, there, and everywhere. But whatever he did, he knew that only the cipher of him was there, nothing was filled in. He went to the theatre; what he heard and saw fell upon a cold surface of consciousness, which was now all that he was, there was nothing behind it, he could have no experience of any sort. Mechanical registering took place in him, no more. He had no being, no contents. Neither had the people he came into contact with. They were mere permutations of known quantities. There was no roundness or fullness in this world he now inhabited, everything was a dead shape mental arrangement, without life or being.

Much of the time, he was with friends and comrades. Then he forgot everything. Their activities made up for his own negation, they engaged his negative horror.

He only became happy when he drank, and he drank a good deal. Then he was just the opposite to what he had been. He became a warm, diffuse, glowing cloud, in a warm, diffuse formless fashion. Everything melted down into a rosy glow, and he was the glow, and everything was the glow, everybody else was the glow, and it was very nice, very nice. He would sing songs, it was so nice.

Ursula went back to Beldover shut and firm. She loved Skrebensky, of that she was resolved. She would allow nothing else.

She read his long, obsessed letter about getting married and going to India, without any particular response. She seemed to ignore what he said about marriage. It did not come home to her. He seemed, throughout the greater part of his letter, to be talking without much meaning.

She replied to him pleasantly and easily. She rarely wrote long letters.

> India sounds lovely. I can just see myself on an elephant swaying between lanes of obsequious natives. But I don't know if father would let me go. We must see.
>
> I keep living over again the lovely times we have had. But I don't think you liked me quite so much towards the end, did you? You did not like me when we left Paris. Why didn't you?
>
> I love you very much. I love your body. It is so clear and fine. I am glad you do not go naked, or all the women would fall in love with you. I am very jealous of it, I love it so much.

He was more or less satisfied with this letter. But day after day he was walking about, dead, non-existent.

He could not come again to Nottingham until the end of April. Then he persuaded her to go with him for a weekend to a friend's house near Oxford. By this time they were engaged. He had written to her father, and the thing was settled. He brought her an emerald ring, of which she was very proud.

Her people treated her now with a little distance, as if she had already left them. They left her very much alone.

She went with him for the three days in the country house near Oxford. It was delicious, and she was very happy. But the thing she remembered most was when, getting up in the morning after he had gone back quietly to his own room, having spent the night with her, she found herself very rich in being alone, and enjoying to the full her solitary room, she drew up her blind and saw the plum trees in the garden below all glittering and snowy and delighted with the sunshine, in full bloom under a blue sky. They threw out their blossom, they flung it out under the blue heavens, the whitest blossom! How excited it made her.

She had to hurry through her dressing to go and walk in the garden under the plum trees, before anyone should come and talk to her. Out she slipped, and paced like a queen in fairy pleasaunces. The blossom was silver-shadowy when she looked up from under the tree at the blue sky. There was a faint scent, a faint noise of bees, a wonderful quickness of happy morning.

She heard the breakfast gong and went indoors.

"Where have you been?" asked the others.

"I had to go out under the plum trees," she said, her face glowing like a flower. "It is so lovely."

A shadow of anger crossed Skrebensky's soul. She had not wanted him to be there. He hardened his will.

At night there was a moon, and the blossom glistened ghostly, they went together to look at it. She saw the moonlight on his face as he waited near her, and his features were like silver and his eyes in shadow were unfathomable. She was in love with him. He was very quiet.

They went indoors and she pretended to be tired. So she went quickly to bed.

"Don't be long coming to me," she whispered, as she was supposed to be kissing him good night.

And he waited, intent, obsessed, for the moment when he could come to her.

She enjoyed him, she made much of him. She liked to put her fingers on the soft skin of his sides, or on the softness of his back, when he made the muscles hard underneath, the muscles developed very strong through riding; and she had a great thrill of excitement and passion, because of the unimpressible hardness of his body, that was so soft and smooth under her fingers, that came to her with such absolute service.

She owned his body and enjoyed it with all the delight and carelessness of a possessor. But he had become gradually afraid of her body. He wanted her, he wanted her endlessly. But there had come a tension into his desire, a constraint which prevented his enjoying the delicious approach and the lovable close of the endless embrace. He was afraid. His will was always tense, fixed.

Her final examination was at midsummer. She insisted on sitting for it, although she had neglected her work during the past months. He also wanted her to go in for the degree. Then, he thought, she would be satisfied. Secretly he hoped she would fail, so that she would be more glad of him.

"Would you rather live in India or in England when we are married?" he asked her.

"Oh, in India, by far," she said, with a careless lack of consideration which annoyed him.

Once she said, with heat:

"I shall be glad to leave England. Everything is so meagre and paltry, it is so unspiritual—I hate democracy."

He became angry to hear her talk like this, he did not know why. Somehow, he could not bear it, when she attacked things. It was as if she were attacking him.

"What do you mean?" he asked her, hostile. "Why do you hate democracy?"

"Only the greedy and ugly people come to the top in a democracy," she said, "because they're the only people who will push themselves there. Only degenerate races are democratic."

"What do you want then—an aristocracy?" he asked, secretly moved. He always felt that by rights he belonged to the ruling aristocracy. Yet to hear her speak for his class pained him with a curious, painful pleasure. He felt he was acquiescing in something illegal, taking to himself some wrong, reprehensible advantages.

"I *do* want an aristocracy," she cried. "And I'd far rather have an aristocracy of birth than of money. Who are the aristocrats now—who are chosen as the best to rule? Those who have money and the brains for money. It doesn't matter what else they have: but they must have money-brains,—because they are ruling in the name of money."

"The people elect the government," he said.

"I know they do. But what are the people? Each one of them is a money-interest. I hate it, that anybody is my equal who has the same amount of money as I have. I *know* I am better than all of them. I hate them. They are not my equals. I hate equality on a money basis. It is the equality of dirt."

Her eyes blazed at him, he felt as if she wanted to destroy him. She had gripped him and was trying to break him. His anger sprang up, against her. At least he would fight for his existence with her. A hard, blind resistance possessed him.

"I don't care about money," he said, "neither do I want to put my finger in the pie. I am too sensitive about my finger."

"What is your finger to me?" she cried, in a passion. "You with your dainty fingers, and your going to India because you will be one of the somebodies there! It's a mere dodge, your going to India."

"In what way a dodge?" he cried, white with anger and fear.

"You think the Indians are simpler than us, and so you'll enjoy being near them and being a lord over them," she said. "And you'll feel so righteous, governing them for their own good. Who are you, to feel righteous? What are you righteous about, in your governing? Your governing stinks. What do you govern for, but to make things there as dead and mean as they are here!"

"I don't feel righteous in the least," he said.

"Then what *do* you feel? It's all such a nothingness, what you feel and what you don't feel."

"What do you feel yourself?" he said. "Aren't you righteous in your own mind?"

"Yes, I am, because I'm against you, and all your old, dead things," she cried.

She seemed, with the last words, uttered in hard knowledge, to strike down the flag that he kept flying. He felt cut off at the knees, a figure made worthless. A horrible sickness gripped him, as if his legs were really cut away, and he could not move, but remained a crippled trunk, dependent, worthless. The ghastly sense of helplessness, as if he were a mere figure that did not exist vitally, made him mad, beside himself.

Now, even whilst he was with her, this death of himself came over him, when he walked about like a body from which all individual life is gone. In this state he neither heard nor saw nor felt, only the mechanism of his life continued.

He hated her, as far as, in this state, he could hate. His cunning suggested to him all the ways of making her esteem him. For she did not esteem him. He left her and did not write to her. He flirted with other women, with Gudrun.

This last made her very fierce. She was still fiercely jealous of his body. In passionate anger she upbraided him because, not being man enough to satisfy one woman, he hung round others. She lifted her shoulders and turned aside her face in a motion of cold, indifferent worthlessness. He felt he would kill her.

When she had roused him to a pitch of madness, when she saw his eyes all dark and mad with suffering, then a great suffering overcame her soul, a great, inconquerable suffering. And she loved him. For, oh, she wanted to love him. Stronger than life or death was her craving to be able to love him.

And at such moments, when he was mad with her destroying him, when all his complacency was destroyed, all his everyday self was broken, and only the stripped, rudimentary, primal man remained, demented with torture, her passion to love him became love, she took him again, they came together in an overwhelming passion, in which he knew he satisfied her.

But it all contained a developing germ of death. After each contact, her anguished desire for him or for that which she never had from him was stronger, her love was more hopeless. After each contact his mad dependence on her was deepened, his hope of standing strong and taking her in his own strength was weakened. He felt himself a mere attribute of her.

Whitsuntide came, just before her examination. She was to have a few days of rest. Dorothy had inherited her patrimony, and had taken a cottage in Sussex. She invited them to stay with her.

They went down to Dorothy's neat, low cottage at the foot of the downs. Here they could do as they liked. Ursula was always yearning to go to the top of the downs. The white track wound up to the rounded summit. And she must go.

Up there, she could see the Channel a few miles away, the sea raised up and faintly glittering in the sky, the Isle of Wight a shadow lifted in the far distance, the river winding bright through the patterned plain to seaward, Arundel Castle a shadowy bulk, and then the rolling of the high, smooth downs, making a high, smooth land under heaven, acknowledging only the heavens in their great, sun-glowing strength, and suffering only a few bushes to trespass on the intercourse between their great, unabateable body and the changeful body of the sky.

Below she saw the villages and the woods of the weald, and the train running bravely, a gallant little thing, running with all the importance of the world over the water meadows and into the gap of the downs, waving its white steam, yet all the while so little. So little, yet its courage carried it from end to end of the earth, till there was no place where it did not go. Yet the downs, in magnificent indifference, bearing limbs and body to the sun, drinking sunshine and sea-wind and sea-wet cloud into its golden skin, with superb stillness and calm of being, was not the downs still more wonderful? The blind, pathetic, energetic courage of the train as it steamed tinily away through the patterned levels to the sea's dimness, so fast and so energetic, made her weep. Where was it going? It was going nowhere, it was just going. So blind, so without goal or aim, yet so hasty! She sat on an old prehistoric earth-work and cried, and the tears ran down her face. The train had tunnelled all the earth, blindly, and uglily.

And she lay face downwards on the downs, that were so strong, that cared only for their intercourse with the everlasting skies, and she wished she could become a strong mound smooth under the sky, bosom and limbs bared to all winds and clouds and bursts of sunshine.

But she must get up again and look down from her foothold of sunshine, down and away at the patterned, level earth, with its villages and its smoke and its energy. So shortsighted the train seemed, running to the distance, so terrifying in their littleness the villages, with such pettiness in their activity.

Skrebensky wandered dazed, not knowing where he was or what he was doing with her. All her passion seemed to be to wander up there on the downs, and when she must descend to earth, she was heavy. Up there she was exhilarated and free.

She would not love him in a house any more. She said she hated houses, and particularly she hated beds. There was something distasteful in his coming to her bed.

She would stay the night on the downs, up there, he with her. It was midsummer, the days were glamorously long. At about half-past ten, when the bluey-black darkness had at last fallen, they took rugs and climbed the steep track to the summit of the downs, he and she.

Up there, the stars were big, the earth below was gone into darkness. She was free up there with the stars. Far out they saw tiny yellow lights—but it was very far out, at sea, or on land. She was free up among the stars.

She took off her clothes, and made him take off all his, and they ran over the smooth, moonless turf, a long way, more than a mile from where they had left their clothing, running in the dark, soft wind, utterly naked, as naked as the downs themselves. Her hair was loose and blew about her shoulders, she ran swiftly, wearing sandals when she set off on the long run to the dew-pond.

In the round dew-pond the stars were untroubled. She ventured softly into the water, grasping at the stars with her hands.

And then suddenly she started back, running swiftly. He was there, beside her, but only on sufferance. He was a screen for her fears. He served her. She took him, she clasped him, clenched him close, but her eyes were open looking at the stars, it was as if the stars were lying with her and entering the unfathomable darkness of her womb, fathoming her at last. It was not him.

The dawn came. They stood together on a high place, an earthwork of the stone-age men, watching for the light. It came over the land. But the land was dark. She watched a pale rim on the sky, away against the darkened land. The darkness became bluer. A little wind was running in from the sea behind. It seemed to be running to the pale rift of the dawn. And she and he darkly, on an outpost of the darkness, stood watching for the dawn.

The light grew stronger, gushing up against the dark sapphire of the transparent night. The light grew stronger, whiter, then over it hovered a flush of rose. A flush of rose, and then yellow, pale, new-created yellow, the whole quivering and poising momentarily over the fountain on the sky's rim.

The rose hovered and quivered, burned, fused to flame, to a transient red, while the yellow surged out in great waves, thrown from the ever-increasing fountain, great waves of yellow flinging into the sky, scattering its spray over the darkness, which became bluer and bluer, paler, till soon it would itself be a radiance, which had been darkness.

The sun was coming. There was a quivering, a powerful, terrifying swim of molten light. Then the molten source itself surged forth, revealing itself. The sun was in the sky, too powerful to look at.

And the ground beneath lay so still, so peaceful. Only now and again a cock crew. Otherwise, from the distant yellow hills to the pine trees at the foot of the downs, everything was newly washed into being, in a flood of new, golden creation.

It was so unutterably still and perfect with promise, the golden-lighted, distinct land, that Ursula's soul rocked and wept. Suddenly he glanced at her. The tears were running over her cheeks, her mouth was working strangely.

"What is the matter?" he asked.

After a moment's struggle with her voice.

"It is so beautiful," she said, looking at the glowing, beautiful land. It was so beautiful, so perfect, and so unsullied.

He too realised what England would be in a few hours' time—a blind, sordid, strenuous activity, all for nothing, fuming with dirty smoke and running trains and groping in the bowels of the earth, all for nothing. A ghastliness came over him.

He looked at Ursula. Her face was wet with tears, very bright, like a transfiguration in the refulgent light. Nor was his the hand to wipe away the burning, bright tears. He stood apart, overcome by a cruel ineffectuality.

Gradually a great, helpless sorrow was rising in him. But as yet he was fighting it away, he was struggling for his own life. He became very quiet and unaware of the things about him, awaiting, as it were, her judgment on him.

They returned to Nottingham, the time of her examination came. She must go to London. But she would not stay with him in an hotel. She would go to a quiet little pension near the British Museum.

Those quiet residential squares of London made a great impression on her mind. They were very complete. Her mind seemed imprisoned in their quietness. Who was going to liberate her?

In the evening, her practical examinations being over, he went with her to dinner at one of the hotels down the river, near Richmond. It was golden and beautiful, with yellow water and white and scarlet-striped boat-awnings, and blue shadows under the trees.

"When shall we be married?" he asked her, quietly, simply, as if it were a mere question of comfort.

She watched the changing pleasure-traffic of the river. He looked at her golden, puzzled *museau*. The knot gathered in his throat.

"I don't know," she said.

A hot grief gripped his throat.

"Why don't you know—don't you want to be married?" he asked her.

Her head turned slowly, her face, puzzled, like a boy's face, expressionless because she was trying to think, looked towards his face. She did not see him, because she was pre-occupied. She did not quite know what she was going to say.

"I don't think I want to be married," she said, and her naïve, troubled, puzzled eyes rested a moment on his, then travelled away, pre-occupied.

"Do you mean never, or not just yet?" he asked.

The knot in his throat grew harder, his face was drawn as if he were being strangled.

"I mean never," she said, out of some far self which spoke for once beyond her.

His drawn, strangled face watched her blankly for a few moments, then a strange sound took place in his throat. She started, came to herself, and, horrified, saw him. His head made a queer motion, the chin jerked back against the throat, the curious, crowing, hiccupping sound came again, his face twisted like insanity, and he was crying, crying blind and twisted as if something were broken which kept him in control.

"Tony—don't," she cried, starting up.

It tore every one of her nerves to see him. He made groping movements to get out of his chair. But he was crying uncontrollably, noiselessly, with his face twisted like a mask, contorted and the tears running down the amazing grooves in his cheeks. Blindly, his face always this horrible working mask, he groped for his hat, for his way down from the terrace. It was eight o'clock, but still brightly light. The other people were staring. In great agitation, part of which was exasperation, she stayed behind, paid the waiter with a half-sovereign, took her yellow silk coat, then followed Skrebensky.

She saw him walking with brittle, blind steps along the path by the river. She could tell by the strange stiffness and brittleness of his figure that he was still crying. Hurrying after him, running, she took his arm.

"Tony," she cried, "don't! Why are you like this? What are you doing this for? Don't. It's not necessary."

He heard, and his manhood was cruelly, coldly defaced. Yet it was no good. He could not gain control of his face. His face, his breast, were weeping violently, as if automatically. His will, his knowledge had nothing to do with it. He simply could not stop.

She walked holding his arm, silent with exasperation and perplexity and pain. He took the uncertain steps of a blind man, because his mind was blind with weeping.

"Shall we go home? Shall we have a taxi?" she said.

He could pay no attention. Very flustered, very agitated, she signalled indefinitely to a taxi-cab that was going slowly by. The driver saluted and drew up. She opened the door and pushed Skrebensky in, then took her own place. Her face was uplifted, the mouth closed down, she looked hard and cold and ashamed. She winced as the driver's dark red face was thrust round upon her, a full-blooded, animal face with black eyebrows and a thick, short-cut moustache.

"Where to, lady?" he said, his white teeth showing. Again for a moment she was flustered.

"Forty, Rutland Square," she said.

He touched his cap and stolidly set the car in motion. He seemed to have a league with her to ignore Skrebensky.

The latter sat as if trapped within the taxi-cab, his face still working, whilst occasionally he made quick slight movements of the head, to shake away his tears. He never moved his hands. She could not bear to look at him. She sat with face uplifted and averted to the window.

At length, when she had regained some control over herself, she turned again to him. He was much quieter. His face was wet, and twitched occasionally, his hands still lay motionless. But his eyes were quite still, like a washed sky after rain, full of a wan light, and quite steady, almost ghost-like.

A pain flamed in her womb, for him.

"I didn't think I should hurt you," she said, laying her hand very lightly, tentatively, on his arm. "The words came without my knowing. They didn't mean anything, really."

He remained quite still, hearing, but washed all wan and without feeling. She waited, looking at him, as if he were some curious, not-understandable creature.

"You won't cry again, will you, Tony?"

Some shame and bitterness against her burned him in the question. She noticed how his moustache was soddened wet with tears. Taking her handkerchief, she wiped his face. The driver's heavy, stolid back remained always turned to them, as if conscious but indifferent. Skrebensky sat motionless whilst Ursula wiped his face, softly, carefully, and yet clumsily, not as well as he would have wiped it himself.

Her handkerchief was too small. It was soon wet through. She groped in his pocket for his own. Then, with its more ample capacity, she carefully dried his face. He remained motionless all the while. Then she drew his cheek to hers and kissed him. His face was cold. Her heart was hurt. She saw the tears welling quickly to his eyes again. As if he were a child, she again wiped away his tears.

By now she herself was on the point of weeping. Her underlip was caught between her teeth.

So she sat still, for fear of her own tears, sitting close by him, holding his hand warm and close and loving. Meanwhile the car ran on, and a soft, midsummer dusk began to gather. For a long while they sat motionless. Only now and again her hand closed more closely, lovingly, over his hand, then gradually relaxed.

The dusk began to fall. One or two lights appeared. The driver drew up to light his lamps. Skrebensky moved for the first time, leaning forward to watch the driver. His face had always the same still, clarified, almost childlike look, impersonal.

They saw the driver's strange, full, dark face peering into the lamps under drawn brows. Ursula shuddered. It was the face almost of an animal yet of a quick, strong, wary animal that had them within its knowledge, almost within its power. She clung closer to Skrebensky.

"My love?" she said to him, questioningly, when the car was again running in full motion.

He made no movement or sound. He let her hold his hand, he let her reach forward, in the gathering darkness, and kiss his still cheek. The crying had gone by—he would not cry any more. He was whole and himself again.

"My love," she repeated, trying to make him notice her. But as yet he could not.

He watched the road. They were running by Kensington Gardens. For the first time his lips opened.

"Shall we get out and go into the park," he asked.

"Yes," she said, quietly, not sure what was coming.

After a moment he took the tube from its peg. She saw the stout, strong, self-contained driver lean his head.

"Stop at Hyde Park Corner."

The dark head nodded, the car ran on just the same.

Presently they pulled up. Skrebensky paid the man. Ursula stood back. She saw the driver salute as he received his tip, and then, before he set the car in motion, turn and look at her, with his quick, powerful, animal's look, his eyes very concentrated and the whites of his eyes flickering. Then he drove away into the crowd. He had let her go. She had been afraid.

Skrebensky turned with her into the park. A band was still playing and the place was thronged with people. They listened to the ebbing music, then went aside to a dark seat, where they sat closely, hand in hand.

Then at length, as out of the silence, she said to him, wondering:

"What hurt you so?"

She really did not know, at this moment.

"When you said you wanted never to marry me," he replied, with a childish simplicity.

"But why did that hurt you so?" she said. "You needn't mind everything I say so particularly."

"I don't know—I didn't want to do it," he said, humbly, ashamed.

She pressed his hand warmly. They sat close together, watching the soldiers go by with their sweethearts, the lights trailing in myriads down the great thoroughfares that beat on the edge of the park.

"I didn't know you cared so much," she said, also humbly.

"I didn't," he said. "I was knocked over myself.—But I care—all the world."

His voice was so quiet and colourless, it made her heart go pale with fear.

"My love!" she said, drawing near to him. But she spoke out of fear, not out of love.

"I care all the world—I care for nothing else—neither in life nor in death," he said, in the same steady, colourless voice of essential truth.

"Than for what?" she murmured duskily.

"Than for you—to be with me."

And again she was afraid. Was she to be conquered by this? She cowered close to him, very close to him. They sat perfectly still, listening to the great, heavy, beating sound of the town, the murmur of lovers going by, the footsteps of soldiers.

She shivered against him.

"You are cold?" he said.

"A little."

"We will go and have some supper."

He was now always quiet and decided and remote, very beautiful. He seemed to have some strange, cold power over her.

They went to a restaurant, and drank chianti. But his pale, wan look did not go away.

"Don't leave me to-night," he said at length, looking at her, pleading. He was so strange and impersonal, she was afraid.

"But the people of my place," she said, quivering.

"I will explain to them—they know we are engaged."

She sat pale and mute. He waited.

"Shall we go?" he said at length.

"Where?"

"To an hotel."

Her heart was hardened. Without answering, she rose to acquiesce. But she was now cold and unreal. Yet she could not refuse him. It seemed like fate, a fate she did not want.

They went to an Italian hotel somewhere, and had a sombre bedroom with a very large bed, clean, but sombre. The ceiling was painted with a bunch of flowers in a big medallion over the bed. She thought it was pretty.

He came to her, and cleaved to her very close, like steel cleaving and clinching on to her. Her passion was roused, it was fierce but cold. But it was fierce, and extreme, and good, their passion this night. He slept with her fast in his arms. All night long he held her fast against him. She was passive, acquiescent. But her sleep was not very deep nor very real.

She woke in the morning to a sound of water dashed on a courtyard, to sunlight streaming through a lattice. She thought she was in a foreign country. And Skrebensky was there an incubus upon her.

She lay still, thinking, whilst his arm was round her, his head against her shoulders, his body against hers, just behind her. He was still asleep.

She watched the sunshine coming in bars through the *persiennes,* and her immediate surroundings again melted away.

She was in some other land, some other world, where the old restraints had dissolved and vanished, where one moved freely, not afraid of one's fellow men, nor wary, nor on the defensive, but calm, indifferent, at one's ease. Vaguely, in a sort of silver light, she wandered at large and at ease. The bonds of the world were broken. This world of England had vanished away. She heard a voice in the yard below calling:

"O Giovann'—O'-O'-O'-Giovann'—!"

And she knew she was in a new country, in a new life. It was very delicious to lie thus still, with one's soul wandering freely and simply in the silver light of some other, simpler, more finely natural world.

But always there was a foreboding waiting to command her. She became more aware of Skrebensky. She knew he was waking up. She must modify her soul, depart from her further world, for him.

She knew he was awake. He lay still, with a concrete stillness, not as when he slept. Then his arm tightened almost convulsively upon her, and he said, half timidly:

"Did you sleep well?"

"Very well."

"So did I."

There was a pause.

"And do you love me?" he asked.

She turned and looked at him searchingly. He seemed outside her.

"I do," she said.

But she said it out of complacency and a desire not to be harried. There was a curious breach of silence between them, which frightened him.

They lay rather late, then he rang for breakfast. She wanted to be able to go straight downstairs and away from the place, when she got up. She was happy in this room, but the thought of the publicity of the hall downstairs rather troubled her.

A young Italian, a Sicilian, dark and slightly pock-marked, buttoned up in a sort of grey tunic, appeared with the tray. His face had an almost African imperturbability, impassive, incomprehensible.

"One might be in Italy," Skrebensky said to him, genially. A vacant look, almost like fear, came on the fellow's face. He did not understand.

"This is like Italy," Skrebensky explained.

The face of the Italian flashed with a non-comprehending smile, he finished setting out the tray, and was gone. He did not understand: he would understand nothing: he disappeared from the door like a half-domesticated wild animal. It made Ursula shudder slightly, the quick, sharp-sighted, intent animality of the man.

Skrebensky was beautiful to her this morning, his face softened and transfused with suffering and with love, his movements very still and gentle. He was beautiful to her, but she was detached from him by a chill distance. Always she seemed to be bearing up against the distance that separated them. But he was unaware. This morning he was transfused and beautiful. She admired his movements, the way he spread honey on his roll, or poured out the coffee.

When breakfast was over, she lay still again on the pillows, whilst he went through his toilet. She watched him, as he sponged himself, and quickly dried himself with the towel. His body was beautiful, his movements intent and quick, she admired him and she appreciated him without reserve. He seemed completed now. He aroused no fruitful fecundity in her. He seemed added up, finished. She knew him all round, not on any side did he lead into the unknown. Poignant, almost passionate appreciation she felt for him, but none of the dreadful wonder, none of the rich fear, the connection with the unknown, or the reverence of love. He was, however, unaware this morning. His body was quiet and fulfilled, his veins complete with satisfaction, he was happy, finished.

Again she went home. But this time he went with her. He wanted to stay by her. He wanted her to marry him. It was already July. In early September he must sail for India. He could not bear to think of going alone. She must come with him. Nervously, he kept beside her.

Her examination was finished, her college career was over. There remained for her now to marry or to work again. She applied for no post. It was concluded she would marry. India tempted her—the strange, strange land. But with the thought of Calcutta, or Bombay, or of Simla, and of the European population, India was no more attractive to her than Nottingham.

She had failed in her examination: she had gone down: she had not taken her degree. It was a blow to her. It hardened her soul.

"It doesn't matter," he said. "What are the odds, whether you are a Bachelor of Arts or not, according to the London University? All you know, you know, and if you are Mrs. Skrebensky, the B.A. is meaningless."

Instead of consoling her, this made her harder, more ruthless. She was now up against her own fate. It was for her to choose between being Mrs. Skrebensky, even Baroness Skrebensky, wife of a lieutenant in the Royal Engineers, the Sappers, as he called them, living with the European population in India—or being Ursula Brangwen, spinster, school-mistress. She was qualified by her Intermediate Arts examination. She would probably even now get a post quite easily as assistant in one of the higher grade schools, or even in Willey Green School. Which was she to do?

She hated most of all entering the bondage of teaching once more. Very heartily she detested it. Yet at the thought of marriage and living with Skrebensky amid the European population in India, her soul was locked and would not budge. She had very little feeling about it: only there was a deadlock.

Skrebensky waited, she waited, everybody waited for the decision. When Anton talked to her, and seemed insidiously to suggest himself as a husband to her, she knew how utterly locked out he was. On the other hand, when she saw Dorothy, and discussed the matter, she felt she would marry him promptly, at once, as a sharp disavowal of adherence with Dorothy's views.

The situation was almost ridiculous.

"But do you love him?" asked Dorothy.

"It isn't a question of loving him," said Ursula. "I love him well enough—certainly more than I love anybody else in the world. And I shall never love anybody else the same again. We have had the flower of each other. But I don't *care* about love. I don't value it. I don't care whether I love or whether I don't, whether I have love or whether I haven't. What is it to me?"

And she shrugged her shoulders in fierce, angry contempt.

Dorothy pondered, rather angry and afraid.

"Then what *do* you care about?" she asked, exasperated.

"I don't know," said Ursula. "But something impersonal. Love—love—love—what does it mean—what does it amount to? So much personal gratification. It doesn't lead anywhere."

"It isn't supposed to lead anywhere, is it?" said Dorothy, satirically. "I thought it was the one thing which is an end in itself."

"Then what does it matter to me?" cried Ursula. "As an end in itself, I could love a hundred men, one after the other. Why should I end with a Skrebensky? Why should I not go on, and love all the types I fancy, one after another, if love is an end in itself? There are plenty of men who aren't Anton, whom I could love—whom I would like to love."

"Then you don't love *him*," said Dorothy.

"I tell you I do;—quite as much, and perhaps more than I should love any of the others. Only there are plenty of things that aren't in Anton that I would love in the other men."

"What, for instance?"

"It doesn't matter. But a sort of strong understanding, in some men, and then a dignity, a directness, something unquestioned that there is in working men, and then a jolly, reckless passionateness that you see—a man who could really let go——"

Dorothy could feel that Ursula was already hankering after something else, something that this man did not give her.

"The question is, what *do* you want," propounded Dorothy. "Is it just other men?"

Ursula was silenced. This was her own dread. Was she just promiscuous?

"Because if it is," continued Dorothy, "you'd better marry Anton. The other can only end badly."

So out of fear of herself Ursula was to marry Skrebensky.

He was very busy now, preparing to go to India. He must visit relatives and contract business. He was almost sure of Ursula now. She seemed to have given in. And she seemed to become again an important, self-assured man.

It was the first week in August, and he was one of a large party in a bungalow on the Lincolnshire coast. It was a tennis, golf, motor-car, motor-boat party, given by his great-aunt, a lady of social pretensions. Ursula was invited to spend the week with the party.

She went rather reluctantly. Her marriage was more or less fixed for the twenty-eighth of the month. They were to sail for India on September the fifth. One thing she knew, in her subconsciousness, and that was, she would never sail for India.

She and Anton, being important guests on account of the coming marriage, had rooms in the large bungalow. It was a big place, with a great central hall, two smaller writing-rooms, and then two corridors from which opened eight or nine bedrooms. Skrebensky was put on one corridor, Ursula on the other. They felt very lost, in the crowd.

Being lovers, however, they were allowed to be out alone together as much as they liked. Yet she felt very strange, in this crowd of strange people, uneasy, as if she had no privacy. She was not used to these homogeneous crowds. She was afraid.

She felt different from the rest of them, with their hard, easy, shallow intimacy, that seemed to cost them so little. She felt she was not pronounced enough. It was a kind of hold-your-own unconventional atmosphere. She did not like it. In crowds, in assemblies of people, she liked formality. She felt she did not produce the right effect. She was not effective: she was not beautiful: she was nothing. Even before Skrebensky she felt unimportant, almost inferior. He could take his part very well with the rest.

He and she went out into the night. There was a moon behind clouds, shedding a diffused light, gleaming now and again in bits of smoky mother-of-pearl. So they walked together on the wet, ribbed sands near the sea, hearing the run of the long, heavy waves, that made a ghostly whiteness and a whisper.

He was sure of himself. As she walked, the soft silk of her dress—she wore a blue shantung, full-skirted—blew away from the sea and flapped and clung to her legs. She wished it would not. Everything seemed to give her away, and she could not rouse herself to deny, she was so confused.

He would lead her away to a pocket in the sand-hills, secret amid the grey thorn-bushes and the grey, glassy grass. He held her close against him, felt all her firm, unutterably desirable mould of body through the fine fibre of the silk that fell about her limbs. The silk, slipping fierily on the hidden, yet revealed roundness and firmness of her body, her loins, seemed to run in him like fire, make his brain burn like brimstone. She liked it, the electric fire of the silk under his hands upon her limbs, the fire flew over her, as he drew nearer and nearer to discovery. She vibrated like a jet of electric, firm fluid in response. Yet she did not feel beautiful. All the time, she felt she was not beautiful to him, only exciting.

She did not know how she suffered in this house. She was healthy and exorbitantly full of interest. So she played tennis and learned golf, she rowed out and swam in the deep sea, and enjoyed it very much indeed, full of zest. Yet all the time, among those others, she felt shocked and wincing, as if her violently-sensitive nakedness were exposed to the hard, brutal, material impact of the rest of the people.

The days went by unmarked, in a full, almost strenuous enjoyment of one's own physique. Skrebensky was one among the others, till evening came, and he took her for himself. She was allowed a great deal of freedom and was treated with a good deal of respect, as a girl on the eve of marriage, about to depart for another continent.

The trouble began at evening. Then a yearning for something unknown came over her, a passion for something she knew not what. She would walk the foreshore alone after dusk, expecting, expecting something, as if she had gone to a rendezvous. The salt, bitter passion of the sea, its indifference to the earth, its swinging, definite motion, its strength, its attack, and its salt burning, seemed to provoke her to a pitch of madness, tantalizing her with vast suggestions of fulfilment. And then, for personification, would come Skrebensky, Skrebensky, whom she knew, whom she was fond of, who was attractive, but whose soul could not contain her in its waves of strength, nor his breast compel her in burning, salty passion.

One evening they went out after dinner, across the low golf links to the dunes and the sea. The sky had small, faint stars, all was still and faintly dark. They walked together in silence, then ploughed, labouring, through the heavy loose sand of the gap between the dunes. They went in silence under the even, faint darkness, in the darker shadow of the sandhills.

Suddenly, cresting the heavy, sandy pass, Ursula lifted her head, and shrank back, momentarily frightened. There was a great whiteness confronting her, the moon was incandescent as a round furnace door, out of which came the high blast of moonlight, over the seaward half of the world, a dazzling, terrifying glare of white light. They shrank back for a moment into shadow, uttering a cry. He felt his chest laid bare, where the secret was heavily hidden. He felt himself fusing down to nothingness, like a bead that rapidly disappears in an incandescent flame.

"How wonderful!" cried Ursula, in low, calling tones. "How wonderful!" And she went forward, plunging into it. He followed behind. She too seemed to melt into the glare, towards the moon.

The sands were as ground silver, the sea moved in solid brightness, coming towards them, and she went to meet the advance of the flashing, buoyant water. He stood behind, encompassed, a shadow ever dissolving.

She stood on the edge of the water, at the edge of the solid, flashing body of the sea, and the wave rushed over her feet.

"I want to go," she cried, in a strong, dominant voice. "I want to go."

He saw the moonlight on her face, so she was like metal, he heard her ringing, metallic voice, like the voice of a harpy to him.

She prowled, ranging on the edge of the water like a possessed creature, and he followed her. He saw the froth of the wave followed by the hard, bright water swirl over her feet and her ankles, she swung out her arms, to balance, he expected every moment to see her walk into the sea, dressed as she was, and be carried swimming out.

But she turned, she walked to him.

"I want to go," she cried again, in the high, hard voice, like the scream of gulls.

"Where?" he asked.

"I don't know."

And she seized hold of his arm, held him fast, as if captive, and walked him a little way by the edge of the dazzling, dazing water.

Then there in the great flare of light, she clinched hold of him, hard, as if suddenly she had the strength of destruction, she fastened her arms round him and tightened him in her grip, whilst her mouth sought his in a hard, rending, ever-increasing kiss, till his body was powerless in her grip, his heart melted in fear from the fierce, beaked, harpy's kiss. The water washed again over their feet, but she took no notice. She seemed unaware, she seemed to be pressing in her beaked mouth till she had the heart of him. Then, at last, she drew away and looked at him—looked at him. He knew what she wanted. He took her by the hand and led her across the foreshore, back to the sandhills. She went silently. He felt as if the ordeal of proof was upon him, for life or death. He led her to a dark hollow.

"No, here," she said, going out to the slope full under the moonshine. She lay motionless, with wide-open eyes looking at the moon. He came direct to her, without preliminaries. She held him pinned down at the chest, awful. The fight, the struggle for consummation was terrible. It lasted till it was agony to his soul, till he succumbed, till he gave way as if dead, lay with his face buried, partly in her hair, partly in the sand, motionless, as if he would be motionless now for ever, hidden away in the dark, buried, only buried, he only wanted to be buried in the goodly darkness, only that, and no more.

He seemed to swoon. It was a long time before he came to himself. He was aware of an unusual motion of her breast. He looked up. Her face lay like an image in the moonlight, the eyes wide open, rigid. But out of the eyes, slowly, there rolled a tear, that glittered in the moonlight as it ran down her cheek.

He felt as if the knife were being pushed into his already dead body. With head strained back, he watched, drawn tense, for some minutes, watched the unaltering, rigid face like metal in the moonlight, the fixed, unseeing eye, in which slowly the water gathered, shook with glittering moonlight, then surcharged, brimmed over and ran trickling, a tear with its burden of moonlight, into the darkness, to fall in the sand.

He drew gradually away as if afraid, drew away—she did not move. He glanced at her—she lay the same. Could he break away? He turned, saw the open foreshore, clear in front of him, and he plunged away, on and on, ever farther from the horrible figure that lay stretched in the moonlight on the sands with the tears gathering and travelling on the motionless, eternal face.

He felt, if ever he must see her again, his bones must be broken, his body crushed, obliterated for ever. And as yet, he had the love of his own living body. He wandered on a long, long way, till his brain grew dark and he was unconscious with weariness. Then he curled in the deepest darkness he could find, under the sea-grass, and lay there without consciousness.

She broke from her tense cramp of agony gradually, though each movement was a goad of heavy pain. Gradually, she lifted her dead body from the sands, and rose at last. There was now no moon for her, no sea. All had passed away. She trailed her dead body to the house, to her room, where she lay down inert.

Morning brought her a new access of superficial life. But all within her was cold, dead, inert. Skrebensky appeared at breakfast. He was white and obliterated. They did not look at each other nor speak to each other. Apart from the ordinary, trivial talk of civil people, they were separate, they did not speak of what was between them during the remaining two days of their stay. They were like two dead people who dare not recognise, dare not see each other.

Then she packed her bag and put on her things. There were several guests leaving together, for the same train. He would have no opportunity to speak to her.

He tapped at her bedroom door at the last minute. She stood with her umbrella in her hand. He closed the door. He did not know what to say.

"Have you done with me?" he asked her at length, lifting his head.

"It isn't me," she said. "You have done with me—we have done with each other."

He looked at her, at the closed face, which he thought so cruel. And he knew he could never touch her again. His will was broken, he was seared, but he clung to the life of his body.

"Well, what have I done?" he asked, in a rather querulous voice.

"I don't know," she said, in the same dull, feelingless voice. "It is finished. It had been a failure."

He was silent. The words still burned his bowels.

"Is it my fault?" he said, looking up at length, challenging the last stroke.

"You couldn't——" she began. But she broke down.

He turned away, afraid to hear more. She began to gather her bag, her handkerchief, her umbrella. She must be gone now. He was waiting for her to be gone.

At length the carriage came and she drove away with the rest. When she was out of sight, a great relief came over him, a pleasant banality. In an instant, everything was obliterated. He was childishly amiable and companionable all the day long. He was astonished that life could be so nice. It was better than it had been before. What a simple thing it was to be rid of her! How friendly and simple everything felt to him. What false thing had she been forcing on him?

But at night he dared not be alone. His room-mate had gone, and the hours of darkness were an agony to him. He watched the window in suffering and terror. When would this horrible darkness be lifted off him? Setting all his nerves, he endured it. He went to sleep with the dawn.

He never thought of her. Only his terror of the hours of night grew on him, obsessed him like a mania. He slept fitfully, with constant wakings of anguish. The fear wore away the core of him.

His plan was to sit up very late: drink in company until one or half-past one in the morning: then he would get three hours of sleep, of oblivion. It was light by five o'clock. But he was shocked almost to madness if he opened his eyes on the darkness.

In the daytime he was all right, always occupied with the thing of the moment, adhering to the trivial present, which seemed to him ample and satisfying. No matter how little and futile his occupations were, he gave himself to them entirely, and felt normal and fulfilled. He was always active, cheerful, gay, charming, trivial. Only he dreaded the darkness and silence of his own bedroom, when the darkness should challenge him upon his own soul. That he could not bear, as he could not bear to think about Ursula. He had no soul, no background. He never thought of Ursula, not once, he gave her no sign. She was the darkness, the challenge, the horror. He turned to immediate things. He wanted to marry quickly, to screen himself from the darkness, the challenge of his own soul. He would marry his Colonel's daughter. Quickly, without hesitation, pursued by his obsession for activity, he wrote to this girl, telling her his engagement was broken—it had been a temporary infatuation which he less than any one else could understand now it was over—and could he see his very dear friend soon? He would not be happy till he had an answer.

He received a rather surprised reply from the girl, but she would be glad to see him. She was living with her aunt. He went down to her at once, and proposed to her the first evening. He was accepted. The marriage took place quietly within fourteen days' time. Ursula was not notified of the event. In another week, Skrebensky sailed with his new wife to India.

XVI

THE RAINBOW

Ursula went home to Beldover faint, dim, closed up. She could scarcely speak or notice. It was as if her energy were frozen. Her people asked her what was the matter. She told them she had broken off the engagement with Skrebensky. They looked blank and angry. But she could not feel any more.

The weeks crawled by in apathy. He would have sailed for India now. She was scarcely interested. She was inert, without strength or interest.

Suddenly a shock ran through her, so violent that she thought she was struck down. Was she with child? She had been so stricken under the pain of herself and of him, this had never occurred to her. Now like a flame it took hold of her limbs and body. Was she with child?

In the first flaming hours of wonder, she did not know what she felt. She was as if tied to the stake. The flames were licking her and devouring her. But the flames were also good. They seemed to wear her away to rest. What she felt in her heart and her womb she did not know. It was a kind of swoon.

Then gradually the heaviness of her heart pressed and pressed into consciousness. What was she doing? Was she bearing a child? Bearing a child? To what?

Her flesh thrilled, but her soul was sick. It seemed, this child, like the seal set on her own nullity. Yet she was glad in her flesh that she was with child. She began to think, that she would write to Skrebensky, that she would go out to him, and marry him, and live simply as a good wife to him. What did the self, the form of life matter? Only the living from day to day mattered, the beloved existence in the body, rich, peaceful, complete, with no beyond, no further trouble, no further complication. She had been wrong, she had been arrogant and wicked, wanting that other thing, that fantastic freedom, that illusory, conceited fulfilment which she had imagined she could not have with Skrebensky. Who was she to be wanting some fantastic fulfilment in her life? Was it not enough that she had her man, her children, her place of shelter under the sun? Was it not enough for her, as it had been enough for her mother? She would marry and love her husband and fill her place simply. That was the ideal.

Suddenly she saw her mother in a just and true light. Her mother was simple and radically true. She had taken the life that was given. She had not, in her arrogant conceit, insisted on creating life to fit herself. Her mother was right, profoundly right, and she herself had been false, trashy, conceited.

A great mood of humility came over her, and in this humility a bondaged sort of peace. She gave her limbs to the bondage, she loved the bondage, she called it peace. In this state she sat down to write to Skrebensky.

> *Since you left me I have suffered a great deal, and so have come to myself. I cannot tell you the remorse I feel for my wicked, perverse behaviour. It was given to me to love you, and to know your love for me. But instead of thankfully, on my knees, taking what God had given me, I must have the moon in my keeping, I must insist on having the moon for my own. Because I could not have it, everything else must go.*
>
> *I do not know if you can ever forgive me. I could die with shame to think of my behaviour with you during our last times, and I don't know if I could ever bear to look you in the face again. Truly the best thing would be for me to die, and cover my fantasies for ever. But I find I am with child, so that cannot be.*
>
> *It is your child, and for that reason I must revere it and submit my body entirely to its welfare, entertaining no thought of death, which once more is largely conceit. Therefore, because you once loved me, and because this child is your child, I ask you to have me back. If you will cable me one word, I will come to you as soon as I can. I swear to you to be a dutiful wife, and to serve you in all things. For now I only hate myself and my own conceited foolishness. I love you—I love the thought of you—you were natural and decent all through, whilst I was so false. Once I am with you again, I shall ask no more than to rest in your shelter all my life——*

This letter she wrote, sentence by sentence, as if from her deepest, sincerest heart. She felt that now, now, she was at the depths of herself. This was her true self, forever. With this document she would appear before God at the Judgment Day.

For what had a woman but to submit? What was her flesh but for childbearing, her strength for her children and her husband, the giver of life? At last she was a woman.

She posted her letter to his club, to be forwarded to him in Calcutta. He would receive it soon after his arrival in India—within three weeks of his arrival there. In a month's time she would receive word from him. Then she would go.

She was quite sure of him. She thought only of preparing her garments and of living quietly, peacefully, till the time when she should join him again and her history would be concluded for ever. The peace held like an unnatural calm for a long time. She was aware, however, of a gathering restiveness, a tumult impending within her. She tried to run away from it. She wished she could hear from Skrebensky, in answer to her letter, so that her course should be resolved, she should be engaged in fulfilling her fate. It was this inactivity which made her liable to the revulsion she dreaded.

It was curious how little she cared about his not having written to her before. It was enough that she had sent her letter. She would get the required answer, that was all.

One afternoon in early October, feeling the seething rising to madness within her, she slipped out in the rain, to walk abroad, lest the house should suffocate her. Everywhere was drenched wet and deserted, the grimed houses glowed dull red, the butt houses burned scarlet in a gleam of light, under the glistening, blackish purple slates. Ursula went on towards Willey Green. She lifted her face and walked swiftly, seeing the passage of light across the shallow valley, seeing the colliery and its clouds of steam for a moment visionary in dim brilliance, away in the chaos of rain. Then the veils closed again. She was glad of the rain's privacy and intimacy.

Making on towards the wood, she saw the pale gleam of Willey Water through the cloud below, she walked the open space where hawthorn trees streamed like hair on the wind and round bushes were presences slowing through the atmosphere. It was very splendid, free and chaotic.

Yet she hurried to the wood for shelter. There, the vast booming overhead vibrated down and encircled her, tree-trunks spanned the circle of tremendous sound, myriads of tree-trunks, enormous and streaked black with water, thrust like stanchions upright between the roaring overhead and the sweeping of the circle underfoot. She glided between the tree-trunks, afraid of them. They might turn and shut her in as she went through their martialled silence.

So she flitted along, keeping an illusion that she was unnoticed. She felt like a bird that has flown in through the window of a hall where vast warriors sit at the board. Between their grave, booming ranks she was hastening, assuming she was unnoticed, till she emerged, with beating heart, through the far window and out into the open, upon the vivid green, marshy meadow.

She turned under the shelter of the common, seeing the great veils of rain swinging with slow, floating waves across the landscape. She was very wet and a long way from home, far enveloped in the rain and the waving landscape. She must beat her way back through all this fluctuation, back to stability and security.

A solitary thing, she took the track straight across the wilderness, going back. The path was a narrow groove in the turf between high, sere, tussocky grass; it was scarcely more than a rabbit run. So she moved swiftly along, watching her footing, going like a bird on the wind, with no thought, contained in motion. But her heart had a small, living seed of fear, as she went through the wash of hollow space.

Suddenly she knew there was something else. Some horses were looming in the rain, not near yet. But they were going to be near. She continued her path, inevitably. They were horses in the lee of a clump of trees beyond, above her. She pursued her way with bent head. She did not want to lift her face to them. She did not want to know they were there. She went on in the wild track.

She knew the heaviness on her heart. It was the weight of the horses. But she would circumvent them. She would bear the weight steadily, and so escape. She would go straight on, and on, and be gone by.

Suddenly the weight deepened and her heart grew tense to bear it. Her breathing was laboured. But this weight also she could bear. She knew without looking that the horses were moving nearer. What were they? She felt the thud of their heavy hoofs on the ground. What was it that was drawing near her, what weight oppressing her heart? She did not know, she did not look.

Yet now her way was cut off. They were blocking her back. She knew they had gathered on a log bridge over the sedgy dike, a dark, heavy, powerfully heavy knot. Yet her feet went on and on. They would burst before her. They would burst before her. Her feet went on and on. And tense, and more tense became her nerves and her veins, they ran hot, they ran white hot, they must fuse and she must die.

But the horses had burst before her. In a sort of lightning of knowledge their movement travelled through her, the quiver and strain and thrust of their powerful flanks, as they burst before her and drew on, beyond.

She knew they had not gone, she knew they awaited her still. But she went on over the log bridge that their hoofs had churned and drummed, she went on, knowing things about them. She was aware of their breasts gripped, clenched narrow in a hold that never relaxed, she was aware of their red nostrils flaming with long endurance, and of their haunches, so rounded, so massive, pressing, pressing, pressing to burst the grip upon their breasts, pressing for ever till they went mad, running against the walls of time, and never bursting free. Their great haunches were smoothed and darkened with rain. But the darkness and wetness of rain could not put out the hard, urgent, massive fire that was locked within these flanks, never, never.

She went on, drawing near. She was aware of the great flash of hoofs, a bluish, iridescent flash surrounding a hollow of darkness. Large, large seemed the bluish, incandescent flash of the hoof-iron, large as a halo of lightning round the knotted darkness of the flanks. Like circles of lightning came the flash of hoofs from out of the powerful flanks.

They were awaiting her again. They had gathered under an oak tree, knotting their awful, blind, triumphing flanks together, and waiting, waiting. They were waiting for her approach. As if from a far distance she was drawing near, towards the line of twiggy oak trees where they made their intense darkness, gathered on a single bank.

She must draw near. But they broke away, they cantered round, making a wide circle to avoid noticing her, and cantered back into the open hillside behind her.

They were behind her. The way was open before her, to the gate in the high hedge in the near distance, so she could pass into the smaller, cultivated field, and so out to the high-road and the ordered world of man. Her way was clear. She lulled her heart. Yet her heart was couched with fear, couched with fear all along.

Suddenly she hesitated as if seized by lightning. She seemed to fall, yet found herself faltering forward with small steps. The thunder of horses galloping down the path behind her shook her, the weight came down upon her, down to the moment of extinction. She could not look round, so the horses thundered upon her.

Cruelly, they swerved and crashed by on her left hand. She saw the fierce flanks crinkled and as yet inadequate, the great hoofs flashing bright as yet only brandished about her, and one by one the horses crashed by, intent, working themselves up.

They had gone by, brandishing themselves thunderously about her, enclosing her. They slackened their burst transport, they slowed down, and cantered together into a knot once more, in the corner by the gate and the trees ahead of her. They stirred, they moved uneasily, they settled their uneasy flanks into one group, one purpose. They were up against her.

Her heart was gone, she had no more heart. She knew she dare not draw near. That concentrated, knitted flank of the horse-group had conquered. It stirred uneasily, awaiting her, knowing its triumph. It stirred uneasily, with the uneasiness of awaited triumph. Her heart was gone, her limbs were dissolved, she was dissolved like water. All the hardness and looming power was in the massive body of the horse-group.

Her feet faltered, she came to a standstill. It was the crisis. The horses stirred their flanks uneasily. She looked away, failing. On her left, two hundred yards down the slope, the thick hedge ran parallel. At one point there was an oak tree. She might climb into the boughs of that oak tree, and so round and drop on the other side of the hedge.

Shuddering, with limbs like water, dreaded every moment to fall, she began to work her way as if making a wide detour round the horse-mass. The horses stirred their flanks in a knot against her. She trembled forward as if in a trance.

Then suddenly, in a flame of agony, she darted, seized the rugged knots of the oak tree and began to climb. Her body was weak but her hands were as hard as steel. She knew she was strong. She struggled in a great effort till she hung on the bough. She knew the horses were aware. She gained her foot-hold on the bough. The horses were loosening their knot, stirring, trying to realise. She was working her way round to the other side of the tree. As they started to canter towards her, she fell in a heap on the other side of the hedge.

For some moments she could not move. Then she saw through the rabbit-cleared bottom of the hedge the great, working hoofs of the horses as they cantered near. She could not bear it. She rose and walked swiftly, diagonally across the field. The horses galloped along the other side of the hedge to the corner, where they were held up. She could feel them there in their huddled group all the while she hastened across the bare field. They were almost pathetic, now. Her will alone carried her, till, trembling, she climbed the fence under a leaning thorn tree that overhung the grass by the high-road. The use went from her, she sat on the fence leaning back against the trunk of the thorn tree, motionless.

As she sat there, spent, time and the flux of change passed away from her, she lay as if unconscious upon the bed of the stream, like a stone, unconscious, unchanging, unchangeable, whilst everything rolled by in transience, leaving her there, a stone at rest on the bed of the stream, inalterable and passive, sunk to the bottom of all change.

She lay still a long time, with her back against the thorn tree trunk, in her final isolation. Some colliers passed, tramping heavily up the wet road, their voices sounding out, their shoulders up to their ears, their figures blotched and spectral in the rain. Some did not see her. She opened her eyes languidly as they passed by. Then one man going alone saw her. The whites of his eyes showed in his black face as he looked in wonderment at her. He hesitated in his walk, as if to speak to her, out of frightened concern for her. How she dreaded his speaking to her, dreaded his questioning her.

She slipped from her seat and went vaguely along the path—vaguely. It was a long way home. She had an idea that she must walk for the rest of her life, wearily, wearily. Step after step, step after step, and always along the wet, rainy road between the hedges. Step after step, step after step, the monotony produced a deep, cold sense of nausea in her. How profound was her cold nausea, how profound! That too plumbed the bottom. She seemed destined to find the bottom of all things to-day: the bottom of all things. Well, at any rate she was walking along the bottom-most bed—she was quite safe: quite safe, if she had to go on and on for ever, seeing this was the very bottom, and there was nothing deeper. There was nothing deeper, you see, so one could not but feel certain, passive.

She arrived home at last. The climb up the hill to Beldover had been very trying. Why must one climb the hill? Why must one climb? Why not stay below? Why force one's way up the slope? Why force one's way up and up, when one is at the bottom? Oh, it was very trying, very wearying, very burden-some. Always burdens, always, always burdens. Still, she must get to the top and go home to bed. She must go to bed.

She got in and went upstairs in the dusk without its being noticed she was in such a sodden condition. She was too tired to go downstairs again. She got into bed and lay shuddering with cold, yet too apathetic to get up or call for relief. Then gradually she became more ill.

She was very ill for a fortnight, delirious, shaken and racked. But always, amid the ache of delirium, she had a dull firmness of being, a sense of perma-nency. She was in some way like the stone at the bottom of the river, inviolable and unalterable, no matter what storm raged in her body. Her soul lay still and permanent, full of pain, but itself for ever. Under all her illness, persisted a deep, inalterable knowledge.

She knew, and she cared no more. Throughout her illness, distorted into vague forms, persisted the question of herself and Skrebensky, like a gnawing ache that was still superficial, and did not touch her isolated, impregnable core of reality. But the corrosion of him burned in her till it burned itself out.

Must she belong to him, must she adhere to him? Something compelled her, and yet it was not real. Always the ache, the ache of unreality, of her belonging to Skrebensky. What bound her to him when she was not bound to him? Why did the falsity persist? Why did the falsity gnaw, gnaw, gnaw at her, why could she not wake up to clarity, to reality. If she could but wake up, if she could but wake up, the falsity of the dream, of her connection with Skrebensky, would be gone. But the sleep, the delirium pinned her down. Even when she was calm and sober she was in its spell.

Yet she was never in its spell. What extraneous thing bound her to him? There was some bond put upon her. Why could she not break it through? What was it? What was it?

In her delirium she beat and beat at the question. And at last her weariness gave her the answer—it was the child. The child bound her to him. The child was like a bond round her brain, tightened on her brain. It bound her to Skre-bensky.

But why, why did it bind her to Skrebensky? Could she not have a child of herself? Was not the child her own affair? all her own affair? What had it to do with him? Why must she be bound, aching and cramped with the bondage, to Skrebensky and Skrebensky's world? Anton's world: it became in her feverish brain a compression which enclosed her. If she could not get out of the com-pression she would go mad. The compression was Anton and Anton's world, not the Anton she possessed, but the Anton she did not possess, that which was owned by some other influence, by the world.

She fought and fought and fought all through her illness to be free of him and his world, to put it aside, to put it aside, into its place. Yet ever anew it gained ascendency over her, it laid new hold on her. Oh, the unutterable weariness of her flesh, which she could not cast off, nor yet extricate. If she could but extri-cate herself, if she could but disengage herself from feeling, from her body, from all the vast encumbrances of the world that was in contact with her, from her father, and her mother, and her lover, and all her acquaintance.

Repeatedly, in an ache of utter weariness she repeated: "I have no father nor mother nor lover, I have no allocated place in the world of things, I do not belong to Beldover nor to Nottingham nor to England nor to this world, they none of them exist, I am trammelled and entangled in them, but they are all unreal. I must break out of it, like a nut from its shell which is an unreality."

And again, to her feverish brain, came the vivid reality of acorns in February lying on the floor of a wood with their shells burst and discarded and the kernel issued naked to put itself forth. She was the naked, clear kernel thrusting forth the clear, powerful shoot, and the world was a bygone winter, discarded, her mother and father and Anton, and college and all her friends, all cast off like a year that has gone by, whilst the kernel was free and naked and striving to take new root, to create a new knowledge of Eternity in the flux of Time. And the kernel was the only reality; the rest was cast off into oblivion.

This grew and grew upon her. When she opened her eyes in the afternoon and saw the window of her room and the faint, smoky landscape beyond, this was all husk and shell lying by, all husk and shell, she could see nothing else, she was enclosed still, but loosely enclosed. There was a space between her and the shell. It was burst, there was a rift in it. Soon she would have her root fixed in a new Day, her nakedness would take itself the bed of a new sky and a new air, this old, decaying, fibrous husk would be gone.

Gradually she began really to sleep. She slept in the confidence of her new reality. She slept breathing with her soul the new air of a new world. The peace was very deep and enrichening. She had her root in new ground, she was gradually absorbed into growth.

When she woke at last it seemed as if a new day had come on the earth. How long, how long had she fought through the dust and obscurity, for this new dawn? How frail and fine and clear she felt, like the most fragile flower that opens in the end of winter. But the pole of night was turned and the dawn was coming in.

Very far off was her old experience—Skrebensky, her parting with him—very far off. Some things were real; those first glamorous weeks. Before, these had seemed like hallucination. Now they seemed like common reality. The rest was unreal. She knew that Skrebensky had never become finally real. In the weeks of passionate ecstasy he had been with her in her desire, she had created him for the time being. But in the end he had failed and broken down.

Strange, what a void separated him and her. She liked him now, as she liked a memory, some bygone self. He was something of the past, finite. He was that which is known. She felt a poignant affection for him, as for that which is past. But, when she looked with her face forward, he was not. Nay, when she looked ahead, into the undiscovered land before her, what was there she could recognise but a fresh glow of light and inscrutable trees going up from the earth like smoke. It was the unknown, the unexplored, the undiscovered upon whose shore she had landed, alone, after crossing the void, the darkness which washed the New World and the Old.

There would be no child: she was glad. If there had been a child, it would have made little difference, however. She would have kept the child and herself, she would not have gone to Skrebensky. Anton belonged to the past.

There came the cablegram from Skrebensky: "I am married." An old pain and anger and contempt stirred in her. Did he belong so utterly to the cast-off past? She repudiated him. He was as he was. It was good that he was as he was. Who was she to have a man according to her own desire? It was not for her to create, but to recognise a man created by God. The man should come from the

Infinite and she should hail him. She was glad she could not create her man. She was glad she had nothing to do with his creation. She was glad that this lay within the scope of that vaster power in which she rested at last. The man would come out of Eternity to which she herself belonged.

As she grew better, she sat to watch a new creation. As she sat at her window, she saw the people go by in the street below, colliers, women, children, walking each in the husk of an old fruition, but visible through the husk, the swelling and the heaving contour of the new germination. In the still, silenced forms of the colliers she saw a sort of suspense, a waiting in pain for the new liberation; she saw the same in the false hard confidence of the women. The confidence of the women was brittle. It would break quickly to reveal the strength and patient effort of the new germination.

In everything she saw she grasped and groped to find the creation of the living God, instead of the old, hard barren form of bygone living. Sometimes great terror possessed her. Sometimes she lost touch, she lost her feeling, she could only know the old horror of the husk which bound in her and all mankind. They were all in prison, they were all going mad.

She saw the stiffened bodies of the colliers, which seemed already enclosed in a coffin, she saw their unchanging eyes, the eyes of those who are buried alive: she saw the hard, cutting edges of the new houses, which seemed to spread over the hillside in their insentient triumph, the triumph of horrible, amorphous angles and straight lines, the expression of corruption triumphant and unopposed, corruption so pure that it is hard and brittle: she saw the dun atmosphere over the blackened hills opposite, the dark blotches of houses, slate roofed and amorphous, the old church-tower standing up in hideous obsoleteness above raw new houses on the crest of the hill, the amorphous, brittle, hard edged new houses advancing from Beldover to meet the corrupt new houses from Lethley, the houses of Lethley advancing to mix with the houses of Hainor, a dry, brittle, terrible corruption spreading over the face of the land, and she was sick with a nausea so deep that she perished as she sat. And then, in the blowing clouds, she saw a band of faint iridescence colouring in faint colours a portion of the hill. And forgetting, startled, she looked for the hovering colour and saw a rainbow forming itself. In one place it gleamed fiercely, and, her heart anguished with hope, she sought the shadow of iris where the bow should be. Steadily the colour gathered, mysteriously, from nowhere, it took presence upon itself, there was a faint, vast rainbow. The arc bended and strengthened itself till it arched indomitable, making great architecture of light and colour and the space of heaven, its pedestals luminous in the corruption of new houses on the low hill, its arch the top of heaven.

And the rainbow stood on the earth. She knew that the sordid people who crept hard-scaled and separate on the face of the world's corruption were living still, that the rainbow was arched in their blood and would quiver to life in their spirit, that they would cast off their horny covering of disintegration, that new, clean, naked bodies would issue to a new germination, to a new growth, rising to the light and the wind and the clean rain of heaven. She saw in the rainbow the earth's new architecture, the old, brittle corruption of houses and factories swept away, the world built up in a living fabric of Truth, fitting to the over-arching heaven.

Sons
and
Lovers

Contents

Part One

I

THE EARLY MARRIED LIFE OF THE MORELS

The Bottoms" succeeded to "Hell Row". Hell Row was a block of thatched, bulging cottages that stood by the brookside on Greenhill Lane. There lived the colliers who worked in the little gin-pits two fields away. The brook ran under the alder trees, scarcely soiled by these small mines, whose coal was drawn to the surface by donkeys that plodded wearily in a circle round a gin. And all over the countryside were these same pits, some of which had been worked in the time of Charles II, the few colliers and the donkeys burrowing down like ants into the earth, making queer mounds and little black places among the corn-fields and the meadows. And the cottages of these coal-miners, in blocks and pairs here and there, together with odd farms and homes of the stockingers, straying over the parish, formed the village of Bestwood.

Then, some sixty years ago, a sudden change took place. The gin-pits were elbowed aside by the large mines of the financiers. The coal and iron field of Nottinghamshire and Derbyshire was discovered. Carston, Waite and Co. appeared. Amid tremendous excitement, Lord Palmerston formally opened the company's first mine at Spinney Park, on the edge of Sherwood Forest.

About this time the notorious Hell Row, which through growing old had acquired an evil reputation, was burned down, and much dirt was cleansed away.

Carston, Waite & Co. found they had struck on a good thing, so, down the valleys of the brooks from Selby and Nuttall, new mines were sunk, until soon there were six pits working. From Nuttall, high up on the sandstone among the woods, the railway ran, past the ruined priory of the Carthusians and past Robin Hood's Well, down to Spinney Park, then on to Minton, a large mine among corn-fields; from Minton across the farmlands of the valleyside to Bunker's Hill, branching off there, and running north to Beggarlee and Selby, that looks over at Crich and the hills of Derbyshire: six mines like black studs on the country-side, linked by a loop of fine chain, the railway.

To accommodate the regiments of miners, Carston, Waite and Co. built the Squares, great quadrangles of dwellings on the hillside of Bestwood, and then, in the brook valley, on the site of Hell Row, they erected the Bottoms.

The Bottoms consisted of six blocks of miners' dwellings, two rows of three, like the dots on a blank-six domino, and twelve houses in a block. This double row of dwellings sat at the foot of the rather sharp slope from Bestwood, and looked out, from the attic windows at least, on the slow climb of the valley towards Selby.

The houses themselves were substantial and very decent. One could walk all round, seeing little front gardens with auriculas and saxifrage in the shadow of the bottom block, sweet-williams and pinks in the sunny top block; seeing neat front windows, little porches, little privet hedges, and dormer windows for the attics. But that was outside; that was the view on to the uninhabited parlours of all the colliers' wives. The dwelling-room, the kitchen, was at the back of the house, facing inward between the blocks, looking at a scrubby back garden, and then at the ash-pits. And between the rows, between the long lines of ash-pits, went the alley, where the children played and the women gossiped and the men smoked. So, the actual conditions of living in the Bottoms, that was so well built and that looked so nice, were quite unsavoury because people must live in the kitchen, and the kitchens opened on to that nasty alley of ash-pits.

Mrs. Morel was not anxious to move into the Bottoms, which was already twelve years old and on the downward path, when she descended to it from Bestwood. But it was the best she could do. Moreover, she had an end house in one of the top blocks, and thus had only one neighbour; on the other side an extra strip of garden. And, having an end house, she enjoyed a kind of aristocracy among the other women of the "between" houses, because her rent was five shillings and sixpence instead of five shillings a week. But this superiority in station was not much consolation to Mrs. Morel.

She was thirty-one years old, and had been married eight years. A rather small woman, of delicate mould but resolute bearing, she shrank a little from the first contact with the Bottoms women. She came down in the July, and in the September expected her third baby.

Her husband was a miner. They had only been in their new home three weeks when the wakes, or fair, began. Morel, she knew, was sure to make a holiday of it. He went off early on the Monday morning, the day of the fair. The two children were highly excited. William, a boy of seven, fled off immediately after breakfast, to prowl round the wakes ground, leaving Annie, who was only five, to whine all morning to go also. Mrs. Morel did her work. She scarcely knew her neighbours yet, and knew no one with whom to trust the little girl. So she promised to take her to the wakes after dinner.

William appeared at half-past twelve. He was a very active lad, fair-haired, freckled, with a touch of the Dane or Norwegian about him.

"Can I have my dinner, mother?" he cried, rushing in with his cap on. " 'Cause it begins at half-past one, the man says so."

"You can have your dinner as soon as it's done," replied the mother.

"Isn't it done?" he cried, his blue eyes staring at her in indignation. "Then I'm goin' be-out it."

"You'll do nothing of the sort. It will be done in five minutes. It is only half-past twelve."

"They'll be beginnin'," the boy half cried, half shouted.

"You won't die if they do," said the mother. "Besides, it's only half-past twelve, so you've a full hour."

The lad began hastily to lay the table, and directly the three sat down. They were eating batter-pudding and jam, when the boy jumped off his chair and stood perfectly still. Some distance away could be heard the first small braying of a merry-go-round, and the tooting of a horn. His face quivered as he looked at his mother.

"I told you!" he said, running to the dresser for his cap.

"Take your pudding in your hand—and it's only five past one, so you were wrong—you haven't got your twopence," cried the mother in a breath.

The boy came back, bitterly disappointed, for his twopence, then went off without a word.

"I want to go, I want to go," said Annie, beginning to cry.

"Well, and you shall go, whining, wizzening little stick!" said the mother. And later in the afternoon she trudged up the hill under the tall hedge with her child. The hay was gathered from the fields, and cattle were turned on to the eddish. It was warm, peaceful.

Mrs. Morel did not like the wakes. There were two sets of horses, one going by steam, one pulled round by a pony; three organs were grinding, and there came odd cracks of pistol-shots, fearful screeching of the cocoanut man's rattle, shouts of the Aunt Sally man, screeches from the peep-show lady. The mother perceived her son gazing enraptured outside the Lion Wallace booth, at the pictures of this famous lion that had killed a negro and maimed for life two white men. She left him alone, and went to get Annie a spin of toffee. Presently the lad stood in front of her, wildly excited.

"You never said you was coming—isn't the' a lot of things?—that lion's killed three men—I've spent my tuppence—an' look here."

He pulled from his pocket two egg-cups, with pink moss-roses on them.

"I got these from that stall where y'ave ter get them marbles in them holes. An' I got these two in two goes—'aepenny a go—they've got moss-roses on, look here. I wanted these."

She knew he wanted them for her.

"H'm!" she said, pleased. "They *are* pretty!"

"Shall you carry 'em, 'cause I'm frightened o' breakin' 'em?"

He was tipful of excitement now she had come, led her about the ground, showed her everything. Then, at the peep-show, she explained the pictures, in a sort of story, to which he listened as if spellbound. He would not leave her. All the time he stuck close to her, bristling with a small boy's pride of her. For no other woman looked such a lady as she did, in her little black bonnet and her cloak. She smiled when she saw women she knew. When she was tired she said to her son:

"Well, are you coming now, or later?"

"Are you goin' a'ready?" he cried, his face full of reproach.

"Already? It is past four, I know."

"What are you goin' a'ready for?" he lamented.

"You needn't come if you don't want," she said.

And she went slowly away with her little girl, whilst her son stood watching her, cut to the heart to let her go, and yet unable to leave the wakes. As she crossed the open ground in front of the Moon and Stars she heard men shouting, and smelled the beer, and hurried a little, thinking her husband was probably in the bar.

At about half-past six her son came home, tired now, rather pale, and somewhat wretched. He was miserable, though he did not know it, because he had let her go alone. Since she had gone, he had not enjoyed his wakes.

"Has my dad been?" he asked.

"No," said the mother.

"He's helping to wait at the Moon and Stars. I seed him through that black tin stuff wi' holes in, on the window, wi' his sleeves rolled up."

"Ha!" exclaimed the mother shortly. "He's got no money. An' he'll be satisfied if he gets his 'lowance, whether they give him more or not."

When the light was fading, and Mrs. Morel could see no more to sew, she rose and went to the door. Everywhere was the sound of excitement, the restlessness of the holiday, that at last infected her. She went out into the side garden. Women were coming home from the wakes, the children hugging a white lamb with green legs, or a wooden horse. Occasionally a man lurched past, almost as full as he could carry. Sometimes a good husband came along with his family, peacefully. But usually the women and children were alone. The stay-at-home mothers stood gossiping at the corners of the alley, as the twilight sank, folding their arms under their white aprons.

Mrs. Morel was alone, but she was used to it. Her son and her little girl slept upstairs; so, it seemed, her home was there behind her, fixed and stable. But she felt wretched with the coming child. The world seemed a dreary place, where nothing else would happen for her—at least until William grew up. But for herself, nothing but this dreary endurance—till the children grew up. And the children! She could not afford to have this third. She did not want it. The father was serving beer in a public-house, swilling himself drunk. She despised him, and was tied to him. This coming child was too much for her. If it were not for William and Annie, she was sick of it, the struggle with poverty and ugliness and meanness.

She went into the front garden, feeling too heavy to take herself out, yet unable to stay indoors. The heat suffocated her. And looking ahead, the prospect of her life made her feel as if she were buried alive.

The front garden was a small square with a privet hedge. There she stood, trying to soothe herself with the scent of flowers and the fading, beautiful evening. Opposite her small gate was the stile that led uphill, under the tall hedge, between the burning glow of the cut pastures. The sky overhead throbbed and pulsed with light. The glow sank quickly off the field; the earth and the hedges smoked dusk. As it grew dark, a ruddy glare came out on the hilltop, and out of the glare the diminished commotion of the fair.

Sometimes, down the trough of darkness formed by the path under the hedges, men came lurching home. One young man lapsed into a run down the steep bit that ended the hill, and went with a crash into the stile. Mrs. Morel shuddered. He picked himself up, swearing viciously, rather pathetically, as if he thought the stile had wanted to hurt him.

She went indoors, wondering if things were never going to alter. She was beginning by now to realise that they would not. She seemed so far away from her girlhood, she wondered if it were the same person walking heavily up the back garden at the Bottoms as had run so lightly up the breakwater at Sheerness ten years before.

"What have *I* to do with it?" she said to herself. "What have I to do with all this? Even the child I am going to have! It doesn't seem as if *I* were taken into account."

Sometimes life takes hold of one, carries the body along, accomplishes one's history, and yet is not real, but leaves oneself as it were slurred over.

"I wait," Mrs. Morel said to herself—"I wait, and what I wait for can never come."

Then she straightened the kitchen, lit the lamp, mended the fire, looked out the washing for the next day, and put it to soak. After which she sat down to her sewing. Through the long hours her needle flashed regularly through the stuff. Occasionally she sighed, moving to relieve herself. And all the time she was thinking how to make the most of what she had, for the children's sakes.

At half-past eleven her husband came. His cheeks were very red and very shiny above his black moustache. His head nodded slightly. He was pleased with himself.

"Oh! Oh! waitin' for me, lass? I've bin 'elpin' Anthony, an' what's think he's gen me? Nowt b'r a lousy hae'f-crown, an' that's ivry penny——"

"He thinks you've made the rest up in beer," she said shortly.

"An' I 'aven't—that I 'aven't. You b'lieve me, I've 'ad very little this day, I have an' all." His voice went tender. "Here, an' I browt thee a bit o' brandys-nap, an' a cocoanut for th' children." He laid the gingerbread and the cocoanut, a hairy object, on the table. "Nay, tha niver said thankyer for nowt i' thy life, did ter?"

As a compromise, she picked up the cocoanut and shook it, to see if it had any milk.

"It's a good 'un, you may back yer life o' that. I got it fra' Bill Hodgkisson. 'Bill,' I says, 'tha non wants them three nuts, does ter? Arena ter for gi'ein' me one for my bit of a lad an' wench?' 'I ham, Walter, my lad,' 'e says; 'ta'e which on 'em ter's a mind.' An' so I took one, an' thanked 'im. I didn't like ter shake it afore 'is eyes, but 'e says, 'Tha'd better ma'e sure it's a good un, Walt.' An' so, yer see, I knowed it was. He's a nice chap, is Bill Hodgkisson, 'e's a nice chap!"

"A man will part with anything so long as he's drunk, and you're drunk along with him," said Mrs. Morel.

"Eh, tha mucky little 'ussy, who's drunk, I sh'd like ter know?" said Morel. He was extraordinarily pleased with himself, because of his day's helping to wait in the Moon and Stars. He chattered on.

Mrs. Morel, very tired, and sick of his babble, went to bed as quickly as possible, while he raked the fire.

Mrs. Morel came of a good old burgher family, famous independents who had fought with Colonel Hutchinson, and who remained stout Congregation-alists. Her grandfather had gone bankrupt in the lace-market at a time when so many lace-manufacturers were ruined in Nottingham. Her father, George Coppard, was an engineer—a large, handsome, haughty man, proud of his fair skin and blue eyes, but more proud still of his integrity. Gertrude resembled her mother in her small build. But her temper, proud and unyielding, she had from the Coppards.

George Coppard was bitterly galled by his own poverty. He became foreman of the engineers in the dockyard at Sheerness. Mrs. Morel—Gertrude—was the second daughter. She favoured her mother, loved her mother best of all; but she had the Coppards' clear, defiant blue eyes and their broad brow. She remem-bered to have hated her father's overbearing manner towards her gentle, hu-morous, kindly-souled mother. She remembered running over the breakwater at Sheerness and finding the boat. She remembered to have been petted and flattered by all the men when she had gone to the dockyard, for she was a delicate, rather proud child. She remembered the funny old mistress, whose assistant she had become, whom she had loved to help in the private school. And she still had the Bible that John Field had given her. She used to walk home from chapel with John Field when she was nineteen. He was the son of a well-to-do tradesman, had been to college in London, and was to devote himself to business.

She could always recall in detail a September Sunday afternoon, when they had sat under the vine at the back of her father's house. The sun came through the chinks of the vine-leaves and made beautiful patterns, like a lace scarf, falling on her and on him. Some of the leaves were clean yellow, like yellow flat flowers.

"Now sit still," he had cried. "Now your hair, I don't know what it *is* like! It's as bright as copper and gold, as red as burnt copper, and it has gold threads where the sun shines on it. Fancy their saying it's brown. Your mother calls it mouse-colour."

She had met his brilliant eyes, but her clear face scarcely showed the elation which rose within her.

"But you say you don't like business," she pursued.

"I don't. I hate it!" he cried hotly.

"And you would like to go into the ministry," she half implored.

"I should. I should love it, if I thought I could make a first-rate preacher."

"Then why don't you—why *don't* you?" Her voice rang with defiance. "If *I* were a man, nothing would stop me."

She held her head erect. He was rather timid before her.

"But my father's so stiff-necked. He means to put me into the business, and I know he'll do it."

"But if you're a *man?*" she had cried.

"Being a man isn't everything," he replied, frowning with puzzled helplessness.

Now, as she moved about her work at the Bottoms, with some experience of what being a man meant, she knew that it was *not* everything.

At twenty, owing to her health, she had left Sheerness. Her father had retired home to Nottingham. John Field's father had been ruined; the son had gone as a teacher in Norwood. She did not hear of him until, two years later, she made determined inquiry. He had married his landlady, a woman of forty, a widow with property.

And still Mrs. Morel preserved John Field's Bible. She did not now believe him to be—— Well, she understood pretty well what he might or might not have been. So she preserved his Bible, and kept his memory intact in her heart, for her own sake. To her dying day, for thirty-five years, she did not speak of him.

When she was twenty-three years old, she met, at a Christmas party, a young man from the Erewash Valley. Morel was then twenty-seven years old. He was well set-up, erect, and very smart. He had wavy black hair that shone again, and a vigorous black beard that had never been shaved. His cheeks were ruddy, and his red, moist mouth was noticeable because he laughed so often and so heartily. He had that rare thing, a rich, ringing laugh. Gertrude Coppard had watched him, fascinated. He was so full of colour and animation, his voice ran so easily into comic grotesque, he was so ready and so pleasant with everybody. Her own father had a rich fund of humour, but it was satiric. This man's was different: soft, non-intellectual, warm, a kind of gambolling.

She herself was opposite. She had a curious, receptive mind which found much pleasure and amusement in listening to other folk. She was clever in leading folk to talk. She loved ideas, and was considered very intellectual. What she liked most of all was an argument on religion or philosophy or politics with some educated man. This she did not often enjoy. So she always had people tell her about themselves, finding her pleasure so.

In her person she was rather small and delicate, with a large brow, and dropping bunches of brown silk curls. Her blue eyes were very straight, honest, and searching. She had the beautiful hands of the Coppards. Her dress was always subdued. She wore dark blue silk, with a peculiar silver chain of silver scallops. This, and a heavy brooch of twisted gold, was her only ornament. She was still perfectly intact, deeply religious, and full of beautiful candour.

Walter Morel seemed melted away before her. She was to the miner that thing of mystery and fascination, a lady. When she spoke to him, it was with a southern pronounciation and a purity of English which thrilled him to hear. She watched him. He danced well, as if it were natural and joyous in him to dance. His grandfather was a French refugee who had married an English barmaid—if it had been a marriage. Gertrude Coppard watched the young miner as he danced, a certain subtle exultation like glamour in his movement, and his face the flower of his body, ruddy, with tumbled black hair, and laughing alike whatever partner he bowed above. She thought him rather wonderful, never having met anyone like him. Her father was to her the type of all men. And George Coppard, proud in his bearing, handsome, and rather bitter; who preferred theology in reading, and who drew near in sympathy only to one man, the Apostle Paul; who was harsh in government, and in familiarity ironic; who ignored all sensuous pleasure:—he was very different from the miner. Gertrude herself was rather contemptuous of dancing; she had not the slightest inclination towards that accomplishment, and had never learned even a Roger de Coverley. She was puritan, like her father, high-minded, and really stern. Therefore the dusky, golden softness of this man's sensuous flame of life, that flowed off his flesh like the flame from a candle, not baffled and gripped into incandescence by thought and spirit as her life was, seemed to her something wonderful, beyond her.

He came and bowed above her. A warmth radiated through her as if she had drunk wine.

"Now do come and have this one wi' me," he said caressively. "It's easy, you know. I'm pining to see you dance."

She had told him before she could not dance. She glanced at his humility and smiled. Her smile was very beautiful. It moved the man so that he forgot everything.

"No, I won't dance," she said softly. Her words came clean and ringing.

Not knowing what he was doing—he often did the right thing by instinct— he sat beside her, inclining reverentially.

"But you mustn't miss your dance," she reproved.

"Nay, I don't want to dance that—it's not one as I care about."

"Yet you invited me to it."

He laughed very heartily at this.

"I never thought o' that. Tha'rt not long in taking the curl out of me."

It was her turn to laugh quickly.

"You don't look as if you'd come much uncurled," she said.

"I'm like a pig's tail, I curl because I canna help it," he laughed, rather boisterously.

"And you are a miner!" she exclaimed in surprise.

"Yes. I went down when I was ten."

She looked at him in wondering dismay.

"When you were ten! And wasn't it very hard?" she asked.

"You soon get used to it. You live like th' mice, an' you pop out at night to see what's going on."

"It makes me feel blind," she frowned.

"Like a moudiwarp!" he laughed. "Yi, an' there's some chaps as does go round like moudiwarps." He thrust his face forward in the blind, snout-like way of a mole, seeming to sniff and peer for direction. "They dun though!" he protested naïvely. "Tha niver seed such a way they get in. But tha mun let me ta'e thee down some time, an' tha can see for thysen."

She looked at him, startled. This was a new tract of life suddenly opened before her. She realised the life of the miners, hundreds of them toiling below earth and coming up at evening. He seemed to her noble. He risked his life daily, and with gaiety. She looked at him, with a touch of appeal in her pure humility.

"Shouldn't ter like it?" he asked tenderly. " 'Appen not, it 'ud dirty thee." She had never been "thee'd" and "thou'd" before.

The next Christmas they were married, and for three months she was per-fectly happy: for six months she was very happy.

He had signed the pledge, and wore the blue ribbon of a tee-totaller: he was nothing if not showy. They lived, she thought, in his own house. It was small, but convenient enough, and quite nicely furnished, with solid, worthy stuff that suited her honest soul. The women, her neighbours, were rather foreign to her, and Morel's mother and sisters were apt to sneer at her ladylike ways. But she could perfectly well live by herself, so long as she had her husband close.

Sometimes, when she herself wearied of love-talk, she tried to open her heart seriously to him. She saw him listen deferentially, but without understand-ing. This killed her efforts at a finer intimacy, and she had flashes of fear. Some-times he was restless of an evening: it was not enough for him just to be near her, she realised. She was glad when he set himself to little jobs.

He was a remarkably handy man—could make or mend anything. So she would say:

"I do like that coal-rake of your mother's—it is small and natty."

"Does ter, my wench? Well, I made that, so I can make thee one!"

"What! why, it's a steel one!"

"An' what if it is! Tha s'lt ha'e one very similar, if not exactly same."

She did not mind the mess, nor the hammering and noise. He was busy and happy.

But in the seventh month, when she was brushing his Sunday coat, she felt papers in the breast pocket, and, seized with a sudden curiosity, took them out to read. He very rarely wore the frock-coat he was married in: and it had not occurred to her before to feel curious concerning the papers. They were the bills of the household furniture, still unpaid.

"Look here," she said at night, after he was washed and had had his dinner. "I found these in the pocket of your wedding-coat. Haven't you settled the bills yet?"

"No. I haven't had a chance."

"But you told me all was paid. I had better go into Nottingham on Saturday and settle them. I don't like sitting on another man's chairs and eating from an unpaid table."

He did not answer.

"I can have your bank-book, can't I?"

"Tha can ha'e it, for what good it'll be to thee."

"I thought——" she began. He had told her had a good bit of money left over. But she realised it was no use asking questions. She sat rigid with bitterness and indignation.

The next day she went down to see his mother.

"Didn't you buy the furniture for Walter?" she asked.

"Yes, I did," tartly retorted the elder woman.

"And how much did he give you to pay for it?"

The elder woman was stung with fine indignation.

"Eighty pound, if you're so keen on knowin'," she replied.

"Eighty pounds! But there are forty-two pounds still owing!"

"I can't help that."

"But where has it all gone?"

"You'll find all the papers, I think, if you look—beside ten pound as he owed me, an' six pound as the wedding cost down here."

"Six pounds!" echoed Gertrude Morel. It seemed to her monstrous that, after her own father had paid so heavily for her wedding, six pounds more should have been squandered in eating and drinking at Walter's parents' house, at his expense.

"And how much has he sunk in his houses?" she asked.

"His houses—which houses?"

Gertrude Morel went white to the lips. He had told her the house he lived in, and the next one, was his own.

"I thought the house we live in——" she began.

"They're my houses, those two," said the mother-in-law. "And not clear either. It's as much as I can do to keep the mortgage interest paid."

Gertrude sat white and silent. She was her father now.

"Then we ought to be paying you rent," she said coldly.

"Walter is paying me rent," replied the mother.

"And what rent?" asked Gertrude.

"Six and six a week," retorted the mother.

It was more than the house was worth. Gertrude held her head erect, looked straight before her.

"It is lucky to be you," said the elder woman, bitingly, "to have a husband as takes all the worry of the money, and leaves you a free hand."

The young wife was silent.

She said very little to her husband, but her manner had changed towards him. Something in her proud, honourable soul had crystallised out hard as rock.

When October came in, she thought only of Christmas. Two years ago, at Christmas, she had met him. Last Christmas she had married him. This Christmas she would bear him a child.

"You don't dance yourself, do you, missis?" asked her nearest neighbour, in October, when there was great talk of opening a dancing-class over the Brick and Tile Inn at Bestwood.

"No—I never had the least inclination to," Mrs. Morel replied.

"Fancy! An' how funny as you should ha' married your Mester. You know he's quite a famous one for dancing."

"I didn't know he was famous," laughed Mrs. Morel.

"Yea, he is though! Why, he ran that dancing-class in the Miners' Arms club-room for over five year."

"Did he?"

"Yes, he did." The other woman was defiant. "An' it was thronged every Tuesday, and Thursday, an' Sat'day—an' there *was* carryin's-on, accordin' to all accounts."

This kind of thing was gall and bitterness to Mrs. Morel, and she had a fair share of it. The women did not spare her, at first; for she was superior, though she could not help it.

He began to be rather late in coming home.

"They're working very late now, aren't they?" she said to her washer-woman.

"No later than they allers do, I don't think. But they stop to have their pint at Ellen's, an' they get talkin', an' there you are! Dinner stone cold—an' it serves 'em right."

"But Mr. Morel does not take any drink."

The woman dropped the clothes, looked at Mrs. Morel, then went on with her work, saying nothing.

Gertrude Morel was very ill when the boy was born. Morel was good to her, as good as gold. But she felt very lonely, miles away from her own people. She felt lonely with him now, and his presence only made it more intense.

The boy was small and frail at first, but he came on quickly. He was a beautiful child, with dark gold ringlets, and dark-blue eyes which changed gradually to a clear grey. His mother loved him passionately. He came just when her own bitterness of disillusion was hardest to bear; when her faith in life was shaken, and her soul felt dreary and lonely. She made much of the child, and the father was jealous.

At last Mrs. Morel despised her husband. She turned to the child; she turned from the father. He had begun to neglect her; the novelty of his own home was gone. He had no grit, she said bitterly to herself. What he felt just at the minute, that was all to him. He could not abide by anything. There was nothing at the back of all his show.

There began a battle between the husband and wife—a fearful, bloody battle that ended only with the death of one. She fought to make him undertake his own responsibilities, to make him fulfil his obligations. But he was too different from her. His nature was purely sensuous, and she strove to make him moral, religious. She tried to force him to face things. He could not endure it—it drove him out of his mind.

While the baby was still tiny, the father's temper had become so irritable that it was not to be trusted. The child had only to give a little trouble when the man began to bully. A little more, and the hard hands of the collier hit the baby. Then Mrs. Morel loathed her husband, loathed him for days; and he went out and drank; and she cared very little what he did. Only, on his return, she scathed him with her satire.

The estrangement between them caused him, knowingly or unknowingly, grossly to offend her where he would not have done.

William was only one year old, and his mother was proud of him, he was so pretty. She was not well off now, but her sisters kept the boy in clothes. Then, with his little white hat curled with an ostrich feather, and his white coat, he was a joy to her, the twining wisps of hair clustering round his head. Mrs. Morel lay listening, one Sunday morning, to the chatter of the father and child downstairs. Then she dozed off. When she came downstairs, a great fire glowed in the grate, the room was hot, the breakfast was roughly laid, and seated in his arm-chair, against the chimney-piece, sat Morel, rather timid; and standing between his legs, the child—cropped like a sheep, with such an odd round poll—looking wondering at her; and on a newspaper spread out upon the hearthrug, a myriad of crescent-shaped curls, like the petals of a marigold scattered in the reddening firelight.

Mrs. Morel stood still. It was her first baby. She went very white, and was unable to speak.

"What dost think o' 'im?" Morel laughed uneasily.

She gripped her two fists, lifted them, and came forward. Morel shrank back. "I could kill you, I could!" she said. She choked with rage, her two fists uplifted.

"Yer non want ter make a wench on 'im," Morel said, in a frightened tone, bending his head to shield his eyes from hers. His attempt at laughter had vanished.

The mother looked down at the jagged, close-clipped head of her child. She put her hands on his hair, and stroked and fondled his head.

"Oh—my boy!" she faltered. Her lip trembled, her face broke, and, snatching up the child, she buried her face in his shoulder and cried painfully. She was one of those women who cannot cry; whom it hurts as it hurts a man. It was like ripping something out of her, her sobbing.

Morel sat with his elbows on his knees, his hands gripped together till the knuckles were white. He gazed in the fire, feeling almost stunned, as if he could not breathe.

Presently she came to an end, soothed the child and cleared away the breakfast-table. She left the newspaper, littered with curls, spread upon the hearth-rug. At last her husband gathered it up and put it at the back of the fire. She went about her work with closed mouth and very quiet. Morel was subdued. He crept about wretchedly, and his meals were a misery that day. She spoke to him civilly, and never alluded to what he had done. But he felt something final had happened.

Afterwards she said she had been silly, that the boy's hair would have had to be cut, sooner or later. In the end, she even brought herself to say to her husband it was just as well he had played barber when he did. But she knew, and Morel knew, that that act had caused something momentous to take place in her soul. She remembered the scene all her life, as one in which she had suffered the most intensely.

This act of masculine clumsiness was the spear through the side of her love for Morel. Before, while she had striven against him bitterly, she had fretted after him, as if he had gone astray from her. Now she ceased to fret for his love: he was an outsider to her. This made life much more bearable.

Nevertheless, she still continued to strive with him. She still had her high moral sense, inherited from generations of Puritans. It was now a religious instinct, and she was almost a fanatic with him, because she loved him, or had loved him. If he sinned, she tortured him. If he drank, and lied, was often a poltroon, sometimes a knave, she wielded the lash unmercifully.

The pity was, she was too much his opposite. She could not be content with the little he might be; she would have him the much that he ought to be. So, in seeking to make him nobler than he could be, she destroyed him. She injured and hurt and scarred herself, but she lost none of her worth. She also had the children.

He drank rather heavily, though not more than many miners, and always beer, so that whilst his health was affected, it was never injured. The week-end was his chief carouse. He sat in the Miners' Arms until turning-out time every Friday, every Saturday, and every Sunday evening. On Monday and Tuesday he had to get up and reluctantly leave towards ten o'clock. Sometimes he stayed at home on Wednesday and Thursday evenings, or was only out for an hour. He practically never had to miss work owing to his drinking.

But although he was very steady at work, his wages fell off. He was blabmouthed, a tongue-wagger. Authority was hateful to him, therefore he could only abuse the pit-managers. He would say, in the Palmerston:

"Th' gaffer come down to our stall this morning, an' 'e says, 'You know, Walter, this 'ere'll not do. What about these props?' An' I says to him, 'Why, what art talkin' about? What d'st mean about th' props?' 'It'll never do, this 'ere,' 'e says. 'You'll be havin' th' roof in, one o' these days.' An' I says, 'Tha'd better stan' on a bit o' clunch, then, an' hold it up wi' thy 'ead.' So 'e wor that mad, 'e cossed an' 'e swore, an' t'other chaps they did laugh." Morel was a good mimic. He imitated the manager's fat, squeaky voice, with its attempt at good English.

" 'I shan't have it, Walter. Who knows more about it, me or you?' So I says, 'I've niver fun out how much tha' knows, Alfred. It'll 'appen carry thee ter bed an' back.' "

So Morel would go on to the amusement of his boon companions. And some of this would be true. The pit-manager was not an educated man. He had been a boy along with Morel, so that, while the two disliked each other, they more or less took each other for granted. But Alfred Charlesworth did not forgive the butty these public-house sayings. Consequently, although Morel was a good miner, sometimes earning as much as five pounds a week when he married, he came gradually to have worse and worse stalls, where the coal was thin, and hard to get, and unprofitable.

Also, in summer, the pits are slack. Often, on bright sunny mornings, the men are seen trooping home again at ten, eleven, or twelve o'clock. No empty trucks stand at the pit-mouth. The women on the hillside look across as they shake the hearth-rug against the fence, and count the wagons the engine is taking along the line up the valley. And the children, as they come from school at dinner-time, looking down the fields and seeing the wheels on the headstocks standing, say:

"Minton's knocked off. My dad'll be at home."

And there is a sort of shadow over all, women and children and men, because money will be short at the end of the week.

Morel was supposed to give his wife thirty shillings a week, to provide everything—rent, food, clothes, clubs, insurance, doctors. Occasionally, if he were flush, he gave her thirty-five. But these occasions by no means balanced those when he gave her twenty-five. In winter, with a decent stall, the miner might earn fifty or fifty-five shillings a week. Then he was happy. On Friday night, Saturday, and Sunday, he spent royally, getting rid of his sovereign or thereabouts. And out of so much, he scarcely spared the children an extra penny or bought them a pound of apples. It all went in drink. In the bad times, matters were more worrying, but he was not so often drunk, so that Mrs. Morel used to say:

"I'm not sure I wouldn't rather be short, for when he's flush, there isn't a minute of peace."

If he earned forty shillings he kept ten; from thirty-five he kept five; from thirty-two he kept four; from twenty-eight he kept three; from twenty-four he kept two; from twenty he kept one-and-six; from eighteen he kept a shilling; from sixteen he kept sixpence. He never saved a penny, and he gave his wife no opportunity of saving; instead, she had occasionally to pay his debts; not public-house debts, for those never were passed on to the women, but debts when he had bought a canary, or a fancy walking-stick.

At the wakes time Morel was working badly, and Mrs. Morel was trying to save against her confinement. So it galled her bitterly to think he should be out taking his pleasure and spending money, whilst she remained at home, harassed.

There were two days' holiday. On the Tuesday morning Morel rose early. He was in good spirits. Quite early, before six o'clock, she heard him whistling away to himself downstairs. He had a pleasant way of whistling, lively and musical. He nearly always whistled hymns. He had been a choir-boy with a beautiful voice, and had taken solos in Southwell cathedral. His morning whistling alone betrayed it.

His wife lay listening to him tinkering away in the garden, his whistling ringing out as he sawed and hammered away. It always gave her a sense of warmth and peace to hear him thus as she lay in bed, the children not yet awake, in the bright early morning, happy in his man's fashion.

At nine o'clock, while the children with bare legs and feet were sitting playing on the sofa, and the mother was washing up, he came in from his carpentry, his sleeves rolled up, his waistcoat hanging open. He was still a good-looking man, with black, wavy hair, and a large black moustache. His face was perhaps too much inflamed, and there was about him a look almost of peevishness. But now he was jolly. He went straight to the sink where his wife was washing up.

"What, are thee there!" he said boisterously. "Sluthe off an' let me wesh mysen."

"You may wait till I've finished," said his wife.

"Oh, mun I? An' what if I shonna?"

This good-humoured threat amused Mrs. Morel.

"Then you can go and wash yourself in the soft-water tub."

"Ha! I can' an' a', tha mucky little 'ussy."

With which he stood watching her a moment, then went away to wait for her.

When he chose he could still make himself again a real gallant. Usually he preferred to go out with a scarf round his neck. Now, however, he made a toilet. There seemed so much gusto in the way he puffed and swilled as he washed himself, so much alacrity with which he hurried to the mirror in the kitchen, and, bending because it was too low for him, scrupulously parted his wet black hair, that it irritated Mrs. Morel. He put on a turn-down collar, a black bow, and wore his Sunday tail-coat. As such, he looked spruce, and what his clothes would not do, his instinct for making the most of his good looks would.

At half-past nine Jerry Purdy came to call for his pal. Jerry was Morel's bosom friend, and Mrs. Morel disliked him. He was a tall, thin man, with a rather foxy face, the kind of face that seems to lack eyelashes. He walked with a stiff, brittle dignity, as if his head were on a wooden spring. His nature was cold and shrewd. Generous where he intended to be generous, he seemed to be very fond of Morel, and more or less to take charge of him.

Mrs. Morel hated him. She had known his wife, who had died of consumption, and who had, at the end, conceived such a violent dislike of her husband, that if he came into her room it caused her hæmorrhage. None of which Jerry had seemed to mind. And now his eldest daughter, a girl of fifteen, kept a poor house for him, and looked after the two younger children.

"A mean, wizzen-hearted stick!" Mrs. Morel said of him.

"I've never known Jerry mean in *my* life," protested Morel. "A opener-handed and more freer chap you couldn't find anywhere, accordin' to my knowledge."

"Open-handed to you," retorted Mrs. Morel. "But his fist is shut tight enough to his children, poor things."

"Poor things! And what for are they poor things, I should like to know."

But Mrs. Morel would not be appeased on Jerry's score.

The subject of argument was seen, craning his thin neck over the scullery curtain. He caught Mrs. Morel's eye.

"Mornin', missis! Mester in?"

"Yes—he is."

Jerry entered unasked, and stood by the kitchen doorway. He was not invited to sit down, but stood there, coolly asserting the rights of men and husbands.

"A nice day," he said to Mrs. Morel.

"Yes."

"Grand out this morning—grand for a walk."

"Do you mean *you're* going for a walk?" she asked.

"Yes. We mean walkin' to Nottingham," he replied.

"H'm!"

The two men greeted each other, both glad: Jerry, however, full of assurance, Morel rather subdued, afraid to seem too jubilant in presence of his wife. But he laced his boots quickly, with spirit. They were going for a ten-mile walk across the fields to Nottingham. Climbing the hillside from the Bottoms, they mounted gaily into the morning. At the Moon and Stars they had their first drink, then on to the Old Spot. Then a long five miles of drought to carry them into Bulwell to a glorious pint of bitter. But they stayed in a field with some haymakers whose gallon bottle was full, so that, when they came in sight of the city, Morel was sleepy. The town spread upwards before them, smoking vaguely in the midday glare, fridging the crest away to the south with spires and factory bulks and chimneys. In the last field Morel lay down under an oak tree and slept soundly for over an hour. When he rose to go forward he felt queer.

The two had dinner in the Meadows, with Jerry's sister, then repaired to the Punch Bowl, where they mixed in the excitement of pigeon-racing. Morel never in his life played cards, considering them as having some occult, malevolent power—"the devil's pictures," he called them! But he was a master of skittles and of dominoes. He took a challenge from a Newark man, on skittles. All the men in the old, long bar took sides, betting either one way or the other. Morel took off his coat. Jerry held the hat containing the money. The men at the tables watched. Some stood with their mugs in their hands. Morel felt his big wooden ball carefully, then launched it. He played havoc among the nine-pins, and won half a crown, which restored him to solvency.

By seven o'clock the two were in good condition. They caught the 7.30 train home.

In the afternoon the Bottoms was intolerable. Every inhabitant remaining was out of doors. The women, in twos and threes, bareheaded and in white aprons, gossiped in the alley between the blocks. Men, having a rest between drinks, sat on their heels and talked. The place smelled stale; the slate roofs glistered in the arid heat.

Mrs. Morel took the little girl down to the brook in the meadows, which were not more than two hundred yards away. The water ran quickly over stones and broken pots. Mother and child leaned on the rail of the old sheep-bridge, watching. Up at the dipping-hole, at the other end of the meadow, Mrs. Morel could see the naked forms of boys flashing round the deep yellow water, or an occasional bright figure dart glittering over the blackish stagnant meadow. She knew William was at the dipping-hole, and it was the dread of her life lest he should get drowned. Annie played under the tall old hedge, picking up alder cones, that she called currants. The child required much attention, and the flies were teasing.

The children were put to bed at seven o'clock. Then she worked awhile.

When Walter Morel and Jerry arrived at Bestwood they felt a load off their minds; a railway journey no longer impended, so they could put the finishing touches to a glorious day. They entered the Nelson with the satisfaction of returned travellers.

The next day was a work-day, and the thought of it put a damper on the men's spirits. Most of them, moreover, had spent their money. Some were already rolling dismally home, to sleep in preparation for the morrow. Mrs. Morel, listening to their mournful singing, went indoors. Nine o'clock passed, and ten, and still "the pair" had not returned. On a doorstep somewhere a man was singing loudly, in a drawl: "Lead, kindly Light." Mrs. Morel was always indignant with the drunken men that they must sing that hymn when they got maudlin.

"As if 'Genevieve' weren't good enough," she said.

The kitchen was full of the scent of boiled herbs and hops. On the hob a large black saucepan steamed slowly. Mrs. Morel took a panchion, a great bowl of thick red earth, streamed a heap of white sugar into the bottom, and then, straining herself to the weight, was pouring in the liquor.

Just then Morel came in. He had been very jolly in the Nelson, but coming home had grown irritable. He had not quite got over the feeling of irritability and pain, after having slept on the ground when he was so hot; and a bad conscience afflicted him as he neared the house. He did not know he was angry. But when the garden gate resisted his attempts to open it, he kicked it and broke the latch. He entered just as Mrs. Morel was pouring the infusion of herbs out of the saucepan. Swaying slightly, he lurched against the table. The boiling liquor pitched. Mrs. Morel started back.

"Good gracious," she cried, "coming home in his drunkenness!"

"Comin' home in his what?" he snarled, his hat over his eye.

Suddenly her blood rose in a jet.

"Say you're *not* drunk!" she flashed.

She had put down her saucepan, and was stirring the sugar into the beer. He dropped his two hands heavily on the table, and thrust his face forwards at her.

" 'Say you're not drunk,' " he repeated. "Why, nobody but a nasty little bitch like you 'ud 'ave such a thought."

He thrust his face forward at her.

"There's money to bezzle with, if there's money for nothing else."

"I've not spent a two-shillin' bit this day," he said.

"You don't get as drunk as a lord on nothing," she replied. "And," she cried, flashing into sudden fury, "if you've been sponging on your beloved Jerry, why, let him look after his children, for they need it."

"It's a lie, it's a lie. Shut your face, woman."

They were now at battle-pitch. Each forgot everything save the hatred of the other and the battle between them. She was fiery and furious as he. They went on till he called her a liar.

"No," she cried, starting up, scarce able to breathe. "Don't call me that— you, the most despicable liar that ever walked in shoe-leather." She forced the last words out of suffocated lungs.

"You're a liar!" he yelled, banging the table with his fist. "You're a liar, you're a liar."

She stiffened herself, with clenched fists.

"The house is filthy with you," she cried.

"Then get out on it—it's mine. Get out on it!" he shouted. "It's me as brings th' money whoam, not thee. It's my house, not thine. Then ger out on't—ger out on't!"

"And I would," she cried, suddenly shaken into tears of impotence. "Ah, wouldn't I, wouldn't I have gone long ago, but for those children. Ay, haven't I repented not going years ago, when I'd only the one"—suddenly drying into rage. "Do you think it's for *you* I stop—do you think I'd stop one minute for *you?*"

"Go, then," he shouted, beside himself. "Go!"

"No!" She faced round. "No," she cried loudly, "you shan't have it *all* your own way; you shan't do *all* you like. I've got those children to see to. My word," she laughed, "I should look well to leave them to you."

"Go," he cried thickly, lifting his fist. He was afraid of her. "Go!"

"I should be only too glad. I should laugh, laugh, my lord, if I could get away from you," she replied.

He came up to her, his red face, with its bloodshot eyes, thrust forward, and gripped her arms. She cried in fear of him, struggled to be free. Coming slightly to himself, panting, he pushed her roughly to the outer door, and thrust her forth, slotting the bolt behind her with a bang. Then he went back into the kitchen, dropped into his arm-chair, his head, bursting full of blood, sinking between his knees. Thus he dipped gradually into a stupor, from exhaustion and intoxication.

The moon was high and magnificent in the August night. Mrs. Morel, seared with passion, shivered to find herself out there in a great white light, that fell cold on her, and gave a shock to her inflamed soul. She stood for a few moments helplessly staring at the glistening great rhubarb leaves near the door. Then she got the air into her breast. She walked down the garden path, trembling in every limb, while the child boiled within her. For a while she could not control her consciousness; mechanically she went over the last scene, then over it again, certain phrases, certain moments coming each time like a brand red-hot down on her soul; and each time she enacted again the past hour, each time the brand came down at the same points, till the mark was burnt in, and the pain burnt out, and at last she came to herself. She must have been half an hour in this delirious condition. Then the presence of the night came again to her. She glanced round in fear. She had wandered to the side garden, where she was walking up and down the path beside the currant bushes under the long wall. The garden was a narrow strip, bounded from the road, that cut transversely between the blocks, by a thick thorn hedge.

She hurried out of the side garden to the front, where she could stand as if in an immense gulf of white light, the moon streaming high in face of her, the moonlight standing up from the hills in front, and filling the valley where the Bottoms crouched, almost blindingly. There, panting and half weeping in reaction from the stress, she murmured to herself over and over again: "The nuisance! the nuisance!"

She became aware of something about her. With an effort she roused herself to see what it was that penetrated her consciousness. The tall white lilies were reeling in the moonlight, and the air was charged with their perfume, as with a presence. Mrs. Morel gasped slightly in fear. She touched the big, pallid flowers on their petals, then shivered. They seemed to be stretching in the moonlight.

She put her hand into one white bin: the gold scarcely showed on her fingers by moonlight. She bent down to look at the binful of yellow pollen; but it only appeared dusky. Then she drank a deep draught of the scent. It almost made her dizzy.

Mrs. Morel leaned on the garden gate, looking out, and she lost herself awhile. She did not know what she thought. Except for a slight feeling of sickness, and her consciousness in the child, herself melted out like scent into the shiny, pale air. After a time the child, too, melted with her in the mixing-pot of moonlight, and she rested with the hills and lilies and houses, all swum together in a kind of swoon.

When she came to herself she was tired for sleep. Languidly she looked about her; the clumps of white phlox seemed like bushes spread with linen; a moth ricochetted over them, and right across the garden. Following it with her eye roused her. A few whiffs of the raw, strong scent of phlox invigorated her. She passed along the path, hesitating at the white rose-bush. It smelled sweet and simple. She touched the white ruffles of the roses. Their fresh scent and cool, soft leaves reminded her of the morning-time and sunshine. She was very fond of them. But she was tired, and wanted to sleep. In the mysterious out-of-doors she felt forlorn.

There was no noise anywhere. Evidently the children had not been wakened, or had gone to sleep again. A train, three miles away, roared across the valley. The night was very large, and very strange, stretching its hoary distances infinitely. And out of the silver-grey fog of darkness came sounds vague and hoarse: a corncrake not far off, sound of a train like a sigh, and distant shouts of men.

Her quietened heart beginning to beat quickly again, she hurried down the side garden to the back of the house. Softly she lifted the latch; the door was still bolted, and hard against her. She rapped gently, waited, then rapped again. She must not rouse the children, nor the neighbours. He must be asleep, and he would not wake easily. Her heart began to burn to be indoors. She clung to the door-handle. Now it was cold; she would take a chill, and in her present condition!

Putting her apron over her head and her arms, she hurried again to the side garden, to the window of the kitchen. Leaning on the sill, she could just see, under the blind, her husband's arms spread out on the table, and his black head on the board. He was sleeping with his face lying on the table. Something in his attitude made her feel tired of things. The lamp was burning smokily; she could tell by the copper colour of the light. She tapped at the window more and more noisily. Almost it seemed as if the glass would break. Still he did not wake up.

After vain efforts, she began to shiver, partly from contact with the stone, and from exhaustion. Fearful always for the unborn child, she wondered what she could do for warmth. She went down to the coal-house, where there was an old hearth-rug she had carried out for the rag-man the day before. This she wrapped over her shoulders. It was warm, if grimy. Then she walked up and down the garden path, peeping every now and then under the blind, knocking, and telling herself that in the end the very strain of his position must wake him.

At last, after about an hour, she rapped long and low at the window. Gradually the sound penetrated to him. When, in despair, she had ceased to tap, she saw him stir, then lift his face blindly. The labouring of his heart hurt him into consciousness. She rapped imperatively at the window. He started awake. Instantly she saw his fists set and his eyes glare. He had not a grain of physical fear.

If it had been twenty burglars, he would have gone blindly for them. He glared round, bewildered, but prepared to fight.

"Open the door, Walter," she said coldly.

His hands relaxed. It dawned on him what he had done. His head dropped, sullen and dogged. She saw him hurry to the door, heard the bolt chock. He tried the latch. It opened—and there stood the silver-grey night, fearful to him, after the tawny light of the lamp. He hurried back.

When Mrs. Morel entered, she saw him almost running through the door to the stairs. He had ripped his collar off his neck in his haste to be gone ere she came in, and there it lay with bursten button-holes. It made her angry.

She warmed and soothed herself. In her weariness forgetting everything, she moved about at the little tasks that remained to be done, set his breakfast, rinsed his pit-bottle, put his pit-clothes on the hearth to warm, set his pit-boots beside them, put him out a clean scarf and snap-bag and two apples, raked the fire, and went to bed. He was already dead asleep. His narrow black eyebrows were drawn up in a sort of peevish misery into his forehead while his cheeks' downstrokes, and his sulky mouth, seemed to be saying: "I don't care who you are nor what you are, I *shall* have my own way."

Mrs. Morel knew him too well to look at him. As she unfastened her brooch at the mirror, she smiled faintly to see her face all smeared with the yellow dust of lilies. She brushed it off, and at last lay down. For some time her mind continued snapping and jetting sparks, but she was asleep before her husband awoke from the first sleep of his drunkenness.

II

The Birth of Paul, and Another Battle

After such a scene as the last, Walter Morel was for some days abashed and ashamed, but he soon regained his old bullying indifference. Yet there was a slight shrinking, a diminishing in his assurance. Physically even, he shrank, and his fine full presence waned. He never grew in the least stout, so that, as he sank from his erect, assertive bearing, his physique seemed to contract along with his pride and moral strength.

But now he realised how hard it was for his wife to drag about at her work, and, his sympathy quickened by penitence, hastened forward with his help. He came straight home from the pit, and stayed in at evening till Friday, and then he could not remain at home. But he was back again by ten o'clock, almost quite sober.

He always made his own breakfast. Being a man who rose early and had plenty of time he did not, as some miners do, drag his wife out of bed at six o'clock. At five, sometimes earlier, he woke, got straight out of bed, and went downstairs. When she could not sleep, his wife lay waiting for this time, as for a period of peace. The only real rest seemed to be when he was out of the house.

He went downstairs in his shirt and then struggled into his pit-trousers, which were left on the hearth to warm all night. There was always a fire, because Mrs. Morel raked. And the first sound in the house was the bang, bang of the poker against the raker, as Morel smashed the remainder of the coal to make the kettle, which was filled and left on the hob, finally boil. His cup and knife and fork, all he wanted except just the food, was laid ready on the table on a newspaper. Then he got his breakfast, made the tea, packed the bottom of the doors with rugs to shut out the draught, piled a big fire, and sat down to an hour of joy. He toasted his bacon on a fork and caught the drops of fat on his bread; then he put the rasher on his thick slice of bread, and cut off chunks with a clasp-knife, poured his tea into his saucer, and was happy. With his family about, meals were never so pleasant. He loathed a fork: it is a modern introduction which has still scarcely reached common people. What Morel preferred was a clasp-knife. Then, in solitude, he ate and drank, often sitting, in cold weather, on a little stool with his back to the warm chimney-piece, his food on the fender, his cup on the hearth. And then he read the last night's newspaper— what of it he could—spelling it over laboriously. He preferred to keep the blinds down and the candle lit even when it was daylight; it was the habit of the mine.

At a quarter to six he rose, cut two thick slices of bread and butter, and put them in the white calico snap-bag. He filled his tin bottle with tea. Cold tea without milk or sugar was the drink he preferred for the pit. Then he pulled off his shirt, and put on his pit-singlet, a vest of thick flannel cut low round the neck, and with short sleeves like a chemise.

Then he went upstairs to his wife with a cup of tea because she was ill, and because it occurred to him.

"I've brought thee a cup o' tea, lass," he said.

"Well, you needn't, for you know I don't like it," she replied.

"Drink it up; it'll pop thee off to sleep again."

She accepted the tea. It pleased him to see her take it and sip it.

"I'll back my life there's no sugar in," she said.

"Yi—there's one big 'un," he replied, injured.

"It's a wonder," she said, sipping again.

She had a winsome face when her hair was loose. He loved her to grumble at him in this manner. He looked at her again, and went, without any sort of leave-taking. He never took more than two slices of bread and butter to eat in the pit, so an apple or an orange was a treat to him. He always liked it when she put one out for him. He tied a scarf round his neck, put on his great, heavy boots, his coat, with the big pocket, that carried his snap-bag and his bottle of tea, and went forth into the fresh morning air, closing, without locking, the door behind him. He loved the early morning, and the walk across the fields. So he appeared at the pit-top, often with a stalk from the hedge between his teeth, which he chewed all day to keep his mouth moist, down the mine, feeling quite as happy as when he was in the field.

Later, when the time for the baby grew nearer, he would bustle round in his slovenly fashion, poking out the ashes, rubbing the fireplace, sweeping the house before he went to work. Then, feeling very self-righteous, he went upstairs.

"Now I'm cleaned up for thee: tha's no 'casions ter stir a peg all day, but sit and read thy books."

Which made her laugh, in spite of her indignation.

"And the dinner cooks itself?" she answered.

"Eh, I know nowt about th' dinner."

"You'd know if there weren't any."

"Ay, 'appen so," he answered, departing.

When she got downstairs, she would find the house tidy, but dirty. She could not rest until she had thoroughly cleaned; so she went down to the ash-pit with her dust-pan. Mrs. Kirk, spying her, would contrive to have to go to her own coal-place at that minute. Then, across the wooden fence, she would call:

"So you keep wagging on, then?"

"Ay," answered Mrs. Morel deprecatingly. "There's nothing else for it."

"Have you seen Hose?" called a very small woman from across the road. It was Mrs. Anthony, a black-haired, strange little body, who always wore a brown velvet dress, tight fitting.

"I haven't," said Mrs. Morel.

"Eh, I wish he'd come. I've got a copperful of clothes, an' I'm sure I heered his bell."

"Hark! He's at the end."

The two women looked down the alley. At the end of the Bottoms a man stood in a sort of old-fashioned trap, bending over bundles of cream-coloured stuff; while a cluster of women held up their arms to him, some with bundles. Mrs. Anthony herself had a heap of creamy, undyed stockings hanging over her arm.

"I've done ten dozen this week," she said proudly to Mrs. Morel.

"T-t-t!" went the other. "I don't know how you can find time."

"Eh!" said Mrs. Anthony. "You can find time if you make time."

"I don't know how you do it," said Mrs. Morel. "And how much shall you get for those many?"

"Tuppence-ha'penny a dozen," replied the other.

"Well," said Mrs. Morel. "I'd starve before I'd sit down and seam twenty-four stockings for twopence ha'penny."

"Oh, I don't know," said Mrs. Anthony. "You can rip along with 'em."

Hose was coming along, ringing his bell. Women were waiting at the yard-ends with their seamed stockings hanging over their arms. The man, a common fellow, made jokes with them, tried to swindle them, and bullied them. Mrs. Morel went up her yard disdainfully.

It was an understood thing that if one woman wanted her neighbour, she should put the poker in the fire and bang at the back of the fireplace, which, as the fires were back to back, would make a great noise in the adjoining house. One morning Mrs. Kirk, mixing a pudding, nearly started out of her skin as she heard the thud, thud, in her grate. With her hands all floury, she rushed to the fence.

"Did you knock, Mrs. Morel?"

"If you wouldn't mind, Mrs. Kirk."

Mrs. Kirk climbed on to her copper, got over the wall on to Mrs. Morel's copper, and ran in to her neighbour.

"Eh, dear, how are you feeling?" she cried in concern.

"You might fetch Mrs. Bower," said Mrs. Morel.

Mrs. Kirk went into the yard, lifted up her strong, shrill voice, and called: "Ag-gie—Ag-gie!"

The sound was heard from one end of the Bottoms to the other. At last Aggie came running up, and was sent for Mrs. Bower, whilst Mrs. Kirk left her pudding and stayed with her neighbour.

Mrs. Morel went to bed. Mrs. Kirk had Annie and William for dinner. Mrs. Bower, fat and waddling, bossed the house.

"Hash some cold meat up for the master's dinner, and make him an apple-charlotte pudding," said Mrs. Morel.

"He may go without pudding *this* day," said Mrs. Bower.

Morel was not as a rule one of the first to appear at the bottom of the pit, ready to come up. Some men were there before four o'clock, when the whistle blew loose-all; but Morel, whose stall, a poor one, was at this time about a mile and a half away from the bottom, worked usually till the first mate stopped, then he finished also. This day, however, the miner was sick of the work. At two o'clock he looked at his watch, by the light of the green candle—he was in a safe working—and again at half-past two. He was hewing at a piece of rock that was in the way for the next day's work. As he sat on his heels, or kneeled, giving hard blows with his pick, "Uszza—uszza!" he went.

"Shall ter finish, Sorry?" cried Barker, his fellow butty.

"Finish? Niver while the world stands!" growled Morel.

And he went on striking. He was tired.

"It's a heart-breaking job," said Barker.

But Morel was too exasperated, at the end of his tether, to answer. Still he struck and hacked with all his might.

"Tha might as well leave it, Walter," said Barker. "It'll do to-morrow, without thee hackin' thy guts out."

"I'll lay no b—— finger on this to-morrow, Isr'el!" cried Morel.

"Oh, well, if tha wunna, someb'dy else'll ha'e to," said Israel.

Then Morel continued to strike.

"Hey-up there—*loose-a'!*" cried the men, leaving the next stall.

Morel continued to strike.

"Tha'll happen catch me up," said Barker, departing.

When he had gone, Morel, left alone, felt savage. He had not finished his job. He had overworked himself into a frenzy. Rising, wet with sweat, he threw his tool down, pulled on his coat, blew out his candle, took his lamp, and went. Down the main road the lights of the other men went swinging. There was a hollow sound of many voices. It was a long, heavy tramp underground.

He sat at the bottom of the pit, where the great drops of water fell plash. Many colliers were waiting their turns to go up, talking noisily. Morel gave his answers short and disagreeable.

"It's rainin', Sorry," said old Giles, who had had the news from the top.

Morel found one comfort. He had his old umbrella, which he loved, in the lamp cabin. At last he took his stand on the chair, and was at the top in a moment. Then he handed in his lamp and got his umbrella, which he had bought at an auction for one-and-six. He stood on the edge of the pit-bank for a moment, looking out over the fields; grey rain was falling. The trucks stood full of wet, bright coal. Water ran down the sides of the waggons, over the white "C.W. and Co.". Colliers, walking indifferent to the rain, were streaming down the line and up the field, a grey, dismal host. Morel put up his umbrella, and took pleasure from the peppering of the drops thereon.

All along the road to Bestwood the miners tramped, wet and grey and dirty, but their red mouths talking with animation. Morel also walked with a gang, but he said nothing. He frowned peevishly as he went. Many men passed into the Prince of Wales or into Ellen's. Morel, feeling sufficiently disagreeable to resist temptation, trudged along under the dripping trees that overhung the park wall, and down the mud of Greenhill Lane.

Mrs. Morel lay in bed, listening to the rain, and the feet of the colliers from Minton, their voices, and the bang, bang of the gates as they went through the stile up the field.

"There's some herb beer behind the pantry door," she said. "Th' master 'll want a drink, if he doesn't stop."

But he was late, so she concluded he had called for a drink, since it was raining. What did he care about the child or her?

She was very ill when her children were born.

"What is it?" she asked, feeling sick to death.

"A boy."

And she took consolation in that. The thought of being the mother of men was warming to her heart. She looked at the child. It had blue eyes, and a lot of fair hair, and was bonny. Her love came up hot, in spite of everything. She had it in bed with her.

Morel, thinking nothing, dragged his way up the garden path, wearily and angrily. He closed his umbrella, and stood it in the sink; then he sluthered his heavy boots into the kitchen. Mrs. Bower appeared in the inner doorway.

"Well," she said, "she's about as bad as she can be. It's a boy childt."

The miner grunted, put his empty snap-bag and his tin bottle on the dresser, went back into the scullery and hung up his coat, then came and dropped into his chair.

"Han yer got a drink?" he asked.

The woman went into the pantry. There was heard the pop of a cork. She set the mug, with a little, disgusted rap, on the table before Morel. He drank, gasped, wiped his big moustache on the end of his scarf, drank, gasped, and lay back in his chair. The woman would not speak to him again. She set his dinner before him, and went upstairs.

"Was that the master?" asked Mrs. Morel.

"I've gave him his dinner," replied Mrs. Bower.

After he had sat with his arms on the table—he resented the fact that Mrs. Bower put no cloth on for him, and gave him a little plate, instead of a full-sized dinner-plate—he began to eat. The fact that his wife was ill, that he had another boy, was nothing to him at that moment. He was too tired; he wanted his dinner; he wanted to sit with his arms lying on the board; he did not like having Mrs. Bower about. The fire was too small to please him.

After he had finished his meal, he sat for twenty minutes; then he stoked up a big fire. Then, in his stockinged feet, he went reluctantly upstairs. It was a struggle to face his wife at this moment, and he was tired. His face was black, and smeared with sweat. His singlet had dried again, soaking the dirt in. He had a dirty woollen scarf round his throat. So he stood at the foot of the bed.

"Well, how are ter, then?" he asked.

"I s'll be all right," she answered.

"H'm!"

He stood at a loss what to say next. He was tired, and this bother was rather a nuisance to him, and he didn't quite know where he was.

"A lad, tha says," he stammered.

She turned down the sheet and showed the child.

"Bless him!" he murmured. Which made her laugh, because he blessed by rote—pretending paternal emotion, which he did not feel just then.

"Go now," she said.

"I will, my lass," he answered, turning away.

Dismissed, he wanted to kiss her, but he dared not. She half wanted him to kiss her, but could not bring herself to give any sign. She only breathed freely when he was gone out of the room again, leaving behind him a faint smell of pit-dirt.

Mrs. Morel had a visit every day from the Congregational clergyman. Mr.

Heaton was young, and very poor. His wife had died at the birth of his first baby, so he remained alone in the manse. He was a Bachelor of Arts of Cambridge, very shy, and no preacher. Mrs. Morel was fond of him, and he depended on her. For hours he talked to her, when she was well. He became the god-parent of the child.

Occasionally the minister stayed to tea with Mrs. Morel. Then she laid the cloth early, got out her best cups, with a little green rim, and hoped Morel would not come too soon; indeed, if he stayed for a pint, she would not mind this day. She had always two dinners to cook, because she believed children should have their chief meal at midday, whereas Morel needed his at five o'-clock. So Mr. Heaton would hold the baby, whilst Mrs. Morel beat up a batter-pudding or peeled the potatoes, and he, watching her all the time, would discuss his next sermon. His ideas were quaint and fantastic. She brought him judiciously to earth. It was a discussion of the wedding at Cana.

"When He changed the water into wine at Cana," he said, "that is a symbol that the ordinary life, even the blood, of the married husband and wife, which had before been uninspired, like water, became filled with the Spirit, and was as wine, because, when love enters, the whole spiritual constitution of a man changes, is filled with the Holy Ghost, and almost his form is altered."

Mrs. Morel thought to herself:

"Yes, poor fellow, his young wife is dead; that is why he makes his love into the Holy Ghost."

They were halfway down their first cup of tea when they heard the sluther of pit-boots.

"Good gracious!" exclaimed Mrs. Morel, in spite of herself.

The minister looked rather scared. Morel entered. He was feeling rather savage. He nodded a "How d'yer do" to the clergyman, who rose to shake hands with him.

"Nay," said Morel, showing his hand, "look thee at it! Tha niver wants ter shake hands wi' a hand like that, does ter? There's too much pick-haft and shovel-dirt on it."

The minister flushed with confusion, and sat down again. Mrs. Morel rose, carried out the steaming saucepan. Morel took off his coat, dragged his arm-chair to table, and sat down heavily.

"Are you tired?" asked the clergyman.

"Tired? I ham that," replied Morel. *"You* don't know what it is to be tired, as *I'm* tired."

"No," replied the clergyman.

"Why, look yer 'ere," said the miner, showing the shoulders of his singlet. "It's a bit dry now, but it's wet as a clout with sweat even yet. Feel it."

"Goodness!" cried Mrs. Morel. "Mr. Heaton doesn't want to feel your nasty singlet."

The clergyman put out his hand gingerly.

"No, perhaps he doesn't," said Morel; "but it's all come out of me, whether or not. An' iv'ry day alike my singlet's wringin' wet. 'Aven't you got a drink, Missis, for a man when he comes home barkled up from the pit."

"You know you drank all the beer," said Mrs. Morel, pouring out his tea.

"An' was there no more to be got?" Turning to the clergyman—"A man gets that caked up wi' th' dust, you know,—that clogged up down a coal-mine, he *needs* a drink when he comes home."

"I am sure he does," said the clergyman.

"But it's ten to one if there's owt for him."

"There's water—and there's tea," said Mrs. Morel.

"Water! It's not water as'll clear his throat."

He poured out a saucerful of tea, blew it, and sucked it up through his great black moustache, sighing afterwards. Then he poured out another saucerful, and stood his cup on the table.

"My cloth!" said Mrs. Morel, putting it on a plate.

"A man as comes home as I do 's too tired to care about cloths," said Morel.

"Pity!" exclaimed his wife, sarcastically.

The room was full of the smell of meat and vegetables and pit-clothes.

He leaned over to the minister, his great moustache thrust forward, his mouth very red in his black face.

"Mr. Heaton," he said, "a man as has been down the black hole all day, dingin' away at a coal-face, yi, a sight harder than that wall——'

"Needn't make a moan of it," put in Mrs. Morel.

She hated her husband because, whenever he had an audience, he whined and played for sympathy. William, sitting nursing the baby, hated him, with a boy's hatred for false sentiment, and for the stupid treatment of his mother. Annie had never liked him; she merely avoided him.

When the minister had gone, Mrs. Morel looked at her cloth.

"A fine mess!" she said.

"Dos't think I'm goin' to sit wi' my arms danglin', cos tha's got a parson for tea wi' thee?" he bawled.

They were both angry, but she said nothing. The baby began to cry, and Mrs. Morel, picking up a saucepan from the hearth, accidentally knocked Annie on the head, whereupon the girl began to whine, and Morel to shout at her. In the midst of this pandemonium, William looked up at the big glazed text over the mantelpiece and read distinctly:

"God Bless Our Home!"

Whereupon Mrs. Morel, trying to soothe the baby, jumped up, rushed at him, boxed his ears, saying:

"What are *you* putting in for?"

And then she sat down and laughed, till tears ran over her cheeks, while William kicked the stool he had been sitting on, and Morel growled:

"I canna see what there is so much to laugh at."

One evening, directly after the parson's visit, feeling unable to bear herself after another display from her husband, she took Annie and the baby and went out. Morel had kicked William, and the mother would never forgive him.

She went over the sheep-bridge and across a corner of the meadow to the cricket-ground. The meadows seemed one space of ripe, evening light, whispering with the distant mill-race. She sat on a seat under the alders in the cricket-ground, and fronted the evening. Before her, level and solid, spread the big green cricket-field, like the bed of a sea of light. Children played in the bluish shadow of the pavilion. Many rooks, high up, came cawing home across the softly-woven sky. They stooped in a long curve down into the golden glow, concentrating, cawing, wheeling, like black flakes on a slow vortex, over a tree clump that made a dark boss among the pasture.

A few gentlemen were practising, and Mrs. Morel could hear the chock of the ball, and the voices of men suddenly roused; could see the white forms of men shifting silently over the green, upon which already the under shadows were smouldering. Away at the grange, one side of the haystacks was lit up, the other sides blue-grey. A waggon of sheaves rocked small across the melting yellow light.

The sun was going down. Every open evening, the hills of Derbyshire were blazed over with red sunset. Mrs. Morel watched the sun sink from the glistening sky, leaving a soft flower-blue overhead, while the western space went red, as if all the fire had swum down there, leaving the bell cast flawless blue. The mountain-ash berries across the field stood fierily out from the dark leaves, for a moment. A few shocks of corn in a corner of the fallow stood up as if alive; she imagined them bowing; perhaps her son would be a Joseph. In the east, a mirrored sunset floated pink opposite the west's scarlet. The big haystacks on the hillside, that butted into the glare, went cold.

With Mrs. Morel it was one of those still moments when the small frets vanish, and the beauty of things stands out, and she had the peace and the strength to see herself. Now and again, a swallow cut close to her. Now and again, Annie came up with a handful of alder-currants. The baby was restless on his mother's knee, clambering with his hands at the light.

Mrs. Morel looked down at him. She had dreaded this baby like a catastrophe, because of her feeling for her husband. And now she felt strangely towards the infant. Her heart was heavy because of the child, almost as if it were unhealthy, or malformed. Yet it seemed quite well. But she noticed the peculiar knitting of the baby's brows, and the peculiar heaviness of its eyes, as if it were trying to understand something that was pain. She felt, when she looked at her child's dark, brooding pupils, as if a burden were on her heart.

"He looks as if he was thinking about something—quite sorrowful," said Mrs. Kirk.

Suddenly, looking at him, the heavy feeling at the mother's heart melted into passionate grief. She bowed over him, and a few tears shook swiftly out of her very heart. The baby lifted his fingers.

"My lamb!" she cried softly.

And at that moment she felt, in some far inner place of her soul, that she and her husband were guilty.

The baby was looking up at her. It had blue eyes like her own, but its look was heavy, steady, as if it had realised something that had stunned some point of its soul.

In her arms lay the delicate baby. Its deep blue eyes, always looking up at her unblinking, seemed to draw her innermost thoughts out of her. She no longer loved her husband; she had not wanted this child to come, and there it lay in her arms and pulled at her heart. She felt as if the navel string that had connected its frail little body with hers had not been broken. A wave of hot love went over her to the infant. She held it close to her face and breast. With all her force, with all her soul she would make up to it for having brought it into the world unloved. She would love it all the more now it was here; carry it in her love. Its clear, knowing eyes gave her pain and fear. Did it know all about her? When it lay under her heart, had it been listening then? Was there a reproach in the look? She felt the marrow melt in her bones, with fear and pain.

Once more she was aware of the sun lying red on the rim of the hill opposite. She suddenly held up the child in her hands.

"Look!" she said. "Look, my pretty!"

She thrust the infant forward to the crimson, throbbing sun, almost with relief. She saw him lift his little fist. Then she put him to her bosom again, ashamed almost of her impulse to give him back again whence he came.

"If he lives," she thought to herself, "what will become of him—what will he be?"

Her heart was anxious.

"I will call him Paul," she said suddenly; she knew not why.

After a while she went home. A fine shadow was flung over the deep green meadow, darkening all.

As she expected, she found the house empty. But Morel was home by ten o'clock, and that day, at least, ended peacefully.

Walter Morel was, at this time, exceedingly irritable. His work seemed to exhaust him. When he came home he did not speak civilly to anybody. If the fire were rather low he bullied about that; he grumbled about his dinner; if the children made a chatter he shouted at them in a way that made their mother's blood boil, and made them hate him.

On the Friday, he was not home by eleven o'clock. The baby was unwell, and was restless, crying if he were put down. Mrs. Morel, tired to death, and still weak, was scarcely under control.

"I wish the nuisance would come," she said wearily to herself.

The child at last sank down to sleep in her arms. She was too tired to carry him to the cradle.

"But I'll say nothing, whatever time he comes," she said. "It only works me up; I won't say anything. But I know if he does anything it'll make my blood boil," she added to herself.

She sighed, hearing him coming, as if it were something she could not bear. He, taking his revenge, was nearly drunk. She kept her head bent over the child as he entered, not wishing to see him. But it went through her like a flash of hot fire when, in passing, he lurched against the dresser, setting the tins rattling, and clutched at the white pot knobs for support. He hung up his hat and coat, then returned, stood glowering from a distance at her, as she sat bowed over the child.

"Is there nothing to eat in the house?" he asked, insolently, as if to a servant. In certain stages of his intoxication he affected the clipped, mincing speech of the towns. Mrs. Morel hated him most in this condition.

"You know what there is in the house," she said, so coldly, it sounded impersonal.

He stood and glared at her without moving a muscle.

"I asked a civil question, and I expect a civil answer," he said affectedly.

"And you got it," she said, still ignoring him.

He glowered again. Then he came unsteadily forward. He leaned on the table with one hand, and with the other jerked at the table drawer to get a knife to cut bread. The drawer stuck because he pulled sideways. In a temper he dragged it, so that it flew out bodily, and spoons, forks, knives, a hundred metallic things, splashed with a clatter and a clang upon the brick floor. The baby gave a little convulsed start.

"What are you doing, clumsy, drunken fool?" the mother cried.

"Then tha should get the flamin' thing thysen. Tha should get up, like other women have to, an' wait on a man."

"Wait on you—wait on you?" she cried. "Yes, I see myself."

"Yis, an' I'll learn thee tha's got to. Wait on me, yes tha sh'lt wait on me——"

"Never, milord. I'd wait on a dog at the door first."

"What—what?"

He was trying to fit in the drawer. At her last speech he turned round. His face was crimson, his eyes bloodshot. He stared at her one silent second in threat.

"P-h!" she went quickly, in contempt.

He jerked at the drawer in his excitement. It fell, cut sharply on his shin, and on the reflex he flung it at her.

One of the corners caught her brow as the shallow drawer crashed into the fireplace. She swayed, almost fell stunned from her chair. To her very soul she was sick; she clasped the child tightly to her bosom. A few moments elapsed; then, with an effort, she brought herself to. The baby was crying plaintively. Her left brow was bleeding rather profusely. As she glanced down at the child, her brain reeling, some drops of blood soaked into its white shawl; but the baby was at least not hurt. She balanced her head to keep equilibrium, so that the blood ran into her eye.

Walter Morel remained as he had stood, leaning on the table with one hand, looking blank. When he was sufficiently sure of his balance, he went across to her, swayed, caught hold of the back of her rocking-chair, almost tipping her out; then leaning forward over her, and swaying as he spoke, he said, in a tone of wondering concern:

"Did it catch thee?"

He swayed again, as if he would pitch on to the child. With the catastrophe he had lost all balance.

"Go away," she said, struggling to keep her presence of mind.

He hiccoughed. "Let's—let's look at it," he said, hiccoughing again.

"Go away!" she cried.

"Lemme—lemme look at it, lass."

She smelled him of drink, felt the unequal pull of his swaying grasp on the back of her rocking-chair.

"Go away," she said, and weakly she pushed him off.

He stood, uncertain in balance, gazing upon her. Summoning all her strength she rose, the baby on one arm. By a cruel effort of will, moving as if in sleep, she went across to the scullery, where she bathed her eye for a minute in cold water; but she was too dizzy. Afraid lest she should swoon, she returned to her rocking-chair, trembling in every fibre. By instinct, she kept the baby clasped.

Morel, bothered, had succeeded in pushing the drawer back into its cavity, and was on his knees, groping, with numb paws, for the scattered spoons.

Her brow was still bleeding. Presently Morel got up and came craning his neck towards her.

"What has it done to thee, lass?" he asked, in a very wretched, humble tone.

"You can see what it's done," she answered.

He stood, bending forward, supported on his hands, which grasped his legs just above the knee. He peered to look at the wound. She drew away from the thrust of his face with its great moustache, averting her own face as much as possible. As he looked at her, who was cold and impassive as stone, with mouth shut tight, he sickened with feebleness and hopelessness of spirit. He was turning drearily away, when he saw a drop of blood fall from the averted wound into the baby's fragile, glistening hair. Fascinated, he watched the heavy dark drop hang in the glistening cloud, and pull down the gossamer. Another drop fell. It would soak through to the baby's scalp. He watched, fascinated, feeling it soak in; then, finally, his manhood broke.

"What of this child?" was all his wife said to him. But her low, intense tones brought his head lower. She softened: "Get me some wadding out of the middle drawer," she said.

He stumbled away very obediently, presently returning with a pad, which she singed before the fire, then put on her forehead, as she sat with the baby on her lap.

"Now that clean pit-scarf." ·

Again he rummaged and fumbled in the drawer, returning presently with a red, narrow scarf. She took it, and with trembling fingers proceeded to bind it round her head.

"Let me tie it for thee," he said humbly.

"I can do it myself," she replied. When it was done she went upstairs, telling him to rake the fire and lock the door.

In the morning Mrs. Morel said:

"I knocked against the latch of the coal-place, when I was getting a raker in the dark, because the candle blew out." Her two small children looked up at her with wide, dismayed eyes. They said nothing, but their parted lips seemed to express the unconscious tragedy they felt.

Walter Morel lay in bed next day until nearly dinner-time. He did not think of the previous evening's work. He scarcely thought of anything, but he would not think of that. He lay and suffered like a sulking dog. He had hurt himself most; and he was the more damaged because he would never say a word to her, or express his sorrow. He tried to wriggle out of it. "It was her own fault," he said to himself. Nothing, however, could prevent his inner consciousness inflicting on him the punishment which ate into his spirit like rust, and which he could only alleviate by drinking.

He felt as if he had not the initiative to get up, or to say a word, or to move, but could only lie like a log. Moreover, he had himself violent pains in the head. It was Saturday. Towards noon he rose, cut himself food in the pantry, ate with his head dropped, then pulled on his boots, and went out, to return at three o'clock slightly tipsy and relieved; then once more straight to bed. He rose again at six in the evening, had tea and went straight out.

Sunday was the same: bed till noon, the Palmerston Arms till 2.30, dinner, and bed; scarcely a word spoken. When Mrs. Morel went upstairs, towards four o'clock, to put on her Sunday dress, he was fast asleep. She would have felt sorry for him, if he had once said, "Wife, I'm sorry." But no; he insisted to himself it was her fault. And so he broke himself. So she merely left him alone. There was this deadlock of passion between them, and she was stronger.

The family began tea. Sunday was the only day when all sat down to meals together.

"Isn't my father going to get up?" asked William.

"Let him lie," the mother replied.

There was a feeling of misery over all the house. The children breathed the air that was poisoned, and they felt dreary. They were rather disconsolate, did not know what to do, what to play at.

Immediately Morel woke he got straight out of bed. That was characteristic of him all his life. He was all for activity. The prostrated inactivity of two mornings was stifling him.

It was near six o'clock when he got down. This time he entered without hesitation, his wincing sensitiveness having hardened again. He did not care any longer what the family thought or felt.

The tea-things were on the table. William was reading aloud from "The Child's Own", Annie listening and asking eternally "why?" Both children hushed into silence as they heard the approaching thud of their father's stockinged feet, and shrank as he entered. Yet he was usually indulgent to them.

Morel made the meal alone, brutally. He ate and drank more noisily than he had need. No one spoke to him. The family life withdrew, shrank away, and became hushed as he entered. But he cared no longer about his alienation.

Immediately he had finished tea he rose with alacrity to go out. It was this alacrity, this haste to be gone, which so sickened Mrs. Morel. As she heard him sousing heartily in cold water, heard the eager scratch of the steel comb on the side of the bowl, as he wetted his hair, she closed her eyes in disgust. As he bent over, lacing his boots, there was a certain vulgar gusto in his movement that divided him from the reserved, watchful rest of the family. He always ran away from the battle with himself. Even in his own heart's privacy, he excused himself, saying, "If she hadn't said so-and-so, it would never have happened. She asked for what she's got." The children waited in restraint during his preparations. When he had gone, they sighed with relief.

He closed the door behind him, and was glad. It was a rainy evening. The Palmerston would be the cosier. He hastened forward in anticipation. All the slate roofs of the Bottoms shone black with wet. The roads, always dark with coal-dust, were full of blackish mud. He hastened along. The Palmerston windows were steamed over. The passage was paddled with wet feet. But the air was warm, if foul, and full of the sound of voices and the smell of beer and smoke.

"What shollt ha'e, Walter?" cried a voice, as soon as Morel appeared in the doorway.

"Oh, Jim, my lad, wheriver has thee sprung frae?"

The men made a seat for him, and took him in warmly. He was glad. In a minute or two they had thawed all responsibility out of him, all shame, all trouble, and he was clear as a bell for a jolly night.

On the Wednesday following, Morel was penniless. He dreaded his wife. Having hurt her, he hated her. He did not know what to do with himself that evening, having not even twopence with which to go to the Palmerston, and being already rather deeply in debt. So, while his wife was down the garden with the child, he hunted in the top drawer of the dresser where she kept her purse, found it, and looked inside. It contained a half-crown, two halfpennies, and a sixpence. So he took the sixpence, put the purse carefully back, and went out.

The next day, when she wanted to pay the greengrocer, she looked in the purse for her sixpence, and her heart sank to her shoes. Then she sat down and thought: "Was there a sixpence? I hadn't spent it, had I? And I hadn't left it anywhere else?"

She was much put about. She hunted round everywhere for it. And, as she sought, the conviction came into her heart that her husband had taken it. What she had in her purse was all the money she possessed. But that he should sneak it from her thus was unbearable. He had done so twice before. The first time she had not accused him, and at the week-end he had put the shilling again into her purse. So that was how she had known he had taken it. The second time he had not paid back.

This time she felt it was too much. When he had had his dinner—he came home early that day—she said to him coldly:

"Did you take sixpence out of my purse last night?"

"Me!" he said, looking up in an offended way. "No, I didna! I niver clapped eyes on your purse."

But she could detect the lie.

"Why, you know you did," she said quietly.

"I tell you I didna," he shouted. "Yer at me again, are yer? I've had about enough on't."

"So you filch sixpence out of my purse while I'm taking the clothes in."

"I'll may yer pay for this," he said, pushing back his chair in desperation. He bustled and got washed, then went determinedly upstairs. Presently he came down dressed, and with a big bundle in a blue-checked, enormous handkerchief.

"And now," he said, "you'll see me again when you do."

"It'll be before I want to," she replied; and at that he marched out of the house with his bundle. She sat trembling slightly, but her heart brimming with contempt. What would she do if he went to some other pit, obtained work, and got in with another woman? But she knew him too well—he couldn't. She was dead sure of him. Nevertheless her heart was gnawed inside her.

"Where's my dad?" said William, coming in from school.

"He says he's run away," replied the mother.

"Where to?"

"Eh, I don't know. He's taken a bundle in the blue handkerchief, and says he's not coming back."

"What shall we do?" cried the boy.

"Eh, never trouble, he won't go far."

"But if he doesn't come back," wailed Annie.

And she and William retired to the sofa and wept. Mrs. Morel sat and laughed.

"You pair of gabeys!" she exclaimed. "You'll see him before the night's out."

But the children were not to be consoled. Twilight came on. Mrs. Morel grew anxious from very weariness. One part of her said it would be a relief to see the last of him; another part fretted because of keeping the children; and inside her, as yet, she could not quite let him go. At the bottom, she knew very well he could *not* go.

When she went down to the coal-place at the end of the garden, however, she felt something behind the door. So she looked. And there in the dark lay the big blue bundle. She sat on a piece of coal and laughed. Every time she saw it, so fat and yet so ignominious, slunk into its corner in the dark, with its ends flopping like dejected ears from the knots, she laughed again. She was relieved.

Mrs. Morel sat waiting. He had not any money, she knew, so if he stopped he was running up a bill. She was very tired of him—tired to death. He had not even the courage to carry his bundle beyond the yard-end.

As she meditated, at about nine o'clock, he opened the door and came in, slinking, and yet sulky. She said not a word. He took off his coat, and slunk to his arm-chair, where he began to take off his boots.

"You'd better fetch your bundle before you take your boots off," she said quietly.

"You may thank your stars I've come back to-night," he said, looking up from under his dropped head, sulkily, trying to be impressive.

"Why, where should you have gone? You daren't even get your parcel through the yard-end," she said.

He looked such a fool she was not even angry with him. He continued to take his boots off and prepare for bed.

"I don't know what's in your blue handkerchief," she said. "But if you leave it the children shall fetch it in the morning."

Whereupon he got up and went out of the house, returning presently and crossing the kitchen with averted face, hurrying upstairs. As Mrs. Morel saw him slink quickly through the inner doorway, holding his bundle, she laughed to herself: but her heart was bitter, because she had loved him.

III

THE CASTING OFF OF MOREL—

THE TAKING ON OF WILLIAM

During the next week Morel's temper was almost unbearable. Like all miners, he was a great lover of medicines, which, strangely enough, he would often pay for himself.

"You mun get me a drop o' laxy vitral," he said. "It's a winder as we canna ha'e a sup i' th' 'ouse."

So Mrs. Morel bought him elixir of vitriol, his favourite first medicine. And he made himself a jug of wormwood tea. He had hanging in the attic great bunches of dried herbs: wormwood, rue, horehound, elder flowers, parsley-purt, marshmallow, hyssop, dandelion, and centaury. Usually there was a jug of one or other decoction standing on the hob, from which he drank largely.

"Grand!" he said, smacking his lips after wormwood. "Grand!" And he exhorted the children to try.

"It's better than any of your tea or your cocoa stews," he vowed. But they were not to be tempted.

This time, however, neither pills nor vitriol nor all his herbs would shift the "nasty peens in his head". He was sickening for an attack of an inflammation of the brain. He had never been well since his sleeping on the ground when he went with Jerry to Nottingham. Since then he had drunk and stormed. Now he fell seriously ill, and Mrs. Morel had him to nurse. He was one of the worst patients imaginable. But, in spite of all, and putting aside the fact that he was bread-winner, she never quite wanted him to die. Still there was one part of her wanted him for herself.

The neighbours were very good to her: occasionally some had the children in to meals, occasionally some would do the downstairs work for her, one would mind the baby for a day. But it was a great drag, nevertheless. It was not every day the neighbours helped. Then she had nursing of baby and husband, cleaning and cooking, everything to do. She was quite worn out, but she did what was wanted of her.

And the money was just sufficient. She had seventeen shillings a week from clubs, and every Friday Barker and the other butty put by a portion of the stall's profits for Morel's wife. And the neighbours made broths, and gave eggs, and such invalids' trifles. If they had not helped her so generously in those times, Mrs. Morel would never have pulled through, without incurring debts that would have dragged her down.

The weeks passed. Morel, almost against hope, grew better. He had a fine constitution, so that, once on the mend, he went straight forward to recovery.

Soon he was pottering about downstairs. During his illness his wife had spoilt him a little. Now he wanted her to continue. He often put his hand to his head, pulled down the corners of his mouth, and shammed pains he did not feel. But there was no deceiving her. At first she merely smiled to herself. Then she scolded him sharply.

"Goodness, man, don't be so lachrymose."

That wounded him slightly, but still he continued to feign sickness.

"I wouldn't be such a mardy baby," said the wife shortly.

Then he was indignant, and cursed under his breath, like a boy. He was forced to resume a normal tone, and to cease to whine.

Nevertheless, there was a state of peace in the house for some time. Mrs. Morel was more tolerant of him, and he, depending on her almost like a child, was rather happy. Neither knew that she was more tolerant because she loved him less. Up till this time, in spite of all, he had been her husband and her man. She had felt that, more or less, what he did to himself he did to her. Her living depended on him. There were many, many stages in the ebbing of her love for him, but it was always ebbing.

Now, with the birth of this third baby, her self no longer set towards him, helplessly, but was like a tide that scarcely rose, standing off from him. After this she scarcely desired him. And, standing more aloof from him, not feeling him so much part of herself, but merely part of her circumstances, she did not mind so much what he did, could leave him alone.

There was the halt, the wistfulness about the ensuing year, which is like autumn in a man's life. His wife was casting him off, half regretfully, but relentlessly; casting him off and turning now for love and life to the children. Henceforward he was more or less a husk. And he himself acquiesced, as so many men do, yielding their place to their children.

During his recuperation, when it was really over between them, both made an effort to come back somewhat to the old relationship of the first months of their marriage. He sat at home and, when the children were in bed, and she was sewing—she did all her sewing by hand, made all shirts and children's clothing—he would read to her from the newspaper, slowly pronouncing and delivering the words like a man pitching quoits. Often she hurried him on, giving him a phrase in anticipation. And then he took her words humbly.

The silences between them were peculiar. There would be the swift, slight "cluck" of her needle, the sharp "pop" of his lips as he let out the smoke, the warmth, the sizzle on the bars as he spat in the fire. Then her thoughts turned to William. Already he was getting a big boy. Already he was top of the class, and the master said he was the smartest lad in the school. She saw him a man, young, full of vigour, making the world glow again for her.

And Morel sitting there, quite alone, and having nothing to think about, would be feeling vaguely uncomfortable. His soul would reach out in its blind way to her and find her gone. He felt a sort of emptiness, almost like a vacuum in his soul. He was unsettled and restless. Soon he could not live in that atmosphere, and he affected his wife. Both felt an oppression on their breathing when they were left together for some time. Then he went to bed and she settled down to enjoy herself alone, working, thinking, living.

Meanwhile another infant was coming, fruit of this little peace and tenderness between the separating parents. Paul was seventeen months old when the new baby was born. He was then a plump, pale child, quiet, with heavy blue eyes, and still the peculiar slight knitting of the brows. The last child was also a boy, fair and bonny. Mrs. Morel was sorry when she knew she was with child, both for economic reasons and because she did not love her husband; but not for the sake of the infant.

They called the baby Arthur. He was very pretty, with a mop of gold curls, and he loved his father from the first. Mrs. Morel was glad this child loved the father. Hearing the miner's footsteps, the baby would put up his arms and crow. And if Morel were in a good temper, he called back immediately, in his hearty, mellow voice:

"What then, my beauty? I sh'll come to thee in a minute."

And as soon as he had taken off his pit-coat, Mrs. Morel would put an apron round the child, and give him to his father.

"What a sight the lad looks!" she would exclaim sometimes, taking back the baby, that was smutted on the face from his father's kisses and play. Then Morel laughed joyfully.

"He's a little collier, bless his bit o' mutton!" he exclaimed.

And these were the happy moments of her life now, when the children included the father in her heart.

Meanwhile William grew bigger and stronger and more active, while Paul, always rather delicate and quiet, got slimmer, and trotted after his mother like her shadow. He was usually active and interested, but sometimes he would have fits of depression. Then the mother would find the boy of three or four crying on the sofa.

"What's the matter?" she asked, and got no answer.

"What's the matter?" she insisted, getting cross.

"I don't know," sobbed the child.

So she tried to reason him out of it, or to amuse him, but without effect. It made her feel beside herself. Then the father, always impatient, would jump from his chair and shout:

"If he doesn't stop, I'll smack him till he does."

"You'll do nothing of the sort," said the mother coldly. And then she carried the child into the yard, plumped him into his little chair, and said: "Now cry there, Misery!"

And then a butterfly on the rhubarb-leaves perhaps caught his eye, or at last he cried himself to sleep. These fits were not often, but they caused a shadow in Mrs. Morel's heart, and her treatment of Paul was different from that of the other children.

Suddenly one morning as she was looking down the alley of the Bottoms for the barm-man, she heard a voice calling her. It was the thin little Mrs. Anthony in brown velvet.

"Here, Mrs. Morel, I want to tell you about your Willie."

"Oh, do you?" replied Mrs. Morel. "Why, what's the matter?"

"A lad as gets 'old of another an' rips his clothes off'n 'is back," Mrs. Anthony said, "wants showing something."

"Your Alfred's as old as my William," said Mrs. Morel.

" 'Appen 'e is, but that doesn't give him a right to get hold of the boy's collar, an' fair rip it clean off his back."

"Well," said Mrs. Morel, "I don't thrash my children, and even if I did, I should want to hear their side of the tale."

"They'd happen be a bit better if they did get a good hiding," retorted Mrs. Anthony. "When it comes ter rippin' a lad's clean collar off'n 'is back a-purpose——"

"I'm sure he didn't do it on purpose," said Mrs. Morel.

"Make me a liar!" shouted Mrs. Anthony.

Mrs. Morel moved away and closed her gate. Her hand trembled as she held her mug of barm.

"But I s'll let your mester know," Mrs. Anthony cried after her.

At dinner-time, when William had finished his meal and wanted to be off again—he was then eleven years old—his mother said to him:

"What did you tear Alfred Anthony's collar for?"

"When did I tear his collar?"

"I don't know when, but his mother says you did."

"Why—it was yesterday—an' it was torn a'ready."

"But you tore it more."

"Well, I'd got a cobbler as 'ad licked seventeen—an' Alfy Ant'ny 'e says:

> 'Adam an' Eve an' pinch-me,
>   Went down to a river to bade.
> Adam an' Eve got drownded,
>   Who do yer think got saved?'

An' so I says: 'Oh, Pinch-*you*,' an' so I pinched 'im, an' 'e was mad, an' so he snatched my cobbler an' run off with it. An' so I run after 'im, an' when I was gettin' hold of 'im, 'e dodged, an' it ripped 'is collar. But I got my cobbler——"

He pulled from his pocket a black old horse-chestnut hanging on a string. This old cobbler had "cobbled"—hit and smashed—seventeen other cobblers on similar strings. So the boy was proud of his veteran.

"Well," said Mrs. Morel, "you know you've got no right to rip his collar."

"Well, our mother!" he answered. "I never meant tr'a done it—an' it was on'y an old indirrubber collar as was torn a'ready."

"Next time," said his mother, "*you* be more careful. I shouldn't like it if you came home with your collar torn off."

"I don't care, our mother; I never did it a-purpose."

The boy was rather miserable at being reprimanded.

"No—well, you be more careful."

William fled away, glad to be exonerated. And Mrs. Morel, who hated any bother with the neighbours, thought she would explain to Mrs. Anthony, and the business would be over.

But that evening Morel came in from the pit looking very sour. He stood in the kitchen and glared round, but did not speak for some minutes. Then:

"Wheer's that Willy?" he asked.

"What do you want *him* for?" asked Mrs. Morel, who had guessed.

"I'll let 'im know when I get him," said Morel, banging his pit-bottle on to the dresser.

"I suppose Mrs. Anthony's got hold of you and been yarning to you about Alfy's collar," said Mrs. Morel, rather sneering.

"Niver mind who's got hold of me," said Morel. "When I get hold of *'im* I'll make his bones rattle."

"It's a poor tale," said Mrs. Morel, "that you're so ready to side with any snipey vixen who likes to come telling tales against your own children."

"I'll learn 'im!" said Morel. "It none matters to me whose lad 'e is; 'e's none goin' rippin' an' tearin' about just as he's a mind."

" 'Ripping and tearing about!' " repeated Mrs. Morel. "He was running after that Alfy, who'd taken his cobbler, and he accidentally got hold of his collar, because the other dodged—as an Anthony would."

"I know!" shouted Morel threateningly.

"You would, before you're told," replied his wife bitingly.

"Niver you mind," stormed Morel. "I know my business."

"That's more than doubtful," said Mrs. Morel, "supposing some loud-mouthed creature had been getting you to thrash your own children."

"I know," repeated Morel.

And he said no more, but sat and nursed his bad temper. Suddenly William ran in, saying:

"Can I have my tea, mother?"

"Tha can ha'e more than that!" shouted Morel.

"Hold your noise, man," said Mrs. Morel; "and don't look so ridiculous."

"He'll look ridiculous before I've done wi' him!" shouted Morel, rising from his chair and glaring at his son.

William, who was a tall lad for his years, but very sensitive, had gone pale, and was looking in a sort of horror at his father.

"Go out!" Mrs. Morel commanded her son.

William had not the wit to move. Suddenly Morel clenched his fist, and crouched.

"I'll *gi'e* him 'go out'!" he shouted like an insane thing.

"What!" cried Mrs. Morel, panting with rage. "You shall not touch him for *her* telling, you shall not!"

"Shonna I?" shouted Morel. "Shonna I?"

And, glaring at the boy, he ran forward. Mrs. Morel sprang in between them, with her fist lifted.

"Don't you *dare!*" she cried.

"What!" he shouted, baffled for the moment. "What!"

She spun round to her son.

"Go out of the house!" she commanded him in fury.

The boy, as if hypnotised by her, turned suddenly and was gone. Morel rushed to the door, but was too late. He returned, pale under his pit-dirt with fury. But now his wife was fully roused.

"Only dare!" she said in a loud, ringing voice. "Only dare, milord, to lay a finger on that child! You'll regret it for ever."

He was afraid of her. In a towering rage, he sat down.

When the children were old enough to be left, Mrs. Morel joined the Women's Guild. It was a little club of women attached to the Co-operative Wholesale Society, which met on Monday night in the long room over the grocery shop of the Bestwood "Co-op". The women were supposed to discuss the benefits to be derived from co-operation, and other social questions. Sometimes Mrs. Morel read a paper. It seemed queer to the children to see their mother, who was always busy about the house, sitting writing in her rapid fashion, thinking, referring to books, and writing again. They felt for her on such occasions the deepest respect.

But they loved the Guild. It was the only thing to which they did not grudge their mother—and that partly because she enjoyed it, partly because of the treats they derived from it. The Guild was called by some hostile husbands, who found their wives getting too independent, the "clat-fart" shop—that is, the gossip-shop. It is true, from off the basis of the Guild, the women could look at their homes, at the conditions of their own lives, and find fault. So the colliers found their women had a new standard of their own, rather disconcerting. And also, Mrs. Morel always had a lot of news on Monday nights, so that the children liked William to be in when their mother came home, because she told him things.

Then, when the lad was thirteen, she got him a job in the "Co-op." office. He was a very clever boy, frank, with rather rough features and real viking blue eyes.

"What dost want ter ma'e a stool-harsed Jack on 'im for?" said Morel. "All he'll do is to wear his britches behind out, an' earn nowt. What's 'e startin' wi'?"

"It doesn't matter what he's starting with," said Mrs. Morel.

"It wouldna! Put 'im i' th' pit we me, an' 'e'll earn a easy ten shillin' a wik from th' start. But six shillin' wearin' his truck-end out on a stool's better than ten shillin' i' th' pit wi' me, I know."

"He is *not* going in the pit," said Mrs. Morel, "and there's an end of it."

"It wor good enough for me, but it's non good enough for 'im."

"If your mother put you in the pit at twelve, it's no reason why I should do the same with my lad."

"Twelve! It wor a sight afore that!"

"Whenever it was," said Mrs. Morel.

She was very proud of her son. He went to the night school, and learned shorthand, so that by the time he was sixteen he was the best shorthand clerk and book-keeper on the place, except one. Then he taught in the night schools. But he was so fiery that only his good-nature and his size protected him.

All the things that men do—the decent things—William did. He could run like the wind. When he was twelve he won a first prize in a race; an inkstand of glass, shaped like an anvil. It stood proudly on the dresser, and gave Mrs. Morel a keen pleasure. The boy only ran for her. He flew home with his anvil, breathless, with a "Look, mother!" That was the first real tribute to herself. She took it like a queen.

"How pretty!" she exclaimed.

Then he began to get ambitious. He gave all his money to his mother. When he earned fourteen shillings a week, she gave him back two for himself, and, as he never drank, he felt himself rich. He went about with the bourgeois of Bestwood. The townlet contained nothing higher than the clergyman. Then came the bank manager, then the doctors, then the tradespeople, and after that the hosts of colliers. William began to consort with the sons of the chemist, the schoolmaster, and the tradesmen. He played billiards in the Mechanics' Hall. Also he danced—this in spite of his mother. All the life that Bestwood offered he enjoyed, from the sixpenny-hops down Church Street, to sports and billiards.

Paul was treated to dazzling descriptions of all kinds of flower-like ladies, most of whom lived like cut blooms in William's heart for a brief fortnight.

Occasionally some flame would come in pursuit of her errant swain. Mrs. Morel would find a strange girl at the door, and immediately she sniffed the air.

"Is Mr. Morel in?" the damsel would ask appealingly.

"My husband is at home," Mrs. Morel replied.

"I—I mean *young* Mr. Morel," repeated the maiden painfully.

"Which one? There are several."

Whereupon much blushing and stammering from the fair one.

"I—I met Mr. Morel—at Ripley," she explained.

"Oh—at a dance!"

"Yes."

"I don't approve of the girls my son meets at dances. And he is *not* at home."

Then he came home angry with his mother for having turned the girl away so rudely. He was a careless, yet eager-looking fellow, who walked with long strides, sometimes frowning, often with his cap pushed jollily to the back of his head. Now he came in frowning. He threw his cap on to the sofa, and took his strong jaw in his hand, and glared down at his mother. She was small, with her hair taken straight back from her forehead. She had a quiet air of authority, and yet of rare warmth. Knowing her son was angry, she trembled inwardly.

"Did a lady call for me yesterday, mother?" he asked.

"I don't know about a lady. There was a girl came."

"And why didn't you tell me?"

"Because I forgot, simply."

He fumed a little.

"A good-looking girl—seemed a lady?"

"I didn't look at her."

"Big brown eyes?"

"I did *not* look. And tell your girls, my son, that when they're running after you, they're not to come and ask your mother for you. Tell them that—brazen baggages you meet at dancing-classes."

"I'm sure she was a nice girl."

"And I'm sure she wasn't."

There ended the altercation. Over the dancing there was a great strife between the mother and the son. The grievance reached its height when William said he was going to Hucknall Torkard—considered a low town—to a fancy-dress ball. He was to be a Highlander. There was a dress he could hire, which one of his friends had had, and which fitted him perfectly. The Highland suit came home. Mrs. Morel received it coldly and would not unpack it.

"My suit come?" cried William.

"There's a parcel in the front room."

He rushed in and cut the string.

"How do you fancy your son in this!" he said, enraptured, showing her the suit.

"You know I don't want to fancy you in it."

On the evening of the dance, when he had come home to dress, Mrs. Morel put on her coat and bonnet.

"Aren't you going to stop and see me, mother?" he asked.

"No; I don't want to see you," she replied.

She was rather pale, and her face was closed and hard. She was afraid of her son's going the same way as his father. He hesitated a moment, and his heart stood still with anxiety. Then he caught sight of the Highland bonnet with its ribbons. He picked it up gleefully, forgetting her. She went out.

When he was nineteen he suddenly left the Co-op. office and got a situation in Nottingham. In his new place he had thirty shillings a week instead of eighteen. This was indeed a rise. His mother and his father were brimmed up with pride. Everybody praised William. It seemed he was going to get on rapidly. Mrs. Morel hoped, with his aid, to help her younger sons. Annie was now studying to be a teacher. Paul, also very clever, was getting on well, having lessons in French and German from his godfather, the clergyman who was still a friend to Mrs. Morel. Arthur, a spoilt and very good-looking boy, was at the Board school, but there was talk of his trying to get a scholarship for the High School in Nottingham.

William remained a year at his new post in Nottingham. He was studying hard, and growing serious. Something seemed to be fretting him. Still he went out to the dances and the river parties. He did not drink. The children were all rabid teetotallers. He came home very late at night, and sat yet longer studying. His mother implored him to take more care, to do one thing or another.

"Dance, if you want to dance, my son; but don't think you can work in the office, and then amuse yourself, and *then* study on top of all. You can't; the human frame won't stand it. Do one thing or the other—amuse yourself or learn Latin; but don't try to do both."

Then he got a place in London, at a hundred and twenty a year. This seemed a fabulous sum. His mother doubted almost whether to rejoice or to grieve.

"They want me in Lime Street on Monday week, mother," he cried, his eyes blazing as he read the letter. Mrs. Morel felt everything go silent inside her. He read the letter: " 'And will you reply by Thursday whether you accept. Yours faithfully——' They want me, mother, at a hundred and twenty a year, and don't even ask to see me. Didn't I tell you I could do it! Think of me in London! And I can give you twenty pounds a year, mater. We s'll all be rolling in money."

"We shall, my son," she answered sadly.

It never occurred to him that she might be more hurt at his going away than glad of his success. Indeed, as the days drew near for his departure, her heart began to close and grow dreary with despair. She loved him so much! More than that, she hoped in him so much. Almost she lived by him. She liked to do things for him: she liked to put a cup for his tea and to iron his collars, of which he was so proud. It was a joy to her to have him proud of his collars. There was no laundry. So she used to rub away at them with her little convex iron, to polish them, till they shone from the sheer pressure of her arm. Now she would not do it for him. Now he was going away. She felt almost as if he were going as well out of her heart. He did not seem to leave her inhabited with himself. That was the grief and the pain to her. He took nearly all himself away.

A few days before his departure—he was just twenty—he burned his love-letters. They had hung on a file at the top of the kitchen cupboard. From some of them he had read extracts to his mother. Some of them she had taken the trouble to read herself. But most were too trivial.

Now, on the Saturday morning he said:

"Come on, Postle, let's go through my letters, and you can have the birds and flowers."

Mrs. Morel had done her Saturday's work on the Friday, because he was having a last day's holiday. She was making him a rice cake, which he loved, to take with him. He was scarcely conscious that she was so miserable.

He took the first letter off the file. It was mauve-tinted, and had purple and green thistles. William sniffed the page.

"Nice scent! Smell."

And he thrust the sheet under Paul's nose.

"Um!" said Paul, breathing in. "What d'you call it? Smell, mother."

His mother ducked her small, fine nose down to the paper.

"*I* don't want to smell their rubbish," she said, sniffing.

"This girl's father," said William, "is as rich as Crœsus. He owns property without end. She calls me Lafayette, because I know French. 'You will see, I've forgiven you'—I like *her* forgiving me. 'I told mother about you this morning, and she will have much pleasure if you come to tea on Sunday, but she will have to get father's consent also. I sincerely hope he will agree. I will let you know how it transpires. If, however, you——' "

" 'Let you know how it' what?" interrupted Mrs. Morel.

" 'Transpires'—oh yes!"

" 'Transpires!' " repeated Mrs. Morel mockingly. "I thought she was so well educated!"

William felt slightly uncomfortable, and abandoned this maiden, giving Paul the corner with the thistles. He continued to read extracts from his letters, some of which amused his mother, some of which saddened her and made her anxious for him.

"My lad," she said, "they're very wise. They know they've only got to flatter your vanity, and you press up to them like a dog that has its head scratched."

"Well, they can't go on scratching for ever," he replied. "And when they've done, I trot away."

"But one day you'll find a string round your neck that you can't pull off," she answered.

"Not me! I'm equal to any of 'em, mater, they needn't flatter themselves."

"You flatter *yourself*," she said quietly.

Soon there was a heap of twisted black pages, all that remained of the file of scented letters, except that Paul had thirty or forty pretty tickets from the corners of the notepaper—swallows and forget-me-nots and ivy sprays. And William went to London, to start a new life.

IV

THE YOUNG LIFE OF PAUL

Paul would be built like his mother, slightly and rather small. His fair hair went reddish, and then dark brown; his eyes were grey. He was a pale, quiet child, with eyes that seemed to listen, and with a full, dropping underlip.

As a rule he seemed old for his years. He was so conscious of what other people felt, particularly his mother. When she fretted he understood, and could have no peace. His soul seemed always attentive to her.

As he grew older he became stronger. William was too far removed from him to accept him as a companion. So the smaller boy belonged at first almost entirely to Annie. She was a tomboy and a "flybie-skybie", as her mother called her. But she was intensely fond of her second brother. So Paul was towed round at the heels of Annie, sharing her game. She raced wildly at lerky with the other young wild-cats of the Bottoms. And always Paul flew beside her, living her share of the game, having as yet no part of his own. He was quiet and not noticeable. But his sister adored him. He always seemed to care for things if she wanted him to.

She had a big doll of which she was fearfully proud, though not so fond. So she laid the doll on the sofa, and covered it with an antimacassar, to sleep. Then she forgot it. Meantime Paul must practise jumping off the sofa arm. So he jumped crash into the face of the hidden doll. Annie rushed up, uttered a loud wail, and sat down to weep a dirge. Paul remained quite still.

"You couldn't tell it was there, mother; you couldn't tell it was there," he repeated over and over. So long as Annie wept for the doll he sat helpless with misery. Her grief wore itself out. She forgave her brother—he was so much upset. But a day or two afterwards she was shocked.

"Let's make a sacrifice of Arabella," he said. "Let's burn her."

She was horrified, yet rather fascinated. She wanted to see what the boy would do. He made an altar of bricks, pulled some of the shavings out of Arabella's body, put the waxen fragments into the hollow face, poured on a little paraffin, and set the whole thing alight. He watched with wicked satisfaction the drops of wax melt off the broken forehead of Arabella, and drop like sweat into the flame. So long as the stupid big doll burned he rejoiced in silence. At the end he poked among the embers with a stick, fished out the arms and legs, all blackened, and smashed them under stones.

"That's the sacrifice of Missis Arabella," he said. "An' I'm glad there's nothing left of her."

Which disturbed Annie inwardly, although she could say nothing. He seemed to hate the doll so intensely, because he had broken it.

All the children, but particularly Paul, were peculiarly *against* their father, along with their mother. Morel continued to bully and to drink. He had periods, months at a time, when he made the whole life of the family a misery. Paul never forgot coming home from the Band of Hope one Monday evening and finding his mother with her eye swollen and discoloured, his father standing on the hearth-rug, feet astride, his head down, and William, just home from work, glaring at his father. There was a silence as the young children entered, but none of the elders looked round.

William was white to the lips, and his fists were clenched. He waited until the children were silent, watching with children's rage and hate; then he said:

"You coward, you daren't do it when I was in."

But Morel's blood was up. He swung round on his son. William was bigger, but Morel was hard-muscled, and mad with fury.

"Dossn't I?" he shouted. "Dossn't I? Ha'e much more o' thy chelp, my young jockey, an' I'll rattle my fist about thee. Ay, an' I sholl that, dost see?"

Morel crouched at the knees and showed his fist in an ugly, almost beast-like fashion. William was white with rage.

"Will yer?" he said, quiet and intense. "It 'ud be the last time, though."

Morel danced a little nearer, crouching, drawing back his fist to strike. William put his fists ready. A light came into his blue eyes, almost like a laugh. He watched his father. Another word, and the men would have begun to fight. Paul hoped they would. The three children sat pale on the sofa.

"Stop it, both of you," cried Mrs. Morel in a hard voice. "We've had enough for *one* night. And *you*," she said, turning on to her husband, "look at your children!"

Morel glanced at the sofa.

"Look at the children, you nasty little bitch!" he sneered. "Why, what have *I* done to the children, I should like to know? But they're like yourself; you've put 'em up to your own tricks and nasty ways—you've learned 'em in it, you 'ave."

She refused to answer him. No one spoke. After a while he threw his boots under the table and went to bed.

"Why didn't you let me have a go at him?" said William, when his father was upstairs. "I could easily have beaten him."

"A nice thing—your own father," she replied.

" 'Father!' " repeated William. "Call *him* my father!"

"Well, he is—and so——"

"But why don't you let me settle him? I could do, easily."

"The idea!" she cried. "It hasn't come to *that* yet."

"No," he said, "it's come to worse. Look at yourself. *Why* didn't you let me give it him?"

"Because I couldn't bear it, so never think of it," she cried quickly.

And the children went to bed, miserably.

When William was growing up, the family moved from the Bottoms to a house on the brow of the hill, commanding a view of the valley, which spread out like a convex cockle-shell, or a clamp-shell, before it. In front of the house was a huge old ashtree. The west wind, sweeping from Derbyshire, caught the houses with full force, and the tree shrieked again. Morel liked it.

"It's music," he said. "It sends me to sleep."

But Paul and Arthur and Annie hated it. To Paul it became almost a demoniacal noise. The winter of their first year in the new house their father was very bad. The children played in the street, on the brim of the wide, dark valley, until eight o'clock. Then they went to bed. Their mother sat sewing below. Having such a great space in front of the house gave the children a feeling of night, of vastness, and of terror. This terror came in from the shrieking of the tree and the anguish of the home discord. Often Paul would wake up, after he had been asleep a long time, aware of thuds downstairs. Instantly he was wide awake. Then he heard the booming shouts of his father, come home nearly drunk, then the sharp replies of his mother, then the bang, bang of his father's fist on the table, and the nasty snarling shout as the man's voice got higher. And then the whole was drowned in a piercing medley of shrieks and cries from the great, wind-swept ash-tree. The children lay silent in suspense, waiting for a lull in the wind to hear what their father was doing. He might hit their mother again. There was a feeling of horror, a kind of bristling in the darkness, and a sense of blood. They lay with their hearts in the grip of an intense anguish. The wind came through the tree fiercer and fiercer. All the cords of the great harp hummed, whistled, and shrieked. And then came the horror of the sudden silence, silence everywhere, outside and downstairs. What was it? Was it a silence of blood? What had he done?

The children lay and breathed the darkness. And then, at last, they heard their father throw down his boots and tramp upstairs in his stockinged feet. Still they listened. Then at last, if the wind allowed, they heard the water of the tap drumming into the kettle, which their mother was filling for morning, and they could go to sleep in peace.

So they were happy in the morning—happy, very happy playing, dancing at night round the lonely lamp-post in the midst of the darkness. But they had one tight place of anxiety in their hearts, one darkness in their eyes, which showed all their lives.

Paul hated his father. As a boy he had a fervent private religion.

"Make him stop drinking," he prayed every night. "Lord, let my father die," he prayed very often. "Let him not be killed at pit," he prayed when, after tea, the father did not come home from work.

That was another time when the family suffered intensely. The children came from school and had their teas. On the hob the big black saucepan was simmering, the stew-jar was in the oven, ready for Morel's dinner. He was expected at five o'clock. But for months he would stop and drink every night on his way from work.

In the winter nights, when it was cold, and grew dark early, Mrs. Morel would put a brass candlestick on the table, light a tallow candle to save the gas. The children finished their bread-and-butter, or dripping, and were ready to go out to play. But if Morel had not come they faltered. The sense of his sitting in all his pit-dirt, drinking, after a long day's work, not coming home and eating and washing, but sitting, getting drunk, on an empty stomach, made Mrs. Morel unable to bear herself. From her the feeling was transmitted to the other children. She never suffered alone any more: the children suffered with her.

Paul went out to play with the rest. Down in the great trough of twilight, tiny clusters of lights burned where the pits were. A few last colliers straggled up the dim field path. The lamplighter came along. No more colliers came. Darkness shut down over the valley; work was done. It was night.

Then Paul ran anxiously into the kitchen. The one candle still burned on the table, the big fire glowed red. Mrs. Morel sat alone. On the hob the saucepan steamed; the dinner-plate lay waiting on the table. All the room was full of the sense of waiting, waiting for the man who was sitting in his pit-dirt, dinnerless, some mile away from home, across the darkness, drinking himself drunk. Paul stood in the doorway.

"Has my dad come?" he asked.

"You can see he hasn't," said Mrs. Morel, cross with the futility of the question.

Then the boy dawdled about near his mother. They shared the same anxiety. Presently Mrs. Morel went out and strained the potatoes.

"They're ruined and black," she said; "but what do I care?"

Not many words were spoken. Paul almost hated his mother for suffering because his father did not come home from work.

"What do you bother yourself for?" he said. "If he wants to stop and get drunk, why don't you let him?"

"Let him!" flashed Mrs. Morel. "You may well say 'let him'."

She knew that the man who stops on the way home from work is on a quick way to ruining himself and his home. The children were yet young, and depended on the breadwinner. William gave her the sense of relief, providing her at last with someone to turn to if Morel failed. But the tense atmosphere of the room on these waiting evenings was the same.

The minutes ticked away. At six o'clock still the cloth lay on the table, still the dinner stood waiting, still the same sense of anxiety and expectation in the room. The boy could not stand it any longer. He could not go out and play. So he ran in to Mrs. Inger, next door but one, for her to talk to him. She had no children. Her husband was good to her, but was in a shop, and came home late. So, when she saw the lad at the door, she called:

"Come in, Paul."

The two sat talking for some time, when suddenly the boy rose, saying:

"Well, I'll be going and seeing if my mother wants an errand doing."

He pretended to be perfectly cheerful, and did not tell his friend what ailed him. Then he ran indoors.

Morel at these times came in churlish and hateful.

"This is a nice time to come home," said Mrs. Morel.

"Wha's it matter to yo' what time I come whoam?" he shouted.

And everybody in the house was still, because he was dangerous. He ate his food in the most brutal manner possible, and, when he had done, pushed all the pots in a heap away from him, to lay his arms on the table. Then he went to sleep.

Paul hated his father so. The collier's small, mean head, with its black hair slightly soiled with grey, lay on the bare arms, and the face, dirty and inflamed, with a fleshy nose and thin, paltry brows, was turned sideways, asleep with beer and weariness and nasty temper. If anyone entered suddenly, or a noise were made, the man looked up and shouted:

"I'll lay my fist about thy y'ead, I'm tellin' thee, if tha doesna stop that clatter! Dost hear?"

And the two last words, shouted in a bullying fashion, usually at Annie, made the family writhe with hate of the man.

He was shut out from all family affairs. No one told him anything. The children, alone with their mother, told her all about the day's happenings, everything. Nothing had really taken place in them until it was told to their mother. But as soon as the father came in, everything stopped. He was like the scotch in the smooth, happy machinery of the home. And he was always aware of this fall of silence on his entry, the shutting off of life, the unwelcome. But now it was gone too far to alter.

He would dearly have liked the children to talk to him, but they could not. Sometimes Mrs. Morel would say:

"You ought to tell your father."

Paul won a prize in a competition in a child's paper. Everybody was highly jubilant.

"Now you'd better tell your father when he comes in," said Mrs. Morel. "You know how he carries on and says he's never told anything."

"All right," said Paul. But he would almost rather have forfeited the prize than have to tell his father.

"I've won a prize in a competition, dad," he said.

Morel turned round to him.

"Have you, my boy? What sort of a competition?"

"Oh, nothing—about famous women."

"And how much is the prize, then, as you've got?"

"It's a book."

"Oh, indeed!"

"About birds."

"Hm—hm!"

And that was all. Conversation was impossible between the father and any other member of the family. He was an outsider. He had denied the God in him.

The only times when he entered again into the life of his own people was when he worked, and was happy at work. Sometimes, in the evening, he cobbled the boots or mended the kettle or his pit-bottle. Then he always wanted several attendants, and the children enjoyed it. They united with him in the work, in the actual doing of something, when he was his real self again.

He was a good workman, dexterous, and one who, when he was in a good humour, always sang. He had whole periods, months, almost years, of friction and nasty temper. Then sometimes he was jolly again. It was nice to see him run with a piece of red-hot iron into the scullery, crying:

"Out of my road—out of my road!"

Then he hammered the soft, red-glowing stuff on his iron goose, and made the shape he wanted. Or he sat absorbed for a moment, soldering. Then the children watched with joy as the metal sank suddenly molten, and was shoved about against the nose of the soldering-iron, while the room was full of a scent of burnt resin and hot tin, and Morel was silent and intent for a minute. He always sang when he mended boots because of the jolly sound of hammering. And he was rather happy when he sat putting great patches on his moleskin pit trousers, which he would often do, considering them too dirty, and the stuff too hard, for his wife to mend.

But the best time for the young children was when he made fuses. Morel fetched a sheaf of long sound wheat-straws from the attic. These he cleaned with his hand, till each one gleamed like a stalk of gold, after which he cut the straws into lengths of about six inches, leaving, if he could, a notch at the bottom of each piece. He always had a beautifully sharp knife that could cut a straw clean without hurting it. Then he set in the middle of the table a heap of gunpowder, a little pile of black grains upon the white-scrubbed board. He made and trimmed the straws while Paul and Annie filled and plugged them. Paul loved to see the black grains trickle down a crack in his palm into the mouth of the straw, peppering jollily downwards till the straw was full. Then he bunged up the mouth with a bit of soap—which he got on his thumb-nail from a pat in a saucer—and the straw was finished.

"Look, dad!" he said.

"That's right, my beauty," replied Morel, who was peculiarly lavish of endearments to his second son. Paul popped the fuse into the powder-tin, ready for the morning, when Morel would take it to the pit, and use it to fire a shot that would blast the coal down.

Meantime Arthur, still fond of his father, would lean on the arm of Morel's chair and say:

"Tell us about down pit, daddy."

This Morel loved to do.

"Well, there's one little 'oss—we call 'im Taffy," he would begin. "An' he's a fawce 'un!"

Morel had a warm way of telling a story. He made one feel Taffy's cunning.

"He's a brown 'un," he would answer, "an' not very high. Well, he comes i' th' stall wi' a rattle, an' then yo' 'ear 'im sneeze.

" 'Ello, Taff,' you say, 'what art sneezin' for? Bin ta'ein' some snuff?'

"An' 'e sneezes again. Then he slives up an' shoves 'is 'ead on yer, that cadin'.

" 'What's want, Taff?' yo' say."

"And what does he?" Arthur always asked.

"He wants a bit o' bacca, my duckie."

This story of Taffy would go on interminably, and everybody loved it.

Or sometimes it was a new tale.

"An' what dost think, my darlin'? When I went to put my coat on at snap-time, what should go runnin' up my arm but a mouse.

" 'Hey up, theer!' I shouts.

"An' I wor just in time ter get 'im by th' tail."

"And did you kill it?"

"I did, for they're a nuisance. The place is fair snied wi' 'em."

"An' what do they live on?"

"The corn as the 'osses drops—an' they'll get in your pocket an' eat your snap, if you'll let 'em—no matter where yo' hing your coat—the slivin', nibblin' little nuisances, for they are."

These happy evenings could not take place unless Morel had some job to do. And then he always went to bed very early, often before the children. There was nothing remaining for him to stay up for, when he had finished tinkering, and had skimmed the headlines of the newspaper.

And the children felt secure when their father was in bed. They lay and talked softly a while. Then they started as the lights went suddenly sprawling over the ceiling from the lamps that swung in the hands of the colliers tramping by outside, going to take the nine o'clock shift. They listened to the voices of the men, imagined them dipping down into the dark valley. Sometimes they went to the window and watched the three or four lamps growing tinier and tinier, swaying down the fields in the darkness. Then it was a joy to rush back to bed and cuddle closely in the warmth.

Paul was rather a delicate boy, subject to bronchitis. The others were all quite strong; so this was another reason for his mother's difference in feeling for him. One day he came home at dinner-time feeling ill. But it was not a family to make any fuss.

"What's the matter with *you?*" his mother asked sharply.

"Nothing," he replied.

But he ate no dinner.

"If you eat no dinner, you're not going to school," she said.

"Why?" he asked.

"That's why."

So after dinner he lay down on the sofa, on the warm chintz cushions the children loved. Then he fell into a kind of doze. That afternoon Mrs. Morel was ironing. She listened to the small, restless noise the boy made in his throat as she worked. Again rose in her heart the old, almost weary feeling towards him. She had never expected him to live. And yet he had a great vitality in his young body. Perhaps it would have been a little relief to her if he had died. She always felt a mixture of anguish in her love for him.

He, in his semi-conscious sleep, was vaguely aware of the clatter of the iron on the iron-stand, of the faint thud, thud on the ironing-board. Once roused, he opened his eyes to see his mother standing on the hearth-rug with the hot iron near her cheek, listening, as it were, to the heat. Her still face, with the mouth closed tight from suffering and disillusion and self-denial, and her nose the smallest bit on one side, and her blue eyes so young, quick, and warm, made his heart contract with love. When she was quiet, so, she looked brave and rich with life, but as if she had been done out of her rights. It hurt the boy keenly, this feeling about her that she had never had her life's fulfilment: and his own incapability to make up to her hurt him with a sense of impotence, yet made him patiently dogged inside. It was his childish aim.

She spat on the iron, and a little ball of spit bounded, raced off the dark, glossy surface. Then, kneeling, she rubbed the iron on the sack lining of the hearth-rug vigorously. She was warm in the ruddy firelight. Paul loved the way she crouched and put her head on one side. Her movements were light and quick. It was always a pleasure to watch her. Nothing she ever did, no movement she ever made, could have been found fault with by her children. The room was warm and full of the scent of hot linen. Later on the clergyman came and talked softly with her.

Paul was laid up with an attack of bronchitis. He did not mind much. What happened happened, and it was no good kicking against the pricks. He loved the evenings, after eight o'clock, when the light was put out, 'and he could watch the fire-flames spring over the darkness of the walls and ceiling; could watch huge shadows waving and tossing, till the room seemed full of men who battled silently.

On retiring to bed, the father would come into the sickroom. He was always very gentle if anyone were ill. But he disturbed the atmosphere for the boy.

"Are ter asleep, my darlin'?" Morel asked softly.

"No; is my mother comin'?"

"She's just finishin' foldin' the clothes. Do you want anything?" Morel rarely "thee'd" his son.

"I don't want nothing. But how long will she be?"

"Not long, my duckie."

The father waited undecidedly on the hearth-rug for a moment or two. He felt his son did not want him. Then he went to the top of the stairs and said to his wife:

"This childt's axin' for thee; how long art goin' to be?"

"Until I've finished, good gracious! Tell him to go to sleep."

"She says you're to go to sleep," the father repeated gently to Paul.

"Well, I want *her* to come," insisted the boy.

"He says he can't go off till you come," Morel called downstairs.

"Eh, dear! I shan't be long. And do stop shouting downstairs. There's the other children——"

Then Morel came again and crouched before the bedroom fire. He loved a fire dearly.

"She says she won't be long," he said.

He loitered about indefinitely. The boy began to get feverish with irritation. His father's presence seemed to aggravate all his sick impatience. At last Morel, after having stood looking at his son awhile, said softly:

"Good-night, my darling."

"Good-night," Paul replied, turning round in relief to be alone.

Paul loved to sleep with his mother. Sleep is still most perfect, in spite of hygienists, when it is shared with a beloved. The warmth, the security and peace of soul, the utter comfort from the touch of the other, knits the sleep, so that it takes the body and soul completely in its healing. Paul lay against her and slept, and got better; whilst she, always a bad sleeper, fell later on into a profound sleep that seemed to give her faith.

In convalescence he would sit up in bed, see the fluffy horses feeding at the troughs in the field, scattering their hay on the trodden yellow snow; watch the miners troop home—small, black figures trailing slowly in gangs across the white field. Then the night came up in dark blue vapour from the snow.

In convalescence everything was wonderful. The snowflakes, suddenly arriving on the window-pane, clung there a moment like swallows, then were gone, and a drop of water was crawling down the glass. The snowflakes whirled round the corner of the house, like pigeons dashing by. Away across the valley the little black train crawled doubtfully over the great whiteness.

While they were so poor, the children were delighted if they could do anything to help economically. Annie and Paul and Arthur went out early in the morning, in summer, looking for mushrooms, hunting through the wet grass, from which the larks were rising, for the white-skinned, wonderful naked bodies crouched secretly in the green. And if they got half a pound they felt exceedingly happy: there was the joy of finding something, the joy of accepting something straight from the hand of Nature, and the joy of contributing to the family exchequer.

But the most important harvest, after gleaning for frumenty, was the blackberries. Mrs. Morel must buy fruit for puddings on the Saturdays; also she liked blackberries. So Paul and Arthur scoured the coppices and woods and old quarries, so long as a blackberry was to be found, every week-end going on their search. In that region of mining villages blackberries became a comparative rarity. But Paul hunted far and wide. He loved being out in the country, among the bushes. But he also could not bear to go home to his mother empty. That, he felt, would disappoint her, and he would have died rather.

"Good gracious!" she would exclaim as the lads came in, late, and tired to death, and hungry, "wherever have you been?"

"Well," replied Paul, "there wasn't any, so we went over Misk Hills. And look here, our mother!"

She peeped into the basket.

"Now, those are fine ones!" she exclaimed.

"And there's over two pounds—isn't there over two pounds?"

She tried the basket.

"Yes," she answered doubtfully.

Then Paul fished out a little spray. He always brought her one spray, the best he could find.

"Pretty!" she said, in a curious tone, of a woman accepting a love-token.

The boy walked all day, went miles and miles, rather than own himself beaten and come home to her empty-handed. She never realised this, whilst he was young. She was a woman who waited for her children to grow up. And William occupied her chiefly.

But when William went to Nottingham, and was not so much at home, the mother made a companion of Paul. The latter was unconsciously jealous of his brother, and William was jealous of him. At the same time, they were good friends.

Mrs. Morel's intimacy with her second son was more subtle and fine, perhaps not so passionate as with her eldest. It was the rule that Paul should fetch the money on Friday afternoons. The colliers of the five pits were paid on Fridays, but not individually. All the earnings of each stall were put down to the chief butty, as contractor, and he divided the wages again, either in the public-house or in his own home. So that the children could fetch the money, school closed early on Friday afternoons. Each of the Morel children—William, then Annie, then Paul—had fetched the money on Friday afternoons, until they went themselves to work. Paul used to set off at half-past three, with a little calico bag in his pocket. Down all the paths, women, girls, children, and men were seen trooping to the offices.

These offices were quite handsome: a new, red-brick building, almost like a mansion, standing in its own grounds at the end of Greenhill Lane. The waiting-room was the hall, a long, bare room paved with blue brick, and having a seat all round, against the wall. Here sat the colliers in their pit-dirt. They had come up early. The women and children usually loitered about on the red gravel paths. Paul always examined the grass border, and the big grass bank, because in it grew tiny pansies and tiny forget-me-nots. There was a sound of many voices. The women had on their Sunday hats. The girls chattered loudly. Little dogs ran here and there. The green shrubs were silent all around.

Then from inside came the cry "Spinney Park—Spinney Park." All the folk for Spinney Park trooped inside. When it was time for Bretty to be paid, Paul went in among the crowd. The pay-room was quite small. A counter went across, dividing it into half. Behind the counter stood two men—Mr. Braithwaite and his clerk, Mr. Winterbottom. Mr. Braithwaite was large, somewhat of the stern patriarch in appearance, having a rather thin white beard. He was usually muffled in an enormous silk neckerchief, and right up to the hot summer a huge fire burned in the open grate. No window was open. Sometimes in winter the air scorched the throats of the people, coming in from the freshness.

Mr. Winterbottom was rather small and fat, and very bald. He made remarks that were not witty, whilst his chief launched forth patriarchal admonitions against the colliers.

The room was crowded with miners in their pit-dirt, men who had been home and changed, and women, and one or two children, and usually a dog. Paul was quite small, so it was often his fate to be jammed behind the legs of the men, near the fire which scorched him. He knew the order of the names—they went according to stall number.

"Holliday," came the ringing voice of Mr. Braithwaite. Then Mrs. Holliday stepped silently forward, was paid, drew aside.

"Bower—John Bower."

A boy stepped to the counter. Mr. Braithwaite, large and irascible, glowered at him over his spectacles.

"John Bower!" he repeated.

"It's me," said the boy.

"Why, you used to 'ave a different nose than that," said glossy Mr. Winterbottom, peering over the counter. The people tittered, thinking of John Bower senior.

"How is it your father's not come!" said Mr. Braithwaite, in a large and magisterial voice.

"He's badly," piped the boy.

"You should tell him to keep off the drink," pronounced the great cashier.

"An' niver mind if he puts his foot through yer," said a mocking voice from behind.

All the men laughed. The large and important cashier looked down at his next sheet.

"Fred Pilkington!" he called, quite indifferent.

Mr. Braithwaite was an important shareholder in the firm.

Paul knew his turn was next but one, and his heart began to beat. He was pushed against the chimney-piece. His calves were burning. But he did not hope to get through the wall of men.

"Walter Morel!" came the ringing voice.

"Here!" piped Paul, small and inadequate.

"Morel—Walter Morel!" the cashier repeated, his finger and thumb on the invoice, ready to pass on.

Paul was suffering convulsions of self-consciousness, and could not or would not shout. The backs of the men obliterated him. Then Mr. Winterbottom came to the rescue.

"He's here. Where is he? Morel's lad?"

The fat, red, bald little man peered round with keen eyes. He pointed at the fireplace. The colliers looked round, moved aside, and disclosed the boy.

"Here he is!" said Mr. Winterbottom.

Paul went to the counter.

"Seventeen pounds eleven and fivepence. Why don't you shout up when you're called?" said Mr. Braithwaite. He banged on to the invoice a five-pound bag of silver, then in a delicate and pretty movement, picked up a little ten-pound column of gold, and plumped it beside the silver. The gold slid in a bright stream over the paper. The cashier finished counting off the money; the boy dragged the whole down the counter to Mr. Winterbottom, to whom the stoppages for rent and tools must be paid. Here he suffered again.

"Sixteen an' six," said Mr. Winterbottom.

The lad was too much upset to count. He pushed forward some loose silver and half a sovereign.

"How much do you think you've given me?" asked Mr. Winterbottom.

The boy looked at him, but said nothing. He had not the faintest notion.

"Haven't you got a tongue in your head?"

Paul bit his lip, and pushed forward some more silver.

"Don't they teach you to count at the Board-school?" he asked.

"Nowt but algibbra an' French," said a collier.

"An' cheek an' impidence," said another.

Paul was keeping someone waiting. With trembling fingers he got his money into the bag and slid out. He suffered the tortures of the damned on these occasions.

His relief, when he got outside, and was walking along the Mansfield Road, was infinite. On the park wall the mosses were green. There were some gold and some white fowls pecking under the apple trees of an orchard. The colliers were walking home in a stream. The boy went near the wall, self-consciously. He knew many of the men, but could not recognise them in their dirt. And this was a new torture to him.

When he got down to the New Inn, at Bretty, his father was not yet come. Mrs. Wharmby, the landlady, knew him. His grandmother, Morel's mother, had been Mrs. Wharmby's friend.

"Your father's not come yet," said the landlady, in the peculiar half-scornful, half-patronising voice of a woman who talks chiefly to grown men. "Sit you down."

Paul sat down on the edge of the bench in the bar. Some colliers were "reckoning"—sharing out their money—in a corner; others came in. They all glanced at the boy without speaking. At last Morel came; brisk, and with something of an air, even in his blackness.

"Hello!" he said rather tenderly to his son. "Have you bested me? Shall you have a drink of something?"

Paul and all the children were bred up fierce anti-alcoholists, and he would have suffered more in drinking a lemonade before all the men than in having a tooth drawn.

The landlady looked at him *de haut en bas*, rather pitying, and at the same time, resenting his clear, fierce morality. Paul went home, glowering. He entered the house silently. Friday was baking day, and there was usually a hot bun. His mother put it before him.

Suddenly he turned on her in a fury, his eyes flashing:

"I'm *not* going to the office any more," he said.

"Why, what's the matter?" his mother asked in surprise. His sudden rages rather amused her.

"I'm *not* going any more," he declared.

"Oh, very well, tell your father so."

He chewed his bun as if he hated it.

"I'm not—I'm not going to fetch the money."

"Then one of Carlin's children can go; they'd be glad enough of the six-pence," said Mrs. Morel.

This sixpence was Paul's only income. It mostly went in buying birthday presents; but it *was* an income, and he treasured it. But——

"They can have it, then!" he said. "I don't want it."

"Oh, very well," said his mother. "But you needn't bully *me* about it."

"They're hateful, and common, and hateful, they are, and I'm not going any more. Mr. Braithwaite drops his 'h's', an' Mr. Winterbottom says 'You was'."

"And is that why you won't go any more?" smiled Mrs. Morel.

The boy was silent for some time. His face was pale, his eyes dark and furious. His mother moved about at her work, taking no notice of him.

"They always stan' in front of me, so's I can't get out," he said.

"Well, my lad, you've only to *ask* them," she replied.

"An' then Alfred Winterbottom says, 'What do they teach you at the Board-school?' "

"They never taught *him* much," said Mrs. Morel, "that is a fact—neither manners nor wit—and his cunning he was born with."

So, in her own way, she soothed him. His ridiculous hypersensitiveness made her heart ache. And sometimes the fury in his eyes roused her, made her sleeping soul lift up its head a moment, surprised.

"What was the cheque?" she asked.

"Seventeen pounds eleven and fivepence, and sixteen and six stoppages," replied the boy. "It's a good week; and only five shillings stoppages for my father."

So she was able to calculate how much her husband had earned, and could call him to account if he gave her short money. Morel always kept to himself the secret of the week's amount.

Friday was the baking night and market night. It was the rule that Paul should stay at home and bake. He loved to stop in and draw or read; he was very fond of drawing. Annie always "gallivanted" on Friday nights; Arthur was enjoying himself as usual. So the boy remained alone.

Mrs. Morel loved her marketing. In the tiny market-place on the top of the hill, where four roads, from Nottingham and Derby, Ilkeston and Mansfield, meet, many stalls were erected. Brakes ran in from surrounding villages. The market-place was full of women, the streets packed with men. It was amazing to see so many men everywhere in the streets. Mrs. Morel usually quarrelled with her lace woman, sympathised with her fruit man—who was a gabey, but his wife was a bad 'un—laughed with the fish man—who was a scamp but so droll—put the linoleum man in his place, was cold with the odd-wares man, and only went to the crockery man when she was driven—or drawn by the cornflowers on a little dish; then she was coldly polite.

"I wondered how much that little dish was," she said.

"Sevenpence to you."

"Thank you."

She put the dish down and walked away; but she could not leave the market-place without it. Again she went by where the pots lay coldly on the floor, and she glanced at the dish furtively, pretending not to.

She was a little woman, in a bonnet and a black costume. Her bonnet was in its third year; it was a great grievance to Annie.

"Mother!" the girl implored, "don't wear that nubbly little bonnet."

"Then what else shall I wear," replied the mother tartly. "And I'm sure it's right enough."

It had started with a tip; then had had flowers; now was reduced to black lace and a bit of jet.

"It looks rather come down," said Paul. "Couldn't you give it a pick-me-up?"

"I'll jowl your head for impudence," said Mrs. Morel, and she tied the strings of the black bonnet valiantly under her chin.

She glanced at the dish again. Both she and her enemy, the pot man, had an uncomfortable feeling, as if there were something between them. Suddenly he shouted:

"Do you want it for fivepence?"

She started. Her heart hardened; but then she stooped and took up her dish. "I'll have it," she said.

"Yer'll do me the favour, like?" he said. "Yer'd better spit in it, like yer do when y'ave something give yer."

Mrs. Morel paid him the fivepence in a cold manner.

"I don't see you give it me," she said. "You wouldn't let me have it for fivepence if you didn't want to."

"In this flamin', scrattlin' place you may count yerself lucky if you can give your things away," he growled.

"Yes; there are bad times, and good," said Mrs. Morel.

But she had forgiven the pot man. They were friends. She dare now finger his pots. So she was happy.

Paul was waiting for her. He loved her home-coming. She was always her best so—triumphant, tired, laden with parcels, feeling rich in spirit. He heard her quick, light step in the entry and looked up from his drawing.

"Oh!" she sighed, smiling at him from the doorway.

"My word, you *are* loaded!" he exclaimed, putting down his brush.

"I am!" she gasped. "That brazen Annie said she'd meet me. *Such* a weight!"

She dropped her string bag and her packages on the table.

"Is the bread done?" she asked, going to the oven.

"The last one is soaking," he replied. "You needn't look, I've not forgotten it."

"Oh, that pot man!" she said, closing the oven door. "You know what a wretch I've said he was? Well, I don't think he's quite so bad."

"Don't you?"

The boy was attentive to her. She took off her little black bonnet.

"No. I think he can't make any money—well, it's everybody's cry alike nowadays—and it makes him disagreeable."

"It would *me,*" said Paul.

"Well, one can't wonder at it. And he let me have—how much do you think he let me have *this* for?"

She took the dish out of its rag of newspaper, and stood looking on it with joy.

"Show me!" said Paul.

The two stood together gloating over the dish.

"I *love* cornflowers on things," said Paul.

"Yes, and I thought of the teapot you bought me——"

"One and three," said Paul.

"Fivepence!"

"It's not enough, mother."

"No. Do you know, I fairly sneaked off with it. But I'd been extravagant, I couldn't afford any more. And he needn't have let me have it if he hadn't wanted to."

"No, he needn't, need he," said Paul, and the two comforted each other from the fear of having robbed the pot man.

"We c'n have stewed fruit in it," said Paul.

"Or custard, or a jelly," said his mother.

"Or radishes and lettuce," said he.

"Don't forget that bread," she said, her voice bright with glee.

Paul looked in the oven; tapped the loaf on the base.

"It's done," he said, giving it to her.

She tapped it also.

"Yes," she replied, going to unpack her bag. "Oh, and I'm a wicked, extravagant woman. I know I s'll come to want."

He hopped to her side eagerly, to see her latest extravagance. She unfolded another lump of newspaper and disclosed some roots of pansies and of crimson daisies.

"Four penn'orth!" she moaned.

"How *cheap!*" he cried.

"Yes, but I couldn't afford it *this* week of all weeks."

"But lovely!" he cried.

"Aren't they!" she exclaimed, giving way to pure joy. "Paul, look at this yellow one, isn't it—and a face just like an old man!"

"Just!" cried Paul, stooping to sniff. "And smells that nice! But he's a bit splashed."

He ran in the scullery, came back with the flannel, and carefully washed the pansy.

"*Now* look at him now he's wet!" he said.

"Yes!" she exclaimed, brimful of satisfaction.

The children of Scargill Street felt quite select. At the end where the Morels lived there were not many young things. So the few were more united. Boys and girls played together, the girls joining in the fights and the rough games, the boys taking part in the dancing games and rings and make-belief of the girls.

Annie and Paul and Arthur loved the winter evenings, when it was not wet. They stayed indoors till the colliers were all gone home, till it was thick dark, and the street would be deserted. Then they tied their scarves round their necks, for they scorned overcoats, as all the colliers' children did, and went out. The entry was very dark, and at the end the whole great night opened out, in a hollow, with a little tangle of lights below where Minton pit lay, and another far away opposite for Selby. The farthest tiny lights seemed to stretch out the darkness for ever. The children looked anxiously down the road at the one lamp-post, which stood at the end of the field path. If the little, luminous space were deserted, the two boys felt genuine desolation. They stood with their hands in their pockets under the lamp, turning their backs on the night, quite miserable, watching the dark houses. Suddenly a pinafore under a short coat was seen, and a long-legged girl came flying up.

"Where's Billy Pillins an' your Annie an' Eddie Dakin?"

"I don't know."

But it did not matter so much—there were three now. They set up a game round the lamp-post, till the others rushed up, yelling. Then the play went fast and furious.

There was only this one lamp-post. Behind was the great scoop of darkness, as if all the night were there. In front, another wide, dark way opened over the hill brow. Occasionally somebody came out of this way and went into the field down the path. In a dozen yards the night had swallowed them. The children played on.

They were brought exceedingly close together owing to their isolation. If a quarrel took place, the whole play was spoilt. Arthur was very touchy, and Billy Pillins—really Philips—was worse. Then Paul had to side with Arthur, and on

Paul's side went Alice, while Billy Pillins always had Emmie Limb and Eddie Dakin to back him up. Then the six would fight, hate with a fury of hatred, and flee home in terror. Paul never forgot, after one of these fierce internecine fights, seeing a big red moon lift itself up, slowly, between the waste road over the hill-top, steadily, like a great bird. And he thought of the Bible, that the moon should be turned to blood. And the next day he made haste to be friends with Billy Pillins. And then the wild, intense games went on again under the lamp-post, surrounded by so much darkness. Mrs. Morel, going into her parlour, would hear the children singing away:

> "My shoes are made of Spanish leather,
>   My socks are made of silk;
> I wear a ring on every finger,
>   I wash myself in milk."

They sounded so perfectly absorbed in the game as their voices came out of the night, that they had the feel of wild creatures singing. It stirred the mother; and she understood when they came in at eight o'clock, ruddy, with brilliant eyes, and quick, passionate speech.

They all loved the Scargill Street house for its openness, for the great scallop of the world it had in view. On summer evenings the women would stand against the field fence, gossiping, facing the west, watching the sunsets flare quickly out, till the Derbyshire hills ridged across the crimson far away, like the black crest of a newt.

In this summer season the pits never turned full time, particularly the soft coal. Mrs. Dakin, who lived next door to Mrs. Morel, going to the field fence to shake her hearth-rug, would spy men coming slowly up the hill. She saw at once they were colliers. Then she waited, a tall, thin, shrew-faced woman, standing on the hill brow, almost like a menace to the poor colliers who were toiling up. It was only eleven o'clock. From the far-off wooded hills the haze that hangs like fine black crape at the back of a summer morning had not yet dissipated. The first man came to the stile. "Chock-chock!" went the gate under his thrust.

"What, han' yer knocked off?" cried Mrs. Dakin.

"We han, missis."

"It's a pity as they letn yer goo," she said sarcastically.

"It is that," replied the man.

"Nay, you know you're flig to come up again," she said.

And the man went on. Mrs. Dakin, going up her yard, spied Mrs. Morel taking the ashes to the ash-pit.

"I reckon Minton's knocked off, missis," she cried.

"Isn't it sickenin!" exclaimed Mrs. Morel in wrath.

"Ha! But I'n just seed Jont Hutchby."

"They might as well have saved their shoe-leather," said Mrs. Morel. And both women went indoors disgusted.

The colliers, their faces scarcely blackened, were trooping home again. Morel hated to go back. He loved the sunny morning. But he had gone to pit to work, and to be sent home again spoilt his temper.

"Good gracious, at this time!" exclaimed his wife, as he entered.

"Can I help it, woman?" he shouted.

"And I've not done half enough dinner."

"Then I'll eat my bit o' snap as I took with me," he bawled pathetically. He felt ignominious and sore.

And the children, coming home from school, would wonder to see their father eating with his dinner the two thick slices of rather dry and dirty bread-and-butter that had been to pit and back.

"What's my dad eating his snap for now?" asked Arthur.

"I should ha'e it holled at me if I didna," snorted Morel.

"What a story!" exclaimed his wife.

"An' is it goin' to be wasted?" said Morel. "I'm not such a extravagant mortal as you lot, with your waste. If I drop a bit of bread at pit, in all the dust an' dirt, I pick it up an' eat it."

"The mice would eat it," said Paul. "It wouldn't be wasted."

"Good bread-an'-butter's not for mice, either," said Morel. "Dirty or not dirty, I'd eat it rather than it should be wasted."

"You might leave it for the mice and pay for it out of your next pint," said Mrs. Morel.

"Oh, might I?" he exclaimed.

They were very poor that autumn. William had just gone away to London, and his mother missed his money. He sent ten shillings once or twice, but he had many things to pay for at first. His letters came regularly once a week. He wrote a good deal to his mother, telling her all his life, how he made friends, and was exchanging lessons with a Frenchman, how he enjoyed London. His mother felt again he was remaining to her just as when he was at home. She wrote to him every week her direct, rather witty letters. All day long, as she cleaned the house, she thought of him. He was in London: he would do well. Almost, he was like her knight who wore *her* favour in the battle.

He was coming at Christmas for five days. There had never been such preparations. Paul and Arthur scoured the land for holly and evergreens. Annie made the pretty paper hoops in the old-fashioned way. And there was unheard-of extravagance in the larder. Mrs. Morel made a big and magnificent cake. Then, feeling queenly, she showed Paul how to blanch almonds. He skinned the long nuts reverently, counting them all, to see not one was lost. It was said that eggs whisked better in a cold place. So the boy stood in the scullery, where the temperature was nearly at freezing-point, and whisked and whisked, and flew in excitement to his mother as the white of egg grew stiffer and more snowy.

"Just look, mother! Isn't it lovely?"

And he balanced a bit on his nose, then blew it in the air.

"Now, don't waste it," said the mother.

Everybody was mad with excitement. William was coming on Christmas Eve. Mrs. Morel surveyed her pantry. There was a big plum cake, and a rice cake, jam tarts, lemon tarts, and mince-pies—two enormous dishes. She was finishing cooking—Spanish tarts and cheese-cakes. Everywhere was decorated. The kissing bunch of berried holly hung with bright and glittering things, spun slowly over Mrs. Morel's head as she trimmed her little tarts in the kitchen. A great fire roared. There was a scent of cooked pastry. He was due at seven o'clock, but he would be late. The three children had gone to meet him. She was alone. But at a quarter to seven Morel came in again. Neither wife nor husband spoke. He sat in his arm-chair, quite awkward with excitement, and she quietly went on with her baking. Only by the careful way in which she did things could it be told how much moved she was. The clock ticked on.

"What time dost say he's coming?" Morel asked for the fifth time.

"The train gets in at half-past six," she replied emphatically.

"Then he'll be here at ten past seven."

"Eh, bless you, it'll be hours late on the Midland," she said indifferently. But she hoped, by expecting him late, to bring him early. Morel went down the entry to look for him. Then he came back.

"Goodness, man!" she said. "You're like an ill-sitting hen."

"Hadna you better be gettin' him summat t' eat ready?" asked the father.

"There's plenty of time," she answered.

"There's not so much as I can see on," he answered, turning crossly in his chair. She began to clear her table. The kettle was singing. They waited and waited.

Meantime the three children were on the platform at Sethley Bridge, on the Midland main line, two miles from home. They waited one hour. A train came—he was not there. Down the line the red and green lights shone. It was very dark and very cold.

"Ask him if the London train's come," said Paul to Annie, when they saw a man in a tip cap.

"I'm not," said Annie. "You be quiet—he might send us off."

But Paul was dying for the man to know they were expecting someone by the London train: it sounded so grand. Yet he was much too much scared of broaching any man, let alone one in a peaked cap, to dare to ask. The three children could scarcely go into the waiting-room for fear of being sent away, and for fear something should happen whilst they were off the platform. Still they waited in the dark and cold.

"It's an hour an' a half late," said Arthur pathetically.

"Well," said Annie, "it's Christmas Eve."

They all grew silent. He wasn't coming. They looked down the darkness of the railway. There was London! It seemed the uttermost of distance. They thought anything might happen if one came from London. They were all too troubled to talk. Cold, and unhappy, and silent, they huddled together on the platform.

At last, after more than two hours, they saw the lights of an engine peering round, away down the darkness. A porter ran out. The children drew back with beating hearts. A great train, bound for Manchester, drew up. Two doors opened, and from one of them, William. They flew to him. He handed parcels to them cheerily, and immediately began to explain that this great train had stopped for *his* sake at such a small station as Sethley Bridge: it was not booked to stop.

Meanwhile the parents were getting anxious. The table was set, the chop was cooked, everything was ready. Mrs. Morel put on her black apron. She was wearing her best dress. Then she sat, pretending to read. The minutes were a torture to her.

"H'm!" said Morel. "It's an hour an' a ha'ef."

"And those children waiting!" she said.

"Th' train canna ha' come in yet," he said.

"I tell you, on Christmas Eve they're *hours* wrong."

They were both a bit cross with each other, so gnawed with anxiety. The ash tree moaned outside in a cold, raw wind. And all that space of night from London home! Mrs. Morel suffered. The slight click of the works inside the clock irritated her. It was getting so late; it was getting unbearable.

At last there was a sound of voices, and a footstep in the entry.

"Ha's here!" cried Morel, jumping up.

Then he stood back. The mother ran a few steps towards the door and waited. There was a rush and a patter of feet, the door burst open. William was there. He dropped his Gladstone bag and took his mother in his arms.

"Mater!" he said.

"My boy!" she cried.

And for two seconds, no longer, she clasped him and kissed him. Then she withdrew and said, trying to be quite normal:

"But how late you are!"

"Aren't I!" he cried, turning to his father. "Well, dad!"

The two men shook hands.

"Well, my lad!"

Morel's eyes were wet.

"We thought tha'd niver be commin'," he said.

"Oh, I'd come!" exclaimed William.

Then the son turned round to his mother.

"But you look well," she said proudly, laughing.

"Well!" he exclaimed. "I should think so—coming home!"

He was a fine fellow, big, straight, and fearless-looking. He looked round at the evergreens and the kissing bunch, and the little tarts that lay in their tins on the hearth.

"By jove! mother, it's not different!" he said, as if in relief.

Everybody was still for a second. Then he suddenly sprang forward, picked a tart from the hearth, and pushed it whole into his mouth.

"Well, did iver you see such a parish oven!" the father exclaimed.

He had brought them endless presents. Every penny he had he had spent on them. There was a sense of luxury overflowing in the house. For his mother there was an umbrella with gold on the pale handle. She kept it to her dying day, and would have lost anything rather than that. Everybody had something gorgeous, and besides, there were pounds of unknown sweets: Turkish delight, crystallised pineapple, and such-like things which, the children thought, only the splendour of London could provide. And Paul boasted of these sweets among his friends.

"Real pineapple, cut off in slices, and then turned into crystal—fair grand!"

Everybody was mad with happiness in the family. Home was home, and they loved it with a passion of love, whatever the suffering had been. There were parties, there were rejoicings. People came in to see William, to see what difference London had made to him. And they all found him "such a gentleman, and *such* a fine fellow, my word"!

When he went away again the children retired to various places to weep alone. Morel went to bed in misery, and Mrs. Morel felt as if she were numbed by some drug, as if her feelings were paralysed. She loved him passionately.

He was in the office of a lawyer connected with a large shipping firm, and at the midsummer his chief offered him a trip in the Mediterranean on one of the boats, for quite a small cost. Mrs. Morel wrote: "Go, go, my boy. You may never have a chance again, and I should love to think of you cruising there in the Mediterranean almost better than to have you at home." But William came home for his fortnight's holiday. Not even the Mediterranean, which pulled at all his young man's desire to travel, and at his poor man's wonder at the glamorous south, could take him away when he might come home. That compensated his mother for much.

V

PAUL LAUNCHES INTO LIFE

Morel was rather a heedless man, careless of danger. So he had endless accidents. Now, when Mrs. Morel heard the rattle of an empty coal-cart cease at her entry-end, she ran into the parlour to look, expecting almost to see her husband seated in the wagon, his face grey under his dirt, his body limp and sick with some hurt or other. If it were he, she would run out to help.

About a year after William went to London, and just after Paul had left school, before he got work, Mrs. Morel was upstairs and her son was painting in the kitchen—he was very clever with his brush—when there came a knock at the door. Crossly he put down his brush to go. At the same moment his mother opened a window upstairs and looked down.

A pit-lad in his dirt stood on the threshold.

"Is this Walter Morel's?" he asked.

"Yes," said Mrs. Morel. "What is it?"

But she had guessed already.

"Your mester's got hurt," he said.

"Eh, dear me!" she exclaimed. "It's a wonder if he hadn't, lad. And what's he done this time?"

"I don't know for sure, but it's 'is leg somewhere. They ta'ein' 'im ter th' 'ospital."

"Good gracious me!" she exclaimed. "Eh, dear, what a one he is! There's not five minutes of peace, I'll be hanged if there is! His thumb's nearly better, and now—— Did you see him?"

"I seed him at th' bottom. An' I seed 'em bring 'im up in a tub, an' 'e wor in a dead faint. But he shouted like anythink when Doctor Fraser examined him i' th' lamp cabin—an' cossed an' swore, an' said as 'e wor goin' to be ta'en whoam—'e worn't goin' ter th' 'ospital."

The boy faltered to an end.

"He *would* want to come home, so that I can have all the bother. Thank you, my lad. Eh, dear, if I'm not sick—sick and surfeited, I am!"

She came downstairs. Paul had mechanically resumed his painting.

"And it must be pretty bad if they've taken him to the hospital," she went on. "But what a *careless* creature he is! *Other* men don't have all these accidents. Yes, he *would* want to put all the burden on me. Eh, dear, just as we *were* getting easy a bit at last. Put those things away, there's no time to be painting now. What time is there a train? I know I s'll have to go trailing to Keston. I s'll have to leave that bedroom."

"I can finish it," said Paul.

"You needn't. I shall catch the seven o'clock back, I should think. Oh, my blessed heart, the fuss and commotion he'll make! And those granite setts at Tinder Hill—he might well call them kidney pebbles—they'll jolt him almost to bits. I wonder why they can't mend them, the state they're in, an' all the men as go across in that ambulance. You'd think they'd have a hospital here. The men bought the ground, and, my sirs, there'd be accidents enough to keep it going. But no, they must trail them ten miles in a slow ambulance to Notting-ham. It's a crying shame! Oh, and the fuss he'll make! I know he will! I wonder who's with him. Barker, I s'd think. Poor beggar, he'll wish himself anywhere rather. But he'll look after him, I know. Now there's no telling how long he'll be stuck in that hospital—and *won't* he hate it! But if it's only his leg it's not so bad."

All the time she was getting ready. Hurriedly taking off her bodice, she crouched at the boiler while the water ran slowly into her lading-can.

"I wish this boiler was at the bottom of the sea!" she exclaimed, wriggling the handle impatiently. She had very handsome, strong arms, rather surprising on a smallish woman.

Paul cleared away, put on the kettle, and set the table.

"There isn't a train till four-twenty," he said. "You've time enough."

"Oh no, I haven't!" she cried, blinking at him over the towel as she wiped her face.

"Yes, you have. You must drink a cup of tea at any rate. Should I come with you to Keston?"

"Come with me? What for, I should like to know? Now, what have I to take him? Eh, dear! His clean shirt—and it's a blessing it *is* clean. But it had better be aired. And stockings—he won't want them—and a towel, I suppose; and handkerchiefs. Now what else?"

"A comb, a knife and fork and spoon," said Paul. His father had been in the hospital before.

"Goodness knows what sort of state his feet were in," continued Mrs. Morel, as she combed her long brown hair, that was fine as silk, and was touched now with grey. "He's very particular to wash himself to the waist, but below he thinks doesn't matter. But there, I suppose they see plenty like it."

Paul had laid the table. He cut his mother one or two pieces of very thin bread and butter.

"Here you are," he said, putting her cup of tea in her place.

"I can't be bothered!" she exclaimed crossly.

"Well, you've got to, so there, now it's put out ready," he insisted.

So she sat down and sipped her tea, and ate a little, in silence. She was thinking.

In a few minutes she was gone, to walk the two and a half miles to Keston Station. All the things she was taking him she had in her bulging string bag. Paul watched her go up the road between the hedges—a little, quick-stepping figure, and his heart ached for her, that she was thrust forward again into pain and trouble. And she, tripping so quickly in her anxiety, felt at the back of her her son's heart waiting on her, felt him bearing what part of the burden he could, even supporting her. And when she was at the hospital, she thought: "It *will* upset that lad when I tell him how bad it is. I'd better be careful." And when she was trudging home again, she felt he was coming to share her burden.

"Is it bad?" asked Paul, as soon as she entered the house.

"It's bad enough," she replied.

"What?"

She sighed and sat down, undoing her bonnet-strings. Her son watched her face as it was lifted, and her small, work-hardened hands fingering at the bow under her chin.

"Well," she answered, "it's not really dangerous, but the nurse says it's a dreadful smash. You see, a great piece of rock fell on his leg—here—and it's a compound fracture. There are pieces of bone sticking through——"

"Ugh—how horrid!" exclaimed the children.

"And," she continued, "of course he says he's going to die—it wouldn't be him if he didn't. 'I'm done for, my lass!' he said, looking at me. 'Don't be so silly,' I said to him. 'You're not going to die of a broken leg, however badly it's smashed.' 'I s'll niver come out of 'ere but in a wooden box,' he groaned. 'Well,' I said, 'if you want them to carry you into the garden in a wooden box, when you're better, I've no doubt they will.' 'If we think it's good for him,' said the Sister. She's an awfully nice Sister, but rather strict."

Mrs. Morel took off her bonnet. The children waited in silence.

"Of course, he *is* bad," she continued, "and he will be. It's a great shock, and he's lost a lot of blood; and, of course, it *is* a very dangerous smash. It's not at all sure that it will mend so easily. And then there's the fever and the mortification—if it took bad ways he'd quickly be gone. But there, he's a clean-blooded man, with wonderful healing flesh, and so I see no reason why it *should* take bad ways. Of course there's a wound——"

She was pale now with emotion and anxiety. The three children realised that it was very bad for their father, and the house was silent, anxious.

"But he always gets better," said Paul after a while.

"That's what I tell him," said the mother.

Everybody moved about in silence.

"And he really looked nearly done for," she said. "But the Sister says that is the pain."

Annie took away her mother's coat and bonnet.

"And he looked at me when I came away! I said: 'I s'll have to go now, Walter, because of the train—and the children.' And he looked at me. It seems hard."

Paul took up his brush again and went on painting. Arthur went outside for some coal. Annie sat looking dismal. And Mrs. Morel, in her little rocking-chair that her husband had made for her when the first baby was coming, remained motionless, brooding. She was grieved, and bitterly sorry for the man who was hurt so much. But still, in her heart of hearts, where the love should have burned, there was a blank. Now, when all her woman's pity was roused to its full extent, when she would have slaved herself to death to nurse him and to save him, when she would have taken the pain herself, if she could, somewhere far away inside her, she felt indifferent to him and to his suffering. It hurt her most of all, this failure to love him, even when he roused her strong emotions. She brooded a while.

"And there," she said suddenly, "when I'd got half-way to Keston, I found I'd come out in my working boots—and *look* at them." They were an old pair of Paul's, brown and rubbed through at the toes. "I didn't know what to do with myself, for shame," she added.

In the morning, when Annie and Arthur were at school, Mrs. Morel talked again to her son, who was helping her with her housework.

"I found Barker at the hospital. He did look bad, poor little fellow! 'Well,' I said to him, 'what sort of a journey did you have with him?' 'Dunna ax me, missis!' he said. 'Ay,' I said, 'I know what he'd be.' 'But it *wor* bad for him, Mrs. Morel, it *wor* that!' he said. 'I know,' I said. 'At ivry jolt I thought my 'eart would ha' flown clean out o' my mouth,' he said. 'An' the scream 'e gives sometimes! Missis, not for a fortune would I go through wi' it again.' 'I can quite understand it,' I said. 'It's a nasty job, though,' he said, 'an' one as'll be a long while afore it's right again.' 'I'm afraid it will,' I said. I like Mr. Barker—I *do* like him. There's something so manly about him."

Paul resumed his task silently.

"And of course," Mrs. Morel continued, "for a man like your father, the hospital *is* hard. He *can't* understand rules and regulations. And he won't let anybody else touch him, not if he can help it. When he smashed the muscles of his thigh, and it had to be dressed four times a day, *would* he let anybody but me or his mother do it? He wouldn't. So, of course, he'll suffer in there with the nurses. And I didn't like leaving him. I'm sure, when I kissed him an' came away, it seemed a shame."

So she talked to her son, almost as if she were thinking aloud to him, and he took it in as best he could, by sharing her trouble to lighten it. And in the end she shared almost everything with him without knowing.

Morel had a very bad time. For a week he was in a critical condition. Then he began to mend. And then, knowing he was going to get better, the whole family sighed with relief, and proceeded to live happily.

They were not badly off whilst Morel was in the hospital. There were fourteen shillings a week from the pit, ten shillings from the sick club, and five shillings from the Disability Fund; and then every week the butties had something for Mrs. Morel—five or seven shillings—so that she was quite well to do. And whilst Morel was progressing favourably in the hospital, the family was extraordinarily happy and peaceful. On Saturdays and Wednesdays Mrs. Morel went to Nottingham to see her husband. Then she always brought back some little thing: a small tube of paints for Paul, or some thick paper; a couple of postcards for Annie, that the whole family rejoiced over for days before the girl was allowed to send them away; or a fret-saw for Arthur, or a bit of pretty wood. She described her adventures into the big shops with joy. Soon the folk in the picture-shop knew her, and knew about Paul. The girl in the book-shop took a keen interest in her. Mrs. Morel was full of information when she got home from Nottingham. The three sat round till bed-time, listening, putting in, arguing. Then Paul often raked the fire.

"I'm the man in the house now," he used to say to his mother with joy. They learned how perfectly peaceful the home could be. And they almost regretted—though none of them would have owned to such callousness—that their father was soon coming back.

Paul was now fourteen, and was looking for work. He was a rather small and rather finely-made boy, with dark brown hair and light blue eyes. His face had already lost its youthful chubbiness, and was becoming somewhat like William's—rough-featured, almost rugged—and it was extraordinarily mobile. Usually he looked as if he saw things, was full of life, and warm; then his smile, like his mother's, came suddenly and was very lovable; and then, when there was any clog in his soul's quick running, his face went stupid and ugly. He was the sort of boy that becomes a clown and a lout as soon as he is not understood, or feels himself held cheap; and, again, is adorable at the first touch of warmth.

He suffered very much from the first contact with anything. When he was seven, the starting school had been a nightmare and a torture to him. But afterwards he liked it. And now that he felt he had to go out into life, he went through agonies of shrinking self-consciousness. He was quite a clever painter for a boy of his years, and he knew some French and German and mathematics that Mr. Heaton had taught him. But nothing he had was of any commercial value. He was not strong enough for heavy manual work, his mother said. He did not care for making things with his hands, preferred racing about, or making excursions into the country, or reading, or painting.

"What do you want to be?" his mother asked.

"Anything."

"That is no answer," said Mrs. Morel.

But it was quite truthfully the only answer he could give. His ambition, as far as this world's gear went, was quietly to earn his thirty or thirty-five shillings a week somewhere near home, and then, when his father died, have a cottage with his mother, paint and go out as he liked, and live happy ever after. That was his programme as far as doing things went. But he was proud within himself, measuring people against himself, and placing them, inexorably. And he thought that *perhaps* he might also make a painter, the real thing. But that he left alone.

"Then," said his mother, "you must look in the paper for the advertisements."

He looked at her. It seemed to him a bitter humiliation and an anguish to go through. But he said nothing. When he got up in the morning, his whole being was knotted up over this one thought:

"I've got to go and look for advertisements for a job."

It stood in front of the morning, that thought, killing all joy and even life, for him. His heart felt like a tight knot.

And then, at ten o'clock, he set off. He was supposed to be a queer, quiet child. Going up the sunny street of the little town, he felt as if all the folk he met said to themselves: "He's going to the Co-op. reading-room to look in the papers for a place. He can't get a job. I suppose he's living on his mother." Then he crept up the stone stairs behind the drapery shop at the Co-op, and peeped in the reading-room. Usually one or two men were there, either old, useless fellows, or colliers "on the club". So he entered, full of shrinking and suffering when they looked up, seated himself at the table, and pretended to scan the news. He knew they would think: "What does a lad of thirteen want in a reading-room with a newspaper?" and he suffered.

Then he looked wistfully out of the window. Already he was a prisoner of industrialism. Large sunflowers stared over the old red wall of the garden opposite, looking in their jolly way down on the women who were hurrying with something for dinner. The valley was full of corn, brightening in the sun. Two collieries, among the fields, waved their small white plumes of steam. Far off on the hills were the woods of Annesley, dark and fascinating. Already his heart went down. He was being taken into bondage. His freedom in the beloved home valley was going now.

The brewers' waggons came rolling up from Keston with enormous barrels, four a side, like beans in a burst bean-pod. The waggoner, throned aloft, rolling massively in his seat, was not so much below Paul's eye. The man's hair, on his small, bullet head, was bleached almost white by the sun, and on his thick red arms, rocking idly on his sack apron, the white hairs glistened. His red face shone and was almost asleep with sunshine. The horses, handsome and brown, went on by themselves, looking by far the masters of the show.

Paul wished he were stupid. "I wish," he thought to himself, "I was fat like him, and like a dog in the sun. I wish I was a pig and a brewer's waggoner."

Then, the room being at last empty, he would hastily copy an advertisement on a scrap of paper, then another, and slip out in immense relief. His mother would scan over his copies.

"Yes," she said, "you may try."

William had written out a letter of application, couched in admirable busi-

ness language, which Paul copied, with variations. The boy's handwriting was
execrable, so that William, who did all things well, got into a fever of impatience.

The elder brother was becoming quite swanky. In London he found that he
could associate with men far above his Bestwood friends in station. Some of the
clerks in the office had studied for the law, and were more or less going through
a kind of apprenticeship. William always made friends among men wherever he
went, he was so jolly. Therefore he was soon visiting and staying in houses of
men who, in Bestwood, would have looked down on the unapproachable bank
manager, and would merely have called indifferently on the Rector. So he
began to fancy himself as a great gun. He was, indeed, rather surprised at the ease
with which he became a gentleman.

His mother was glad, he seemed so pleased. And his lodging in Walthamstow
was so dreary. But now there seemed to come a kind of fever into the young
man's letters. He was unsettled by all the change, he did not stand firm on his
own feet, but seemed to spin rather giddily on the quick current of the new life.
His mother was anxious for him. She could feel him losing himself. He had
danced and gone to the theatre, boated on the river, been out with friends; and
she knew he sat up afterwards in his cold bedroom grinding away at Latin,
because he intended to get on in his office, and in the law as much as he could.
He never sent his mother any money now. It was all taken, the little he had, for
his own life. And she did not want any, except sometimes, when she was in a
tight corner, and when ten shillings would have saved her much worry. She still
dreamed of William, and of what he would do, with herself behind him. Never
for a minute would she admit to herself how heavy and anxious her heart was
because of him.

Also he talked a good deal now of a girl he had met at a dance, a handsome
brunette, quite young, and a lady, after whom the men were running thick and
fast.

"I wonder if you would run, my boy," his mother wrote to him, "unless you
saw all the other men chasing her too. You feel safe enough and vain enough in
a crowd. But take care, and see how you feel when you find yourself alone, and
in triumph."

William resented these things, and continued the chase. He had taken the
girl on the river. "If you saw her, mother, you would know how I feel. Tall and
elegant, with the clearest of clear, transparent olive complexions, hair as black as
jet, and such grey eyes—bright, mocking, like lights on water at night. It is all
very well to be a bit satirical till you see her. And she dresses as well as any
woman in London. I tell you, your son doesn't half put his head up when she
goes walking down Piccadilly with him."

Mrs. Morel wondered, in her heart, if her son did not go walking down
Piccadilly with an elegant figure and fine clothes, rather than with a woman
who was near to him. But she congratulated him in her doubtful fashion. And,
as she stood over the washing-tub, the mother brooded over her son. She saw
him saddled with an elegant and expensive wife, earning little money, dragging
along and getting draggled in some small, ugly house in a suburb. "But there,"
she told herself, "I am very likely a silly—meeting trouble half-way." Nevertheless, the load of anxiety scarcely ever left her heart, lest William should do the
wrong thing by himself.

Presently, Paul was bidden call upon Thomas Jordan, Manufacturer of Surgical Appliances, at 21, Spaniel Row, Nottingham. Mrs. Morel was all joy.

"There, you see!" she cried, her eyes shining. "You've only written four letters, and the third is answered. You're lucky, my boy, as I always said you were."

Paul looked at the picture of a wooden leg, adorned with elastic stockings and other appliances, that figured on Mr. Jordan's notepaper, and he felt alarmed. He had not known that elastic stockings existed. And he seemed to feel the business world, with its regulated system of values, and its impersonality, and he dreaded it. It seemed monstrous also that a business could be run on wooden legs.

Mother and son set off together one Tuesday morning. It was August and blazing hot. Paul walked with something screwed up tight inside him. He would have suffered much physical pain rather than this unreasonable suffering at being exposed to strangers, to be accepted or rejected. Yet he chattered away with his mother. He would never have confessed to her how he suffered over these things, and she only partly guessed. She was gay, like a sweetheart. She stood in front of the ticket-office at Bestwood, and Paul watched her take from her purse the money for the tickets. As he saw her hands in their old black kid gloves getting the silver out of the worn purse, his heart contracted with pain of love of her.

She was quite excited, and quite gay. He suffered because she *would* talk aloud in presence of the other travellers.

"Now look at that silly cow!" she said, "careering round as if it thought it was a circus."

"It's most likely a bottfly," he said very low.

"A what?" she asked brightly and unashamed.

They thought a while. He was sensible all the time of having her opposite him. Suddenly their eyes met, and she smiled to him—a rare, intimate smile, beautiful with brightness and love. Then each looked out of the window.

The sixteen slow miles of railway journey passed. The mother and son walked down Station Street, feeling the excitement of lovers having an adventure together. In Carrington Street they stopped to hang over the parapet and look at the barges on the canal below.

"It's just like Venice," he said, seeing the sunshine on the water that lay between high factory walls.

"Perhaps," she answered, smiling.

They enjoyed the shops immensely.

"Now you see that blouse," she would say, "wouldn't that just suit our Annie? And for one-and-eleven-three. Isn't that cheap?"

"And made of needlework as well," he said.

"Yes."

They had plenty of time, so they did not hurry. The town was strange and delightful to them. But the boy was tied up inside in a knot of apprehension. He dreaded the interview with Thomas Jordan.

It was nearly eleven o'clock by St. Peter's Church. They turned up a narrow street that led to the Castle. It was gloomy and old-fashioned, having low dark shops and dark green house doors with brass knockers, and yellow-ochred doorsteps projecting on to the pavement; then another old shop whose small window looked like a cunning, half-shut eye. Mother and son went cautiously, looking everywhere for "Thomas Jordan and Son". It was like hunting in some wild place. They were on tiptoe of excitement.

Suddenly they spied a big, dark archway, in which were names of various firms, Thomas Jordan among them.

"Here it is!" said Mrs. Morel. "But now *where* is it?"

They looked round. On one side was a queer, dark, cardboard factory, on the other a Commercial Hotel.

"It's up the entry," said Paul.

And they ventured under the archway, as into the jaws of the dragon. They emerged into a wide yard, like a well, with buildings all round. It was littered with straw and boxes, and cardboard. The sunshine actually caught one crate whose straw was streaming on to the yard like gold. But elsewhere the place was like a pit. There were several doors, and two flights of steps. Straight in front, on a dirty glass door at the top of a staircase, loomed the ominous words "Thomas Jordan and Son—Surgical Appliances." Mrs. Morel went first, her son followed her. Charles I mounted his scaffold with a lighter heart than had Paul Morel as he followed his mother up the dirty steps to the dirty door.

She pushed open the door, and stood in pleased surprise. In front of her was a big warehouse, with creamy paper parcels everywhere, and clerks, with their shirt-sleeves rolled back, were going about in an at-home sort of way. The light was subdued, the glossy cream parcels seemed luminous, the counters were of dark brown wood. All was quiet and very homely. Mrs. Morel took two steps forward, then waited. Paul stood behind her. She had on her Sunday bonnet and a black veil; he wore a boy's broad white collar and a Norfolk suit.

One of the clerks looked up. He was thin and tall, with a small face. His way of looking was alert. Then he glanced round to the other end of the room, where was a glass office. And then he came forward. He did not say anything, but leaned in a gentle, inquiring fashion towards Mrs. Morel.

"Can I see Mr. Jordan?" she asked.

"I'll fetch him," answered the young man.

He went down to the glass office. A red-faced, white-whiskered old man looked up. He reminded Paul of a pomeranian dog. Then the same little man came up the room. He had short legs, was rather stout, and wore an alpaca jacket. So, with one ear up, as it were, he came stoutly and inquiringly down the room.

"Good-morning!" he said, hesitating before Mrs. Morel, in doubt as to whether she were a customer or not.

"Good-morning. I came with my son, Paul Morel. You asked him to call this morning."

"Come this way," said Mr. Jordan, in a rather snappy little manner intended to be business-like.

They followed the manufacturer into a grubby little room, upholstered in black American leather, glossy with the rubbing of many customers. On the table was a pile of trusses, yellow wash-leather hoops tangled together. They looked new and living. Paul sniffed the odour of new wash-leather. He wondered what the things were. By this time he was so much stunned that he only noticed the outside things.

"Sit down!" said Mr. Jordan, irritably pointing Mrs. Morel to a horse-hair chair. She sat on the edge in an uncertain fashion. Then the little old man fidgeted and found a paper.

"Did you write this letter?" he snapped, thrusting what Paul recognised as his own notepaper in front of him.

"Yes," he answered.

At that moment he was occupied in two ways: first, in feeling guilty for telling a lie, since William had composed the letter; second, in wondering why his letter seemed so strange and different, in the fat, red hand of the man, from what it had been when it lay on the kitchen table. It was like part of himself, gone astray. He resented the way the man held it.

"Where did you learn to write?" said the old man crossly.

Paul merely looked at him shamedly, and did not answer.

"He *is* a bad writer," put in Mrs. Morel apologetically. Then she pushed up her veil. Paul hated her for not being prouder with this common little man, and he loved her face clear of the veil.

"And you say you know French?" inquired the little man, still sharply.

"Yes," said Paul.

"What school did you go to?"

"The Board-school."

"And did you learn it there?"

"No—I——" The boy went crimson and got no farther.

"His godfather gave him lessons," said Mrs. Morel, half pleading and rather distant.

Mr. Jordan hesitated. Then, in his irritable manner—he always seemed to keep his hands ready for action—he pulled another sheet of paper from his pocket, unfolded it. The paper made a crackling noise. He handed it to Paul.

"Read that," he said.

It was a note in French, in thin, flimsy foreign handwriting that the boy could not decipher. He stared blankly at the paper.

" 'Monsieur,' " he began; then he looked in great confusion at Mr. Jordan. "It's the—it's the——"

He wanted to say "handwriting", but his wits would no longer work even sufficiently to supply him with the word. Feeling an utter fool, and hating Mr. Jordan, he turned desperately to the paper again.

" 'Sir,—Please send me'—er—er—I can't tell the—er—'two pairs—*gris fil bas*—grey thread stockings'—er—er—'*sans*—without'—er—I can't tell the words—er—'*doigts*—fingers'—er—I can't tell the——"

He wanted to say "handwriting", but the word still refused to come. Seeing him stuck, Mr. Jordan snatched the paper from him.

" 'Please send by return two pairs grey thread stockings without *toes.* ' "

"Well," flashed Paul, " '*doigts*' means 'fingers'—as well—as a rule——"

The little man looked at him. He did not know whether "*doigts*" meant "fingers"; he knew that for all *his* purposes it meant "toes".

"Fingers to stockings!" he snapped.

"Well, it *does* mean fingers," the boy persisted.

He hated the little man, who made such a clod of him. Mr. Jordan looked at the pale, stupid, defiant boy, then at the mother, who sat quiet and with that peculiar shut-off look of the poor who have to depend on the favour of others.

"And when could he come?" he asked.

"Well," said Mrs. Morel, "as soon as you wish. He has finished school now."

"He would live in Bestwood?"

"Yes; but he could be in—at the station—at quarter to eight."

"H'm!"

It ended by Paul's being engaged as junior spiral clerk at eight shillings a week. The boy did not open his mouth to say another word, after having insisted that "*doigts*" meant "fingers". He followed his mother down the stairs. She looked at him with her bright blue eyes full of love and joy.

"I think you'll like it," she said.

" *'Doigts'* does mean 'fingers', mother, and it was the writing. I couldn't read the writing."

"Never mind, my boy. I'm sure he'll be all right, and you won't see much of him. Wasn't that first young fellow nice? I'm sure you'll like them."

"But wasn't Mr. Jordan common, mother? Does he own it all?"

"I suppose he was a workman who has got on," she said. "You mustn't mind people so much. They're not being disagreeable to *you*—it's their way. You always think people are meaning things for you. But they don't."

It was very sunny. Over the big desolate space of the market-place the blue sky shimmered, and the granite cobbles of the paving glistened. Shops down the Long Row were deep in obscurity, and the shadow was full of colour. Just where the horse trams trundled across the market was a row of fruit stalls, with fruit blazing in the sun—apples and piles of reddish oranges, small greengage plums and bananas. There was a warm scent of fruit as mother and son passed. Gradually his feeling of ignominy and of rage sank.

"Where should we go for dinner?" asked the mother.

It was felt to be a reckless extravagance. Paul had only been in an eating-house once or twice in his life, and then only to have a cup of tea and a bun. Most of the people of Bestwood considered that tea and bread-and-butter, and perhaps potted beef, was all they could afford to eat in Nottingham. Real cooked dinner was considered great extravagance. Paul felt rather guilty.

They found a place that looked quite cheap. But when Mrs. Morel scanned the bill of fare, her heart was heavy, things were so dear. So she ordered kidney-pies and potatoes as the cheapest available dish.

"We oughtn't to have come here, mother," said Paul.

"Never mind," she said. "We won't come again."

She insisted on his having a small currant tart, because he liked sweets.

"I don't want it, mother," he pleaded.

"Yes," she insisted; "you'll have it."

And she looked round for the waitress. But the waitress was busy, and Mrs. Morel did not like to bother her then. So the mother and son waited for the girl's pleasure, whilst she flirted among the men.

"Brazen hussy!" said Mrs. Morel to Paul. "Look now, she's taking that man *his* pudding, and he came long after us."

"It doesn't matter, mother," said Paul.

Mrs. Morel was angry. But she was too poor, and her orders were too meagre, so that she had not the courage to insist on her rights just then. They waited and waited.

"Should we go, mother?" he said.

Then Mrs. Morel stood up. The girl was passing near.

"Will you bring one currant tart?" said Mrs. Morel clearly.

The girl looked round insolently.

"Directly," she said.

"We have waited quite long enough," said Mrs. Morel.

In a moment the girl came back with the tart. Mrs. Morel asked coldly for the bill. Paul wanted to sink through the floor. He marvelled at his mother's hardness. He knew that only years of battling had taught her to insist even so little on her rights. She shrank as much as he.

"It's the last time I go *there* for anything!" she declared, when they were outside the place, thankful to be clear.

"We'll go," she said, "and look at Keep's and Boot's, and one or two places, shall we?"

They had discussions over the pictures, and Mrs. Morel wanted to buy him a little sable brush that he hankered after. But this indulgence he refused. He stood in front of milliners' shops and drapers' shops almost bored, but content for her to be interested. They wandered on.

"Now, just look at those black grapes!" she said. "They make your mouth water. I've wanted some of those for years, but I s'll have to wait a bit before I get them."

Then she rejoiced in the florists, standing in the doorway sniffing.

"Oh! oh! Isn't it simply lovely!"

Paul saw, in the darkness of the shop, an elegant young lady in black peering over the counter curiously.

"They're looking at you," he said, trying to draw his mother away.

"But what is it?" she exclaimed, refusing to be moved.

"Stocks!" he answered, sniffing hastily. "Look, there's a tubful."

"So there is—red and white. But really, I never knew stocks to smell like it!" And, to his great relief, she moved out of the doorway, but only to stand in front of the window.

"Paul!" she cried to him, who was trying to get out of sight of the elegant young lady in black—the shop-girl. "Paul! Just look here!"

He came reluctantly back.

"Now, just look at that fuchsia!" she exclaimed, pointing.

"H'm!" He made a curious, interested sound. "You'd think every second as the flowers was going to fall off, they hang so big an' heavy."

"And such an abundance!" she cried.

"And the way they drop downwards with their threads and knots!"

"Yes!" she exclaimed. "Lovely!"

"I wonder who'll buy it!" he said.

"I wonder!" she answered. "Not us."

"It would die in our parlour."

"Yes, beastly cold, sunless hole; it kills every bit of a plant you put in, and the kitchen chokes them to death."

They bought a few things, and set off towards the station. Looking up the canal, through the dark pass of the buildings, they saw the Castle on its bluff of brown, green-bushed rock, in a positive miracle of delicate sunshine.

"Won't it be nice for me to come out at dinner-times?" said Paul. "I can go all round here and see everything. I s'll love it."

"You will," assented his mother.

He had spent a perfect afternoon with his mother. They arrived home in the mellow evening, happy, and glowing, and tired.

In the morning he filled in the form for his season-ticket and took it to the station. When he got back, his mother was just beginning to wash the floor. He sat crouched up on the sofa.

"He says it'll be here on Saturday," he said.

"And how much will it be?"

"About one pound eleven," he said.

She went on washing her floor in silence.

"Is it a lot?" he asked.

"It's no more than I thought," she answered.

"An' I s'll earn eight shillings a week," he said.

She did not answer, but went on with her work. At last she said:

"That William promised me, when he went to London, as he'd give me a pound a month. He has given me ten shillings—twice; and now I know he hasn't a farthing if I asked him. Not that I want it. Only just now you'd think he might be able to help with this ticket, which I'd never expected."

"He earns a lot," said Paul.

"He earns a hundred and thirty pounds. But they're all alike. They're large in promises, but it's precious little fulfilment you get."

"He spends over fifty shillings a week on himself," said Paul.

"And I keep this house on less than thirty," she replied; "and am supposed to find money for extras. But they don't care about helping you, once they've gone. He'd rather spend it on that dressed-up creature."

"She should have her own money if she's so grand," said Paul.

"She should, but she hasn't. I asked him. And I know he doesn't buy her a gold bangle for nothing. I wonder whoever bought me a gold bangle."

William was succeeding with his "Gipsy", as he called her. He asked the girl—her name was Louisa Lily Denys Western—for a photograph to send to his mother. The photo came—a handsome brunette, taken in profile, smirking slightly—and, it might be, quite naked, for on the photograph not a scrap of clothing was to be seen, only a naked bust.

"Yes," wrote Mrs. Morel to her son, "the photograph of Louie is very striking, and I can see she must be attractive. But do you think, my boy, it was very good taste of a girl to give her young man that photo to send to his mother—the first? Certainly the shoulders are beautiful, as you say. But I hardly expected to see so much of them at the first view."

Morel found the photograph standing on the chiffonier in the parlour. He came out with it between his thick thumb and finger.

"Who dost reckon this is?" he asked of his wife.

"It's the girl our William is going with," replied Mrs. Morel.

"H'm! 'Er's a bright spark, from th' look on 'er, an' one as wunna do him owermuch good neither. Who is she?"

"Her name is Louisa Lily Denys Western."

"An' come again to-morrer!" exclaimed the miner. "An' is 'er an actress?"

"She is not. She's supposed to be a lady."

"I'll bet!" he exclaimed, still staring at the photo. "A lady, is she? An' how much does she reckon ter keep up this sort o' game on?"

"On nothing. She lives with an old aunt, whom she hates, and takes what bit of money's given her."

"H'm!" said Morel, laying down the photograph. "Then he's a fool to ha' ta'en up wi' such a one as that."

"Dear Mater," William replied. "I'm sorry you didn't like the photograph. It never occurred to me when I sent it, that you mightn't think it decent. However, I told Gyp that it didn't quite suit your prim and proper notions, so she's going to send you another, that I hope will please you better. She's always being photographed; in fact, the photographers ask her if they may take her for nothing."

Presently the new photograph came, with a little silly note from the girl. This time the young lady was seen in a black satin evening bodice, cut square, with little puff sleeves, and black lace hanging down her beautiful arms.

"I wonder if she ever wears anything except evening clothes," said Mrs. Morel sarcastically. "I'm sure I ought to be impressed."

"You are disagreeable, mother," said Paul. "I think the first one with bare shoulders is lovely."

"Do you?" answered his mother. "Well, I don't."

On the Monday morning the boy got up at six to start work. He had the season-ticket, which had cost such bitterness, in his waistcoat pocket. He loved it with its bars of yellow across. His mother packed his dinner in a small, shut-up basket, and he set off at a quarter to seven to catch the 7.15 train. Mrs. Morel came to the entry-end to see him off.

It was a perfect morning. From the ash tree the slender green fruits that the children call "pigeons" were twinkling gaily down on a little breeze, into the front gardens of the houses. The valley was full of a lustrous dark haze, through which the ripe corn shimmered, and in which the steam from Minton pit melted swiftly. Puffs of wind came. Paul looked over the high woods of Aldersley, where the country gleamed, and home had never pulled at him so powerfully.

"Good-morning, mother," he said, smiling, but feeling very unhappy.

"Good-morning," she replied cheerfully and tenderly.

She stood in her white apron on the open road, watching him as he crossed the field. He had a small, compact body that looked full of life. She felt, as she saw him trudging over the field, that where he determined to go he would get. She thought of William. He would have leaped the fence instead of going round the stile. He was away in London, doing well. Paul would be working in Nottingham. Now she had two sons in the world. She could think of two places, great centres of industry, and feel that she had put a man into each of them, that these men would work out what *she* wanted; they were derived from her, they were of her, and their works also would be hers. All the morning long she thought of Paul.

At eight o'clock he climbed the dismal stairs of Jordan's Surgical Appliance Factory, and stood helplessly against the first great parcel-rack, waiting for somebody to pick him up. The place was still not awake. Over the counters were great dust sheets. Two men only had arrived, and were heard talking in a corner, as they took off their coats and rolled up their shirt-sleeves. It was ten past eight. Evidently there was no rush or punctuality. Paul listened to the voices of the two clerks. Then he heard someone cough, and saw in the office at the end of the room an old, decaying clerk, in a round smoking-cap of black velvet embroidered with red and green, opening letters. He waited and waited. One of the junior clerks went to the old man, greeted him cheerily and loudly. Evidently the old "chief" was deaf. Then the young fellow came striding importantly down to his counter. He spied Paul.

"Hello!" he said. "You the new lad?"

"Yes," said Paul.

"H'm! What's your name?"

"Paul Morel."

"Paul Morel? All right, you come on round here."

Paul followed him round the rectangle of counters. The room was second storey. It had a great hole in the middle of the floor, fenced as with a wall of counters, and down this wide shaft the lifts went, and the light for the bottom storey. Also there was a corresponding big, oblong hole in the ceiling, and one could see above, over the fence of the top floor, some machinery; and right away overhead was the glass roof, and all light for the three storeys came downwards, getting dimmer, so that it was always night on the ground floor and rather gloomy on the second floor. The factory was the top floor, the warehouse the second, the storehouse the ground floor. It was an insanitary, ancient place.

Paul was led round to a very dark corner.

"This is the 'Spiral' corner," said the clerk. "You're Spiral, with Papple-worth. He's your boss, but he's not come yet. He doesn't get here till half-past eight. So you can fetch the letters, if you like, from Mr. Melling down there."

The young man pointed to the old clerk in the office.

"All right," said Paul.

"Here's a peg to hang your cap on. Here are your entry ledgers. Mr. Papple-worth won't be long."

And the thin young man stalked away with long, busy strides over the hollow wooden floor.

After a minute or two Paul went down and stood in the door of the glass office. The old clerk in the smoking-cap looked down over the rim of his spectacles.

"Good-morning," he said, kindly and impressively. "You want the letters for the Spiral department, Thomas?"

Paul resented being called "Thomas". But he took the letters and returned to his dark place, where the counter made an angle, where the great parcel-rack came to an end, and where there were three doors in the corner. He sat on a high stool and read the letters—those whose handwriting was not too difficult. They ran as follows:

"Will you please send me at once a pair of lady's silk spiral thigh-hose, with-out feet, such as I had from you last year; length, thigh to knee, etc." Or, "Major Chamberlain wishes to repeat his previous order for a silk non-elastic suspensory bandage."

Many of these letters, some of them in French or Norwegian, were a great puzzle to the boy. He sat on his stool nervously awaiting the arrival of his "boss". He suffered tortures of shyness when, at half-past eight, the factory girls for upstairs trooped past him.

Mr. Pappleworth arrived, chewing a chlorodyne gum, at about twenty to nine, when all the other men were at work. He was a thin, sallow man with a red nose, quick, staccato, and smartly but stiffly dressed. He was about thirty-six years old. There was something rather "doggy", rather smart, rather 'cute and shrewd, and something warm, and something slightly contemptible about him.

"You my new lad?" he said.

Paul stood up and said he was.

"Fetched the letters?"

Mr. Pappleworth gave a chew to his gum.

"Yes."

"Copied 'em?"

"No."

"Well, come on then, let's look slippy. Changed your coat?"

"No."

"You want to bring an old coat and leave it here." He pronounced the last words with the chlorodyne gum between his side teeth. He vanished into the darkness behind the great parcel-rack, reappeared coatless, turning up a smart striped shirt-cuff over a thin and hairy arm. Then he slipped into his coat. Paul noticed how thin he was, and that his trousers were in folds behind. He seized a stool, dragged it beside the boy's, and sat down.

"Sit down," he said.

Paul took a seat.

Mr. Pappleworth was very close to him. The man seized the letters, snatched

a long entry-book out of a rack in front of him, flung it open, seized a pen, and
said:

"Now look here. You want to copy these letters in here." He sniffed twice,
gave a quick chew at his gum, stared fixedly at a letter, then went very still and
absorbed, and wrote the entry rapidly, in a beautiful flourishing hand. He
glanced quickly at Paul.

"See that?"

"Yes."

"Think you can do it all right?"

"Yes."

"All right then, let's see you."

He sprang off his stool. Paul took a pen. Mr. Pappleworth disappeared. Paul
rather liked copying the letters, but he wrote slowly, laboriously, and exceedingly badly. He was doing the fourth letter, and feeling quite busy and happy,
when Mr Pappleworth reappeared.

"Now then, how'r' yer getting on? Done 'em?"

He leaned over the boy's shoulder, chewing, and smelling of chlorodyne.

"Strike my bob, lad, but you're a beautiful writer!" he exclaimed satirically.
"Ne'er mind, how many h'yer done? Only three! I'd 'a eaten 'em. Get on, my
lad, an' put numbers on 'em. Here, look! Get on!"

Paul ground away at the letters, whilst Mr. Pappleworth fussed over various
jobs. Suddenly the boy started as a shrill whistle sounded near his ear. Mr.
Pappleworth came, took a plug out of a pipe, and said, in an amazingly cross and
bossy voice:

"Yes?"

Paul heard a faint voice, like a woman's, out of the mouth of the tube. He
gazed in wonder, never having seen a speaking-tube before.

"Well," said Mr. Pappleworth disagreeably into the tube, "you'd better get
some of your back work done, then."

Again the woman's tiny voice was heard, sounding pretty and cross.

"I've not time to stand here while you talk," said Mr. Pappleworth, and he
pushed the plug into the tube.

"Come, my lad," he said imploringly to Paul, "there's Polly crying out for
them orders. Can't you buck up a bit? Here, come out!"

He took the book, to Paul's immense chagrin, and began the copying himself. He worked quickly and well. This done, he seized some strips of long
yellow paper, about three inches wide, and made out the day's orders for the
work-girls.

"You'd better watch me," he said to Paul, working all the while rapidly.
Paul watched the weird little drawings of legs, and thighs, and ankles, with the
strokes across and the numbers, and the few brief directions which his chief
made upon the yellow paper. Then Mr. Pappleworth finished and jumped up.

"Come on with me," he said, and the yellow papers flying in his hands, he
dashed through a door and down some stairs, into the basement where the gas
was burning. They crossed the cold, damp storeroom, then a long, dreary room
with a long table on trestles, into a smaller, cosy apartment, not very high,
which had been built on to the main building. In this room a small woman with
a red serge blouse, and her black hair done on top of her head, was waiting like
a proud little bantam.

"Here y'are!" said Pappleworth.

"I think it is 'here you are'!" exclaimed Polly. "The girls have been here nearly half an hour waiting. Just think of the time wasted!"

"*You* think of getting your work done and not talking so much," said Mr. Pappleworth. "You could ha' been finishing off."

"You know quite well we finished everything off on Saturday!" cried Polly, flying at him, her dark eyes flashing.

"Tu–tu–tu–tu–terterter!" he mocked. "Here's your new lad. Don't ruin him as you did the last."

"As we did the last!" repeated Polly. "Yes, *we* do a lot of ruining, we do. My word, a lad would *take* some ruining after he'd been with you."

"It's time for work now, not for talk," said Mr. Pappleworth severely and coldly.

"It was time for work some time back," said Polly, marching away with her head in the air. She was an erect little body of forty.

In that room were two round spiral machines on the bench under the window. Through the inner doorway was another longer room, with six more machines. A little group of girls, nicely dressed in white aprons, stood talking together.

"Have you nothing else to do but talk?" said Mr. Pappleworth.

"Only wait for you," said one handsome girl, laughing.

"Well, get on, get on," he said. "Come on, my lad. You'll know your road down here again."

And Paul ran upstairs after his chief. He was given some checking and invoicing to do. He stood at the desk, labouring in his execrable handwriting. Presently Mr. Jordan came strutting down from the glass office and stood behind him, to the boy's great discomfort. Suddenly a red and fat finger was thrust on the form he was filling in.

"*Mr. J. A. Bates, Esquire!*" exclaimed the cross voice just behind his ear.

Paul looked at "Mr. J. A. Bates, Esquire" in his own vile writing, and wondered what was the matter now.

"Didn't they teach you any better than *that* while they were at it? If you put 'Mr.' you don't put Esquire'—a man can't be both at once."

The boy regretted his too-much generosity in disposing of honours, hesitated, and with trembling fingers, scratched out the "Mr." Then all at once Mr. Jordan snatched away the invoice.

"Make another! Are you going to send *that* to a gentleman?" And he tore up the blue form irritably.

Paul, his ears red with shame, began again. Still Mr. Jordan watched.

"I don't know what they *do* teach in schools. You'll have to write better than that. Lads learn nothing nowadays, but how to recite poetry and play the fiddle. Have you seen his writing?" he asked of Mr. Pappleworth.

"Yes; prime, isn't it?" replied Mr. Pappleworth indifferently.

Mr. Jordan gave a little grunt, not unamiable. Paul divined that his master's bark was worse than his bite. Indeed, the little manufacturer, although he spoke bad English, was quite gentleman enough to leave his men alone and to take no notice of trifles. But he knew he did not look like the boss and owner of the show, so he had to play his role of proprietor at first, to put things on a right footing.

"Let's see, *what's* your name?" asked Mr. Pappleworth of the boy.

"Paul Morel."

It is curious that children suffer so much at having to pronounce their own names.

"Paul Morel, is it? All right, you Paul-Morel through them things there, and then——"

Mr. Pappleworth subsided on to a stool, and began writing. A girl came up from out of a door just behind, put some newly-pressed elastic web appliances on the counter, and returned. Mr. Pappleworth picked up the whitey-blue knee-band, examined it, and its yellow order-paper quickly, and put it on one side. Next was a flesh-pink "leg". He went through the few things, wrote out a couple of orders, and called to Paul to accompany him. This time they went through the door whence the girl had emerged. There Paul found himself at the top of a little wooden flight of steps, and below him saw a room with windows round two sides, and at the farther end half a dozen girls sitting bending over the benches in the light from the window, sewing. They were singing together "Two Little Girls in Blue". Hearing the door opened, they all turned round, to see Mr. Pappleworth and Paul looking down on them from the far end of the room. They stopped singing.

"Can't you make a bit less row?" said Mr. Pappleworth. "Folk'll think we keep cats."

A hunchback woman on a high stool turned her long, rather heavy face towards Mr. Pappleworth, and said, in a contralto voice:

"They're all tom-cats then."

In vain Mr. Pappleworth tried to be impressive for Paul's benefit. He descended the steps into the finishing-off room, and went to the hunchback Fanny. She had such a short body on her high stool that her head, with its great bands of bright brown hair, seemed over large, as did her pale, heavy face. She wore a dress of green-black cashmere, and her wrists, coming out of the narrow cuffs, were thin and flat, as she put down her work nervously. He showed her something that was wrong with a knee-cap.

"Well," she said, "you needn't come blaming it on to me. It's not my fault." Her colour mounted to her cheek.

"I never said it *was* your fault. Will you do as I tell you?" replied Mr. Pappleworth shortly.

"You don't say it's my fault, but you'd like to make out as it was," the hunchback woman cried, almost in tears. Then she snatched the knee-cap from her "boss", saying: "Yes, I'll do it for you, but you needn't be snappy."

"Here's your new lad," said Mr. Pappleworth.

Fanny turned, smiling very gently on Paul.

"Oh!" she said.

"Yes; don't make a softy of him between you."

"It's not us as 'ud make a softy of him," she said indignantly.

"Come on then, Paul," said Mr. Pappleworth.

"*Au revoy*, Paul," said one of the girls.

There was a titter of laughter. Paul went out, blushing deeply, not having spoken a word.

The day was very long. All morning the work-people were coming to speak to Mr. Pappleworth. Paul was writing or learning to make up parcels, ready for the midday post. At one o'clock, or, rather, at a quarter to one, Mr. Pappleworth disappeared to catch his train: he lived in the suburbs. At one o'clock, Paul, feeling very lost, took his dinner-basket down into the stockroom in the basement, that had the long table on trestles, and ate his meal hurriedly, alone in that cellar of gloom and desolation. Then he went out of doors. The brightness and the freedom of the streets made him feel adventurous and happy. But at two o'clock he was back in the corner of the big room. Soon the work-girls went trooping past, making remarks. It was the commoner girls who worked upstairs at the heavy tasks of truss-making and the finishing of artificial limbs. He waited for Mr. Pappleworth, not knowing what to do, sitting scribbling on the yellow order-paper. Mr. Pappleworth came at twenty minutes to three. Then he sat and gossiped with Paul, treating the boy entirely as an equal, even in age.

In the afternoon there was never very much to do, unless it were near the week-end, and the accounts had to be made up. At five o'clock all the men went down into the dungeon with the table on trestles, and there they had tea, eating bread-and-butter on the bare, dirty boards, talking with the same kind of ugly haste and slovenliness with which they ate their meal. And yet upstairs the atmosphere among them was always jolly and clear. The cellar and the trestles affected them.

After tea, when all the gases were lighted, *work* went more briskly. There was the big evening post to get off. The hose came up warm and newly pressed from the workrooms. Paul had made out the invoices. Now he had the packing up and addressing to do, then he had to weigh his stock of parcels on the scales. Everywhere voices were calling weights, there was the chink of metal, the rapid snapping of string, the hurrying to old Mr. Melling for stamps. And at last the postman came with his sack, laughing and jolly. Then everything slacked off, and Paul took his dinner-basket and ran to the station to catch the eight-twenty train. The day in the factory was just twelve hours long.

His mother sat waiting for him rather anxiously. He had to walk from Keston, so was not home until about twenty past nine. And he left the house before seven in the morning. Mrs. Morel was rather anxious about his health. But she herself had had to put up with so much that she expected her children to take the same odds. They must go through with what came. And Paul stayed at Jordan's, although all the time he was there his health suffered from the darkness and lack of air and the long hours.

He came in pale and tired. His mother looked at him. She saw he was rather pleased, and her anxiety all went.

"Well, and how was it?" she asked.

"Ever so funny, mother," he replied. "You don't have to work a bit hard, and they're nice with you."

"And did you get on all right?"

"Yes: they only say my writing's bad. But Mr. Pappleworth—he's my man—said to Mr. Jordan I should be all right. I'm Spiral, mother; you must come and see. It's ever so nice."

Soon he liked Jordan's. Mr. Pappleworth, who had a certain "saloon bar" flavour about him, was always natural, and treated him as if he had been a comrade. Sometimes the "Spiral boss" was irritable, and chewed more lozenges than ever. Even then, however, he was not offensive, but one of those people who hurt themselves by their own irritability more than they hurt other people.

"Haven't you done that *yet?*" he would cry. "Go on, be a month of Sundays."

Again, and Paul could understand him least then, he was jocular and in high spirits.

"I'm going to bring my little Yorkshire terrier bitch to-morrow," he said jubilantly to Paul.

"What's a Yorkshire terrier?"

"*Don't* know what a Yorkshire terrier is? *Don't know a Yorkshire——*" Mr. Pappleworth was aghast.

"Is it a little silky one—colours of iron and rusty silver?"

"*That's* it, my lad. She's a gem. She's had five pounds' worth of pups already, and she's worth over seven pounds herself; and she doesn't weigh twenty ounces."

The next day the bitch came. She was a shivering, miserable morsel. Paul did not care for her; she seemed so like a wet rag that would never dry. Then a man called for her, and began to make coarse jokes. But Mr. Pappleworth nodded his head in the direction of the boy, and the talk went on *sotto voce*.

Mr. Jordan only made one more excursion to watch Paul, and then the only fault he found was seeing the boy lay his pen on the counter.

"Put your pen in your ear, if you're going to be a clerk. Pen in your ear!" And one day he said to the lad: "Why don't you hold your shoulders straighter? Come down here," when he took him into the glass office and fitted him with special braces for keeping the shoulders square.

But Paul liked the girls best. The men seemed common and rather dull. He liked them all, but they were uninteresting. Polly, the little brisk overseer downstairs, finding Paul eating in the cellar, asked him if she could cook him anything on her little stove. Next day his mother gave him a dish that could be heated up. He took it into the pleasant, clean room to Polly. And very soon it grew to be an established custom that he should have dinner with her. When he came in at eight in the morning he took his basket to her, and when he came down at one o'clock she had his dinner ready.

He was not very tall, and pale, with thick chestnut hair, irregular features, and a wide, full mouth. She was like a small bird. He often called her a "robinet". Though naturally rather quiet, he would sit and chatter with her for hours telling her about his home. The girls all liked to hear him talk. They often gathered in a little circle while he sat on a bench, and held forth to them, laughing. Some of them regarded him as a curious little creature, so serious, yet so bright and jolly, and always so delicate in his way with them. They all liked him, and he adored them. Polly he felt he belonged to. Then Connie, with her mane of red hair, her face of apple-blossom, her murmuring voice, such a lady in her shabby black frock, appealed to his romantic side.

"When you sit winding," he said, "it looks as if you were spinning at a spinning-wheel—it looks ever so nice. You remind me of Elaine in the 'Idylls of the King'. I'd draw you if I could."

And she glanced at him blushing shyly. And later on he had a sketch he prized very much: Connie sitting on the stool before the wheel, her flowing mane of red hair on her rusty black frock, her red mouth shut and serious, running the scarlet thread off the hank on to the reel.

With Louie, handsome and brazen, who always seemed to thrust her hip at him, he usually joked.

Emma was rather plain, rather old, and condescending. But to condescend to him made her happy, and he did not mind.

"How do you put needles in?" he asked.

"Go away and don't bother."

"But I ought to know how to put needles in."

She ground at her machine all the while steadily.

"There are many things you ought to know," she replied.

"Tell me, then, how to stick needles in the machine."

"Oh, the boy, what a nuisance he is! Why, *this* is how you do it."

He watched her attentively. Suddenly a whistle piped. Then Polly appeared, and said in a clear voice:

"Mr. Pappleworth wants to know how much longer you're going to be down here playing with the girls, Paul."

Paul flew upstairs, calling "Good-bye!" and Emma drew herself up.

"It wasn't *me* who wanted him to play with the machine," she said.

As a rule, when all the girls came back at two o'clock, he ran upstairs to Fanny, the hunchback, in the finishing-off room. Mr. Pappleworth did not appear till twenty to three, and he often found his boy sitting beside Fanny, talking, or drawing, or singing with the girls.

Often, after a minute's hesitation, Fanny would begin to sing. She had a fine contralto voice. Everybody joined in the chorus, and it went well. Paul was not at all embarrassed, after a while, sitting in the room with the half a dozen work-girls.

At the end of the song Fanny would say:

"I know you've been laughing at me."

"Don't be so soft, Fanny!" cried one of the girls.

Once there was mention of Connie's red hair.

"Fanny's is better, to my fancy," said Emma.

"You needn't try to make a fool of me," said Fanny, flushing deeply.

"No, but she has, Paul; she's got beautiful hair."

"It's a treat of a colour," said he. "That coldish colour like earth, and yet shiny. It's like bog-water."

"Goodness me!" exclaimed one girl, laughing.

"How I do but get criticised," said Fanny.

"But you should see it down, Paul," cried Emma earnestly. "It's simply beautiful. Put it down for him, Fanny, if he wants something to paint."

Fanny would not, and yet she wanted to.

"Then I'll take it down myself," said the lad.

"Well, you can if you like," said Fanny.

And he carefully took the pins out of the knot, and the rush of hair, of uniform dark brown, slid over the humped back.

"What a lovely lot!" he exclaimed.

The girls watched. There was silence. The youth shook the hair loose from the coil.

"It's splendid!" he said, smelling its perfume. "I'll bet it's worth pounds."

"I'll leave it to you when I die, Paul," said Fanny, half joking.

"You look just like anybody else, sitting drying their hair," said one of the girls to the long-legged hunchback.

Poor Fanny was morbidly sensitive, always imagining insults. Polly was curt and business-like. The two departments were for ever at war, and Paul was always finding Fanny in tears. Then he was made the recipient of all her woes, and he had to plead her case with Polly.

So the time went along happily enough. The factory had a homely feel. No one was rushed or driven. Paul always enjoyed it when the work got faster, towards post-time, and all the men united in labour. He liked to watch his fellow-clerks at work. The man was the work and the work was the man, one thing, for the time being. It was different with the girls. The real woman never seemed to be there at the task, but as if left out, waiting.

From the train going home at night he used to watch the lights of the town, sprinkled thick on the hills, fusing together in a blaze in the valleys. He felt rich in life and happy. Drawing farther off, there was a patch of lights at Bulwell like myriad petals shaken to the ground from the shed stars; and beyond was the red glare of the furnaces, playing like hot breath on the clouds.

He had to walk two and more miles from Keston home, up two long hills, down two short hills. He was often tired, and he counted the lamps climbing the hill above him, how many more to pass. And from the hill-top, on pitch-dark nights, he looked round on the villages five or six miles away, that shone like swarms of glittering living things, almost a heaven against his feet. Marlpool and Heanor scattered the far-off darkness with brilliance. And occasionally the black valley space between was traced, violated by a great train rushing south to London or north to Scotland. The trains roared by like projectiles level on the darkness, fuming and burning, making the valley clang with their passage. They were gone, and the lights of the towns and villages glittered in silence.

And then he came to the corner at home, which faced the other side of the night. The ash-tree seemed a friend now. His mother rose with gladness as he entered. He put his eight shillings proudly on the table.

"It'll help, mother?" he asked wistfully.

"There's precious little left," she answered, "after your ticket and dinners and such are taken off."

Then he told her the budget of the day. His life-story, like an Arabian Nights, was told night after night to his mother. It was almost as if it were her own life.

VI

DEATH IN THE FAMILY

Arthur Morel was growing up. He was a quick, careless, impulsive boy, a good deal like his father. He hated study, made a great moan if he had to work, and escaped as soon as possible to his sport again.

In appearance he remained the flower of the family, being well made, grace-ful, and full of life. His dark brown hair and fresh colouring, and his exquisite dark blue eyes shaded with long lashes, together with his generous manner and fiery temper, made him a favourite. But as he grew older his temper became uncertain. He flew into rages over nothing, seemed unbearably raw and irrita-ble.

His mother, whom he loved, wearied of him sometimes. He thought only of himself. When he wanted amusement, all that stood in his way he hated, even if it were she. When he was in trouble he moaned to her ceaselessly.

"Goodness, boy!" she said, when he groaned about a master who, he said, hated him, "if you don't like it, alter it, and if you can't alter it, put up with it."

And his father, whom he had loved and who had worshipped him, he came to detest. As he grew older Morel fell into a slow ruin. His body, which had been beautiful in movement and in being, shrank, did not seem to ripen with the years, but to get mean and rather despicable. There came over him a look of meanness and of paltriness. And when the mean-looking elderly man bullied or ordered the boy about, Arthur was furious. Moreover, Morel's manners got worse and worse, his habits somewhat disgusting. When the children were growing up and in the crucial stage of adolescence, the father was like some ugly irritant to their souls. His manners in the house were the same as he used among the colliers down pit.

"Dirty nuisance!" Arthur would cry, jumping up and going straight out of the house when his father disgusted him. And Morel persisted the more because his children hated it. He seemed to take a kind of satisfaction in disgusting them, and driving them nearly mad, while they were so irritably sensitive at the age of fourteen or fifteen. So that Arthur, who was growing up when his father was degenerate and elderly, hated him worst of all.

Then, sometimes, the father would seem to feel the contemptuous hatred of his children.

"There's not a man tries harder for his family!" he would shout. "He does his best for them, and then gets treated like a dog. But I'm not going to stand it, I tell you!"

But for the threat and the fact that he did not try so hard as he imagined, they would have felt sorry. As it was, the battle now went on nearly all between father and children, he persisting in his dirty and disgusting ways, just to assert his independence. They loathed him.

Arthur was so inflamed and irritable at last, that when he won a scholarship for the Grammar School in Nottingham, his mother decided to let him live in town, with one of her sisters, and only come home at week-ends.

Annie was still a junior teacher in the Board-school, earning about four shillings a week. But soon she would have fifteen shillings, since she had passed her examination, and there would be financial peace in the house.

Mrs. Morel clung now to Paul. He was quiet and not brilliant. But still he stuck to his painting, and still he stuck to his mother. Everything he did was for her. She waited for his coming home in the evening, and then she unburdened herself of all she had pondered, or of all that had occurred to her during the day. He sat and listened with his earnestness. The two shared lives.

William was engaged now to his brunette, and had bought her an engagement ring that cost eight guineas. The children gasped at such a fabulous price.

"Eight guineas!" said Morel. "More fool him! If he'd gen me some on't, it 'ud ha' looked better on 'im."

"Given *you* some of it!" cried Mrs. Morel. "Why give *you* some of it!"

She remembered *he* had bought no engagement ring at all, and she preferred William, who was not mean, if he were foolish. But now the young man talked only of the dances to which he went with his betrothed, and the different resplendent clothes she wore; or he told his mother with glee how they went to the theatre like great swells.

He wanted to bring the girl home. Mrs. Morel said she should come at the Christmas. This time William arrived with a lady, but with no presents. Mrs. Morel had prepared supper. Hearing footsteps, she rose and went to the door. William entered.

"Hello, mother!" He kissed her hastily, then stood aside to present a tall, handsome girl, who was wearing a costume of fine black-and-white check, and furs.

"Here's Gyp!"

Miss Western held out her hand and showed her teeth in a small smile. "Oh, how do you do, Mrs. Morel!" she exclaimed.

"I am afraid you will be hungry," said Mrs. Morel.

"Oh no, we had dinner in the train. Have you got my gloves, Chubby?"

William Morel, big and raw-boned, looked at her quickly.

"How should I?" he said.

"Then I've lost them. Don't be cross with me."

A frown went over his face, but he said nothing. She glanced round the kitchen. It was small and curious to her, with its glittering kissing-bunch, its evergreens behind the pictures, its wooden chairs and little deal table. At that moment Morel came in.

"Hello, dad!"

"Hello, my son! Tha's let on me!"

The two shook hands, and William presented the lady. She gave the same smile that showed her teeth.

"How do you do, Mr. Morel?"

Morel bowed obsequiously.

"I'm very well, and I hope so are you. You must make yourself very welcome."

"Oh, thank you," she replied, rather amused.

"You will like to go upstairs," said Mrs. Morel.

"If you don't mind; but not if it is any trouble to you."

"It is no trouble. Annie will take you. Walter, carry up this box."

"And don't be an hour dressing yourself up," said William to his betrothed.

Annie took a brass candlestick, and, too shy almost to speak, preceded the young lady to the front bedroom, which Mr. and Mrs. Morel had vacated for her. It, too, was small and cold by candle-light. The colliers' wives only lit fires in bedrooms in case of extreme illness.

"Shall I unstrap the box?" asked Annie.

"Oh, thank you very much!"

Annie played the part of maid, then went downstairs for hot water.

"I think she's rather tired, mother," said William. "It's a beastly journey, and we had such a rush."

"Is there anything I can give her?" asked Mrs. Morel.

"Oh no, she'll be all right."

But there was a chill in the atmosphere. After half an hour Miss Western came down, having put on a purplish-coloured dress, very fine for the collier's kitchen.

"I told you you'd no need to change," said William to her.

"Oh, Chubby!" Then she turned with that sweetish smile to Mrs. Morel. "Don't you think he's always grumbling, Mrs. Morel?"

"Is he?" said Mrs. Morel. "That's not very nice of him."

"It isn't, really!"

"You are cold," said the mother. "Won't you come near the fire?"

Morel jumped out of his arm-chair.

"Come and sit you here!" he cried. "Come and sit you here!"

"No, dad, keep your own chair. Sit on the sofa, Gyp," said William.

"No, no!" cried Morel. "This cheer's warmest. Come and sit here, Miss Wesson."

"Thank you so much," said the girl, seating herself in the collier's arm-chair, the place of honour. She shivered, feeling the warmth of the kitchen penetrate her.

"Fetch me a hanky, Chubby dear!" she said, putting up her mouth to him, and using the same intimate tone as if they were alone; which made the rest of the family feel as if they ought not to be present. The young lady evidently did not realise them as people: they were creatures to her for the present. William winced.

In such a household, in Streatham, Miss Western would have been a lady condescending to her inferiors. These people were to her, certainly clownish—

in short, the working classes. How was she to adjust herself?

"I'll go," said Annie.

Miss Western took no notice, as if a servant had spoken. But when the girl came downstairs again with the handkerchief, she said: "Oh, thank you!" in a gracious way.

She sat and talked about the dinner on the train, which had been so poor; about London, about dances. She was really very nervous, and chattered from fear. Morel sat all the time smoking his thick twist tobacco, watching her, and listening to her glib London speech, as he puffed. Mrs. Morel, dressed up in her best black silk blouse, answered quietly and rather briefly. The three children sat round in silence and admiration. Miss Western was the princess. Everything of the best was got out for her: the best cups, the best spoons, the best table cloth, the best coffee-jug. The children thought she must find it quite grand. She felt strange, not able to realize the people, not knowing how to treat them. William joked, and was slightly uncomfortable.

At about ten o'clock he said to her:

"Aren't you tired, Gyp?"

"Rather, Chubby," she answered, at once in the intimate tones and putting her head slightly on one side.

"I'll light her the candle, mother," he said.

"Very well," replied the mother.

Miss Western stood up, held out her hand to Mrs. Morel.

"Good-night, Mrs. Morel," she said.

Paul sat at the boiler, letting the water run from the tap into a stone beer-bottle. Annie swathed the bottle in an old flannel pit-singlet, and kissed her mother good-night. She was to share the room with the lady, because the house was full.

"You wait a minute," said Mrs. Morel to Annie. And Annie sat nursing the hot-water bottle. Miss Western shook hands all round, to everybody's discomfort, and took her departure, preceded by William. In five minutes he was downstairs again. His heart was rather sore; he did not know why. He talked very little till everybody had gone to bed, but himself and his mother. Then he stood with his legs apart, in his old attitude on the hearth-rug, and said hesitatingly:

"Well, mother?"

"Well, my son?"

She sat in the rocking-chair, feeling somehow hurt and humiliated, for his sake.

"Do you like her?"

"Yes," came the slow answer.

"She's shy yet, mother. She's not used to it. It's different from her aunt's house, you know."

"Of course it is, my boy; and she must find it difficult."

"She does." Then he frowned swiftly. "If only she wouldn't put on her *blessed* airs!"

"It's only her first awkwardness, my boy. She'll be all right."

"That's it, mother," he replied gratefully. But his brow was gloomy. "You know, she's not like you, mother. She's not serious, and she can't think."

"She's young, my boy."

"Yes; and she's had no sort of show. Her mother died when she was a child. Since then she's lived with her aunt, whom she can't bear. And her father was a rake. She's had no love."

"No! Well, you must make up to her."

"And so—you have to forgive her a lot of things."

"*What* do you have to forgive her, my boy?"

"I dunno. When she seems shallow, you have to remember she's never had anybody to bring her deeper side out. And she's *fearfully* fond of me."

"Anybody can see that."

"But you know, mother—she's—she's different from us. Those sort of people, like those she lives amongst, they don't seem to have the same principles."

"You mustn't judge too hastily," said Mrs. Morel.

But he seemed uneasy within himself.

In the morning, however, he was up singing and larking round the house.

"Hello!" he called, sitting on the stairs. "Are you getting up?"

"Yes," her voice called faintly.

"Merry Christmas!" he shouted to her.

Her laugh, pretty and tinkling, was heard in the bedroom. She did not come down in half an hour.

"Was she *really* getting up when she said she was?" he asked of Annie.

"Yes, she was," replied Annie.

He waited a while, then went to the stairs again.

"Happy New Year," he called.

"Thank you, Chubby dear!" came the laughing voice, far away.

"Buck up!" he implored.

It was nearly an hour, and still he was waiting for her. Morel, who always rose before six, looked at the clock.

"Well, it's a winder!" he exclaimed.

The family had breakfasted, all but William. He went to the foot of the stairs.

"Shall I have to send you an Easter egg up there?" he called, rather crossly. She only laughed. The family expected, after that time of preparation, something like magic. At last she came, looking very nice in a blouse and skirt.

"Have you *really* been all this time getting ready?" he asked.

"Chubby dear! That question is not permitted, is it, Mrs. Morel?"

She played the grand lady at first. When she went with William to chapel, he in his frock-coat and silk hat, she in her furs and London-made costume, Paul and Arthur and Annie expected everybody to bow to the ground in admiration. And Morel, standing in his Sunday suit at the end of the road, watching the gallant pair go, felt he was the father of princes and princesses.

And yet she was not so grand. For a year now she had been a sort of secretary or clerk in a London office. But while she was with the Morels she queened it. She sat and let Annie or Paul wait on her as if they were her servants. She treated Mrs. Morel with a certain glibness and Morel with patronage. But after a day or so she began to change her tune.

William always wanted Paul or Annie to go along with them on their walks. It was so much more interesting. And Paul really *did* admire "Gipsy" wholeheartedly; in fact, his mother scarcely forgave the boy for the adulation with which he treated the girl.

On the second day, when Lily said: "Oh, Annie, do you know where I left my muff?" William replied:

"You know it is in your bedroom. Why do you ask Annie?"

And Lily went upstairs with a cross, shut mouth. But it angered the young man that she made a servant of his sister.

On the third evening William and Lily were sitting together in the parlour by the fire in the dark. At a quarter to eleven Mrs. Morel was heard raking the fire. William came out to the kitchen, followed by his beloved.

"Is it as late as that, mother?" he said. She had been sitting alone.

"It is not *late,* my boy, but it is as late as I usually sit up."

"Won't you go to bed, then?" he asked.

"And leave you two? No, my boy, I don't believe in it."

"Can't you trust us, mother?"

"Whether I can or not, I won't do it. You can stay till eleven if you like, and I can read."

"Go to bed, Gyp," he said to his girl. "We won't keep mater waiting."

"Annie has left the candle burning, Lily," said Mrs. Morel; "I think you will see."

"Yes, thank you. Good-night, Mrs. Morel."

William kissed his sweetheart at the foot of the stairs, and she went. He returned to the kitchen.

"Can't you trust us, mother?" he repeated, rather offended.

"My boy, I tell you I don't *believe* in leaving two young things like you alone downstairs when everyone else is in bed."

And he was forced to take this answer. He kissed his mother good-night.

At Easter he came over alone. And then he discussed his sweetheart endlessly with his mother.

"You know, mother, when I'm away from her I don't care for her a bit. I shouldn't care if I never saw her again. But, then, when I'm with her in the evenings I am awfully fond of her."

"It's a queer sort of love to marry on," said Mrs. Morel, "if she holds you no more than that!"

"It *is* funny!" he exclaimed. It worried and perplexed him. "But yet—there's so much between us now I couldn't give her up."

"You know best," said Mrs. Morel. "But if it is as you say, I wouldn't call it *love*—at any rate, it doesn't look much like it."

"Oh, I don't know, mother. She's an orphan, and——"

They never came to any sort of conclusion. He seemed puzzled and rather fretted. She was rather reserved. All his strength and money went in keeping this girl. He could scarcely afford to take his mother to Nottingham when he came over.

Paul's wages had been raised at Christmas to ten shillings, to his great joy. He was quite happy at Jordan's, but his health suffered from the long hours and the confinement. His mother, to whom he became more and more significant, thought how to help.

His half-day holiday was on Monday afternoon. On a Monday morning in May, as the two sat alone at breakfast, she said:

"I think it will be a fine day."

He looked up in surprise. This meant something.

"You know Mr. Leivers has gone to live on a new farm. Well, he asked me last week if I wouldn't go and see Mrs. Leivers, and I promised to bring you on Monday if it's fine. Shall we go?"

"I say, little woman, how lovely!" he cried. "And we'll go this afternoon?"

Paul hurried off to the station jubilant. Down Derby Road was a cherry-tree that glistened. The old brick wall by the Statutes ground burned scarlet, spring was a very flame of green. And the steep swoop of highroad lay, in its cool morning dust, splendid with patterns of sunshine and shadow, perfectly still. The trees sloped their great green shoulders proudly; and inside the warehouse all the morning, the boy had a vision of spring outside.

When he came home at dinner-time his mother was rather excited.

"Are we going?" he asked.

"When I'm ready," she replied.

Presently he got up.

"Go and get dressed while I wash up," he said.

She did so. He washed the pots, straightened, and then took her boots. They were quite clean. Mrs. Morel was one of those naturally exquisite people who can walk in mud without dirtying their shoes. But Paul had to clean them for her. They were kid boots at eight shillings a pair. He, however, thought them the most dainty boots in the world, and he cleaned them with as much reverence as if they had been flowers.

Suddenly she appeared in the inner doorway rather shyly. She had got a new cotton blouse on. Paul jumped up and went forward.

"Oh, my stars!" he exclaimed. "What a bobby-dazzler!"

She sniffed in a little haughty way, and put her head up.

"It's not a bobby-dazzler at all!" she replied. "It's very quiet."

She walked forward, whilst he hovered round her.

"Well," she asked, quite shy, but pretending to be high and mighty, "do you like it?"

"Awfully! You *are* a fine little woman to go jaunting out with!"

He went and surveyed her from the back.

"Well," he said, "if I was walking down the street behind you, I should say: 'Doesn't *that* little person fancy herself!' "

"Well, she doesn't," replied Mrs. Morel. "She's not sure it suits her."

"Oh no! she wants to be in dirty black, looking as if she was wrapped in burnt paper. It *does* suit you, and *I* say you look nice."

She sniffed in her little way, pleased, but pretending to know better.

"Well," she said, "it's cost me just three shillings. You couldn't have got it ready-made for that price, could you?"

"I should think you couldn't," he replied.

"And, you know, it's good stuff."

"Awfully pretty," he said.

The blouse was white, with a little sprig of heliotrope and black.

"Too young for me, though, I'm afraid," she said.

"Too young for you!" he exclaimed in disgust. "Why don't you buy some false white hair and stick it on your head."

"I s'll soon have no need," she replied. "I'm going white fast enough."

"Well, you've no business to," he said. "What do I want with a white-haired mother?"

"I'm afraid you'll have to put up with one, my lad," she said rather strangely.

They set off in great style, she carrying the umbrella William had given her, because of the sun. Paul was considerably taller than she, though he was not big. He fancied himself.

On the fallow land the young wheat shone silkily. Minton pit waved its plumes of white steam, coughed, and rattled hoarsely.

"Now look at that!" said Mrs. Morel. Mother and son stood on the road to watch. Along the ridge of the great pit-hill crawled a little group in silhouette against the sky, a horse, a small truck, and a man. They climbed the incline against the heavens. At the end the man tipped the wagon. There was an undue rattle as the waste fell down the sheer slope of the enormous bank.

"You sit a minute, mother," he said, and she took a seat on a bank, whilst he sketched rapidly. She was silent whilst he worked, looking round at the afternoon, the red cottages shining among their greenness.

"The world is a wonderful place," she said, "and wonderfully beautiful."

"And so's the pit," he said. "Look how it heaps together, like something alive almost—a big creature that you don't know."

"Yes," she said. "Perhaps!"

"And all the trucks standing waiting, like a string of beasts to be fed," he said.

"And very thankful I am they *are* standing," she said, "for that means they'll turn middling time this week."

"But I like the feel of *men* on things, while they're alive. There's a feel of men about trucks, because they've been handled with men's hands, all of them."

"Yes," said Mrs. Morel.

They went along under the trees of the highroad. He was constantly informing her, but she was interested. They passed the end of Nethermere, that was tossing its sunshine like petals lightly in its lap. Then they turned on a private road, and in some trepidation approached a big farm. A dog barked furiously. A woman came out to see.

"Is this the way to Willey Farm?" Mrs. Morel asked.

Paul hung behind in terror of being sent back. But the woman was amiable, and directed them. The mother and son went through the wheat and oats, over a little bridge into a wild meadow. Peewits, with their white breasts glistening, wheeled and screamed about them. The lake was still and blue. High overhead a heron floated. Opposite, the wood heaped on the hill, green and still.

"It's a wild road, mother," said Paul. "Just like Canada."

"Isn't it beautiful!" said Mrs. Morel, looking round.

"See that heron—see—see her legs?"

He directed his mother, what she must see and what not. And she was quite content.

"But now," she said, "which way? He told me through the wood."

The wood, fenced and dark, lay on their left.

"I can feel a bit of a path this road," said Paul. "You've got town feet, somehow or other, you have."

They found a little gate, and soon were in a broad green alley of the wood, with a new thicket of fir and pine on one hand, an old oak glade dipping down on the other. And among the oaks the bluebells stood in pools of azure, under the new green hazels, upon a pale fawn floor of oak-leaves. He found flowers for her.

"Here's a bit of new-mown hay," he said; then, again, he brought her forget-me-nots. And, again, his heart hurt with love, seeing her hand, used with work, holding the little bunch of flowers he gave her. She was perfectly happy.

But at the end of the riding was a fence to climb. Paul was over in a second.

"Come," he said, "let me help you."

"No, go away. I will do it in my own way."

He stood below with his hands up ready to help her. She climbed cautiously.

"What a way to climb!" he exclaimed scornfully, when she was safely to earth again.

"Hateful stiles!" she cried.

"Duffer of a little woman," he replied, "who can't get over 'em."

In front, along the edge of the wood, was a cluster of low red farm buildings.

The two hastened forward. Flush with the wood was the apple orchard, where blossom was falling on the grindstone. The pond was deep under a hedge and overhanging oak trees. Some cows stood in the shade. The farm and buildings, three sides of a quadrangle, embraced the sunshine towards the wood. It was very still.

Mother and son went into the small railed garden, where was a scent of red gillivers. By the open door were some floury loaves, put out to cool. A hen was just coming to peck them. Then, in the doorway suddenly appeared a girl in a dirty apron. She was about fourteen years old, had a rosy dark face, a bunch of short black curls, very fine and free, and dark eyes; shy, questioning, a little resentful of the strangers, she disappeared. In a minute another figure appeared, a small, frail woman, rosy, with great dark brown eyes.

"Oh!" she exclaimed, smiling with a little glow, "you've come, then. I *am* glad to see you." Her voice was intimate and rather sad.

The two women shook hands.

"Now are you sure we're not a bother to you?" said Mrs. Morel. "I know what a farming life is."

"Oh no! We're only too thankful to see a new face, it's so lost up here."

"I suppose so," said Mrs. Morel.

They were taken through into the parlour—a long, low room, with a great bunch of guelder-roses in the fireplace. There the women talked, whilst Paul went out to survey the land. He was in the garden smelling the gillivers and looking at the plants, when the girl came out quickly to the heap of coal which stood by the fence.

"I suppose these are cabbage-roses?" he said to her, pointing to the bushes along the fence.

She looked at him with startled, big brown eyes.

"I suppose they are cabbage-roses when they come out?" he said.

"I don't know," she faltered. "They're white with pink middles."

"Then they're maiden-blush."

Miriam flushed. She had a beautiful warm colouring.

"I don't know," she said.

"You don't have *much* in your garden," he said.

"This is our first year here," she answered, in a distant, rather superior way, drawing back and going indoors. He did not notice, but went his round of exploration. Presently his mother came out, and they went through the buildings. Paul was hugely delighted.

"And I suppose you have the fowls and calves and pigs to look after?" said Mrs. Morel to Mrs. Leivers.

"No," replied the little woman. "I can't find time to look after cattle, and I'm not used to it. It's as much as I can do to keep going in the house."

"Well, I suppose it is," said Mrs. Morel.

Presently the girl came out.

"Tea is ready, mother," she said in a musical, quiet voice.

"Oh, thank you, Miriam, then we'll come," replied her mother, almost ingratiatingly. "Would you *care* to have tea now, Mrs. Morel?"

"Of course," said Mrs. Morel. "Whenever it's ready."

Paul and his mother and Mrs. Leivers had tea together. Then they went out into the wood that was flooded with bluebells, while fumy forget-me-nots were in the paths. The mother and son were in ecstasy together.

When they got back to the house, Mr. Leivers and Edgar, the eldest son, were in the kitchen. Edgar was about eighteen. Then Geoffrey and Maurice, big lads of twelve and thirteen, were in from school. Mr. Leivers was a good-looking man in the prime of life, with a golden-brown moustache, and blue eyes screwed up against the weather.

The boys were condescending, but Paul scarcely observed it. They went round for eggs, scrambling into all sorts of places. As they were feeding the fowls Miriam came out. The boys took no notice of her. One hen, with her yellow chickens, was in a coop. Maurice took his hand full of corn and let the hen peck from it.

"Durst you do it?" he asked of Paul.

"Let's see," said Paul.

He had a small hand, warm, and rather capable-looking. Miriam watched. He held the corn to the hen. The bird eyed it with her hard, bright eye, and suddenly made a peck into his hand. He started, and laughed. "Rap, rap, rap!" went the bird's beak in his palm. He laughed again, and the other boys joined.

"She knocks you, and nips you, but she never hurts," said Paul, when the last corn had gone.

"Now, Miriam," said Maurice, "you come an' 'ave a go."

"No," she cried, shrinking back.

"Ha! baby. The mardy-kid!" said her brothers.

"It doesn't hurt a bit," said Paul. "It only just nips rather nicely."

"No," she still cried, shaking her black curls and shrinking.

"She dursn't," said Geoffrey. "She niver durst do anything except recite poitry."

"Dursn't jump off a gate, dursn't tweedle, dursn't go on a slide, dursn't stop a girl hittin' her. She can do nowt but go about thinkin' herself somebody. 'The Lady of the Lake.' Yah!" cried Maurice.

Miriam was crimson with shame and misery.

"I dare do more than you," she cried. "You're never anything but cowards and bullies."

"Oh, cowards and bullies!" they repeated mincingly, mocking her speech.

> "Not such a clown shall anger me,
> A boor is answered silently."

he quoted against her, shouting with laughter.

She went indoors. Paul went with the boys into the orchard, where they had rigged up a parallel bar. They did feats of strength. He was more agile than strong, but it served. He fingered a piece of apple-blossom that hung low on a swinging bough.

"I wouldn't get the apple-blossom," said Edgar, the eldest brother. "There'll be no apples next year."

"I wasn't going to get it," replied Paul, going away.

The boys felt hostile to him; they were more interested in their own pursuits. He wandered back to the house to look for his mother. As he went round the back, he saw Miriam kneeling in front of the hen-coop, some maize in her hand, biting her lip, and crouching in an intense attitude. The hen was eyeing her wickedly. Very gingerly she put forward her hand. The hen bobbed for her. She drew back quickly with a cry, half of fear, half of chagrin.

"It won't hurt you," said Paul.

She flushed crimson and started up.

"I only wanted to try," she said in a low voice.

"See, it doesn't hurt," he said, and, putting only two corns in his palm, he let the hen peck, peck, peck at his bare hand. "It only makes you laugh," he said.

She put her hand forward and dragged it away, tried again, and started back with a cry. He frowned.

"Why, I'd let her take corn from my face," said Paul, "only she bumps a bit. She's ever so neat. If she wasn't, look how much ground she'd peck up every day."

He waited grimly, and watched. At last Miriam let the bird peck from her hand. She gave a little cry—fear, and pain because of fear—rather pathetic. But she had done it, and she did it again.

"There, you see," said the boy. "It doesn't hurt, does it?"

She looked at him with dilated dark eyes.

"No," she laughed, trembling.

Then she rose and went indoors. She seemed to be in some way resentful of the boy.

"He thinks I'm only a common girl," she thought, and she wanted to prove she was a grand person like the "Lady of the Lake".

Paul found his mother ready to go home. She smiled on her son. He took the great bunch of flowers. Mr. and Mrs. Leivers walked down the fields with them. The hills were golden with evening; deep in the woods showed the darkening purple of bluebells. It was everywhere perfectly still, save for the rustling of leaves and birds.

"But it is a beautiful place," said Mrs. Morel.

"Yes," answered Mr. Leivers; "it's a nice little place, if only it weren't for the rabbits. The pasture's bitten down to nothing. I dunno if ever I s'll get the rent off it."

He clapped his hands, and the field broke into motion near the woods, brown rabbits hopping everywhere.

"Would you believe it!" exclaimed Mrs. Morel.

She and Paul went on alone together.

"Wasn't it lovely, mother?" he said quietly.

A thin moon was coming out. His heart was full of happiness till it hurt. His mother had to chatter, because she, too, wanted to cry with happiness.

"Now *wouldn't* I help that man!" she said. *"Wouldn't* I see to the fowls and the young stock! And *I'd* learn to milk, and *I'd* talk with him, and *I'd* plan with him. My word, if I were his wife, the farm would be run, I know! But there, she hasn't the strength—she simply hasn't the strength. She ought never to have been burdened like it, you know. I'm sorry for her, and I'm sorry for him too. My word, if *I'd* had him, I shouldn't have thought him a bad husband! Not that she does either; and she's very lovable."

William came home again with his sweetheart at the Whitsuntide. He had one week of his holidays then. It was beautiful weather. As a rule, William and Lily and Paul went out in the morning together for a walk. William did not talk to his beloved much, except to tell her things from his boyhood. Paul talked endlessly to both of them. They lay down, all three, in a meadow by Minton Church. On one side, by the Castle Farm, was a beautiful quivering screen of poplars. Hawthorn was dropping from the hedges; penny daisies and ragged robin were in the field, like laughter. William, a big fellow of twenty-three, thinner now and even a bit gaunt, lay back in the sunshine and dreamed, while she fingered with his hair. Paul went gathering the big daisies. She had taken off her hat; her hair was black as a horse's mane. Paul came back and threaded daisies in her jet-black hair—big spangles of white and yellow, and just a pink touch of ragged robin.

"Now you look like a young witch-woman," the boy said to her. "Doesn't she, William?"

Lily laughed. William opened his eyes and looked at her. In his gaze was a certain baffled look of misery and fierce appreciation.

"Has he made a sight of me?" she asked, laughing down on her lover.

"That he has!" said William, smiling.

He looked at her. Her beauty seemed to hurt him. He glanced at her flower-decked head and frowned.

"You look nice enough, if that's what you want to know," he said.

And she walked without her hat. In a little while William recovered, and was rather tender to her. Coming to a bridge, he carved her initials and his in a heart.

L . L . W .
W . M .

She watched his strong, nervous hand, with its glistening hairs and freckles, as he carved, and she seemed fascinated by it.

All the time there was a feeling of sadness and warmth, and a certain tenderness in the house, whilst William and Lily were at home. But often he got irritable. She had brought, for an eight-days' stay, five dresses and six blouses.

"Oh, would you mind," she said to Annie, "washing me these two blouses, and these things?"

And Annie stood washing when William and Lily went out the next morning. Mrs. Morel was furious. And sometimes the young man, catching a glimpse of his sweetheart's attitude towards his sister, hated her.

On Sunday morning she looked very beautiful in a dress of foulard, silky and sweeping, and blue as a jay-bird's feather, and in a large cream hat covered with many roses, mostly crimson. Nobody could admire her enough. But in the evening, when she was going out, she asked again:

"Chubby, have you got my gloves?"

"Which?" asked William.

"My new black *suède.*"

"No."

There was a hunt. She had lost them.

"Look here, mother," said William, "that's the fourth pair she's lost since Christmas— at five shillings a pair!"

"You only gave me *two* of them," she remonstrated.

And in the evening, after supper, he stood on the hearth-rug whilst she sat on the sofa, and he seemed to hate her. In the afternoon he had left her whilst he went to see some old friend. She had sat looking at a book. After supper William wanted to write a letter.

"Here is your book, Lily," said Mrs. Morel. "Would you care to go on with it for a few minutes?"

"No, thank you," said the girl. "I will sit still."

"But it is so dull."

William scribbled irritably at a great rate. As he sealed the envelope he said: "Read a book! Why, she's never read a book in her life."

"Oh, go along!" said Mrs. Morel, cross with the exaggeration.

"It's true, mother—she hasn't," he cried, jumping up and taking his old position on the hearth-rug. "She's never read a book in her life."

" 'Er's like me," chimed in Morel. " 'Er canna see what there is i' books, ter sit borin' your nose in 'em for, nor more can I."

"But you shouldn't say these things," said Mrs. Morel to her son.

"But it's true, mother—she *can't* read. What did you give her?"

"Well, I gave her a little thing of Annie Swan's. Nobody wants to read dry stuff on Sunday afternoon."

"Well, I'll bet she didn't read ten lines of it."

"You are mistaken," said his mother.

All the time Lily sat miserably on the sofa. He turned to her swiftly.

"*Did* you read any?" he asked.

"Yes, I did," she replied.

"How much?"

"I don't know how many pages."

"Tell me *one thing* you read."

She could not.

She never got beyond the second page. He read a great deal, and had a quick, active intelligence. She could understand nothing but love-making and chatter. He was accustomed to having all his thoughts sifted through his mother's mind; so, when he wanted companionship, and was asked in reply to be the billing and twittering lover, he hated his betrothed.

"You know, mother," he said, when he was alone with her at night, "she's no idea of money, she's so wessel-brained. When she's paid, she'll suddenly buy such rot as *marrons glacés*, and then *I* have to buy her season ticket, and her extras, even her underclothing. And she wants to get married, and I think myself we might as well get married next year. But at this rate——"

"A fine mess of a marriage it would be," replied his mother. "I should consider it again, my boy."

"Oh, well, I've gone too far to break off now," he said, "and so I shall get married as soon as I can."

"Very well, my boy. If you will, you will, and there's no stopping you; but I tell you, *I* can't sleep when I think about it."

"Oh, she'll be all right, mother. We shall manage."

"And she lets you buy her underclothing?" asked the mother.

"Well," he began apologetically, "she didn't ask me; but one morning—and it *was* cold—I found her on the station shivering, not able to keep still; so I asked her if she was well wrapped up. She said: 'I think so.' So I said: 'Have you got warm underthings on?' And she said: 'No, they were cotton.' I asked her why on earth she hadn't got something thicker on in weather like that, and she said because she *had* nothing. And there she is—a bronchial subject! I *had* to take her and get some warm things. Well, mother, I shouldn't mind the money if we had any. And, you know, she *ought* to keep enough to pay for her season-ticket; but no, she comes to me about that, and I have to find the money."

"It's a poor lookout," said Mrs. Morel bitterly.

He was pale, and his rugged face, that used to be so perfectly careless and laughing, was stamped with conflict and despair.

"But I can't give her up now; it's gone too far," he said. "And, besides, for *some* things I couldn't do without her."

"My boy, remember you're taking your life in your hands," said Mrs. Morel. "*Nothing* is as bad as a marriage that's a hopeless failure. Mine was bad enough,

God knows, and ought to teach you something; but it might have been worse by a long chalk."

He leaned with his back against the side of the chimney-piece, his hands in his pockets. He was a big, raw-boned man, who looked as if he would go to the world's end if he wanted to. But she saw the despair on his face.

"I couldn't give her up now," he said.

"Well," she said, "remember there are worse wrongs than breaking off an engagement."

"I can't give her up *now*," he said.

The clock ticked on; mother and son remained in silence, a conflict between them; but he would say no more. At last she said:

"Well, go to bed, my son. You'll feel better in the morning, and perhaps you'll know better."

He kissed her, and went. She raked the fire. Her heart was heavy now as it had never been. Before, with her husband, things had seemed to be breaking down in her, but they did not destroy her power to live. Now her soul felt lamed in itself. It was her hope that was struck.

And so often William manifested the same hatred towards his betrothed. On the last evening at home he was railing against her.

"Well," he said, "if you don't believe me, what she's like, would you believe she has been confirmed three times?"

"Nonsense!" laughed Mrs. Morel.

"Nonsense or not, she *has!* That's what confirmation means for her—a bit of a theatrical show where she can cut a figure."

"I haven't, Mrs. Morel!" cried the girl—"I haven't! it is not true!"

"What!" he cried, flashing round on her. "Once in Bromley, once in Beckenham, and once somewhere else."

"Nowhere else!" she said, in tears—"nowhere else!"

"It *was!* And if it wasn't why were you confirmed *twice?*"

"Once I was only fourteen, Mrs. Morel," she pleaded, tears in her eyes.

"Yes," said Mrs. Morel; "I can quite understand it, child. Take no notice of him. You ought to be ashamed, William, saying such things."

"But it's true. She's religious—she had blue velvet PrayerBooks—and she's not as much religion, or anything else, in her than that table-leg. Gets confirmed three times for show, to show herself off, and that's how she is in *everything—everything!*"

The girl sat on the sofa, crying. She was not strong.

"As for *love!*" he cried, "you might as well ask a fly to love you! It'll love settling on you——"

"Now, say no more," commanded Mrs. Morel. "If you want to say these things, you must find another place than this. I am ashamed of you, William! Why don't you be more manly. To do nothing but find fault with a girl, and then pretend you're engaged to her!"

Mrs. Morel subsided in wrath and indignation.

William was silent, and later he repented, kissed and comforted the girl. Yet it was true, what he had said. He hated her.

When they were going away, Mrs. Morel accompanied them as far as Nottingham. It was a long way to Keston station.

"You know, mother," he said to her, "Gyp's shallow. Nothing goes deep with her."

"William, I *wish* you wouldn't say these things," said Mrs. Morel, very uncomfortable for the girl who walked beside her.

"But it doesn't, mother. She's very much in love with me now, but if I died she'd have forgotten me in three months."

Mrs. Morel was afraid. Her heart beat furiously, hearing the quiet bitterness of her son's last speech.

"How do you know?" she replied. "You *don't* know, and therefore you've no right to say such a thing."

"He's always saying these things!" cried the girl.

"In three months after I was buried you'd have somebody else, and I should be forgotten," he said. "And that's your love!"

Mrs. Morel saw them into the train in Nottingham, then she returned home.

"There's one comfort," she said to Paul—"he'll never have any money to marry on, that I *am* sure of. And so she'll save him that way."

So she took cheer. Matters were not yet very desperate. She firmly believed William would never marry his Gipsy. She waited, and she kept Paul near to her.

All summer long William's letters had a feverish tone; he seemed unnatural and intense. Sometimes he was exaggeratedly jolly, usually he was flat and bitter in his letter.

"Ah," his mother said, "I'm afraid he's ruining himself against that creature, who isn't worthy of his love—no, no more than a rag doll."

He wanted to come home. The midsummer holiday was gone; it was a long while to Christmas. He wrote in wild excitement, saying he could come for Saturday and Sunday at Goose Fair, the first week in October.

"You are not well, my boy," said his mother, when she saw him.

She was almost in tears at having him to herself again.

"No, I've not been well," he said. "I've seemed to have a dragging cold all the last month, but it's going, I think."

It was sunny October weather. He seemed wild with joy, like a schoolboy escaped; then again he was silent and reserved. He was more gaunt than ever, and there was a haggard look in his eyes.

"You are doing too much," said his mother to him.

He was doing extra work, trying to make some money to marry on, he said. He only talked to his mother once on the Saturday night; then he was sad and tender about his beloved.

"And yet, you know, mother, for all that, if I died she'd be broken-hearted for two months, and then she'd start to forget me. You'd see, she'd never come home here to look at my grave, not even once."

"Why, William," said his mother, "you're not going to die, so why talk about it?"

"But whether or not——" he replied.

"And she can't help it. She is like that, and if you choose her—well, you can't grumble," said his mother.

On the Sunday morning, as he was putting his collar on:

"Look," he said to his mother, holding up his chin, "what a rash my collar's made under my chin!"

Just at the junction of chin and throat was a big red inflamation.

"It ought not to do that," said his mother. "Here, put a bit of this soothing ointment on. You should wear different collars."

He went away on Sunday midnight, seeming better and more solid for his two days at home.

On Tuesday morning came a telegram from London that he was ill. Mrs. Morel got off her knees from washing the floor, read the telegram, called a neighbour, went to her landlady and borrowed a sovereign, put on her things, and set off. She hurried to Keston, caught an express for London in Nottingham. She had to wait in Nottingham nearly an hour. A small figure in her black bonnet, she was anxiously asking the porters if they knew how to get to Elmers End. The journey was three hours. She sat in her corner in a kind of stupor, never moving. At King's Cross still no one could tell her how to get to Elmers End. Carrying her string bag, that contained her nightdress, a comb and brush, she went from person to person. At last they sent her underground to Cannon Street.

It was six o'clock when she arrived at William's lodging. The blinds were not down.

"How is he?" she asked.

"No better," said the landlady.

She followed the woman upstairs. William lay on the bed, with bloodshot eyes, his face rather discoloured. The clothes were tossed about, there was no fire in the room, a glass of milk stood on the stand at his bedside. No one had been with him.

"Why, my son!" said the mother bravely.

He did not answer. He looked at her, but did not see her. Then he began to say, in a dull voice, as if repeating a letter from dictation: "Owing to a leakage in the hold of this vessel, the sugar had set, and become converted into rock. It needed hacking——"

He was quite unconscious. It had been his business to examine some such cargo of sugar in the Port of London.

"How long has he been like this?" the mother asked the landlady.

"He got home at six o'clock on Monday morning, and he seemed to sleep all day; then in the night we heard him talking, and this morning he asked for you. So I wired, and we fetched the doctor."

"Will you have a fire made?"

Mrs. Morel tried to soothe her son, to keep him still.

The doctor came. It was pneumonia, and, he said, a peculiar erysipelas, which had started under the chin where the collar chafed, and was spreading over the face. He hoped it would not get to the brain.

Mrs. Morel settled down to nurse. She prayed for William, prayed that he would recognise her. But the young man's face grew more discoloured. In the night she struggled with him. He raved, and raved, and would not come to consciousness. At two o'clock, in a dreadful paroxysm, he died.

Mrs. Morel sat perfectly still for an hour in the lodging bedroom; then she roused the household.

At six o'clock, with the aid of the charwoman, she laid him out; then she went round the dreary London village to the registrar and the doctor.

At nine o'clock to the cottage on Scargill Street came another wire: "William died last night. Let father come, bring money."

Annie, Paul, and Arthur were at home; Mr. Morel was gone to work. The three children said not a word. Annie began to whimper with fear; Paul set off for his father.

It was a beautiful day. At Brinsley pit the white steam melted slowly in the sunshine of a soft blue sky; the wheels of the headstocks twinkled high up; the screen, shuffling its coal into the trucks, made a busy noise.

"I want my father; he's got to go to London," said the boy to the first man he met on the bank.

"Tha wants Walter Morel? Go in theer an' tell Joe Ward."

Paul went into the little top office.

"I want my father; he's got to go to London."

"Thy feyther? Is he down? What's his name?"

"Mr. Morel."

"What, Walter? Is owt amiss?"

"He's got to go to London."

The man went to the telephone and rang up the bottom office.

"Walter Morel's wanted, number 42, Hard. Summat's amiss; there's his lad here."

Then he turned round to Paul.

"He'll be up in a few minutes," he said.

Paul wandered out to the pit-top. He watched the chair come up, with its wagon of coal. The great iron cage sank back on its rest, a full carfle was hauled off, an empty tram run on to the chair, a bell ting'ed somewhere, the chair heaved, then dropped like a stone.

Paul did not realise William was dead; it was impossible, with such a bustle going on. The puller-off swung the small truck on to the turn-table, another man ran with it along the bank down the curving lines.

"And William is dead, and my mother's in London, and what will she be doing?" the boy asked himself, as if it were a conundrum.

He watched chair after chair come up, and still no father. At last, standing beside a wagon, a man's form! the chair sank on its rests, Morel stepped off. He was slightly lame from an accident.

"Is it thee, Paul? Is 'e worse?"

"You've got to go to London."

The two walked off the pit-bank, where men were watching curiously. As they came out and went along the railway, with the sunny autumn field on one side and a wall of trucks on the other, Morel said in a frightened voice:

" 'E's niver gone, child?"

"Yes."

"When wor't?"

"Last night. We had a telegram from my mother."

Morel walked on a few strides, then leaned up against a truck-side, his hand over his eyes. He was not crying. Paul stood looking round, waiting. On the weighing machine a truck trundled slowly. Paul saw everything, except his father leaning against the truck as if he were tired.

Morel had only once before been to London. He set off, scared and peaked, to help his wife. That was on Tuesday. The children were left alone in the house. Paul went to work, Arthur went to school, and Annie had in a friend to be with her.

On Saturday night, as Paul was turning the corner, coming home from Keston, he saw his mother and father, who had come to Sethley Bridge Station. They were walking in silence in the dark, tired, straggling apart. The boy waited.

"Mother!" he said, in the darkness.

Mrs. Morel's small figure seemed not to observe. He spoke again.

"Paul!" she said, uninterestedly.

She let him kiss her, but she seemed unaware of him.

In the house she was the same—small, white, and mute. She noticed nothing, she said nothing, only:

"The coffin will be here to-night, Walter. You'd better see about some help." Then, turning to the children: "We're bringing him home."

Then she relapsed into the same mute looking into space, her hands folded on her lap. Paul, looking at her, felt he could not breathe. The house was dead silent.

"I went to work, mother," he said plaintively.

"Did you?" she answered, dully.

After half an hour Morel, troubled and bewildered, came in again.

"Wheer s'll we ha'e him when he *does* come?" he asked his wife.

"In the front-room."

"Then I'd better shift th' table?"

"Yes."

"An' ha'e him across th' chairs?"

"You know there—— Yes, I suppose so."

Morel and Paul went, with a candle, into the parlour. There was no gas there. The father unscrewed the top of the big mahogany oval table, and cleared the middle of the room; then he arranged six chairs opposite each other, so that the coffin could stand on their beds.

"You niver seed such a length as he is!" said the miner, and watching anxiously as he worked.

Paul went to the bay window and looked out. The ash-tree stood monstrous and black in front of the wide darkness. It was a faintly luminous night. Paul went back to his mother.

At ten o'clock Morel called:

"He's here!"

Everyone started. There was a noise of unbarring and unlocking the front door, which opened straight from the night into the room.

"Bring another candle," called Morel.

Annie and Arthur went. Paul followed with his mother. He stood with his arm round her waist in the inner doorway. Down the middle of the cleared room waited six chairs, face to face. In the window, against the lace curtains, Arthur held up one candle, and by the open door, against the night, Annie stood leaning forward, her brass candlestick glittering.

There was the noise of wheels. Outside in the darkness of the street below Paul could see horses and a black vehicle, one lamp, and a few pale faces; then some men, miners, all in their shirt-sleeves, seemed to struggle in the obscurity. Presently two men appeared, bowed beneath a great weight. It was Morel and his neighbour.

"Steady!" called Morel, out of breath.

He and his fellow mounted the steep garden step, heaved into the candlelight with their gleaming coffin-end. Limbs of other men were seen struggling behind. Morel and Burns, in front, staggered; the great dark weight swayed.

"Steady, steady!" cried Morel, as if in pain.

All the six bearers were up in the small garden, holding the great coffin aloft. There were three more steps to the door. The yellow lamp of the carriage shone alone down the black road.

"Now then!" said Morel.

The coffin swayed, the men began to mount the three steps with their load. Annie's candle flickered, and she whimpered as the first men appeared, and the limbs and bowed heads of six men struggled to climb into the room, bearing the coffin that rode like sorrow on their living flesh.

"Oh, my son—my son!" Mrs. Morel sang softly, and each time the coffin swung to the unequal climbing of the men: "Oh, my son—my son—my son!"

"Mother!" Paul whimpered, his hand round her waist.

She did not hear.

"Oh, my son—my son!" she repeated.

Paul saw drops of sweat fall from his father's brow. Six men were in the room—six coatless men, with yielding, struggling limbs, filling the room and knocking against the furniture. The coffin veered, and was gently lowered on to the chairs. The sweat fell from Morel's face on its boards.

"My word, he's a weight!" said a man, and the five miners sighed, bowed, and, trembling with the struggle, descended the steps again, closing the door behind them.

The family was alone in the parlour with the great polished box. William, when laid out, was six feet four inches long. Like a monument lay the bright brown, ponderous coffin. Paul thought it would never be got out of the room again. His mother was stroking the polished wood.

They buried him on the Monday in the little cemetery on the hillside that looks over the fields at the big church and the houses. It was sunny, and the white chrysanthemums frilled themselves in the warmth.

Mrs. Morel could not be persuaded, after this, to talk and take her old bright interest in life. She remained shut off. All the way home in the train she had said to herself: "If only it could have been me!"

When Paul came home at night he found his mother sitting, her day's work done, with hands folded in her lap upon her coarse apron. She always used to have changed her dress and put on a black apron, before. Now Annie set his supper, and his mother sat looking blankly in front of her, her mouth shut tight. Then he beat his brains for news to tell her.

"Mother, Miss Jordan was down to-day, and she said my sketch of a colliery at work was beautiful."

But Mrs. Morel took no notice. Night after night he forced himself to tell her things, although she did not listen. It drove him almost insane to have her thus. At last:

"What's a-matter, mother?" he asked.

She did not hear.

"What's a-matter?" he persisted. "Mother, what's a-matter?"

"You know what's the matter," she said irritably, turning away.

The lad—he was sixteen years old—went to bed drearily. He was cut off and wretched through October, November and December. His mother tried, but she could not rouse herself. She could only brood on her dead son; he had been let to die so cruelly.

At last, on December 23, with his five shillings Christmas-box in his pocket, Paul wandered blindly home. His mother looked at him, and her heart stood still.

"What's the matter?" she asked.

"I'm badly, mother!" he replied. "Mr. Jordan gave me five shillings for a Christmas-box!"

He handed it to her with trembling hands. She put it on the table.

"You aren't glad!" he reproached her; but he trembled violently.

"Where hurts you?" she said, unbuttoning his overcoat.

It was the old question.

"I feel badly, mother."

She undressed him and put him to bed. He had pneumonia dangerously, the doctor said.

"Might he never have had it if I'd kept him at home, not let him go to Nottingham?" was one of the first things she asked.

"He might not have been so bad," said the doctor.

Mrs. Morel stood condemned on her own ground.

"I should have watched the living, not the dead," she told herself.

Paul was very ill. His mother lay in bed at nights with him; they could not afford a nurse. He grew worse, and the crisis approached. One night he tossed into consciousness in the ghastly, sickly feeling of dissolution, when all the cells in the body seem in intense irritability to be breaking down, and consciousness makes a last flare of struggle, like madness.

"I s'll die, mother!" he cried, heaving for breath on the pillow.

She lifted him up, crying in a small voice:

"Oh, my son—my son!"

That brought him to. He realised her. His whole will rose up and arrested him. He put his head on her breast, and took ease of her for love.

"For some things," said his aunt, "it was a good thing Paul was ill that Christmas. I believe it saved his mother."

Paul was in bed for seven weeks. He got up white and fragile. His father had bought him a pot of scarlet and gold tulips. They used to flame in the window in the March sunshine as he sat on the sofa chattering to his mother. The two knitted together in perfect intimacy. Mrs. Morel's life now rooted itself in Paul.

William had been a prophet. Mrs. Morel had a little present and a letter from Lily at Christmas. Mrs. Morel's sister had a letter at the New Year.

"I was at a ball last night. Some delightful people were there, and I enjoyed myself thoroughly," said the letter. "I had every dance—did not sit out one."

Mrs. Morel never heard any more of her.

Morel and his wife were gentle with each other for some time after the death of their son. He would go into a kind of daze, staring wide-eyed and blank across the room. Then he got up suddenly and hurried out to the Three Spots, returning in his normal state. But never in his life would he go for a walk up Shepstone, past the office where his son had worked, and he always avoided the cemetery.

Part Two

2

VII

LAD-AND-GIRL LOVE

Paul had been many times up to Willey Farm during the autumn. He was friends with the two youngest boys. Edgar the eldest, would not condescend at first. And Miriam also refused to be approached. She was afraid of being set at nought, as by her own brothers. The girl was romantic in her soul. Everywhere was a Walter Scott heroine being loved by men with helmets or with plumes in their caps. She herself was something of a princess turned into a swine-girl in her own imagination. And she was afraid lest this boy, who, nevertheless, looked something like a Walter Scott hero, who could paint and speak French, and knew what algebra meant, and who went by train to Nottingham every day, might consider her simply as the swine-girl, unable to perceive the princess beneath; so she held aloof.

Her great companion was her mother. They were both brown-eyed, and inclined to be mystical, such women as treasure religion inside them, breathe it in their nostrils, and see the whole of life in a mist thereof. So to Miriam, Christ and God made one great figure, which she loved tremblingly and passionately when a tremendous sunset burned out the western sky, and Ediths, and Lucys, and Rowenas, Brian de Bois Guilberts, Rob Roys, and Guy Mannerings, rustled the sunny leaves in the morning, or sat in her bedroom aloft, alone, when it snowed. That was life to her. For the rest, she drudged in the house, which work she would not have minded had not her clean red floor been mucked up immediately by the trampling farm-boots of her brothers. She madly wanted her little brother of four to let her swathe him and stifle him in her love; she went to church reverently, with bowed head, and quivered in anguish from the vulgarity of the other choir-girls and from the common-sounding voice of the curate; she fought with her brothers, whom she considered brutal louts; and she held not her father in too high esteem because he did not carry any mystical ideals cherished in his heart, but only wanted to have as easy a time as he could, and his meals when he was ready for them.

She hated her position as swine-girl. She wanted to be considered. She wanted to learn, thinking that if she could read, as Paul said he could read, "Colomba", or the "Voyage autour de ma Chambre", the world would have a different face for her and a deepened respect. She could not be princess by wealth or standing. So she was mad to have learning whereon to pride herself. For she was different from other folk, and must not be scooped up among the common fry. Learning was the only distinction to which she thought to aspire.

Her beauty—that of a shy, wild, quiveringly sensitive thing—seemed nothing to her. Even her soul, so strong for rhapsody, was not enough. She must have something to reinforce her pride, because she felt different from other people. Paul she eyed rather wistfully. On the whole, she scorned the male sex. But here was a new specimen, quick, light, graceful, who could be gentle and who could be sad, and who was clever, and who knew a lot, and who had a death in the family. The boy's poor morsel of learning exalted him almost sky-high in her esteem. Yet she tried hard to scorn him, because he would not see in her the princess but only the swine-girl. And he scarcely observed her.

Then he was so ill, and she felt he would be weak. Then she would be stronger than he. Then she could love him. If she could be mistress of him in his weakness, take care of him, if he could depend on her, if she could, as it were, have him in her arms, how she would love him!

As soon as the skies brightened and plum-blossom was out, Paul drove off in the milkman's heavy float up to Willey Farm. Mr. Leivers shouted in a kindly fashion at the boy, then clicked to the horse as they climbed the hill slowly, in the freshness of the morning. White clouds went on their way, crowding to the back of the hills that were rousing in the spring-time. The water of Nethermere lay below, very blue against the seared meadows and the thorn-trees.

It was four and a half miles' drive. Tiny buds on the hedges, vivid as copper-green, were opening into rosettes; and thrushes called, and blackbirds shrieked and scolded. It was a new, glamorous world.

Miriam, peeping through the kitchen window, saw the horse walk through the big white gate into the farmyard that was backed by the oak-wood, still bare. Then a youth in a heavy overcoat climbed down. He put up his hands for the whip and the rug that the good-looking, ruddy farmer handed down to him. Miriam appeared in the doorway. She was nearly sixteen, very beautiful, with her warm colouring, her gravity, her eyes dilating suddenly like an ecstasy.

"I say," said Paul, turning shyly aside, "your daffodils are nearly out. Isn't it early? But don't they look cold?"

"Cold!" said Miriam, in her musical, caressing voice.

"The green on their buds——" and he faltered into silence timidly.

"Let me take the rug," said Miriam over-gently.

"I can carry it," he answered, rather injured. But he yielded it to her.

Then Mrs. Leivers appeared.

"I'm sure you're tired and cold," she said. "Let me take your coat. It *is* heavy. You mustn't walk far in it."

She helped him off with his coat. He was quite unused to such attention. She was almost smothered under its weight.

"Why, mother," laughed the farmer as he passed through the kitchen, swinging the great milk-churns, "you've got almost more than you can manage there."

She beat up the sofa cushions for the youth.

The kitchen was very small and irregular. The farm had been originally a labourer's cottage. And the furniture was old and battered. But Paul loved it—loved the sack-bag that formed the hearthrug, and the funny little corner under the stairs, and the small window deep in the corner, through which, bending a little, he could see the plum trees in the back garden and the lovely round hills beyond.

"Won't you lie down?" said Mrs. Leivers.

"Oh no; I'm not tired," he said. "Isn't it lovely coming out, don't you think? I saw a sloe-bush in blossom and a lot of celandines. I'm glad it's sunny."

"Can I give you anything to eat or to drink?"

"No, thank you."

"How's your mother?"

"I think she's tired now. I think she's had too much to do. Perhaps in a little while she'll go to Skegness with me. Then she'll be able to rest. I s'll be glad if she can."

"Yes," replied Mrs. Leivers. "It's a wonder she isn't ill herself."

Miriam was moving about preparing dinner. Paul watched everything that happened. His face was pale and thin, but his eyes were quick and bright with life as ever. He watched the strange, almost rhapsodic way in which the girl moved about, carrying a great stew-jar to the oven, or looking in the saucepan. The atmosphere was different from that of his own home, where everything seemed so ordinary. When Mr. Leivers called loudly outside to the horse, that was reaching over to feed on the rose-bushes in the garden, the girl started, looked round with dark eyes, as if something had come breaking in on her world. There was a sense of silence inside the house and out. Miriam seemed as in some dreamy tale, a maiden in bondage, her spirit dreaming in a land far away and magical. And her discoloured, old blue frock and her broken boots seemed only like the romantic rags of King Cophetua's beggar-maid.

She suddenly became aware of his keen blue eyes upon her, taking her all in. Instantly her broken boots and her frayed old frock hurt her. She resented his seeing everything. Even he knew that her stocking was not pulled up. She went into the scullery, blushing deeply. And afterwards her hands trembled slightly at her work. She nearly dropped all she handled. When her inside dream was shaken, her body quivered with trepidation. She resented that he saw so much.

Mrs. Leivers sat for some time talking to the boy, although she was needed at her work. She was too polite to leave her. Presently she excused herself and rose. After a while she looked into the tin saucepan.

"Oh *dear*, Miriam," she cried, "these potatoes have boiled dry!"

Miriam started as if she had been stung.

"Have they, mother?" she cried.

"I shouldn't care, Miriam," said the mother, "if I hadn't trusted them to you." She peered into the pan.

The girl stiffened as if from a blow. Her dark eyes dilated; she remained standing in the same spot.

"Well," she answered, gripped tight in self-conscious shame, "I'm sure I looked at them five minutes since."

"Yes," said the mother, "I know it's easily done."

"They're not much burned," said Paul. "It doesn't matter, does it?"

Mrs. Leivers looked at the youth with her brown, hurt eyes.

"It wouldn't matter but for the boys," she said to him. "Only Miriam knows what a trouble they make if the potatoes are 'caught'."

"Then," thought Paul to himself, "you shouldn't let them make a trouble."

After a while Edgar came in. He wore leggings, and his boots were covered with earth. He was rather small, rather formal, for a farmer. He glanced at Paul, nodded to him distantly, and said:

"Dinner ready?"

"Nearly, Edgar," replied the mother apologetically.

"I'm ready for mine," said the young man, taking up the newspaper and reading. Presently the rest of the family trooped in. Dinner was served. The meal went rather brutally. The over-gentleness and apologetic tone of the mother brought out all the brutality of manners in the sons. Edgar tasted the potatoes, moved his mouth quickly like a rabbit, looked indignantly at his mother, and said:

"These potatoes are burnt, mother."

"Yes, Edgar. I forgot them for a minute. Perhaps you'll have bread if you can't eat them."

Edgar looked in anger across at Miriam.

"What was Miriam doing that she couldn't attend to them?" he said.

Miriam looked up. Her mouth opened, her dark eyes blazed and winced, but she said nothing. She swallowed her anger and her shame, bowing her dark head.

"I'm sure she was trying hard," said the mother.

"She hasn't got sense even to boil the potatoes," said Edgar. "What is she kept at home for?"

"On'y for eating everything that's left in th' pantry," said Maurice.

"They don't forget that potato-pie against our Miriam," laughed the father.

She was utterly humiliated. The mother sat in silence, suffering, like some saint out of place at the brutal board.

It puzzled Paul. He wondered vaguely why all this intense feeling went running because of a few burnt potatoes. The mother exalted everything—even a bit of housework—to the plane of a religious trust. The sons resented this; they felt themselves cut away underneath, and they answered with brutality and also with a sneering superciliousness.

Paul was just opening out from childhood into manhood. This atmosphere, where everything took a religious value, came with a subtle fascination to him. There was something in the air. His own mother was logical. Here there was something different, something he loved, something that at times he hated.

Miriam quarrelled with her brothers fiercely. Later in the afternoon, when they had gone away again, her mother said:

"You disappointed me at dinner-time, Miriam."

The girl dropped her head.

"They are such *brutes!*" she suddenly cried, looking up with flashing eyes.

"But hadn't you promised not to answer them?" said the mother. "And I believed in you. I *can't* stand it when you wrangle."

"But they're so hateful!" cried Miriam, "and—and *low.*"

"Yes, dear. But how often have I asked you not to answer Edgar back? Can't you let him say what he likes?"

"But why should he say what he likes?"

"Aren't you strong enough to bear it, Miriam, if even for my sake? Are you so weak that you must wrangle with them?"

Mrs. Leivers stuck unflinchingly to this doctrine of "the other cheek". She could not instil it at all into the boys. With the girls she succeeded better, and Miriam was the child of her heart. The boys loathed the other cheek when it was presented to them. Miriam was often sufficiently lofty to turn it. Then they spat on her and hated her. But she walked in her proud humility, living within herself.

There was always this feeling of jangle and discord in the Leivers family. Although the boys resented so bitterly this eternal appeal to their deeper feelings of resignation and proud humility, yet it had its effect on them. They could not establish between themselves and an outsider just the ordinary human feeling and unexaggerated friendship; they were always restless for the something deeper. Ordinary folk seemed shallow to them, trivial and inconsiderable. And

so they were unaccustomed, painfully uncouth in the simplest social intercourse, suffering, and yet insolent in their superiority. Then beneath was the
yearning for the soul-intimacy to which they could not attain because they were
too dumb, and every approach to close connection was blocked by their clumsy
contempt of other people. They wanted genuine intimacy, but they could not
get even normally near to anyone, because they scorned to take the first steps,
they scorned the triviality which forms common human intercourse.

Paul fell under Mrs. Leivers's spell. Everything had a religious and intensified
meaning when he was with her. His soul, hurt, highly developed, sought her as
if for nourishment. Together they seemed to sift the vital fact from an experience.

Miriam was her mother's daughter. In the sunshine of the afternoon mother
and daughter went down the fields with him. They looked for nests. There was
a jenny wren's in the hedge by the orchard.

"I *do* want you to see this," said Mrs. Leivers.

He crouched down and carefully put his finger through the thorns into the
round door of the nest.

"It's almost as if you were feeling inside the live body of the bird," he said,
"it's so warm. They say a bird makes its nest round like a cup with pressing its
breast on it. Then how did it make the ceiling round, I wonder?"

The nest seemed to start into life for the two women. After that, Miriam
came to see it every day. It seemed so close to her. Again, going down the
hedgeside with the girl, he noticed the celandines, scalloped splashes of gold, on
the side of the ditch.

"I like them," he said, "when their petals go flat back with the sunshine.
They seemed to be pressing themselves at the sun."

And then the celandines ever after drew her with a little spell. An-
thropomorphic as she was, she stimulated him into appreciating things thus, and
then they lived for her. She seemed to need things kindling in her imagination
or in her soul before she felt she had them. And she was cut off from ordinary
life by her religious intensity which made the world for her either a nunnery
garden or a paradise, where sin and knowledge were not, or else an ugly, cruel
thing.

So it was in this atmosphere of subtle intimacy, this meeting in their common feeling for something in Nature, that their love started.

Personally, he was a long time before he realized her. For ten months he had
to stay at home after his illness. For a while he went to Skegness with his
mother, and was perfectly happy. But even from the seaside he wrote long
letters to Mrs. Leivers about the shore and the sea. And he brought back his
beloved sketches of the flat Lincoln coast, anxious for them to see. Almost they
would interest the Leivers more than they interested his mother. It was not his
art Mrs. Morel cared about; it was himself and his achievement. But Mrs. Leivers and her children were almost his disciples. They kindled him and made him
glow to his work, whereas his mother's influence was to make him quietly
determined, patient, dogged, unwearied.

He soon was friends with the boys, whose rudeness was only superficial.
They had all, when they could trust themselves, a strange gentleness and lova-
bleness.

"Will you come with me on to the fallow?" asked Edgar, rather hesitatingly.

Paul went joyfully, and spent the afternoon helping to hoe or to single turnips with his friend. He used to lie with the three brothers in the hay piled up in

the barn and tell them about Nottingham and about Jordan's. In return, they taught him to milk, and let him do little jobs—chopping hay or pulping turnips—just as much as he liked. At midsummer he worked all through hay-harvest with them, and then he loved them. The family was so cut off from the world actually. They seemed, somehow, like *'les derniers fils d'une race épuisée''*. Though the lads were strong and healthy, yet they had all that over-sensitiveness and hanging-back which made them so lonely, yet also such close, delicate friends once their intimacy was won. Paul loved them dearly, and they him.

Miriam came later. But he had come into her life before she made any mark on his. One dull afternoon, when the men were on the land and the rest at school, only Miriam and her mother at home, the girl said to him, after having hesitated for some time:

"Have you seen the swing?"

"No," he answered. "Where?"

"In the cowshed," she replied.

She always hesitated to offer or to show him anything. Men have such different standards of worth from women, and her dear things—the valuable things to her—her brothers had so often mocked or flouted.

"Come on, then," he replied, jumping up.

There were two cowsheds, one on either side of the barn. In the lower, darker shed there was standing for four cows. Hens flew scolding over the manger-wall as the youth and girl went forward for the great thick rope which hung from the beam in the darkness overhead, and was pushed back over a peg in the wall.

"It's something like a rope!" he exclaimed appreciatively; and he sat down on it, anxious to try it. Then immediately he rose.

"Come on, then, and have first go," he said to the girl.

"See," she answered, going into the barn, "we put some bags on the seat"; and she made the swing comfortable for him. That gave her pleasure. He held the rope.

"Come on, then," he said to her.

"No, I won't go first," she answered.

She stood aside in her still, aloof fashion.

"Why?"

"You go," she pleaded.

Almost for the first time in her life she had the pleasure of giving up to a man, of spoiling him. Paul looked at her.

"All right," he said, sitting down. "Mind out!"

He set off with a spring, and in a moment was flying through the air, almost out of the door of the shed, the upper half of which was open, showing outside the drizzling rain, the filthy yard, the cattle standing disconsolate against the black cart-shed, and at the back of all the grey-green wall of the wood. She stood below in her crimson tam-o'-shanter and watched. He looked down at her, and she saw his blue eyes sparkling.

"It's a treat of a swing," he said.

"Yes."

He was swinging through the air, every bit of him swinging, like a bird that swoops for joy of movement. And he looked down at her. Her crimson cap hung over her dark curls, her beautiful warm face, so still in a kind of brooding, was lifted towards him. It was dark and rather cold in the shed. Suddenly a swallow came down from the high roof and darted out of the door.

"I didn't know a bird was watching," he called.

He swung negligently. She could feel him falling and lifting through the air, as if he were lying on some force.

"Now I'll die," he said, in a detached, dreamy voice, as though he were the dying motion of the swing. She watched him, fascinated. Suddenly he put on the brake and jumped out.

"I've had a long turn," he said. "But it's a treat of a swing—it's a real treat of a swing!"

Miriam was amused that he took a swing so seriously and felt so warmly over it.

"No; you go on," she said.

"Why, don't you want one?" he asked, astonished.

"Well, not much. I'll have just a little."

She sat down, whilst he kept the bags in place for her.

"It's so ripping!" he said, setting her in motion. "Keep your heels up, or they'll bang the manger wall."

She felt the accuracy with which he caught her, exactly at the right moment, and the exactly proportionate strength of his thrust, and she was afraid. Down to her bowels went the hot wave of fear. She was in his hands. Again, firm and inevitable came the thrust at the right moment. She gripped the rope, almost swooning.

"Ha!" she laughed in fear. "No higher!"

"But you're not a *bit* high," he remonstrated.

"But no higher."

He heard the fear in her voice, and desisted. Her heart melted in hot pain when the moment came for him to thrust her forward again. But he left her alone. She began to breathe.

"Won't you really go any farther?" he asked. "Should I keep you there?"

"No; let me go by myself," she answered.

He moved aside and watched her.

"Why, you're scarcely moving," he said.

She laughed slightly with shame, and in a moment got down.

"They say if you can swing you won't be sea-sick," he said, as he mounted again. "I don't believe I should ever be sea-sick."

Away he went. There was something fascinating to her in him. For the moment he was nothing but a piece of swinging stuff; not a particle of him that did not swing. She could never lose herself so, nor could her brothers. It roused a warmth in her. It were almost as if he were a flame that had lit a warmth in her whilst he swung in the middle air.

And gradually the intimacy with the family concentrated for Paul on three persons—the mother, Edgar, and Miriam. To the mother he went for that sympathy and that appeal which seemed to draw him out. Edgar was his very close friend. And to Miriam he more or less condescended, because she seemed so humble.

But the girl gradually sought him out. If he brought up his sketch-book, it was she who pondered longest over the last picture. Then she would look up at him. Suddenly, her dark eyes alight like water that shakes with a stream of gold in the dark, she would ask:

"Why do I like this so?"

Always something in his breast shrank from these close, intimate, dazzled looks of hers.

"Why *do* you?" he asked.

"I don't know. It seems so true."

"It's because—it's because there is scarcely any shadow in it; it's more shim-mery, as if I'd painted the shimmering protoplasm in the leaves and everywhere, and not the stiffness of the shape. That seems dead to me. Only this shimmeri-ness is the real living. The shape is a dead crust. The shimmer is inside really."

And she, with her little finger in her mouth, would ponder these sayings. They gave her a feeling of life again, and vivified things which had meant noth-ing to her. She managed to find some meaning in his struggling, abstract speeches. And they were the medium through which she came distinctly at her beloved objects.

Another day she sat at sunset whilst he was painting some pine-trees which caught the red glare from the west. He had been quiet.

"There you are!" he said suddenly. "I wanted that. Now, look at them and tell me, are they pine trunks or are they red coals, standing-up pieces of fire in that darkness? There's God's burning bush for you, that burned not away."

Miriam looked, and was frightened. But the pine trunks were wonderful to her, and distinct. He packed his box and rose. Suddenly he looked at her.

"Why are you always sad?" he asked her.

"Sad!" she exclaimed, looking up at him with startled, wonderful brown eyes.

"Yes," he replied. "You are always sad."

"I am not—oh, not a bit!" she cried.

"But even your joy is like a flame coming off of sadness," he persisted. "You're never jolly, or even just all right."

"No," she pondered. "I wonder—why?"

"Because you're not; because you're different inside, like a pine-tree, and then you flare up; but you're not just like an ordinary tree, with fidgety leaves and jolly——"

He got tangled up in his own speech; but she brooded on it, and he had a strange, roused sensation, as if his feelings were new. She got so near him. It was a strange stimulant.

Then sometimes he hated her. Her youngest brother was only five. He was a frail lad, with immense brown eyes in his quaint fragile face—one of Rey-nolds's "Choir of Angels", with a touch of elf. Often Miriam kneeled to the child and drew him to her.

"Eh, my Hubert!" she sang, in a voice heavy and surcharged with love. "Eh, my Hubert!"

And, folding him in her arms, she swayed slightly from side to side with love, her face half lifted, her eyes half closed, her voice drenched with love.

"Don't!" said the child, uneasy—"don't, Miriam!"

"Yes; you love me, don't you?" she murmured deep in her throat, almost as if she were in a trance, and swaying also as if she were swooned in an ecstasy of love.

"Don't!" repeated the child, a frown on his clear brow.

"You love me, don't you?" she murmured.

"What do you make such a *fuss* for?" cried Paul, all in suffering because of her extreme emotion. "Why can't you be ordinary with him?"

She let the child go, and rose, and said nothing. Her intensity, which would leave no emotion on a normal plane, irritated the youth into a frenzy. And this fearful, naked contact of her on small occasions shocked him. He was used to his mother's reserve. And on such occasions he was thankful in his heart and soul that he had his mother, so sane and wholesome.

All the life of Miriam's body was in her eyes, which were usually dark as a dark church, but could flame with light like a conflagration. Her face scarcely ever altered from its look of brooding. She might have been one of the women who went with Mary when Jesus was dead. Her body was not flexible and living. She walked with a swing, rather heavily, her head bowed forward, pondering. She was not clumsy, and yet none of her movements seemed quite *the* movement. Often, when wiping the dishes, she would stand in bewilderment and chagrin because she had pulled in two halves a cup or a tumbler. It was as if, in her fear and self-mistrust, she put too much strength into the effort. There was no looseness or abandon about her. Everything was gripped stiff with intensity, and her effort, overcharged, closed in on itself.

She rarely varied from her swinging, forward, intense walk. Occasionally she ran with Paul down the fields. Then her eyes blazed naked in a kind of ecstasy that frightened him. But she was physically afraid. If she were getting over a stile, she gripped his hands in a little hard anguish, and began to lose her presence of mind. And he could not persuade her to jump from even a small height. Her eyes dilated, became exposed and palpitating.

"No!" she cried, half laughing in terror—"no!"

"You shall!" he cried once, and, jerking her forward, he brought her falling from the fence. But her wild "Ah!" of pain, as if she were losing consciousness, cut him. She landed on her feet safely, and afterwards had courage in this respect.

She was very much dissatisfied with her lot.

"Don't you like being at home?" Paul asked her, surprised.

"Who would?" she answered, low and intense. "What is it? I'm all day cleaning what the boys make just as bad in five minutes. I don't *want* to be at home."

"What do you want, then?"

"I want to do something. I want a chance like anybody else. Why should I, because I'm a girl, be kept at home and not allowed to be anything? What chance *have* I?"

"Chance of what?"

"Of knowing anything—of learning, of doing anything. It's not fair, because I'm a woman."

She seemed very bitter. Paul wondered. In his own home Annie was almost glad to be a girl. She had not so much responsibility; things were lighter for her. She never wanted to be other than a girl. But Miriam almost fiercely wished she were a man. And yet she hated men at the same time.

"But it's as well to be a woman as a man," he said, frowning.

"Ha! Is it? Men have everything."

"I should think women ought to be as glad to be women as men are to be men," he answered.

"No!"—she shook her head—"no! Everything the men have."

"But what do you want?" he asked.

"I want to learn. Why *should* it be that I know nothing?"

"What! such as mathematics and French?"

"Why *shouldn't* I know mathematics? Yes!" she cried, her eye expanding in a kind of defiance.

"Well, you can learn as much as I know," he said. "I'll teach you, if you like."

Her eyes dilated. She mistrusted him as teacher.

"Would you?" he asked.

Her head had dropped, and she was sucking her finger broodingly.

"Yes," she said hesitatingly.

He used to tell his mother all these things.

"I'm going to teach Miriam algebra," he said.

"Well," replied Mrs. Morel, "I hope she'll get fat on it."

When he went up to the farm on the Monday evening, it was drawing twilight. Miriam was just sweeping up the kitchen, and was kneeling at the hearth when he entered. Everyone was out but her. She looked round at him, flushed, her dark eyes shining, her fine hair falling about her face.

"Hello!" she said, soft and musical. "I knew it was you."

"How?"

"I knew your step. Nobody treads so quick and firm."

He sat down, sighing.

"Ready to do some algebra?" he asked, drawing a little book from his pocket.

"But——"

He could feel her backing away.

"You said you wanted," he insisted.

"To-night, though?" she faltered.

"But I came on purpose. And if you want to learn it, you must begin."

She took up her ashes in the dustpan and looked at him, half tremulously, laughing.

"Yes, but to-night! You see, I haven't thought of it."

"Well, my goodness! Take the ashes and come."

He went and sat on the stone bench in the back-yard, where the big milk-cans were standing, tipped up, to air. The men were in the cowsheds. He could hear the little sing-song of the milk spurting into the pails. Presently she came, bringing some big greenish apples.

"You know you like them," she said.

He took a bite.

"Sit down," he said, with his mouth full.

She was short-sighted, and peered over his shoulder. It irritated him. He gave her the book quickly.

"Here," he said. "It's only letters for figures. You put down 'a' instead of '2' or '6'."

They worked, he talking, she with her head down on the book. He was quick and hasty. She never answered. Occasionally, when he demanded of her, "Do you see?" she looked up at him, her eyes wide with the half-laugh that comes of fear. "Don't you?" he cried.

He had been too fast. But she said nothing. He questioned her more, then got hot. It made his blood rouse to see her there, as it were, at his mercy, her mouth open, her eyes dilated with laughter that was afraid, apologetic, ashamed. Then Edgar came along with two buckets of milk.

"Hello!" he said. "What are you doing?"

"Algebra," replied Paul.

"Algebra!" repeated Edgar curiously. Then he passed on with a laugh. Paul took a bite at his forgotten apple, looked at the miserable cabbages in the garden, pecked into lace by the fowls, and he wanted to pull them up. Then he glanced at Miriam. She was poring over the book, seemed absorbed in it, yet trembling lest she could not get at it. It made him cross. She was ruddy and beautiful. Yet her soul seemed to be intensely supplicating. The algebra-book she closed, shrinking, knowing he was angered; and at the same instant he grew gentle, seeing her hurt because she did not understand.

But things came slowly to her. And when she held herself in a grip, seemed so utterly humble before the lesson, it made his blood rouse. He stormed at her, got ashamed, continued the lesson, and grew furious again, abusing her. She listened in silence. Occasionally, very rarely, she defended herself. Her liquid dark eyes blazed at him.

"You don't give me time to learn it," she said.

"All right," he answered, throwing the book on the table and lighting a cigarette. Then, after a while, he went back to her repentant. So the lessons went. He was always either in a rage or very gentle.

"What do you tremble your *soul* before it for?" he cried. "You don't learn algebra with your blessed soul. Can't you look at it with your clear simple wits?"

Often, when he went again into the kitchen, Mrs. Leivers would look at him reproachfully, saying:

"Paul, don't be so hard on Miriam. She may not be quick, but I'm sure she tries."

"I can't help it," he said rather pitiably. "I go off like it."

"You don't mind me, Miriam, do you?" he asked of the girl later.

"No," she reassured him in her beautiful deep tones—"no, I don't mind."

"Don't mind me; it's my fault."

But, in spite of himself, his blood began to boil with her. It was strange that no one else made him in such fury. He flared against her. Once he threw the pencil in her face. There was a silence. She turned her face slightly aside.

"I didn't——" he began, but got no farther, feeling weak in all his bones. She never reproached him or was angry with him. He was often cruelly ashamed. But still again his anger burst like a bubble surcharged; and still, when he saw her eager, silent, as it were, blind face, he felt he wanted to throw the pencil in it; and still, when he saw her hand trembling and her mouth parted with suffering, his heart was scalded with pain for her. And because of the intensity to which she roused him, he sought her.

Then he often avoided her and went with Edgar. Miriam and her brother were naturally antagonistic. Edgar was a rationalist, who was curious, and had a sort of scientific interest in life. It was a great bitterness to Miriam to see herself deserted by Paul for Edgar, who seemed so much lower. But the youth was very happy with her elder brother. The two men spent afternoons together on the land or in the loft doing carpentry, when it rained. And they talked together, or Paul taught Edgar the songs he himself had learned from Annie at the piano. And often all the men, Mr. Leivers as well, had bitter debates on the nationalizing of the land and similar problems. Paul had already heard his mother's views, and as these were as yet his own, he argued for her. Miriam attended and took part, but was all the time waiting until it should be over and a personal communication might begin.

"After all," she said within herself, "if the land were nationalized, Edgar and Paul and I would be just the same." So she waited for the youth to come back to her.

He was studying for his painting. He loved to sit at home, alone with his mother, at night, working and working. She sewed or read. Then, looking up from his task, he would rest his eyes for a moment on her face, that was bright with living warmth, and he returned gladly to his work.

"I can do my best things when you sit there in your rocking-chair, mother," he said.

"I'm sure!" she exclaimed, sniffing with mock scepticism. But she felt it was so, and her heart quivered with brightness. For many hours she sat still, slightly conscious of him labouring away, whilst she worked or read her book. And he, with all his soul's intensity directing his pencil, could feel her warmth inside him like strength. They were both very happy so, and both unconscious of it. These times, that meant so much, and which were real living, they almost ignored.

He was conscious only when stimulated. A sketch finished, he always wanted to take it to Miriam. Then he was stimulated into knowledge of the work he had produced unconsciously. In contact with Miriam he gained insight; his vision went deeper. From his mother he drew the life-warmth, the strength to produce; Miriam urged this warmth into intensity like a white light.

When he returned to the factory the conditions of work were better. He had Wednesday afternoon off to go to the Art School—Miss Jordan's provision—returning in the evening. Then the factory closed at six instead of eight on Thursday and Friday evenings.

One evening in the summer Miriam and he went over the fields by Herod's Farm on their way from the library home. So it was only three miles to Willey Farm. There was a yellow glow over the mowing-grass, and the sorrel-heads burned crimson. Gradually, as they walked along the high land, the gold in the west sank down to red, the red to crimson, and then the chill blue crept up against the glow.

They came out upon the high road to Alfreton, which ran white between the darkening fields. There Paul hesitated. It was two miles home for him, one mile forward for Miriam. They both looked up the road that ran in shadow right under the glow of the north-west sky. On the crest of the hill, Selby, with its stark houses and the up-pricked headstocks of the pit, stood in black silhouette small against the sky.

He looked at his watch.

"Nine o'clock!" he said.

The pair stood, loth to part, hugging their books.

"The wood is so lovely now," she said. "I wanted you to see it."

He followed her slowly across the road to the white gate.

"They grumble so if I'm late," he said.

"But you're not doing anything wrong," she answered impatiently.

He followed her across the nibbled pasture in the dusk. There was a coolness in the wood, a scent of leaves, of honeysuckle, and a twilight. The two walked in silence. Night came wonderfully there, among the throng of dark tree-trunks. He looked round, expectant.

She wanted to show him a certain wild-rose bush she had discovered. She knew it was wonderful. And yet, till he had seen it, she felt it had not come into her soul. Only he could make it her own, immortal. She was dissatisfied.

Dew was already on the paths. In the old oak-wood a mist was rising, and he hesitated, wondering whether one whiteness were a strand of fog or only campion-flowers pallid in a cloud.

By the time they came to the pine-trees Miriam was getting very eager and very tense. Her bush might be gone. She might not be able to find it; and she wanted it so much. Almost passionately she wanted to be with him when he stood before the flowers. They were going to have a communion together—something that thrilled her, something holy. He was walking beside her in silence. They were very near to each other. She trembled, and he listened, vaguely anxious.

Coming to the edge of the wood, they saw the sky in front, like mother-of-pearl, and the earth growing dark. Somewhere on the outermost branches of the pine-wood the honeysuckle was streaming scent.

"Where?" he asked.

"Down the middle path," she murmured, quivering.

When they turned the corner of the path she stood still. In the wide walk between the pines, gazing rather frightened, she could distinguish nothing for some moments; the greying light robbed things of their colour. Then she saw her bush.

"Ah!" she cried, hastening forward.

It was very still. The tree was tall and straggling. It had thrown its briers over a hawthorn-bush, and its long streamers trailed thick, right down to the grass, splashing the darkness everywhere with great spilt stars, pure white. In bosses of ivory and in large splashed stars the roses gleamed on the darkness of foliage and stems and grass. Paul and Miriam stood close together, silent, and watched. Point after point the steady roses shone out to them, seeming to kindle something in their souls. The dusk came like smoke around, and still did not put out the roses.

Paul looked into Miriam's eyes. She was pale and expectant with wonder, her lips were parted, and her dark eyes lay open to him. His look seemed to travel down into her. Her soul quivered. It was the communion she wanted. He turned aside, as if pained. He turned to the bush.

"They seem as if they walk like butterflies, and shake themselves," he said.

She looked at her roses. They were white, some incurved and holy, others expanded in an ecstasy. The tree was dark as a shadow. She lifted her hand impulsively to the flowers; she went forward and touched them in worship.

"Let us go," he said.

There was a cool scent of ivory roses—a white, virgin scent. Something made him feel anxious and imprisoned. The two walked in silence.

"Till Sunday," he said quietly, and left her; and she walked home slowly, feeling her soul satisfied with the holiness of the night. He stumbled down the path. And as soon as he was out of the wood, in the free open meadow, where he could breathe, he started to run as fast as he could. It was like a delicious delirium in his veins.

Always when he went with Miriam, and it grew rather late, he knew his mother was fretting and getting angry about him—why, he could not understand. As he went into the house, flinging down his cap, his mother looked up at the clock. She had been sitting thinking, because a chill to her eyes prevented her reading. She could feel Paul being drawn away by this girl. And she did not care for Miriam. "She is one of those who will want to suck a man's soul out till he has none of his own left," she said to herself; "and he is just such a gaby as to let himself be absorbed. She will never let him become a man; she never will." So, while he was away with Miriam, Mrs. Morel grew more and more worked up.

She glanced at the clock and said, coldly and rather tired:

"You have been far enough to-night."

His soul, warm and exposed from contact with the girl, shrank.

"You must have been right home with her," his mother continued.

He would not answer. Mrs. Morel, looking at him quickly, saw his hair was damp on his forehead with haste, saw him frowning in his heavy fashion, resentfully.

"She must be wonderfully fascinating, that you can't get away from her, but must go trailing eight miles at this time of night."

He was hurt between the past glamour with Miriam and the knowledge that his mother fretted. He had meant not to say anything, to refuse to answer. But he could not harden his heart to ignore his mother.

"I *do* like to talk to her," he answered irritably.

"Is there nobody else to talk to?"

"You wouldn't say anything if I went with Edgar."

"You know I should. You know, whoever you went with, I should say it was too far for you to go trailing, late at night, when you've been to Nottingham. Besides"—her voice suddenly flashed into anger and contempt—"it is disgusting—bits of lads and girls courting."

"It is *not* courting," he cried.

"I don't know what else you call it."

"It's not! Do you think we *spoon* and do? We only talk."

"Till goodness knows what time and distance," was the sarcastic rejoinder.

Paul snapped at the laces of his boots angrily.

"What are you so mad about?" he asked. "Because you don't like her."

"I don't say I don't like her. But I don't hold with children keeping company, and never did."

"But you don't mind our Annie going out with Jim Inger."

"They've more sense than you two."

"Why?"

"Our Annie's not one of the deep sort."

He failed to see the meaning of this remark. But his mother looked tired. She was never so strong after William's death; and her eyes hurt her.

"Well," he said, "it's so pretty in the country. Mr. Sleath asked about you. He said he'd missed you. Are you a bit better?"

"I ought to have been in bed a long time ago," she replied.

"Why, mother, you know you wouldn't have gone before quarter-past ten."

"Oh, yes, I should!"

"Oh, little woman, you'd say anything now you're disagreeable with me, wouldn't you?"

He kissed her forehead that he knew so well: the deep marks between the brows, the rising of the fine hair, greying now, and the proud setting of the temples. His hand lingered on her shoulder after his kiss. Then he went slowly to bed. He had forgotten Miriam; he only saw how his mother's hair was lifted back from her warm, broad brow. And somehow, she was hurt.

Then the next time he saw Miriam he said to her:

"Don't let me be late to-night—not later than ten o'clock. My mother gets so upset."

Miriam dropped her head, brooding.

"Why does she get upset?" she asked.

"Because she says I oughtn't to be out late when I have to get up early."

"Very well!" said Miriam, rather quietly, with just a touch of a sneer.
He resented that. And he was usually late again.

That there was any love growing between him and Miriam neither of them
would have acknowledged. He thought he was too sane for such sentimentality,
and she thought herself too lofty. They both were late in coming to maturity,
and psychical ripeness was much behind even the physical. Miriam was exceedingly sensitive, as her mother had always been. The slightest grossness made her
recoil almost in anguish. Her brothers were brutal, but never coarse in speech.
The men did all the discussing of farm matters outside. But, perhaps, because of
the continual business of birth and of begetting which goes on upon every farm,
Miriam was the more hypersensitive to the matter, and her blood was chastened
almost to disgust of the faintest suggestion of such intercourse. Paul took his
pitch from her, and their intimacy went on in an utterly blanched and chaste
fashion. It could never be mentioned that the mare was in foal.

When he was nineteen, he was earning only twenty shillings a week, but he
was happy. His painting went well, and life went well enough. On the Good
Friday he organised a walk to the Hemlock Stone. There were three lads of his
own age, then Annie and Arthur, Miriam and Geoffrey. Arthur, apprenticed as
an electrician in Nottingham, was home for the holiday. Morel, as usual, was up
early, whistling and sawing in the yard. At seven o'clock the family heard him
buy threepennyworth of hot-cross buns; he talked with gusto to the little girl
who brought them, calling her "my darling". He turned away several boys who
came with more buns, telling them they had been "kested" by a little lass. Then
Mrs. Morel got up, and the family straggled down. It was an immense luxury to
everybody, this lying in bed just beyond the ordinary time on a weekday. And
Paul and Arthur read before breakfast, and had the meal unwashed, sitting in
their shirt-sleeves. This was another holiday luxury. The room was warm. Everything felt free of care and anxiety. There was a sense of plenty in the house.

While the boys were reading, Mrs. Morel went into the garden. They were
now in another house, an old one, near the Scargill Street home, which had
been left soon after William had died. Directly came an excited cry from the
garden:

"Paul! Paul! come and look!"

It was his mother's voice. He threw down his book and went out. There was
a long garden that ran to a field. It was a grey, cold day, with a sharp wind
blowing out of Derbyshire. Two fields away Bestwood began, with a jumble of
roofs and red house-ends, out of which rose the church tower and the spire of
the Congregational Chapel. And beyond went woods and hills, right away to
the pale grey heights of the Pennine Chain.

Paul looked down the garden for his mother. Her head appeared among the
young currant-bushes.

"Come here!" she cried.

"What for?" he answered.

"Come and see."

She had been looking at the buds on the currant trees. Paul went up.

"To think," she said, "that here I might never have seen them!"

Her son went to her side. Under the fence, in a little bed, was a ravel of poor
grassy leaves, such as come from very immature bulbs, and three scyllas in
bloom. Mrs. Morel pointed to the deep blue flowers.

"Now, just see those!" she exclaimed. "I was looking at the currant bushes,
when, thinks I to myself, 'There's something very blue; is it a bit of sugar-bag?'"

and there, behold you! Sugar-bag! Three glories of the snow, and *such* beauties! But where on earth did they come from?"

"I don't know," said Paul.

"Well, that's a marvel, now! I *thought* I knew every weed and blade in this garden. But *haven't* they done well? You see, that gooseberry-bush just shelters them. Not nipped, not touched!"

He crouched down and turned up the bells of the little blue flowers.

"They're a glorious colour!" he said.

"Aren't they!" she cried. "I guess they come from Switzerland, where they say they have such lovely things. Fancy them against the snow! But where have they come from? They can't have *blown* here, can they?"

Then he remembered having set here a lot of little trash of bulbs to mature.

"And you never told me," she said.

"No! I thought I'd leave it till they might flower."

"And now, you see! I might have missed them. And I've never had a glory of the snow in my garden in my life."

She was full of excitement and elation. The garden was an endless joy to her. Paul was thankful for her sake at last to be in a house with a long garden that went down to a field. Every morning after breakfast she went out and was happy pottering about in it. And it was true, she knew every weed and blade.

Everybody turned up for the walk. Food was packed, and they set off, a merry, delighted party. They hung over the wall of the mill-race, dropped paper in the water on one side of the tunnel and watched it shoot out on the other. They stood on the footbridge over Boathouse Station and looked at the metals gleaming coldly.

"You should see the Flying Scotsman come through at half-past six!" said Leonard, whose father was a signalman. "Lad, but she doesn't half buzz!" and the little party looked up the lines one way, to London, and the other way, to Scotland, and they felt the touch of these two magical places.

In Ilkeston the colliers were waiting in gangs for the public-houses to open. It was a town of idleness and lounging. At Stanton Gate the iron foundry blazed. Over everything there were great discussions. At Trowell they crossed again from Derbyshire into Nottinghamshire. They came to the Hemlock Stone at dinner-time. Its field was crowded with folk from Nottingham and Ilkeston.

They had expected a venerable and dignified monument. They found a little, gnarled, twisted stump of rock, something like a decayed mushroom, standing out pathetically on the side of a field. Leonard and Dick immediately proceeded to carve their initials, "L. W." and "R. P.", in the old red sandstone; but Paul desisted, because he had read in the newspaper satirical remarks about initial-carvers, who could find no other road to immortality. Then all the lads climbed to the top of the rock to look round.

Everywhere in the field below, factory girls and lads were eating lunch or sporting about. Beyond was the garden of an old manor. It had yew-hedges and thick clumps and borders of yellow crocuses round the lawn.

"See," said Paul to Miriam, "what a quiet garden!"

She saw the dark yews and the golden crocuses, then she looked gratefully. He had not seemed to belong to her among all these others; he was different then—not her Paul, who understood the slightest quiver of her innermost soul, but something else, speaking another language than hers. How it hurt her, and deadened her very perceptions. Only when he came right back to her, leaving his other, his lesser self, as she thought, would she feel alive again. And now he asked her to look at this garden, wanting the contact with her again. Impatient of the set in the field, she turned to the quiet lawn, surrounded by sheaves of shut-up crocuses. A feeling of stillness, almost of ecstasy, came over her. It felt almost as if she were alone with him in this garden.

Then he left her again and joined the others. Soon they started home. Miriam loitered behind, alone. She did not fit in with the others; she could very rarely get into human relations with anyone: so her friend, her companion, her lover, was Nature. She saw the sun declining wanly. In the dusky, cold hedgerows were some red leaves. She lingered to gather them, tenderly, passionately. The love in her finger-tips caressed the leaves; the passion in her heart came to a glow upon the leaves.

Suddenly she realised she was alone in a strange road, and she hurried forward. Turning a corner in the lane, she came upon Paul, who stood bent over something, his mind fixed on it, working away steadily, patiently, a little hopelessly. She hesitated in her approach, to watch.

He remained concentrated in the middle of the road. Beyond, one rift of rich gold in that colourless grey evening seemed to make him stand out in dark relief. She saw him, slender and firm, as if the setting sun had given him to her. A deep pain took hold of her, and she knew she must love him. And she had discovered him, discovered in him a rare potentiality, discovered his loneliness. Quivering as at some "annunciation", she went slowly forward.

At last he looked up.

"Why," he exclaimed gratefully, "have you waited for me!"

She saw a deep shadow in his eyes.

"What is it?" she asked.

"The spring broken here;" and he showed her where his umbrella was injured.

Instantly, with some shame, she knew he had not done the damage himself, but that Geoffrey was responsible.

"It is only an old umbrella, isn't it?" she asked.

She wondered why he, who did not usually trouble over trifles, made such a mountain of this molehill.

"But it was William's an' my mother can't help but know," he said quietly, still patiently working at the umbrella.

The words went through Miriam like a blade. This, then, was the confirmation of her vision of him! She looked at him. But there was about him a certain reserve, and she dared not comfort him, not even speak softly to him.

"Come on," he said. "I can't do it;" and they went in silence along the road.

That same evening they were walking along under the trees by Nether Green. He was talking to her fretfully, seemed to be struggling to convince himself.

"You know," he said, with an effort, "if one person loves, the other does."

"Ah!" she answered. "Like mother said to me when I was little, 'Love begets love.'"

"Yes, something like that, I think it *must* be."

"I hope so, because, if it were not, love might be a very terrible thing," she said.

"Yes, but it *is*—at least with most people," he answered.

And Miriam, thinking he had assured himself, felt strong in herself. She always regarded that sudden coming upon him in the lane as a revelation. And this conversation remained graven in her mind as one of the letters of the law.

Now she stood with him and for him. When, about this time, he outraged the family feeling at Willey Farm by some overbearing insult, she stuck to him, and believed he was right. And at this time she dreamed dreams of him, vivid, unforgettable. These dreams came again later on, developed to a more subtle psychological stage.

On the Easter Monday the same party took an excursion to Wingfield Manor. It was great excitement to Miriam to catch a train at Sethley Bridge, amid all the bustle of the Bank Holiday crowd. They left the train at Alfreton. Paul was interested in the street and in the colliers with their dogs. Here was a new race of miners. Miriam did not live till they came to the church. They were all rather timid of entering, with their bags of food, for fear of being turned out. Leonard, a comic, thin fellow, went first; Paul, who would have died rather than be sent back, went last. The place was decorated for Easter. In the font hundreds of white narcissi seemed to be growing. The air was dim and coloured from the windows and thrilled with a subtle scent of lilies and narcissi. In that atmosphere Miriam's soul came into a glow. Paul was afraid of the things he mustn't do; and he was sensitive to the feel of the place. Miriam turned to him. He answered. They were together. He would not go beyond the Communion-rail. She loved him for that. Her soul expanded into prayer beside him. He felt the strange fascination of shadowy religious places. All his latent mysticism quivered into life. She was drawn to him. He was a prayer along with her.

Miriam very rarely talked to the other lads. They at once became awkward in conversation with her. So usually she was silent.

It was past midday when they climbed the steep path to the manor. All things shone softly in the sun, which was wonderfully warm and enlivening. Celandines and violets were out. Everybody was tip-top full with happiness. The glitter of the ivy, the soft, atmospheric grey of the castle walls, the gentleness of everything near the ruin, was perfect.

The manor is of hard, pale grey stone, and the other walls are blank and calm. The young folk were in raptures. They went in trepidation, almost afraid that the delight of exploring this ruin might be denied them. In the first courtyard, within the high broken walls, were farm-carts, with their shafts lying idle on the ground, the tyres of the wheels brilliant with gold-red rust. It was very still.

All eagerly paid their sixpences, and went timidly through the fine clean arch of the inner courtyard. They were shy. Here on the pavement, where the hall had been, an old thorn tree was budding. All kinds of strange openings and broken rooms were in the shadow around them.

After lunch they set off once more to explore the ruin. This time the girls went with the boys, who could act as guides and expositors. There was one tall tower in a corner, rather tottering, where they say Mary Queen of Scots was imprisoned.

"Think of the Queen going up here!" said Miriam in a low voice, as she climbed the hollow stairs.

"If she could get up," said Paul, "for she had rheumatism like anything. I reckon they treated her rottenly."

"You don't think she deserved it?" asked Miriam.

"No, I don't. She was only lively."

They continued to mount the winding staircase. A high wind, blowing through the loopholes, went rushing up the shaft, and filled the girl's skirts like a balloon, so that she was ashamed, until he took the hem of her dress and held it down for her. He did it perfectly simply, as he would have picked up her glove. She remembered this always.

Round the broken top of the tower the ivy bushed out, old and handsome. Also, there were a few chill gillivers, in pale cold bud. Miriam wanted to lean over for some ivy, but he would not let her. Instead, she had to wait behind him, and take from him each spray as he gathered it and held it to her, each one separately, in the purest manner of chivalry. The tower seemed to rock in the wind. They looked over miles and miles of wooded country, and country with gleams of pasture.

The crypt underneath the manor was beautiful, and in perfect preservation. Paul made a drawing: Miriam stayed with him. She was thinking of Mary Queen of Scots looking with her strained, hopeless eyes, that could not understand misery, over the hills whence no help came, or sitting in this crypt, being told of a God as cold as the place she sat in.

They set off again gaily, looking round on their beloved manor that stood so clean and big on its hill.

"Supposing you could have *that* farm," said Paul to Miriam.

"Yes!"

"Wouldn't it be lovely to come and see you!"

They were now in the bare country of stone walls, which he loved, and which, though only ten miles from home, seemed so foreign to Miriam. The party was straggling. As they were crossing a large meadow that sloped away from the sun, along a path embedded with innumerable tiny glittering points, Paul, walking alongside, laced his fingers in the strings of the bag Miriam was carrying, and instantly she felt Annie behind, watchful and jealous. But the meadow was bathed in a glory of sunshine, and the path was jewelled, and it was seldom that he gave her any sign. She held her fingers very still among the strings of the bag, his fingers touching; and the place was golden as a vision.

At last they came into the straggling grey village of Crich, that lies high. Beyond the village was the famous Crich Stand that Paul could see from the garden at home. The party pushed on. Great expanse of country spread around and below. The lads were eager to get to the top of the hill. It was capped by a round knoll, half of which was by now cut away, and on the top of which stood an ancient monument, sturdy and squat, for signalling in old days far down into the level lands of Nottinghamshire and Leicestershire.

It was blowing so hard, high up there in the exposed place, that the only way to be safe was to stand nailed by the wind to the wall of the tower. At their feet fell the precipice where the limestone was quarried away. Below was a jumble of hills and tiny villages—Matlock, Ambergate, Stoney Middleton. The lads were eager to spy out the church of Bestwood, far away among the rather crowded country on the left. They were disgusted that it seemed to stand on a plain. They saw the hills of Derbyshire fall into the monotony of the Midlands that swept away South.

Miriam was somewhat scared by the wind, but the lads enjoyed it. They went on, miles and miles, to Whatstandwell. All the food was eaten, everybody was hungry, and there was very little money to get home with. But they managed to procure a loaf and a currant-loaf, which they hacked to pieces with shut-knives, and ate sitting on the wall near the bridge, watching the bright Derwent rushing by, and the brakes from Matlock pulling up at the inn.

Paul was now pale with weariness. He had been responsible for the party all day, and now he was done. Miriam understood, and kept close to him, and he left himself in her hands.

They had an hour to wait at Ambergate Station. Trains came, crowded with excursionists returning to Manchester, Birmingham, and London.

"We might be going there—folk easily might think we're going that far," said Paul.

They got back rather late. Miriam, walking home with Geoffrey, watched the moon rise big and red and misty. She felt something was fulfilled in her.

She had an elder sister, Agatha, who was a school-teacher. Between the two girls was a feud. Miriam considered Agatha worldly. And she wanted herself to be a school-teacher.

One Saturday afternoon Agatha and Miriam were upstairs dressing. Their bedroom was over the stable. It was a low room, not very large, and bare. Miriam had nailed on the wall a reproduction of Veronese's "St. Catherine". She loved the woman who sat in the window, dreaming. Her own windows were too small to sit in. But the front one was dripped over with honeysuckle and virginia creeper, and looked upon the tree-tops of the oak-wood across the yard, while the little back window, no bigger than a handkerchief, was a loop-hole to the east, to the dawn beating up against the beloved round hills.

The two sisters did not talk much to each other. Agatha, who was fair and small and determined, had rebelled against the home atmosphere, against the doctrine of "the other cheek". She was out in the world now, in a fair way to be independent. And she insisted on worldly values, on appearance, on manners, on position, which Miriam would fain have ignored.

Both girls liked to be upstairs, out of the way, when Paul came. They preferred to come running down, open the stair-foot door, and see him watching, expectant of them. Miriam stood painfully pulling over her head a rosary he had given her. It caught in the fine mesh of her hair. But at last she had it on, and the red-brown wooden beads looked well against her cool brown neck. She was a well-developed girl, and very handsome. But in the little looking-glass nailed against the whitewashed wall she could only see a fragment of herself at a time. Agatha had bought a little mirror of her own, which she propped up to suit herself. Miriam was near the window. Suddenly she heard the well-known click of the chain, and she saw Paul fling open the gate, push his bicycle into the yard. She saw him look at the house, and she shrank away. He walked in a nonchalant fashion, and his bicycle went with him as if it were a live thing.

"Paul's come!" she exclaimed.

"Aren't you glad?" said Agatha cuttingly.

Miriam stood still in amazement and bewilderment.

"Well, aren't you?" she asked.

"Yes, but I'm not going to let him see it, and think I wanted him."

Miriam was startled. She heard him putting his bicycle in the stable underneath, and talking to Jimmy, who had been a pit-horse, and who was seedy.

"Well, Jimmy my lad, how are ter? Nobbut sick an' sadly, like? Why, then, it's a shame, my owd lad."

She heard the rope run through the hole as the horse lifted its head from the lad's caress. How she loved to listen when he thought only the horse could hear. But there was a serpent in her Eden. She searched earnestly in herself to see if she wanted Paul Morel. She felt there would be some disgrace in it. Full of twisted feeling, she was afraid she did want him. She stood self-convicted. Then came an agony of new shame. She shrank within herself in a coil of torture. Did she want Paul Morel, and did he know she wanted him? What a subtle infamy upon her. She felt as if her whole soul coiled into knots of shame.

Agatha was dressed first, and ran downstairs. Miriam heard her greet the lad gaily, knew exactly how brilliant her grey eyes became with that tone. She herself would have felt it bold to have greeted him in such wise. Yet there she stood under the self-accusation of wanting him, tied to that stake of torture. In bitter perplexity she kneeled down and prayed:

"O Lord, let me not love Paul Morel. Keep me from loving him, if I ought not to love him."

Something anomalous in the prayer arrested her. She lifted her head and pondered. How could it be wrong to love him? Love was God's gift. And yet it caused her shame. That was because of him, Paul Morel. But, then, it was not his affair, it was her own, between herself and God. She was to be a sacrifice. But it was God's sacrifice, not Paul Morel's or her own. After a few minutes she hid her face in the pillow again, and said:

"But, Lord, if it is Thy will that I should love him, make me love him—as Christ would, who died for the souls of men. Make me love him splendidly, because he is Thy son."

She remained kneeling for some time, quite still, and deeply moved, her black hair against the red squares and the lavender-sprigged squares of the patchwork quilt. Prayer was almost essential to her. Then she fell into that rapture of self-sacrifice, identifying herself with a God who was sacrificed, which gives to so many human souls their deepest bliss.

When she went downstairs Paul was lying back in an arm-chair, holding forth with much vehemence to Agatha, who was scorning a little painting he had brought to show her. Miriam glanced at the two, and avoided their levity. She went into the parlour to be alone.

It was tea-time before she was able to speak to Paul, and then her manner was so distant he thought he had offended her.

Miriam discontinued her practice of going each Thursday evening to the library in Bestwood. After calling for Paul regularly during the whole spring, a number of trifling incidents and tiny insults from his family awakened her to their attitude towards her, and she decided to go no more. So she announced to Paul one evening she would not call at his house again for him on Thursday nights.

"Why?" he asked, very short.

"Nothing. Only I'd rather not."

"Very well."

"But," she faltered, "if you'd care to meet me, we could still go together."

"Meet you where?"

"Somewhere—where you like."

"I shan't meet you anywhere. I don't see why you shouldn't keep calling for me. But if you won't, I don't want to meet you."

So the Thursday evenings which had been so precious to her, and to him, were dropped. He worked instead. Mrs. Morel sniffed with satisfaction at this arrangement.

He would not have it that they were lovers. The intimacy between them had been kept so abstract, such a matter of the soul, all thought and weary struggle into consciousness, that he saw it only as a platonic friendship. He stoutly denied there was anything else between them. Miriam was silent, or else she very quietly agreed. He was a fool who did not know what was happening to himself. By tacit agreement they ignored the remarks and insinuations of their acquaintances.

"We aren't lovers, we are friends," he said to her. "We know it. Let them talk. What does it matter what they say."

Sometimes, as they were walking together, she slipped her arm timidly into his. But he always resented it, and she knew it. It caused a violent conflict in him. With Miriam he was always on the high plane of abstraction, when his natural fire of love was transmitted into the fine stream of thought. She would have it so. If he were jolly and, as she put it, flippant, she waited till he came back to her, till the change had taken place in him again, and he was wrestling with his own soul, frowning, passionate in his desire for understanding. And in this passion for understanding her soul lay close to his; she had him all to herself. But he must be made abstract first.

Then, if she put her arm in his, it caused him almost torture. His consciousness seemed to split. The place where she was touching him ran hot with friction. He was one internecine battle, and he became cruel to her because of it.

One evening in midsummer Miriam called at the house, warm from climbing. Paul was alone in the kitchen; his mother could be heard moving about upstairs.

"Come and look at the sweet-peas," he said to the girl.

They went into the garden. The sky behind the townlet and the church was orange-red; the flower-garden was flooded with a strange warm light that lifted every leaf into significance. Paul passed along a fine row of sweet-peas, gathering a blossom here and there, all cream and pale blue. Miriam followed, breathing the fragrance. To her, flowers appealed with such strength she felt she must make them part of herself. When she bent and breathed a flower, it was as if she and the flower were loving each other. Paul hated her for it. There seemed a sort of exposure about the action, something too intimate.

When he had got a fair bunch, they returned to the house. He listened for a moment to his mother's quiet movement upstairs, then he said:

"Come here, and let me pin them in for you." He arranged them two or three at a time in the bosom of her dress, stepping back now and then to see the effect. "You know," he said, taking the pin out of his mouth, "a woman ought always to arrange her flowers before her glass."

Miriam laughed. She thought flowers ought to be pinned in one's dress without any care. That Paul should take pains to fix her flowers for her was his whim.

He was rather offended at her laughter.

"Some women do—those who look decent," he said.

Miriam laughed again, but mirthlessly, to hear him thus mix her up with women in a general way. From most men she would have ignored it. But from him it hurt her.

He had nearly finished arranging the flowers when he heard his mother's footstep on the stairs. Hurriedly he pushed in the last pin and turned away.

"Don't let mater know," he said.

Miriam picked up her books and stood in the doorway looking with chagrin at the beautiful sunset. She would call for Paul no more, she said.

"Good-evening, Mrs. Morel," she said, in a deferential way. She sounded as if she felt she had no right to be there.

"Oh, is it you, Miriam?" replied Mrs. Morel coolly.

But Paul insisted on everybody's accepting his friendship with the girl, and Mrs. Morel was too wise to have any open rupture.

It was not till he was twenty years old that the family could ever afford to go away for a holiday. Mrs. Morel had never been away for a holiday, except to see her sister, since she had been married. Now at last Paul had saved enough money, and they were all going. There was to be a party: some of Annie's friends, one friend of Paul's, a young man in the same office where William had previously been, and Miriam.

It was great excitement writing for rooms. Paul and his mother debated it endlessly between them. They wanted a furnished cottage for two weeks. She thought one week would be enough, but he insisted on two.

At last they got an answer from Mablethorpe, a cottage such as they wished for thirty shillings a week. There was immense jubilation. Paul was wild with joy for his mother's sake. She would have a real holiday now. He and she sat at evening picturing what it would be like. Annie came in, and Leonard, and Alice, and Kitty. There was wild rejoicing and anticipation. Paul told Miriam. She seemed to brood with joy over it. But the Morel's house rang with excitement.

They were to go on Saturday morning by the seven train. Paul suggested that Miriam should sleep at his house, because it was so far for her to walk. She came down for supper. Everybody was so excited that even Miriam was accepted with warmth. But almost as soon as she entered the feeling in the family became close and tight. He had discovered a poem by Jean Ingelow which mentioned Mablethorpe, and so he must read it to Miriam. He would never have got so far in the direction of sentimentality as to read poetry to his own family. But now they condescended to listen. Miriam sat on the sofa absorbed in him. She always seemed absorbed in him, and by him, when he was present. Mrs. Morel sat jealously in her own chair. She was going to hear also. And even Annie and the father attended, Morel with his head cocked on one side, like somebody listening to a sermon and feeling conscious of the fact. Paul ducked his head over the book. He had got now all the audience he cared for. And Mrs. Morel and Annie almost contested with Miriam who should listen best and win his favour. He was in very high feather.

"But," interrupted Mrs. Morel, "what *is* the 'Bride of Enderby' that the bells are supposed to ring?"

"It's an old tune they used to play on the bells for a warning against water. I suppose the Bride of Enderby was drowned in a flood," he replied. He had not the faintest knowledge what it really was, but he would never have sunk so low as to confess that to his womenfolk. They listened and believed him. He believed himself.

"And the people knew what that tune meant?" said his mother.

"Yes—just like the Scotch when they heard 'The Flowers o' the Forest'—and when they used to ring the bells backward for alarm."

"How?" said Annie. "A bell sounds the same whether it's rung backwards or forwards."

"But," he said, "if you start with the deep bell and ring up to the high one—der—der—der—der—der—der—der—der!"

He ran up the scale. Everybody thought it clever. He thought so too. Then, waiting a minute, he continued the poem.

"Hm!" said Mrs. Morel curiously, when he finished. "But I wish everything that's written weren't so sad."

"*I* canna see what they want drownin' theirselves for," said Morel.

There was a pause. Annie got up to clear the table.

Miriam rose to help with the pots.

"Let *me* help to wash up," she said.

"Certainly not," cried Annie. "You sit down again. There aren't many."

And Miriam, who could not be familiar and insist, sat down again to look at the book with Paul.

He was master of the party; his father was no good. And great tortures he suffered lest the tin box should be put out at Firsby instead of at Mablethorpe. And he wasn't equal to getting a carriage. His bold little mother did that.

"Here!" she cried to a man. "Here!"

Paul and Annie got behind the rest, convulsed with shamed laughter.

"How much will it be to drive to Brook Cottage?" said Mrs. Morel.

"Two shillings."

"Why, how far is it?"

"A good way."

"I don't believe it," she said.

But she scrambled in. There were eight crowded in one old seaside carriage. "You see," said Mrs. Morel, "it's only threepence each, and if it were a tram-car——"

They drove along. Each cottage they came to, Mrs. Morel cried:

"Is it this? Now, this is it!"

Everybody sat breathless. They drove past. There was a universal sigh.

"I'm thankful it wasn't that brute," said Mrs. Morel. "I *was* frightened." They drove on and on.

At last they descended at a house that stood alone over the dyke by the highroad. There was wild excitement because they had to cross a little bridge to get into the front garden. But they loved the house that lay so solitary, with a sea-meadow on one side, and immense expanse of land patched in white barley, yellow oats, red wheat, and green root-crops, flat and stretching level to the sky.

Paul kept accounts. He and his mother ran the show. The total expenses— lodging, food, everything—was sixteen shillings a week per person. He and Leonard went bathing in the morning. Morel was wandering abroad quite early.

"You, Paul," his mother called from the bedroom, "eat a piece of bread-and-butter."

"All right," he answered.

And when he got back he saw his mother presiding in state at the breakfast-table. The woman of the house was young. Her husband was blind, and she did laundry work. So Mrs. Morel always washed the pots in the kitchen and made the beds.

"But you said you'd have a real holiday," said Paul, "and now you work."

"Work!" she exclaimed. "What are you talking about!"

He loved to go with her across the fields to the village and the sea. She was afraid of the plank bridge, and he abused her for being a baby. On the whole he stuck to her as if he were *her* man.

Miriam did not get much of him, except, perhaps, when all the others went to the "Coons". Coons were insufferably stupid to Miriam, so he thought they were to himself also, and he preached priggishly to Annie about the fatuity of listening to them. Yet he, too, knew all their songs, and sang them along the roads roisterously. And if he found himself listening, the stupidity pleased him very much. Yet to Annie he said:

"Such rot! there isn't a grain of intelligence in it. Nobody with more gumption than a grasshopper could go and sit and listen." And to Miriam he said, with much scorn of Annie and the others: "I suppose they're at the 'Coons'."

It was queer to see Miriam singing coon songs. She had a straight chin that went in a perpendicular line from the lower lip to the turn. She always reminded Paul of some sad Botticelli angel when she sang, even when it was:

"Come down lover's lane
For a walk with me, talk with me."

Only when he sketched, or at evening when the others were at the "Coons", she had him to herself. He talked to her endlessly about his love of horizontals: how they, the great levels of sky and land in Lincolnshire, meant to him the eternality of the will, just as the bowed Norman arches of the church, repeating themselves, meant the dogged leaping forward of the persistent human soul, on and on, nobody knows where; in contradiction to the perpendicular lines and to the Gothic arch, which, he said, leapt up at heaven and touched the ecstasy and lost itself in the divine. Himself, he said, was Norman, Miriam was Gothic. She bowed in consent even to that.

One evening he and she went up the great sweeping shore of sand towards Theddlethorpe. The long breakers plunged and ran in a hiss of foam along the coast. It was a warm evening. There was not a figure but themselves on the far reaches of sand, no noise but the sound of the sea. Paul loved to see it clanging at the land. He loved to feel himself between the noise of it and the silence of the sandy shore. Miriam was with him. Everything grew very intense. It was quite dark when they turned again. The way home was through a gap in the sandhills, and then along a raised grass road between two dykes. The country was black and still. From behind the sandhills came the whisper of the sea. Paul and Miriam walked in silence. Suddenly he started. The whole of his blood seemed to burst into flame, and he could scarcely breathe. An enormous orange moon was staring at them from the rim of the sandhills. He stood still, looking at it.

"Ah!" cried Miriam, when she saw it.

He remained perfectly still, staring at the immense and ruddy moon, the only thing in the far-reaching darkness of the level. His heart beat heavily, the muscles of his arms contracted.

"What is it?" murmured Miriam, waiting for him.

He turned and looked at her. She stood beside him, for ever in shadow. Her face, covered with the darkness of her hat, was watching him unseen. But she was brooding. She was slightly afraid—deeply moved and religious. That was her best state. He was impotent against it. His blood was concentrated like a flame in his chest. But he could not get across to her. There were flashes in his blood. But somehow she ignored them. She was expecting some religious state in him. Still yearning, she was half aware of his passion, and gazed at him, troubled.

"What is it?" she murmured again.

"It's the moon," he answered, frowning.

"Yes," she assented. "Isn't it wonderful?" She was curious about him. The crisis was past.

He did not know himself what was the matter. He was naturally so young, and their intimacy was so abstract, he did not know he wanted to crush her on to his breast to ease the ache there. He was afraid of her. The fact that he might want her as a man wants a woman had in him been suppressed into a shame. When she shrank in her convulsed, coiled torture from the thought of such a thing, he had winced to the depths of his soul. And now this "purity" prevented even their first love-kiss. It was as if she could scarcely stand the shock of physical love, even a passionate kiss, and then he was too shrinking and sensitive to give it.

As they walked along the dark fen-meadow he watched the moon and did not speak. She plodded beside him. He hated her, for she seemed in some way to make him despise himself. Looking ahead—he saw the one light in the darkness, the window of their lamp-lit cottage.

He loved to think of his mother, and the other jolly people.

"Well, everybody else has been in long ago!" said his mother as they entered.

"What does that matter!" he cried irritably. "I can go a walk if I like, can't I?"

"And I should have thought you could get in to supper with the rest," said Mrs. Morel.

"I shall please myself," he retorted. "It's not *late*. I shall do as I like."

"Very well," said his mother cuttingly, "then *do* as you like." And she took no further notice of him that evening. Which he pretended neither to notice nor to care about, but sat reading. Miriam read also, obliterating herself. Mrs. Morel hated her for making her son like this. She watched Paul growing irritable, priggish, and melancholic. For this she put the blame on Miriam. Annie and all her friends joined against the girl. Miriam had no friend of her own, only Paul. But she did not suffer so much, because she despised the triviality of these other people.

And Paul hated her because, somehow, she spoilt his ease and naturalness. And he writhed himself with a feeling of humiliation.

VIII

STRIFE IN LOVE

Arthur finished his apprenticeship, and got a job on the electrical plant at Minton Pit. He earned very little, but had a good chance of getting on. But he was wild and restless. He did not drink nor gamble. Yet he somehow contrived to get into endless scrapes, always through some hot-headed thoughtlessness. Either he went rabbiting in the woods, like a poacher, or he stayed in Nottingham all night instead of coming home, or he miscalculated his dive into the canal at Bestwood, and scored his chest into one mass of wounds on the raw stones and tins at the bottom.

He had not been at his work many months when again he did not come home one night.

"Do you know where Arthur is?" asked Paul at breakfast.

"I do not," replied his mother.

"He is a fool," said Paul. "And if he *did* anything I shouldn't mind. But no, he simply can't come away from a game of whist, or else he must see a girl home from the skating-rink—quite proprietously—and so can't get home. He's a fool."

"I don't know that it would make it any better if he did something to make us all ashamed," said Mrs. Morel.

"Well, *I* should respect him more," said Paul.

"I very much doubt it," said his mother coldly.

They went on with breakfast.

"Are you fearfully fond of him?" Paul asked his mother.

"What do you ask that for?"

"Because they say a woman always like the youngest best."

"She may do—but I don't. No, he wearies me."

"And you'd actually rather he was good?"

"I'd rather he showed some of a man's common sense."

Paul was raw and irritable. He also wearied his mother very often. She saw the sunshine going out of him, and she resented it.

As they were finishing breakfast came the postman with a letter from Derby. Mrs. Morel screwed up her eyes to look at the address.

"Give it here, blind eye!" exclaimed her son, snatching it away from her. She started, and almost boxed his ears.

"It's from your son, Arthur," he said.

"What now——!" cried Mrs. Morel.

" 'My dearest Mother,' " Paul read, " 'I don't know what made me such a fool. I want you to come and fetch me back from here. I came with Jack Bredon yesterday, instead of going to work, and enlisted. He said he was sick of wearing the seat of a stool out, and, like the idiot you know I am, I came away with him.

" 'I have taken the King's shilling, but perhaps if you came for me they would let me go back with you. I was a fool when I did it. I don't want to be in the army. My dear mother, I am nothing but a trouble to you. But if you get me out of this, I promise I will have more sense and consideration. . . .' "

Mrs. Morel sat down in her rocking-chair.

"Well, *now,*" she cried, "let him stop!"

"Yes," said Paul, "let him stop."

There was silence. The mother sat with her hands folded in her apron, her face set, thinking.

"If I'm not *sick!*" she cried suddenly. "Sick!"

"Now," said Paul, beginning to frown, "you're not going to worry your soul out about this, do you hear."

"I suppose I'm to take it as a blessing," she flashed, turning on her son.

"You're not going to mount it up to a tragedy, so there," he retorted.

"The *fool!*—the young fool!" she cried.

"He'll look well in uniform," said Paul irritatingly.

His mother turned on him like a fury.

"Oh, will he!" she cried. "Not in my eyes!"

"He should get in a cavalry regiment; he'll have the time of his life, and will look an awful swell."

"Swell!—*swell!*—a mighty swell idea indeed!—a common soldier!"

"Well," said Paul, "what am I but a common clerk?"

"A good deal, my boy!" cried his mother, stung.

"What?"

"At any rate, a *man,* and not a thing in a red coat."

"I shouldn't mind being in a red coat—or dark blue, that would suit me better—if they didn't boss me about too much."

But his mother had ceased to listen.

"Just as he was getting on, or might have been getting on, at his job—a young nuisance—here he goes and ruins himself for life. What good will he be, do you think, after *this?*"

"It may lick him into shape beautifully," said Paul.

"Lick him into shape!—lick what marrow there *was* out of his bones. A *soldier!*—a common *soldier!*—nothing but a body that makes movements when it hears a shout! It's a fine thing!"

"I can't understand why it upsets you," said Paul.

"No, perhaps you can't. But *I* understand;" and she sat back in her chair, her chin in one hand, holding her elbow with the other, brimmed up with wrath and chagrin.

"And shall you go to Derby?" asked Paul.

"Yes."

"It's no good."

"I'll see for myself."

"And why on earth don't you let him stop. It's just what he wants."

"Of course," cried the mother, "*you* know what he wants!"

She got ready and went by the first train to Derby, where she saw her son and the sergeant. It was, however, no good.

When Morel was having his dinner in the evening, she said suddenly: "I've had to go to Derby to-day."

The miner turned up his eyes, showing the whites in his black face.

"Has ter, lass. What took thee there?"

"That Arthur!"

"Oh—an' what's agate now?"

"He's only enlisted."

Morel put down his knife and leaned back in his chair.

"Nay," he said, "that he niver 'as!"

"And is going down to Aldershot to-morrow."

"Well!" exclaimed the miner. "That's a winder." He considered it a moment, said "H'm!" and proceeded with his dinner. Suddenly his face contracted with wrath. "I hope he may never set foot i' my house again," he said.

"The idea!" cried Mrs. Morel. "Saying such a thing!"

"I do," repeated Morel. "A fool as runs away for a soldier, let 'im look after 'issen; I s'll do no more for 'im."

"A fat sight you have done as it is," she said.

And Morel was almost ashamed to go to his public-house that evening.

"Well, did you go?" said Paul to his mother when he came home.

"I did."

"And could you see him?"

"Yes."

"And what did he say?"

"He blubbered when I came away."

"H'm!"

"And so did I, so you needn't 'h'm'!"

Mrs. Morel fretted after her son. She knew he would not like the army. He did not. The discipline was intolerable to him.

"But the doctor," she said with some pride to Paul, "said he was perfectly proportioned—almost exactly; all his measurements were correct. He *is* good-looking, you know."

"He's awfully nice-looking. But he doesn't fetch the girls like William, does he?"

"No; it's a different character. He's a good deal like his father, irresponsible."

To console his mother, Paul did not go much to Willey Farm at this time. And in the autumn exhibition of students' work in the Castle he had two studies, a landscape in water-colour and a still life in oil, both of which had first-prize awards. He was highly excited.

"What do you think I've got for my pictures, mother?" he asked, coming home one evening. She saw by his eyes he was glad. Her face flushed.

"Now, how should I know, my boy!"

"A first prize for those glass jars——"

"H'm!"

"And a first prize for that sketch up at Willey Farm."

"Both first?"

"Yes."

"H'm!"

There was a rosy, bright look about her, though she said nothing.

"It's nice," he said, "isn't it?"

"It is."

"Why don't you praise me up to the skies?"

She laughed.

"I should have the trouble of dragging you down again," she said.

But she was full of joy, nevertheless. William had brought her his sporting trophies. She kept them still, and she did not forgive his death. Arthur was handsome—at least, a good specimen—and warm and generous, and probably would do well in the end. But Paul was going to distinguish himself. She had a great belief in him, the more because he was unaware of his own powers. There was so much to come out of him. Life for her was rich with promise. She was to see herself fulfilled. Not for nothing had been her struggle.

Several times during the exhibition Mrs. Morel went to the Castle unknown to Paul. She wandered down the long room looking at the other exhibits. Yes, they were good. But they had not in them a certain something which she demanded for her satisfaction. Some made her jealous, they were so good. She looked at them a long time trying to find fault with them. Then suddenly she had a shock that made her heart beat. There hung Paul's picture! She knew it as if it were printed on her heart.

"Name—Paul Morel—First Prize."

It looked so strange, there in public, on the walls of the Castle gallery, where in her lifetime she had seen so many pictures. And she glanced round to see if anyone had noticed her again in front of the same sketch.

But she felt a proud woman. When she met well-dressed ladies going home to the Park, she thought to herself:

"Yes, you look very well—but I wonder if *your* son has two first prizes in the Castle."

And she walked on, as proud a little woman as any in Nottingham. And Paul felt he had done something for her, if only a trifle. All his work was hers.

One day, as he was going up Castle Gate, he met Miriam. He had seen her on the Sunday, and had not expected to meet her in town. She was walking with a rather striking woman, blonde, with a sullen expression, and a defiant carriage. It was strange how Miriam, in her bowed, meditative bearing, looked dwarfed beside this woman with the handsome shoulders. Miriam watched Paul searchingly. His gaze was on the stranger, who ignored him. The girl saw his masculine spirit rear its head.

"Hello!" he said, "you didn't tell me you were coming to town."

"No," replied Miriam, half apologetically. "I drove in to Cattle Market with father."

He looked at her companion.

"I've told you about Mrs. Dawes," said Miriam huskily; she was nervous. "Clara, do you know Paul?"

"I think I've seen him before," replied Mrs. Dawes indifferently, as she shook hands with him. She had scornful grey eyes, a skin like white honey, and a full mouth, with a slightly lifted upper lip that did not know whether it was raised in scorn of all men or out of eagerness to be kissed, but which believed the former. She carried her head back, as if she had drawn away in contempt, perhaps from men also. She wore a large, dowdy hat of black beaver, and a sort of slightly affected simple dress that made her look rather sack-like. She was evidently poor, and had not much taste. Miriam usually looked nice.

"Where have you seen me?" Paul asked of the woman.

She looked at him as if she would not trouble to answer. Then:

"Walking with Louie Travers," she said.

Louie was one of the "Spiral" girls.

"Why, do you know her?" he asked.

She did not answer. He turned to Miriam.

"Where are you going?" he asked.

"To the Castle."

"What train are you going home by?"

"I am driving with father. I wish you could come too. What time are you free?"

"You know not till eight to-night, damn it!"

And directly the two women moved on.

Paul remembered that Clara Dawes was the daughter of an old friend of Mrs. Leivers. Miriam had sought her out because she had once been Spiral overseer at Jordan's, and because her husband, Baxter Dawes, was smith for the factory, making the irons for cripple instruments, and so on. Through her Miriam felt she got into direct contact with Jordan's, and could estimate better Paul's position. But Mrs. Dawes was separated from her husband, and had taken up Women's Rights. She was supposed to be clever. It interested Paul.

Baxter Dawes he knew and disliked. The smith was a man of thirty-one or thirty-two. He came occasionally through Paul's corner—a big, well-set man, also striking to look at, and handsome. There was a peculiar similarity between himself and his wife. He had the same white skin, with a clear, golden tinge. His hair was of soft brown, his moustache was golden. And he had a similar defiance in his bearing and manner. But then came the difference. His eyes, dark brown and quick-shifting, were dissolute. They protruded very slightly, and his eyelids hung over them in a way that was half hate. His mouth, too, was sensual. His whole manner was of cowed defiance, as if he were ready to knock anybody down who disapproved of him—perhaps because he really disapproved of himself.

From the first day he had hated Paul. Finding the lad's impersonal, deliberate gaze of an artist on his face, he got into a fury.

"What are yer lookin' at?" he sneered, bullying.

The boy glanced away. But the smith used to stand behind the counter and talk to Mr. Pappleworth. His speech was dirty, with a kind of rottenness. Again he found the youth with his cool, critical gaze fixed on his face. The smith started round as if he had been stung.

"What'r yer lookin' at, three hap'orth o' pap?" he snarled.

The boy shrugged his shoulders slightly.

"Why yer——!" shouted Dawes.

"Leave him alone," said Mr. Pappleworth, in that insinuating voice which means, "He's only one of your good little sops who can't help it."

Since that time the boy used to look at the man every time he came through with the same curious criticism, glancing away before he met the smith's eye. It made Dawes furious. They hated each other in silence.

Clara Dawes had no children. When she had left her husband the home had been broken up, and she had gone to live with her mother. Dawes lodged with his sister. In the same house was a sister-in-law, and somehow Paul knew that this girl, Louie Travers, was now Dawes's woman. She was a handsome, insolent hussy, who mocked at the youth, and yet flushed if he walked along to the station with her as she went home.

The next time he went to see Miriam it was Saturday evening. She had a fire in the parlour, and was waiting for him. The others, except her father and mother and the young children, had gone out, so the two had the parlour together. It was a long, low, warm room. There were three of Paul's small sketches on the wall, and his photo was on the mantelpiece. On the table and on the high old rosewood piano were bowls of coloured leaves. He sat in the arm-chair, she crouched on the hearthrug near his feet. The glow was warm on her handsome, pensive face as she kneeled there like a devotee.

"What did you think of Mrs. Dawes?" she asked quietly.

"She doesn't look very amiable," he replied.

"No, but don't you think she's a fine woman?" she said, in a deep tone.

"Yes—in stature. But without a grain of taste. I like her for some things. Is she disagreeable?"

"I don't think so. I think she's dissatisfied."

"What with?"

"Well—how would *you* like to be tied for life to a man like that?"

"Why did she marry him, then, if she was to have revulsions so soon?"

"Ay, why did she!" repeated Miriam bitterly.

"And I should have thought she had enough fight in her to match him," he said.

Miriam bowed her head.

"Ay?" she queried satirically. "What makes you think so?"

"Look at her mouth—made for passion—and the very setback of her throat——" He threw his head back in Clara's defiant manner.

Miriam bowed a little lower.

"Yes," she said.

There was a silence for some moments, while he thought of Clara.

"And what were the things you liked about her?" she asked.

"I don't know—her skin and the texture of her—and her—I don't know—there's a sort of fierceness somewhere in her. I appreciate her as an artist, that's all."

"Yes."

He wondered why Miriam crouched there brooding in that strange way. It irritated him.

"You don't really like her, do you?" he asked the girl.

She looked at him with her great, dazzled dark eyes.

"I do," she said.

"You don't—you can't—not really."

"Then what?" she asked slowly.

"Eh, I don't know—perhaps you like her because she's got a grudge against men."

That was more probably one of his own reasons for liking Mrs. Dawes, but this did not occur to him. They were silent. There had come into his forehead a knitting of the brows which was becoming habitual with him, particularly when he was with Miriam. She longed to smooth it away, and she was afraid of it. It seemed the stamp of a man who was not her man in Paul Morel.

There were some crimson berries among the leaves in the bowl. He reached over and pulled out a bunch.

"If you put red berries in your hair," he said, "why would you look like some witch or priestess, and never like a reveller?"

She laughed with a naked, painful sound.

"I don't know," she said.

His vigorous warm hands were playing excitedly with the berries.

"Why can't you laugh?" he said. "You never laugh laughter. You only laugh when something is odd or incongruous, and then it almost seems to hurt you."

She bowed her head as if he were scolding her.

"I wish you could laugh at me just for one minute—just for one minute. I feel as if it would set something free."

"But"—and she looked up at him with eyes frightened and struggling—"I do laugh at you—I *do*."

"Never! There's always a kind of intensity. When you laugh I could always cry; it seems as if it shows up your suffering. Oh, you make me knit the brows of my very soul and cogitate."

Slowly she shook her head despairingly.

"I'm sure I don't want to," she said.

"I'm so damned spiritual with *you* always!" he cried.

She remained silent, thinking. "Then why don't you be otherwise." But he saw her crouching, brooding figure, and it seemed to tear him in two.

"But, there, it's autumn," he said, "and everybody feels like a disembodied spirit then."

There was still another silence. This peculiar sadness between them thrilled her soul. He seemed so beautiful with his eyes gone dark, and looking as if they were deep as the deepest well.

"You make me so spiritual!" he lamented. "And I don't want to be spiritual."

She took her finger from her mouth with a little pop, and looked up at him almost challenging. But still her soul was naked in her great dark eyes, and there was the same yearning appeal upon her. If he could have kissed her in abstract purity he would have done so. But he could not kiss her thus—and she seemed to leave no other way. And she yearned to him.

He gave a brief laugh.

"Well," he said, "get that French and we'll do some—some Verlaine."

"Yes," she said in a deep tone, almost of resignation. And she rose and got the books. And her rather red, nervous hands looked so pitiful, he was mad to comfort her and kiss her. But then he dared not—or could not. There was something prevented him. His kisses were wrong for her. They continued the reading till ten o'clock, when they went into the kitchen, and Paul was natural and jolly again with the father and mother. His eyes were dark and shining; there was a kind of fascination about him.

When he went into the barn for his bicycle he found the front wheel punctured.

"Fetch me a drop of water in a bowl," he said to her. "I shall be late, and then I s'll catch it."

He lighted the hurricane lamp, took off his coat, turned up the bicycle, and set speedily to work. Miriam came with the bowl of water and stood close to him, watching. She loved to see his hands doing things. He was slim and vigorous, with a kind of easiness even in his most hasty movements. And busy at his work he seemed to forget her. She loved him absorbedly. She wanted to run her hands down his sides. She always wanted to embrace him, so long as he did not want her.

"There!" he said, rising suddenly. "Now, could you have done it quicker?"

"No!" she laughed.

He straightened himself. His back was towards her. She put her two hands on his sides, and ran them quickly down.

"You are so *fine!*" she said.

He laughed, hating her voice, but his blood roused to a wave of flame by her hands. She did not seem to realise *him* in all this. He might have been an object. She never realised the male he was.

He lighted his bicycle-lamp, bounced the machine on the barn floor to see that the tyres were sound, and buttoned his coat.

"That's all right!" he said.

She was trying the brakes, that she knew were broken.

"Did you have them mended?" she asked.

"No!"

"But why didn't you?"

"The back one goes on a bit."

"But it's not safe."

"I can use my toe."

"I wish you'd had them mended," she murmured.

"Don't worry—come to tea to-morrow, with Edgar."

"Shall we?"

"Do—about four. I'll come to meet you."

"Very well."

She was pleased. They went across the dark yard to the gate. Looking across, he saw through the uncurtained window of the kitchen the heads of Mr. and Mrs. Leivers in the warm glow. It looked very cosy. The road, with pine trees, was quite black in front.

"Till to-morrow," he said, jumping on his bicycle.

"You'll take care, won't you?" she pleaded.

"Yes."

His voice already came out of the darkness. She stood a moment watching the light from his lamp race into obscurity along the ground. She turned very slowly indoors. Orion was wheeling up over the wood, his dog twinkling after him, half smothered. For the rest the world was full of darkness, and silent, save for the breathing of cattle in their stalls. She prayed earnestly for his safety that night. When he left her, she often lay in anxiety, wondering if he had got home safely.

He dropped down the hills on his bicycle. The roads were greasy, so he had to let it go. He felt a pleasure as the machine plunged over the second, steeper drop in the hill. "Here goes!" he said. It was risky, because of the curve in the darkness at the bottom, and because of the brewers' waggons with drunken waggoners asleep. His bicycle seemed to fall beneath him, and he loved it. Recklessness is almost a man's revenge on his woman. He feels he is not valued, so he will risk destroying himself to deprive her altogether.

The stars on the lake seemed to leap like grasshoppers, silver upon the blackness, as he spun past. Then there was the long climb home.

"See, mother!" he said, as he threw her the berries and leaves on to the table.

"H'm!" she said, glancing at them, then away again. She sat reading, alone, as she always did.

"Aren't they pretty?"

"Yes."

He knew she was cross with him. After a few minutes he said:

"Edgar and Miriam are coming to tea to-morrow."

She did not answer.

"You don't mind?"

Still she did not answer.

"Do you?" he asked.

"You know whether I mind or not."

"I don't see why you should. I have plenty of meals there."

"You do."

"Then why do you begrudge them tea?"

"I begrudge whom tea?"

"What are you so horrid for?"

"Oh, say no more! You've asked her to tea, it's quite sufficient. She'll come."

He was very angry with his mother. He knew it was merely Miriam she objected to. He flung off his boots and went to bed.

Paul went to meet his friends the next afternoon. He was glad to see them coming. They arrived home at about four o'clock. Everywhere was clean and still for Sunday afternoon. Mrs. Morel sat in her black dress and black apron. She rose to meet the visitors. With Edgar she was cordial, but with Miriam cold and rather grudging. Yet Paul thought the girl looked so nice in her brown cashmere frock.

He helped his mother to get the tea ready. Miriam would have gladly proffered, but was afraid. He was rather proud of his home. There was about it now, he thought, a certain distinction. The chairs were only wooden, and the sofa was old. But the hearthrug and cushions were cosy; the pictures were prints in good taste; there was a simplicity in everything, and plenty of books. He was never ashamed in the least of his home, nor was Miriam of hers, because both were what they should be, and warm. And then he was proud of the table; the china was pretty, the cloth was fine. It did not matter that the spoons were not silver nor the knives ivory-handled; everything looked nice. Mrs. Morel had managed wonderfully while her children were growing up, so that nothing was out of place.

Miriam talked books a little. That was her unfailing topic. But Mrs. Morel was not cordial, and turned soon to Edgar.

At first Edgar and Miriam used to go into Mrs. Morel's pew. Morel never went to chapel, preferring the public-house. Mrs. Morel, like a little champion, sat at the head of her pew, Paul at the other end; and at first Miriam sat next to him. Then the chapel was like home. It was a pretty place, with dark pews and slim, elegant pillars, and flowers. And the same people had sat in the same places ever since he was a boy. It was wonderfully sweet and soothing to sit there for an hour and a half, next to Miriam, and near to his mother, uniting his two loves under the spell of the place of worship. Then he felt warm and happy and religious at once. And after chapel he walked home with Miriam, whilst Mrs. Morel spent the rest of the evening with her old friend, Mrs. Burns. He was keenly alive on his walks on Sunday nights with Edgar and Miriam. He never went past the pits at night, by the lighted lamp-house, the tall black head-stocks and lines of trucks, past the fans spinning slowly like shadows, without the feeling of Miriam returning to him, keen and almost unbearable.

She did not very long occupy the Morels' pew. Her father took one for themselves once more. It was under the little gallery, opposite the Morels'. When Paul and his mother came in the chapel the Leivers's pew was always empty. He was anxious for fear she would not come: it was so far, and there were so many rainy Sundays. Then, often very late indeed, she came in, with her long stride, her head bowed, her face hidden under her hat of dark green velvet. Her face, as she sat opposite, was always in shadow. But it gave him a very keen feeling, as if all his soul stirred within him, to see her there. It was not the same glow, happiness, and pride, that he felt in having his mother in charge: something more wonderful, less human, and tinged to intensity by a pain, as if there were something he could not get to.

At this time he was beginning to question the orthodox creed. He was twenty-one, and she was twenty. She was beginning to dread the spring: he became so wild, and hurt her so much. All the way he went cruelly smashing her beliefs. Edgar enjoyed it. He was by nature critical and rather dispassionate. But Miriam suffered exquisite pain, as, with an intellect like a knife, the man she loved examined her religion in which she lived and moved and had her being. But he did not spare her. He was cruel. And when they went alone he was even more fierce, as if he would kill her soul. He bled her beliefs till she almost lost consciousness.

"She exults—she exults as she carries him off from me," Mrs. Morel cried in her heart when Paul had gone. "She's not like an ordinary woman, who can leave me my share in him. She wants to absorb him. She wants to draw him out and absorb him till there is nothing left of him, even for himself. He will never be a man on his own feet—she will suck him up." So the mother sat, and battled and brooded bitterly.

And he, coming home from his walks with Miriam, was wild with torture. He walked biting his lips and with clenched fists, going at a great rate. Then, brought up against a stile, he stood for some minutes, and did not move. There was a great hollow of darkness fronting him, and on the black upslopes patches of tiny lights, and in the lowest trough of the night, a flare of the pit. It was all weird and dreadful. Why was he torn so, almost bewildered, and unable to move? Why did his mother sit at home and suffer? He knew she suffered badly. But why should she? And why did he hate Miriam, and feel so cruel towards her, at the thought of his mother. If Miriam caused his mother suffering, then he hated her—and he easily hated her. Why did she make him feel as if he were uncertain of himself, insecure, an indefinite thing, as if he had not sufficient sheathing to prevent the night and the space breaking into him? How he hated her! And then, what a rush of tenderness and humility!

Suddenly he plunged on again, running home. His mother saw on him the marks of some agony, and she said nothing. But he had to make her talk to him. Then she was angry with him for going so far with Miriam.

"Why don't you like her, mother?" he cried in despair.

"I don't know, my boy," she replied piteously. "I'm sure I've tried to like her. I've tried and tried, but I can't—I can't!"

And he felt dreary and hopeless between the two.

Spring was the worst time. He was changeable, and intense and cruel. So he decided to stay away from her. Then came the hours when he knew Miriam was expecting him. His mother watched him growing restless. He could not go on with his work. He could do nothing. It was as if something were drawing his soul out towards Willey Farm. Then he put on his hat and went, saying nothing. And his mother knew he was gone. And as soon as he was on the way he sighed with relief. And when he was with her he was cruel again.

One day in March he lay on the bank of Nethermere, with Miriam sitting beside him. It was a glistening, white-and-blue day. Big clouds, so brilliant, went by overhead, while shadows stole along on the water. The clear spaces in the sky were of clean, cold blue. Paul lay on his back in the old grass, looking up. He could not bear to look at Miriam. She seemed to want him, and he resisted. He resisted all the time. He wanted now to give her passion and tenderness, and he could not. He felt that she wanted the soul out of his body, and not him. All his strength and energy she drew into herself through some channel which united them. She did not want to meet him, so that there were two of them, man and woman together. She wanted to draw all of him into her. It urged him to an intensity like madness, which fascinated him, as drug-taking might.

He was discussing Michael Angelo. It felt to her as if she were fingering the very quivering tissue, the very protoplasm of life, as she heard him. It gave her deepest satisfaction. And in the end it frightened her. There he lay in the white intensity of his search, and his voice gradually filled her with fear, so level it was, almost inhuman, as if in a trance.

"Don't talk any more," she pleaded softly, laying her hand on his forehead.

He lay quite still, almost unable to move. His body was somewhere discarded.

"Why not? Are you tired?"

"Yes, and it wears you out."

He laughed shortly, realising.

"Yet you always make me like it," he said.

"I don't wish to," she said, very low.

"Not when you've gone too far, and you feel you can't bear it. But your unconscious self always asks it of me. And I suppose I want it."

He went on, in his dead fashion:

"If only you could want me, and not want what I can reel off for you!"

"I!" she cried bitterly—"I! Why, when would you let me take you?"

"Then it's my fault," he said, and, gathering himself together, he got up and began to talk trivialities. He felt insubstantial. In a vague way he hated her for it. And he knew he was as much to blame himself. This, however, did not prevent his hating her.

One evening about this time he had walked along the home road with her. They stood by the pasture leading down to the wood, unable to part. As the stars came out the clouds closed. They had glimpses of their own constellation, Orion, towards the west. His jewels glimmered for a moment, his dog ran low, struggling with difficulty through the spume of cloud.

Orion was for them chief in significance among the constellations. They had gazed at him in their strange, surcharged hours of feeling, until they seemed themselves to live in every one of his stars. This evening Paul had been moody and perverse. Orion had seemed just an ordinary constellation to him. He had fought against his glamour and fascination. Miriam was watching her lover's mood carefully. But he said nothing that gave him away, till the moment came to part, when he stood frowning gloomily at the gathered clouds, behind which the great constellation must be striding still.

There was to be a little party at his house the next day, at which she was to attend.

"I shan't come and meet you," he said.

"Oh, very well; it's not very nice out," she replied slowly.

"It's not that—only they don't like me to. They say I care more for you than for them. And you understand, don't you? You know it's only friendship."

Miriam was astonished and hurt for him. It had cost him an effort. She left him, wanting to spare him any further humiliation. A fine rain blew in her face as she walked along the road. She was hurt deep down; and she despised him for being blown about by any wind of authority. And in her heart of hearts, unconsciously, she felt that he was trying to get away from her. This she would never have acknowledged. She pitied him.

At this time Paul became an important factor in Jordan's warehouse. Mr. Pappleworth left to set up a business of his own, and Paul remained with Mr. Jordan as Spiral overseer. His wages were to be raised to thirty shillings at the year-end, if things went well.

Still on Friday night Miriam often came down for her French lesson. Paul did not go so frequently to Willey Farm, and she grieved at the thought of her education's coming to end; moreover, they both loved to be together, in spite of discords. So they read Balzac, and did compositions, and felt highly cultured.

Friday night was reckoning night for the miners. Morel "reckoned"—shared up the money of the stall—either in the New Inn at Bretty or in his own house, according as his fellow-butties wished. Barker had turned a non-drinker, so now the men reckoned at Morel's house.

Annie, who had been teaching away, was at home again. She was still a tomboy; and she was engaged to be married. Paul was studying design.

Morel was always in good spirits on Friday evening, unless the week's earnings were small. He bustled immediately after his dinner, prepared to get washed. It was decorum for the women to absent themselves while the men reckoned. Women were not supposed to spy into such a masculine privacy as the butties' reckoning, nor were they to know the exact amount of the week's earnings. So, whilst her father was spluttering in the scullery, Annie went out to spend an hour with a neighbour. Mrs. Morel attended to her baking.

"Shut that doo-er!" bawled Morel furiously.

Annie banged it behind her, and was gone.

"If tha oppens it again while I'm weshin' me, I'll ma'e thy jaw rattle," he threatened from the midst of his soap-suds. Paul and the mother frowned to hear him.

Presently he came running out of the scullery, with the soapy water dripping from him, dithering with cold.

"Oh, my sirs!" he said. "Wheer's my towel?"

It was hung on a chair to warm before the fire, otherwise he would have bullied and blustered. He squatted on his heels before the hot baking-fire to dry himself.

"F-ff-f!" he went, pretending to shudder with cold.

"Goodness, man, don't be such a kid!" said Mrs. Morel. "It's not cold."

"Thee strip thysen stark nak'd to wesh thy flesh i' that scullery," said the miner, as he rubbed his hair; "nowt b'r a ice-'ouse!"

"And I shouldn't make that fuss," replied his wife.

"No, tha'd drop down stiff, as dead as a door-knob, wi' thy nesh sides."

"Why is a door-knob deader than anything else?" asked Paul, curious.

"Eh, I dunno; that's what they say," replied his father. "But there's that much draught i' yon scullery, as it blows through your ribs like through a five-barred gate."

"It would have some difficulty in blowing through yours," said Mrs. Morel. Morel looked down ruefully at his sides.

"Me!" he exclaimed. "I'm nowt b'r a skinned rabbit. My bones fair juts out on me."

"I should like to know where," retorted his wife.

"Iv'ry-wheer! I'm nobbut a sack o' faggots."

Mrs. Morel laughed. He had still a wonderfully young body, muscular, without any fat. His skin was smooth and clear. It might have been the body of a man of twenty-eight, except that there were, perhaps, too many blue scars, like tattoo-marks, where the coal-dust remained under the skin, and that his chest was too hairy. But he put his hand on his side ruefully. It was his fixed belief that, because he did not get fat, he was as thin as a starved rat.

Paul looked at his father's thick, brownish hands all scarred, with broken nails, rubbing the fine smoothness of his sides, and the incongruity struck him. It seemed strange they were the same flesh.

"I suppose," he said to his father, "you had a good figure once."

"Eh!" exclaimed the miner, glancing round, startled and timid, like a child.

"He had," exclaimed Mrs. Morel, "if he didn't hurtle himself up as if he was trying to get in the smallest space he could."

"Me!" exclaimed Morel—"me a good figure! I wor niver much more n'r a skeleton."

"Man!" cried his wife, "don't be such a pulamiter!"

" 'Strewth!" he said. "Tha's niver knowed me but what I looked as if I wor goin' off in a rapid decline."

She sat and laughed.

"You've had a constitution like iron," she said; "and never a man had a better start, if it was body that counted. You should have seen him as a young man," she cried suddenly to Paul, drawing herself up to imitate her husband's once handsome bearing.

Morel watched her shyly. He saw again the passion she had had for him. It blazed upon her for a moment. He was shy, rather scared, and humble. Yet again he felt his old glow. And then immediately he felt the ruin he had made during these years. He wanted to bustle about, to run away from it.

"Gi'e my back a bit of a wesh," he asked her.

His wife brought a well-soaped flannel and clapped it on his shoulders. He gave a jump.

"Eh, tha mucky little 'ussy!" he cried. "Cowd as death!"

"You ought to have been a salamander," she laughed, washing his back. It was very rarely she would do anything so personal for him. The children did those things.

"The next world won't be half hot enough for you," she added.

"No," he said; "tha'lt see as it's draughty for me."

But she had finished. She wiped him in a desultory fashion, and went upstairs, returning immediately with his shifting-trousers. When he was dried he struggled into his shirt. Then, ruddy and shiny, with hair on end, and his flannelette shirt hanging over his pit-trousers, he stood warming the garments he was going to put on. He turned them, he pulled them inside out, he scorched them.

"Goodness, man!" cried Mrs. Morel, "get dressed!"

"Should thee like to clap thysen into britches as cowd as a tub o' water?" he said.

At last he took off his pit-trousers and donned decent black. He did all this on the hearth-rug, as he would have done if Annie and her familiar friends had been present.

Mrs. Morel turned the bread in the oven. Then from the red earthenware panchion of dough that stood in a corner she took another handful of paste, worked it to the proper shape, and dropped it into a tin. As she was doing so Barker knocked and entered. He was a quiet, compact little man, who looked as if he would go through a stone wall. His black hair was cropped short, his head was bony. Like most miners, he was pale, but healthy and taut.

"Evenin', missis," he nodded to Mrs. Morel, and he seated himself with a sigh.

"Good-evening," she replied cordially.

"Tha's made thy heels crack," said Morel.

"I dunno as I have," said Barker.

He sat, as the men always did in Morel's kitchen, effacing himself rather.

"How's missis?" she asked of him.

He had told her some time back:

"We're expectin' us third just now, you see."

"Well," he answered, rubbing his head, "she keeps pretty middlin', I think."

"Let's see—when?" asked Mrs. Morel.

"Well, I shouldn't be surprised any time now."

"Ah! And she's kept fairly?"

"Yes, tidy."

"That's a blessing, for she's none too strong."

"No. An' I've done another silly trick."

"What's that?"

Mrs. Morel knew Barker wouldn't do anything very silly.

"I'm come be-out th' market-bag."

"You can have mine."

"Nay, you'll be wantin' that yourself."

"I shan't. I take a string bag always."

She saw the determined little collier buying in the week's groceries and meat on the Friday nights, and she admired him. "Barker's little, but he's ten times the man you are," she said to her husband.

Just then Wesson entered. He was thin, rather frail-looking, with a boyish ingenuousness and a slightly foolish smile, despite his seven children. But his wife was a passionate woman.

"I see you've kested me," he said, smiling rather vapidly.

"Yes," replied Barker.

The newcomer took off his cap and his big woollen muffler. His nose was pointed and red.

"I'm afraid you're cold, Mr. Wesson," said Mrs. Morel.

"It's a bit nippy," he replied.

"Then come to the fire."

"Nay, I s'll do where I am."

Both colliers sat away back. They could not be induced to come on to the hearth. The hearth is sacred to the family.

"Go thy ways i' th' arm-chair," cried Morel cheerily.

"Nay, thank yer; I'm very nicely here."

"Yes, come, of course," insisted Mrs. Morel.

He rose and went awkwardly. He sat in Morel's arm-chair awkwardly. It was too great a familiarity. But the fire made him blissfully happy.

"And how's that chest of yours?" demanded Mrs. Morel.

He smiled again, with his blue eyes rather sunny.

"Oh, it's very middlin'," he said.

"Wi' a rattle in it like a kettle-drum," said Barker shortly.

"T-t-t-t!" went Mrs. Morel rapidly with her tongue. "Did you have that flannel singlet made?"

"Not yet," he smiled.

"Then, why didn't you?" she cried.

"It'll come," he smiled.

"Ah, an' Doomsday!" exclaimed Barker.

Barker and Morel were both impatient of Wesson. But, then, they were both as hard as nails, physically.

When Morel was nearly ready he pushed the bag of money to Paul.

"Count it, boy," he asked humbly.

Paul impatiently turned from his books and pencil, tipped the bag upside down on the table. There was a five-pound bag of silver, sovereigns and loose money. He counted quickly, referred to the checks—the written papers giving amount of coal—put the money in order. Then Barker glanced at the checks.

Mrs. Morel went upstairs, and the three men came to table. Morel, as master of the house, sat in his arm-chair, with his back to the hot fire. The two butties had cooler seats. None of them counted the money.

"What did we say Simpson's was?" asked Morel; and the butties cavilled for a minute over the dayman's earnings. Then the amount was put aside.

"An' Bill Naylor's?"

This money also was taken from the pack.

Then, because Wesson lived in one of the company's houses, and his rent had been deducted, Morel and Barker took four-and-six each. And because Morel's coals had come, and the leading was stopped, Barker and Wesson took four shillings each. Then it was plain sailing. Morel gave each of them a sovereign till there were no more sovereigns; each half a crown till there were no more half-crowns; each a shilling till there were no more shillings. If there was anything at the end that wouldn't split, Morel took it and stood drinks.

Then the three men rose and went. Morel scuttled out of the house before his wife came down. She heard the door close, and descended. She looked hastily at the bread in the oven. Then, glancing on the table, she saw her money lying. Paul had been working all the time. But now he felt his mother counting the week's money, and her wrath rising.

"T-t-t-t!" went her tongue.

He frowned. He could not work when she was cross. She counted again.

"A measly twenty-five shillings!" she exclaimed. "How much was the cheque?"

"Ten pounds eleven," said Paul irritably. He dreaded what was coming.

"And he gives me a scrattlin' twenty-five, an' his club this week! But I know him. He thinks because you're earning he needn't keep the house any longer. No, all he has to do with his money is to guttle it. But I'll show him!"

"Oh, mother, don't!" cried Paul.

"Don't what, I should like to know?" she exclaimed.

"Don't carry on again. I can't work."

She went very quiet.

"Yes, it's all very well," she said; "but how do you think I'm going to manage?"

"Well, it won't make it any better to whittle about it."

"I should like to know what you'd do if you had it to put up with."

"It won't be long. You can have my money. Let him go to hell."

He went back to his work, and she tied her bonnet-strings grimly. When she was fretted he could not bear it. But now he began to insist on her recognizing him.

"The two loaves at the top," she said, "will be done in twenty minutes. Don't forget them."

"All right," he answered; and she went to market.

He remained alone working. But his usual intense concentration became unsettled. He listened for the yard-gate. At a quarter-past seven came a low knock, and Miriam entered.

"All alone?" she said.

"Yes."

As if at home, she took off her tam-o'-shanter and her long coat, hanging them up. It gave him a thrill. This might be their own house, his and hers. Then she came back and peered over his work.

"What is it?" she asked.

"Still design, for decorating stuffs, and for embroidery."

She bent short-sightedly over the drawings.

It irritated him that she peered so into everything that was his, searching him out. He went into the parlour and returned with a bundle of brownish linen. Carefully unfolding it, he spread it on the floor. It proved to be a curtain or *portière*, beautifully stencilled with a design on roses.

"Ah, how beautiful!" she cried.

The spread cloth, with its wonderful reddish roses and dark green stems, all so simple, and somehow so wicked-looking, lay at her feet. She went on her knees before it, her dark curls dropping. He saw her crouched voluptuously before his work, and his heart beat quickly. Suddenly she looked up at him.

"Why does it seem cruel?" she asked.

"What?"

"There seems a feeling of cruelty about it," she said.

"It's jolly good, whether or not," he replied, folding up his work with a lover's hands.

She rose slowly, pondering.

"And what will you do with it?" she asked.

"Send it to Liberty's. I did it for my mother, but I think she'd rather have the money."

"Yes," said Miriam. He had spoken with a touch of bitterness, and Miriam sympathised. Money would have been nothing to *her*.

He took the cloth back into the parlour. When he returned he threw to Miriam a smaller piece. It was a cushion-cover with the same design.

"I did that for you," he said.

She fingered the work with trembling hands, and did not speak. He became embarrassed.

"By Jove, the bread!" he cried.

He took the top loaves out, tapped them vigorously. They were done. He put them on the hearth to cool. Then he went to the scullery, wetted his hands, scooped the last white dough out of the punchion, and dropped it in a baking-tin. Miriam was still bent over her painted cloth. He stood rubbing the bits of dough from his hands.

"You do like it?" he asked.

She looked up at him, with her dark eyes one flame of love. He laughed uncomfortably. Then he began to talk about the design. There was for him the most intense pleasure in talking about his work to Miriam. All his passion, all his wild blood, went into this intercourse with her, when he talked and conceived his work. She brought forth to him his imaginations. She did not understand, any more than a woman understands when she conceives a child in her womb. But this was life for her and for him.

While they were talking, a young woman of about twenty-two, small and pale, hollow-eyed, yet with a relentless look about her, entered the room. She was a friend at the Morel's.

"Take your things off," said Paul.

"No, I'm not stopping."

She sat down in the arm-chair opposite Paul and Miriam, who were on the sofa. Miriam moved a little farther from him. The room was hot, with a scent of new bread. Brown, crisp loaves stood on the hearth.

"I shouldn't have expected to see you here to-night, Miriam Leivers," said Beatrice wickedly.

"Why not?" murmured Miriam huskily.

"Why, let's look at your shoes."

Miriam remained uncomfortably still.

"If tha doesna tha durs'na," laughed Beatrice.

Miriam put her feet from under her dress. Her boots had that queer, irreso-lute, rather pathetic look about them, which showed how self-conscious and self-mistrustful she was. And they were covered with mud.

"Glory! You're a positive muck-heap," exclaimed Beatrice. "Who cleans your boots?"

"I clean them myself."

"Then you wanted a job," said Beatrice. "It would ha' taken a lot of men to ha' brought me down here to-night. But love laughs at sludge, doesn't it, 'Postle my duck?"

"*Inter alia*," he said.

"Oh, Lord! are you going to spout foreign languages? What does it mean, Miriam?"

There was a fine sarcasm in the last question, but Miriam did not see it.

" 'Among other things,' I believe," she said humbly.

Beatrice put her tongue between her teeth and laughed wickedly.

" 'Among other things,' 'Postle?" she repeated. "Do you mean love laughs at mothers, and fathers, and sisters, and brothers, and men friends, and lady friends, and even at the b'loved himself?"

She affected a great innocence.

"In fact, it's one big smile," he replied.

"Up its sleeve, 'Postle Morel—you believe me," she said; and she went off into another burst of wicked, silent laughter.

Miriam sat silent, withdrawn into herself. Every one of Paul's friends de-lighted in taking sides against her, and he left her in the lurch—seemed almost to have a sort of revenge upon her then.

"Are you still at school?" asked Miriam of Beatrice.

"Yes."

"You've not had your notice, then?"

"I expect it at Easter."

"Isn't it an awful shame, to turn you off merely because you didn't pass the exam.?"

"I don't know," said Beatrice coldly.

"Agatha says you're as good as any teacher anywhere. It seems to me ridiculous. I wonder why you didn't pass."

"Short of brains, eh, 'Postle?" said Beatrice briefly.

"Only brains to bite with," replied Paul, laughing.

"Nuisance!" she cried; and, springing from her seat, she rushed and boxed his ears. She had beautiful small hands. He held her wrists while she wrestled with him. At last she broke free, and seized two handfuls of his thick, dark brown hair, which she shook.

"Beat!" he said, as he pulled his hair straight with his fingers. "I hate you!" She laughed with glee.

"Mind!" she said. "I want to sit next to you."

"I'd as lief be neighbours with a vixen," he said, nevertheless making place for her between him and Miriam.

"Did it ruffle his pretty hair, then!" she cried; and, with her hair-comb, she combed him straight. "And his nice little moustache!" she exclaimed. She tilted his head back and combed his young moustache, "It's a wicked moustache, 'Postle," she said. "It's a red for danger. Have you got any of those cigarettes?"

He pulled his cigarette-case from his pocket. Beatrice looked inside it.

"And fancy me having Connie's last cig.," said Beatrice, putting the thing between her teeth. He held a lit match to her, and she puffed daintily.

"Thanks so much, darling," she said mockingly.

It gave her a wicked delight.

"Don't you think he does it nicely, Miriam?" she asked.

"Oh, very!" said Miriam.

He took a cigarette for himself.

"Light, old boy?" said Beatrice, tilting her cigarette at him.

He bent forward to her to light his cigarette at hers. She was winking at him as he did so. Miriam saw his eyes trembling with mischief, and his full, almost sensual, mouth quivering. He was not himself, and she could not bear it. As he was now, she had no connection with him; she might as well not have existed. She saw the cigarette dancing on his full red lips. She hated his thick hair for being tumbled loose on his forehead.

"Sweet boy!" said Beatrice, tipping up his chin and giving him a little kiss on the cheek.

"I s'll kiss thee back, Beat," he said.

"Tha wunna!" she giggled, jumping up and going away. "Isn't he shameless, Miriam?"

"Quite," said Miriam. "By the way, aren't you forgetting the bread?"

"By Jove!" he cried, flinging open the oven door.

Out puffed the bluish smoke and a smell of burned bread.

"Oh, golly!" cried Beatrice, coming to his side. He crouched before the oven, she peered over his shoulder. "This is what comes of the oblivion of love, my boy."

Paul was ruefully removing the loaves. One was burnt black on the hot side; another was hard as a brick.

"Poor mater!" said Paul.

"You want to grate it," said Beatrice. "Fetch me the nutmeg-grater."

She arranged the bread in the oven. He brought the grater, and she grated the bread on to a newspaper on the table. He set the doors open to blow away the smell of burned bread. Beatrice grated away, puffing her cigarette, knocking the charcoal off the poor loaf.

"My word, Miriam! you're in for it this time," said Beatrice.

"I!" exclaimed Miriam in amazement.

"You'd better be gone when his mother comes in. *I* know why King Alfred burned the cakes. Now I see it! 'Postle would fix up a tale about his work making him forget, if he thought it would wash. If that old woman had come in a bit sooner, she'd have boxed the brazen thing's ears who made the oblivion, instead of poor Alfred's."

She giggled as she scraped the loaf. Even Miriam laughed in spite of herself. Paul mended the fire ruefully.

The garden gate was heard to bang.

"Quick!" cried Beatrice, giving Paul the scraped loaf. "Wrap it up in a damp towel."

Paul disappeared into the scullery. Beatrice hastily blew her scrapings into the fire, and sat down innocently. Annie came bursting in. She was an abrupt, quite smart young woman. She blinked in the strong light.

"Smell of burning!" she exclaimed.

"It's the cigarettes," replied Beatrice demurely.

"Where's Paul?"

Leonard had followed Annie. He had a long comic face and blue eyes, very sad.

"I suppose he's left you to settle it between you," he said. He nodded sympathetically to Miriam, and became gently sarcastic to Beatrice.

"No," said Beatrice, "he's gone off with number nine."

"I just met number five inquiring for him," said Leonard.

"Yes—we're going to share him up like Solomon's baby," said Beatrice. Annie laughed.

"Oh, ay," said Leonard. "And which bit should you have?"

"I don't know," said Beatrice. "I'll let all the others pick first."

"An' you'd have the leavings, like?" said Leonard, twisting up a comic face. Annie was looking in the oven. Miriam sat ignored. Paul entered.

"This bread's a fine sight, our Paul," said Annie.

"Then you should stop an' look after it," said Paul.

"You mean *you* should do what you're reckoning to do," replied Annie.

"He should, shouldn't he!" cried Beatrice.

"I s'd think he'd got plenty on hand," said Leonard.

"You had a nasty walk, didn't you, Miriam?" said Annie.

"Yes—but I'd been in all week——"

"And you wanted a bit of a change, like," insinuated Leonard kindly.

"Well, you can't be stuck in the house for ever," Annie agreed. She was quite amiable. Beatrice pulled on her coat, and went out with Leonard and Annie. She would meet her own boy.

"Don't forget that bread, our Paul," cried Annie. "Good-night, Miriam. I don't think it will rain."

When they had all gone, Paul fetched the swathed loaf, unwrapped it, and surveyed it sadly.

"It's a mess!" he said.

"But," answered Miriam impatiently, "what is it, after all—twopence ha'penny."

"Yes, but—it's the mater's precious baking, and she'll take it to heart. However, it's no good bothering."

He took the loaf back into the scullery. There was a little distance between him and Miriam. He stood balanced opposite her for some moments considering, thinking of his behaviour with Beatrice. He felt guilty inside himself, and yet glad. For some inscrutable reason it served Miriam right. He was not going to repent. She wondered what he was thinking of as he stood suspended. His thick hair was tumbled over his forehead. Why might she not push it back for him, and remove the marks of Beatrice's comb? Why might she not press his body with her two hands. It looked so firm, and every whit living. And he would let other girls, why not her?

Suddenly he started into life. It made her quiver almost with terror as he quickly pushed the hair off his forehead and came towards her.

"Half-past eight!" he said. "We'd better buck up. Where's your French?"

Miriam shyly and rather bitterly produced her exercise-book. Every week she wrote for him a sort of diary of her inner life, in her own French. He had found this was the only way to get her to do compositions. And her diary was mostly a love-letter. He would read it now; she felt as if her soul's history were going to be desecrated by him in his present mood. He sat beside her. She watched his hand, firm and warm, rigorously scoring her work. He was reading only the French, ignoring her soul that was there. But gradually his hand forgot its work. He read in silence, motionless. She quivered.

" 'Ce matin les oiseaux m'ont éveillé,' " he read. " 'Il faisait encore un crépuscule. Mais la petite fenêtre de ma chambre était blême, et puis, jaûne, et tous les oiseaux du bois éclatèrent dans un chanson vif et résonnant. Toute l'aûbe tressaillit. J'avais rêvé de vous. Est-ce que vous voyez aussi l'aûbe? Les oiseaux m'éveillent presque tous les matins, et toujours il y a quelque chose de terreur dans le cri des grives. Il est si clair——' "

Miriam sat tremulous, half ashamed. He remained quite still, trying to understand. He only knew she loved him. He was afraid of her love for him. It was too good for him, and he was inadequate. His own love was at fault, not hers. Ashamed, he corrected her work, humbly writing above her words.

"Look," he said quietly, "the past participle conjugated with *avoir* agrees with the direct object when it precedes."

She bent forward, trying to see and to understand. Her free, fine curls tickled his face. He started as if they had been red hot, shuddering. He saw her peering forward at the page, her red lips parted piteously, the black hair springing in fine strands across her tawny, ruddy cheek. She was coloured like a pomegranate for richness. His breath came short as he watched her. Suddenly she looked up at him. Her dark eyes were naked with their love, afraid, and yearning. His eyes, too, were dark, and they hurt her. They seemed to master her. She lost all her self-control, was exposed in fear. And he knew, before he could kiss her, he must drive something out of himself. And a touch of hate for her crept back again into his heart. He returned to her exercise.

Suddenly he flung down the pencil, and was at the oven in a leap, turning the bread. For Miriam he was too quick. She started violently, and it hurt her with real pain. Even the way he crouched before the oven hurt her. There seemed to be something cruel in it, something cruel in the swift way he pitched the bread out of the tins, caught it up again. If only he had been gentle in his movements she would have felt so rich and warm. As it was, she was hurt.

He returned and finished the exercise.

"You've done well this week," he said.

She saw he was flattered by her diary. It did not repay her entirely.

"You really do blossom out sometimes," he said. "You ought to write poetry."

She lifted her head with joy, then she shook it mistrustfully.

"I don't trust myself," she said.

"You should try!"

Again she shook her head.

"Shall we read, or is it too late?" he asked.

"It is late—but we can read just a little," she pleaded.

She was really getting now the food for her life during the next week. He made her copy Baudelaire's "Le Balcon". Then he read it for her. His voice was soft and caressing, but growing almost brutal. He had a way of lifting his lips and showing his teeth, passionately and bitterly, when he was much moved. This he did now. It made Miriam feel as if he were trampling on her. She dared not look at him, but sat with her head bowed. She could not understand why he got into such a tumult and fury. It made her wretched. She did not like Baudelaire, on the whole—nor Verlaine.

> "Behold her singing in the field
> Yon solitary highland lass."

That nourished her heart. So did "Fair Ines". And—

> "It was a beauteous evening, calm and pure,
> And breathing holy quiet like a nun."

These were like herself. And there was he, saying in his throat bitterly:

> *"Tu te rappelleras la beauté des caresses."*

The poem was finished; he took the bread out of the oven, arranging the burnt loaves at the bottom of the panchion, the good ones at the top. The desiccated loaf remained swathed up in the scullery.

"Mater needn't know till morning," he said. "It won't upset her so much then as at night."

Miriam looked in the bookcase, saw what postcards and letters he had received, saw what books were there. She took one that had interested him. Then he turned down the gas and they set off. He did not trouble to lock the door.

He was not home again until a quarter to eleven. His mother was seated in the rocking-chair. Annie, with a rope of hair hanging down her back, remained sitting on a low stool before the fire, her elbows on her knees, gloomily. On the table stood the offending loaf unswathed. Paul entered rather breathless. No one spoke. His mother was reading the little local newspaper. He took off his coat, and went to sit down on the sofa. His mother moved curtly aside to let him pass. No one spoke. He was very uncomfortable. For some minutes he sat pretending to read a piece of paper he found on the table. Then——

"I forgot that bread, mother," he said.

There was no answer from either woman.

"Well," he said, "it's only twopence ha'penny. I can pay you for that."

Being angry, he put three pennies on the table and slid them towards his mother. She turned away her head. Her mouth was shut tightly.

"Yes," said Annie, "you don't know how badly my mother is!"

The girl sat staring glumly into the fire.

"Why is she badly?" asked Paul, in his overbearing way.

"Well!" said Annie. "She could scarcely get home."

He looked closely at his mother. She looked ill.

"*Why* could you scarcely get home?" he asked her, still sharply. She would not answer.

"I found her as white as a sheet sitting here," said Annie, with a suggestion of tears in her voice.

"Well, *why?*" insisted Paul. His brows were knitting, his eyes dilating passionately.

"It was enough to upset anybody," said Mrs. Morel, "hugging those parcels—meat, and green-groceries, and a pair of curtains——"

"Well, why *did* you hug them; you needn't have done."

"Then who would?"

"Let Annie fetch the meat."

"Yes, and I *would* fetch the meat, but how was I to know. You were off with Miriam, instead of being in when my mother came."

"And what was the matter with you?" asked Paul of his mother.

"I suppose it's my heart," she replied. Certainly she looked bluish round the mouth.

"And have you felt it before?"

"Yes—often enough."

"Then why haven't you told me?—and why haven't you seen a doctor?"

Mrs. Morel shifted in her chair, angry with him for his hectoring.

"You'd never notice anything," said Annie. "You're too eager to be off with Miriam."

"Oh, am I—and any worse than you with Leonard?"

"*I* was in at a quarter to ten."

There was silence in the room for a time.

"I should have thought," said Mrs. Morel bitterly, "that she wouldn't have occupied you so entirely as to burn a whole ovenful of bread."

"Beatrice was here as well as she."

"Very likely. But we know why the bread is spoilt."

"Why?" he flashed.

"Because you were engrossed with Miriam," replied Mrs. Morel hotly.

"Oh, very well—then it was *not!*" he replied angrily.

He was distressed and wretched. Seizing a paper, he began to read. Annie, her blouse unfastened, her long ropes of hair twisted into a plait, went up to bed, bidding him a very curt good-night.

Paul sat pretending to read. He knew his mother wanted to upbraid him. He also wanted to know what had made her ill, for he was troubled. So, instead of running away to bed, as he would have liked to do, he sat and waited. There was a tense silence. The clock ticked loudly.

"You'd better go to bed before your father comes in," said the mother harshly. "And if you're going to have anything to eat, you'd better get it."

"I don't want anything."

It was his mother's custom to bring him some trifle for supper on Friday night, the night of luxury for the colliers. He was too angry to go and find it in the pantry this night. This insulted her.

"If I *wanted* you to go to Selby on Friday night, I can imagine the scene," said Mrs. Morel. "But you're never too tired to go if *she* will come for you. Nay, you neither want to eat nor drink then."

"I can't let her go alone."

"Can't you? And why does she come?"

"Not because I ask her."

"She doesn't come without you want her——"

"Well, what if I *do* want her——" he replied.

"Why, nothing, if it was sensible or reasonable. But to go trapseing up there miles and miles in the mud, coming home at midnight, and got to go to Nottingham in the morning——"

"If I hadn't, you'd be just the same."

"Yes, I should, because there's no sense in it. Is she *so* fascinating that you must follow her all that way?" Mrs. Morel was bitterly sarcastic. She sat still, with averted face, stroking with a rhythmic, jerked movement, the black sateen of her apron. It was a movement that hurt Paul to see.

"I do like her," he said, "but——"

"*Like* her!" said Mrs. Morel, in the same biting tones. "It seems to me you like nothing and nobody else. There's neither Annie, nor me, nor anyone now for you."

"What nonsense, mother—you know I don't love her—I—I tell you I *don't* love her—she doesn't even walk with my arm, because I don't want her to."

"Then why do you fly to her so often?"

"I *do* like to talk to her—I never said I didn't. But I *don't* love her."

"Is there nobody else to talk to?"

"Not about the things we talk of. There's a lot of things that you're not interested in, that——"

"What things?"

Mrs. Morel was so intense that Paul began to pant.

"Why—painting—and books. *You* don't care about Herbert Spencer."

"No," was the sad reply. "And *you* won't at my age."

"Well, but I do now—and Miriam does——"

"And how do you know," Mrs. Morel flashed defiantly, "that *I* shouldn't. Do you ever try me!"

"But you don't, mother, you know you don't care whether a picture's decorative or not; you don't care what *manner* it is in."

"How do you know I don't care? Do you ever try me? Do you ever talk to me about these things, to try?"

"But it's not that that matters to you, mother, you know it's not."

"What is it, then—what is it, then, that matters to me?" she flashed. He knitted his brows with pain.

"You're old, mother, and we're young."

He only meant that the interests of *her* age were not the interests of his. But he realised the moment he had spoken that he had said the wrong thing.

"Yes, I know it well—I am old. And therefore I may stand aside; I have nothing more to do with you. You only want me to wait on you—the rest is for Miriam."

He could not bear it. Instinctively he realised that he was life to her. And, after all, she was the chief thing to him, the only supreme thing.

"You know it isn't, mother, you know it isn't!"

She was moved to pity by his cry.

"It looks a great deal like it," she said, half putting aside her despair.

"No, mother—I really *don't* love her. I talk to her, but I want to come home to you."

He had taken off his collar and tie, and rose, bare-throated, to go to bed. As he stooped to kiss his mother, she threw her arms round his neck, hid her face on his shoulder, and cried, in a whimpering voice, so unlike her own that he writhed in agony:

"I can't bear it. I could let another woman—but not her. She'd leave me no room, not a bit of room——"

And immediately he hated Miriam bitterly.

"And I've never—you know, Paul—I've never had a husband—not really——"

He stroked his mother's hair, and his mouth was on her throat.

"And she exults so in taking you from me—she's not like ordinary girls."

"Well, I don't love her, mother," he murmured, bowing his head and hiding his eyes on her shoulder in misery. His mother kissed him a long, fervent kiss.

"My boy!" she said, in a voice trembling with passionate love.

Without knowing, he gently stroked her face.

"There," said his mother, "now go to bed. You'll be *so* tired in the morning." As she was speaking she heard her husband coming. "There's your father—now go." Suddenly she looked at him almost as if in fear. "Perhaps I'm selfish. If you want her, take her, my boy."

His mother looked so strange, Paul kissed her, trembling.

"Ha—mother!" he said softly.

Morel came in, walking unevenly. His hat was over one corner of his eye. He balanced in the doorway.

"At your mischief again?" he said venomously.

Mrs. Morel's emotion turned into sudden hate of the drunkard who had come in thus upon her.

"At any rate, it is sober," she said.

"H'm—h'm! h'm—h'm!" he sneered. He went into the passage, hung up his hat and coat. Then they heard him go down three steps to the pantry. He returned with a piece of pork-pie in his fist. It was what Mrs. Morel had bought for her son.

"Nor was that bought for you. If you can give me no more than twenty-five shillings, I'm sure I'm not going to buy you pork-pie to stuff, after you've swilled a bellyful of beer."

"Wha-at—wha-at!" snarled Morel, toppling in his balance. "Wha-at—not for me?" He looked at the piece of meat and crust, and suddenly, in a vicious spurt of temper, flung it into the fire.

Paul started to his feet.

"Waste your own stuff!" he cried.

"What—what!" suddenly shouted Morel, jumping up and clenching his fist. "I'll show yer, yer young jockey!"

"All right!" said Paul viciously, putting his head on one side. "Show me!"

He would at that moment dearly have loved to have a smack at something. Morel was half crouching, fists up, ready to spring. The young man stood, smiling with his lips.

"Ussha!" hissed the father, swiping round with a great stroke just past his son's face. He dared not, even though so close, really touch the young man, but swerved an inch away.

"Right!" said Paul, his eyes upon the side of his father's mouth, where in another instant his fist would have hit. He ached for that stroke. But he heard a faint moan from behind. His mother was deadly pale and dark at the mouth. Morel was dancing up to deliver another blow.

"Father!" said Paul, so that the word rang.

Morel started, and stood at attention.

"Mother!" moaned the boy. "Mother!"

She began to struggle with herself. Her open eyes watched him, although she could not move. Gradually she was coming to herself. He laid her down on the sofa, and ran upstairs for a little whisky, which at last she could sip. The tears were hopping down his face. As he kneeled in front of her he did not cry, but the tears ran down his face quickly. Morel, on the opposite side of the room, sat with his elbows on his knees glaring across.

"What's a-matter with 'er?" he asked.

"Faint!" replied Paul.

"H'm!"

The elderly man began to unlace his boots. He stumbled off to bed. His last fight was fought in that home.

Paul kneeled there, stroking his mother's hand.

"Don't be poorly, mother—don't be poorly!" he said time after time.

"It's nothing, my boy," she murmured.

At last he rose, fetched in a large piece of coal, and raked the fire. Then he cleared the room, put everything straight, laid the things for breakfast, and brought his mother's candle.

"Can you go to bed, mother?"

"Yes, I'll come."

"Sleep with Annie, mother, not with him."

"No. I'll sleep in my own bed."

"Don't sleep with him, mother."

"I'll sleep in my own bed."

She rose, and he turned out the gas, then followed her closely upstairs, carrying her candle. On the landing he kissed her close.

"Good-night, mother."

"Good-night!" she said.

He pressed his face upon the pillow in a fury of misery. And yet, somewhere in his soul, he was at peace because he still loved his mother best. It was the bitter peace of resignation.

The efforts of his father to conciliate him next day were a great humiliation to him.

Everybody tried to forget the scene.

IX

DEFEAT OF MIRIAM

Paul was dissatisfied with himself and with everything. The deepest of his love belonged to his mother. When he felt he had hurt her, or wounded his love for her, he could not bear it. Now it was spring, and there was battle between him and Miriam. This year he had a good deal against her. She was vaguely aware of it. The old feeling that she was to be a sacrifice to this love, which she had had when she prayed, was mingled in all her emotions. She did not at the bottom believe she ever would have him. She did not believe in herself primarily: doubted whether she could ever be what he would demand of her. Certainly she never saw herself living happily through a lifetime with him. She saw tragedy, sorrow, and sacrifice ahead. And in sacrifice she was proud, in renunciation she was strong, for she did not trust herself to support everyday life. She was prepared for the big things and the deep things, like tragedy. It was the sufficiency of the small day-life she could not trust.

The Easter holidays began happily. Paul was his own frank self. Yet she felt it would go wrong. On the Sunday afternoon she stood at her bedroom window, looking across at the oak-trees of the wood, in whose branches a twilight was tangled, below the bright sky of the afternoon. Grey-green rosettes of honey-suckle leaves hung before the window, some already, she fancied, showing bud. It was spring, which she loved and dreaded.

Hearing the clack of the gate she stood in suspense. It was a bright grey day. Paul came into the yard with his bicycle, which glittered as he walked. Usually he rang his bell and laughed towards the house. To-day he walked with shut lips and cold, cruel bearing, that had something of a slouch and a sneer in it. She knew him well by now, and could tell from that keen-looking, aloof young body of his what was happening inside him. There was a cold correctness in the way he put his bicycle in its place, that made her heart sink.

She came downstairs nervously. She was wearing a new net blouse that she thought became her. It had a high collar with a tiny ruff, reminding her of Mary, Queen of Scots, and making her, she thought, look wonderfully a woman, and dignified. At twenty she was full-breasted and luxuriously formed. Her face was still like a soft rich mask, unchangeable. But her eyes, once lifted, were wonderful. She was afraid of him. He would notice her new blouse.

He, being in a hard, ironical mood, was entertaining the family to a description of a service given in the Primitive Methodist Chapel, conducted by one of the well-known preachers of the sect. He sat at the head of the table, his mobile face, with the eyes that could be so beautiful, shining with tenderness or dancing with laughter, now taking on one expression and then another, in imitation of various people he was mocking. His mockery always hurt her; it was too near the reality. He was too clever and cruel. She felt that when his eyes were like this, hard with mocking hate, he would spare neither himself nor anybody else. But Mrs. Leivers was wiping her eyes with laughter, and Mr. Leivers, just awake from his Sunday nap, was rubbing his head in amusement. The three brothers sat with ruffled, sleepy appearance in their shirt-sleeves, giving a guffaw from time to time. The whole family loved a "take-off" more than anything.

He took no notice of Miriam. Later, she saw him remark her new blouse, saw that the artist approved, but it won from him not a spark of warmth. She was nervous, could hardly reach the teacups from the shelves.

When the men went out to milk, she ventured to address him personally.

"You were late," she said.

"Was I?" he answered.

There was silence for a while.

"Was it rough riding?" she asked.

"I didn't notice it."

She continued quickly to lay the table. When she had finished——

"Tea won't be for a few minutes. Will you come and look at the daffodils?" she said.

He rose without answering. They went out into the back garden under the budding damson-trees. The hills and the sky were clean and cold. Everything looked washed, rather hard. Miriam glanced at Paul. He was pale and impassive. It seemed cruel to her that his eyes and brows, which she loved, could look so hurting.

"Has the wind made you tired?" she asked. She detected an underneath feeling of weariness about him.

"No, I think not," he answered.

"It must be rough on the road—the wood moans so."

"You can see by the clouds it's a south-west wind; that helps me here."

"You see, I don't cycle, so I don't understand," she murmured.

"Is there need to cycle to know that!" he said.

She thought his sarcasms were unnecessary. They went forward in silence. Round the wild, tussocky lawn at the back of the house was a thorn hedge, under which daffodils were craning forward from among their sheaves of grey-green blades. The cheeks of the flowers were greenish with cold. But still some had burst, and their gold ruffled and glowed. Miriam went on her knees before one cluster, took a wild-looking daffodil between her hands, turned up its face of gold to her, and bowed down, caressing it with her mouth and cheeks and brow. He stood aside, with his hands in his pockets, watching her. One after another she turned up to him the faces of the yellow, bursten flowers appealingly, fondling them lavishly all the while.

"Aren't they magnificent?" she murmured.

"Magnificent! It's a bit thick—they're pretty!"

She bowed again to her flowers at his censure of her praise. He watched her crouching, sipping the flowers with fervid kisses.

"Why must you always be fondling things?" he said irritably.

"But I love to touch them," she replied, hurt.

"Can you never like things without clutching them as if you wanted to pull the heart out of them? Why don't you have a bit more restraint, or reserve, or something?"

She looked up at him full of pain, then continued slowly to stroke her lips against a ruffled flower. Their scent, as she smelled it, was so much kinder than he; it almost made her cry.

"You wheedle the soul out of things," he said. "I would never wheedle—at any rate, I'd go straight."

He scarcely knew what he was saying. These things came from him mechanically. She looked at him. His body seemed one weapon, firm and hard against her.

"You're always begging things to love you," he said, "as if you were a beggar for love. Even the flowers, you have to fawn on them——"

Rhythmically, Miriam was swaying and stroking the flower with her mouth, inhaling the scent which ever after made her shudder as it came to her nostrils.

"You don't want to love—your eternal and abnormal craving is to be loved. You aren't positive, you're negative. You absorb, absorb, as if you must fill yourself up with love, because you've got a shortage somewhere."

She was stunned by his cruelty, and did not hear. He had not the faintest notion of what he was saying. It was as if his fretted, tortured soul, run hot by thwarted passion, jetted off these sayings like sparks from electricity. She did not grasp anything he said. She only sat crouched beneath his cruelty and his hatred of her. She never realised in a flash. Over everything she brooded and brooded.

After tea he stayed with Edgar and the brothers, taking no notice of Miriam. She, extremely unhappy on this looked-for holiday, waited for him. And at last he yielded and came to her. She was determined to track this mood of his to its origin. She counted it not much more than a mood.

"Shall we go through the wood a little way?" she asked him, knowing he never refused a direct request.

They went down to the warren. On the middle path they passed a trap, a narrow horseshoe hedge of small fir-boughs, baited with the guts of a rabbit. Paul glanced at it frowning. She caught his eye.

"Isn't it dreadful?" she asked.

"I don't know! Is it worse than a weasel with its teeth in a rabbit's throat? One weasel or many rabbits? One or the other must go!"

He was taking the bitterness of life badly. She was rather sorry for him.

"We will go back to the house," he said. "I don't want to walk out."

They went past the lilac-tree, whose bronze leaf-buds were coming unfastened. Just a fragment remained of the haystack, a monument squared and brown, like a pillar of stone. There was a little bed of hay from the last cutting.

"Let us sit here a minute," said Miriam.

He sat down against his will, resting his back against the hard wall of hay. They faced the amphitheatre of round hills that glowed with sunset, tiny white farms standing out, the meadows golden, the woods dark and yet luminous, tree-tops folded over tree-tops, distinct in the distance. The evening had cleared, and the east was tender with a magenta flush under which the land lay still and rich.

"Isn't it beautiful?" she pleaded.

But he only scowled. He would rather have had it ugly just then.

At that moment a big bull-terrier came rushing up, open-mouthed, pranced his two paws on the youth's shoulders, licking his face. Paul drew back, laughing. Bill was a great relief to him. He pushed the dog aside, but it came leaping back.

"Get out," said the lad, "or I'll dot thee one."

But the dog was not to be pushed away. So Paul had a little battle with the creature, pitching poor Bill away from him, who, however, only floundered tumultously back again, wild with joy. The two fought together, the man laughing grudgingly, the dog grinning all over. Miriam watched them. There was something pathetic about the man. He wanted so badly to love, to be tender. The rough way he bowled the dog over was really loving. Bill got up, panting with happiness, his brown eyes rolling in his white face, and lumbered back again. He adored Paul. The lad frowned.

"Bill, I've had enough o' thee," he said.

But the dog only stood with two heavy paws, that quivered with love, upon his thigh, and flickered a red tongue at him. He drew back.

"No," he said—"no—I've had enough."

And in a minute the dog trotted off happily, to vary the fun.

He remained staring miserably across at the hills, whose still beauty he begrudged. He wanted to go and cycle with Edgar. Yet he had not the courage to leave Miriam.

"Why are you sad?" she asked humbly.

"I'm not sad; why should I be," he answered. "I'm only normal."

She wondered why he always claimed to be normal when he was disagreeable.

"But what is the matter?" she pleaded, coaxing him soothingly.

"Nothing!"

"Nay!" she murmured.

He picked up a stick and began to stab the earth with it.

"You'd far better not talk," he said.

"But I wish to know——" she replied.

He laughed resentfully.

"You always do," he said.

"It's not fair to me," she murmured.

He thrust, thrust, thrust at the ground with the pointed stick, digging up little clods of earth as if he were in a fever of irritation. She gently and firmly laid her hand on his wrist.

"Don't!" she said. "Put it away."

He flung the stick into the currant-bushes, and leaned back. Now he was bottled up.

"What is it?" she pleaded softly.

He lay perfectly still, only his eyes alive, and they full of torment.

"You know," he said at length, rather wearily—"you know—we'd better break off."

It was what she dreaded. Swiftly everything seemed to darken before her eyes.

"Why!" she murmured. "What has happened?"

"Nothing has happened. We only realise where we are. It's no good——"

She waited in silence, sadly, patiently. It was no good being impatient with him. At any rate, he would tell her now what ailed him.

"We agreed on friendship," he went on in a dull, monotonous voice. "How often *have* we agreed for friendship! And yet—it neither stops there, nor gets anywhere else."

He was silent again. She brooded. What did he mean? He was so wearying. There was something he would not yield. Yet she must be patient with him.

"I can only give friendship—it's all I'm capable of—it's a flaw in my make-up. The thing overbalances to one side—I hate a toppling balance. Let us have done."

There was warmth of fury in his last phrases. He meant she loved him more than he her. Perhaps he could not love her. Perhaps she had not in herself that which he wanted. It was the deepest motive of her soul, this self-mistrust. It was so deep she dared neither realise nor acknowledge. Perhaps she was deficient. Like an infinitely subtle shame, it kept her always back. If it were so, she would do without him. She would never let herself want him. She would merely see.

"But what has happened?" she said.

"Nothing—it's all in myself—it only comes out just now. We're always like this towards Easter-time."

He grovelled so helplessly, she pitied him. At least she never floundered in such a pitiable way. After all, it was he who was chiefly humiliated.

"What do you want?" she asked him.

"Why—I mustn't come often—that's all. Why should I monopolise you when I'm not—— You see, I'm deficient in something with regard to you——"

He was telling her he did not love her, and so ought to leave her a chance with another man. How foolish and blind and shamefully clumsy he was! What were other men to her! What were men to her at all! But he, ah! she loved his soul. Was *he* deficient in something? Perhaps he was.

"But I don't understand," she said huskily. "Yesterday——"

The night was turning jangled and hateful to him as the twilight faded. And she bowed under her suffering.

"I know," he cried, "you never will! You'll never believe that I can't—can't physically, any more than I can fly up like a skylark——"

"What?" she murmured. Now she dreaded.

"Love you."

He hated her bitterly at that moment because he made her suffer. Love her! She knew he loved her. He really belonged to her. This about not loving her, physically, bodily, was a mere perversity on his part, because he knew she loved him. He was stupid like a child. He belonged to her. His soul wanted her. She guessed somebody had been influencing him. She felt upon him the hardness, the foreignness of another influence.

"What have they been saying at home?" she asked.

"It's not that," he answered.

And then she knew it was. She despised them for their commonness, his people. They did not know what things were really worth.

He and she talked very little more that night. After all he left her to cycle with Edgar.

He had come back to his mother. Hers was the strongest tie in his life. When he thought round, Miriam shrank away. There was a vague, unreal feel about her. And nobody else mattered. There was one place in the world that stood solid and did not melt into unreality: the place where his mother was. Everybody else could grow shadowy, almost non-existent to him, but she could not. It was as if the pivot and pole of his life, from which he could not escape, was his mother.

And in the same way she waited for him. In him was established her life now. After all, the life beyond offered very little to Mrs. Morel. She saw that our chance for *doing* is here, and doing counted with her. Paul was going to prove that she had been right; he was going to make a man whom nothing should shift off his feet; he was going to alter the face of the earth in some way which mattered. Wherever he went she felt her soul went with him. Whatever he did she felt her soul stood by him, ready, as it were, to hand him his tools. She could not bear it when he was with Miriam. William was dead. She would fight to keep Paul.

And he came back to her. And in his soul was a feeling of the satisfaction of self-sacrifice because he was faithful to her. She loved him first; he loved her first. And yet it was not enough. His new young life, so strong and imperious, was urged towards something else. It made him mad with restlessness. She saw this, and wished bitterly that Miriam had been a woman who could take this new life of his, and leave her the roots. He fought against his mother almost as he fought against Miriam.

It was a week before he went again to Willey Farm. Miriam had suffered a great deal, and was afraid to see him again. Was she now to endure the ignominy of his abandoning her? That would only be superficial and temporary. He would come back. She held the keys to his soul. But meanwhile, how he would torture her with his battle against her. She shrank from it.

However, the Sunday after Easter he came to tea. Mrs. Leivers was glad to see him. She gathered something was fretting him, that he found things hard. He seemed to drift to her for comfort. And she was good to him. She did him that great kindness of treating him almost with reverence.

He met her with the young children in the front garden.

"I'm glad you've come," said the mother, looking at him with her great appealing brown eyes. "It is such a sunny day. I was just going down the fields for the first time this year."

He felt she would like him to come. That soothed him. They went, talking simply, he gentle and humble. He could have wept with gratitude that she was deferential to him. He was feeling humiliated.

At the bottom of the Mow Close they found a thrush's nest.

"Shall I show you the eggs?" he said.

"Do!" replied Mrs. Leivers. "They seem *such* a sign of spring, and so hopeful."

He put aside the thorns, and took out the eggs, holding them in the palm of his hand.

"They are quite hot—I think we frightened her off them," he said.

"Ay, poor thing!" said Mrs. Leivers.

Miriam could not help touching the eggs, and his hand which, it seemed to her, cradled them so well.

"Isn't it a strange warmth!" she murmured, to get near him.

"Blood heat," he answered.

She watched him putting them back, his body pressed against the hedge, his arm reaching slowly through the thorns, his hand folded carefully over the eggs. He was concentrated on the act. Seeing him so, she loved him; he seemed so simple and sufficient to himself. And she could not get to him.

After tea she stood hesitating at the bookshelf. He took "Tartarin de Tarascon". Again they sat on the bank of hay at the foot of the stack. He read a couple of pages, but without any heart for it. Again the dog came racing up to repeat the fun of the other day. He shoved his muzzle in the man's chest. Paul fingered his ear for a moment. Then he pushed him away.

"Go away, Bill," he said. "I don't want you."

Bill slunk off, and Miriam wondered and dreaded what was coming. There was a silence about the youth that made her still with apprehension. It was not his furies, but his quiet resolutions that she feared.

Turning his face a little to one side, so that she could not see him, he began, speaking slowly and painfully:

"Do you think—if I didn't come up so much—you might get to like somebody else—another man?"

So this was what he was still harping on.

"But I don't know any other men. Why do you ask?" she replied, in a low tone that should have been a reproach to him.

"Why," he blurted, "because they say I've no right to come up like this—without we mean to marry——"

Miriam was indignant at anybody's forcing the issues between them. She had been furious with her own father for suggesting to Paul, laughingly, that he knew why he came so much.

"Who says?" she asked, wondering if her people had anything to do with it. They had not.

"Mother—and the others. They say at this rate everybody will consider me engaged, and I ought to consider myself so, because it's not fair to you. And I've tried to find out—and I don't think I love you as a man ought to love his wife. What do *you* think about it?"

Miriam bowed her head moodily. She was angry at having this struggle. People should leave him and her alone.

"I don't know," she murmured.

"Do you think we love each other enough to marry?" he asked definitely. It made her tremble.

"No," she answered truthfully. "I don't think so—we're too young."

"I thought perhaps," he went on miserably, "that you, with your intensity in things, might have given me more—than I could ever make up to you. And even now—if you think it better—we'll be engaged."

Now Miriam wanted to cry. And she was angry, too. He was always such a child for people to do as they liked with.

"No, I don't think so," she said firmly.

He pondered a minute.

"You see," he said, "with me—I don't think one person would ever monopolize me—be everything to me—I think never."

This she did not consider.

"No," she murmured. Then, after a pause, she looked at him, and her dark eyes flashed.

"This is your mother," she said. "I know she never liked me."

"No, no, it isn't," he said hastily. "It was for your sake she spoke this time. She only said, if I was going on, I ought to consider myself engaged." There was a silence. "And if I ask you to come down any time, you won't stop away, will you?"

She did not answer. By this time she was very angry.

"Well, what shall we do?" she said shortly. "I suppose I'd better drop French. I was just beginning to get on with it. But I suppose I can go on alone."

"I don't see that we need," he said. "I can give you a French lesson, surely."

"Well—and there are Sunday nights. I shan't stop coming to chapel, because I enjoy it, and it's all the social life I get. But you've no need to come home with me. I can go alone."

"All right," he answered, rather taken aback. "But if I ask Edgar, he'll always come with us, and then they can say nothing."

There was silence. After all, then, she would not lose much. For all their talk down at his home there would not be much difference. She wished they would mind their own business.

"And you won't think about it, and let it trouble you, will you?" he asked.

"Oh no," replied Miriam, without looking at him.

He was silent. She thought him unstable. He had no fixity of purpose, no anchor of righteousness that held him.

"Because," he continued, "a man gets across his bicycle—and goes to work—and does all sorts of things. But a woman broods."

"No, I shan't bother," said Miriam. And she meant it.

It had gone rather chilly. They went indoors.

"How white Paul looks!" Mrs. Leivers exclaimed. "Miriam, you shouldn't have let him sit out of doors. Do you think you've taken cold, Paul?"

"Oh, no!" he laughed.

But he felt done up. It wore him out, the conflict in himself. Miriam pitied him now. But quite early, before nine o'clock, he rose to go.

"You're not going home, are you?" asked Mrs. Leivers anxiously.

"Yes," he replied. "I said I'd be early." He was very awkward.

"But this *is* early," said Mrs. Leivers.

Miriam sat in the rocking-chair, and did not speak. He hesitated, expecting her to rise and go with him to the barn as usual for his bicycle. She remained as she was. He was at a loss.

"Well—good-night, all!" he faltered.

She spoke her good-night along with all the others. But as he went past the window he looked in. She saw him pale, his brows knit slightly in a way that had become constant with him, his eyes dark with pain.

She rose and went to the doorway to wave good-bye to him as he passed through the gate. He rode slowly under the pine-trees, feeling a cur and a miserable wretch. His bicycle went tilting down the hills at random. He thought it would be a relief to break one's neck.

Two days later he sent her up a book and a little note, urging her to read and be busy.

At this time he gave all his friendship to Edgar. He loved the family so much, he loved the farm so much; it was the dearest place on earth to him. His home was not so lovable. It was his mother. But then he would have been just as happy with his mother anywhere. Whereas Willey Farm he loved passionately. He loved the little pokey kitchen, where men's boots tramped, and the dog slept with one eye open for fear of being trodden on; where the lamp hung over the table at night, and everything was so silent. He loved Miriam's long, low parlour, with its atmosphere of romance, its flowers, its books, its high rose-wood piano. He loved the gardens and the buildings that stood with their scarlet roofs on the naked edges of the fields, crept towards the wood as if for cosiness, the wild country scooping down a valley and up the uncultured hills of the other side. Only to be there was an exhilaration and a joy to him. He loved Mrs. Leivers, with her unworldliness and her quaint cynicism; he loved Mr. Leivers, so warm and young and lovable; he loved Edgar, who lit up when he came, and the boys and the children and Bill—even the sow Circe and the Indian game-cock called Tippoo. All this besides Miriam. He could not give it up.

So he went as often, but he was usually with Edgar. Only all the family, including the father, joined in charades and games at evening. And later, Miriam drew them together, and they read "Macbeth" out of penny books, taking parts. It was great excitement. Miriam was glad, and Mrs. Leivers was glad, and Mr. Leivers enjoyed it. Then they all learned songs together from tonic sol-fa, singing in a circle round the fire. But now Paul was very rarely alone with Miriam. She waited. When she and Edgar and he walked home together from chapel or from the literary society in Bestwood, she knew his talk, so passionate and so unorthodox nowadays, was for her. She did envy Edgar, however, his cycling with Paul, his Friday nights, his days working in the fields. For her Friday nights and her French lessons were gone. She was nearly always alone, walking, pondering in the wood, reading, studying, dreaming, waiting. And he wrote to her frequently.

One Sunday evening they attained to their old rare harmony. Edgar had stayed to Communion—he wondered what it was like—with Mrs. Morel. So Paul came on alone with Miriam to his home. He was more or less under her spell again. As usual, they were discussing the sermon. He was setting now full sail towards Agnosticism, but such a religious Agnosticism that Miriam did not suffer so badly. They were at the Renan "Vie de Jésus" stage. Miriam was the threshing-floor on which he threshed out all his beliefs. While he trampled his ideas upon her soul, the truth came out for him. She alone was his threshing-floor. She alone helped him towards realization. Almost impassive, she submitted to his argument and expounding. And somehow, because of her, he gradually realized where he was wrong. And what he realized, she realized. She felt he could not do without her.

They came to the silent house. He took the key out of the scullery window, and they entered. All the time he went on with his discussion. He lit the gas, mended the fire, and brought her some cakes from the pantry. She sat on the sofa, quietly, with a plate on her knee. She wore a large white hat with some pinkish flowers. It was a cheap hat, but he liked it. Her face beneath was still and pensive, golden-brown and ruddy. Always her ears were hid in her short curls. She watched him.

She liked him on Sundays. Then he wore a dark suit that showed the lithe movement of his body. There was a clean, clear-cut look about him. He went on with his thinking to her. Suddenly he reached for a Bible. Miriam liked the way he reached up—so sharp, straight to the mark. He turned the pages quickly, and read her a chapter of St. John. As he sat in the arm-chair reading, intent, his voice only thinking, she felt as if he were using her unconsciously as a man uses his tools at some work he is bent on. She loved it. And the wistfulness of his voice was like a reaching to something, and it was as if she were what he reached with. She sat back on the sofa away from him, and yet feeling herself the very instrument his hand grasped. It gave her great pleasure.

Then he began to falter and to get self-conscious. And when he came to the verse, "A woman, when she is in travail, hath sorrow because her hour is come", he missed it out. Miriam had felt him growing uncomfortable. She shrank when the well-known words did not follow. He went on reading, but she did not hear. A grief and shame made her bend her head. Six months ago he would have read it simply. Now there was a scotch in his running with her. Now she felt there was really something hostile between them, something of which they were ashamed.

She ate her cake mechanically. He tried to go on with his argument, but could not get back the right note. Soon Edgar came in. Mrs. Morel had gone to her friends'. The three set off to Willey Farm.

Miriam brooded over his split with her. There was something else he wanted. He could not be satisfied; he could give her no peace. There was between them now always a ground for strife. She wanted to prove him. She believed that his chief need in life was herself. If she could prove it, both to herself and to him, the rest might go; she could simply trust to the future.

So in May she asked him to come to Willey Farm and meet Mrs. Dawes. There was something he hankered after. She saw him, whenever they spoke of Clara Dawes, rouse and get slightly angry. He said he did not like her. Yet he was keen to know about her. Well, he should put himself to the test. She believed that there were in him desires for higher things, and desires for lower, and that the desire for the higher would conquer. At any rate, he should try. She forgot that her "higher" and "lower" were arbitrary.

He was rather excited at the idea of meeting Clara at Willey Farm. Mrs. Dawes came for the day. Her heavy, dun-coloured hair was coiled on top of her head. She wore a white blouse and navy skirt, and somehow, wherever she was, seemed to make things look paltry and insignificant. When she was in the room, the kitchen seemed too small and mean altogether. Miriam's beautiful twilightly parlour looked stiff and stupid. All the Leivers were eclipsed like candles. They found her rather hard to put up with. Yet she was perfectly amiable, but indifferent, and rather hard.

Paul did not come till afternoon. He was early. As he swung off his bicycle, Miriam saw him look round at the house eagerly. He would be disappointed if the visitor had not come. Miriam went out to meet him, bowing her head because of the sunshine. Nasturtiums were coming out crimson under the cool green shadow of their leaves. The girl stood, dark-haired, glad to see him.

"Hasn't Clara come?" he asked.

"Yes," replied Miriam in her musical tone. "She's reading."

He wheeled his bicycle into the barn. He had put on a handsome tie, of which he was rather proud, and socks to match.

"She came this morning?" he asked.

"Yes," replied Miriam, as she walked at his side. "You said you'd bring me that letter from the man at Liberty's. Have you remembered?"

"Oh, dash, no!" he said. "But nag at me till you get it."

"I don't like to nag at you."

"Do it whether or not. And is she any more agreeable?" he continued.

"You know I always think she is quite agreeable."

He was silent. Evidently his eagerness to be early to-day had been the new-comer. Miriam already began to suffer. They went together towards the house.
‘ He took the clips off his trousers, but was too lazy to brush the dust from his shoes, in spite of the socks and tie.

Clara sat in the cool parlour reading. He saw the nape of her white neck, and the fine hair lifted from it. She rose, looking at him indifferently. To shake hands she lifted her arm straight, in a manner that seemed at once to keep him at a distance, and yet to fling something to him. He noticed how her breasts swelled inside her blouse, and how her shoulder curved handsomely under the thin muslin at the top of her arm.

"You have chosen a fine day," he said.

"It happens so," she said.

"Yes," he said; "I am glad."

She sat down, not thanking him for his politeness.

"What have you been doing all morning?" asked Paul of Miriam.

"Well, you see," said Miriam, coughing huskily, "Clara only came with father—and so—she's not been here very long."

Clara sat leaning on the table, holding aloof. He noticed her hands were large, but well kept. And the skin on them seemed almost coarse, opaque, and white, with fine golden hairs. She did not mind if he observed her hands. She intended to scorn him. Her heavy arm lay negligently on the table. Her mouth was closed as if she were offended, and she kept her face slightly averted.

"You were at Margaret Bonford's meeting the other evening," he said to her.

Miriam did not know this courteous Paul. Clara glanced at him.

"Yes," she said.

"Why," asked Miriam, "how do you know?"

"I went in for a few minutes before the train came," he answered.

Clara turned away again rather disdainfully.

"I think she's a lovable little woman," said Paul.

"Margaret Bonford!" exclaimed Clara. "She's a great deal cleverer than most men."

"Well, I didn't say she wasn't," he said, deprecating. "She's lovable for all that."

"And, of course, that is all that matters," said Clara witheringly.

He rubbed his head, rather perplexed, rather annoyed.

"I suppose it matters more than her cleverness," he said; "which, after all, would never get her to heaven."

"It's not heaven she wants to get—it's her fair share on earth," retorted Clara. She spoke as if he were responsible for some deprivation which Miss Bonford suffered.

"Well," he said, "I thought she was warm, and awfully nice—only too frail. I wished she was sitting comfortably in peace——"

" 'Darning her husband's stockings,' " said Clara scathingly.

"I'm sure she wouldn't mind darning even my stockings," he said. "And I'm sure she'd do them well. Just as I wouldn't mind blacking her boots if she wanted me to."

But Clara refused to answer this sally of his. He talked to Miriam for a little while. The other woman held aloof.

"Well," he said, "I think I'll go and see Edgar. Is he on the land?"

"I believe," said Miriam, "he's gone for a load of coal. He should be back directly."

"Then," he said, "I'll go and meet him."

Miriam dared not propose anything for the three of them. He rose and left them.

On the top road, where the gorse was out, he saw Edgar walking lazily beside the mare, who nodded her white-starred forehead as she dragged the clanking load of coal. The young farmer's face lighted up as he saw his friend. Edgar was good-looking, with dark, warm eyes. His clothes were old and rather disreputable, and he walked with considerable pride.

"Hello!" he said, seeing Paul bareheaded. "Where are you going?"

"Came to meet you. Can't stand 'Nevermore'."

Edgar's teeth flashed in a laugh of amusement.

"Who is 'Nevermore'?" he asked.

"The lady—Mrs. Dawes—it ought to be Mrs. The Raven that quothed 'Nevermore'."

Edgar laughed with glee.

"Don't you like her?" he asked.

"Not a fat lot," said Paul. "Why, do you?"

"No!" The answer came with a deep ring of conviction. "No!" Edgar pursed up his lips. "I can't say she's much in my line." He mused a little. Then: "But why do you call her 'Nevermore'?" he asked.

"Well," said Paul, "if she looks at a man she says haughtily 'Nevermore', and if she looks at herself in the looking-glass she says disdainfully 'Nevermore', and if she thinks back she says it in disgust, and if she looks forward she says it cynically."

Edgar considered this speech, failed to make much out of it, and said, laughing:

"You think she's a man-hater?"

"She thinks she is," replied Paul.

"But you don't think so?"

"No," replied Paul.

"Wasn't she nice with you, then?"

"Could you imagine her *nice* with anybody?" asked the young man.

Edgar laughed. Together they unloaded the coal in the yard. Paul was rather self-conscious, because he knew Clara could see if she looked out of the window. She didn't look.

On Saturday afternoons the horses were brushed down and groomed. Paul and Edgar worked together, sneezing with the dust that came from the pelts of Jimmy and Flower.

"Do you know a new song to teach me?" said Edgar.

He continued to work all the time. The back of his neck was sun-red when he bent down, and his fingers that held the brush were thick. Paul watched him sometimes.

" 'Mary Morrison'?" suggested the younger.

Edgar agreed. He had a good tenor voice, and he loved to learn all the songs his friend could teach him, so that he could sing whilst he was carting. Paul had a very indifferent baritone voice, but a good ear. However, he sang softly, for fear of Clara. Edgar repeated the line in a clear tenor. At times they both broke off to sneeze, and first one, then the other, abused his horse.

Miriam was impatient of men. It took so little to amuse them—even Paul. She thought it anomalous in him that he could be so thoroughly absorbed in a triviality.

It was tea-time when they had finished.

"What song was that?" asked Miriam.

Edgar told her. The conversation turned to singing.

"We have such jolly times," Miriam said to Clara.

Mrs. Dawes ate her meal in a slow, dignified way. Whenever the men were present she grew distant.

"Do you like singing?" Miriam asked her.

"If it is good," she said.

Paul, of course, coloured.

"You mean if it is high-class and trained?" he said.

"I think a voice needs training before the singing is anything," she said.

"You might as well insist on having people's voices trained before you allowed them to talk," he replied. "Really, people sing for their own pleasure, as a rule."

"And it may be for other people's discomfort."

"Then the other people should have flaps to their ears," he replied.

The boys laughed. There was a silence. He flushed deeply, and ate in silence.

After tea, when all the men had gone but Paul, Mrs. Leivers said to Clara:

"And you find life happier now?"

"Infinitely."

"And you are satisfied?"

"So long as I can be free and independent."

"And you don't *miss* anything in your life?" asked Mrs. Leivers gently.

"I've put all that behind me."

Paul had been feeling uncomfortable during this discourse. He got up.

"You'll find you're always tumbling over the things you've put behind you," he said. Then he took his departure to the cow-sheds. He felt he had been witty, and his manly pride was high. He whistled as he went down the brick track.

Miriam came for him a little while later to know if he would go with Clara and her for a walk. They set off down to Strelley Mill Farm. As they were going beside the brook, on the Willey Water side, looking through the brake at the edge of the wood, where pink campions glowed under a few sunbeams, they saw, beyond the tree-trunks and the thin hazel bushes, a man leading a great bay horse through the gullies. The big red beast seemed to dance romantically through that dimness of green hazel drift, away there where the air was shadowy, as if it were in the past, among the fading bluebells that might have bloomed for Deidre or Iseult.

The three stood charmed.

"What a treat to be a knight," he said, "and to have a pavilion here."

"And to have us shut up safely?" replied Clara.

"Yes," he answered, "singing with your maids at your broidery. I would carry your banner of white and green and heliotrope. I would have 'W.S.P.U.' emblazoned on my shield, beneath a woman rampant."

"I have no doubt," said Clara, "that you would much rather fight for a woman than let her fight for herself."

"I would. When she fights for herself she seems like a dog before a looking-glass, gone into a mad fury with its own shadow."

"And *you* are the looking-glass?" she asked, with a curl of the lip.

"Or the shadow," he replied.

"I am afraid," she said, "that you are too clever."

"Well, I leave it to you to be *good,*" he retorted, laughing. "Be good, sweet maid, and just let *me* be clever."

But Clara wearied of his flippancy. Suddenly, looking at her, he saw that the upward lifting of her face was misery and not scorn. His heart grew tender for everybody. He turned and was gentle with Miriam, whom he had neglected till then.

At the wood's edge they met Limb, a thin, swarthy man of forty, tenant of Strelley Mill, which he ran as a cattle-raising farm. He held the halter of the powerful stallion indifferently, as if he were tired. The three stood to let him pass over the stepping-stones of the first brook. Paul admired that so large an animal should walk on such springy toes, with an endless excess of vigour. Limb pulled up before them.

"Tell your father, Miss Leivers," he said, in a peculiar piping voice, "that his young beas'es 'as broke that bottom fence three days an' runnin'."

"Which?" asked Miriam, tremulous.

The great horse breathed heavily, shifting round its red flanks, and looking suspiciously with its wonderful big eyes upwards from under its lowered head and falling mane.

"Come along a bit," replied Limb, "an' I'll show you."

The man and the stallion went forward. It danced sideways, shaking its white fetlocks and looking frightened, as it felt itself in the brook.

"No hanky-pankyin'," said the man affectionately to the beast.

It went up the bank in little leaps, then splashed finely through the second brook. Clara, walking with a kind of sulky abandon, watched it half-fascinated, half-contemptuous. Limb stopped and pointed to the fence under some willows.

"There, you see where they got through," he said. "My man's druv 'em back three times."

"Yes," answered Miriam, colouring as if she were at fault.

"Are you comin' in?" asked the man.

"No, thanks; but we should like to go by the pond."

"Well, just as you've a mind," he said.

The horse gave little whinneys of pleasure at being so near home.

"He is glad to be back," said Clara, who was interested in the creature.

"Yes—'e's been a tidy step to-day."

They went through the gate, and saw approaching them from the big farmhouse a smallish, dark, excitable-looking woman of about thirty-five. Her hair was touched with grey, her dark eyes looked wild. She walked with her hands behind her back. Her brother went forward. As it saw her, the big bay stallion whinneyed again. She came up excitedly.

"Are you home again, my boy!" she said tenderly to the horse, not to the man. The great beast shifted round to her, ducking his head. She smuggled into his mouth the wrinkled yellow apple she had been hiding behind her back, then she kissed him near the eyes. He gave a big sigh of pleasure. She held his head in her arms against her breast.

"Isn't he splendid!" said Miriam to her.

Miss Limb looked up. Her dark eyes glanced straight at Paul.

"Oh, good-evening, Miss Leivers," she said. "It's ages since you've been down."

Miriam introduced her friends.

"Your horse is a fine fellow!" said Clara.

"Isn't he!" Again she kissed him. "As loving as any man!"

"More loving than most men, I should think," replied Clara.

"He's a nice boy!" cried the woman, again embracing the horse.

Clara, fascinated by the big beast, went up to stroke his neck.

"He's quite gentle," said Miss Limb. "Don't you think big fellows are?"

"He's a beauty!" replied Clara.

She wanted to look in his eyes. She wanted him to look at her.

"It's a pity he can't talk," she said.

"Oh, but he can—all but," replied the other woman.

Then her brother moved on with the horse.

"Are you coming in? Do come in, Mr.—I didn't catch it."

"Morel," said Miriam. "No, we won't come in, but we should like to go by the mill-pond."

"Yes—yes, do. Do you fish, Mr. Morel?"

"No," said Paul.

"Because if you do you might come and fish any time," said Miss Limb. "We scarcely see a soul from week's end to week's end. I should be thankful."

"What fish are there in the pond?" he asked.

They went through the front garden, over the sluice, and up the steep bank to the pond, which lay in shadow, with its two wooded islets. Paul walked with Miss Limb.

"I shouldn't mind swimming here," he said.

"Do," she replied. "Come when you like. My brother will be awfully pleased to talk with you. He is so quiet, because there is no one to talk to. Do come and swim."

Clara came up.

"It's a fine depth," she said, "and so clear."

"Yes," said Miss Limb.

"Do you swim?" said Paul. "Miss Limb was just saying we could come when we liked."

"Of course there's the farm-hands," said Miss Limb.

They talked a few moments, then went on up the wild hill, leaving the lonely, haggard-eyed woman on the bank.

The hillside was all ripe with sunshine. It was wild and tussocky, given over to rabbits. The three walked in silence. Then:

"She makes me feel uncomfortable," said Paul.

"You mean Miss Limb?" asked Miriam. "Yes."

"What's a matter with her? Is she going dotty with being too lonely?"

"Yes," said Miriam. "It's not the right sort of life for her. I think it's cruel to bury her there. I really ought to go and see her more. But—she upsets me."

"She makes me feel sorry for her—yes, and she bothers me," he said.

"I suppose," blurted Clara suddenly, "she wants a man."

The other two were silent for a few moments.

"But it's the loneliness sends her cracked," said Paul.

Clara did not answer, but strode on uphill. She was walking with her hand hanging, her legs swinging as she kicked through the dead thistles and the tussocky grass, her arms hanging loose. Rather than walking, her handsome body seemed to be blundering up the hill. A hot wave went over Paul. He was curious about her. Perhaps life had been cruel to her. He forgot Miriam, who was walking beside him talking to him. She glanced at him, finding he did not answer her. His eyes were fixed ahead on Clara.

"Do you still think she is disagreeable?" she asked.

He did not notice that the question was sudden. It ran with his thoughts.

"Something's the matter with her," he said.

"Yes," answered Miriam.

They found at the top of the hill a hidden wild field, two sides of which were backed by the wood, the other sides by high loose hedges of hawthorn and elder bushes. Between these overgrown bushes were gaps that the cattle might have walked through had there been any cattle now. There the turf was smooth as velveteen, padded and holed by the rabbits. The field itself was coarse, and crowded with tall, big cow-slips that had never been cut. Clusters of strong flowers rose everywhere above the coarse tussocks of bent. It was like a roadstead crowded with tall, fairy shipping.

"Ah!" cried Miriam, and she looked at Paul, her dark eyes dilating. He smiled. Together they enjoyed the field of flowers. Clara, a little way off, was looking at the cowslips disconsolately. Paul and Miriam stayed close together, talking in subdued tones. He kneeled on one knee, quickly gathering the best blossoms, moving from tuft to tuft restlessly, talking softly all the time. Miriam plucked the flowers lovingly, lingering over them. He always seemed to her too quick and almost scientific. Yet his bunches had a natural beauty more than hers. He loved them, but as if they were his and he had a right to them. She had more reverence for them: they held something she had not.

The flowers were very fresh and sweet. He wanted to drink them. As he gathered them, he ate the little yellow trumpets. Clara was still wandering about disconsolately. Going towards her, he said:

"Why don't you get some?"

"I don't believe in it. They look better growing."

"But you'd like some?"

"They want to be left."

"I don't believe they do."

"I don't want the corpses of flowers about me," she said.

"That's a stiff, artificial notion," he said. "They don't die any quicker in water than on their roots. And besides, they *look* nice in a bowl—they look jolly. And you only call a thing a corpse because it looks corpse-like."

"Whether it is one or not?" she argued.

"It isn't one to me. A dead flower isn't a corpse of a flower."

Clara now ignored him.

"And even so—what right have you to pull them?" she asked.

"Because I like them, and want them—and there's plenty of them."

"And that is sufficient?"

"Yes. Why not? I'm sure they'd smell nice in your room in Nottingham."

"And I should have the pleasure of watching them die."

"But then—it does not matter if they do die."

Whereupon he left her, and went stooping over the clumps of tangled flowers which thickly sprinkled the field like pale, luminous foam-clots. Miriam had come close. Clara was kneeling, breathing some scent from the cowslips.

"I think," said Miriam, "if you treat them with reverence you don't do them any harm. It is the spirit you pluck them in that matters."

"Yes," he said. "But no, you get 'em because you want 'em, and that's all." He held out his bunch.

Miriam was silent. He picked some more.

"Look at these!" he continued; "sturdy and lusty like little trees and like boys with fat legs."

Clara's hat lay on the grass not far off. She was kneeling, bending forward still to smell the flowers. Her neck gave him a sharp pang, such a beautiful thing, yet not proud of itself just now. Her breasts swung slightly in her blouse. The arching curve of her back was beautiful and strong; she wore no stays. Suddenly, without knowing, he was scattering a handful of cowslips over her hair and neck, saying:

> "Ashes to ashes, and dust to dust,
> If the Lord won't have you the devil must."

The chill flowers fell on her neck. She looked up at him, with almost pitiful, scared grey eyes, wondering what he was doing. Flowers fell on her face, and she shut her eyes.

Suddenly, standing there above her, he felt awkward.

"I thought you wanted a funeral," he said, ill at ease.

Clara laughed strangely, and rose, picking the cowslips from her hair. She took up her hat and pinned it on. One flower had remained tangled in her hair. He saw, but would not tell her. He gathered up the flowers he had sprinkled over her.

At the edge of the wood the bluebells had flowed over into the field and stood there like flood-water. But they were fading now. Clara strayed up to them. He wandered after her. The bluebells pleased him.

"Look how they've come out of the wood!" he said.

Then she turned with a flash of warmth and of gratitude.

"Yes," she smiled.

His blood beat up.

"It makes me think of the wild men of the woods, how terrified they would be when they got breast to breast with the open space."

"Do you think they were?" she asked.

"I wonder which was more frightened among old tribes—those bursting out of their darkness of woods upon all the space of light, or those from the open tiptoeing into the forests."

"I should think the second," she answered.

"Yes, you *do* feel like one of the open space sort, trying to force yourself into the dark, don't you?"

"How should I know?" she answered queerly.

The conversation ended there.

The evening was deepening over the earth. Already the valley was full of shadow. One tiny square of light stood opposite at Crossleigh Bank Farm. Brightness was swimming on the tops of the hills. Miriam came up slowly, her face in her big, loose bunch of flowers, walking ankle-deep through the scattered froth of the cowslips. Beyond her the trees were coming into shape, all shadow.

"Shall we go?" she asked.

And the three turned away. They were all silent. Going down the path they could see the light of home right across, and on the ridge of the hill a thin dark outline with little lights, where the colliery village touched the sky.

"It has been nice, hasn't it?" he asked.

Miriam murmured assent. Clara was silent.

"Don't you think so?" he persisted.

But she walked with her head up, and still did not answer. He could tell by the way she moved, as if she didn't care, that she suffered.

At this time Paul took his mother to Lincoln. She was bright and enthusiastic as ever, but as he sat opposite her in the railway carriage, she seemed to look frail. He had a momentary sensation as if she were slipping away from him. Then he wanted to get hold of her, to fasten her, almost to chain her. He felt he must keep hold of her with his hand.

They drew near to the city. Both were at the window looking for the cathedral.

"There she is, mother!" he cried.

They saw the great cathedral lying couchant above the plain.

"Ah!" she exclaimed. "So she is!"

He looked at his mother. Her blue eyes were watching the cathedral quietly. She seemed again to be beyond him. Something in the eternal repose of the uplifted cathedral, blue and noble against the sky, was reflected in her, something of the fatality. What was, *was*. With all his young will he could not alter it. He saw her face, the skin still fresh and pink and downy, but crow's-feet near her eyes, her eyelids steady, sinking a little, her mouth always closed with disillusion; and there was on her the same eternal look, as if she knew fate at last. He beat against it with all the strength of his soul.

"Look, mother, how big she is above the town! Think, there are streets and streets below her! She looks bigger than the city altogether."

"So she does!" exclaimed his mother, breaking bright into life again. But he had seen her sitting, looking steady out of the window at the cathedral, her face and eyes fixed, reflecting the relentlessness of life. And the crow's-feet near her eyes, and her mouth shut so hard, made him feel he would go mad.

They ate a meal that she considered wildly extravagant.

"Don't imagine I like it," she said, as she ate her cutlet. "I *don't* like it, I really don't! Just *think* of your money wasted!"

"You never mind my money," he said. "You forget I'm a fellow taking his girl for an outing."

And he bought her some blue violets.

"Stop it at once, sir!" she commanded. "How can I do it?"

"You've got nothing to do. Stand still!"

And in the middle of High Street he stuck the flowers in her coat.

"An old thing like me!" she said, sniffing.

"You see," he said, "I want people to think we're awful swells. So look ikey."

"I'll jowl your head," she laughed.

"Strut!" he commanded. "Be a fantail pigeon."

It took him an hour to get her through the street. She stood above Glory Hole, she stood before Stone Bow, she stood everywhere, and exclaimed.

A man came up, took off his hat, and bowed to her.

"Can I show you the town, madam?"

"No, thank you," she answered. "I've got my son."

Then Paul was cross with her for not answering with more dignity.

"You go away with you!" she exclaimed. "Ha! that's the Jew's House. Now, do you remember that lecture, Paul———?"

But she could scarcely climb the cathedral hill. He did not notice. Then suddenly he found her unable to speak. He took her into a little public-house, where she rested.

"It's nothing," she said. "My heart is only a bit old; one must expect it."

He did not answer, but looked at her. Again his heart was crushed in a hot grip. He wanted to cry, he wanted to smash things in fury.

They set off again, pace by pace, so slowly. And every step seemed like a weight on his chest. He felt as if his heart would burst. At last they came to the top. She stood enchanted, looking at the castle gate, looking at the cathedral front. She had quite forgotten herself.

"Now *this* is better than I thought it could be!" she cried.

But he hated it. Everywhere he followed her, brooding. They sat together in the cathedral. They attended a little service in the choir. She was timid.

"I suppose it is open to anybody?" she asked him.

"Yes," he replied. "Do you think they'd have the damned cheek to send us away."

"Well, I'm sure," she exclaimed, "they would if they heard your language."

Her face seemed to shine again with joy and peace during the service. And all the time he was wanting to rage and smash things and cry.

Afterwards, when they were leaning over the wall, looking at the town below, he blurted suddenly:

"Why can't a man have a *young* mother? What is she old for?"

"Well," his mother laughed, "she can scarcely help it."

"And why wasn't I the oldest son? Look—they say the young ones have the advantage—but look, *they* had the young mother. You should have had me for your eldest son."

"*I* didn't arrange it," she remonstrated. "Come to consider, you're as much to blame as me."

He turned on her, white, his eyes furious.

"What are you old for!" he said, mad with his impotence. "*Why* can't you walk? *Why* can't you come with me to places?"

"At one time," she replied, "I could have run up that hill a good deal better than you."

"What's the good of that to *me?*" he cried, hitting his fist on the wall. Then he became plaintive. "It's too bad of you to be ill, Little, it is——"

"Ill!" she cried. "I'm a bit old, and you'll have to put up with it, that's all."

They were quiet. But it was as much as they could bear. They got jolly again over tea. As they sat by Brayford, watching the boats, he told her about Clara. His mother asked him innumerable questions.

"Then who does she live with?"

"With her mother, on Bluebell Hill."

"And have they enough to keep them?"

"I don't think so. I think they do lace work."

"And wherein lies her charm, my boy?"

"I don't know that she's charming, mother. But she's nice. And she seems straight, you know—not a bit deep, not a bit."

"But she's a good deal older than you."

"She's thirty, I'm going of twenty-three."

"You haven't told me what you like her for."

"Because I don't know—a sort of defiant way she's got—a sort of angry way."

Mrs. Morel considered. She would have been glad now for her son to fall in love with some woman who would—she did not know what. But he fretted so, got so furious suddenly, and again was melancholic. She wished he knew some nice woman—— She did not know what she wished, but left it vague. At any rate, she was not hostile to the idea of Clara.

Annie, too, was getting married. Leonard had gone away to work in Birmingham. One week-end when he was home she had said to him:

"You don't look very well, my lad."

"I dunno," he said. "I feel anyhow or nohow, ma."

He called her "ma" already in his boyish fashion.

"Are you sure they're good lodgings?" she asked.

"Yes—yes. Only—it's a winder when you have to pour your own tea out—an' nobody to grouse if you team it in your saucer and sup it up. It somehow takes a' the taste out of it."

Mrs. Morel laughed.

"And so it knocks you up?" she said.

"I dunno. I want to get married," he blurted, twisting his fingers and looking down at his boots. There was a silence.

"But," she exclaimed, "I thought you said you'd wait another year."

"Yes, I did say so," he replied stubbornly.

Again she considered.

"And you know," she said, "Annie's a bit of a spendthrift. She's saved no more than eleven pounds. And I know, lad, you haven't had much chance."

He coloured up to the ears.

"I've got thirty-three quid," he said.

"It doesn't go far," she answered.

He said nothing, but twisted his fingers.

"And you know," she said, "I've nothing——"

"I didn't want, ma!" he cried, very red, suffering and remonstrating.

"No, my lad, I know. I was only wishing I had. And take away five pounds for the wedding and things—it leaves twenty-nine pounds. You won't do much on that."

He twisted still, impotent, stubborn, not looking up.

"But do you really want to get married?" she asked. "Do you feel as if you ought?"

He gave her one straight look from his blue eyes.

"Yes," he said.

"Then," she replied, "we must all do the best we can for it, lad."

The next time he looked up there were tears in his eyes.

"I don't want Annie to feel handicapped," he said, struggling.

"My lad," she said, "you're steady—you've got a decent place. If a man had *needed* me I'd have married him on his last week's wages. She may find it a bit hard to start humbly. Young girls *are* like that. They look forward to the fine home they think they'll have. But *I* had expensive furniture. It's not everything."

So the wedding took place almost immediately. Arthur came home, and was splendid in uniform. Annie looked nice in a dove-grey dress that she could take for Sundays. Morel called her a fool for getting married, and was cool with his son-in-law. Mrs. Morel had white tips in her bonnet, and some white on her blouse, and was teased by both her sons for fancying herself so grand. Leonard was jolly and cordial, and felt a fearful fool. Paul could not quite see what Annie wanted to get married for. He was fond of her, and she of him. Still, he hoped rather lugubriously that it would turn out all right. Arthur was astonishingly handsome in his scarlet and yellow, and he knew it well, but was secretly ashamed of the uniform. Annie cried her eyes up in the kitchen, on leaving her mother. Mrs. Morel cried a little, then patted her on the back and said:

"But don't cry, child, he'll be good to you."

Morel stamped and said she was a fool to go and tie herself up. Leonard looked white and overwrought. Mrs. Morel said to him:

"I s'll trust her to you, my lad, and hold you responsible for her."

"You can," he said, nearly dead with the ordeal. And it was all over.

When Morel and Arthur were in bed, Paul sat talking, as he often did, with his mother.

"You're not sorry she's married, mother, are you?" he asked.

"I'm not sorry she's married—but—it seems strange that she should go from me. It even seems to me hard that she can prefer to go with her Leonard. That's how mothers are—I know it's silly."

"And shall you be miserable about her?"

"When I think of my own wedding day," his mother answered, "I can only hope her life will be different."

"But you can trust him to be good to her?"

"Yes, yes. They say he's not good enough for her. But I say if a man is *genuine,* as he is, and a girl is fond of him—then—it should be all right. He's as good as she."

"So you don't mind?"

"I would *never* have let a daughter of mine marry a man I didn't *feel* to be genuine through and through. And yet, there's a gap now she's gone."

They were both miserable, and wanted her back again. It seemed to Paul his mother looked lonely, in her new black silk blouse with its bit of white trimming.

"At any rate, mother, I s'll never marry," he said.

"Ay, they all say that, my lad. You've not met the one yet. Only wait a year or two."

"But I shan't marry, mother. I shall live with you, and we'll have a servant."

"Ay, my lad, it's easy to talk. We'll see when the time comes."

"What time? I'm nearly twenty-three."

"Yes, you're not one that would marry young. But in three years' time——"

"I shall be with you just the same."

"We'll see, my boy, we'll see."

"But you don't want me to marry?"

"I shouldn't like to think of you going through your life without anybody to care for you and do—no."

"And you think I ought to marry?"

"Sooner or later every man ought."

"But you'd rather it were later."

"It would be hard—and very hard. It's as they say:

" 'A son's my son till he takes him a wife,
But my daughter's my daughter the whole of her life.' "

"And you think I'd let a wife take me from you?"

"Well, you wouldn't ask her to marry your mother as well as you," Mrs. Morel smiled.

"She could do what she liked; she wouldn't have to interfere."

"She wouldn't—till she'd got you—and then you'd see."

"I never will see. I'll never marry while I've got you—I won't."

"But I shouldn't like to leave you with nobody, my boy," she cried.

"You're not going to leave me. What are you? Fifty-three! I'll give you till seventy-five. There you are, I'm fat and forty-four. Then I'll marry a staid body. See!"

His mother sat and laughed.

"Go to bed," she said—"go to bed."

"And we'll have a pretty house, you and me, and a servant, and it'll be just all right. I s'll perhaps be rich with my painting."

"Will you go to bed!"

"And then you s'll have a pony-carriage. See yourself—a little Queen Victoria trotting round."

"I tell you to go to bed," she laughed.

He kissed her and went. His plans for the future were always the same.

Mrs. Morel sat brooding—about her daughter, about Paul, about Arthur. She fretted at losing Annie The family was very closely bound. And she felt she *must* live now, to be with her children. Life was so rich for her. Paul wanted her, and so did Arthur. Arthur never knew how deeply he loved her. He was a creature of the moment. Never yet had he been forced to realise himself. The army had disciplined his body, but not his soul. He was in perfect health and very handsome. His dark, vigorous hair sat close to his smallish head. There was something childish about his nose, something almost girlish about his dark blue eyes. But he had the full red mouth of a man under his brown moustache, and his jaw was strong. It was his father's mouth; it was the nose and eyes of her own mother's people—good-looking, weak-principled folk. Mrs. Morel was anxious about him. Once he had really run the rig he was safe. But how far would he go?

The army had not really done him any good. He resented bitterly the authority of the officers. He hated having to obey as if he were an animal. But he had too much sense to kick. So he turned his attention to getting the best out of it. He could sing, he was a boon-companion. Often he got into scrapes, but they were the manly scrapes that are easily condoned. So he made a good time out of it, whilst his self-respect was in suppression. He trusted to his good looks and handsome figure, his refinement, his decent education to get him most of what he wanted, and he was not disappointed. Yet he was restless. Something seemed to gnaw him inside. He was never still, he was never alone. With his mother he was rather humble. Paul he admired and loved and despised slightly. And Paul admired and loved and despised him slightly.

Mrs. Morel had had a few pounds left to her by her father, and she decided to buy her son out of the army. He was wild with joy. Now he was like a lad taking a holiday.

He had always been fond of Beatrice Wyld, and during his furlough he picked up with her again. She was stronger and better in health. The two often went long walks together, Arthur taking her arm in soldier's fashion, rather stiffly. And she came to play the piano whilst he sang. Then Arthur would unhook his tunic collar. He grew flushed, his eyes were bright, he sang in a manly tenor. Afterwards they sat together on the sofa. He seemed to flaunt his body: she was aware of him so—the strong chest, the sides, the thighs in their close-fitting trousers.

He liked to lapse into the dialect when he talked to her. She would sometimes smoke with him. Occasionally she would only take a few whiffs at his cigarette.

"Nay," he said to her one evening, when she reached for his cigarette. "Nay, tha doesna. I'll gi'e thee a smoke kiss if ter's a mind."

"I wanted a whiff, no kiss at all," she answered.

"Well, an' tha s'lt ha'e a whiff," he said, "along wi' t' kiss."

"I want a draw at thy fag," she cried, snatching for the cigarette between his lips.

He was sitting with his shoulder touching her. She was small and quick as lightning. He just escaped.

"I'll gi'e thee a smoke kiss," he said.

"Tha'rt a knivey nuisance, Arty Morel," she said, sitting back.

"Ha'e a smoke kiss?"

The soldier leaned forward to her, smiling. His face was near hers.

"Shonna!" she replied, turning away her head.

He took a draw at his cigarette, and pursed up his mouth, and put his lips close to her. His dark-brown cropped moustache stood out like a brush. She looked at the puckered crimson lips, then suddenly snatched the cigarette from his fingers and darted away. He, leaping after her, seized the comb from her back hair. She turned, threw the cigarette at him. He picked it up, put it in his mouth, and sat down.

"Nuisance!" she cried. "Give me my comb!"

She was afraid that her hair, specially done for him, would come down. She stood with her hands to her head. He hid the comb between his knees.

"I've non got it," he said.

The cigarette trembled between his lips with laughter as he spoke.

"Liar!" she said.

" 'S true as I'm here!" he laughed, showing his hands.

"You brazen imp!" she exclaimed, rushing and scuffling for the comb, which he had under his knees. As she wrestled with him, pulling at his smooth, tight-covered knees, he laughed till he lay back on the sofa shaking with laughter. The cigarette fell from his mouth almost singeing his throat. Under his delicate tan the blood flushed up, and he laughed till his blue eyes were blinded, his throat swollen almost to choking. Then he sat up. Beatrice was putting in her comb.

"Tha tickled me, Beat," he said thickly.

Like a flash her small white hand went out and smacked his face. He started up, glaring at her. They stared at each other. Slowly the flush mounted her cheek, she dropped her eyes, then her head. He sat down sulkily. She went into the scullery to adjust her hair. In private there she shed a few tears, she did not know what for.

When she returned she was pursed up close. But it was only a film over her fire. He, with ruffled hair, was sulking upon the sofa. She sat down opposite, in the arm-chair, and neither spoke. The clock ticked in the silence like blows.

"You are a little cat, Beat," he said at length, half apologetically.

"Well, you shouldn't be brazen," she replied.

There was again a long silence. He whistled to himself like a man much agitated but defiant. Suddenly she went across to him and kissed him.

"Did it, pore fing!" she mocked.

He lifted his face, smiling curiously.

"Kiss?" he invited her.

"Daren't I?" she asked.

"Go on!" he challenged, his mouth lifted to her.

Deliberately, and with a peculiar quivering smile that seemed to overspread her whole body, she put her mouth on his. Immediately his arms folded round her. As soon as the long kiss was finished she drew back her head from him, put her delicate fingers on his neck, through the open collar. Then she closed her eyes, giving herself up again in a kiss.

She acted of her own free will. What she would do she did, and made nobody responsible.

Paul felt life changing around him. The conditions of youth were gone. Now it was a home of grown-up people. Annie was a married woman, Arthur was following his own pleasure in a way unknown to his folk. For so long they had all lived at home, and gone out to pass their time. But now, for Annie and Arthur, life lay outside their mother's house. They came home for holiday and for rest. So there was that strange, half-empty feeling about the house, as if the birds had flown. Paul became more and more unsettled. Annie and Arthur had gone. He was restless to follow. Yet home was for him beside his mother. And still there was something else, something outside, something he wanted.

He grew more and more restless. Miriam did not satisfy him. His old mad desire to be with her grew weaker. Sometimes he met Clara in Nottingham, sometimes he went to meetings with her, sometimes he saw her at Willey Farm. But on these last occasions the situation became strained. There was a triangle of antagonism between Paul and Clara and Miriam. With Clara he took on a smart, worldly, mocking tone very antagonistic to Miriam. It did not matter what went before. She might be intimate and sad with him. Then as soon as Clara appeared, it all vanished, and he played to the newcomer.

Miriam had one beautiful evening with him in the hay. He had been on the horse-rake, and having finished, came to help her to put the hay in cocks. Then he talked to her of his hopes and despairs, and his whole soul seemed to lie bare before her. She felt as if she watched the very quivering stuff of life in him. The moon came out: they walked home together: he seemed to have come to her because he needed her so badly, and she listened to him, gave him all her love and her faith. It seemed to her he brought her the best of himself to keep, and that she would guard it all her life. Nay, the sky did not cherish the stars more surely and eternally than she would guard the good in the soul of Paul Morel. She went on home alone, feeling exalted, glad in her faith.

And then, the next day, Clara came. They were to have tea in the hayfield. Miriam watched the evening drawing to gold and shadow. And all the time Paul was sporting with Clara. He made higher and higher heaps of hay that they were jumping over. Miriam did not care for the game, and stood aside. Edgar and Geoffrey and Maurice and Clara and Paul jumped. Paul won, because he was light. Clara's blood was roused. She could run like an Amazon. Paul loved the determined way she rushed at the haycock and leaped, landed on the other side, her breasts shaken, her thick hair come undone.

"You touched!" he cried. "You touched!"

"No!" she flashed, turning to Edgar. "I didn't touch, did I? Wasn't I clear?"

"I couldn't say," laughed Edgar.

None of them could say.

"But you touched," said Paul. "You're beaten."

"I did *not* touch!" she cried.

"As plain as anything," said Paul.

"Box his ears for me!" she cried to Edgar.

"Nay," Edgar laughed. "I daren't. You must do it yourself."

"And nothing can alter the fact that you touched," laughed Paul.

She was furious with him. Her little triumph before these lads and men was gone. She had forgotten herself in the game. Now he was to humble her.

"I think you are despicable!" she said.

And again he laughed, in a way that tortured Miriam.

"And I *knew* you couldn't jump that heap," he teased.

She turned her back on him. Yet everybody could see that the only person she listened to, or was conscious of, was he, and he of her. It pleased the men to see this battle between them. But Miriam was tortured.

Paul could choose the lesser in place of the higher, she saw. He could be unfaithful to himself, unfaithful to the real, deep Paul Morel. There was a danger of his becoming frivolous, of his running after his satisfaction like any Arthur, or like his father. It made Miriam bitter to think that he should throw away his soul for this flippant traffic of triviality with Clara. She walked in bitterness and silence, while the other two rallied each other, and Paul sported.

And afterwards, he would not own it, but he was rather ashamed of himself, and prostrated himself before Miriam. Then again he rebelled.

"It's not religious to be religious," he said. "I reckon a crow is religious when it sails across the sky. But it only does it because it feels itself carried to where it's going, not because it thinks it is being eternal."

But Miriam knew that one should be religious in everything, have God, whatever God might be, present in everything.

"I don't believe God knows such a lot about Himself," he cried. "God doesn't *know* things, He *is* things. And I'm sure He's not soulful."

And then it seemed to her that Paul was arguing God on to his own side, because he wanted his own way and his own pleasure. There was a long battle between him and her. He was utterly unfaithful to her even in her own presence; then he was ashamed, then repentant; then he hated her, and went off again. Those were the ever-recurring conditions.

She fretted him to the bottom of his soul. There she remained—sad, pensive, a worshipper. And he caused her sorrow. Half the time he grieved for her, half the time he hated her. She was his conscience; and he felt, somehow, he had got a conscience that was too much for him. He could not leave her, because in one way she did hold the best of him. He could not stay with her because she did not take the rest of him, which was three-quarters. So he chafed himself into rawness over her.

When she was twenty-one he wrote her a letter which could only have been written to her.

"May I speak of our old, worn love, this last time. It, too, is changing, is it not? Say, has not the body of that love died, and left you its invulnerable soul? You see, I can give you a spirit love, I have given it you this long, long time; but not embodied passion. See, you are a nun. I have given you what I would give a holy nun—as a mystic monk to a mystic nun. Surely you esteem it best. Yet you regret—no, have regretted—the other. In all our relations no body enters. I do not talk to you through the senses—rather through the spirit. That is why we cannot love in the common sense. Ours is not an everyday affection. As yet we are mortal, and to live side by side with one another would be dreadful, for somehow with you I cannot long be trivial, and, you know, to be always beyond this mortal state would be to lose it. If people marry, they must live together as affectionate humans, who may be commonplace with each other without feeling awkward—not as two souls. So I feel it.

"Ought I to send this letter?—I doubt it. But there—it is best to understand. *Au revoir.*"

Miriam read this letter twice, after which she sealed it up. A year later she broke the seal to show her mother the letter.

"You are a nun—you are a nun." The words went into her heart again and again. Nothing he ever had said had gone into her so deeply, fixedly, like a mortal wound.

She answered him two days after the party.

" 'Our intimacy would have been all-beautiful but for one little mistake,' " she quoted. "Was the mistake mine?"

Almost immediately he replied to her from Nottingham, sending her at the same time a little "Omar Khayyám".

"I am glad you answered; you are so calm and natural you put me to shame. What a ranter I am! We are often out of sympathy. But in fundamentals we may always be together I think.

"I must thank you for your sympathy with my painting and drawing. Many a sketch is dedicated to you. I do look forward to your criticisms, which, to my shame and glory, are always grand appreciations. It is a lovely joke, that. *Au revoir.*"

This was the end of the first phase of Paul's love affair. He was now about twenty-three years old, and, though still virgin, the sex instinct that Miriam had over-refined for so long now grew particularly strong. Often, as he talked to Clara Dawes, came that thickening and quickening of his blood, that peculiar concentration in the breast, as if something were alive there, a new self or a new centre of consciousness, warning him that sooner or later he would have to ask one woman or another. But he belonged to Miriam. Of that she was so fixedly sure that he allowed her right.

X

CLARA

When he was twenty-three years old, Paul sent in a landscape to the winter exhibition at Nottingham Castle. Miss Jordan had taken a good deal of interest in him, and invited him to her house, where he met other artists. He was beginning to grow ambitious.

One morning the postman came just as he was washing in the scullery. Suddenly he heard a wild noise from his mother. Rushing into the kitchen, he found her standing on the hearth-rug wildly waving a letter and crying "Hurrah!" as if she had gone mad. He was shocked and frightened.

"Why, mother!" he exclaimed.

She flew to him, flung her arms round him for a moment, then waved the letter, crying:

"Hurrah, my boy! I knew we should do it!"

He was afraid of her—the small, severe woman with greying hair suddenly bursting out in such frenzy. The postman came running back, afraid something had happened. They saw his tipped cap over the short curtains. Mrs. Morel rushed to the door.

"His picture's got first prize, Fred," she cried, "and is sold for twenty guineas."

"My word, that's something like!" said the young postman, whom they had known all his life.

"And Major Moreton has bought it!" she cried.

"It looks like meanin' something, that does, Mrs. Morel," said the postman, his blue eyes bright. He was glad to have brought such a lucky letter. Mrs. Morel went indoors and sat down, trembling. Paul was afraid lest she might have misread the letter, and might be disappointed after all. He scrutinised it once, twice. Yes, he became convinced it was true. Then he sat down, his heart beating with joy.

"Mother!" he exclaimed.

"Didn't I *say* we should do it!" she said, pretending she was not crying.

He took the kettle off the fire and mashed the tea.

"You didn't think, mother——" he began tentatively.

"No, my son—not so much—but I expected a good deal."

"But not so much," he said.

"No—no—but I knew we should do it."

And then she recovered her composure, apparently at least. He sat with his shirt turned back, showing his young throat almost like a girl's, and the towel in his hand, his hair sticking up wet.

"Twenty guineas, mother! That's just what you wanted to buy Arthur out. Now you needn't borrow any. It'll just do."

"Indeed, I shan't take it all," she said.

"But why?"

"Because I shan't."

"Well—you have twelve pounds, I'll have nine."

They cavilled about sharing the twenty guineas. She wanted to take only the five pounds she needed. He would not hear of it. So they got over the stress of emotion by quarrelling.

Morel came home at night from the pit, saying:

"They tell me Paul's got first prize for his picture, and sold it to Lord Henry Bentley for fifty pound."

"Oh, what stories people do tell!" she cried.

"Ha!" he answered. "I said I wor sure it wor a lie. But they said tha'd told Fred Hodgkisson."

"As if I would tell him such stuff!"

"Ha!" assented the miner.

But he was disappointed nevertheless.

"It's true he has got the first prize," said Mrs. Morel.

The miner sat heavily in his chair.

"Has he, beguy!" he exclaimed.

He stared across the room fixedly.

"But as for fifty pounds—such nonsense!" She was silent awhile. "Major Moreton bought it for twenty guineas, that's true."

"Twenty guineas! Tha niver says!" exclaimed Morel.

"Yes, and it was worth it."

"Ay!" he said. "I don't misdoubt it. But twenty guineas for a bit of a paintin' as he knocked off in an hour or two!"

He was silent with conceit of his son. Mrs. Morel sniffed, as if it were nothing.

"And when does he handle th' money?" asked the collier.

"That I couldn't tell you. When the picture is sent home, I suppose."

There was silence. Morel stared at the sugar-basin instead of eating his dinner. His black arm, with the hand all gnarled with work lay on the table. His wife pretended not to see him rub the back of his hand across his eyes, nor the smear in the coal-dust on his black face.

"Yes, an' that other lad 'ud 'a done as much if they hadna ha' killed 'im," he said quietly.

The thought of William went through Mrs. Morel like a cold blade. It left her feeling she was tired, and wanted rest.

Paul was invited to dinner at Mr. Jordan's. Afterwards he said:

"Mother, I want an evening suit."

"Yes, I was afraid you would," she said. She was glad. There was a moment or two of silence. "There's that one of William's," she continued, "that I know cost four pounds ten and which he'd only worn three times."

"Should you like me to wear it, mother?" he asked.

"Yes. I think it would fit you—at least the coat. The trousers would want shortening."

He went upstairs and put on the coat and vest. Coming down, he looked strange in a flannel collar and a flannel shirt-front, with an evening coat and vest. It was rather large.

"The tailor can make it right," she said, smoothing her hand over his shoulder. "It's beautiful stuff. I never could find in my heart to let your father wear the trousers, and very glad I am now."

And as she smoothed her hand over the silk collar she thought of her eldest son. But this son was living enough inside the clothes. She passed her hand down his back to feel him. He was alive and hers. The other was dead.

He went out to dinner several times in his evening suit that had been William's. Each time his mother's heart was firm with pride and joy. He was started now. The studs she and the children had bought for William were in his shirt-front; he wore one of William's dress shirts. But he had an elegant figure. His face was rough, but warm-looking and rather pleasing. He did not look particularly a gentleman, but she thought he looked quite a man.

He told her everything that took place, everything that was said. It was as if she had been there. And he was dying to introduce her to these new friends who had dinner at seven-thirty in the evening.

"Go along with you!" she said. "What do they want to know me for?"

"They do!" he cried indignantly. "If they want to know me—and they say they do—then they want to know you, because you are quite as clever as I am."

"Go along with you, child!" she laughed.

But she began to spare her hands. They, too, were work-gnarled now. The skin was shiny with so much hot water, the knuckles rather swollen. But she began to be careful to keep them out of soda. She regretted what they had been—so small and exquisite. And when Annie insisted on her having more stylish blouses to suit her age, she submitted. She even went so far as to allow a black velvet bow to be placed on her hair. Then she sniffed in her sarcastic manner, and was sure she looked a sight. But she looked a lady, Paul declared, as much as Mrs. Major Moreton, and far, far nicer. The family was coming on. Only Morel remained unchanged, or rather, lapsed slowly.

Paul and his mother now had long discussions about life. Religion was fading into the background. He had shovelled away all the beliefs that would hamper him, had cleared the ground, and come more or less to the bedrock of belief that one should feel inside oneself for right and wrong, and should have the patience to gradually realise one's God. Now life interested him more.

"You know," he said to his mother, "I don't want to belong to the well-to-do middle class. I like my common people best. I belong to the common people."

"But if anyone else said so, my son, wouldn't you be in a tear. *You* know you consider yourself equal to any gentleman."

"In myself," he answered, "not in my class or my education or my manners. But in myself I am."

"Very well, then. Then why talk about the common people?"

"Because—the difference between people isn't in their class, but in themselves. Only from the middle classes one gets ideas, and from the common people—life itself, warmth. You feel their hates and loves."

"It's all very well, my boy. But, then, why don't you go and talk to your father's pals?"

"But they're rather different."

"Not at all. They're the common people. After all, whom do you mix with now—among the common people? Those that exchange ideas, like the middle classes. The rest don't interest you."

"But—there's the life——"

"I don't believe there's a jot more life from Miriam than you could get from any educated girl—say Miss Moreton. It is *you* who are snobbish about class."

She frankly *wanted* him to climb into the middle classes, a thing not very difficult, she knew. And she wanted him in the end to marry a lady.

Now she began to combat him in his restless fretting. He still kept up his connection with Miriam, could neither break free nor go the whole length of engagement. And this indecision seemed to bleed him of his energy. Moreover, his mother suspected him of an unrecognised leaning towards Clara, and, since the latter was a married woman, she wished he would fall in love with one of the girls in a better station of life. But he was stupid, and would refuse to love or even to admire a girl much, just because she was his social superior.

"My boy," said his mother to him, "all your cleverness, your breaking away from old things, and taking life in your own hands, doesn't seem to bring you much happiness."

"What is happiness!" he cried. "It's nothing to me! How *am* I to be happy?"

The plump question disturbed her.

"That's for you to judge, my lad. But if you could meet some *good* woman who would *make* you happy—and you began to think of settling your life—when you have the means—so that you could work without all this fretting—it would be much better for you."

He frowned. His mother caught him on the raw of his wound of Miriam. He pushed the tumbled hair off his forehead, his eyes full of pain and fire.

"You mean easy, mother," he cried. "That's a woman's whole doctrine for life—ease of soul and physical comfort. And I do despise it."

"Oh, do you!" replied his mother. "And do you call yours a divine discontent?"

"Yes. I don't care about its divinity. But damn your happiness! So long as life's full, it doesn't matter whether it's happy or not. I'm afraid your happiness would bore me."

"You never give it a chance," she said. Then suddenly all her passion of grief over him broke out. "But it does matter!" she cried. "And you *ought* to be happy, you ought to try to be happy, to live to be happy. How could I bear to think your life wouldn't be a happy one!"

"Your own's been bad enough, mater, but it hasn't left you so much worse off than the folk who've been happier. I reckon you've done well. And I am the same. Aren't I well enough off?"

"You're not, my son. Battle—battle—and suffer. It's about all you do, as far as I can see."

"But why not, my dear? I tell you it's the best——"

"It isn't. And one *ought* to be happy, one *ought*."

By this time Mrs. Morel was trembling violently. Struggles of this kind often took place between her and her son, when she seemed to fight for his very life against his own will to die. He took her in his arms. She was ill and pitiful.

"Never mind, Little," he murmured. "So long as you don't feel life's paltry and a miserable business, the rest doesn't matter, happiness or unhappiness."

She pressed him to her.

"But I want you to be happy," she said pathetically.

"Eh, my dear—say rather you want me to live."

Mrs. Morel felt as if her heart would break for him. At this rate she knew he would not live. He had that poignant carelessness about himself, his own suffering, his own life, which is a form of slow suicide. It almost broke her heart. With all the passion of her strong nature she hated Miriam for having in this subtle way undermined his joy. It did not matter to her that Miriam could not help it. Miriam did it, and she hated her.

She wished so much he would fall in love with a girl equal to be his mate— educated and strong. But he would not look at anybody above him in station. He seemed to like Mrs. Dawes. At any rate that feeling was wholesome. His mother prayed and prayed for him, that he might not be wasted. That was all her prayer—not for his soul or his righteousness, but that he might not be wasted. And while he slept, for hours and hours she thought and prayed for him.

He drifted away from Miriam imperceptibly, without knowing he was going. Arthur only left the army to be married. The baby was born six months after his wedding. Mrs. Morel got him a job under the firm again, at twenty-one shillings a week. She furnished for him, with the help of Beatrice's mother, a little cottage of two rooms. He was caught now. It did not matter how he kicked and struggled, he was fast. For a time he chafed, was irritable with his young wife, who loved him; he went almost distracted when the baby, which was delicate, cried or gave trouble. He grumbled for hours to his mother. She only said: "Well, my lad, you did it yourself, now you must make the best of it." And then the grit came out in him. He buckled to work, undertook his responsibilities, acknowledged that he belonged to his wife and child, and did make a good best of it. He had never been very closely inbound into the family. Now he was gone altogether.

The months went slowly along. Paul had more or less got into connection with the Socialist, Suffragette, Unitarian people in Nottingham, owing to his acquaintance with Clara. One day a friend of his and of Clara's, in Bestwood, asked him to take a message to Mrs. Dawes. He went in the evening across Sneinton Market to Bluebell Hill. He found the house in a mean little street paved with granite cobbles and having causeways of dark blue, grooved bricks. The front door went up a step from off this rough pavement, where the feet of the passers-by rasped and clattered. The brown paint on the door was so old that the naked wood showed between the rents. He stood on the street below and knocked. There came a heavy footstep; a large, stout woman of about sixty towered above him. He looked up at her from the pavement. She had a rather severe face.

She admitted him into the parlour, which opened on to the street. It was a small, stuffy, defunct room, of mahogany, and deathly enlargements of photographs of departed people done in carbon. Mrs. Radford left him. She was stately, almost martial. In a moment Clara appeared. She flushed deeply, and he was covered with confusion. It seemed as if she did not like being discovered in her home circumstances.

"I thought it couldn't be your voice," she said.

But she might as well be hung for a sheep as for a lamb. She invited him out of the mausoleum of a parlour into the kitchen.

That was a little, darkish room too, but it was smothered in white lace. The mother had seated herself again by the cupboard, and was drawing thread from a vast web of lace. A clump of fluff and ravelled cotton was at her right hand, a heap of three-quarter-inch lace lay on her left, whilst in front of her was the mountain of lace web, piling the hearthrug. Threads of curly cotton, pulled out from between the lengths of lace, strewed over the fender and the fireplace. Paul dared not go forward, for fear of treading on piles of white stuff.

On the table was a jenny for carding the lace. There was a pack of brown cardboard squares, a pack of cards of lace, a little box of pins, and on the sofa lay a heap of drawn lace.

The room was all lace, and it was so dark and warm that the white, snowy stuff seemed the more distinct.

"If you're coming in you won't have to mind the work," said Mrs. Radford. "I know we're about blocked up. But sit you down."

Clara, much embarrassed, gave him a chair against the wall opposite the white heaps. Then she herself took her place on the sofa, shamedly.

"Will you drink a bottle of stout?" Mrs. Radford asked. "Clara, get him a bottle of stout."

He protested, but Mrs. Radford insisted.

"You look as if you could do with it," she said. "Haven't you never any more colour than that?"

"It's only a thick skin I've got that doesn't show the blood through," he answered.

Clara, ashamed and chagrined, brought him a bottle of stout and a glass. He poured out some of the black stuff.

"Well," he said, lifting the glass, "here's health!"

"And thank you," said Mrs. Radford.

He took a drink of stout.

"And light yourself a cigarette, so long as you don't set the house on fire," said Mrs. Radford.

"Thank you," he replied.

"Nay, you needn't thank me," she answered. "I s'll be glad to smell a bit of smoke in th' 'ouse again. A house o' women is as dead as a house wi' no fire, to my thinkin'. I'm not a spider as likes a corner to myself. I like a man about, if he's only something to snap at."

Clara began to work. Her jenny spun with a subdued buzz; the white lace hopped from between her fingers on to the card. It was filled; she snipped off the length, and pinned the end down to the banded lace. Then she put a new card in her jenny. Paul watched her. She sat square and magnificent. Her throat and arms were bare. The blood still mantled below her ears; she bent her head in shame of her humility. Her face was set on her work. Her arms were creamy and full of life beside the white lace; her large, well-kept hands worked with a balanced movement, as if nothing would hurry them. He, not knowing, watched her all the time. He saw the arch of her neck from the shoulder, as she bent her head; he saw the coil of dun hair; he watched her moving, gleaming arms.

"I've heard a bit about you from Clara," continued the mother. "You're in Jordan's, aren't you?" She drew her lace unceasing.

"Yes."

"Ay, well, and I can remember when Thomas Jordan used to ask me for one of my toffies."

"Did he?" laughed Paul. "And did he get it?"

"Sometimes he did, sometimes he didn't—which was latterly. For he's the sort that takes all and gives naught, he is—or used to be."

"I think he's very decent," said Paul.

"Yes; well, I'm glad to hear it."

Mrs. Radford looked across at him steadily. There was something determined about her that he liked. Her face was falling loose, but her eyes were calm, and there was something strong in her that made it seem she was not old; merely her wrinkles and loose cheeks were an anachronism. She had the strength and sang-froid of a woman in the prime of life. She continued drawing the lace with slow, dignified movements. The big web came up inevitably over her apron; the length of lace fell away at her side. Her arms were finely shapen, but glossy and yellow as old ivory. They had not the peculiar dull gleam that made Clara's so fascinating to him.

"And you've been going with Miriam Leivers?" the mother asked him.

"Well——" he answered.

"Yes, she's a nice girl," she continued. "She's very nice, but she's a bit too much above this world to suit my fancy."

"She is a bit like that," he agreed.

"She'll never be satisfied till she's got wings and can fly over everybody's head, she won't," she said.

Clara broke in, and he told her his message. She spoke humbly to him. He had surprised her in her drudgery. To have her humble made him feel as if he were lifting his head in expectation.

"Do you like jennying?" he asked.

"What can a woman do!" she replied bitterly.

"Is it sweated?"

"More or less. Isn't *all* woman's work? That's another trick the men have played, since we force ourselves into the labour market."

"Now then, you shut up about the men," said her mother. "If the women wasn't fools, the men wouldn't be bad uns, that's what I say. No man was ever that bad wi' me but what he got it back again. Not but what they're a lousy l there's no denying it."

"But they're all right really, aren't they?" he asked.

"Well, they're a bit different from women," she answered.

"Would you care to be back at Jordan's?" he asked Clara.

"I don't think so," she replied.

"Yes, she would!" cried her mother; "thank her stars if she could get back. Don't you listen to her. She's for ever on that 'igh horse of hers, an' it's back's that thin an' starved it'll cut her i' two one of these days."

Clara suffered badly from her mother. Paul felt as if his eyes were coming very wide open. Wasn't he to take Clara's fulminations so seriously, after all? She spun steadily at her work. He experienced a thrill of joy, thinking she might need his help. She seemed denied and deprived of so much. And her arm moved mechanically, that should never have been subdued to a mechanism, and her head was bowed to the lace, that never should have been bowed. She seemed to be stranded there among the refuse that life has thrown away, doing her jennying. It was a bitter thing to her to be put aside by life, as if it had no use for her. No wonder she protested.

She came with him to the door. He stood below in the mean street, looking up at her. So fine she was in her stature and her bearing, she reminded him of Juno dethroned. As she stood in the doorway, she winced from the street, from her surroundings.

"And you will go with Mrs. Hodgkisson to Hucknall?"

He was talking quite meaninglessly, only watching her. Her grey eyes at last met his. They looked dumb with humiliation, pleading with a kind of captive misery. He was shaken and at a loss. He had thought her high and mighty.

When he left her, he wanted to run. He went to the station in a sort of dream, and was at home without realising he had moved out of her street.

He had an idea that Susan, the overseer of the Spiral girls, was about to be married. He asked her the next day.

"I say, Susan, I heard a whisper of your getting married. What about it?" Susan flushed red.

"Who's been talking to you?" she replied.

"Nobody. I merely heard a whisper that you *were* thinking——"

"Well, I am, though you needn't tell anybody. What's more, I wish I wasn't!"

"Nay, Susan, you won't make me believe that."

"Shan't I? You *can* believe it, though. I'd rather stop here a thousand times." Paul was perturbed.

"Why, Susan?"

The girl's colour was high, and her eyes flashed.

"That's why!"

"And must you?"

For answer, she looked at him. There was about him a candour and gentleness which made the women trust him. He understood.

"Ah, I'm sorry," he said.

Tears came to her eyes.

"But you'll see it'll turn out all right. You'll make the best of it," he continued rather wistfully.

"There's nothing else for it."

"Yea, there's making the worst of it. Try and make it all right."

He soon made occasion to call again on Clara.

"Would you," he said, "care to come back to Jordan's?"

She put down her work, laid her beautiful arms on the table, and looked at him for some moments without answering. Gradually the flush mounted her cheek.

"Why?" she asked.

Paul felt rather awkward.

"Well, because Susan is thinking of leaving," he said.

Clara went on with her jennying. The white lace leaped in little jumps and bounds on to the card. He waited for her. Without raising her head, she said at last, in a peculiar low voice:

"Have you said anything about it?"

"Except to you, not a word."

There was again a long silence.

"I will apply when the advertisement is out," she said.

"You will apply before that. I will let you know exactly when."

She went on spinning her little machine, and did not contradict him.

Clara came to Jordan's. Some of the older hands, Fanny among them, remembered her earlier rule, and cordially disliked the memory. Clara had always been "ikey", reserved, and superior. She had never mixed with the girls as one of themselves. If she had occasion to find fault, she did it coolly and with perfect politeness, which the defaulter felt to be a bigger insult than crossness. Towards Fanny, the poor, overstrung hunchback, Clara was unfailingly compassionate and gentle, as a result of which Fanny shed more bitter tears than ever the rough tongues of the other overseers had caused her.

There was something in Clara that Paul disliked, and much that piqued him. If she were about, he always watched her strong throat or her neck, upon which the blonde hair grew low and fluffy. There was a fine down, almost invisible, upon the skin of her face and arms, and when once he had perceived it, he saw it always.

When he was at his work, painting in the afternoon, she would come and stand near to him, perfectly motionless. Then he felt her, though she neither spoke nor touched him. Although she stood a yard away he felt as if he were in contact with her. Then he could paint no more. He flung down the brushes, and turned to talk to her.

Sometimes she praised his work; sometimes she was critical and cold.

"You are affected in that piece," she would say; and, as there was an element of truth in her condemnation, his blood boiled with anger.

Again: "What of this?" he would ask enthusiastically.

"H'm!" She made a small doubtful sound. "It doesn't interest me much."

"Because you don't understand it," he retorted.

"Then why ask me about it?"

"Because I thought you would understand."

She would shrug her shoulders in scorn of his work. She maddened him. He was furious. Then he abused her, and went into passionate exposition of his stuff. This amused and stimulated her. But she never owned that she had been wrong.

During the ten years that she had belonged to the women's movement she had acquired a fair amount of education, and, having had some of Miriam's passion to be instructed, had taught herself French, and could read in that language with a struggle. She considered herself as a woman apart, and particularly apart, from her class. The girls in the Spiral department were all of good homes. It was a small, special industry, and had a certain distinction. There was an air of refinement in both rooms. But Clara was aloof also from her fellow-workers.

None of these things, however, did she reveal to Paul. She was not the one to give herself away. There was a sense of mystery about her. She was so reserved, he felt she had much to reserve. Her history was open on the surface, but its inner meaning was hidden from everybody. It was exciting. And then sometimes he caught her looking at him from under her brows with an almost furtive, sullen scrutiny, which made him move quickly. Often she met his eyes. But then her own were, as it were, covered over, revealing nothing. She gave him a little, lenient smile. She was to him extraordinarily provocative, because of the knowledge she seemed to possess, and gathered fruit of experience he could not attain.

One day he picked up a copy of *Lettres de mon Moulin* from her work-bench.

"You read French, do you?" he cried.

Clara glanced round negligently. She was making an elastic stocking of heliotrope silk, turning the Spiral machine with slow, balanced regularity, occasionally bending down to see her work or to adjust the needles; then her magnificent neck, with its down and fine pencils of hair, shone white against the lavender, lustrous silk. She turned a few more rounds, and stopped.

"What did you say?" she asked, smiling sweetly.

Paul's eyes glittered at her insolent indifference to him.

"I did not know you read French," he said, very polite.

"Did you not?" she replied, with a faint, sarcastic smile.

"Rotten swank!" he said, but scarcely loud enough to be heard.

He shut his mouth angrily as he watched her. She seemed to scorn the work she mechanically produced; yet the hose she made were as nearly perfect as possible.

"You don't like Spiral work," he said.

"Oh, well, all work is work," she answered, as if she knew all about it.

He marvelled at her coldness. He had to do everything hotly. She must be something special.

"What would you prefer to do?" he asked.

She laughed at him indulgently, as she said:

"There is so little likelihood of my ever being given a choice, that I haven't wasted time considering."

"Pah!" he said, contemptuous on his side now. "You only say that because you're too proud to own up what you want and can't get."

"You know me very well," she replied coldly.

"I know you think you're terrific great shakes, and that you live under the eternal insult of working in a factory."

He was very angry and very rude. She merely turned away from him in disdain. He walked whistling down the room, flirted and laughed with Hilda.

Later on he said to himself:

"What was I so impudent to Clara for?" He was rather annoyed with himself, at the same time glad. "Serve her right; she stinks with silent pride," he said to himself angrily.

In the afternoon he came down. There was a certain weight on his heart which he wanted to remove. He thought to do it by offering her chocolates.

"Have one?" he said. "I bought a handful to sweeten me up."

To his great relief, she accepted. He sat on the work-bench beside her machine, twisting a piece of silk round his finger. She loved him for his quick, unexpected movements, like a young animal. His feet swung as he pondered. The sweets lay strewn on the bench. She bent over her machine, grinding rhythmically, then stooping to see the stocking that hung beneath, pulled down by the weight. He watched the handsome crouching of her back, and the apron-strings curling on the floor.

"There is always about you," he said, "a sort of waiting. Whatever I see you doing, you're not really there: you are waiting—like Penelope when she did her weaving." He could not help a spurt of wickedness. "I'll call you Penelope," he said.

"Would it make any difference?" she said, carefully removing one of her needles.

"That doesn't matter, so long as it pleases me. Here, I say, you seem to forget I'm your boss. It just occurs to me."

"And what does that mean?" she asked coolly.

"It means I've got a right to boss you."

"Is there anything you want to complain about?"

"Oh, I say, you needn't be nasty," he said angrily.

"I don't know what you want," she said, continuing her task.

"I want you to treat me nicely and respectfully."

"Call you 'sir', perhaps?" she asked quietly.

"Yes, call me 'sir'. I should love it."

"Then I wish you would go upstairs, sir."

His mouth closed, and a frown came on his face. He jumped suddenly down. "You're too blessed superior for anything," he said.

And he went away to the other girls. He felt he was being angrier than he had any need to be. In fact, he doubted slightly that he was showing off. But if he were, then he would. Clara heard him laughing, in a way she hated, with the girls down the next room.

When at evening he went through the department after the girls had gone, he saw his chocolates lying untouched in front of Clara's machine. He left them. In the morning they were still there, and Clara was at work. Later on Minnie, a little brunette they called Pussy, called to him:

"Hey, haven't you got a chocolate for anybody?"

"Sorry, Pussy," he replied. "I meant to have offered them; then I went and forgot 'em."

"I think you did," she answered.

"I'll bring you some this afternoon. You don't want them after they've been lying about, do you?"

"Oh, I'm not particular," smiled Pussy.

"Oh no," he said. "They'll be dusty."

He went up to Clara's bench.

"Sorry I left these things littering about," he said.

She flushed scarlet. He gathered them together in his fist.

"They'll be dirty now," he said. "You should have taken them. I wonder why you didn't. I meant to have told you I wanted you to."

He flung them out of the window into the yard below. He just glanced at her. She winced from his eyes.

In the afternoon he brought another packet.

"Will you take some?" he said, offering them first to Clara. "These are fresh."

She accepted one, and put it on to the bench.

"Oh, take several—for luck," he said.

She took a couple more, and put them on the bench also. Then she turned in confusion to her work. He went on up the room.

"Here you are, Pussy," he said. "Don't be greedy!"

"Are they all for her?" cried the others, rushing up.

"Of course they're not," he said.

The girls clamoured round. Pussy drew back from her mates.

"Come out!" she cried. "I can have first pick, can't I, Paul?"

"Be nice with 'em," he said, and went away.

"You *are* a dear," the girls cried.

"Tenpence," he answered.

He went past Clara without speaking. She felt the three chocolate creams would burn her if she touched them. It needed all her courage to slip them into the pocket of her apron.

The girls loved him and were afraid of him. He was so nice while he was nice, but if he were offended, so distant, treating them as if they scarcely existed, or not more than the bobbins of thread. And then, if they were impudent, he said quietly: "Do you mind going on with your work," and stood and watched.

When he celebrated his twenty-third birthday, the house was in trouble. Arthur was just going to be married. His mother was not well. His father, getting an old man, and lame from his accidents, was given a paltry, poor job. Miriam was an eternal reproach. He felt he owed himself to her, yet could not give himself. The house, moreover, needed his support. He was pulled in all directions. He was not glad it was his birthday. It made him bitter.

He got to work at eight o'clock. Most of the clerks had not turned up. The girls were not due till 8:30. As he was changing his coat, he heard a voice behind him say:

"Paul, Paul, I want you."

It was Fanny, the hunchback, standing at the top of her stairs, her face radiant with a secret. Paul looked at her in astonishment.

"I want you," she said.

He stood, at a loss.

"Come on," she coaxed. "Come before you begin on the letters."

He went down the half-dozen steps into her dry, narrow, "finishing-off" room. Fanny walked before him: her black bodice was short—the waist was under her armpits—and her green-black cashmere skirt seemed very long, as she strode with big strides before the young man, himself so graceful. She went to her seat at the narrow end of the room, where the window opened on to chimney-pots. Paul watched her thin hands and her flat red wrists as she excitedly twitched her white apron, which was spread on the bench in front of her. She hesitated.

"You didn't think we'd forgot you?" she asked, reproachful.

"Why?" he asked. He had forgotten his birthday himself.

" 'Why,' he says! 'Why!' Why, look here!" She pointed to the calendar, and he saw, surrounding the big black number "21", hundreds of little crosses in black-lead.

"Oh, kisses for my birthday," he laughed. "How did you know?"

"Yes, you want to know, don't you?" Fanny mocked, hugely delighted. "There's one from everybody—except Lady Clara—and two from some. But I shan't tell you how many I put."

"Oh, I know, you're spooney," he said.

"There you are mistaken!" she cried, indignant. "I could never be so soft." Her voice was strong and contralto.

"You always pretend to be such a hard-hearted hussy," he laughed. "And you know you're as sentimental——"

"I'd rather be called sentimental than frozen meat," Fanny blurted. Paul knew she referred to Clara, and he smiled.

"Do you say such nasty things about me?" he laughed.

"No, my duck," the hunchback woman answered, lavishly tender. She was thirty-nine. "No, my duck, because you don't think yourself a fine figure in marble and us nothing but dirt. I'm as good as you, aren't I, Paul?" and the question delighted her.

"Why, we're not better than one another, are we?" he replied.

"But I'm as good as you, aren't I, Paul?" she persisted daringly.

"Of course you are. If it comes to goodness, you're better."

She was rather afraid of the situation. She might get hysterical.

"I thought I'd get here before the others—won't they say I'm deep! Now shut your eyes——" she said.

"And open your mouth, and see what God sends you," he continued, suiting action to words, and expecting a piece of chocolate. He heard the rustle of the apron, and a faint clink of metal. "I'm going to look," he said.

He opened his eyes. Fanny, her long cheeks flushed, her blue eyes shining, was gazing at him. There was a little bundle of paint-tubes on the bench before him. He turned pale.

"No, Fanny," he said quickly.

"From us all," she answered hastily.

"No, but——"

"Are they the right sort?" she asked, rocking herself with delight.

"Jove! they're the best in the catalogue."

"But they're the right sorts?" she cried.

"They're off the little list I'd made to get when my ship came in." He bit his lip.

Fanny was overcome with emotion. She must turn the conversation.

"They was all on thorns to do it; they all paid their shares, all except the Queen of Sheba."

The Queen of Sheba was Clara.

"And wouldn't she join?" Paul asked.

"She didn't get the chance; we never told her; we wasn't going to have *her* bossing *this* show. We didn't *want* her to join."

Paul laughed at the woman. He was much moved. At last he must go. She was very close to him. Suddenly she flung her arms round his neck and kissed him vehemently.

"I can give you a kiss to-day," she said apologetically. "You've looked so white, it's made my heart ache."

Paul kissed her, and left her. Her arms were so pitifully thin that his heart ached also.

That day he met Clara as he ran downstairs to wash his hands at dinner-time.

"You have stayed to dinner!" he exclaimed. It was unusual for her.

"Yes; and I seem to have dined on old surgical-appliance stock. I *must* go out now, or I shall feel stale india-rubber right through."

She lingered. He instantly caught at her wish.

"You are going anywhere?" he asked.

They went together up to the Castle. Outdoors she dressed very plainly, down to ugliness; indoors she always looked nice. She walked with hesitating steps alongside Paul, bowing and turning away from him. Dowdy in dress, and drooping, she showed to great disadvantage. He could scarcely recognise her strong form, that seemed to slumber with power. She appeared almost insignificant, drowning her stature in her stoop, as she shrank from the public gaze.

The Castle grounds were very green and fresh. Climbing the precipitous ascent, he laughed and chattered, but she was silent, seeming to brood over something. There was scarcely time to go inside the squat, square building that crowns the bluff of rock. They leaned upon the wall where the cliff runs sheer down to the Park. Below them, in their holes in the sandstone, pigeons preened themselves and cooed softly. Away down upon the boulevard at the foot of the rock, tiny trees stood in their own pools of shadow, and tiny people went scurrying about in almost ludicrous importance.

"You feel as if you could scoop up the folk like tadpoles, and have a handful of them," he said.

She laughed, answering:

"Yes; it is not necessary to get far off in order to see us proportionately. The trees are much more significant."

"Bulk only," he said.

She laughed cynically.

Away beyond the boulevard the thin stripes of the metals showed upon the railway-track, whose margin was crowded with little stacks of timber, beside which smoking toy engines fussed. Then the silver string of the canal lay at random among the black heaps. Beyond, the dwellings, very dense on the river flat, looked like black, poisonous herbage, in thick rows and crowded beds, stretching right away, broken now and then by taller plants, right to where the river glistened in a hieroglyph across the country. The steep scarp cliffs across the river looked puny. Great stretches of country darkened with trees and faintly brightened with corn-land, spread towards the haze, where the hills rose blue beyond grey.

"It is comforting," said Mrs. Dawes, "to think the town goes no farther. It is only a *little* sore upon the country yet."

"A little scab," Paul said.

She shivered. She loathed the town. Looking drearily across at the country which was forbidden her, her impassive face, pale and hostile, she reminded Paul of one of the bitter, remorseful angels.

"But the town's all right," he said; "it's only temporary. This is the crude, clumsy make-shift we've practised on, till we find out what the idea is. The town will come all right."

The pigeons in the pockets of rock, among the perched bushes, cooed comfortably. To the left the large church of St. Mary rose into space, to keep close company with the Castle, above the heaped rubble of the town. Mrs. Dawes smiled brightly as she looked across the country.

"I feel better," she said.

"Thank you," he replied. "Great compliment!"

"Oh, my brother!" she laughed.

"H'm! that's snatching back with the left hand what you gave with the right, and no mistake," he said.

She laughed in amusement at him.

"But what was the matter with you?" he asked. "I know you were brooding something special. I can see the stamp of it on your face yet."

"I think I will not tell you," she said.

"All right, hug it," he answered.

She flushed and bit her lip.

"No," she said, "it was the girls."

"What about 'em?" Paul asked.

"They have been plotting something for a week now, and today they seem particularly full of it. All alike; they insult me with their secrecy."

"Do they?" he asked in concern.

"I should not mind," she went on, in the metallic, angry tone, "if they did not thrust it into my face—the fact that they have a secret."

"Just like women," said he.

"It is hateful, their mean gloating," she said intensely.

Paul was silent. He knew what the girls gloated over. He was sorry to be the cause of this new dissension.

"They can have all the secrets in the world," she went on, brooding bitterly; "but they might refrain from glorying in them, and making me feel more out of it than ever. It is—it is almost unbearable."

Paul thought for a few minutes. He was much perturbed.

"I will tell you what it's all about," he said, pale and nervous. "It's my birthday, and they've bought me a fine lot of paints, all the girls. They're jealous of you"—he felt her stiffen coldly at the word 'jealous'—"merely because I sometimes bring you a book," he added slowly. "But, you see, it's only a trifle. Don't bother about it, will you—because"—he laughed quickly—"well, what would they say if they saw us here now, in spite of their victory?"

She was angry with him for his clumsy reference to their present intimacy. It was almost insolent of him. Yet he was so quiet, she forgave him, although it cost her an effort.

Their two hands lay on the rough stone parapet of the Castle wall. He had inherited from his mother a fineness of mould, so that his hands were small and vigorous. Hers were large, to match her large limbs, but white and powerful looking. As Paul looked at them he knew her. "She is wanting somebody to take her hands—for all she is so contemptuous of us," he said to himself. And she saw nothing but his two hands, so warm and alive, which seemed to live for her. He was brooding now, staring out over the country from under sullen brows. The little, interesting diversity of shapes had vanished from the scene; all that remained was a vast, dark matrix of sorrow and tragedy, the same in all the houses and the river-flats and the people and the birds; they were only shapen differently. And now that the forms seemed to have melted away, there remained the mass from which all the landscape was composed, a dark mass of struggle and pain. The factory, the girls, his mother, the large, uplifted church, the thicket of the town, merged into one atmosphere—dark, brooding, and sorrowful, every bit.

"Is that two o'clock striking?" Mrs. Dawes said in surprise.

Paul started, and everything sprang into form, regained its individuality, its forgetfulness, and its cheerfulness.

They hurried back to work.

When he was in the rush of preparing for the night's post, examining the work up from Fanny's room, which smelt of ironing, the evening postman came in.

"'Mr. Paul Morel,'" he said, smiling, handing Paul a package. "A lady's handwriting! Don't let the girls see it."

The postman, himself a favourite, was pleased to make fun of the girls' affection for Paul.

It was a volume of verse with a brief note: "You will allow me to send you this, and so spare me my isolation. I also sympathise and wish you well.—C.D." Paul flushed hot.

"Good Lord! Mrs. Dawes. She can't afford it. Good Lord, who ever'd have thought it!"

He was suddenly intensely moved. He was filled with the warmth of her. In the glow he could almost feel her as if she were present—her arms, her shoulders, her bosom, see them, feel them, almost contain them.

This move on the part of Clara brought them into closer intimacy. The other girls noticed that when Paul met Mrs. Dawes his eyes lifted and gave that peculiar bright greeting which they could interpret. Knowing he was unaware, Clara made no sign, save that occasionally she turned aside her face from him when he came upon her.

They walked out together very often at dinner-time; it was quite open, quite frank. Everybody seemed to feel that he was quite unaware of the state of his own feeling, and that nothing was wrong. He talked to her now with some of the old fervour with which he had talked to Miriam, but he cared less about the talk; he did not bother about his conclusions.

One day in October they went out to Lambley for tea. Suddenly they came to a halt on top of the hill. He climbed and sat on a gate, she sat on the stile. The afternoon was perfectly still, with a dim haze, and yellow sheaves glowing through. They were quiet.

"How old were you when you married?" he asked quietly.

"Twenty-two."

Her voice was subdued, almost submissive. She would tell him now.

"It is eight years ago?"

"Yes."

"And when did you leave him?"

"Three years ago."

"Five years! Did you love him when you married him?"

She was silent for some time; then she said slowly:

"I thought I did—more or less. I didn't think much about it. And he wanted me. I was very prudish then."

"And you sort of walked into it without thinking?"

"Yes. I seemed to have been asleep nearly all my life."

"Somnambule? But—when did you wake up?"

"I don't know that I ever did, or ever have—since I was a child."

"You went to sleep as you grew to be a woman? How queer! And he didn't wake you?"

"No; he never got there," she replied, in a monotone.

The brown birds dashed over the hedges where the rose-hips stood naked and scarlet.

"Got where?" he asked.

"At me. He never really mattered to me."

The afternoon was so gently warm and dim. Red roofs of the cottages burned among the blue haze. He loved the day. He could feel, but he could not understand, what Clara was saying.

"But why did you leave him? Was he horrid to you?"

She shuddered lightly.

"He—he sort of degraded me. He wanted to bully me because he hadn't got me. And then I felt as if I wanted to run, as if I was fastened and bound up. And he seemed dirty."

"I see."

He did not at all see.

"And was he always dirty?" he asked.

"A bit," she replied slowly. "And then he seemed as if he couldn't get *at* me, really. And then he got brutal—he *was* brutal!"

"And why did you leave him finally?"

"Because—because he was unfaithful to me——"

They were both silent for some time. Her hand lay on the gate-post as she balanced. He put his own over it. His heart beat quickly.

"But did you—were you ever—did you ever give him a chance?"

"Chance? How?"

"To come near to you."

"I married him—and I was willing——"

They both strove to keep their voices steady.

"I believe he loves you," he said.

"It looks like it," she replied.

He wanted to take his hand away, and could not. She saved him by removing her own. After a silence, he began again:

"Did you leave him out of count all along?"

"He left me," she said.

"And I suppose he couldn't *make* himself mean everything to you?"

"He tried to bully me into it."

But the conversation had got them both out of their depth. Suddenly Paul jumped down.

"Come on," he said. "Let's go and get some tea."

They found a cottage, where they sat in the cold parlour. She poured out his tea. She was very quiet. He felt she had withdrawn again from him. After tea, she stared broodingly into her tea-cup, twisting her wedding ring all the time. In her abstraction she took the ring off her finger, stood it up, and spun it upon the table. The gold became a diaphanous, glittering globe. It fell, and the ring was quivering upon the table. She spun it again and again. Paul watched, fascinated.

But she was a married woman, and he believed in simple friendship. And he considered that he was perfectly honourable with regard to her. It was only a friendship between man and woman, such as any civilised persons might have.

He was like so many young men of his own age. Sex had become so complicated in him that he would have denied that he ever could want Clara or Miriam or any woman whom he *knew*. Sex desire was a sort of detached thing, that did not belong to a woman. He loved Miriam with his soul. He grew warm at the thought of Clara, he battled with her, he knew the curves of her breast and shoulders as if they had been moulded inside him; and yet he did not positively desire her. He would have denied it for ever. He believed himself really bound to Miriam. If ever he should marry, some time in the far future, it would be his duty to marry Miriam. That he gave Clara to understand, and she said nothing, but left him to his courses. He came to her, Mrs. Dawes, whenever he could. Then he wrote frequently to Miriam, and visited the girl occasionally. So he went on through the winter; but he seemed not so fretted. His mother was easier about him. She thought he was getting away from Miriam.

Miriam knew now how strong was the attraction of Clara for him; but still she was certain that the best in him would triumph. His feeling for Mrs. Dawes—who, moreover, was a married woman—was shallow and temporal, compared with his love for herself. He would come back to her, she was sure; with some of his young freshness gone, perhaps, but cured of his desire for the lesser things which other women than herself could give him. She could bear all if he were inwardly true to her and must come back.

He saw none of the anomaly of his position. Miriam was his old friend, lover, and she belonged to Bestwood and home and his youth. Clara was a newer friend, and she belonged to Nottingham, to life, to the world. It seemed to him quite plain.

Mrs. Dawes and he had many periods of coolness, when they saw little of each other; but they always came together again.

"Were you horrid with Baxter Dawes?" he asked her. It was a thing that seemed to trouble him.

"In what way?"

"Oh, I don't know. But weren't you horrid with him? Didn't you do something that knocked him to pieces?"

"What, pray?"

"Making him feel as if he were nothing—*I* know," Paul declared.

"You are so clever, my friend," she said coolly.

The conversation broke off there. But it made her cool with him for some time.

She very rarely saw Miriam now. The friendship between the two women was not broken off, but considerably weakened.

"Will you come in to the concert on Sunday afternoon?" Clara asked him just after Christmas.

"I promised to go up to Willey Farm," he replied.

"Oh, very well."

"You don't mind, do you?" he asked.

"Why should I?" she answered.

Which almost annoyed him.

"You know," he said, "Miriam and I have been a lot to each other ever since I was sixteen—that's seven years now."

"It's a long time," Clara replied.

"Yes; but somehow she—it doesn't go right——"

"How?" asked Clara.

"She seems to draw me and draw me, and she wouldn't leave a single hair of me free to fall out and blow away—she'd keep it."

"But you like to be kept."

"No," he said, "I don't. I wish it could be normal, give and take—like me and you. I want a woman to keep me, but not in her pocket."

"But if you love her, it couldn't be normal, like me and you."

"Yes; I should love her better then. She sort of wants me so much that I can't give myself."

"Wants you how?"

"Wants the soul out of my body. I can't help shrinking back from her."

"And yet you love her!"

"No, I don't love her. I never even kiss her."

"Why not?" Clara asked.

"I don't know."

"I suppose you're afraid," she said.

"I'm not. Something in me shrinks from her like hell—she so good, when I'm not good."

"How do you know what she is?"

"I do! I know she wants a sort of soul union."

"But how do you know what she wants?"

"I've been with her for seven years."

"And you haven't found out the very first thing about her."

"What's that?"

"That she doesn't want any of your soul communion. That's your own imagination. She wants you."

He pondered over this. Perhaps he was wrong.

"But she seems——" he began.

"You've never tried," she answered.

XI

THE TEST ON MIRIAM

With the spring came again the old madness and battle. Now he knew he would have to go to Miriam. But what was his reluctance? He told himself it was only a sort of overstrong virginity in her and him which neither could break through. He might have married her; but his circumstances at home made it difficult, and, moreover, he did not want to marry. Marriage was for life, and because they had become close companions, he and she, he did not see that it should inevitably follow they should be man and wife. He did not feel that he wanted marriage with Miriam. He wished he did. He would have given his head to have felt a joyous desire to marry her and to have her. Then why couldn't he bring it off? There was some obstacle; and what was the obstacle? It lay in the physical bondage. He shrank from the physical contact. But why? With her he felt bound up inside himself. He could not go out to her. Something struggled in him, but he could not get to her. Why? She loved him. Clara said she even wanted him; then why couldn't he go to her, make love to her, kiss her? Why, when she put her arm in his, timidly, as they walked, did he feel he would burst forth in brutality and recoil? He owed himself to her; he wanted to belong to her. Perhaps the recoil and the shrinking from her was love in its first fierce modesty. He had no aversion for her. No, it was the opposite; it was a strong desire battling with a still stronger shyness and virginity. It seemed as if virginity were a positive force, which fought and won in both of them. And with her he felt it so hard to overcome; yet he was nearest to her, and with her alone could he deliberately break through. And he owed himself to her. Then, if they could get things right, they could marry; but he would not marry unless he could feel strong in the joy of it—never. He could not have faced his mother. It seemed to him that to sacrifice himself in a marriage he did not want would be degrading, and would undo all his life, make it a nullity. He would try what he *could* do.

And he had a great tenderness for Miriam. Always, she was sad, dreaming her religion; and he was nearly a religion to her. He could not bear to fail her. It would all come right if they tried.

He looked round. A good many of the nicest men he knew were like himself, bound in by their own virginity, which they could not break out of. They were so sensitive to their women that they would go without them for ever rather than do them a hurt, an injustice. Being the sons of mothers whose husbands had blundered rather brutally through their feminine sanctities, they were themselves too diffident and shy. They could easier deny themselves than incur any reproach from a woman; for a woman was like their mother, and they were full of the sense of their mother. They preferred themselves to suffer the misery of celibacy, rather than risk the other person.

He went back to her. Something in her, when he looked at her, brought the tears almost to his eyes. One day he stood behind her as she sang. Annie was playing a song on the piano. As Miriam sang her mouth seemed hopeless. She sang like a nun singing to heaven. It reminded him so much of the mouth and eyes of one who sings beside a Botticelli Madonna, so spiritual. Again, hot as steel, came up the pain in him. Why must he ask her for the other thing? Why was there his blood battling with her? If only he could have been always gentle, tender with her, breathing with her the atmosphere of reverie and religious dreams, he would give his right hand. It was not fair to hurt her. There seemed an eternal maidenhood about her; and when he thought of her mother, he saw the great brown eyes of a maiden who was nearly scared and shocked out of her virgin maidenhood, but not quite, in spite of her seven children. They had been born almost leaving her out of count, not of her, but upon her. So she could never let them go, because she never had possessed them.

Mrs. Morel saw him going again frequently to Miriam, and was astonished. He said nothing to his mother. He did not explain nor excuse himself. If he came home late, and she reproached him, he frowned and turned on her in an overbearing way:

"I shall come home when I like," he said; "I am old enough."

"Must she keep you till this time?"

"It is I who stay," he answered.

"And she lets you? But very well," she said.

And she went to bed, leaving the door unlocked for him; but she lay listening until he came, often long after. It was a great bitterness to her that he had gone back to Miriam. She recognised, however, the uselessness of any further interference. He went to Willey Farm as a man now, not as a youth. She had no right over him. There was a coldness between him and her. He hardly told her anything. Discarded, she waited on him, cooked for him still, and loved to slave for him; but her face closed again like a mask. There was nothing for her to do now but the housework; for all the rest he had gone to Miriam. She could not forgive him. Miriam killed the joy and the warmth in him. He had been such a jolly lad, and full of the warmest affection; now he grew colder, more and more irritable and gloomy. It reminded her of William; but Paul was worse. He did things with more intensity, and more realisation of what he was about. His mother knew how he was suffering for want of a woman, and she saw him going to Miriam. If he had made up his mind, nothing on earth would alter him. Mrs. Morel was tired. She began to give up at last; she had finished. She was in the way.

He went on determinedly. He realised more or less what his mother felt. It only hardened his soul. He made himself callous towards her; but it was like being callous to his own health. It undermined him quickly; yet he persisted.

He lay back in the rocking-chair at Willey Farm one evening. He had been talking to Miriam for some weeks, but had not come to the point. Now he said suddenly:

"I am twenty-four, almost."

She had been brooding. She looked up at him suddenly in surprise.

"Yes. What makes you say it?"

There was something in the charged atmosphere that she dreaded.

"Sir Thomas More says one can marry at twenty-four."

She laughed quaintly, saying:

"Does it need Sir Thomas More's sanction?"

"No; but one ought to marry about then."

"Ay," she answered broodingly; and she waited.

"I can't marry you," he continued slowly, "not now, because we've no money, and they depend on me at home."

She sat half-guessing what was coming.

"But I want to marry now——"

"You want to marry?" she repeated.

"A woman—you know what I mean."

She was silent.

"Now, at last, I must," he said.

"Ay," she answered.

"And you love me?"

She laughed bitterly.

"Why are you ashamed of it," he answered. "You wouldn't be ashamed before your God, why are you before people?"

"Nay," she answered deeply, "I am not ashamed."

"You are," he replied bitterly; "and it's my fault. But you know I can't help being—as I am—don't you?"

"I know you can't help it," she replied.

"I love you an awful lot—then there is something short."

"Where?" she answered, looking at him.

"Oh, in me! It is I who ought to be ashamed—like a spiritual cripple. And I am ashamed. It is misery. Why is it?"

"I don't know," replied Miriam.

"And I don't know," he repeated. "Don't you think we have been too fierce in our what they call purity? Don't you think that to be so much afraid and averse is a sort of dirtiness?"

She looked at him with startled dark eyes.

"You recoiled away from anything of the sort, and I took the motion from you, and recoiled also, perhaps worse."

There was silence in the room for some time.

"Yes," she said, "it is so."

"There is between us," he said, "all these years of intimacy. I feel naked enough before you. Do you understand?"

"I think so," she answered.

"And you love me?"

She laughed.

"Don't be bitter," he pleaded.

She looked at him and was sorry for him; his eyes were dark with torture. She was sorry for him; it was worse for him to have this deflated love than for herself, who could never be properly mated. He was restless, for ever urging forward and trying to find a way out. He might do as he liked, and have what he liked of her.

"Nay," she said softly, "I am not bitter."

She felt she could bear anything for him; she would suffer for him. She put her hand on his knee as he leaned forward in his chair. He took it and kissed it; but it hurt to do so. He felt he was putting himself aside. He sat there sacrificed to her purity, which felt more like nullity. How could he kiss her hand passionately, when it would drive her away, and leave nothing but pain? Yet slowly he drew her to him and kissed her.

They knew each other too well to pretend anything. As she kissed him, she watched his eyes; they were staring across the room, with a peculiar dark blaze in them that fascinated her. He was perfectly still. She could feel his heart throbbing heavily in his breast.

"What are you thinking about?" she asked.

The blaze in his eyes shuddered, became uncertain.

"I was thinking, all the while, I love you. I have been obstinate."

She sank her head on his breast.

"Yes," she answered.

"That's all," he said, and his voice seemed sure, and his mouth was kissing her throat.

Then she raised her head and looked into his eyes with her full gaze of love. The blaze struggled, seemed to try to get away from her, and then was quenched. He turned his head quickly aside. It was a moment of anguish.

"Kiss me," she whispered.

He shut his eyes, and kissed her, and his arms folded her closer and closer.

When she walked home with him over the fields, he said:

"I am glad I came back to you. I feel so simple with you—as if there was nothing to hide. We will be happy?"

"Yes," she murmured, and the tears came to her eyes.

"Some sort of perversity in our souls," he said, "makes us not want, get away from, the very thing we want. We have to fight against that."

"Yes," she said, and she felt stunned.

As she stood under the drooping-thorn tree, in the darkness by the roadside, he kissed her, and his fingers wandered over her face. In the darkness, where he could not see her but only feel her, his passion flooded him. He clasped her very close.

"Sometime you will have me?" he murmured, hiding his face on her shoulder. It was so difficult.

"Not now," she said.

His hopes and his heart sunk. A dreariness came over him.

"No," he said.

His clasp of her slackened.

"I love to feel your arm *there!*" she said, pressing his arm against her back, where it went round her waist. "It rests me so."

He tightened the pressure of his arm upon the small of her back to rest her.

"We belong to each other," he said.

"Yes."

"Then why shouldn't we belong to each other altogether?"

"But——" she faltered.

"I know it's a lot to ask," he said; "but there's not much risk for you really—not in the Gretchen way. You can trust me there?"

"Oh, I can trust you." The answer came quick and strong. "It's not that—it's not that at all—but——"

"What?"

She hid her face in his neck with a little cry of misery.

"I don't know!" she cried.

She seemed slightly hysterical, but with a sort of horror. His heart died in him.

"You don't think it ugly?" he asked.

"No, not now. You have *taught* me it isn't."

"You are afraid?"

She calmed herself hastily.

"Yes, I am only afraid," she said.

He kissed her tenderly.

"Never mind," he said. "You should please yourself."

Suddenly she gripped her arms round her, and clenched her body stiff.

"You *shall* have me," she said, through her shut teeth.

His heart beat up again like fire. He folded her close, and his mouth was on her throat. She could not bear it. She drew away. He disengaged her.

"Won't you be late?" she asked gently.

He sighed, scarcely hearing what she said. She waited, wishing he would go. At last he kissed her quickly and climbed the fence. Looking round he saw the pale blotch of her face down in the darkness under the hanging tree. There was no more of her but this pale blotch.

"Good-bye!" she called softly. She had no body, only a voice and a dim face. He turned away and ran down the road, his fists clenched; and when he came to the wall over the lake he leaned there, almost stunned, looking up the black water.

Miriam plunged home over the meadows. She was not afraid of people, what they might say; but she dreaded the issue with him. Yes, she would let him

have her if he insisted; and then, when she thought of it afterwards, her heart
went down. He would be disappointed, he would find no satisfaction, and then
he would go away. Yet he was so insistent; and over this, which did not seem so
all-important to her, was their love to break down. After all, he was only like
other men, seeking his satisfaction. Oh, but there was something more in him,
something deeper! She could trust to it, in spite of all desires. He said that
possession was a great moment in life. All strong emotions concentrated there.
Perhaps it was so. There was something divine in it; then she would submit,
religiously, to the sacrifice. He should have her. And at the thought her whole
body clenched itself involuntarily, hard, as if against something; but Life forced
her through this gate of suffering, too, and she would submit. At any rate, it
would give him what he wanted, which was her deepest wish. She brooded and
brooded and brooded herself towards accepting him.

He courted her now like a lover. Often, when he grew hot, she put his face
from her, held it between her hands, and looked in his eyes. He could not meet
her gaze. Her dark eyes, full of love, earnest and searching, made him turn away.
Not for an instant would she let him forget. Back again he had to torture himself
into a sense of his responsibility and hers. Never any relaxing, never any leaving
himself to the great hunger and impersonality of passion; he must be brought
back to a deliberate, reflective creature. As if from a swoon of passion she called
him back to the littleness, the personal relationship. He could not bear it.
"Leave me alone—leave me alone!" he wanted to cry; but she wanted him to
look at her with eyes full of love. His eyes, full of the dark, impersonal fire of
desire, did not belong to her.

There was a great crop of cherries at the farm. The trees at the back of the
house, very large and tall, hung thick with scarlet and crimson drops, under the
dark leaves. Paul and Edgar were gathering the fruit one evening. It had been a
hot day, and now the clouds were rolling in the sky, dark and warm. Paul
climbed high in the tree, above the scarlet roofs of the buildings. The wind,
moaning steadily, made the whole tree rock with a subtle, thrilling motion that
stirred the blood. The young man, perched insecurely in the slender branches,
rocked till he felt slightly drunk, reached down the boughs, where the scarlet
beady cherries hung thick underneath, and tore off handful after handful of the
sleek, cool-fleshed fruit. Cherries touched his ears and his neck as he stretched
forward, their chill finger-tips sending a flash down his blood. All shades of red,
from a golden vermilion to a rich crimson, glowed and met his eyes under a
darkness of leaves.

The sun, going down, suddenly caught the broken clouds. Immense piles of
gold flared out in the south-east, heaped in soft, glowing yellow right up the
sky. The world, till now dusk and grey, reflected the gold glow, astonished.
Everywhere the trees, and the grass, and the far-off water, seemed roused from
the twilight and shining.

Miriam came out wondering.

"Oh!" Paul heard her mellow voice call, "isn't it wonderful?"

He looked down. There was a faint gold glimmer on her face, that looked
very soft, turned up to him.

"How high you are!" she said.

Beside her, on the rhubarb leaves, were four dead birds, thieves that had
been shot. Paul saw some cherry stones hanging quite bleached, like skeletons,
picked clear of flesh. He looked down again to Miriam.

"Clouds are on fire," he said.

"Beautiful!" she cried.

She seemed so small, so soft, so tender, down there. He threw a handful of cherries at her. She was startled and frightened. He laughed with a low, chuckling sound, and pelted her. She ran for shelter, picking up some cherries. Two fine red pairs she hung over her ears; then she looked up again.

"Haven't you got enough?" she asked.

"Nearly. It is like being on a ship up here."

"And how long will you stay?"

"While the sunset lasts."

She went to the fence and sat there, watching the gold clouds fall to pieces, and go in immense, rose-coloured ruin towards the darkness. Gold flamed to scarlet, like pain in its intense brightness. Then the scarlet sank to rose, and rose to crimson, and quickly the passion went out of the sky. All the world was dark grey. Paul scrambled quickly down with his basket, tearing his shirt-sleeve as he did so.

"They are lovely," said Miriam, fingering the cherries.

"I've torn my sleeve," he answered.

She took the three-cornered rip, saying:

"I shall have to mend it." It was near the shoulder. She put her fingers through the tear. "How warm!" she said.

He laughed. There was a new, strange note in his voice, one that made her pant.

"Shall we stay out?" he said.

"Won't it rain?" she asked.

"No, let us walk a little way."

They went down the fields and into the thick plantation of fir-trees and pines.

"Shall we go in among the trees?" he asked.

"Do you want to?"

"Yes."

It was very dark among the firs, and the sharp spines pricked her face. She was afraid. Paul was silent and strange.

"I like the darkness," he said. "I wish it were thicker—good, thick darkness."

He seemed to be almost unaware of her as a person: she was only to him then a woman. She was afraid.

He stood against a pine-tree trunk and took her in his arms. She relinquished herself to him, but it was a sacrifice in which she felt something of horror. This thick-voiced, oblivious man was a stranger to her.

Later it began to rain. The pine-trees smelled very strong. Paul lay with his head on the ground, on the dead pine needles, listening to the sharp hiss of the rain—a steady, keen noise. His heart was down, very heavy. Now he realised that she had not been with him all the time, that her soul had stood apart, in a sort of horror. He was physically at rest, but no more. Very dreary at heart, very sad, and very tender, his fingers wandered over her face pitifully. Now again she loved him deeply. He was tender and beautiful.

"The rain!" he said.

"Yes—is it coming on you?"

She put her hands over him, on his hair, on his shoulders, to feel if the raindrops fell on him. She loved him dearly. He, as he lay with his face on the dead pine-leaves, felt extraordinarily quiet. He did not mind if the raindrops came on him: he would have lain and got wet through: he felt as if nothing mattered, as if his living were smeared away into the beyond, near and quite lovable. This strange, gentle reaching-out to death was new to him.

"We must go," said Miriam.

"Yes," he answered, but did not move.

To him now, life seemed a shadow, day a white shadow; night, and death, and stillness, and inaction, this seemed like *being*. To be alive, to be urgent and insistent—that was *not-to-be*. The highest of all was to melt out into the darkness and sway there, identified with the great Being.

"The rain is coming in on us," said Miriam.

He rose, and assisted her.

"It is a pity," he said.

"What?"

"To have to go. I feel so still."

"Still!" she repeated.

"Stiller than I have ever been in my life."

He was walking with his hand in hers. She pressed his fingers, feeling a slight fear. Now he seemed beyond her; she had a fear lest she should lose him.

"The fir-trees are like presences on the darkness: each one only a presence."

She was afraid, and said nothing.

"A sort of hush: the whole night wondering and asleep: I suppose that's what we do in death—sleep in wonder."

She had been afraid before of the brute in him: now of the mystic. She trod beside him in silence. The rain fell with a heavy "Hush!" on the trees. At last they gained the cart-shed.

"Let us stay here awhile," he said.

There was a sound of rain everywhere, smothering everything.

"I feel so strange and still," he said; "along with everything."

"Ay," she answered patiently.

He seemed again unaware of her, though he held her hand close.

"To be rid of our individuality, which is our will, which is our effort—to live effortless, a kind of curious sleep—that is very beautiful, I think; that is our after-life—our immortality."

"Yes?"

"Yes—and very beautiful to have."

"You don't usually say that."

"No."

In a while they went indoors. Everybody looked at them curiously. He still kept the quiet, heavy look in his eyes, the stillness in his voice. Instinctively, they all left him alone.

About this time Miriam's grandmother, who lived in a tiny cottage in Woodlinton, fell ill, and the girl was sent to keep house. It was a beautiful little place. The cottage had a big garden in front, with red brick walls, against which the plum trees were nailed. At the back another garden was separated from the fields by a tall old hedge. It was very pretty. Miriam had not much to do, so she found time for her beloved reading, and for writing little introspective pieces which interested her.

At the holiday-time her grandmother, being better, was driven to Derby to stay with her daughter for a day or two. She was a crotchety old lady, and might return the second day or the third; so Miriam stayed alone in the cottage, which also pleased her.

Paul used often to cycle over, and they had as a rule peaceful and happy times. He did not embarrass her much; but then on the Monday of the holiday he was to spend a whole day with her.

It was perfect weather. He left his mother, telling her where he was going. She would be alone all the day. It cast a shadow over him; but he had three days that were all his own, when he was going to do as he liked. It was sweet to rush through the morning lanes on his bicycle.

He got to the cottage at about eleven o'clock. Miriam was busy preparing dinner. She looked so perfectly in keeping with the little kitchen, ruddy and busy. He kissed her and sat down to watch. The room was small and cosy. The sofa was covered all over with a sort of linen in squares of red and pale blue, old, much washed, but pretty. There was a stuffed owl in a case over a corner cupboard. The sunlight came through the leaves of the scented geraniums in the window. She was cooking a chicken in his honour. It was their cottage for the day, and they were man and wife. He beat the eggs for her and peeled the potatoes. He thought she gave a feeling of home almost like his mother; and no one could look more beautiful, with her tumbled curls, when she was flushed from the fire.

The dinner was a great success. Like a young husband, he carved. They talked all the time with unflagging zest. Then he wiped the dishes she had washed, and they went out down the fields. There was a bright little brook that ran into a bog at the foot of a very steep bank. Here they wandered, picking still a few marsh-marigolds and many big blue forget-me-nots. Then she sat on the bank with her hands full of flowers, mostly golden water-blobs. As she put her face down into the marigolds, it was all overcast with a yellow shine.

"Your face is bright," he said, "like a transfiguration."

She looked at him, questioning. He laughed pleadingly to her, laying his hands on hers. Then he kissed her fingers, then her face.

The world was all steeped in sunshine, and quite still, yet not asleep, but quivering with a kind of expectancy.

"I have never seen anything more beautiful than this," he said. He held her hand fast all the time.

"And the water singing to itself as it runs—do you love it?" She looked at him full of love. His eyes were very dark, very bright.

"Don't you think it's a great day?" he asked.

She murmured her assent. She *was* happy, and he saw it.

"And our day—just between us," he said.

They lingered a little while. Then they stood up upon the sweet thyme, and he looked down at her simply.

"Will you come?" he asked.

They went back to the house, hand in hand, in silence. The chickens came scampering down the path to her. He locked the door, and they had the little house to themselves.

He never forgot seeing her as she lay on the bed, when he was unfastening his collar. First he saw only her beauty, and was blind with it. She had the most beautiful body he had ever imagined. He stood unable to move or speak, looking at her, his face half-smiling with wonder. And then he wanted her, but as he went forward to her, her hands lifted in a little pleading movement, and he looked at her face, and stopped. Her big brown eyes were watching him, still and resigned and loving; she lay as if she had given herself up to sacrifice: there was her body for him; but the look at the back of her eyes, like a creature awaiting immolation, arrested him, and all his blood fell back.

"You are sure you want me?" he asked, as if a cold shadow had come over him.

"Yes, quite sure."

She was very quiet, very calm. She only realised that she was doing something for him. He could hardly bear it. She lay to be sacrificed for him because she loved him so much. And he had to sacrifice her. For a second, he wished he were sexless or dead. Then he shut his eyes again to her, and his blood beat back again.

And afterwards he loved her—loved her to the last fibre of his being. He loved her. But he wanted, somehow, to cry. There was something he could not bear for her sake. He stayed with her till quite late at night. As he rode home he felt that he was finally initiated. He was a youth no longer. But why had he the dull pain in his soul? Why did the thought of death, the after-life, seem so sweet and consoling?

He spent the week with Miriam, and wore her out with his passion before it was gone. He had always, almost wilfully, to put her out of count, and act from the brute strength of his own feelings. And he could not do it often, and there remained afterwards always the sense of failure and of death. If he were really with her, he had to put aside himself and his desire. If he would have her, he had to put her aside.

"When I come to you," he asked her, his eyes dark with pain and shame, "you don't really want me, do you?"

"Ah, yes!" she replied quickly.

He looked at her.

"Nay," he said.

She began to tremble.

"You see," she said, taking his face and shutting it out against her shoulder—"you see—as we are—how can I get used to you? It would come all right if we were married."

He lifted her head, and looked at her.

"You mean, now, it is always too much shock?"

"Yes—and—"

"You are always clenched against me."

She was trembling with agitation.

"You see," she said, "I'm not used to the thought——"

"You are lately," he said.

"But all my life. Mother said to me: 'There is one thing in marriage that is always dreadful, but you have to bear it.' And I believed it."

"And still believe it," he said.

"No!" she cried hastily. "I believe, as you do, that loving, even in *that* way, is the high-water mark of living."

"That doesn't alter the fact that you never *want* it."

"No," she said, taking his head in her arms and rocking in despair. "Don't say so! You don't understand." She rocked with pain. "Don't I want your children?"

"But not me."

"How can you say so? But we must be married to have children——"

"Shall we be married, then? *I* want you to have my children."

He kissed her hand reverently. She pondered sadly, watching him.

"We are too young," she said at length.

"Twenty-four and twenty-three——"

"Not yet," she pleaded, as she rocked herself in distress.

"When you will," he said.

She bowed her head gravely. The tone of hopelessness in which he said these things grieved her deeply. It had always been a failure between them. Tacitly, she acquiesced in what he felt.

And after a week of love he said to his mother suddenly one Sunday night, just as they were going to bed:

"I shan't go so much to Miriam's, mother."

She was surprised, but she would not ask him anything.

"You please yourself," she said.

So he went to bed. But there was a new quietness about him which she had wondered at. She almost guessed. She would leave him alone, however. Precipitation might spoil things. She watched him in his loneliness, wondering where he would end. He was sick, and much too quiet for him. There was a perpetual little knitting of his brows, such as she had seen when he was a small baby, and which had been gone for many years. Now it was the same again. And she could do nothing for him. He had to go on alone, make his own way.

He continued faithful to Miriam. For one day he had loved her utterly. But it never came again. The sense of failure grew stronger. At first it was only a sadness. Then he began to feel he could not go on. He wanted to run, to go abroad, anything. Gradually he ceased to ask her to have him. Instead of drawing them together, it put them apart. And then he realised, consciously, that it was no good. It was useless trying: it would never be a success between them.

For some months he had seen very little of Clara. They had occasionally walked out for half an hour at dinner-time. But he always reserved himself for Miriam. With Clara, however, his brow cleared, and he was gay again. She treated him indulgently, as if he were a child. He thought he did not mind. But deep below the surface it piqued him.

Sometimes Miriam said:

"What about Clara? I hear nothing of her lately."

"I walked with her about twenty minutes yesterday," he replied.

"And what did she talk about?"

"I don't know. I suppose I did all the jawing—I usually do. I think I was telling her about the strike, and how the women took it."

"Yes."

So he gave the account of himself.

But insidiously, without his knowing it, the warmth he felt for Clara drew him away from Miriam, for whom he felt responsible, and to whom he felt he belonged. He thought he was being quite faithful to her. It was not easy to estimate exactly the strength and warmth of one's feelings for a woman till they have run away with one.

He began to give more time to his men friends. There was Jessop, at the art school; Swain, who was chemistry demonstrator at the university; Newton, who was a teacher; besides Edgar and Miriam's younger brothers. Pleading work, he sketched and studied with Jessop. He called in the University for Swain, and the two went "down town" together. Having come home in the train with Newton, he called and had a game of billiards with him in the Moon and Stars. If he gave to Miriam the excuse of his men friends, he felt quite justified. His mother began to be relieved. He always told her where he had been.

During the summer Clara wore sometimes a dress of soft cotton stuff with loose sleeves. When she lifted her hands, her sleeves fell back, and her beautiful strong arms shone out.

"Half a minute," he cried. "Hold your arm still."

He made sketches of her hand and arm, and the drawings contained some of the fascination the real thing had for him. Miriam, who always went scrupulously through his books and papers, saw the drawings.

"I think Clara has such beautiful arms," he said.

"Yes! When did you draw them?"

"On Tuesday, in the work-room. You know, I've got a corner where I can work. Often I can do every single thing they need in the department, before dinner. Then I work for myself in the afternoon, and just see to things at night."

"Yes," she said, turning the leaves of his sketch-book.

Frequently he hated Miriam. He hated her as she bent forward and pored over his things. He hated her way of patiently casting him up, as if he were an endless psychological account. When he was with her, he hated her for having got him, and yet not got him, and he tortured her. She took all and gave nothing, he said. At least, she gave no living warmth. She was never alive, and giving off life. Looking for her was like looking for something which did not exist. She was only his conscience, not his mate. He hated her violently, and was more cruel to her. They dragged on till the next summer. He saw more and more of Clara.

At last he spoke. He had been sitting working at home one evening. There was between him and his mother a peculiar condition of people frankly finding fault with each other. Mrs. Morel was strong on her feet again. He was not going to stick to Miriam. Very well; then she would stand aloof till he said something. It had been coming a long time, this bursting of the storm in him, when he would come back to her. This evening there was between them a peculiar condition of suspense. He worked feverishly and mechanically, so that he could escape from himself. It grew late. Through the open door, stealthily, came the scent of madonna lilies, almost as if it were prowling abroad. Suddenly he got up and went out of doors.

The beauty of the night made him want to shout. A half-moon, dusky gold, was sinking behind the black sycamore at the end of the garden, making the sky dull purple with its glow. Nearer, a dim white fence of lilies went across the garden, and the air all round seemed to stir with scent, as if it were alive. He went across the bed of pinks, whose keen perfume came sharply across the rocking, heavy scent of the lilies, and stood alongside the white barrier of flowers. They flagged all loose, as if they were panting. The scent made him drunk. He went down to the field to watch the moon sink under.

A corncrake in the hay-close called insistently. The moon slid quite quickly downwards, growing more flushed. Behind him the great flowers leaned as if they were calling. And then, like a shock, he caught another perfume, something raw and coarse. Hunting round, he found the purple iris, touched their fleshy throats and their dark, grasping hands. At any rate, he had found something. They stood stiff in the darkness. Their scent was brutal. The moon was melting down upon the crest of the hill. It was gone; all was dark. The corncrake called still.

Breaking off a pink, he suddenly went indoors.

"Come, my boy," said his mother. "I'm sure it's time you went to bed."

He stood with the pink against his lips.

"I shall break off with Miriam, mother," he answered calmly.

She looked up at him over her spectacles. He was staring back at her, unswerving. She met his eyes for a moment, then took off her glasses. He was white. The male was up in him, dominant. She did not want to see him too clearly.

"But I thought——" she began.

"Well," he answered, "I don't love her. I don't want to marry her—so I shall have done."

"But," exclaimed his mother, amazed, "I thought lately you had made up your mind to have her, and so I said nothing."

"I had—I wanted to—but now I don't want. It's no good. I shall break off on Sunday. I ought to, oughtn't I?"

"You know best. You know I said so long ago."

"I can't help that now. I shall break off on Sunday."

"Well," said his mother, "I think it will be best. But lately I decided you had made up your mind to have her, so I said nothing, and should have said nothing. But I say as I have always said, I *don't* think she is suited to you."

"On Sunday I break off," he said, smelling the pink. He put the flower in his mouth. Unthinking, he bared his teeth, closed them on the blossom slowly, and had a mouthful of petals. These he spat into the fire, kissed his mother, and went to bed.

On Sunday he went up to the farm in the early afternoon. He had written Miriam that they would walk over the fields to Hucknall. His mother was very tender with him. He said nothing. But she saw the effort it was costing. The peculiar set look on his face stilled her.

"Never mind, my son," she said. "You will be so much better when it is all over."

Paul glanced swiftly at his mother in surprise and resentment. He did not want sympathy.

Miriam met him at the lane-end. She was wearing a new dress of figured muslin that had short sleeves. Those short sleeves, and Miriam's brown-skinned arms beneath them—such pitiful, resigned arms—gave him so much pain that they helped to make him cruel. She had made herself look so beautiful and fresh for him. She seemed to blossom for him alone. Every time he looked at her—a mature young woman now, and beautiful in her new dress—it hurt so much that his heart seemed almost to be bursting with the restraint he put on it. But he had decided, and it was irrevocable.

On the hills they sat down, and he lay with his head in her lap, whilst she fingered his hair. She knew that "he was not there," as she put it. Often, when she had him with her, she looked for him, and could not find him. But this afternoon she was not prepared.

It was nearly five o'clock when he told her. They were sitting on the bank of a stream, where the lip of turf hung over a hollow bank of yellow earth, and he was hacking away with a stick, as he did when he was perturbed and cruel.

"I have been thinking," he said, "we ought to break off."

"Why?" she cried in surprise.

"Because it's no good going on."

"Why is it no good?"

"It isn't. I don't want to marry. I don't want ever to marry. And if we're not going to marry, it's no good going on."

"But why do you say this now?"

"Because I've made up my mind."

"And what about these last months, and the things you told me then?"

"I can't help it! I don't want to go on."

"You don't want any more of me?"

"I want us to break off—you be free of me, I free of you."

"And what about these last months?"

"I don't know. I've not told you anything but what I thought was true."

"Then why are you different now?"

"I'm not—I'm the same—only I know it's no good going on."

"You haven't told me why it's no good."

"Because I don't want to go on—and I don't want to marry."

"How many times have you offered to marry me, and I wouldn't?"

"I know; but I want us to break off."

There was silence for a moment or two, while he dug viciously at the earth. She bent her head, pondering. He was an unreasonable child. He was like an infant which, when it has drunk its fill, throws away and smashes the cup. She looked at him, feeling she could get hold of him and *wring* some consistency out of him. But she was helpless. Then she cried:

"I have said you were only fourteen—you are only *four!*"

He still dug at the earth viciously. He heard.

"You are a child of four," she repeated in her anger.

He did not answer, but said in his heart: "All right; if I'm a child of four, what do you want me for? I don't want another mother." But he said nothing to her, and there was silence.

"And have you told your people?" she asked.

"I have told my mother."

There was another long interval of silence.

"Then what do you *want?*" she asked.

"Why, I want us to separate. We have lived on each other all these years; now let us stop. I will go my own way without you, and you will go your way without me. You will have an independent life of your own then."

There was in it some truth that, in spite of her bitterness, she could not help registering. She knew she felt in a sort of bondage to him, which she hated because she could not control it. She hated her love for him from the moment it grew too strong for her. And, deep down, she had hated him because she loved him and he dominated her. She had resisted his domination. She had fought to keep herself free of him in the last issue. And she *was* free of him, even more than he of her.

"And," he continued, "we shall always be more or less each other's work. You have done a lot for me, I for you. Now let us start and live by ourselves."

"What do you want to do?" she asked.

"Nothing—only to be free," he answered.

She, however, knew in her heart that Clara's influence was over him to liberate him. But she said nothing.

"And what have I to tell my mother?" she asked.

"I told my mother," he answered, "that I was breaking off—clean and altogether."

"I shall not tell them at home," she said.

Frowning, "You please yourself," he said.

He knew he had landed her in a nasty hole, and was leaving her in the lurch. It angered him.

"Tell them you wouldn't and won't marry me, and have broken off," he said. "It's true enough."

She bit her finger moodily. She thought over their whole affair. She had known it would come to this; she had seen it all along. It chimed with her bitter expectation.

"Always—it has always been so!" she cried. "It has been one long battle between us—you fighting away from me."

It came from her unawares, like a flash of lightning. The man's heart stood still. Was this how she saw it?

"But we've had *some* perfect hours, *some* perfect times, when we were together!" he pleaded.

"Never!" she cried; "never! It has always been you fighting me off."

"Not always—not at first!" he pleaded.

"Always, from the very beginning—always the same!"

She had finished, but she had done enough. He sat aghast. He had wanted to say: "It has been good, but it is at an end." And she—she whose love he had believed in when he had despised himself—denied that their love had ever been love. "He had always fought away from her?" Then it had been monstrous. There had never been anything really between them; all the time he had been imagining something where there was nothing. And she had known. She had known so much, and had told him so little. She had known all the time. All the time this was at the bottom of her!

He sat silent in bitterness. At last the whole affair appeared in a cynical aspect to him. She had really played with him, not he with her. She had hidden all her condemnation from him, had flattered him, and despised him. She despised him now. He grew intellectual and cruel.

"You ought to marry a man who worships you," he said; "then you could do as you liked with him. Plenty of men will worship you, if you get on the private side of their natures. You ought to marry one such. They would never fight you off."

"Thank you!" she said. "But don't advise me to marry someone else any more. You've done it before."

"Very well," he said; "I will say no more."

He sat still, feeling as if he had had a blow, instead of giving one. Their eight years of friendship and love, *the* eight years of his life, were nullified.

"When did you think of this?" she asked.

"I thought definitely on Thursday night."

"I knew it was coming," she said.

That pleased him bitterly. "Oh, very well! If she knew then it doesn't come as a surprise to her," he thought.

"And have you said anything to Clara?" she asked.

"No; but I shall tell her now."

There was a silence.

"Do you remember the things you said this time last year, in my grandmother's house—nay last month even?"

"Yes," he said; "I do! And I meant them! I can't help that it's failed."

"It has failed because you want something else."

"It would have failed whether or not. *You* never believed in me."

She laughed strangely.

He sat in silence. He was full of a feeling that she had deceived him. She had despised him when he thought she worshipped him. She had let him say wrong things, and had not contradicted him. She had let him fight alone. But it stuck in his throat that she had despised him whilst he thought she worshipped him. She should have told him when she found fault with him. She had not played fair. He hated her. All these years she had treated him as if he were a hero, and thought of him secretly as an infant, a foolish child. Then why had she left the foolish child to his folly? His heart was hard against her.

She sat full of bitterness. She had known—oh, well she had known! All the time he was away from her she had summed him up, seen his littleness, his meanness, and his folly. Even she had guarded her soul against him. She was not overthrown, not prostrated, not even much hurt. She had known. Only why, as he sat there, had he still this strange dominance over her? His very movements fascinated her as if she were hypnotised by him. Yet he was despicable, false, inconsistent, and mean. Why this bondage for her? Why was it the movement of his arm stirred her as nothing else in the world could? Why was she fastened to him? Why, even now, if he looked at her and commanded her, would she have to obey? She would obey him in his trifling commands. But once he was obeyed, then she had him in her power, she knew, to lead him where she would. She was sure of herself. Only, this new influence! Ah, he was not a man! He was a baby that cries for the newest toy. And all the attachment of his soul would not keep him. Very well, he would have to go. But he would come back when he had tired of his new sensation.

He hacked at the earth till she was fretted to death. She rose. He sat flinging lumps of earth in the stream.

"We will go and have tea here?" he asked.

"Yes," she answered.

They chattered over irrelevant subjects during tea. He held forth on the love of ornament—the cottage parlour moved him thereto—and its connection with aesthetics. She was cold and quiet. As they walked home, she asked:

"And we shall not see each other?"

"No—or rarely," he answered.

"Nor write?" she asked, almost sarcastically.

"As you will," he answered. "We're not strangers—never should be, whatever happened. I will write to you now and again. You please yourself."

"I see!" she answered cuttingly.

But he was at that stage at which nothing else hurts. He had made a great cleavage in his life. He had had a great shock when she had told him their love had been always a conflict. Nothing more mattered. If it never had been much, there was no need to make a fuss that it was ended.

He left her at the lane-end. As she went home, solitary, in her new frock, having her people to face at the other end, he stood still with shame and pain in the highroad, thinking of the suffering he caused her.

In the reaction towards restoring his self-esteem, he went into the Willow Tree for a drink. There were four girls who had been out for the day, drinking a modest glass of port. They had some chocolates on the table. Paul sat near with his whisky. He noticed the girls whispering and nudging. Presently one, a bonny dark hussy, leaned to him and said:

"Have a chocolate?"

The others laughed loudly at her impudence.

"All right," said Paul. "Give me a hard one—nut. I don't like creams."

"Here you are, then," said the girl; "here's an almond for you."

She held the sweet between her fingers. He opened his mouth. She popped it in, and blushed.

"You *are* nice!" he said.

"Well," she answered, "we thought you looked overcast, and they dared me offer you a chocolate."

"I don't mind if I have another—another sort," he said.

And presently they were all laughing together.

It was nine o'clock when he got home, falling dark. He entered the house in silence. His mother, who had been waiting, rose anxiously.

"I told her," he said.

"I'm glad," replied the mother, with great relief.

He hung up his cap wearily.

"I said we'd have done altogether," he said.

"That's right, my son," said the mother. "It's hard for her now, but best in the long run. I know. You weren't suited for her."

He laughed shakily as he sat down.

"I've had such a lark with some girls in a pub," he said.

His mother looked at him. He had forgotten Miriam now. He told her about the girls in the Willow Tree. Mrs. Morel looked at him. It seemed unreal, his gaiety. At the back of it was too much horror and misery.

"Now have some supper," she said very gently.

Afterwards he said wistfully:

"She never thought she'd have me, mother, not from the first, and so she's not disappointed."

"I'm afraid," said his mother, "she doesn't give up hopes of you yet."

"No," he said, "perhaps not."

"You'll find it's better to have done," she said.

"I don't know," he said desperately.

"Well, leave her alone," replied his mother.

So he left her, and she was alone. Very few people cared for her, and she for very few people. She remained alone with herself, waiting.

XII

PASSION

He was gradually making it possible to earn a livelihood by his art. Liberty's had taken several of his painted designs on various stuffs, and he could sell designs for embroideries, for altar-cloths, and similar things, in one or two places. It was not very much he made at present, but he might extend it. He had also made friends with the designer for a pottery firm, and was gaining some knowledge of his new acquaintance's art. The applied arts interested him very much. At the same time he laboured slowly at his pictures. He loved to paint large figures, full of light, but not merely made up of lights and cast shadows, like the impressionists; rather definite figures that had a certain luminous quality, like some of Michael Angelo's people. And these he fitted into a landscape, in what he thought true proportion. He worked a great deal from memory, using everybody he knew. He believed firmly in his work, that it was good and valuable. In spite of fits of depression, shrinking, everything, he believed in his work.

He was twenty-four when he said his first confident thing to his mother.

"Mother," he said, "I s'll make a painter that they'll attend to."

She sniffed in her quaint fashion. It was like a half-pleased shrug of the shoulders.

"Very well, my boy, we'll see," she said.

"You shall see, my pigeon! You see if you're not swanky one of these days!"

"I'm quite content, my boy," she smiled.

"But you'll have to alter. Look at you with Minnie!"

Minnie was the small servant, a girl of fourteen.

"And what about Minnie?" asked Mrs. Morel, with dignity.

"I heard her this morning: 'Eh, Mrs. Morel! I was going to do that,' when you went out in the rain for some coal," he said. "That looks a lot like your being able to manage servants!"

"Well, it was only the child's niceness," said Mrs. Morel.

"And you apologising to her: 'You can't do two things at once, can you?' "

"She *was* busy washing up," replied Mrs. Morel.

"And what did she say? 'It could easy have waited a bit. Now look how your feet paddle!' "

"Yes—brazen young baggage!" said Mrs. Morel, smiling.

He looked at his mother, laughing. She was quite warm and rosy again with love of him. It seemed as if all the sunshine were on her for a moment. He continued his work gladly. She seemed so well when she was happy that he forgot her grey hair.

And that year she went with him to the Isle of Wight for a holiday. It was too exciting for them both, and too beautiful. Mrs. Morel was full of joy and wonder. But he would have her walk with him more than she was able. She had a bad fainting bout. So grey her face was, so blue her mouth! It was agony to him. He felt as if someone were pushing a knife in his chest. Then she was better again, and he forgot. But the anxiety remained inside him, like a wound that did not close.

After leaving Miriam he went almost straight to Clara. On the Monday following the day of the rupture he went down to the work-room. She looked up at him and smiled. They had grown very intimate unawares. She saw a new brightness about him.

"Well, Queen of Sheba!" he said, laughing.

"But why?" she asked.

"I think it suits you. You've got a new frock on."

She flushed, asking:

"And what of it?"

"Suits you—awfully! *I* could design you a dress."

"How would it be?"

He stood in front of her, his eyes glittering as he expounded. He kept her eyes fixed with his. Then suddenly he took hold of her. She half-started back. He drew the stuff of her blouse tighter, smoothed it over her breast.

"More *so*!" he explained.

But they were both of them flaming with blushes, and immediately he ran away. He had touched her. His whole body was quivering with the sensation.

There was already a sort of secret understanding between them. The next evening he went to the cinematograph with her for a few minutes before train-time. As they sat, he saw her hand lying near him. For some moments he dared not touch it. The pictures danced and dithered. Then he took her hand in his. It was large and firm; it filled his grasp. He held it fast. She neither moved nor made any sign. When they came out his train was due. He hesitated.

"Good-night," she said. He darted away across the road.

The next day he came again, talking to her. She was rather superior with him.

"Shall we go a walk on Monday?" he asked.

She turned her face aside.

"Shall you tell Miriam?" she replied sarcastically.

"I have broken off with her," he said.

"When?"

"Last Sunday."

"You quarrelled?"

"No! I had made up my mind. I told her quite definitely I should consider myself free."

Clara did not answer, and he returned to his work. She was so quiet and so superb!

On the Saturday evening he asked her to come and drink coffee with him in a restaurant, meeting him after work was over. She came, looking very reserved and very distant. He had three-quarters of an hour to train-time.

"We will walk a little while," he said.

She agreed, and they went past the Castle into the Park. He was afraid of her. She walked moodily at his side, with a kind of resentful, reluctant, angry walk. He was afraid to take her hand.

"Which way shall we go?" he asked as they walked in darkness.

"I don't mind."

"Then we'll go up the steps."

He suddenly turned round. They had passed the Park steps. She stood still in resentment at his suddenly abandoning her. He looked for her. She stood aloof. He caught her suddenly in his arms, held her strained for a moment, kissed her. Then he let her go.

"Come along," he said, penitent.

She followed him. He took her hand and kissed her finger-tips. They went in silence. When they came to the light, he let go her hand. Neither spoke till they reached the station. Then they looked each other in the eyes.

"Good-night," she said.

And he went for his train. His body acted mechanically. People talked to him. He heard faint echoes answering them. He was in a delirium. He felt that he would go mad if Monday did not come at once. On Monday he would see her again. All himself was pitched there, ahead. Sunday intervened. He could not bear it. He could not see her till Monday. And Sunday intervened—hour after hour of tension. He wanted to beat his head against the door of the carriage. But he sat still. He drank some whisky on the way home, but it only made it worse. His mother must not be upset, that was all. He dissembled, and got quickly to bed. There he sat, dressed, with his chin on his knees, staring out of the window at the far hill, with its few lights. He neither thought nor slept, but sat perfectly still, staring. And when at last he was so cold that he came to himself, he found his watch had stopped at half-past two. It was after three o'clock. He was exhausted, but still there was the torment of knowing it was only Sunday morning. He went to bed and slept. Then he cycled all day long, til he was fagged out. And he scarcely knew where he had been. But the day after was Monday. He slept till four o'clock. Then he lay and thought. He was coming nearer to himself—he could see himself, real, somewhere in front. She would go a walk with him in the afternoon. Afternoon! It seemed years ahead.

Slowly the hours crawled. His father got up; he heard him pottering about. Then the miner set off to the pit, his heavy boots scraping the yard. Cocks were still crowing. A cart went down the road. His mother got up. She knocked the fire. Presently she called him softly. He answered as if he were asleep. This shell of himself did well.

He was walking to the station—another mile! The train was near Nottingham. Would it stop before the tunnels? But it did not matter; it would get there before dinner-time. He was at Jordan's. She would come in half an hour. At any rate, she would be near. He had done the letters. She would be there. Perhaps she had not come. He ran downstairs. Ah! he saw her through the glass door. Her shoulders stooping a little to her work made him feel he could not go forward; he could not stand. He went in. He was pale, nervous, awkward, and quite cold. Would she misunderstand him? He could not write his real self with this shell.

"And this afternoon," he struggled to say. "You will come?"

"I think so," she replied, murmuring.

He stood before her, unable to say a word. She hid her face from him. Again came over him the feeling that he would lose consciousness. He set his teeth and went upstairs. He had done everything correctly yet, and he would do so. All the morning things seemed a long way off, as they do to a man under chloroform. He himself seemed under a tight band of constraint. Then there was his other self, in the distance, doing things, entering stuff in a ledger, and he watched that far-off him carefully to see he made no mistake.

But the ache and strain of it could not go on much longer. He worked incessantly. Still it was only twelve o'clock. As if he had nailed his clothing against the desk, he stood there and worked, forcing every stroke out of himself. It was a quarter to one; he could clear away. Then he ran downstairs.

"You will meet me at the Fountain at two o'clock," he said.

"I can't be there till half-past."

"Yes!" he said.

She saw his dark, mad eyes.

"I will try at a quarter past."

And he had to be content. He went and got some dinner. All the time he was still under chloroform, and every minute was stretched out indefinitely. He walked miles of streets. Then he thought he would be late at the meeting-place. He was at the Fountain at five past two. The torture of the next quarter of an hour was refined beyond expression. It was the anguish of combining the living self with the shell. Then he saw her. She came! And he was there.

"You are late," he said.

"Only five minutes," she answered.

"I'd never have done it to you," he laughed.

She was in a dark blue costume. He looked at her beautiful figure.

"You want some flowers," he said, going to the nearest florist's.

She followed him in silence. He bought her a bunch of scarlet, brick-red carnations. She put them in her coat, flushing.

"That's a fine colour!" he said.

"I'd rather have had something softer," she said.

He laughed.

"Do you feel like a blot of vermilion walking down the street?" he said.

She hung her head, afraid of the people they met. He looked sideways at her as they walked. There was a wonderful close down on her face near the ear that he wanted to touch. And a certain heaviness, the heaviness of a very full ear of corn that dips slightly in the wind, that there was about her, made his brain spin. He seemed to be spinning down the street, everything going round.

As they sat in the tramcar, she leaned her heavy shoulder against him, and he took her hand. He felt himself coming round from the anaesthetic, beginning to breathe. Her ear, half-hidden among her blonde hair, was near to him. The temptation to kiss it was almost too great. But there were other people on top of the car. It still remained to him to kiss it. After all, he was not himself, he was some attribute of hers, like the sunshine that fell on her.

He looked quickly away. It had been raining. The big bluff of the Castle rock was streaked with rain, as it reared above the flat of the town. They crossed the wide, black space of the Midland Railway, and passed the cattle enclosure that stood out white. Then they ran down sordid Wilford Road.

She rocked slightly to the tram's motion, and as she leaned against him, rocked upon him. He was a vigorous, slender man, with exhaustless energy. His face was rough, with rough-hewn features, like the common people's; but his eyes under the deep brows were so full of life that they fascinated her. They seemed to dance, and yet they were still trembling on the finest balance of laughter. His mouth the same was just going to spring into a laugh of triumph, yet did not. There was a sharp suspense about him. She bit her lip moodily. His hand was hard clenched over hers.

They paid their two halfpennies at the turnstile and crossed the bridge. The Trent was very full. It swept silent and insidious under the bridge, travelling in a soft body. There had been a great deal of rain. On the river levels were flat gleams of flood water. The sky was grey, with glisten of silver here and there. In Wilford churchyard the dahlias were sodden with rain—wet black-crimson balls. No one was on the path that went along the green river meadow, along the elm-tree colonnade.

There was the faintest haze over the silvery-dark water and the green meadow-bank, and the elm-trees that were spangled with gold. The river slid by in a body, utterly silent and swift, intertwining among itself like some subtle, complex creature. Clara walked moodily beside him.

"Why," she asked at length, in rather a jarring tone, "did you leave Miriam?"

He frowned.

"Because I *wanted* to leave her," he said.

"Why?"

"Because I didn't want to go on with her. And I didn't want to marry."

She was silent for a moment. They picked their way down the muddy path. Drops of water fell from the elm-trees.

"You didn't want to marry Miriam, or you didn't want to marry at all?" she asked.

"Both," he answered—"both!"

They had to manoeuvre to get to the stile, because of the pools of water.

"And what did she say?" Clara asked.

"Miriam? She said I was a baby of four, and that I always *had* battled her off."

Clara pondered over this for a time.

"But you have really been going with her for some time?" she asked.

"Yes."

"And now you don't want any more of her?"

"No. I know it's no good."

She pondered again.

"Don't you think you've treated her rather badly?" she asked.

"Yes; I ought to have dropped it years back. But it would have been no good going on. Two wrongs don't make a right."

"How old *are* you?" Clara asked.

"Twenty-five."

"And I am thirty," she said.

"I know you are."

"I shall be thirty-one—or *am* I thirty-one?"

"I neither know nor care. What does it matter!"

They were at the entrance to the Grove. The wet, red track, already sticky with fallen leaves, went up the steep bank between the grass. On either side stood the elm-trees like pillars along a great aisle, arching over and making high up a roof from which the dead leaves fell. All was empty and silent and wet. She stood on top of the stile, and he held both her hands. Laughing, she looked down into his eyes. Then she leaped. Her breast came against his; he held her, and covered her face with kisses.

They went on up the slippery, steep red path. Presently she released his hand and put it round her waist.

"You press the vein in my arm, holding it so tightly," she said.

They walked along. His finger-tips felt the rocking of her breast. All was silent and deserted. On the left the red wet plough-land showed through the doorways between the elm-boles and their branches. On the right, looking down, they could see the tree-tops of elms growing far beneath them, hear occasionally the gurgle of the river. Sometimes there below they caught glimpses of the full, soft-sliding Trent, and of water-meadows dotted with small cattle.

"It has scarcely altered since little Kirke White used to come," he said.

But he was watching her throat below the ear, where the flush was fusing into the honey-white, and her mouth that pouted disconsolate. She stirred against him as she walked, and his body was like a taut string.

Half-way up the big colonnade of elms, where the Grove rose highest above the river, their forward movement faltered to an end. He led her across to the grass, under the trees at the edge of the path. The cliff of red earth sloped swiftly down, through trees and bushes, to the river that glimmered and was dark between the foliage. The far-below water-meadows were very green. He and she stood leaning against one another, silent, afraid, their bodies touching all along. There came a quick gurgle from the river below.

"Why," he asked at length, "did you hate Baxter Dawes?"

She turned to him with a splendid movement. Her mouth was offered him, and her throat; her eyes were half-shut; her breast was tilted as if it asked for him. He flashed with a small laugh, shut his eyes, and met her in a long, whole kiss. Her mouth fused with his; their bodies were sealed and annealed. It was some minutes before they withdrew. They were standing beside the public path.

"Will you go down to the river?" he asked.

She looked at him, leaving herself in his hands. He went over the brim of the declivity and began to climb down.

"It is slippery," he said.

"Never mind," she replied.

The red clay went down almost sheer. He slid, went from one tuft of grass to the next, hanging on to the bushes, making for a little platform at the foot of a tree. There he waited for her, laughing with excitement. Her shoes were clogged with red earth. It was hard for her. He frowned. At last he caught her hand, and she stood beside him. The cliff rose above them and fell away below. Her colour was up, her eyes flashed. He looked at the big drop below them.

"It's risky," he said; "or messy, at any rate. Shall we go back?"

"Not for my sake," she said quickly.

"All right. You see, I can't help you; I should only hinder. Give me that little parcel and your gloves. Your poor shoes!"

They stood perched on the face of the declivity, under the trees.

"Well, I'll go again," he said.

Away he went, slipping, staggering, sliding to the next tree, into which he fell with a slam that nearly shook the breath out of him. She came after cautiously, hanging on to the twigs and grasses. So they descended, stage by stage, to the river's brink. There, to his disgust, the flood had eaten away the path, and the red decline ran straight into the water. He dug in his heels and brought himself up violently. The string of the parcel broke with a snap; the brown parcel bounded down, leaped into the water, and sailed smoothly away. He hung on to his tree.

"Well, I'll be damned!" he cried crossly. Then he laughed. She was coming perilously down.

"Mind!" he warned her. He stood with his back to the tree, waiting. "Come now," he called, opening his arms.

She let herself run. He caught her, and together they stood watching the dark water scoop at the raw edge of the bank. The parcel had sailed out of sight.

"It doesn't matter," she said.

He held her close and kissed her. There was only room for their four feet.

"It's a swindle!" he said. "But there's a rut where a man has been, so if we go on I guess we shall find the path again."

The river slid and twined its great volume. On the other bank cattle were feeding on the desolate flats. The cliff rose high above Paul and Clara on their right hand. They stood against the tree in the watery silence.

"Let us try going forward," he said; and they struggled in the red clay along the groove a man's nailed boots had made. They were hot and flushed. Their barkled shoes hung heavy on their steps. At last they found the broken path. It was littered with rubble from the water, but at any rate it was easier. They cleaned their boots with twigs. His heart was beating thick and fast.

Suddenly, coming on to the little level, he saw two figures of men standing silent at the water's edge. His heart leaped. They were fishing. He turned and put his hand up warningly to Clara. She hesitated, buttoned her coat. The two went on together.

The fishermen turned curiously to watch the two intruders on their privacy and solitude. They had had a fire, but it was nearly out. All kept perfectly still. The men turned again to their fishing, stood over the grey glinting river like statues. Clara went with bowed head, flushing; he was laughing to himself. Directly they passed out of sight behind the willows.

"Now they ought to be drowned," said Paul softly.

Clara did not answer. They toiled forward along a tiny path on the river's lip. Suddenly it vanished. The bank was sheer red solid clay in front of them, sloping straight into the river. He stood and cursed beneath his breath, setting his teeth.

"It's impossible!" said Clara.

He stood erect, looking round. Just ahead were two islets in the stream, covered with osiers. But they were unattainable. The cliff came down like a sloping wall from far above their heads. Behind, not far back, were the fishermen. Across the river the distant cattle fed silently in the desolate afternoon. He cursed again deeply under his breath. He gazed up the great steep bank. Was there no hope but to scale back to the public path?

"Stop a minute," he said, and, digging his heels sideways into the steep bank of red clay, he began nimbly to mount. He looked across at every tree-foot. At last he found what he wanted. Two beech-trees side by side on the hill held a little level on the upper face between their roots. It was littered with damp leaves, but it would do. The fishermen were perhaps sufficiently out of sight. He threw down his rainproof and waved to her to come.

She toiled to his side. Arriving there, she looked at him heavily, dumbly, and laid her head on his shoulder. He held her fast as he looked round. They were safe enough from all but the small, lonely cows over the river. He sunk his mouth on her throat, where he felt her heavy pulse beat under his lips. Everything was perfectly still. There was nothing in the afternoon but themselves.

When she arose, he, looking on the ground all the time, saw suddenly sprinkled on the black wet beech-roots many scarlet carnation petals, like splashed drops of blood; and red, small splashes fell from her bosom, streaming down her dress to her feet.

"Your flowers are smashed," he said.

She looked at him heavily as she put back her hair. Suddenly he put his finger-tips on her cheek.

"Why dost look so heavy?" he reproached her.

She smiled sadly, as if she felt alone in herself. He caressed her cheek with his fingers, and kissed her.

"Nay!" he said. "Never thee bother!"

She gripped his fingers tight, and laughed shakily. Then she dropped her hand. He put the hair back from her brows, stroking her temples, kissing them lightly.

"But tha shouldna worrit!" he said softly, pleading.

"No, I don't worry!" she laughed tenderly and resigned.

"Yea, tha does! Dunna thee worrit," he implored, caressing.

"No!" she consoled him, kissing him.

They had a stiff climb to get to the top again. It took them a quarter of an hour. When he got on to the level grass, he threw off his cap, wiped the sweat from his forehead, and sighed.

"Now we're back at the ordinary level," he said.

She sat down, panting, on the tussocky grass. Her cheeks were flushed pink. He kissed her, and she gave way to joy.

"And now I'll clean thy boots and make thee fit for respectable folk," he said.

He kneeled at her feet, worked away with a stick and tufts of grass. She put her fingers in his hair, drew his head to her, and kissed it.

"What am I supposed to be doing," he said, looking at her laughing; "cleaning shoes or dibbling with love? Answer me that!"

"Just whichever I please," she replied.

"I'm your boot-boy for the time being, and nothing else!" But they remained looking into each other's eyes and laughing. Then they kissed with little nibbling kisses.

"T-t-t-t!" he went with his tongue, like his mother. "I tell you, nothing gets done when there's a woman about."

And he returned to his boot-cleaning, singing softly. She touched his thick hair, and he kissed her fingers. He worked away at her shoes. At last they were quite presentable.

"There you are, you see!" he said. "Aren't I a great hand at restoring you to respectability? Stand up! There, you look as irreproachable as Britannia herself!"

He cleaned his own boots a little, washed his hands in a puddle, and sang. They went on into Clifton village. He was madly in love with her; every movement she made, every crease in her garments, sent a hot flash through him and seemed adorable.

The old lady at whose house they had tea was roused into gaiety by them.

"I could wish you'd had something of a better day," she said, hovering round.

"Nay!" he laughed. "We've been saying how nice it is."

The old lady looked at him curiously. There was a peculiar glow and charm about him. His eyes were dark and laughing. He rubbed his moustache with a glad movement.

"Have you been saying *so!*" she exclaimed, a light rousing in her old eyes.

"Truly!" he laughed.

"Then I'm sure the day's good enough," said the old lady.

She fussed about, and did not want to leave them.

"I don't know whether you'd like some radishes as well," she said to Clara; "but I've got some in the garden—*and* a cucumber."

Clara flushed. She looked very handsome.

"I should like some radishes," she answered.

And the old lady pottered off gleefully.

"If she knew!" said Clara quietly to him.

"Well, she doesn't know; and it shows we're nice in ourselves, at any rate. You look quite enough to satisfy an archangel, and I'm sure I feel harmless—so—if it makes you look nice, and makes folk happy when they have us, and makes us happy—why, we're not cheating them out of much!"

They went on with the meal. When they were going away, the old lady came timidly with three tiny dahlias in full blow, neat as bees, and speckled scarlet and white. She stood before Clara, pleased with herself, saying:

"I don't know whether—" and holding the flowers forward in her old hand.

"Oh, how pretty!" cried Clara, accepting the flowers.

"Shall she have them all?" asked Paul reproachfully of the old woman.

"Yes, she shall have them all," she replied, beaming with joy. "You have got enough for your share."

"Ah, but I shall ask her to give me one!" he teased.

"Then she does as she pleases," said the old lady, smiling. And she bobbed a little curtsey of delight.

Clara was rather quiet and uncomfortable. As they walked along, he said:

"You don't feel criminal, do you?"

She looked at him with startled grey eyes.

"Criminal!" she said. "No."

"But you seem to feel you have done a wrong?"

"No," she said. "I only think, 'If they knew!'"

"If they knew, they'd cease to understand. As it is, they do understand, and they like it. What do they matter? Here, with only the trees and me, you don't feel not the least bit wrong, do you?"

He took her by the arm, held her facing him, holding her eyes with his. Something fretted him.

"Not sinners, are we?" he said, with an uneasy little frown.

"No," she replied.

He kissed her, laughing.

"You like your little bit of guiltiness, I believe," he said. "I believe Eve enjoyed it, when she went cowering out of Paradise."

But there was a certain glow and quietness about her that made him glad. When he was alone in the railway-carriage, he found himself tumultuously happy, and the people exceedingly nice, and the night lovely, and everything good.

Mrs. Morel was sitting reading when he got home. Her health was not good now, and there had come that ivory pallor into her face which he never noticed, and which afterwards he never forgot. She did not mention her own ill-health to him. After all, she thought, it was not much.

"You are late!" she said, looking at him.

His eyes were shining; his face seemed to glow. He smiled to her.

"Yes; I've been down Clifton Grove with Clara."

His mother looked at him again.

"But won't people talk?" she said.

"Why? They know she's a suffragette, and so on. And what if they do talk!"

"Of course, there may be nothing wrong in it," said his mother. "But you know what folks are, and if once she gets talked about——"

"Well, I can't help it. Their jaw isn't so almighty important, after all."

"I think you ought to consider *her.*"

"So I *do!* What can people say?—that we take a walk together. I believe you're jealous."

"You know I should be *glad* if she weren't a married woman."

"Well, my dear, she lives separate from her husband, and talks on platforms; so she's already singled out from the sheep, and, as far as I can see, hasn't much to lose. No; her life's nothing to her, so what's the worth of nothing? She goes with me—it becomes something. Then she must pay—we both must pay! Folk are so frightened of paying; they'd rather starve and die."

"Very well, my son. We'll see how it will end."

"Very well, my mother. I'll abide by the end."

"We'll see!"

"And she's—she's *awfully* nice, mother; she is really! You don't know!"

"That's not the same as marrying her."

"It's perhaps better."

There was silence for a while. He wanted to ask his mother something, but was afraid.

"Should you like to know her?" He hesitated.

"Yes," said Mrs. Morel coolly. "I should like to know what she's like."

"But she's nice, mother, she is! And not a bit common!"

"I never suggested she was."

"But you seem to think she's—not as good as—— She's better than ninety-nine folk out of a hundred, I tell you! She's *better,* she is! She's fair, she's honest, she's straight! There isn't anything underhand or superior about her. Don't be mean about her!"

Mrs. Morel flushed.

"I am sure I am not mean about her. She may be quite as you say, but——"

"You don't approve," he finished.

"And do you expect me to?" she answered coldly.

"Yes!—yes!—if you'd anything about you, you'd be glad! Do you *want* to see her?"

"I said I did."

"Then I'll bring her—shall I bring her here?"

"You please yourself."

"Then I *will* bring her here—one Sunday—to tea. If you think a horrid thing about her, I shan't forgive you."

His mother laughed.

"As if it would make any difference!" she said. He knew he had won.

"Oh, but it feels so fine, when she's there! She's such a queen in her way."

Occasionally he still walked a little way from chapel with Miriam and Edgar. He did not go up to the farm. She, however, was very much the same with him, and he did not feel embarrassed in her presence. One evening she was alone when he accompanied her. They began by talking books: it was their unfailing topic. Mrs. Morel had said that his and Miriam's affair was like a fire fed on books—if there were no more volumes it would die out. Miriam, for her part, boasted that she could read him like a book, could place her finger any minute on the chapter and the line. He, easily taken in, believed that Miriam knew more about him than anyone else. So it pleased him to talk to her about himself, like the simplest egoist. Very soon the conversation drifted to his own doings. It flattered him immensely that he was of such supreme interest.

"And what have you been doing lately?"

"I—oh, not much! I made a sketch of Bestwood from the garden, that is nearly right at last. It's the hundredth try."

So they went on. Then she said:

"You've not been out, then, lately?"

"Yes; I went up Clifton Grove on Monday afternoon with Clara."

"It was not very nice weather," said Miriam, "was it?"

"But I wanted to go out, and it was all right. The Trent *is* full."

"And did you go to Barton?" she asked.

"No; we had tea in Clifton."

"Did you! That would be nice."

"It was! The jolliest old woman! She gave us several pom-pom dahlias, as pretty as you like."

Miriam bowed her head and brooded. He was quite unconscious of concealing anything from her.

"What made her give them you?" she asked.

He laughed.

"Because she liked us—because we were jolly, I should think."

Miriam put her finger in her mouth.

"Were you late home?" she asked.

At last he resented her tone.

"I caught the seven-thirty."

"Ha!"

They walked on in silence, and he was angry.

"And how *is* Clara?" asked Miriam.

"Quite all right, I think."

"That's good!" she said, with a tinge of irony. "By the way, what of her husband? One never hears anything of him."

"He's got some other woman, and is also quite all right," he replied. "At least, so I think."

"I see—you don't know for certain. Don't you think a position like that is hard on a woman?"

"Rottenly hard!"

"It's so unjust!" said Miriam. "The man does as he likes——"

"Then let the woman also," he said.

"How can she? And if she does, look at her position!"

"What of it?"

"Why, it's impossible! You don't understand what a woman forfeits——"

"No, I don't. But if a woman's got nothing but her fair fame to feed on, why, it's thin tack, and a donkey would die of it!"

So she understood his moral attitude, at least, and she knew he would act accordingly.

She never asked him anything direct, but she got to know enough.

Another day, when he saw Miriam, the conversation turned to marriage, then to Clara's marriage with Dawes.

"You see," he said, "she never knew the fearful importance of marriage. She thought it was all in the day's march—it would have to come—and Dawes—well, a good many women would have given their souls to get him; so why not him? Then she developed into the *femme incomprise,* and treated him badly, I'll bet my boots."

"And she left him because he didn't understand her?"

"I suppose so. I suppose she had to. It isn't altogether a question of understanding; it's a question of living. With him, she was only half-alive; the rest was dormant, deadened. And the dormant woman was the *femme incomprise,* and she *had* to be awakened."

"And what about him."

"I don't know. I rather think he loves her as much as he can, but he's a fool."

"It was something like your mother and father," said Miriam.

"Yes; but my mother, I believe, got real joy and satisfaction out of my father at first. I believe she had a passion for him; that's why she stayed with him. After all, they were bound to each other."

"Yes," said Miriam.

"That's what one *must have,* I think," he continued—"the real, real flame of feeling through another person—once, only once, if it only lasts three months. See, my mother looks as if she'd *had* everything that was necessary for her living and developing. There's not a tiny bit of feeling of sterility about her."

"No," said Miriam.

"And with my father, at first, I'm sure she had the real thing. She knows; she has been there. You can feel it about her, and about him, and about hundreds of people you meet every day; and, once it has happened to you, you can go on with anything and ripen."

"What happened, exactly?" asked Miriam.

"It's so hard to say, but the something big and intense that changes you when you really come together with somebody else. It almost seems to fertilise your soul and make it that you can go on and mature."

"And you think your mother had it with your father?"

"Yes; and at the bottom she feels grateful to him for giving it her, even now, though they are miles apart."

"And you think Clara never had it?"

"I'm sure."

Miriam pondered this. She saw what he was seeking—a sort of baptism of fire in passion, it seemed to her. She realised that he would never be satisfied till he had it. Perhaps it was essential to him, as to some men, to sow wild oats; and afterwards, when he was satisfied, he would not rage with restlessness any more, but could settle down and give her his life into her hands. Well, then, if he must go, let him go and have his fill—something big and intense, he called it. At any rate, when he had got it, he would not want it—that he said himself; he would want the other thing that she could give him. He would want to be owned, so that he could work. It seemed to her a bitter thing that he must go, but she could let him go into an inn for a glass of whisky, so she could let him go to Clara, so long as it was something that would satisfy a need in him, and leave him free for herself to possess.

"Have you told your mother about Clara?" she asked.

She knew this would be a test of the seriousness of his feeling for the other woman: she knew he was going to Clara for something vital, not as a man goes for pleasure to a prostitute, if he told his mother.

"Yes," he said, "and she is coming to tea on Sunday."

"To your house?"

"Yes; I want mater to see her."

"Ah!"

There was a silence. Things had gone quicker than she thought. She felt a sudden bitterness that he could leave her so soon and so entirely. And was Clara to be accepted by his people, who had been so hostile to herself?

"I may call in as I go to chapel," she said. "It is a long time since I saw Clara."

"Very well," he said, astonished, and unconsciously angry.

On the Sunday afternoon he went to Keston to meet Clara at the station. As he stood on the platform he was trying to examine in himself if he had a premonition.

"Do I *feel* as if she'd come?" he said to himself, and he tried to find out. His heart felt queer and contracted. That seemed like foreboding. Then he *had* a foreboding she would not come! Then she would not come, and instead of taking her over the fields home, as he had imagined, he would have to go alone. The train was late; the afternoon would be wasted, and the evening. He hated her for not coming. Why had she promised, then, if she could not keep her promise? Perhaps she had missed her train—he himself was always missing trains—but that was no reason why she should miss this particular one. He was angry with her; he was furious.

Suddenly he saw the train crawling, sneaking round the corner. Here, then, was the train, but of course she had not come. The green engine hissed along the platform, the row of brown carriages drew up, several doors opened. No; she had not come! No! Yes; ah, there she was! She had a big black hat on! He was at her side in a moment.

"I thought you weren't coming," he said.

She was laughing rather breathlessly as she put out her hand to him; their eyes met. He took her quickly along the platform, talking at a great rate to hide his feeling. She looked beautiful. In her hat were large silk roses, coloured like tarnished gold. Her costume of dark cloth fitted so beautifully over her breast and shoulders. His pride went up as he walked with her. He felt the station people, who knew him, eyed her with awe and admiration.

"I was sure you weren't coming," he laughed shakily.

She laughed in answer, almost with a little cry.

"And I wondered, when I was in the train, what*ever* I should do if you weren't there!" she said.

He caught her hand impulsively, and they went along the narrow twitchel. They took the road into Nuttall and over the Reckoning House Farm. It was a blue, mild day. Everywhere the brown leaves lay scattered; many scarlet hips stood upon the hedge beside the wood. He gathered a few for her to wear.

"Though, really," he said, as he fitted them into the breast of her coat, "you ought to object to my getting them, because of the birds. But they don't care much for rose-hips in this part, where they can get plenty of stuff. You often find the berries going rotten in the springtime."

So he chattered, scarcely aware of what he said, only knowing he was putting berries in the bosom of her coat, while she stood patiently for him. And she watched his quick hands, so full of life, and it seemed to her she had never *seen* anything before. Till now, everything had been indistinct.

They came near to the colliery. It stood quite still and black among the corn-fields, its immense heap of slag seen rising almost from the oats.

"What a pity there is a coal-pit here where it is so pretty!" said Clara.

"Do you think so?" he answered. "You see, I am so used to it I should miss it. No; and I like the pits here and there. I like the rows of trucks, and the headstocks, and the steam in the daytime, and the lights at night. When I was a boy, I always thought a pillar of cloud by day and a pillar of fire by night was a pit, with its steam, and its lights, and the burning bank,—and I thought the Lord was always at the pit-top."

As they drew near home she walked in silence, and seemed to hang back. He pressed her fingers in his own. She flushed, but gave no response.

"Don't you want to come home?" he asked.

"Yes, I want to come," she replied.

It did not occur to him that her position in his home would be rather a peculiar and difficult one. To him it seemed just as if one of his men friends were going to be introduced to his mother, only nicer.

The Morels lived in a house in an ugly street that ran down a steep hill. The street itself was hideous. The house was rather superior to most. It was old, grimy, with a big bay window, and it was semi-detached; but it looked gloomy. Then Paul opened the door to the garden, and all was different. The sunny afternoon was there, like another land. By the path grew tansy and little trees. In front of the window was a plot of sunny grass, with old lilacs round it. And away went the garden, with heaps of dishevelled chrysanthemums in the sunshine, down to the sycamore-tree, and the field, and beyond one looked over a few red-roofed cottages to the hills with all the glow of the autumn afternoon.

Mrs. Morel sat in her rocking-chair, wearing her black silk blouse. Her grey-brown hair was taken smooth back from her brow and her high temples; her face was rather pale. Clara, suffering, followed Paul into the kitchen. Mrs. Morel rose. Clara thought her a lady, even rather stiff. The young woman was very nervous. She had almost a wistful look, almost resigned.

"Mother—Clara," said Paul.

Mrs. Morel held out her hand and smiled.

"He has told me a good deal about you," she said.

The blood flamed in Clara's cheek.

"I hope you don't mind my coming," she faltered.

"I was pleased when he said he would bring you," replied Mrs. Morel.

Paul, watching, felt his heart contract with pain. His mother looked so small, and sallow, and done-for beside the luxuriant Clara.

"It's such a pretty day, mother!" he said. "And we saw a jay."

His mother looked at him; he had turned to her. She thought what a man he seemed, in his dark, well-made clothes. He was pale and detached-looking; it would be hard for any woman to keep him. Her heart glowed; then she was sorry for Clara.

"Perhaps you'll leave your things in the parlour," said Mrs. Morel nicely to the young woman.

"Oh, thank you," she replied.

"Come on," said Paul, and he led the way into the little front room, with its old piano, its mahogany furniture, its yellowing marble mantelpiece. A fire was burning; the place was littered with books and drawing-boards. "I leave my things lying about," he said. "It's so much easier."

She loved his artist's paraphernalia, and the books, and the photos of people. Soon he was telling her: this was William's young lady in the evening dress, this was Annie and her husband, this was Arthur and his wife and the baby. She felt as if she were being taken into the family. He showed her photos, books, sketches, and they talked a little while. Then they returned to the kitchen. Mrs. Morel put aside her book. Clara wore a blouse of fine silk chiffon, with narrow black-and-white stripes; her hair was done simply, coiled on top of her head. She looked rather stately and reserved.

"You have gone to live down Sneinton Boulevard?" said Mrs. Morel. "When I was a girl—girl, I say!—when I was a young woman *we* lived in Minerva Terrace."

"Oh, did you!" said Clara. "I have a friend in number 6."

And the conversation had started. They talked Nottingham and Nottingham people; it interested them both. Clara was still rather nervous; Mrs. Morel was still somewhat on her dignity. She clipped her language very clear and precise. But they were going to get on well together, Paul saw.

Mrs. Morel measured herself against the younger woman, and found herself easily stronger. Clara was deferential. She knew Paul's surprising regard for his mother, and she had dreaded the meeting, expecting someone rather hard and cold. She was surprised to find this little interested woman chatting with such readiness; and then she felt, as she felt with Paul, that she would not care to stand in Mrs. Morel's way. There was something so hard and certain in his mother, as if she never had a misgiving in her life.

Presently Morel came down, ruffled and yawning, from his afternoon sleep. He scratched his grizzled head, he podded in his stocking feet, his waistcoat hung open over his shirt. He seemed incongruous.

"This is Mrs. Dawes, father," said Paul.

Then Morel pulled himself together. Clara saw Paul's manner of bowing and shaking hands.

"Oh, indeed!" exclaimed Morel. "I am very glad to see you—I am, I assure you. But don't disturb yourself. No, no make yourself quite comfortable, and be very welcome."

Clara was astonished at this flood of hospitality from the old collier. He was so courteous, so gallant! She thought him most delightful.

"And may you have come far?" he asked.

"Only from Nottingham," she said.

"From Nottingham! Then you have had a beautiful day for your journey."

Then he strayed into the scullery to wash his hands and face, and from force of habit came on to the hearth with the towel to dry himself.

At tea Clara felt the refinement and sang-froid of the household. Mrs. Morel was perfectly at her ease. The pouring out the tea and attending to the people went on unconsciously, without interrupting her in her talk. There was a lot of room at the oval table; the china of dark blue willow-pattern looked pretty on the glossy cloth. There was a little bowl of small, yellow chrysanthemums. Clara felt she completed the circle, and it was a pleasure to her. But she was rather afraid of the self-possession of the Morels, father and all. She took their tone; there was a feeling of balance. It was a cool, clear atmosphere, where everyone was himself, and in harmony. Clara enjoyed it, but there was a fear deep at the bottom of her.

Paul cleared the table whilst his mother and Clara talked. Clara was conscious of his quick, vigorous body as it came and went, seeming blown quickly by a wind at its work. It was almost like the hither and thither of a leaf that comes unexpected. Most of herself went with him. By the way she leaned forward, as if listening, Mrs. Morel could see she was possessed elsewhere as she talked, and again the elder woman was sorry for her.

Having finished, he strolled down the garden, leaving the two women to talk. It was a hazy, sunny afternoon, mild and soft. Clara glanced through the window after him as he loitered among the chrysanthemums. She felt as if something almost tangible fastened her to him; yet he seemed so easy in his graceful, indolent movement, so detached as he tied up the too-heavy flower branches to their stakes, that she wanted to shriek in her helplessness.

Mrs. Morel rose.

"You will let me help you wash up," said Clara.

"Eh, there are so few, it will only take a minute," said the other.

Clara, however, dried the tea-things, and was glad to be on such good terms with his mother; but it was torture not to be able to follow him down the garden. At last she allowed herself to go; she felt as if a rope were taken off her ankle.

The afternoon was golden over the hills of Derbyshire. He stood across in the other garden, beside a bush of pale Michaelmas daisies, watching the last bees crawl into the hive. Hearing her coming, he turned to her with an easy motion, saying:

"It's the end of the run with these chaps."

Clara stood near him. Over the low red wall in front was the country and the far-off hills, all golden dim.

At that moment Miriam was entering through the garden-door. She saw Clara go up to him, saw him turn, and saw them come to rest together. Something in their perfect isolation together made her know that it was accomplished between them, that they were, as she put it, married. She walked very slowly down the cinder-track of the long garden.

Clara had pulled a button from a hollyhock spire, and was breaking it to get the seeds. Above her bowed head the pink flowers stared, as if defending her. The last bees were falling down to the hive.

"Count your money," laughed Paul, as she broke the flat seeds one by one from the roll of coin. She looked at him.

"I'm well off," she said, smiling.

"How much? Pf!" He snapped his fingers. "Can I turn them into gold?"

"I'm afraid not," she laughed.

They looked into each other's eyes, laughing. At that moment they became aware of Miriam. There was a click, and everything had altered.

"Hello, Miriam!" he exclaimed. "You said you'd come!"

"Yes. Had you forgotten?"

She shook hands with Clara, saying:

"It seems strange to see you here."

"Yes," replied the other; "it seems strange to be here."

There was a hesitation.

"This is pretty, isn't it?" said Miriam.

"I like it very much," replied Clara.

Then Miriam realised that Clara was accepted as she had never been.

"Have you come down alone?" asked Paul.

"Yes; I went to Agatha's to tea. We are going to chapel. I only called in for a moment to see Clara."

"You should have come in here to tea," he said.

Miriam laughed shortly, and Clara turned impatiently aside.

"Do you like the chrysanthemums?" he asked.

"Yes; they are very fine," replied Miriam.

"Which sort do you like best?" he asked.

"I don't know. The bronze, I think."

"I don't think you've seen all the sorts. Come and look. Come and see which are *your* favourites, Clara."

He led the two women back to his own garden, where the towsled bushes of flowers of all colours stood raggedly along the path down to the field. The situation did not embarrass him, to his knowledge.

"Look, Miriam; these are the white ones that came from your garden. They aren't so fine here, are they?"

"No," said Miriam.

"But they're hardier. You're so sheltered; things grow big and tender, and then die. These little yellow ones I like. Will you have some?"

While they were out there the bells began to ring in the church, sounding loud across the town and the field. Miriam looked at the tower, proud among the clustering roofs, and remembered the sketches he had brought her. It had been different then, but he had not left her even yet. She asked him for a book to read. He ran indoors.

"What! is that Miriam?" asked his mother coldly.

"Yes; she said she'd call and see Clara."

"You told her, then?" came the sarcastic answer.

"Yes; why shouldn't I?"

"There's certainly no reason why you shouldn't," said Mrs. Morel, and she returned to her book. He winced from his mother's irony, frowned irritably, thinking: "Why can't I do as I like?"

"You've not seen Mrs. Morel before?" Miriam was saying to Clara.

"No; but she's *so* nice!"

"Yes," said Miriam, dropping her head; "in some ways she's very fine."

"I should think so."

"Had Paul told you much about her?"

"He had talked a good deal."

"Ha!"

There was silence until he returned with the book.

"When will you want it back?" Miriam asked.

"When you like," he answered.

Clara turned to go indoors, whilst he accompanied Miriam to the gate.

"When will you come up to Willey Farm?" the latter asked.

"I couldn't say," replied Clara.

"Mother asked me to say she'd be pleased to see you any time, if you cared to come."

"Thank you; I should like to, but I can't say when."

"Oh, very well!" exclaimed Miriam rather bitterly, turning away.

She went down the path with her mouth to the flowers he had given her.

"You're sure you won't come in?" he said.

"No, thanks."

"We are going to chapel."

"Ah, I shall see you, then!" Miriam was very bitter.

"Yes."

They parted. He felt guilty towards her. She was bitter, and she scorned him. He still belonged to herself, she believed; yet he could have Clara, take her home, sit with her next his mother in chapel, give her the same hymn-book he had given herself years before. She heard him running quickly indoors.

But he did not go straight in. Halting on the plot of grass, he heard his mother's voice, then Clara's answer:

"What I hate is the bloodhound quality in Miriam."

"Yes," said his mother quickly, "yes; *doesn't it* make you hate her, now!"

His heart went hot, and he was angry with them for talking about the girl. What right had they to say that? Something in the speech itself stung him into a flame of hate against Miriam. Then his own heart rebelled furiously at Clara's taking the liberty of speaking so about Miriam. After all, the girl was the better woman of the two, he thought, if it came to goodness. He went indoors. His mother looked excited. She was beating with her hand rhythmically on the sofa-arm, as women do who are wearing out. He could never bear to see the movement. There was a silence; then he began to talk.

In chapel Miriam saw him find the place in the hymn-book for Clara, in exactly the same way as he used for herself. And during the sermon he could see the girl across the chapel, her hat throwing a dark shadow over her face. What did she think, seeing Clara with him? He did not stop to consider. He felt himself cruel towards Miriam.

After chapel he went over Pentrich with Clara. It was a dark autumn night. They had said good-bye to Miriam, and his heart had smitten him as he left the girl alone. "But it serves her right," he said inside himself, and it almost gave him pleasure to go off under her eyes with this other handsome woman.

There was a scent of damp leaves in the darkness. Clara's hand lay warm and inert in his own as they walked. He was full of conflict. The battle that raged inside him made him feel desperate.

Up Pentrich Hill Clara leaned against him as he went. He slid his arm round her waist. Feeling the strong motion of her body under his arm as she walked, the tightness in his chest because of Miriam relaxed, and the hot blood bathed him. He held her closer and closer.

Then: "You still keep on with Miriam," she said quietly.

"Only talk. There never *was* a great deal more than talk between us," he said bitterly.

"Your mother doesn't care for her," said Clara.

"No, or I might have married her. But it's all up really!"

Suddenly his voice went passionate with hate.

"If I was with her now, we should be jawing about the 'Christian Mystery', or some such tack. Thank God, I'm not!"

They walked on in silence for some time.

"But you can't really give her up," said Clara.

"I don't give her up, because there's nothing to give," he said.

"There is for her."

"I don't know why she and I shouldn't be friends as long as we live," he said. "But it'll only be friends."

Clara drew away from him, leaning away from contact with him.

"What are you drawing away for?" he asked.

She did not answer, but drew farther from him.

"Why do you want to walk alone?" he asked.

Still there was no answer. She walked resentfully, hanging her head.

"Because I said I would be friends with Miriam!" he exclaimed.

She would not answer him anything.

"I tell you it's only words that go between us," he persisted, trying to take her again.

She resisted. Suddenly he strode across in front of her, barring her way.

"Damn it!" he said. "What do you want now?"

"You'd better run after Miriam," mocked Clara.

The blood flamed up in him. He stood showing his teeth. She drooped sulkily. The lane was dark, quite lonely. He suddenly caught her in his arms, stretched forward, and put his mouth on her face in a kiss of rage. She turned frantically to avoid him. He held her fast. Hard and relentless his mouth came for her. Her breasts hurt against the wall of his chest. Helpless, she went loose in his arms, and he kissed her, and kissed her.

He heard people coming down the hill.

"Stand up! stand up!" he said thickly, gripping her arm till it hurt. If he had let go, she would have sunk to the ground.

She sighed and walked dizzily beside him. They went on in silence.

"We will go over the fields," he said; and then she woke up.

But she let herself be helped over the stile, and she walked in silence with him over the first dark field. It was the way to Nottingham and to the station, she knew. He seemed to be looking about. They came out on a bare hilltop where stood the dark figure of the ruined windmill. There he halted. They stood together high up in the darkness, looking at the lights scattered on the night before them, handfuls of glittering points, villages lying high and low on the dark, here and there.

"Like treading among the stars," he said, with a quaky laugh.

Then he took her in his arms, and held her fast. She moved aside her mouth to ask, dogged and low:

"What time is it?"

"It doesn't matter," he pleaded thickly.

"Yes it does—yes! I must go!"

"It's early yet," he said.

"What time is it?" she insisted.

All round lay the black night, speckled and spangled with lights.

"I don't know."

She put her hand on his chest, feeling for his watch. He felt the joints fuse into fire. She groped in his waistcoat pocket, while he stood panting. In the darkness she could see the round, pale face of the watch, but not the figures. She stooped over it. He was panting till he could take her in his arms again.

"I can't see," she said.

"Then don't bother."

"Yes; I'm going!" she said, turning away.

"Wait! I'll look!" But he could not see. "I'll strike a match."

He secretly hoped it was too late to catch the train. She saw the glowing lantern of his hands as he cradled the light: then his face lit up, his eyes fixed on the watch. Instantly all was dark again. All was black before her eyes; only a glowing match was red near her feet. Where was he?"

"What is it?" she asked, afraid.

"You can't do it," his voice answered out of the darkness.

There was a pause. She felt in his power. She had heard the ring in his voice. It frightened her.

"What time is it?" she asked, quiet, definite, hopeless.

"Two minutes to nine," he replied, telling the truth with a struggle.

"And can I get from here to the station in fourteen minutes?"

"No. At any rate——"

She could distinguish his dark form again a yard or so away. She wanted to escape.

"But can't I do it?" she pleaded.

"If you hurry," he said brusquely. "But you could easily walk it, Clara; it's only seven miles to the tram. I'll come with you."

"No; I want to catch the train."

"But why?"

"I do—I want to catch the train."

Suddenly his voice altered.

"Very well," he said, dry and hard. "Come along, then."

And he plunged ahead into the darkness. She ran after him, wanting to cry. Now he was hard and cruel to her. She ran over the rough, dark fields behind him, out of breath, ready to drop. But the double row of lights at the station drew nearer. Suddenly:

"There she is!" he cried, breaking into a run.

There was a faint rattling noise. Away to the right the train, like a luminous caterpillar, was threading across the night. The rattling ceased.

"She's over the viaduct. You'll just do it."

Clara ran, quite out of breath, and fell at last into the train. The whistle blew. He was gone. Gone!—and she was in a carriage full of people. She felt the cruelty of it.

He turned round and plunged home. Before he knew where he was he was in the kitchen at home. He was very pale. His eyes were dark and dangerous-looking, as if he were drunk. His mother looked at him.

"Well, I must say your boots are in a nice state!" she said.

He looked at his feet. Then he took off his overcoat. His mother wondered if he were drunk.

"She caught the train then?" she said.

"Yes."

"I hope *her* feet weren't so filthy. Where on earth you dragged her I don't know!"

He was silent and motionless for some time.

"Did you like her?" he asked grudgingly at last.

"Yes, I liked her. But you'll tire of her, my son; you know you will."

He did not answer. She noticed how he laboured in his breathing.

"Have you been running?" she asked.

"We had to run for the train."

"You'll go and knock yourself up. You'd better drink hot milk."

It was as good a stimulant as he could have, but he refused and went to bed. There he lay face down on the counterpane, and shed tears of rage and pain. There was a physical pain that made him bite his lips till they bled, and the chaos inside him left him unable to think, almost to feel.

"This is how she serves me, is it?" he said in his heart, over and over, pressing his face in the quilt. And he hated her. Again he went over the scene, and again he hated her.

The next day there was a new aloofness about him. Clara was very gentle, almost loving. But he treated her distantly, with a touch of contempt. She sighed, continuing to be gentle. He came round.

One evening of that week Sarah Bernhardt was at the Theatre Royal in Nottingham, giving *"La Dame aux Camélias"*. Paul wanted to see this old and famous actress, and he asked Clara to accompany him. He told his mother to leave the key in the window for him.

"Shall I book seats?" he asked of Clara.

"Yes. And put on an evening suit, will you? I've never seen you in it."

"But, good Lord, Clara! Think of *me* in evening suit at the theatre!" he remonstrated.

"Would you rather not?" she asked.

"I will if you *want* me to; but I s'll feel a fool."

She laughed at him.

"Then feel a fool for my sake, once, won't you?"

The request made his blood flush up.

"I suppose I s'll have to."

"What are you taking a suitcase for?" his mother asked.

He blushed furiously.

"Clara asked me," he said.

"And what seats are you going in?"

"Circle—three-and-six each!"

"Well, I'm sure!" exclaimed his mother sarcastically.

"It's only once in the bluest of blue moons," he said.

He dressed at Jordan's, put on an overcoat and a cap, and met Clara in a café. She was with one of her suffragette friends. She wore an old long coat, which did not suit her, and had a little wrap over her head, which he hated. The three went to the theatre together.

Clara took off her coat on the stairs, and he discovered she was in a sort of semi-evening dress, that left her arms and neck and part of her breast bare. Her hair was done fashionably. The dress, a simple thing of green crape, suited her. She looked quite grand, he thought. He could see her figure inside the frock, as if that were wrapped closely round her. The firmness and the softness of her upright body could almost be felt as he looked at her. He clenched his fists.

And he was to sit all the evening beside her beautiful naked arm, watching the strong throat rise from the strong chest, watching the breasts under the green stuff, the curve of her limbs in the tight dress. Something in him hated her again for submitting him to this torture of nearness. And he loved her as she balanced her head and stared straight in front of her, pouting, wistful, immobile, as if she yielded herself to her fate because it was too strong for her. She could not help herself; she was in the grip of something bigger than herself. A kind of eternal look about her, as if she were a wistful sphinx, made it necessary for him to kiss her. He dropped his programme, and crouched down on the floor to get it, so that he could kiss her hand and wrist. Her beauty was a torture to him. She sat immobile. Only, when the lights went down, she sank a little against him, and he caressed her hand and arm with his fingers. He could smell her faint perfume. All the time his blood kept sweeping up in great white-hot waves that killed his consciousness momentarily.

The drama continued. He saw it all in the distance, going on somewhere; he did not know where, but it seemed far away inside him. He was Clara's white heavy arms, her throat, her moving bosom. That seemed to be himself. Then away somewhere the play went on, and he was identified with that also. There was no himself. The grey and black eyes of Clara, her bosom coming down on him, her arm that he held gripped between his hands, were all that existed. Then he felt himself small and helpless, her towering in her force above him.

Only the intervals, when the lights came up, hurt him expressibly. He wanted to run anywhere, so long at it would be dark again. In a maze, he wandered out for a drink. Then the lights were out, and the strange, insane reality of Clara and the drama took hold of him again.

The play went on. But he was obsessed by the desire to kiss the tiny blue vein that nestled in the bend of her arm. He could feel it. His whole face seemed suspended till he had put his lips there. It must be done. And the other people! At last he bent quickly forward and touched it with his lips. His moustache brushed the sensitive flesh. Clara shivered, drew away her arm.

When all was over, the lights up, the people clapping, he came to himself and looked at his watch. His train was gone.

"I s'll have to walk home!" he said.

Clara looked at him.

"It is too late?" she asked.

He nodded. Then he helped her on with her coat.

"I love you! You look beautiful in that dress," he murmured over her shoulder, among the throng of bustling people.

She remained quiet. Together they went out of the theatre. He saw the cabs waiting, the people passing. It seemed he met a pair of brown eyes which hated him. But he did not know. He and Clara turned away, mechanically taking the direction to the station.

The train had gone. He would have to walk the ten miles home.

"It doesn't matter," he said. "I shall enjoy it."

"Won't you," she said, flushing, "come home for the night? I can sleep with mother."

He looked at her. Their eyes met.

"What will your mother say?" he asked.

"She won't mind."

"You're sure?"

"Quite!"

"*Shall* I come?"

"If you will."

"Very well."

And they turned away. At the first stopping-place they took the car. The wind blew fresh in their faces. The town was dark; the tram tipped in its haste. He sat with her hand fast in his.

"Will your mother be gone to bed?" he asked.

"She may be. I hope not."

They hurried along the silent, dark little street, the only people out of doors. Clara quickly entered the house. He hesitated.

He leaped up the step and was in the room. Her mother appeared in the inner doorway, large and hostile.

"Who have you got there?" she asked.

"It's Mr. Morel; he has missed his train. I thought we might put him up for the night, and save him a ten-mile walk."

"H'm" exclaimed Mrs. Radford. "That's your look-out! If you've invited him, he's very welcome as far as I'm concerned. *You* keep the house!"

"If you don't like me, I'll go away again," he said.

"Nay, nay, you needn't! Come along in! I dunno what you'll think of the supper I'd got her."

It was a little dish of chip potatoes and a piece of bacon. The table was roughly laid for one.

"You can have some more bacon," continued Mrs. Radford. "More chips you can't have."

"It's a shame to bother you," he said.

"Oh, don't you be apologetic! It doesn't *do* wi' me! You treated her to the theatre, didn't you?" There was a sarcasm in the last question.

"Well?" laughed Paul uncomfortably.

"Well, and what's an inch of bacon! Take your coat off."

The big, straight-standing woman was trying to estimate the situation. She moved about the cupboard. Clara took his coat. The room was very warm and cosy in the lamplight.

"My sirs!" exclaimed Mrs. Radford; "but you two's a pair of bright beauties, I must say! What's all that get-up for?"

"I believe we don't know," he said, feeling a victim.

"There isn't room in *this* house for two such bobby-dazzlers, if you fly your kites *that* high!" she rallied them. It was a nasty thrust.

He in his dinner jacket, and Clara in her green dress and bare arms, were confused. They felt they must shelter each other in that little kitchen.

"And look at *that* blossom!" continued Mrs. Radford, pointing to Clara. "What does she reckon she did it for?"

Paul looked at Clara. She was rosy; her neck was warm with blushes. There was a moment of silence.

"You like to see it, don't you?" he asked.

The mother had them in her power. All the time his heart was beating hard, and he was tight with anxiety. But he would fight her.

"Me like to see it!" exclaimed the old woman. "What should I like to see her make a fool of herself for?"

"I've seen people look bigger fools," he said. Clara was under his protection now.

"Oh, ay! and when was that?" came the sarcastic rejoinder.

"When they made frights of themselves," he answered.

Mrs. Radford, large and threatening, stood suspended on the hearthrug, holding her fork.

"They're fools either road," she answered at length, turning to the Dutch oven.

"No," he said, fighting stoutly. "Folk ought to look as well as they can."

"And do you call *that* looking nice!" cried the mother, pointing a scornful fork at Clara. "That—that looks as if it wasn't properly dressed!"

"I believe you're jealous that you can't swank as well," he said laughing.

"Me! I could have worn evening dress with anybody, if I'd wanted to!" came the scornful answer.

"And why didn't you want to?" he asked pertinently. "Or *did* you wear it?"

There was a long pause. Mrs. Radford readjusted the bacon in the Dutch oven. His heart beat fast, for fear he had offended her.

"Me!" she exclaimed at last. "No, I didn't! And when I was in service, I knew as soon as one of the maids came out in bare shoulders what sort *she* was, going to her sixpenny hop!"

"Were you too good to go to a sixpenny hop?" he said.

Clara sat with bowed head. His eyes were dark and glittering. Mrs. Radford took the Dutch oven from the fire, and stood near him, putting bits of bacon on his plate.

"*There's* a nice crozzly bit!" she said.

"Don't give me the best!" he said.

"*She's* got what *she* wants," was the answer.

There was a sort of scornful forbearance in the woman's tone that made Paul know she was mollified.

"But *do* have some!" he said to Clara.

She looked up at him with her grey eyes, humiliated and lonely.

"No thanks!" she said.

"Why won't you?" he answered carelessly.

The blood was beating up like fire in his veins. Mrs. Radford sat down again, large and impressive and aloof. He left Clara altogether to attend to the mother.

"They say Sarah Bernhardt's fifty," he said.

"Fifty! She's turned sixty!" came the scornful answer.

"Well," he said, "you'd never think it! She made me want to howl even now."

"I should like to see myself howling at *that* bad old baggage!" said Mrs. Radford. "It's time she began to think herself a grandmother, not a shrieking catamaran——"

He laughed.

"A catamaran is a boat the Malays use," he said.

"And it's a word as *I* use," she retorted.

"My mother does sometimes, and it's no good my telling her," he said.

"I s'd think she boxes your ears," said Mrs. Radford, good-humouredly.

"She'd like to, and she says she will, so I give her a little stool to stand on."

"That's the worst of my mother," said Clara. "She never wants a stool for anything."

"But she often can't touch *that* lady with a long prop," retorted Mrs. Radford to Paul.

"I s'd think she doesn't want touching with a prop," he laughed. "*I* shouldn't."

"It might do the pair of you good to give you a crack on the head with one," said the mother, laughing suddenly.

"Why are you so vindictive towards me?" he said. "I've not stolen anything from you."

"No; I'll watch that," laughed the older woman.

Soon the supper was finished. Mrs. Radford sat guard in her chair. Paul lit a cigarette. Clara went upstairs, returning with a sleeping-suit, which she spread on the fender to air.

"Why, I'd forgot all about *them!*" said Mrs. Radford. "Where have they sprung from?"

"Out of my drawer."

"H'm! You bought 'em for Baxter, an' he wouldn't wear 'em, would he?"— laughing. "Said he reckoned to do wi'out trousers i' bed." She turned confidentially to Paul, saying: "He couldn't *bear* 'em, them pyjama things."

The young man sat making rings of smoke.

"Well, it's everyone to his taste," he laughed.

Then followed a little discussion of the merits of pyjamas.

"My mother loves me in them," he said. "She says I'm a pierrot."

"I can imagine they'd suit you," said Mrs. Radford.

After a while he glanced at the little clock that was ticking on the mantelpiece. It was half-past twelve.

"It is funny," he said, "but it takes hours to settle down to sleep after the theatre."

"It's about time you did," said Mrs. Radford, clearing the table.

"Are *you* tired?" he asked of Clara.

"Not the least bit," she answered, avoiding his eyes.

"Shall we have a game at cribbage?" he said.

"I've forgotten it."

"Well, I'll teach you again. May we play crib, Mrs. Radford?" he asked.

"You'll please yourselves," she said; "but it's pretty late."

"A game or so will make us sleepy," he answered.

Clara brought the cards, and sat spinning her wedding-ring whilst he shuffled them. Mrs. Radford was washing up in the scullery. As it grew later Paul felt the situation getting more and more tense.

"Fifteen two, fifteen four, fifteen six, and two's eight——!"

The clock struck one. Still the game continued. Mrs. Radford had done all the little jobs preparatory to going to bed, had locked the door and filled the kettle. Still Paul went on dealing and counting. He was obsessed by Clara's arms and throat. He believed he could see where the division was just beginning for her breasts. He could not leave her. She watched his hands, and felt her joints melt as they moved quickly. She was so near; it was almost as if he touched her, and yet not quite. His mettle was roused. He hated Mrs. Radford. She sat on, nearly dropping asleep, but determined and obstinate in her chair. Paul glanced at her, then at Clara. She met his eyes, that were angry, mocking, and hard as steel. Her own answered him in shame. He knew *she,* at any rate, was of his mind. He played on.

At last Mrs. Radford roused herself stiffly, and said:

"Isn't it nigh on time you two was thinking o' bed?"

Paul played on without answering. He hated her sufficiently to murder her.

"Half a minute," he said.

The elder woman rose and sailed stubbornly into the scullery, returning with his candle, which she put on the mantelpiece. Then she sat down again. The hatred of her went so hot down his veins, he dropped his cards.

"We'll stop, then," he said, but his voice was still a challenge.

Clara saw his mouth shut hard. Again he glanced at her. It seemed like an agreement. She bent over the cards, coughing, to clear her throat.

"Well, I'm glad you've finished," said Mrs. Radford. "Here, take your things"—she thrust the warm suit in his hand—"and this is your candle. Your room's over this; there's only two, so you can't go far wrong. Well, good-night. I hope you'll rest well."

"I'm sure I shall; I always do," he said.

"Yes; and so you ought at your age," she replied.

He bade good-night to Clara, and went. The twisting stairs of white, scrubbed wood creaked and clanged at every step. He went doggedly. The two doors faced each other. He went in his room, pushed the door to, without fastening the latch.

It was a small room with a large bed. Some of Clara's hairpins were on the dressing-table—her hair-brush. Her clothes and some skirts hung under a cloth in a corner. There was actually a pair of stockings over a chair. He explored the room. Two books of his own were there on the shelf. He undressed, folded his suit, and sat on the bed, listening. Then he blew out the candle, lay down, and in two minutes was almost asleep. Then click!—he was wide awake and writhing in torment. It was as if, when he had nearly got to sleep, something had bitten him suddenly and sent him mad. He sat up and looked at the room in the darkness, his feet doubled under him, perfectly motionless, listening. He heard a cat somewhere away outside; then the heavy, poised tread of the mother; then Clara's distinct voice:

"Will you unfasten my dress?"

There was silence for some time. At last the mother said:

"Now then! aren't you coming up?"

"No, not yet," replied the daughter calmly.

"Oh, very well then! If it's not late enough, stop a bit longer. Only you needn't come waking me up when I've got to sleep."

"I shan't be long," said Clara.

Immediately afterwards Paul heard the mother slowly mounting the stairs. The candlelight flashed through the cracks in his door. Her dress brushed the door, and his heart jumped. Then it was dark, and he heard the clatter of her latch. She was very leisurely indeed in her preparations for sleep. After a long time it was quite still. He sat strung up on the bed, shivering slightly. His door was an inch open. As Clara came upstairs, he would intercept her. He waited. All was dead silence. The clock struck two. Then he heard a slight scrape of the fender downstairs. Now he could not help himself. His shivering was uncontrollable. He felt he must go or die.

He stepped off the bed, and stood a moment, shuddering. Then he went straight to the door. He tried to step lightly. The first stair cracked like a shot. He listened. The old woman stirred in her bed. The staircase was dark. There was a slit of light under the stair-foot door, which opened into the kitchen. He stood a moment. Then he went on, mechanically. Every step creaked, and his back was creeping, lest the old woman's door should open behind him up above. He fumbled with the door at the bottom. The latch opened with a loud clack. He went through into the kitchen, and shut the door noisily behind him. The old woman daren't come now.

Then he stood, arrested. Clara was kneeling on a pile of white underclothing on the hearth-rug, her back towards him, warming herself. She did not look round, but sat crouching on her heels, and her rounded beautiful back was towards him, and her face was hidden. She was warming her body at the fire for consolation. The glow was rosy on one side, the shadow was dark and warm on the other. Her arms hung slack.

He shuddered violently, clenching his teeth and fists hard to keep control. Then he went forward to her. He put one hand on her shoulder, the fingers of the other hand under her chin to raise her face. A convulsed shiver ran through her, once, twice, at his touch. She kept her head bent.

"Sorry!" he murmured, realising that his hands were very cold.

Then she looked up at him, frightened, like a thing that is afraid of death.

"My hands are so cold," he murmured.

"I like it," she whispered, closing her eyes.

The breath of her words were on his mouth. Her arms clasped his knees. The cord of his sleeping-suit dangled against her and made her shiver. As the warmth went into him, his shuddering became less.

At length, unable to stand so any more, he raised her, and she buried her head on his shoulder. His hands went over her slowly with an infinite tenderness of caress. She clung close to him, trying to hide herself against him. He clasped her very fast. Then at last she looked at him, mute, imploring, looking to see if she must be ashamed.

His eyes were dark, very deep, and very quiet. It was as if her beauty and his taking it hurt him, made him sorrowful. He looked at her with a little pain, and was afraid. He was so humble before her. She kissed him fervently on the eyes, first one, then the other, and she folded herself to him. She gave herself. He held her fast. It was a moment intense almost to agony.

She stood letting him adore her and tremble with joy of her. It healed her hurt pride. It healed her; it made her glad. It made her feel erect and proud again. Her pride had been wounded inside her. She had been cheapened. Now she radiated with joy and pride again. It was her restoration and her recognition.

Then he looked at her, his face radiant. They laughed to each other, and he strained her to his chest. The seconds ticked off, the minutes passed, and still the two stood clasped rigid together, mouth to mouth, like a statue in one block.

But again his fingers went seeking over her, restless, wandering, dissatisfied. The hot blood came up wave upon wave. She laid her head on his shoulder.

"Come you to my room," he murmured.

She looked at him and shook her head, her mouth pouting disconsolately, her eyes heavy with passion. He watched her fixedly.

"Yes!" he said.

Again she shook her head.

"Why not?" he asked.

She looked at him still heavily, sorrowfully, and again she shook her head. His eyes hardened, and he gave way.

When, later on, he was back in bed, he wondered why she had refused to come to him openly, so that her mother would know. At any rate, then things would have been definite. And she could have stayed with him the night, without having to go, as she was, to her mother's bed. It was strange, and he could not understand it. And then almost immediately he fell asleep.

He awoke in the morning with someone speaking to him. Opening his eyes, he saw Mrs. Radford, big and stately, looking down on him. She held a cup of tea in her hand.

"Do you think you're going to sleep till Doomsday?" she said.

He laughed at once.

"It ought only to be about five o'clock," he said.

"Well," she answered, "it's half-past seven, whether or not. Here, I've brought you a cup of tea."

He rubbed his face, pushed the tumbled hair off his forehead, and roused himself.

"What's it so late for!" he grumbled.

He resented being wakened. It amused her. She saw his neck in the flannel sleeping-jacket, as white and round as a girl's. He rubbed his hair crossly.

"It's no good your scratching your head," she said. "It won't make it no earlier. Here, an' how long d'you think I'm going to stand waiting wi' this here cup?"

"Oh, dash the cup!" he said.

"You should go to bed earlier," said the woman.

He looked up at her, laughing with impudence.

"I went to bed before *you* did," he said.

"Yes, my Guyney, you did!" she exclaimed.

"Fancy," he said, stirring his tea, "having tea brought to bed to me! My mother'll think I'm ruined for life."

"Don't she never do it?" asked Mrs. Radford.

"She'd as leave think of flying."

"Ah, I always spoilt my lot! That's why they've turned out such bad uns," said the elderly woman.

"You'd only Clara," he said. "And Mr. Radford's in heaven. So I suppose there's only you left to be the bad un."

"I'm not bad; I'm only soft," she said, as she went out of the bedroom. "I'm only a fool, I am!"

Clara was very quiet at breakfast, but she had a sort of air of proprietorship over him that pleased him infinitely. Mrs. Radford was evidently fond of him. He began to talk of his painting.

"What's the good," exclaimed the mother, "of your whittling and worrying and twistin' and too-in' at that painting of yours? What *good* does it do you, I should like to know? You'd better be enjoyin' yourself."

"Oh, but," exclaimed Paul, "I made over thirty guineas last year."

"Did you! Well, that's a consideration, but it's nothing to the time you put in."

"And I've got four pounds owing. A man said he'd give me five pounds if I'd paint him and his missis and the dog and the cottage. And I went and put the fowls in instead of the dog, and he was waxy, so I had to knock a quid off. I was sick of it, and I didn't like the dog. I made a picture of it. What shall I do when he pays me the four pounds?"

"Nay! you know your own uses for your money," said Mrs. Radford.

"But I'm going to bust this four pounds. Should we go to the seaside for a day or two?"

"Who?"

"You and Clara and me."

"What, on your money!" she exclaimed, half-wrathful.

"Why not?"

"*You* wouldn't be long in breaking your neck at a hurdle race!" she said.

"So long as I get a good run for my money! Will you?"

"Nay; you may settle that atween you."

"And you're willing?" he asked, amazed and rejoicing.

"You'll do as you like," said Mrs. Radford, "whether I'm willing or not."

XIII

BAXTER DAWES

Soon after Paul had been to the theatre with Clara, he was drinking in the Punch Bowl with some friends of his when Dawes came in. Clara's husband was growing stout; his eyelids were getting slack over his brown eyes; he was losing his healthy firmness of flesh. He was very evidently on the downward track. Having quarrelled with his sister, he had gone into cheap lodgings. His mistress had left him for a man who would marry her. He had been in prison one night for fighting when he was drunk, and there was a shady betting episode in which he was concerned.

Paul and he were confirmed enemies, and yet there was between them that peculiar feeling of intimacy, as if they were secretly near to each other, which sometimes exists between two people, although they never speak to one another. Paul often thought of Baxter Dawes, often wanted to get at him and be friends with him. He knew that Dawes often thought about him, and that the man was drawn to him by some bond or other. And yet the two never looked at each other save in hostility.

Since he was a superior employee at Jordan's, it was the thing for Paul to offer Dawes a drink.

"What'll you have?" he asked of him.

"Nowt wi' a bleeder like you!" replied the man.

Paul turned away with a slight disdainful movement of the shoulders, very irritating.

"The aristocracy," he continued, "is really a military institution. Take Germany, now. She's got thousands of aristocrats whose only means of existence is the army. They're deadly poor, and life's deadly slow. So they hope for a war. They look for war as a chance of getting on. Till there's a war they are idle good-for-nothings. When there's a war, they are leaders and commanders. There you are, then—they *want* war!"

He was not a favourite debater in the public-house, being too quick and overbearing. He irritated the older men by his assertive manner, and his cocksureness. They listened in silence, and were not sorry when he finished.

Dawes interrupted the young man's flow of eloquence by asking, in a loud sneer:

"Did you learn all that at th' theatre th' other night?"

Paul looked at him; their eyes met. Then he knew Dawes had seen him coming out of the theatre with Clara.

"Why, what about th' theatre?" asked one of Paul's associates, glad to get a dig at the young fellow, and sniffing something tasty.

"Oh, him in a bob-tailed evening suit, on the lardy-da!" sneered Dawes, jerking his head contemptuously at Paul.

"That's comin' it strong," said the mutual friend. "Tart an' all?"

"Tart, begod!" said Dawes.

"Go on; let's have it!" cried the mutual friend.

"You've got it," said Dawes, "an' I reckon Morelly had it an' all."

"Well, I'll be jiggered!" said the mutual friend. "An' was it a proper tart?"

"Tart, God blimey—yes!"

"How do you know?"

"Oh," said Dawes, "I reckon he spent t' night——"

There was a good deal of laughter at Paul's expense.

"But who *was* she? D'you know her?" asked the mutual friend.

"I should *shay sho,*" said Dawes.

This brought another burst of laughter.

"Then spit it out," said the mutual friend.

Dawes shook his head, and took a gulp of beer.

"It's a wonder he hasn't let on himself," he said. "He'll be braggin' of it in a bit."

"Come on, Paul," said his friend; "it's no good. You might just as well own up."

"Own up what? That I happened to take a friend to the theatre?"

"Oh well, if it was all right, tell us who she was, lad," said the friend.

"She *was* all right," said Dawes.

Paul was furious. Dawes wiped his golden moustache with his fingers, sneering.

"Strike me——! One o' that sort?" said the mutual friend. "Paul, boy, I'm surprised at you. And do you know her, Baxter?"

"Just a bit, like!"

He winked at the other men.

"Oh well," said Paul, "I'll be going!"

The mutual friend laid a detaining hand on his shoulder.

"Nay," he said, "you don't get off as easy as that, my lad. We've got to have a full account of this business."

"Then get it from Dawes!" he said.

"You shouldn't funk your own deeds, man," remonstrated the friend.

Then Dawes made a remark which caused Paul to throw half a glass of beer in his face.

"Oh, Mr. Morel!" cried the barmaid, and she rang the bell for the "chucker-out".

Dawes spat and rushed for the young man. At that minute a brawny fellow with his shirt-sleeves rolled up and his trousers tight over his haunches intervened.

"Now, then!" he said, pushing his chest in front of Dawes.

"Come out!" cried Dawes.

Paul was leaning, white and quivering, against the brass rail of the bar. He hated Dawes, wished something could exterminate him at that minute; and at the same time, seeing the wet hair on the man's forehead, he thought he looked pathetic. He did not move.

"Come out, you——," said Dawes.

"That's enough, Dawes," cried the barmaid.

"Come on," said the "chucker-out", with kindly insistence, "you'd better be getting on."

And, by making Dawes edge away from his own close proximity, he worked him to the door.

"*That's* the little sod as started it!" cried Dawes, half-cowed, pointing to Paul Morel.

"Why, what a story, Mr. Dawes!" said the barmaid. "You know it was you all the time."

Still the "chucker-out" kept thrusting his chest forward at him, still he kept edging back, until he was in the doorway and on the steps outside; then he turned round.

"All right," he said, nodding straight at his rival.

Paul had a curious sensation of pity, almost of affection, mingled with violent hate, for the man. The coloured door swung to; there was silence in the bar.

"Serve him jolly well right!" said the barmaid.

"But it's a nasty thing to get a glass of beer in your eyes," said the mutual friend.

"I tell you I was glad he did," said the barmaid. "Will you have another, Mr. Morel?"

She held up Paul's glass questioningly. He nodded.

"He's a man as doesn't care for anything, is Baxter Dawes," said one.

"Pooh! is he?" said the barmaid. "He's a loud-mouthed one, he is, and they're never much good. Give me a pleasant-spoken chap, if you want a devil!"

"Well, Paul, my lad," said the friend, "you'll have to take care of yourself now for a while."

"You won't have to give him a chance over you, that's all," said the barmaid.

"Can you box?" asked a friend.

"Not a bit," he answered, still very white.

"I might give you a turn or two," said the friend.

"Thanks, I haven't time."

And presently he took his departure.

"Go along with him, Mr. Jenkinson," whispered the barmaid, tipping Mr. Jenkinson the wink.

The man nodded, took his hat, said: "Good-night all!" very heartily, and followed Paul, calling:

"Half a minute, old man. You an' me's going the same road, I believe."

"Mr. Morel doesn't like it," said the barmaid. "You'll see, we shan't have him in much more. I'm sorry; he's good company. And Baxter Dawes wants locking up, that's what he wants."

Paul would have died rather than his mother should get to know of this affair. He suffered tortures of humiliation and self-consciousness. There was now a good deal of his life of which necessarily he could not speak to his mother. He had a life apart from her—his sexual life. The rest she still kept. But he felt he had to conceal something from her, and it irked him. There was a certain silence between them, and he felt he had, in that silence, to defend himself against her; he felt condemned by her. Then sometimes he hated her, and pulled at her bondage. His life wanted to free itself of her. It was like a circle where life turned back on itself, and got no farther. She bore him, loved him, kept him, and his love turned back into her, so that he could not be free to go forward with his own life, really love another woman. At this period, unknowingly, he resisted his mother's influence. He did not tell her things; there was a distance between them.

Clara was happy, almost sure of him. She felt she had at last got him for herself; and then again came the uncertainty. He told her jestingly of the affair with her husband. Her colour came up, her grey eyes flashed.

"That's him to a 'T'," she cried—"like a navvy! He's not fit for mixing with decent folk."

"Yet you married him," he said.

It made her furious that he reminded her.

"I did!" she cried. "But how was I to know?"

"I think he might have been rather nice," he said.

"You think *I* made him what he is!" she exclaimed.

"Oh no! he made himself. But there's something about him——"

Clara looked at her lover closely. There was something in him she hated, a sort of detached criticism of herself, a coldness which made her woman's soul harden against him.

"And what are you going to do?" she asked.

"How?"

"About Baxter."

"There's nothing to do, is there?" he replied.

"You can fight him if you have to, I suppose?" she said.

"No; I haven't the least sense of the 'fist'. It's funny. With most men there's the instinct to clench the fist and hit. It's not so with me. I should want a knife or a pistol or something to fight with."

"Then you'd better carry something," she said.

"Nay," he laughed; "I'm not daggeroso."

"But he'll do something to you. You don't know him."

"All right," he said, "we'll see."

"And you'll let him?"

"Perhaps, if I can't help it."

"And if he kills you?" she said.

"I should be sorry, for his sake and mine."

Clara was silent for a moment.

"You *do* make me angry!" she exclaimed.

"That's nothing afresh," he laughed.

"But why are you so silly? You don't know him."

"And don't want."

"Yes, but you're not going to let a man do as he likes with you?"

"What must I do?" he replied, laughing.

"*I* should carry a revolver," she said. "I'm sure he's dangerous."

"I might blow my fingers off," he said.

"No; but won't you?" she pleaded.

"No."

"Not anything?"

"No."

"And you'll leave him to——?"

"Yes."

"You are a fool!"

"Fact!"

She set her teeth with anger.

"I could *shake* you!" she cried, trembling with passion.

"Why?"

"Let a man like *him* do as he likes with you."

"You can go back to him if he triumphs," he said.

"Do you want me to hate you?" she asked.

"Well, I only tell you," he said.

"And *you* say you *love* me!" she exclaimed, low and indignant.

"Ought I to slay him to please you?" he said. "But if I did, see what a hold he'd have over me."

"Do you think I'm a fool!" she exclaimed.

"Not at all. But you don't understand me, my dear."

There was a pause between them.

"But you ought *not* to expose yourself," she pleaded.

He shrugged his shoulders.

    " 'The man in righteousness arrayed,
      The pure and blameless liver,
    Needs not the keen Toledo blade,
      Nor venom-freighted quiver,' "

he quoted.

She looked at him searchingly.

"I wish I could understand you," she said.

"There's simply nothing to understand," he laughed.

She bowed her head, brooding.

He did not see Dawes for several days; then one morning as he ran upstairs from the Spiral room he almost collided with the burly metal-worker.

"What the——!" cried the smith.

"Sorry!" said Paul, and passed on.

"Sorry!" sneered Dawes.

Paul whistled lightly, "Put Me among the Girls".

"I'll stop your whistle, my jockey!" he said.

The other took no notice.

"You're goin' to answer for that job of the other night."

Paul went to his desk in his corner, and turned over the leaves of the ledger.

"Go and tell Fanny I want order 097, quick!" he said to his boy.

Dawes stood in the doorway, tall and threatening, looking at the top of the young man's head.

"Six and five's eleven and seven's one-and-six," Paul added aloud.

"An' you hear, do you!" said Dawes.

"Five and ninepence!" He wrote a figure. "What's that?" he said.

"I'm going to show you what it is," said the smith.

The other went on adding the figures aloud.

"Yer crawlin' little——, yer daresn't face me proper!"

Paul quickly snatched the heavy ruler. Dawes started. The young man ruled some lines in his ledger. The elder man was infuriated.

"But wait till I light on you, no matter where it is, I'll settle your hash for a bit, yer little swine!"

"All right," said Paul.

At that the smith started heavily from the doorway. Just then a whistle piped shrilly. Paul went to the speaking-tube.

"Yes!" he said, and he listened. "Er—yes!" He listened, then he laughed. "I'll come down directly. I've got a visitor just now."

Dawes knew from his tone that he had been speaking to Clara. He stepped forward.

"Yer little devil!" he said. "I'll visitor you, inside of two minutes! Think I'm goin' to have *you* whipperty-snappin' round?"

The other clerks in the warehouse looked up. Paul's office-boy appeared, holding some white article.

"Fanny says you could have had it last night if you'd let her know," he said.

"All right," answered Paul, looking at the stocking. "Get it off."

Dawes stood frustrated, helpless with rage. Morel turned round.

"Excuse me a minute," he said to Dawes, and he would have run downstairs.

"By God, I'll stop your gallop!" shouted the smith, seizing him by the arm. He turned quickly.

"Hey! Hey!" cried the office-boy, alarmed.

Thomas Jordan started out of his little glass office, and came running down the room.

"What's a-matter, what's a-matter?" he said, in his old man's sharp voice.

"I'm just goin' ter settle this little——, that's all," said Dawes desperately.

"What do you mean?" snapped Thomas Jordan.

"What I say," said Dawes, but he hung fire.

Morel was leaning against the counter, ashamed, half-grinning.

"What's it all about?" snapped Thomas Jordan.

"Couldn't say," said Paul, shaking his head and shrugging his shoulders.

"Couldn't yer, couldn't yer!" cried Dawes, thrusting forward his handsome, furious face, and squaring his fist.

"Have you finished?" cried the old man, strutting. "Get off about your business, and don't come here tipsy in the morning."

Dawes turned his big frame slowly upon him.

"Tipsy!" he said. "Who's tipsy? I'm no more tipsy than *you* are!"

"We've heard that song before," snapped the old man. "Now you get off, and don't be long about it. Comin' *here* with your rowdying."

The smith looked down contemptuously on his employer. His hands, large, and grimy, and yet well shaped for his labour, worked restlessly. Paul remembered they were the hands of Clara's husband, and a flash of hate went through him.

"Get out before you're turned out!" snapped Thomas Jordan.

"Why, who'll turn me out?" said Dawes, beginning to sneer.

Mr. Jordan started, marched up to the smith, waving him off, thrusting his stout little figure at the man, saying:

"Get off my premises—get off!"

He seized and twitched Dawes's arm.

"Come off!" said the smith, and with a jerk of the elbow he sent the little manufacturer staggering backwards.

Before anyone could help him, Thomas Jordan had collided with the flimsy spring-door. It had given way, and let him crash down the half-dozen steps into Fanny's room. There was a second of amazement; then men and girls were running. Dawes stood a moment looking bitterly on the scene, then he took his departure.

Thomas Jordan was shaken and bruised, not otherwise hurt. He was, however, beside himself with rage. He dismissed Dawes from his employment, and summoned him for assault.

At the trial Paul Morel had to give evidence. Asked how the trouble began, he said:

"Dawes took occasion to insult Mrs. Dawes and me because I accompanied her to the theatre one evening; then I threw some beer at him, and he wanted his revenge."

"*Cherchez la femme!*" smiled the magistrate.

The case was dismissed after the magistrate had told Dawes he thought him a skunk.

"You gave the case away," snapped Mr. Jordan to Paul.

"I don't think I did," replied the latter. "Besides, you didn't really want a conviction, did you?"

"What do you think I took the case up for?"

"Well," said Paul, "I'm sorry if I said the wrong thing." Clara was also very angry.

"Why need *my* name have been dragged in?" she said.

"Better speak it openly than leave it to be whispered."

"There was no need for anything at all," she declared.

"We are none the poorer," he said indifferently.

"*You* may not be," she said.

"And you?" he asked.

"I need never have been mentioned."

"I'm sorry," he said; but he did not sound sorry.

He told himself easily: "She will come round." And she did.

He told his mother about the fall of Mr. Jordan and the trial of Dawes. Mrs. Morel watched him closely.

"And what do you think of it all?" she asked him.

"I think he's a fool," he said.

But he was very uncomfortable, nevertheless.

"Have you ever considered where it will end?" his mother said.

"No," he answered; "things work out of themselves."

"They do, in a way one doesn't like, as a rule," said his mother.

"And then one has to put up with them," he said.

"You'll find you're not as good at 'putting up' as you imagine," she said.

He went on working rapidly at his design.

"Do you ever ask *her* opinion?" she said at length.

"What of?"

"Of you, and the whole thing."

"I don't care what her opinion of me is. She's fearfully in love with me, but it's not very deep."

"But quite as deep as your feeling for her."

He looked up at his mother curiously.

"Yes," he said. "You know, mother, I think there must be something the matter with me, that I *can't* love. When she's there, as a rule, I *do* love her. Sometimes, when I see her just as *the woman,* I love her, mother; but then, when she talks and criticises, I often don't listen to her."

"Yet she's as much sense as Miriam."

"Perhaps; and I love her better than Miriam. But *why* don't they hold me?"

The last question was almost a lamentation. His mother turned away her face, sat looking across the room, very quiet, grave, with something of renunciation.

"But you wouldn't want to marry Clara?" she said.

"No; at first perhaps I would. But why—why don't I want to marry her or anybody? I feel sometimes as if I wronged my women, mother."

"How wronged them, my son?"

"I don't know."

He went on painting rather despairingly; he had touched the quick of the trouble.

"And as for wanting to marry," said his mother, "there's plenty of time yet."

"But no, mother. I even love Clara, and I did Miriam; but to *give* myself to them in marriage I couldn't. I couldn't belong to them. They seem to want *me*, and I can't ever give it them."

"You haven't met the right woman."

"And I never shall meet the right woman while you live," he said.

She was very quiet. Now she began to feel again tired, as if she were done. "We'll see, my son," she answered.

The feeling that things were going in a circle made him mad.

Clara was, indeed, passionately in love with him, and he with her, as far as passion went. In the daytime he forgot her a good deal. She was working in the same building, but he was not aware of it. He was busy, and her existence was of no matter to him. But all the time she was in her spiral room she had a sense that he was upstairs, a physical sense of his person in the same building. Every second she expected him to come through the door, and when he came it was a shock to her. But he was often short and offhand with her. He gave her his directions in an official manner, keeping her at bay. With what wits she had left she listened to him. She dared not misunderstand or fail to remember, but it was a cruelty to her. She wanted to touch his chest. She knew exactly how his breast was shapen under the waistcoat, and she wanted to touch it. It maddened her to hear his mechanical voice giving orders about the work. She wanted to break through the sham of it, smash the trivial coating of business which covered him with hardness, get at the man again; but she was afraid, and before she could feel one touch of his warmth he was gone, and she ached again.

He knew that she was dreary every evening she did not see him, so he gave her a good deal of his time. The days were often a misery to her, but the evenings and the nights were usually a bliss to them both. Then they were silent. For hours they sat together, or walked together in the dark, and talked only a few, almost meaningless words. But he had her hand in his, and her bosom left its warmth in his chest, making him feel whole.

One evening they were walking down by the canal, and something was troubling him. She knew she had not got him. All the time he whistled softly and persistently to himself. She listened, feeling she could learn more from his whistling than from his speech. It was a sad dissatisfied tune—a tune that made her feel he would not stay with her. She walked on in silence. When they came to the swing bridge he sat down on the great pole, looking at the stars in the water. He was a long way from her. She had been thinking.

"Will you always stay at Jordan's?" she asked.

"No," he answered without reflecting. "No; I s'll leave Nottingham and go abroad—soon."

"Go abroad! What for?"

"I dunno! I feel restless."

"But what shall you do?"

"I shall have to get some steady designing work, and some sort of sale for my pictures first," he said. "I am gradually making my way. I know I am."

"And when do you think you'll go?"

"I don't know. I shall hardly go for long, while there's my mother."

"You couldn't leave her?"

"Not for long."

She looked at the stars in the black water. They lay very white and staring. It was an agony to know he would leave her, but it was almost an agony to have him near her.

"And if you made a nice lot of money, what would you do?" she asked.

"Go somewhere in a pretty house near London with my mother."

"I see."

There was a long pause.

"I could still come and see you," he said. "I don't know. Don't ask me what I should do; I don't know."

There was a silence. The stars shuddered and broke upon the water. There came a breath of wind. He went suddenly to her, and put his hand on her shoulder.

"Don't ask me anything about the future," he said miserably. "I don't know anything. Be with me now, will you, no matter what it is?"

And she took him in her arms. After all, she was a married woman, and she had no right even to what he gave her. He needed her badly. She had him in her arms, and he was miserable. With her warmth she folded him over, consoled him, loved him. She would let the moment stand for itself.

After a moment he lifted his head as if he wanted to speak.

"Clara," he said, struggling.

She caught him passionately to her, pressed his head down on her breast with her hand. She could not bear the suffering in his voice. She was afraid in her soul. He might have anything of her—anything; but she did not want to *know*. She felt she could not bear it. She wanted him to be soothed upon her— soothed. She stood clasping him and caressing him, and he was something unknown to her—something almost uncanny. She wanted to soothe him into forgetfulness.

And soon the struggle went down in his soul, and he forgot. But then Clara was not there for him, only a woman, warm, something he loved and almost worshipped, there in the dark. But it was not Clara, and she submitted to him. The naked hunger and inevitability of his loving her, something strong and blind and ruthless in its primitiveness, made the hour almost terrible to her. She knew how stark and alone he was, and she felt it was great that he came to her; and she took him simply because his need was bigger either than her or him, and her soul was still within her. She did this for him in his need, even if he left her, for she loved him.

All the while the peewits were screaming in the field. When he came to, he wondered what was near his eyes, curving and strong with life in the dark, and what voice it was speaking. Then he realised it was the grass, and the peewit was calling. The warmth was Clara's breathing heaving. He lifted his head, and looked into her eyes. They were dark and shining and strange, life wild at the source staring into his life, stranger to him, yet meeting him; and he put his face down on her throat, afraid. What was she? A strong, strange, wild life, that breathed with his in the darkness through this hour. It was all so much bigger than themselves that he was hushed. They had met, and included in their meeting the thrust of the manifold grass stems, the cry of the peewit, the wheel of the stars.

When they stood up they saw other lovers stealing down the opposite hedge. It seemed natural they were there; the night contained them.

And after such an evening they both were very still, having known the immensity of passion. They felt small, half-afraid, childish and wondering, like Adam and Eve when they lost their innocence and realised the magnificence of the power which drove them out of Paradise and across the great night and the great day of humanity. It was for each of them an initiation and a satisfaction. To know their own nothingness, to know the tremendous living flood which carried them always, gave them rest within themselves. If so great a magnificent power could overwhelm them, identify them altogether with itself, so that they knew they were only grains in the tremendous heave that lifted every grass blade its little height, and every tree, and living thing, then why fret about themselves? They could let themselves be carried by life, and they felt a sort of peace each in the other. There was a verification which they had had together. Nothing could nullify it, nothing could take it away; it was almost their belief in life.

But Clara was not satisfied. Something great was there, she knew; something great enveloped her. But it did not keep her. In the morning it was not the same. They had *known,* but she could not keep the moment. She wanted it again; she wanted something permanent. She had not realised fully. She thought it was he whom she wanted. He was not safe to her. This that had been between them might never be again; he might leave her. She had not got him; she was not satisfied. She had been there, but she had not gripped the—the something—she knew not what—which she was mad to have.

In the morning he had considerable peace, and was happy in himself. It seemed almost as if he had known the baptism of fire in passion, and it left him at rest. But it was not Clara. It was something that happened because of her, but it was not her. They were scarcely any nearer each other. It was as if they had been blind agents of a great force.

When she saw him that day at the factory her heart melted like a drop of fire. It was his body, his brows. The drop of fire grew more intense in her breast; she must hold him. But he, very quiet, very subdued this morning, went on giving his instruction. She followed him into the dark, ugly basement, and lifted her arms to him. He kissed her, and the intensity of passion began to burn him again. Somebody was at the door. He ran upstairs; she returned to her room, moving as if in a trance.

After that the fire slowly went down. He felt more and more that his experience had been impersonal, and not Clara. He loved her. There was a big tenderness, as after a strong emotion they had known together; but it was not she who could keep his soul steady. He had wanted her to be something she could not be.

And she was mad with desire of him. She could not see him without touching him. In the factory, as he talked to her about Spiral hose, she ran her hand secretly along his side. She followed him out into the basement for a quick kiss; her eyes, always mute and yearning, full of unrestrained passion, she kept fixed on his. He was afraid of her, lest she should too flagrantly give herself away before the other girls. She invariably waited for him at dinner-time for him to embrace her before she went. He felt as if she were helpless, almost a burden to him, and it irritated him.

"But what do you always want to be kissing and embracing for?" he said. "Surely there's a time for everything."

She looked up at him, and the hate came into her eyes.

'*Do* I always want to be kissing you?" she said.

"Always, even if I come to ask you about the work. I don't want anything to do with love when I'm at work. Work's work——"

"And what is love?" she asked. "Has it to have special hours?"

"Yes; out of work hours."

"And you'll regulate it according to Mr. Jordan's closing time?"

"Yes; and according to the freedom from business of any sort."

"It is only to exist in spare time?"

"That's all, and not always then—not the kissing sort of love."

"And that's all you think of it?"

"It's quite enough."

"I'm glad you think so."

And she was cold to him for some time—she hated him; and while she was cold and contemptuous, he was uneasy till she had forgiven him again. But when they started afresh they were not any nearer. He kept her because he never satisfied her.

In the spring they went together to the seaside. They had rooms at a little cottage near Theddlethorpe, and lived as man and wife. Mrs. Radford sometimes went with them.

It was known in Nottingham that Paul Morel and Mrs. Dawes were going together, but as nothing was very obvious, and Clara always a solitary person, and he seemed so simple and innocent, it did not make much difference.

He loved the Lincolnshire coast, and she loved the sea. In the early morning they often went out together to bathe. The grey of the dawn, the far, desolate reaches of the fenland smitten with winter, the sea-meadows rank with herbage, were stark enough to rejoice his soul. As they stepped on to the highroad from their plank bridge, and looked round at the endless monotony of levels, the land a little darker than the sky, the sea sounding small beyond the sandhills, his heart filled strong with the sweeping relentlessness of life. She loved him then. He was solitary and strong, and his eyes had a beautiful light.

They shuddered with cold; then he raced her down the road to the green turf bridge. She could run well. Her colour soon came, her throat was bare, her eyes shone. He loved her for being so luxuriously heavy, and yet so quick. Himself was light; she went with a beautiful rush. They grew warm, and walked hand in hand.

A flush came into the sky, the wan moon, half-way down the west, sank into insignificance. On the shadowy land things began to take life, plants with great leaves became distinct. They came through a pass in the big, cold sandhills on to the beach. The long waste of foreshore lay moaning under the dawn and the sea; the ocean was a flat dark strip with a white edge. Over the gloomy sea the sky grew red. Quickly the fire spread among the clouds and scattered them. Crimson burned to orange, orange to dull gold, and in a golden glitter the sun came up, dribbling fierily over the waves in little splashes, as if someone had gone along and the light had spilled from her pail as she walked.

The breakers ran down the shore in long, hoarse strokes. Tiny seagulls, like specks of spray, wheeled above the line of surf. Their crying seemed larger than they. Far away the coast reached out, and melted into the morning, the tussocky sandhills seemed to sink to a level with the beach. Mablethorpe was tiny on their right. They had alone the space of all this level shore, the sea, and the upcoming sun, the faint noise of the waters, the sharp crying of the gulls.

They had a warm hollow in the sandhills where the wind did not come. He stood looking out to sea.

"It's very fine," he said.

"Now don't get sentimental," she said.

It irritated her to see him standing gazing at the sea, like a solitary and poetic person. He laughed. She quickly undressed.

"There are some fine waves this morning," she said triumphantly.

She was a better swimmer than he; he stood idly watching her.

"Aren't you coming?" she said.

"In a minute," he answered.

She was white and velvet skinned, with heavy shoulders. A little wind, coming from the sea, blew across her body and ruffled her hair.

The morning was of a lovely limpid gold colour. Veils of shadow seemed to be drifting away on the north and the south. Clara stood shrinking slightly from the touch of the wind, twisting her hair. The sea-grass rose behind the white stripped woman. She glanced at the sea, then looked at him. He was watching her with dark eyes which she loved and could not understand. She hugged her breasts between her arms, cringing, laughing:

"Oo, it will be so cold!" she said.

He bent forward and kissed her, held her suddenly close, and kissed her again. She stood waiting. He looked into her eyes, then away at the pale sands.

"Go, then!" he said quietly.

She flung her arms round his neck, drew him against her, kissed him passionately, and went, saying:

"But you'll come in?"

"In a minute."

She went plodding heavily over the sand that was soft as velvet. He, on the sandhills, watched the great pale coast envelop her. She grew smaller, lost proportion, seemed only like a large white bird toiling forward.

"Not much more than a big white pebble on the beach, not much more than a clot of foam being blown and rolled over the sand," he said to himself.

She seemed to move very slowly across the vast sounding shore. As he watched, he lost her. She was dazzled out of sight by the sunshine. Again he saw her, the merest white speck moving against the white, muttering sea-edge.

"Look how little she is!" he said to himself. "She's lost like a grain of sand in the beach—just a concentrated speck blown along, a tiny white foam-bubble, almost nothing among the morning. Why does she absorb me?"

The morning was altogether uninterrupted: she was gone in the water. Far and wide the beach, the sandhills with their blue marrain, the shining water, glowed together in immense, unbroken solitude.

"What is she, after all?" he said to himself. "Here's the seacoast morning, big and permanent and beautiful; there is she, fretting, always unsatisfied, and temporary as a bubble of foam. What does she mean to me, after all? She represents something, like a bubble of foam represents the sea. But what is *she?* It's not her I care for."

Then, startled by his own unconscious thoughts, that seemed to speak so distinctly that all the morning could hear, he undressed and ran quickly down the sands. She was watching for him. Her arm flashed up to him, she heaved on a wave, subsided, her shoulders in a pool of liquid silver. He jumped through the breakers, and in a moment her hand was on his shoulder.

He was a poor swimmer, and could not stay long in the water. She played round him in triumph, sporting with her superiority, which he begrudged her. The sunshine stood deep and fine on the water. They laughed in the sea for a minute or two, then raced each other back to the sandhills.

When they were drying themselves, panting heavily, he watched her laughing, breathless face, her bright shoulders, her breasts that swayed and made him frightened as she rubbed them, and he thought again:

"But she is magnificent, and even bigger than the morning and the sea. Is she——? Is she——"

She, seeing his dark eyes fixed on her, broke off from her drying with a laugh.

"What are you looking at?" she said.

"You," he answered, laughing.

Her eyes met his, and in a moment he was kissing her white "goose-fleshed" shoulder, and thinking:

"What is she? What is she?"

She loved him in the morning. There was something detached, hard, and elemental about his kisses then, as if he were only conscious of his own will, not in the least of her and her wanting him.

Later in the day he went out sketching.

"You," he said to her, "go with your mother to Sutton. I am so dull."

She stood and looked at him. He knew she wanted to come with him, but he preferred to be alone. She made him feel imprisoned when she was there, as if he could not get a free deep breath, as if there were something on top of him. She felt his desire to be free of her.

In the evening he came back to her. They walked down the shore in the darkness, then sat for awhile in the shelter of the sandhills.

"It seems," she said, as they stared over the darkness of the sea, where no light was to be seen—"it seemed as if you only loved me at night—as if you didn't love me in the daytime."

He ran the cold sand through his fingers, feeling guilty under the accusation.

"The night is free to you," he replied. "In the daytime I want to be by myself."

"But why?" she said. "Why, even now, when we are on this short holiday?"

"I don't know. Love-making stifles me in the daytime."

"But it needn't be always love-making," she said.

"It always is," he answered, "when you and I are together."

She sat feeling very bitter.

"Do you ever want to marry me?" he asked curiously.

"Do you me?" she replied.

"Yes, yes; I should like us to have children," he answered slowly.

She sat with her head bent, fingering the sand.

"But you don't really want a divorce from Baxter, do you?" he said.

It was some minute before she replied.

"No," she said, very deliberately; "I don't think I do."

"Why?"

"I don't know."

"Do you feel as if you belonged to him?"

"No; I don't think so."

"What, then?"

"I think he belongs to me," she replied.

He was silent for some minutes, listening to the wind blowing over the hoarse, dark sea.

"And you never really intended to belong to *me?*" he said.

"Yes, I do belong to you," she answered.

"No," he said; "because you don't want to be divorced."

It was a knot they could not untie, so they left it, took what they could get, and what they could not attain they ignored.

"I consider you treated Baxter rottenly," he said another time.

He half-expected Clara to answer him, as his mother would: "You consider your own affairs, and don't know so much about other people's." But she took him seriously, almost to his own surprise.

"Why?" she said.

"I suppose you thought he was a lily of the valley, and so you put him in an appropriate pot, and tended him according. You made up your mind he was a lily of the valley and it was no good his being a cow-parsnip. You wouldn't have it."

"I certainly never imagined him a lily of the valley."

"You imagined him something he wasn't. That's just what a woman is. She thinks she knows what's good for a man, and she's going to see he gets it; and no matter if he's starving, he may sit and whistle for what he needs, while she's got him, and is giving him what's good for him."

"And what are you doing?" she asked.

"I'm thinking what tune I shall whistle," he laughed.

And instead of boxing his ears, she considered him in earnest.

"You think I want to give you what's good for you?" she asked.

"I hope so; but love should give a sense of freedom, not of prison. Miriam made me feel tied up like a donkey to a stake. I must feed on her patch, and nowhere else. It's sickening!"

"And would *you* let a *woman* do as she likes?"

"Yes; I'll see that she *likes* to love me. If she doesn't—well, I don't hold her."

"If you were as wonderful as you say——," replied Clara.

"I should be the marvel I am," he laughed.

There was a silence in which they hated each other, though they laughed.

"Love's a dog in a manger," he said.

"And which of us is the dog?" she asked.

"Oh well, you, of course."

So there went on a battle between them. She knew she never fully had him. Some part, big and vital in him, she had no hold over; nor did she ever try to get it, or even to realise what it was. And he knew in some way that she held herself still as Mrs. Dawes. She did not love Dawes, never had loved him; but she believed he loved her, at least depended on her. She felt a certain surety about him that she never felt with Paul Morel. Her passion for the young man had filled her soul, given her a certain satisfaction, eased her of her self-mistrust, her doubt. Whatever else she was, she was inwardly assured. It was almost as if she had gained *herself*, and stood now distinct and complete. She had received her confirmation; but she never believed that her life belonged to Paul Morel, nor his to her. They would separate in the end, and the rest of her life would be an ache after him. But at any rate, she *knew* now, she was sure of herself. And the same could almost be said of him. Together they had received the baptism of life, each through the other; but now their missions were separate. Where he wanted to go she could not come with him. They would have to part sooner or later. Even if they married, and were faithful to each other, still he would have to leave her, go on alone, and she would only have to attend to him when he came home. But it was not possible. Each wanted a mate to go side by side with.

Clara had gone to live with her mother upon Mapperley Plains. One evening, as Paul and she were walking along Woodborough Road, they met Dawes. Morel knew something about the bearing of the man approaching, but he was absorbed in his thinking at the moment, so that only his artist's eye watched the form of the stranger. Then he suddenly turned to Clara with a laugh, and put his hand on her shoulder, saying, laughing:

"But we walk side by side, and yet I'm in London arguing with an imaginary Orpen; and where are you?"

At that instant Dawes passed, almost touching Morel. The young man glanced, saw the dark brown eyes burning, full of hate and yet tired.

"Who was that?" he asked of Clara.

"It was Baxter," she replied.

Paul took his hand from her shoulder and glanced round; then he saw again distinctly the man's form as it approached him. Dawes still walked erect, with his fine shoulders flung back, and his face lifted; but there was a furtive look in his eyes that gave one the impression he was trying to get unnoticed past every person he met, glancing suspiciously to see what they thought of him. And his hands seemed to be wanting to hide. He wore old clothes, the trousers were torn at the knee, and the handkerchief tied round his throat was dirty; but his cap was still defiantly over one eye. As she saw him, Clara felt guilty. There was a tiredness and despair on his face that made her hate him, because it hurt her.

"He looks shady," said Paul.

But the note of pity in his voice reproached her, and made her feel hard.

"His true commonness comes out," she answered.

"Do you hate him?" he asked.

"You talk," she said, "about the cruelty of women; I wish you knew the cruelty of men in their brute force. They simply don't know that the woman exists."

"Don't *I?*" he said.

"No," she answered.

"Don't I know you exist?"

"About *me* you know nothing," she said bitterly—"about *me!*"

"No more than Baxter knew?" he asked.

"Perhaps not as much."

He felt puzzled, and helpless, and angry. There she walked unknown to him, though they had been through such experience together.

"But you know *me* pretty well," he said.

She did not answer.

"Did you know Baxter as well as you know me?" he asked.

"He wouldn't let me," she said.

"And I have let you know me?"

"It's what men *won't* let you do. They won't let you get really near to them," she said.

"And haven't I let you?"

"Yes," she answered slowly; "but you've never come near to me. You can't come out of yourself, you can't. Baxter could do that better than you."

He walked on pondering. He was angry with her for preferring Baxter to him.

"You begin to value Baxter now you've not got him," he said.

"No; I can only see where he was different from you."

But he felt she had a grudge against him.

One evening, as they were coming home over the fields, she startled him by asking:

"Do you think it's worth it—the—the sex part?"

"The act of loving, itself?"

"Yes; is it worth anything to you?"

"But how can you separate it?" he said. "It's the culmination of everything. All our intimacy culminates then."

"Not for me," she said.

He was silent. A flash of hate for her came up. After all, she was dissatisfied with him, even there, where he thought they fulfilled each other. But he believed her too implicitly.

"I feel," she continued slowly, "as if I hadn't got you, as if all of you weren't there, and as if it weren't *me* you were taking——"

"Who, then?"

"Something just for yourself. It has been fine, so that I daren't think of it. But is it *me* you want, or is it *It?*"

He again felt guilty. Did he leave Clara out of count, and take simply women? But he thought that was splitting a hair.

"When I had Baxter, actually had him, then I *did* feel as if I had all of him," she said.

"And it was better?" he asked.

"Yes, yes; it was more whole. I don't say you haven't given me more than he ever gave me."

"Or could give you."

"Yes, perhaps; but you've never given me yourself."

He knitted his brows angrily.

"If I start to make love to you," he said, "I just go like a leaf down the wind."

"And leave me out of count," she said.

"And then is it nothing to you?" he asked, almost rigid with chagrin.

"It's something; and sometimes you have carried me away—right away—I know—and—I reverence you for it—but——"

"Don't 'but' me," he said, kissing her quickly, as a fire ran through him.

She submitted, and was silent.

It was true as he said. As a rule, when he started love-making, the emotion was strong enough to carry with it everything—reason, soul, blood—in a great sweep, like the Trent carries bodily its back-swirls and intertwinings, noiselessly. Gradually the little criticisms, the little sensations, were lost, thought also went, everything borne along in one flood. He became, not a man with a mind, but a great instinct. His hands were like creatures, living; his limbs, his body, were all life and consciousness, subject to no will of his, but living in themselves. Just as he was, so it seemed the vigorous, wintry stars were strong also with life. He and they struck with the same pulse of fire, and the same joy of strength which held the bracken-frond stiff near his eyes held his own body firm. It was as if he, and the stars, and the dark herbage, and Clara were licked up in an immense tongue of flame, which tore onwards and upwards. Everything rushed along in living beside him; everything was still, perfect in itself, along with him. This wonderful stillness in each thing in itself, while it was being borne along in a very ecstasy of living, seemed the highest point of bliss.

And Clara knew this held him to her, so she trusted altogether to the passion. It, however, failed her very often. They did not often reach again the height of that once when the peewits had called. Gradually, some mechanical effort spoilt their loving, or, when they had splendid moments, they had them separately, and not so satisfactorily. So often he seemed merely to be running on alone; often they realised it had been a failure, not what they had wanted. He left her, knowing *that* evening had only made a little split between them. Their loving grew more mechanical, without the marvellous glamour. Gradually they began to introduce novelties, to get back some of the feeling of satisfaction. They would be very near, almost dangerously near to the river, so that the black water ran not far from his face, and it gave a little thrill; or they loved sometimes in a little hollow below the fence of the path where people were passing occasionally, on the edge of the town, and they heard footsteps coming, almost felt the vibration of the tread, and they heard what the passers-by said—strange little things that were never intended to be heard. And afterwards each of them was rather ashamed, and these things caused a distance between the two of them. He began to despise her a little, as if she had merited it!

One night he left her to go to Daybrook Station over the fields. It was very dark, with an attempt at snow, although the spring was so far advanced. Morel had not much time; he plunged forward. The town ceases almost abruptly on the edge of a steep hollow; there the houses with their yellow lights stand up against the darkness. He went over the stile, and dropped quickly into the hollow of the fields. Under the orchard one warm window shone in Swineshead Farm. Paul glanced round. Behind, the houses stood on the brim of the dip, black against the sky, like wild beasts glaring curiously with yellow eyes down into the darkness. It was the town that seemed savage and uncouth, glaring on the clouds at the back of him. Some creature stirred under the willows of the farm pond. It was too dark to distinguish anything.

He was close up to the next stile before he saw a dark shape leaning against it. The man moved aside.

"Good-evening!" he said.

"Good-evening!" Morel answered, not noticing.

"Paul Morel?" said the man.

Then he knew it was Dawes. The man stopped his way.

"I've got yer, have I?" he said awkwardly.

"I shall miss my train," said Paul.

He could see nothing of Dawes's face. The man's teeth seemed to chatter as he talked.

"You're going to get it from me now," said Dawes.

Morel attempted to move forward; the other man stepped in front of him.

"Are yer goin' to take that top-coat off," he said, "or are you goin' to lie down to it?"

Paul was afraid the man was mad.

"But," he said, "I don't know how to fight."

"All right, then," answered Dawes, and before the younger man knew where he was, he was staggering backwards from a blow across the face.

The whole night went black. He tore off his overcoat and coat, dodging a blow, and flung the garments over Dawes. The latter swore savagely. Morel, in his shirt-sleeves, was now alert and furious. He felt his whole body unsheath itself like a claw. He could not fight, so he would use his wits. The other man became more distinct to him; he could see particularly the shirt-breast. Dawes stumbled over Paul's coats, then came rushing forward. The young man's mouth was bleeding. It was the other man's mouth he was dying to get at, and the desire was anguish in its strength. He stepped quickly through the stile, and as Dawes was coming through after him, like a flash he got a blow in over the other's mouth. He shivered with pleasure. Dawes advanced slowly, spitting. Paul was afraid; he moved round to get to the stile again. Suddenly, from out of nowhere, came a great blow against his ear, that sent him falling helpless backwards. He heard Dawes's heavy panting, like a wild beast's, then came a kick on the knee, giving him such agony that he got up and, quite blind, leapt clean under his enemy's guard. He felt blows and kicks, but they did not hurt. He hung on to the bigger man like a wild cat, till at last Dawes fell with a crash, losing his presence of mind. Paul went down with him. Pure instinct brought his hands to the man's neck and before Dawes, in frenzy and agony, could wrench him free, he had got his fists twisted in the scarf and his knuckles dug in the throat of the other man. He was a pure instinct, without reason or feeling. His body, hard and wonderful in itself, cleaved against the struggling body of the other man; not a muscle in him relaxed. He was quite unconscious, only his body had taken upon itself to kill this man. For himself, he had never feeling nor reason. He lay pressed hard against his adversary, his body adjusting itself to its one pure purpose of choking the other man, resisting exactly at the right moment, with exactly the right amount of strength, the struggles of the other, silent, intent, unchanging, gradually pressing its knuckles deeper, feeling the struggles of the other body become wilder and more frenzied. Tighter and tighter grew his body, like a screw that is gradually increasing in pressure, till something breaks.

Then suddenly he relaxed, full of wonder and misgiving. Dawes had been yielding. Morel felt his body flame with pain, as he realised what he was doing; he was all bewildered. Dawes's struggles suddenly renewed themselves in a furious spasm. Paul's hands were wrenched, torn out of the scarf in which they were knotted, and he was flung away, helpless. He heard the horrid sound of the other's gasping, but he lay stunned; then, still dazed, he felt the blows of the other's feet, and lost consciousness.

Dawes, grunting with pain like a beast, was kicking the prostrate body of his rival. Suddenly the whistle of the train shrieked two fields away. He turned round and glared suspiciously. What was coming? He saw the lights of the train draw across his vision. It seemed to him people were approaching. He made off across the field into Nottingham, and dimly in his consciousness as he went, he felt on his foot the place where his boot had knocked against one of the lad's bones. The knock seemed to re-echo inside him; he hurried to get away from it.

Morel gradually came to himself. He knew where he was and what had happened, but he did not want to move. He lay still, with tiny bits of snow tickling his face. It was pleasant to lie quite, quite still. The time passed. It was the bits of snow that kept rousing him when he did not want to be roused. At last his will clicked into action.

"I mustn't lie here," he said; "it's silly."

But still he did not move.

"I said I was going to get up," he repeated. "Why don't I?"

And still it was some time before he had sufficiently pulled himself together to stir; then gradually he got up. Pain made him sick and dazed, but his brain was clear. Reeling, he groped for his coats and got them on, buttoning his overcoat up to his ears. It was some time before he found his cap. He did not know whether his face was still bleeding. Walking blindly, every step making him sick with pain, he went back to the pond and washed his face and hands. The icy water hurt, but helped to bring him back to himself. He crawled back up the hill to the tram. He wanted to get to his mother—he must get to his mother—that was his blind intention. He covered his face as much as he could, and struggled sickly along. Continually the ground seemed to fall away from him as he walked, and he felt himself dropping with a sickening feeling into space; so, like a nightmare, he got through with the journey home.

Everybody was in bed. He looked at himself. His face was discoloured and smeared with blood, almost like a dead man's face. He washed it, and went to bed. The night went by in delirium. In the morning he found his mother looking at him. Her blue eyes—they were all he wanted to see. She was there; he was in her hands.

"It's not much, mother," he said. "It was Baxter Dawes."

"Tell me where it hurts you," she said quietly.

"I don't know—my shoulder. Say it was a bicycle accident, mother."

He could not move his arm. Presently Minnie, the little servant, came upstairs with some tea.

"Your mother's nearly frightened me out of my wits—fainted away," she said.

He felt he could not bear it. His mother nursed him; he told her about it.

"And now I should have done with them all," she said quietly.

"I will, mother."

She covered him up.

"And don't think about it," she said—"only try to go to sleep. The doctor won't be here till eleven."

He had a dislocated shoulder, and the second day acute bronchitis set in. His mother was pale as death now, and very thin. She would sit and look at him, then away into space. There was something between them that neither dared mention. Clara came to see him. Afterwards he said to his mother:

"She makes me tired, mother."

"Yes; I wish she wouldn't come," Mrs. Morel replied.

Another day Miriam came, but she seemed almost like a stranger to him.

"You know, I don't care about them, mother," he said.

"I'm afraid you don't, my son," she replied sadly.

It was given out everywhere that it was a bicycle accident. Soon he was able to go to work again, but now there was a constant sickness and gnawing at his heart. He went to Clara, but there seemed, as it were, nobody there. He could not work. He and his mother seemed almost to avoid each other. There was some secret between them which they could not bear. He was not aware of it. He only knew that his life seemed unbalanced, as if it were going to smash into pieces.

Clara did not know what was the matter with him. She realised that he seemed unaware of her. Even when he came to her he seemed unaware of her; always he was somewhere else. She felt she was clutching for him, and he was somewhere else. It tortured her, and so she tortured him. For a month at a time she kept him at arm's length. He almost hated her, and was driven to her in spite of himself. He went mostly into the company of men, was always at the George or the White Horse. His mother was ill, distant, quiet, shadowy. He was terrified of something; he dared not look at her. Her eyes seemed to grow darker, her face more waxen; still she dragged about at her work.

At Whitsuntide he said he would go to Blackpool for four days with his friend Newton. The latter was a big, jolly fellow, with a touch of the bounder about him. Paul said his mother must go to Sheffield to stay a week with Annie, who lived there. Perhaps the change would do her good. Mrs. Morel was attending a woman's doctor in Nottingham. He said her heart and her digestion were wrong. She consented to go to Sheffield, though she did not want to; but now she would do everything her son wished of her. Paul said he would come for her on the fifth day, and stay also in Sheffield till the holiday was up. It was agreed.

The two young men set off gaily for Blackpool. Mrs. Morel was quite lively as Paul kissed her and left her. Once at the station, he forgot everything. Four days were clear—not an anxiety, not a thought. The two young men simply enjoyed themselves. Paul was like another man. None of himself remained—no Clara, no Miriam, no mother that fretted him. He wrote to them all, and long letters to his mother; but they were jolly letters that made her laugh. He was having a good time, as young fellows will in a place like Blackpool. And underneath it all was a shadow for her.

Paul was very gay, excited at the thought of staying with his mother in Sheffield. Newton was to spend the day with them. Their train was late. Joking, laughing, with their pipes between their teeth, the young men swung their bags on to the tram-car. Paul had bought his mother a little collar of real lace that he wanted to see her wear, so that he could tease her about it.

Annie lived in a nice house, and had a little maid. Paul ran gaily up the steps. He expected his mother laughing in the hall, but it was Annie who opened to him. She seemed distant to him. He stood a second in dismay. Annie let him kiss her cheek.

"Is my mother ill?" he said.

"Yes; she's not very well. Don't upset her."

"Is she in bed?"

"Yes."

And then the queer feeling went over him, as if all the sunshine had gone out of him, and it was all shadow. He dropped the bag and ran upstairs. Hesitating, he opened the door. His mother sat up in bed, wearing a dressing-gown of old-rose colour. She looked at him almost as if she were ashamed of herself, pleading to him, humble. He saw the ashy look about her.

"Mother!" he said.

"I thought you were never coming," she answered gaily.

But he only fell on his knees at the bedside, and buried his face in the bedclothes, crying in agony, and saying:

"Mother—mother—mother!"

She stroked his hair slowly with her thin hand.

"Don't cry," she said. "Don't cry—it's nothing."

But he felt as if his blood was melting into tears, and he cried in terror and pain.

"Don't—don't cry," his mother faltered.

Slowly she stroked his hair. Shocked out of himself, he cried, and the tears hurt in every fibre of his body. Suddenly he stopped, but he dared not lift his face out of the bedclothes.

"You are late. Where have you been?" his mother asked.

"The train was late," he replied, muffled in the sheet.

"Yes; that miserable Central! Is Newton come?"

"Yes."

"I'm sure you must be hungry, and they've kept dinner waiting."

With a wrench he looked up at her.

"What is it, mother?" he asked brutally.

She averted her eyes as she answered:

"Only a bit of a tumour, my boy. You needn't trouble. It's been there—the lump has—a long time."

Up came the tears again. His mind was clear and hard, but his body was crying.

"Where?" he said.

She put her hand on her side.

"Here. But you know they can sweal a tumour away."

He stood feeling dazed and helpless, like a child. He thought perhaps it was as she said. Yes; he reassured himself it was so. But all the while his blood and his body knew definitely what it was. He sat down on the bed, and took her hand. She had never had but the one ring—her wedding-ring.

"When were you poorly?" he asked.

"It was yesterday it began," she answered submissively.

"Pains?"

"Yes; but not more than I've often had at home. I believe Dr. Ansell is an alarmist."

"You ought not to have travelled alone," he said, to himself more than to her.

"As if that had anything to do with it!" she answered quickly.

They were silent for a while.

"Now go and have your dinner," she said. "You *must* be hungry."

"Have you had yours?"

"Yes; a beautiful sole I had. Annie *is* good to me."

They talked a little while, then he went downstairs. He was very white and strained. Newton sat in miserable sympathy.

After dinner he went into the scullery to help Annie to wash up. The little maid had gone on an errand.

"Is it really a tumour?" he asked.

Annie began to cry again.

"The pain she had yesterday—I never saw anybody suffer like it!" she cried. "Leonard ran like a madman for Dr. Ansell, and when she'd got to bed she said to me: 'Annie, look at this lump on my side. I wonder what it is?' And there I looked, and I thought I should have dropped. Paul, as true as I'm here, it's a lump as big as my double fist. I said: 'Good gracious, mother, whenever did that come?' 'Why, child,' she said, 'it's been there a long time.' I thought I should have died, our Paul, I did. She's been having these pains for months at home, and nobody looking after her."

The tears came to his eyes, then dried suddenly.

"But she's been attending the doctor in Nottingham—and she never told me," he said.

"If I'd have been at home," said Annie, "I should have seen for myself."

He felt like a man walking in unrealities. In the afternoon he went to see the doctor. The latter was a shrewd, lovable man.

"But what is it?" he said.

The doctor looked at the young man, then knitted his fingers.

"It may be a large tumour which has formed in the membrane," he said slowly, "and which we *may* be able to make go away."

"Can't you operate?" asked Paul.

"Not there," replied the doctor.

"Are you sure?"

"*Quite!*"

Paul meditated a while.

"Are you sure it's a tumour?" he asked. "Why did Dr. Jameson in Nottingham never find out anything about it? She's been going to him for weeks, and he's treated her for heart and indigestion."

"Mrs. Morel never told Dr. Jameson about the lump," said the doctor.

"And do you *know* it's a tumour?"

"No, I am not sure."

"What else *might* it be? You asked my sister if there was cancer in the family. Might it be cancer?"

"I don't know."

"And what shall you do?"

"I should like an examination, with Dr. Jameson."

"Then have one."

"You must arrange about that. His fee wouldn't be less than ten guineas to come here from Nottingham."

"When would you like him to come?"

"I will call in this evening, and we will talk it over."

Paul went away, biting his lip.

His mother could come downstairs for tea, the doctor said. Her son went upstairs to help her. She wore the old-rose dressing-gown that Leonard had given Annie, and, with a little colour in her face, was quite young again.

"But you look quite pretty in that," he said.

"Yes; they make me so fine, I hardly know myself," she answered.

But when she stood up to walk, the colour went. Paul helped her, half-carrying her. At the top of the stairs she was gone. He lifted her up and carried her quickly downstairs; laid her on the couch. She was light and frail. Her face looked as if she were dead, with blue lips shut tight. Her eyes opened—her blue, unfailing eyes—and she looked at him pleadingly, almost wanting him to forgive her. He held brandy to her lips, but her mouth would not open. All the time she watched him lovingly. She was only sorry for him. The tears ran down his face without ceasing, but not a muscle moved. He was intent on getting a little brandy between her lips. Soon she was able to swallow a teaspoonful. She lay back, so tired. The tears continued to run down his face.

"But," she panted, "it'll go off. Don't cry!"

"I'm not doing," he said.

After a while she was better again. He was kneeling beside the couch. They looked into each other's eyes.

"I don't want you to make a trouble of it," she said.

"No, mother. You'll have to be quite still, and then you'll get better soon."

But he was white to the lips, and their eyes as they looked at each other understood. Her eyes were so blue—such a wonderful forget-me-not blue! He felt if only they had been of a different colour he could have borne it better. His heart seemed to be ripping slowly in his breast. He kneeled there, holding her hand, and neither said anything. Then Annie came in.

"Are you all right?" she murmured timidly to her mother.

"Of course," said Mrs. Morel.

Paul sat down and told her about Blackpool. She was curious.

A day or two after, he went to see Dr. Jameson in Nottingham, to arrange for a consultation. Paul had practically no money in the world. But he could borrow.

His mother had been used to go to the public consultation on Saturday morning, when she could see the doctor for only a nominal sum. Her son went on the same day. The waiting-room was full of poor women, who sat patiently on a bench around the wall. Paul thought of his mother, in her little black costume, sitting waiting likewise. The doctor was late. The women all looked rather frightened. Paul asked the nurse in attendance if he could see the doctor immediately he came. It was arranged so. The women sitting patiently round the walls of the room eyed the young man curiously.

At last the doctor came. He was about forty, good-looking, brown-skinned. His wife had died, and he, who had loved her, had specialised on women's ailments. Paul told his name and his mother's. The doctor did not remember.

"Number forty-six M.," said the nurse; and the doctor looked up the case in his book.

"There is a big lump that may be a tumour," said Paul. "But Dr. Ansell was going to write you a letter."

"Ah, yes!" replied the doctor, drawing the letter from his pocket. He was very friendly, affable, busy, kind. He would come to Sheffield the next day.

"What is your father?" he asked.

"He is a coal-miner," replied Paul.

"Not very well off, I suppose?"

"This—I see after this," said Paul.

"And you?" smiled the doctor.

"I am a clerk in Jordan's Appliance Factory."

The doctor smiled at him.

"Er—to go to Sheffield!" he said, putting the tips of his fingers together, and smiling with his eyes. "Eight guineas?"

"Thank you!" said Paul, flushing and rising. "And you'll come to-morrow?"

"To-morrow—Sunday? Yes! Can you tell me about what time there is a train in the afternoon?"

"There is a Central gets in at four-fifteen."

"And will there be any way of getting up to the house? Shall I have to walk?" The doctor smiled.

"There is the tram," said Paul; "the Western Park tram."

The doctor made a note of it.

"Thank you!" he said, and shook hands.

Then Paul went on home to see his father, who was left in the charge of Minnie. Walter Morel was getting very grey now. Paul found him digging in the garden. He had written him a letter. He shook hands with his father.

"Hello, son! Tha has landed, then?" said the father.

"Yes," replied the son. "But I'm going back to-night."

"Are ter, beguy!" exclaimed the collier. "An' has ter eaten owt?"

"No."

"That's just like thee," said Morel. "Come thy ways in."

The father was afraid of the mention of his wife. The two went indoors. Paul ate in silence; his father, with earthy hands, and sleeves rolled up, sat in the arm-chair opposite and looked at him.

"Well, an' how is she?" asked the miner at length, in a little voice.

"She can sit up; she can be carried down for tea," said Paul.

"That's a blessin'!" exclaimed Morel. "I hope we s'll soon be havin' her whoam, then. An' what's that Nottingham doctor say?"

"He's going to-morrow to have an examination of her."

"Is he beguy! That's a tidy penny, I'm thinkin'!"

"Eight guineas."

"Eight guineas!" the miner spoke breathlessly. "Well, we mun find it from somewhere."

"I can pay that," said Paul.

There was silence between them for some time.

"She says she hopes you're getting on all right with Minnie," Paul said.

"Yes, I'm all right, an' I wish as she was," answered Morel.

"But Minnie's a good little wench, bless 'er heart!" He sat looking dismal.

"I s'll have to be going at half-past three," said Paul.

"It's a trapse for thee, lad! Eight guineas! An' when dost think she'll be able to get as far as this?"

"We must see what the doctors say to-morrow," Paul said.

Morel sighed deeply. The house seemed strangely empty, and Paul thought his father looked lost, forlorn, and old.

"You'll have to go and see her next week, father," he said.

"I hope she'll be a-whoam by that time," said Morel.

"If she's not," said Paul, "then you must come."

"I dunno wheer I s'll find th' money," said Morel.

"And I'll write to you what the doctor says," said Paul.

"But tha writes i' such a fashion, I canna ma'e it out," said Morel.

"Well, I'll write plain."

It was no good asking Morel to answer, for he could scarcely do more than write his own name.

The doctor came. Leonard felt it his duty to meet him with a cab. The examination did not take long. Annie, Arthur, Paul, and Leonard were waiting in the parlour anxiously. The doctors came down. Paul glanced at them. He had never had any hope, except when he had deceived himself.

"It *may* be a tumour; we must wait and see," said Dr. Jameson.

"And if it is," said Annie, "can you sweal it away?"

"Probably," said the doctor.

Paul put eight sovereigns and half a sovereign on the table. The doctor counted them, took a florin out of his purse, and put that down.

"Thank you!" he said. "I'm sorry Mrs. Morel is so ill. But we must see what we can do."

"There can't be an operation?" said Paul.

The doctor shook his head.

"No," he said; "and even if there could, her heart wouldn't stand it."

"Is her heart risky?" asked Paul.

"Yes; you must be careful with her."

"Very risky?"

"No—er—no, no! Just take care."

And the doctor was gone.

Then Paul carried his mother downstairs. She lay simply, like a child. But when he was on the stairs, she put her arms round his neck, clinging.

"I'm so frightened of these beastly stairs," she said.

And he was frightened, too. He would let Leonard do it another time. He felt he could not carry her.

"He thinks it's only a tumour!" cried Annie to her mother. "And he can sweal it away."

"I *knew* he could," protested Mrs. Morel scornfully.

She pretended not to notice that Paul had gone out of the room. He sat in the kitchen, smoking. Then he tried to brush some grey ash off his coat. He looked again. It was one of his mother's grey hairs. It was so long! He held it up, and it drifted into the chimney. He let go. The long grey hair floated and was gone in the blackness of the chimney.

The next day he kissed her before going back to work. It was very early in the morning, and they were alone.

"You won't fret, my boy!" she said.

"No, mother."

"No; it would be silly. And take care of yourself."

"Yes," he answered. Then, after a while: "And I shall come next Saturday, and shall bring my father?"

"I suppose he wants to come," she replied. "At any rate, if he does you'll have to let him."

He kissed her again, and stroked the hair from her temples, gently, tenderly, as if she were a lover.

"Shan't you be late?" she murmured.

"I'm going," he said, very low.

Still he sat a few minutes, stroking the brown and grey hair from her temples.

"And you won't be any worse, mother?"

"No, my son."

"You promise me?"

"Yes; I won't be any worse."

He kissed her, held her in his arms for a moment, and was gone. In the early sunny morning he ran to the station, crying all the way; he did not know what for. And her blue eyes were wide and staring as she thought of him.

In the afternoon he went a walk with Clara. They sat in the little wood where bluebells were standing. He took her hand.

"You'll see," he said to Clara, "she'll never be better."

"Oh, you don't know!" replied the other.

"I do," he said.

She caught him impulsively to her breast.

"Try and forget it, dear," she said; "try and forget it."

"I will," he answered.

Her breast was there, warm for him; her hands were in his hair. It was comforting, and he held his arms round her. But he did not forget. He only talked to Clara of something else. And it was always so. When she felt it coming, the agony, she cried to him:

"Don't think of it, Paul! Don't think of it, my darling!"

And she pressed him to her breast, rocked him, soothed him like a child. So he put the trouble aside for her sake, to take it up again immediately he was alone. All the time, as he went about, he cried mechanically. His mind and hands were busy. He cried, he did not know why. It was his blood weeping. He was just as much alone whether he was with Clara or with the men in the White Horse. Just himself and this pressure inside him, that was all that existed. He read sometimes. He had to keep his mind occupied. And Clara was a way of occupying his mind.

On the Saturday Walter Morel went to Sheffield. He was a forlorn figure, looking rather as if nobody owned him. Paul ran upstairs.

"My father's come," he said, kissing his mother.

"Has he?" she answered wearily.

The old collier came rather frightened into the bedroom.

"How dun I find thee, lass?" he said, going forward and kissing her in a hasty, timid fashion.

"Well, I'm middlin'," she replied.

"I see tha art," he said. He stood looking down on her. Then he wiped his eyes with his handkerchief. Helpless, and as if nobody owned him, he looked.

"Have you gone on all right?" asked the wife, rather wearily, as if it were an effort to talk to him.

"Yis," he answered. " 'Er's a bit behint-hand now and again, as yer might expect."

"Does she have your dinner ready?" asked Mrs. Morel.

"Well, I've 'ad to shout at 'er once or twice," he said.

"And you *must* shout at her if she's not ready. She *will* leave things to the last minute."

She gave him a few instructions. He sat looking at her as if she were almost a stranger to him, before whom he was awkward and humble, and also as if he had lost his presence of mind, and wanted to run. This feeling that he wanted to run away, that he was on thorns to be gone from so trying a situation, and yet must linger because it looked better, made his presence so trying. He put up his eyebrows for misery, and clenched his fists on his knees, feeling so awkward in presence of big trouble.

Mrs. Morel did not change much. She stayed in Sheffield for two months. If anything, at the end she was rather worse. But she wanted to go home. Annie had her children. Mrs. Morel wanted to go home. So they got a motor-car from Nottingham—for she was too ill to go by train—and she was driven through the sunshine. It was just August; everything was bright and warm. Under the blue sky they could all see she was dying. Yet she was jollier than she had been for weeks. They all laughed and talked.

"Annie," she exclaimed, "I saw a lizard dart on that rock!"

Her eyes were so quick; she was still so full of life.

Morel knew she was coming. He had the front door open. Everybody was on tiptoe. Half the street turned out. They heard the sound of the great motor-car. Mrs. Morel, smiling, drove home down the street.

"And just look at them all come out to see me!" she said. "But there, I suppose I should have done the same. How do you do, Mrs. Matthews? How are you, Mrs. Harrison?"

They none of them could hear, but they saw her smile and nod. And they all saw death on her face, they said. It was a great event in the street.

Morel wanted to carry her indoors, but he was too old. Arthur took her as if she were a child. They had set her a big, deep chair by the hearth where her rocking-chair used to stand. When she was unwrapped and seated, and had drunk a little brandy, she looked round the room.

"Don't think I don't like your house, Annie," she said; "but it's nice to be in my own home again."

And Morel answered huskily:

"It is, lass, it is."

And Minnie, the little quaint maid, said:

"An' we glad t' 'ave yer."

There was a lovely yellow ravel of sunflowers in the garden. She looked out of the window.

"There are my sunflowers!" she said.

XIV

THE RELEASE

By the way," said Dr. Ansell one evening when Morel was in Sheffield, "we've got a man in the fever hospital here who comes from Nottingham—Dawes. He doesn't seem to have many belongings in this world."

"Baxter Dawes!" Paul exclaimed.

"That's the man—has been a fine fellow, physically, I should think. Been in a bit of a mess lately. You know him?"

"He used to work at the place where I am."

"Did he? Do you know anything about him? He's just sulking, or he'd be a lot better than he is by now."

"I don't know anything of his home circumstances, except that he's separated from his wife and has been a bit down, I believe. But tell him about me, will you? Tell him I'll come and see him."

The next time Morel saw the doctor he said:

"And what about Dawes?"

"I said to him," answered the other, " 'Do you know a man from Nottingham named Morel?' and he looked at me as if he'd jump at my throat. So I said: 'I see you know the name; it's Paul Morel.' Then I told him about your saying you would go and see him. 'What does he want?' he said, as if you were a policeman.."

"And did he say he would see me?" asked Paul.

"He wouldn't say anything—good, bad or indifferent," replied the doctor.

"Why not?"

"That's what I want to know. There he lies and sulks, day in, day out. Can't get a word of information out of him."

"Do you think I might go?" asked Paul.

"You might."

There was a feeling of connection between the rival men, more than ever since they had fought. In a way Morel felt guilty towards the other, and more or less responsible. And being in such a state of soul himself, he felt an almost painful nearness to Dawes, who was suffering and despairing, too. Besides, they had met in a naked extremity of hate, and it was a bond. At any rate, the elemental man in each had met.

He went down to the isolation hospital, with Dr. Ansell's card. This sister, a healthy young Irishwoman, led him down the ward.

"A visitor to see you, Jim Crow," she said.

Dawes turned over suddenly with a startled grunt.

"Eh?"

"Caw!" she mocked. "He can only say 'Caw!' I have brought you a gentleman to see you. Now say 'Thank you,' and show some manners."

Dawes looked swiftly with his dark, startled eyes beyond the sister at Paul. His look was full of fear, mistrust, hate, and misery. Morel met the swift, dark eyes, and hesitated. The two men were afraid of the naked selves they had been.

"Dr. Ansell told me you were here," said Morel, holding out his hand.

Dawes mechanically shook hands.

"So I thought I'd come in," continued Paul.

There was no answer. Dawes lay staring at the opposite wall.

"Say 'Caw!' " mocked the nurse. "Say 'Caw!' Jim Crow."

"He is getting on all right?" said Paul to her.

"Oh yes! He lies and imagines he's going to die," said the nurse, "and it frightens every word out of his mouth."

"And you *must* have somebody to talk to," laughed Morel.

"That's it!" laughed the nurse. "Only two old men and a boy who always cries. It *is* hard lines! Here am I dying to hear Jim Crow's voice, and nothing but an odd 'Caw!' will he give!"

"So rough on you!" said Morel.

"Isn't it?" said the nurse.

"I suppose I am a godsend," he laughed.

"Oh, dropped straight from heaven!" laughed the nurse.

Presently she left the two men alone. Dawes was thinner, and handsome again, but life seemed low in him. As the doctor said, he was lying sulking, and would not move forward towards convalescence. He seemed to grudge every beat of his heart.

"Have you had a bad time?" asked Paul.

Suddenly again Dawes looked at him.

"What are you doing in Sheffield?" he asked.

"My mother was taken ill at my sister's in Thurston Street. What are you doing here?"

There was no answer.

"How long have you been in?" Morel asked.

"I couldn't say for sure," Dawes answered grudgingly.

He lay staring across at the wall opposite, as if trying to believe Morel was not there. Paul felt his heart go hard and angry.

"Dr. Ansell told me you were here," he said coldly.

The other man did not answer.

"Typhoid's pretty bad, I know," Morel persisted.

Suddenly Dawes said:

"What did you come for?"

"Because Dr. Ansell said you didn't know anybody here. Do you?"

"I know nobody nowhere," said Dawes.

"Well," said Paul, "it's because you don't choose to, then."

There was another silence.

"We s'll be taking my mother home as soon as we can," said Paul.

"What's a-matter with her?" asked Dawes, with a sick man's interest in illness.

"She's got a cancer."

There was another silence.

"But we want to get her home," said Paul. "We s'll have to get a motor-car."

Dawes lay thinking."

"Why don't you ask Thomas Jordan to lend you his?" said Dawes.

"It's not big enough," Morel answered.

Dawes blinked his dark eyes as he lay thinking.

"Then ask Jack Pilkington; he'd lend it you. You know him."

"I think I s'll hire one," said Paul.

"You're a fool if you do," said Dawes.

The sick man was gaunt and handsome again. Paul was sorry for him because his eyes looked so tired.

"Did you get a job here?" he asked.

"I was only here a day or two before I was taken bad," Dawes replied.

"You want to get in a convalescent home," said Paul.

The other's face clouded again.

"I'm goin' in no convalescent home," he said.

"My father's been in one at Seathorpe, an' he liked it. Dr. Ansell would get you a recommend."

Dawes lay thinking. It was evident he dared not face the world again.

"The seaside would be all right just now," Morel said. "Sun on those sand-hills, and the waves not far out."

The other did not answer.

"By Gad!" Paul concluded, too miserable to bother much; "it's all right when you know you're going to walk again, and swim!"

Dawes glanced at him quickly. The man's dark eyes were afraid to meet any other eyes in the world. But the real misery and helplessness in Paul's tone gave him a feeling of relief.

"Is she far gone?" he asked.

"She's going like wax," Paul answered; "but cheerful—lively!"

He bit his lip. After a minute he rose.

"Well, I'll be going," he said. "I'll leave you this half-crown."

"I don't want it," Dawes muttered.

Morel did not answer, but left the coin on the table.

"Well," he said, "I'll try and run in when I'm back in Sheffield. Happen you might like to see my brother-in-law? He works in Pyecrofts."

"I don't know him," said Dawes.

"He's all right. Should I tell him to come? He might bring you some papers to look at."

The other man did not answer. Paul went. The strong emotion that Dawes aroused in him, repressed, made him shiver.

He did not tell his mother, but next day he spoke to Clara about this inter-view. It was in the dinner-hour. The two did not often go out together now, but this day he asked her to go with him to the Castle grounds. There they sat while the scarlet geraniums and the yellow calceolarias blazed in the sunlight. She was now always rather protective, and rather resentful towards him.

"Did you know Baxter was in Sheffield Hospital with typhoid?" he asked.

She looked at him with startled grey eyes, and her face went pale.

"No," she said, frightened.

"He's getting better. I went to see him yesterday—the doctor told me."

Clara seemed stricken by the news.

"Is he very bad?" she asked guiltily.

"He has been. He's mending now."

"What did he say to you?"

"Oh, nothing! He seems to be sulking."

There was a distance between the two of them. He gave her more informa-tion.

She went about shut up and silent. The next time they took a walk together, she disengaged herself from his arm, and walked at a distance from him. He was wanting her comfort badly.

"Won't you be nice with me?" he asked.

She did not answer.

"What's the matter?" he said, putting his arm across her shoulder.

"Don't!" she said, disengaging herself.

He left her alone, and returned to his own brooding.

"Is it Baxter that upsets you?" he asked at length.

"I *have* been *vile* to him!" she said.

"I've said many a time you haven't treated him well," he replied.

And there was a hostility between them. Each pursued his own train of thought.

"I've treated him—no, I've treated him badly," she said. "And now you treat *me* badly. It serves me right."

"How do I treat you badly?" he said.

"It serves me right," she repeated. "I never considered him worth having, and now you don't consider *me*. But it serves me right. He loved me a thousand times better than you ever did."

"He didn't!" protested Paul.

"He did! At any rate, he did respect me, and that's what you don't do."

"It looked as if he respected you!" he said.

"He did! And I *made* him horrid—I know I did! You've taught me that. And he loved me a thousand times better than ever you do."

"All right," said Paul.

He only wanted to be left alone now. He had his own trouble, which was almost too much to bear. Clara only tormented him and made him tired. He was not sorry when he left her.

She went on the first opportunity to Sheffield to see her husband. The meeting was not a success. But she left him roses and fruit and money. She wanted to make restitution. It was not that she loved him. As she looked at him lying there her heart did not warm with love. Only she wanted to humble herself to him, to kneel before him. She wanted now to be self-sacrificial. After all, she had failed to make Morel really love her. She was morally frightened. She wanted to do penance. So she kneeled to Dawes, and it gave him a subtle pleasure. But the distance between them was still very great—too great. It frightened the man. It almost pleased the woman. She liked to feel she was serving him across an insuperable distance. She was proud now.

Morel went to see Dawes once or twice. There was a sort of friendship between the two men, who were all the while deadly rivals. But they never mentioned the woman who was between them.

Mrs. Morel got gradually worse. At first they used to carry her downstairs, sometimes even into the garden. She sat propped in her chair, smiling, and so pretty. The gold wedding-ring shone on her white hand; her hair was carefully brushed. And she watched the tangled sunflowers dying, the chrysanthemums coming out, and the dahlias.

Paul and she were afraid of each other. He knew, and she knew, that she was dying. But they kept up a pretence of cheerfulness. Every morning, when he got up, he went into her room in his pyjamas.

"Did you sleep, my dear?" he asked.

"Yes," she answered.

"Not very well?"

"Well, yes!"

Then he knew she had lain awake. He saw her hand under the bedclothes, pressing the place on her side where the pain was.

"Has it been bad?" he asked.

"No. It hurt a bit, but nothing to mention."

And she sniffed in her old scornful way. As she lay she looked like a girl. And all the while her blue eyes watched him. But there were the dark pain-circles beneath that made him ache again.

"It's a sunny day," he said.

"It's a beautiful day."

"Do you think you'll be carried down?"

"I shall see."

Then he went away to get her breakfast. All day long he was conscious of nothing but her. It was a long ache that made him feverish. Then, when he got home in the early evening, he glanced through the kitchen window. She was not there; she had not got up.

He ran straight upstairs and kissed her. He was almost afraid to ask:

"Didn't you get up, pigeon?"

"No," she said. "It was that morphia; it made me tired."

"I think he gives you too much," he said.

"I think he does," she answered.

He sat down by the bed, miserably. She had a way of curling and lying on her side, like a child. The grey and brown hair was loose over her ear.

"Doesn't it tickle you?" he said, gently putting it back.

"It does," she replied.

His face was near hers. Her blue eyes smiled straight into his, like a girl's—warm, laughing with tender love. It made him pant with terror, agony, and love.

"You want your hair doing in a plait," he said. "Lie still."

And going behind her, he carefully loosened her hair, brushed it out. It was like fine long silk of brown and grey. Her head was snuggled between her shoulders. As he lightly brushed and plaited her hair, he bit his lip and felt dazed. It all seemed unreal, he could not understand it.

At night he often worked in her room, looking up from time to time. And so often he found her blue eyes fixed on him. And when their eyes met, she smiled. He worked away again mechanically, producing good stuff without knowing what he was doing.

Sometimes he came in, very pale and still, with watchful, sudden eyes, like a man who is drunk almost to death. They were both afraid of the veils that were ripping between them.

Then she pretended to be better, chattered to him gaily, made a great fuss over some scraps of news. For they had both come to the condition when they had to make much of the trifles, lest they should give in to the big thing, and their human independence would go smash. They were afraid, so they made light of things and were gay.

Sometimes as she lay he knew she was thinking of the past. Her mouth gradually shut hard in a line. She was holding herself rigid, so that she might die without ever uttering the great cry that was tearing from her. He never forgot that hard, utterly lonely and stubborn clenching of her mouth, which persisted for weeks. Sometimes, when it was lighter, she talked about her husband. Now she hated him. She did not forgive him. She could not bear him to be in the room. And a few things, the things that had been most bitter to her, came up again so strongly that they broke from her, and she told her son.

He felt as if his life were being destroyed, piece by piece, within him. Often the tears came suddenly. He ran to the station, the tear-drops falling on the pavement. Often he could not go on with his work. The pen stopped writing. He sat staring, quite unconscious. And when he came round again he felt sick and trembled in his limbs. He never questioned what it was. His mind did not try to analyse or understand. He merely submitted, and kept his eyes shut; let the thing go over him.

His mother did the same. She thought of the pain, of the morphia, of the next day; hardly ever of the death. That was coming, she knew. She had to submit to it. But she would never entreat it or make friends with it. Blind, with her face shut hard and blind, she was pushed towards the door. The days passed, the weeks, the months.

Sometimes, in the sunny afternoons, she seemed almost happy.

"I try to think of the nice times—when we went to Mablethorpe, and Robin Hood's Bay, and Shanklin," she said. "After all, not everybody has seen those beautiful places. And wasn't it beautiful! I try to think of that, not of the other things."

Then, again, for a whole evening she spoke not a word; neither did he. They were together, rigid, stubborn, silent. He went into his room at last to go to bed, and leaned against the doorway as if paralysed, unable to go any farther. His consciousness went. A furious storm, he knew not what, seemed to ravage inside him. He stood leaning there, submitting, never questioning.

In the morning they were both normal again, though her face was grey with the morphia, and her body felt like ash. But they were bright again, nevertheless. Often, especially if Annie or Arthur were at home, he neglected her. He did not see much of Clara. Usually he was with men. He was quick and active and lively; but when his friends saw him go white to the gills, his eyes dark and glittering, they had a certain mistrust of him. Sometimes he went to Clara, but she was almost cold to him.

"Take me!" he said simply.

Occasionally she would. But she was afraid. When he had her then, there was something in it that made her shrink away from him—something unnatural. She grew to dread him. He was so quiet, yet so strange. She was afraid of the man who was not there with her, whom she could feel behind this makebelief lover; somebody sinister, that filled her with horror. She began to have a kind of horror of him. It was almost as if he were a criminal. He wanted her—he had her—and it made her feel as if death itself had her in its grip. She lay in horror. There was no man there loving her. She almost hated him. Then came little bouts of tenderness. But she dared not pity him.

Dawes had come to Colonel Seely's Home near Nottingham. There Paul visited him sometimes, Clara very occasionally. Between the two men the friendship developed peculiarly. Dawes, who mended very slowly and seemed very feeble, seemed to leave himself in the hands of Morel.

In the beginning of November Clara reminded Paul that it was her birthday.

"I'd nearly forgotten," he said.

"I'd thought quite," she replied.

"No. Shall we go to the seaside for the week-end?"

They went. It was cold and rather dismal. She waited for him to be warm and tender with her, instead of which he seemed hardly aware of her. He sat in the railway-carriage, looking out, and was startled when she spoke to him. He was not definitely thinking. Things seemed as if they did not exist. She went across to him.

"What is it dear?" she asked.

"Nothing!" he said. "Don't those windmill sails look monotonous?"

He sat holding her hand. He could not talk nor think. It was a comfort, however, to sit holding her hand. She was dissatisfied and miserable. He was not with her; she was nothing.

And in the evening they sat among the sandhills, looking at the black, heavy sea.

"She will never give in," he said quietly.

Clara's heart sank.

"No," she replied.

"There are different ways of dying. My father's people are frightened, and have to be hauled out of life into death like cattle into a slaughter-house, pulled by the neck; but my mother's people are pushed from behind, inch by inch. They are stubborn people, and won't die."

"Yes," said Clara.

"And she won't die. She can't. Mr. Renshaw, the parson, was in the other day. 'Think!' he said to her; 'you will have your mother and father, and your sisters, and your son, in the Other Land.' And she said: 'I have done without them for a long time, and *can* do without them now. It is the living I want, not the dead.' She wants to live even now."

"Oh, how horrible!" said Clara, too frightened to speak.

"And she looks at me, and she wants to stay with me," he went on monotonously. "She's got such a will, it seems as if she would never go—never!"

"Don't think of it!" cried Clara.

"And she was religious—she is religious now—but it is no good. She simply won't give in. And do you know, I said to her on Thursday: 'Mother, if I had to die, I'd die. I'd *will* to die.' And she said to me, sharp: 'Do you think I haven't? Do you think you can die when you like?'"

His voice ceased. He did not cry, only went on speaking monotonously. Clara wanted to run. She looked round. There was the black, re-echoing shore, the dark sky down on her. She got up terrified. She wanted to be where there was light, where there were other people. She wanted to be away from him. He sat with his head dropped, not moving a muscle.

"And I don't want her to eat," he said, "and she knows it. When I ask her: 'Shall you have anything' she's almost afraid to say 'Yes.' 'I'll have a cup of Benger's,' she says. 'It'll only keep your strength up,' I said to her. 'Yes'—and she almost cried—'but there's such a gnawing when I eat nothing, I can't bear it.' So I went and made her the food. It's the cancer that gnaws like that at her. I wish she'd die!"

"Come!" said Clara roughly. "I'm going."

He followed her down the darkness of the sands. He did not come to her. He seemed scarcely aware of her existence. And she was afraid of him, and disliked him.

In the same acute daze they went back to Nottingham. He was always busy, always doing something, always going from one to the other of his friends.

On the Monday he went to see Baxter Dawes. Listless and pale, the man rose to greet the other, clinging to his chair as he held out his hand.

"You shouldn't get up," said Paul.

Dawes sat down heavily, eyeing Morel with a sort of suspicion.

"Don't you waste your time on me," he said, "if you've owt better to do."

"I wanted to come," said Paul. "Here! I brought you some sweets."

The invalid put them aside.

"It's not been much of a week-end," said Morel.

"How's your mother?" asked the other.

"Hardly any different."

"I thought she was perhaps worse, being as you didn't come on Sunday."

"I was at Skegness," said Paul. "I wanted a change."

The other looked at him with dark eyes. He seemed to be waiting, not quite daring to ask, trusting to be told.

"I went with Clara," said Paul.

"I knew as much," said Dawes quietly.

"It was an old promise," said Paul.

"You have it your own way," said Dawes.

This was the first time Clara had been definitely mentioned between them.

"Nay," said Morel slowly; "she's tired of me."

Again Dawes looked at him.

"Since August she's been getting tired of me," Morel repeated.

The two men were very quiet together. Paul suggested a game of draughts. They played in silence.

"I s'll go abroad when my mother's dead," said Paul.

"Abroad!" repeated Dawes.

"Yes; I don't care what I do."

They continued the game. Dawes was winning.

"I s'll have to begin a new start of some sort," said Paul; "and you as well, I suppose."

He took one of Dawes's pieces.

"I dunno where," said the other.

"Things have to happen," Morel said. "It's no good doing anything—at least—no, I don't know. Give me some toffee."

The two men ate sweets, and began another game of draughts.

"What made that scar on your mouth?" asked Dawes.

Paul put his hand hastily to his lips, and looked over the garden.

"I had a bicycle accident," he said.

Dawes's hand trembled as he moved the piece.

"You shouldn't ha' laughed at me," he said, very low.

"When?"

"That night on Woodborough Road, when you and her passed me—you with your hand on her shoulder."

"I never laughed at you," said Paul.

Dawes kept his fingers on the draught-piece.

"I never knew you were there till the very second when you passed," said Morel.

"It was that as did me," Dawes said, very low.

Paul took another sweet.

"I never laughed," he said, "except as I'm always laughing."

They finished the game.

That night Morel walked home from Nottingham, in order to have something to do. The furnaces flared in a red blotch over Bulwell; the black clouds were like a low ceiling. As he went along the ten miles of highroad, he felt as if he were walking out of life, between the black levels of the sky and the earth. But at the end was only the sick-room. If he walked and walked for ever, there was only that place to come to.

He was not tired when he got near home, or he did not know it. Across the fields he could see the red firelight leaping in her bedroom window.

"When she's dead," he said to himself, "that fire will go out."

He took off his boots quietly and crept upstairs. His mother's door was wide open, because she slept alone still. The red firelight dashed its glow on the landing. Soft as a shadow, he peeped in her doorway.

"Paul!" she murmured.

His heart seemed to break again. He went in and sat by the bed.

"How late you are!" she murmured.

"Not very," he said.

"Why, what time is it?" The murmur came plaintive and helpless.

"It's only just gone eleven."

That was not true; it was nearly one o'clock.

"Oh!" she said; "I thought it was later."

And he knew the unutterable misery of her nights that would not go.

"Can't you sleep, my pigeon?" he said.

"No, I can't," she wailed.

"Never mind, Little!" he said crooning. "Never mind, my love. I'll stop with you half an hour, my pigeon; then perhaps it will be better."

And he sat by the bedside, slowly, rhythmically stroking her brows with his finger-tips, stroking her eyes shut, soothing her, holding her fingers in his free hand. They could hear the sleepers' breathing in the other rooms.

"Now go to bed," she murmured, lying quite still under his fingers and his love.

"Will you sleep?" he asked.

"Yes, I think so."

"You feel better, my Little, don't you?"

"Yes," she said, like a fretful, half-soothed child.

Still the days and the weeks went by. He hardly ever went to see Clara now. But he wandered restlessly from one person to another for some help, and there was none anywhere. Miriam had written to him tenderly. He went to see her. Her heart was very sore when she saw him, white, gaunt, with his eyes dark and bewildered. Her pity came up, hurting her till she could not bear it.

"How is she?" she asked.

"The same—the same!" he said. "The doctor says she can't last, but I know she will. She'll be here at Christmas."

Miriam shuddered. She drew him to her; she pressed him to her bosom; she kissed him and kissed him. He submitted, but it was torture. She could not kiss his agony. That remained alone and apart. She kissed his face, and roused his blood, while his soul was apart writhing with the agony of death. And she kissed him and fingered his body, till at last, feeing he would go mad, he got away from her. It was not that he wanted just then—not that. And she thought she had soothed him and done him good.

December came, and some snow. He stayed at home all the while now. They could not afford a nurse. Annie came to look after her mother; the parish nurse, whom they loved, came in morning and evening. Paul shared the nursing with Annie. Often, in the evenings, when friends were in the kitchen with them, they all laughed together and shook with laughter. It was reaction. Paul was so comical, Annie was so quaint. The whole party laughed till they cried, trying to subdue the sound. And Mrs. Morel, lying alone in the darkness heard them, and among her bitterness was a feeling of relief.

Then Paul would go upstairs gingerly, guiltily, to see if she had heard.

"Shall I give you some milk?" he asked.

"A little," she replied plaintively.

And he would put some water with it, so that it should not nourish her. Yet he loved her more than his own life.

She had morphia every night, and her heart got fitful. Annie slept beside her. Paul would go in in the early morning, when his sister got up. His mother was wasted and almost ashen in the morning with the morphia. Darker and darker grew her eyes, all pupil, with the torture. In the mornings the weariness and ache was too much to bear. Yet she could not—would not—weep, or even complain much.

"You slept a bit later this morning, little one," he would say to her.

"Did I?" she answered, with fretful weariness.

"Yes; it's nearly eight o'clock."

He stood looking out of the window. The whole country was bleak and pallid under the snow. Then he felt her pulse. There was a strong stroke and a weak one, like a sound and its echo. That was supposed to betoken the end. She let him feel her wrist, knowing what he wanted.

Sometimes they looked in each other's eyes. Then they almost seemed to make an agreement. It was almost as if he were agreeing to die also. But she did not consent to die; she would not. Her body was wasted to a fragment of ash. Her eyes were dark and full of torture.

"Can't you give her something to put an end to it?" he asked the doctor at last.

But the doctor shook his head.

"She can't last many days now, Mr. Morel," he said.

Paul went indoors.

"I can't bear it much longer; we shall all go mad," said Annie.

The two sat down to breakfast.

"Go and sit with her while we have breakfast, Minnie," said Annie. But the girl was frightened.

Paul went through the country, through the woods, over the snow. He saw the marks of rabbits and birds in the white snow. He wandered miles and miles. A smoky red sunset came on slowly, painfully, lingering. He thought she would die that day. There was a donkey that came up to him over the snow by the wood's edge, and put its head against him, and walked with him alongside. He put his arms round the donkey's neck, and stroked his cheeks against his ears.

His mother, silent, was still alive, with her hard mouth gripped grimly, her eyes of dark torture only living.

It was nearing Christmas; there was more snow. Annie and he felt as if they could go on no more. Still her dark eyes were alive. Morel, silent and frightened, obliterated himself. Sometimes he would go into the sick-room and look at her. Then he backed out, bewildered.

She kept her hold on life still. The miners had been out on strike, and returned a fortnight or so before Christmas. Minnie went upstairs with the feeding-cup. It was two days after the men had been in.

"Have the men been saying their hands are sore, Minnie?" she asked, in the faint, querulous voice that would not give in. Minnie stood surprised.

"Not as I know of, Mrs. Morel," she answered.

"But I'll bet they are sore," said the dying woman, as she moved her head ⌐h a sigh of weariness. But, at any rate, there'll be something to buy in with ⌐week."

⌐t a thing did she let slip.

⌐ur father's pit things will want well airing, Annie," she said, when the ⌐re going back to work.

"Don't you bother about that, my dear," said Annie.

One night Annie and Paul were alone. Nurse was upstairs.

"She'll live over Christmas," said Annie. They were both full of horror.

"She won't," he replied grimly. "I s'll give her morphia."

"Which?" said Annie.

"All that came from Sheffield," said Paul.

"Ay—do!" said Annie.

The next day he was painting in the bedroom. She seemed to be asleep. He stepped softly backwards and forwards at his painting. Suddenly her small voice wailed:

"Don't walk about, Paul."

He slipped out of bed. A bud of gas was burning in the sick chamber. His mother lay with her cheek on her hand, curled up as she had gone to sleep. But her mouth had fallen open, and she breathed with great, hoarse breaths, like snoring, and there were long intervals between.

"She's going!" he whispered.

"Yes," said Annie.

"How long has she been like it?"

"I only just woke up."

Annie huddled into the dressing-gown, Paul wrapped himself in a brown blanket. It was three o'clock. He mended the fire. Then the two sat waiting. The great, snoring breath was taken—held awhile—then given back. There was a space—a long space. Then they started. The great, snoring breath was taken again. He bent close down and looked at her.

"Isn't it awful!" whispered Annie.

He nodded. They sat down again helplessly. Again came the great, snoring breath. Again they hung suspended. Again it was given back, long and harsh. The sound, so irregular, at such wide intervals, sounded through the house. Morel, in his room, slept on. Paul and Annie sat crouched, huddled, motionless. The great snoring sound began again—there was a painful pause while the breath was held—back came the rasping breath. Minute after minute passed. Paul looked at her again, bending low over her.

"She may last like this," he said.

They were both silent. He looked out of the window, and could faintly discern the snow on the garden.

"You go to my bed," he said to Annie. "I'll sit up."

"No," she said, "I'll stop with you."

"I'd rather you didn't," he said.

At last Annie crept out of the room, and he was alone. He hugged himself in his brown blanket, crouched in front of his mother, watching. She looked dreadful, with the bottom jaw fallen back. He watched. Sometimes he thought the great breath would never begin again. He could not bear it—the waiting. Then suddenly, startling him, came the great harsh sound. He mended the fire again, noiselessly. She must not be disturbed. The minutes went by. The night was going, breath by breath. Each time the sound came he felt it wring him, til' at last he could not feel so much.

His father got up. Paul heard the miner drawing his stocking on, yawni` Then Morel, in shirt and stockings, entered.

"Hush!" said Paul.

Morel stood watching. Then he looked at his son, helplessly, and in h

"Had I better stop a-whoam?" he whispered.

"No. Go to work. She'll last through to-morrow."

"I don't think so."

"Yes. Go to work."

The miner looked at her again, in fear, and went obediently out of the room. Paul saw the tape of his garters swinging against his legs.

After another half-hour Paul went downstairs and drank a cup of tea, then returned. Morel, dressed for the pit, came upstairs again.

"Am I to go?" he said.

"Yes."

And in a few minutes Paul heard his father's heavy steps go thudding over the deadening snow. Miners called in the streets as they tramped in gangs to work. The terrible, long-drawn breaths continued—heave—heave—heave; then a long pause—then—ah-h-h-h-h! as it came back. Far away over the snow sounded the hooters of the ironworks. One after another they crowed and boomed, some small and far away, some near, the blowers of the collieries and the other works. Then there was silence. He mended the fire. The great breaths broke the silence—she looked just the same. He put back the blind and peered out. Still it was dark. Perhaps there was a lighter tinge. Perhaps the snow was bluer. He drew up the blind and got dressed. Then, shuddering, he drank brandy from the bottle on the wash-stand. The snow *was* growing blue. He heard a cart clanking down the street. Yes, it was seven o'clock, and it was coming a little bit light. He heard some people calling. The world was waking. A grey, deathly dawn crept over the snow. Yes, he could see the houses. He put out the gas. It seemed very dark. The breathing came still, but he was almost used to it. He could see her. She was just the same. He wondered if he piled heavy clothes on top of her it would stop. He looked at her. That was not her—not her a bit. If he piled the blanket and heavy coats on her——

Suddenly the door opened, and Annie entered. She looked at him questioningly.

"Just the same," he said calmly.

They whispered together a minute, then went downstairs to get breakfast. It was twenty to eight. Soon Annie came down.

"Isn't it awful! Doesn't she look awful!" she whispered, dazed with horror. He nodded.

"If she looks like that!" said Annie.

"Drink some tea," he said.

They went upstairs again. Soon the neighbours came with their frightened question:

"How is she?"

It went on just the same. She lay with her cheek in her hand, her mouth fallen open, and the great, ghastly snores came and went.

At ten o'clock nurse came. She looked strange and woebegone.

"Nurse," cried Paul, "she'll last like this for days?"

"She can't, Mr. Morel," said nurse. "She can't."

There was a silence.

"Isn't it dreadful!" wailed the nurse. "Who would have thought she could nd it? Go down now, Mr. Morel, go down."

At last, at about eleven o'clock, he went downstairs and sat in the neigh-
's house. Annie was downstairs also. Nurse and Arthur were upstairs. Paul
ith his head in his hands. Suddenly Annie came flying across the yard
half mad:
l—Paul—she's gone!"

In a second he was back in his own house and upstairs. She lay curled up and still, with her face on her hand, and nurse was wiping her mouth. They all stood back. He kneeled down, and put his face to hers and his arms round her:

"My love—my love—oh, my love!" he whispered again and again. "My love—oh, my love!"

Then he heard the nurse behind him, crying, saying:

"She's better, Mr. Morel, she's better."

When he took his face up from his warm, dead mother he went straight downstairs and began blacking his boots.

There was a good deal to do, letters to write, and so on. The doctor came and glanced at her, and sighed.

"Ay—poor thing!" he said, then turned away. "Well, call at the surgery about six for the certificate."

The father came home from work at about four o'clock. He dragged silently into the house and sat down. Minnie bustled to give him his dinner. Tired, he laid his black arms on the table. There were swede turnips for his dinner, which he liked. Paul wondered if he knew. It was some time, and nobody had spoken. At last the son said:

"You noticed the blinds were down?"

Morel looked up.

"No," he said. "Why—has she gone?"

"Yes."

"When wor that?"

"About twelve this morning."

"H'm!"

The miner sat still for a moment, then began his dinner. It was as if nothing had happened. He ate his turnips in silence. Afterwards he washed and went upstairs to dress. The door of her room was shut.

"Have you seen her?" Annie asked of him when he came down.

"No," he said.

In a little while he went out. Annie went away, and Paul called on the undertaker, the clergyman, the doctor, the registrar. It was a long business. He got back at nearly eight o'clock. The undertaker was coming soon to measure for the coffin. The house was empty except for her. He took a candle and went upstairs.

The room was cold, that had been warm for so long. Flowers, bottles, plates, all sick-room litter was taken away; everything was harsh and austere. She lay raised on the bed, the sweep of the sheet from the raised feet was like a clean curve of snow, so silent. She lay like a maiden asleep. With his candle in his hand, he bent over her. She lay like a girl asleep and dreaming of her love. The mouth was a little open as if wondering from the suffering, but her face was young, her brow clear and white as if life had never touched it. He looked again at the eyebrows, at the small, winsome nose a bit on one side. She was young again. Only the hair as it arched so beautifully from her temples was mixed with silver, and the two simple plaits that lay on her shoulders were filigree of silver and brown. She would wake up. She would lift her eyelids. She was with him still. He bent and kissed her passionately. But there was coldness against his mouth. He bit his lips with horror. Looking at her, he felt he could never, never let her go. No! He stroked the hair from her temples. That, too, was cold. He saw the mouth so dumb and wondering at the hurt. Then he crouched on the floor, whispering to her:

"Mother, mother!"

He was still with her when the undertakers came, young men who had been to school with him. They touched her reverently, and in a quiet, businesslike fashion. They did not look at her. He watched jealously. He and Annie guarded her fiercely. They would not let anybody come to see her, and the neighbours were offended.

After a while Paul went out of the house, and played cards at a friend's. It was midnight when he got back. His father rose from the couch as he entered, saying in a plaintive way:

"I thought tha wor niver comin', lad."

"I didn't think you'd sit up," said Paul.

His father looked so forlorn. Morel had been a man without fear—simply nothing frightened him. Paul realised with a start that he had been afraid to go to bed, alone in the house with his dead. He was sorry.

"I forgot you'd be alone, father," he said.

"Dost want owt to eat?" asked Morel.

"No."

"Sithee—I made thee a drop o' hot milk. Get it down thee; it's cold enough for owt."

Paul drank it.

After a while Morel went to bed. He hurried past the closed door, and left his own door open. Soon the son came upstairs also. He went in to kiss her goodnight, as usual. It was cold and dark. He wished they had kept her fire burning. Still she dreamed her young dream. But she would be cold.

"My dear!" he whispered. "My dear!"

And he did not kiss her, for fear she should be cold and strange to him. It eased him she slept so beautifully. He shut her door softly, not to wake her, and went to bed.

In the morning Morel summoned his courage, hearing Annie downstairs and Paul coughing in the room across the landing. He opened her door, and went into the darkened room. He saw the white uplifted form in the twilight, but her he dared not see. Bewildered, too frightened to possess any of his faculties, he got out of the room again and left her. He never looked at her again. He had not seen her for months, because he had not dared to look. And she looked like his young wife again.

"Have you seen her?" Annie asked of him sharply after breakfast.

"Yes," he said.

"And don't you think she looks nice?"

"Yes."

He went out of the house soon after. And all the time he seemed to be creeping aside to avoid it.

Paul went about from place to place, doing the business of the death. He met Clara in Nottingham, and they had tea together in a café, when they were quite jolly again. She was infinitely relieved to find he did not take it tragically.

Later, when the relatives began to come for the funeral, the affair became public, and the children became social beings. They put themselves aside. They buried her in a furious storm of rain and wind. The wet clay glistened, all the white flowers were soaked. Annie gripped his arm and leaned forward. Down below she saw a dark corner of William's coffin. The oak box sank steadily. She was gone. The rain poured in the grave. The procession of black, with its umbrellas glistening, turned away. The cemetery was deserted under the drenching

Paul went home and busied himself supplying the guests with drinks. His father sat in the kitchen with Mrs. Morel's relatives, "superior" people, and wept, and said what a good lass she'd been, and how he'd tried to do everything he could for her—everything. He had striven all his life to do what he could for her, and he'd nothing to reproach himself with. She was gone, but he'd done his best for her. He wiped his eyes with his white handkerchief. He'd nothing to reproach himself for, he repeated. All his life he'd done his best for her.

And that was how he tried to dismiss her. He never thought of her personally. Everything deep in him he denied. Paul hated his father for sitting sentimentalising over her. He knew he would do it in the public-houses. For the real tragedy went on in Morel in spite of himself. Sometimes, later, he came down from his afternoon sleep, white and cowering.

"I *have* been dreaming of thy mother," he said in a small voice.

"Have you, father? When I dream of her it's always just as she was when she was well. I dream of her often, but it seems quite nice and natural, as if nothing had altered."

But Morel crouched in front of the fire in terror.

The weeks passed half-real, not much pain, not much of anything, perhaps a little relief, mostly a *nuit blanche*. Paul went restless from place to place. For some months, since his mother had been worse, he had not made love to Clara. She was, as it were, dumb to him, rather distant. Dawes saw her very occasionally, but the two could not get an inch across the great distance between them. The three of them were drifting forward.

Dawes mended very slowly. He was in the convalescent home at Skegness at Christmas, nearly well again. Paul went to the seaside for a few days. His father was with Annie in Sheffield. Dawes came to Paul's lodgings. His time in the home was up. The two men, between whom was such a big reserve, seemed faithful to each other. Dawes depended on Morel now. He knew Paul and Clara had practically separated.

Two days after Christmas Paul was to go back to Nottingham. The evening before he sat with Dawes smoking before the fire.

"You know Clara's coming down for the day to-morrow?" he said.

The other man glanced at him.

"Yes, you told me," he replied.

Paul drank the remainder of his glass of whisky.

"I told the landlady your wife was coming," he said.

"Did you?" said Dawes, shrinking, but almost leaving himself in the other's hands. He got up rather stiffly, and reached for Morel's glass.

"Let me fill you up," he said.

Paul jumped up.

"You sit still," he said.

But Dawes, with rather shaky hand, continued to mix the drink.

"Say when," he said.

"Thanks!" replied the other. "But you've no business to get up."

"It does me good, lad," replied Dawes. "I begin to think I'm right again then."

"You are about right, you know."

"I am, certainly I am," said Dawes, nodding to him.

"And Len says he can get you on in Sheffield."

Dawes glanced at him again, with dark eyes that agreed with everythi[ng] other would say, perhaps a trifle dominated by him.

"It's funny," said Paul, "starting again. I feel in a lot bigger mess th[an]

"In what way, lad?"

"I don't know. I don't know. It's as if I was in a tangled sort of hole, rather dark and dreary, and no road anywhere."

"I know—I understand it," Dawes said, nodding. "But you'll find it'll come all right."

He spoke caressingly.

"I suppose so," said Paul.

Dawes knocked his pipe in a hopeless fashion.

"You've not done for yourself like I have," he said.

Morel saw the wrist and the white hand of the other man gripping the stem of the pipe and knocking out the ash, as if he had given up.

"How old are you?" Paul asked.

"Thirty-nine," replied Dawes, glancing at him.

Those brown eyes, full of the consciousness of failure, almost pleading for reassurance, for someone to re-establish the man in himself, to warm him, to set him up firm again, troubled Paul.

"You'll just be in your prime," said Morel. "You don't look as if much life had gone out of you."

The brown eyes of the other flashed suddenly.

"It hasn't," he said. "The go is there."

Paul looked up and laughed.

"We've both got plenty of life in us yet to make things fly," he said.

The eyes of the two men met. They exchanged one look. Having recognised the stress of passion each in the other, they both drank their whisky.

"Yes, begod!" said Dawes, breathless.

There was a pause.

"And I don't see," said Paul, "why you shouldn't go on where you left off."

"What——" said Dawes, suggestively.

"Yes—fit your old home together again."

Dawes hid his face and shook his head.

"Couldn't be done," he said, and looked up with an ironic smile.

"Why? Because you don't want?"

"Perhaps."

They smoked in silence. Dawes showed his teeth as he bit his pipe stem.

"You mean you don't want her?" asked Paul.

Dawes stared up at the picture with a caustic expression on his face.

"I hardly know," he said.

The smoke floated softly up.

"I believe she wants you," said Paul.

"Do you?" replied the other, soft, satirical, abstract.

"Yes. She never really hitched on to me—you were always there in the background. That's why she wouldn't get a divorce."

Dawes continued to stare in a satirical fashion at the picture over the mantelpiece.

"That's how women are with me," said Paul. "They want me like mad, but they don't want to belong to me. And she *belonged* to you all the time. I knew."

The triumphant male came up in Dawes. He showed his teeth more distinctly.

"Perhaps I was a fool," he said.

"You were a big fool," said Morel.

"But perhaps even *then* you were a bigger fool," said Dawes.

There was a touch of triumph and malice in it.

"Do you think so?" said Paul.

They were silent for some time.

"At any rate, I'm clearing out to-morrow," said Morel.

"I see," answered Dawes.

Then they did not talk any more. The instinct to murder each other had returned. They almost avoided each other.

They shared the same bedroom. When they retired Dawes seemed abstract, thinking of something. He sat on the side of the bed in his shirt, looking at his legs.

"Aren't you getting cold?" asked Morel.

"I was lookin' at these legs," replied the other.

"What's up with 'em? They look all right," replied Paul, from his bed.

"They look all right. But there's some water in 'em yet."

"And what about it?"

"Come and look."

Paul reluctantly got out of bed and went to look at the rather handsome legs of the other man that were covered with glistening, dark gold hair.

"Look here," said Dawes, pointing to his shin. "Look at the water under here."

"Where?" said Paul.

The man pressed in his finger-tips. They left little dents that filled up slowly.

"It's nothing," said Paul.

"You feel," said Dawes.

Paul tried with his fingers. It made little dents.

"H'm!" he said.

"Rotten, isn't it?" said Dawes.

"Why? It's nothing much."

"You're not much of a man with water in your legs."

"I can't see as it makes any difference," said Morel. "I've got a weak chest." He returned to his own bed.

"I suppose the rest of me's all right," said Dawes, and he put out the light.

In the morning it was raining. Morel packed his bag. The sea was grey and shaggy and dismal. He seemed to be cutting himself off from life more and more. It gave him a wicked pleasure to do it.

The two men were at the station. Clara stepped out of the train, and came along the platform, very erect and coldly composed. She wore a long coat and a tweed hat. Both men hated her for her composure. Paul shook hands with her at the barrier. Dawes was leaning against the bookstall, watching. His black overcoat was buttoned up to the chin because of the rain. He was pale, with almost a touch of nobility in his quietness. He came forward, limping slightly.

"You ought to look better than this," she said.

"Oh, I'm all right now."

The three stood at a loss. She kept the two men hesitating near her.

"Shall we go to the lodging straight off," said Paul, "or somewhere else?"

"We may as well go home," said Dawes.

Paul walked on the outside of the pavement, then Dawes, then Clara. made polite conversation. The sitting-room faced the sea, whole tide, gr shaggy, hissed not far off.

Morel swung up the big arm-chair.

"Sit down, Jack," he said.

"I don't want that chair," said Dawes.

"Sit down!" Morel repeated.

Clara took off her things and laid them on the couch. She had a slight air of resentment. Lifting her hair with her fingers, she sat down, rather aloof and composed. Paul ran downstairs to speak to the landlady.

"I should think you're cold," said Dawes to his wife. "Come nearer to the fire."

"Thank you, I'm quite warm," she answered.

She looked out of the window at the rain and at the sea.

"When are you going back?" she asked.

"Well, the rooms are taken until to-morrow, so he wants me to stop. He's going back to-night."

"And then you're thinking of going to Sheffield?"

"Yes."

"Are you fit to start work?"

"I'm going to start."

"You've really got a place?"

"Yes—begin on Monday."

"You don't look fit."

"Why don't I?"

She looked again out of the window instead of answering.

"And have you got lodgings in Sheffield?"

"Yes."

Again she looked away out of the window. The panes were blurred with streaming rain.

"And can you manage all right?" she asked.

"I s'd think so. I s'll have to!"

They were silent when Morel returned.

"I shall go by the four-twenty," he said as he entered.

Nobody answered.

"I wish you'd take your boots off," he said to Clara.

"There's a pair of slippers of mine."

"Thank you," she said. "They aren't wet."

He put the slippers near her feet. She left them there.

Morel sat down. Both the men seemed helpless, and each of them had a rather hunted look. But Dawes now carried himself quietly, seemed to yield himself, while Paul seemed to screw himself up. Clara thought she had never seen him look so small and mean. He was as if trying to get himself into the smallest possible compass. And as he went about arranging, and as he sat talking, there seemed something false about him and out of tune. Watching him unknown, she said to herself there was no stability about him. He was fine in his way, passionate, and able to give her drinks of pure life when he was in one mood. And now he looked paltry and insignificant. There was nothing stable about him. Her husband had more manly dignity. At any rate he did not waft about with any wind. There was something evanescent about Morel, she thought, something shifting and false. He would never make sure ground for woman to stand on. She despised him rather for his shrinking together, getting smaller. Her husband at least was manly, and when he was beaten gave up; this other would never own to being beaten. He would shift round and prowl, get smaller. She despised him. And yet she watched him rather than the others, and it seemed as if their three fates lay in his hands. She hated him

She seemed to understand better now about men, and what they could or would do. She was less afraid of them, more sure of herself. That they were not the small egoists she had imagined them made her more comfortable. She had learned a good deal—almost as much as she wanted to learn. Her cup had been full. It was still as full as she could carry. On the whole, she would not be sorry when he was gone.

They had dinner, and sat eating nuts and drinking by the fire. Not a serious word had been spoken. Yet Clara realised that Morel was withdrawing from the circle, leaving her the option to stay with her husband. It angered her. He was a mean fellow, after all, to take what he wanted and then give her back. She did not remember that she herself had had what she wanted, and really, at the bottom of her heart, wished to be given back.

Paul felt crumpled up and lonely. His mother had really supported his life. He had loved her; they two had, in fact, faced the world together. Now she was gone, and for ever behind him was the gap in life, the tear in the veil, through which his life seemed to drift slowly, as if he were drawn towards death. He wanted someone of their own free initiative to help him. The lesser things he began to let go from him, for fear of this big thing, the lapse towards death, following in the wake of his beloved. Clara could not stand for him to hold on to. She wanted him, but not to understand him. He felt she wanted the man on top, not the real him that was in trouble. That would be too much trouble to her; he dared not give it her. She could not cope with him. It made him ashamed. So, secretly ashamed because he was in such a mess, because his own hold on life was so unsure, because nobody held him, feeling unsubstantial, shadowy, as if he did not count for much in this concrete world, he drew himself together smaller and smaller. He did not want to die; he would not give in. But he was not afraid of death. If nobody would help, he would go on alone.

Dawes had been driven to the extremity of life, until he was afraid. He could go to the brink of death, he could lie on the edge and look in. Then, cowed, afraid, he had to crawl back, and like a beggar take what offered. There was a certain nobility in it. As Clara saw, he owned himself beaten, and he wanted to be taken back whether or not. That she could do for him.

It was three o'clock.

"I am going by the four-twenty," said Paul again to Clara. "Are you coming then or later?"

"I don't know," she said.

"I'm meeting my father in Nottingham at seven-fifteen," he said.

"Then," she answered, "I'll come later."

Dawes jerked suddenly, as if he had been held on a strain. He looked out over the sea, but he saw nothing.

"There are one or two books in the corner," said Morel. "I've done with 'em."

At about four o'clock he went.

"I shall see you both later," he said, as he shook hands.

"I suppose so," said Dawes. "An' perhaps—one day—I s'll be able to pay you back the money as——"

"I shall come for it, you'll see," laughed Paul. "I s'll be on the rocks befo' I'm very much older."

"Ay—well——" said Dawes.

"Good-bye," he said to Clara.

"Good-bye," she said, giving him her hand. Then she glanced at him f last time, dumb and humble.

He was gone. Dawes and his wife sat down again.

"It's a nasty day for travelling," said the man.

"Yes," she answered.

They talked in a desultory fashion until it grew dark. The landlady brought in the tea. Dawes drew up his chair to the table without being invited, like a husband. Then he sat humbly waiting for his cup. She served him as she would, like a wife, not consulting his wish.

After tea, as it drew near to six o'clock, he went to the window. All was dark outside. The sea was roaring.

"It's raining yet," he said.

"Is it?" she answered.

"You won't go to-night, shall you?" he said, hesitating.

She did not answer. He waited.

"I shouldn't go in this rain," he said.

"Do you *want* me to stay?" she asked.

His hand as he held the dark curtain trembled.

"Yes," he said.

He remained with his back to her. She rose and went slowly to him. He let go the curtain, turned, hesitating, towards her. She stood with her hands behind her back, looking up at him in a heavy, inscrutable fashion.

"Do you want me, Baxter?" she asked.

His voice was hoarse as he answered:

"Do you want to come back to me?"

She made a moaning noise, lifted her arms, and put them round his neck, drawing him to her. He hid his face on her shoulder, holding her clasped.

"Take me back!" she whispered, ecstatic. "Take me back, take me back!" And she put her fingers through his fine, thin dark hair, as if she were only semi-conscious. He tightened his grasp on her.

"Do you want me again?" he murmured, broken.

XV

DERELICT

Clara went with her husband to Sheffield, and Paul scarcely saw her again. Walter Morel seemed to have let all the trouble go over him, and there he was, crawling about on the mud of it, just the same. There was scarcely any bond between father and son, save that each felt he must not let the other go in any actual want. As there was no one to keep on the home, and as they could neither of them bear the emptiness of the house, Paul took lodgings in Nottingham, and Morel went to live with a friendly family in Bestwood.

Everything seemed to have gone smash for the young man. He could not paint. The picture he finished on the day of his mother's death—one that satisfied him—was the last thing he did. At work there was no Clara. When he came home he could not take up his brushes again. There was nothing left.

So he was always in the town at one place or another, drinking, knocking out with the men he knew. It really wearied him. He talked to barmaids, to most any woman, but there was that dark, strained look in his eyes, as if he were hunting something.

Everything seemed so different, so unreal. There seemed no reason why people should go along the street, and houses pile up in the daylight. There seemed no reason why these things should occupy the space, instead of leaving it empty. His friends talked to him: he heard the sounds, and he answered. But why there should be the noise of speech he could not understand.

He was most himself when he was alone, or working hard and mechanically at the factory. In the latter case there was pure forgetfulness, when he lapsed from consciousness. But it had to come to an end. It hurt him so, that things had lost their reality. The first snowdrops came. He saw the tiny drop-pearls among the grey. They would have given him the liveliest emotion at one time. Now they were there, but they did not seem to mean anything. In a few moments they would cease to occupy that place, and just the space would be, where they had been. Tall, brilliant tram-cars ran along the street at night. It seemed almost a wonder they should trouble to rustle backwards and forwards. "Why trouble to go tilting down to Trent Bridges?" he asked of the big trams. It seemed they just as well might *not* be as be.

The realest thing was the thick darkness at night. That seemed to him whole and comprehensible and restful. He could leave himself to it. Suddenly a piece of paper started near his feet and blew along down the pavement. He stood still, rigid, with clenched fists, a flame of agony going over him. And he saw again the sick-room, his mother, her eyes. Unconsciously he had been with her, in her company. The swift hop of the paper reminded him she was gone. But he had been with her. He wanted everything to stand still, so that he could be with her again.

The days passed, the weeks. But everything seemed to have fused, gone into a conglomerated mass. He could not tell one day from another, one week from another, hardly one place from another. Nothing was distinct or distinguishable. Often he lost himself for an hour at a time, could not remember what he had done.

One evening he came home late to his lodging. The fire was burning low; everybody was in bed. He threw on some more coal, glanced at the table, and decided he wanted no supper. Then he sat down in the arm-chair. It was perfectly still. He did not know anything, yet he saw the dim smoke wavering up the chimney. Presently two mice came out, cautiously, nibbling the fallen crumbs. He watched them as it were from a long way off. The church clock struck two. Far away he could hear the sharp clinking of the trucks on the railway. No, it was not they that were far away. They were there in their places. But where was he himself?

The time passed. The two mice, careering wildly, scampered cheekily over his slippers. He had not moved a muscle. He did not want to move. He was not thinking of anything. It was easier so. There was no wrench of knowing anything. Then, from time to time, some other consciousness, working mechanically, flashed into sharp phrases.

"What am I doing?"

And out of the semi-intoxicated trance came the answer:

"Destroying myself."

Then a dull, live feeling, gone in an instant, told him that it was wrong. After a while, suddenly came the question:

"Why wrong?"

Again there was no answer, but a stroke of hot stubbornness inside his c' resisted his own annihilation.

There was a sound of a heavy cart clanking down the road. Sudder electric light went out; there was a bruising thud in the penny-in-the-slot meter. He did not stir, but sat gazing in front of him. Only the mice had scuttled, and the fire glowed red in the dark room.

Then, quite mechanically and more distinctly, the conversation began again inside him.

"She's dead. What was it all for—her struggle?"

That was his despair wanting to go after her.

"You're alive."

"She's not."

"She is—in you."

Suddenly he felt tired with the burden of it.

"You've got to keep alive for her sake," said his will in him.

Something felt sulky, as if it would not rouse.

"You've got to carry forward her living, and what she had done, go on with it."

But he did not want to. He wanted to give up.

"But you can go on with your painting," said the will in him. "Or else you can beget children. They both carry on her effort."

"Painting is not living."

"Then live."

"Marry whom?" came the sulky question.

"As best you can.

"Miriam?"

But he did not trust that.

He rose suddenly, went straight to bed. When he got inside his bedroom and closed the door, he stood with clenched fist.

"Mater, my dear——" he began, with the whole force of his soul. Then he stopped. He would not say it. He would not admit that he wanted to die, to have done. He would not own that life had beaten him, or that death had beaten him. Going straight to bed, he slept at once, abandoning himself to the sleep.

So the weeks went on. Always alone, his soul oscillated, first on the side of death, then on the side of life, doggedly. The real agony was that he had nowhere to go, nothing to do, nothing to say, and *was* nothing himself. Sometimes he ran down the streets as if he were mad: sometimes he was mad; things weren't there, things were there. It made him pant. Sometimes he stood before the bar of the public-house where he called for a drink. Everything suddenly stood back away from him. He saw the face of the barmaid, the gabbling drinkers, his own glass on the slopped, mahogany board, in the distance. There was something between him and them. He could not get into touch. He did not want them; he did not want his drink. Turning abruptly, he went out. On the threshold he stood and looked at the lighted street. But he was not of it or in it. Something separated him. Everything went on there below those lamps, shut away from him. He could not get at them. He felt he couldn't touch the lamp-posts, not if he reached. Where could he go? There was nowhere to go, neither back into the inn, or forward anywhere. He felt stifled. There was nowhere for him. The stress grew inside him; he felt he should smash.

"I mustn't," he said; and, turning blindly, he went in and drank. Sometimes the drink did him good; sometimes it made him worse. He ran down the road. Ever restless, he went here, there, everywhere. He determined to work. But when he had made six strokes, he loathed the pencil violently, got up, and went hurried off to a club where he could play cards or billiards, to a place

where he could flirt with a barmaid who was no more to him than the brass
pump-handle she drew.

He was very thin and lantern-jawed. He dared not meet his own eyes in the
mirror; he never looked at himself. He wanted to get away from himself, but
there was nothing to get hold of. In despair he thought of Miriam. Perhaps—
perhaps——?

Then, happening to go into the Unitarian Church one Sunday evening,
when they stood up to sing the second hymn he saw her before him. The light
glistened on her lower lip as she sang. She looked as if she had got something, at
any rate: some hope in heaven, if not in earth. Her comfort and her life seemed
in the after-world. A warm, strong feeling for her came up. She seemed to
yearn, as she sang, for the mystery and comfort. He put his hope in her. He
longed for the sermon to be over, to speak to her.

The throng carried her out just before him. He could nearly touch her. She
did not know he was there. He saw the brown, humble nape of her neck under
its black curls. He would leave himself to her. She was better and bigger than he.
He would depend on her.

She went wandering, in her blind way, through the little throngs of people
outside the church. She always looked so lost and out of place among people.
He went forward and put his hand on her arm. She started violently. Her great
brown eyes dilated in fear, then went questioning at the sight of him. He shrank
slightly from her.

"I didn't know——" she faltered.

"Nor I," he said.

He looked away. His sudden, flaring hope sank again.

"What are you doing in town?" he asked.

"I'm staying at Cousin Anne's."

"Ha! For long?"

"No; only till to-morrow."

"Must you go straight home?"

She looked at him, then hid her face under her hat-brim.

"No," she said—"no; it's not necessary."

He turned away, and she went with him. They threaded through the throng
of church people. The organ was still sounding in St. Mary's. Dark figures came
through the lighted doors; people were coming down the steps. The large coloured windows glowed up in the night. The church was like a great lantern
suspended. They went down Hollow Stone, and he took the car for the
Bridges.

"You will just have supper with me," he said: "then I'll bring you back."

"Very well," she replied, low and husky.

They scarcely spoke while they were on the car. The Trent ran dark and full
under the bridge. Away towards Colwick all was black night. He lived down
Holme Road, on the naked edge of the town, facing across the river meadows
towards Sneinton Hermitage and the steep scrap of Colwick Wood. The floods
were out. The silent water and the darkness spread away on their left. Almo
afraid, they hurried along by the houses.

Supper was laid. He swung the curtain over the window. There was a b
of freesias and scarlet anemones on the table. She bent to them. Still touc
them with her fingertips, she looked up at him, saying:

"Aren't they beautiful?"

"Yes," he said. "What will you drink—coffee?"

"I should like it," she said.

"Then excuse me a moment."

He went out to the kitchen.

Miriam took off her things and looked round. It was a bare, severe room. Her photo, Clara's, Annie's, were on the wall. She looked on the drawing-board to see what he was doing. There were only a few meaningless lines. She looked to see what books he was reading. Evidently just an ordinary novel. The letters in the rack she saw were from Annie, Arthur, and from some man or other she did not know. Everything he had touched, everything that was in the least personal to him, she examined with lingering absorption. He had been gone from her for so long, she wanted to rediscover him, his position, what he was now. But there was not much in the room to help her. It only made her feel rather sad, it was so hard and comfortless.

She was curiously examining a sketch-book when he returned with the coffee.

"There's nothing new in it," he said, "and nothing very interesting."

He put down the tray, and went to look over her shoulder. She turned the pages slowly, intent on examining everything.

"H'm!" he said, as she paused at a sketch. "I'd forgotten that. It's not bad, is it?"

"No," she said. "I don't quite understand it."

He took the book from her and went through it. Again he made a curious sound of surprise and pleasure.

"There's some not bad stuff in there," he said.

"Not at all bad," she answered gravely.

He felt again her interest in his work. Or was it for himself? Why was she always most interested in him as he appeared in his work?

They sat down to supper.

"By the way," he said, "didn't I hear something about your earning your own living?"

"Yes," she replied, bowing her dark head over her cup.

"And what of it?"

"I'm merely going to the farming college at Broughton for three months, and I shall probably be kept on as a teacher there."

"I say—that sounds all right for you! You always wanted to be independent."

"Yes."

"Why didn't you tell me?"

"I only knew last week."

"But I heard a month ago," he said.

"Yes; but nothing was settled then."

"I should have thought," he said, "you'd have told me you were trying."

She ate her food in the deliberate, constrained way, almost as if she recoiled little from doing anything so publicly, that he knew so well.

"I suppose you're glad," he said.

"Very glad."

"Yes—it will be something."

was rather disappointed.

think it will be a great deal," she said, almost haughtily, resentfully.

ughed shortly.

do you think it won't?" she asked.

"Oh, I don't think it won't be a great deal. Only you'll find earning your own living isn't everything."

"No," she said, swallowing with difficulty; "I don't suppose it is."

"I suppose work *can* be nearly everything to a man," he said, "though it isn't to me. But a woman only works with a part of herself. The real and vital part is covered up."

"But a man can give *all* himself to work?" she asked.

"Yes, practically."

"And a woman only the unimportant part of herself?"

"That's it."

She looked up at him, and her eyes dilated with anger.

"Then," she said, "if it's true, it's a great shame."

"It is. But I don't know everything," he answered.

After supper they drew up to the fire. He swung her a chair facing him, and they sat down. She was wearing a dress of dark claret colour, that suited her dark complexion and her large features. Still, the curls were fine and free, but her face was much older, the brown throat much thinner. She seemed old to him, older than Clara. Her bloom of youth had quickly gone. A sort of stiffness, almost of woodenness, had come upon her. She meditated a little while, then looked at him.

"And how are things with you?" she asked.

"About all right," he answered.

She looked at him, waiting.

"Nay," she said, very low.

Her brown, nervous hands were clasped over her knee. They had still the lack of confidence or repose, the almost hysterical look. He winced as he saw them. Then he laughed mirthlessly. She put her fingers between her lips. His slim, black, tortured body lay quite still in the chair. She suddenly took her finger from her mouth and looked at him.

"And you have broken off with Clara?"

"Yes."

His body lay like an abandoned thing, strewn in the chair.

"You know," she said, "I think we ought to be married."

He opened his eyes for the first time since many months, and attended to her with respect.

"Why?" he said.

"See," she said, "how you waste yourself! You might be ill, you might die, and I never know—be no more then than if I had never know you."

"And if we married?" he asked.

"At any rate, I could prevent you wasting yourself and being a prey to other women—like—like Clara."

"A prey?" he repeated, smiling.

She bowed her head in silence. He lay feeling his despair come up again.

"I'm not sure," he said slowly, "that marriage would be much good."

"I only think of you," she replied.

"I know you do. But—you love me so much, you want to put me in ▾ pocket. And I should die there smothered."

She bent her head, put her fingers between her lips, while the bit▾ surged up in her heart.

"And what will you do otherwise?" she asked.

"I don't know—go on, I suppose. Perhaps I shall soon go abroac'

The despairing doggedness in his tone made her go on her knees on the rug before the fire, very near to him. There she crouched as if she were crushed by something, and could not raise her head. His hands lay quite inert on the arms of his chair. She was aware of them. She felt that now he lay at her mercy. If she could rise, take him, put her arms round him, and say, "You are mine," then he would leave himself to her. But dare she? She could easily sacrifice herself. But dare she assert herself? She was aware of his dark-clothed, slender body, that seemed one stroke of life, sprawled in the chair close to her. But no; she dared not put her arms round it, take it up, and say, "It is mine, this body. Leave it to me." And she wanted to. It called to all her woman's instinct. But she crouched, and dared not. She was afraid he would not let her. She was afraid it was too much. It lay there, his body, abandoned. She knew she ought to take it up and claim it, and claim every right to it. But—could she do it? Her impotence before him, before the strong demand of some unknown thing in him, was her extremity. Her hands fluttered; she half-lifted her head. Her eyes, shuddering, appealing, gone almost distracted, pleaded to him suddenly. His heart caught with pity. He took her hands, drew her to him, and comforted her.

"Will you have me, to marry me?" he said very low.

Oh, why did not he take her? Her very soul belonged to him. Why would he not take what was his? She had borne so long the cruelty of belonging to him and not being claimed by him. Now he was straining her again. It was too much for her. She drew back her head, held his face between her hands, and looked him in the eyes. No, he was hard. He wanted something else. She pleaded to him with all her love not to make it *her* choice. She could not cope with it, with him, she knew not with what. But it strained her till she felt she would break.

"Do you want it?" she asked, very gravely.

"Not much," he replied, with pain.

She turned her face aside; then, raising herself with dignity, she took his head to her bosom, and rocked him softly. She was not to have him, then! So she could comfort him. She put her fingers through his hair. For her, the anguished sweetness of self-sacrifice. For him, the hate and misery of another failure. He could not bear it—that breast which was warm and which cradled him without taking the burden of him. So much he wanted to rest on her that the feint of rest only tortured him. He drew away.

"And without marriage we can do nothing?" he asked.

His mouth was lifted from his teeth with pain. She put her little finger between her lips.

"No," she said, low and like the toll of a bell. "No, I think not."

It was the end then between them. She could not take him and relieve him of the responsibility of himself. She could only sacrifice herself to him—sacrifice herself every day, gladly. And that he did not want. He wanted her to hold him and say, with joy and authority: "Stop all this restlessness and beating against death. You are mine for a mate." She had not the strength. Or was it a mate she wanted? or did she want a Christ in him?

He felt, in leaving her, he was defrauding her of life. But he knew that, in ing, stifling the inner, desperate man, he was denying his own life. And he ot hope to give life to her by denying his own.

 sat very quiet. He lit a cigarette. The smoke went up from it, wavering. thinking of his mother, and had forgotten Miriam. She suddenly looked er bitterness came surging up. Her sacrifice, then, was useless. He lay f, careless about her. Suddenly she saw again his lack of religion, his restless instability. He would destroy himself like a perverse child. Well, then, he would!

"I think I must go," she said softly.

By her tone he knew she was despising him. He rose quietly.

"I'll come along with you," he answered.

She stood before the mirror pinning on her hat. How bitter, how unutterably bitter, it made her that he rejected her sacrifice! Life ahead looked dead, as if the glow were gone out. She bowed her face over the flowers—the freesias so sweet and spring-like, the scarlet anemones flaunting over the table. It was like him to have those flowers.

He moved about the room with a certain sureness of touch, swift and relentless and quiet. She knew she could not cope with him. He would escape like a weasel out of her hands. Yet without him her life would trail on lifeless. Brooding, she touched the flowers.

"Have them!" he said; and he took them out of the jar, dripping as they were, and went quickly into the kitchen. She waited for him, took the flowers, and they went out together, he talking, she feeling dead.

She was going from him now. In her misery she leaned against him as they sat on the car. He was unresponsive. Where would he go? What would be the end of him? She could not bear it, the vacant feeling where he should be. He was so foolish, so wasteful, never at peace with himself. And now where would he go? And what did he care that he wasted her? He had no religion; it was all for the moment's attraction that he cared, nothing else, nothing deeper. Well, she would wait and see how it turned out with him. When he had had enough he would give in and come to her.

He shook hands and left her at the door of her cousin's house. When he turned away he felt the last hold for him had gone. The town, as he sat upon the car, stretched away over the bay of railway, a level fume of lights. Beyond the town the country, little smouldering spots for more towns—the sea—the night—on and on! And he had no place in it! Whatever spot he stood on, there he stood alone. From his breast, from his mouth, sprang the endless space, and it was there behind him, everywhere. The people hurrying along the streets offered no obstruction to the void in which he found himself. They were small shadows whose footsteps and voices could be heard, but in each of them the same night, the same silence. He got off the car. In the country all was dead still. Little stars shone high up; little stars spread far away in the flood-waters, a firmament below. Everywhere the vastness and terror of the immense night which is roused and stirred for a brief while by the day, but which returns, and will remain at last eternal, holding everything in its silence and its living gloom. There was no Time, only Space. Who could say his mother had lived and did not live? She had been in one place, and was in another; that was all. And his soul could not leave her, wherever she was. Now she was gone abroad into the night, and he was with her still. They were together. But yet there was his body, his chest, that leaned against the stile, his hands on the wooden bar. They seemed something. Where was he?—one tiny upright speck of flesh, less than an ear of wheat lost in the field. He could not bear it. On every side the immense dark silence seemed pressing him, so tiny a spark, into extinction, and yet, almost nothing, he could not be extinct. Night, in which everything was lost, went reaching out, beyond stars and sun. Stars and sun, a few bright grains, went spinning round for terror, and holding each other in embrace, there in a darkness that outpassed them all, and left them tiny and daunted. So much himself, infinitesimal, at the core a nothingness, and yet not nothing.

"Mother!" he whispered—"mother!"

She was the only thing that held him up, himself, amid all this. And she was gone, intermingled herself. He wanted her to touch him, have him alongside with her.

But no, he would not give in. Turning sharply, he walked towards the city's gold phosphorescence. His fists were shut, his mouth set fast. He would not take that direction, to the darkness, to follow her. He walked towards the faintly humming, glowing town, quickly.